The Terror

and other Writings of Machen
By Arthur Machen
Edited by Anthony Uyl

Devoted Publishing
Woodstock, Ontario, 2017

Arthur Machen

The Terror and other Writings of Machen
By Arthur Machen
Edited by Anthony Uyl

What kind of philosophies do you have?
Let us know!

Contact us at: devotedpub@hotmail.com
Visit our shop on Facebook: @DevotedPublishing

Published in Woodstock, Ontario, Canada 2017

For bulk educational rates, please contact us at the above email address.

ISBN: 978-1-77356-070-0

Table of Contents

THE TERROR

A MYSTERY
BY ARTHUR MACHEN
AUTHOR OF "THE BOWMEN"

NEW YORK, ROBERT M. MCBRIDE & COMPANY, UNION SQUARE, NORTH, 1917

CHAPTER I - The Coming of the Terror

After two years we are turning once more to the morning's news with a sense of appetite and glad expectation. There were thrills at the beginning of the war; the thrill of horror and of a doom that seemed at once incredible and certain; this was when Namur fell and the German host swelled like a flood over the French fields, and drew very near to the walls of Paris. Then we felt the thrill of exultation when the good news came that the awful tide had been turned back, that Paris and the world were safe; for awhile at all events.

Then for days we hoped for more news as good as this or better. Has Von Kluck been surrounded? Not to-day, but perhaps he will be surrounded to-morrow. But the days became weeks, the weeks drew out to months; the battle in the West seemed frozen. Now and again things were done that seemed hopeful, with promise of events still better. But Neuve Chapelle and Loos dwindled into disappointments as their tale was told fully; the lines in the West remained, for all practical purposes of victory, immobile. Nothing seemed to happen; there was nothing to read save the record of operations that were clearly trifling and insignificant. People speculated as to the reason of this inaction; the hopeful said that Joffre had a plan, that he was "nibbling," others declared that we were short of munitions, others again that the new levies were not yet ripe for battle. So the months went by, and almost two years of war had been completed before the motionless English line began to stir and quiver as if it awoke from a long sleep, and began to roll onward, overwhelming the enemy.

The secret of the long inaction of the British Armies has been well kept. On the one hand it was rigorously protected by the censorship, which severe, and sometimes severe to the point of absurdity--"the captains and the ... depart," for instance--became in this particular matter ferocious. As soon as the real significance of that which was happening, or beginning to happen, was perceived by the authorities, an underlined circular was issued to the newspaper proprietors of Great Britain and Ireland. It warned each proprietor that he might impart the contents of this circular to one other person only, such person being the responsible editor of his paper, who was to keep the communication secret under the severest penalties. The circular forbade any mention of certain events that had taken place, that might take place; it forbade any kind of allusion to these events or any hint of their existence, or of the possibility of their existence, not only in the Press, but in any form whatever. The subject was not to be alluded to in conversation, it was not to be hinted at, however obscurely, in letters; the very existence of the circular, its subject apart, was to be a dead secret.

These measures were successful. A wealthy newspaper proprietor of the North, warmed a little at the end of the Throwsters' Feast (which was held as usual, it will be remembered), ventured to say to the man next to him: "How awful it would be, wouldn't it, if...." His words were repeated, as proof, one regrets to say, that it was time for "old Arnold" to "pull himself together"; and he was fined a thousand pounds. Then, there was the case of an obscure weekly paper published in the county town of an agricultural district in Wales. The Meiros Observer (we will call it) was issued from a stationer's back premises, and filled its four pages with accounts of local flower shows, fancy fairs at vicarages, reports of parish councils, and rare bathing fatalities. It also issued a visitors' list, which has been known to contain six names.

This enlightened organ printed a paragraph, which nobody noticed, which was very like paragraphs that small country newspapers have long been in the habit of printing, which could hardly give so much as a hint to any one--to any one, that is, who was not fully instructed in the secret. As a matter of fact, this piece of intelligence got into the paper because the proprietor, who was also the editor, incautiously left the last processes of this particular issue to the staff, who was the Lord-High-Every-thing-Else of the establishment; and the staff put in a bit of gossip he had heard in the market to fill up two inches on the back page. But the result was that the Meiros Observer ceased to appear, owing to "untoward circumstances" as the proprietor said; and he would say no more. No more, that is, by way of explanation, but a great deal more by way of execration of "damned, prying busybodies."

***

Now a censorship that is sufficiently minute and utterly remorseless can do amazing things in the way of hiding ... what it wants to hide. Before the war, one would have thought otherwise; one would have said that, censor or no censor, the fact of the murder at X or the fact of the bank robbery at Y would certainly become known; if not through the Press, at all events through rumor and the passage of the news from mouth to mouth. And this would be true--of England three hundred years ago, and of savage tribelands of to-day. But we have grown of late to such a reverence for the printed word and such a reliance on it, that the old faculty of disseminating news by word of mouth has become atrophied. Forbid the Press to mention the fact that Jones has been murdered, and it is marvelous how few people will hear of it, and of those who hear how few will credit the story that they have heard. You meet a man in the train who remarks that he has been told something about a murder in Southwark; there is all the difference in the world between the impression you receive from such a chance communication and that given by half a dozen lines of print with name, and street and date and all the facts of the case. People in trains repeat all sorts of tales, many of them false; newspapers do not print accounts of murders that have not been committed.

Then another consideration that has made for secrecy. I may have seemed to say that the old office of rumor no longer exists; I shall be reminded of the strange legend of "the Russians" and the mythology of the "Angels of Mons." But let me point out, in the first place, that both these absurdities depended on the papers for their wide dissemination. If there had been no newspapers or magazines Russians and Angels would have made but a brief, vague appearance of the most shadowy kind--a few would have heard of them, fewer still would have believed in them, they would have been gossiped about for a bare week or two, and so they would have vanished away.

And, then, again, the very fact of these vain rumors and fantastic tales having been so widely believed for a time was fatal to the credit of any stray mutterings that may have got abroad. People had been taken in twice; they had seen how grave persons, men of credit, had preached and lectured about the shining forms that had saved the British Army at Mons, or had testified to the trains, packed with gray-coated Muscovites, rushing through the land at dead of night: and now there was a hint of something more amazing than either of the discredited legends. But this time there was no word of confirmation to be found in daily paper, or weekly review, or parish magazine, and so the few that heard either laughed, or, being serious, went home and jotted down notes for essays on "War-time Psychology: Collective Delusions."

***

I followed neither of these courses. For before the secret circular had been issued my curiosity had somehow been aroused by certain paragraphs concerning a "Fatal Accident to Well-known Airman." The propeller of the airplane had been shattered, apparently by a collision with a flight of pigeons; the blades had been broken and the machine had fallen like lead to the earth. And soon after I had seen this account, I heard of some very odd circumstances relating to an explosion in a great munition factory in the Midlands. I thought I saw the possibility of a connection between two very different events.

***

It has been pointed out to me by friends who have been good enough to read this record, that certain phrases I have used may give the impression that I ascribe all the delays of the war on the Western front to the extraordinary circumstances which occasioned the issue of the Secret Circular. Of course this is not the case, there were many reasons for the immobility of our lines from October 1914 to July 1916. These causes have been evident enough and have been openly discussed and deplored. But behind them was something of infinitely greater moment. We lacked men, but men were pouring into the new army; we were short of shells, but when the shortage was proclaimed the nation set itself to mend this matter with all its energy. We could undertake to supply the defects of our army both in men and munitions--if the new and incredible danger could be overcome. It has been overcome; rather, perhaps, it has ceased to exist; and the secret may now be told.

I have said my attention was attracted by an account of the death of a well-known airman. I have not the habit of preserving cuttings, I am sorry to say, so that I cannot be precise as to the date of this event. To the best of my belief it was either towards the end of May or the beginning of June 1915. The newspaper paragraph announcing the death of Flight-Lieutenant Western-Reynolds was brief enough; accidents, and fatal accidents, to the men who are storming the air for us are, unfortunately, by no means so rare as to demand an elaborated notice. But the manner in which Western-Reynolds met his death struck me as extraordinary, inasmuch as it revealed a new danger in the element that we have lately conquered. He was brought down, as I said, by a flight of birds; of pigeons, as appeared by what was found on the bloodstained and shattered blades of the propeller. An eye-witness of the accident, a fellow-officer, described how Western-Reynolds set out from the aerodrome on a fine afternoon, there being hardly any wind. He was going to France; he had made the journey to and fro half a dozen times or more, and felt perfectly secure and at ease.

"'Wester' rose to a great height at once, and we could scarcely see the machine. I was turning to go when one of the fellows called out, 'I say! What's this?' He pointed up, and we saw what looked like a black cloud coming from the south at a tremendous rate. I saw at once it wasn't a cloud; it came with a swirl and a rush quite different from any cloud I've ever seen. But for a second I couldn't make out exactly what it was. It altered its shape and turned into a great crescent, and wheeled and veered about as if it was looking for something. The man who had called out had got his glasses, and was staring for all he was worth. Then he shouted that it was a tremendous flight of birds, 'thousands of them.' They went on wheeling and beating about high up in the air, and we were watching them, thinking it was interesting, but not supposing that they would make any difference to 'Wester,' who was just about out of sight. His machine was just a speck. Then the two arms of the crescent drew in as quick as lightning, and these thousands of birds shot in a solid mass right up there across the sky, and flew away somewhere about nor'-nor'-by-west. Then Henley, the man with the glasses, called out, 'He's down!' and started running, and I went after him. We got a car and as we were going along Henley told me that he'd seen the machine drop dead, as if it came out of that cloud of birds. He thought then that they must have mucked up the propeller somehow. That turned out to be the case. We found the propeller blades all broken and covered with blood and pigeon feathers, and carcasses of the birds had got wedged in between the blades, and were sticking to them."

This was the story that the young airman told one evening in a small company. He did not speak "in confidence," so I have no hesitation in reproducing what he said. Naturally, I did not take a verbatim note of his conversation, but I have something of a knack of remembering talk that interests me, and I think my reproduction is very near to the tale that I heard. And let it be noted that the flying man told his story without any sense or indication of a sense that the incredible, or all but the incredible, had happened. So far as he knew, he said, it was the first accident of the kind. Airmen in France had been bothered once or twice by birds--he thought they were eagles--flying viciously at them, but poor old "Wester" had been the first man to come up against a flight of some thousands of pigeons.

"And perhaps I shall be the next," he added, "but why look for trouble? Anyhow, I'm going to see Toodle-oo to-morrow afternoon."

***

Well, I heard the story, as one hears all the varied marvels and terrors of the air; as one heard some years ago of "air pockets," strange gulfs or voids in the atmosphere into which airmen fell with great peril; or as one heard of the experience of the airman who flew over the Cumberland mountains in the burning summer of 1911, and as he swam far above the heights was suddenly and vehemently blown upwards, the hot air from the rocks striking his plane as if it had been a blast from a furnace chimney. We have just begun to navigate a strange region; we must expect to encounter strange adventures, strange perils. And here a new chapter in the chronicles of these perils and adventures had been opened by the death of Western-Reynolds; and no doubt invention and contrivance would presently hit on some way of countering the new danger.

It was, I think, about a week or ten days after the airman's death that my business called me to a northern town, the name of which, perhaps, had better remain unknown. My mission was to inquire into certain charges of extravagance which had been laid against the working people, that is, the munition workers of this especial town. It was said that the men who used to earn £2 10s. a week were now getting from seven to eight pounds, that "bits of girls" were being paid two pounds instead of seven or eight shillings, and that, in consequence, there was an orgy of foolish extravagance. The girls, I was told, were eating chocolates at four, five, and six shillings a pound, the women were ordering thirty-pound pianos which they couldn't play, and the men bought gold chains at ten and twenty guineas apiece.

I dived into the town in question and found, as usual, that there was a mixture of truth and exaggeration in the stories that I had heard. Gramophones, for example: they cannot be called in strictness necessaries, but they were undoubtedly finding a ready sale, even in the more expensive brands. And I thought that there were a great many very spick and span perambulators to be seen on the pavement; smart perambulators, painted in tender shades of color and expensively fitted.

"And how can you be surprised if people will have a bit of a fling?" a worker said to me. "We're seeing money for the first time in our lives, and it's bright. And we work hard for it, and we risk our lives to get it. You've heard of explosion yonder?"

He mentioned certain works on the outskirts of the town. Of course, neither the name of the works nor of the town had been printed; there had been a brief notice of "Explosion at Munition Works in the Northern District: Many Fatalities." The working man told me about it, and added some dreadful details.

"They wouldn't let their folks see bodies; screwed them up in coffins as they found them in shop. The gas had done it."

"Turned their faces black, you mean?"

"Nay. They were all as if they had been bitten to pieces."

This was a strange gas.

I asked the man in the northern town all sorts of questions about the extraordinary explosion of which he had spoken to me. But he had very little more to say. As I have noted already, secrets that may not be printed are often deeply kept; last summer there were very few people outside high official circles who knew anything about the "Tanks," of which we have all been talking lately, though these strange instruments of war were being exercised and tested in a park not far from London. So the man who told me of the explosion in the munition factory was most likely genuine in his profession that he knew nothing more of the disaster. I found out that he was a smelter employed at a furnace on the other side of the town to the ruined factory; he didn't know even what they had been making there; some very dangerous high explosive, he supposed. His information was really nothing more than a bit of gruesome gossip, which he had heard probably at third or fourth or fifth hand. The horrible detail of faces "as if they had been bitten to pieces" had made its violent impression on him, that was all.

I gave him up and took a tram to the district of the disaster; a sort of industrial suburb, five miles from the center of the town. When I asked for the factory, I was told that it was no good my going to it as there was nobody there. But I found it; a raw and hideous shed with a walled yard about it, and a shut gate. I looked for signs of destruction, but there was nothing. The roof was quite undamaged; and again it struck me that this had been a strange accident. There had been an explosion of sufficient violence to kill workpeople in the building, but the building itself showed no wounds or scars.

A man came out of the gate and locked it behind him. I began to ask him some sort of question, or rather, I began to "open" for a question with "A terrible business here, they tell me," or some such phrase of convention. I got no farther. The man asked me if I saw a policeman walking down the street. I said I did, and I was given the choice of getting about my business forthwith or of being instantly given in charge as a spy. "Th'ast better be gone and quick about it," was, I think, his final advice, and I took it.

Well, I had come literally up against a brick wall. Thinking the problem over, I could only suppose that the smelter or his informant had twisted the phrases of the story. The smelter had said the dead men's faces were "bitten to pieces"; this might be an unconscious perversion of "eaten away." That phrase might describe well enough the effect of strong acids, and, for all I knew of the processes of munition-making, such acids might be used and might explode with horrible results in some perilous stage of their admixture.

It was a day or two later that the accident to the airman, Western-Reynolds, came into my mind. For one of those instants which are far shorter than any measure of time there flashed out the possibility of a link between the two disasters. But here was a wild impossibility, and I drove it away. And yet I think that the thought, mad as it seemed, never left me; it was the secret light that at last guided me through a somber grove of enigmas.

***

It was about this time, so far as the date can be fixed, that a whole district, one might say a whole county, was visited by a series of extraordinary and terrible calamities, which were the more terrible inasmuch as they continued for some time to be inscrutable mysteries. It is, indeed, doubtful whether these awful events do not still remain mysteries to many of those concerned; for before the inhabitants of this part of the country had time to join one link of evidence to another the circular was issued, and thenceforth no one knew how to distinguish undoubted fact from wild and extravagant surmise.

The district in question is in the far west of Wales; I shall call it, for convenience, Meirion. In it there is one seaside town of some repute with holiday-makers for five or six weeks in the summer, and dotted about the county there are three or four small old towns that seem drooping in a slow decay, sleepy and gray with age and forgetfulness. They remind me of what I have read of towns in the west of Ireland. Grass grows between the uneven stones of the pavements, the signs above the shop windows decline, half the letters of these signs are missing, here and there a house has been pulled down, or has been allowed to slide into ruin, and wild greenery springs up through the fallen stones, and there is silence in all the streets. And, it is to be noted, these are not places that were once magnificent. The Celts have never had the art of building, and so far as I can see, such towns as Towy and Merthyr Tegveth and Meiros must have been always much as they are now, clusters of poorish, meanly-built houses, ill-kept and down at heel.

And these few towns are thinly scattered over a wild country where north is divided from south by a wilder mountain range. One of these places is sixteen miles from any station; the others are doubtfully and deviously connected by single-line railways served by rare trains that pause and stagger and hesitate on their slow journey up mountain passes, or stop for half an hour or more at lonely sheds called stations, situated in the midst of desolate marshes. A few years ago I traveled with an Irishman on one of these queer lines, and he looked to right and saw the bog with its yellow and blue grasses and stagnant pools, and he looked to left and saw a ragged hillside, set with gray stone walls. "I can hardly believe," he said, "that I'm not still in the wilds of Ireland."

Here, then, one sees a wild and divided and scattered region a land of outland hills and secret and hidden valleys. I know white farms on this coast which must be separate by two hours of hard, rough walking from any other habitation, which are invisible from any other house. And inland, again, the farms are often ringed about by thick groves of ash, planted by men of old days to shelter their roof-trees from rude winds of the mountain and stormy winds of the sea; so that these places, too, are hidden away, to be surmised only by the wood smoke that rises from the green surrounding leaves. A Londoner must see them to believe in them; and even then he can scarcely credit their utter isolation.

Such, then in the main is Meirion, and on this land in the early summer of last year terror descended--a terror without shape, such as no man there had ever known.

It began with the tale of a little child who wandered out into the lanes to pick flowers one sunny afternoon, and never came back to the cottage on the hill.

CHAPTER II - Death in the Village

The child who was lost came from a lonely cottage that stands on the slope of a steep hillside called the Allt, or the height. The land about it is wild and ragged; here the growth of gorse and bracken, here a marshy hollow of reeds and rushes, marking the course of the stream from some hidden well, here thickets of dense and tangled undergrowth, the outposts of the wood. Down through this broken and uneven ground a path leads to the lane at the bottom of the valley; then the land rises again and swells up to the cliffs over the sea, about a quarter of a mile away. The little girl, Gertrude Morgan, asked her mother if she might go down to the lane and pick the purple flowers--that grew there, and her mother gave her leave, telling her she must be sure to be back by tea-time, as there was apple-tart for tea.

She never came back. It was supposed that she must have crossed the road and gone to the cliff's edge, possibly in order to pick the sea-pinks that were then in full blossom. She must have slipped, they said, and fallen into the sea, two hundred feet below. And, it may be said at once, that there was no doubt some truth in this conjecture, though it stopped very far short of the whole truth. The child's body must have been carried out by the tide, for it was never found.

The conjecture of a false step or of a fatal slide on the slippery turf that slopes down to the rocks was accepted as being the only explanation possible. People thought the accident a strange one because, as a rule, country children living by the cliffs and the sea become wary at an early age, and Gertrude Morgan was almost ten years old. Still, as the neighbors said, "that's how it must have happened, and it's a great pity, to be sure." But this would not do when in a week's time a strong young laborer failed to come to his cottage after the day's work. His body was found on the rocks six or seven miles from the cliffs where the child was supposed to have fallen; he was going home by a path that he had used every night of his life for eight or nine years, that he used of dark nights in perfect security, knowing every inch of it. The police asked if he drank, but he was a teetotaler; if he were subject to fits, but he wasn't. And he was not murdered for his wealth, since agricultural laborers are not wealthy. It was only possible again to talk of slippery turf and a false step; but people began to be frightened. Then a woman was found with her neck broken at the bottom of a disused quarry near Llanfihangel, in the middle of the county. The "false step" theory was eliminated here, for the quarry was guarded with a natural hedge of gorse bushes. One would have to struggle and fight through sharp thorns to destruction in such a place as this; and indeed the gorse bushes were broken as if some one had rushed furiously through them, just above the place where the woman's body was found. And this was strange: there was a dead sheep lying beside her in the pit, as if the woman and the sheep together had been chased over the brim of the quarry. But chased by whom, or by what? And then there was a new form of terror.

This was in the region of the marshes under the mountain. A man and his son, a lad of fourteen or fifteen, set out early one morning to work and never reached the farm where they were bound. Their way skirted the marsh, but it was broad, firm and well metalled, and it had been raised about two feet above the bog. But when search was made in the evening of the same day Phillips and his son were found dead in the marsh, covered with black slime and pondweed. And they lay some ten yards from the path, which, it would seem, they must have left deliberately. It was useless of course, to look for tracks in the black ooze, for if one threw a big stone into it a few seconds removed all marks of the disturbance. The men who found the two bodies beat about the verges and purlieus of the marsh in hope of finding some trace of the murderers; they went to and fro over the rising ground where the black cattle were grazing, they searched the alder thickets by the brook; but they discovered nothing.

***

Most horrible of all these horrors, perhaps, was the affair of the Highway, a lonely and unfrequented by-road that winds for many miles on high and lonely land. Here, a mile from any other dwelling, stands a cottage on the edge of a dark wood. It was inhabited by a laborer named Williams, his wife, and their three children. One hot summer's evening, a man who had been doing a day's gardening at a rectory three or four miles away, passed the cottage, and stopped for a few minutes to chat with Williams, the laborer, who was pottering about his garden, while the children were playing on the path by the door. The two talked of their neighbors and of the potatoes till Mrs. Williams appeared at the doorway and said supper was ready, and Williams turned to go into the house. This was about eight o'clock, and in the ordinary course the family would have their supper and be in bed by nine, or by half-past nine at latest. At ten o'clock that night the local doctor was driving home along the Highway. His horse shied violently and then stopped dead just opposite the gate to the cottage. The doctor got down, frightened at what he saw; and there on the roadway lay Williams, his wife, and the three children, stone dead, all of them. Their skulls were battered in as if by some heavy iron instrument; their faces were beaten into a pulp.

CHAPTER III - The Doctors Theory

It is not easy to make any picture of the horror that lay dark on the hearts of the people of Meirion. It was no longer possible to believe or to pretend to believe that these men and women and children had met their deaths through strange accidents. The little girl and the young laborer might have slipped and fallen over the cliffs, but the woman who lay dead with the dead sheep at the bottom of the quarry, the two men who had been lured into the ooze of the marsh, the family who were found murdered on the Highway before their own cottage door; in these cases there could be no room for the supposition of accident. It seemed as if it were impossible to frame any conjecture or outline of a conjecture that would account for these hideous and, as it seemed, utterly purposeless crimes. For a time people said that there must be a madman at large, a sort of country variant of Jack the Ripper, some horrible pervert who was possessed by the passion of death, who prowled darkling about that lonely land, hiding in woods and in wild places, always watching and seeking for the victims of his desire.

Indeed, Dr. Lewis, who found poor Williams, his wife and children miserably slaughtered on the Highway, was convinced at first that the presence of a concealed madman in the countryside offered the only possible solution to the difficulty.

"I felt sure," he said to me afterwards, "that the Williams's had been killed by a homicidal maniac. It was the nature of the poor creatures' injuries that convinced me that this was the case. Some years ago thirty-seven or thirty-eight years ago as a matter of fact--I had something to do with a case which on the face of it had a strong likeness to the Highway murder. At that time I had a practice at Usk, in Monmouthshire. A whole family living in a cottage by the roadside were murdered one evening; it was called, I think, the Llangibby murder; the cottage was near the village of that name. The murderer was caught in Newport; he was a Spanish sailor, named Garcia, and it

11

appeared that he had killed father, mother, and the three children for the sake of the brass works of an old Dutch clock, which were found on him when he was arrested.

"Garcia had been serving a month's imprisonment in Usk Jail for some small theft, and on his release he set out to walk to Newport, nine or ten miles away; no doubt to get another ship. He passed the cottage and saw the man working in his garden. Garcia stabbed him with his sailor's knife. The wife rushed out; he stabbed her. Then he went into the cottage and stabbed the three children, tried to set the place on fire, and made off with the clockworks. That looked like the deed of a madman, but Garcia wasn't mad--they hanged him, I may say--he was merely a man of a very low type, a degenerate who hadn't the slightest value for human life. I am not sure, but I think he came from one of the Spanish islands, where the people are said to be degenerates, very likely from too much inter-breeding.

"But my point is that Garcia stabbed to kill and did kill, with one blow in each case. There was no senseless hacking and slashing. Now those poor people on the Highway had their heads smashed to pieces by what must have been a storm of blows. Any one of them would have been fatal, but the murderer must have gone on raining blows with his iron hammer on people who were already stone dead. And that sort of thing is the work of a madman, and nothing but a madman. That's how I argued the matter out to myself just after the event.

"I was utterly wrong, monstrously wrong. But who could have suspected the truth?"

Thus Dr. Lewis, and I quote him, or the substance of him, as representative of most of the educated opinion of the district at the beginnings of the terror. People seized on this theory largely because it offered at least the comfort of an explanation, and any explanation, even the poorest, is better than an intolerable and terrible mystery. Besides, Dr. Lewis's theory was plausible; it explained the lack of purpose that seemed to characterize the murders. And yet--there were difficulties even from the first. It was hardly possible that a strange madman should be able to keep hidden in a countryside where any stranger is instantly noted and noticed; sooner or later he would be seen as he prowled along the lanes or across the wild places. Indeed, a drunken, cheerful, and altogether harmless tramp was arrested by a farmer and his man in the fact and act of sleeping off beer under a hedge; but the vagrant was able to prove complete and undoubted alibis, and was soon allowed to go on his wandering way.

Then another theory, or rather a variant of Dr. Lewis's theory, was started. This was to the effect that the person responsible for the outrages was, indeed, a madman; but a madman only at intervals. It was one of the members of the Porth Club, a certain Mr. Remnant, who was supposed to have originated this more subtle explanation. Mr. Remnant was a middle-aged man, who, having nothing particular to do, read a great many books by way of conquering the hours. He talked to the club--doctors, retired colonels, parsons, lawyers--about "personality," quoted various psychological textbooks in support of his contention that personality was sometimes fluid and unstable, went back to "Dr. Jekyll and Mr. Hyde" as good evidence of this proposition, and laid stress on Dr. Jekyll's speculation that the human soul, so far from being one and indivisible, might, possibly turn out to be a mere polity, a state in which dwelt many strange and incongruous citizens, whose characters were not merely unknown but altogether unsurmised by that form of consciousness which so rashly assumed that it was not only the president of the republic but also its sole citizen.

"The long and the short of it is," Mr. Remnant concluded, "that any one of us may be the murderer, though he hasn't the faintest notion of the fact. Take Llewelyn there."

Mr. Payne Llewelyn was an elderly lawyer, a rural Tulkinghorn. He was the hereditary solicitor to the Morgans of Pentwyn. This does not sound anything tremendous to the Saxons of London; but the style is far more than noble to the Celts of West Wales; it is immemorial; Teilo Sant was of the collaterals of the first known chief of the race. And Mr. Payne Llewelyn did his best to look like the legal adviser of this ancient house. He was weighty, he was cautious, he was sound, he was secure. I have compared him to Mr. Tulkinghorn of Lincoln's Inn Fields; but Mr. Llewelyn would most certainly never have dreamed of employing his leisure in peering into the cupboards where the family skeletons were hidden. Supposing such cupboards to have existed, Mr. Payne Llewelyn would have risked large out-of-pocket expenses to furnish them with double, triple, impregnable locks. He was a new man, an advena, certainly; for he was partly of the Conquest, being descended on one side from Sir Payne Turberville; but he meant to stand by the old stock.

"Take Llewelyn now," said Mr. Remnant. "Look here, Llewelyn, can you produce evidence to show where you were on the night those people were murdered on the Highway? I thought not."

Mr. Llewelyn, an elderly man, as I have said, hesitated before speaking.

"I thought not," Remnant went on. "Now I say that it is perfectly possible that Llewelyn may be dealing death throughout Meirion, although in his present personality he may not have the faintest suspicion that there is another Llewelyn within him, a Llewelyn who follows murder as a fine art."

***

Mr. Payne Llewelyn did not at all relish Mr. Remnant's suggestion that he might well be a secret murderer, ravening for blood, remorseless as a wild beast. He thought the phrase about his following murder as a fine art was both nonsensical and in the worst taste, and his opinion was not changed when Remnant pointed out that it was used by De Quincey in the title of one of his most famous essays.

"If you had allowed me to speak," he said with some coldness of manner, "I would have told you that on Tuesday last, the night on which those unfortunate people were murdered on the Highway I was staying at the Angel Hotel, Cardiff. I had business in Cardiff, and I was detained till Wednesday afternoon."

Having given this satisfactory alibi, Mr. Payne Llewelyn left the club, and did not go near it for the rest of the week.

Remnant explained to those who stayed in the smoking room that, of course, he had merely used Mr. Llewelyn as a concrete example of his theory, which, he persisted, had the support of a considerable body of evidence.

"There are several cases of double personality on record," he declared. "And I say again that it is quite possible that these murders may have been committed by one of us in his secondary personality. Why, I may be the murderer in my Remnant B. state, though Remnant A. knows nothing whatever about it, and is perfectly convinced that he could not kill a fowl, much less a whole family. Isn't it so, Lewis?"

Dr. Lewis said it was so, in theory, but he thought not in fact.

"Most of the cases of double or multiple personality that have been investigated," he said, "have been in connection with the very dubious experiments of hypnotism, or the still more dubious experiments of spiritualism. All that sort of thing, in my opinion, is like tinkering with the works of a clock--amateur tinkering, I mean. You fumble about with the wheels and cogs and bits of mechanism that you don't really know anything about; and then you find your clock going backwards or striking 240 at tea-time. And I believe it's just the same thing with these psychical research experiments; the secondary personality is very likely the result of the tinkering and fumbling with a very delicate apparatus that we know nothing about. Mind, I can't say that it's impossible for one of us to be the Highway murderer in his B. state, as Remnant puts it. But I think it's extremely improbable. Probability is the guide of life, you know, Remnant," said Dr. Lewis, smiling at that gentleman, as if to say that he also had done a little reading in his day. "And it follows" therefore, that improbability is also the guide of life. When you get a very high degree of probability, that is, you are justified in taking it as a certainty; and on the other hand, if a supposition is highly improbable, you are justified in treating it as an impossible one. That is, in nine hundred and ninety-nine cases out of a thousand."

"How about the thousandth case?" said Remnant. "Supposing these extraordinary crimes constitute the thousandth case?"

The doctor smiled and shrugged his shoulders, being tired of the subject. But for some little time highly respectable members of Porth society would look suspiciously at one another wondering whether, after all, there mightn't be "something in it." However, both Mr. Remnant's somewhat crazy theory and Dr. Lewis's plausible theory became untenable when two more victims of an awful and mysterious death were offered up in, sacrifice, for a man was found dead in the Llanfihangel quarry, where the woman had been discovered. And on the same day a girl of fifteen was found broken on the jagged rocks under the cliffs near Porth. Now, it appeared that these two deaths must have occurred at about the same time, within an hour of one another, certainly; and the distance between the quarry and the cliffs by Black Rock is certainly twenty miles.

"A motor could do it," one man said.

But it was pointed out that there was no high road between the two places; indeed, it might be said that there was no road at all between them. There was a network of deep, narrow, and tortuous lands that wandered into one another at all manner of queer angles for, say, seventeen miles; this in the middle, as it were, between Black Rock and the quarry at Llanfihangel. But to get to the high land of the cliffs one had to take a path that went through two miles of fields; and the quarry lay a mile away from the nearest by-road in the midst of gorse and bracken and broken land. And, finally, there was no track of motor-car or motor-bicycle in the lanes which must have been followed to pass from one place to the other.

"What about an airplane, then?" said the man of the motor-car theory. Well, there was certainly an aerodrome not far from one of the two places of death; but somehow, nobody believed that the Flying Corps harbored a homicidal maniac. It seemed clear, therefore, that there must be more than one person concerned in the terror of Meirion. And Dr. Lewis himself abandoned his own theory.

"As I said to Remnant at the Club," he remarked, "improbability is the guide of life. I can't believe that there are a pack of madmen or even two madmen at large in the country. I give it up."

And now a fresh circumstance or set of circumstances became manifest to confound judgment and to awaken new and wild surmises. For at about this time people realized that none of the dreadful events that were happening all about them was so much as mentioned in the Press. I have already spoken of the fate of the Meiros Observer. This paper was suppressed by the authorities because it had inserted a brief paragraph about some person who had been "found dead under mysterious circumstances"; I think that paragraph referred to the first death of Llanfihangel quarry. Thenceforth, horror followed on horror, but no word was printed in any of the local journals. The curious went to the newspaper offices--there were two left in the county--but found nothing save a firm refusal to discuss the matter. And the Cardiff papers were drawn and found blank; and the London Press was apparently ignorant of the fact that crimes that had no parallel were terrorizing a whole countryside. Everybody wondered what could have happened, what was happening; and then it was whispered that the coroner would allow no inquiry to be made as to these deaths of darkness.

"In consequence of instructions received from the Home Office," one coroner was understood to have said, "I have to tell the jury that their business will be to hear the medical evidence and to bring in a verdict immediately in accordance with that evidence. I shall disallow all questions."

One jury protested. The foreman refused to bring in any verdict at all.

"Very good," said the coroner. "Then I beg to inform you, Mr. Foreman and gentlemen of the jury, that under the Defense of the Realm Act, I have power to supersede your functions, and to enter a verdict according to the evidence which has been laid before the Court as if it had been the verdict of you all."

The foreman and jury collapsed and accepted what they could not avoid. But the rumors that got abroad of all this, added to the known fact that the terror was ignored in the Press, no doubt by official command, increased the panic that was now; arising, and gave it a new direction. Clearly, people reasoned, these Government restrictions and prohibitions could only refer to the war, to some great danger in connection with the war. And that being so, it followed that the outrages which must be kept so secret were the work of the enemy, that is of concealed German agents.

CHAPTER IV - The Spread of the Terror

It is time, I think, for me to make one point clear. I began this history with certain references to an extraordinary accident to an airman whose machine fell to the ground after collision with a huge flock of pigeons; and then to an explosion in a northern munition factory, an explosion, as I noted, of a very singular kind. Then I deserted the neighborhood of London, and the northern district, and dwelt on a mysterious and terrible series of events which occurred in the summer of 1915 in a Welsh county, which I have named, for convenience, Meirion.

Well, let it be understood at once that all this detail that I have given about the occurrences in Meirion does not imply that the county in the far west was alone or especially afflicted by the terror that was over the land. They tell me that in the villages about Dartmoor the stout Devonshire hearts sank as men's hearts used to sink in the time of plague and pestilence. There was horror, too, about the Norfolk Broads, and far up by Perth no one would venture on the path that leads by Scone to the wooded heights above the Tay. And in the industrial districts: I met a man by chance one day in an odd London corner who spoke with horror of what a friend had told him.

"'Ask no questions, Ned,' he says to me, 'but I tell yow a' was in Bairnigan t'other day, and a' met a pal who'd seen three hundred coffins going out of a works not far from there.'"

And then the ship that hovered outside the mouth of the Thames with all sails set and beat to and fro in the wind, and never answered any hail, and showed no light! The forts shot at her and brought down one of the masts, but she went suddenly about with a change of wind under what sail still stood, and then veered down Channel, and drove ashore at last on the sandbanks and pinewoods of Arcachon, and not a man alive on her, but only rattling heaps of bones! That last voyage of the Semiramis would be something horribly worth telling; but I only heard it at a distance as a yarn, and only believed it because it squared with other things that I knew for certain.

This, then, is my point; I have written of the terror as it fell on Meirion, simply because I have had opportunities of getting close there to what really happened. Third or fourth or fifth hand in the other places; but round about Porth and Merthyr Tegveth I have spoken with people who have seen the tracks of the terror with their own eyes.

Well, I have said that the people of that far western county realized, not only that death was abroad in their quiet lanes and on their peaceful hills, but that for some reason it was to be kept all secret. Newspapers might not print any news of it, the very juries summoned to investigate it were allowed to investigate nothing. And so they concluded that this veil of secrecy must somehow be connected with the war; and from this position it was not a long way to a further inference: that the murderers of innocent men and women and children were either Germans or agents of Germany. It would be just like the Huns, everybody agreed, to think out such a devilish scheme as this; and they always thought out their schemes beforehand. They hoped to seize Paris in a few weeks, but when they were beaten on the Marne they had their trenches on the Aisne ready to fall back on: it had all been prepared years before the war. And so, no doubt, they had devised this terrible plan against England in case they could not beat us in open fight: there were people ready, very likely, all over the country, who were prepared to murder and destroy everywhere as soon as they got the word. In this way the Germans intended to sow terror throughout England and fill our hearts with panic and dismay, hoping so to weaken their enemy at home that he would lose all heart over the war abroad. It was the Zeppelin notion, in another form; they were committing these horrible and mysterious outrages thinking that we should be frightened out of our wits.

It all seemed plausible enough; Germany had by this time perpetrated so many horrors and had so excelled in devilish ingenuities that no abomination seemed too abominable to be probable, or too ingeniously wicked to be beyond the tortuous malice of the Hun. But then came the questions as to who the agents of this terrible design were, as to where they lived, as to how they contrived to move unseen from field to field, from lane to lane. All sorts of fantastic attempts were made to answer these questions; but it was felt that they remained unanswered. Some suggested that the murderers landed from submarines, or flew from hiding places on the West Coast of Ireland, coming and going by night; but there were seen to be flagrant impossibilities in both these suggestions. Everybody agreed that the evil work was no doubt the work of Germany; but nobody could begin to guess how it was done. Somebody at the Club asked Remnant for his theory.

"My theory," said that ingenious person, "is that human progress is simply a long march from one inconceivable to another. Look at that airship of ours that came over Porth yesterday: ten years ago that would have been an inconceivable sight. Take the steam engine, stake printing, take the theory of gravitation: they were all inconceivable till somebody thought of them. So it is, no doubt, with this infernal dodgery that we're talking about: the Huns have found it out, and we haven't; and there you are. We can't conceive how these poor people have been murdered, because the method's inconceivable to us."

The club listened with some awe to this high argument. After Remnant had gone, one member said:

"Wonderful man, that." "Yes," said Dr. Lewis. "He was asked whether he knew something. And his reply really amounted to 'No, I don't,' But I have never heard it better put."

***

It was, I suppose, at about this time when the people were puzzling their heads as to the secret methods used by the Germans or their agents to accomplish their crimes that a very singular circumstance became known to a few of the Porth people. It related to the murder of the Williams family on the Highway in front of their cottage door. I do not know that I have made it plain that the old Roman road called the Highway follows the course of a long, steep hill that goes steadily westward till it slants down and droops towards the sea. On either side of the road the ground falls away, here into deep shadowy woods, here to high pastures, now and again into a field of corn, but for the most part into the wild and broken land that is characteristic of Arfon. The fields are long and narrow, stretching up the steep hillside; they fall into sudden dips and hollows, a well springs up in the midst of one and a grove of ash and thorn bends over it, shading it; and beneath it the ground is thick with reeds and rushes. And then may come on either side of such a field territories glistening with the deep growth of bracken, and rough with gorse and rugged with thickets of blackthorn, green lichen hanging strangely from the branches; such are the lands on either side of the Highway.

Now on the lower slopes of it, beneath the Williams's cottage, some three or four fields down the hill, there is a military camp. The place has been used as a camp for many years, and lately the site has been extended and huts have been erected. But a considerable number of the men were under canvas here in the summer of 1915.

On the night of the Highway murder this camp, as it appeared afterwards, was the scene of the extraordinary panic of the horses.

***

A good many men in the camp were asleep in their tents soon after 9:30, when the Last Post was sounded. They woke up in panic. There was a thundering sound on the steep hillside above them, and down upon the tents came half a dozen horses, mad with fright, trampling the canvas, trampling the men, bruising dozens of them and killing two.

Everything was in wild confusion, men groaning and screaming in the darkness, struggling with the canvas and the twisted ropes, shouting out, some of them, raw lads enough, that the Germans had landed, others wiping the blood from their eyes, a few, roused suddenly from heavy sleep, hitting out at one another, officers coming up at the double roaring out orders to the sergeants, a party of soldiers who were just returning to camp from the village seized with fright at what they could scarcely see or distinguish, at the wildness of the shouting and cursing and groaning that they could not understand, bolting out of the camp again and racing for their lives back to the village: everything in the maddest confusion of wild disorder.

Some of the men had seen the horses galloping down the hill as if terror itself was driving them. They scattered off into the darkness, and somehow or another found their way back in the night to their pasture above the camp. They were grazing there peacefully in the morning, and the only sign of the panic of the night before was the mud they had scattered all over themselves as they pelted through a patch of wet ground. The farmer said they were as quiet a lot as any in Meirion; he could make nothing of it.

"Indeed," he said, "I believe they must have seen the devil himself to be in such a fright as that: save the people!"

Now all this was kept as quiet as might be at the time when it happened; it became known to the men of the Porth Club in the days when they were discussing the difficult question of the German outrages, as the murders were commonly called. And this wild stampede of the farm horses was held by some to be evidence of the extraordinary and unheard of character of the dreadful agency that was at work. One of the members of the club had been told by an officer who was in the camp at the time of the panic that the horses that came charging down were in a perfect fury of fright, that he had never seen horses in such a state, and so there was endless speculation as to the nature of the sight or the sound that had driven half a dozen quiet beasts into raging madness.

Then, in the middle of this talk, two or three other incidents, quite as odd and incomprehensible, came to be known, borne on chance trickles of gossip that came into the towns from outland farms, or were carried by cottagers tramping into Porth on market day with a fowl or two and eggs and garden stuff; scraps and fragments of talk gathered by servants from the country folk and repeated--to their mistresses. And in such ways it came out that up at Plas Newydd there had been a terrible business over swarming the bees; they had turned as wild as wasps and much more savage. They had come about the people who were taking the swarms like a cloud. They settled on one man's face so that you could not see the flesh for the bees crawling all over it, and they had stung him so badly that the doctor did not know whether he would get over it, and they had chased a girl who had come out to see the swarming, and settled on her and stung her to death. Then they had gone off to a brake below the farm and got into a hollow tree there, and it was not safe to go near it, for they would come out at you by day or by night.

And much the same thing had happened, it seemed, at three or four farms and cottages where bees were kept. And there were stories, hardly so clear or so credible, of sheep dogs, mild and trusted beasts, turning as savage as wolves and injuring the farm boys in a horrible manner--in one case it was said with fatal results. It was certainly true that old Mrs. Owen's favorite Brahma-Dorking cock had gone mad; she came into Porth one Saturday morning with her face and her neck all bound up and plastered. She had gone out to her bit of a field to feed the poultry the night before, and the bird had flown at her and attacked her most savagely, inflicting some very nasty wounds before she could beat it off.

"There was a stake handy, lucky for me," she said, "and I did beat him and beat him till the life was out of him. But what is come to the world, whatever?"

***

Now Remnant, the man of theories, was also a man of extreme leisure. It was understood that he had succeeded to ample means when he was quite a young man, and after tasting the savors of the law, as it were, for half a dozen terms at the board of the Middle Temple, he had decided that it would be senseless to bother himself with passing examinations for a profession which he had not the faintest intention of practising. So he turned a deaf ear to the call of "Manger" ringing through the Temple Courts, and set himself out to potter amiably through the world. He had pottered all over Europe, he had looked at Africa, and had even put his head in at the door of the East, on a trip which included the Greek isles and Constantinople. Now getting into the middle fifties, he had settled at Porth for the sake, as he said, of the Gulf Stream and the fuchsia hedges, and pottered over his books and his theories and the local gossip. He was no more brutal than the general public, which revels in the details of mysterious crime; but it must be said that the terror, black though it was, was a boon to him. He peered and investigated and poked about with the relish of a man to whose life a new zest has been added. He listened attentively to the strange tales of bees and dogs and poultry that came into Porth with the country baskets of butter, rabbits, and green peas; and he evolved at last a most extraordinary theory.

Full of this discovery, as he thought it, he went one night to see Dr. Lewis and take his view of the matter.

"I want to talk to you," said Remnant to the doctor, "about what I have called provisionally, the Z Ray."

CHAPTER V - The Incident of the Unknown Tree

Dr. Lewis, smiling indulgently, and quite prepared for some monstrous piece of theorizing, led Remnant into the room that overlooked the terraced garden and the sea.

The doctor's house, though it was only a ten minutes' walk from the center of the town, seemed remote from all other habitations. The drive to it from the road came through a deep grove of trees and a dense shrubbery, trees were about the house on either side, mingling with neighboring groves, and below, the garden fell down, terrace by green terrace, to wild growth, a twisted path amongst red rocks, and at last to the yellow sand of a little cove. The room to which the doctor took Remnant looked over these terraces and across the water to the dim boundaries of the bay. It had French windows that were thrown wide open, and the two men sat in the soft light of the lamp--this was before the days of severe lighting regulations in the Far West--and enjoyed the sweet odors and the sweet vision of the summer evening. Then Remnant began:

"I suppose, Lewis, you've heard these extraordinary stories of bees and dogs and things that have been going about lately?"

"Certainly I have heard them. I was called in at Plas Newydd, and treated Thomas Trevor, who's only just out of danger, by the way. I certified for the poor child, Mary Trevor. She was dying when I got to the place. There was no doubt she was stung to death by bees, and I believe there were other very similar cases at Llantarnam and Morwen; none fatal, I think. What about them?"

"Well: then there are the stories of good-tempered old sheepdogs turning wicked and 'savaging' children?"

"Quite so. I haven't seen any of these cases professionally; but I believe the stories are accurate enough."

"And the old woman assaulted by her own poultry?"

"That's perfectly true. Her daughter put some stuff of their own concoction on her face and neck, and then she came to me. The wounds seemed going all right, so I told her to continue the treatment, whatever it might be."

"Very good," said Mr. Remnant. He spoke now with an italic impressiveness. "Don't you see the link between all this and the horrible things that have been happening about here for the last month?"

Lewis stared at Remnant in amazement. He lifted his red eyebrows and lowered them in a kind of scowl. His speech showed traces of his native accent.

"Great burning!" he exclaimed. "What on earth are you getting at now? It is madness. Do you mean to tell me that you think there is some connection between a swarm or two of bees that have turned nasty, a cross dog, and a wicked old barn-door cock and these poor people that have been pitched over the cliffs and hammered to death on the road? There's no sense in it, you know."

"I am strongly inclined to believe that there is a great deal of sense in it," replied Remnant, with extreme calmness. "Look here, Lewis, I saw you grinning the other day at the club when I was telling the fellows that in my opinion all these outrages had been committed, certainly by the Germans, but by some method of which we have no conception. But what I meant to say when I talked about inconceivables was just this: that the Williams's and the rest of them have been killed in some way that's not in theory at all, not in our theory, at all events, some way we've not contemplated, not thought of for an instant. Do you see my point?"

"Well, in a sort of way. You mean there's an absolute originality in the method? I suppose that is so. But what next?"

Remnant seemed to hesitate, partly from a sense of the portentous nature of what he was about to say, partly from a sort of half-unwillingness to part with so profound a secret.

"Well," he said, "you will allow that we have two sets of phenomena of a very extraordinary kind occurring at the same time. Don't you think that it's only reasonable to connect the two sets with one another."

"So the philosopher of Tenterden steeple and the Goodwin Sands thought, certainly," said Lewis. "But what is the connection? Those poor folks on the Highway weren't stung by bees or worried by a dog. And horses don't throw people over cliffs or stifle them in marshes."

"No; I never meant to suggest anything so absurd. It is evident to me that in all these cases of animals turning suddenly savage the cause has been terror, panic, fear. The horses that went charging into the camp were mad with fright, we know. And I say that in the other instances we have been discussing the cause was the same. The creatures were exposed to an infection of fear, and a frightened beast or bird or insect uses its weapons, whatever they may be. If, for example, there had been anybody with those horses when they took their panic they would have lashed out at him with their heels."

"Yes, I dare say that that is so. Well."

"Well; my belief is that the Germans have made an extraordinary discovery. I have called it the Z Ray. You know that the ether is merely an hypothesis; we have to suppose that it's there to account for the passage of the Marconi current from one place to another. Now, suppose that there is a psychic ether as well as a material ether, suppose that it is possible to direct irresistible impulses across this medium, suppose that these impulses are towards murder or suicide; then I think that you have an explanation of the terrible series of events that have been happening in Meirion for the last few weeks. And it is quite clear to my mind that the horses and the other creatures have been exposed to this Z Ray, and that it has produced on them the effect of terror, with ferocity as the result of terror. Now what do you say to that? Telepathy, you know, is well established; so is hypnotic suggestion. You have only to look in the Encyclopædia Britannica' to see that, and suggestion is so strong in some cases as to be an irresistible imperative. Now don't you feel that putting telepathy and suggestion together, as it were, you have more than the elements of what I call the Z Ray? I feel myself that I have more to go on in making my hypothesis than the inventor of the steam engine had in making his hypothesis when he saw the lid of the kettle bobbing up and down. What do you say?"

Dr. Lewis made no answer. He was watching the growth of a new, unknown tree in his garden.

***

The doctor made no answer to Remnant's question. For one thing, Remnant was profuse in his eloquence--he has been rigidly condensed in this history--and Lewis was tired of the sound of his voice. For another thing, he found the Z Ray theory almost too extravagant to be bearable, wild enough to tear patience to tatters. And then as the tedious argument continued Lewis became conscious that there was something strange about the night.

It was a dark summer night. The moon was old and faint, above the Dragon's Head across the bay, and the air was very still. It was so still that Lewis had noted that not a leaf stirred on the very tip of a high tree that stood out against the sky; and yet he knew that he was listening to some sound that he could not determine or define. It was not the wind in the leaves, it was not the gentle wash of the water of the sea against the rocks; that latter sound he could distinguish quite easily. But there was something else. It was scarcely a sound; it was as if the air itself trembled and fluttered, as the air trembles in a church when they open the great pedal pipes of the organ.

The doctor listened intently. It was not an illusion, the sound was not in his own head, as he had suspected for a moment; but for the life of him he could not make out whence it came or what it was. He gazed down into the night over the terraces of his garden, now sweet with the scent of the flowers of the night; tried to peer over the tree-tops across the sea towards the Dragon's Head. It struck him suddenly that this strange fluttering vibration of the air might be the noise of a distant aeroplane or airship; there was not the usual droning hum, but this sound might be caused by a new type of engine. A new type of engine? Possibly it was an enemy airship; their range, it had been said, was getting longer; and Lewis was just going to call Remnant's attention to the sound, to its possible cause, and to the possible danger that might be hovering over them, when he saw something that caught his breath and his heart with wild amazement and a touch of terror.

He had been staring upward into the sky, and, about to speak to Remnant, he had let his eyes drop for an instant. He looked down towards the trees in the garden, and saw with utter astonishment that one had changed its shape in the few hours that had passed since the setting of the sun. There was a thick grove of ilexes bordering the lowest terrace, and above them rose one tall pine, spreading its head of sparse, dark branches dark against the sky.

As Lewis glanced down over the terraces he saw that the tall pine tree was no longer there. In its place there rose above the ilexes what might have been a greater ilex; there was the blackness of a dense growth of foliage rising like a broad and far-spreading and rounded cloud over the lesser trees.

Here, then was a sight wholly incredible, impossible. It is doubtful whether the process of the human mind in such a case has ever been analyzed and registered; it is doubtful whether it ever can be registered. It is hardly fair to bring in the mathematician, since he deals with absolute truth (so far as mortality can conceive absolute truth); but how would a mathematician feel if he were suddenly confronted with a two-sided triangle? I suppose he would instantly become a raging madman; and Lewis, staring wide-eyed and wild-eyed at a dark and spreading tree which his own experience informed him was not there, felt for an instant that shock which should affront us all when we first realize the intolerable antinomy of Achilles and the Tortoise. Common sense tells us that Achilles will flash past the tortoise almost with the speed of the lightning; the inflexible truth of mathematics assures us that till the earth boils and the heavens cease to endure the Tortoise must still be in advance; and thereupon we should, in common decency, go mad. We do not go mad, because, by special grace, we are certified that, in the final: court of appeal, all science is a lie, even the highest science of all; and so we simply grin at Achilles and the Tortoise, as we grin at Darwin, deride Huxley, and laugh at Herbert Spencer.

Dr. Lewis did not grin. He glared into the dimness of the night, at the great spreading tree that he knew could not be there. And as he gazed he saw that what at first appeared the dense blackness of foliage was fretted and starred with wonderful appearances of lights and colors.

Afterwards he said to me: "I remember thinking to myself: 'Look here, I am not delirious; my temperature is perfectly normal. I am not drunk; I only had a pint of Graves with my dinner, over three hours ago. I have not eaten any poisonous fungus; I have not taken Anhelonium Lewinii experimentally. So, now then! What is happening?'"

The night had gloomed over; clouds obscured the faint moon and the misty stars. Lewis rose, with some kind of warning and inhibiting gesture to Remnant, who, he was conscious was gaping at him in astonishment. He walked to the open French window, and took a pace forward on to the path outside, and looked, very intently, at the dark shape of the tree, down below the sloping garden, above the washing of the waves. He shaded the light of the lamp behind him by holding his hands on each side of his eyes.

The mass of the tree--the tree that couldn't be there--stood out against the sky, but not so clearly, now that the clouds had rolled up. Its edges, the limits of its leafage, were not so distinct. Lewis thought that he could detect some sort of quivering movement in it; though the air was at a dead calm. It was a night on which one might hold up a lighted match and watch it burn without any wavering or inclination of the flame.

"You know," said Lewis, "how a bit of burnt paper will sometimes hang over the coals before it goes up the chimney, and little worms of fire will shoot through it. It was like that, if you should be standing some distance away. Just threads and hairs of yellow light I saw, and specks and sparks of fire, and then a twinkling of a ruby no bigger than a pin point, and a green wandering in the black, as if an emerald were crawling, and then little veins of deep blue. 'Woe is me!' I said to myself in Welsh, 'What is all this color and burning?'

"And, then, at that very moment there came a thundering rap at the door of the room inside, and there was my man telling me that I was wanted directly up at the Garth, as old Mr. Trevor Williams had been taken very bad. I knew his heart was not worth much, so I had to go off directly, and leave Remnant to make what he could of it all."

CHAPTER VI - Mr. Remnant's Z Ray

Dr. Lewis was kept some time at the Garth. It was past twelve when he got back to his house.

He went quickly to the room that overlooked the garden and the sea and threw open the French window and peered into the darkness. There, dim indeed against the dim sky but unmistakable, was the tall pine with its sparse branches, high above the dense growth of the ilex trees. The strange boughs which had amazed him had vanished; there was no appearance now of colors or of fires.

He drew his chair up to the open window and sat there gazing and wondering far into the night, till brightness came upon the sea and sky, and the forms of the trees in the garden grew clear and evident. He went up to his bed at last filled with a great perplexity, still asking questions to which there was no answer.

The doctor did not say anything about the strange tree to Remnant. When they next met, Lewis said that he had thought there was a man hiding amongst the bushes--this in explanation of that warning gesture he had used, and of his going out into the garden and staring into the night. He concealed the truth because he dreaded the Remnant doctrine that would undoubtedly be produced; indeed, he hoped that he had heard the last of the theory of the Z Ray. But Remnant firmly reopened this subject.

"We were interrupted just as I was putting my case to you," he said. "And to sum it all up, it amounts to this: that the Huns have made one of the great leaps of science. They are sending 'suggestions' (which amount to irresistible commands) over here, and the persons affected are seized with suicidal or homicidal mania. The people who were killed by falling over the cliffs or into the quarry probably committed suicide; and so with the man and boy who were found in the bog. As to the Highway case, you remember that Thomas Evans said that he stopped and talked to Williams on the night of the murder. In my opinion Evans was the murderer. He came under the influence of the Ray, became a homicidal maniac in an instant, snatched Williams's spade from his hand and killed him and the others."

"The bodies were found by me on the road."

"It is possible that the first impact of the Ray produces violent nervous excitement, which would manifest itself externally. Williams might have called to his wife to come and see what was the matter with Evans. The children would naturally follow their mother. It seems to me simple. And as for the animals--the horses, dogs, and so forth, they as I say, were no doubt panic stricken by the Ray, and hence driven to frenzy."

"Why should Evans have murdered Williams instead of Williams murdering Evans? Why should the impact of the Ray affect one and not the other?"

"Why does one man react violently to a certain drug, while it makes no impression on another man? Why is A able to drink a bottle of whisky and remain sober, while B is turned into something very like a lunatic after he has drunk three glasses?"

"It is a question of idiosyncrasy," said the doctor.

"Is idiosyncrasy Greek for 'I don't know'?" asked Remnant.

"Not at all," said Lewis, smiling blandly. "I mean that in some diatheses whisky--as you have mentioned whisky--appears not to be pathogenic, or at all events not immediately pathogenic. In other cases, as you very justly observed, there seems to be a very marked cachexia associated with the exhibition of the spirit in question, even in comparatively small doses."

Under this cloud of professional verbiage Lewis escaped from the Club and from Remnant. He did not want to hear any more about that Dreadful Ray, because he felt sure that the Ray was all nonsense. But asking himself why he felt this certitude in the matter he had to confess that he didn't know. An aeroplane, he reflected, was all nonsense before it was made; and he remembered talking in the early nineties to a friend of his about the newly discovered X Rays. The friend laughed incredulously, evidently didn't believe a word of it, till Lewis told him that there was an article on the subject in the current number of the Saturday Review; whereupon the unbeliever said, "Oh, is that so? Oh, really. I see," and was converted on the X Ray faith on the spot. Lewis, remembering this talk, marveled at the strange processes of the human mind, its illogical and yet all-compelling ergos, and wondered whether he himself was only waiting for an article on the Z Ray in the Saturday Review to become a devout believer in the doctrine of Remnant.

But he wondered with far more fervor as to the extraordinary thing he had seen in his own garden with his own eyes. The tree that changed all its shape for an hour or two of the night, the growth of strange boughs, the apparition of secret fires among them, the sparkling of emerald and ruby lights: how could one fail to be afraid with great amazement at the thought of such a mystery?

***

Dr. Lewis's thoughts were distracted from the incredible adventure of the tree by the visit of his sister and her husband. Mr. and Mrs. Merritt lived in a well-known manufacturing town of the Midlands, which was now, of course, a center of munition work. On the day of their arrival at Porth, Mrs. Merritt, who was tired after the long, hot journey, went to bed early, and Merritt and Lewis went into the room by the garden for their talk and tobacco. They spoke of the year that had passed since their last meeting, of the weary dragging of the war, of friends that had perished in it, of the hopelessness of an early ending of all this misery. Lewis said nothing of the terror that was on the land. One does not greet a tired man who is come to a quiet, sunny place for relief from black smoke and work and worry with a tale of horror. Indeed, the doctor saw that his brother-in-law looked far from well. And he seemed "jumpy"; there was an occasional twitch of his mouth that Lewis did not like at all.

"Well," said the doctor, after an interval of silence and port wine, "I am glad to see you here again. Porth always suits you. I don't think you're looking quite up to your usual form. But three weeks of Meirion air will do wonders."

"Well, I hope it will," said the other. "I am not up to the mark. Things are not going well at

Midlingham."

"Business is all right, isn't it?"

"Yes. Business is all right. But there are other things that are all wrong. We are living under a reign of terror. It comes to that."

"What on earth do you mean?"

"Well, I suppose I may tell you what I know. It's not much. I didn't dare write it. But do you know that at every one of the munition works in Midlingham and all about it there's a guard of soldiers with drawn bayonets and loaded rifles day and night? Men with bombs, too. And machine-guns at the big factories."

"German spies?"

"You don't want Lewis guns to fight spies with. Nor bombs. Nor a platoon of men. I woke up last night. It was the machine-gun at Benington's Army Motor Works. Firing like fury. And then bang! bang! bang! That was the hand bombs."

"But what against?"

"Nobody knows."

"Nobody knows what is happening," Merritt repeated, and he went on to describe the bewilderment and terror that hung like a cloud over the great industrial city in the Midlands, how the feeling of concealment, of some intolerable secret danger that must not be named, was worst of all.

"A young fellow I know," he said, "was on short leave the other day from the front, and he spent it with his people at Belmont--that's about four miles out of Midlingham, you know. 'Thank God,' he said to me, 'I am going back to-morrow. It's no good saying that the Wipers salient is nice, because it isn't. But it's a damned sight better than this. At the front you know what you're up against anyhow.' At Midlingham everybody has the feeling that we're up against something awful and we don't know what; it's that that makes people inclined to whisper. There's terror in the air."

Merritt made a sort of picture of the great town cowering in its fear of an unknown danger.

"People are afraid to go about alone at nights in the outskirts. They make up parties at the stations to go home together if it's anything like dark, or if there are any lonely bits on their way."

"But why? I don't understand. What are they afraid of?"

"Well, I told you about my being awakened up the other night with the machine-guns at the motor works rattling away, and the bombs exploding and making the most terrible noise. That sort of thing alarms one, you know. It's only natural."

"Indeed, it must be very terrifying. You mean, then, there is a general nervousness about, a vague sort of apprehension that makes people inclined to herd together?"

"There's that, and there's more. People have gone out that have never come back. There were a couple of men in the train to Holme, arguing about the quickest way to get to Northend, a sort of outlying part of Holme where they both lived. They argued all the way out of Midlingham, one saying that the high road was the quickest though it was the longest. 'It's the quickest going because it's the cleanest going,' he said."

"The other chap fancied a short cut across the fields, by the canal. 'It's half the distance,' he kept on. 'Yes, if you don't lose your way,' said the other. Well, it appears they put an even half-crown on it, and each was to try his own way when they got out of the train. It was arranged that they were to meet at the 'Wagon' in Northend. 'I shall be at the "Wagon" first,' said the man who believed in the short cut, and with that he climbed over the stile and made off across the fields. It wasn't late enough to be really dark, and a lot of them thought he might win the stakes. But he never turned up at the Wagon--or anywhere else for the matter of that."

"What happened to him?"

"He was found lying on his back in the middle of a field--some way from the path. He was dead. The doctors said he'd-been suffocated. Nobody knows how. Then there have been other cases. We whisper about them at Midlingham, but we're afraid to speak out."

Lewis was ruminating all this profoundly. Terror in Meirion and terror far away in the heart of England; but at Midlingham, so far as he could gather from these stories of soldiers on guard, of crackling machine-guns, it was a case of an organized attack on the munitioning of the army. He felt that he did not know enough to warrant his deciding that the terror of Meirion and of Stratfordshire were one.

Then Merritt began again:

"There's a queer story going about, when the door's shut and the curtain's drawn, that is, as to a place right out in the country over the other side of Midlingham; on the opposite side to Dunwich. They've built one of the new factories out there, a great red brick town of sheds they tell me it is, with a tremendous chimney. It's not been finished more than a month or six weeks. They plumped it down right in the middle of the fields, by the line, and they're building huts for the workers as fast as they can but up to the present the men are billeted all about, up and down the line.

"About two hundred yards from this place there's an old footpath, leading from the station and the main road up to a small hamlet on the hillside. Part of the way this path goes by a pretty large wood, most of it thick undergrowth. I should think there must be twenty acres of wood, more or less. As it happens, I used this path once long ago; and I can tell you it's a black place of nights."

"A man had to go this way one night. He got along all right till he came to the wood. And then he said his heart dropped out of his body. It was awful to hear the noises in that wood. Thousands of men were in it, he swears that. It was full of rustling, and pattering of feet trying to go dainty, and the crack of dead boughs lying on the ground as some one trod on them, and swishing of the grass, and some sort of chattering speech going on, that sounded, so he said, as if the dead sat in their bones and talked! He ran for his life, anyhow; across fields, over hedges, through brooks. He must have run, by his tale, ten miles out of his way before he got home to his wife, and beat at the door, and broke in, and bolted it behind him.".

"There is something rather alarming about any wood at night," said Dr. Lewis.

Merritt shrugged his shoulders.

"People say that the Germans have landed, and that they are hiding in underground places all over the country."

CHAPTER VII - The Case of the Hidden Germans

Lewis gasped for a moment, silent in contemplation of the magnificence of rumor. The Germans already landed, hiding underground, striking by night, secretly, terribly, at the power of England! Here was a conception which made the myth of "The Russians" a paltry fable; before which the Legend of Mons was an ineffectual thing.

It was monstrous. And yet--

He looked steadily at Merritt; a square-headed, black-haired, solid sort of man. He had symptoms of nerves about him for the moment, certainly, but one could not wonder at that, whether the tales he told were true, or whether he merely believed them to be true. Lewis had known his brother-in-law for twenty years or more, and had always found him a sure man in his own small world. "But then," said the doctor to himself, "those men, if they once get out of the ring of that little world of theirs, they are lost. Those are the men that believed in Madame Blavatsky."

"Well," he said, "what do you think yourself? The Germans landed and hiding somewhere about the country: there's something extravagant in the notion, isn't there?"

"I don't know what to think. You can't get over the facts. There are the soldiers with their rifles and their guns at the works all over Stratfordshire, and those guns go off. I told you I'd heard them. Then who are the soldiers shooting at? That's what we ask ourselves at Midlingham."

"Quite so; I quite understand. It's an extraordinary state of things."

"It's more than extraordinary; it's an awful state of things. It's terror in the dark, and there's nothing worse than that. As that young fellow I was telling you about said, 'At the front you do know what you're up against.'"

"And people really believe that a number of Germans have somehow got over to England and have hid themselves underground?"

"People say they've got a new kind of poison-gas. Some think that they dig underground places and make the gas there, and lead it by secret pipes into the shops; others say that they throw gas bombs into the factories. It must be worse than anything they've used in France, from what the authorities say."

"The authorities? Do they admit that there are Germans in hiding about Midlingham?"

"No. They call it 'explosions.' But we know it isn't explosions. We know in the Midlands what an explosion sounds like and looks like. And we know that the people killed in these 'explosions' are put into their coffins in the works. Their own relations are not allowed to see them."

"And so you believe in the German theory?"

"If I do, it's because one must believe in something. Some say they've seen the gas. I heard that a man living in Dunwich saw it one night like a black cloud with sparks of fire in it floating over the tops of the trees by Dunwich Common."

The light of an ineffable amazement came into Lewis's eyes. The night of Remnant's visit, the trembling vibration of the air, the dark tree that had grown in his garden since the setting of the sun, the strange leafage that was starred with burning, with emerald and ruby fires, and all vanished away when he returned from his visit to the Garth; and such a leafage had appeared as a burning cloud far in the heart of England: what intolerable mystery, what tremendous doom was signified in this? But one thing was clear and certain: that the terror of Meirion was also the terror of the Midlands.

Lewis made up his mind most firmly that if possible all this should be kept from his brother-in-law. Merritt had come to Porth as to a city of refuge from the horrors of Midlingham; if it could be managed he should be spared the knowledge that the cloud of terror had gone before him and hung black over the western land. Lewis passed the port and said in an even voice:

"Very strange, indeed; a black cloud with sparks of fire?"

"I can't answer for it, you know; it's only a rumor."

"Just so; and you think or you're inclined to think that this and all the rest you've told me is to be put down to the hidden Germans?"

"As I say; because one must think something."

"I quite see your point. No doubt, if it's true, it's the most awful blow that has ever been dealt at any nation in the whole history of man. The enemy established in our vitals! But is it possible, after all? How could it have been worked?"

Merritt told Lewis how it had been worked, or rather, how people said it had been worked. The idea, he said, was that this was a part, and a most important part, of the great German plot to destroy England and the British Empire.

The scheme had been prepared years ago, some thought soon after the Franco-Prussian War. Moltke had seen that the invasion of England (in the ordinary sense of the term invasion) presented very great difficulties. The matter was constantly in discussion in the inner military and high political circles, and the general trend of opinion in these quarters was that at the best, the invasion of England would involve Germany in the gravest difficulties, and leave France in the position of the tertius gaudens. This was the state of affairs when a very high Prussian personage was approached by the Swedish professor, Huvelius.

Thus Merritt, and here I would say in parenthesis that this Huvelius was by all accounts an extraordinary man. Considered personally and apart from his writings he would appear to have been a most amiable individual. He was richer than the generality of Swedes, certainly far richer than the average university professor in Sweden. But his shabby, green frock-coat, and his battered, furry hat were notorious in the university town where he lived. No one laughed, because it was well known that Professor Huvelius spent every penny of his private means and a large portion of his official stipend on works of kindness and charity. He hid his head in a garret, some one said, in order that others might be able to swell on the first floor. It was told of him that he restricted himself to a diet of dry bread and coffee for a month in order that a poor woman of the streets, dying of consumption, might enjoy luxuries in hospital.

And this was the man who wrote the treatise "De Facinore Humano"; to prove the infinite corruption of the human race.

Oddly enough, Professor Huvelius wrote the most cynical book in the world--Hobbes preaches rosy sentimentalism in comparison--with the very highest motives. He held that a very large part of human misery, misadventure, and sorrow was due to the false convention that the heart of man was naturally and in the main well disposed and kindly, if not exactly righteous. "Murderers, thieves, assassins, violators, and all the host of the abominable," he says in one passage, "are created by the false pretense and foolish credence of human virtue. A lion in a cage is a fierce beast, indeed; but what will he be if we declare him to be a lamb and open the doors of his den? Who will be guilty of the deaths of the men, women and children whom he will surely devour, save those who unlocked the cage?" And he goes on to show that kings and the rulers of the peoples could decrease the sum of human misery to a vast extent by acting on the doctrine of human wickedness. "War," he declares, "which is one of the worst of evils, will always continue to exist. But a wise king will desire a brief war rather than a lengthy one, a short evil rather than a long evil. And this not from the benignity of his heart towards his enemies, for we have seen that the human heart is naturally malignant, but because he desires to conquer, and to conquer easily, without a great expenditure of men or of treasure, knowing that if he can accomplish this feat his people will love him and his crown will be secure. So he will wage brief victorious wars, and not only spare his own nation, but the nation of the enemy, since in a short war the loss is less on both sides than in a long war. And so from evil will come good."

And how, asks Huvelius, are such wars to be waged? The wise prince, he replies, will begin by assuming the enemy to be infinitely corruptible and infinitely stupid, since stupidity and corruption are the chief characteristics of man. So the prince will make himself friends in the very councils of his enemy, and also amongst the populace, bribing the wealthy by proffering to them the opportunity of still greater wealth, and winning the poor by swelling words. "For, contrary to the common opinion, it is the wealthy who are greedy of wealth; while the populace are to be gained by talking to them about liberty, their unknown god. And so much are they enchanted by the words liberty, freedom, and such like, that the wise can go to the poor, rob them of what little they have, dismiss them with a hearty kick, and win their hearts and their votes for ever, if only they will assure them that the treatment which they have received is called liberty."

Guided by these principles, says Huvelius, the wise prince will entrench himself in the country that he desires to conquer; "nay, with but little trouble, he may actually and literally throw his garrisons into the heart of the enemy country before war has begun."

***

This is a long and tiresome parenthesis; but it is necessary as explaining the long tale which Merritt told his brother-in-law, he having received it from some magnate of the Midlands, who had traveled in Germany. It is probable that the story was suggested in the first place by the passage from Huvelius which I have just quoted.

Merritt knew nothing of the real Huvelius, who was all but a saint; he thought of the Swedish professor as a monster of iniquity, "worse," as he said, "than Neech"--meaning, no doubt, Nietzsche.

So he told the story of how Huvelius had sold his plan to the Germans; a plan for filling England with German soldiers. Land was to be bought in certain suitable and well-considered places, Englishmen were to be bought as the apparent owners of such land, and secret excavations were to be made, till the country was literally undermined. A subterranean Germany, in fact, was to be dug under selected districts of England; there were to be great caverns, underground cities, well drained, well ventilated, supplied with water, and in these places vast stores both of food and of munitions were to be accumulated, year after year, till "the Day" dawned. And then, warned in time, the secret garrison would leave shops, hotels, offices, villas, and vanish underground, ready to begin their work of bleeding England at the heart.

"That's what Henson told me," said Merritt at the end of his long story. "Henson, head of the Buckley Iron and Steel Syndicate. He has been a lot in Germany."

"Well," said Lewis, "of course, it may be so. If it is so, it is terrible beyond words."

Indeed, he found something horribly plausible in the story. It was an extraordinary plan, of course; an unheard of scheme; but it did not seem impossible. It was the Trojan Horse on a gigantic scale; indeed, he reflected, the story of the horse with the warriors concealed within it which was dragged into the heart of Troy by the deluded Trojans themselves might be taken as a prophetic parable of what had happened to England--if Henson's theory were well founded. And this theory certainly squared with what one had heard of German preparations in Belgium and in France: emplacements for guns ready for the invader, German manufactories which were really German forts on Belgian soil, the caverns by the Aisne made ready for the cannon; indeed, Lewis thought he remembered something about suspicious concrete tennis-courts on the heights commanding London. But a German army hidden under English ground! It was a thought to chill the stoutest heart.

And it seemed from that wonder of the burning tree, that the enemy mysteriously and terribly present at Midlingham, was present also in Meirion. Lewis, thinking of the country as he knew it, of its wild and desolate hillsides, its deep woods, its wastes and solitary places, could not but confess that no more fit region could be found for the deadly enterprise of secret men. Yet, he thought again, there was but little harm to be done in Meirion to the armies of England or to their munitionment. They were working for panic terror? Possibly that might be so; but the camp under the Highway? That should be their first object, and no harm had been done there.

Lewis did not know that since the panic of the horses men had died terribly in that camp; that it was now a fortified place, with a deep, broad trench, a thick tangle of savage barbed wire about it, and a machine-gun planted at each corner.

CHAPTER VIII - What Mr. Merritt Found

Mr. Merritt began to pick up his health and spirits a good deal. For the first morning or two of his stay at the doctor's he contented himself with a very comfortable deck chair close to the house, where he sat under the shade of an old mulberry tree beside his wife and watched the bright sunshine on the green lawns, on the creamy crests of the waves, on the headlands of that glorious coast, purple even from afar with the imperial glow of the heather, on the white farmhouses gleaming in the sunlight, high over the sea, far from any turmoil, from any troubling of men.

The sun was hot, but the wind breathed all the while gently, incessantly, from the east, and Merritt, who had come to this quiet place, not only from dismay, but from the stifling and oily airs of the smoky Midland town, said that that east wind, pure and clear and like well water from the rock, was new life to him. He ate a capital dinner, at the end of his first day at Porth and took rosy views. As to what they had been talking about the night before, he said to Lewis, no doubt there must be trouble of some sort, and perhaps bad trouble; still, Kitchener would soon put it all right.

So things went on very well. Merritt began to stroll about the garden, which was full of the comfortable spaces, groves, and surprises that only country gardens know. To the right of one of the terraces he found an arbor or summer-house covered with white roses, and he was as pleased as if he had discovered the Pole. He spent a whole day there, smoking and lounging and reading a rubbishy sensational story, and declared that the Devonshire roses had taken many years off his age. Then on the other side of the garden there was a filbert grove that he had never explored on any of his former visits; and again there was a find. Deep in the shadow of the filberts was a bubbling well, issuing from rocks, and all manner of green, dewy ferns growing about it and above it, and an angelica springing beside it. Merritt knelt on his knees, and hollowed his hand and drank the well water. He said (over his port) that night that if all water were like the water of the filbert well the world would turn to teetotalism. It takes a townsman to relish the manifold and exquisite joys of the country.

It was not till he began to venture abroad that Merritt found that something was lacking of the old rich peace that used to dwell in Meirion. He had a favorite walk which he never neglected, year after year. This walk led along the cliffs towards Meiros, and then one could turn inland and return to Porth by deep winding lanes that went over the Allt. So Merritt set out early one morning and got as far as a sentry-box at the foot of the path that led up to the cliff. There was a sentry pacing up and down in front of the box, and he called on Merritt to produce his pass, or to turn back to the main road. Merritt was a good deal put out, and asked the doctor about this strict guard. And the doctor was surprised.

"I didn't know they had put their bar up there," he said. "I suppose it's wise. We are certainly in the far West here; still, the Germans might slip round and raid us and do a lot of damage just because Meirion is the last place we should expect them to go for."

"But there are no fortifications, surely, on the cliff?"

"Oh, no; I never heard of anything of the kind there."

"Well, what's the point of forbidding the public to go on the cliff, then? I can quite understand putting a sentry on the top to keep a look-out for the enemy. What I don't understand is a sentry at the bottom who can't keep a look-out for anything, as he can't see the sea. And why warn the public off the cliffs? I couldn't facilitate a German landing by standing on Pengareg, even if I wanted to."

"It is curious," the doctor agreed. "Some military reasons, I suppose."

He let the matter drop, perhaps because the matter did not affect him. People who live in the country all the year round, country doctors certainly, are little given to desultory walking in search of the picturesque.

Lewis had no suspicion that sentries whose object was equally obscure were being dotted all over the country. There was a sentry, for example, by the quarry at Llanfihangel, where the dead woman and the dead sheep had been found some weeks before. The path by the quarry was used a good deal, and its closing would have inconvenienced the people of the neighborhood very considerably. But the sentry had his box by the side of the track and had his orders to keep everybody strictly to the path, as if the quarry were a secret fort.

It was not known till a month or two ago that one of these sentries was himself a victim of the terror. The men on duty at this place were given certain very strict orders, which from the nature of the case, must have seemed to them unreasonable. For old soldiers, orders are orders; but here was a young bank clerk, scarcely in training for a couple of months, who had not begun to appreciate the necessity of hard, literal obedience to an order which seemed to him meaningless. He found himself on a remote and lonely hillside, he had not the faintest notion that his every movement was watched; and he disobeyed a certain instruction that had been given him. The post was found deserted by the relief; the sentry's dead body was found at the bottom of the quarry.

This by the way; but Mr. Merritt discovered again and again that things happened to hamper his walks and his wanderings. Two or three miles from Porth there is a great marsh made by the Afon river before it falls into the sea, and here Merritt had been accustomed to botanize mildly. He had learned pretty accurately the causeways of solid ground that lead through the sea of swamp and ooze and soft yielding soil, and he set out one hot afternoon determined to make a thorough exploration of the marsh, and this time to find that rare Bog Bean, that he felt sure, must grow somewhere in its wide extent.

He got into the by-road that skirts the marsh, and to the gate which he had always used for entrance.

There was the scene as he had known it always, the rich growth of reeds and flags and rushes, the mild black cattle grazing on the "islands" of firm turf, the scented procession of the meadowsweet, the royal glory of the loosestrife, flaming pennons, crimson and golden, of the giant dock.

But they were bringing out a dead man's body through the gate.

A laboring man was holding open the gate on the marsh. Merritt, horrified, spoke to him and asked who it was, and how it had happened.

"They do say he was a visitor at Porth. Somehow he has been drowned in the marsh, whatever."

"But it's perfectly safe. I've been all over it a dozen times."

"Well, indeed, we did always think so. If you did slip by accident, like, and fall into the water, it was not so deep; it was easy enough to climb out again. And this gentleman was quite young, to look at him, poor man; and he has come to Meirion for his pleasure and holiday and found his death in it!"

"Did he do it on purpose? Is it suicide?"

"They say he had no reasons to do that."

Here the sergeant of police in charge of the party interposed, according to orders, which he himself did not understand.

"A terrible thing, sir, to be sure, and a sad pity; and I am sure this is not the sort of sight you have come to see down in Meirion this beautiful summer. So don't you think, sir, that it would be more pleasant like, if you would leave us to this sad business of ours? I have heard many gentlemen staying in Porth say that there is nothing to beat the view from the hill over there, not in the whole of Wales."

Every one is polite in Meirion, but somehow Merritt understood that, in English, this speech meant "move on."

***

Merritt moved back to Porth--he was not in the humor for any idle, pleasurable strolling after so dreadful a meeting with death. He made some inquiries in the town about the dead man, but nothing seemed known of him. It was said that he had been on his honeymoon, that he had been staying at the Porth Castle Hotel; but the people of the hotel declared that they had never heard of such a person. Merritt got the local paper at the end of the week; there was not a word in it of any fatal accident in the marsh. He met the sergeant of police in the street. That officer touched his helmet with the utmost politeness and a "hope you are enjoying yourself, sir; indeed you do look a lot better already"; but as to the poor man who was found drowned or stifled in the marsh, he knew nothing.

The next day Merritt made up his mind to go to the marsh to see whether he could find anything to account for so strange a death. What he found was a man with an armlet standing by the gate. The armlet had the letters "C.W." on it, which are understood to mean Coast Watcher. The Watcher "said he had strict instructions to keep everybody away from the marsh. Why? He didn't know, but some said that the river was changing its course since the new railway embankment was built, and the marsh had become dangerous to people who didn't know it thoroughly.

"Indeed, sir," he added, "it is part of my orders not to set foot on the other side of that gate myself, not for one scrag-end of a minute."

Merritt glanced over the gate incredulously. The marsh looked as it had always looked; there was plenty of sound, hard ground to walk on; he could see the track that he used to follow as firm as ever. He did not believe in the story of the changing course of the river, and Lewis said he had never heard of anything of the kind. But Merritt had put the question in the middle of general conversation; he had not led up to it from any discussion of the death in the marsh, and so the doctor was taken unawares. If he had known of the connection in Merritt's mind between the alleged changing of the Afon's course and the tragical event in the marsh, no doubt he would have confirmed the official explanation. He was, above all things, anxious to prevent his sister and her husband from finding out that the invisible hand of terror that ruled at Midlingham was ruling also in Meirion.

Lewis himself had little doubt that the man who was found dead in the marsh had been struck down by the secret agency, whatever it was, that had already accomplished so much of evil; but it was a chief part of the terror that no one knew for certain that this or that particular event was to be ascribed to it. People do occasionally fall over cliffs through their own carelessness, and as the case of Garcia, the Spanish sailor, showed, cottagers and their wives and children are now and then the victims of savage and purposeless violence. Lewis had never wandered about the marsh himself; but Remnant had pottered round it and about it, and declared that the man who met his death there-- his name was never known, in Porth at all events--must either have committed suicide by deliberately lying prone in the ooze and stifling himself, or else must have been held down in it. There were no details available, so it was clear that the authorities had classified this death with the others; still, the man might have committed suicide, or he might have had a sudden seizure and fallen in the slimy water face-downwards. And so on: it was possible to believe that case A or B or C was in the category of ordinary accidents or ordinary crimes. But it was not possible to believe that A and B and C were all in that category. And thus it was to the end, and thus it is now. We know that the terror reigned, and how it reigned, but there were many dreadful events ascribed to its rule about which there must always be room for doubt.

For example, there was the case of the Mary Ann, the rowing-boat which came to grief in so strange a manner, almost under Merritt's eyes. In my opinion he was quite wrong in associating the sorry fate of the boat and her occupants with a system of signaling by flashlights which he detected or thought that he detected, on the afternoon in which the Mary Ann was capsized. I believe his signaling theory to be all nonsense, in spite of the naturalized German governess who was lodging with her employers in the suspected house. But, on the other hand, there is no doubt in my own mind that the boat was overturned and those in it drowned by the work of the terror.

CHAPTER IX - The Light on the Water

Let it be noted carefully that so far Merritt had not the slightest suspicion that the terror of Midlingham was quick over. Meirion. Lewis had watched and shepherded him carefully. He had let out no suspicion of what had happened in Meirion, and before taking his brother-in-law to the club he had passed round a hint among the members. He did not tell the truth about Midlingham--and here again is a point of interest, that as the terror deepened the general public cooperated voluntarily, and, one would say, almost subconsciously, with the authorities in concealing what they knew from one another--but he gave out a desirable portion of the truth: that his brother-in-law was "nervy," not by any means up to the mark, and that it was therefore desirable that he should be spared the knowledge of the intolerable and tragic mysteries which were being enacted all about them.

"He knows about that poor fellow who was found in the marsh," said Lewis, "and he has a kind of vague suspicion that there is something out of the common about the case; but no more than that."

"A clear case of suggested, or rather commanded suicide," said Remnant. "I regard it as a strong confirmation of my theory."

"Perhaps so," said the doctor, dreading lest he might have to hear about the Z Ray all over again. "But please don't let anything out to him; I want him to get built up thoroughly before he goes back to Midlingham."

Then, on the other hand, Merritt was as still as death about the doings of the Midlands; he hated to think of them, much more to speak of them; and thus, as I say, he and the men at the Porth Club kept their secrets from one another; and thus, from the beginning to the end of the terror, the links were not drawn together. In many cases, no doubt, A and B met every day and talked familiarly, it may be confidentially, on other matters of all sorts, each having in his possession half of the truth, which he concealed from the other. So the two halves were never put together to make a whole.

Merritt, as the doctor guessed, had a kind of uneasy feeling--it scarcely amounted to a suspicion--as to the business of the marsh; chiefly because he thought the official talk about the railway embankment and the course of the river rank nonsense. But finding that nothing more happened, he let the matter drop from his mind, and settled himself down to enjoy his holiday.

He found to his delight that there were no sentries or watchers to hinder him from the approach to Larnac Bay, a delicious cove, a place where the ashgrove and the green meadow and the glistening bracken sloped gently down to red rocks and firm yellow sands. Merritt remembered a rock that formed a comfortable seat, and here he established himself of a golden afternoon, and gazed at the blue of the sea and the crimson bastions and bays of the coast as it bent inward to Sarnau and swept out again southward to the odd-shaped promontory called the Dragon's Head. Merritt gazed on, amused by the antics of the porpoises who were tumbling and splashing and gamboling a little way out at sea, charmed by the pure and radiant air that was so different from the oily smoke that often stood for heaven at Midlingham, and charmed, too, by the white farmhouses dotted here and there on the heights of the curving coast.

Then he noticed a little row-boat at about two hundred yards from the shore. There were two or three people aboard, he could not quite make out how many, and they seemed to be doing something with a line; they were no doubt fishing, and Merritt (who disliked fish) wondered how people could spoil such an afternoon, such a sea, such pellucid and radiant air by trying to catch white, flabby, offensive, evil-smelling creatures that would be excessively nasty when cooked. He puzzled over this problem and turned away from it to the contemplation of the crimson headlands. And then he says that he noticed that signaling was going on. Flashing lights of intense brilliance, he declares, were coming from one of those farms on the heights of the coast; it was as if white fire was spouting from it. Merritt was certain, as the light appeared and disappeared, that some message was being sent, and he regretted that he knew nothing of heliography. Three short flashes, a long and very brilliant flash, then two short flashes. Merritt fumbled in his pocket for pencil and paper so that he might record these signals, and, bringing his eyes down to the sea level, he became aware, with amazement and horror, that the boat had disappeared. All that he could see was some vague, dark object far to westward, running out with the tide.

Now it is certain, unfortunately, that the Mary Ann was capsized and that two schoolboys and the sailor in charge were drowned. The bones of the boat were found amongst the rocks far along the coast, and the three bodies were also washed ashore. The sailor could not swim at all, the boys only a little, and it needs an exceptionally fine swimmer to fight against the outward suck of the tide as it rushes past Pengareg Point.

But I have no belief whatever in Merritt's theory. He held (and still holds, for all I know), that the flashes of light which he saw coming from Penyrhaul, the farmhouse oh the height, had some connection with the disaster to the Mary Ann. When it was ascertained that a family were spending their summer at the farm, and that the governess was a German, though a long naturalized German, Merritt could not see that there was anything left to argue about, though there might be many details to discover. But, in my opinion, all this was a mere mare's nest; the flashes of brilliant light were caused, no doubt, by the sun lighting up one window of the farmhouse after the other.

Still, Merritt was convinced from the very first, even before the damning circumstance of the German governess was brought to light; and on the evening of the disaster, as Lewis and he sat together after dinner, he was endeavoring to put what he called the common sense of the matter to the doctor.

"If you hear a shot," said Merritt, "and you see a man fall, you know pretty well what killed him."

There was a flutter of wild wings in the room. A great moth beat to and fro and dashed itself madly against the ceiling, the walls, the glass bookcase. Then a sputtering sound, a momentary dimming of the lamp. The moth had succeeded in its mysterious quest.

"Can you tell me," said Lewis as if he were answering Merritt, "why moths rush into the flame?"

***

Lewis had put his question as to the strange habits of the common moth to Merritt with the deliberate intent of closing the debate on death by heliograph. The query was suggested, of course, by the incident of the moth in the lamp, and Lewis thought that he had said, "Oh, shut up!" in a somewhat elegant manner. And, in fact Merritt looked dignified, remained silent, and helped himself to port.

That was the end that the doctor had desired. He had no doubt in his own mind that the affair of the Mary Ann was but one more item in the long account of horrors that grew larger almost with every day; and he was in no humor to listen to wild and futile theories as to the manner in which the disaster had been accomplished. Here was a proof that the terror that was upon them was mighty not only on the land but on the waters; for Lewis could not see that the boat could have been attacked by any ordinary means of destruction. From Merritt's story, it must have been in shallow water. The shore of Larnac Bay shelves very gradually, and the Admiralty charts showed the depth of water two hundred yards out to be only two fathoms; this would be too shallow for a submarine. And it could not have been shelled, and it could not have been torpedoed; there was no explosion. The disaster might have been due to carelessness; boys, he considered, will play the fool anywhere, even in a boat; but he did not think so; the sailor would have stopped them. And, it may be mentioned, that the two boys were as a matter of fact extremely steady, sensible young fellows, not in the least likely to play foolish tricks of any kind.

Lewis was immersed in these reflections, having successfully silenced his brother-in-law; he was trying in vain to find some clue to the horrible enigma. The Midlingham theory of a concealed German force, hiding in places under the earth, was extravagant enough, and yet it seemed the only solution that approached plausibility; but then again even a subterranean German host would hardly account for this wreckage of a boat, floating on a calm sea. And then what of the tree with the burning in it that had appeared in the garden there a few weeks ago, and the cloud with a burning in it that had shown over the trees of the Midland village?

I think I have, already written something of the probable emotions of the mathematician confronted suddenly with an undoubted two-sided triangle. I said, if I remember, that he would be forced, in decency, to go mad; and I believe that Lewis was very near to this point. He felt himself confronted with an intolerable problem that most instantly demanded solution, and yet, with the same breath, as it were, denied the possibility of there being any solution. People were being killed in an inscrutable manner by some inscrutable means, day after day, and one asked "why" and "how"; and there seemed no answer. In the Midlands, where every kind of munitionment was manufactured, the explanation of German agency was plausible; and even if the subterranean notion was to be rejected as savoring altogether too much of the fairytale, or rather of the sensational romance, yet it was possible that the backbone of the theory was true; the Germans might have planted their agents in some way or another in the midst of our factories. But here in Meirion, what serious effect could be produced by the casual and indiscriminate slaughter of a couple of schoolboys in a boat, of a harmless holiday-maker in a marsh? The creation of an atmosphere of terror and dismay? It was possible, of course, but it hardly seemed tolerable, in spite of the enormities of Louvain and of the Lusitania.

Into these meditations, and into the still dignified silence of Merritt broke the rap on the door of Lewis's man, and those words which harass the ease of the country doctor when he tries to take any ease: "You're wanted in the surgery, if you please, sir." Lewis bustled out, and appeared no more that night.

The doctor had been summoned to a little hamlet on the outskirts of Porth, separated from it by half a mile or three-quarters of road. One dignifies, indeed, this settlement without a name in calling it a hamlet; it was a mere row of four cottages, built about a hundred years ago for the accommodation of the workers in a quarry long since disused. In one of these cottages the doctor found a father and mother weeping and crying out to "doctor bach, doctor bach," and two frightened children, and one little body, still and dead. It was the youngest of the three, little Johnnie, and he was dead.

The doctor found that the child had been asphyxiated. He felt the clothes; they were dry; it was not a case of drowning. He looked at the neck; there was no mark of strangling. He asked the father how it had happened, and father and mother, weeping most lamentably, declared they had no knowledge of how their child had been killed: "unless it was the People that had done it." The Celtic fairies are still malignant. Lewis asked what had happened that evening; where had the child been?

"Was he with his brother and sister? Don't they know anything about it?"

Reduced into some sort of order from its original piteous confusion, this is the story that the doctor gathered.

All three children had been well and happy through the day. They had walked in with the mother, Mrs. Roberts, to Porth on a marketing expedition in the afternoon; they had returned to the cottage, had had their tea, and afterwards played about on the road in front of the house. John Roberts had come home somewhat late from his work, and it was after dusk when the family sat down to supper. Supper over, the three children went out again to play with other children from the cottage next door, Mrs. Roberts telling them that they might have half an hour before going to bed.

The two mothers came to the cottage gates at the same moment and called out to their children to come along and be quick about it. The two small families had been playing on the strip of turf across the road, just by the stile into the fields. The children ran across the road; all of them except Johnnie Roberts. His brother Willie said that just as their mother called them he heard Johnnie cry out:

"Oh, what is that beautiful shiny thing over the stile?"

CHAPTER X - The Child and the Moth

The little Roberts's ran across the road, up the path, and into the lighted room. Then they noticed that Johnnie had not followed them. Mrs. Roberts was doing something in the back kitchen, and Mr. Roberts had gone out to the shed to bring in some sticks for the next morning's fire. Mrs. Roberts heard the children run in and went on with her work. The children whispered to one another that Johnnie would "catch it" when their mother came out of the back room and found him missing; but they expected he would run in through the open door any minute. But six or seven, perhaps ten, minutes passed, and there was no Johnnie. Then the father and mother came into the kitchen together, and saw that their little boy was not there.

They thought it was some small piece of mischief--that the two other children had hidden the boy somewhere in the room: in the big cupboard perhaps.

"What have you done with him then?" said Mrs. Roberts. "Come out, you little rascal, directly in a minute."

There was no little rascal to come out, and Margaret Roberts, the girl, said that Johnnie had not come across the road with them: he must be still playing all by himself by the hedge.

"What did you let him stay like that for?" said Mrs. Roberts. "Can't I trust you for two minutes together? Indeed to goodness, you are all of you more trouble than you are worth." She went to the open door:

"Johnnie! Come you in directly, or you will be sorry for it. Johnnie!"

The poor woman called at the door. She went out to the gate and called there:

"Come you, little Johnnie. Come you, bachgen, there's a good boy. I do see you hiding there."

She thought he must be hiding in the shadow of the hedge, and that he would come running and laughing--"he was always such a happy little fellow"--to her across the road. But no little merry figure danced out of the gloom of the still, dark night; it was all silence.

It was then, as the mother's heart began to chill, though she still called cheerfully to the missing child, that the elder boy told how Johnnie had said there was something beautiful by the stile: "and perhaps he did climb over, and he is running now about the meadow, and has lost his way."

The father got his lantern then, and the whole family went crying and calling about the meadow, promising cakes and sweets and a fine toy to poor Johnnie if he would come to them.

They found the little body, under the ashgrove in the middle of the field. He was quite still and dead, so still that a great moth had settled on his forehead, fluttering away when they lifted him up.

Dr. Lewis heard this story. There was nothing to be done; little to be said to these most unhappy people.

"Take care of the two that you have left to you," said the doctor as he went away. "Don't let them out of your sight if you can help it. It is dreadful times that we are living in."

It is curious to record, that all through these dreadful times the simple little "season" went through its accustomed course at Porth. The war and its consequences had somewhat thinned the numbers of the summer visitors; still a very fair contingent of them occupied the hotels and boarding-houses and lodging-houses and bathed from the old-fashioned machines on one beach, or from the new-fashioned tents on the other, and sauntered in the sun, or lay stretched out in the shade under the trees that grow down almost to the water's edge. Porth never tolerated Ethiopians or shows of any kind on its sands, but "The Rockets" did very well during that summer in their garden entertainment, given in the castle grounds, and the fit-up companies that came to the Assembly Rooms are said to have paid their bills to a woman and to a man.

Porth depends very largely on its midland and northern custom, custom of a prosperous, well-established sort. People who think Llandudno overcrowded and Colwyn Bay too raw and red and new, come year after year to the placid old town in the southwest and delight in its peace; and as I say, they enjoyed themselves much as usual there in the summer of 1915. Now and then they became conscious, as Mr. Merritt became conscious, that they could not wander about quite in the old way; but they accepted sentries and coast-watchers and people who politely pointed out the advantages of seeing the view from this point rather than from that as very necessary consequences of the dreadful war that was being waged; nay, as a Manchester man said, after having been turned back from his favorite walk to Castell Coch, it was gratifying to think that they were so well looked after.

"So far as I can see," he added, "there's nothing to prevent a submarine from standing out there by Ynys Sant and landing half a dozen men in a collapsible boat in any of these little coves. And pretty fools we should look, shouldn't we, with our throats cut on the sands; or carried back to Germany in the submarine?" He tipped the coast-watcher half-a-crown.

"That's right, lad," he said, "you give us the tip."

Now here was a strange thing. The north-countryman had his thoughts on elusive submarines and German raiders; the watcher had simply received instructions to keep people off the Castell Coch fields, without reason assigned. And there can be no doubt that the authorities themselves, while they marked out the fields as in the "terror zone," gave their orders in the dark and were themselves profoundly in the dark as to the manner of the slaughter that had been done there; for if they had understood what had happened, they would have understood also that their restrictions were useless.

The Manchester man was warned off his walk about ten days after Johnnie Roberts's death. The Watcher had been placed at his post because, the night before, a young farmer had been found by his wife lying in the grass close to the Castle, with no scar on him, nor any mark of violence, but stone dead.

The wife of the dead man, Joseph Cradock, finding her husband lying motionless on the dewy turf, went white and stricken up the path to the village and got two men who bore the body to the farm. Lewis was sent for, and knew, at once when he saw the dead man that he had perished in the way that the little Roberts boy had perished--whatever that awful way might be. Cradock had been asphyxiated; and here again there was no mark of a grip on the throat. It might have been a piece of work by Burke and Hare, the doctor reflected; a pitch plaster might have been clapped over the man's mouth and nostrils and held there.

Then a thought struck him; his brother-in-law had talked of a new kind of poison gas that was said to be used against the munition workers in the Midlands: was it possible that the deaths of the man and the boy were due to some such instrument? He applied his tests but could find no trace of any gas having been employed. Carbonic acid gas? A man could not be killed with that in the open air; to be fatal that required a confined space, such a position as the bottom of a huge vat or of a well.

He did not know how Cradock had been killed; he confessed it to himself. He had been suffocated; that was all he could say.

It seemed that the man had gone out at about half-past nine to look after some beasts. The field in which they were was about five minutes' walk from the house. He told his wife he would be back in a quarter of an hour or twenty minutes. He did not return, and when he had been gone for three-quarters of an hour Mrs. Cradock went out to look for him. She went into the field where the beasts were, and everything seemed all right, but there was no trace of Cradock. She called out; there was no answer.

Now the meadow in which the cattle were pastured is high ground; a hedge divides it from the fields which fall gently down to the castle and the sea. Mrs. Cradock hardly seemed able to say why, having failed to find her husband among his beasts, she turned to the path which led to Castell Coch. She said at first that she had thought that one of the oxen might have broken through the hedge and strayed, and that Cradock had perhaps gone after it. And then, correcting herself, she said:

"There was that; and then there was something else that I could not make out at all. It seemed to me that the hedge did look different from usual. To be sure, things do look different at night, and there was a bit of sea mist about, but somehow it did look odd to me, and I said to myself, 'have I lost my way, then?'"

She declared that the shape of the trees in the hedge appeared to have changed, and besides, it had a look "as if it was lighted up, somehow," and so she went on towards the stile to see what all this could be, and when she came near everything was as usual. She looked over the stile and called and hoped to see her husband coming towards her or to hear his voice; but there was no answer, and glancing down the path she saw, or thought she saw, some sort of brightness on the ground, "a dim sort of light like a bunch of glow-worms in a hedge-bank.

"And so I climbed over the stile and went down the path, and the light seemed to melt away; and there was my poor husband lying on his back, saying not a word to me when I spoke to him and touched him."

***

So for Lewis the terror blackened and became altogether intolerable, and others, he perceived, felt as he did. He did not know, he never asked whether the men at the club had heard of these deaths of the child and the young farmer; but no one spoke of them. Indeed, the change was evident; at the beginning of the terror men spoke of nothing else; now it had become all too awful for ingenious chatter or labored and grotesque theories. And Lewis had received a letter from his brother-in-law at Midlingham; it contained the sentence, "I am afraid Fanny's health has not greatly benefited by her visit to Porth; there are still several symptoms I don't at all like." And this told him, in a phraseology that the doctor and Merritt had agreed upon, that the terror remained heavy in the Midland town.

***

It was soon after the death of Cradock that people began to tell strange tales of a sound that was to be heard of nights about the hills and valleys to the northward of Porth. A man who had missed the last train from Meiros and had been forced to tramp the ten miles between Meiros and Porth seems to have been the first to hear it. He said he had got to the top of the hill by Tredonoc, somewhere between half-past ten and eleven, when he first noticed an odd noise that he could not make out at all; it was like a shout, a long, drawn-out, dismal wail coming from a great way off, faint with distance. He stopped to listen, thinking at first that it might be owls hooting in the woods; but it was different, he said, from that: it was a long cry, and then there was silence and then it began over again. He could make nothing of it, and feeling frightened, he did not quite know of what, he walked on briskly and was glad to see the lights of Porth station.

He told his wife of this dismal sound that night, and she told the neighbors, and most of them thought that it was "all fancy"--or drink, or the owls after all. But the night after, two or three people, who had been to some small merrymaking in a cottage just off the Meiros road, heard the sound as they were going home, soon after ten. They, too, described it as a long, wailing cry, indescribably dismal in the stillness of the autumn night; "like the ghost of a voice," said one; "as if it came up from the bottom of the earth," said another.

31

Arthur Machen

CHAPTER XI - At Treff Loyne Farm

Let it be remembered, again and again, that, all the while that the terror lasted, there was no common stock of information as to the dreadful things that were being done. The press had not said one word upon it, there was no criterion by which the mass of the people could separate fact from mere vague rumor, no test by which ordinary misadventure or disaster could be distinguished from the achievements of the secret and awful force that was at work.

And so with every event of the passing day. A harmless commercial traveler might show himself in the course of his business in the tumbledown main street of Meiros and find himself regarded with looks of fear and suspicion as a possible worker of murder, while it is likely enough that the true agents of the terror went quite unnoticed. And since the real nature of all this mystery of death was unknown, it followed easily that the signs and warnings and omens of it were all the more unknown. Here was horror, there was horror; but there was no links to join one horror with another; no common basis of knowledge from which the connection between this horror and that horror might be inferred.

So there was no one who suspected at all that this dismal and hollow sound that was now heard of nights in the region to the north of Porth, had any relation at all to the case of the little girl who went out one afternoon to pick purple flowers and never returned, or to the case of the man whose body was taken out of the peaty slime of the marsh, or to the case of Cradock, dead in his fields, with a strange glimmering of light about his body, as his wife reported. And it is a question as to how far the rumor of this melancholy, nocturnal summons got abroad at all. Lewis heard of it, as a country doctor hears of most things, driving up and down the lanes, but he heard of it without much interest, with no sense that it was in any sort of relation to the terror. Remnant had been given the story of the hollow and echoing voice of the darkness in a colored and picturesque form; he employed a Tredonoc man to work in his garden once a week. The gardener had not heard the summons himself, but he knew a man who had done so.

"Thomas Jenkins, Pentoppin, he did put his head out late last night to see what the weather was like, as he was cutting a field of corn the next day, and he did tell me that when he was with the Methodists in Cardigan he did never hear no singing eloquence in the chapels that was like to it. He did declare it was like a wailing of Judgment Day."

Remnant considered the matter, and was inclined to think that the sound must be caused by a subterranean inlet of the sea; there might be, he supposed, an imperfect or half-opened or tortuous blow-hole in the Tredonoc woods, and the noise of the tide, surging up below, might very well produce that effect of a hollow wailing, far away. But neither he nor any one else paid much attention to the matter, save the few who heard the call at dead of night, as it echoed awfully over the black hills.

The sound had been heard for three or perhaps four nights, when the people coming out of Tredonoc church after morning service on Sunday noticed that there was a big yellow sheepdog in the churchyard. The dog, it appeared, had been waiting for the congregation; for it at once attached itself to them, at first to the whole body, and then to a group of half a dozen who took the turning to the right. Two of these presently went off over the fields to their respective houses, and four strolled on in the leisurely Sunday-morning manner of the country, and these the dog followed, keeping to heel all the time. The men were talking hay, corn and markets and paid no attention to the animal, and so they strolled along the autumn lane till they came to a gate in the hedge, whence a roughly made farm road went through the fields, and dipped down into the woods and to Treff Loyne farm.

Then the dog became like a possessed creature. He barked furiously. He ran up to one of the men and looked up at him, "as if he were begging for his life," as the man said, and then rushed to the gate and stood by it, wagging his tail and barking at intervals. The men stared and laughed.

"Whose dog will that be?" said one of them.

"It will be Thomas Griffith's, Treff Loyne," said another.

"Well, then, why doesn't he go home? Go home then!" He went through the gesture of picking up a stone from the road and throwing it at the dog. "Go home, then! Over the gate with you."

But the dog never stirred. He barked and whined and ran up to the men and then back to the gate. At last he came to one of them, and crawled and abased himself on the ground and then took hold of the man's coat and tried to pull him in the direction of the gate. The farmer shook the dog off, and the four went on their way; and the dog stood in the road and watched them and then put up its head and uttered a long and dismal howl that was despair.

The four farmers thought nothing of it; sheepdogs in the country are dogs to look after sheep, and their whims and fancies are not studied. But the yellow dog--he was a kind of degenerate collie--haunted the Tredonoc lanes from that day. He came to a cottage door one night and scratched at it, and when it was opened lay down, and then, barking, ran to the garden gate and waited, entreating, as it seemed, the cottager to follow him. They drove him away and again he gave that long howl of anguish. It was almost as bad, they said, as the noise that they had heard a few nights before. And then it occurred to somebody, so far as I can make out with no particular reference to the odd conduct of the Treff Loyne sheepdog, that Thomas Griffith had not been seen for some time past. He had missed market day at Porth, he had not been at Tredonoc church, where he was a pretty regular attendant on Sunday; and then, as heads were put together, it appeared that nobody had seen any of the Griffith family for days and days.

Now in a town, even in a small town, this process of putting heads together is a pretty quick business. In the country, especially in a countryside of wild lands and scattered and lonely farms and cottages, the affair takes time. Harvest was going on, everybody was busy in his own fields, and after the long day's hard work neither the farmer nor his men felt inclined to stroll about in search of news or gossip. A harvester at the day's end is ready for supper and sleep and for nothing else.

And so it was late in that week when it was discovered that Thomas Griffith and all his house had vanished from this world.

I have often been reproached for my curiosity over questions which are apparently of slight importance, or of no importance at all. I love to inquire, for instance, into the question of the visibility of a lighted candle at a distance. Suppose, that is, a candle lighted on a still, dark night in the country; what is the greatest distance at which you can see that there is a light at all? And then as to the human voice; what is its carrying distance, under good conditions, as a mere sound, apart from any matter of making out words that may be uttered?

They are trivial questions, no doubt, but they have always interested me, and the latter point has its application to the strange business of Treff Loyne. That melancholy and hollow sound, that wailing summons that appalled the hearts of those who heard it was, indeed, a human voice, produced in a very exceptional manner; and it seems to have been heard at points varying from a mile and a half to two miles from the farm. I do not know whether this is anything extraordinary; I do not know whether the peculiar method of production was calculated to increase or to diminish the carrying power of the sound.

Again and again I have laid emphasis in this story of the terror on the strange isolation of many of the farms and cottages in Meirion. I have done so in the effort to convince the townsman of something that he has never known. To the Londoner a house a quarter of a mile from the outlying suburban lamp, with no other dwelling within two hundred yards, is a lonely house, a place to fit with ghosts and mysteries and terrors. How can he understand then, the true loneliness of the white farmhouses of Meirion, dotted here and there, for the most part not even on the little lanes and deep winding byways, but set in the very heart of the fields, or alone on huge bastioned headlands facing the sea, and whether on the high verge of the sea or on the hills or in the hollows of the inner country, hidden from the sight of men, far from the sound of any common call. There is Penyrhaul, for example, the farm from which the foolish Merritt thought he saw signals of light being made: from seaward it is of course, widely visible; but from landward, owing partly to the curving and indented configuration of the bay, I doubt whether any other habitation views it from a nearer distance than three miles.

And of all these hidden and remote places, I doubt if any is so deeply buried as Treff Loyne. I have little or no Welsh, I am sorry to say, but I suppose that the name is corrupted from Trellwyn, or Tref-y-llwyn, "the place in the grove," and, indeed, it lies in the very heart of dark, overhanging woods. A deep, narrow valley runs down from the high lands of the Allt, through these woods, through steep hillsides of bracken and gorse, right down to the great marsh, whence Merritt saw the dead man being carried. The valley lies away from any road, even from that by-road, little better than a bridlepath, where the four farmers, returning from church were perplexed by the strange antics of the sheepdog. One cannot say that the valley is overlooked, even from a distance, for so narrow is it that the ashgroves that rim it on either side seem to meet and shut it in. I, at all events, have never found any high place from which Treff Loyne is visible; though, looking down from the Allt, I have seen blue wood-smoke rising from its hidden chimneys.

Such was the place, then, to which one September afternoon a party went up to discover what had happened to Griffith and his family. There were half a dozen farmers, a couple of policemen, and four soldiers, carrying their arms; those last had been lent by the officer commanding at the camp. Lewis, too, was of the party; he had heard by chance that no one knew what had become of Griffith and his family; and he was anxious about a young fellow, a painter, of his acquaintance, who had been lodging at Treff Loyne all the summer.

They all met by the gate of Tredonoc churchyard, and tramped solemnly along the narrow lane; all of them, I think, with some vague discomfort of mind, with a certain shadowy fear, as of men who do not quite know what they may encounter. Lewis heard the corporal and the three soldiers arguing over their orders.

"The Captain says to me," muttered the corporal, "'Don't hesitate to shoot if there's any trouble.' 'Shoot what, sir,' I says. 'The trouble,' says he, and that's all I could get out of him."

The men grumbled in reply; Lewis thought he heard some obscure reference to ratpoison, and wondered what they were talking about.

They came to the gate in the hedge, where the farm road led down to Treff Loyne. They followed this track, roughly made, with grass growing up between its loosely laid stones, down by the hedge from field to wood, till at last they came to the sudden walls of the valley, and the sheltering groves of the ash trees. Here the way curved down the steep hillside, and bent southward, and followed henceforward the hidden hollow of the valley, under the shadow of the trees.

Here was the farm enclosure; the outlying walls of the yard and the barns and sheds and outhouses. One of the farmers threw open the gate and walked into the yard, and forthwith began bellowing at the top of his voice:

"Thomas Griffith! Thomas Griffith! Where be you, Thomas Griffith?"

The rest followed him. The corporal snapped out an order over his shoulder, and there was a rattling metallic noise as the men fixed their bayonets and became in an instant dreadful dealers out of death, in place of harmless fellows with a feeling for beer.

"Thomas Griffith!" again bellowed the farmer.

There was no answer to this summons. But they found poor Griffith lying on his face at the edge of the pond in the middle of the yard. There was a ghastly wound in his side, as if a sharp stake had been driven into his body.

CHAPTER XII - *The Letter of Wrath*

It was a still September afternoon. No wind stirred in the hanging woods that were dark all about the ancient house of Treff Loyne; the only sound in the dim air was the lowing of the cattle; they had wandered, it seemed, from the fields and had come in by the gate of the farmyard and stood there melancholy, as if they mourned for their dead master. And the horses; four great, heavy, patient-looking beasts they were there too, and in the lower field the sheep were standing, as if they waited to be fed.

"You would think they all knew there was something wrong," one of the soldiers muttered to another. A pale sun showed for a moment and glittered on their bayonets. They were standing about the body of poor, dead Griffith, with a certain grimness growing on their faces and hardening there. Their corporal snapped something at them again; they were quite ready. Lewis knelt down by the dead man and looked closely at the great gaping wound in his side.

"He's been dead a long time," he said. "A week, two weeks, perhaps. He was killed by some sharp pointed weapon. How about the family? How many are there of them? I never attended them."

"There was Griffith, and his wife, and his son Thomas and Mary Griffith, his daughter. And I do think there was a gentleman lodging with them this summer."

That was from one of the farmers. They all looked at one another, this party of rescue, who knew nothing of the danger that had smitten this house of quiet people, nothing of the peril which had brought them to this pass of a farmyard with a dead man in it, and his beasts standing patiently about him, as if they waited for the farmer to rise up and give them their food. Then the party turned to the house. It was an old, sixteenth century building, with the singular round, "Flemish" chimney that is characteristic of Meirion. The walls were snowy with whitewash, the windows were deeply set and stone mullioned, and a solid, stone-tiled porch sheltered the doorway from any winds that might penetrate to the hollow of that hidden valley. The windows were shut tight. There was no sign of any life or movement about the place. The party of men looked at one another, and the churchwarden amongst the farmers, the sergeant of police, Lewis, and the corporal drew together.

"What is it to goodness, doctor?" said the churchwarden.

"I can tell you nothing at all--except that that poor man there has been pierced to the heart," said Lewis.

"Do you think they are inside and they will shoot us?" said another farmer. He had no notion of what he meant by "they," and no one of them knew better than he. They did not know what the danger was, or where it might strike them, or whether it was from without or from within. They stared at the murdered man, and gazed dismally at one another.

"Come!" said Lewis, "we must do something. We must get into the house and see what is wrong."

"Yes, but suppose they are at us while we are getting in," said the sergeant. "Where shall we be then, Doctor Lewis?"

The corporal put one of his men by the gate at the top of the farmyard, another at the gate by the bottom of the farmyard, and told them to challenge and shoot. The doctor and the rest opened the little gate of the front garden and went up to the porch and stood listening by the door. It was all dead silence. Lewis took an ash stick from one of the farmers and beat heavily three times on the old, black, oaken door studded with antique nails.

He struck three thundering blows, and then they all waited. There was no answer from within. He beat again, and still silence. He shouted to the people within, but there was no answer. They all turned and looked at one another, that party of quest and rescue who knew not what they sought, what enemy they were to encounter. There was an iron ring on the door. Lewis turned it but the door stood fast; it was evidently barred and bolted. The sergeant of police called out to open, but again there was no answer.

They consulted together. There was nothing for it but to blow the door open, and some one of them called in a loud voice to anybody that might be within to stand away from the door, or they would be killed. And at this very moment the yellow sheepdog came bounding up the yard from the woods and licked their hands and fawned on them and barked joyfully.

"Indeed now," said one of the farmers; "he did know that there was something amiss. A pity it was, Thomas Williams, that we did not follow him when he implored us last Sunday."

The corporal motioned the rest of the party back, and they stood looking fearfully about them at the entrance to the porch. The corporal disengaged his bayonet and shot into the keyhole, calling out once more before he fired. He shot and shot again; so heavy and firm was the ancient door, so stout its bolts and fastenings. At last he had to fire at the massive hinges, and then they all pushed together and the door lurched open and fell forward. The corporal raised his left hand and stepped back a few paces. He hailed his two men at the top and bottom of the farmyard. They were all right, they said. And so the party climbed and struggled over the fallen door into the passage, and into the kitchen of the farmhouse.

Young Griffith was lying dead before the hearth, before a dead fire of white wood ashes. They went on towards the "parlor," and in the doorway of the room was the body of the artist, Secretan, as if he had fallen in trying to get to the kitchen. Upstairs the two women, Mrs. Griffith and her daughter, a girl of eighteen, were lying together on the bed in the big bedroom, clasped in each others' arms.

They went about the house, searched the pantries, the back kitchen and the cellars; there was no life in it.

"Look!" said Dr. Lewis, when they came back to the big kitchen, "look! It is as if they had been besieged. Do you see that piece of bacon, half gnawed through?"

Then they found these pieces of bacon, cut from the sides on the kitchen wall, here and there about the house. There was no bread in the place, no milk, no water.

"And," said one of the farmers, "they had the best water here in all Meirion. The well is down there in the wood; it is most famous water. The old people did use to call it Ffynnon Teilo; it was Saint Teilo's Well, they did say."

"They must have died of thirst," said Lewis. "They have been dead for days and days."

The group of men stood in the big kitchen and stared at one another, a dreadful perplexity in their eyes. The dead were all about them, within the house and without it; and it was in vain to ask why they had died thus. The old man had been killed with the piercing thrust of some sharp weapon; the rest had perished, it seemed probable, of thirst; but what possible enemy was this that besieged the farm and shut in its inhabitants? There was no answer.

The sergeant of police spoke of getting a cart and taking the bodies into Porth, and Dr. Lewis went into the parlor that Secretan had used as a sitting-room, intending to gather any possessions or effects of the dead artist that he might find there. Half a dozen portfolios were piled up in one corner, there were some books on a side table, a fishing-rod and basket behind the door--that seemed all. No doubt there would be clothes and such matters upstairs, and Lewis was about to rejoin the rest of the party in the kitchen, when he looked down at some scattered papers lying with the books on the side table. On one of the sheets he read to his astonishment the words: "Dr. James Lewis, Porth." This was written in a staggering trembling scrawl, and examining the other leaves he saw that they were covered with writing.

The table stood in a dark corner of the room, and Lewis gathered up the sheets of paper and took them to the window-ledge and began to read, amazed at certain phrases that had caught his eye. But the manuscript was in disorder; as if the dead man who had written it had not been equal to the task of gathering the leaves into their proper sequence; it was some time before the doctor had each page in its place. This was the statement that he read, with ever-growing wonder, while a couple of the farmers were harnessing one of the horses in the yard to a cart, and the others were bringing down the dead women.

***

"I do not think that I can last much longer. We shared out the last drops of water a long time ago. I do not know how many days ago. We fall asleep and dream and walk about the house in our dreams, and I am often not sure whether I am awake or still dreaming, and so the days and nights are confused in my mind. I awoke not long ago, at least I suppose I awoke and found I was lying in the passage. I had a confused feeling that I had had an awful dream which seemed horribly real, and I thought for a moment what a relief it was to know that it wasn't true, whatever it might have been. I made up my mind to have a good long walk to freshen myself up, and then I looked round and found that I had been lying on the stones of the passage; and it all came back to me. There was no walk for me.

"I have not seen Mrs. Griffith or her daughter for a long while. They said they were going upstairs to have a rest. I heard them moving about the room at first, now I can hear nothing. Young Griffith is lying in the kitchen, before the hearth. He was talking to himself about the harvest and the weather when I last went into the kitchen. He didn't seem to know I was there, as he went gabbling on in a low voice very fast, and then he began to call the dog, Tiger.

"There seems no hope for any of us. We are in the dream of death...."

Here the manuscript became unintelligible for half a dozen lines. Secretan had written the words "dream of death" three or four times over. He had begun a fresh word and had scratched it out and then followed strange, unmeaning characters, the script, as Lewis thought, of a terrible language. And then the writing became clear, clearer than it was at the beginning of the manuscript, and the sentences flowed more easily, as if the cloud on Secretan's mind had lifted for a while. There was a fresh start, as it were, and the writer began again, in ordinary letter-form:

"DEAR LEWIS,

"I hope you will excuse all this confusion and wandering. I intended to begin a proper letter to you, and now I find all that stuff that you have been reading--if this ever gets into your hands. I have not the energy even to tear it up. If you read it you will know to what a sad pass I had come when it was written. It looks like delirium or a bad dream, and even now, though my mind seems to have cleared up a good deal, I have to hold myself in tightly to be sure that the experiences of the last days in this awful place are true, real things, not a long nightmare from which I shall wake up presently and find myself in my rooms at Chelsea.

"I have said of what I am writing, 'if it ever gets into your hands,' and I am not at all sure that it ever will. If what is happening here is happening everywhere else, then I suppose, the world is coming to an end. I cannot understand it, even now I can hardly believe it. I know that I dream such wild dreams and walk in such mad fancies that I have to look out and look about me to make sure that I am not still dreaming.

"Do you remember that talk we had about two months ago when I dined with you? We got on, somehow or other, to space and time, and I think we agreed that as soon as one tried to reason about space and time one was landed in a maze of contradictions. You said something to the effect that it was very curious but this was just like a dream. 'A man will sometimes wake himself from his crazy dream,' you said, 'by realizing that he is thinking nonsense.' And we both wondered whether these contradictions that one can't avoid if one begins to think of time and space may not really be proofs that the whole of life is a dream, and the moon and the stars bits of nightmare. I have often thought over that lately. I kick at the walls as Dr. Johnson kicked at the stone, to make sure that the things about me are there. And then that other question gets into my mind--is the world really coming to an end, the world as we have always known it; and what on earth will this new world be like? I can't imagine it; it's a story like Noah's Ark and the Flood. People used to talk about the end of the world and fire, but no one ever thought of anything like this.

"And then there's another thing that bothers me. Now and then I wonder whether we are not all mad together in this house. In spite of what I see and know, or, perhaps, I should say, because what I see and know is so impossible, I wonder whether we are not all suffering from a delusion. Perhaps we are our own gaolers, and we are really free to go out and live. Perhaps what we think we see is not there at all. I believe I have heard of whole families going mad together, and I may have come under the influence of the house, having lived in it for the last four months. I know there have been people who have been kept alive by their keepers forcing food down their throats, because they are quite sure that their throats are closed, so that they feel they are unable to swallow a morsel. I wonder now and then whether we are all like this in Treff Loyne; yet in my heart I feel sure that it is not so.

"Still, I do not want to leave a madman's letter behind me, and so I will not tell you the full story of what I have seen, or believe I have seen. If I am a sane man you will be able to fill in the blanks for yourself from your own knowledge. If I am mad, burn the letter and say nothing about it.

Or perhaps--and indeed, I am not quite sure--I may wake up and hear Mary Griffith calling to me in her cheerful sing-song that breakfast will be ready 'directly, in a minute,' and I shall enjoy it and walk over to Porth and tell you the queerest, most horrible dream that a man ever had, and ask what I had better take.

"I think that it was on a Tuesday that we first noticed that there was something queer about, only at the time we didn't know that there was anything really queer in what we noticed. I had been out since nine o'clock in the morning trying to paint the marsh, and I found it a very tough job. I came home about five or six o'clock and found the family at Treff Loyne laughing at old Tiger, the sheepdog. He was making short runs from the farmyard to the door of the house, barking, with quick, short yelps. Mrs. Griffith and Miss Griffith were standing by the porch, and the dog would go to them, look in their faces, and then run up the farmyard to the gate, and then look back with that eager yelping bark, as if he were waiting for the women to follow him. Then, again and again, he ran up to them and tugged at their skirts as if he would pull them by main force away from the house.

"Then the men came home from the fields and he repeated this performance. The dog was running all up and down the farmyard, in and out of the barn and sheds yelping, barking; and always with that eager run to the person he addressed, and running away directly, and looking back as, if to see whether we were following him. When the house door was shut and they all sat down to supper, he would give them no peace, till at last they turned him out of doors. And then he sat in the porch and scratched at the door with his claws, barking all the while. When the daughter brought in my meal, she said: 'We can't think what is come to old Tiger, and indeed, he has always been a good dog, too.'

"The dog barked and yelped and whined and scratched at the door all through the evening. They let him in once, but he seemed to have become quite frantic. He ran up to one member of the family after another; his eyes were bloodshot and his mouth was foaming, and he tore at their clothes till they drove him out again into the darkness. Then he broke into a long, lamentable howl of anguish, and we heard no more of him."

CHAPTER XIII - The Last Words of Mr. Secretan

"I slept ill that night I awoke again and again from uneasy M dreams, and I seemed in my sleep to hear strange calls and noises and a sound of murmurs and beatings on the door. There were deep, hollow voices, too, that echoed in my sleep, and when I woke I could hear the autumn wind, mournful, on the hills above us. I started up once with a dreadful scream in my ears; but then the house was all still, and I fell again into uneasy sleep.

"It was soon after dawn when I finally roused myself. The people in the house were talking to each other in high voices, arguing about something that I did not understand.

"'It is those damned gipsies, I tell you,' said old Griffith.

"'What would they do a thing like that for?' asked Mrs. Griffith. 'If it was stealing now--'"

"'It is more likely that John Jenkins has done it out of spite,' said the son. 'He said that he would remember you when we did catch him poaching.'"

"They seemed puzzled and angry, so far as I could make out, but not at all frightened. I got up and began to dress. I don't think I looked out of the window. The glass on my dressing-table is high and broad, and the window is small; one would have to poke one's head round the glass to see anything.

"The voices were still arguing downstairs. I heard the old man say, 'Well, here's for a beginning anyhow,' and then the door slammed.

"A minute later the old man shouted, I think, to his son. Then there was a great noise which I will not describe more particularly, and a dreadful screaming and crying inside the house and a sound of rushing feet. They all cried out at once to each other. I heard the daughter crying, 'it is no good, mother, he is dead, indeed they have killed him,' and Mrs. Griffith screaming to the girl to let her go. And then one of them rushed out of the kitchen and shot the great bolts of oak across the door, just as something beat against it with a thundering crash.

"I ran downstairs. I found them all in wild confusion, in an agony of grief and horror and amazement. They were like people who had seen something so awful that they had gone mad.

"I went to the window looking out on the farmyard. I won't tell you all that I saw. But I saw poor old Griffith lying by the pond, with the blood pouring out of his side.

"I wanted to go out to him and bring him in. But they told me that he must be stone dead, and such things also that it was quite plain that any one who went out of the house would not live more than a moment. We could not believe it, even as we gazed at the body of the dead man; but it was there. I used to wonder sometimes what one would feel like if one saw an apple drop from the tree and shoot up into the air and disappear. I think I know now how one would feel.

"Even then we couldn't believe that it would last. We were not seriously afraid for ourselves. We spoke of getting out in an hour or two, before dinner anyhow. It couldn't last, because it was impossible. Indeed, at twelve o'clock young Griffith said he would go down to the well by the back way and draw another pail of water. I went to the door and stood by it. He had not gone a dozen yards before they were on him. He ran for his life, and we had all we could do to bar the door in time. And then I began to get frightened.

"Still we could not believe in it. Somebody would come along shouting in an hour or two and it would all melt away and vanish. There could not be any real danger. There was plenty of bacon in the house, and half the weekly baking of loaves and some beer in the cellar and a pound or so of tea, and a whole pitcher of water that had been drawn from the well the night before. We could do all right for the day and in the morning it would have all gone away.

"But day followed day and it was still there. I knew Treff Loyne was a lonely place--that was why I had gone there, to have a long rest from all the jangle and rattle and turmoil of London, that makes a man alive and kills him too. I went to Treff Loyne because it was buried in the narrow valley under the ash trees, far away from any track. There was not so much as a footpath that was near it; no one ever came that way. Young Griffith had told me that it was a mile and a half to the nearest house, and the thought of the silent peace and retirement of the farm used to be a delight to me.

"And now this thought came back without delight, with terror. Griffith thought that a shout might be heard on a still night up away on the Allt, 'if a man was listening for it,' he added, doubtfully. My voice was clearer and stronger than his, and on the second night I said I would go up to my bedroom and call for help through the open window. I waited till it was all dark and still, and looked out through the window before opening it. And then I saw over the ridge of the long barn across the yard what looked like a tree, though I knew there was no tree there. It was a dark mass against the sky, with wide-spread boughs, a tree of thick, dense growth. I wondered what this could be, and I threw open the window, not only because I was going to call for help, but because I wanted to see more clearly what the dark growth over the barn really was.

"I saw in the depth of the dark of it points of fire, and colors in light, all glowing and moving, and the air trembled. I stared out into the night, and the dark tree lifted over the roof of the barn and rose up in the air and floated towards me. I did not move till at the last moment when it was close to the house; and then I saw what it was and banged the window down only just in time. I had to fight, and I saw the tree that was like a burning cloud rise up in the night and sink again and settle over the barn.

"I told them downstairs of this. They sat with white faces, and Mrs. Griffith said that ancient devils were let loose and had come out of the trees and out of the old hills because of the wickedness that was on the earth. She began to, murmur something to herself, something that sounded to me like broken-down Latin.

"I went up to my room again an hour later, but the dark tree swelled over the barn. Another day went by, and at dusk I looked out, but the eyes of fire were watching me. I dared not open the window.

"And then I thought of another plan. There was the great old fireplace, with the round Flemish chimney going high above the house. If I stood beneath it and shouted I thought perhaps the sound might be carried better than if I called out of the window; for all I knew the round chimney might act as a sort of megaphone. Night after night, then, I stood in the hearth and called for help from nine o'clock to eleven. I thought of the lonely place, deep in the valley of the ashtrees, of the lonely hills and lands about it. I thought of the little cottages far away and hoped that my voice might reach to those within them. I thought of the winding lane high on the Allt, and of the few men that came there of nights; but I hoped that my cry might come to one of them.

"But we had drunk up the beer, and we would only let ourselves have water by little drops, and on the fourth night my throat was dry, and I began to feel strange and weak; I knew that all the voice I had in my lungs would hardly reach the length of the field by the farm.

"It was then we began to dream of wells and fountains, and water coming very cold, in little drops, out of rocky places in the middle of a cool wood. We had given up all meals; now and then one would cut a lump from the sides of bacon on the kitchen wall and chew a bit of it, but the saltness was like fire.

"There was a great shower of rain one night. The girl said we might open a window and hold out bowls and basins and catch the rain. I spoke of the cloud with burning eyes. She said 'we will go to the window in the dairy at the back, and one of us can get some water at all events,' She stood up with her basin on the stone slab in the dairy and looked out and heard the plashing of the rain, falling very fast. And she unfastened the catch of the window and had just opened it gently with one hand, for about an inch, and had her basin in the other hand. 'And then,' said she, 'there was something that began to tremble and shudder and shake as it did when we went to the Choral Festival at St. Teilo's, and the organ played, and there was the cloud and the burning close before me.'

"And then we began to dream, as I say. I woke up in my sitting-room one hot afternoon when the sun was shining, and I had been looking and searching in my dream all through the house, and I had gone down to the old cellar that wasn't used, the cellar with the pillars and the vaulted room, with an iron pike in my hand. Something said to me that there was water there, and in my dream I went to a heavy stone by the middle pillar and raised it up, and there beneath was a bubbling well of cold, clear water, and I had just hollowed my hand to drink it when I woke. I went into the kitchen and told young Griffith. I said I was sure there was water there. He shook his head, but he took up the great kitchen poker and we went down to the old cellar. I showed him the stone by the pillar, and he raised it up. But there was no well.

"Do you know, I reminded myself of many people whom I have met in life? I would not be convinced. I was sure that, after all, there was a well there. They had a butcher's cleaver in the kitchen and I took it down to the old cellar and hacked at the ground with it. The others didn't interfere with me. We were getting past that. We hardly ever spoke to one another. Each one would be wandering about the house, upstairs and downstairs, each one of us, I suppose, bent on his own foolish plan and mad design, but we hardly ever spoke. Years ago, I was an actor for a bit, and I remember how it was on first nights; the actors treading softly up and down the wings, by their entrance, their lips moving and muttering over the words of their parts, but without a word for one another. So it was with us. I came upon young Griffith one evening evidently trying to make a subterranean passage under one of the walls of the house. I knew he was mad, as he knew I was mad when he saw me digging for a well in the cellar; but neither said anything to the other.

"Now we are past all this. We are too weak. We dream when we are awake and when we dream we think we wake. Night and day come and go and we mistake one for another; I hear Griffith murmuring to himself about the stars when the sun is high at noonday, and at midnight I have found myself thinking that I walked in bright sunlit meadows beside cold, rushing streams that flowed from high rocks.

"Then at the dawn figures in black robes, carrying lighted tapers in their hands pass slowly about and about; and I hear great rolling organ music that sounds as if some tremendous rite were to begin, and voices crying in an ancient song shrill from the depths of the earth.

"Only a little while ago I heard a voice which sounded as if it were at my very ears, but rang and echoed and resounded as if it were rolling and reverberated from the vault of some cathedral, chanting in terrible modulations. I heard the words quite clearly.

***

"Incipit liber iræ Domini Dei nostri. (Here beginneth The Book of the Wrath of the Lord our God.)

"And then the voice sang the word Aleph, prolonging it, it seemed through ages, and a light was extinguished as it began the chapter:

"In that day, saith the Lord, there shall be a cloud over the land, and in the cloud a burning and a shape of fire, and out of the cloud shall issue forth my messengers; they shall run all together, they shall not turn aside; this shall be a day of exceeding bitterness, without salvation. And on every high hill, saith the Lord of Hosts, I will set my sentinels, and my armies shall encamp in the place of every valley; in the house that is amongst rushes I will execute judgment, and in vain shall they fly for refuge to the munitions of the rocks. In the groves of the woods, in the places where the leaves are as a tent above them, they shall find the sword of the slayer; and they that put their trust in walled cities shall be confounded. Woe unto the armed man, woe unto him that taketh pleasure in the strength of his artillery, for a little thing shall smite him, and by one that hath no might shall he be brought down into the dust. That which is low shall be set on high; I will make the lamb and the young sheep to be as the lion from the swellings of Jordan; they shall not spare, saith the Lord, and the doves shall be as eagles on the hill Engedi; none shall be found that may abide the onset of their battle.

"Even now I can hear the voice rolling far away, as if it came from the altar of a great church and I stood at the door. There are lights very far away in the hollow of a vast darkness, and one by one they are put out. I hear a voice chanting again with that endless modulation that climbs and aspires to the stars, and shines there, and rushes down to the dark depths of the earth, again to ascend; the word is Zain."

Here the manuscript lapsed again, and finally into utter, lamentable confusion. There were scrawled lines wavering across the page on which Secretan seemed to have been trying to note the unearthly music that swelled in his dying ears. As the scrapes and scratches of ink showed, he had tried hard to begin a new sentence. The pen had dropped at last out of his hand upon the paper, leaving a blot and a smear upon it.

Lewis heard the tramp of feet along the passage; they were carrying out the dead to the cart.

CHAPTER XIV - The End of the Terror

Dr. Lewis maintained that we should never begin to understand the real significance of life until we began to study just those aspects of it which we now dismiss and overlook as utterly inexplicable, and therefore, unimportant.

We were discussing a few months ago the awful shadow of the terror which at length had passed away from the land. I had formed my opinion, partly from observation, partly from certain facts which had been communicated to me, and the pass-words having been exchanged, I found that Lewis had come by very different ways to the same end.

"And yet," he said, "it is not a true end, or rather, it is like all the ends of human inquiry, it leads one to a great mystery. We must confess that what has happened might have happened at any time in the history of the world. It did not happen till a year ago as a matter of fact, and therefore we made up our minds that it never could happen; or, one would better say, it was outside the range even of imagination. But this is our way. Most people are quite sure that the Black Death--otherwise the Plague--will never invade Europe again. They have made up their complacent minds that it was due to dirt and bad drainage. As a matter of fact the Plague had nothing to do with dirt or with drains; and there is nothing to prevent its ravaging England to-morrow. But if you tell people so, they won't believe you. They won't believe in anything that isn't there at the particular moment when you are talking to them. As with the Plague, so with the Terror. We could not believe that such a thing could ever happen. Remnant said, truly enough, that whatever it was, it was outside theory, outside our theory. Flatland cannot believe in the cube or the sphere."

I agreed with all this. I added that sometimes the world was incapable of seeing, much less believing, that which was before its own eyes.

"Look," I said, "at any eighteenth century print of a Gothic cathedral. You will find that the trained artistic eye even could not behold in any true sense the building that was before it. I have seen an old print of Peterborough Cathedral that looks as if the artist had drawn it from a clumsy model, constructed of bent wire and children's bricks.

"Exactly; because Gothic was outside the aesthetic theory (and therefore vision) of the time. You can't believe what you don't see: rather, you can't see what you don't believe. It was so during the time of the Terror. All this bears out what Coleridge said as to the necessity of having the idea before the facts could be of any service to one. Of course, he was right; mere facts, without the correlating idea, are nothing and lead to no conclusion. We had plenty of facts, but we could make nothing of them. I went home at the tail of that dreadful procession from Treff Loyne in a state of mind very near to madness. I heard one of the soldiers saying to the other: 'There's no rat that'll spike a man to the heart, Bill.' I don't know why, but I felt that if I heard any more of such talk as that I should go crazy; it seemed to me that the anchors of reason were parting. I left the party and took the short cut across the fields into Porth. I looked up Davies in the High Street and arranged with him that he should take on any cases I might have that evening, and then I went home and gave my man his instructions to send people on. And then I shut myself up to think it all out--if I could.

"You must not suppose that my experiences of that afternoon had afforded me the slightest illumination. Indeed, if it had not been that I had seen poor old Griffith's body lying pierced in his own farmyard, I think I should have been inclined to accept one of Secretan's hints, and to believe that the whole family had fallen a victim to a collective delusion or hallucination, and had shut themselves up and died of thirst through sheer madness. I think there have been such cases. It's the insanity of inhibition, the belief that you can't do something which you are really perfectly capable of doing. But; I had seen the body of the murdered man and the wound that had killed him.

"Did the manuscript left by Secretan give me no hint? Well, it seemed to me to make confusion worse confounded. You have seen it; you know that in certain places it is evidently mere delirium, the wanderings of a dying mind. How was I to separate the facts from the phantasms--lacking the key to the whole enigma. Delirium is often a sort of cloud-castle, a sort of magnified and distorted shadow of actualities, but it is a very difficult thing, almost an impossible thing, to reconstruct the real house from the distortion of it, thrown on the clouds of the patient's brain. You see, Secretan in writing that extraordinary document almost insisted on the fact that he was not in his proper sense; that for days he had been part asleep, part awake, part delirious. How was one to judge his statement, to separate delirium from fact? In one thing he stood confirmed; you remember he speaks of calling for help up the old chimney of Treff Loyne; that did seem to fit in with the tales of a hollow, moaning cry that had been heard upon the Allt: so far one could take him as a recorder of actual experiences. And I looked in the old cellars of the farm and found a frantic sort of rabbit-hole dug by one of the pillars; again he was confirmed. But what was one to make of that story of the chanting voice, and the letters of the Hebrew alphabet, and the chapter out of some unknown Minor Prophet? When one has the key it is easy enough to sort out the facts, or the hints of facts from the delusions; but I hadn't the key on that September evening. I was forgetting the 'tree' with lights and fires in it; that, I think, impressed me more than anything with the feeling that Secretan's story was, in the main, a true story. I had seen a like appearance down there in my own garden; but what was it?

"Now, I was saying that, paradoxically, it is only by the inexplicable things that life can be explained. We are apt to say, you know, 'a very odd coincidence' and pass the matter by, as if there were no more to be said, or as if that were the end of it. Well, I believe that the only real path lies through the blind alleys."

"How do you mean?"

"Well, this is an instance of what I mean. I told you about Merritt, my brother-in-law, and the capsizing of that boat, the Mary Ann. He had seen, he said, signal lights flashing from one of the farms on the coast, and he was quite certain that the two things were intimately connected as cause and effect. I thought it all nonsense, and I was wondering how I was going to shut him up when a big moth flew into the room through that window, fluttered about, and succeeded in burning itself alive in the lamp. That gave me my cue; I asked Merritt if he knew why moths made for lamps or something of the kind; I thought it would be a hint to him that I was sick of his flashlights and his half-baked theories. So it was--he looked sulky and held his tongue.

"But a few minutes later I was called out by a man who had found his little boy dead in a field near his cottage about an hour before. The child was so still, they said, that a great moth had settled on his forehead and only fluttered away when they lifted up the body. It was absolutely illogical; but it was this odd 'coincidence' of the moth in my lamp and the moth on the dead boy's forehead that first set me on the track. I can't say that it guided me in any real sense; it was more like a great flare of red paint on a wall; it rang up my attention, if I may say so; it was a sort of shock like a bang on the big drum. No doubt Merritt was talking great nonsense that evening so far as his particular instance went; the flashes of light from the farm had nothing to do with the wreck of the boat. But his general principle was sound; when you hear a gun go off and see a man fall it is idle to talk of 'a mere coincidence.' I think a very interesting book might be written on this question: I would call it 'A Grammar of Coincidence.'

"But as you will remember, from having read my notes on the matter, I was called in about ten days later to see a man named Cradock, who had been found in a field near his farm quite dead. This also was at night. His wife found him, and there were some very queer things in her story. She said that the hedge of the field looked as if it were changed; she began to be afraid that she had lost her way and got into the wrong field. Then she said the hedge was lighted up as if there were a lot of glow-worms in it, and when she peered over the stile there seemed to be some kind of glimmering upon the ground, and then the glimmering melted away, and she found her husband's body near where this light had been. Now this man Cradock had been suffocated just as the little boy Roberts had been suffocated, and as that man in the Midlands who took a short cut one night had been suffocated. Then I remembered that poor Johnnie Roberts had called out about 'something shiny' over the stile just before he played truant. Then, on my part, I had to contribute the very remarkable sight I witnessed here, as I looked down over the garden; the appearance as of a spreading tree where I knew there was no such tree, and then the shining and burning of lights and moving colors. Like the poor child and Mrs. Cradock, I had seen something shiny, just as some man in Stratfordshire had seen a dark cloud with points of fire in it floating over the trees. And Mrs. Cradock thought that the shape of the trees in the hedge had changed.

"My mind almost uttered the word that was wanted; but you see the difficulties. This set of circumstances could not, so far as I could see, have any relation with the other circumstances of the Terror. How could I connect all this with the bombs and machine-guns of the Midlands, with the armed men who kept watch about the munition shops by day and night. Then there was the long list of people here who had fallen over the cliffs or into the quarry; there were the cases of the men stifled in the slime of the marshes; there was the affair of the family murdered in front of their cottage on the Highway; there was the capsized Mary Ann. I could not see any thread that could bring all these incidents together; they seemed to me to be hopelessly disconnected. I could not make out any relation between the agency that beat out the brains of the Williams's and the agency, that overturned the boat. I don't know, but I think it's very likely if nothing more had happened that I should have put the whole thing down as an unaccountable series of crimes and accidents which chanced to occur in Meirion in the summer of 1915. Well, of course, that would have been an impossible standpoint in view of certain incidents in Merritt's story. Still, if one is confronted by the insoluble, one lets it go at last. If the mystery is inexplicable, one pretends that there isn't any mystery. That is the justification for what is called free thinking.

"Then came that extraordinary business of Treff Loyne. I couldn't put that on one side. I couldn't pretend that nothing strange or out of the way had happened. There was no getting over it or getting round it. I had seen with my eyes that there was a mystery, and a most horrible mystery. I have forgotten my logic, but one might say that Treff Loyne demonstrated the existence of a mystery in the figure of Death.

"I took it all home, as I have told you, and sat down for the evening before it. It appalled me, not only by its horror, but here again by the discrepancy between its terms. Old Griffith, so far as I could judge, had been killed by the thrust of a pike or perhaps of a sharpened stake: how could one relate this to the burning tree that had floated over the ridge of the barn. It was as if I said to you: 'here is a man drowned, and here is a man burned alive: show that each death was caused by the same agency!' And the moment that I left this particular case of Treff Loyne, and tried to get some light on it from other instances of the Terror, I would think of the man in the midlands who heard the feet of a thousand men rustling in the wood, and their voices as if dead men sat up in their bones and talked. And then I would say to myself, 'and how about that boat overturned in a calm sea?' There seemed no end to it, no hope of any solution.

"It was, I believe, a sudden leap of the mind that liberated me from the tangle. It was quite beyond logic. I went back to that evening when Merritt was boring me with his flashlights, to the moth in the candle, and to the moth on the forehead of poor Johnnie Roberts. There was no sense in it; but I suddenly determined that the child and Joseph Cradock the farmer, and that unnamed Stratfordshire man, all found at night, all asphyxiated, had been choked by vast swarms of moths. I don't pretend even now that this is demonstrated, but I'm sure it's true.

"Now suppose you encounter a swarm of these creatures in the dark. Suppose the smaller ones fly up your nostrils. You will gasp for breath and open your mouth. Then, suppose some hundreds of them fly into your mouth, into your gullet, into your windpipe, what will happen to you? You will be dead in a very short time, choked, asphyxiated."

"But the moths would be dead too. They would be found in the bodies."

"The moths? Do you know that it is extremely difficult to kill a moth with cyanide of potassium? Take a frog, kill it, open its stomach. There you will find its dinner of moths and small beetles, and the 'dinner' will shake itself and walk off cheerily, to resume an entirely active existence. No; that is no difficulty.

"Well, now I came to this. I was shutting out all the other cases. I was confining myself to those that came under the one formula. I got to the assumption or conclusion, whichever you like, that certain people had been asphyxiated by the action of moths. I had accounted for that extraordinary appearance of burning or colored lights that I had witnessed myself, when I saw the growth of that strange tree in my garden. That was clearly the cloud with points of fire in it that the Stratfordshire man took for a new and terrible kind of poison gas, that was the shiny something that poor little Johnnie Roberts had seen over the stile, that was the glimmering light that had led Mrs. Cradock to her husband's dead body, that was the assemblage of terrible eyes that had watched over Treff Loyne by night. Once on the right track I understood all this, for coming into this room in the dark, I have been amazed by the wonderful burning and the strange fiery colors of the eyes of a single moth, as it crept up the pane of glass, outside. Imagine the effect of myriads of such eyes, of the movement of these lights and fires in a vast swarm of moths, each insect being in constant motion while it kept its place in the mass: I felt that all this was clear and certain.

"Then the next step. Of course, we know nothing really about moths; rather, we know nothing of moth reality. For all I know there may be hundreds of books which treat of moth and nothing but moth. But these are scientific books, and science only deals with surfaces; it has nothing to do with realities--it is impertinent if it attempts to do with realities. To take a very minor matter; we don't even know why the moth desires the flame. But we do know what the moth does not do; it does not gather itself into swarms with the object of destroying human life. But here, by the hypothesis, were cases in which the moth had done this very thing; the moth race had entered, it seemed, into a malignant conspiracy against the human race. It was quite impossible, no doubt--that is to say, it had never happened before--but I could see no escape from this conclusion.

"These insects, then, were definitely hostile to man; and then I stopped, for I could not see the next step, obvious though it seems to me now. I believe that the soldiers' scraps of talk on the way to Treff Loyne and back flung the next plank over the gulf. They had spoken of 'rat poison,' of no rat being able to spike a man through the heart; and then, suddenly, I saw my way clear. If the moths were infected with hatred of men, and possessed the design and the power of combining against him; why not suppose this hatred, this design, this power shared by other non-human creatures.

"The secret of the Terror might be condensed into a sentence: the animals had revolted against men.

"Now, the puzzle became easy enough; one had only to classify. Take the cases of the people who met their deaths by falling over cliffs or over the edge of quarries. We think of sheep as timid creatures, who always ran away. But suppose sheep that don't run away; and, after all, in reason why should they run away? Quarry or no quarry, cliff or no cliff; what would happen to you if a hundred sheep ran after you instead of running from you? There would be no help for it; they would have you down and beat you to death or stifle you. Then suppose man, woman, or child near a cliff's edge or a quarry-side, and a sudden rush of sheep. Clearly there is no help; there is nothing for it but to go over. There can be no doubt that that, is what happened in all these cases.

"And again; you know the country and you know how a herd of cattle will sometimes pursue people through the fields in a solemn, stolid sort of way. They behave as if they wanted to close in on you. Townspeople sometimes get frightened and scream and run; you or I would take no notice, or at the utmost, wave our sticks at the herd, which will stop dead or lumber off. But suppose they don't lumber off. The mildest old cow, remember, is stronger than any man. What can one man or half a dozen men do against half a hundred of these beasts no longer restrained by that mysterious inhibition, which has made for ages the strong the humble slaves of the weak? But if you are botanizing in the marsh, like that poor fellow who was staying at Porth, and forty or fifty young cattle gradually close round you, and refuse to move when you shout and wave your stick, but get closer and closer instead, and get you into the slime. Again, where is your help? If you haven't got an automatic pistol, you must go down and stay down, while the beasts lie quietly on you for five minutes. It was a quicker death for poor Griffith of Treff Loyne--one of his own beasts gored him to death with one sharp thrust of its horn into his heart. And from that morning those within the house were closely besieged by their own cattle and horses and sheep; and when those unhappy people within opened a window to call for help or to catch a few drops of rain water to relieve their burning thirst, the cloud waited for them with its myriad eyes of fire. Can you wonder that Secretan's statement reads in places like mania? You perceive the horrible position of those people in Treff Loyne; not only did they see death advancing on them, but advancing with incredible steps, as if one were to die not only in nightmare but by nightmare. But no one in his wildest, most fiery dreams had ever imagined such a fate. I am not astonished that Secretan at one moment suspected the evidence of his own senses, at another surmised that the world's end had come."

"And how about the Williams's who were murdered on the Highway near here?"

"The horses were the murderers; the horses that afterwards stampeded the camp below. By some means which is still obscure to me they lured that family into the road and beat their brains out; their shod hoofs were the instruments of execution. And, as for the Mary Ann, the boat that was capsized, I have no doubt that it was overturned by a sudden rush of the porpoises that were gamboling about in the water of Larnac Bay. A porpoise is a heavy beast--half a dozen of them could easily upset a light rowing-boat. The munition works? Their enemy was rats. I believe that it has been calculated that in 'greater London' the number of rats is about equal to the number of human beings, that is, there are about seven millions of them. The proportion would be about the same in all the great centers of population; and the rat, moreover, is, on occasion, migratory in its habits. You can understand now that story of the Semiramis, beating about the mouth of the Thames, and at last cast away by Arcachon, her only crew dry heaps of bones. The rat is an expert boarder of ships. And so one can understand the tale told by the frightened man who took the path by the wood that led up from the new munition works. He thought he heard a thousand men treading softly through the wood and chattering to one another in some horrible tongue; what he did hear was the marshaling of an army of rats--their array before the battle.

"And conceive the terror of such an attack. Even one rat in a fury is said to be an ugly customer to meet; conceive then, the irruption of these terrible, swarming myriads, rushing upon the helpless, unprepared, astonished workers in the munition shops."

***

There can be no doubt, I think, that Dr. Lewis was entirely justified in these extraordinary conclusions. As I say, I had arrived at pretty much the same end, by different ways; but this rather as to the general situation, while Lewis had made his own particular study of those circumstances of the Terror that were within his immediate purview, as a physician in large practice in the southern part of Meirion. Of some of the cases which he reviewed he had, no doubt, no immediate or first-hand knowledge; but he judged these instances by their similarity to the facts which had come under his personal notice. He spoke of the affairs of the quarry at Llanfihangel on the analogy of the people who were found dead at the bottom of the cliffs near Porth, and he was no doubt justified in doing so. He told me that, thinking the whole matter over, he was hardly more astonished by the Terror in itself than by the strange way in which he had arrived at his conclusions.

"You know," he said, "those certain evidences of animal malevolence which we knew of, the bees that stung the child to death, the trusted sheepdog's turning savage, and so forth. Well, I got no light whatever from all this; it suggested nothing to me--simply because I had not got that 'idea' which Coleridge rightly holds necessary in all inquiry; facts qua facts, as we said, mean nothing and, come to nothing. You do not believe, therefore you cannot see.

"And then, when the truth at last appeared it was through the whimsical 'coincidence' as we call such signs, of the moth in my lamp and the moth on the dead child's forehead. This, I think, is very extraordinary."

"And there seems to have been one beast that remained faithful; the dog at Treff Loyne. That is strange."

"That remains a mystery."

***

It would not be wise, even now, to describe too closely the terrible scenes that were to be seen in the munition areas of the north and the midlands during the black months of the Terror. Out of the factories issued at black midnight the shrouded dead in their coffins, and their very kinsfolk did not know how they had come by their deaths. All the towns were full of houses of mourning, were full of dark and terrible rumors; incredible, as the incredible reality. There were things done and suffered that perhaps never will be brought to light, memories and secret traditions of these things will be whispered in families, delivered from father to son, growing wilder with the passage of the years, but never growing wilder than the truth.

It is enough to say that the cause of the Allies was for awhile in deadly peril. The men at the front called in their extremity for guns and shells. No one told them what was happening in the places where these munitions were made.

At first the position was nothing less than desperate; men in high places were almost ready to cry "mercy" to the enemy. But, after the first panic, measures were taken such as those described by Merritt in his account of the matter. The workers were armed with special weapons, guards were mounted, machine-guns were placed in position, bombs and liquid flame were ready against the obscene hordes of the enemy, and the "burning clouds" found a fire fiercer than their own. Many deaths occurred amongst the airmen; but they, too, were given special guns, arms that scattered shot broadcast, and so drove away the dark flights that threatened the airplanes.

And, then, in the winter of 1915-16, the Terror ended suddenly as it had begun. Once more a sheep was a frightened beast that ran instinctively from a little child; the cattle were again solemn, stupid creatures, void of harm; the spirit and the convention of malignant design passed out of the hearts of all the animals. The chains that they had cast off for awhile were thrown again about them.

And, finally, there comes the inevitable "why?" Why did the beasts who had been humbly and patiently subject to man, or affrighted by his presence, suddenly know their strength and learn how to league together, and declare bitter war against their ancient master?

It is a most difficult and obscure question. I give what explanation I have to give with very great diffidence, and an eminent disposition to be corrected, if a clearer light can be found.

Some friends of mine, for whose judgment I have very great respect, are inclined to think that there was a certain contagion of hate. They hold that the fury of the whole world at war, the great passion of death that seems driving all humanity to destruction, infected at last these lower creatures, and in place of their native instinct of submission, gave them rage and wrath and ravening.

This may be the explanation. I cannot say that it is not so, because I do not profess to understand the working of the universe. But I confess that the theory strikes me as fanciful. There may be a contagion of hate as there is a contagion of smallpox; I do not know, but I hardly believe it.

In my opinion, and it is only an opinion, the source of the great revolt of the beasts is to be sought in a much subtler region of inquiry. I believe that the subjects revolted because the king abdicated. Man has dominated the beasts throughout the ages, the spiritual has reigned over the rational through the peculiar quality and grace of spirituality that men possess, that makes a man to be that which he is. And when he maintained this power and grace, I think it is pretty clear that between him and the animals there was a certain treaty and alliance. There was supremacy on the one hand, and submission on the other; but at the same time there was between the two that cordiality which exists between lords and subjects in a well-organized state. I know a socialist who maintains that Chaucer's "Canterbury Tales" give a picture of true democracy. I do not know about that, but I see that knight and miller were able to get on quite pleasantly together, just because the knight knew that he was a knight and the miller knew that he was a miller. If the knight had had conscientious objections to his knightly grade, while the miller saw no reason why he should not be a knight, I am sure that their intercourse would have been difficult, unpleasant, and perhaps murderous.

So with man. I believe in the strength and truth of tradition. A learned man said to me a few weeks ago: "When I have to choose between the evidence of tradition and the evidence of a document, I always believe the evidence of tradition. Documents may be falsified, and often are falsified; tradition is never falsified." This is true; and, therefore, I think, one may put trust in the vast body of folklore which asserts that there was once a worthy and friendly alliance between man and the beasts. Our popular tale of Dick Whittington and his Cat no doubt represents the adaptation of a very ancient legend to a comparatively modern personage, but we may go back into the ages and find the popular tradition asserting that not only are the animals the subjects, but also the friends of man.

All that was in virtue of that singular spiritual element in man which the rational animals do not possess. Spiritual does not mean respectable, it does not even mean moral, it does not mean "good" in the ordinary acceptation of the word. It signifies the royal prerogative of man, differentiating him from the beasts.

For long ages he has been putting off this royal robe, he has been wiping the balm of consecration from his own breast. He has declared, again and again, that he is not spiritual, but rational, that is, the equal of the beasts over whom he was once sovereign. He has vowed that he is not Orpheus but Caliban.

But the beasts also have within them something which corresponds to the spiritual quality in men--we are content to call it instinct. They perceived that the throne was vacant--not even friendship was possible between them and the self-deposed monarch. If he were not king he was a sham, an imposter, a thing to be destroyed.

Hence, I think, the Terror. They have risen once--they may rise again.

THE END

THE GREAT GOD PAN

I - THE EXPERIMENT

"I am glad you came, Clarke; very glad indeed. I was not sure you could spare the time."

"I was able to make arrangements for a few days; things are not very lively just now. But have you no misgivings, Raymond? Is it absolutely safe?"

The two men were slowly pacing the terrace in front of Dr. Raymond's house. The sun still hung above the western mountain-line, but it shone with a dull red glow that cast no shadows, and all the air was quiet; a sweet breath came from the great wood on the hillside above, and with it, at intervals, the soft murmuring call of the wild doves. Below, in the long lovely valley, the river wound in and out between the lonely hills, and, as the sun hovered and vanished into the west, a faint mist, pure white, began to rise from the hills. Dr. Raymond turned sharply to his friend.

"Safe? Of course it is. In itself the operation is a perfectly simple one; any surgeon could do it."

"And there is no danger at any other stage?"

"None; absolutely no physical danger whatsoever, I give you my word. You are always timid, Clarke, always; but you know my history. I have devoted myself to transcendental medicine for the last twenty years. I have heard myself called quack and charlatan and impostor, but all the while I knew I was on the right path. Five years ago I reached the goal, and since then every day has been a preparation for what we shall do tonight."

"I should like to believe it is all true." Clarke knit his brows, and looked doubtfully at Dr. Raymond. "Are you perfectly sure, Raymond, that your theory is not a phantasmagoria--a splendid vision, certainly, but a mere vision after all?"

Dr. Raymond stopped in his walk and turned sharply. He was a middle-aged man, gaunt and thin, of a pale yellow complexion, but as he answered Clarke and faced him, there was a flush on his cheek.

"Look about you, Clarke. You see the mountain, and hill following after hill, as wave on wave, you see the woods and orchard, the fields of ripe corn, and the meadows reaching to the reed-beds by the river. You see me standing here beside you, and hear my voice; but I tell you that all these things--yes, from that star that has just shone out in the sky to the solid ground beneath our feet--I say that all these are but dreams and shadows; the shadows that hide the real world from our eyes. There is a real world, but it is beyond this glamour and this vision, beyond these 'chases in Arras, dreams in a career,' beyond them all as beyond a veil. I do not know whether any human being has ever lifted that veil; but I do know, Clarke, that you and I shall see it lifted this very night from before another's eyes. You may think this all strange nonsense; it may be strange, but it is true, and the ancients knew what lifting the veil means. They called it seeing the god Pan."

Clarke shivered; the white mist gathering over the river was chilly.

"It is wonderful indeed," he said. "We are standing on the brink of a strange world, Raymond, if what you say is true. I suppose the knife is absolutely necessary?"

"Yes; a slight lesion in the grey matter, that is all; a trifling rearrangement of certain cells, a microscopical alteration that would escape the attention of ninety-nine brain specialists out of a hundred. I don't want to bother you with 'shop,' Clarke; I might give you a mass of technical detail which would sound very imposing, and would leave you as enlightened as you are now. But I suppose you have read, casually, in out-of-the-way corners of your paper, that immense strides have been made recently in the physiology of the brain. I saw a paragraph the other day about Digby's theory, and Browne Faber's discoveries. Theories and discoveries! Where they are standing now, I stood fifteen years ago, and I need not tell you that I have not been standing still for the last fifteen years. It will be enough if I say that five years ago I made the discovery that I alluded to when I said that ten years ago I reached the goal. After years of labour, after years of toiling and groping in the dark, after days and nights of disappointments and sometimes of despair, in which I used now and then to tremble and grow cold with the thought that perhaps there were others seeking for what I sought, at last, after so long, a pang of sudden joy thrilled my soul, and I knew the long journey was at an end. By what seemed then and still seems a chance, the suggestion of a moment's idle thought followed up upon familiar lines and paths that I had tracked a hundred times already, the great truth burst upon me, and I saw, mapped out in lines of sight, a whole world, a sphere unknown; continents and islands, and great oceans in which no ship has sailed (to my belief) since a Man first lifted up his eyes and beheld the sun, and the stars of heaven, and the quiet earth beneath. You will think this all high-flown language, Clarke, but it is hard to be literal. And yet; I do not know whether what I am hinting at cannot be set forth in plain and lonely terms. For instance, this world of ours is pretty well girded now with the telegraph wires and cables; thought, with something less than the speed of thought, flashes from sunrise to sunset, from north to south, across the floods and the desert places. Suppose that an electrician of today were suddenly to perceive that he and his friends have merely been playing with pebbles and mistaking them for the foundations of the world; suppose that such a man saw uttermost space lie open before the current, and words of men flash forth to the sun and beyond the sun into the systems beyond, and the voice of articulate-speaking men echo in the waste void that bounds our thought. As analogies go, that is a pretty good analogy of what I have done; you can understand now a little of what I felt as I stood here one evening; it was a summer evening, and the valley looked much as it does now; I stood here, and saw before me the unutterable, the unthinkable gulf that yawns profound between two worlds, the world of matter and the world of spirit; I saw the great empty deep stretch dim before me, and in that instant a bridge of light leapt from the earth to the unknown shore, and the abyss was spanned. You may look in Browne Faber's book, if you like, and you will find that to the present day men of science are unable to account for the presence, or to specify the functions of a certain group of nerve-cells in the brain. That group is, as it were, land to let, a mere waste place for fanciful theories. I am not in the position of Browne Faber and the specialists, I am perfectly instructed as to the possible functions of those nerve-centers in the scheme of things. With a touch I can bring them into play, with a touch, I say, I can set free the current, with a touch I can complete the communication between this world of sense and--we shall be able to finish the sentence later on. Yes, the knife is necessary; but think what that knife will effect. It will level utterly the solid wall of sense, and probably, for the first time since man was made, a spirit will gaze on a spirit-world. Clarke, Mary will see the god Pan!"

"But you remember what you wrote to me? I thought it would be requisite that she--"

He whispered the rest into the doctor's ear.

"Not at all, not at all. That is nonsense. I assure you. Indeed, it is better as it is; I am quite certain of that."

"Consider the matter well, Raymond. It's a great responsibility. Something might go wrong; you would be a miserable man for the rest of your days."

"No, I think not, even if the worst happened. As you know, I rescued Mary from the gutter, and from almost certain starvation, when she was a child; I think her life is mine, to use as I see fit. Come, it's getting late; we had better go in."

Dr. Raymond led the way into the house, through the hall, and down a long dark passage. He took a key from his pocket and opened a heavy door, and motioned Clarke into his laboratory. It had once been a billiard-room, and was lighted by a glass dome in the centre of the ceiling, whence there still shone a sad grey light on the figure of the doctor as he lit a lamp with a heavy shade and placed it on a table in the middle of the room.

Clarke looked about him. Scarcely a foot of wall remained bare; there were shelves all around laden with bottles and phials of all shapes and colours, and at one end stood a little Chippendale book-case. Raymond pointed to this.

"You see that parchment Oswald Crollius? He was one of the first to show me the way, though I don't think he ever found it himself. That is a strange saying of his: 'In every grain of wheat there lies hidden the soul of a star.'"

There was not much furniture in the laboratory. The table in the centre, a stone slab with a drain in one corner, the two armchairs on which Raymond and Clarke were sitting; that was all, except an odd-looking chair at the furthest end of the room. Clarke looked at it, and raised his eyebrows.

"Yes, that is the chair," said Raymond. "We may as well place it in position." He got up and wheeled the chair to the light, and began raising and lowering it, letting down the seat, setting the back at various angles, and adjusting the foot-rest. It looked comfortable enough, and Clarke passed his hand over the soft green velvet, as the doctor manipulated the levers.

"Now, Clarke, make yourself quite comfortable. I have a couple hours' work before me; I was obliged to leave certain matters to the last."

Raymond went to the stone slab, and Clarke watched him drearily as he bent over a row of phials and lit the flame under the crucible. The doctor had a small hand-lamp, shaded as the larger one, on a ledge above his apparatus, and Clarke, who sat in the shadows, looked down at the great shadowy room, wondering at the bizarre effects of brilliant light and undefined darkness contrasting with one another. Soon he became conscious of an odd odour, at first the merest suggestion of odour, in the room, and as it grew more decided he felt surprised that he was not reminded of the chemist's shop or the surgery. Clarke found himself idly endeavouring to analyse the sensation, and half conscious, he began to think of a day, fifteen years ago, that he had spent roaming through the woods and meadows near his own home. It was a burning day at the beginning of August, the heat had dimmed the outlines of all things and all distances with a faint mist, and people who observed the thermometer spoke of an abnormal register, of a temperature that was almost tropical. Strangely that wonderful hot day of the fifties rose up again in Clarke's imagination; the sense of dazzling all-pervading sunlight seemed to blot out the shadows and the lights of the laboratory, and he felt again the heated air beating in gusts about his face, saw the shimmer rising from the turf, and heard the myriad murmur of the summer.

˙ "I hope the smell doesn't annoy you, Clarke; there's nothing unwholesome about it. It may make you a bit sleepy, that's all."

Clarke heard the words quite distinctly, and knew that Raymond was speaking to him, but for the life of him he could not rouse himself from his lethargy. He could only think of the lonely walk he had taken fifteen years ago; it was his last look at the fields and woods he had known since he was a child, and now it all stood out in brilliant light, as a picture, before him. Above all there came to his nostrils the scent of summer, the smell of flowers mingled, and the odour of the woods, of cool shaded places, deep in the green depths, drawn forth by the sun's heat; and the scent of the good earth, lying as it were with arms stretched forth, and smiling lips, overpowered all. His fancies made him wander, as he had wandered long ago, from the fields into the wood, tracking a little path between the shining undergrowth of beech-trees; and the trickle of water dropping from the limestone rock sounded as a clear melody in the dream. Thoughts began to go astray and to mingle with other thoughts; the beech alley was transformed to a path between ilex-trees, and here and there a vine climbed from bough to bough, and sent up waving tendrils and drooped with purple grapes, and the sparse grey-green leaves of a wild olive-tree stood out against the dark shadows of the ilex. Clarke, in the deep folds of dream, was conscious that the path from his father's house had led him into an undiscovered country, and he was wondering at the strangeness of it all, when suddenly, in place of the hum and murmur of the summer, an infinite silence seemed to fall on all things, and the wood was hushed, and for a moment in time he stood face to face there with a presence, that was neither man nor beast, neither the living nor the dead, but all things mingled, the form of all things but devoid of all form. And in that moment, the sacrament of body and soul was dissolved, and a voice seemed to cry "Let us go hence," and then the darkness of darkness beyond the stars, the darkness of everlasting.

When Clarke woke up with a start he saw Raymond pouring a few drops of some oily fluid into a green phial, which he stoppered tightly.

"You have been dozing," he said; "the journey must have tired you out. It is done now. I am going to fetch Mary; I shall be back in ten minutes."

Clarke lay back in his chair and wondered. It seemed as if he had but passed from one dream into another. He half expected to see the walls of the laboratory melt and disappear, and to awake in London, shuddering at his own sleeping fancies. But at last the door opened, and the doctor returned, and behind him came a girl of about seventeen, dressed all in white. She was so beautiful that Clarke did not wonder at what the doctor had written to him. She was blushing now over face and neck and arms, but Raymond seemed unmoved.

"Mary," he said, "the time has come. You are quite free. Are you willing to trust yourself to me entirely?"

"Yes, dear."

"Do you hear that, Clarke? You are my witness. Here is the chair, Mary. It is quite easy. Just sit in it and lean back. Are you ready?"

"Yes, dear, quite ready. Give me a kiss before you begin."

The doctor stooped and kissed her mouth, kindly enough. "Now shut your eyes," he said. The girl closed her eyelids, as if she were tired, and longed for sleep, and Raymond placed the green phial to her nostrils. Her face grew white, whiter than her dress; she struggled faintly, and then with the feeling of submission strong within her, crossed her arms upon her breast as a little child about to say her prayers. The bright light of the lamp fell full upon her, and Clarke watched changes fleeting over her face as the changes of the hills when the summer clouds float across the sun. And then she lay all white and still, and the doctor turned up one of her eyelids. She was quite unconscious. Raymond pressed hard on one of the levers and the chair instantly sank back. Clarke saw him cutting away a circle, like a tonsure, from her hair, and the lamp was moved nearer. Raymond took a small glittering instrument from a little case, and Clarke turned away shudderingly. When he looked again the doctor was binding up the wound he had made.

"She will awake in five minutes." Raymond was still perfectly cool. "There is nothing more to be done; we can only wait."

The minutes passed slowly; they could hear a slow, heavy, ticking. There was an old clock in the passage. Clarke felt sick and faint; his knees shook beneath him, he could hardly stand.

Suddenly, as they watched, they heard a long-drawn sigh, and suddenly did the colour that had vanished return to the girl's cheeks, and suddenly her eyes opened. Clarke quailed before them. They shone with an awful light, looking far away, and a great wonder fell upon her face, and her hands stretched out as if to touch what was invisible; but in an instant the wonder faded, and gave place to the most awful terror. The muscles of her face were hideously convulsed, she shook from head to foot; the soul seemed struggling and shuddering within the house of flesh. It was a horrible sight, and Clarke rushed forward, as she fell shrieking to the floor.

Three days later Raymond took Clarke to Mary's bedside. She was lying wide-awake, rolling her head from side to side, and grinning vacantly.

"Yes," said the doctor, still quite cool, "it is a great pity; she is a hopeless idiot. However, it could not be helped; and, after all, she has seen the Great God Pan."

II - MR. CLARKE'S MEMOIRS

Mr. Clarke, the gentleman chosen by Dr. Raymond to witness the strange experiment of the god Pan, was a person in whose character caution and curiosity were oddly mingled; in his sober moments he thought of the unusual and eccentric with undisguised aversion, and yet, deep in his heart, there was a wide-eyed inquisitiveness with respect to all the more recondite and esoteric elements in the nature of men. The latter tendency had prevailed when he accepted Raymond's invitation, for though his considered judgment had always repudiated the doctor's theories as the wildest nonsense, yet he secretly hugged a belief in fantasy, and would have rejoiced to see that belief confirmed. The horrors that he witnessed in the dreary laboratory were to a certain extent salutary; he was conscious of being involved in an affair not altogether reputable, and for many years afterwards he clung bravely to the commonplace, and rejected all occasions of occult investigation. Indeed, on some homeopathic principle, he for some time attended the seances of distinguished mediums, hoping that the clumsy tricks of these gentlemen would make him altogether disgusted with mysticism of every kind, but the remedy, though caustic, was not efficacious. Clarke knew that he still pined for the unseen, and little by little, the old passion began to reassert itself, as the face of Mary, shuddering and convulsed with an unknown terror, faded slowly from his memory. Occupied all day in pursuits both serious and lucrative, the temptation to relax in the evening was too great, especially in the winter months, when the fire cast a warm glow over his snug bachelor apartment, and a bottle of some choice claret stood ready by his elbow. His dinner digested, he would make a brief pretence of reading the evening paper, but the mere catalogue of news soon palled upon him, and Clarke would find himself casting glances of warm desire in the direction of an old Japanese bureau, which stood at a pleasant distance from the hearth. Like a boy before a jam-closet, for a few minutes he would hover indecisive, but lust always prevailed, and Clarke ended by drawing up his chair, lighting a candle, and sitting down before the bureau. Its pigeon-holes and drawers teemed with documents on the most morbid subjects, and in the well reposed a large manuscript volume, in which he had painfully entered the gems of his collection. Clarke had a fine contempt for published literature; the most ghostly story ceased to interest him if it happened to be printed; his sole pleasure was in the reading, compiling, and rearranging what he called his "Memoirs to prove the Existence of the Devil," and engaged in this pursuit the evening seemed to fly and the night appeared too short.

On one particular evening, an ugly December night, black with fog, and raw with frost, Clarke hurried over his dinner, and scarcely deigned to observe his customary ritual of taking up the paper and laying it down again. He paced two or three times up and down the room, and opened the bureau, stood still a moment, and sat down. He leant back, absorbed in one of those dreams to which he was subject, and at length drew out his book, and opened it at the last entry. There were three or four pages densely covered with Clarke's round, set penmanship, and at the beginning he had written in a somewhat larger hand:

Singular Narrative told me by my Friend, Dr. Phillips.

He assures me that all the facts related therein are strictly and wholly True, but refuses to give either the Surnames of the Persons Concerned, or the Place where these Extraordinary Events occurred.

Mr. Clarke began to read over the account for the tenth time, glancing now and then at the pencil notes he had made when it was told him by his friend. It was one of his humours to pride himself on a certain literary ability; he thought well of his style, and took pains in arranging the circumstances in dramatic order. He read the following story:--

The persons concerned in this statement are Helen V., who, if she is still alive, must now be a woman of twenty-three, Rachel M., since deceased, who was a year younger than the above, and Trevor W., an imbecile, aged eighteen. These persons were at the period of the story inhabitants of a village on the borders of Wales, a place of some importance in the time of the Roman occupation, but now a scattered hamlet, of not more than five hundred souls. It is situated on rising ground, about six miles from the sea, and is sheltered by a large and picturesque forest.

Some eleven years ago, Helen V. came to the village under rather peculiar circumstances. It is understood that she, being an orphan, was adopted in her infancy by a distant relative, who brought her up in his own house until she was twelve years old. Thinking, however, that it would be better for the child to have playmates of her own age, he advertised in several local papers for a good home in a comfortable farmhouse for a girl of twelve, and this advertisement was answered by Mr. R., a well-to-do farmer in the above-mentioned village. His references proving satisfactory, the gentleman sent his adopted daughter to Mr. R., with a letter, in which he stipulated that the girl should have a room to herself, and stated that her guardians need be at no trouble in the matter of education, as she was already sufficiently educated for the position in life which she would occupy. In fact, Mr. R. was given to understand that the girl was allowed to find her own occupations and to spend her time almost as she liked. Mr. R. duly met her at the nearest station, a town seven miles away from his house, and seems to have remarked nothing extraordinary about the child except that she was reticent as to her former life and her adopted father. She was, however, of a very different type from the inhabitants of the village; her skin was a pale, clear olive, and her features were strongly marked, and of a somewhat foreign character. She appears to have settled down easily enough into farmhouse life, and became a favourite with the children, who sometimes went with her on her rambles in the forest, for this was her amusement. Mr. R. states that he has known her to go out by herself directly after their early breakfast, and not return till after dusk, and that, feeling uneasy at a young girl being out alone for so many hours, he communicated with her adopted father, who replied in a brief note that Helen must do as she chose. In the winter, when the forest paths are impassable, she spent most of her time in her bedroom, where she slept alone, according to the instructions of her relative. It was on one of these expeditions to the forest that the first of the singular incidents with which this girl is connected occurred, the date being about a year after her arrival at the village. The preceding winter had been remarkably severe, the snow drifting to a great depth, and the frost continuing for an unexampled period, and the summer following was as noteworthy for its extreme heat. On one of the very hottest days in this summer, Helen V. left the farmhouse for one of her long rambles in the forest, taking with her, as usual, some bread and meat for lunch. She was seen by some men in the fields making for the old Roman Road, a green causeway which traverses the highest part of the wood, and they were astonished to observe that the girl had taken off her hat, though the heat of the sun was already tropical. As it happened, a labourer, Joseph W. by name, was working in the forest near the Roman Road, and at twelve o'clock his little son, Trevor, brought the man his dinner of bread and cheese. After the meal, the boy, who was about seven years old at the time, left his father at work, and, as he said, went to look for flowers in the wood, and the man, who could hear him shouting with delight at his discoveries, felt no uneasiness. Suddenly, however, he was horrified at hearing the most dreadful screams, evidently the result of great terror, proceeding from the direction in which his son had gone, and he hastily threw down his tools and ran to see what had happened. Tracing his path by the sound, he met the little boy, who was running headlong, and was evidently terribly frightened, and on questioning him the man elicited that after picking a posy of flowers he felt tired, and lay down on the grass and fell asleep. He was suddenly awakened, as he stated, by a peculiar noise, a sort of singing he called it, and on peeping through the branches he saw Helen V. playing on the grass with a "strange naked man," who he seemed unable to describe more fully. He said he felt dreadfully frightened and ran away crying for his father. Joseph W. proceeded in the direction indicated by his son, and found Helen V. sitting on the grass in the middle of a glade or open space left by charcoal burners. He angrily charged her with frightening his little boy, but she entirely denied the accusation and laughed at the child's story of a "strange man," to which he himself did not attach much credence. Joseph W. came to the conclusion that the boy had woke up with a sudden fright, as children sometimes do, but Trevor persisted in his story, and continued in such evident distress that at last his father took him home, hoping that his mother would be able to soothe him. For many weeks, however, the boy gave his parents much anxiety; he became nervous and strange in his manner, refusing to leave the cottage by himself, and constantly alarming the household by waking in the night with cries of "The man in the wood! father! father!"

In course of time, however, the impression seemed to have worn off, and about three months later he accompanied his father to the home of a gentleman in the neighborhood, for whom Joseph W. occasionally did work. The man was shown into the study, and the little boy was left sitting in the hall, and a few minutes later, while the gentleman was giving W. his instructions, they were both horrified by a piercing shriek and the sound of a fall, and rushing out they found the child lying senseless on the floor, his face contorted with terror. The doctor was immediately summoned, and after some examination he pronounced the child to be suffering form a kind of fit, apparently produced by a sudden shock. The boy was taken to one of the bedrooms, and after some time recovered consciousness, but only to pass into a condition described by the medical man as one of violent hysteria. The doctor exhibited a strong sedative, and in the course of two hours pronounced him fit to walk home, but in passing through the hall the paroxysms of fright returned and with additional violence. The father perceived that the child was pointing at some object, and heard the old cry, "The man in the wood," and looking in the direction indicated saw a stone head of grotesque appearance, which had been built into the wall above one of the doors. It seems the owner of the house had recently made alterations in his premises, and on digging the foundations for some offices, the men had found a curious head, evidently of the Roman period, which had been placed in the manner described. The head is pronounced by the most experienced archaeologists of the district to be that of a faun or satyr. [Dr. Phillips tells me that he has seen the head in question, and assures me that he has never received such a vivid presentment of intense evil.]

From whatever cause arising, this second shock seemed too severe for the boy Trevor, and at the present date he suffers from a weakness of intellect, which gives but little promise of amending. The matter caused a good deal of sensation at the time, and the girl Helen was closely questioned by Mr. R., but to no purpose, she steadfastly denying that she had frightened or in any way molested Trevor.

The second event with which this girl's name is connected took place about six years ago, and is of a still more extraordinary character.

At the beginning of the summer of 1882, Helen contracted a friendship of a peculiarly intimate character with Rachel M., the daughter of a prosperous farmer in the neighbourhood. This girl, who was a year younger than Helen, was considered by most people to be the prettier of the two, though Helen's features had to a great extent softened as she became older. The two girls, who were together on every available opportunity, presented a singular contrast, the one with her clear, olive skin and almost Italian appearance, and the other of the proverbial red and white of our rural districts. It must be stated that the payments made to Mr. R. for the maintenance of Helen were known in the village for their excessive liberality, and the impression was general that she would one day inherit a large sum of money from her relative. The parents of Rachel were therefore not averse from their daughter's friendship with the girl, and even encouraged the intimacy, though they now bitterly regret having done so. Helen still retained her extraordinary fondness for the forest, and on several occasions Rachel accompanied her, the two friends setting out early in the morning, and remaining in the wood until dusk. Once or twice after these excursions Mrs. M. thought her daughter's manner rather peculiar; she seemed languid and dreamy, and as it has been expressed, "different from herself," but these peculiarities seem to have been thought too trifling for remark. One evening, however, after Rachel had come home, her mother heard a noise which sounded like suppressed weeping in the girl's room, and on going in found her lying, half undressed, upon the bed, evidently in the greatest distress. As soon as she saw her mother, she exclaimed, "Ah, mother, mother, why did you let me go to the forest with Helen?" Mrs. M. was astonished at so strange a question, and proceeded to make inquiries. Rachel told her a wild story. She said--

Clarke closed the book with a snap, and turned his chair towards the fire. When his friend sat one evening in that very chair, and told his story, Clarke had interrupted him at a point a little subsequent to this, had cut short his words in a paroxysm of horror. "My God!" he had exclaimed, "think, think what you are saying. It is too incredible, too monstrous; such things can never be in this quiet world, where men and women live and die, and struggle, and conquer, or maybe fail, and fall down under sorrow, and grieve and suffer strange fortunes for many a year; but not this, Phillips, not such things as this. There must be some explanation, some way out of the terror. Why, man, if such a case were possible, our earth would be a nightmare."

But Phillips had told his story to the end, concluding:

"Her flight remains a mystery to this day; she vanished in broad sunlight; they saw her walking in a meadow, and a few moments later she was not there."

Clarke tried to conceive the thing again, as he sat by the fire, and again his mind shuddered and shrank back, appalled before the sight of such awful, unspeakable elements enthroned as it were, and triumphant in human flesh. Before him stretched the long dim vista of the green causeway in the forest, as his friend had described it; he saw the swaying leaves and the quivering shadows on the grass, he saw the sunlight and the flowers, and far away, far in the long distance, the two figures moved toward him. One was Rachel, but the other?

Clarke had tried his best to disbelieve it all, but at the end of the account, as he had written it in his book, he had placed the inscription:

ET DIABOLUS INCARNATE EST. ET HOMO FACTUS EST.

III - THE CITY OF RESURRECTIONS

"Herbert! Good God! Is it possible?"

"Yes, my name's Herbert. I think I know your face, too, but I don't remember your name. My memory is very queer."

"Don't you recollect Villiers of Wadham?"

"So it is, so it is. I beg your pardon, Villiers, I didn't think I was begging of an old college friend. Good-night."

"My dear fellow, this haste is unnecessary. My rooms are close by, but we won't go there just yet. Suppose we walk up Shaftesbury Avenue a little way? But how in heaven's name have you come to this pass, Herbert?"

"It's a long story, Villiers, and a strange one too, but you can hear it if you like."

"Come on, then. Take my arm, you don't seem very strong."

The ill-assorted pair moved slowly up Rupert Street; the one in dirty, evil-looking rags, and the other attired in the regulation uniform of a man about town, trim, glossy, and eminently well-to-do. Villiers had emerged from his restaurant after an excellent dinner of many courses, assisted by an ingratiating little flask of Chianti, and, in that frame of mind which was with him almost chronic, had delayed a moment by the door, peering round in the dimly-lighted street in search of those mysterious incidents and persons with which the streets of London teem in every quarter and every hour. Villiers prided himself as a practised explorer of such obscure mazes and byways of London life, and in this unprofitable pursuit he displayed an assiduity which was worthy of more serious employment. Thus he stood by the lamp-post surveying the passers-by with undisguised curiosity, and with that gravity known only to the systematic diner, had just enunciated in his mind the formula: "London has been called the city of encounters; it is more than that, it is the city of Resurrections," when these reflections were suddenly interrupted by a piteous whine at his elbow, and a deplorable appeal for alms. He looked around in some irritation, and with a sudden shock found himself confronted with the embodied proof of his somewhat stilted fancies. There, close beside him, his face altered and disfigured by poverty and disgrace, his body barely covered by greasy ill-fitting rags, stood his old friend Charles Herbert, who had matriculated on the same day as himself, with whom he had been merry and wise for twelve revolving terms. Different occupations and varying interests had interrupted the friendship, and it was six years since Villiers had seen Herbert; and now he looked upon this wreck of a man with grief and dismay, mingled with a certain inquisitiveness as to what dreary chain of circumstances had dragged him down to such a doleful pass. Villiers felt together with compassion all the relish of the amateur in mysteries, and congratulated himself on his leisurely speculations outside the restaurant.

They walked on in silence for some time, and more than one passer-by stared in astonishment at the unaccustomed spectacle of a well-dressed man with an unmistakable beggar hanging on to his arm, and, observing this, Villiers led the way to an obscure street in Soho. Here he repeated his question.

"How on earth has it happened, Herbert? I always understood you would succeed to an excellent position in Dorsetshire. Did your father disinherit you? Surely not?"

"No, Villiers; I came into all the property at my poor father's death; he died a year after I left Oxford. He was a very good father to me, and I mourned his death sincerely enough. But you know what young men are; a few months later I came up to town and went a good deal into society. Of course I had excellent introductions, and I managed to enjoy myself very much in a harmless sort of way. I played a little, certainly, but never for heavy stakes, and the few bets I made on races brought me in money--only a few pounds, you know, but enough to pay for cigars and such petty pleasures. It was in my second season that the tide turned. Of course you have heard of my marriage?"

"No, I never heard anything about it."

"Yes, I married, Villiers. I met a girl, a girl of the most wonderful and most strange beauty, at the house of some people whom I knew. I cannot tell you her age; I never knew it, but, so far as I can guess, I should think she must have been about nineteen when I made her acquaintance. My friends had come to know her at Florence; she told them she was an orphan, the child of an English father and an Italian mother, and she charmed them as she charmed me. The first time I saw her was at an evening party. I was standing by the door talking to a friend, when suddenly above the hum and babble of conversation I heard a voice which seemed to thrill to my heart. She was singing an Italian song. I was introduced to her that evening, and in three months I married Helen. Villiers, that woman, if I can call her woman, corrupted my soul. The night of the wedding I found myself sitting in her bedroom in the hotel, listening to her talk. She was sitting up in bed, and I listened to her as she spoke in her beautiful voice, spoke of things which even now I would not dare whisper in the blackest night, though I stood in the midst of a wilderness. You, Villiers, you may think you know life, and London, and what goes on day and night in this dreadful city; for all I can say you may have heard the talk of the vilest, but I tell you you can have no conception of what I know, not in your most fantastic, hideous dreams can you have imaged forth the faintest shadow of what I have heard--and seen. Yes, seen. I have seen the incredible, such horrors that even I myself sometimes stop in the middle of the street and ask whether it is possible for a man to behold such things and live. In a year, Villiers, I was a ruined man, in body and soul--in body and soul."

"But your property, Herbert? You had land in Dorset."

"I sold it all; the fields and woods, the dear old house--everything."

"And the money?"

"She took it all from me."

"And then left you?"

"Yes; she disappeared one night. I don't know where she went, but I am sure if I saw her again it would kill me. The rest of my story is of no interest; sordid misery, that is all. You may think, Villiers, that I have exaggerated and talked for effect; but I have not told you half. I could tell you certain things which would convince you, but you would never know a happy day again. You would pass the rest of your life, as I pass mine, a haunted man, a man who has seen hell."

Villiers took the unfortunate man to his rooms, and gave him a meal. Herbert could eat little, and scarcely touched the glass of wine set before him. He sat moody and silent by the fire, and seemed relieved when Villiers sent him away with a small present of money.

"By the way, Herbert," said Villiers, as they parted at the door, "what was your wife's name? You said Helen, I think? Helen what?"

"The name she passed under when I met her was Helen Vaughan, but what her real name was I can't say. I don't think she had a name. No, no, not in that sense. Only human beings have names, Villiers; I can't say anymore. Good-bye; yes, I will not fail to call if I see any way in which you can help me. Good-night."

The man went out into the bitter night, and Villiers returned to his fireside. There was something about Herbert which shocked him inexpressibly; not his poor rags nor the marks which poverty had set upon his face, but rather an indefinite terror which hung about him like a mist. He had acknowledged that he himself was not devoid of blame; the woman, he had avowed, had corrupted him body and soul, and Villiers felt that this man, once his friend, had been an actor in scenes evil beyond the power of words. His story needed no confirmation: he himself was the embodied proof of it. Villiers mused curiously over the story he had heard, and wondered whether he had heard both the first and the last of it. "No," he thought, "certainly not the last, probably only the beginning. A case like this is like a nest of Chinese boxes; you open one after the other and find a quainter workmanship in every box. Most likely poor Herbert is merely one of the outside boxes; there are stranger ones to follow."

Villiers could not take his mind away from Herbert and his story, which seemed to grow wilder as the night wore on. The fire seemed to burn low, and the chilly air of the morning crept into the room; Villiers got up with a glance over his shoulder, and, shivering slightly, went to bed.

A few days later he saw at his club a gentleman of his acquaintance, named Austin, who was famous for his intimate knowledge of London life, both in its tenebrous and luminous phases. Villiers, still full of his encounter in Soho and its consequences, thought Austin might possibly be able to shed some light on Herbert's history, and so after some casual talk he suddenly put the question:

"Do you happen to know anything of a man named Herbert--Charles Herbert?"

Austin turned round sharply and stared at Villiers with some astonishment.

"Charles Herbert? Weren't you in town three years ago? No; then you have not heard of the Paul Street case? It caused a good deal of sensation at the time."

"What was the case?"

"Well, a gentleman, a man of very good position, was found dead, stark dead, in the area of a certain house in Paul Street, off Tottenham Court Road. Of course the police did not make the discovery; if you happen to be sitting up all night and have a light in your window, the constable will ring the bell, but if you happen to be lying dead in somebody's area, you will be left alone. In this instance, as in many others, the alarm was raised by some kind of vagabond; I don't mean a common tramp, or a public-house loafer, but a gentleman, whose business or pleasure, or both, made him a spectator of the London streets at five o'clock in the morning. This individual was, as he said, 'going home,' it did not appear whence or whither, and had occasion to pass through Paul Street between four and five a.m. Something or other caught his eye at Number 20; he said, absurdly enough, that the house had the most unpleasant physiognomy he had ever observed, but, at any rate, he glanced down the area and was a good deal astonished to see a man lying on the stones, his limbs all huddled together, and his face turned up. Our gentleman thought his face looked peculiarly ghastly, and so set off at a run in search of the nearest policeman. The constable was at first inclined to treat the matter lightly, suspecting common drunkenness; however, he came, and after looking at the man's face, changed his tone, quickly enough. The early bird, who had picked up this fine worm, was sent off for a doctor, and the policeman rang and knocked at the door till a slatternly servant girl came down looking more than half asleep. The constable pointed out the contents of the area to the maid, who screamed loudly enough to wake up the street, but she knew nothing of the man; had never seen him at the house, and so forth. Meanwhile, the original discoverer had come back with a medical man, and the next thing was to get into the area. The gate was open, so the whole quartet stumped down the steps. The doctor hardly needed a moment's examination; he said the poor fellow had been dead for several hours, and it was then the case began to get interesting. The dead man had not been robbed, and in one of his pockets were papers identifying him as--well, as a man of good family and means, a favourite in society, and nobody's enemy, as far as could be known. I don't give his name, Villiers, because it has nothing to do with the story, and because it's no good raking up these affairs about the dead when there are no relations living. The next curious point was that the medical men couldn't agree as to how he met his death. There were some slight bruises on his shoulders, but they were so slight that it looked as if he had been pushed roughly out of the kitchen door, and not thrown over the railings from the street or even dragged down the steps. But there were positively no other marks of violence about him, certainly none that would account for his death; and when they came to the autopsy there wasn't a trace of poison of any kind. Of course the police wanted to know all about the people at Number 20, and here again, so I have heard from private sources, one or two other very curious points came out. It appears that the occupants of the house were a Mr. and Mrs. Charles Herbert; he was said to be a landed proprietor, though it struck most people that Paul Street was not exactly the place to look for country gentry. As for Mrs. Herbert, nobody seemed to know who or what she was, and, between ourselves, I fancy the divers after her history found themselves in rather strange waters. Of course they both denied knowing anything about the deceased, and in default of any evidence against them they were discharged. But some very odd things came out about them. Though it was between five and six in the morning when the dead man was removed, a large crowd had collected, and several of the neighbours ran to see what was going on. They were pretty free with their comments, by all accounts, and from these it appeared that Number 20 was in very bad odour in Paul Street. The detectives tried to trace down these rumours to some solid foundation of fact, but could not get hold of anything. People shook their heads and raised their eyebrows and thought the Herberts rather 'queer,' 'would rather not be seen going into their house,' and so on, but there was nothing tangible. The authorities were morally certain the man met his death in some way or another in the house and was thrown out by the kitchen door, but they couldn't prove it, and the absence of any indications of violence or poisoning left them helpless. An odd case, wasn't it? But curiously enough, there's something more that I haven't told you. I happened to know one of the doctors who was consulted as to the cause of death, and some time after the inquest I met him, and asked him about it. 'Do you really mean to tell me,' I said, 'that you were baffled by the case, that you actually don't know what the man died of?' 'Pardon me,' he replied, 'I know perfectly well what caused death. Blank died of fright, of sheer, awful terror; I never saw features so hideously contorted in the entire course of my practice, and I have seen the faces of a whole host of dead.' The doctor was usually a cool customer enough, and a certain vehemence in his manner struck me, but I couldn't get anything more out of him. I suppose the Treasury didn't see their way to prosecuting the Herberts for frightening a man to death; at any rate, nothing was done, and the case dropped out of men's minds. Do you happen to know anything of Herbert?"

"Well," replied Villiers, "he was an old college friend of mine."

"You don't say so? Have you ever seen his wife?"

"No, I haven't. I have lost sight of Herbert for many years."

"It's queer, isn't it, parting with a man at the college gate or at Paddington, seeing nothing of him for years, and then finding him pop up his head in such an odd place. But I should like to have seen Mrs. Herbert; people said extraordinary things about her."

"What sort of things?"

"Well, I hardly know how to tell you. Everyone who saw her at the police court said she was at once the most beautiful woman and the most repulsive they had ever set eyes on. I have spoken to a man who saw her, and I assure you he positively shuddered as he tried to describe the woman, but he couldn't tell why. She seems to have been a sort of enigma; and I expect if that one dead man could have told tales, he would have told some uncommonly queer ones. And there you are again in another puzzle; what could a respectable country gentleman like Mr. Blank (we'll call him that if you don't mind) want in such a very queer house as Number 20? It's altogether a very odd case, isn't it?"

"It is indeed, Austin; an extraordinary case. I didn't think, when I asked you about my old friend, I should strike on such strange metal. Well, I must be off; good-day."

Villiers went away, thinking of his own conceit of the Chinese boxes; here was quaint workmanship indeed.

IV - THE DISCOVERY IN PAUL STREET

A few months after Villiers' meeting with Herbert, Mr. Clarke was sitting, as usual, by his after-dinner hearth, resolutely guarding his fancies from wandering in the direction of the bureau. For more than a week he had succeeded in keeping away from the "Memoirs," and he cherished hopes of a complete self-reformation; but, in spite of his endeavours, he could not hush the wonder and the strange curiosity that the last case he had written down had excited within him. He had put the case, or rather the outline of it, conjecturally to a scientific friend, who shook his head, and thought Clarke getting queer, and on this particular evening Clarke was making an effort to rationalize the story, when a sudden knock at the door roused him from his meditations.

"Mr. Villiers to see you sir."

"Dear me, Villiers, it is very kind of you to look me up; I have not seen you for many months; I should think nearly a year. Come in, come in. And how are you, Villiers? Want any advice about investments?"

"No, thanks, I fancy everything I have in that way is pretty safe. No, Clarke, I have really come to consult you about a rather curious matter that has been brought under my notice of late. I am afraid you will think it all rather absurd when I tell my tale. I sometimes think so myself, and that's just what I made up my mind to come to you, as I know you're a practical man."

Mr. Villiers was ignorant of the "Memoirs to prove the Existence of the Devil."

"Well, Villiers, I shall be happy to give you my advice, to the best of my ability. What is the nature of the case?"

"It's an extraordinary thing altogether. You know my ways; I always keep my eyes open in the streets, and in my time I have chanced upon some queer customers, and queer cases too, but this, I think, beats all. I was coming out of a restaurant one nasty winter night about three months ago; I had had a capital dinner and a good bottle of Chianti, and I stood for a moment on the pavement, thinking what a mystery there is about London streets and the companies that pass along them. A bottle of red wine encourages these fancies, Clarke, and I dare say I should have thought a page of small type, but I was cut short by a beggar who had come behind me, and was making the usual appeals. Of course I looked round, and this beggar turned out to be what was left of an old friend of mine, a man named Herbert. I asked him how he had come to such a wretched pass, and he told me. We walked up and down one of those long and dark Soho streets, and there I listened to his story. He said he had married a beautiful girl, some years younger than himself, and, as he put it, she had corrupted him body and soul. He wouldn't go into details; he said he dare not, that what he had seen and heard haunted him by night and day, and when I looked in his face I knew he was speaking the truth. There was something about the man that made me shiver. I don't know why, but it was there. I gave him a little money and sent him away, and I assure you that when he was gone I gasped for breath. His presence seemed to chill one's blood."

"Isn't this all just a little fanciful, Villiers? I suppose the poor fellow had made an imprudent marriage, and, in plain English, gone to the bad."

"Well, listen to this." Villiers told Clarke the story he had heard from Austin.

"You see," he concluded, "there can be but little doubt that this Mr. Blank, whoever he was, died of sheer terror; he saw something so awful, so terrible, that it cut short his life. And what he saw, he most certainly saw in that house, which, somehow or other, had got a bad name in the neighbourhood. I had the curiosity to go and look at the place for myself. It's a saddening kind of street; the houses are old enough to be mean and dreary, but not old enough to be quaint. As far as I could see most of them are let in lodgings, furnished and unfurnished, and almost every door has three bells to it. Here and there the ground floors have been made into shops of the commonest kind; it's a dismal street in every way. I found Number 20 was to let, and I went to the agent's and got the key. Of course I should have heard nothing of the Herberts in that quarter, but I asked the man, fair and square, how long they had left the house and whether there had been other tenants in the meanwhile. He looked at me queerly for a minute, and told me the Herberts had left immediately after the unpleasantness, as he called it, and since then the house had been empty."

Mr. Villiers paused for a moment.

"I have always been rather fond of going over empty houses; there's a sort of fascination about the desolate empty rooms, with the nails sticking in the walls, and the dust thick upon the window-sills. But I didn't enjoy going over Number 20, Paul Street. I had hardly put my foot inside the passage when I noticed a queer, heavy feeling about the air of the house. Of course all empty houses are stuffy, and so forth, but this was something quite different; I can't describe it to you, but it seemed to stop the breath. I went into the front room and the back room, and the kitchens downstairs; they were all dirty and dusty enough, as you would expect, but there was something strange about them all. I couldn't define it to you, I only know I felt queer. It was one of the rooms on the first floor, though, that was the worst. It was a largish room, and once on a time the paper must have been cheerful enough, but when I saw it, paint, paper, and everything were most doleful. But the room was full of horror; I felt my teeth grinding as I put my hand on the door, and when I went in, I thought I should have fallen fainting to the floor. However, I pulled myself together, and stood against the end wall, wondering what on earth there could be about the room to make my limbs tremble, and my heart beat as if I were at the hour of death. In one corner there was a pile of newspapers littered on the floor, and I began looking at them; they were papers of three or four years ago, some of them half torn, and some crumpled as if they had been used for packing. I turned the whole pile over, and amongst them I found a curious drawing; I will show it to you presently. But I couldn't stay in the room; I felt it was overpowering me. I was thankful to come out, safe and sound, into the open air. People stared at me as I walked along the street, and one man said I was drunk. I was staggering about from one side of the pavement to the other, and it was as much as I could do to take the key back to the agent and get home. I was in bed for a week, suffering from what my doctor called nervous shock and exhaustion. One of those days I was reading the evening paper, and happened to notice a paragraph headed: 'Starved to Death.' It was the usual style of thing; a model lodging-house in Marylebone, a door locked for several days, and a dead man in his chair when they broke in. 'The deceased,' said the paragraph, 'was known as Charles Herbert, and is believed to have been once a prosperous country gentleman. His name was familiar to the public three years ago in connection with the mysterious death in Paul Street, Tottenham Court Road, the deceased being the tenant of the house Number 20, in the area of which a gentleman of good position was found dead under circumstances not devoid of suspicion.' A tragic ending, wasn't it? But after all, if what he told me were true, which I am sure it was, the man's life was all a tragedy, and a tragedy of a stranger sort than they put on the boards."

"And that is the story, is it?" said Clarke musingly.

"Yes, that is the story."

"Well, really, Villiers, I scarcely know what to say about it. There are, no doubt, circumstances in the case which seem peculiar, the finding of the dead man in the area of Herbert's house, for instance, and the extraordinary opinion of the physician as to the cause of death; but, after all, it is conceivable that the facts may be explained in a straightforward manner. As to your own sensations, when you went to see the house, I would suggest that they were due to a vivid imagination; you must have been brooding, in a semi-conscious way, over what you had heard. I don't exactly see what more can be said or done in the matter; you evidently think there is a mystery of some kind, but Herbert is dead; where then do you propose to look?"

"I propose to look for the woman; the woman whom he married. She is the mystery."

The two men sat silent by the fireside; Clarke secretly congratulating himself on having successfully kept up the character of advocate of the commonplace, and Villiers wrapped in his gloomy fancies.

"I think I will have a cigarette," he said at last, and put his hand in his pocket to feel for the cigarette-case.

"Ah!" he said, starting slightly, "I forgot I had something to show you. You remember my saying that I had found a rather curious sketch amongst the pile of old newspapers at the house in Paul Street? Here it is."

Villiers drew out a small thin parcel from his pocket. It was covered with brown paper, and secured with string, and the knots were troublesome. In spite of himself Clarke felt inquisitive; he bent forward on his chair as Villiers painfully undid the string, and unfolded the outer covering. Inside was a second wrapping of tissue, and Villiers took it off and handed the small piece of paper to Clarke without a word.

There was dead silence in the room for five minutes or more; the two men sat so still that they could hear the ticking of the tall old-fashioned clock that stood outside in the hall, and in the mind of one of them the slow monotony of sound woke up a far, far memory. He was looking intently at the small pen-and-ink sketch of the woman's head; it had evidently been drawn with great care, and by a true artist, for the woman's soul looked out of the eyes, and the lips were parted with a strange smile. Clarke gazed still at the face; it brought to his memory one summer evening, long ago; he saw again the long lovely valley, the river winding between the hills, the meadows and the cornfields, the dull red sun, and the cold white mist rising from the water. He heard a voice speaking to him across the waves of many years, and saying "Clarke, Mary will see the god Pan!" and then he was standing in the grim room beside the doctor, listening to the heavy ticking of the clock, waiting and watching, watching the figure lying on the green chair beneath the lamplight. Mary rose up, and he looked into her eyes, and his heart grew cold within him.

"Who is this woman?" he said at last. His voice was dry and hoarse.

"That is the woman who Herbert married."

Clarke looked again at the sketch; it was not Mary after all. There certainly was Mary's face, but there was something else, something he had not seen on Mary's features when the white-clad girl entered the laboratory with the doctor, nor at her terrible awakening, nor when she lay grinning on the bed. Whatever it was, the glance that came from those eyes, the smile on the full lips, or the expression of the whole face, Clarke shuddered before it at his inmost soul, and thought, unconsciously, of Dr. Phillip's words, "the most vivid presentment of evil I have ever seen." He turned the paper over mechanically in his hand and glanced at the back.

"Good God! Clarke, what is the matter? You are as white as death."

Villiers had started wildly from his chair, as Clarke fell back with a groan, and let the paper drop from his hands.

"I don't feel very well, Villiers, I am subject to these attacks. Pour me out a little wine; thanks, that will do. I shall feel better in a few minutes."

Villiers picked up the fallen sketch and turned it over as Clarke had done.

"You saw that?" he said. "That's how I identified it as being a portrait of Herbert's wife, or I should say his widow. How do you feel now?"

"Better, thanks, it was only a passing faintness. I don't think I quite catch your meaning. What did you say enabled you to identify the picture?"

"This word--'Helen'--was written on the back. Didn't I tell you her name was Helen? Yes; Helen Vaughan."

Clarke groaned; there could be no shadow of doubt.

"Now, don't you agree with me," said Villiers, "that in the story I have told you to-night, and in the part this woman plays in it, there are some very strange points?"

"Yes, Villiers," Clarke muttered, "it is a strange story indeed; a strange story indeed. You must give me time to think it over; I may be able to help you or I may not. Must you be going now? Well, good-night, Villiers, good-night. Come and see me in the course of a week."

V - THE LETTER OF ADVICE

"Do you know, Austin," said Villiers, as the two friends were pacing sedately along Piccadilly one pleasant morning in May, "do you know I am convinced that what you told me about Paul Street and the Herberts is a mere episode in an extraordinary history? I may as well confess to you that when I asked you about Herbert a few months ago I had just seen him."

"You had seen him? Where?"

"He begged of me in the street one night. He was in the most pitiable plight, but I recognized the man, and I got him to tell me his history, or at least the outline of it. In brief, it amounted to this--he had been ruined by his wife."

"In what manner?"

"He would not tell me; he would only say that she had destroyed him, body and soul. The man is dead now."

"And what has become of his wife?"

"Ah, that's what I should like to know, and I mean to find her sooner or later. I know a man named Clarke, a dry fellow, in fact a man of business, but shrewd enough. You understand my meaning; not shrewd in the mere business sense of the word, but a man who really knows something about men and life. Well, I laid the case before him, and he was evidently impressed. He said it needed consideration, and asked me to come again in the course of a week. A few days later I received this extraordinary letter."

Austin took the envelope, drew out the letter, and read it curiously. It ran as follows:--

"MY DEAR VILLIERS,--I have thought over the matter on which you consulted me the other night, and my advice to you is this. Throw the portrait into the fire, blot out the story from your mind. Never give it another thought, Villiers, or you will be sorry. You will think, no doubt, that I am in possession of some secret information, and to a certain extent that is the case. But I only know a little; I am like a traveller who has peered over an abyss, and has drawn back in terror.

What I know is strange enough and horrible enough, but beyond my knowledge there are depths and horrors more frightful still, more incredible than any tale told of winter nights about the fire. I have resolved, and nothing shall shake that resolve, to explore no whit farther, and if you value your happiness you will make the same determination.

"Come and see me by all means; but we will talk on more cheerful topics than this."

Austin folded the letter methodically, and returned it to Villiers.

"It is certainly an extraordinary letter," he said, "what does he mean by the portrait?"

"Ah! I forgot to tell you I have been to Paul Street and have made a discovery."

Villiers told his story as he had told it to Clarke, and Austin listened in silence. He seemed puzzled.

"How very curious that you should experience such an unpleasant sensation in that room!" he said at length. "I hardly gather that it was a mere matter of the imagination; a feeling of repulsion, in short."

"No, it was more physical than mental. It was as if I were inhaling at every breath some deadly fume, which seemed to penetrate to every nerve and bone and sinew of my body. I felt racked from head to foot, my eyes began to grow dim; it was like the entrance of death."

"Yes, yes, very strange certainly. You see, your friend confesses that there is some very black story connected with this woman. Did you notice any particular emotion in him when you were telling your tale?"

"Yes, I did. He became very faint, but he assured me that it was a mere passing attack to which he was subject."

"Did you believe him?"

"I did at the time, but I don't now. He heard what I had to say with a good deal of indifference, till I showed him the portrait. It was then that he was seized with the attack of which I spoke. He looked ghastly, I assure you."

"Then he must have seen the woman before. But there might be another explanation; it might have been the name, and not the face, which was familiar to him. What do you think?"

"I couldn't say. To the best of my belief it was after turning the portrait in his hands that he nearly dropped from the chair. The name, you know, was written on the back."

"Quite so. After all, it is impossible to come to any resolution in a case like this. I hate melodrama, and nothing strikes me as more commonplace and tedious than the ordinary ghost story of commerce; but really, Villiers, it looks as if there were something very queer at the bottom of all this."

The two men had, without noticing it, turned up Ashley Street, leading northward from Piccadilly. It was a long street, and rather a gloomy one, but here and there a brighter taste had illuminated the dark houses with flowers, and gay curtains, and a cheerful paint on the doors. Villiers glanced up as Austin stopped speaking, and looked at one of these houses; geraniums, red and white, drooped from every sill, and daffodil-coloured curtains were draped back from each window.

"It looks cheerful, doesn't it?" he said.

"Yes, and the inside is still more cheery. One of the pleasantest houses of the season, so I have heard. I haven't been there myself, but I've met several men who have, and they tell me it's uncommonly jovial."

"Whose house is it?"

"A Mrs. Beaumont's."

"And who is she?"

"I couldn't tell you. I have heard she comes from South America, but after all, who she is is of little consequence. She is a very wealthy woman, there's no doubt of that, and some of the best people have taken her up. I hear she has some wonderful claret, really marvellous wine, which must have cost a fabulous sum. Lord Argentine was telling me about it; he was there last Sunday evening. He assures me he has never tasted such a wine, and Argentine, as you know, is an expert. By the way, that reminds me, she must be an oddish sort of woman, this Mrs. Beaumont. Argentine asked her how old the wine was, and what do you think she said? 'About a thousand years, I believe.' Lord Argentine thought she was chaffing him, you know, but when he laughed she said she was speaking quite seriously and offered to show him the jar. Of course, he couldn't say anything more after that; but it seems rather antiquated for a beverage, doesn't it? Why, here we are at my rooms. Come in, won't you?"

"Thanks, I think I will. I haven't seen the curiosity-shop for a while."

It was a room furnished richly, yet oddly, where every jar and bookcase and table, and every rug and jar and ornament seemed to be a thing apart, preserving each its own individuality.

"Anything fresh lately?" said Villiers after a while.

"No; I think not; you saw those queer jugs, didn't you? I thought so. I don't think I have come across anything for the last few weeks."

Austin glanced around the room from cupboard to cupboard, from shelf to shelf, in search of some new oddity. His eyes fell at last on an odd chest, pleasantly and quaintly carved, which stood in a dark corner of the room.

"Ah," he said, "I was forgetting, I have got something to show you." Austin unlocked the chest, drew out a thick quarto volume, laid it on the table, and resumed the cigar he had put down.

"Did you know Arthur Meyrick the painter, Villiers?"

"A little; I met him two or three times at the house of a friend of mine. What has become of him? I haven't heard his name mentioned for some time."

"He's dead."

"You don't say so! Quite young, wasn't he?"

"Yes; only thirty when he died."

"What did he die of?"

"I don't know. He was an intimate friend of mine, and a thoroughly good fellow. He used to come here and talk to me for hours, and he was one of the best talkers I have met. He could even talk about painting, and that's more than can be said of most painters. About eighteen months ago he was feeling rather overworked, and partly at my suggestion he went off on a sort of roving expedition, with no very definite end or aim about it. I believe New York was to be his first port, but I never heard from him. Three months ago I got this book, with a very civil letter from an English doctor practising at Buenos Ayres, stating that he had attended the late Mr. Meyrick during his illness, and that the deceased had expressed an earnest wish that the enclosed packet should be sent to me after his death. That was all."

"And haven't you written for further particulars?"

"I have been thinking of doing so. You would advise me to write to the doctor?"

"Certainly. And what about the book?"

"It was sealed up when I got it. I don't think the doctor had seen it."

"It is something very rare? Meyrick was a collector, perhaps?"

"No, I think not, hardly a collector. Now, what do you think of these Ainu jugs?"

"They are peculiar, but I like them. But aren't you going to show me poor Meyrick's legacy?"

"Yes, yes, to be sure. The fact is, it's rather a peculiar sort of thing, and I haven't shown it to any one. I wouldn't say anything about it if I were you. There it is."

Villiers took the book, and opened it at haphazard.

"It isn't a printed volume, then?" he said.

"No. It is a collection of drawings in black and white by my poor friend Meyrick."

Villiers turned to the first page, it was blank; the second bore a brief inscription, which he read:

Silet per diem universus, nec sine horrore secretus est; lucet nocturnis ignibus, chorus Aegipanum undique personatur: audiuntur et cantus tibiarum, et tinnitus cymbalorum per oram maritimam.

On the third page was a design which made Villiers start and look up at Austin; he was gazing abstractedly out of the window. Villiers turned page after page, absorbed, in spite of himself, in the frightful Walpurgis Night of evil, strange monstrous evil, that the dead artist had set forth in hard black and white. The figures of Fauns and Satyrs and Aegipans danced before his eyes, the darkness of the thicket, the dance on the mountain-top, the scenes by lonely shores, in green vineyards, by rocks and desert places, passed before him: a world before which the human soul seemed to shrink back and shudder. Villiers whirled over the remaining pages; he had seen enough, but the picture on the last leaf caught his eye, as he almost closed the book.

"Austin!"

"Well, what is it?"

"Do you know who that is?"

It was a woman's face, alone on the white page.

"Know who it is? No, of course not."

"I do."

"Who is it?"

"It is Mrs. Herbert."

"Are you sure?"

"I am perfectly sure of it. Poor Meyrick! He is one more chapter in her history."

"But what do you think of the designs?"

"They are frightful. Lock the book up again, Austin. If I were you I would burn it; it must be a terrible companion even though it be in a chest."

"Yes, they are singular drawings. But I wonder what connection there could be between Meyrick and Mrs. Herbert, or what link between her and these designs?"

"Ah, who can say? It is possible that the matter may end here, and we shall never know, but in my own opinion this Helen Vaughan, or Mrs. Herbert, is only the beginning. She will come back to London, Austin; depend on it, she will come back, and we shall hear more about her then. I doubt it will be very pleasant news."

VI - THE SUICIDES

Lord Argentine was a great favourite in London Society. At twenty he had been a poor man, decked with the surname of an illustrious family, but forced to earn a livelihood as best he could, and the most speculative of money-lenders would not have entrusted him with fifty pounds on the chance of his ever changing his name for a title, and his poverty for a great fortune. His father had been near enough to the fountain of good things to secure one of the family livings, but the son, even if he had taken orders, would scarcely have obtained so much as this, and moreover felt no vocation for the ecclesiastical estate. Thus he fronted the world with no better armour than the bachelor's gown and the wits of a younger son's grandson, with which equipment he contrived in some way to make a very tolerable fight of it. At twenty-five Mr. Charles Aubernon saw himself still a man of struggles and of warfare with the world, but out of the seven who stood before him and the high places of his family three only remained. These three, however, were "good lives," but yet not proof against the Zulu assegais and typhoid fever, and so one morning Aubernon woke up and found himself Lord Argentine, a man of thirty who had faced the difficulties of existence, and had conquered. The situation amused him immensely, and he resolved that riches should be as pleasant to him as poverty had always been. Argentine, after some little consideration, came to the conclusion that dining, regarded as a fine art, was perhaps the most amusing pursuit open to fallen humanity, and thus his dinners became famous in London, and an invitation to his table a thing covetously desired. After ten years of lordship and dinners Argentine still declined to be jaded, still persisted in enjoying life, and by a kind of infection had become recognized as the cause of joy in others, in short, as the best of company. His sudden and tragical death therefore caused a wide and deep sensation. People could scarcely believe it, even though the newspaper was before their eyes, and the cry of "Mysterious Death of a Nobleman" came ringing up from the street. But there stood the brief paragraph: "Lord Argentine was found dead this morning by his valet under distressing circumstances. It is stated that there can be no doubt that his lordship committed suicide, though no motive can be assigned for the act. The deceased nobleman was widely known in society, and much liked for his genial manner and sumptuous hospitality. He is succeeded by," etc., etc.

By slow degrees the details came to light, but the case still remained a mystery. The chief witness at the inquest was the deceased's valet, who said that the night before his death Lord Argentine had dined with a lady of good position, whose name was suppressed in the newspaper reports. At about eleven o'clock Lord Argentine had returned, and informed his man that he should not require his services till the next morning. A little later the valet had occasion to cross the hall and was somewhat astonished to see his master quietly letting himself out at the front door. He had taken off his evening clothes, and was dressed in a Norfolk coat and knickerbockers, and wore a low brown hat. The valet had no reason to suppose that Lord Argentine had seen him, and though his master rarely kept late hours, thought little of the occurrence till the next morning, when he knocked at the bedroom door at a quarter to nine as usual. He received no answer, and, after knocking two or three times, entered the room, and saw Lord Argentine's body leaning forward at an angle from the bottom of the bed. He found that his master had tied a cord securely to one of the short bed-posts, and, after making a running noose and slipping it round his neck, the unfortunate man must have resolutely fallen forward, to die by slow strangulation. He was dressed in the light suit in which the valet had seen him go out, and the doctor who was summoned pronounced that life had been extinct for more than four hours. All papers, letters, and so forth seemed in perfect order, and nothing was discovered which pointed in the most remote way to any scandal either great or small. Here the evidence ended; nothing more could be discovered. Several persons had been present at the dinner-party at which Lord Argentine had assisted, and to all these he seemed in his usual genial spirits. The valet, indeed, said he thought his master appeared a little excited when he came home, but confessed that the alteration in his manner was very slight, hardly noticeable, indeed. It seemed hopeless to seek for any clue, and the suggestion that Lord Argentine had been suddenly attacked by acute suicidal mania was generally accepted.

It was otherwise, however, when within three weeks, three more gentlemen, one of them a nobleman, and the two others men of good position and ample means, perished miserably in the almost precisely the same manner. Lord Swanleigh was found one morning in his dressing-room, hanging from a peg affixed to the wall, and Mr. Collier-Stuart and Mr. Herries had chosen to die as Lord Argentine. There was no explanation in either case; a few bald facts; a living man in the evening, and a body with a black swollen face in the morning. The police had been forced to confess themselves powerless to arrest or to explain the sordid murders of Whitechapel; but before the horrible suicides of Piccadilly and Mayfair they were dumbfoundered, for not even the mere ferocity which did duty as an explanation of the crimes of the East End, could be of service in the West. Each of these men who had resolved to die a tortured shameful death was rich, prosperous, and to all appearances in love with the world, and not the acutest research should ferret out any shadow of a lurking motive in either case. There was a horror in the air, and men looked at one another's faces when they met, each wondering whether the other was to be the victim of the fifth nameless tragedy. Journalists sought in vain for their scrapbooks for materials whereof to concoct reminiscent articles; and the morning paper was unfolded in many a house with a feeling of awe; no man knew when or where the next blow would light.

A short while after the last of these terrible events, Austin came to see Mr. Villiers. He was curious to know whether Villiers had succeeded in discovering any fresh traces of Mrs. Herbert, either through Clarke or by other sources, and he asked the question soon after he had sat down.

"No," said Villiers, "I wrote to Clarke, but he remains obdurate, and I have tried other channels, but without any result. I can't find out what became of Helen Vaughan after she left Paul Street, but I think she must have gone abroad. But to tell the truth, Austin, I haven't paid much attention to the matter for the last few weeks; I knew poor Herries intimately, and his terrible death has been a great shock to me."

"I can well believe it," answered Austin gravely, "you know Argentine was a friend of mine. If I remember rightly, we were speaking of him that day you came to my rooms."

"Yes; it was in connection with that house in Ashley Street, Mrs. Beaumont's house. You said something about Argentine's dining there."

"Quite so. Of course you know it was there Argentine dined the night before--before his death."

"No, I had not heard that."

"Oh, yes; the name was kept out of the papers to spare Mrs. Beaumont. Argentine was a great favourite of hers, and it is said she was in a terrible state for sometime after."

A curious look came over Villiers' face; he seemed undecided whether to speak or not. Austin began again.

"I never experienced such a feeling of horror as when I read the account of Argentine's death. I didn't understand it at the time, and I don't now. I knew him well, and it completely passes my understanding for what possible cause he--or any of the others for the matter of that--could have resolved in cold blood to die in such an awful manner. You know how men babble away each other's characters in London, you may be sure any buried scandal or hidden skeleton would have been brought to light in such a case as this; but nothing of the sort has taken place. As for the theory of mania, that is very well, of course, for the coroner's jury, but everybody knows that it's all nonsense. Suicidal mania is not small-pox."

Austin relapsed into gloomy silence. Villiers sat silent, also, watching his friend. The expression of indecision still fleeted across his face; he seemed as if weighing his thoughts in the balance, and the considerations he was resolving left him still silent. Austin tried to shake off the remembrance of tragedies as hopeless and perplexed as the labyrinth of Daedalus, and began to talk in an indifferent voice of the more pleasant incidents and adventures of the season.

"That Mrs. Beaumont," he said, "of whom we were speaking, is a great success; she has taken London almost by storm. I met her the other night at Fulham's; she is really a remarkable woman."

"You have met Mrs. Beaumont?"

"Yes; she had quite a court around her. She would be called very handsome, I suppose, and yet there is something about her face which I didn't like. The features are exquisite, but the expression is strange. And all the time I was looking at her, and afterwards, when I was going home, I had a curious feeling that very expression was in some way or another familiar to me."

"You must have seen her in the Row."

"No, I am sure I never set eyes on the woman before; it is that which makes it puzzling. And to the best of my belief I have never seen anyone like her; what I felt was a kind of dim far-off memory, vague but persistent. The only sensation I can compare it to, is that odd feeling one sometimes has in a dream, when fantastic cities and wondrous lands and phantom personages appear familiar and accustomed."

Villiers nodded and glanced aimlessly round the room, possibly in search of something on which to turn the conversation. His eyes fell on an old chest somewhat like that in which the artist's strange legacy lay hid beneath a Gothic scutcheon.

"Have you written to the doctor about poor Meyrick?" he asked.

"Yes; I wrote asking for full particulars as to his illness and death. I don't expect to have an answer for another three weeks or a month. I thought I might as well inquire whether Meyrick knew an Englishwoman named Herbert, and if so, whether the doctor could give me any information about her. But it's very possible that Meyrick fell in with her at New York, or Mexico, or San Francisco; I have no idea as to the extent or direction of his travels."

"Yes, and it's very possible that the woman may have more than one name."

"Exactly. I wish I had thought of asking you to lend me the portrait of her which you possess. I might have enclosed it in my letter to Dr. Matthews."

"So you might; that never occurred to me. We might send it now. Hark! what are those boys calling?"

While the two men had been talking together a confused noise of shouting had been gradually growing louder. The noise rose from the eastward and swelled down Piccadilly, drawing nearer and nearer, a very torrent of sound; surging up streets usually quiet, and making every window a frame for a face, curious or excited. The cries and voices came echoing up the silent street where Villiers lived, growing more distinct as they advanced, and, as Villiers spoke, an answer rang up from the pavement:

"The West End Horrors; Another Awful Suicide; Full Details!"

Austin rushed down the stairs and bought a paper and read out the paragraph to Villiers as the uproar in the street rose and fell. The window was open and the air seemed full of noise and terror.

"Another gentleman has fallen a victim to the terrible epidemic of suicide which for the last month has prevailed in the West End. Mr. Sidney Crashaw, of Stoke House, Fulham, and King's Pomeroy, Devon, was found, after a prolonged search, hanging dead from the branch of a tree in his garden at one o'clock today. The deceased gentleman dined last night at the Carlton Club and seemed in his usual health and spirits. He left the club at about ten o'clock, and was seen walking leisurely up St. James's Street a little later. Subsequent to this his movements cannot be traced. On the discovery of the body medical aid was at once summoned, but life had evidently been long extinct. So far as is known, Mr. Crashaw had no trouble or anxiety of any kind. This painful suicide, it will be remembered, is the fifth of the kind in the last month. The authorities at Scotland Yard are unable to suggest any explanation of these terrible occurrences."

Austin put down the paper in mute horror.

"I shall leave London to-morrow," he said, "it is a city of nightmares. How awful this is, Villiers!"

Mr. Villiers was sitting by the window quietly looking out into the street. He had listened to the newspaper report attentively, and the hint of indecision was no longer on his face.

"Wait a moment, Austin," he replied, "I have made up my mind to mention a little matter that occurred last night. It stated, I think, that Crashaw was last seen alive in St. James's Street shortly after ten?"

"Yes, I think so. I will look again. Yes, you are quite right."

"Quite so. Well, I am in a position to contradict that statement at all events. Crashaw was seen after that; considerably later indeed."

"How do you know?"

"Because I happened to see Crashaw myself at about two o'clock this morning."

"You saw Crashaw? You, Villiers?"

"Yes, I saw him quite distinctly; indeed, there were but a few feet between us."

"Where, in Heaven's name, did you see him?"

"Not far from here. I saw him in Ashley Street. He was just leaving a house."

"Did you notice what house it was?"

"Yes. It was Mrs. Beaumont's."

"Villiers! Think what you are saying; there must be some mistake. How could Crashaw be in Mrs. Beaumont's house at two o'clock in the morning? Surely, surely, you must have been dreaming, Villiers; you were always rather fanciful."

"No; I was wide awake enough. Even if I had been dreaming as you say, what I saw would have roused me effectually."

"What you saw? What did you see? Was there anything strange about Crashaw? But I can't believe it; it is impossible."

"Well, if you like I will tell you what I saw, or if you please, what I think I saw, and you can judge for yourself."

"Very good, Villiers."

The noise and clamour of the street had died away, though now and then the sound of shouting still came from the distance, and the dull, leaden silence seemed like the quiet after an earthquake or a storm. Villiers turned from the window and began speaking.

"I was at a house near Regent's Park last night, and when I came away the fancy took me to walk home instead of taking a hansom. It was a clear pleasant night enough, and after a few minutes I had the streets pretty much to myself. It's a curious thing, Austin, to be alone in London at night, the gas-lamps stretching away in perspective, and the dead silence, and then perhaps the rush and clatter of a hansom on the stones, and the fire starting up under the horse's hoofs. I walked along pretty briskly, for I was feeling a little tired of being out in the night, and as the clocks were striking two I turned down Ashley Street, which, you know, is on my way. It was quieter than ever there, and the lamps were fewer; altogether, it looked as dark and gloomy as a forest in winter. I had done about half the length of the street when I heard a door closed very softly, and naturally I looked up to see who was abroad like myself at such an hour. As it happens, there is a street lamp close to the house in question, and I saw a man standing on the step. He had just shut the door and his face was towards me, and I recognized Crashaw directly. I never knew him to speak to, but I had often seen him, and I am positive that I was not mistaken in my man. I looked into his face for a moment, and then--I will confess the truth--I set off at a good run, and kept it up till I was within my own door."

"Why?"

"Why? Because it made my blood run cold to see that man's face. I could never have supposed that such an infernal medley of passions could have glared out of any human eyes; I almost fainted as I looked. I knew I had looked into the eyes of a lost soul, Austin, the man's outward form remained, but all hell was within it. Furious lust, and hate that was like fire, and the loss of all hope and horror that seemed to shriek aloud to the night, though his teeth were shut; and the utter blackness of despair. I am sure that he did not see me; he saw nothing that you or I can see, but what he saw I hope we never shall. I do not know when he died; I suppose in an hour, or perhaps two, but when I passed down Ashley Street and heard the closing door, that man no longer belonged to this world; it was a devil's face I looked upon."

There was an interval of silence in the room when Villiers ceased speaking. The light was failing, and all the tumult of an hour ago was quite hushed. Austin had bent his head at the close of the story, and his hand covered his eyes.

"What can it mean?" he said at length.

"Who knows, Austin, who knows? It's a black business, but I think we had better keep it to ourselves, for the present at any rate. I will see if I cannot learn anything about that house through private channels of information, and if I do light upon anything I will let you know."

VII - THE ENCOUNTER IN SOHO

Three weeks later Austin received a note from Villiers, asking him to call either that afternoon or the next. He chose the nearer date, and found Villiers sitting as usual by the window, apparently lost in meditation on the drowsy traffic of the street. There was a bamboo table by his side, a fantastic thing, enriched with gilding and queer painted scenes, and on it lay a little pile of papers arranged and docketed as neatly as anything in Mr. Clarke's office.

"Well, Villiers, have you made any discoveries in the last three weeks?"

"I think so; I have here one or two memoranda which struck me as singular, and there is a statement to which I shall call your attention."

"And these documents relate to Mrs. Beaumont? It was really Crashaw whom you saw that night standing on the doorstep of the house in Ashley Street?"

"As to that matter my belief remains unchanged, but neither my inquiries nor their results have any special relation to Crashaw. But my investigations have had a strange issue. I have found out who Mrs. Beaumont is!"

"Who is she? In what way do you mean?"

"I mean that you and I know her better under another name."

"What name is that?"

"Herbert."

"Herbert!" Austin repeated the word, dazed with astonishment.

"Yes, Mrs. Herbert of Paul Street, Helen Vaughan of earlier adventures unknown to me. You had reason to recognize the expression of her face; when you go home look at the face in Meyrick's book of horrors, and you will know the sources of your recollection."

"And you have proof of this?"

"Yes, the best of proof; I have seen Mrs. Beaumont, or shall we say Mrs. Herbert?"

"Where did you see her?"

"Hardly in a place where you would expect to see a lady who lives in Ashley Street, Piccadilly. I saw her entering a house in one of the meanest and most disreputable streets in Soho. In fact, I had made an appointment, though not with her, and she was precise to both time and place."

"All this seems very wonderful, but I cannot call it incredible. You must remember, Villiers, that I have seen this woman, in the ordinary adventure of London society, talking and laughing, and sipping her coffee in a commonplace drawing-room with commonplace people. But you know what you are saying."

"I do; I have not allowed myself to be led by surmises or fancies. It was with no thought of finding Helen Vaughan that I searched for Mrs. Beaumont in the dark waters of the life of London, but such has been the issue."

"You must have been in strange places, Villiers."

"Yes, I have been in very strange places. It would have been useless, you know, to go to Ashley Street, and ask Mrs. Beaumont to give me a short sketch of her previous history. No; assuming, as I had to assume, that her record was not of the cleanest, it would be pretty certain that at some previous time she must have moved in circles not quite so refined as her present ones. If you see mud at the top of a stream, you may be sure that it was once at the bottom. I went to the bottom. I have always been fond of diving into Queer Street for my amusement, and I found my knowledge of that locality and its inhabitants very useful. It is, perhaps, needless to say that my friends had never heard the name of Beaumont, and as I had never seen the lady, and was quite unable to describe her, I had to set to work in an indirect way. The people there know me; I have been able to do some of them a service now and again, so they made no difficulty about giving their information; they were aware I had no communication direct or indirect with Scotland Yard. I had to cast out a good many lines, though, before I got what I wanted, and when I landed the fish I did not for a moment suppose it was my fish. But I listened to what I was told out of a constitutional liking for useless information, and I found myself in possession of a very curious story, though, as I imagined, not the story I was looking for. It was to this effect. Some five or six years ago, a woman named Raymond suddenly made her appearance in the neighbourhood to which I am referring. She was described to me as being quite young, probably not more than seventeen or eighteen, very handsome, and looking as if she came from the country. I should be wrong in saying that she found her level in going to this particular quarter, or associating with these people, for from what I was told, I should think the worst den in London far too good for her. The person from whom I got my information, as you may suppose, no great Puritan, shuddered and grew sick in telling me of the nameless infamies which were laid to her charge. After living there for a year, or perhaps a little more, she disappeared as suddenly as she came, and they saw nothing of her till about the time of the Paul Street case. At first she came to her old haunts only occasionally, then more frequently, and finally took up her abode there as before, and remained for six or eight months. It's of no use my going into details as to the life that woman led; if you want particulars you can look at Meyrick's legacy. Those designs were not drawn from his imagination. She again disappeared, and the people of the place saw nothing of her till a few months ago. My informant told me that she had taken some rooms in a house which he pointed out, and these rooms she was in the habit of visiting two or three times a week and always at ten in the morning. I was led to expect that one of these visits would be paid on a certain day about a week ago, and I accordingly managed to be on the look-out in company with my cicerone at a quarter to ten, and the hour and the lady came with equal punctuality. My friend and I were standing under an archway, a little way back from the street, but she saw us, and gave me a glance that I shall be long in forgetting. That look was quite enough for me; I knew Miss Raymond to be Mrs. Herbert; as for Mrs. Beaumont she had quite gone out of my head. She went into the house, and I watched it till four o'clock, when she came out, and then I followed her. It was a long chase, and I had to be very careful to keep a long way in the background, and yet not lose sight of the woman. She took me down to the Strand, and then to Westminster, and then up St. James's Street, and along Piccadilly. I felt queerish when I saw her turn up Ashley Street; the thought that Mrs. Herbert was Mrs. Beaumont came into my mind, but it seemed too impossible to be true. I waited at the corner, keeping my eye on her all the time, and I took particular care to note the house at which she stopped. It was the house with the gay curtains, the home of flowers, the house out of which Crashaw came the night he hanged himself in his garden. I was just going away with my discovery, when I saw an empty carriage come round and draw up in front of the house, and I came to the conclusion that Mrs. Herbert was going out for a drive, and I was right. There, as it happened, I met a man I know, and we stood talking together a little distance from the carriage-way, to which I had my back. We had not been there for ten minutes when my friend took off his hat, and I glanced round and saw the lady I had been following all day. 'Who is that?' I said, and his answer was 'Mrs. Beaumont; lives in Ashley Street.' Of course there could be no doubt after that. I don't know whether she saw me, but I don't think she did. I went home at once, and, on consideration, I thought that I had a sufficiently good case with which to go to Clarke."

"Why to Clarke?"

"Because I am sure that Clarke is in possession of facts about this woman, facts of which I know nothing."

"Well, what then?"

Mr. Villiers leaned back in his chair and looked reflectively at Austin for a moment before he answered:

"My idea was that Clarke and I should call on Mrs. Beaumont."

"You would never go into such a house as that? No, no, Villiers, you cannot do it. Besides, consider; what result..."

"I will tell you soon. But I was going to say that my information does not end here; it has been completed in an extraordinary manner.

"Look at this neat little packet of manuscript; it is paginated, you see, and I have indulged in the civil coquetry of a ribbon of red tape. It has almost a legal air, hasn't it? Run your eye over it, Austin. It is an account of the entertainment Mrs. Beaumont provided for her choicer guests. The man who wrote this escaped with his life, but I do not think he will live many years. The doctors tell him he must have sustained some severe shock to the nerves."

Austin took the manuscript, but never read it. Opening the neat pages at haphazard his eye was caught by a word and a phrase that followed it; and, sick at heart, with white lips and a cold sweat pouring like water from his temples, he flung the paper down.

"Take it away, Villiers, never speak of this again. Are you made of stone, man? Why, the dread and horror of death itself, the thoughts of the man who stands in the keen morning air on the black platform, bound, the bell tolling in his ears, and waits for the harsh rattle of the bolt, are as nothing compared to this. I will not read it; I should never sleep again."

"Very good. I can fancy what you saw. Yes; it is horrible enough; but after all, it is an old story, an old mystery played in our day, and in dim London streets instead of amidst the vineyards and the olive gardens. We know what happened to those who chanced to meet the Great God Pan, and those who are wise know that all symbols are symbols of something, not of nothing. It was, indeed, an exquisite symbol beneath which men long ago veiled their knowledge of the most awful, most secret forces which lie at the heart of all things; forces before which the souls of men must wither and die and blacken, as their bodies blacken under the electric current. Such forces cannot be named, cannot be spoken, cannot be imagined except under a veil and a symbol, a symbol to the most of us appearing a quaint, poetic fancy, to some a foolish tale. But you and I, at all events, have known something of the terror that may dwell in the secret place of life, manifested under human flesh; that which is without form taking to itself a form. Oh, Austin, how can it be? How is it that the very sunlight does not turn to blackness before this thing, the hard earth melt and boil beneath such a burden?"

Villiers was pacing up and down the room, and the beads of sweat stood out on his forehead. Austin sat silent for a while, but Villiers saw him make a sign upon his breast.

"I say again, Villiers, you will surely never enter such a house as that? You would never pass out alive."

"Yes, Austin, I shall go out alive--I, and Clarke with me."

"What do you mean? You cannot, you would not dare..."

"Wait a moment. The air was very pleasant and fresh this morning; there was a breeze blowing, even through this dull street, and I thought I would take a walk. Piccadilly stretched before me a clear, bright vista, and the sun flashed on the carriages and on the quivering leaves in the park. It was a joyous morning, and men and women looked at the sky and smiled as they went about their work or their pleasure, and the wind blew as blithely as upon the meadows and the scented gorse. But somehow or other I got out of the bustle and the gaiety, and found myself walking slowly along a quiet, dull street, where there seemed to be no sunshine and no air, and where the few foot-passengers loitered as they walked, and hung indecisively about corners and archways. I walked along, hardly knowing where I was going or what I did there, but feeling impelled, as one sometimes is, to explore still further, with a vague idea of reaching some unknown goal. Thus I forged up the street, noting the small traffic of the milk-shop, and wondering at the incongruous medley of penny pipes, black tobacco, sweets, newspapers, and comic songs which here and there jostled one another in the short compass of a single window. I think it was a cold shudder that suddenly passed through me that first told me that I had found what I wanted. I looked up from the pavement and stopped before a dusty shop, above which the lettering had faded, where the red bricks of two hundred years ago had grimed to black; where the windows had gathered to themselves the dust of winters innumerable. I saw what I required; but I think it was five minutes before I had steadied myself and could walk in and ask for it in a cool voice and with a calm face. I think there must even then have been a tremor in my words, for the old man who came out of the back parlour, and fumbled slowly amongst his goods, looked oddly at me as he tied the parcel. I paid what he asked, and stood leaning by the counter, with a strange reluctance to take up my goods and go. I asked about the business, and learnt that trade was bad and the profits cut down sadly; but then the street was not what it was before traffic had been diverted, but that was done forty years ago, 'just before my father died,' he said. I got away at last, and walked along sharply; it was a dismal street indeed, and I was glad to return to the bustle and the noise. Would you like to see my purchase?"

Austin said nothing, but nodded his head slightly; he still looked white and sick. Villiers pulled out a drawer in the bamboo table, and showed Austin a long coil of cord, hard and new; and at one end was a running noose.

"It is the best hempen cord," said Villiers, "just as it used to be made for the old trade, the man told me. Not an inch of jute from end to end."

Austin set his teeth hard, and stared at Villiers, growing whiter as he looked.

"You would not do it," he murmured at last. "You would not have blood on your hands. My God!" he exclaimed, with sudden vehemence, "you cannot mean this, Villiers, that you will make yourself a hangman?"

"No. I shall offer a choice, and leave Helen Vaughan alone with this cord in a locked room for fifteen minutes. If when we go in it is not done, I shall call the nearest policeman. That is all."

"I must go now. I cannot stay here any longer; I cannot bear this. Good-night."

"Good-night, Austin."

The door shut, but in a moment it was open again, and Austin stood, white and ghastly, in the entrance.

"I was forgetting," he said, "that I too have something to tell. I have received a letter from Dr. Harding of Buenos Ayres. He says that he attended Meyrick for three weeks before his death."

"And does he say what carried him off in the prime of life? It was not fever?"

"No, it was not fever. According to the doctor, it was an utter collapse of the whole system, probably caused by some severe shock. But he states that the patient would tell him nothing, and that he was consequently at some disadvantage in treating the case."

"Is there anything more?"

"Yes. Dr. Harding ends his letter by saying: 'I think this is all the information I can give you about your poor friend. He had not been long in Buenos Ayres, and knew scarcely any one, with the exception of a person who did not bear the best of characters, and has since left--a Mrs. Vaughan.'"

VIII - THE FRAGMENTS

[Amongst the papers of the well-known physician, Dr. Robert Matheson, of Ashley Street, Piccadilly, who died suddenly, of apoplectic seizure, at the beginning of 1892, a leaf of manuscript paper was found, covered with pencil jottings. These notes were in Latin, much abbreviated, and had evidently been made in great haste. The MS. was only deciphered with difficulty, and some words have up to the present time evaded all the efforts of the expert employed. The date, "XXV Jul. 1888," is written on the right-hand corner of the MS. The following is a translation of Dr. Matheson's manuscript.]

"Whether science would benefit by these brief notes if they could be published, I do not know, but rather doubt. But certainly I shall never take the responsibility of publishing or divulging one word of what is here written, not only on account of my oath given freely to those two persons who were present, but also because the details are too abominable. It is probably that, upon mature consideration, and after weighting the good and evil, I shall one day destroy this paper, or at least leave it under seal to my friend D., trusting in his discretion, to use it or to burn it, as he may think fit.

"As was befitting, I did all that my knowledge suggested to make sure that I was suffering under no delusion. At first astounded, I could hardly think, but in a minute's time I was sure that my pulse was steady and regular, and that I was in my real and true senses. I then fixed my eyes quietly on what was before me.

"Though horror and revolting nausea rose up within me, and an odour of corruption choked my breath, I remained firm. I was then privileged or accursed, I dare not say which, to see that which was on the bed, lying there black like ink, transformed before my eyes. The skin, and the flesh, and the muscles, and the bones, and the firm structure of the human body that I had thought to be unchangeable, and permanent as adamant, began to melt and dissolve.

"I know that the body may be separated into its elements by external agencies, but I should have refused to believe what I saw. For here there was some internal force, of which I knew nothing, that caused dissolution and change.

"Here too was all the work by which man had been made repeated before my eyes. I saw the form waver from sex to sex, dividing itself from itself, and then again reunited. Then I saw the body descend to the beasts whence it ascended, and that which was on the heights go down to the depths, even to the abyss of all being. The principle of life, which makes organism, always remained, while the outward form changed.

"The light within the room had turned to blackness, not the darkness of night, in which objects are seen dimly, for I could see clearly and without difficulty. But it was the negation of light; objects were presented to my eyes, if I may say so, without any medium, in such a manner that if there had been a prism in the room I should have seen no colours represented in it.

"I watched, and at last I saw nothing but a substance as jelly. Then the ladder was ascended again... [here the MS. is illegible] ...for one instance I saw a Form, shaped in dimness before me, which I will not farther describe. But the symbol of this form may be seen in ancient sculptures, and in paintings which survived beneath the lava, too foul to be spoken of... as a horrible and unspeakable shape, neither man nor beast, was changed into human form, there came finally death.

"I who saw all this, not without great horror and loathing of soul, here write my name, declaring all that I have set on this paper to be true.

"ROBERT MATHESON, Med. Dr."

***

...Such, Raymond, is the story of what I know and what I have seen. The burden of it was too heavy for me to bear alone, and yet I could tell it to none but you. Villiers, who was with me at the last, knows nothing of that awful secret of the wood, of how what we both saw die, lay upon the smooth, sweet turf amidst the summer flowers, half in sun and half in shadow, and holding the girl Rachel's hand, called and summoned those companions, and shaped in solid form, upon the earth we tread upon, the horror which we can but hint at, which we can only name under a figure. I would not tell Villiers of this, nor of that resemblance, which struck me as with a blow upon my heart, when I saw the portrait, which filled the cup of terror at the end. What this can mean I dare not guess. I know that what I saw perish was not Mary, and yet in the last agony Mary's eyes looked into mine. Whether there can be any one who can show the last link in this chain of awful mystery, I do not know, but if there be any one who can do this, you, Raymond, are the man. And if you know the secret, it rests with you to tell it or not, as you please.

I am writing this letter to you immediately on my getting back to town. I have been in the country for the last few days; perhaps you may be able to guess in which part. While the horror and wonder of London was at its height--for "Mrs. Beaumont," as I have told you, was well known in society--I wrote to my friend Dr. Phillips, giving some brief outline, or rather hint, of what happened, and asking him to tell me the name of the village where the events he had related to me occurred. He gave me the name, as he said with the less hesitation, because Rachel's father and mother were dead, and the rest of the family had gone to a relative in the State of Washington six months before. The parents, he said, had undoubtedly died of grief and horror caused by the terrible death of their daughter, and by what had gone before that death. On the evening of the day which I received Phillips' letter I was at Caermaen, and standing beneath the mouldering Roman walls, white with the winters of seventeen hundred years, I looked over the meadow where once had stood the older temple of the "God of the Deeps," and saw a house gleaming in the sunlight. It was the house where Helen had lived. I stayed at Caermaen for several days. The people of the place, I found, knew little and had guessed less. Those whom I spoke to on the matter seemed surprised that an antiquarian (as I professed myself to be) should trouble about a village tragedy, of which they gave a very commonplace version, and, as you may imagine, I told nothing of what I knew. Most of my time was spent in the great wood that rises just above the village and climbs the hillside, and goes down to the river in the valley; such another long lovely valley, Raymond, as that on which we looked one summer night, walking to and fro before your house. For many an hour I strayed through the maze of the forest, turning now to right and now to left, pacing slowly down long alleys of undergrowth, shadowy and chill, even under the midday sun, and halting beneath great oaks; lying on the short turf of a clearing where the faint sweet scent of wild roses came to me on the wind and mixed with the heavy perfume of the elder, whose mingled odour is like the odour of the room of the dead, a vapour of incense and corruption. I stood at the edges of the wood, gazing at all the pomp and procession of the foxgloves towering amidst the bracken and shining red in the broad sunshine, and beyond them into deep thickets of close undergrowth where springs boil up from the rock and nourish the water-weeds, dank and evil. But in all my wanderings I avoided one part of the wood; it was not till yesterday that I climbed to the summit of the hill, and stood upon the ancient Roman road that threads the highest ridge of the wood. Here they had walked, Helen and Rachel, along this quiet causeway, upon the pavement of green turf, shut in on either side by high banks of red earth, and tall hedges of shining beech, and here I followed in their steps, looking out, now and again, through partings in the boughs, and seeing on one side the sweep of the wood stretching far to right and left, and sinking into the broad level, and beyond, the yellow sea, and the land over the sea. On the other side was the valley and the river and hill following hill as wave on wave, and wood and meadow, and cornfield, and white houses gleaming, and a great wall of mountain, and far blue peaks in the north. And so at last I came to the place. The track went up a gentle slope, and widened out into an open space with a wall of thick undergrowth around it, and then, narrowing again, passed on into the distance and the faint blue mist of summer heat. And into this pleasant summer glade Rachel passed a girl, and left it, who shall say what? I did not stay long there.

In a small town near Caermaen there is a museum, containing for the most part Roman remains which have been found in the neighbourhood at various times. On the day after my arrival in Caermaen I walked over to the town in question, and took the opportunity of inspecting the museum. After I had seen most of the sculptured stones, the coffins, rings, coins, and fragments of tessellated pavement which the place contains, I was shown a small square pillar of white stone, which had been recently discovered in the wood of which I have been speaking, and, as I found on inquiry, in that open space where the Roman road broadens out. On one side of the pillar was an inscription, of which I took a note. Some of the letters have been defaced, but I do not think there can be any doubt as to those which I supply. The inscription is as follows:

DEVOMNODENT--i--
FLA--v--IVSSENILISPOSSV--it--
PROPTERNVP--tias--
--qua--SVIDITSVBVMB--ra--

"To the great god Nodens (the god of the Great Deep or Abyss) Flavius Senilis has erected this pillar on account of the marriage which he saw beneath the shade."

The custodian of the museum informed me that local antiquaries were much puzzled, not by the inscription, or by any difficulty in translating it, but as to the circumstance or rite to which allusion is made.

***

...And now, my dear Clarke, as to what you tell me about Helen Vaughan, whom you say you saw die under circumstances of the utmost and almost incredible horror. I was interested in your account, but a good deal, nay all, of what you told me I knew already. I can understand the strange likeness you remarked in both the portrait and in the actual face; you have seen Helen's mother. You remember that still summer night so many years ago, when I talked to you of the world beyond the shadows, and of the god Pan. You remember Mary. She was the mother of Helen Vaughan, who was born nine months after that night.

Mary never recovered her reason. She lay, as you saw her, all the while upon her bed, and a few days after the child was born she died. I fancy that just at the last she knew me; I was standing by the bed, and the old look came into her eyes for a second, and then she shuddered and groaned and died. It was an ill work I did that night when you were present; I broke open the door of the house of life, without knowing or caring what might pass forth or enter in. I recollect your telling me at the time, sharply enough, and rightly too, in one sense, that I had ruined the reason of a human being by a foolish experiment, based on an absurd theory. You did well to blame me, but my theory was not all absurdity. What I said Mary would see she saw, but I forgot that no human eyes can look on such a sight with impunity. And I forgot, as I have just said, that when the house of life is thus thrown open, there may enter in that for which we have no name, and human flesh may become the veil of a horror one dare not express. I played with energies which I did not understand, you have seen the ending of it. Helen Vaughan did well to bind the cord about her neck and die, though the death was horrible. The blackened face, the hideous form upon the bed, changing and melting before your eyes from woman to man, from man to beast, and from beast to worse than beast, all the strange horror that you witness, surprises me but little. What you say the doctor whom you sent for saw and shuddered at I noticed long ago; I knew what I had done the moment the child was born, and when it was scarcely five years old I surprised it, not once or twice but several times with a playmate, you may guess of what kind. It was for me a constant, an incarnate horror, and after a few years I felt I could bear it no more, and I sent Helen Vaughan away. You know now what frightened the boy in the wood. The rest of the strange story, and all else that you tell me, as discovered by your friend, I have contrived to learn from time to time, almost to the last chapter. And now Helen is with her companions...

The House of Souls

Short Story Index Reprint Series
AYER COMPANY PUBLISHERS, INC. NORTH STRATFORD, NH 03590
First Published 1922

Introduction

It was somewhere, I think, towards the autumn of the year 1889 that the thought occurred to me that I might perhaps try to write a little in the modern way. For, hitherto, I had been, as it were, wearing costume in literature. The rich, figured English of the earlier part of the seventeenth century had always had a peculiar attraction for me. I accustomed myself to write in it, to think in it; I kept a diary in that manner, and half-unconsciously dressed up my every day thoughts and common experiences in the habit of the Cavalier or of the Caroline Divine. Thus, when in 1884 I got a commission to translate the Heptameron, I wrote quite naturally in the language of my favourite period, and, as some critics declare, made my English version somewhat more antique and stiff than the original. And so "The Anatomy of Tobacco" was an exercise in the antique of a different kind; and "The Chronicle of Clemendy" was a volume of tales that tried their hardest to be mediæval; and the translation of the "Moyen de Parvenir" was still a thing in the ancient mode.

It seemed, in fine, to be settled that in literature I was to be a hanger on of the past ages; and I don't quite know how I managed to get away from them. I had finished translating "Casanova"--more modern, but not thoroughly up to date--and I had nothing particular on hand, and, somehow or other, it struck me that I might try a little writing for the papers. I began with a "turnover" as it was called, for the old vanished Globe, a harmless little article on old English proverbs; and I shall never forget my pride and delight when one day, being at Dover, with a fresh autumn wind blowing from the sea, I bought a chance copy of the paper and saw my essay on the front page. Naturally, I was encouraged to persevere, and I wrote more turnovers for the Globe and then tried the St. James's Gazette and found that they paid two pounds instead of the guinea of the Globe, and again, naturally enough, devoted most of my attention to the St. James's Gazette. From the essay or literary paper, I somehow got into the habit of the short story, and did a good many of these, still for the St. James's, till in the autumn of 1890, I wrote a tale called "The Double Return." Well, Oscar Wilde asked: "Are you the author of that story that fluttered the dovecotes? I thought it was very good." But: it did flutter the dovecotes, and the St. James's Gazette and I parted.

But I still wrote short stories, now chiefly for what were called "society" papers, which have become extinct. And one of these appeared in a paper, the name of which I have long forgotten. I had called the tale "Resurrectio Mortuorum," and the editor had very sensibly rendered the title into "The Resurrection of the Dead."

I do not clearly remember how the story began. I am inclined to think something in this way:

"Old Mr. Llewellyn, the Welsh antiquary, threw his copy of the morning paper on the floor and banged the breakfast-table, exclaiming: 'Good God! Here's the last of the Caradocs of the Garth, has been married in a Baptist Chapel by a dissenting preacher; somewhere in Peckham.'" Or, did I take up the tale a few years after this happy event and shew the perfectly cheerful contented young commercial clerk running somewhat too fast to catch the bus one morning, and feeling dazed all day long over the office work, and going home in a sort of dimness, and then at his very doorstep, recovering as it were, his ancestral consciousness. I think it was the sight of his wife and the tones of her voice that suddenly announced to him with the sound of a trumpet that he had nothing to do with this woman with the Cockney accent, or the pastor who was coming to supper, or the red brick villa, or Peckham or the City of London. Though the old place on the banks of the Usk had been sold fifty years before, still, he was Caradoc of the Garth. I forget how I ended the story: but here was one of the sources of "A Fragment of Life."

And somehow, though the tale was written and printed and paid for; it stayed with me as a tale half told in the years from 1890 to 1899. I was in love with the notion: this contrast between the raw London suburb and its mean limited life and its daily journeys to the City; its utter banality and lack of significance; between all this and the old, grey mullioned house under the forest near the river, the armorial bearings on the Jacobean porch, and noble old traditions: all this captivated me and I thought of my mistold tale at intervals, while I was writing "The Great God Pan," "The Red Hand," "The Three Impostors," "The Hill of Dreams," "The White People," and "Hieroglyphics." It was at the back of my head, I suppose, all the time, and at last in '99 I began to write it all over again from a somewhat different standpoint.

The fact was that one grey Sunday afternoon in the March of that year, I went for a long walk with a friend. I was living in Gray's Inn in those days, and we stravaged up Gray's Inn Road on one of those queer, unscientific explorations of the odd corners of London in which I have always delighted. I don't think that there was any definite scheme laid down; but we resisted manifold temptations. For on the right of Gray's Inn Road is one of the oddest quarters of London--to those, that is, with the unsealed eyes. Here are streets of 1800-1820 that go down into a valley--Flora in "Little Dorrit" lived in one of them--and then crossing King's Cross Road climb very steeply up to heights which always suggest to me that I am in the hinder and poorer quarter of some big seaside place, and that there is a fine view of the sea from the attic windows. This place was once called Spa Fields, and has very properly an old meeting house of the Countess of Huntingdon's Connection as one of its attractions. It is one of the parts of London which would attract me if I wished to hide; not to escape arrest, perhaps, but rather to escape the possibility of ever meeting anybody who had ever seen me before.

But: my friend and I resisted it all. We strolled along to the parting of many ways at King's Cross Station, and struck boldly up Pentonville. Again: on our left was Barnsbury, which is like Africa. In Barnsbury semper aliquid novi, but our course was laid for us by some occult influence, and we came to Islington and chose the right hand side of the way. So far, we were tolerably in the region of the known, since every year there is the great Cattle Show at Islington, and many men go there. But, trending to the right, we got into Canonbury, of which there are only Travellers' Tales. Now and then, perhaps, as one sits about the winter fire, while the storm howls without and the snow falls fast, the silent man in the corner has told how he had a great aunt who lived in Canonbury in 1860; so in the fourteenth century you might meet men who had talked with those who had been in Cathay and had seen the splendours of the Grand Cham. Such is Canonbury; I hardly dare speak of its dim squares, of the deep, leafy back-gardens behind the houses, running down into obscure alleyways with discreet, mysterious postern doors: as I say, "Travellers' Tales"; things not much credited.

But, he who adventures in London has a foretaste of infinity. There is a region beyond Ultima Thule. I know not how it was, but on this famous Sunday afternoon, my friend and I, passing through Canonbury came into something called the Balls Pond Road--Mr. Perch, the messenger of Dombey & Son, lived somewhere in this region--and so I think by Dalston down into Hackney where caravans, or trams, or, as I think you say in America, trolley cars set out at stated intervals to the limits of the western world.

But in the course of that walk which had become an exploration of the unknown, I had seen two common things which had made a profound impression upon me. One of these things was a street, the other a small family party. The street was somewhere in that vague, uncharted, Balls Pond-Dalston region. It was a long street and a grey street. Each house was exactly like every other house. Each house had a basement, the sort of story which house-agents have grown to call of late a "lower ground floor." The front windows of these basements were half above the patch of black, soot-smeared soil and coarse grass that named itself a garden, and so, passing along at the hour of four o'clock or four-thirty, I could see that in everyone of these "breakfast rooms"--their technical name--the tea tray and the tea cups were set out in readiness. I received from this trivial and natural circumstance an impression of a dull life, laid out in dreadful lines of patterned uniformity, of a life without adventure of body or soul.

Then, the family party. It got into the tram down Hackney way. There were father, mother and baby; and I should think that they came from a small shop, probably from a small draper's shop. The parents were young people of twenty-five to thirty-five. He wore a black shiny frock coat--an "Albert" in America?--a high hat, little side whiskers and dark moustache and a look of amiable vacuity. His wife was oddly bedizened in black satin, with a wide spreading hat, not ill-looking, simply unmeaning. I fancy that she had at times, not too often, "a temper of her own." And the very small baby sat upon her knee. The party was probably going forth to spend the Sunday evening with relations or friends.

And yet, I said to myself, these two have partaken together of the great mystery, of the great sacrament of nature, of the source of all that is magical in the wide world. But have they discerned the mysteries? Do they know that they have been in that place which is called Syon and Jerusalem?--I am quoting from an old book and a strange book.

It was thus that, remembering the old story of the "Resurrection of the Dead," I was furnished with the source of "A Fragment of Life." I was writing "Hieroglyphics" at the time, having just finished "The White People"; or rather, having just decided that what now appears in print under that heading was all that would ever be written, that the Great Romance that should have been written--in manifestation of the idea--would never be written at all. And so, when Hieroglyphics was finished, somewhere about May 1899, I set about "A Fragment of Life" and wrote the first chapter with the greatest relish and the utmost ease. And then my own life was dashed into fragments. I ceased to write. I travelled. I saw Syon and Bagdad and other strange places--see "Things Near and Far" for an explanation of this obscure passage--and found myself in the lighted world of floats and battens, entering L. U. E., crossing R and exiting R 3; and doing all sorts of queer things.

But still, in spite of all these shocks and changes, the "notion" would not leave me. I went at it again, I suppose in 1904; consumed with a bitter determination to finish what I had begun. Everything now had become difficult. I tried this way and that way and the other way. They all failed and I broke down on every one of them; and I tried and tried again. At last I cobbled up some sort of an end, an utterly bad one, as I realized as I wrote every single line and word of it, and the story appeared, in 1904 or 1905, in Horlick's Magazine under the editorship of my old and dear friend, A. E. Waite.

Still; I was not satisfied. That end was intolerable and I knew it. Again, I sat down to the work, night after night I wrestled with it. And I remember an odd circumstance which may or may not be of some physiological interest. I was then living in a circumscribed "upper part" of a house in Cosway Street, Marylebone Road. That I might struggle by myself, I wrote in the little kitchen; and night after night as I fought grimly, savagely, all but hopelessly for some fit close for "A Fragment of Life," I was astonished and almost alarmed to find that my feet developed a sensation of most deadly cold. The room was not cold; I had lit the oven burners of the little gas cooking stove. I was not cold; but my feet were chilled in a quite extraordinary manner, as if they had been packed in ice. At last I took off my slippers with a view of poking my toes into the oven of the stove, and feeling my feet with my hand, I perceived that, in fact, they were not cold at all! But the sensation remained; there, I suppose, you have an odd case of a transference of something that was happening in the brain to the extremities. My feet were quite warm to the palm of my hand, but to my sense they were frozen. But what a testimony to the fitness of the American idiom, "cold feet," as signifying a depressed and desponding mood! But, somehow or other, the tale was finished and the "notion" was at last out of my head. I have gone into all this detail about "A Fragment of Life" because I have been assured in many quarters that it is the best thing that I have ever done, and students of the crooked ways of literature may be interested to hear of the abominable labours of doing it.

"The White People" belongs to the same year as the first chapter of "A Fragment of Life," 1899, which was also the year of "Hieroglyphics." The fact was I was in high literary spirits, just then. I had been harassed and worried for a whole year in the office of Literature, a weekly paper published by The Times, and getting free again, I felt like a prisoner released from chains; ready to dance in letters to any extent. Forthwith I thought of "A Great Romance," a highly elaborate and elaborated piece of work, full of the strangest and rarest things. I have forgotten how it was that this design broke down; but I found by experiment that the great romance was to go on that brave shelf of the unwritten books, the shelf where all the splendid books are to be found in their golden bindings. "The White People" is a small piece of salvage from the wreck. Oddly enough, as is insinuated in the Prologue, the mainspring of the story is to be sought in a medical textbook. In the Prologue reference is made to a review article by Dr. Coryn. But I have since found out that Dr. Coryn was merely quoting from a scientific treatise that case of the lady whose fingers became violently inflamed because she saw a heavy window sash descend on the fingers of her child. With this instance, of course, are to be considered all cases of stigmata, both ancient and modern: and then the question is obvious enough: what limits can we place to the powers of the imagination? Has not the imagination the potentiality at least of performing any miracle, however marvelous, however incredible, according to our ordinary standards? As to the decoration of the story, that is a mingling which I venture to think somewhat ingenious of odds and ends of folk lore and witch lore with pure inventions of my own. Some years later I was amused to receive a letter from a gentleman who was, if I remember, a schoolmaster somewhere in Malaya. This gentleman, an earnest student of folklore, was writing an article on some singular things he had observed amongst the Malayans, and chiefly a kind of were-wolf state into which some of them were able to conjure themselves. He had found, as he said, startling resemblances between the magic ritual of Malaya and some of the ceremonies and practices hinted at in "The White People." He presumed that all this was not fancy but fact; that is that I was describing practices actually in use among superstitious people on the Welsh border; he was going to quote from me in the article for the Journal of the Folk Lore Society, or whatever it was called, and he just wanted to let me know. I wrote in a hurry to the folklore journal to bid them beware: for the instances selected by the student were all fictions of my own brain!

"The Great God Pan" and "The Inmost Light" are tales of an earlier date, going back to 1890, '91, '92. I have written a good deal about them in "Far Off Things," and in a preface to an edition of "The Great God Pan," published by Messrs. Simpkin, Marshall in 1916, I have described at length the origins of the book. But I must quote anew some extracts from the reviews which welcomed "The Great God Pan" to my extraordinary entertainment, hilarity and refreshment. Here are a few of the best:

"It is not Mr. Machen's fault but his misfortune, that one shakes with laughter rather than with dread over the contemplation of his psychological bogey."--Observer.

"His horror, we regret to say, leaves us quite cold ... and our flesh obstinately refuses to creep."--Chronicle.

"His bogies don't scare."--Sketch.

"We are afraid he only succeeds in being ridiculous."--Manchester Guardian.

"Gruesome, ghastly and dull."--Lady's Pictorial.

"Incoherent nightmare of sex ... which would soon lead to insanity if unrestrained ... innocuous from its absurdity."--Westminster Gazette.

And so on, and so on. Several papers, I remember, declared that "The Great God Pan" was simply a stupid and incompetent rehash of Huysmans' "Là-Bas" and "À Rebours." I had not read these books so I got them both. Thereon, I perceived that my critics had not read them either.

A Fragment of Life

I

Edward Darnell awoke from a dream of an ancient wood, and of a clear well rising into grey film and vapour beneath a misty, glimmering heat; and as his eyes opened he saw the sunlight bright in the room, sparkling on the varnish of the new furniture. He turned and found his wife's place vacant, and with some confusion and wonder of the dream still lingering in his mind, he rose also, and began hurriedly to set about his dressing, for he had overslept a little, and the 'bus passed the corner at 9.15. He was a tall, thin man, dark-haired and dark-eyed, and in spite of the routine of the City, the counting of coupons, and all the mechanical drudgery that had lasted for ten years, there still remained about him the curious hint of a wild grace, as if he had been born a creature of the antique wood, and had seen the fountain rising from the green moss and the grey rocks.

The breakfast was laid in the room on the ground floor, the back room with the French windows looking on the garden, and before he sat down to his fried bacon he kissed his wife seriously and dutifully. She had brown hair and brown eyes, and though her lovely face was grave and quiet, one would have said that she might have awaited her husband under the old trees, and bathed in the pool hollowed out of the rocks.

They had a good deal to talk over while the coffee was poured out and the bacon eaten, and Darnell's egg brought in by the stupid, staring servant-girl of the dusty face. They had been married for a year, and they had got on excellently, rarely sitting silent for more than an hour, but for the past few weeks Aunt Marian's present had afforded a subject for conversation which seemed inexhaustible. Mrs. Darnell had been Miss Mary Reynolds, the daughter of an auctioneer and estate agent in Notting Hill, and Aunt Marian was her mother's sister, who was supposed rather to have lowered herself by marrying a coal merchant, in a small way, at Turnham Green. Marian had felt the family attitude a good deal, and the Reynoldses were sorry for many things that had been said, when the coal merchant saved money and took up land on building leases in the neighbourhood of Crouch End, greatly to his advantage, as it appeared. Nobody had thought that Nixon could ever do very much; but he and his wife had been living for years in a beautiful house at Barnet, with bow-windows, shrubs, and a paddock, and the two families saw but little of each other, for Mr. Reynolds was not very prosperous. Of course, Aunt Marian and her husband had been asked to Mary's wedding, but they had sent excuses with a nice little set of silver apostle spoons, and it was feared that nothing more was to be looked for. However, on Mary's birthday her aunt had written a most affectionate letter, enclosing a cheque for a hundred pounds from 'Robert' and herself, and ever since the receipt of the money the Darnells had discussed the question of its judicious disposal. Mrs. Darnell had wished to invest the whole sum in Government securities, but Mr. Darnell had pointed out that the rate of interest was absurdly low, and after a good deal of talk he had persuaded his wife to put ninety pounds of the money in a safe mine, which was paying five per cent. This was very well, but the remaining ten pounds, which Mrs. Darnell had insisted on reserving, gave rise to legends and discourses as interminable as the disputes of the schools.

At first Mr. Darnell had proposed that they should furnish the 'spare' room. There were four bedrooms in the house: their own room, the small one for the servant, and two others overlooking the garden, one of which had been used for storing boxes, ends of rope, and odd numbers of 'Quiet Days' and 'Sunday Evenings,' besides some worn suits belonging to Mr. Darnell which had been carefully wrapped up and laid by, as he scarcely knew what to do with them. The other room was frankly waste and vacant, and one Saturday afternoon, as he was coming home in the 'bus, and while he revolved that difficult question of the ten pounds, the unseemly emptiness of the spare room suddenly came into his mind, and he glowed with the idea that now, thanks to Aunt Marian, it could be furnished. He was busied with this delightful thought all the way home, but when he let himself in, he said nothing to his wife, since he felt that his idea must be matured. He told Mrs. Darnell that, having important business, he was obliged to go out again directly, but that he should be back without fail for tea at half-past six; and Mary, on her side, was not sorry to be alone, as she was a little behindhand with the household books. The fact was, that Darnell, full of the design of furnishing the spare bedroom, wished to consult his friend Wilson, who lived at Fulham, and had often given him judicious advice as to the laying out of money to the very best advantage. Wilson was connected with the Bordeaux wine trade, and Darnell's only anxiety was lest he should not be at home.

However, it was all right; Darnell took a tram along the Goldhawk Road, and walked the rest of the way, and was delighted to see Wilson in the front garden of his house, busy amongst his flower-beds.

'Haven't seen you for an age,' he said cheerily, when he heard Darnell's hand on the gate; 'come in. Oh, I forgot,' he added, as Darnell still fumbled with the handle, and vainly attempted to enter. 'Of course you can't get in; I haven't shown it you.'

It was a hot day in June, and Wilson appeared in a costume which he had put on in haste as soon as he arrived from the City. He wore a straw hat with a neat pugaree protecting the back of his neck, and his dress was a Norfolk jacket and knickers in heather mixture.

'See,' he said, as he let Darnell in; 'see the dodge. You don't turn the handle at all. First of all push hard, and then pull. It's a trick of my own, and I shall have it patented. You see, it keeps undesirable characters at a distance--such a great thing in the suburbs. I feel I can leave Mrs. Wilson alone now; and, formerly, you have no idea how she used to be pestered.'

'But how about visitors?' said Darnell. 'How do they get in?'

'Oh, we put them up to it. Besides,' he said vaguely, 'there is sure to be somebody looking out. Mrs. Wilson is nearly always at the window. She's out now; gone to call on some friends. The Bennetts' At Home day, I think it is. This is the first Saturday, isn't it? You know J. W. Bennett, don't you? Ah, he's in the House; doing very well, I believe. He put me on to a very good thing the other day.'

'But, I say,' said Wilson, as they turned and strolled towards the front door, 'what do you wear those black things for? You look hot. Look at me. Well, I've been gardening, you know, but I feel as cool as a cucumber. I dare say you don't know where to get these things? Very few men do. Where do you suppose I got 'em?'

'In the West End, I suppose,' said Darnell, wishing to be polite.

'Yes, that's what everybody says. And it is a good cut. Well, I'll tell you, but you needn't pass it on to everybody. I got the tip from Jameson--you know him, "Jim-Jams," in the China trade, 39 Eastbrook--and he said he didn't want everybody in the City to know about it. But just go to Jennings, in Old Wall, and mention my name, and you'll be all right. And what d'you think they cost?'

'I haven't a notion,' said Darnell, who had never bought such a suit in his life.

'Well, have a guess.'

Darnell regarded Wilson gravely.

The jacket hung about his body like a sack, the knickerbockers drooped lamentably over his calves, and in prominent positions the bloom of the heather seemed about to fade and disappear.

'Three pounds, I suppose, at least,' he said at length.

'Well, I asked Dench, in our place, the other day, and he guessed four ten, and his father's got something to do with a big business in Conduit Street. But I only gave thirty-five and six. To measure? Of course; look at the cut, man.'

Darnell was astonished at so low a price.

'And, by the way,' Wilson went on, pointing to his new brown boots, 'you know where to go for shoe-leather? Oh, I thought everybody was up to that! There's only one place. "Mr. Bill," in Gunning Street,--nine and six.'

They were walking round and round the garden, and Wilson pointed out the flowers in the beds and borders. There were hardly any blossoms, but everything was neatly arranged.

'Here are the tuberous-rooted Glasgownias,' he said, showing a rigid row of stunted plants; 'those are Squintaceæ; this is a new introduction, Moldavia Semperflorida Andersonii; and this is Prattsia.'

'When do they come out?' said Darnell.

'Most of them in the end of August or beginning of September,' said Wilson briefly. He was slightly annoyed with himself for having talked so much about his plants, since he saw that Darnell cared nothing for flowers; and, indeed, the visitor could hardly dissemble vague recollections that came to him; thoughts of an old, wild garden, full of odours, beneath grey walls, of the fragrance of the meadowsweet beside the brook.

'I wanted to consult you about some furniture,' Darnell said at last. 'You know we've got a spare room, and I'm thinking of putting a few things into it. I haven't exactly made up my mind, but I thought you might advise me.'

'Come into my den,' said Wilson. 'No; this way, by the back'; and he showed Darnell another ingenious arrangement at the side door whereby a violent high-toned bell was set pealing in the house if one did but touch the latch. Indeed, Wilson handled it so briskly that the bell rang a wild alarm, and the servant, who was trying on her mistress's things in the bedroom, jumped madly to the window and then danced a hysteric dance. There was plaster found on the drawing-room table on Sunday afternoon, and Wilson wrote a letter to the 'Fulham Chronicle,' ascribing the phenomenon 'to some disturbance of a seismic nature.'

For the moment he knew nothing of the great results of his contrivance, and solemnly led the way towards the back of the house. Here there was a patch of turf, beginning to look a little brown, with a background of shrubs. In the middle of the turf, a boy of nine or ten was standing all alone, with something of an air.

'The eldest,' said Wilson. 'Havelock. Well, Lockie, what are ye doing now? And where are your brother and sister?'

The boy was not at all shy. Indeed, he seemed eager to explain the course of events.

'I'm playing at being Gawd,' he said, with an engaging frankness. 'And I've sent Fergus and Janet to the bad place. That's in the shrubbery. And they're never to come out any more. And they're burning for ever and ever.'

'What d'you think of that?' said Wilson admiringly. 'Not bad for a youngster of nine, is it? They think a lot of him at the Sunday-school. But come into my den.'

The den was an apartment projecting from the back of the house. It had been designed as a back kitchen and washhouse, but Wilson had draped the 'copper' in art muslin and had boarded over the sink, so that it served as a workman's bench.

'Snug, isn't it?' he said, as he pushed forward one of the two wicker chairs. 'I think out things here, you know; it's quiet. And what about this furnishing? Do you want to do the thing on a grand scale?'

'Oh, not at all. Quite the reverse. In fact, I don't know whether the sum at our disposal will be sufficient. You see the spare room is ten feet by twelve, with a western exposure, and I thought if we could manage it, that it would seem more cheerful furnished. Besides, it's pleasant to be able to ask a visitor; our aunt, Mrs. Nixon, for example. But she is accustomed to have everything very nice.'

'And how much do you want to spend?'

'Well, I hardly think we should be justified in going much beyond ten pounds. That isn't enough, eh?'

Wilson got up and shut the door of the back kitchen impressively.

'Look here,' he said, 'I'm glad you came to me in the first place. Now you'll just tell me where you thought of going yourself.'

'Well, I had thought of the Hampstead Road,' said Darnell in a hesitating manner.

'I just thought you'd say that. But I'll ask you, what is the good of going to those expensive shops in the West End? You don't get a better article for your money. You're merely paying for fashion.'

'I've seen some nice things in Samuel's, though. They get a brilliant polish on their goods in those superior shops. We went there when we were married.'

'Exactly, and paid ten per cent more than you need have paid. It's throwing money away. And how much did you say you had to spend? Ten pounds. Well, I can tell you where to get a beautiful bedroom suite, in the very highest finish, for six pound ten. What d'you think of that? China included, mind you; and a square of carpet, brilliant colours, will only cost you fifteen and six. Look here, go any Saturday afternoon to Dick's, in the Seven Sisters Road, mention my name, and ask for Mr. Johnston. The suite's in ash, "Elizabethan" they call it. Six pound ten, including the china, with one of their "Orient" carpets, nine by nine, for fifteen and six. Dick's.'

Wilson spoke with some eloquence on the subject of furnishing. He pointed out that the times were changed, and that the old heavy style was quite out of date.

'You know,' he said, 'it isn't like it was in the old days, when people used to buy things to last hundreds of years. Why, just before the wife and I were married, an uncle of mine died up in the North and left me his furniture. I was thinking of furnishing at the time, and I thought the things might come in handy; but I assure you there wasn't a single article that I cared to give house-room to. All dingy, old mahogany; big bookcases and bureaus, and claw-legged chairs and tables. As I said to the wife (as she was soon afterwards), "We don't exactly want to set up a chamber of horrors, do we?" So I sold off the lot for what I could get. I must confess I like a cheerful room.'

Darnell said he had heard that artists liked the old-fashioned furniture.

'Oh, I dare say. The "unclean cult of the sunflower," eh? You saw that piece in the "Daily Post"? I hate all that rot myself. It isn't healthy, you know, and I don't believe the English people will stand it. But talking of curiosities, I've got something here that's worth a bit of money.'

He dived into some dusty receptacle in a corner of the room, and showed Darnell a small, worm-eaten Bible, wanting the first five chapters of Genesis and the last leaf of the Apocalypse. It bore the date of 1753.

'It's my belief that's worth a lot,' said Wilson. 'Look at the worm-holes. And you see it's "imperfect," as they call it. You've noticed that some of the most valuable books are "imperfect" at the sales?'

The interview came to an end soon after, and Darnell went home to his tea. He thought seriously of taking Wilson's advice, and after tea he told Mary of his idea and of what Wilson had said about Dick's.

Mary was a good deal taken by the plan when she had heard all the details. The prices struck her as very moderate. They were sitting one on each side of the grate (which was concealed by a pretty cardboard screen, painted with landscapes), and she rested her cheek on her hand, and her beautiful dark eyes seemed to dream and behold strange visions. In reality she was thinking of Darnell's plan.

'It would be very nice in some ways,' she said at last. 'But we must talk it over. What I am afraid of is that it will come to much more than ten pounds in the long run. There are so many things to be considered. There's the bed. It would look shabby if we got a common bed without brass mounts. Then the bedding, the mattress, and blankets, and sheets, and counterpane would all cost something.'

She dreamed again, calculating the cost of all the necessaries, and Darnell stared anxiously; reckoning with her, and wondering what her conclusion would be. For a moment the delicate colouring of her face, the grace of her form, and the brown hair, drooping over her ears and clustering in little curls about her neck, seemed to hint at a language which he had not yet learned; but she spoke again.

'The bedding would come to a great deal, I am afraid. Even if Dick's are considerably cheaper than Boon's or Samuel's. And, my dear, we must have some ornaments on the mantelpiece. I saw some very nice vases at eleven-three the other day at Wilkin and Dodd's. We should want six at least, and there ought to be a centre-piece. You see how it mounts up.'

Darnell was silent. He saw that his wife was summing up against his scheme, and though he had set his heart on it, he could not resist her arguments.

'It would be nearer twelve pounds than ten,' she said.

'The floor would have to be stained round the carpet (nine by nine, you said?), and we should want a piece of linoleum to go under the washstand. And the walls would look very bare without any pictures.'

'I thought about the pictures,' said Darnell; and he spoke quite eagerly. He felt that here, at least, he was unassailable. 'You know there's the "Derby Day" and the "Railway Station," ready framed, standing in the corner of the box-room already. They're a bit old-fashioned, perhaps, but that doesn't matter in a bedroom. And couldn't we use some photographs? I saw a very neat frame in natural oak in the City, to hold half a dozen, for one and six. We might put in your father, and your brother James, and Aunt Marian, and your grandmother, in her widow's cap--and any of the others in the album. And then there's that old family picture in the hair-trunk--that might do over the mantelpiece.'

'You mean your great-grandfather in the gilt frame? But that's very old-fashioned, isn't it? He looks so queer in his wig. I don't think it would quite go with the room, somehow.'

Darnell thought a moment. The portrait was a 'kitcat' of a young gentleman, bravely dressed in the fashion of 1750, and he very faintly remembered some old tales that his father had told him about this ancestor--tales of the woods and fields, of the deep sunken lanes, and the forgotten country in the west.

'No,' he said, 'I suppose it is rather out of date. But I saw some very nice prints in the City, framed and quite cheap.'

'Yes, but everything counts. Well, we will talk it over, as you say. You know we must be careful.'

The servant came in with the supper, a tin of biscuits, a glass of milk for the mistress, and a modest pint of beer for the master, with a little cheese and butter. Afterwards Edward smoked two pipes of honeydew, and they went quietly to bed; Mary going first, and her husband following a quarter of an hour later, according to the ritual established from the first days of their marriage. Front and back doors were locked, the gas was turned off at the meter, and when Darnell got upstairs he found his wife already in bed, her face turned round on the pillow.

She spoke softly to him as he came into the room.

'It would be impossible to buy a presentable bed at anything under one pound eleven, and good sheets are dear, anywhere.'

He slipped off his clothes and slid gently into bed, putting out the candle on the table. The blinds were all evenly and duly drawn, but it was a June night, and beyond the walls, beyond that desolate world and wilderness of grey Shepherd's Bush, a great golden moon had floated up through magic films of cloud, above the hill, and the earth was filled with a wonderful light between red sunset lingering over the mountain and that marvellous glory that shone into the woods from the summit of the hill. Darnell seemed to see some reflection of that wizard brightness in the room; the pale walls and the white bed and his wife's face lying amidst brown hair upon the pillow were illuminated, and listening he could almost hear the corncrake in the fields, the fern-owl sounding his strange note from the quiet of the rugged place where the bracken grew, and, like the echo of a magic song, the melody of the nightingale that sang all night in the alder by the little brook. There was nothing that he could say, but he slowly stole his arm under his wife's neck, and played with the ringlets of brown hair. She never moved, she lay there gently breathing, looking up to the blank ceiling of the room with her beautiful eyes, thinking also, no doubt, thoughts that she could not utter, kissing her husband obediently when he asked her to do so, and he stammered and hesitated as he spoke.

They were nearly asleep, indeed Darnell was on the very eve of dreaming, when she said very softly--

'I am afraid, darling, that we could never afford it.' And he heard her words through the murmur of the water, dripping from the grey rock, and falling into the clear pool beneath.

Sunday morning was always an occasion of idleness. Indeed, they would never have got breakfast if Mrs. Darnell, who had the instincts of the housewife, had not awoke and seen the bright sunshine, and felt that the house was too still. She lay quiet for five minutes, while her husband slept beside her, and listened intently, waiting for the sound of Alice stirring down below. A golden tube of sunlight shone through some opening in the Venetian blinds, and it shone on the brown hair that lay about her head on the pillow, and she looked steadily into the room at the 'duchesse' toilet-table, the coloured ware of the washstand, and the two photogravures in oak frames, 'The Meeting' and 'The Parting,' that hung upon the wall. She was half dreaming as she listened for the servant's footsteps, and the faint shadow of a shade of a thought came over her, and she imagined dimly, for the quick moment of a dream, another world where rapture was wine, where one wandered in a deep and happy valley, and the moon was always rising red above the trees. She was thinking of Hampstead, which represented to her the vision of the world beyond the walls, and the thought of the heath led her away to Bank Holidays, and then to Alice. There was not a sound in the house; it might have been midnight for the stillness if the drawling cry of the Sunday paper had not suddenly echoed round the corner of Edna Road, and with it came the warning clank and shriek of the milkman with his pails.

Mrs. Darnell sat up, and wide awake, listened more intently. The girl was evidently fast asleep, and must be roused, or all the work of the day would be out of joint, and she remembered how Edward hated any fuss or discussion about household matters, more especially on a Sunday, after his long week's work in the City. She gave her husband an affectionate glance as he slept on, for she was very fond of him, and so she gently rose from the bed and went in her nightgown to call the maid.

The servant's room was small and stuffy, the night had been very hot, and Mrs. Darnell paused for a moment at the door, wondering whether the girl on the bed was really the dusty-faced servant who bustled day by day about the house, or even the strangely bedizened creature, dressed in purple, with a shiny face, who would appear on the Sunday afternoon, bringing in an early tea, because it was her 'evening out.' Alice's hair was black and her skin was pale, almost of the olive tinge, and she lay asleep, her head resting on one arm, reminding Mrs. Darnell of a queer print of a 'Tired Bacchante' that she had seen long ago in a shop window in Upper Street, Islington. And a cracked bell was ringing; that meant five minutes to eight, and nothing done.

She touched the girl gently on the shoulder, and only smiled when her eyes opened, and waking with a start, she got up in sudden confusion. Mrs. Darnell went back to her room and dressed slowly while her husband still slept, and it was only at the last moment, as she fastened her cherry-coloured bodice, that she roused him, telling him that the bacon would be overdone unless he hurried over his dressing.

Over the breakfast they discussed the question of the spare room all over again. Mrs. Darnell still admitted that the plan of furnishing it attracted her, but she could not see how it could be done for the ten pounds, and as they were prudent people they did not care to encroach on their savings. Edward was highly paid, having (with allowances for extra work in busy weeks) a hundred and forty pounds a year, and Mary had inherited from an old uncle, her godfather, three hundred pounds, which had been judiciously laid out in mortgage at 4-1/2 per cent. Their total income, then, counting in Aunt Marian's present, was a hundred and fifty-eight pounds a year, and they were clear of debt, since Darnell had bought the furniture for the house out of money which he had saved for five or six years before. In the first few years of his life in the City his income had, of course, been smaller, and at first he had lived very freely, without a thought of laying by. The theatres and music-halls had attracted him, and scarcely a week passed without his going (in the pit) to one or the other; and he had occasionally bought photographs of actresses who pleased him. These he had solemnly burnt when he became engaged to Mary; he remembered the evening well; his heart had been so full of joy and wonder, and the landlady had complained bitterly of the mess in the grate when he came home from the City the next night. Still, the money was lost, as far as he could recollect, ten or twelve shillings; and it annoyed him all the more to reflect that if he had put it by, it would have gone far towards the purchase of an 'Orient' carpet in brilliant colours. Then there had been other expenses of his youth: he had purchased threepenny and even fourpenny cigars, the latter rarely, but the former frequently, sometimes singly, and sometimes in bundles of twelve for half-a-crown. Once a meerschaum pipe had haunted him for six weeks; the tobacconist had drawn it out of a drawer with some air of secrecy as he was buying a packet of 'Lone Star.' Here was another useless expense, these American-manufactured tobaccos; his 'Lone Star,' 'Long Judge,' 'Old Hank,' 'Sultry Clime,' and the rest of them cost from a shilling to one and six the two-ounce packet; whereas now he got excellent loose honeydew for threepence halfpenny an ounce. But the crafty tradesman, who had marked him down as a buyer of expensive fancy goods, nodded with his air of mystery, and, snapping open the case, displayed the meerschaum before the dazzled eyes of Darnell. The bowl was carved in the likeness of a female figure, showing the head and torso, and the mouthpiece was of the very best amber--only twelve and six, the man said, and the amber alone, he declared, was worth more than that. He explained that he felt some delicacy about showing the pipe to any but a regular customer, and was willing to take a little under cost price and 'cut the loss.' Darnell resisted for the time, but the pipe troubled him, and at last he bought it. He was pleased to show it to the younger men in the office for a while, but it never smoked very well, and he gave it away just before his marriage, as from the nature of the carving it would have been impossible to use it in his wife's presence. Once, while he was taking his holidays at Hastings, he had purchased a malacca cane--a useless thing that had cost seven shillings--and he reflected with sorrow on the innumerable evenings on which he had rejected his landlady's plain fried chop, and had gone out to flaner among the Italian restaurants in Upper Street, Islington (he lodged in Holloway), pampering himself with expensive delicacies: cutlets and green peas, braised beef with tomato sauce, fillet steak and chipped potatoes, ending the banquet very often with a small wedge of Gruyère, which cost twopence. One night, after receiving a rise in his salary, he had actually drunk a quarter-flask of Chianti and had added the enormities of Benedictine, coffee, and cigarettes to an expenditure already disgraceful, and sixpence to the waiter made the bill amount to four shillings instead of the shilling that would have provided him with a wholesome and sufficient repast at home. Oh, there were many other items in this account of extravagance, and Darnell had often regretted his way of life, thinking that if he had been more careful, five or six pounds a year might have been added to their income.

And the question of the spare room brought back these regrets in an exaggerated degree. He persuaded himself that the extra five pounds would have given a sufficient margin for the outlay that he desired to make; though this was, no doubt, a mistake on his part. But he saw quite clearly that, under the present conditions, there must be no levies made on the very small sum of money that they had saved. The rent of the house was thirty-five, and rates and taxes added another ten pounds--nearly a quarter of their income for house-room. Mary kept down the housekeeping bills to the very best of her ability, but meat was always dear, and she suspected the maid of cutting surreptitious slices from the joint and eating them in her bedroom with bread and treacle in the dead of night, for the girl had disordered and eccentric appetites. Mr. Darnell thought no more of restaurants, cheap or dear; he took his lunch with him to the City, and joined his wife in the evening at high tea--chops, a bit of steak, or cold meat from the Sunday's dinner. Mrs. Darnell ate bread and jam and drank a little milk in the middle of the day; but, with the utmost economy, the effort to live within their means and to save for future contingencies was a very hard one. They had determined to do without change of air for at least three years, as the honeymoon at Walton-on-the-Naze had cost a good deal; and it was on this ground that they had, somewhat illogically, reserved the ten pounds, declaring that as they were not to have any holiday they would spend the money on something useful.

And it was this consideration of utility that was finally fatal to Darnell's scheme. They had calculated and recalculated the expense of the bed and bedding, the linoleum, and the ornaments, and by a great deal of exertion the total expenditure had been made to assume the shape of 'something very little over ten pounds,' when Mary said quite suddenly--

'But, after all, Edward, we don't really want to furnish the room at all. I mean it isn't necessary. And if we did so it might lead to no end of expense. People would hear of it and be sure to fish for invitations. You know we have relatives in the country, and they would be almost certain, the Mallings, at any rate, to give hints.'

Darnell saw the force of the argument and gave way. But he was bitterly disappointed.

'It would have been very nice, wouldn't it?' he said with a sigh.

'Never mind, dear,' said Mary, who saw that he was a good deal cast down. 'We must think of some other plan that will be nice and useful too.'

She often spoke to him in that tone of a kind mother, though she was by three years the younger.

'And now,' she said, 'I must get ready for church. Are you coming?'

Darnell said that he thought not. He usually accompanied his wife to morning service, but that day he felt some bitterness in his heart, and preferred to lounge under the shade of the big mulberry tree that stood in the middle of their patch of garden--relic of the spacious lawns that had once lain smooth and green and sweet, where the dismal streets now swarmed in a hopeless labyrinth.

So Mary went quietly and alone to church. St. Paul's stood in a neighbouring street, and its Gothic design would have interested a curious inquirer into the history of a strange revival. Obviously, mechanically, there was nothing amiss. The style chosen was 'geometrical decorated,' and the tracery of the windows seemed correct. The nave, the aisles, the spacious chancel, were reasonably proportioned; and, to be quite serious, the only feature obviously wrong was the substitution of a low 'chancel wall' with iron gates for the rood screen with the loft and rood. But this, it might plausibly be contended, was merely an adaptation of the old idea to modern requirements, and it would have been quite difficult to explain why the whole building, from the mere mortar setting between the stones to the Gothic gas standards, was a mysterious and elaborate blasphemy. The canticles were sung to Joll in B flat, the chants were 'Anglican,' and the sermon was the gospel for the day, amplified and rendered into the more modern and graceful English of the preacher. And Mary came away.

After their dinner (an excellent piece of Australian mutton, bought in the 'World Wide' Stores, in Hammersmith), they sat for some time in the garden, partly sheltered by the big mulberry tree from the observation of their neighbours. Edward smoked his honeydew, and Mary looked at him with placid affection.

'You never tell me about the men in your office,' she said at length. 'Some of them are nice fellows, aren't they?'

'Oh, yes, they're very decent. I must bring some of them round, one of these days.'

He remembered with a pang that it would be necessary to provide whisky. One couldn't ask the guest to drink table beer at tenpence the gallon.

'Who are they, though?' said Mary. 'I think they might have given you a wedding present.'

'Well, I don't know. We never have gone in for that sort of thing. But they're very decent chaps. Well, there's Harvey; "Sauce" they call him behind his back. He's mad on bicycling. He went in last year for the Two Miles Amateur Record. He'd have made it, too, if he could have got into better training.

'Then there's James, a sporting man. You wouldn't care for him. I always think he smells of the stable.'

'How horrid!' said Mrs. Darnell, finding her husband a little frank, lowering her eyes as she spoke.

'Dickenson might amuse you,' Darnell went on. 'He's always got a joke. A terrible liar, though. When he tells a tale we never know how much to believe. He swore the other day he'd seen one of the governors buying cockles off a barrow near London Bridge, and Jones, who's just come, believed every word of it.'

Darnell laughed at the humorous recollection of the jest.

'And that wasn't a bad yarn about Salter's wife,' he went on. 'Salter is the manager, you know. Dickenson lives close by, in Notting Hill, and he said one morning that he had seen Mrs. Salter, in the Portobello Road, in red stockings, dancing to a piano organ.'

'He's a little coarse, isn't he?' said Mrs. Darnell. 'I don't see much fun in that.'

'Well, you know, amongst men it's different. You might like Wallis; he's a tremendous photographer. He often shows us photos he's taken of his children--one, a little girl of three, in her bath. I asked him how he thought she'd like it when she was twenty-three.'

Mrs. Darnell looked down and made no answer.

There was silence for some minutes while Darnell smoked his pipe. 'I say, Mary,' he said at length, 'what do you say to our taking a paying guest?'

'A paying guest! I never thought of it. Where should we put him?'

'Why, I was thinking of the spare room. The plan would obviate your objection, wouldn't it? Lots of men in the City take them, and make money of it too. I dare say it would add ten pounds a year to our income. Redgrave, the cashier, finds it worth his while to take a large house on purpose. They have a regular lawn for tennis and a billiard-room.'

Mary considered gravely, always with the dream in her eyes. 'I don't think we could manage it, Edward,' she said; 'it would be inconvenient in many ways.' She hesitated for a moment. 'And I don't think I should care to have a young man in the house. It is so very small, and our accommodation, as you know, is so limited.'

She blushed slightly, and Edward, a little disappointed as he was, looked at her with a singular longing, as if he were a scholar confronted with a doubtful hieroglyph, either wholly wonderful or altogether commonplace. Next door children were playing in the garden, playing shrilly, laughing, crying, quarrelling, racing to and fro. Suddenly a clear, pleasant voice sounded from an upper window.

'Enid! Charles! Come up to my room at once!'

There was an instant sudden hush. The children's voices died away.

'Mrs. Parker is supposed to keep her children in great order,' said Mary. 'Alice was telling me about it the other day. She had been talking to Mrs. Parker's servant. I listened to her without any remark, as I don't think it right to encourage servants' gossip; they always exaggerate everything. And I dare say children often require to be corrected.'

The children were struck silent as if some ghastly terror had seized them.

Darnell fancied that he heard a queer sort of cry from the house, but could not be quite sure. He turned to the other side, where an elderly, ordinary man with a grey moustache was strolling up and down on the further side of his garden. He caught Darnell's eye, and Mrs. Darnell looking towards him at the same moment, he very politely raised his tweed cap. Darnell was surprised to see his wife blushing fiercely.

'Sayce and I often go into the City by the same 'bus,' he said, 'and as it happens we've sat next to each other two or three times lately. I believe he's a traveller for a leather firm in Bermondsey. He struck me as a pleasant man. Haven't they got rather a good-looking servant?'

'Alice has spoken to me about her--and the Sayces,' said Mrs. Darnell. 'I understand that they are not very well thought of in the neighbourhood. But I must go in and see whether the tea is ready. Alice will be wanting to go out directly.'

Darnell looked after his wife as she walked quickly away. He only dimly understood, but he could see the charm of her figure, the delight of the brown curls clustering about her neck, and he again felt that sense of the scholar confronted by the hieroglyphic. He could not have expressed his emotion, but he wondered whether he would ever find the key, and something told him that before she could speak to him his own lips must be unclosed. She had gone into the house by the back kitchen door, leaving it open, and he heard her speaking to the girl about the water being 'really boiling.' He was amazed, almost indignant with himself; but the sound of the words came to his ears as strange, heart-piercing music, tones from another, wonderful sphere. And yet he was her husband, and they had been married nearly a year; and yet, whenever she spoke, he had to listen to the sense of what she said, constraining himself, lest he should believe she was a magic creature, knowing the secrets of immeasurable delight.

He looked out through the leaves of the mulberry tree. Mr. Sayce had disappeared from his view, but he saw the light-blue fume of the cigar that he was smoking floating slowly across the shadowed air. He was wondering at his wife's manner when Sayce's name was mentioned, puzzling his head as to what could be amiss in the household of a most respectable personage, when his wife appeared at the dining-room window and called him in to tea. She smiled as he looked up, and he rose hastily and walked in, wondering whether he were not a little 'queer,' so strange were the dim emotions and the dimmer impulses that rose within him.

Alice was all shining purple and strong scent, as she brought in the teapot and the jug of hot water. It seemed that a visit to the kitchen had inspired Mrs. Darnell in her turn with a novel plan for disposing of the famous ten pounds. The range had always been a trouble to her, and when sometimes she went into the kitchen, and found, as she said, the fire 'roaring halfway up the chimney,' it was in vain that she reproved the maid on the ground of extravagance and waste of coal. Alice was ready to admit the absurdity of making up such an enormous fire merely to bake (they called it 'roast') a bit of beef or mutton, and to boil the potatoes and the cabbage; but she was able to show Mrs. Darnell that the fault lay in the defective contrivance of the range, in an oven which 'would not get hot.' Even with a chop or a steak it was almost as bad; the heat seemed to escape up the chimney or into the room, and Mary had spoken several times to her husband on the shocking waste of coal, and the cheapest coal procurable was never less than eighteen shillings the ton. Mr. Darnell had written to the landlord, a builder, who had replied in an illiterate but offensive communication, maintaining the excellence of the stove and charging all the faults to the account of 'your good lady,' which really implied that the Darnells kept no servant, and that Mrs. Darnell did everything. The range, then, remained, a standing annoyance and expense. Every morning, Alice said, she had the greatest difficulty in getting the fire to light at all, and once lighted it 'seemed as if it fled right up the chimney.' Only a few nights before Mrs. Darnell had spoken seriously to her husband about it; she had got Alice to weigh the coals expended in cooking a cottage pie, the dish of the evening, and deducting what remained in the scuttle after the pie was done, it appeared that the wretched thing had consumed nearly twice the proper quantity of fuel.

'You remember what I said the other night about the range?' said Mrs. Darnell, as she poured out the tea and watered the leaves. She thought the introduction a good one, for though her husband was a most amiable man, she guessed that he had been just a little hurt by her decision against his furnishing scheme.

'The range?' said Darnell. He paused as he helped himself to the marmalade and considered for a moment. 'No, I don't recollect. What night was it?'

'Tuesday. Don't you remember? You had "overtime," and didn't get home till quite late.'

She paused for a moment, blushing slightly; and then began to recapitulate the misdeeds of the range, and the outrageous outlay of coal in the preparation of the cottage pie.

'Oh, I recollect now. That was the night I thought I heard the nightingale (people say there are nightingales in Bedford Park), and the sky was such a wonderful deep blue.'

He remembered how he had walked from Uxbridge Road Station, where the green 'bus stopped, and in spite of the fuming kilns under Acton, a delicate odour of the woods and summer fields was mysteriously in the air, and he had fancied that he smelt the red wild roses, drooping from the hedge. As he came to his gate he saw his wife standing in the doorway, with a light in her hand, and he threw his arms violently about her as she welcomed him, and whispered something in her ear, kissing her scented hair. He had felt quite abashed a moment afterwards, and he was afraid that he had frightened her by his nonsense; she seemed trembling and confused. And then she had told him how they had weighed the coal.

'Yes, I remember now,' he said. 'It is a great nuisance, isn't it? I hate to throw away money like that.'

'Well, what do you think? Suppose we bought a really good range with aunt's money? It would save us a lot, and I expect the things would taste much nicer.'

Darnell passed the marmalade, and confessed that the idea was brilliant.

'It's much better than mine, Mary,' he said quite frankly. 'I am so glad you thought of it. But we must talk it over; it doesn't do to buy in a hurry. There are so many makes.'

Each had seen ranges which looked miraculous inventions; he in the neighbourhood of the City; she in Oxford Street and Regent Street, on visits to the dentist. They discussed the matter at tea, and afterwards they discussed it walking round and round the garden, in the sweet cool of the evening.

'They say the "Newcastle" will burn anything, coke even,' said Mary.

'But the "Glow" got the gold medal at the Paris Exhibition,' said Edward.

'But what about the "Eutopia" Kitchener? Have you seen it at work in Oxford Street?' said Mary. 'They say their plan of ventilating the oven is quite unique.'

'I was in Fleet Street the other day,' answered Edward, 'and I was looking at the "Bliss" Patent Stoves. They burn less fuel than any in the market--so the makers declare.'

He put his arm gently round her waist. She did not repel him; she whispered quite softly--
'I think Mrs. Parker is at her window,' and he drew his arm back slowly.

'But we will talk it over,' he said. 'There is no hurry. I might call at some of the places near the City, and you might do the same thing in Oxford Street and Regent Street and Piccadilly, and we could compare notes.'

Mary was quite pleased with her husband's good temper. It was so nice of him not to find fault with her plan; 'He's so good to me,' she thought, and that was what she often said to her brother, who did not care much for Darnell. They sat down on the seat under the mulberry, close together, and she let Darnell take her hand, and as she felt his shy, hesitating fingers touch her in the shadow, she pressed them ever so softly, and as he fondled her hand, his breath was on her neck, and she heard his passionate, hesitating voice whisper, 'My dear, my dear,' as his lips touched her cheek. She trembled a little, and waited. Darnell kissed her gently on the cheek and drew away his hand, and when he spoke he was almost breathless.

'We had better go in now,' he said. 'There is a heavy dew, and you might catch cold.'

A warm, scented gale came to them from beyond the walls. He longed to ask her to stay out with him all night beneath the tree, that they might whisper to one another, that the scent of her hair might inebriate him, that he might feel her dress still brushing against his ankles. But he could not find the words, and it was absurd, and she was so gentle that she would do whatever he asked, however foolish it might be, just because he asked her. He was not worthy to kiss her lips; he bent down and kissed her silk bodice, and again he felt that she trembled, and he was ashamed, fearing that he had frightened her.

They went slowly into the house, side by side, and Darnell lit the gas in the drawing-room, where they always sat on Sunday evenings. Mrs. Darnell felt a little tired and lay down on the sofa, and Darnell took the arm-chair opposite. For a while they were silent, and then Darnell said suddenly--

'What's wrong with the Sayces? You seemed to think there was something a little strange about them. Their maid looks quite quiet.'

'Oh, I don't know that one ought to pay any attention to servants' gossip. They're not always very truthful.'

'It was Alice told you, wasn't it?'

'Yes. She was speaking to me the other day, when I was in the kitchen in the afternoon.'

'But what was it?'

'Oh, I'd rather not tell you, Edward. It's not pleasant. I scolded Alice for repeating it to me.'

Darnell got up and took a small, frail chair near the sofa.

'Tell me,' he said again, with an odd perversity. He did not really care to hear about the household next door, but he remembered how his wife's cheeks flushed in the afternoon, and now he was looking at her eyes.

'Oh, I really couldn't tell you, dear. I should feel ashamed.'

'But you're my wife.'

'Yes, but it doesn't make any difference. A woman doesn't like to talk about such things.'

Darnell bent his head down. His heart was beating; he put his ear to her mouth and said, 'Whisper.'

Mary drew his head down still lower with her gentle hand, and her cheeks burned as she whispered--

'Alice says that--upstairs--they have only--one room furnished. The maid told her--herself.'

With an unconscious gesture she pressed his head to her breast, and he in turn was bending her red lips to his own, when a violent jangle clamoured through the silent house. They sat up, and Mrs. Darnell went hurriedly to the door.

'That's Alice,' she said. 'She is always in in time. It has only just struck ten.'

Darnell shivered with annoyance. His lips, he knew, had almost been opened. Mary's pretty handkerchief, delicately scented from a little flagon that a school friend had given her, lay on the floor, and he picked it up, and kissed it, and hid it away.

The question of the range occupied them all through June and far into July. Mrs. Darnell took every opportunity of going to the West End and investigating the capacity of the latest makes, gravely viewing the new improvements and hearing what the shopmen had to say; while Darnell, as he said, 'kept his eyes open' about the City. They accumulated quite a literature of the subject, bringing away illustrated pamphlets, and in the evenings it was an amusement to look at the pictures. They viewed with reverence and interest the drawings of great ranges for hotels and public institutions, mighty contrivances furnished with a series of ovens each for a different use, with wonderful apparatus for grilling, with batteries of accessories which seemed to invest the cook almost with the dignity of a chief engineer. But when, in one of the lists, they encountered the images of little toy 'cottage' ranges, for four pounds, and even for three pounds ten, they grew scornful, on the strength of the eight or ten pound article which they meant to purchase--when the merits of the divers patents had been thoroughly thrashed out.

The 'Raven' was for a long time Mary's favourite. It promised the utmost economy with the highest efficiency, and many times they were on the point of giving the order. But the 'Glow' seemed equally seductive, and it was only £8. 5s. as compared with £9. 7s. 6d., and though the 'Raven' was supplied to the Royal Kitchen, the 'Glow' could show more fervent testimonials from continental potentates.

It seemed a debate without end, and it endured day after day till that morning, when Darnell woke from the dream of the ancient wood, of the fountains rising into grey vapour beneath the heat of the sun. As he dressed, an idea struck him, and he brought it as a shock to the hurried breakfast, disturbed by the thought of the City 'bus which passed the corner of the street at 9.15.

'I've got an improvement on your plan, Mary,' he said, with triumph. 'Look at that,' and he flung a little book on the table.

He laughed. 'It beats your notion all to fits. After all, the great expense is the coal. It's not the stove--at least that's not the real mischief. It's the coal is so dear. And here you are. Look at those oil stoves. They don't burn any coal, but the cheapest fuel in the world--oil; and for two pounds ten you can get a range that will do everything you want.'

'Give me the book,' said Mary, 'and we will talk it over in the evening, when you come home. Must you be going?'

Darnell cast an anxious glance at the clock.

'Good-bye,' and they kissed each other seriously and dutifully, and Mary's eyes made Darnell think of those lonely water-pools, hidden in the shadow of the ancient woods.

So, day after day, he lived in the grey phantasmal world, akin to death, that has, somehow, with most of us, made good its claim to be called life. To Darnell the true life would have seemed madness, and when, now and again, the shadows and vague images reflected from its splendour fell across his path, he was afraid, and took refuge in what he would have called the sane 'reality' of common and usual incidents and interests. His absurdity was, perhaps, the more evident, inasmuch as 'reality' for him was a matter of kitchen ranges, of saving a few shillings; but in truth the folly would have been greater if it had been concerned with racing stables, steam yachts, and the spending of many thousand pounds.

But so went forth Darnell, day by day, strangely mistaking death for life, madness for sanity, and purposeless and wandering phantoms for true beings. He was sincerely of opinion that he was a City clerk, living in Shepherd's Bush--having forgotten the mysteries and the far-shining glories of the kingdom which was his by legitimate inheritance.

II

All day long a fierce and heavy heat had brooded over the City, and as Darnell neared home he saw the mist lying on all the damp lowlands, wreathed in coils about Bedford Park to the south, and mounting to the west, so that the tower of Acton Church loomed out of a grey lake. The grass in the squares and on the lawns which he overlooked as the 'bus lumbered wearily along was burnt to the colour of dust. Shepherd's Bush Green was a wretched desert, trampled brown, bordered with monotonous poplars, whose leaves hung motionless in air that was still, hot smoke. The foot passengers struggled wearily along the pavements, and the reek of the summer's end mingled with the breath of the brickfields made Darnell gasp, as if he were inhaling the poison of some foul sick-room.

He made but a slight inroad into the cold mutton that adorned the tea-table, and confessed that he felt rather 'done up' by the weather and the day's work.

'I have had a trying day, too,' said Mary. 'Alice has been very queer and troublesome all day, and I have had to speak to her quite seriously. You know I think her Sunday evenings out have a rather unsettling influence on the girl. But what is one to do?'

'Has she got a young man?'

'Of course: a grocer's assistant from the Goldhawk Road--Wilkin's, you know. I tried them when we settled here, but they were not very satisfactory.'

'What do they do with themselves all the evening? They have from five to ten, haven't they?'

'Yes; five, or sometimes half-past, when the water won't boil. Well, I believe they go for walks usually. Once or twice he has taken her to the City Temple, and the Sunday before last they walked up and down Oxford Street, and then sat in the Park. But it seems that last Sunday they went to tea with his mother at Putney. I should like to tell the old woman what I really think of her.'

'Why? What happened? Was she nasty to the girl?'

'No; that's just it. Before this, she has been very unpleasant on several occasions. When the young man first took Alice to see her--that was in March--the girl came away crying; she told me so herself. Indeed, she said she never wanted to see old Mrs. Murry again; and I told Alice that, if she had not exaggerated things, I could hardly blame her for feeling like that.'

'Why? What did she cry for?'

'Well, it seems that the old lady--she lives in quite a small cottage in some Putney back street--was so stately that she would hardly speak. She had borrowed a little girl from some neighbour's family, and had managed to dress her up to imitate a servant, and Alice said nothing could be sillier than to see that mite opening the door, with her black dress and her white cap and apron, and she hardly able to turn the handle, as Alice said. George (that's the young man's name) had told Alice that it was a little bit of a house; but he said the kitchen was comfortable, though very plain and old-fashioned. But, instead of going straight to the back, and sitting by a big fire on the old settle that they had brought up from the country, that child asked for their names (did you ever hear such nonsense?) and showed them into a little poky parlour, where old Mrs. Murry was sitting "like a duchess," by a fireplace full of coloured paper, and the room as cold as ice. And she was so grand that she would hardly speak to Alice.'

'That must have been very unpleasant.'

'Oh, the poor girl had a dreadful time. She began with: "Very pleased to make your acquaintance, Miss Dill. I know so very few persons in service." Alice imitates her mincing way of talking, but I can't do it. And then she went on to talk about her family, how they had farmed their own land for five hundred years--such stuff! George had told Alice all about it: they had had an old cottage with a good strip of garden and two fields somewhere in Essex, and that old woman talked almost as if they had been country gentry, and boasted about the Rector, Dr. Somebody, coming to see them so often, and of Squire Somebody Else always looking them up, as if they didn't visit them out of kindness. Alice told me it was as much as she could do to keep from laughing in Mrs. Murry's face, her young man having told her all about the place, and how small it was, and how the Squire had been so kind about buying it when old Murry died and George was a little boy, and his mother not able to keep things going. However, that silly old woman "laid it on thick," as you say, and the young man got more and more uncomfortable, especially when she went on to speak about marrying in one's own class, and how unhappy she had known young men to be who had married beneath them, giving some very pointed looks at Alice as she talked. And then such an amusing thing happened: Alice had noticed George looking about him in a puzzled sort of way, as if he couldn't make out something or other, and at last he burst out and asked his mother if she had been buying up the neighbours' ornaments, as he remembered the two green cut-glass vases on the mantelpiece at Mrs. Ellis's, and the wax flowers at Miss Turvey's. He was going on, but his mother scowled at him, and upset some books, which he had to pick up; but Alice quite understood she had been borrowing things from her neighbours, just as she had borrowed the little girl, so as to look grander. And then they had tea--water bewitched, Alice calls it--and very thin bread and butter, and rubbishy foreign pastry from the Swiss shop in the High Street--all sour froth and rancid fat, Alice declares. And then Mrs. Murry began boasting again about her family, and snubbing Alice and talking at her, till the girl came away quite furious, and very unhappy, too. I don't wonder at it, do you?'

'It doesn't sound very enjoyable, certainly,' said Darnell, looking dreamily at his wife. He had not been attending very carefully to the subject-matter of her story, but he loved to hear a voice that was incantation in his ears, tones that summoned before him the vision of a magic world.

'And has the young man's mother always been like this?' he said after a long pause, desiring that the music should continue.

'Always, till quite lately, till last Sunday in fact. Of course Alice spoke to George Murry at once, and said, like a sensible girl, that she didn't think it ever answered for a married couple to live with the man's mother, "especially," she went on, "as I can see your mother hasn't taken much of a fancy to me." He told her, in the usual style, it was only his mother's way, that she didn't really mean anything, and so on; but Alice kept away for a long time, and rather hinted, I think, that it might come to having to choose between her and his mother. And so affairs went on all through the spring and summer, and then, just before the August Bank Holiday, George spoke to Alice again about it, and told her how sorry the thought of any unpleasantness made him, and how he wanted his mother and her to get on with each other, and how she was only a bit old-fashioned and queer in her ways, and had spoken very nicely to him about her when there was nobody by. So the long and the short of it was that Alice said she might come with them on the Monday, when they had settled to go to Hampton Court--the girl was always talking about Hampton Court, and wanting to see it. You remember what a beautiful day it was, don't you?'

'Let me see,' said Darnell dreamily. 'Oh yes, of course--I sat out under the mulberry tree all day, and we had our meals there: it was quite a picnic. The caterpillars were a nuisance, but I enjoyed the day very much.' His ears were charmed, ravished with the grave, supernal melody, as of antique song, rather of the first made world in which all speech was descant, and all words were sacraments of might, speaking not to the mind but to the soul. He lay back in his chair, and said--

'Well, what happened to them?'

'My dear, would you believe it; but that wretched old woman behaved worse than ever. They met as had been arranged, at Kew Bridge, and got places, with a good deal of difficulty, in one of those char-à-banc things, and Alice thought she was going to enjoy herself tremendously. Nothing of the kind. They had hardly said "Good morning," when old Mrs. Murry began to talk about Kew Gardens, and how beautiful it must be there, and how much more convenient it was than Hampton, and no expense at all; just the trouble of walking over the bridge. Then she went on to say, as they were waiting for the char-à-banc, that she had always heard there was nothing to see at Hampton, except a lot of nasty, grimy old pictures, and some of them not fit for any decent woman, let alone girl, to look at, and she wondered why the Queen allowed such things to be shown, putting all kinds of notions into girls' heads that were light enough already; and as she said that she looked at Alice so nastily--horrid old thing--that, as she told me afterwards, Alice would have slapped her face if she hadn't been an elderly woman, and George's mother. Then she talked about Kew again, saying how wonderful the hot-houses were, with palms and all sorts of wonderful things, and a lily as big as a parlour table, and the view over the river. George was very good, Alice told me. He was quite taken aback at first, as the old woman had promised faithfully to be as nice as ever she could be; but then he said, gently but firmly, "Well, mother, we must go to Kew some other day, as Alice has set her heart on Hampton for to-day, and I want to see it myself!" All Mrs. Murry did was to snort, and look at the girl like vinegar, and just then the char-à-banc came up, and they had to scramble for their seats. Mrs. Murry grumbled to herself in an indistinct sort of voice all the way to Hampton Court. Alice couldn't very well make out what she said, but now and then she seemed to hear bits of sentences, like: Pity to grow old, if sons grow bold; and Honour thy father and mother; and Lie on the shelf, said the housewife to the old shoe, and the wicked son to his mother; and I gave you milk and you give me the go-by. Alice thought they must be proverbs (except the Commandment, of course), as George was always saying how old-fashioned his mother is; but she says there were so many of them, and all pointed at her and George, that she thinks now Mrs. Murry must have made them up as they drove along. She says it would be just like her to do it, being old-fashioned, and ill-natured too, and fuller of talk than a butcher on Saturday night. Well, they got to Hampton at last, and Alice thought the place would please her, perhaps, and they might have some enjoyment. But she did nothing but grumble, and out loud too, so that people looked at them, and a woman said, so that they could hear, "Ah well, they'll be old themselves some day," which made Alice very angry, for, as she said, they weren't doing anything. When they showed her the chestnut avenue in Bushey Park, she said it was so long and straight that it made her quite dull to look at it, and she thought the deer (you know how pretty they are, really) looked thin and miserable, as if they would be all the better for a good feed of hog-wash, with plenty of meal in it. She said she knew they weren't happy by the look in their eyes, which seemed to tell her that their keepers beat them. It was the same with everything; she said she remembered market-gardens in Hammersmith and Gunnersbury that had a better show of flowers, and when they took her to the place where the water is, under the trees, she burst out with its being rather hard to tramp her off her legs to show her a common canal, with not so much as a barge on it to liven it up a bit. She went on like that the whole day, and Alice told me she was only too thankful to get home and get rid of her. Wasn't it wretched for the girl?'

'It must have been, indeed. But what happened last Sunday?'

'That's the most extraordinary thing of all. I noticed that Alice was rather queer in her manner this morning; she was a longer time washing up the breakfast things, and she answered me quite sharply when I called to her to ask when she would be ready to help me with the wash; and when I went into the kitchen to see about something, I noticed that she was going about her work in a sulky sort of way. So I asked her what was the matter, and then it all came out. I could scarcely believe my own ears when she mumbled out something about Mrs. Murry thinking she could do very much better for herself; but I asked her one question after another till I had it all out of her. It just shows one how foolish and empty-headed these girls are. I told her she was no better than a weather-cock. If you will believe me, that horrid old woman was quite another person when Alice went to see her the other night. Why, I can't think, but so she was. She told the girl how pretty she was; what a neat figure she had; how well she walked; and how she'd known many a girl not half so clever or well-looking earning her twenty-five or thirty pounds a year, and with good families. She seems to have gone into all sorts of details, and made elaborate calculations as to what she would be able to save, "with decent folks, who don't screw, and pinch, and lock up everything in the house," and then she went off into a lot of hypocritical nonsense about how fond she was of Alice, and how she could go to her grave in peace, knowing how happy her dear George would be with such a good wife, and about her savings from good wages helping to set up a little home, ending up with "And, if you take an old woman's advice, deary, it won't be long before you hear the marriage bells."'

'I see,' said Darnell; 'and the upshot of it all is, I suppose, that the girl is thoroughly dissatisfied?'

'Yes, she is so young and silly. I talked to her, and reminded her of how nasty old Mrs. Murry had been, and told her that she might change her place and change for the worse. I think I have persuaded her to think it over quietly, at all events. Do you know what it is, Edward? I have an idea. I believe that wicked old woman is trying to get Alice to leave us, that she may tell her son how changeable she is; and I suppose she would make up some of her stupid old proverbs: "A changeable wife, a troublesome life," or some nonsense of the kind. Horrid old thing!'

'Well, well,' said Darnell, 'I hope she won't go, for your sake. It would be such a bother for you, hunting for a fresh servant.'

He refilled his pipe and smoked placidly, refreshed somewhat after the emptiness and the burden of the day. The French window was wide open, and now at last there came a breath of quickening air, distilled by the night from such trees as still wore green in that arid valley. The song to which Darnell had listened in rapture, and now the breeze, which even in that dry, grim suburb still bore the word of the woodland, had summoned the dream to his eyes, and he meditated over matters that his lips could not express.

'She must, indeed, be a villainous old woman,' he said at length.

'Old Mrs. Murry? Of course she is; the mischievous old thing! Trying to take the girl from a comfortable place where she is happy.'

'Yes; and not to like Hampton Court! That shows how bad she must be, more than anything.'

'It is beautiful, isn't it?'

'I shall never forget the first time I saw it. It was soon after I went into the City; the first year. I had my holidays in July, and I was getting such a small salary that I couldn't think of going away to the seaside, or anything like that. I remember one of the other men wanted me to come with him on a walking tour in Kent. I should have liked that, but the money wouldn't run to it. And do you know what I did? I lived in Great College Street then, and the first day I was off, I stayed in bed till past dinner-time, and lounged about in an arm-chair with a pipe all the afternoon. I had got a new kind of tobacco--one and four for the two-ounce packet--much dearer than I could afford to smoke, and I was enjoying it immensely. It was awfully hot, and when I shut the window and drew down the red blind it grew hotter; at five o'clock the room was like an oven. But I was so pleased at not having to go into the City, that I didn't mind anything, and now and again I read bits from a queer old book that had belonged to my poor dad. I couldn't make out what a lot of it meant, but it fitted in somehow, and I read and smoked till tea-time. Then I went out for a walk, thinking I should be better for a little fresh air before I went to bed; and I went wandering away, not much noticing where I was going, turning here and there as the fancy took me. I must have gone miles and miles, and a good many of them round and round, as they say they do in Australia if they lose their way in the bush; and I am sure I couldn't have gone exactly the same way all over again for any money. Anyhow, I was still in the streets when the twilight came on, and the lamp-lighters were trotting round from one lamp to another. It was a wonderful night: I wish you had been there, my dear.'

'I was quite a girl then.'

'Yes, I suppose you were. Well, it was a wonderful night. I remember, I was walking in a little street of little grey houses all alike, with stucco copings and stucco door-posts; there were brass plates on a lot of the doors, and one had "Maker of Shell Boxes" on it, and I was quite pleased, as I had often wondered where those boxes and things that you buy at the seaside came from. A few children were playing about in the road with some rubbish or other, and men were singing in a small public-house at the corner, and I happened to look up, and I noticed what a wonderful colour the sky had turned. I have seen it since, but I don't think it has ever been quite what it was that night, a dark blue, glowing like a violet, just as they say the sky looks in foreign countries. I don't know why, but the sky or something made me feel quite queer; everything seemed changed in a way I couldn't understand. I remember, I told an old gentleman I knew then--a friend of my poor father's, he's been dead for five years, if not more--about how I felt, and he looked at me and said something about fairyland; I don't know what he meant, and I dare say I didn't explain myself properly. But, do you know, for a moment or two I felt as if that little back street was beautiful, and the noise of the children and the men in the public-house seemed to fit in with the sky and become part of it. You know that old saying about "treading on air" when one is glad! Well, I really felt like that as I walked, not exactly like air, you know, but as if the pavement was velvet or some very soft carpet. And then--I suppose it was all my fancy--the air seemed to smell sweet, like the incense in Catholic churches, and my breath came queer and catchy, as it does when one gets very excited about anything. I felt altogether stranger than I've ever felt before or since.'

Darnell stopped suddenly and looked up at his wife. She was watching him with parted lips, with eager, wondering eyes.

'I hope I'm not tiring you, dear, with all this story about nothing. You have had a worrying day with that stupid girl; hadn't you better go to bed?'

'Oh, no, please, Edward. I'm not a bit tired now. I love to hear you talk like that. Please go on.'

'Well, after I had walked a bit further, that queer sort of feeling seemed to fade away. I said a bit further, and I really thought I had been walking about five minutes, but I had looked at my watch just before I got into that little street, and when I looked at it again it was eleven o'clock. I must have done about eight miles. I could scarcely believe my own eyes, and I thought my watch must have gone mad; but I found out afterwards it was perfectly right. I couldn't make it out, and I can't now; I assure you the time passed as if I walked up one side of Edna Road and down the other. But there I was, right in the open country, with a cool wind blowing on me from a wood, and the air full of soft rustling sounds, and notes of birds from the bushes, and the singing noise of a little brook that ran under the road. I was standing on the bridge when I took out my watch and struck a wax light to see the time; and it came upon me suddenly what a strange evening it had been. It was all so different, you see, to what I had been doing all my life, particularly for the year before, and it almost seemed as if I couldn't be the man who had been going into the City every day in the morning and coming back from it every evening after writing a lot of uninteresting letters. It was like being pitched all of a sudden from one world into another. Well, I found my way back somehow or other, and as I went along I made up my mind how I'd spend my holiday. I said to myself, "I'll have a walking tour as well as Ferrars, only mine is to be a tour of London and its environs," and I had got it all settled when I let myself into the house about four o'clock in the morning, and the sun was shining, and the street almost as still as the wood at midnight!'

'I think that was a capital idea of yours. Did you have your tour? Did you buy a map of London?'

'I had the tour all right. I didn't buy a map; that would have spoilt it, somehow; to see everything plotted out, and named, and measured. What I wanted was to feel that I was going where nobody had been before. That's nonsense, isn't it? as if there could be any such places in London, or England either, for the matter of that.'

'I know what you mean; you wanted to feel as if you were going on a sort of voyage of discovery. Isn't that it?'

'Exactly, that's what I was trying to tell you. Besides, I didn't want to buy a map. I made a map.'

'How do you mean? Did you make a map out of your head?'

'I'll tell you about it afterwards. But do you really want to hear about my grand tour?'

'Of course I do; it must have been delightful. I call it a most original idea.'

'Well, I was quite full of it, and what you said just now about a voyage of discovery reminds me of how I felt then. When I was a boy I was awfully fond of reading of great travellers--I suppose all boys are--and of sailors who were driven out of their course and found themselves in latitudes where no ship had ever sailed before, and of people who discovered wonderful cities in strange countries; and all the second day of my holidays I was feeling just as I used to when I read these books. I didn't get up till pretty late. I was tired to death after all those miles I had walked; but when I had finished my breakfast and filled my pipe, I had a grand time of it. It was such nonsense, you know; as if there could be anything strange or wonderful in London.'

'Why shouldn't there be?'

'Well, I don't know; but I have thought afterwards what a silly lad I must have been. Anyhow, I had a great day of it, planning what I would do, half making-believe--just like a kid--that I didn't know where I might find myself, or what might happen to me. And I was enormously pleased to think it was all my secret, that nobody else knew anything about it, and that, whatever I might see, I would keep to myself. I had always felt like that about the books. Of course, I loved reading them, but it seemed to me that, if I had been a discoverer, I would have kept my discoveries a secret. If I had been Columbus, and, if it could possibly have been managed, I would have found America all by myself, and never have said a word about it to anybody. Fancy! how beautiful it would be to be walking about in one's own town, and talking to people, and all the while to have the thought that one knew of a great world beyond the seas, that nobody else dreamed of. I should have loved that!

'And that is exactly what I felt about the tour I was going to make. I made up my mind that nobody should know; and so, from that day to this, nobody has heard a word of it.'

'But you are going to tell me?'

'You are different. But I don't think even you will hear everything; not because I won't, but because I can't tell many of the things I saw.'

'Things you saw? Then you really did see wonderful, strange things in London?'

'Well, I did and I didn't. Everything, or pretty nearly everything, that I saw is standing still, and hundreds of thousands of people have looked at the same sights--there were many places that the fellows in the office knew quite well, I found out afterwards. And then I read a book called "London and its Surroundings." But (I don't know how it is) neither the men at the office nor the writers of the book seem to have seen the things that I did. That's why I stopped reading the book; it seemed to take the life, the real heart, out of everything, making it as dry and stupid as the stuffed birds in a museum.

'I thought about what I was going to do all that day, and went to bed early, so as to be fresh. I knew wonderfully little about London, really; though, except for an odd week now and then, I had spent all my life in town. Of course I knew the main streets--the Strand, Regent Street, Oxford Street, and so on--and I knew the way to the school I used to go to when I was a boy, and the way into the City. But I had just kept to a few tracks, as they say the sheep do on the mountains; and that made it all the easier for me to imagine that I was going to discover a new world.'

Darnell paused in the stream of his talk. He looked keenly at his wife to see if he were wearying her, but her eyes gazed at him with unabated interest--one would have almost said that they were the eyes of one who longed and half expected to be initiated into the mysteries, who knew not what great wonder was to be revealed. She sat with her back to the open window, framed in the sweet dusk of the night, as if a painter had made a curtain of heavy velvet behind her; and the work that she had been doing had fallen to the floor. She supported her head with her two hands placed on each side of her brow, and her eyes were as the wells in the wood of which Darnell dreamed in the night-time and in the day.

'And all the strange tales I had ever heard were in my head that morning,' he went on, as if continuing the thoughts that had filled his mind while his lips were silent. 'I had gone to bed early, as I told you, to get a thorough rest, and I had set my alarum clock to wake me at three, so that I might set out at an hour that was quite strange for the beginning of a journey. There was a hush in the world when I awoke, before the clock had rung to arouse me, and then a bird began to sing and twitter in the elm tree that grew in the next garden, and I looked out of the window, and everything was still, and the morning air breathed in pure and sweet, as I had never known it before. My room was at the back of the house, and most of the gardens had trees in them, and beyond these trees I could see the backs of the houses of the next street rising like the wall of an old city; and as I looked the sun rose, and the great light came in at my window, and the day began.

'And I found that when I was once out of the streets just about me that I knew, some of the queer feeling that had come to me two days before came back again. It was not nearly so strong, the streets no longer smelt of incense, but still there was enough of it to show me what a strange world I passed by. There were things that one may see again and again in many London streets: a vine or a fig tree on a wall, a lark singing in a cage, a curious shrub blossoming in a garden, an odd shape of a roof, or a balcony with an uncommon-looking trellis-work in iron. There's scarcely a street, perhaps, where you won't see one or other of such things as these; but that morning they rose to my eyes in a new light, as if I had on the magic spectacles in the fairy tale, and just like the man in the fairy tale, I went on and on in the new light. I remember going through wild land on a high place; there were pools of water shining in the sun, and great white houses in the middle of dark, rocking pines, and then on the turn of the height I came to a little lane that went aside from the main road, a lane that led to a wood, and in the lane was a little old shadowed house, with a bell turret in the roof, and a porch of trellis-work all dim and faded into the colour of the sea; and in the garden there were growing tall, white lilies, just as we saw them that day we went to look at the old pictures; they were shining like silver, and they filled the air with their sweet scent. It was from near that house I saw the valley and high places far away in the sun. So, as I say, I went "on and on," by woods and fields, till I came to a little town on the top of a hill, a town full of old houses bowing to the ground beneath their years, and the morning was so still that the blue smoke rose up straight into the sky from all the roof-tops, so still that I heard far down in the valley the song of a boy who was singing an old song through the streets as he went to school, and as I passed through the awakening town, beneath the old, grave houses, the church bells began to ring.

'It was soon after I had left this town behind me that I found the Strange Road. I saw it branching off from the dusty high road, and it looked so green that I turned aside into it, and soon I felt as if I had really come into a new country. I don't know whether it was one of the roads the old Romans made that my father used to tell me about; but it was covered with deep, soft turf, and the great tall hedges on each side looked as if they had not been touched for a hundred years; they had grown so broad and high and wild that they met overhead, and I could only get glimpses here and there of the country through which I was passing, as one passes in a dream. The Strange Road led me on and on, up and down hill; sometimes the rose bushes had grown so thick that I could scarcely make my way between them, and sometimes the road broadened out into a green, and in one valley a brook, spanned by an old wooden bridge, ran across it. I was tired, and I found a soft and shady place beneath an ash tree, where I must have slept for many hours, for when I woke up it was late in the afternoon. So I went on again, and at last the green road came out into the highway, and I looked up and saw another town on a high place with a great church in the middle of it, and when I went up to it there was a great organ sounding from within, and the choir was singing.'

There was a rapture in Darnell's voice as he spoke, that made his story well-nigh swell into a song, and he drew a long breath as the words ended, filled with the thought of that far-off summer day, when some enchantment had informed all common things, transmuting them into a great sacrament, causing earthly works to glow with the fire and the glory of the everlasting light.

And some splendour of that light shone on the face of Mary as she sat still against the sweet gloom of the night, her dark hair making her face more radiant. She was silent for a little while, and then she spoke--

'Oh, my dear, why have you waited so long to tell me these wonderful things? I think it is beautiful. Please go on.'

'I have always been afraid it was all nonsense,' said Darnell. 'And I don't know how to explain what I feel. I didn't think I could say so much as I have to-night.'

'And did you find it the same day after day?'

'All through the tour? Yes, I think every journey was a success. Of course, I didn't go so far afield every day; I was too tired. Often I rested all day long, and went out in the evening, after the lamps were lit, and then only for a mile or two. I would roam about old, dim squares, and hear the wind from the hills whispering in the trees; and when I knew I was within call of some great glittering street, I was sunk in the silence of ways where I was almost the only passenger, and the lamps were so few and faint that they seemed to give out shadows instead of light. And I would walk slowly, to and fro, perhaps for an hour at a time, in such dark streets, and all the time I felt what I told you about its being my secret--that the shadow, and the dim lights, and the cool of the evening, and trees that were like dark low clouds were all mine, and mine alone, that I was living in a world that nobody else knew of, into which no one could enter.

'I remembered one night I had gone farther. It was somewhere in the far west, where there are orchards and gardens, and great broad lawns that slope down to trees by the river. A great red moon rose that night through mists of sunset, and thin, filmy clouds, and I wandered by a road that passed through the orchards, till I came to a little hill, with the moon showing above it glowing like a great rose. Then I saw figures pass between me and the moon, one by one, in a long line, each bent double, with great packs upon their shoulders. One of them was singing, and then in the middle of the song I heard a horrible shrill laugh, in the thin cracked voice of a very old woman, and they disappeared into the shadow of the trees. I suppose they were people going to work, or coming from work in the gardens; but how like it was to a nightmare!

'I can't tell you about Hampton; I should never finish talking. I was there one evening, not long before they closed the gates, and there were very few people about. But the grey-red, silent, echoing courts, and the flowers falling into dreamland as the night came on, and the dark yews and shadowy-looking statues, and the far, still stretches of water beneath the avenues; and all melting into a blue mist, all being hidden from one's eyes, slowly, surely, as if veils were dropped, one by one, on a great ceremony! Oh! my dear, what could it mean? Far away, across the river, I heard a soft bell ring three times, and three times, and again three times, and I turned away, and my eyes were full of tears.

'I didn't know what it was when I came to it; I only found out afterwards that it must have been Hampton Court. One of the men in the office told me he had taken an A. B. C. girl there, and they had great fun. They got into the maze and couldn't get out again, and then they went on the river and were nearly drowned. He told me there were some spicy pictures in the galleries; his girl shrieked with laughter, so he said.'

Mary quite disregarded this interlude.

'But you told me you had made a map. What was it like?'

'I'll show it you some day, if you want to see it. I marked down all the places I had gone to, and made signs--things like queer letters--to remind me of what I had seen. Nobody but myself could understand it. I wanted to draw pictures, but I never learnt how to draw, so when I tried nothing was like what I wanted it to be. I tried to draw a picture of that town on the hill that I came to on the evening of the first day; I wanted to make a steep hill with houses on top, and in the middle, but high above them, the great church, all spires and pinnacles, and above it, in the air, a cup with rays coming from it. But it wasn't a success. I made a very strange sign for Hampton Court, and gave it a name that I made up out of my head.'

The Darnells avoided one another's eyes as they sat at breakfast the next morning. The air had lightened in the night, for rain had fallen at dawn; and there was a bright blue sky, with vast white clouds rolling across it from the south-west, and a fresh and joyous wind blew in at the open window; the mists had vanished. And with the mists there seemed to have vanished also the sense of strange things that had possessed Mary and her husband the night before; and as they looked out into the clear light they could scarcely believe that the one had spoken and the other had listened a few hours before to histories very far removed from the usual current of their thoughts and of their lives. They glanced shyly at one another, and spoke of common things, of the question whether Alice would be corrupted by the insidious Mrs. Murry, or whether Mrs. Darnell would be able to persuade the girl that the old woman must be actuated by the worst motives.

'And I think, if I were you,' said Darnell, as he went out, 'I should step over to the stores and complain of their meat. That last piece of beef was very far from being up to the mark--full of sinew.'

III

It might have been different in the evening, and Darnell had matured a plan by which he hoped to gain much. He intended to ask his wife if she would mind having only one gas, and that a good deal lowered, on the pretext that his eyes were tired with work; he thought many things might happen if the room were dimly lit, and the window opened, so that they could sit and watch the night, and listen to the rustling murmur of the tree on the lawn. But his plans were made in vain, for when he got to the garden gate his wife, in tears, came forth to meet him.

'Oh, Edward,' she began, 'such a dreadful thing has happened! I never liked him much, but I didn't think he would ever do such awful things.'

'What do you mean? Who are you talking about? What has happened? Is it Alice's young man?'

'No, no. But come in, dear. I can see that woman opposite watching us: she's always on the look out.'

'Now, what is it?' said Darnell, as they sat down to tea. 'Tell me, quick! you've quite frightened me.'

'I don't know how to begin, or where to start. Aunt Marian has thought that there was something queer for weeks. And then she found--oh, well, the long and short of it is that Uncle Robert has been carrying on dreadfully with some horrid girl, and aunt has found out everything!'

'Lord! you don't say so! The old rascal! Why, he must be nearer seventy than sixty!'

'He's just sixty-five; and the money he has given her----'

The first shock of surprise over, Darnell turned resolutely to his mince.

'We'll have it all out after tea,' he said; 'I am not going to have my meals spoilt by that old fool of a Nixon. Fill up my cup, will you, dear?'

'Excellent mince this,' he went on, calmly. 'A little lemon juice and a bit of ham in it? I thought there was something extra. Alice all right to-day? That's good. I expect she's getting over all that nonsense.'

He went on calmly chattering in a manner that astonished Mrs. Darnell, who felt that by the fall of Uncle Robert the natural order had been inverted, and had scarcely touched food since the intelligence had arrived by the second post. She had started out to keep the appointment her aunt had made early in the morning, and had spent most of the day in a first-class waiting-room at Victoria Station, where she had heard all the story.

'Now,' said Darnell, when the table had been cleared, 'tell us all about it. How long has it been going on?'

'Aunt thinks now, from little things she remembers, that it must have been going on for a year at least. She says there has been a horrid kind of mystery about uncle's behaviour for a long time, and her nerves were quite shaken, as she thought he must be involved with Anarchists, or something dreadful of the sort.'

'What on earth made her think that?'

'Well, you see, once or twice when she was out walking with her husband, she has been startled by whistles, which seemed to follow them everywhere. You know there are some nice country walks at Barnet, and one in particular, in the fields near Totteridge, that uncle and aunt rather made a point of going to on fine Sunday evenings. Of course, this was not the first thing she noticed, but, at the time, it made a great impression on her mind; she could hardly get a wink of sleep for weeks and weeks.'

'Whistling?' said Darnell. 'I don't quite understand. Why should she be frightened by whistling?'

'I'll tell you. The first time it happened was one Sunday in last May. Aunt had a fancy they were being followed a Sunday or two before, but she didn't see or hear anything, except a sort of crackling noise in the hedge. But this particular Sunday they had hardly got through the stile into the fields, when she heard a peculiar kind of low whistle. She took no notice, thinking it was no concern of hers or her husband's, but as they went on she heard it again, and then again, and it followed them the whole walk, and it made her so uncomfortable, because she didn't know where it was coming from or who was doing it, or why. Then, just as they got out of the fields into the lane, uncle said he felt quite faint, and he thought he would try a little brandy at the "Turpin's Head," a small public-house there is there. And she looked at him and saw his face was quite purple--more like apoplexy, as she says, than fainting fits, which make people look a sort of greenish-white. But she said nothing, and thought perhaps uncle had a peculiar way of fainting of his own, as he always was a man to have his own way of doing everything. So she just waited in the road, and he went ahead and slipped into the public, and aunt says she thought she saw a little figure rise out of the dusk and slip in after him, but she couldn't be sure. And when uncle came out he looked red instead of purple, and said he felt much better; and so they went home quietly together, and nothing more was said. You see, uncle had said nothing about the whistling, and aunt had been so frightened that she didn't dare speak, for fear they might be both shot.

'She wasn't thinking anything more about it, when two Sundays afterwards the very same thing happened just as it had before. This time aunt plucked up a spirit, and asked uncle what it could be. And what do you think he said? "Birds, my dear, birds." Of course aunt said to him that no bird that ever flew with wings made a noise like that: sly, and low, with pauses in between; and then he said that many rare sorts of birds lived in North Middlesex and Hertfordshire. "Nonsense, Robert," said aunt, "how can you talk so, considering it has followed us all the way, for a mile or more?" And then uncle told her that some birds were so attached to man that they would follow one about for miles sometimes; he said he had just been reading about a bird like that in a book of travels. And do you know that when they got home he actually showed her a piece in the "Hertfordshire Naturalist" which they took in to oblige a friend of theirs, all about rare birds found in the neighbourhood, all the most outlandish names, aunt says, that she had never heard or thought of, and uncle had the impudence to say that it must have been a Purple Sandpiper, which, the paper said, had "a low shrill note, constantly repeated." And then he took down a book of Siberian Travels from the bookcase and showed her a page which told how a man was followed by a bird all day long through a forest. And that's what Aunt Marian says vexes her more than anything almost; to think that he should be so artful and ready with those books, twisting them to his own wicked ends. But, at the time, when she was out walking, she simply couldn't make out what he meant by talking about birds in that random, silly sort of way, so unlike him, and they went on, that horrible whistling following them, she looking straight ahead and walking fast, really feeling more huffy and put out than frightened. And when they got to the next stile, she got over and turned round, and 'lo and behold," as she says, there was no Uncle Robert to be seen! She felt herself go quite white with alarm, thinking of that whistle, and making sure he'd been spirited away or snatched in some way or another, and she had just screamed out "Robert" like a mad woman, when he came quite slowly round the corner, as cool as a cucumber, holding something in his hand. He said there were some flowers he could never pass, and when aunt saw that he had got a dandelion torn up by the roots, she felt as if her head were going round.'

Mary's story was suddenly interrupted. For ten minutes Darnell had been writhing in his chair, suffering tortures in his anxiety to avoid wounding his wife's feelings, but the episode of the dandelion was too much for him, and he burst into a long, wild shriek of laughter, aggravated by suppression into the semblance of a Red Indian's war-whoop. Alice, who was washing-up in the scullery, dropped some three shillings' worth of china, and the neighbours ran out into their gardens wondering if it were murder. Mary gazed reproachfully at her husband.

'How can you be so unfeeling, Edward?' she said, at length, when Darnell had passed into the feebleness of exhaustion. 'If you had seen the tears rolling down poor Aunt Marian's cheeks as she told me, I don't think you would have laughed. I didn't think you were so hard-hearted.'

'My dear Mary,' said Darnell, faintly, through sobs and catching of the breath, 'I am awfully sorry. I know it's very sad, really, and I'm not unfeeling; but it is such an odd tale, now, isn't it? The Sandpiper, you know, and then the dandelion!'

His face twitched and he ground his teeth together. Mary looked gravely at him for a moment, and then she put her hands to her face, and Darnell could see that she also shook with merriment.

'I am as bad as you,' she said, at last. 'I never thought of it in that way. I'm glad I didn't, or I should have laughed in Aunt Marian's face, and I wouldn't have done that for the world. Poor old thing; she cried as if her heart would break. I met her at Victoria, as she asked me, and we had some soup at a confectioner's. I could scarcely touch it; her tears kept dropping into the plate all the time; and then we went to the waiting-room at the station, and she cried there terribly.'

'Well,' said Darnell, 'what happened next? I won't laugh any more.'

'No, we mustn't; it's much too horrible for a joke. Well, of course aunt went home and wondered and wondered what could be the matter, and tried to think it out, but, as she says, she could make nothing of it. She began to be afraid that uncle's brain was giving way through overwork, as he had stopped in the City (as he said) up to all hours lately, and he had to go to Yorkshire (wicked old story-teller!), about some very tiresome business connected with his leases. But then she reflected that however queer he might be getting, even his queerness couldn't make whistles in the air, though, as she said, he was always a wonderful man. So she had to give that up; and then she wondered if there were anything the matter with her, as she had read about people who heard noises when there was really nothing at all. But that wouldn't do either, because though it might account for the whistling, it wouldn't account for the dandelion or the Sandpiper, or for fainting fits that turned purple, or any of uncle's queerness. So aunt said she could think of nothing but to read the Bible every day from the beginning, and by the time she got into Chronicles she felt rather better, especially as nothing had happened for three or four Sundays. She noticed uncle seemed absent-minded, and not as nice to her as he might be, but she put that down to too much work, as he never came home before the last train, and had a hansom twice all the way, getting there between three and four in the morning. Still, she felt it was no good bothering her head over what couldn't be made out or explained anyway, and she was just settling down, when one Sunday evening it began all over again, and worse things happened. The whistling followed them just as it did before, and poor aunt set her teeth and said nothing to uncle, as she knew he would only tell her stories, and they were walking on, not saying a word, when something made her look back, and there was a horrible boy with red hair, peeping through the hedge just behind, and grinning. She said it was a dreadful face, with something unnatural about it, as if it had been a dwarf, and before she had time to have a good look, it popped back like lightning, and aunt all but fainted away.'

'A red-headed boy?' said Darnell. 'I thought——What an extraordinary story this is. I've never heard of anything so queer. Who was the boy?'

'You will know in good time,' said Mrs. Darnell. 'It is very strange, isn't it?'

'Strange!' Darnell ruminated for a while.

'I know what I think, Mary,' he said at length. 'I don't believe a word of it. I believe your aunt is going mad, or has gone mad, and that she has delusions. The whole thing sounds to me like the invention of a lunatic.'

'You are quite wrong. Every word is true, and if you will let me go on, you will understand how it all happened.'

'Very good, go ahead.'

'Let me see, where was I? Oh, I know, aunt saw the boy grinning in the hedge. Yes, well, she was dreadfully frightened for a minute or two; there was something so queer about the face, but then she plucked up a spirit and said to herself, "After all, better a boy with red hair than a big man with a gun," and she made up her mind to watch Uncle Robert closely, as she could see by his look he knew all about it; he seemed as if he were thinking hard and puzzling over something, as if he didn't know what to do next, and his mouth kept opening and shutting, like a fish's. So she kept her face straight, and didn't say a word, and when he said something to her about the fine sunset, she took no notice. "Don't you hear what I say, Marian?" he said, speaking quite crossly, and bellowing as if it were to somebody in the next field. So aunt said she was very sorry, but her cold made her so deaf, she couldn't hear much. She noticed uncle looked quite pleased, and relieved too, and she knew he thought she hadn't heard the whistling. Suddenly uncle pretended to see a beautiful spray of honeysuckle high up in the hedge, and he said he must get it for aunt, only she must go on ahead, as it made him nervous to be watched. She said she would, but she just stepped aside behind a bush where there was a sort of cover in the hedge, and found she could see him quite well, though she scratched her face terribly with poking it into a rose bush. And in a minute or two out came the boy from behind the hedge, and she saw uncle and him talking, and she knew it was the same boy, as it wasn't dark enough to hide his flaming red head. And uncle put out his hand as if to catch him, but he just darted into the bushes and vanished. Aunt never said a word at the time, but that night when they got home she charged uncle with what she'd seen and asked him what it all meant. He was quite taken aback at first, and stammered and stuttered and said a spy wasn't his notion of a good wife, but at last he made her swear secrecy, and told her that he was a very high Freemason, and that the boy was an emissary of the order who brought him messages of the greatest importance. But aunt didn't believe a word of it, as an uncle of hers was a mason, and he never behaved like that. It was then she began to be afraid that it was really Anarchists, or something of the kind, and every time the bell rang she thought that uncle had been found out, and the police had come for him.'

'What nonsense! As if a man with house property would be an Anarchist.'

'Well, she could see there must be some horrible secret, and she didn't know what else to think. And then she began to have the things through the post.'

'Things through the post! What do you mean by that?'

'All sorts of things; bits of broken bottle-glass, packed carefully as if it were jewellery; parcels that unrolled and unrolled worse than Chinese boxes, and then had "cat" in large letters when you came to the middle; old artificial teeth, a cake of red paint, and at last cockroaches.'

'Cockroaches by post! Stuff and nonsense; your aunt's mad.'

'Edward, she showed me the box; it was made to hold cigarettes, and there were three dead cockroaches inside. And when she found a box of exactly the same kind, half-full of cigarettes, in uncle's great-coat pocket, then her head began to turn again.'

Darnell groaned, and stirred uneasily in his chair, feeling that the tale of Aunt Marian's domestic troubles was putting on the semblance of an evil dream.

'Anything else?' he asked.

'My dear, I haven't repeated half the things poor aunt told me this afternoon. There was the night she thought she saw a ghost in the shrubbery. She was anxious about some chickens that were just due to hatch out, so she went out after dark with some egg and bread-crumbs, in case they might be out. And just before her she saw a figure gliding by the rhododendrons. It looked like a short, slim man dressed as they used to be hundreds of years ago; she saw the sword by his side, and the feather in his cap. She thought she should have died, she said, and though it was gone in a minute, and she tried to make out it was all her fancy, she fainted when she got into the house. Uncle was at home that night, and when she came to and told him he ran out, and stayed out for half-an-hour or more, and then came in and said he could find nothing; and the next minute aunt heard that low whistle just outside the window, and uncle ran out again.'

'My dear Mary, do let us come to the point. What on earth does it all lead to?'

'Haven't you guessed? Why, of course it was that girl all the time.'

'Girl? I thought you said it was a boy with a red head?'

'Don't you see? She's an actress, and she dressed up. She won't leave uncle alone. It wasn't enough that he was with her nearly every evening in the week, but she must be after him on Sundays too. Aunt found a letter the horrid thing had written, and so it has all come out. Enid Vivian she calls herself, though I don't suppose she has any right to one name or the other. And the question is, what is to be done?'

'Let us talk of that again. I'll have a pipe, and then we'll go to bed.'

They were almost asleep when Mary said suddenly--

'Doesn't it seem queer, Edward? Last night you were telling me such beautiful things, and to-night I have been talking about that disgraceful old man and his goings on.'

'I don't know,' answered Darnell, dreamily. 'On the walls of that great church upon the hill I saw all kinds of strange grinning monsters, carved in stone.'

The misdemeanours of Mr. Robert Nixon brought in their train consequences strange beyond imagination. It was not that they continued to develop on the somewhat fantastic lines of these first adventures which Mrs. Darnell had related; indeed, when 'Aunt Marian' came over to Shepherd's Bush, one Sunday afternoon, Darnell wondered how he had had the heart to laugh at the misfortunes of a broken-hearted woman.

He had never seen his wife's aunt before, and he was strangely surprised when Alice showed her into the garden where they were sitting on the warm and misty Sunday in September. To him, save during these latter days, she had always been associated with ideas of splendour and success: his wife had always mentioned the Nixons with a tinge of reverence; he had heard, many times, the epic of Mr. Nixon's struggles and of his slow but triumphant rise. Mary had told the story as she had received it from her parents, beginning with the flight to London from some small, dull, and unprosperous town in the flattest of the Midlands, long ago, when a young man from the country had great chances of fortune. Robert Nixon's father had been a grocer in the High Street, and in after days the successful coal merchant and builder loved to tell of that dull provincial life, and while he glorified his own victories, he gave his hearers to understand that he came of a race which had also known how to achieve. That had been long ago, he would explain: in the days when that rare citizen who desired to go to London or to York was forced to rise in the dead of night, and make his way, somehow or other, by ten miles of quagmirish, wandering lanes to the Great North Road, there to meet the 'Lightning' coach, a vehicle which stood to all the countryside as the visible and tangible embodiment of tremendous speed--'and indeed,' as Nixon would add, 'it was always up to time, which is more than can be said of the Dunham Branch Line nowadays!' It was in this ancient Dunham that the Nixons had waged successful trade for perhaps a hundred years, in a shop with bulging bay windows looking on the market-place. There was no competition, and the townsfolk, and well-to-do farmers, the clergy and the country families, looked upon the house of Nixon as an institution fixed as the town hall (which stood on Roman pillars) and the parish church. But the change came: the railway crept nearer and nearer, the farmers and the country gentry became less well-to-do; the tanning, which was the local industry, suffered from a great business which had been established in a larger town, some twenty miles away, and the profits of the Nixons grew less and less. Hence the hegira of Robert, and he would dilate on the poorness of his beginnings, how he saved, by little and little, from his sorry wage of City clerk, and how he and a fellow clerk, 'who had come into a hundred pounds,' saw an opening in the coal trade--and filled it. It was at this stage of Robert's fortunes, still far from magnificent, that Miss Marian Reynolds had encountered him, she being on a visit to friends in Gunnersbury. Afterwards, victory followed victory; Nixon's wharf became a landmark to bargemen; his power stretched abroad, his dusky fleets went outwards to the sea, and inward by all the far reaches of canals. Lime, cement, and bricks were added to his merchandise, and at last he hit upon the great stroke--that extensive taking up of land in the north of London. Nixon himself ascribed this coup to native sagacity, and the possession of capital; and there were also obscure rumours to the effect that some one or other had been 'done' in the course of the transaction. However that might be, the Nixons grew wealthy to excess, and Mary had often told her husband of the state in which they dwelt, of their liveried servants, of the glories of their drawing-room, of their broad lawn, shadowed by a splendid and ancient cedar. And so Darnell had somehow been led into conceiving the lady of this demesne as a personage of no small pomp. He saw her, tall, of dignified port and presence, inclining, it might be, to some measure of obesity, such a measure as was not unbefitting in an elderly lady of position, who lived well and lived at ease. He even imagined a slight ruddiness of complexion, which went very well with hair that was beginning to turn grey, and when he heard the door-bell ring, as he sat under the mulberry on the Sunday afternoon, he bent forward to catch sight of this stately figure, clad, of course, in the richest, blackest silk, girt about with heavy chains of gold.

He started with amazement when he saw the strange presence that followed the servant into the garden. Mrs. Nixon was a little, thin old woman, who bent as she feebly trotted after Alice; her eyes were on the ground, and she did not lift them when the Darnells rose to greet her. She glanced to the right, uneasily, as she shook hands with Darnell, to the left when Mary kissed her, and when she was placed on the garden seat with a cushion at her back, she looked away at the back of the houses in the next street. She was dressed in black, it was true, but even Darnell could see that her gown was old and shabby, that the fur trimming of her cape and the fur boa which was twisted about her neck were dingy and disconsolate, and had all the melancholy air which fur wears when it is seen in a second-hand clothes-shop in a back street. And her gloves--they were black kid, wrinkled with much wear, faded to a bluish hue at the finger-tips, which showed signs of painful mending. Her hair, plastered over her forehead, looked dull and colourless, though some greasy matter had evidently been used with a view of producing a becoming gloss, and on it perched an antique bonnet, adorned with black pendants that rattled paralytically one against the other.

And there was nothing in Mrs. Nixon's face to correspond with the imaginary picture that Darnell had made of her. She was sallow, wrinkled, pinched; her nose ran to a sharp point, and her red-rimmed eyes were a queer water-grey, that seemed to shrink alike from the light and from encounter with the eyes of others. As she sat beside his wife on the green garden-seat, Darnell, who occupied a wicker-chair brought out from the drawing-room, could not help feeling that this shadowy and evasive figure, muttering replies to Mary's polite questions, was almost impossibly remote from his conceptions of the rich and powerful aunt, who could give away a hundred pounds as a mere birthday gift. She would say little at first; yes, she was feeling rather tired, it had been so hot all the way, and she had been afraid to put on lighter things as one never knew at this time of year what it might be like in the evenings; there were apt to be cold mists when the sun went down, and she didn't care to risk bronchitis.

'I thought I should never get here,' she went on, raising her voice to an odd querulous pipe. 'I'd no notion it was such an out-of-the-way place, it's so many years since I was in this neighbourhood.'

She wiped her eyes, no doubt thinking of the early days at Turnham Green, when she married Nixon; and when the pocket-handkerchief had done its office she replaced it in a shabby black bag which she clutched rather than carried. Darnell noticed, as he watched her, that the bag seemed full, almost to bursting, and he speculated idly as to the nature of its contents: correspondence, perhaps, he thought, further proofs of Uncle Robert's treacherous and wicked dealings. He grew quite uncomfortable, as he sat and saw her glancing all the while furtively away from his wife and himself, and presently he got up and strolled away to the other end of the garden, where he lit his pipe and walked to and fro on the gravel walk, still astounded at the gulf between the real and the imagined woman.

Presently he heard a hissing whisper, and he saw Mrs. Nixon's head inclining to his wife's. Mary rose and came towards him.

'Would you mind sitting in the drawing-room, Edward?' she murmured. 'Aunt says she can't bring herself to discuss such a delicate matter before you. I dare say it's quite natural.'

'Very well, but I don't think I'll go into the drawing-room. I feel as if a walk would do me good. You mustn't be frightened if I am a little late,' he said; 'if I don't get back before your aunt goes, say good-bye to her for me.'

He strolled into the main road, where the trams were humming to and fro. He was still confused and perplexed, and he tried to account for a certain relief he felt in removing himself from the presence of Mrs. Nixon. He told himself that her grief at her husband's ruffianly conduct was worthy of all pitiful respect, but at the same time, to his shame, he had felt a certain physical aversion from her as she sat in his garden in her dingy black, dabbing her red-rimmed eyes with a damp pocket-handkerchief. He had been to the Zoo when he was a lad, and he still remembered how he had shrunk with horror at the sight of certain reptiles slowly crawling over one another in their slimy pond. But he was enraged at the similarity between the two sensations, and he walked briskly on that level and monotonous road, looking about him at the unhandsome spectacle of suburban London keeping Sunday.

There was something in the tinge of antiquity which still exists in Acton that soothed his mind and drew it away from those unpleasant contemplations, and when at last he had penetrated rampart after rampart of brick, and heard no more the harsh shrieks and laughter of the people who were enjoying themselves, he found a way into a little sheltered field, and sat down in peace beneath a tree, whence he could look out on a pleasant valley. The sun sank down beneath the hills, the clouds changed into the likeness of blossoming rose-gardens; and he still sat there in the gathering darkness till a cool breeze blew upon him, and he rose with a sigh, and turned back to the brick ramparts and the glimmering streets, and the noisy idlers sauntering to and fro in the procession of their dismal festival. But he was murmuring to himself some words that seemed a magic song, and it was with uplifted heart that he let himself into his house.

Mrs. Nixon had gone an hour and a half before his return, Mary told him. Darnell sighed with relief, and he and his wife strolled out into the garden and sat down side by side.

They kept silence for a time, and at last Mary spoke, not without a nervous tremor in her voice.

'I must tell you, Edward,' she began, 'that aunt has made a proposal which you ought to hear. I think we should consider it.'

'A proposal? But how about the whole affair? Is it still going on?'

'Oh, yes! She told me all about it. Uncle is quite unrepentant. It seems he has taken a flat somewhere in town for that woman, and furnished it in the most costly manner. He simply laughs at aunt's reproaches, and says he means to have some fun at last. You saw how broken she was?'

'Yes; very sad. But won't he give her any money? Wasn't she very badly dressed for a woman in her position?'

'Aunt has no end of beautiful things, but I fancy she likes to hoard them; she has a horror of spoiling her dresses. It isn't for want of money, I assure you, as uncle settled a very large sum on her two years ago, when he was everything that could be desired as a husband. And that brings me to what I want to say. Aunt would like to live with us. She would pay very liberally. What do you say?'

'Would like to live with us?' exclaimed Darnell, and his pipe dropped from his hand on to the grass. He was stupefied by the thought of Aunt Marian as a boarder, and sat staring vacantly before him, wondering what new monster the night would next produce.

'I knew you wouldn't much like the idea,' his wife went on. 'But I do think, dearest, that we ought not to refuse without very serious consideration. I am afraid you did not take to poor aunt very much.'

Darnell shook his head dumbly.

'I thought you didn't; she was so upset, poor thing, and you didn't see her at her best. She is really so good. But listen to me, dear. Do you think we have the right to refuse her offer? I told you she has money of her own, and I am sure she would be dreadfully offended if we said we wouldn't have her. And what would become of me if anything happened to you? You know we have very little saved.'

Darnell groaned.

'It seems to me,' he said, 'that it would spoil everything. We are so happy, Mary dear, by ourselves. Of course I am extremely sorry for your aunt. I think she is very much to be pitied. But when it comes to having her always here----'

'I know, dear. Don't think I am looking forward to the prospect; you know I don't want anybody but you. Still, we ought to think of the future, and besides we shall be able to live so very much better. I shall be able to give you all sorts of nice things that I know you ought to have after all that hard work in the City. Our income would be doubled.'

'Do you mean she would pay us £150 a year?'

'Certainly. And she would pay for the spare room being furnished, and any extra she might want. She told me, specially, that if a friend or two came now and again to see her, she would gladly bear the cost of a fire in the drawing-room, and give something towards the gas bill, with a few shillings for the girl for any additional trouble. We should certainly be more than twice as well off as we are now. You see, Edward, dear, it's not the sort of offer we are likely to have again. Besides, we must think of the future, as I said. Do you know aunt took a great fancy to you?'

He shuddered and said nothing, and his wife went on with her argument.

'And, you see, it isn't as if we should see so very much of her. She will have her breakfast in bed, and she told me she would often go up to her room in the evening directly after dinner. I thought that very nice and considerate. She quite understands that we shouldn't like to have a third person always with us. Don't you think, Edward, that, considering everything, we ought to say we will have her?'

'Oh, I suppose so,' he groaned. 'As you say, it's a very good offer, financially, and I am afraid it would be very imprudent to refuse. But I don't like the notion, I confess.'

'I am so glad you agree with me, dear. Depend upon it, it won't be half so bad as you think. And putting our own advantage on one side, we shall really be doing poor aunt a very great kindness. Poor old dear, she cried bitterly after you were gone; she said she had made up her mind not to stay any longer in Uncle Robert's house, and she didn't know where to go, or what would become of her, if we refused to take her in. She quite broke down.'

'Well, well; we will try it for a year, anyhow. It may be as you say; we shan't find it quite so bad as it seems now. Shall we go in?'

He stooped for his pipe, which lay as it had fallen, on the grass. He could not find it, and lit a wax match which showed him the pipe, and close beside it, under the seat, something that looked like a page torn from a book. He wondered what it could be, and picked it up.

The gas was lit in the drawing-room, and Mrs. Darnell, who was arranging some notepaper, wished to write at once to Mrs. Nixon, cordially accepting her proposal, when she was startled by an exclamation from her husband.

'What is the matter?' she said, startled by the tone of his voice. 'You haven't hurt yourself?'

'Look at this,' he replied, handing her a small leaflet; 'I found it under the garden seat just now.'

Mary glanced with bewilderment at her husband and read as follows:--

THE NEW AND CHOSEN SEED OF ABRAHAM PROPHECIES TO BE FULFILLED IN THE PRESENT YEAR

1. The Sailing of a Fleet of One hundred and Forty and Four Vessels for Tarshish and the Isles.

2. Destruction of the Power of the Dog, including all the instruments of anti-Abrahamic legislation.

3. Return of the Fleet from Tarshish, bearing with it the gold of Arabia, destined to be the

Foundation of the New City of Abraham.

4. The Search for the Bride, and the bestowing of the Seals on the Seventy and Seven.

5. The Countenance of FATHER to become luminous, but with a greater glory than the face of Moses.

6. The Pope of Rome to be stoned with stones in the valley called Berek-Zittor.

7. FATHER to be acknowledged by Three Great Rulers. Two Great Rulers will deny FATHER, and will immediately perish in the Effluvia of FATHER'S Indignation.

8. Binding of the Beast with the Little Horn, and all Judges cast down.

9. Finding of the Bride in the Land of Egypt, which has been revealed to FATHER as now existing in the western part of London.

10. Bestowal of the New Tongue on the Seventy and Seven, and on the One Hundred and Forty and Four. FATHER proceeds to the Bridal Chamber.

11. Destruction of London and rebuilding of the City called No, which is the New City of Abraham.

12. FATHER united to the Bride, and the present Earth removed to the Sun for the space of half an hour.

Mrs. Darnell's brow cleared as she read matter which seemed to her harmless if incoherent. From her husband's voice she had been led to fear something more tangibly unpleasant than a vague catena of prophecies.

'Well,' she said, 'what about it?'

'What about it? Don't you see that your aunt dropped it, and that she must be a raging lunatic?'

'Oh, Edward! don't say that. In the first place, how do you know that aunt dropped it at all? It might easily have blown over from any of the other gardens. And, if it were hers, I don't think you should call her a lunatic. I don't believe, myself, that there are any real prophets now; but there are many good people who think quite differently. I knew an old lady once who, I am sure, was very good, and she took in a paper every week that was full of prophecies and things very like this. Nobody called her mad, and I have heard father say that she had one of the sharpest heads for business he had ever come across.'

'Very good; have it as you like. But I believe we shall both be sorry.'

They sat in silence for some time. Alice came in after her 'evening out,' and they sat on, till Mrs. Darnell said she was tired and wanted to go to bed.

Her husband kissed her. 'I don't think I will come up just yet,' he said; 'you go to sleep, dearest. I want to think things over. No, no; I am not going to change my mind: your aunt shall come, as I said. But there are one or two things I should like to get settled in my mind.'

He meditated for a long while, pacing up and down the room. Light after light was extinguished in Edna Road, and the people of the suburb slept all around him, but still the gas was alight in Darnell's drawing-room, and he walked softly up and down the floor. He was thinking that about the life of Mary and himself, which had been so quiet, there seemed to be gathering on all sides grotesque and fantastic shapes, omens of confusion and disorder, threats of madness; a strange company from another world. It was as if into the quiet, sleeping streets of some little ancient town among the hills there had come from afar the sound of drum and pipe, snatches of wild song, and there had burst into the market-place the mad company of the players, strangely bedizened, dancing a furious measure to their hurrying music, drawing forth the citizens from their sheltered homes and peaceful lives, and alluring them to mingle in the significant figures of their dance.

Yet afar and near (for it was hidden in his heart) he beheld the glimmer of a sure and constant star. Beneath, darkness came on, and mists and shadows closed about the town. The red, flickering flame of torches was kindled in the midst of it. The song grew louder, with more insistent, magical tones, surging and falling in unearthly modulations, the very speech of incantation; and the drum beat madly, and the pipe shrilled to a scream, summoning all to issue forth, to leave their peaceful hearths; for a strange rite was preconized in their midst. The streets that were wont to be so still, so hushed with the cool and tranquil veils of darkness, asleep beneath the patronage of the evening star, now danced with glimmering lanterns, resounded with the cries of those who hurried forth, drawn as by a magistral spell; and the songs swelled and triumphed, the reverberant beating of the drum grew louder, and in the midst of the awakened town the players, fantastically arrayed, performed their interlude under the red blaze of torches. He knew not whether they were players, men that would vanish suddenly as they came, disappearing by the track that climbed the hill; or whether they were indeed magicians, workers of great and efficacious spells, who knew the secret word by which the earth may be transformed into the hall of Gehenna, so that they that gazed and listened, as at a passing spectacle, should be entrapped by the sound and the sight presented to them, should be drawn into the elaborated figures of that mystic dance, and so should be whirled away into those unending mazes on the wild hills that were abhorred, there to wander for evermore.

But Darnell was not afraid, because of the Daystar that had risen in his heart. It had dwelt there all his life, and had slowly shone forth with clearer and clearer light, and he began to see that though his earthly steps might be in the ways of the ancient town that was beset by the Enchanters, and resounded with their songs and their processions, yet he dwelt also in that serene and secure world of brightness, and from a great and unutterable height looked on the confusion of the mortal pageant, beholding mysteries in which he was no true actor, hearing magic songs that could by no means draw him down from the battlements of the high and holy city.

His heart was filled with a great joy and a great peace as he lay down beside his wife and fell asleep, and in the morning, when he woke up, he was glad.

IV

In a haze as of a dream Darnell's thoughts seemed to move through the opening days of the next week. Perhaps nature had not intended that he should be practical or much given to that which is usually called 'sound common sense,' but his training had made him desirous of good, plain qualities of the mind, and he uneasily strove to account to himself for his strange mood of the Sunday night, as he had often endeavoured to interpret the fancies of his boyhood and early manhood. At first he was annoyed by his want of success; the morning paper, which he always secured as the 'bus delayed at Uxbridge Road Station, fell from his hands unread, while he vainly reasoned, assuring himself that the threatened incursion of a whimsical old woman, though tiresome enough, was no rational excuse for those curious hours of meditation in which his thoughts seemed to have dressed themselves in unfamiliar, fantastic habits, and to parley with him in a strange speech, and yet a speech that he had understood.

With such arguments he perplexed his mind on the long, accustomed ride up the steep ascent of Holland Park, past the incongruous hustle of Notting Hill Gate, where in one direction a road shows the way to the snug, somewhat faded bowers and retreats of Bayswater, and in another one sees the portal of the murky region of the slums. The customary companions of his morning's journey were in the seats about him; he heard the hum of their talk, as they disputed concerning politics, and the man next to him, who came from Acton, asked him what he thought of the Government now. There was a discussion, and a loud and excited one, just in front, as to whether rhubarb was a fruit or vegetable, and in his ear he heard Redman, who was a near neighbour, praising the economy of 'the wife.'

'I don't know how she does it. Look here; what do you think we had yesterday? Breakfast: fish-cakes, beautifully fried--rich, you know, lots of herbs, it's a receipt of her aunt's; you should just taste 'em. Coffee, bread, butter, marmalade, and, of course, all the usual etceteras. Dinner: roast beef, Yorkshire, potatoes, greens, and horse-radish sauce, plum tart, cheese. And where will you get a better dinner than that? Well, I call it wonderful, I really do.'

But in spite of these distractions he fell into a dream as the 'bus rolled and tossed on its way Citywards, and still he strove to solve the enigma of his vigil of the night before, and as the shapes of trees and green lawns and houses passed before his eyes, and as he saw the procession moving on the pavement, and while the murmur of the streets sounded in his ears, all was to him strange and unaccustomed, as if he moved through the avenues of some city in a foreign land. It was, perhaps, on these mornings, as he rode to his mechanical work, that vague and floating fancies that must have long haunted his brain began to shape themselves, and to put on the form of definite conclusions, from which he could no longer escape, even if he had wished it. Darnell had received what is called a sound commercial education, and would therefore have found very great difficulty in putting into articulate speech any thought that was worth thinking; but he grew certain on these mornings that the 'common sense' which he had always heard exalted as man's supremest faculty was, in all probability, the smallest and least-considered item in the equipment of an ant of average intelligence. And with this, as an almost necessary corollary, came a firm belief that the whole fabric of life in which he moved was sunken, past all thinking, in the grossest absurdity; that he and all his friends and acquaintances and fellow-workers were interested in matters in which men were never meant to be interested, were pursuing aims which they were never meant to pursue, were, indeed, much like fair stones of an altar serving as a pigsty wall. Life, it seemed to him, was a great search for--he knew not what; and in the process of the ages one by one the true marks upon the ways had been shattered, or buried, or the meaning of the words had been slowly forgotten; one by one the signs had been turned awry, the true entrances had been thickly overgrown, the very way itself had been diverted from the heights to the depths, till at last the race of pilgrims had become hereditary stone-breakers and ditch-scourers on a track that led to destruction--if it led anywhere at all. Darnell's heart thrilled with a strange and trembling joy, with a sense that was all new, when it came to his mind that this great loss might not be a hopeless one, that perhaps the difficulties were by no means insuperable. It might be, he considered, that the stone-breaker had merely to throw down his hammer and set out, and the way would be plain before him; and a single step would free the delver in rubbish from the foul slime of the ditch.

It was, of course, with difficulty and slowly that these things became clear to him. He was an English City clerk, 'flourishing' towards the end of the nineteenth century, and the rubbish heap that had been accumulating for some centuries could not be cleared away in an instant. Again and again the spirit of nonsense that had been implanted in him as in his fellows assured him that the true world was the visible and tangible world, the world in which good and faithful letter-copying was exchangeable for a certain quantum of bread, beef, and house-room, and that the man who copied letters well, did not beat his wife, nor lose money foolishly, was a good man, fulfilling the end for which he had been made. But in spite of these arguments, in spite of their acceptance by all who were about him, he had the grace to perceive the utter falsity and absurdity of the whole position. He was fortunate in his entire ignorance of sixpenny 'science,' but if the whole library had been projected into his brain it would not have moved him to 'deny in the darkness that which he had known in the light.' Darnell knew by experience that man is made a mystery for mysteries and visions, for the realization in his consciousness of ineffable bliss, for a great joy that transmutes the whole world, for a joy that surpasses all joys and overcomes all sorrows. He knew this certainly, though he knew it dimly; and he was apart from other men, preparing himself for a great experiment.

With such thoughts as these for his secret and concealed treasure, he was able to bear the threatened invasion of Mrs. Nixon with something approaching indifference. He knew, indeed, that her presence between his wife and himself would be unwelcome to him, and he was not without grave doubts as to the woman's sanity; but after all, what did it matter? Besides, already a faint glimmering light had risen within him that showed the profit of self-negation, and in this matter he had preferred his wife's will to his own. Et non sua poma; to his astonishment he found a delight in denying himself his own wish, a process that he had always regarded as thoroughly detestable. This was a state of things which he could not in the least understand; but, again, though a member of a most hopeless class, living in the most hopeless surroundings that the world has ever seen, though he knew as much of the askesis as of Chinese metaphysics; again, he had the grace not to deny the light that had begun to glimmer in his soul.

And he found a present reward in the eyes of Mary, when she welcomed him home after his foolish labours in the cool of the evening. They sat together, hand in hand, under the mulberry tree, at the coming of the dusk, and as the ugly walls about them became obscure and vanished into the formless world of shadows, they seemed to be freed from the bondage of Shepherd's Bush, freed to wander in that undisfigured, undefiled world that lies beyond the walls. Of this region Mary knew little or nothing by experience, since her relations had always been of one mind with the modern world, which has for the true country an instinctive and most significant horror and dread. Mr. Reynolds had also shared in another odd superstition of these later days--that it is necessary to leave London at least once a year; consequently Mary had some knowledge of various seaside resorts on the south and east coasts, where Londoners gather in hordes, turn the sands into one vast, bad music-hall, and derive, as they say, enormous benefit from the change. But experiences such as these give but little knowledge of the country in its true and occult sense; and yet Mary, as she sat in the dusk beneath the whispering tree, knew something of the secret of the wood, of the valley shut in by high hills, where the sound of pouring water always echoes from the clear brook. And to Darnell these were nights of great dreams; for it was the hour of the work, the time of transmutation, and he who could not understand the miracle, who could scarcely believe in it, yet knew, secretly and half consciously, that the water was being changed into the wine of a new life. This was ever the inner music of his dreams, and to it he added on these still and sacred nights the far-off memory of that time long ago when, a child, before the world had overwhelmed him, he journeyed down to the old grey house in the west, and for a whole month heard the murmur of the forest through his bedroom window, and when the wind was hushed, the washing of the tides about the reeds; and sometimes awaking very early he had heard the strange cry of a bird as it rose from its nest among the reeds, and had looked out and had seen the valley whiten to the dawn, and the winding river whiten as it swam down to the sea. The memory of all this had faded and become shadowy as he grew older and the chains of common life were riveted firmly about his soul; all the atmosphere by which he was surrounded was well-nigh fatal to such thoughts, and only now and again in half-conscious moments or in sleep he had revisited that valley in the far-off west, where the breath of the wind was an incantation, and every leaf and stream and hill spoke of great and ineffable mysteries. But now the broken vision was in great part restored to him, and looking with love in his wife's eyes he saw the gleam of water-pools in the still forest, saw the mists rising in the evening, and heard the music of the winding river.

They were sitting thus together on the Friday evening of the week that had begun with that odd and half-forgotten visit of Mrs. Nixon, when, to Darnell's annoyance, the door-bell gave a discordant peal, and Alice with some disturbance of manner came out and announced that a gentleman wished to see the master. Darnell went into the drawing-room, where Alice had lit one gas so that it flared and burnt with a rushing sound, and in this distorting light there waited a stout, elderly gentleman, whose countenance was altogether unknown to him. He stared blankly, and hesitated, about to speak, but the visitor began.

'You don't know who I am, but I expect you'll know my name. It's Nixon.'

He did not wait to be interrupted. He sat down and plunged into narrative, and after the first few words, Darnell, whose mind was not altogether unprepared, listened without much astonishment.

'And the long and the short of it is,' Mr. Nixon said at last, 'she's gone stark, staring mad, and we had to put her away to-day--poor thing.'

His voice broke a little, and he wiped his eyes hastily, for though stout and successful he was not unfeeling, and he was fond of his wife. He had spoken quickly, and had gone lightly over many details which might have interested specialists in certain kinds of mania, and Darnell was sorry for his evident distress.

'I came here,' he went on after a brief pause, 'because I found out she had been to see you last Sunday, and I knew the sort of story she must have told.'

Darnell showed him the prophetic leaflet which Mrs. Nixon had dropped in the garden. 'Did you know about this?' he said.

'Oh, him,' said the old man, with some approach to cheerfulness; 'oh yes, I thrashed him black and blue the day before yesterday.'

'Isn't he mad? Who is the man?'

'He's not mad, he's bad. He's a little Welsh skunk named Richards. He's been running some sort of chapel over at New Barnet for the last few years, and my poor wife--she never could find the parish church good enough for her--had been going to his damned schism shop for the last twelve-month. It was all that finished her off. Yes; I thrashed him the day before yesterday, and I'm not afraid of a summons either. I know him, and he knows I know him.'

Old Nixon whispered something in Darnell's ear, and chuckled faintly as he repeated for the third time his formula--

'I thrashed him black and blue the day before yesterday.'

Darnell could only murmur condolences and express his hope that Mrs. Nixon might recover. The old man shook his head.

'I'm afraid there's no hope of that,' he said. 'I've had the best advice, but they couldn't do anything, and told me so.'

Presently he asked to see his niece, and Darnell went out and prepared Mary as well as he could. She could scarcely take in the news that her aunt was a hopeless maniac, for Mrs. Nixon, having been extremely stupid all her days, had naturally succeeded in passing with her relations as typically sensible. With the Reynolds family, as with the great majority of us, want of imagination is always equated with sanity, and though many of us have never heard of Lombroso we are his ready-made converts. We have always believed that poets are mad, and if statistics unfortunately show that few poets have really been inhabitants of lunatic asylums, it is soothing to learn that nearly all poets have had whooping-cough, which is doubtless, like intoxication, a minor madness.

'But is it really true?' she asked at length. 'Are you certain uncle is not deceiving you? Aunt seemed so sensible always.'

She was helped at last by recollecting that Aunt Marian used to get up very early of mornings, and then they went into the drawing-room and talked to the old man. His evident kindliness and honesty grew upon Mary, in spite of a lingering belief in her aunt's fables, and when he left, it was with a promise to come to see them again.

Mrs. Darnell said she felt tired, and went to bed; and Darnell returned to the garden and began to pace to and fro, collecting his thoughts. His immeasurable relief at the intelligence that, after all, Mrs. Nixon was not coming to live with them taught him that, despite his submission, his dread of the event had been very great. The weight was removed, and now he was free to consider his life without reference to the grotesque intrusion that he had feared. He sighed for joy, and as he paced to and fro he savoured the scent of the night, which, though it came faintly to him in that brick-bound suburb, summoned to his mind across many years the odour of the world at night as he had known it in that short sojourn of his boyhood; the odour that rose from the earth when the flame of the sun had gone down beyond the mountain, and the afterglow had paled in the sky and on the fields. And as he recovered as best he could these lost dreams of an enchanted land, there came to him other images of his childhood, forgotten and yet not forgotten, dwelling unheeded in dark places of the memory, but ready to be summoned forth. He remembered one fantasy that had long haunted him. As he lay half asleep in the forest on one hot afternoon of that memorable visit to the country, he had 'made believe' that a little companion had come to him out of the blue mists and the green light beneath the leaves--a white girl with long black hair, who had played with him and whispered her secrets in his ear, as his father lay sleeping under a tree; and from that summer afternoon, day by day, she had been beside him; she had visited him in the wilderness of London, and even in recent years there had come to him now and again the sense of her presence, in the midst of the heat and turmoil of the City. The last visit he remembered well; it was a few weeks before he married, and from the depths of some futile task he had looked up with puzzled eyes, wondering why the close air suddenly grew scented with green leaves, why the murmur of the trees and the wash of the river on the reeds came to his ears; and then that sudden rapture to which he had given a name and an individuality possessed him utterly. He knew then how the dull flesh of man can be like fire; and now, looking back from a new standpoint on this and other experiences, he realized how all that was real in his life had been unwelcomed, uncherished by him, had come to him, perhaps, in virtue of merely negative qualities on his part. And yet, as he reflected, he saw that there had been a chain of witnesses all through his life: again and again voices had whispered in his ear words in a strange language that he now recognized as his native tongue; the common street had not been lacking in visions of the true land of his birth; and in all the passing and repassing of the world he saw that there had been emissaries ready to guide his feet on the way of the great journey.

A week or two after the visit of Mr. Nixon, Darnell took his annual holiday.

There was no question of Walton-on-the-Naze, or of anything of the kind, as he quite agreed with his wife's longing for some substantial sum put by against the evil day. But the weather was still fine, and he lounged away the time in his garden beneath the tree, or he sauntered out on long aimless walks in the western purlieus of London, not unvisited by that old sense of some great ineffable beauty, concealed by the dim and dingy veils of grey interminable streets. Once, on a day of heavy rain he went to the 'box-room,' and began to turn over the papers in the old hair trunk-- scraps and odds and ends of family history, some of them in his father's handwriting, others in faded ink, and there were a few ancient pocket-books, filled with manuscript of a still earlier time, and in these the ink was glossier and blacker than any writing fluids supplied by stationers of later days. Darnell had hung up the portrait of the ancestor in this room, and had bought a solid kitchen table and a chair; so that Mrs. Darnell, seeing him looking over his old documents, half thought of naming the room 'Mr. Darnell's study.' He had not glanced at these relics of his family for many years, but from the hour when the rainy morning sent him to them, he remained constant to research till the end of the holidays. It was a new interest, and he began to fashion in his mind a faint picture of his forefathers, and of their life in that grey old house in the river valley, in the western land of wells and streams and dark and ancient woods. And there were stranger things than mere notes on family history amongst that odd litter of old disregarded papers, and when he went back to his work in the City some of the men fancied that he was in some vague manner changed in appearance; but he only laughed when they asked him where he had been and what he had been doing with himself. But Mary noticed that every evening he spent at least an hour in the box-room; she was rather sorry at the waste of time involved in reading old papers about dead people. And one afternoon, as they were out together on a somewhat dreary walk towards Acton, Darnell stopped at a hopeless second- hand bookshop, and after scanning the rows of shabby books in the window, went in and purchased two volumes. They proved to be a Latin dictionary and grammar, and she was surprised to hear her husband declare his intention of acquiring the Latin language.

But, indeed, all his conduct impressed her as indefinably altered; and she began to be a little alarmed, though she could scarcely have formed her fears in words. But she knew that in some way that was all indefined and beyond the grasp of her thought their lives had altered since the summer, and no single thing wore quite the same aspect as before. If she looked out into the dull street with its rare loiterers, it was the same and yet it had altered, and if she opened the window in the early morning the wind that entered came with a changed breath that spoke some message that she could not understand. And day by day passed by in the old course, and not even the four walls were altogether familiar, and the voices of men and women sounded with strange notes, with the echo, rather, of a music that came over unknown hills. And day by day as she went about her household work, passing from shop to shop in those dull streets that were a network, a fatal labyrinth of grey desolation on every side, there came to her sense half-seen images of some other world, as if she walked in a dream, and every moment must bring her to light and to awakening, when the grey should fade, and regions long desired should appear in glory. Again and again it seemed as if that which was hidden would be shown even to the sluggish testimony of sense; and as she went to and fro from street to street of that dim and weary suburb, and looked on those grey material walls, they seemed as if a light glowed behind them, and again and again the mystic fragrance of incense was blown to her nostrils from across the verge of that world which is not so much impenetrable as ineffable, and to her ears came the dream of a chant that spoke of hidden choirs about all her ways. She struggled against these impressions, refusing her assent to the testimony of them, since all the pressure of credited opinion for three hundred years has been directed towards stamping out real knowledge, and so effectually has this been accomplished that we can only recover the truth through much anguish. And so Mary passed the days in a strange perturbation, clinging to common things and common thoughts, as if she feared that one morning she would wake up in an unknown world to a changed life. And Edward Darnell went day by day to his labour and returned in the evening, always with that shining of light within his eyes and upon his face, with the gaze of wonder that was greater day by day, as if for him the veil grew thin and soon would disappear.

From these great matters both in herself and in her husband Mary shrank back, afraid, perhaps, that if she began the question the answer might be too wonderful. She rather taught herself to be troubled over little things; she asked herself what attraction there could be in the old records over which she supposed Edward to be poring night after night in the cold room upstairs. She had glanced over the papers at Darnell's invitation, and could see but little interest in them; there were one or two sketches, roughly done in pen and ink, of the old house in the west: it looked a shapeless and fantastic place, furnished with strange pillars and stranger ornaments on the projecting porch; and on one side a roof dipped down almost to the earth, and in the centre there was something that might almost be a tower rising above the rest of the building. Then there were documents that seemed all names and dates, with here and there a coat of arms done in the margin, and she came upon a string of uncouth Welsh names linked together by the word 'ap' in a chain that looked endless. There was a paper covered with signs and figures that meant nothing to her, and then there were the pocket-books, full of old-fashioned writing, and much of it in Latin, as her husband told her--it was a collection as void of significance as a treatise on conic sections, so far as Mary was concerned. But night after night Darnell shut himself up with the musty rolls, and more than ever when he rejoined her he bore upon his face the blazonry of some great adventure. And one night she asked him what interested him so much in the papers he had shown her.

He was delighted with the question. Somehow they had not talked much together for the last few weeks, and he began to tell her of the records of the old race from which he came, of the old strange house of grey stone between the forest and the river. The family went back and back, he said, far into the dim past, beyond the Normans, beyond the Saxons, far into the Roman days, and for many hundred years they had been petty kings, with a strong fortress high up on the hill, in the heart of the forest; and even now the great mounds remained, whence one could look through the trees towards the mountain on one side and across the yellow sea on the other. The real name of the family was not Darnell; that was assumed by one Iolo ap Taliesin ap Iorwerth in the sixteenth century--why, Darnell did not seem to understand. And then he told her how the race had dwindled in prosperity, century by century, till at last there was nothing left but the grey house and a few acres of land bordering the river.

'And do you know, Mary,' he said, 'I suppose we shall go and live there some day or other. My great-uncle, who has the place now, made money in business when he was a young man, and I believe he will leave it all to me. I know I am the only relation he has. How strange it would be. What a change from the life here.'

'You never told me that. Don't you think your great-uncle might leave his house and his money to somebody he knows really well? You haven't seen him since you were a little boy, have you?'

'No; but we write once a year. And from what I have heard my father say, I am sure the old man would never leave the house out of the family. Do you think you would like it?'

'I don't know. Isn't it very lonely?'

'I suppose it is. I forget whether there are any other houses in sight, but I don't think there are any at all near. But what a change! No City, no streets, no people passing to and fro; only the sound of the wind and the sight of the green leaves and the green hills, and the song of the voices of the earth.'... He checked himself suddenly, as if he feared that he was about to tell some secret that must not yet be uttered; and indeed, as he spoke of the change from the little street in Shepherd's Bush to that ancient house in the woods of the far west, a change seemed already to possess himself, and his voice put on the modulation of an antique chant. Mary looked at him steadily and touched his arm, and he drew a long breath before he spoke again.

'It is the old blood calling to the old land,' he said. 'I was forgetting that I am a clerk in the City.'

It was, doubtless, the old blood that had suddenly stirred in him; the resurrection of the old spirit that for many centuries had been faithful to secrets that are now disregarded by most of us, that now day by day was quickened more and more in his heart, and grew so strong that it was hard to conceal. He was indeed almost in the position of the man in the tale, who, by a sudden electric shock, lost the vision of the things about him in the London streets, and gazed instead upon the sea and shore of an island in the Antipodes; for Darnell only clung with an effort to the interests and the atmosphere which, till lately, had seemed all the world to him; and the grey house and the wood and the river, symbols of the other sphere, intruded as it were into the landscape of the London suburb.

But he went on, with more restraint, telling his stories of far-off ancestors, how one of them, the most remote of all, was called a saint, and was supposed to possess certain mysterious secrets often alluded to in the papers as the 'Hidden Songs of Iolo Sant.' And then with an abrupt transition he recalled memories of his father and of the strange, shiftless life in dingy lodgings in the backwaters of London, of the dim stucco streets that were his first recollections, of forgotten squares in North London, and of the figure of his father, a grave bearded man who seemed always in a dream, as if he too sought for the vision of a land beyond the strong walls, a land where there were deep orchards and many shining hills, and fountains and water-pools gleaming under the leaves of the wood.

'I believe my father earned his living,' he went on, 'such a living as he did earn, at the Record Office and the British Museum. He used to hunt up things for lawyers and country parsons who wanted old deeds inspected. He never made much, and we were always moving from one lodging to another--always to out-of-the-way places where everything seemed to have run to seed. We never knew our neighbours--we moved too often for that--but my father had about half a dozen friends, elderly men like himself, who used to come to see us pretty often; and then, if there was any money, the lodging-house servant would go out for beer, and they would sit and smoke far into the night.

'I never knew much about these friends of his, but they all had the same look, the look of longing for something hidden. They talked of mysteries that I never understood, very little of their own lives, and when they did speak of ordinary affairs one could tell that they thought such matters as money and the want of it were unimportant trifles. When I grew up and went into the City, and met other young fellows and heard their way of talking, I wondered whether my father and his friends were not a little queer in their heads; but I know better now.'

So night after night Darnell talked to his wife, seeming to wander aimlessly from the dingy lodging-houses, where he had spent his boyhood in the company of his father and the other seekers, to the old house hidden in that far western valley, and the old race that had so long looked at the setting of the sun over the mountain. But in truth there was one end in all that he spoke, and Mary felt that beneath his words, however indifferent they might seem, there was hidden a purpose, that they were to embark on a great and marvellous adventure.

So day by day the world became more magical; day by day the work of separation was being performed, the gross accidents were being refined away. Darnell neglected no instruments that might be useful in the work; and now he neither lounged at home on Sunday mornings, nor did he accompany his wife to the Gothic blasphemy which pretended to be a church. They had discovered a little church of another fashion in a back street, and Darnell, who had found in one of the old notebooks the maxim Incredibilia sola Credenda, soon perceived how high and glorious a thing was that service at which he assisted. Our stupid ancestors taught us that we could become wise by studying books on 'science,' by meddling with test-tubes, geological specimens, microscopic preparations, and the like; but they who have cast off these follies know that they must read not 'science' books, but mass-books, and that the soul is made wise by the contemplation of mystic ceremonies and elaborate and curious rites. In such things Darnell found a wonderful mystery language, which spoke at once more secretly and more directly than the formal creeds; and he saw that, in a sense, the whole world is but a great ceremony or sacrament, which teaches under visible forms a hidden and transcendent doctrine. It was thus that he found in the ritual of the church a perfect image of the world; an image purged, exalted, and illuminate, a holy house built up of shining and translucent stones, in which the burning torches were more significant than the wheeling stars, and the fuming incense was a more certain token than the rising of the mist. His soul went forth with the albed procession in its white and solemn order, the mystic dance that signifies rapture and a joy above all joys, and when he beheld Love slain and rise again victorious he knew that he witnessed, in a figure, the consummation of all things, the Bridal of all Bridals, the mystery that is beyond all mysteries, accomplished from the foundation of the world. So day by day the house of his life became more magical.

And at the same time he began to guess that if in the New Life there are new and unheard-of joys, there are also new and unheard-of dangers. In his manuscript books which professed to deliver the outer sense of those mysterious 'Hidden Songs of Iolo Sant' there was a little chapter that bore the heading: Fons Sacer non in communem Vsum convertendus est, and by diligence, with much use of the grammar and dictionary, Darnell was able to construe the by no means complex Latin of his ancestor. The special book which contained the chapter in question was one of the most singular in the collection, since it bore the title Terra de Iolo, and on the surface, with an ingenious concealment of its real symbolism, it affected to give an account of the orchards, fields, woods, roads, tenements, and waterways in the possession of Darnell's ancestors. Here, then, he read of the Holy Well, hidden in the Wistman's Wood--Sylva Sapientum--'a fountain of abundant water, which no heats of summer can ever dry, which no flood can ever defile, which is as a water of life, to them that thirst for life, a stream of cleansing to them that would be pure, and a medicine of such healing virtue that by it, through the might of God and the intercession of His saints, the most grievous wounds are made whole.' But the water of this well was to be kept sacred perpetually, it was not to be used for any common purpose, nor to satisfy any bodily thirst; but ever to be esteemed as holy, 'even as the water which the priest hath hallowed.' And in the margin a comment in a later hand taught Darnell something of the meaning of these prohibitions. He was warned not to use the Well of Life as a mere luxury of mortal life, as a new sensation, as a means of making the insipid cup of everyday existence more palatable. 'For,' said the commentator, 'we are not called to sit as the spectators in a theatre, there to watch the play performed before us, but we are rather summoned to stand in the very scene itself, and there fervently to enact our parts in a great and wonderful mystery.'

Darnell could quite understand the temptation that was thus indicated. Though he had gone but a little way on the path, and had barely tested the over-runnings of that mystic well, he was already aware of the enchantment that was transmuting all the world about him, informing his life with a strange significance and romance. London seemed a city of the Arabian Nights, and its labyrinths of streets an enchanted maze; its long avenues of lighted lamps were as starry systems, and its immensity became for him an image of the endless universe. He could well imagine how pleasant it might be to linger in such a world as this, to sit apart and dream, beholding the strange pageant played before him; but the Sacred Well was not for common use, it was for the cleansing of the soul, and the healing of the grievous wounds of the spirit. There must be yet another transformation: London had become Bagdad; it must at last be transmuted to Syon, or in the phrase of one of his old documents, the City of the Cup.

And there were yet darker perils which the Iolo MSS. (as his father had named the collection) hinted at more or less obscurely. There were suggestions of an awful region which the soul might enter, of a transmutation that was unto death, of evocations which could summon the utmost forces of evil from their dark places--in a word, of that sphere which is represented to most of us under the crude and somewhat childish symbolism of Black Magic. And here again he was not altogether without a dim comprehension of what was meant. He found himself recalling an odd incident that had happened long ago, which had remained all the years in his mind unheeded, amongst the many insignificant recollections of his childhood, and now rose before him, clear and distinct and full of meaning. It was on that memorable visit to the old house in the west, and the whole scene returned, with its smallest events, and the voices seemed to sound in his ears. It was a grey, still day of heavy heat that he remembered: he had stood on the lawn after breakfast, and wondered at the great peace and silence of the world. Not a leaf stirred in the trees on the lawn, not a whisper came from the myriad leaves of the wood; the flowers gave out sweet and heavy odours as if they breathed the dreams of the summer night; and far down the valley, the winding river was like dim silver under that dim and silvery sky, and the far hills and woods and fields vanished in the mist. The stillness of the air held him as with a charm; he leant all the morning against the rails that parted the lawn from the meadow, breathing the mystic breath of summer, and watching the fields brighten as with a sudden blossoming of shining flowers as the high mist grew thin for a moment before the hidden sun. As he watched thus, a man weary with heat, with some glance of horror in his eyes, passed him on his way to the house; but he stayed at his post till the old bell in the turret rang, and they dined all together, masters and servants, in the dark cool room that looked towards the still leaves of the wood. He could see that his uncle was upset about something, and when they had finished dinner he heard him tell his father that there was trouble at a farm; and it was settled that they should all drive over in the afternoon to some place with a strange name. But when the time came Mr. Darnell was too deep in old books and tobacco smoke to be stirred from his corner, and Edward and his uncle went alone in the dog-cart. They drove swiftly down the narrow lane, into the road that followed the winding river, and crossed the bridge at Caermaen by the mouldering Roman walls, and then, skirting the deserted, echoing village, they came out on a broad white turnpike road, and the limestone dust followed them like a cloud. Then, suddenly, they turned to the north by such a road as Edward had never seen before. It was so narrow that there was barely room for the cart to pass, and the footway was of rock, and the banks rose high above them as they slowly climbed the long, steep way, and the untrimmed hedges on either side shut out the light. And the ferns grew thick and green upon the banks, and hidden wells dripped down upon them; and the old man told him how the lane in winter was a torrent of swirling water, so that no one could pass by it. On they went, ascending and then again descending, always in that deep hollow under the wild woven boughs, and the boy wondered vainly what the country was like on either side. And now the air grew darker, and the hedge on one bank was but the verge of a dark and rustling wood, and the grey limestone rocks had changed to dark-red earth flecked with green patches and veins of marl, and suddenly in the stillness from the depths of the wood a bird began to sing a melody that charmed the heart into another world, that sang to the child's soul of the blessed faery realm beyond the woods of the earth, where the wounds of man are healed. And so at last, after many turnings and windings, they came to a high bare land where the lane broadened out into a kind of common, and along the edge of this place there were scattered three or four old cottages, and one of them was a little tavern. Here they stopped, and a man came out and tethered the tired horse to a post and gave him water; and old Mr. Darnell took the child's hand and led him by a path across the fields. The boy could see the country now, but it was all a strange, undiscovered land; they were in the heart of a wilderness of hills and valleys that he had never looked upon, and they were going down a wild, steep hillside, where the narrow path wound in and out amidst gorse and towering bracken, and the sun gleaming out for a moment, there was a gleam of white water far below in a narrow valley, where a little brook poured and rippled from stone to stone. They went down the hill, and through a brake, and then, hidden in dark-green orchards, they came upon a long, low whitewashed house, with a stone roof strangely coloured by the growth of moss and lichens. Mr. Darnell knocked at a heavy oaken door, and they came into a dim room where but little light entered through the thick glass in the deep-set window. There were heavy beams in the ceiling, and a great fireplace sent out an odour of burning wood that Darnell never forgot, and the room seemed to him full of women who talked all together in frightened tones. Mr. Darnell beckoned to a tall, grey old man, who wore corduroy knee-breeches, and the boy, sitting on a high straight-backed chair, could see the old man and his uncle passing to and fro across the window-panes, as they walked together on the garden path. The women stopped their talk for a moment, and one of them brought him a glass of milk and an apple from some cold inner chamber; and then, suddenly, from a room above there rang out a shrill and terrible shriek, and then, in a young girl's voice, a more terrible song. It was not like anything the child had ever heard, but as the man recalled it to his memory, he knew to what song it might be compared--to a certain chant indeed that summons the angels and archangels to assist in the great Sacrifice. But as this song chants of the heavenly army, so did that seem to summon all the hierarchy of evil, the hosts of Lilith and Samael; and the words that rang out with such awful modulations--neumata inferorum--were in some unknown tongue that few men have ever heard on earth.

The women glared at one another with horror in their eyes, and he saw one or two of the oldest of them clumsily making an old sign upon their breasts. Then they began to speak again, and he remembered fragments of their talk.

'She has been up there,' said one, pointing vaguely over her shoulder.

'She'd never know the way,' answered another. 'They be all gone that went there.'

'There be nought there in these days.'

'How can you tell that, Gwenllian? 'Tis not for us to say that.'

'My great-grandmother did know some that had been there,' said a very old woman. 'She told me how they was taken afterwards.'

And then his uncle appeared at the door, and they went their way as they had come. Edward Darnell never heard any more of it, nor whether the girl died or recovered from her strange attack; but the scene had haunted his mind in boyhood, and now the recollection of it came to him with a certain note of warning, as a symbol of dangers that might be in the way.

***

It would be impossible to carry on the history of Edward Darnell and of Mary his wife to a greater length, since from this point their legend is full of impossible events, and seems to put on the semblance of the stories of the Graal. It is certain, indeed, that in this world they changed their lives, like King Arthur, but this is a work which no chronicler has cared to describe with any amplitude of detail. Darnell, it is true, made a little book, partly consisting of queer verse which might have been written by an inspired infant, and partly made up of 'notes and exclamations' in an odd dog-Latin which he had picked up from the 'Iolo MSS.', but it is to be feared that this work, even if published in its entirety, would cast but little light on a perplexing story. He called this piece of literature 'In Exitu Israel,' and wrote on the title page the motto, doubtless of his own composition, 'Nunc certe scio quod omnia legenda; omnes historiæ, omnes fabulæ, omnis Scriptura sint de ME narrata.' It is only too evident that his Latin was not learnt at the feet of Cicero; but in this dialect he relates the great history of the 'New Life' as it was manifested to him. The 'poems' are even stranger. One, headed (with an odd reminiscence of old-fashioned books) 'Lines written on looking down from a Height in London on a Board School suddenly lit up by the Sun' begins thus:-

One day when I was all alone
I found a wondrous little stone,
It lay forgotten on the road
Far from the ways of man's abode.
When on this stone mine eyes I cast
I saw my Treasure found at last.
I pressed it hard against my face,
I covered it with my embrace,
I hid it in a secret place.
And every day I went to see
This stone that was my ecstasy;
And worshipped it with flowers rare,
And secret words and sayings fair.
O stone, so rare and red and wise
O fragment of far Paradise,
O Star, whose light is life! O Sea,
Whose ocean is infinity!
Thou art a fire that ever burns,
And all the world to wonder turns;
And all the dust of the dull day
By thee is changed and purged away,
So that, where'er I look, I see
A world of a Great Majesty.
The sullen river rolls all gold,
The desert park's a faery wold,
When on the trees the wind is borne
I hear the sound of Arthur's horn
I see no town of grim grey ways,
But a great city all ablaze
With burning torches, to light up
The pinnacles that shrine the Cup.
Ever the magic wine is poured,
Ever the Feast shines on the board,
Ever the song is borne on high
That chants the holy Magistry--
Etc. etc. etc.

From such documents as these it is clearly impossible to gather any very definite information. But on the last page Darnell has written--

'So I awoke from a dream of a London suburb, of daily labour, of weary, useless little things; and as my eyes were opened I saw that I was in an ancient wood, where a clear well rose into grey film and vapour beneath a misty, glimmering heat. And a form came towards me from the hidden places of the wood, and my love and I were united by the well.'

The White People

PROLOGUE

'Sorcery and sanctity,' said Ambrose, 'these are the only realities. Each is an ecstasy, a withdrawal from the common life.'

Cotgrave listened, interested. He had been brought by a friend to this mouldering house in a northern suburb, through an old garden to the room where Ambrose the recluse dozed and dreamed over his books.

'Yes,' he went on, 'magic is justified of her children. There are many, I think, who eat dry crusts and drink water, with a joy infinitely sharper than anything within the experience of the "practical" epicure.'

'You are speaking of the saints?'

'Yes, and of the sinners, too. I think you are falling into the very general error of confining the spiritual world to the supremely good; but the supremely wicked, necessarily, have their portion in it. The merely carnal, sensual man can no more be a great sinner than he can be a great saint. Most of us are just indifferent, mixed-up creatures; we muddle through the world without realizing the meaning and the inner sense of things, and, consequently, our wickedness and our goodness are alike second-rate, unimportant.'

'And you think the great sinner, then, will be an ascetic, as well as the great saint?'

'Great people of all kinds forsake the imperfect copies and go to the perfect originals. I have no doubt but that many of the very highest among the saints have never done a "good action" (using the words in their ordinary sense). And, on the other hand, there have been those who have sounded the very depths of sin, who all their lives have never done an "ill deed."'

He went out of the room for a moment, and Cotgrave, in high delight, turned to his friend and thanked him for the introduction.

'He's grand,' he said. 'I never saw that kind of lunatic before.'

Ambrose returned with more whisky and helped the two men in a liberal manner. He abused the teetotal sect with ferocity, as he handed the seltzer, and pouring out a glass of water for himself, was about to resume his monologue, when Cotgrave broke in--

'I can't stand it, you know,' he said, 'your paradoxes are too monstrous. A man may be a great sinner and yet never do anything sinful! Come!'

'You're quite wrong,' said Ambrose. 'I never make paradoxes; I wish I could. I merely said that a man may have an exquisite taste in Romanée Conti, and yet never have even smelt four ale. That's all, and it's more like a truism than a paradox, isn't it? Your surprise at my remark is due to the fact that you haven't realized what sin is. Oh, yes, there is a sort of connexion between Sin with the capital letter, and actions which are commonly called sinful: with murder, theft, adultery, and so forth. Much the same connexion that there is between the A, B, C and fine literature. But I believe that the misconception--it is all but universal--arises in great measure from our looking at the matter through social spectacles. We think that a man who does evil to us and to his neighbours must be very evil. So he is, from a social standpoint; but can't you realize that Evil in its essence is a lonely thing, a passion of the solitary, individual soul? Really, the average murderer, quâ murderer, is not by any means a sinner in the true sense of the word. He is simply a wild beast that we have to get rid of to save our own necks from his knife. I should class him rather with tigers than with sinners.'

'It seems a little strange.'

'I think not. The murderer murders not from positive qualities, but from negative ones; he lacks something which non-murderers possess. Evil, of course, is wholly positive--only it is on the wrong side. You may believe me that sin in its proper sense is very rare; it is probable that there have been far fewer sinners than saints. Yes, your standpoint is all very well for practical, social purposes; we are naturally inclined to think that a person who is very disagreeable to us must be a very great sinner! It is very disagreeable to have one's pocket picked, and we pronounce the thief to be a very great sinner. In truth, he is merely an undeveloped man. He cannot be a saint, of course; but he may be, and often is, an infinitely better creature than thousands who have never broken a single commandment. He is a great nuisance to us, I admit, and we very properly lock him up if we catch him; but between his troublesome and unsocial action and evil--Oh, the connexion is of the weakest.'

It was getting very late. The man who had brought Cotgrave had probably heard all this before, since he assisted with a bland and judicious smile, but Cotgrave began to think that his 'lunatic' was turning into a sage.

'Do you know,' he said, 'you interest me immensely? You think, then, that we do not understand the real nature of evil?'

'No, I don't think we do. We over-estimate it and we under-estimate it. We take the very numerous infractions of our social "bye-laws"--the very necessary and very proper regulations which keep the human company together--and we get frightened at the prevalence of "sin" and "evil." But this is really nonsense. Take theft, for example. Have you any horror at the thought of Robin Hood, of the Highland caterans of the seventeenth century, of the moss-troopers, of the company promoters of our day?

'Then, on the other hand, we underrate evil. We attach such an enormous importance to the "sin" of meddling with our pockets (and our wives) that we have quite forgotten the awfulness of real sin.'

'And what is sin?' said Cotgrave.

'I think I must reply to your question by another. What would your feelings be, seriously, if your cat or your dog began to talk to you, and to dispute with you in human accents? You would be overwhelmed with horror. I am sure of it. And if the roses in your garden sang a weird song, you would go mad. And suppose the stones in the road began to swell and grow before your eyes, and if the pebble that you noticed at night had shot out stony blossoms in the morning?

'Well, these examples may give you some notion of what sin really is.'

'Look here,' said the third man, hitherto placid, 'you two seem pretty well wound up. But I'm going home. I've missed my tram, and I shall have to walk.'

Ambrose and Cotgrave seemed to settle down more profoundly when the other had gone out into the early misty morning and the pale light of the lamps.

'You astonish me,' said Cotgrave. 'I had never thought of that. If that is really so, one must turn everything upside down. Then the essence of sin really is----'

'In the taking of heaven by storm, it seems to me,' said Ambrose. 'It appears to me that it is simply an attempt to penetrate into another and higher sphere in a forbidden manner. You can understand why it is so rare. There are few, indeed, who wish to penetrate into other spheres, higher or lower, in ways allowed or forbidden. Men, in the mass, are amply content with life as they find it. Therefore there are few saints, and sinners (in the proper sense) are fewer still, and men of genius, who partake sometimes of each character, are rare also. Yes; on the whole, it is, perhaps, harder to be a great sinner than a great saint.'

'There is something profoundly unnatural about sin? Is that what you mean?'

'Exactly. Holiness requires as great, or almost as great, an effort; but holiness works on lines that were natural once; it is an effort to recover the ecstasy that was before the Fall. But sin is an effort to gain the ecstasy and the knowledge that pertain alone to angels, and in making this effort man becomes a demon. I told you that the mere murderer is not therefore a sinner; that is true, but the sinner is sometimes a murderer. Gilles de Raiz is an instance. So you see that while the good and the evil are unnatural to man as he now is--to man the social, civilized being--evil is unnatural in a much deeper sense than good. The saint endeavours to recover a gift which he has lost; the sinner tries to obtain something which was never his. In brief, he repeats the Fall.'

'But are you a Catholic?' said Cotgrave.

'Yes; I am a member of the persecuted Anglican Church.'

'Then, how about those texts which seem to reckon as sin that which you would set down as a mere trivial dereliction?'

'Yes; but in one place the word "sorcerers" comes in the same sentence, doesn't it? That seems to me to give the key-note. Consider: can you imagine for a moment that a false statement which saves an innocent man's life is a sin? No; very good, then, it is not the mere liar who is excluded by those words; it is, above all, the "sorcerers" who use the material life, who use the failings incidental to material life as instruments to obtain their infinitely wicked ends. And let me tell you this: our higher senses are so blunted, we are so drenched with materialism, that we should probably fail to recognize real wickedness if we encountered it.'

'But shouldn't we experience a certain horror--a terror such as you hinted we would experience if a rose tree sang--in the mere presence of an evil man?'

'We should if we were natural: children and women feel this horror you speak of, even animals experience it. But with most of us convention and civilization and education have blinded and deafened and obscured the natural reason. No, sometimes we may recognize evil by its hatred of the good--one doesn't need much penetration to guess at the influence which dictated, quite unconsciously, the "Blackwood" review of Keats--but this is purely incidental; and, as a rule, I suspect that the Hierarchs of Tophet pass quite unnoticed, or, perhaps, in certain cases, as good but mistaken men.'

'But you used the word "unconscious" just now, of Keats' reviewers. Is wickedness ever unconscious?'

'Always. It must be so. It is like holiness and genius in this as in other points; it is a certain rapture or ecstasy of the soul; a transcendent effort to surpass the ordinary bounds. So, surpassing these, it surpasses also the understanding, the faculty that takes note of that which comes before it. No, a man may be infinitely and horribly wicked and never suspect it. But I tell you, evil in this, its certain and true sense, is rare, and I think it is growing rarer.'

'I am trying to get hold of it all,' said Cotgrave. 'From what you say, I gather that the true evil differs generically from that which we call evil?'

'Quite so. There is, no doubt, an analogy between the two; a resemblance such as enables us to use, quite legitimately, such terms as the "foot of the mountain" and the "leg of the table." And, sometimes, of course, the two speak, as it were, in the same language. The rough miner, or "puddler," the untrained, undeveloped "tiger-man," heated by a quart or two above his usual measure, comes home and kicks his irritating and injudicious wife to death. He is a murderer. And Gilles de Raiz was a murderer. But you see the gulf that separates the two? The "word," if I may so speak, is accidentally the same in each case, but the "meaning" is utterly different. It is flagrant "Hobson Jobson" to confuse the two, or rather, it is as if one supposed that Juggernaut and the Argonauts had something to do etymologically with one another. And no doubt the same weak likeness, or analogy, runs between all the "social" sins and the real spiritual sins, and in some cases, perhaps, the lesser may be "schoolmasters" to lead one on to the greater--from the shadow to the reality. If you are anything of a Theologian, you will see the importance of all this.'

'I am sorry to say,' remarked Cotgrave, 'that I have devoted very little of my time to theology. Indeed, I have often wondered on what grounds theologians have claimed the title of Science of Sciences for their favourite study; since the "theological" books I have looked into have always seemed to me to be concerned with feeble and obvious pieties, or with the kings of Israel and Judah. I do not care to hear about those kings.'

Ambrose grinned.

'We must try to avoid theological discussion,' he said. 'I perceive that you would be a bitter disputant. But perhaps the "dates of the kings" have as much to do with theology as the hobnails of the murderous puddler with evil.'

'Then, to return to our main subject, you think that sin is an esoteric, occult thing?'

'Yes. It is the infernal miracle as holiness is the supernal. Now and then it is raised to such a pitch that we entirely fail to suspect its existence; it is like the note of the great pedal pipes of the organ, which is so deep that we cannot hear it. In other cases it may lead to the lunatic asylum, or to still stranger issues. But you must never confuse it with mere social misdoing. Remember how the Apostle, speaking of the "other side," distinguishes between "charitable" actions and charity. And as one may give all one's goods to the poor, and yet lack charity; so, remember, one may avoid every crime and yet be a sinner.'

'Your psychology is very strange to me,' said Cotgrave, 'but I confess I like it, and I suppose that one might fairly deduce from your premises the conclusion that the real sinner might very possibly strike the observer as a harmless personage enough?'

'Certainly; because the true evil has nothing to do with social life or social laws, or if it has, only incidentally and accidentally. It is a lonely passion of the soul--or a passion of the lonely soul-- whichever you like. If, by chance, we understand it, and grasp its full significance, then, indeed, it will fill us with horror and with awe. But this emotion is widely distinguished from the fear and the disgust with which we regard the ordinary criminal, since this latter is largely or entirely founded on the regard which we have for our own skins or purses. We hate a murderer, because we know that we should hate to be murdered, or to have any one that we like murdered. So, on the "other side," we venerate the saints, but we don't "like" them as we like our friends. Can you persuade yourself that you would have "enjoyed" St. Paul's company? Do you think that you and I would have "got on" with Sir Galahad?

'So with the sinners, as with the saints. If you met a very evil man, and recognized his evil; he would, no doubt, fill you with horror and awe; but there is no reason why you should "dislike" him. On the contrary, it is quite possible that if you could succeed in putting the sin out of your mind you might find the sinner capital company, and in a little while you might have to reason yourself back into horror. Still, how awful it is. If the roses and the lilies suddenly sang on this coming morning; if the furniture began to move in procession, as in De Maupassant's tale!'

'I am glad you have come back to that comparison,' said Cotgrave, 'because I wanted to ask you what it is that corresponds in humanity to these imaginary feats of inanimate things. In a word--what is sin? You have given me, I know, an abstract definition, but I should like a concrete example.'

'I told you it was very rare,' said Ambrose, who appeared willing to avoid the giving of a direct answer. 'The materialism of the age, which has done a good deal to suppress sanctity, has done perhaps more to suppress evil. We find the earth so very comfortable that we have no inclination either for ascents or descents. It would seem as if the scholar who decided to "specialize" in Tophet, would be reduced to purely antiquarian researches. No palæontologist could show you a live pterodactyl.'

'And yet you, I think, have "specialized," and I believe that your researches have descended to our modern times.'

'You are really interested, I see. Well, I confess, that I have dabbled a little, and if you like I can show you something that bears on the very curious subject we have been discussing.'

Ambrose took a candle and went away to a far, dim corner of the room. Cotgrave saw him open a venerable bureau that stood there, and from some secret recess he drew out a parcel, and came back to the window where they had been sitting.

Ambrose undid a wrapping of paper, and produced a green pocket-book.

'You will take care of it?' he said. 'Don't leave it lying about. It is one of the choicer pieces in my collection, and I should be very sorry if it were lost.'

He fondled the faded binding.

'I knew the girl who wrote this,' he said. 'When you read it, you will see how it illustrates the talk we have had to-night. There is a sequel, too, but I won't talk of that.'

'There was an odd article in one of the reviews some months ago,' he began again, with the air of a man who changes the subject. 'It was written by a doctor--Dr. Coryn, I think, was the name. He says that a lady, watching her little girl playing at the drawing-room window, suddenly saw the heavy sash give way and fall on the child's fingers. The lady fainted, I think, but at any rate the doctor was summoned, and when he had dressed the child's wounded and maimed fingers he was summoned to the mother. She was groaning with pain, and it was found that three fingers of her hand, corresponding with those that had been injured on the child's hand, were swollen and inflamed, and later, in the doctor's language, purulent sloughing set in.'

Ambrose still handled delicately the green volume.

'Well, here it is,' he said at last, parting with difficulty, it seemed, from his treasure.

'You will bring it back as soon as you have read it,' he said, as they went out into the hall, into the old garden, faint with the odour of white lilies.

There was a broad red band in the east as Cotgrave turned to go, and from the high ground where he stood he saw that awful spectacle of London in a dream.

THE GREEN BOOK

The morocco binding of the book was faded, and the colour had grown faint, but there were no stains nor bruises nor marks of usage. The book looked as if it had been bought 'on a visit to London' some seventy or eighty years ago, and had somehow been forgotten and suffered to lie away out of sight. There was an old, delicate, lingering odour about it, such an odour as sometimes haunts an ancient piece of furniture for a century or more. The end-papers, inside the binding, were oddly decorated with coloured patterns and faded gold. It looked small, but the paper was fine, and there were many leaves, closely covered with minute, painfully formed characters.

I found this book (the manuscript began) in a drawer in the old bureau that stands on the landing. It was a very rainy day and I could not go out, so in the afternoon I got a candle and rummaged in the bureau. Nearly all the drawers were full of old dresses, but one of the small ones looked empty, and I found this book hidden right at the back. I wanted a book like this, so I took it to write in. It is full of secrets. I have a great many other books of secrets I have written, hidden in a safe place, and I am going to write here many of the old secrets and some new ones; but there are some I shall not put down at all. I must not write down the real names of the days and months which I found out a year ago, nor the way to make the Aklo letters, or the Chian language, or the great beautiful Circles, nor the Mao Games, nor the chief songs. I may write something about all these things but not the way to do them, for peculiar reasons. And I must not say who the Nymphs are, or the Dôls, or Jeelo, or what voolas mean. All these are most secret secrets, and I am glad when I remember what they are, and how many wonderful languages I know, but there are some things that I call the secrets of the secrets of the secrets that I dare not think of unless I am quite alone, and then I shut my eyes, and put my hands over them and whisper the word, and the Alala comes. I only do this at night in my room or in certain woods that I know, but I must not describe them, as they are secret woods. Then there are the Ceremonies, which are all of them important, but some are more delightful than others--there are the White Ceremonies, and the Green Ceremonies, and the Scarlet Ceremonies. The Scarlet Ceremonies are the best, but there is only one place where they can be performed properly, though there is a very nice imitation which I have done in other places. Besides these, I have the dances, and the Comedy, and I have done the Comedy sometimes when the others were looking, and they didn't understand anything about it. I was very little when I first knew about these things.

When I was very small, and mother was alive, I can remember remembering things before that, only it has all got confused. But I remember when I was five or six I heard them talking about me when they thought I was not noticing. They were saying how queer I was a year or two before, and how nurse had called my mother to come and listen to me talking all to myself, and I was saying words that nobody could understand. I was speaking the Xu language, but I only remember a very few of the words, as it was about the little white faces that used to look at me when I was lying in my cradle. They used to talk to me, and I learnt their language and talked to them in it about some great white place where they lived, where the trees and the grass were all white, and there were white hills as high up as the moon, and a cold wind. I have often dreamed of it afterwards, but the faces went away when I was very little. But a wonderful thing happened when I was about five. My nurse was carrying me on her shoulder; there was a field of yellow corn, and we went through it, it was very hot. Then we came to a path through a wood, and a tall man came after us, and went with us till we came to a place where there was a deep pool, and it was very dark and shady. Nurse put me down on the soft moss under a tree, and she said: 'She can't get to the pond now.' So they left me there, and I sat quite still and watched, and out of the water and out of the wood came two wonderful white people, and they began to play and dance and sing. They were a kind of creamy white like the old ivory figure in the drawing-room; one was a beautiful lady with kind dark eyes, and a grave face, and long black hair, and she smiled such a strange sad smile at the other, who laughed and came to her. They played together, and danced round and round the pool, and they sang a song till I fell asleep. Nurse woke me up when she came back, and she was looking something like the lady had looked, so I told her all about it, and asked her why she looked like that. At first she cried, and then she looked very frightened, and turned quite pale. She put me down on the grass and stared at me, and I could see she was shaking all over. Then she said I had been dreaming, but I knew I hadn't. Then she made me promise not to say a word about it to anybody, and if I did I should be thrown into the black pit. I was not frightened at all, though nurse was, and I never forgot about it, because when I shut my eyes and it was quite quiet, and I was all alone, I could see them again, very faint and far away, but very splendid; and little bits of the song they sang came into my head, but I couldn't sing it.

I was thirteen, nearly fourteen, when I had a very singular adventure, so strange that the day on which it happened is always called the White Day. My mother had been dead for more than a year, and in the morning I had lessons, but they let me go out for walks in the afternoon. And this afternoon I walked a new way, and a little brook led me into a new country, but I tore my frock getting through some of the difficult places, as the way was through many bushes, and beneath the low branches of trees, and up thorny thickets on the hills, and by dark woods full of creeping thorns. And it was a long, long way. It seemed as if I was going on for ever and ever, and I had to creep by a place like a tunnel where a brook must have been, but all the water had dried up, and the floor was rocky, and the bushes had grown overhead till they met, so that it was quite dark. And I went on and on through that dark place; it was a long, long way. And I came to a hill that I never saw before. I was in a dismal thicket full of black twisted boughs that tore me as I went through them, and I cried out because I was smarting all over, and then I found that I was climbing, and I went up and up a long way, till at last the thicket stopped and I came out crying just under the top of a big bare place, where there were ugly grey stones lying all about on the grass, and here and there a little twisted, stunted tree came out from under a stone, like a snake. And I went up, right to the top, a long way. I never saw such big ugly stones before; they came out of the earth some of them, and some looked as if they had been rolled to where they were, and they went on and on as far as I could see, a long, long way. I looked out from them and saw the country, but it was strange. It was winter time, and there were black terrible woods hanging from the hills all round; it was like seeing a large room hung with black curtains, and the shape of the trees seemed quite different from any I had ever seen before. I was afraid. Then beyond the woods there were other hills round in a great ring, but I had never seen any of them; it all looked black, and everything had a voor over it. It was all so still and silent, and the sky was heavy and grey and sad, like a wicked voorish dome in Deep Dendo. I went on into the dreadful rocks. There were hundreds and hundreds of them. Some were like horrid-grinning men; I could see their faces as if they would jump at me out of the stone, and catch hold of me, and drag me with them back into the rock, so that I should always be there. And there were other rocks that were like animals, creeping, horrible animals, putting out their tongues, and others were like words that I could not say, and others like dead people lying on the grass. I went on among them, though they frightened me, and my heart was full of wicked songs that they put into it; and I wanted to make faces and twist myself about in the way they did, and I went on and on a long way till at last I liked the rocks, and they didn't frighten me any more. I sang the songs I thought of; songs full of words that must not be spoken or written down. Then I made faces like the faces on the rocks, and I twisted myself about like the twisted ones, and I lay down flat on the ground like the dead ones, and I went up to one that was grinning, and put my arms round him and hugged him. And so I went on and on through the rocks till I came to a round mound in the middle of them. It was higher than a mound, it was nearly as high as our house, and it was like a great basin turned upside down, all smooth and round and green, with one stone, like a post, sticking up at the top. I climbed up the sides, but they were so steep I had to stop or I should have rolled all the way down again, and I should have knocked against the stones at the bottom, and perhaps been killed. But I wanted to get up to the very top of the big round mound, so I lay down flat on my face, and took hold of the grass with my hands and drew myself up, bit by bit, till I was at the top. Then I sat down on the stone in the middle, and looked all round about. I felt I had come such a long, long way, just as if I were a hundred miles from home, or in some other country, or in one of the strange places I had read about in the 'Tales of the Genie' and the 'Arabian Nights,' or as if I had gone across the sea, far away, for years and I had found another world that nobody had ever seen or heard of before, or as if I had somehow flown through the sky and fallen on one of the stars I had read about where everything is dead and cold and grey, and there is no air, and the wind doesn't blow. I sat on the stone and looked all round and down and round about me. It was just as if I was sitting on a tower in the middle of a great empty town, because I could see nothing all around but the grey rocks on the ground. I couldn't make out their shapes any more, but I could see them on and on for a long way, and I looked at them, and they seemed as if they had been arranged into patterns, and shapes, and figures. I knew they couldn't be, because I had seen a lot of them coming right out of the earth, joined to the deep rocks below, so I looked again, but still I saw nothing but circles, and small circles inside big ones, and pyramids, and domes, and spires, and they seemed all to go round and round the place where I was sitting, and the more I looked, the more I saw great big rings of rocks, getting bigger and bigger, and I stared so long that it felt as if they were all moving and turning, like a great wheel, and I was turning, too, in the middle. I got quite dizzy and queer in the head, and everything began to be hazy and not clear, and I saw little sparks of blue light, and the stones looked as if they were springing and dancing and twisting as they went round and round and round. I was frightened again, and I cried out loud, and jumped up from the stone I was sitting on, and fell down. When I got up I was so glad they all looked still, and I sat down on the top and slid down the mound, and went on again. I danced as I went in the peculiar way the rocks had danced when I got giddy, and I was so glad I could do it quite well, and I danced and danced along, and sang extraordinary songs that came into my head. At last I came to the edge of that great flat hill, and there were no more rocks, and the way went again through a dark thicket in a hollow. It was just as bad as the other one I went through climbing up, but I didn't mind this one, because I was so glad I had seen those singular dances and could imitate them. I went down, creeping through the bushes, and a tall nettle stung me on my leg, and made me burn, but I didn't mind it, and I tingled with the boughs and the thorns, but I only laughed and sang. Then I got out of the thicket into a close valley, a little secret place like a dark passage that nobody ever knows of, because it was so narrow and deep and the woods were so thick round it. There is a steep bank with trees hanging over it, and there the ferns keep green all through the winter, when they are dead and brown upon the hill, and the ferns there have a sweet, rich smell like what oozes out of fir trees. There was a little stream of water running down this valley, so small that I could easily step across it. I drank the water with my hand, and it tasted like bright, yellow wine, and it sparkled and bubbled as it ran down over beautiful red and yellow and green stones, so that it seemed alive and all colours at once. I drank it, and I drank more with my hand, but I couldn't drink enough, so I lay down and bent my head and sucked the water up with my lips. It tasted much better, drinking it that way, and a ripple would come up to my mouth and give me a kiss, and I laughed, and drank again, and pretended there was a nymph, like the one in the old picture at home, who lived in the water and was kissing me. So I bent low down to the water, and put my lips softly to it, and whispered to the nymph that I would come again. I felt sure it could not be common water, I was so glad when I got up and went on; and I danced again and went up and up the valley, under hanging hills. And when I came to the top, the ground rose up in front of me, tall and steep as a wall, and there was nothing but the green wall and the sky. I thought of 'for ever and for ever, world without end, Amen'; and I thought I must have really found the end of the world, because it was like the end of everything, as if there could be nothing at all beyond, except the kingdom of Voor, where the light goes when it is put out, and the water goes when the sun takes it away. I began to think of all the long, long way I had journeyed, how I had found a brook and followed it, and followed it on, and gone through bushes and thorny thickets, and dark woods full of creeping thorns. Then I had crept up a tunnel under trees, and climbed a thicket, and seen all the grey rocks, and sat in the middle of them when they turned round, and then I had gone on through the grey rocks and come down the hill through the stinging thicket and up the dark valley, all a long, long way. I wondered how I should get home again, if I could ever find the way, and if my home was there any more, or if it were turned and everybody in it into grey rocks, as in the 'Arabian Nights.' So I sat down on the grass and thought what I should do next. I was tired, and my feet were hot with walking, and as I looked about I saw there was a wonderful well just under the high, steep wall of grass. All the ground round it was covered with bright, green, dripping moss; there was every kind of moss there, moss like beautiful little ferns, and like palms and fir trees, and it was all green as jewellery, and drops of water hung on it like diamonds. And in the middle was the great well, deep and shining and beautiful, so clear that it looked as if I could touch the red sand at the bottom, but it was far below. I stood by it and looked in, as if I were looking in a glass. At the bottom of the well, in the middle of it, the red grains of sand were moving and stirring all the time, and I saw how the water bubbled up, but at the top it was quite smooth, and full and brimming. It was a great well, large like a bath, and with the shining, glittering green moss about it, it looked like a great white jewel, with green jewels all round. My feet were so hot and tired that I took off my boots and stockings, and let my feet down into the water, and the water was soft and cold, and when I got up I wasn't tired any more, and I felt I must go on, farther and farther, and see what was on the other side of the wall. I climbed up it very slowly, going sideways all the time, and when I got to the top and looked over, I was in the queerest country I had seen, stranger even than the hill of the grey rocks. It looked as if earth-children had been playing there with their spades, as it was all hills and hollows, and castles and walls made of earth and covered with grass. There were two mounds like big beehives, round and great and solemn, and then hollow basins, and then a steep mounting wall like the ones I saw once by the seaside where the big guns and the soldiers were. I nearly fell into one of the round hollows, it went away from under my feet so suddenly, and I ran fast down the side and stood at the bottom and looked up. It was strange and solemn to look up. There was nothing but the grey, heavy sky and the sides of the hollow; everything else had gone away, and the hollow was the whole world, and I thought that at night it must be full of ghosts and moving shadows and pale things when the moon shone down to the bottom at the dead of the night, and the wind wailed up above. It was so strange and solemn and lonely, like a hollow temple of dead heathen gods. It reminded me of a tale my nurse had told me when I was quite little; it was the same nurse that took me into the wood where I saw the beautiful white people. And I remembered how nurse had told me the story one winter night, when the wind was beating the trees against the wall, and crying and moaning in the nursery chimney. She said there was, somewhere or other, a hollow pit, just like the one I was standing in, everybody was afraid to go into it or near it, it was such a bad place. But once upon a time there was a poor girl who said she would go into the hollow pit, and everybody tried to stop her, but she would go. And she went down into the pit and came back laughing, and said there was nothing there at all, except green grass and red stones, and white stones and yellow flowers. And soon after people saw she had most beautiful emerald earrings, and they asked how she got them, as she and her mother were quite poor. But she laughed, and said her earrings were not made of emeralds at all, but only of green grass. Then, one day, she wore on her breast the reddest ruby that any one had ever seen, and it was as big as a hen's egg, and glowed and sparkled like a hot burning coal of fire. And they asked how she got it, as she and her mother were quite poor. But she laughed, and said it was not a ruby at all, but only a red stone. Then one day she wore round her neck the loveliest necklace that any one had ever seen, much finer than the queen's finest, and it was made of great bright diamonds, hundreds of them, and they shone like all the stars on a night in June. So they asked her how she got it, as she and her mother were quite poor. But she laughed, and said they were not diamonds at all, but only white stones. And one day she went to the Court, and she wore on her head a crown of pure angel-gold, so nurse said, and it shone like the sun, and it was much more splendid than the crown the king was wearing himself, and in her ears she wore the emeralds, and the big ruby was the brooch on her breast, and the great diamond necklace was sparkling on her neck. And the king and queen thought she was some great princess from a long way off, and got down from their thrones and went to meet her, but somebody told the king and queen who she was, and that she was quite poor. So the king asked why she wore a gold crown, and how she got it, as she and her mother were so poor. And she laughed, and said it wasn't a gold crown at all, but only some yellow flowers she had put in her hair. And the king thought it was very strange, and said she should stay at the Court, and they would see what would happen next. And she was so lovely that everybody said that her eyes were greener than the emeralds, that her lips were redder than the ruby, that her skin was whiter than the diamonds, and that her hair was brighter than the golden crown. So the king's son said he would marry her, and the king said he might. And the bishop married them, and there was a great supper, and afterwards the king's son went to his wife's room.

But just when he had his hand on the door, he saw a tall, black man, with a dreadful face, standing in front of the door, and a voice said--

Venture not upon your life,
This is mine own wedded wife.

Then the king's son fell down on the ground in a fit. And they came and tried to get into the room, but they couldn't, and they hacked at the door with hatchets, but the wood had turned hard as iron, and at last everybody ran away, they were so frightened at the screaming and laughing and shrieking and crying that came out of the room. But next day they went in, and found there was nothing in the room but thick black smoke, because the black man had come and taken her away. And on the bed there were two knots of faded grass and a red stone, and some white stones, and some faded yellow flowers. I remembered this tale of nurse's while I was standing at the bottom of the deep hollow; it was so strange and solitary there, and I felt afraid. I could not see any stones or flowers, but I was afraid of bringing them away without knowing, and I thought I would do a charm that came into my head to keep the black man away. So I stood right in the very middle of the hollow, and I made sure that I had none of those things on me, and then I walked round the place, and touched my eyes, and my lips, and my hair in a peculiar manner, and whispered some queer words that nurse taught me to keep bad things away. Then I felt safe and climbed up out of the hollow, and went on through all those mounds and hollows and walls, till I came to the end, which was high above all the rest, and I could see that all the different shapes of the earth were arranged in patterns, something like the grey rocks, only the pattern was different. It was getting late, and the air was indistinct, but it looked from where I was standing something like two great figures of people lying on the grass. And I went on, and at last I found a certain wood, which is too secret to be described, and nobody knows of the passage into it, which I found out in a very curious manner, by seeing some little animal run into the wood through it. So I went after the animal by a very narrow dark way, under thorns and bushes, and it was almost dark when I came to a kind of open place in the middle. And there I saw the most wonderful sight I have ever seen, but it was only for a minute, as I ran away directly, and crept out of the wood by the passage I had come by, and ran and ran as fast as ever I could, because I was afraid, what I had seen was so wonderful and so strange and beautiful. But I wanted to get home and think of it, and I did not know what might not happen if I stayed by the wood. I was hot all over and trembling, and my heart was beating, and strange cries that I could not help came from me as I ran from the wood. I was glad that a great white moon came up from over a round hill and showed me the way, so I went back through the mounds and hollows and down the close valley, and up through the thicket over the place of the grey rocks, and so at last I got home again. My father was busy in his study, and the servants had not told about my not coming home, though they were frightened, and wondered what they ought to do, so I told them I had lost my way, but I did not let them find out the real way I had been. I went to bed and lay awake all through the night, thinking of what I had seen. When I came out of the narrow way, and it looked all shining, though the air was dark, it seemed so certain, and all the way home I was quite sure that I had seen it, and I wanted to be alone in my room, and be glad over it all to myself, and shut my eyes and pretend it was there, and do all the things I would have done if I had not been so afraid. But when I shut my eyes the sight would not come, and I began to think about my adventures all over again, and I remembered how dusky and queer it was at the end, and I was afraid it must be all a mistake, because it seemed impossible it could happen. It seemed like one of nurse's tales, which I didn't really believe in, though I was frightened at the bottom of the hollow; and the stories she told me when I was little came back into my head, and I wondered whether it was really there what I thought I had seen, or whether any of her tales could have happened a long time ago. It was so queer; I lay awake there in my room at the back of the house, and the moon was shining on the other side towards the river, so the bright light did not fall upon the wall. And the house was quite still. I had heard my father come upstairs, and just after the clock struck twelve, and after the house was still and empty, as if there was nobody alive in it. And though it was all dark and indistinct in my room, a pale glimmering kind of light shone in through the white blind, and once I got up and looked out, and there was a great black shadow of the house covering the garden, looking like a prison where men are hanged; and then beyond it was all white; and the wood shone white with black gulfs between the trees. It was still and clear, and there were no clouds on the sky. I wanted to think of what I had seen but I couldn't, and I began to think of all the tales that nurse had told me so long ago that I thought I had forgotten, but they all came back, and mixed up with the thickets and the grey rocks and the hollows in the earth and the secret wood, till I hardly knew what was new and what was old, or whether it was not all dreaming. And then I remembered that hot summer afternoon, so long ago, when nurse left me by myself in the shade, and the white people came out of the water and out of the wood, and played, and danced, and sang, and I began to fancy that nurse told me about something like it before I saw them, only I couldn't recollect exactly what she told me. Then I wondered whether she had been the white lady, as I remembered she was just as white and beautiful, and had the same dark eyes and black hair; and sometimes she smiled and looked like the lady had looked, when she was telling me some of her stories, beginning with 'Once on a time,' or 'In the time of the fairies.' But I thought she couldn't be the lady, as she seemed to have gone a different way into the wood, and I didn't think the man who came after us could be the other, or I couldn't have seen that wonderful secret in the secret wood. I thought of the moon: but it was afterwards when I was in the middle of the wild land, where the earth was made into the shape of great figures, and it was all walls, and mysterious hollows, and smooth round mounds, that I saw the great white moon come up over a round hill. I was wondering about all these things, till at last I got quite frightened, because I was afraid something had happened to me, and I remembered nurse's tale of the poor girl who went into the hollow pit, and was carried away at last by the black man. I knew I had gone into a hollow pit too, and perhaps it was the same, and I had done something dreadful. So I did the charm over again, and touched my eyes and my lips and my hair in a peculiar manner, and said the old words from the fairy language, so that I might be sure I had not been carried away. I tried again to see the secret wood, and to creep up the passage and see what I had seen there, but somehow I couldn't, and I kept on thinking of nurse's stories. There was one I remembered about a young man who once upon a time went hunting, and all the day he and his hounds hunted everywhere, and they crossed the rivers and went into all the woods, and went round the marshes, but they couldn't find anything at all, and they hunted all day till the sun sank down and began to set behind the mountain. And the young man was angry because he couldn't find anything, and he was going to turn back, when just as the sun touched the mountain, he saw come out of a brake in front of him a beautiful white stag. And he cheered to his hounds, but they whined and would not follow, and he cheered to his horse, but it shivered and stood stock still, and the young man jumped off the horse and left the hounds and began to follow the white stag all alone. And soon it was quite dark, and the sky was black, without a single star shining in it, and the stag went away into the darkness. And though the man had brought his gun with him he never shot at the stag, because he wanted to catch it, and he was afraid he would lose it in the night. But he never lost it once, though the sky was so black and the air was so dark, and the stag went on and on till the young man didn't know a bit where he was. And they went through enormous woods where the air was full of whispers and a pale, dead light came out from the rotten trunks that were lying on the ground, and just as the man thought he had lost the stag, he would see it all white and shining in front of him, and he would run fast to catch it, but the stag always ran faster, so he did not catch it. And they went through the enormous woods, and they swam across rivers, and they waded through black marshes where the ground bubbled, and the air was full of will-o'-the-wisps, and the stag fled away down into rocky narrow valleys, where the air was like the smell of a vault, and the man went after it. And they went over the great mountains and the man heard the wind come down from the sky, and the stag went on and the man went after. At last the sun rose and the young man found he was in a country that he had never seen before; it was a beautiful valley with a bright stream running through it, and a great, big round hill in the middle. And the stag went down the valley, towards the hill, and it seemed to be getting tired and went slower and slower, and though the man was tired, too, he began to run faster, and he was sure he would catch the stag at last. But just as they got to the bottom of the hill, and the man stretched out his hand to catch the stag, it vanished into the earth, and the man began to cry; he was so sorry that he had lost it after all his long hunting. But as he was crying he saw there was a door in the hill, just in front of him, and he went in, and it was quite dark, but he went on, as he thought he would find the white stag. And all of a sudden it got light, and there was the sky, and the sun shining, and birds singing in the trees, and there was a beautiful fountain. And by the fountain a lovely lady was sitting, who was the queen of the fairies, and she told the man that she had changed herself into a stag to bring him there because she loved him so much. Then she brought out a great gold cup, covered with jewels, from her fairy palace, and she offered him wine in the cup to drink. And he drank, and the more he drank the more he longed to drink, because the wine was enchanted. So he kissed the lovely lady, and she became his wife, and she stayed all that day and all that night in the hill where she lived, and when he woke he found he was lying on the ground, close to where he had seen the stag first, and his horse was there and his hounds were there waiting, and he looked up, and the sun sank behind the mountain. And he went home and lived a long time, but he would never kiss any other lady because he had kissed the queen of the fairies, and he would never drink common wine any more, because he had drunk enchanted wine. And sometimes nurse told me tales that she had heard from her great-grandmother, who was very old, and lived in a cottage on the mountain all alone, and most of these tales were about a hill where people used to meet at night long ago, and they used to play all sorts of strange games and do queer things that nurse told me of, but I couldn't understand, and now, she said, everybody but her great-grandmother had forgotten all about it, and nobody knew where the hill was, not even her great-grandmother. But she told me one very strange story about the hill, and I trembled when I remembered it. She said that people always went there in summer, when it was very hot, and they had to dance a good deal. It would be all dark at first, and there were trees there, which made it much darker, and people would come, one by one, from all directions, by a secret path which nobody else knew, and two persons would keep the gate, and every one as they came up had to give a very curious sign, which nurse showed me as well as she could, but she said she couldn't show me properly. And all kinds of people would come; there would be gentle folks and village folks, and some old people and boys and girls, and quite small children, who sat and watched. And it would all be dark as they came in, except in one corner where some one was burning something that smelt strong and sweet, and made them laugh, and there one would see a glaring of coals, and the smoke mounting up red. So they would all come in, and when the last had come there was no door any more, so that no one else could get in, even if they knew there was anything beyond. And once a gentleman who was a stranger and had ridden a long way, lost his path at night, and his horse took him into the very middle of the wild country, where everything was upside down, and there were dreadful marshes and great stones everywhere, and holes underfoot, and the trees looked like gibbet-posts, because they had great black arms that stretched out across the way. And this strange gentleman was very frightened, and his horse began to shiver all over, and at last it stopped and wouldn't go any farther, and the gentleman got down and tried to lead the horse, but it wouldn't move, and it was all covered with a sweat, like death. So the gentleman went on all alone, going farther and farther into the wild country, till at last he came to a dark place, where he heard shouting and singing and crying, like nothing he had ever heard before. It all sounded quite close to him, but he couldn't get in, and so he began to call, and while he was calling, something came behind him, and in a minute his mouth and arms and legs were all bound up, and he fell into a swoon. And when he came to himself, he was lying by the roadside, just where he had first lost his way, under a blasted oak with a black trunk, and his horse was tied beside him. So he rode on to the town and told the people there what had happened, and some of them were amazed; but others knew. So when once everybody had come, there was no door at all for anybody else to pass in by. And when they were all inside, round in a ring, touching each other, some one began to sing in the darkness, and some one else would make a noise like thunder with a thing they had on purpose, and on still nights people would hear the thundering noise far, far away beyond the wild land, and some of them, who thought they knew what it was, used to make a sign on their breasts when they woke up in their beds at dead of night and heard that terrible deep noise, like thunder on the mountains. And the noise and the singing would go on and on for a long time, and the people who were in a ring swayed a little to and fro; and the song was in an old, old language that nobody knows now, and the tune was queer. Nurse said her great-grandmother had known some one who remembered a little of it, when she was quite a little girl, and nurse tried to sing some of it to me, and it was so strange a tune that I turned all cold and my flesh crept as if I had put my hand on something dead. Sometimes it was a man that sang and sometimes it was a woman, and sometimes the one who sang it did it so well that two or three of the people who were there fell to the ground shrieking and tearing with their hands. The singing went on, and the people in the ring kept swaying to and fro for a long time, and at last the moon would rise over a place they called the Tole Deol, and came up and showed them swinging and swaying from side to side, with the sweet thick smoke curling up from the burning coals, and floating in circles all around them. Then they had their supper. A boy and a girl brought it to them; the boy carried a great cup of wine, and the girl carried a cake of bread, and they passed the bread and the wine round and round, but they tasted quite different from common bread and common wine, and changed everybody that tasted them. Then they all rose up and danced, and secret things were brought out of some hiding place, and they played extraordinary games, and danced round and round and round in the moonlight, and sometimes people would suddenly disappear and never be heard of afterwards, and nobody knew what had happened to them. And they drank more of that curious wine, and they made images and worshipped them, and nurse showed me how the images were made one day when we were out for a walk, and we passed by a place where there was a lot of wet clay. So nurse asked me if I would like to know what those things were like that they made on the hill, and I said yes. Then she asked me if I would promise never to tell a living soul a word about it, and if I did I was to be thrown into the black pit with the dead people, and I said I wouldn't tell anybody, and she said the same thing again and again, and I promised. So she took my wooden spade and dug a big lump of clay and put it in my tin bucket, and told me to say if any one met us that I was going to make pies when I went home. Then we went on a little way till we came to a little brake growing right down into the road, and nurse stopped, and looked up the road and down it, and then peeped through the hedge into the field on the other side, and then she said, 'Quick!' and we ran into the brake, and crept in and out among the bushes till we had gone a good way from the road. Then we sat down under a bush, and I wanted so much to know what nurse was going to make with the clay, but before she would begin she made me promise again not to say a word about it, and she went again and peeped through the bushes on every side, though the lane was so small and deep that hardly anybody ever went there. So we sat down, and nurse took the clay out of the bucket, and began to knead it with her hands, and do queer things with it, and turn it about. And she hid it under a big dock-leaf for a minute or two and then she brought it out again, and then she stood up and sat down, and walked round the clay in a peculiar manner, and all the time she was softly singing a sort of rhyme, and her face got very red. Then she sat down again, and took the clay in her hands and began to shape it into a doll, but not like the dolls I have at home, and she made the queerest doll I had ever seen, all out of the wet clay, and hid it under a bush to get dry and hard, and all the time she was making it she was singing these rhymes to herself, and her face got redder and redder. So we left the doll there, hidden away in the bushes where nobody would ever find it. And a few days later we went the same walk, and when we came to that narrow, dark part of the lane where the brake runs down to the bank, nurse made me promise all over again, just as she had done before, and we crept into the bushes till we got to the green place where the little clay man was hidden. I remember it all so well, though I was only eight, and it is eight years ago now as I am writing it down, but the sky was a deep violet blue, and in the middle of the brake where we were sitting there was a great elder tree covered with blossoms, and on the other side there was a clump of meadowsweet, and when I think of that day the smell of the meadowsweet and elder blossom seems to fill the room, and if I shut my eyes I can see the glaring blue sky, with little clouds very white floating across it, and nurse who went away long ago sitting opposite me and looking like the beautiful white lady in the wood. So we sat down and nurse took out the clay doll from the secret place where she had hidden it, and she said we must 'pay our respects,' and she would show me what to do, and I must watch her all the time. So she did all sorts of queer things with the little clay man, and I noticed she was all streaming with perspiration, though we had walked so slowly, and then she told me to 'pay my respects,' and I did everything she did because I liked her, and it was such an odd game. And she said that if one loved very much, the clay man was very good, if one did certain things with it, and if one hated very much, it was just as good, only one had to do different things with it, and we played with it a long time, and pretended all sorts of things. Nurse said her great-grandmother had told her all about these images, but what we did was no harm at all, only a game. But she told me a story about these images that frightened me very much, and that was what I remembered that night when I was lying awake in my room in the pale, empty darkness, thinking of what I had seen and the secret wood. Nurse said there was once a young lady of the high gentry, who lived in a great castle. And she was so beautiful that all the gentlemen wanted to marry her, because she was the loveliest lady that anybody had ever seen, and she was kind to everybody, and everybody thought she was very good. But though she was polite to all the gentlemen who wished to marry her, she put them off, and said she couldn't make up her mind, and she wasn't sure she wanted to marry anybody at all. And her father, who was a very great lord, was angry, though he was so fond of her, and he asked her why she wouldn't choose a bachelor out of all the handsome young men who came to the castle. But she only said she didn't love any of them very much, and she must wait, and if they pestered her, she said she would go and be a nun in a nunnery. So all the gentlemen said they would go away and wait for a year and a day, and when a year and a day were gone, they would come back again and ask her to say which one she would marry. So the day was appointed and they all went away; and the lady had promised that in a year and a day it would be her wedding day with one of them. But the truth was, that she was the queen of the people who danced on the hill on summer nights, and on the proper nights she would lock the door of her room, and she and her maid would steal out of the castle by a secret passage that only they knew of, and go away up to the hill in the wild land. And she knew more of the secret things than any one else, and more than any one knew before or after, because she would not tell anybody the most secret secrets. She knew how to do all the awful things, how to destroy young men, and how to put a curse on people, and other things that I could not understand. And her real name was the Lady Avelin, but the dancing people called her Cassap, which meant somebody very wise, in the old language. And she was whiter than any of them and taller, and her eyes shone in the dark like burning rubies; and she could sing songs that none of the others could sing, and when she sang they all fell down on their faces and worshipped her. And she could do what they called shib-show, which was a very wonderful enchantment. She would tell the great lord, her father, that she wanted to go into the woods to gather flowers, so he let her go, and she and her maid went into the woods where nobody came, and the maid would keep watch. Then the lady would lie down under the trees and begin to sing a particular song, and she stretched out her arms, and from every part of the wood great serpents would come, hissing and gliding in and out among the trees, and shooting out their forked tongues as they crawled up to the lady. And they all came to her, and twisted round her, round her body, and her arms, and her neck, till she was covered with writhing serpents, and there was only her head to be seen. And she whispered to them, and she sang to them, and they writhed round and round, faster and faster, till she told them to go. And they all went away directly, back to their holes, and on the lady's breast there would be a most curious, beautiful stone, shaped something like an egg, and coloured dark blue and yellow, and red, and green, marked like a serpent's scales. It was called a glame stone, and with it one could do all sorts of wonderful things, and nurse said her great-grandmother had seen a glame stone with her own eyes, and it was for all the world shiny and scaly like a snake. And the lady could do a lot of other things as well, but she was quite fixed that she would not be married. And there were a great many gentlemen who wanted to marry her, but there were five of them who were chief, and their names were Sir Simon, Sir John, Sir Oliver, Sir Richard, and Sir Rowland. All the others believed she spoke the truth, and that she would choose one of them to be her man when a year and a day was done; it was only Sir Simon, who was very crafty, who thought she was deceiving them all, and he vowed he would watch and try if he could find out anything. And though he was very wise he was very young, and he had a smooth, soft face like a girl's, and he pretended, as the rest did, that he would not come to the castle for a year and a day, and he said he was going away beyond the sea to foreign parts. But he really only went a very little way, and came back dressed like a servant girl, and so he got a place in the castle to wash the dishes. And he waited and watched, and he listened and said nothing, and he hid in dark places, and woke up at night and looked out, and he heard things and he saw things that he thought were very strange. And he was so sly that he told the girl that waited on the lady that he was really a young man, and that he had dressed up as a girl because he loved her so very much and wanted to be in the same house with her, and the girl was so pleased that she told him many things, and he was more than ever certain that the Lady Avelin was deceiving him and the others. And he was so clever, and told the servant so many lies, that one night he managed to hide in the Lady Avelin's room behind the curtains. And he stayed quite still and never moved, and at last the lady came. And she bent down under the bed, and raised up a stone, and there was a hollow place underneath, and out of it she took a waxen image, just like the clay one that I and nurse had made in the brake. And all the time her eyes were burning like rubies. And she took the little wax doll up in her arms and held it to her breast, and she whispered and she murmured, and she took it up and she laid it down again, and she held it high, and she held it low, and she laid it down again. And she said, 'Happy is he that begat the bishop, that ordered the clerk, that married the man, that had the wife, that fashioned the hive, that harboured the bee, that gathered the wax that my own true love was made of.' And she brought out of an aumbry a great golden bowl, and she brought out of a closet a great jar of wine, and she poured some of the wine into the bowl, and she laid her mannikin very gently in the wine, and washed it in the wine all over. Then she went to a cupboard and took a small round cake and laid it on the image's mouth, and then she bore it softly and covered it up. And Sir Simon, who was watching all the time, though he was terribly frightened, saw the lady bend down and stretch out her arms and whisper and sing, and then Sir Simon saw beside her a handsome young man, who kissed her on the lips. And they drank wine out of the golden bowl together, and they ate the cake together. But when the sun rose there was only the little wax doll, and the lady hid it again under the bed in the hollow place. So Sir Simon knew quite well what the lady was, and he waited and he watched, till the time she had said was nearly over, and in a week the year and a day would be done. And one night, when he was watching behind the curtains in her room, he saw her making more wax dolls. And she made five, and hid them away. And the next night she took one out, and held it up, and filled the golden bowl with water, and took the doll by the neck and held it under the water. Then she said--

Sir Dickon, Sir Dickon, your day is done,
You shall be drowned in the water wan.

And the next day news came to the castle that Sir Richard had been drowned at the ford. And at night she took another doll and tied a violet cord round its neck and hung it up on a nail. Then she said--

Sir Rowland, your life has ended its span,
High on a tree I see you hang.

And the next day news came to the castle that Sir Rowland had been hanged by robbers in the wood. And at night she took another doll, and drove her bodkin right into its heart. Then she said--

Sir Noll, Sir Noll, so cease your life,
Your heart piercèd with the knife.

And the next day news came to the castle that Sir Oliver had fought in a tavern, and a stranger had stabbed him to the heart. And at night she took another doll, and held it to a fire of charcoal till it was melted. Then she said--

Sir John, return, and turn to clay,
In fire of fever you waste away.

And the next day news came to the castle that Sir John had died in a burning fever. So then Sir Simon went out of the castle and mounted his horse and rode away to the bishop and told him everything. And the bishop sent his men, and they took the Lady Avelin, and everything she had done was found out. So on the day after the year and a day, when she was to have been married, they carried her through the town in her smock, and they tied her to a great stake in the market-place, and burned her alive before the bishop with her wax image hung round her neck. And people said the wax man screamed in the burning of the flames. And I thought of this story again and again as I was lying awake in my bed, and I seemed to see the Lady Avelin in the market-place, with the yellow flames eating up her beautiful white body. And I thought of it so much that I seemed to get into the story myself, and I fancied I was the lady, and that they were coming to take me to be burnt with fire, with all the people in the town looking at me. And I wondered whether she cared, after all the strange things she had done, and whether it hurt very much to be burned at the stake. I tried again and again to forget nurse's stories, and to remember the secret I had seen that afternoon, and what was in the secret wood, but I could only see the dark and a glimmering in the dark, and then it went away, and I only saw myself running, and then a great moon came up white over a dark round hill. Then all the old stories came back again, and the queer rhymes that nurse used to sing to me; and there was one beginning 'Halsy cumsy Helen musty,' that she used to sing very softly when she wanted me to go to sleep. And I began to sing it to myself inside of my head, and I went to sleep.

The next morning I was very tired and sleepy, and could hardly do my lessons, and I was very glad when they were over and I had had my dinner, as I wanted to go out and be alone. It was a warm day, and I went to a nice turfy hill by the river, and sat down on my mother's old shawl that I had brought with me on purpose. The sky was grey, like the day before, but there was a kind of white gleam behind it, and from where I was sitting I could look down on the town, and it was all still and quiet and white, like a picture. I remembered that it was on that hill that nurse taught me to play an old game called 'Troy Town,' in which one had to dance, and wind in and out on a pattern in the grass, and then when one had danced and turned long enough the other person asks you questions, and you can't help answering whether you want to or not, and whatever you are told to do you feel you have to do it. Nurse said there used to be a lot of games like that that some people knew of, and there was one by which people could be turned into anything you liked, and an old man her great-grandmother had seen had known a girl who had been turned into a large snake. And there was another very ancient game of dancing and winding and turning, by which you could take a person out of himself and hide him away as long as you liked, and his body went walking about quite empty, without any sense in it. But I came to that hill because I wanted to think of what had happened the day before, and of the secret of the wood. From the place where I was sitting I could see beyond the town, into the opening I had found, where a little brook had led me into an unknown country. And I pretended I was following the brook over again, and I went all the way in my mind, and at last I found the wood, and crept into it under the bushes, and then in the dusk I saw something that made me feel as if I were filled with fire, as if I wanted to dance and sing and fly up into the air, because I was changed and wonderful. But what I saw was not changed at all, and had not grown old, and I wondered again and again how such things could happen, and whether nurse's stories were really true, because in the daytime in the open air everything seemed quite different from what it was at night, when I was frightened, and thought I was to be burned alive. I once told my father one of her little tales, which was about a ghost, and asked him if it was true, and he told me it was not true at all, and that only common, ignorant people believed in such rubbish. He was very angry with nurse for telling me the story, and scolded her, and after that I promised her I would never whisper a word of what she told me, and if I did I should be bitten by the great black snake that lived in the pool in the wood. And all alone on the hill I wondered what was true. I had seen something very amazing and very lovely, and I knew a story, and if I had really seen it, and not made it up out of the dark, and the black bough, and the bright shining that was mounting up to the sky from over the great round hill, but had really seen it in truth, then there were all kinds of wonderful and lovely and terrible things to think of, so I longed and trembled, and I burned and got cold. And I looked down on the town, so quiet and still, like a little white picture, and I thought over and over if it could be true. I was a long time before I could make up my mind to anything; there was such a strange fluttering at my heart that seemed to whisper to me all the time that I had not made it up out of my head, and yet it seemed quite impossible, and I knew my father and everybody would say it was dreadful rubbish. I never dreamed of telling him or anybody else a word about it, because I knew it would be of no use, and I should only get laughed at or scolded, so for a long time I was very quiet, and went about thinking and wondering; and at night I used to dream of amazing things, and sometimes I woke up in the early morning and held out my arms with a cry. And I was frightened, too, because there were dangers, and some awful thing would happen to me, unless I took great care, if the story were true. These old tales were always in my head, night and morning, and I went over them and told them to myself over and over again, and went for walks in the places where nurse had told them to me; and when I sat in the nursery by the fire in the evenings I used to fancy nurse was sitting in the other chair, and telling me some wonderful story in a low voice, for fear anybody should be listening. But she used to like best to tell me about things when we were right out in the country, far from the house, because she said she was telling me such secrets, and walls have ears. And if it was something more than ever secret, we had to hide in brakes or woods; and I used to think it was such fun creeping along a hedge, and going very softly, and then we would get behind the bushes or run into the wood all of a sudden, when we were sure that none was watching us; so we knew that we had our secrets quite all to ourselves, and nobody else at all knew anything about them. Now and then, when we had hidden ourselves as I have described, she used to show me all sorts of odd things. One day, I remember, we were in a hazel brake, overlooking the brook, and we were so snug and warm, as though it was April; the sun was quite hot, and the leaves were just coming out. Nurse said she would show me something funny that would make me laugh, and then she showed me, as she said, how one could turn a whole house upside down, without anybody being able to find out, and the pots and pans would jump about, and the china would be broken, and the chairs would tumble over of themselves. I tried it one day in the kitchen, and I found I could do it quite well, and a whole row of plates on the dresser fell off it, and cook's little work-table tilted up and turned right over 'before her eyes,' as she said, but she was so frightened and turned so white that I didn't do it again, as I liked her. And afterwards, in the hazel copse, when she had shown me how to make things tumble about, she showed me how to make rapping noises, and I learnt how to do that, too. Then she taught me rhymes to say on certain occasions, and peculiar marks to make on other occasions, and other things that her great-grandmother had taught her when she was a little girl herself. And these were all the things I was thinking about in those days after the strange walk when I thought I had seen a great secret, and I wished nurse were there for me to ask her about it, but she had gone away more than two years before, and nobody seemed to know what had become of her, or where she had gone. But I shall always remember those days if I live to be quite old, because all the time I felt so strange, wondering and doubting, and feeling quite sure at one time, and making up my mind, and then I would feel quite sure that such things couldn't happen really, and it began all over again. But I took great care not to do certain things that might be very dangerous. So I waited and wondered for a long time, and though I was not sure at all, I never dared to try to find out. But one day I became sure that all that nurse said was quite true, and I was all alone when I found it out. I trembled all over with joy and terror, and as fast as I could I ran into one of the old brakes where we used to go-- it was the one by the lane, where nurse made the little clay man--and I ran into it, and I crept into it; and when I came to the place where the elder was, I covered up my face with my hands and lay down flat on the grass, and I stayed there for two hours without moving, whispering to myself delicious, terrible things, and saying some words over and over again. It was all true and wonderful and splendid, and when I remembered the story I knew and thought of what I had really seen, I got hot and I got cold, and the air seemed full of scent, and flowers, and singing. And first I wanted to make a little clay man, like the one nurse had made so long ago, and I had to invent plans and stratagems, and to look about, and to think of things beforehand, because nobody must dream of anything that I was doing or going to do, and I was too old to carry clay about in a tin bucket. At last I thought of a plan, and I brought the wet clay to the brake, and did everything that nurse had done, only I made a much finer image than the one she had made; and when it was finished I did everything that I could imagine and much more than she did, because it was the likeness of something far better. And a few days later, when I had done my lessons early, I went for the second time by the way of the little brook that had led me into a strange country. And I followed the brook, and went through the bushes, and beneath the low branches of trees, and up thorny thickets on the hill, and by dark woods full of creeping thorns, a long, long way. Then I crept through the dark tunnel where the brook had been and the ground was stony, till at last I came to the thicket that climbed up the hill, and though the leaves were coming out upon the trees, everything looked almost as black as it was on the first day that I went there. And the thicket was just the same, and I went up slowly till I came out on the big bare hill, and began to walk among the wonderful rocks. I saw the terrible voor again on everything, for though the sky was brighter, the ring of wild hills all around was still dark, and the hanging woods looked dark and dreadful, and the strange rocks were as grey as ever; and when I looked down on them from the great mound, sitting on the stone, I saw all their amazing circles and rounds within rounds, and I had to sit quite still and watch them as they began to turn about me, and each stone danced in its place, and they seemed to go round and round in a great whirl, as if one were in the middle of all the stars and heard them rushing through the air. So I went down among the rocks to dance with them and to sing extraordinary songs; and I went down through the other thicket, and drank from the bright stream in the close and secret valley, putting my lips down to the bubbling water; and then I went on till I came to the deep, brimming well among the glittering moss, and I sat down. I looked before me into the secret darkness of the valley, and behind me was the great high wall of grass, and all around me there were the hanging woods that made the valley such a secret place. I knew there was nobody here at all besides myself, and that no one could see me. So I took off my boots and stockings, and let my feet down into the water, saying the words that I knew. And it was not cold at all, as I expected, but warm and very pleasant, and when my feet were in it I felt as if they were in silk, or as if the nymph were kissing them. So when I had done, I said the other words and made the signs, and then I dried my feet with a towel I had brought on purpose, and put on my stockings and boots. Then I climbed up the steep wall, and went into the place where there are the hollows, and the two beautiful mounds, and the round ridges of land, and all the strange shapes. I did not go down into the hollow this time, but I turned at the end, and made out the figures quite plainly, as it was lighter, and I had remembered the story I had quite forgotten before, and in the story the two figures are called Adam and Eve, and only those who know the story understand what they mean. So I went on and on till I came to the secret wood which must not be described, and I crept into it by the way I had found. And when I had gone about halfway I stopped, and turned round, and got ready, and I bound the handkerchief tightly round my eyes, and made quite sure that I could not see at all, not a twig, nor the end of a leaf, nor the light of the sky, as it was an old red silk handkerchief with large yellow spots, that went round twice and covered my eyes, so that I could see nothing. Then I began to go on, step by step, very slowly. My heart beat faster and faster, and something rose in my throat that choked me and made me want to cry out, but I shut my lips, and went on. Boughs caught in my hair as I went, and great thorns tore me; but I went on to the end of the path. Then I stopped, and held out my arms and bowed, and I went round the first time, feeling with my hands, and there was nothing. I went round the second time, feeling with my hands, and there was nothing. Then I went round the third time, feeling with my hands, and the story was all true, and I wished that the years were gone by, and that I had not so long a time to wait before I was happy for ever and ever.

Nurse must have been a prophet like those we read of in the Bible. Everything that she said began to come true, and since then other things that she told me of have happened. That was how I came to know that her stories were true and that I had not made up the secret myself out of my own head. But there was another thing that happened that day. I went a second time to the secret place. It was at the deep brimming well, and when I was standing on the moss I bent over and looked in, and then I knew who the white lady was that I had seen come out of the water in the wood long ago when I was quite little. And I trembled all over, because that told me other things. Then I remembered how sometime after I had seen the white people in the wood, nurse asked me more about them, and I told her all over again, and she listened, and said nothing for a long, long time, and at last she said, 'You will see her again.' So I understood what had happened and what was to happen. And I understood about the nymphs; how I might meet them in all kinds of places, and they would always help me, and I must always look for them, and find them in all sorts of strange shapes and appearances. And without the nymphs I could never have found the secret, and without them none of the other things could happen. Nurse had told me all about them long ago, but she called them by another name, and I did not know what she meant, or what her tales of them were about, only that they were very queer. And there were two kinds, the bright and the dark, and both were very lovely and very wonderful, and some people saw only one kind, and some only the other, but some saw them both. But usually the dark appeared first, and the bright ones came afterwards, and there were extraordinary tales about them. It was a day or two after I had come home from the secret place that I first really knew the nymphs. Nurse had shown me how to call them, and I had tried, but I did not know what she meant, and so I thought it was all nonsense. But I made up my mind I would try again, so I went to the wood where the pool was, where I saw the white people, and I tried again. The dark nymph, Alanna, came, and she turned the pool of water into a pool of fire....

EPILOGUE

'That's a very queer story,' said Cotgrave, handing back the green book to the recluse, Ambrose. 'I see the drift of a good deal, but there are many things that I do not grasp at all. On the last page, for example, what does she mean by "nymphs"?'

'Well, I think there are references throughout the manuscript to certain "processes" which have been handed down by tradition from age to age. Some of these processes are just beginning to come within the purview of science, which has arrived at them--or rather at the steps which lead to them--by quite different paths. I have interpreted the reference to "nymphs" as a reference to one of these processes.'

'And you believe that there are such things?'

'Oh, I think so. Yes, I believe I could give you convincing evidence on that point. I am afraid you have neglected the study of alchemy? It is a pity, for the symbolism, at all events, is very beautiful, and moreover if you were acquainted with certain books on the subject, I could recall to your mind phrases which might explain a good deal in the manuscript that you have been reading.'

'Yes; but I want to know whether you seriously think that there is any foundation of fact beneath these fancies. Is it not all a department of poetry; a curious dream with which man has indulged himself?'

'I can only say that it is no doubt better for the great mass of people to dismiss it all as a dream. But if you ask my veritable belief--that goes quite the other way. No; I should not say belief, but rather knowledge. I may tell you that I have known cases in which men have stumbled quite by accident on certain of these "processes," and have been astonished by wholly unexpected results. In the cases I am thinking of there could have been no possibility of "suggestion" or sub-conscious action of any kind. One might as well suppose a schoolboy "suggesting" the existence of Æschylus to himself, while he plods mechanically through the declensions.

'But you have noticed the obscurity,' Ambrose went on, 'and in this particular case it must have been dictated by instinct, since the writer never thought that her manuscripts would fall into other hands. But the practice is universal, and for most excellent reasons. Powerful and sovereign medicines, which are, of necessity, virulent poisons also, are kept in a locked cabinet. The child may find the key by chance, and drink herself dead; but in most cases the search is educational, and the phials contain precious elixirs for him who has patiently fashioned the key for himself.'

'You do not care to go into details?'

'No, frankly, I do not. No, you must remain unconvinced. But you saw how the manuscript illustrates the talk we had last week?'

'Is this girl still alive?'

'No. I was one of those who found her. I knew the father well; he was a lawyer, and had always left her very much to herself. He thought of nothing but deeds and leases, and the news came to him as an awful surprise. She was missing one morning; I suppose it was about a year after she had written what you have read. The servants were called, and they told things, and put the only natural interpretation on them--a perfectly erroneous one.

'They discovered that green book somewhere in her room, and I found her in the place that she described with so much dread, lying on the ground before the image.'

'It was an image?'

'Yes, it was hidden by the thorns and the thick undergrowth that had surrounded it. It was a wild, lonely country; but you know what it was like by her description, though of course you will understand that the colours have been heightened. A child's imagination always makes the heights higher and the depths deeper than they really are; and she had, unfortunately for herself, something more than imagination. One might say, perhaps, that the picture in her mind which she succeeded in a measure in putting into words, was the scene as it would have appeared to an imaginative artist. But it is a strange, desolate land.'

'And she was dead?'

'Yes. She had poisoned herself--in time. No; there was not a word to be said against her in the ordinary sense. You may recollect a story I told you the other night about a lady who saw her child's fingers crushed by a window?'

'And what was this statue?'

'Well, it was of Roman workmanship, of a stone that with the centuries had not blackened, but had become white and luminous. The thicket had grown up about it and concealed it, and in the Middle Ages the followers of a very old tradition had known how to use it for their own purposes. In fact it had been incorporated into the monstrous mythology of the Sabbath. You will have noted that those to whom a sight of that shining whiteness had been vouchsafed by chance, or rather, perhaps, by apparent chance, were required to blindfold themselves on their second approach. That is very significant.'

'And is it there still?'

'I sent for tools, and we hammered it into dust and fragments.'

'The persistence of tradition never surprises me,' Ambrose went on after a pause. 'I could name many an English parish where such traditions as that girl had listened to in her childhood are still existent in occult but unabated vigour. No, for me, it is the "story" not the "sequel," which is strange and awful, for I have always believed that wonder is of the soul.'

The Inmost Light

I

One evening in autumn, when the deformities of London were veiled in faint blue mist, and its vistas and far-reaching streets seemed splendid, Mr. Charles Salisbury was slowly pacing down Rupert Street, drawing nearer to his favourite restaurant by slow degrees. His eyes were downcast in study of the pavement, and thus it was that as he passed in at the narrow door a man who had come up from the lower end of the street jostled against him.

'I beg your pardon--wasn't looking where I was going. Why, it's Dyson!'

'Yes, quite so. How are you, Salisbury?'

'Quite well. But where have you been, Dyson? I don't think I can have seen you for the last five years?'

'No; I dare say not. You remember I was getting rather hard up when you came to my place at Charlotte Street?'

'Perfectly. I think I remember your telling me that you owed five weeks' rent, and that you had parted with your watch for a comparatively small sum.'

'My dear Salisbury, your memory is admirable. Yes, I was hard up. But the curious thing is that soon after you saw me I became harder up. My financial state was described by a friend as "stone broke." I don't approve of slang, mind you, but such was my condition. But suppose we go in; there might be other people who would like to dine--it's a human weakness, Salisbury.'

'Certainly; come along. I was wondering as I walked down whether the corner table were taken. It has a velvet back, you know.'

'I know the spot; it's vacant. Yes, as I was saying, I became even harder up.'

'What did you do then?' asked Salisbury, disposing of his hat, and settling down in the corner of the seat, with a glance of fond anticipation at the menu.

'What did I do? Why, I sat down and reflected. I had a good classical education, and a positive distaste for business of any kind: that was the capital with which I faced the world. Do you know, I have heard people describe olives as nasty! What lamentable Philistinism! I have often thought, Salisbury, that I could write genuine poetry under the influence of olives and red wine. Let us have Chianti; it may not be very good, but the flasks are simply charming.'

'It is pretty good here. We may as well have a big flask.'

'Very good. I reflected, then, on my want of prospects, and I determined to embark in literature.'

'Really; that was strange. You seem in pretty comfortable circumstances, though.'

'Though! What a satire upon a noble profession. I am afraid, Salisbury, you haven't a proper idea of the dignity of an artist. You see me sitting at my desk--or at least you can see me if you care to call--with pen and ink, and simple nothingness before me, and if you come again in a few hours you will (in all probability) find a creation!'

'Yes, quite so. I had an idea that literature was not remunerative.'

'You are mistaken; its rewards are great. I may mention, by the way, that shortly after you saw me I succeeded to a small income. An uncle died, and proved unexpectedly generous.'

'Ah, I see. That must have been convenient.'

'It was pleasant--undeniably pleasant. I have always considered it in the light of an endowment of my researches. I told you I was a man of letters; it would, perhaps, be more correct to describe myself as a man of science.'

'Dear me, Dyson, you have really changed very much in the last few years. I had a notion, don't you know, that you were a sort of idler about town, the kind of man one might meet on the north side of Piccadilly every day from May to July.'

'Exactly. I was even then forming myself, though all unconsciously. You know my poor father could not afford to send me to the University. I used to grumble in my ignorance at not having completed my education. That was the folly of youth, Salisbury; my University was Piccadilly. There I began to study the great science which still occupies me.'

'What science do you mean?'

'The science of the great city; the physiology of London; literally and metaphysically the greatest subject that the mind of man can conceive. What an admirable salmi this is; undoubtedly the final end of the pheasant. Yet I feel sometimes positively overwhelmed with the thought of the vastness and complexity of London. Paris a man may get to understand thoroughly with a reasonable amount of study; but London is always a mystery. In Paris you may say: "Here live the actresses, here the Bohemians, and the Ratés"; but it is different in London. You may point out a street, correctly enough, as the abode of washerwomen; but, in that second floor, a man may be studying Chaldee roots, and in the garret over the way a forgotten artist is dying by inches.'

'I see you are Dyson, unchanged and unchangeable,' said Salisbury, slowly sipping his Chianti. 'I think you are misled by a too fervid imagination; the mystery of London exists only in your fancy. It seems to me a dull place enough. We seldom hear of a really artistic crime in London, whereas I believe Paris abounds in that sort of thing.'

'Give me some more wine. Thanks. You are mistaken, my dear fellow, you are really mistaken. London has nothing to be ashamed of in the way of crime. Where we fail is for want of Homers, not Agamemnons. Carent quia vate sacro, you know.'

'I recall the quotation. But I don't think I quite follow you.'

'Well, in plain language, we have no good writers in London who make a speciality of that kind of thing. Our common reporter is a dull dog; every story that he has to tell is spoilt in the telling. His idea of horror and of what excites horror is so lamentably deficient. Nothing will content the fellow but blood, vulgar red blood, and when he can get it he lays it on thick, and considers that he has produced a telling article. It's a poor notion. And, by some curious fatality, it is the most commonplace and brutal murders which always attract the most attention and get written up the most. For instance, I dare say that you never heard of the Harlesden case?'

'No; no, I don't remember anything about it.'

'Of course not. And yet the story is a curious one. I will tell it you over our coffee. Harlesden, you know, or I expect you don't know, is quite on the out-quarters of London; something curiously different from your fine old crusted suburb like Norwood or Hampstead, different as each of these is from the other. Hampstead, I mean, is where you look for the head of your great China house with his three acres of land and pine-houses, though of late there is the artistic substratum; while Norwood is the home of the prosperous middle-class family who took the house "because it was near the Palace," and sickened of the Palace six months afterwards; but Harlesden is a place of no character. It's too new to have any character as yet. There are the rows of red houses and the rows of white houses and the bright green Venetians, and the blistering doorways, and the little backyards they call gardens, and a few feeble shops, and then, just as you think you're going to grasp the physiognomy of the settlement, it all melts away.'

'How the dickens is that? the houses don't tumble down before one's eyes, I suppose!'

'Well, no, not exactly that. But Harlesden as an entity disappears. Your street turns into a quiet lane, and your staring houses into elm trees, and the back-gardens into green meadows. You pass instantly from town to country; there is no transition as in a small country town, no soft gradations of wider lawns and orchards, with houses gradually becoming less dense, but a dead stop. I believe the people who live there mostly go into the City. I have seen once or twice a laden 'bus bound thitherwards. But however that may be, I can't conceive a greater loneliness in a desert at midnight than there is there at midday. It is like a city of the dead; the streets are glaring and desolate, and as you pass it suddenly strikes you that this too is part of London. Well, a year or two ago there was a doctor living there; he had set up his brass plate and his red lamp at the very end of one of those shining streets, and from the back of the house, the fields stretched away to the north. I don't know what his reason was in settling down in such an out-of-the-way place, perhaps Dr. Black, as we will call him, was a far-seeing man and looked ahead. His relations, so it appeared afterwards, had lost sight of him for many years and didn't even know he was a doctor, much less where he lived. However, there he was settled in Harlesden, with some fragments of a practice, and an uncommonly pretty wife. People used to see them walking out together in the summer evenings soon after they came to Harlesden, and, so far as could be observed, they seemed a very affectionate couple. These walks went on through the autumn, and then ceased; but, of course, as the days grew dark and the weather cold, the lanes near Harlesden might be expected to lose many of their attractions. All through the winter nobody saw anything of Mrs. Black; the doctor used to reply to his patients' inquiries that she was a "little out of sorts, would be better, no doubt, in the spring." But the spring came, and the summer, and no Mrs. Black appeared, and at last people began to rumour and talk amongst themselves, and all sorts of queer things were said at "high teas," which you may possibly have heard are the only form of entertainment known in such suburbs. Dr. Black began to surprise some very odd looks cast in his direction, and the practice, such as it was, fell off before his eyes. In short, when the neighbours whispered about the matter, they whispered that Mrs. Black was dead, and that the doctor had made away with her. But this wasn't the case;

Mrs. Black was seen alive in June. It was a Sunday afternoon, one of those few exquisite days that an English climate offers, and half London had strayed out into the fields, north, south, east, and west to smell the scent of the white May, and to see if the wild roses were yet in blossom in the hedges. I had gone out myself early in the morning, and had had a long ramble, and somehow or other as I was steering homeward I found myself in this very Harlesden we have been talking about. To be exact, I had a glass of beer in the "General Gordon," the most flourishing house in the neighbourhood, and as I was wandering rather aimlessly about, I saw an uncommonly tempting gap in a hedgerow, and resolved to explore the meadow beyond. Soft grass is very grateful to the feet after the infernal grit strewn on suburban sidewalks, and after walking about for some time I thought I should like to sit down on a bank and have a smoke. While I was getting out my pouch, I looked up in the direction of the houses, and as I looked I felt my breath caught back, and my teeth began to chatter, and the stick I had in one hand snapped in two with the grip I gave it. It was as if I had had an electric current down my spine, and yet for some moment of time which seemed long, but which must have been very short, I caught myself wondering what on earth was the matter. Then I knew what had made my very heart shudder and my bones grind together in an agony. As I glanced up I had looked straight towards the last house in the row before me, and in an upper window of that house I had seen for some short fraction of a second a face. It was the face of a woman, and yet it was not human. You and I, Salisbury, have heard in our time, as we sat in our seats in church in sober English fashion, of a lust that cannot be satiated and of a fire that is unquenchable, but few of us have any notion what these words mean. I hope you never may, for as I saw that face at the window, with the blue sky above me and the warm air playing in gusts about me, I knew I had looked into another world--looked through the window of a commonplace, brand-new house, and seen hell open before me. When the first shock was over, I thought once or twice that I should have fainted; my face streamed with a cold sweat, and my breath came and went in sobs, as if I had been half drowned. I managed to get up at last, and walked round to the street, and there I saw the name "Dr. Black" on the post by the front gate. As fate or my luck would have it, the door opened and a man came down the steps as I passed by. I had no doubt it was the doctor himself. He was of a type rather common in London; long and thin, with a pasty face and a dull black moustache. He gave me a look as we passed each other on the pavement, and though it was merely the casual glance which one foot-passenger bestows on another, I felt convinced in my mind that here was an ugly customer to deal with. As you may imagine, I went my way a good deal puzzled and horrified too by what I had seen; for I had paid another visit to the "General Gordon," and had got together a good deal of the common gossip of the place about the Blacks. I didn't mention the fact that I had seen a woman's face in the window; but I heard that Mrs. Black had been much admired for her beautiful golden hair, and round what had struck me with such a nameless terror, there was a mist of flowing yellow hair, as it were an aureole of glory round the visage of a satyr. The whole thing bothered me in an indescribable manner; and when I got home I tried my best to think of the impression I had received as an illusion, but it was no use. I knew very well I had seen what I have tried to describe to you, and I was morally certain that I had seen Mrs. Black. And then there was the gossip of the place, the suspicion of foul play, which I knew to be false, and my own conviction that there was some deadly mischief or other going on in that bright red house at the corner of Devon Road: how to construct a theory of a reasonable kind out of these two elements. In short, I found myself in a world of mystery; I puzzled my head over it and filled up my leisure moments by gathering together odd threads of speculation, but I never moved a step towards any real solution, and as the summer days went on the matter seemed to grow misty and indistinct, shadowing some vague terror, like a nightmare of last month. I suppose it would before long have faded into the background of my brain--I should not have forgotten it, for such a thing could never be forgotten--but one morning as I was looking over the paper my eye was caught by a heading over some two dozen lines of small type. The words I had seen were simply, "The Harlesden Case," and I knew what I was going to read. Mrs. Black was dead. Black had called in another medical man to certify as to cause of death, and something or other had aroused the strange doctor's suspicions and there had been an inquest and post-mortem. And the result? That, I will confess, did astonish me considerably; it was the triumph of the unexpected. The two doctors who made the autopsy were obliged to confess that they could not discover the faintest trace of any kind of foul play; their most exquisite tests and reagents failed to detect the presence of poison in the most infinitesimal quantity. Death, they found, had been caused by a somewhat obscure and scientifically interesting form of brain disease. The tissue of the brain and the molecules of the grey matter had undergone a most extraordinary series of changes; and the younger of the two doctors, who has some reputation, I believe, as a specialist in brain trouble, made some remarks in giving his evidence which struck me deeply at the time, though I did not then grasp their full significance. He said: "At the commencement of the examination I was astonished to find appearances of a character entirely new to me, notwithstanding my somewhat large experience. I need not specify these appearances at present, it will be sufficient for me to state that as I proceeded in my task I could scarcely believe that the brain before me was that of a human being at all." There was some surprise at this statement, as you may imagine, and the coroner asked the doctor if he meant to say that the brain resembled that of an animal. "No," he replied, "I should not put it in that way. Some of the appearances I noticed seemed to point in that direction, but others, and these were the more surprising, indicated a nervous organization of a wholly different character from that either of man or the lower animals." It was a curious thing to say, but of course the jury brought in a verdict of death from natural causes, and, so far as the public was concerned, the case came to an end. But after I had read what the doctor said I made up my mind that I should like to know a good deal more, and I set to work on what seemed likely to prove an interesting investigation. I had really a good deal of trouble, but I was successful in a measure. Though why--my dear fellow, I had no notion at the time. Are you aware that we have been here nearly four hours? The waiters are staring at us. Let's have the bill and be gone.'

The two men went out in silence, and stood a moment in the cool air, watching the hurrying traffic of Coventry Street pass before them to the accompaniment of the ringing bells of hansoms and the cries of the newsboys; the deep far murmur of London surging up ever and again from beneath these louder noises.

'It is a strange case, isn't it?' said Dyson at length. 'What do you think of it?'

'My dear fellow, I haven't heard the end, so I will reserve my opinion. When will you give me the sequel?'

'Come to my rooms some evening; say next Thursday. Here's the address. Good-night; I want to get down to the Strand.' Dyson hailed a passing hansom, and Salisbury turned northward to walk home to his lodgings.

II

Mr. Salisbury, as may have been gathered from the few remarks which he had found it possible to introduce in the course of the evening, was a young gentleman of a peculiarly solid form of intellect, coy and retiring before the mysterious and the uncommon, with a constitutional dislike of paradox. During the restaurant dinner he had been forced to listen in almost absolute silence to a strange tissue of improbabilities strung together with the ingenuity of a born meddler in plots and mysteries, and it was with a feeling of weariness that he crossed Shaftesbury Avenue, and dived into the recesses of Soho, for his lodgings were in a modest neighbourhood to the north of Oxford Street. As he walked he speculated on the probable fate of Dyson, relying on literature, unbefriended by a thoughtful relative, and could not help concluding that so much subtlety united to a too vivid imagination would in all likelihood have been rewarded with a pair of sandwich-boards or a super's banner. Absorbed in this train of thought, and admiring the perverse dexterity which could transmute the face of a sickly woman and a case of brain disease into the crude elements of romance, Salisbury strayed on through the dimly-lighted streets, not noticing the gusty wind which drove sharply round corners and whirled the stray rubbish of the pavement into the air in eddies, while black clouds gathered over the sickly yellow moon. Even a stray drop or two of rain blown into his face did not rouse him from his meditations, and it was only when with a sudden rush the storm tore down upon the street that he began to consider the expediency of finding some shelter. The rain, driven by the wind, pelted down with the violence of a thunderstorm, dashing up from the stones and hissing through the air, and soon a perfect torrent of water coursed along the kennels and accumulated in pools over the choked-up drains. The few stray passengers who had been loafing rather than walking about the street had scuttered away, like frightened rabbits, to some invisible places of refuge, and though Salisbury whistled loud and long for a hansom, no hansom appeared. He looked about him, as if to discover how far he might be from the haven of Oxford Street, but strolling carelessly along, he had turned out of his way, and found himself in an unknown region, and one to all appearance devoid even of a public-house where shelter could be bought for the modest sum of twopence. The street lamps were few and at long intervals, and burned behind grimy glasses with the sickly light of oil, and by this wavering glimmer Salisbury could make out the shadowy and vast old houses of which the street was composed. As he passed along, hurrying, and shrinking from the full sweep of the rain, he noticed the innumerable bell-handles, with names that seemed about to vanish of old age graven on brass plates beneath them, and here and there a richly carved penthouse overhung the door, blackening with the grime of fifty years. The storm seemed to grow more and more furious; he was wet through, and a new hat had become a ruin, and still Oxford Street seemed as far off as ever; it was with deep relief that the dripping man caught sight of a dark archway which seemed to promise shelter from the rain if not from the wind. Salisbury took up his position in the driest corner and looked about him; he was standing in a kind of passage contrived under part of a house, and behind him stretched a narrow footway leading between blank walls to regions unknown. He had stood there for some time, vainly endeavouring to rid himself of some of his superfluous moisture, and listening for the passing wheel of a hansom, when his attention was aroused by a loud noise coming from the direction of the passage behind, and growing louder as it drew nearer. In a couple of minutes he could make out the shrill, raucous voice of a woman, threatening and renouncing, and making the very stones echo with her accents, while now and then a man grumbled and expostulated. Though to all appearance devoid of romance, Salisbury had some relish for street rows, and was, indeed, somewhat of an amateur in the more amusing phases of drunkenness; he therefore composed himself to listen and observe with something of the air of a subscriber to grand opera. To his annoyance, however, the tempest seemed suddenly to be composed, and he could hear nothing but the impatient steps of the woman and the slow lurch of the man as they came towards him. Keeping back in the shadow of the wall, he could see the two drawing nearer; the man was evidently drunk, and had much ado to avoid frequent collision with the wall as he tacked across from one side to the other, like some bark beating up against a wind. The woman was looking straight in front of her, with tears streaming from her eyes, but suddenly as they went by the flame blazed up again, and she burst forth into a torrent of abuse, facing round upon her companion.

'You low rascal, you mean, contemptible cur,' she went on, after an incoherent storm of curses, 'you think I'm to work and slave for you always, I suppose, while you're after that Green Street girl and drinking every penny you've got? But you're mistaken, Sam--indeed, I'll bear it no longer. Damn you, you dirty thief, I've done with you and your master too, so you can go your own errands, and I only hope they'll get you into trouble.'

The woman tore at the bosom of her dress, and taking something out that looked like paper, crumpled it up and flung it away. It fell at Salisbury's feet. She ran out and disappeared in the darkness, while the man lurched slowly into the street, grumbling indistinctly to himself in a perplexed tone of voice. Salisbury looked out after him and saw him maundering along the pavement, halting now and then and swaying indecisively, and then starting off at some fresh tangent. The sky had cleared, and white fleecy clouds were fleeting across the moon, high in the heaven. The light came and went by turns, as the clouds passed by, and, turning round as the clear, white rays shone into the passage, Salisbury saw the little ball of crumpled paper which the woman had cast down. Oddly curious to know what it might contain, he picked it up and put it in his pocket, and set out afresh on his journey.

III

Salisbury was a man of habit. When he got home, drenched to the skin, his clothes hanging lank about him, and a ghastly dew besmearing his hat, his only thought was of his health, of which he took studious care. So, after changing his clothes and encasing himself in a warm dressing-gown, he proceeded to prepare a sudorific in the shape of a hot gin and water, warming the latter over one of those spirit-lamps which mitigate the austerities of the modern hermit's life. By the time this preparation had been exhibited, and Salisbury's disturbed feelings had been soothed by a pipe of tobacco, he was able to get into bed in a happy state of vacancy, without a thought of his adventure in the dark archway, or of the weird fancies with which Dyson had seasoned his dinner. It was the same at breakfast the next morning, for Salisbury made a point of not thinking of any thing until that meal was over; but when the cup and saucer were cleared away, and the morning pipe was lit, he remembered the little ball of paper, and began fumbling in the pockets of his wet coat. He did not remember into which pocket he had put it, and as he dived now into one and now into another, he experienced a strange feeling of apprehension lest it should not be there at all, though he could not for the life of him have explained the importance he attached to what was in all probability mere rubbish. But he sighed with relief when his fingers touched the crumpled surface in an inside pocket, and he drew it out gently and laid it on the little desk by his easy-chair with as much care as if it had been some rare jewel. Salisbury sat smoking and staring at his find for a few minutes, an odd temptation to throw the thing in the fire and have done with it struggling with as odd a speculation as to its possible contents, and as to the reason why the infuriated woman should have flung a bit of paper from her with such vehemence. As might be expected, it was the latter feeling that conquered in the end, and yet it was with something like repugnance that he at last took the paper and unrolled it, and laid it out before him. It was a piece of common dirty paper, to all appearance torn out of a cheap exercise-book, and in the middle were a few lines written in a queer cramped hand. Salisbury bent his head and stared eagerly at it for a moment, drawing a long breath, and then fell back in his chair gazing blankly before him, till at last with a sudden revulsion he burst into a peal of laughter, so long and loud and uproarious that the landlady's baby on the floor below awoke from sleep and echoed his mirth with hideous yells. But he laughed again and again, and took the paper up to read a second time what seemed such meaningless nonsense.

'Q. has had to go and see his friends in Paris,' it began. 'Traverse Handle S. "Once around the grass, and twice around the lass, and thrice around the maple tree."'

Salisbury took up the paper and crumpled it as the angry woman had done, and aimed it at the fire. He did not throw it there, however, but tossed it carelessly into the well of the desk, and laughed again. The sheer folly of the thing offended him, and he was ashamed of his own eager speculation, as one who pores over the high-sounding announcements in the agony column of the daily paper, and finds nothing but advertisement and triviality. He walked to the window, and stared out at the languid morning life of his quarter; the maids in slatternly print dresses washing door-steps, the fish-monger and the butcher on their rounds, and the tradesmen standing at the doors of their small shops, drooping for lack of trade and excitement. In the distance a blue haze gave some grandeur to the prospect, but the view as a whole was depressing, and would only have interested a student of the life of London, who finds something rare and choice in its very aspect. Salisbury turned away in disgust, and settled himself in the easy-chair, upholstered in a bright shade of green, and decked with yellow gimp, which was the pride and attraction of the apartments. Here he composed himself to his morning's occupation--the perusal of a novel that dealt with sport and love in a manner that suggested the collaboration of a stud-groom and a ladies' college. In an ordinary way, however, Salisbury would have been carried on by the interest of the story up to lunch-time, but this morning he fidgeted in and out of his chair, took the book up and laid it down again, and swore at last to himself and at himself in mere irritation. In point of fact the jingle of the paper found in the archway had 'got into his head,' and do what he would he could not help muttering over and over, 'Once around the grass, and twice around the lass, and thrice around the maple tree.' It became a positive pain, like the foolish burden of a music-hall song, everlastingly quoted, and sung at all hours of the day and night, and treasured by the street-boys as an unfailing resource for six months together. He went out into the streets, and tried to forget his enemy in the jostling of the crowds and the roar and clatter of the traffic, but presently he would find himself stealing quietly aside, and pacing some deserted byway, vainly puzzling his brains, and trying to fix some meaning to phrases that were meaningless. It was a positive relief when Thursday came, and he remembered that he had made an appointment to go and see Dyson; the flimsy reveries of the self-styled man of letters appeared entertaining when compared with this ceaseless iteration, this maze of thought from which there seemed no possibility of escape. Dyson's abode was in one of the quietest of the quiet streets that led down from the Strand to the river, and when Salisbury passed from the narrow stairway into his friend's room, he saw that the uncle had been beneficent indeed. The floor glowed and flamed with all the colours of the East; it was, as Dyson pompously remarked, 'a sunset in a dream,' and the lamplight, the twilight of London streets, was shut out with strangely worked curtains, glittering here and there with threads of gold. In the shelves of an oak armoire stood jars and plates of old French china, and the black and white of etchings not to be found in the Haymarket or in Bond Street, stood out against the splendour of a Japanese paper. Salisbury sat down on the settle by the hearth, and sniffed the mingled fumes of incense and tobacco, wondering and dumb before all this splendour after the green rep and the oleographs, the gilt-framed mirror, and the lustres of his own apartment.

'I am glad you have come,' said Dyson. 'Comfortable little room, isn't it? But you don't look very well, Salisbury. Nothing disagreed with you, has it?'

'No; but I have been a good deal bothered for the last few days. The fact is I had an odd kind of--of--adventure, I suppose I may call it, that night I saw you, and it has worried me a good deal. And the provoking part of it is that it's the merest nonsense--but, however, I will tell you all about it, by and by. You were going to let me have the rest of that odd story you began at the restaurant.'

'Yes. But I am afraid, Salisbury, you are incorrigible. You are a slave to what you call matter of fact. You know perfectly well that in your heart you think the oddness in that case is of my making, and that it is all really as plain as the police reports. However, as I have begun, I will go on. But first we will have something to drink, and you may as well light your pipe.'

Dyson went up to the oak cupboard, and drew from its depths a rotund bottle and two little glasses, quaintly gilded.

'It's Benedictine,' he said. 'You'll have some, won't you?'

Salisbury assented, and the two men sat sipping and smoking reflectively for some minutes before Dyson began.

'Let me see,' he said at last, 'we were at the inquest, weren't we? No, we had done with that. Ah, I remember. I was telling you that on the whole I had been successful in my inquiries, investigation, or whatever you like to call it, into the matter. Wasn't that where I left off?'

'Yes, that was it. To be precise, I think "though" was the last word you said on the matter.'

'Exactly. I have been thinking it all over since the other night, and I have come to the conclusion that that "though" is a very big "though" indeed. Not to put too fine a point on it, I have had to confess that what I found out, or thought I found out, amounts in reality to nothing. I am as far away from the heart of the case as ever. However, I may as well tell you what I do know. You may remember my saying that I was impressed a good deal by some remarks of one of the doctors who gave evidence at the inquest. Well, I determined that my first step must be to try if I could get something more definite and intelligible out of that doctor. Somehow or other I managed to get an introduction to the man, and he gave me an appointment to come and see him. He turned out to be a pleasant, genial fellow; rather young and not in the least like the typical medical man, and he began the conference by offering me whisky and cigars. I didn't think it worth while to beat about the bush, so I began by saying that part of his evidence at the Harlesden Inquest struck me as very peculiar, and I gave him the printed report, with the sentences in question underlined. He just glanced at the slip, and gave me a queer look. "It struck you as peculiar, did it?" said he. "Well, you must remember that the Harlesden case was very peculiar. In fact, I think I may safely say that in some features it was unique--quite unique." "Quite so," I replied, "and that's exactly why it interests me, and why I want to know more about it. And I thought that if anybody could give me any information it would be you. What is your opinion of the matter?"

'It was a pretty downright sort of question, and my doctor looked rather taken aback.

'"Well," he said, "as I fancy your motive in inquiring into the question must be mere curiosity, I think I may tell you my opinion with tolerable freedom. So, Mr., Mr. Dyson? if you want to know my theory, it is this: I believe that Dr. Black killed his wife."

'"But the verdict," I answered, "the verdict was given from your own evidence."

'"Quite so; the verdict was given in accordance with the evidence of my colleague and myself, and, under the circumstances, I think the jury acted very sensibly. In fact, I don't see what else they could have done. But I stick to my opinion, mind you, and I say this also. I don't wonder at Black's doing what I firmly believe he did. I think he was justified."

'"Justified! How could that be?" I asked. I was astonished, as you may imagine, at the answer I had got. The doctor wheeled round his chair and looked steadily at me for a moment before he answered.

'"I suppose you are not a man of science yourself? No; then it would be of no use my going into detail. I have always been firmly opposed myself to any partnership between physiology and psychology. I believe that both are bound to suffer. No one recognizes more decidedly than I do the impassable gulf, the fathomless abyss that separates the world of consciousness from the sphere of matter. We know that every change of consciousness is accompanied by a rearrangement of the molecules in the grey matter; and that is all. What the link between them is, or why they occur together, we do not know, and most authorities believe that we never can know. Yet, I will tell you that as I did my work, the knife in my hand, I felt convinced, in spite of all theories, that what lay before me was not the brain of a dead woman--not the brain of a human being at all. Of course I saw the face; but it was quite placid, devoid of all expression. It must have been a beautiful face, no doubt, but I can honestly say that I would not have looked in that face when there was life behind it for a thousand guineas, no, nor for twice that sum."

'"My dear sir," I said, "you surprise me extremely. You say that it was not the brain of a human being. What was it then?"

'"The brain of a devil." He spoke quite coolly, and never moved a muscle. "The brain of a devil," he repeated, "and I have no doubt that Black found some way of putting an end to it. I don't blame him if he did. Whatever Mrs. Black was, she was not fit to stay in this world. Will you have anything more? No? Good-night, good-night."

'It was a queer sort of opinion to get from a man of science, wasn't it? When he was saying that he would not have looked on that face when alive for a thousand guineas, or two thousand guineas, I was thinking of the face I had seen, but I said nothing. I went again to Harlesden, and passed from one shop to another, making small purchases, and trying to find out whether there was anything about the Blacks which was not already common property, but there was very little to hear. One of the tradesmen to whom I spoke said he had known the dead woman well; she used to buy of him such quantities of grocery as were required for their small household, for they never kept a servant, but had a charwoman in occasionally, and she had not seen Mrs. Black for months before she died. According to this man Mrs. Black was "a nice lady," always kind and considerate, and so fond of her husband and he of her, as every one thought. And yet, to put the doctor's opinion on one side, I knew what I had seen. And then after thinking it all over, and putting one thing with another, it seemed to me that the only person likely to give me much assistance would be Black himself, and I made up my mind to find him. Of course he wasn't to be found in Harlesden; he had left, I was told, directly after the funeral. Everything in the house had been sold, and one fine day Black got into the train with a small portmanteau, and went, nobody knew where. It was a chance if he were ever heard of again, and it was by a mere chance that I came across him at last. I was walking one day along Gray's Inn Road, not bound for anywhere in particular, but looking about me, as usual, and holding on to my hat, for it was a gusty day in early March, and the wind was making the treetops in the Inn rock and quiver. I had come up from the Holborn end, and I had almost got to Theobald's Road when I noticed a man walking in front of me, leaning on a stick, and to all appearance very feeble. There was something about his look that made me curious, I don't know why, and I began to walk briskly with the idea of overtaking him, when of a sudden his hat blew off and came bounding along the pavement to my feet. Of course I rescued the hat, and gave it a glance as I went towards its owner. It was a biography in itself; a Piccadilly maker's name in the inside, but I don't think a beggar would have picked it out of the gutter. Then I looked up and saw Dr. Black of Harlesden waiting for me. A queer thing, wasn't it? But, Salisbury, what a change! When I saw Dr. Black come down the steps of his house at Harlesden he was an upright man, walking firmly with well-built limbs; a man, I should say, in the prime of his life. And now before me there crouched this wretched creature, bent and feeble, with shrunken cheeks, and hair that was whitening fast, and limbs that trembled and shook together, and misery in his eyes. He thanked me for bringing him his hat, saying, "I don't think I should ever have got it, I can't run much now. A gusty day, sir, isn't it?" and with this he was turning away, but by little and little I contrived to draw him into the current of conversation, and we walked together eastward. I think the man would have been glad to get rid of me; but I didn't intend to let him go, and he stopped at last in front of a miserable house in a miserable street. It was, I verily believe, one of the most wretched quarters I have ever seen: houses that must have been sordid and hideous enough when new, that had gathered foulness with every year, and now seemed to lean and totter to their fall. "I live up there," said Black, pointing to the tiles, "not in the front--in the back. I am very quiet there. I won't ask you to come in now, but perhaps some other day----" I caught him up at that, and told him I should be only too glad to come and see him. He gave me an odd sort of glance, as if he were wondering what on earth I or anybody else could care about him, and I left him fumbling with his latch-key. I think you will say I did pretty well when I tell you that within a few weeks I had made myself an intimate friend of Black's. I shall never forget the first time I went to his room; I hope I shall never see such abject, squalid misery again. The foul paper, from which all pattern or trace of a pattern had long vanished, subdued and penetrated with the grime of the evil street, was hanging in mouldering pennons from the wall. Only at the end of the room was it possible to stand upright, and the sight of the wretched bed and the odour of corruption that pervaded the place made me turn faint and sick. Here I found him munching a piece of bread; he seemed surprised to find that I had kept my promise, but he gave me his chair and sat on the bed while we talked. I used to go to see him often, and we had long conversations together, but he never mentioned Harlesden or his wife. I fancy that he supposed me ignorant of the matter, or thought that if I had heard of it, I should never connect the respectable Dr. Black of Harlesden with a poor garreteer in the backwoods of London. He was a strange man, and as we sat together smoking, I often wondered whether he were mad or sane, for I think the wildest dreams of Paracelsus and the Rosicrucians would appear plain and sober fact compared with the theories I have heard him earnestly advance in that grimy den of his. I once ventured to hint something of the sort to him. I suggested that something he had said was in flat contradiction to all science and all experience. "No," he answered, "not all experience, for mine counts for something. I am no dealer in unproved theories; what I say I have proved for myself, and at a terrible cost. There is a region of knowledge which you will never know, which wise men seeing from afar off shun like the plague, as well they may, but into that region I have gone. If you knew, if you could even dream of what may be done, of what one or two men have done in this quiet world of ours, your very soul would shudder and faint within you. What you have heard from me has been but the merest husk and outer covering of true science--that science which means death, and that which is more awful than death, to those who gain it. No, when men say that there are strange things in the world, they little know the awe and the terror that dwell always with them and about them." There was a sort of fascination about the man that drew me to him, and I was quite sorry to have to leave London for a month or two; I missed his odd talk. A few days after I came back to town I thought I would look him up, but when I gave the two rings at the bell that used to summon him, there was no answer. I rang and rang again, and was just turning to go away, when the door opened and a dirty woman asked me what I wanted. From her look I fancy she took me for a plain-clothes officer after one of her lodgers, but when I inquired if Mr. Black were in, she gave me a stare of another kind. "There's no Mr. Black lives here," she said. "He's gone. He's dead this six weeks. I always thought he was a bit queer in his head, or else had been and got into some trouble or other. He used to go out every morning from ten till one, and one Monday morning we heard him come in, and go into his room and shut the door, and a few minutes after, just as we was a-sitting down to our dinner, there was such a scream that I thought I should have gone right off. And then we heard a stamping, and down he came, raging and cursing most dreadful, swearing he had been robbed of something that was worth millions. And then he just dropped down in the passage, and we thought he was dead. We got him up to his room, and put him on his bed, and I just sat there and waited, while my 'usband he went for the doctor. And there was the winder wide open, and a little tin box he had lying on the floor open and empty, but of course nobody could possible have got in at the winder, and as for him having anything that was worth anything, it's nonsense, for he was often weeks and weeks behind with his rent, and my 'usband he threatened often and often to turn him into the street, for, as he said, we've got a living to myke like other people--and, of course, that's true; but, somehow, I didn't like to do it, though he was an odd kind of a man, and I fancy had been better off. And then the doctor came and looked at him, and said as he couldn't do nothing, and that night he died as I was a-sitting by his bed; and I can tell you that, with one thing and another, we lost money by him, for the few bits of clothes as he had were worth next to nothing when they came to be sold." I gave the woman half a sovereign for her trouble, and went home thinking of Dr. Black and the epitaph she had made him, and wondering at his strange fancy that he had been robbed. I take it that he had very little to fear on that score, poor fellow; but I suppose that he was really mad, and died in a sudden access of his mania. His landlady said that once or twice when she had had occasion to go into his room (to dun the poor wretch for his rent, most likely), he would keep her at the door for about a minute, and that when she came in she would find him putting away his tin box in the corner by the window; I suppose he had become possessed with the idea of some great treasure, and fancied himself a wealthy man in the midst of all his misery. Explicit, my tale is ended, and you see that though I knew Black, I know nothing of his wife or of the history of her death.--That's the Harlesden case, Salisbury, and I think it interests me all the more deeply because there does not seem the shadow of a possibility that I or any one else will ever know more about it. What do you think of it?'

'Well, Dyson, I must say that I think you have contrived to surround the whole thing with a mystery of your own making. I go for the doctor's solution: Black murdered his wife, being himself in all probability an undeveloped lunatic.'

'What? Do you believe, then, that this woman was something too awful, too terrible to be allowed to remain on the earth? You will remember that the doctor said it was the brain of a devil?'

'Yes, yes, but he was speaking, of course, metaphorically. It's really quite a simple matter if you only look at it like that.'

'Ah, well, you may be right; but yet I am sure you are not. Well, well, it's no good discussing it any more. A little more Benedictine? That's right; try some of this tobacco. Didn't you say that you had been bothered by something--something which happened that night we dined together?'

'Yes, I have been worried, Dyson, worried a great deal. I----But it's such a trivial matter-- indeed, such an absurdity--that I feel ashamed to trouble you with it.'

'Never mind, let's have it, absurd or not.'

With many hesitations, and with much inward resentment of the folly of the thing, Salisbury told his tale, and repeated reluctantly the absurd intelligence and the absurder doggerel of the scrap of paper, expecting to hear Dyson burst out into a roar of laughter.

'Isn't it too bad that I should let myself be bothered by such stuff as that?' he asked, when he had stuttered out the jingle of once, and twice, and thrice.

Dyson listened to it all gravely, even to the end, and meditated for a few minutes in silence.

'Yes,' he said at length, 'it was a curious chance, your taking shelter in that archway just as those two went by. But I don't know that I should call what was written on the paper nonsense; it is bizarre certainly, but I expect it has a meaning for somebody. Just repeat it again, will you, and I will write it down. Perhaps we might find a cipher of some sort, though I hardly think we shall.'

Again had the reluctant lips of Salisbury slowly to stammer out the rubbish that he abhorred, while Dyson jotted it down on a slip of paper.

'Look over it, will you?' he said, when it was done; 'it may be important that I should have every word in its place. Is that all right?'

'Yes; that is an accurate copy. But I don't think you will get much out of it. Depend upon it, it is mere nonsense, a wanton scribble. I must be going now, Dyson. No, no more; that stuff of yours is pretty strong. Good-night.'

'I suppose you would like to hear from me, if I did find out anything?'

'No, not I; I don't want to hear about the thing again. You may regard the discovery, if it is one, as your own.'

'Very well. Good-night.'

IV

A good many hours after Salisbury had returned to the company of the green rep chairs, Dyson still sat at his desk, itself a Japanese romance, smoking many pipes, and meditating over his friend's story. The bizarre quality of the inscription which had annoyed Salisbury was to him an attraction, and now and again he took it up and scanned thoughtfully what he had written, especially the quaint jingle at the end. It was a token, a symbol, he decided, and not a cipher, and the woman who had flung it away was in all probability entirely ignorant of its meaning; she was but the agent of the 'Sam' she had abused and discarded, and he too was again the agent of some one unknown, possibly of the individual styled Q, who had been forced to visit his French friends. But what to make of 'Traverse Handle S.' Here was the root and source of the enigma, and not all the tobacco of Virginia seemed likely to suggest any clue here. It seemed almost hopeless, but Dyson regarded himself as the Wellington of mysteries, and went to bed feeling assured that sooner or later he would hit upon the right track For the next few days he was deeply engaged in his literary labours, labours which were a profound mystery even to the most intimate of his friends, who searched the railway bookstalls in vain for the result of so many hours spent at the Japanese bureau in company with strong tobacco and black tea. On this occasion Dyson confined himself to his room for four days, and it was with genuine relief that he laid down his pen and went out into the streets in quest of relaxation and fresh air. The gas-lamps were being lighted, and the fifth edition of the evening papers was being howled through the streets, and Dyson, feeling that he wanted quiet, turned away from the clamorous Strand, and began to trend away to the north-west. Soon he found himself in streets that echoed to his footsteps, and crossing a broad new thoroughfare, and verging still to the west, Dyson discovered that he had penetrated to the depths of Soho. Here again was life; rare vintages of France and Italy, at prices which seemed contemptibly small, allured the passer-by; here were cheeses, vast and rich, here olive oil, and here a grove of Rabelaisian sausages; while in a neighbouring shop the whole Press of Paris appeared to be on sale. In the middle of the roadway a strange miscellany of nations sauntered to and fro, for there cab and hansom rarely ventured; and from window over window the inhabitants looked forth in pleased contemplation of the scene. Dyson made his way slowly along, mingling with the crowd on the cobble-stones, listening to the queer babel of French and German, and Italian and English, glancing now and again at the shop-windows with their levelled batteries of bottles, and had almost gained the end of the street, when his attention was arrested by a small shop at the corner, a vivid contrast to its neighbours. It was the typical shop of the poor quarter; a shop entirely English. Here were vended tobacco and sweets, cheap pipes of clay and cherry-wood; penny exercise-books and penholders jostled for precedence with comic songs, and story papers with appalling cuts showed that romance claimed its place beside the actualities of the evening paper, the bills of which fluttered at the doorway. Dyson glanced up at the name above the door, and stood by the kennel trembling, for a sharp pang, the pang of one who has made a discovery, had for a moment left him incapable of motion. The name over the shop was Travers. Dyson looked up again, this time at the corner of the wall above the lamp-post, and read in white letters on a blue ground the words 'Handel Street, W. C.,' and the legend was repeated in fainter letters just below. He gave a little sigh of satisfaction, and without more ado walked boldly into the shop, and stared full in the face the fat man who was sitting behind the counter. The fellow rose to his feet, and returned the stare a little curiously, and then began in stereotyped phrase--

'What can I do for you, sir?'

Dyson enjoyed the situation and a dawning perplexity on the man's face. He propped his stick carefully against the counter and leaning over it, said slowly and impressively--

'Once around the grass, and twice around the lass, and thrice around the maple-tree.'

Dyson had calculated on his words producing an effect, and he was not disappointed. The vendor of miscellanies gasped, open-mouthed like a fish, and steadied himself against the counter. When he spoke, after a short interval, it was in a hoarse mutter, tremulous and unsteady.

'Would you mind saying that again, sir? I didn't quite catch it.'

'My good man, I shall most certainly do nothing of the kind. You heard what I said perfectly well. You have got a clock in your shop, I see; an admirable timekeeper, I have no doubt. Well, I give you a minute by your own clock.'

The man looked about him in a perplexed indecision, and Dyson felt that it was time to be bold.

'Look here, Travers, the time is nearly up. You have heard of Q, I think. Remember, I hold your life in my hands. Now!'

Dyson was shocked at the result of his own audacity. The man shrank and shrivelled in terror, the sweat poured down a face of ashy white, and he held up his hands before him.

'Mr. Davies, Mr. Davies, don't say that--don't for Heaven's sake. I didn't know you at first, I didn't indeed. Good God! Mr. Davies, you wouldn't ruin me? I'll get it in a moment.'

'You had better not lose any more time.'

The man slunk piteously out of his own shop, and went into a back parlour. Dyson heard his trembling fingers fumbling with a bunch of keys, and the creak of an opening box. He came back presently with a small package neatly tied up in brown paper in his hands, and, still full of terror, handed it to Dyson.

'I'm glad to be rid of it,' he said. 'I'll take no more jobs of this sort.'

Dyson took the parcel and his stick, and walked out of the shop with a nod, turning round as he passed the door. Travers had sunk into his seat, his face still white with terror, with one hand over his eyes, and Dyson speculated a good deal as he walked rapidly away as to what queer chords those could be on which he had played so roughly. He hailed the first hansom he could see and drove home, and when he had lit his hanging lamp, and laid his parcel on the table, he paused for a moment, wondering on what strange thing the lamplight would soon shine. He locked his door, and cut the strings, and unfolded the paper layer after layer, and came at last to a small wooden box, simply but solidly made. There was no lock, and Dyson had simply to raise the lid, and as he did so he drew a long breath and started back. The lamp seemed to glimmer feebly like a single candle, but the whole room blazed with light--and not with light alone, but with a thousand colours, with all the glories of some painted window; and upon the walls of his room and on the familiar furniture, the glow flamed back and seemed to flow again to its source, the little wooden box. For there upon a bed of soft wool lay the most splendid jewel, a jewel such as Dyson had never dreamed of, and within it shone the blue of far skies, and the green of the sea by the shore, and the red of the ruby, and deep violet rays, and in the middle of all it seemed aflame as if a fountain of fire rose up, and fell, and rose again with sparks like stars for drops. Dyson gave a long deep sigh, and dropped into his chair, and put his hands over his eyes to think. The jewel was like an opal, but from a long experience of the shop-windows he knew there was no such thing as an opal one-quarter or one-eighth of its size. He looked at the stone again, with a feeling that was almost awe, and placed it gently on the table under the lamp, and watched the wonderful flame that shone and sparkled in its centre, and then turned to the box, curious to know whether it might contain other marvels. He lifted the bed of wool on which the opal had reclined, and saw beneath, no more jewels, but a little old pocket-book, worn and shabby with use. Dyson opened it at the first leaf, and dropped the book again appalled. He had read the name of the owner, neatly written in blue ink:

STEVEN BLACK, M. D.,
Oranmore,
Devon Road,
Harlesden.

It was several minutes before Dyson could bring himself to open the book a second time; he remembered the wretched exile in his garret; and his strange talk, and the memory too of the face he had seen at the window, and of what the specialist had said, surged up in his mind, and as he held his finger on the cover, he shivered, dreading what might be written within. When at last he held it in his hand, and turned the pages, he found that the first two leaves were blank, but the third was covered with clear, minute writing, and Dyson began to read with the light of the opal flaming in his eyes.

V

'Ever since I was a young man'--the record began--'I devoted all my leisure and a good deal of time that ought to have been given to other studies to the investigation of curious and obscure branches of knowledge. What are commonly called the pleasures of life had never any attractions for me, and I lived alone in London, avoiding my fellow-students, and in my turn avoided by them as a man self-absorbed and unsympathetic. So long as I could gratify my desire of knowledge of a peculiar kind, knowledge of which the very existence is a profound secret to most men, I was intensely happy, and I have often spent whole nights sitting in the darkness of my room, and thinking of the strange world on the brink of which I trod. My professional studies, however, and the necessity of obtaining a degree, for some time forced my more obscure employment into the background, and soon after I had qualified I met Agnes, who became my wife. We took a new house in this remote suburb, and I began the regular routine of a sober practice, and for some months lived happily enough, sharing in the life about me, and only thinking at odd intervals of that occult science which had once fascinated my whole being. I had learnt enough of the paths I had begun to tread to know that they were beyond all expression difficult and dangerous, that to persevere meant in all probability the wreck of a life, and that they led to regions so terrible, that the mind of man shrinks appalled at the very thought. Moreover, the quiet and the peace I had enjoyed since my marriage had wiled me away to a great extent from places where I knew no peace could dwell. But suddenly--I think indeed it was the work of a single night, as I lay awake on my bed gazing into the darkness--suddenly, I say, the old desire, the former longing, returned, and returned with a force that had been intensified ten times by its absence; and when the day dawned and I looked out of the window, and saw with haggard eyes the sunrise in the east, I knew that my doom had been pronounced; that as I had gone far, so now I must go farther with unfaltering steps. I turned to the bed where my wife was sleeping peacefully, and lay down again, weeping bitter tears, for the sun had set on our happy life and had risen with a dawn of terror to us both. I will not set down here in minute detail what followed; outwardly I went about the day's labour as before, saying nothing to my wife. But she soon saw that I had changed; I spent my spare time in a room which I had fitted up as a laboratory, and often I crept upstairs in the grey dawn of the morning, when the light of many lamps still glowed over London; and each night I had stolen a step nearer to that great abyss which I was to bridge over, the gulf between the world of consciousness and the world of matter. My experiments were many and complicated in their nature, and it was some months before I realized whither they all pointed, and when this was borne in upon me in a moment's time, I felt my face whiten and my heart still within me. But the power to draw back, the power to stand before the doors that now opened wide before me and not to enter in, had long ago been absent; the way was closed, and I could only pass onward. My position was as utterly hopeless as that of the prisoner in an utter dungeon, whose only light is that of the dungeon above him; the doors were shut and escape was impossible. Experiment after experiment gave the same result, and I knew, and shrank even as the thought passed through my mind, that in the work I had to do there must be elements which no laboratory could furnish, which no scales could ever measure. In that work, from which even I doubted to escape with life, life itself must enter; from some human being there must be drawn that essence which men call the soul, and in its place (for in the scheme of the world there is no vacant chamber)--in its place would enter in what the lips can hardly utter, what the mind cannot conceive without a horror more awful than the horror of death itself. And when I knew this, I knew also on whom this fate would fall; I looked into my wife's eyes. Even at that hour, if I had gone out and taken a rope and hanged myself, I might have escaped, and she also, but in no other way. At last I told her all. She shuddered, and wept, and called on her dead mother for help, and asked me if I had no mercy, and I could only sigh. I concealed nothing from her; I told her what she would become, and what would enter in where her life had been; I told her of all the shame and of all the horror. You who will read this when I am dead--if indeed I allow this record to survive,--you who have opened the box and have seen what lies there, if you could understand what lies hidden in that opal! For one night my wife consented to what I asked of her, consented with the tears running down her beautiful face, and hot shame flushing red over her neck and breast, consented to undergo this for me. I threw open the window, and we looked together at the sky and the dark earth for the last time; it was a fine star-light night, and there was a pleasant breeze blowing, and I kissed her on her lips, and her tears ran down upon my face. That night she came down to my laboratory, and there, with shutters bolted and barred down, with curtains drawn thick and close, so that the very stars might be shut out from the sight of that room, while the crucible hissed and boiled over the lamp, I did what had to be done, and led out what was no longer a woman. But on the table the opal flamed and sparkled with such light as no eyes of man have ever gazed on, and the rays of the flame that was within it flashed and glittered, and shone even to my heart. My wife had only asked one thing of me; that when there came at last what I had told her, I would kill her. I have kept that promise.'

***

There was nothing more. Dyson let the little pocket-book fall, and turned and looked again at the opal with its flaming inmost light, and then with unutterable irresistible horror surging up in his heart, grasped the jewel, and flung it on the ground, and trampled it beneath his heel. His face was white with terror as he turned away, and for a moment stood sick and trembling, and then with a start he leapt across the room and steadied himself against the door. There was an angry hiss, as of steam escaping under great pressure, and as he gazed, motionless, a volume of heavy yellow smoke was slowly issuing from the very centre of the jewel, and wreathing itself in snake-like coils above it. And then a thin white flame burst forth from the smoke, and shot up into the air and vanished; and on the ground there lay a thing like a cinder, black and crumbling to the touch.

THE THREE IMPOSTORS

or The Transmutations

TRANSLATOR OF 'L'HEPTAMERON' AND 'LE MOYEN DE PARVENIR';
AUTHOR OF 'THE CHRONICLE OF CLEMENDY' AND 'THE GREAT GOD PAN'

BOSTON: Roberts Bros, 1895
LONDON: John Lane, Vigo st.

PROLOGUE

"And Mr. Joseph Walters is going to stay the night?" said the smooth clean-shaven man to his companion, an individual not of the most charming appearance, who had chosen to make his ginger-colored mustache merge into a pair of short chin-whiskers.

The two stood at the hall door, grinning evilly at each other; and presently a girl ran quickly down, the stairs, and joined them. She was quite young, with a quaint and piquant rather than a beautiful face, and her eyes were of a shining hazel. She held a neat paper parcel in one hand, and laughed with her friends.

"Leave the door open," said the smooth man to the other, as they were going out. "Yes, by----," he went on with an ugly oath. "We'll leave the front door on the jar. He may like to see company, you know."

The other man looked doubtfully about him. "Is it quite prudent do you think, Davies?" he said, pausing with his hand on the mouldering knocker. "I don't think Lipsius would like it. What do you say, Helen?"

"I agree with Davies. Davies is an artist, and you are commonplace, Richmond, and a bit of a coward. Let the door stand open, of course. But what a pity Lipsius had to go away! He would have enjoyed himself."

"Yes," replied the smooth Mr. Davies, "that summons to the west was very hard on the doctor."

The three passed out, leaving the hall door, cracked and riven with frost and wet, half open, and they stood silent for a moment under the ruinous shelter of the porch.

"Well," said the girl, "it is done at last. I shall hurry no more on the track of the young man with spectacles."

"We owe a great deal to you," said Mr. Davies politely; "the doctor said so before he left. But have we not all three some farewells to make? I, for my part, propose to say good-by, here, before this picturesque but mouldy residence, to my friend Mr. Burton, dealer in the antique and curious," and the man lifted his hat with an exaggerated bow.

"And I," said Richmond, "bid adieu to Mr. Wilkins, the private secretary, whose company has, I confess, become a little tedious."

"Farewell to Miss Lally, and to Miss Leicester also," said the girl, making as she spoke a delicious courtesy. "Farewell to all occult adventure; the farce is played."

Mr. Davies and the lady seemed full of grim enjoyment, but Richmond tugged at his whiskers nervously.

"I feel a bit shaken up," he said. "I've seen rougher things in the States, but that crying noise he made gave me a sickish feeling. And then the smell--But my stomach was never very strong."

The three friends moved away from the door, and began to walk slowly up and down what had been a gravel path, but now lay green and pulpy with damp mosses. It was a fine autumn evening, and a faint sunlight shone on the yellow walls of the old deserted house, and showed the patches of gangrenous decay, and all the stains, the black drift of rain from the broken pipes, the scabrous blots where the bare bricks were exposed, the green weeping of a gaunt laburnum that stood beside the porch, and ragged marks near the ground where the reeking clay was gaining on the worn foundations. It was a queer rambling old place, the centre perhaps two hundred years old, with dormer windows sloping from the tiled roof, and on each side there were Georgian wings; bow windows had been carried up to the first floor, and two dome-like cupolas that had once been painted a bright green were now gray and neutral. Broken urns lay upon the path, and a heavy mist seemed to rise from the unctuous clay; the neglected shrubberies, grown all tangled and unshapen, smelt dank and evil, and there was an atmosphere all about the deserted mansion that proposed thoughts of an opened grave. The three friends looked dismally at the rough grasses and the nettles that grew thick over lawn and flower-beds; and at the sad water-pool in the midst of the weeds. There, above green and oily scum instead of lilies, stood a rusting Triton on the rocks, sounding a dirge through a shattered horn; and beyond, beyond the sunk fence and the far meadows; the sun slid down and shone red through the bars of the elm trees.

Richmond shivered and stamped his foot. "We had better be going soon," he said; "there is nothing else to be done here."

"No," said Davies, "it is finished at last. I thought for some time we should never get hold of the gentleman with the spectacles. He was a clever fellow, but, Lord! he broke up badly at last. I can tell you he looked white at me when I touched him on the arm in the bar. But where could he have hidden the thing? We can all swear it was not on him."

The girl laughed, and they turned away, when Richmond gave a violent start. "Ah!" he cried, turning to the girl, "what have you got there? Look, Davies, look! it's all oozing and dripping."

The young woman glanced down at the little parcel she was carrying, and partially unfolded the paper.

"Yes, look both of you," she said; "it's my own idea. Don't you think it will do nicely for the doctor's museum? It comes from the right hand, the hand that took the gold Tiberius."

Mr. Davies nodded with a good deal of approbation, and Richmond lifted his ugly high-crowned bowler, and wiped his forehead with a dingy handkerchief.

"I'm going," he said; "you two can stay if you like."

The three went round by the stable path, past the withered wilderness of the old kitchen garden, and struck off by a hedge at the back, making for a particular point in the road. About five minutes later two gentlemen, whom idleness had led to explore these forgotten outskirts of London, came sauntering up the shadowy carriage drive. They had spied the deserted house from the road, and as they observed all the heavy desolation of the place they began to moralize in the great style, with considerable debts to Jeremy Taylor.

"Look, Dyson," said the one as they drew nearer, "look at those upper windows; the sun is setting, and though the panes are dusty, yet

> *"The grimy sash an oriel burns."*

"Phillipps," replied the elder and (it must be said) the more pompous of the two, "I yield to fantasy, I cannot withstand the influence of the grotesque. Here, where all is falling into dimness and dissolution, and we walk in cedarn gloom, and the very air of heaven goes mouldering to the lungs, I cannot remain commonplace. I look at that deep glow on the panes, and the house lies all enchanted; that very room, I tell you, is within all blood and fire."

ADVENTURE OF THE GOLD TIBERIUS

The acquaintance between Mr. Dyson and Mr. Charles Phillipps arose from one of those myriad chances which are every day doing their work in the streets of London. Mr. Dyson was a man of letters, and an unhappy instance of talents misapplied. With gifts that might have placed him in the flower of his youth among the most favored of Bentley's favorite novelists, he had chosen to be perverse; he was, it is true, familiar with scholastic logic, but he knew nothing of the logic of life, and he flattered himself with the title of artist, when he was in fact but an idle and curious spectator of other men's endeavors. Amongst many delusions, he cherished one most fondly, that he was a strenuous worker; and it was with a gesture of supreme weariness that he would enter his favorite resort, a small tobacco shop in Great Queen Street, and proclaim to any one who cared to listen that he had seen the rising and setting of two successive suns. The proprietor of the shop, a middle-aged man of singular civility, tolerated Dyson partly out of good nature, and partly because he was a regular customer; he was allowed to sit on an empty cask, and to express his sentiments on literary and artistic matters till he was tired or the time for closing came; and if no fresh customers were attracted, it is believed that none were turned away by his eloquence. Dyson, was addicted to wild experiments in tobacco; he never wearied of trying new combinations, and one evening he had just entered the shop and given utterance to his last preposterous formula, when a young fellow, of about his own age, who had come in a moment later, asked the shopman to duplicate the order on his account, smiling politely, as he spoke, to Mr. Dyson's address. Dyson felt profoundly flattered, and after a few phrases the two entered into conversation, and in an hour's time the tobacconist saw the new friends sitting side by side on a couple of casks, deep in talk.

"My dear sir," said Dyson, "I will give you the task of the literary man in a phrase. He has got to do simply this: to invent a wonderful story, and to tell it in a wonderful manner."

"I will grant you that," said Mr. Phillipps, "but you will allow me to insist that in the hands of the true artist in words all stories are marvellous, and every circumstance has its peculiar wonder. The matter is of little consequence, the manner is everything. Indeed, the highest skill is shown in taking matter apparently commonplace and transmuting it by the high alchemy of style into the pure gold of art."

"That is indeed a proof of great skill, but it is great skill exerted foolishly, or at least unadvisedly. It is as if a great violinist were to show us what marvellous harmonies he could draw from a child's banjo."

"No, no, you are really wrong. I see you take a radically mistaken view of life. But we must thresh this out. Come to my rooms; I live not far from here."

It was thus that Mr. Dyson became the associate of Mr. Charles Phillipps, who lived in a quiet square not far from Holborn. Thenceforth they haunted each other's rooms at intervals, sometimes regular, and occasionally the reverse, and made appointments to meet at the shop in Queen Street, where their talk robbed the tobacconist's profit of half its charm. There was a constant jarring of literary formulas, Dyson exalting the claims of the pure imagination, while Phillipps, who was a student of physical science and something of an ethnologist, insisted that all literature ought to have a scientific basis. By the mistaken benevolence of deceased relatives both young men were placed out of reach of hunger, and so, meditating high achievements, idled their time pleasantly away, and revelled in the careless joys of a Bohemianism devoid of the sharp seasoning of adversity.

One night in June Mr. Phillipps was sitting in his room in the calm retirement of Red Lion Square. He had opened the window, and was smoking placidly, while he watched the movement of life below. The sky was clear, and the afterglow of sunset had lingered long about it; and the flushing twilight of a summer evening, vying with the gas-lamps in the square, had fashioned a chiaroscuro that had in it something unearthly; and the children, racing to and fro upon the pavement, the lounging idlers by the public, and the casual passers-by rather flickered, and hovered in the play of lights than stood out substantial things. By degrees in the houses opposite one window after another leaped out a square of light, now and again a figure would shape itself against a blind and vanish, and to all this semi-theatrical magic the runs and flourishes of brave Italian opera played a little distance off on a piano-organ seemed an appropriate accompaniment, while the deep-muttered bass of the traffic of Holborn never ceased. Phillipps enjoyed the scene and its effects; the light in the sky faded and turned to darkness, and the square gradually grew silent, and still he sat dreaming at the window, till the sharp peal of the house bell roused him, and looking at his watch he found that it was past ten o'clock. There was a knock at the door, and his friend Mr. Dyson entered, and, according to his custom, sat down in an armchair and began to smoke in silence.

"You know, Phillipps," he said at length, "that I have always battled for the marvellous. I remember your maintaining in that chair that one has no business to make use of the wonderful, the improbable, the odd coincidence in literature, and you took the ground that it was wrong to do so, because, as a matter of fact, the wonderful and the improbable don't happen, and men's lives are not really shaped by odd coincidence. Now, mind you, if that were so, I would not grant your conclusion, because I think the "criticism-of-life" theory is all nonsense; but I deny your premise. A most singular thing has happened to me to-night."

"Really, Dyson, I am very glad to hear it. Of course I oppose your argument, whatever it may be; but if you would be good enough to tell me of your adventure I should be delighted."

"Well, it came about like this. I have had a very hard day's work; indeed, I have scarcely moved from my old bureau since seven o'clock last night. I wanted to work out that idea we discussed last Tuesday, you know, the notion of the fetish-worshipper."

"Yes, I remember. Have you been able to do anything with it?"

"Yes; it came out better than I expected; but there were great difficulties, the usual agony between the conception and the execution. Anyhow I got it done at about seven o'clock to-night, and I thought I should like a little of the fresh air. I went out and wandered rather aimlessly about the streets; my head was full of my tale, and I didn't much notice where I was going. I got into those quiet places to the north of Oxford Street as you go west, the genteel residential neighborhood of stucco and prosperity. I turned east again without knowing it, and it was quite dark when I passed along a sombre little by-street, ill lighted and empty. I did not know at the time in the least where I was, but I found out afterwards that it was not very far from Tottenham Court Road. I strolled idly along, enjoying the stillness; on one side there seemed to be the back premises of some great shop; tier after tier of dusty windows lifted up into the night, with gibbet-like contrivances for raising heavy goods, and below large doors, fast closed and bolted, all dark and desolate. Then there came a huge pantechnicon warehouse; and over the way a grim blank wall, as forbidding as the wall of a jail, and then the headquarters of some volunteer regiment, and afterwards a passage leading to a court where wagons were standing to be hired. It was, one might almost say, a street devoid of inhabitants, and scarce a window showed the glimmer of a light. I was wondering at the strange peace and dimness there, where it must be close to some roaring main artery of London life, when suddenly I heard the noise of dashing feet tearing along the pavement at full speed, and from a narrow passage, a mews or something of that kind, a man was discharged as from a catapult under my very nose and rushed past me, flinging something from him as he ran. He was gone and down another street in an instant, almost before I knew what had happened, but I didn't much bother about him, I was watching something else. I told you he had thrown something away; well, I watched what seemed a line of flame flash through the air and fly quivering over the pavement, and in spite of myself I could not help tearing after it. The impetus lessened, and I saw something like a bright half-penny roll slower and slower, and then deflect towards the gutter, hover for a moment on the edge, and dance down into a drain. I believe I cried out in positive despair, though I hadn't the least notion what I was hunting; and then to my joy I saw that, instead of dropping into the sewer, it had fallen flat across two bars. I stooped down and picked it up and whipped it into my pocket, and I was just about to walk on when I heard again that sound of dashing footsteps. I don't know why I did it, but as a matter of fact I dived down into the mews, or whatever it was, and stood as much in the shadow as possible. A man went by with a rush a few paces from where I was standing, and I felt uncommonly pleased that I was in hiding. I couldn't make out much feature, but I saw his eyes gleaming and his teeth showing, and he had an ugly-looking knife in one hand, and I thought things would be very unpleasant for gentleman number one if the second robber, or robbed, or what you like, caught him up. I can tell you, Phillipps, a fox hunt is exciting enough, when the horn blows clear on a winter morning, and the hounds give tongue, and the red-coats charge away, but it's nothing to a man hunt, and that's what I had a slight glimpse of to-night. There was murder in the fellow's eyes as he went by, and I don't think there was much more than fifty seconds between the two. I only hope it was enough."

Dyson leant back in his armchair and relit his pipe, and puffed thoughtfully. Phillipps began to walk up and down the room, musing over the story of violent death fleeting in chase along the pavement, the knife shining in the lamplight, the fury of the pursuer, and the terror of the pursued.

"Well," he said at last, "and what was it, after all, that you rescued from the gutter?"

Dyson jumped up, evidently quite startled. "I really haven't a notion. I didn't think of looking. But we shall see."

He fumbled in his waistcoat pocket and drew out a small and shining object, and laid it on the table. It glowed there beneath the lamp with the radiant glory of rare old gold; and the image and the letters stood out in high relief, clear and sharp, as if it had but left the mint a month before. The two men bent over it, and Phillipps took it up and examined it closely.

"Imp. Tiberius Cæsar Augustus," he read the legend, and then, looking at the reverse of the coin, he stared in amazement, and at last turned to Dyson with a look of exultation.

"Do you know what you have found?" he said.

"Apparently a gold coin of some antiquity," said Dyson, coolly.

"Quite so, a gold Tiberius. No, that is wrong. You have found the gold Tiberius. Look at the reverse."

Dyson looked and saw the coin was stamped with the figure of a faun standing amidst reeds and flowing water. The features, minute as they were, stood out in delicate outline; it was a face lovely and yet terrible, and Dyson thought of the well-known passage of the lad's playmate, gradually growing with his growth and increasing with his stature, till the air was filled with the rank fume of the goat.

"Yes," he said, "it is a curious coin. Do you know it?"

"I know about it. It is one of the comparatively few historical objects in existence; it is all storied like those jewels we have read of. A whole cycle of legend has gathered round the thing; the tale goes that it formed part of an issue struck by Tiberius to commemorate an infamous excess. You see the legend on the reverse: 'Victoria.' It is said that by an extraordinary accident the whole issue was thrown into the melting pot, and that only this one coin escaped. It glints through history and legend, appearing and disappearing, with intervals of a hundred years in time and continents in place. It was discovered by an Italian humanist, and lost and rediscovered. It has not been heard of since 1727, when Sir Joshua Byrde, a Turkey merchant, brought it home from Aleppo, and vanished with it a month after he had shown it to the virtuosi, no man knew or knows where. And here it is!"

"Put it into your pocket, Dyson," he said, after a pause. "I would not let any one have a glimpse of the thing, if I were you. I would not talk about it. Did either of the men you saw see you?"

"Well, I think not. I don't think the first man, the man who was vomited out of the dark passage, saw anything at all; and I am sure that the second could not have seen me."

"And you didn't really see them. You couldn't recognize either the one or the other if you met him in the street to-morrow?"

"No, I don't think I could. The street, as I said, was dimly lighted, and they ran like mad-men."

The two men sat silent for some time, each weaving his own fancies of the story; but lust of the marvellous was slowly overpowering Dyson's more sober thoughts.

"It is all more strange than I fancied," he said at last. "It was queer enough what I saw; a man is sauntering along a quiet, sober, every-day London street, a street of gray houses and blank walls, and there, for a moment, a veil seems drawn aside, and the very fume of the pit steams up through the flagstones, the ground glows, red hot, beneath his feet, and he seems to hear the hiss of the infernal caldron. A man flying in mad terror for his life, and furious hate pressing hot on his steps with knife drawn ready; here indeed is horror. But what is all that to what you have told me? I tell you, Phillipps, I see the plot thicken, our steps will henceforth be dogged with mystery, and the most ordinary incidents will teem with significance. You may stand out against it, and shut your eyes, but they will be forced open; mark my words, you will have to yield to the inevitable. A clue, tangled if you like, has been placed by chance in our hands; it will be our business to follow it up. As for the guilty person or persons in this strange case, they will be unable to escape us, our nets will be spread far and wide over this great city, and suddenly, in the streets and places of public resort, we shall in some way or other be made aware that we are in touch with the unknown criminal. Indeed, I almost fancy I see him slowly approaching this quiet square of yours; he is loitering at street corners, wandering, apparently without aim, down far-reaching thoroughfares, but all the while coming nearer and nearer, drawn by an irresistible magnetism, as ships were drawn to the Loadstone Rock in the Eastern tale."

"I certainly think," replied Phillipps, "that, if you pull out that coin and flourish it under people's noses as you are doing at the present moment, you will very probably find yourself in touch with the criminal, or a criminal. You will undoubtedly be robbed with violence. Otherwise, I see no reason why either of us should be troubled. No one saw you secure the coin, and no one knows you have it. I, for my part, shall sleep peacefully, and go about my business with a sense of security and a firm dependence on the natural order of things. The events of the evening, the adventure in the street, have been odd, I grant you, but I resolutely decline to have any more to do with the matter, and, if necessary, I shall consult the police. I will not be enslaved by a gold Tiberius, even though it swims into my ken in a manner which is somewhat melodramatic."

"And I for my part," said Dyson, "go forth like a knight-errant in search of adventure. Not that I shall need to seek; rather adventure will seek me; I shall be like a spider in the midst of his web, responsive to every movement, and ever on the alert."

Shortly afterwards Dyson took his leave, and Mr. Phillipps spent the rest of the night in examining some flint arrow-heads which he had purchased. He had every reason to believe that they were the work of a modern and not a palæolithic man, still he was far from gratified when a close scrutiny showed him that his suspicions were well founded. In his anger at the turpitude which would impose on an ethnologist, he completely forgot Dyson and the gold Tiberius; and when he went to bed at first sunlight, the whole tale had faded utterly from his thoughts.

THE ENCOUNTER OF THE PAVEMENT

Mr. Dyson, walking leisurely along Oxford. Street, and staring with bland inquiry at whatever caught his attention, enjoyed in all its rare flavors the sensation that he was really very hard at work. His observation of mankind, the traffic, and the shop-windows tickled his faculties with an exquisite bouquet; he looked serious, as one looks on whom charges of weight and moment are laid, and he was attentive in his glances to right and left, for fear lest he should miss some circumstance of more acute significance. He had narrowly escaped being run over at a crossing by a charging van, for he hated to hurry his steps, and indeed the afternoon was warm; and he had just halted by a place of popular refreshment, when the astounding gestures of a well dressed individual on the opposite pavement held him enchanted and gasping like a fish. A treble line of hansoms, carriages, vans, cabs, and omnibuses, was tearing east and west, and not the most daring adventurer of the crossings would have cared to try his fortune; but the person who had attracted Dyson's attention seemed to rage on the very edge of the pavement, now and then darting forward at the hazard of instant death, and at each repulse absolutely dancing with excitement, to the rich amusement of the passers-by. At last, a gap that would, have tried the courage of a street-boy appeared between the serried lines of vehicles, and the man rushed across in a frenzy, and escaping by a hair's breadth pounced upon Dyson as a tiger pounces on her prey. "I saw you looking about you," he said, sputtering out his words in his intense eagerness; "would you mind telling me this? Was the man who came out of the Aerated Bread Shop and jumped, into the hansom three minutes ago a youngish looking man with dark whiskers and spectacles? Can't you speak, man? For Heaven's sake can't you speak? Answer me; it's a matter of life and death."

The words bubbled and boiled out of the man's mouth in the fury of his emotion, his face went from red to white, and the beads of sweat stood out on his forehead, and he stamped his feet as he spoke and tore with his hand at his coat, as if something swelled and choked him, stopping the passage of his breath.

"My dear sir," said Dyson, "I always like to be accurate. Your observation was perfectly correct. As you say, a youngish man, a man, I should say, of somewhat timid bearing, ran rapidly out of the shop here, and bounced into a hansom that must have been waiting for him, as it went eastwards at once. Your friend also wore spectacles, as you say. Perhaps you would like me to call a hansom for you to follow the gentleman?"

"No, thank you; it would be waste of time." The man gulped down something which appeared to rise in his throat, and Dyson was alarmed to see him shaking with hysterical laughter, and he clung hard to a lamp-post and swayed and staggered like a ship in a heavy gale.

"How shall I face the doctor?" he murmured to himself. "It is too hard to fail at the last moment." Then he seemed to recollect himself, and stood straight again, and looked quietly at Dyson. I owe you an apology for my violence, he said at last. "Many men would not be so patient as you have been. Would you mind adding to your kindness by walking with me a little way? I feel a little sick; I think it's the sun."

Dyson nodded assent, and devoted himself to a quiet scrutiny of this strange personage as they moved on together. The man was dressed in quiet taste, and the most scrupulous observer could find nothing amiss with the fashion or make of his clothes, yet, from his hat to his boots, everything seemed inappropriate. His silk hat, Dyson thought, should have been a high bowler of odious pattern worn with a baggy morning-coat, and an instinct told him that the fellow did not commonly carry a clean pocket-handkerchief. The face was not of the most agreeable pattern, and was in no way improved by a pair of bulbous chin-whiskers of a ginger hue, into which mustaches of light color merged imperceptibly. Yet in spite of these signals hung out by nature, Dyson felt that the individual beside him was something more than compact of vulgarity. He was struggling with himself, holding his feelings in check, but now and again passion would mount black to his face, and it was evidently by a supreme effort that he kept himself from raging like a madman. Dyson found something curious and a little terrible in the spectacle of an occult emotion thus striving for the mastery, and threatening to break out at every instant with violence, and they had gone some distance before the person whom he had met by so odd a hazard was able to speak quietly.

"You are really very good," he said. "I apologize again; my rudeness was really most unjustifiable. I feel my conduct demands an explanation, and I shall be happy to give it you. Do you happen to know of any place near here where one could sit down? I should really be very glad."

"My dear sir," said Dyson, solemnly, "the only café in London is close by. Pray do not consider yourself as bound to offer me any explanation, but at the same time I should be most happy to listen to you. Let us turn down here."

They walked down a sober street and turned into what seemed a narrow passage past an iron-barred gate thrown back. The passage was paved with flagstones, and decorated with handsome shrubs in pots on either side, and the shadow of the high walls made a coolness which was very agreeable after the hot breath of the sunny street. Presently the passage opened out into a tiny square, a charming place, a morsel of France transplanted into the heart of London. High walls rose on either side, covered with glossy creepers, flower-beds beneath were gay with nasturtiums, geraniums, and marigolds, and odorous with mignonette, and in the centre of the square a fountain hidden by greenery sent a cool shower continually plashing into the basin beneath, and the very noise made this retreat delightful. Chairs and tables were disposed at convenient intervals, and at the other end of the court broad doors had been thrown back; beyond was a long, dark room, and the turmoil of traffic had become a distant murmur. Within the room one or two men were sitting at the tables, writing and sipping, but the courtyard was empty.

"You see, we shall be quiet," said Dyson. "Pray sit down here, Mr.--?"

"Wilkins. My name is Henry Wilkins."

"Sit here, Mr. Wilkins. I think you will find that a comfortable seat. I suppose you have not been here before? This is the quiet time; the place will be like a hive at six o'clock, and the chairs and tables will overflow into that little alley there."

A waiter came in response to the bell; and after Dyson had politely inquired after the health of M. Annibault, the proprietor, he ordered a bottle of the wine of Champigny.

"The wine of Champigny," he observed to Mr. Wilkins, who was evidently a good deal composed by the influence of the place, "is a Tourainian wine of great merit. Ah, here it is; let me fill your glass. How do you find it?"

"Indeed," said Mr. Wilkins, "I should have pronounced it a fine Burgundy. The bouquet is very exquisite. I am fortunate in lighting upon such a good Samaritan as yourself. I wonder you did not think me mad. But if you knew the terrors that assailed me, I am sure you would no longer be surprised at conduct which was certainly most unjustifiable."

He sipped his wine, and leant back in his chair, relishing the drip and trickle of the fountain, and the cool greenness that hedged in this little port of refuge.

"Yes," he said at last, "that is indeed an admirable wine. Thank you; you will allow me to offer you another bottle?"

The waiter was summoned, and descended through a trap-door in the floor of the dark apartment, and brought up the wine. Mr. Wilkins lit a cigarette, and Dyson pulled out his pipe.

"Now," said Mr. Wilkins, "I promised to give you an explanation of my strange behavior. It is rather a long story, but I see, sir, that you are no mere cold observer of the ebb and flow of life. You take, I think, a warm and an intelligent interest in the chances of your fellow-creatures, and I believe you will find what I have to tell not devoid of interest."

Mr. Dyson signified his assent to these propositions, and though he thought Mr. Wilkins's diction a little pompous, prepared to interest himself in his tale. The other, who had so raged with passion half an hour before, was now perfectly cool, and when he had smoked out his cigarette, he began in an even voice to relate the

NOVEL OF THE DARK VALLEY

I am the son of a poor but learned clergyman in the West of England,--but I am forgetting, these details are not of special interest. I will briefly state, then, that my father, who was, as I have said, a learned man, had never learnt the specious arts by which the great are flattered, and would never condescend to the despicable pursuit of self-advertisement. Though his fondness for ancient ceremonies and quaint customs, combined with a kindness of heart that was unequalled and a primitive and fervent piety, endeared him to his moor-land parishioners, such were not the steps by which clergy then rose in the Church, and at sixty my father was still incumbent of the little benefice he had accepted in his thirtieth year. The income of the living was barely sufficient to support life in the decencies which are expected of the Anglican parson; and when my father died a few years ago, I, his only child, found myself thrown upon the world with a slender capital of less than a hundred pounds, and all the problem of existence before me. I felt that there was nothing for me to do in the country, and as usually happens in such cases, London drew me like a magnet. One day in August, in the early morning, while the dew still glittered on the turf, and on the high green banks of the lane, a neighbor drove me to the railway station, and I bade good-bye to the land of the broad moors and unearthly battlements of the wild tors. It was six o'clock as we neared London; the faint sickly fume of the brickfields about Acton came in puffs through the open window, and a mist was rising from the ground. Presently the brief view of successive streets, prim and uniform, struck me with a sense of monotony; the hot air seemed to grow hotter; and when we had rolled beneath the dismal and squalid houses, whose dirty and neglected back yards border the line near Paddington, I felt as if I should be stifled in this fainting breath of London. I got a hansom and drove off, and every street increased my gloom; gray houses with blinds drawn down, whole thoroughfares almost desolate, and the foot-passengers who seemed to stagger wearily along rather than walk, all made me feel a sinking at heart. I put up for the night at a small hotel in a street leading from the Strand, where my father had stayed on his few brief visits to town; and when I went out after dinner, the real gayety and bustle of the Strand and Fleet Street could cheer me but little, for in all this great city there was no single human being whom I could claim even as an acquaintance. I will not weary you with the history of the next year, for the adventures of a man who sinks are too trite to be worth recalling. My money did not last me long; I found that I must be neatly dressed, or no one to whom I applied would so much as listen to me; and I must live in a street of decent reputation if I wished to be treated with common civility. I applied for various posts, for which, as I now see, I was completely devoid of qualification; I tried to become a clerk without having the smallest notion of business habits, and I found, to my cost, that a general knowledge of literature and an execrable style of penmanship are far from being looked upon with favor in commercial circles. I had read one of the most charming of the works of a famous novelist of the present day, and I frequented the Fleet Street taverns in the hope of making literary friends, and so getting the introductions which I understood were indispensable in the career of letters. I was disappointed; I once or twice ventured to address gentlemen who were sitting in adjoining boxes, and I was answered, politely indeed, but in a manner that told me my advances were unusual. Pound by pound, my small resources melted; I could no longer think of appearances; I migrated to a shy quarter, and my meals became mere observances. I went out at one and returned to my room at two, but nothing but a milk-cake had occurred in the interval. In short, I became acquainted with misfortune; and as I sat amidst slush and ice on a seat in Hyde Park, munching a piece of bread, I realized the bitterness of poverty, and the feelings of a gentleman reduced to something far below the condition of a vagrant. In spite of all discouragement I did not desist in my efforts to earn a living. I consulted advertisement columns, I kept my eyes open for a chance, I looked in at the windows of stationers' shops, but all in vain. One evening I was sitting in a Free Library, and I saw an advertisement in one of the papers. It was something like this: "Wanted, by a gentleman a person of literary taste and abilities as secretary and amanuensis. Must not object to travel." Of course I knew that such an advertisement would have answers by the hundred, and I thought my own chances of securing the post extremely small; however, I applied at the address given, and wrote to Mr. Smith, who was staying at a large hotel at the West End. I must confess that my heart gave a jump when I received a note a couple of days later, asking me to call at the Cosmopole at my earliest convenience. I do not know, sir, what your experiences of life may have been, and so I cannot tell whether you have known such moments. A slight sickness, my heart beating rather more rapidly than usual, a choking in the throat, and a difficulty of utterance; such were my sensations as I walked to the Cosmopole. I had to mention the name twice before the hall porter could understand me, and as I went upstairs my hands were wet. I was a good deal struck by Mr. Smith's appearance; he looked younger than I did, and there was something mild and hesitating about his expression. He was reading when I came in, and he looked up when I gave my name. "My dear sir," he said, "I am really delighted to see you. I have read very carefully the letter you were good enough to send me. Am I to understand that this document is in your own handwriting?" He showed me the letter I had written, and I told him I was not so fortunate as to be able to keep a secretary myself. "Then, sir," he went on, "the post I advertised is at your service. You have no objection to travel, I presume?" As you may imagine, I closed pretty eagerly with the offer he made, and thus I entered the service of Mr. Smith. For the first few weeks I had no special duties; I had received a quarter's salary, and a handsome allowance was made me in lieu of board and lodging. One morning, however, when I called at the hotel according to instructions, my master informed me that I must hold myself in readiness for a sea-voyage, and, to spare unnecessary detail, in the course of a fortnight we had landed at New York. Mr. Smith told me that he was engaged on a work of a special nature, in the compilation of which some peculiar researches had to be made; in short, I was given to understand that we were to travel to the far West.

After about a week had been spent in New York we took our seats in the cars, and began a journey tedious beyond all conception. Day after day, and night after night, the great train rolled on, threading its way through cities the very names of which were strange to me, passing at slow speed over perilous viaducts, skirting mountain ranges and pine forests, and plunging into dense tracts of wood, where mile after mile and hour after hour the same monotonous growth of brushwood met the eye, and all along the continual clatter and rattle of the wheels upon the ill-laid lines made it difficult to hear the voices of our fellow-passengers. We were a heterogeneous and ever-changing company; often I woke up in the dead of night with the sudden grinding jar of the brakes, and looking out found that we had stopped in the shabby street of some frame-built town, lighted chiefly by the flaring windows of the saloon. A few rough-looking fellows would often come out to stare at the cars, and sometimes passengers got down, and sometimes there was a party of two or three waiting on the wooden sidewalk to get on board. Many of the passengers were English; humble households torn up from the moorings of a thousand years, and bound for some problematical paradise in the alkali desert or the Rockies. I heard the men talking to one another of the great profits to be made on the virgin soil of America, and two or three, who were mechanics, expatiated on the wonderful wages given to skilled labor on the railways and in the factories of the States. This talk usually fell dead after a few minutes, and I could see a sickness and dismay in the faces of these men as they looked at the ugly brush or at the desolate expanse of the prairie, dotted here and there with frame-houses, devoid of garden, or flowers or trees, standing all alone in what might have been a great gray sea frozen into stillness. Day after day the waving sky line, and the desolation of a land without form or color or variety, appalled the hearts of such of us as were Englishmen, and once in the night as I lay awake I heard a woman weeping and sobbing, and asking what she had done to come to such a place. Her husband tried to comfort her in the broad speech of Gloucestershire, telling her the ground was so rich that one had only to plough it up and it would grow sunflowers of itself, but she cried for her mother and their old cottage and the beehives, like a little child. The sadness of it all overwhelmed me, and I had no heart to think of other matters; the question of what Mr. Smith could have to do in such a country, and of what manner of literary research could be carried on in the wilderness, hardly troubled me. Now and again my situation struck me as peculiar; I had been engaged as a literary assistant at a handsome salary, and yet my master was still almost a stranger to me; sometimes he would come to where I was sitting in the cars and make a few banal remarks about the country, but for the most part of the journey he sat by himself, not speaking to any one, and so far as I could judge, deep in his thoughts. It was I think on the fifth day from New York when I received, the intimation that we should shortly leave the cars; I had been watching some distant mountains which rose wild and savage before us, and I was wondering if there were human beings so unhappy as to speak of home in connection with those piles of lumbered rock, when Mr. Smith touched me lightly on the shoulder. "You will be glad to be done with, the cars, I have no doubt, Mr. Wilkins," he said. "You were looking at the mountains, I think? Well, I hope we shall be there to-night. The train stops at Reading, and I dare say we shall manage to find our way."

A few hours later the brakeman brought the tram to a standstill at the Reading depot and we got out. I noticed that the town, though of course built almost entirely of frame-houses, was larger and busier than any we had passed for the last two days. The depot was crowded, and as the bell and whistle sounded, I saw that a number of persons were preparing to leave the cars, while an even greater number were waiting to get on board. Besides the passengers, there was a pretty dense crowd of people, some of whom had come to meet or to see off their friends and relatives, while others were mere loafers. Several of our English fellow passengers got down at Reading, but the confusion was so great that they were lost to my sight almost immediately. Mr. Smith beckoned to me to follow him, and we were soon in the thick of the mass; and the continual ringing of bells, the hubbub of voices, the shrieking of whistles, and the hiss of escaping steam, confused my senses, and I wondered dimly as I struggled after my employer, where we were going, and how we should be able to find our way through an unknown country. Mr. Smith had put on a wide-brimmed hat, which he had sloped over his eyes, and as all the men wore hats of the same pattern, it was with some difficulty that I distinguished him in the crowd. We got free at last, and he struck down a side street, and made one or two sharp turns to right and left. It was getting dusk, and we seemed to be passing through a shy portion of the town, there were few people about in the ill-lighted streets, and these few were men of the most unprepossessing pattern. Suddenly we stopped before a corner house, a man was standing at the door, apparently on the look-out for some one, and I noticed that he and Smith gave sharp glances one to the other.

"From New York City, I expect, mister?"

"From New York!"

"All right; they 're ready, and you can have 'em when you choose. I know my orders, you see, and I mean to run this business through."

"Very well, Mr. Evans, that is what we want. Our money is good, you know. Bring them round."

I had stood silent, listening to this dialogue, and wondering what it meant. Smith began to walk impatiently up and down the street, and the man Evans was still standing at his door. He had given a sharp whistle, and I saw him looking me over in a quiet leisurely way, as if to make sure of my face for another time. I was thinking what all this could mean, when an ugly, slouching lad came up a side passage, leading two raw-boned horses.

"Get up, Mr. Wilkins, and be quick about it," said Smith. "We ought to be on our way."

We rode off together into the gathering darkness, and before long I looked back and saw the far plain behind us, with the lights of the town glimmering faintly; and in front rose the mountains. Smith guided his horse on the rough track as surely as if he had been riding along Piccadilly, and I followed him as well as I could. I was weary and exhausted, and scarcely took note of anything; I felt that the track was a gradual ascent, and here and there I saw great boulders by the road. The ride made but little impression on me; I have a faint recollection of passing through a dense black pine forest, where our horses had to pick their way among the rocks, and I remember the peculiar effect of the rarefied air as we kept still mounting higher and higher. I think I must have been half asleep for the latter half of the ride, and it was with a shock that I heard Smith saying--

"Here we are, Wilkins. This is Blue-Rock Park. You will enjoy the view to-morrow. To-night we will have something to eat, and then go to bed."

A man came out of a rough-looking house and took the horses, and we found some fried steak and coarse whiskey awaiting us inside. I had come to a strange place. There were three rooms,--the room in which we had supper, Smith's room and my own. The deaf old man who did the work slept in a sort of shed, and when I woke up the next morning and walked out I found that the house stood in a sort of hollow amongst the mountains; the clumps of pines and some enormous bluish-gray rocks that stood here and there between the trees had given the place the name of Blue-Rock Park. On every side the snow-covered mountains surrounded us, the breath of the air was as wine, and when I climbed the slope and looked down, I could see that, so far as any human fellowship was concerned I might as well have been wrecked on some small island in mid-Pacific. The only trace of man I could see was the rough log-house where I had slept, and in my ignorance I did not know that there were similar houses within comparatively easy distance, as distance is reckoned in the Rockies. But at the moment, the utter, dreadful loneliness rushed upon me, and the thought of the great plain and the great sea that parted me from the world I knew, caught me by the throat, and I wondered if I should die there in that mountain hollow. It was a terrible instant, and I have not yet forgotten it. Of course I managed to conquer my horror; I said I should be all the stronger for the experience, and I made up my mind to make the best of everything. It was a rough life enough, and rough enough board and lodging. I was left entirely to myself. Smith I scarcely ever saw, nor did I know when he was in the house. I have often thought he was far away, and have been surprised to see him walking out of his room, locking the door behind him and putting the key in his pocket; and on several occasions when I fancied he was busy in his room, I have seen him come in with his boots covered with dust and dirt. So far as work went I enjoyed a complete sinecure; I had nothing to do but to walk about the valley, to eat, and to sleep. With one thing and another I grew accustomed, to the life, and managed to make myself pretty comfortable, and by degrees I began to venture farther away from the house, and to explore the country. One day I had contrived to get into a neighboring valley, and suddenly I came upon a group of men sawing timber. I went up to them, hoping that perhaps some of them might be Englishmen; at all events they were human beings, and I should hear articulate speech, for the old man I have mentioned, besides being half blind and stone deaf, was wholly dumb so far as I was concerned. I was prepared to be welcomed in a rough and ready fashion, without much, of the forms of politeness, but the grim glances and the short gruff answers I received astonished me. I saw the men glancing oddly at each other, and one of them who had stopped work began fingering a gun, and I was obliged to return on my path uttering curses on the fate which had brought me into a land where men were more brutish than the very brutes. The solitude of the life began to oppress me as with a nightmare, and a few days later I determined to walk to a kind of station some miles distant, where a rough inn was kept for the accommodation of hunters and tourists. English gentlemen occasionally stopped there for the night, and I thought I might perhaps fall in with some one of better manners than the inhabitants of the country. I found as I had expected a group of men lounging about the door of the log-house that served as a hotel, and as I came nearer I could see that heads were put together and looks interchanged, and when I walked up the six or seven trappers stared at me in stony ferocity, and with something of the disgust that one eyes a loathsome and venomous snake. I felt that I could bear it no longer, and I called out:--

"Is there such a thing as an Englishman here, or any one with a little civilization?"

One of the men put his hand to his belt, but his neighbor checked him and answered me.

"You'll find we've got some of the resources of civilization before very long, mister, and I expect you'll not fancy them extremely. But anyway, there's an Englishman tarrying here, and I've no doubt he'll be glad to see you. There you are, that's Mr. D'Aubernoun."

A young man, dressed like an English country squire, came and stood at the door, and looked at me. One of the men pointed to me and said:--

"That's the individual we were talking about last night. Thought you might like to have a look at him, squire, and here he is."

The young fellow's good-natured English face clouded over, and he glanced sternly at me, and turned away with a gesture of contempt and aversion.

"Sir," I cried, "I do not know what I have done to be treated in this manner. You are my fellow-countryman, and I expected some courtesy."

He gave me a black look and made as if he would go in, but he changed his mind, and faced me.

"You are rather imprudent, I think, to behave in this manner. You must be counting on a forbearance which cannot last very long; which may last a very short time, indeed. And let me tell you this, sir, you may call yourself an Englishman and drag the name of England through the dirt, but you need not count on any English influence to help you. If I were you, I would not stay here much longer."

He went into the inn, and the men quietly watched my face, as I stood there, wondering whether I was going mad. The woman of the house came out and stared at me as if I were a wild beast or a savage, and I turned to her, and spoke quietly.

"I am very hungry and thirsty, I have walked a long way. I have plenty of money. Will you give me something to eat and drink?"

"No, I won't," she said. "You had better quit this."

I crawled home like a wounded beast, and lay down on my bed. It was all a hopeless puzzle to me. I knew nothing but rage and shame and terror, and I suffered little more when I passed by a house in an adjacent valley, and some children who were playing outside ran from me shrieking. I was forced to walk to find some occupation. I should have died if I had sat down quietly in Blue

Rock Park and looked all day at the mountains; but wherever I saw a human being I saw the same glance of hatred and aversion, and once as I was crossing a thick brake I heard a shot, and the venomous hiss of a bullet close to my ear.

One day I heard a conversation which astounded me; I was sitting behind a rock resting, and two men came along the track and halted. One of them had got his feet entangled in some wild vines, and swore fiercely, but the other laughed, and said they were useful things sometimes.

"What the hell do you mean?"

"Oh, nothing much. But they 're uncommon tough, these here vines, and sometimes rope is skerse and dear."

The man who had sworn chuckled at this, and I heard them sit down and light their pipes.

"Have you seen him lately?" asked the humorist.

"I sighted him the other day, but the darned bullet went high. He's got his master's luck, I expect, sir, but it can't last much longer. You heard about him going to Jinks's and trying his brass, but the young Britisher downed him pretty considerable, I can tell you."

"What the devil is the meaning of it?"

"I don't know, but I believe it'll have to be finished, and done in the old style, too. You know how they fix the niggers?"

"Yes, sir, I've seen a little of that. A couple of gallons of kerosene'll cost a dollar at Brown's store, but I should say it's cheap anyway."

They moved off after this, and I lay still behind the rock, the sweat pouring down my face. I was so sick that I could barely stand, and I walked home as slowly as an old man, leaning on my stick. I knew that the two men had been talking about me, and I knew that some terrible death was in store for me. That night I could not sleep. I tossed on the rough bed and tortured myself to find out the meaning of it all. At last in the very dead of night I rose from the bed, and put on my clothes, and went out. I did not care where I went, but I felt that I must walk till I had tired myself out. It was a clear moonlight night, and in a couple of hours I found I was approaching a place of dismal reputation in the mountains, a deep cleft in the rocks, known as Black Gulf Cañon. Many years before, an unfortunate party of Englishmen and Englishwomen had camped here and had been surrounded by Indians. They were captured, outraged, and put to death with almost inconceivable tortures, and the roughest of the trappers or woodsmen gave the cañon a wide berth even in the day-time. As I crushed through the dense brushwood which grew above the cañon, I heard voices, and wondering who could be in such a place at such a time, I went on, walking more carefully and making as little noise as possible. There was a great tree growing on the very edge of the rocks, and I lay down and looked out from behind the trunk. Black Gulf Cañon was below me, the moonlight shining bright into its very depths from midheaven, and casting shadows as black as death from the pointed rock, and all the sheer rock on the other side, overhanging the cañon, was in darkness. At intervals a light veil obscured the moonlight, as a filmy cloud fleeted across the moon; and a bitter wind blew shrill across the gulf. I looked down as I have said, and saw twenty men standing in a semicircle round a rock; I counted them one by one, and knew most of them. They were the very vilest of the vile, more vile than any den in London could show, and there was murder and worse than murder on the heads of not a few. Facing them and me stood Mr. Smith with the rock before him, and on the rock was a great pair of scales, such, as are used in the stores. I heard his voice ringing down the cañon as I lay beside the tree, and my heart turned cold as I heard it.

"Life for gold," he cried, "a life for gold. The blood and the life of an enemy for every pound of gold."

A man stepped out and raised one hand, and with the other flung a bright lump of something into the pan of the scales, which clanged down, and Smith muttered something in his ear. Then he cried again:--

"Blood for gold; for a pound of gold, the life of an enemy. For every pound of gold upon the scales, a life."

One by one the men came forward, each lifting up his right hand; and the gold was weighed in the scales, and each time Smith leaned forward and spoke to each man in his ear. Then he cried again:--

"Desire and lust, for gold on the scales. For every pound of gold, enjoyment of desire."

I saw the same thing happen as before; the uplifted hand, and the metal weighed, and the mouth whispering, and black passion on every face.

Then, one by one, I saw the men again step up to Smith. A muttered conversation seemed to take place; I could see that Smith was explaining and directing, and I noticed that he gesticulated a little as one who points out the way, and once or twice he moved his hands quickly as if he would show that the path was clear and could not be missed. I kept my eyes so intently on his figure that I noted little else, and at last it was with a start that I realized that the cañon was empty. A moment before I thought I had seen the group of villainous faces, and the two standing, a little apart by the rock; I had looked down a moment, and when I glanced again into the cañon there was no one there. In dumb terror I made my way home, and I fell asleep in an instant from exhaustion. No doubt I should have slept on for many hours, but when I woke up, the sun was only rising, and the light shone in on my bed. I had started up from sleep with the sensation of having received a violent shock, and as I looked in confusion about me I saw to my amazement that there were three men in the room. One of them had his hand on my shoulder and spoke to me.

"Come, mister, wake up. Your time's up now, I reckon, and the boys are waiting for you outside, and they 're in a big hurry. Come on; you can put on your clothes, it's kind of chilly this morning."

I saw the other two men smiling sourly at each other, but I understood nothing. I simply pulled on my clothes, and said I was ready.

"All right, come on then. You go first, Nichols, and Jim and I will give the gentleman an arm."

They took me out into the sunlight, and then I understood the meaning of a dull murmur that had vaguely perplexed me while I was dressing. There were about two hundred men waiting outside, and some women too, and when they saw me there was a low muttering growl. I did not know what I had done, but that noise made my heart beat and the sweat come out on my face. I saw confusedly, as through a veil, the tumult and tossing of the crowd, discordant voices were speaking, and amongst all those faces there was not one glance of mercy, but a fury of lust that I did not understand. I found myself presently walking in a sort of procession up the slope of the valley, and on every side of me there were men with revolvers in their hands. Now and then a voice struck me, and I heard words and sentences of which I could form no connected story. But I understood that there was one sentence of execration; I heard scraps of stories that seemed strange and improbable. Some one was talking of men, lured by cunning devices from their homes and murdered with hideous tortures, found writhing like wounded snakes in dark and lonely places, only crying for some one to stab them to the heart, and so end their torments; and I heard another voice speaking of innocent girls who had vanished for a day or two, and then had come back and died, blushing red with shame even in the agonies of death. I wondered what it all meant, and what was to happen, but I was so weary that I walked on in a dream, scarcely longing for anything but sleep. At last we stopped. We had reached the summit of the hill, overlooking Blue Rock Valley, and I saw that I was standing beneath a clump of trees where I had often sat. I was in the midst of a ring of armed men, and I saw that two or three men were very busy with piles of wood, while others were fingering a rope. Then there was a stir in the crowd, and a man was pushed forward. His hands and feet were tightly bound with cord, and though his face was unutterably villainous I pitied him for the agony that worked his features and twisted his lips. I knew him; he was amongst those that had gathered round Smith in Black Gulf Cañon. In an instant he was unbound, and stripped naked; and borne beneath one of the trees, and his neck encircled by a noose that went around the trunk. A hoarse voice gave some kind of order; there was a rush of feet, and the rope tightened; and there before me I saw the blackened face and the writhing limbs and the shameful agony of death. One after another, half a dozen men, all of whom I had seen in the cañon the night before, were strangled before me, and their bodies were flung forth on the ground. Then there was a pause, and the man who had roused me a short while before, came up to me and said:--

"Now, mister, it's your turn. We give you five minutes to cast up your accounts, and when that's clocked, by the living God we will burn you alive at that tree."

It was then I awoke and understood. I cried out:--

"Why, what have I done? Why should you hurt me? I am a harmless man, I never did you any wrong." I covered my face with my hands; it seemed so pitiful, and it was such a terrible death.

"What have I done?" I cried again. "You must take me for some other man. You cannot know me."

"You black-hearted devil," said the man at my side, "we know you well enough. There's not a man within thirty miles of this that won't curse Jack Smith when you are burning in hell."

"My name is not Smith," I said, with some hope left in me. "My name is Wilkins. I was Mr. Smith's secretary, but I knew nothing of him."

"Hark at the black liar," said the man. "Secretary be damned! You were clever enough, I dare say, to slink out at night, and keep your face in the dark, but we've tracked you out at last. But your time's up. Come along."

I was dragged to the tree and bound to it with chains, and I saw the piles of wood heaped all about me, and shut my eyes. Then I felt myself drenched all over with some liquid, and looked again, and a woman grinned at me. She had just emptied a great can of petroleum over me and over the wood. A voice shouted, "Fire away," and I fainted and knew nothing more.

When I opened my eyes I was lying on a bed in a bare comfortless room. A doctor was holding some strong salts to my nostrils, and a gentleman standing by the bed, whom I afterwards found to be the sheriff, addressed me:--

"Say, mister," he began, "you've had an uncommon narrow squeak for it. The boys were just about lighting up when I came along with the posse, and I had as much as I could do to bring you off, I can tell you. And, mind you, I don't blame them; they had made up their minds, you see, that you were the head of the Black Gulf gang, and at first nothing I could say would persuade them you weren't Jack Smith. Luckily, a man from here named Evans, that came along with us, allowed he had seen you with Jack Smith, and that you were yourself. So we brought you along and jailed you, but you can go if you like, when you're through with this faint turn."

I got on the cars the next day, and in three weeks I was in London; again almost penniless. But from that time my fortune seemed to change. I made influential friends in all directions; bank directors courted my company, and editors positively flung themselves into my arms. I had only to choose my career, and after a while I determined that I was meant by nature for a life of comparative leisure. With an ease that seemed almost ridiculous I obtained a well-paid position in connection with a prosperous political club. I have charming chambers in a central neighborhood close to the parks; the club chef exerts himself when I lunch or dine, and the rarest vintages in the cellar are always at my disposal. Yet, since my return to London, I have never known a day's security or peace; I tremble when I awake lest Smith should be standing at my bed, and every step I take seems to bring me nearer to the edge of the precipice. Smith, I knew, had escaped free from the raid of the vigilantes, and I grew faint at the thought that he would in all probability return to London, and that suddenly and unprepared I should meet him face to face. Every morning as I left my house, I would peer up and down the street, expecting to see that dreaded figure awaiting me; I have delayed at street corners, my heart in my mouth, sickening at the thought that a few quick steps might bring us together; I could not bear to frequent the theatres or music halls, lest by some bizarre chance he should prove to be my neighbor. Sometimes, I have been forced, against my will, to walk out at night, and then in silent squares the shadows have made me shudder, and in the medley of meetings in the crowded thoroughfares, I have said to myself, "It must come sooner or later; he will surely return to town, and I shall see him when I feel most secure." I scanned the newspapers for hint or intimation of approaching danger, and no small type nor report of trivial interest was allowed to pass unread. Especially I read and re-read the advertisement columns, but without result. Months passed by and I was undisturbed till, though I felt far from safe, I no longer suffered from the intolerable oppression of instant and ever present terror. This afternoon as I was walking quietly along Oxford Street, I raised my eyes, and looked across the road, and then at last I saw the man who had so long haunted my thoughts.

***

Mr. Wilkins finished his wine, and leaned back in his chair, looking sadly at Dyson; and then, as if a thought struck him, fished out of an inner pocket a leather letter case, and handed a newspaper cutting across the table.

Dyson glanced closely at the slip, and saw that it had been extracted from the columns of an evening paper. It ran as follows:--

WHOLESALE LYNCHING.
SHOCKING STORY.

A Dalziel telegram from Reading (Colorado) states that advices received there from Blue Bock Park report a frightful instance of popular vengeance. For some time the neighborhood has been terrorized by the crimes of a gang of desperadoes, who, under the cover of a carefully planned organization, have perpetrated the most infamous cruelties on men and women. A Vigilance Committee was formed, and it was found that the leader of the gang was a person named Smith, living in Blue Rock Park. Action was taken, and six of the worst in the band were summarily strangled in the presence of two or three hundred men and women. Smith is said to have escaped.

***

"This is a terrible story," said Dyson; "I can well believe that your days and nights are haunted by such fearful scenes as you have described. But surely you have no need to fear Smith? He has much, more cause to fear you. Consider, you have only to lay your information before the police, and a warrant would be immediately issued for his arrest. Besides, you will, I am sure, excuse me for what I am going to say."

"My dear sir," said Mr. Wilkins, "I hope you will speak to me with perfect freedom."

"Well, then, I must confess that my impression was that you were rather disappointed at not being able to stop the man before he drove off. I thought you seemed annoyed that you could not get across the street."

"Sir, I did not know what I was about. I caught sight of the man, but it was only for a moment, and the agony you witnessed was the agony of suspense. I was not perfectly certain of the face; and the horrible thought that Smith was again in London overwhelmed me. I shuddered at the idea of this incarnate fiend, whose soul is black with shocking crimes, mingling free and unobserved amongst the harmless crowds, meditating perhaps a new and more fearful cycle of infamies. I tell you, sir, that an awful being stalks through the streets, a being before whom the sunlight itself should blacken, and the summer air grow chill and dank. Such thoughts as these rushed upon me with the force of a whirlwind; I lost my senses."

"I see. I partly understand your feelings, but I would impress on you that you have nothing really to fear. Depend upon it, Smith will not molest you in any way. You must remember he himself has had a warning; and indeed from the brief glance I had of him, he seemed to me to be a frightened-looking man. However, I see it is getting late, and if you will excuse me, Mr. Wilkins, I think I will be going. I dare say we shall often meet here."

Dyson walked off smartly, pondering the strange story chance had brought him, and finding on cool reflection that there was something a little strange in Mr. Wilkins's manner, for which not even so weird a catalogue of experiences could altogether account.

ADVENTURE OF THE MISSING BROTHER

Mr. Charles Phillipps was, as has been hinted, a gentleman of pronounced scientific tastes. In his early days he had devoted himself with fond enthusiasm to the agreeable study of biology, and a brief monograph on the Embryology of the Microscopic Holothuria had formed his first contribution to the belles lettres. Later, he had somewhat relaxed the severity of his pursuits, and had dabbled in the more frivolous subjects of palæontology and ethnology; he had a cabinet in his sitting-room whose drawers were stuffed with rude flint implements, and a charming fetish from the South Seas was the dominant note in the decorative scheme of the apartment. Flattering himself with the title of materialist, he was in truth one of the most credulous of men, but he required a marvel to be neatly draped in the robes of science before he would give it any credit, and the wildest dreams took solid shape to him if only the nomenclature were severe and irreproachable; he laughed at the witch, but quailed before the powers of the hypnotist, lifting his eyebrows when Christianity was mentioned, but adoring protyle and the ether. For the rest, he prided himself on a boundless scepticism; the average tale of wonder he heard with nothing but contempt, and he would certainly not have credited a word or syllable of Dyson's story of the pursuer and pursued unless the gold coin had been produced as visible and tangible evidence. As it was he half suspected that Dyson had imposed on him; he knew his friend's disordered fancies, and his habit of conjuring up the marvellous to account for the entirely commonplace; and on the whole he was inclined to think that the so-called facts in the odd adventure had been gravely distorted in the telling. Since the evening on which he had listened to the tale, he had paid Dyson a visit, and had delivered himself of some serious talk on the necessity of accurate observation, and the folly, as he put it, of using a kaleidoscope instead of a telescope in the view of things, to which remarks his friend had listened with a smile that was extremely sardonic "My dear fellow," Dyson had remarked at last, "you will allow me to tell you that I see your drift perfectly. However, you will be astonished to hear that I consider you to be the visionary, while I am a sober and serious spectator of human life. You have gone round the circle, and while you fancy yourself far in the golden land of new philosophies, you are in reality a dweller in a metaphorical Clapham; your scepticism has defeated itself and become a monstrous credulity; you are in fact in the position of the bat or owl, I forget which it was, who denied the existence of the sun at noonday, and I shall be astonished if you do not one day come to me full of contrition for your manifold intellectual errors, with a humble resolution to see things in their true light for the future." This tirade had left Mr. Phillipps unimpressed; he considered Dyson as hopeless, and he went home to gloat over some primitive stone implements that a friend had sent him from India. He found that his landlady, seeing them displayed in all their rude formlessness upon the table, had removed the collection to the dustbin, and had replaced it by lunch; and the afternoon was spent in malodorous research. Mrs. Brown, hearing these stones spoken of as very valuable knives, had called him in his hearing "poor Mr. Phillipps," and between rage and evil odors he spent a sorry afternoon. It was four o'clock before he had completed his work of rescue; and, overpowered with the flavors of decaying cabbage-leaves, Phillipps felt that he must have a walk to gain an appetite for the evening meal. Unlike Dyson, he walked fast, with his eyes on the pavement, absorbed in his thoughts and oblivious of the life around him; and he could not have told by what streets he had passed, when he suddenly lifted up his eyes and found himself in Leicester Square. The grass and flowers pleased him, and he welcomed the opportunity of resting for a few minutes, and glancing round, he saw a bench which had only one occupant, a lady, and as she was seated at one end, Phillipps took up a position at the other extremity, and began to pass in angry review the events of the afternoon. He had noticed as he came up to the bench that the person already there was neatly dressed, and to all appearance young; her face he could not see, as it was turned away in apparent contemplation of the shrubs, and moreover shielded with her hand; but it would be doing wrong to Mr. Phillipps to imagine that his choice of a seat was dictated by any hopes of an affair of the heart; he had simply preferred the company of one lady to that of five dirty children, and having seated himself was immersed directly in thoughts of his misfortunes. He had meditated changing his lodgings; but now, on a judicial review of the case in all its bearings, his calmer judgment told him that the race of landladies is like to the race of the leaves, and that there was but little to choose between them. He resolved, however, to talk to Mrs. Brown, the offender, very coolly and yet severely, to point out the extreme indiscretion of her conduct, and to express a hope for better things in the future. With this decision registered in his mind, Phillipps was about to get up from the seat and move off, when he was intensely annoyed to hear a stifled sob, evidently from the lady, who still continued her contemplation of the shrubs and flower-beds. He clutched his stick desperately, and in a moment would have been in full retreat, when the lady turned her face towards him, and with a mute entreaty bespoke his attention. She was a young girl with a quaint and piquant rather than a beautiful face, and she was evidently in the bitterest distress, and Mr. Phillipps sat down again, and cursed his chances heartily. The young lady looked at him with a pair of charming eyes of a shining hazel, which showed no trace of tears, though a handkerchief was in her hand; she bit her lip, and seemed to struggle with some overpowering grief, and her whole attitude was all beseeching and imploring. Phillipps sat on the edge of the bench gazing awkwardly at her, and wondering what was to come next, and she looked at him still without speaking.

"Well, madam," he said at last, "I understood from your gesture that you wished to speak to me. Is there anything I can do for you? Though, if you will pardon me, I cannot help saying that that seems highly improbable."

"Ah, sir," she said in a low murmuring voice, "do not speak harshly to me. I am in sore straits, and I thought from your face that I could safely ask your sympathy, if not your help."

"Would you kindly tell me what is the matter?" said Phillipps. "Perhaps you would like some tea?"

"I knew I could not be mistaken," the lady replied. "That offer of refreshment bespeaks a generous mind. But tea, alas! is powerless to console me. If you will let me, I will endeavor to explain my trouble."

"I should be glad if you would."

"I will do so, and I will try and be brief, in spite of the numerous complications which have made me, young as I am, tremble before what seems the profound and terrible mystery of existence. Yet the grief which now racks my very soul is but too simple; I have lost my brother."

"Lost your brother! How on earth can that be?"

"I see I must trouble you with a few particulars. My brother, then, who is by some years my elder, is a tutor in a private school in the extreme north of London. The want of means deprived him of the advantages of a University education; and lacking the stamp of a degree, he could not hope for that position which his scholarship and his talents entitled him to claim. He was thus forced to accept the post of classical master at Dr. Saunderson's Highgate Academy for the sons of gentlemen, and he has performed his duties with perfect satisfaction to his principal for some years. My personal history need not trouble you; if will be enough if I tell you that for the last month I have been governess in a family residing at Tooting. My brother and I have always cherished the warmest mutual affection; and though circumstances into which I need not enter have kept us apart for some time, yet we have never lost sight of one another. We made up our minds that unless one of us was absolutely unable to rise from a bed of sickness, we would never let a week pass by without meeting, and some time ago we chose this square as our rendezvous on account of its central position and its convenience of access. And indeed, after a week of distasteful toil, my brother felt little inclination for much walking, and we have often spent two or three hours on this bench, speaking of our prospects and of happier days, when we were children. In the early spring it was cold and chilly; still we enjoyed the short respite, and I think that we were often taken for a pair of lovers, as we sat close together, eagerly talking. Saturday after Saturday we have met each other here, and though the doctor told him it was madness, my brother would not allow the influenza to break the appointment. That was some time ago; last Saturday we had a long and happy afternoon, and separated more cheerfully than usual, feeling that the coming week would be bearable, and resolving that our next meeting should be if possible still more pleasant. I arrived here at the time agreed upon, four o'clock, and sat down and watched for my brother, expecting every moment to see him advancing towards me from that gate at the north side of the square. Five minutes passed by, and he had not arrived; I thought he must have missed his train, and the idea that our interview would be cut short by twenty minutes, or perhaps half an hour, saddened me; I had hoped we should be so happy together to-day. Suddenly, moved by I know not what impulse, I turned abruptly round, and how can I describe to you my astonishment when I saw my brother advancing slowly towards me from the southern side of the square, accompanied by another person. My first thought, I remember, had in it something of resentment that this man, whoever he was, should intrude himself into our meeting; I wondered who it could possibly be, for my brother had, I may say, no intimate friends. Then as I looked still at the advancing figures, another feeling took possession of me; it was a sensation of bristling fear, the fear of the child in the dark, unreasonable and unreasoning, but terrible, clutching at my heart as with the cold grip of a dead man's hands. Yet I overcame the feeling, and looked steadily at my brother, waiting for him to speak, and more closely at his companion. Then I noticed that this man was leading my brother rather than walking arm-in-arm with him; he was a tall man, dressed in quite ordinary fashion. He wore a high bowler hat, and, in spite of the warmth of the day, a plain black overcoat, tightly buttoned, and I noticed his trousers, of a quiet black and gray stripe. The face was commonplace too, and indeed I cannot recall any special features, or any trick of expression; for though I looked at him as he came near, curiously enough his face made no impression on me, it was as though I had seen a well-made mask. They passed in front of me, and to my unutterable astonishment I heard my brother's voice speaking to me, though his lips did not move, nor his eyes look into mine. It was a voice I cannot describe, though I knew it, but the words came to my ears as if mingled with plashing water and the sound of a shallow brook flowing amidst stones. I heard, then, the words, 'I cannot stay,' and for a moment the heavens and the earth seemed to rush together with the sound of thunder, and I was thrust forth from the world into a black void without beginning and without end. For, as my brother passed me, I saw the hand that held him by the arm, and seemed to guide him, and in one moment of horror I realized that it was as a formless thing that has mouldered for many years in the grave. The flesh was peeled in strips from the bones, and hung apart dry and granulated, and the fingers that encircled my brother's arm were all unshapen, claw-like things, and one was but a stump from which the end had rotted off. When I recovered my senses I saw the two passing out by that gate. I paused for a moment, and then with a rush as of fire to my heart I knew that no horror could, stay me, but that I must follow my brother and save him, even though all hell rose up against me. I ran out and looked up the pavement, and saw the two figures walking amidst the crowd. I ran across the road, and saw them turn up that side street, and I reached the corner a moment later. In vain I looked to right and left, for neither my brother nor his strange guardian was in sight; two elderly men were coming down arm-in-arm, and a telegraph boy was walking lustily along whistling. I remained there a moment horror-struck, and then I bowed my head and returned to this seat, where you found me. Now, sir, do you wonder at my grief? Oh, tell me what has happened to my brother, or I feel I shall go mad."

Mr. Phillipps, who had listened with exemplary patience to this tale, hesitated a moment before he spoke.

"My dear madam," he said at length, "you have known how to engage me in your service, not only as a man, but as a student of science. As a fellow-creature I pity you most profoundly; you must have suffered extremely from what you saw, or rather from what you fancied you saw. For, as a scientific observer, it is my duty to tell you the plain truth, which, indeed, besides being true, must also console you. Allow me to ask you then to describe your brother."

"Certainly," said the lady, eagerly; "I can describe him accurately. My brother is a somewhat young-looking man; he is pale, has small black whiskers, and wears spectacles. He has rather a timid, almost a frightened expression, and looks about him nervously from side to side. Think, think! Surely you must have seen him. Perhaps you are an habitué of this engaging quarter; you may have met him on some previous Saturday. I may have been mistaken in supposing that he turned up that side street; he may have gone on, and you may have passed each other. Oh, tell me, sir, whether you have not seen him?"

"I am afraid I do not keep a very sharp lookout when I am walking," said Phillipps, who would have passed his mother unnoticed; "but I am sure your description is admirable. And now will you describe the person, who, you say, held your brother by the arm?"

"I cannot do so. I told you, his face seemed devoid of expression or salient feature. It was like a mask."

"Exactly; you cannot describe what you have never seen. I need hardly point out to you the conclusion to be drawn; you have been the victim of an hallucination. You expected to see your brother, you were alarmed because you did not see him, and unconsciously, no doubt, your brain went to work, and finally you saw a mere projection of your own morbid thoughts; a vision of your absent brother, and a mere confusion of terrors incorporated in a figure which you can't describe.

Of course your brother has been in some way prevented from coming to meet you as usual. I expect you will hear from him in a day or two."

The lady looked seriously at Mr. Phillipps, and then for a second there seemed almost a twinkling as of mirth about her eyes, but her face clouded sadly at the dogmatic conclusions to which the scientist was led so irresistibly.

"Ah," she said, "you do not know. I cannot doubt the evidence of my waking senses. Besides, perhaps I have had experiences even more terrible. I acknowledge the force of your arguments, but a woman has intuitions which never deceive her. Believe me, I am not hysterical; feel my pulse, it is quite regular."

She stretched out her hand with a dainty gesture, and a glance that enraptured Phillipps in spite of himself. The hand held out to him was soft and white and warm, and as, in some confusion, he placed his fingers on the purple vein, he felt profoundly touched by the spectacle of love and grief before him.

"No," he said, as he released her wrist, "as you say, you are evidently quite yourself. Still, you must be aware that living men do not possess dead hands. That sort of thing doesn't happen. It is, of course, barely possible that you did see your brother with another gentleman, and that important business prevented him from stopping. As for the wonderful hand, there may have been some deformity, a finger shot off by accident, or something of that sort."

The lady shook her head mournfully.

"I see you are a determined rationalist," she said. "Did you not hear me say that I have had experiences even more terrible? I too was once a sceptic, but after what I have known I can no longer affect to doubt."

"Madam," replied Mr. Phillipps, "no one shall make me deny my faith. I will never believe, nor will I pretend to believe, that two and two make five, nor will I on any pretences admit the existence of two-sided triangles."

"You are a little hasty," rejoined the lady. "But may I ask you if you ever heard the name of Professor Gregg, the authority on ethnology and kindred subjects?"

"I have done much more than merely hear of Professor Gregg," said Phillipps. "I always regarded him as one of our most acute and clear-headed observers; and his last publication, the 'Text-book of Ethnology,' struck me as being quite admirable in its kind. Indeed, the book had but come into my hands when I heard of the terrible accident which cut short Gregg's career. He had, I think, taken a country house in the West of England for the summer, and is supposed to have fallen into a river. So far as I remember, his body was never recovered."

"Sir, I am sure that you are discreet. Your conversation seems to declare as much, and the very title of that little work of yours which you mentioned, assures me that you are no empty trifler. In a word, I feel that I may depend on you. You appear to be under the impression that Professor Gregg is dead; I have no reason to believe that is the case."

"What?" cried Phillipps, astonished and perturbed. "You do not hint that there was anything disgraceful? I cannot believe it. Gregg was a man of clearest character; his private life was one of great benevolence; and though I myself am free from delusions, I believe him to have been a sincere and devout Christian. Surely you cannot mean to insinuate that some disreputable history forced him to flee the country?"

"Again you are in a hurry," replied the lady. "I said nothing of all this. Briefly, then, I must tell you that Professor Gregg left his house one morning in full health both of mind and body. He never returned, but his watch and chain, a purse containing three sovereigns in gold and some loose silver, with a ring that he wore habitually, were found three days later on a wild and savage hillside, many miles from the river. These articles were placed beside a limestone rock of fantastic form; they had been wrapped into a parcel with a kind of rough parchment which was secured with gut. The parcel was opened, and the inner side of the parchment bore an inscription done with some red substance; the characters were undecipherable, but seemed to be a corrupt cuneiform."

"You interest me intensely," said Phillips. "Would you mind continuing your story? The circumstance you have mentioned seems to me of the most inexplicable character, and I thirst for an elucidation."

The young lady seemed to meditate for a moment, and she then proceeded to relate the

Arthur Machen

NOVEL OF THE BLACK SEAL

I must now give you some fuller particulars of my history. I am the daughter of a civil engineer, Steven Lally by name, who was so unfortunate as to die suddenly at the outset of his career, and before he had accumulated sufficient means to support his wife and her two children. My mother contrived to keep the small household going on resources which must have been incredibly small; we lived in a remote country village, because most of the necessaries of life were cheaper than in a town, but even so we were brought up with the severest economy. My father was a clever and well-read man, and left behind him a small but select collection of books, containing the best Greek, Latin, and English classics, and these books were the only amusement we possessed. My brother, I remember, learned Latin out of Descartes' "Meditations," and I, in place of the little tales which children are usually told to read, had nothing more charming than a translation of the "Gesta Romanorum." We grew up thus, quiet and studious children, and in course of time my brother provided for himself in the manner I have mentioned. I continued to live at home; my poor mother had become an invalid, and demanded my continual care, and about two years ago she died after many months of painful illness. My situation was a terrible one; the shabby furniture barely sufficed to pay the debts I had been forced to contract, and the books I despatched to my brother, knowing how he would value them. I was absolutely alone. I was aware how poorly my brother was paid; and though I came up to London in the hope of finding employment, with the understanding that he would defray my expenses, I swore it should only be for a month, and that if I could not in that time find some work, I would starve rather than deprive him of the few miserable pounds he had laid by for his day of trouble. I took a little room in a distant suburb, the cheapest that I could find. I lived on bread and tea, and I spent my time in vain answering of advertisements, and vainer walks to addresses I had noted. Day followed on day, and week on week, and still I was unsuccessful, till at last the term I had appointed drew to a close, and I saw before me the grim prospect of slowly dying of starvation. My landlady was good-natured in her way; she knew the slenderness of my means, and I am sure that she would not have turned me out of doors. It remained for me then to go away, and to try and die in some quiet place. It was winter then, and a thick white fog gathered in the early part of the afternoon, becoming more dense as the day wore on; it was a Sunday, I remember, and the people of the house were at chapel. At about three o'clock I crept out and walked away as quickly as I could, for I was weak from abstinence. The white mist wrapped all the streets in silence, and a hard frost had gathered thick upon the bare branches of the trees, and frost crystals glittered on the wooden fences, and on the cold cruel ground beneath my feet. I walked on, turning to right and left in utter haphazard, without caring to look up at the names of the streets, and all that I remember of my walk on that Sunday afternoon seems but the broken fragments of an evil dream. In a confused vision I stumbled on, through roads half town and half country; gray fields melting into the cloudy world of mist on one side of me, and on the other comfortable villas with a glow of firelight flickering on the walls; but all unreal, red brick walls, and lighted windows, vague trees, and glimmering country, gas-lamps beginning to star the white shadows, the vanishing perspectives of the railway line beneath high embankments, the green and red of the signal lamps,--all these were but momentary pictures flashed on my tired brain and senses numbed by hunger. Now and then I would hear a quick step ringing on the iron road, and men would pass me well wrapped up, walking fast for the sake of warmth, and no doubt eagerly foretasting the pleasures of a glowing hearth, with curtains tightly drawn about the frosted panes, and the welcomes of their friends; but as the early evening darkened and night approached, foot-passengers got fewer and fewer, and I passed through street after street alone. In the white silence I stumbled on, as desolate as if I trod the streets of a buried city; and as I grew more weak and exhausted, something of the horror of death was folding thickly round my heart. Suddenly, as I turned a corner, some one accosted me courteously beneath the lamp-post, and I heard a voice asking if I could kindly point the way to Avon Road. At the sudden shock of human accents I was prostrated and my strength gave way, and I fell all huddled on the side-walk and wept and sobbed and laughed in violent hysteria. I had gone out prepared to die, and as I stepped across the threshold that had sheltered me, I consciously bade adieu to all hopes and all remembrances; the door clanged behind me with the noise of thunder, and I felt that an iron curtain had fallen on the brief passages of my life, and that henceforth I was to walk a little way in a world, of gloom and shadow; I entered on the stage of the first act of death. Then came my wandering in the mist, the whiteness wrapping all things, the void streets, and muffled silence, till when that voice spoke to me, it was as if I had died and life returned to me. In a few minutes I was able to compose my feelings, and as I rose I saw that I was confronted by a middle-aged gentleman of specious appearance, neatly and correctly dressed. He looked at me with an expression of great pity, but before I could stammer out my ignorance of the neighborhood, for indeed I had not the slightest notion of where I had wandered, he spoke.

"My dear madam," he said, "you seem in some terrible distress. You cannot think how you alarmed me. But may I inquire the nature of your trouble? I assure you that you can safely confide in me."

"You are very kind," I replied; "but, I fear there is nothing to be done. My condition seems a hopeless one."

"Oh, nonsense, nonsense! You are too young to talk like that. Come, let us walk down here, and you must tell me your difficulty. Perhaps I may be able to help you."

There was something very soothing and persuasive in his manner, and as we walked together, I gave him an outline of my story, and told of the despair that had oppressed me almost to death.

"You were wrong to give in so completely," he said, when I was silent. "A month is too short a time in which to feel one's way in London. London, let me tell you, Miss Lally, does not lie open and undefended; it is a fortified place, fossed and double-moated with curious intricacies. As must always happen in large towns, the conditions of life have become hugely artificial; no mere simple palisade is run up to oppose the man or woman who would take the place by storm, but serried lines of subtle contrivances, mines, and pitfalls which it needs a strange skill to overcome. You, in your simplicity, fancied you had only to shout for these walls to sink into nothingness, but the time is gone for such startling victories as these. Take courage; you will learn the secret of success before very long."

"Alas, sir," I replied, "I have no doubt your conclusions are correct, but at the present moment I seem to be in a fair way to die of starvation. You spoke of a secret; for heaven's sake, tell it me, if you have any pity for my distress."

He laughed genially. "There lies the strangeness of it all. Those who know the secret cannot tell it if they would; it is positively as ineffable as the central doctrine of Freemasonry. But I may say this, that you yourself have penetrated at least the outer husk of the mystery," and he laughed again.

"Pray do not jest with me," I said. "What have I done, que sais-je? I am so far ignorant that I have not the slightest idea of how my next meal is to be provided."

"Excuse me. You ask what you have done? You have met me. Come, we will fence no longer. I see you have self-education, the only education which is not infinitely pernicious, and I am in want of a governess for my two children. I have been a widower for some years; my name is Gregg. I offer you the post I have named, and shall we say a salary of a hundred a year?"

I could only stutter out my thanks, and slipping a card with his address and a bank-note by way of earnest into my hand, Mr. Gregg bade me good-bye, asking me to call in a day or two.

Such was my introduction to Professor Gregg, and can you wonder that the remembrance of despair and the cold blast that had blown from the gates of death upon me, made me regard him as a second father? Before the close of the week. I was installed in my new duties; the professor had leased an old brick manor house in a western suburb of London, and here, surrounded by pleasant lawns and orchards, and soothed with the murmur of the ancient elms that rocked their boughs above the roof, the new chapter of my life began. Knowing as you do the nature of the professor's occupations, you will not be surprised to hear that the house teemed with books; and cabinets full of strange and even hideous objects filled every available nook in the vast low rooms. Gregg was a man whose one thought was for knowledge, and I too before long caught something of his enthusiasm, and strove to enter into his passion for research. In a few months I was perhaps more his secretary than the governess of the two children, and many a night I have sat at the desk in the glow of the shaded lamp while he, pacing up and down in the rich, gloom of the firelight, dictated to me the substance of his "Text-book of Ethnology." But amidst these more sober and accurate studies I always detected a something hidden, a longing and desire for some object to which he did not allude, and now and then he would break short in what he was saying and lapse into revery, entranced, as it seemed to me, by some distant prospect of adventurous discovery. The text-book was at last finished, and we began to receive proofs from the printers, which were intrusted to me for a first reading, and then underwent the final revision of the professor. All the while his weariness of the actual business he was engaged on increased, and it was with the joyous laugh of a schoolboy when term is over that he one day handed me a copy of the book. "There," he said, "I have kept my word; I promised to write it, and it is done with. Now I shall be free to live for stranger things; I confess it, Miss Lally, I covet the renown of Columbus. You will, I hope, see me play the part of an explorer."

"Surely," I said, "there is little left to explore. You have been born a few hundred years too late for that."

"I think you are wrong," he replied; "there are still, depend upon it, quaint undiscovered countries and continents of strange extent. Ah, Miss Lally, believe me, we stand amidst sacraments and mysteries full of awe, and it doth not yet appear what we shall be. Life, believe me, is no simple thing, no mass of gray matter and congeries of veins and muscles to be laid naked by the surgeon's knife; man is the secret which I am about to explore, and before I can discover him I must cross over weltering seas indeed, and oceans and the mists of many thousand years. You know the myth of the lost Atlantis; what if it be true, and I am destined to be called the discoverer of that wonderful land?"

I could see excitement boiling beneath his words, and in his face was the heat of the hunter; before me stood a man who believed himself summoned to tourney with the unknown. A pang of joy possessed me when I reflected that I was to be in a way associated with him in the adventure, and I too burned with the lust of the chase, not pausing to consider that I knew not what we were to unshadow.

The next morning Professor Gregg took me into his inner study, where ranged against the wall stood a nest of pigeon-holes, every drawer neatly labelled, and the results of years of toil classified in a few feet of space.

"Here," he said, "is my life; here are all the facts which I have gathered together with so much pains, and yet it is all nothing. No, nothing to what I am about to attempt. Look at this;" and he took me to an old bureau, a piece fantastic and faded, which stood in a corner of the room. He unlocked the front and opened one of the drawers.

"A few scraps of paper," he went on, pointing to the drawer, "and a lump of black stone, rudely annotated with queer marks and scratches,--that is all that drawer holds. Here you see is an old envelope with the dark red stamp of twenty years ago, but I have pencilled a few lines at the back; here is a sheet of manuscript, and here some cuttings from obscure local journals. And if you ask me the subject matter of the collection, it will not seem extraordinary. A servant girl at a farmhouse, who disappeared from her place and has never been heard of, a child supposed to have slipped down some old working on the mountains, some queer scribbling on a limestone rock, a man murdered with a blow from a strange weapon; such is the scent I have to go upon. Yes, as you say, there is a ready explanation for all this; the girl may have run away to London, or Liverpool, or New York; the child may be at the bottom of the disused shaft; and the letters on the rock may be the idle whims of some vagrant. Yes, yes, I admit all that; but I know I hold the true key. Look!" and he held me out a slip of yellow paper.

"Characters found inscribed on a limestone rock on the Gray Hills," I read, and then there was a word erased, presumably the name of a county, and a date some fifteen years back. Beneath was traced a number of uncouth characters, shaped somewhat like wedges or daggers, as strange and outlandish as the Hebrew alphabet.

"Now the seal," said Professor Gregg, and he handed me the black stone, a thing about two inches long, and something like an old-fashioned tobacco stopper, much enlarged.

I held it up to the light, and saw to my surprise the characters on the paper repeated on the seal.

"Yes," said the professor, "they are the same. And the marks on the limestone rock were made fifteen years ago, with some red substance. And the characters on the seal are four thousand years old at least. Perhaps much more."

"Is it a hoax?" I said.

"No, I anticipated that. I was not to be led to give my life to a practical joke. I have tested the matter very carefully. Only one person besides myself knows of the mere existence of that black seal. Besides, there are other reasons which I cannot enter into now."

"But what does it all mean?" I said. "I cannot understand to what conclusion all this leads."

"My dear Miss Lally, that is a question I would rather leave unanswered for some little time. Perhaps I shall never be able to say what secrets are held here in solution; a few vague hints, the outlines of village tragedies, a few marks done with red earth upon a rock, and an ancient seal. A queer set of data to go upon? Half-a-dozen pieces of evidence, and twenty years before even so much could be got together; and who knows what mirage or terra incognita may be beyond all this? I look across deep waters, Miss Lally, and the land beyond may be but a haze after all. But still I believe it is not so, and a few months will show whether I am right or wrong."

He left me, and alone I endeavored to fathom the mystery, wondering to what goal such eccentric odds and ends of evidence could lead. I myself am not wholly devoid of imagination, and I had reason to respect the professor's solidity of intellect; yet I saw in the contents of the drawer but the materials of fantasy, and vainly tried to conceive what theory could be founded on the fragments that had been placed before me. Indeed, I could discover in what I had heard and seen but the first chapter of an extravagant romance; and yet deep in my heart I burned with curiosity, and day after day I looked eagerly in Professor Gregg's face for some hint of what was to happen.

It was one evening after dinner that the word came.

"I hope you can make your preparations without much trouble," he said suddenly to me. "We shall be leaving here in a week's time."

"Really!" I said in astonishment. "Where are we going?"

"I have taken a country house in the west of England, not far from Caermaen, a quiet little town, once a city, and the headquarters of a Roman legion. It is very dull there, but the country is pretty, and the air is wholesome."

I detected a glint in his eyes, and guessed that this sudden move had some relation to our conversation of a few days before.

"I shall just take a few books with me," said Professor Gregg, "that is all. Everything else will remain here for our return. I have got a holiday," he went on, smiling at me, "and I shan't be sorry to be quit for a time of my old bones and stones and rubbish. Do you know," he went on, "I have been grinding away at facts for thirty years; it is time for fancies."

The days passed quickly; I could see that the professor was all quivering with suppressed excitement, and I could scarce credit the eager appetence of his glance as we left the old manor house behind us, and began our journey. We set out at mid-day, and it was in the dusk of the evening that we arrived at a little country station. I was tired, and excited, and the drive through, the lanes seems all a dream. First the deserted streets of a forgotten village, while I heard Professor Gregg's voice talking of the Augustan Legion and the clash of arms, and all the tremendous pomp that followed the eagles; then the broad river swimming to full tide with the last afterglow glimmering duskily in the yellow water, the wide meadows, and the cornfields whitening, and the deep lane winding on the slope between the hills and the water. At last we began to ascend, and the air grew rarer; I looked down and saw the pure white mist tracking the outline of the river like a shroud, and a vague and shadowy country, imaginations and fantasy of swelling hills and hanging woods, and half-shaped outlines of hills beyond, stand in the distance the glare of the furnace fire on the mountain, growing by turns a pillar of shining flame, and fading to a dull point of red. We were slowly mounting a carriage drive, and then there came to me the cool breath and the scent of the great wood that was above us; I seemed to wander in its deepest depths, and there was the sound of trickling water, the scent of the green leaves, and the breath of the summer night. The carriage stopped at last, and I could scarcely distinguish the form of the house as I waited a moment at the pillared porch; and the rest of the evening seemed a dream of strange things bounded by the great silence of the wood and the valley and the river.

The next morning when I awoke and looked out of the bow window of the big old-fashioned bedroom, I saw under a gray sky a country that was still all mystery. The long, lovely valley, with the river winding in and out below, crossed, in mid vision by a mediæval bridge of vaulted and buttressed stone, the clear presence of the rising ground beyond, and the woods that I had only seen in shadow the night before, seemed tinged with enchantment, and the soft breath, of air that sighed in at the opened pane was like no other wind. I looked across the valley, and beyond, hill followed on hill as wave on wave, and here a faint blue pillar of smoke rose still in the morning air from the chimney of an ancient gray farmhouse, there was a rugged height crowned with dark firs, and in the distance I saw the white streak of a road that climbed and vanished into some unimagined country. But the boundary of all was a great wall of mountain, vast in the west, and ending like a fortress with a steep ascent and a domed tumulus clear against the sky.

I saw Professor Gregg walking up and down the terrace path below the windows, and it was evident that he was revelling in the sense of liberty, and the thought that he had, for a while, bidden good-bye to task-work. When I joined him there was exultation in his voice as he pointed out the sweep of valley and the river that wound beneath the lovely hills.

"Yes," he said, "it is a strangely beautiful country; and to me, at least, it seems full of mystery. You have not forgotten the drawer I showed you, Miss Lally? No; and you have guessed that I have come here not merely for the sake of the children and the fresh air?"

"I think I have guessed as much as that," I replied; "but you must remember I do not know the mere nature of your investigations; and as for the connection between the search and this wonderful valley, it is past my guessing."

He smiled queerly at me. "You must not think I am making a mystery for the sake of mystery," he said. "I do not speak out because, so far, there is nothing to be spoken, nothing definite I mean, nothing that can be set down in hard black and white, as dull and sure and irreproachable as any blue book. And then I have another reason: many years ago a chance paragraph in a newspaper caught my attention, and focussed in an instant the vagrant thoughts and half-formed fancies of many idle and speculative hours into a certain hypothesis. I saw at once that I was treading on a thin crust; my theory was wild and fantastic in the extreme, and I would not for any consideration have written a hint of it for publication. But I thought that in the company of scientific men like myself, men who knew the course of discovery, and were aware that the gas that blazes and flares in the gin-palace was once a wild hypothesis; I thought that with such men as these I might hazard my dream--let us say Atlantis, or the philosopher's stone, or what you like-- without danger of ridicule. I found I was grossly mistaken; my friends looked blankly at me and at one another, and I could see something of pity, and something also of insolent contempt, in the glances they exchanged. One of them called on me next day, and hinted that I must be suffering from overwork and brain exhaustion. 'In plain terms,' I said, 'you think I am going mad. I think not;' and I showed him out with some little appearance of heat. Since that day I vowed that I would never whisper the nature of my theory to any living soul; to no one but yourself have I ever shown the contents of that drawer. After all, I may be following a rainbow; I may have been misled by the play of coincidence; but as I stand here in this mystic hush and silence amidst the woods and wild hills, I am more than ever sure that I am hot on the scent. Come, it is time we went in."

To me in all this there was something both of wonder and excitement; I knew how in his ordinary work Professor Gregg moved step by step, testing every inch of the way, and never venturing on assertion without proof that was impregnable. Yet I divined more from his glance and the vehemence of his tone than from the spoken word that he had in his every thought the vision of the almost incredible continually with him; and I, who was with some share of imagination no little of a sceptic, offended at a hint of the marvellous, could not help asking myself whether he was cherishing a monomania, and barring out from this one subject all the scientific method of his other life.

Yet, with, this image of mystery haunting my thoughts, I surrendered wholly to the charm of the country. Above the faded house on the hillside began the great forest; a long dark line seen from the opposing hills, stretching above the river for many a mile from north to south, and yielding in the north to even wilder country, barren and savage hills, and ragged common land, a territory all strange and unvisited, and more unknown to Englishmen than the very heart of Africa. The space of a couple of steep fields alone separated the house from the wood, and the children were delighted to follow me up the long alleys of undergrowth, between smooth pleached walls of shining beech, to the highest point in the wood, whence one looked on one side across the river and the rise and fall of the country to the great western mountain wall, and on the other, over the surge and dip of the myriad trees of the forest, over level meadows and the shining yellow sea to the faint coast beyond. I used to sit at this point on the warm sunlit turf which marked the track of the Roman Road, while the two children raced about hunting for the whinberries that grew here and there on the banks. Here beneath the deep blue sky and the great clouds rolling, like olden galleons with sails full-bellied, from the sea to the hills, as I listened to the whispered charm of the great and ancient wood, I lived solely for delight, and only remembered strange things when we would return to the house, and find Professor Gregg either shut up in the little room he had made his study, or else pacing the terrace with the look, patient and enthusiastic, of the determined seeker.

One morning, some eight or nine days after our arrival, I looked out of my window and saw the whole landscape transmuted before me. The clouds had dipped low and hidden the mountain in the west, and a southern wind was driving the rain in shifting pillars up the valley, and the little brooklet that burst the hill below the house now raged, a red torrent, down to the river. We were perforce obliged to keep snug within doors, and when I had attended to my pupils, I sat down in the morning-room where the ruins of a library still encumbered an old-fashioned bookcase. I had inspected the shelves once or twice, but their contents had failed to attract me; volumes of eighteenth century sermons, an old book on farriery, a collection of "Poems" by "persons of quality," Prideaux's "Connection," and an odd volume of Pope were the boundaries of the library, and there seemed little doubt that everything of interest or value had been removed. Now, however, in desperation, I began to re-examine the musty sheepskin and calf bindings, and found, much to my delight, a fine old quarto printed by the Stephani, containing the three books of Pomponius Mela, "De Situ Orbis," and other of the ancient geographers. I knew enough of Latin to steer my way through an ordinary sentence, and I soon became absorbed in the odd mixture of fact and fancy; light shining on a little of the space of the world, and beyond mist and shadow and awful forms. Glancing over the clear-printed pages, my attention was caught by the heading of a chapter in Solinus, and I read the words:--

MIRA DE INTIMIS GENTIBUS LIBYAE, DE LAPIDE
HEXECONTALITHO.

"The wonders of the people that inhabit the inner parts of Libya, and of the stone called Sixtystone."

The odd title attracted me and I read on:--

"Gens ista avia et secreta habitat, in montibus horrendis foeda mysteria celebrat. De hominibus nihil aliud illi præferunt quam figuram, ab humano ritu prorsus exulant, oderunt deum lucis. Stridunt potius quam loquuntur; vox absona nec sine horrore auditur. Lapide quodam gloriantur, quem Hexecontalithon vocant, dicunt enim hunc lapidem sexaginta notas ostendere. Cujus lapidis nomen secretum ineffabile colunt: quod Ixaxar."

"This folk," I translated to myself, "dwells in remote and secret places, and celebrates foul mysteries on savage hills. Nothing have they in common with men save the face, and the customs of humanity are wholly strange to them; and they hate the sun. They hiss rather than speak; their voices are harsh, and not to be heard without fear. They boast of a certain stone, which they call Sixtystone; for they say that it displays sixty characters. And this stone has a secret unspeakable name; which is Ixaxar."

I laughed at the queer inconsequence of all this, and thought it fit for Sinbad the Sailor or other of the supplementary Nights. When I saw Professor Gregg in the course of the day, I told him of my find in the bookcase, and the fantastic rubbish I had been reading. To my surprise, he looked up at me with an expression of great interest.

"That is really very curious," he said. "I have never thought it worth while to look into the old geographers, and I daresay I have missed a good deal. Ah, that is the passage, is it. It seems a shame to rob you of your entertainment, but I really think I must carry off the book."

The next day the professor called to me to come to the study. I found him sitting at a table in the full light of the window, scrutinizing something very attentively with a magnifying-glass.

"Ah, Miss Lally," he began, "I want to use your eyes. This glass is pretty good, but not like my old one that I left in town. Would you mind examining the thing yourself, and telling me how many characters are cut on it?"

He handed me the object in his hand, and I saw that it was the black seal he had shown me in London, and my heart began to beat with the thought that I was presently to know something. I took the seal, and holding it up to the light checked off the grotesque dagger-shaped characters one by one.

"I make sixty-two," I said at last.

"Sixty-two? Nonsense; it's impossible. Ah, I see what you have done, you have counted that and that," and he pointed to two marks which I had certainly taken as letters with the rest.

"Yes, yes," Professor Gregg went on; "but those are obvious scratches, done accidentally; I saw that at once. Yes, then that's quite right. Thank you very much, Miss Lally."

I was going away, rather disappointed at my having been called in merely to count a number of marks on the black seal, when suddenly there flashed into my mind what I had read in the morning.

"But, Professor Gregg, I cried, breathless, the seal, the seal. Why, it is the stone Hexecontalithos that Solinus writes of; it is Ixaxar."

"Yes," he said, "I suppose it is. Or it maybe a mere coincidence. It never does to be too sure, you know, in these matters. Coincidence killed the professor."

I went away puzzled by what I had heard, and as much as ever at a loss to find the ruling clew in this maze of strange evidence. For three days the bad weather lasted, changing from driving rain to a dense mist, fine and dripping, and we seemed to be shut up in a white cloud that veiled all the world away from us. All the while Professor Gregg was darkling in his room, unwilling, it appeared, to dispense confidences or talk of any kind, and I heard him walking to and fro with a quick, impatient step, as if he were in some way wearied of inaction. The fourth morning was fine, and at breakfast the professor said briskly:--

"We want some extra help about the house; a boy of fifteen or sixteen, you know. There are a lot of little odd jobs that take up the maids' time, which a boy could do much better."

"The girls have not complained to me in any way," I replied. "Indeed, Anne said there was much less work than in London, owing to there being so little dust."

"Ah, yes, they are very good girls. But I think we shall do much better with a boy. In fact, that is what has been bothering me for the last two days."

"Bothering you?" I said in astonishment, for as a matter of fact the professor never took the slightest interest in the affairs of the house.

"Yes," he said, "the weather, you know. I really couldn't go out in that Scotch mist; I don't know the country very well, and I should have lost my way. But I am going to get the boy this morning."

"But how do you know there is such a boy as you want anywhere about?"

"Oh, I have no doubt as to that. I may have to walk a mile or two at the most, but I am sure to find just the boy I require."

I thought the professor was poking, but though his tone was airy enough there was something grim and set about his features that puzzled me. He got his stick, and stood at the door looking meditatively before him, and as I passed through the hall he called to me.

"By the way, Miss Lally, there was one thing I wanted to say to you. I daresay you may have heard that some of these country lads are not over bright; idiotic would be a harsh word to use, and they are usually called 'naturals,' or something of the kind, I hope you won't mind if the boy I am after should turn out not too keen-witted; he will be perfectly harmless, of course, and blacking boots doesn't need much mental effort."

With that he was gone, striding up the road that led to the wood; and I remained stupefied, and then for the first time my astonishment was mingled with a sudden note of terror, arising I knew not whence, and all unexplained even to myself, and yet I felt about my heart for an instant something of the chill of death, and that shapeless, formless dread of the unknown that is worse than death itself. I tried to find courage in the sweet air that blew up from the sea, and in the sunlight after rain, but the mystic woods seemed to darken around me; and the vision of the river coiling between the reeds, and the silver gray of the ancient bridge, fashioned in my mind symbols of vague dread, as the mind of a child fashions terror from things harmless and familiar.

Two hours later Professor Gregg returned. I met him as he came down the road, and asked quietly if he had been able to find a boy.

"Oh, yes," he answered; "I found one easily enough. His name is Jervase Cradock, and I expect he will make himself very useful. His father has been dead for many years, and the mother, whom I saw, seemed very glad at the prospect of a few shillings extra coming in on Saturday nights. As I expected, he is not too sharp, has fits at times, the mother said; but as he will not be trusted with the china, that doesn't much matter, does it? And he is not in any way dangerous, you know, merely a little weak."

"When is he coming?"

"To-morrow morning at eight o'clock. Anne will show him what he has to do, and how to do it. At first he will go home every night, but perhaps it may ultimately turn out more convenient for him to sleep here, and only go home for Sundays."

I found nothing to say to all this. Professor Gregg spoke in a quiet tone of matter-of-fact, as indeed was warranted by the circumstance; and yet I could not quell my sensation of astonishment at the whole affair. I knew that in reality no assistance was wanted in the housework, and the professor's prediction that the boy he was to engage might prove a little "simple," followed by so exact a fulfilment, struck me as bizarre in the extreme. The next morning I heard from, the housemaid that the boy Cradock had come at eight, and that she had been trying to make him useful. "He doesn't seem quite all there, I don't think, miss," was her comment; and later in the day I saw him helping the old man who worked in the garden. He was a youth of about fourteen, with black hair and black eyes, and an olive skin, and I saw at once from the curious vacancy of his expression that he was mentally weak. He touched his forehead awkwardly as I went by, and I heard him answering the gardener in a queer, harsh voice that caught my attention; it gave me the impression of some one speaking deep below under the earth, and there was a strange sibilance, like the hissing of the phonograph as the pointer travels over the cylinder. I heard that he seemed anxious to do what he could, and was quite docile and obedient, and Morgan the gardener, who knew his mother, assured me he was perfectly harmless. "He's always been a bit queer," he said, "and no wonder, after what his mother went through before he was born. I did know his father, Thomas Cradock, well, and a very fine workman he was too, indeed. He got something wrong with his lungs owing to working in the wet woods, and never got over it, and went off quite sudden like. And they do say as how Mrs. Cradock was quite off her head; anyhow, she was found by Mr. Hillyer, Ty Coch, all crouched up on the Gray Hills, over there, crying and weeping like a lost soul. And Jervase he was born about eight months afterwards, and as I was saying, he was a bit queer always; and they do say when he could scarcely walk he would frighten the other children into fits with the noises he would make."

A word in the story had stirred up some remembrance within me, and vaguely curious, I asked the old man where the Gray Hills were.

"Up there," he said, with the same gesture he had used before; "you go past the Fox and Hounds, and through the forest, by the old ruins. It's a good five mile from here, and a strange sort of a place. The poorest soil between this and Monmouth, they do say, though it's good feed for sheep. Yes, it was a sad thing for poor Mrs. Cradock."

The old man turned to his work, and I strolled on down the path between the espaliers, gnarled and gouty with age, thinking of the story I had heard, and groping for the point in it that had some key to my memory. In an instant it came before me; I had seen the phrase "Gray Hills" on the slip of yellowed paper that Professor Gregg had taken from the drawer in his cabinet. Again I was seized with pangs of mingled curiosity and fear; I remembered the strange characters copied from the limestone rock, and then again their identity with the inscription on the age-old seal, and the fantastic fables of the Latin geographer. I saw beyond doubt that, unless coincidence had set all the scene and disposed all these bizarre events with curious art, I was to be a spectator of things far removed from the usual and customary traffic and jostle of life. Professor Gregg I noted day by day. He was hot on his trail, growing lean with eagerness; and in the evenings, when the sun was swimming on the verge of the mountain, he would pace the terrace to and fro with his eyes on the ground, while the mist grew white in the valley, and the stillness of the evening brought far voices near, and the blue smoke rose a straight column from the diamond-shaped chimney of the gray farmhouse, just as I had seen it on the first morning. I have told you I was of sceptical habit; but though I understood little or nothing, I began to dread, vainly proposing to myself the iterated dogmas of science that all life is material, and that in the system of things there is no undiscovered land even beyond the remotest stars, where the supernatural can find a footing. Yet there struck in on this the thought that matter is as really awful and unknown as spirit, that science itself but dallies on the threshold, scarcely gaining more than a glimpse of the wonders of the inner place.

There is one day that stands up from amidst the others as a grim red beacon, betokening evil to come. I was sitting on a bench in the garden, watching the boy Cradock weeding, when I was suddenly alarmed by a harsh and choking sound, like the cry of a wild beast in anguish, and I was unspeakably shocked to see the unfortunate lad standing in full view before me, his whole body quivering and shaking at short intervals as though shocks of electricity were passing through him, and his teeth grinding, and foam gathering on his lips, and his face all swollen and blackened to a hideous mask of humanity. I shrieked with terror, and Professor Gregg came running; and as I pointed to Cradock, the boy with one convulsive shudder fell face forward, and lay on the wet earth, his body writhing like a wounded blind-worm, and an inconceivable babble of sounds bursting and rattling and hissing from his lips; he seemed to pour forth an infamous jargon, with words, or what seemed words, that might have belonged to a tongue dead since untold ages, and buried deep beneath Nilotic mud, or in the inmost recesses of the Mexican forest. For a moment the thought passed through my mind, as my ears were still revolted with that infernal clamor, "Surely this is the very speech of hell," and then I cried out again and again, and ran away shuddering to my inmost soul. I had seen Professor Gregg's face as he stooped over the wretched boy and raised him, and I was appalled by the glow of exultation that shone on every lineament and feature. As I sat in my room with drawn blinds, and my eyes hidden in my hands, I heard heavy steps beneath, and I was told afterwards that Professor Gregg had carried Cradock to his study, and had locked the door. I heard voices murmur indistinctly, and I trembled to think of what might be passing within a few feet of where I sat; I longed to escape to the woods and sunshine, and yet I dreaded the sights that might confront me on the way. And at last, as I held the handle of the door nervously, I heard Professor Gregg's voice calling to me with a cheerful ring: "It's all right now, Miss Lally," he said. "The poor fellow has got over it, and I have been arranging for him to sleep here after to-morrow. Perhaps I may be able to do something for him."

"Yes," he said later, "it was a very painful sight, and I don't wonder you were alarmed. We may hope that good food will build him up a little, but I am afraid he will never be really cured;" and he affected the dismal and conventional air with which one speaks of hopeless illness, and yet beneath it I detected the delight that leapt up rampant within him, and fought and struggled to find utterance. It was as if one glanced down on the even surface of the sea, clear and immobile, and saw beneath raging depths, and a storm of contending billows. It was indeed to me a torturing and offensive problem that this man, who had so bounteously rescued me from the sharpness of death, and showed himself in all the relations of life full of benevolence and pity and kindly forethought, should so manifestly be for once on the side of the demons, and take a ghastly pleasure in the torments of an afflicted fellow-creature. Apart, I struggled with the horned difficulty, and strove to find the solution, but without the hint of a clue; beset by mystery and contradiction, I saw nothing that might help me, and began to wonder whether, after all, I had not escaped from the white mist of the suburb at too dear a rate. I hinted something of my thought to the professor; I said enough to let him know that I was in the most acute perplexity, but the moment after regretted what I had done, when I saw his face contort with a spasm of pain.

"My dear Miss Lally," he said, "you surely do not wish to leave us? No, no, you would not do it. You do not know how I rely on you; how confidently I go forward, assured that you are here to watch over my children. You, Miss Lally, are my rear-guard; for, let me tell you, that the business in which I am engaged is not wholly devoid of peril. You have not forgotten what I said the first morning here; my lips are shut by an old and firm resolve, till they can open to utter no ingenious hypothesis or vague surmise but irrefragable fact, as certain as a demonstration in mathematics. Think over it, Miss Lally, not for a moment would I endeavor to keep you here against your own instincts, and yet I tell you frankly that I am persuaded that it is here, here amidst the woods, that your duty lies."

I was touched by the eloquence of his tone, and by the remembrance that the man, after all, had been my salvation, and I gave him my hand on a promise to serve him loyally and without question. A few days later the rector of our church, a little church, gray and severe and quaint, that hovered on the very banks of the river and watched the tides swim and return, came to see us, and Professor Gregg easily persuaded him to stay and share our dinner. Mr. Meyrick was a member of an antique family of squires, whose old manor house stood amongst the hills some seven miles away, and thus rooted in the soil, the rector was a living store of all the old fading customs and lore of the country. His manner, genial with a deal of retired oddity, won on Professor Gregg; and towards the cheese, when a curious Burgundy had begun its incantations, the two men glowed like the wine, and talked of philology with the enthusiasm of a burgess over the peerage. The parson was expounding the pronunciation of the Welsh ll, and producing sounds like the gurgle of his native brooks, when Professor Gregg struck in.

"By the way," he said, "that was a very odd word I met with the other day. You know my boy, poor Jervase Cradock. Well, he has got the bad habit of talking to himself, and the day before yesterday I was walking in the garden here and heard him; he was evidently quite unconscious of my presence. A lot of what he said I couldn't make out, but one word, struck me distinctly. It was such an odd sound; half-sibilant, half-guttural, and as quaint as those double ll's you have been demonstrating. I do not know whether I can give you an idea of the sound. "Ishakshar" is perhaps as near as I can get; but the k ought to be a Greek chi or a Spanish j. Now what does it mean in Welsh?"

"In Welsh?" said the parson. "There is no such word in Welsh, nor any word remotely resembling it. I know the book-Welsh, as they call it, and the colloquial dialects as well as any man, but there's no word like that from Anglesea to Usk. Besides, none of the Cradocks speak a word of Welsh; it's dying out about here."

"Really. You interest me extremely, Mr. Meyrick. I confess the word didn't strike me as having the Welsh ring. But I thought it might be some local corruption."

"No, I never heard such a word, or anything like it. Indeed," he added, smiling whimsically, "if it belongs to any language, I should say it must be that of the fairies,--the Tylwydd Têg, as we call them."

The talk went on to the discovery of a Roman villa in the neighborhood; and soon after I left the room, and sat down apart to wonder at the drawing together of such strange clues of evidence. As the professor had spoken of the curious word, I had caught the glint of his eye upon me; and though the pronunciation he gave was grotesque in the extreme, I recognized the name of the stone of sixty characters mentioned by Solinus, the black seal shut up in some secret drawer of the study, stamped forever by a vanished race with signs that no man could read, signs that might, for all I knew, be the veils of awful things done long ago, and forgotten before the hills were moulded into form.

When, the next morning, I came down, I found Professor Gregg pacing the terrace in his eternal walk.

"Look at that bridge," he said when he saw me, "observe the quaint and Gothic design, the angles between the arches, and the silvery gray of the stone in the awe of the morning light. I confess it seems to me symbolic; it should illustrate a mystical allegory of the passage from one world to another."

"Professor Gregg," I said quietly, "it is time that I knew something of what has happened, and of what is to happen."

For the moment he put me off, but I returned again with the same question in the evening, and then Professor Gregg flamed with excitement. "Don't you understand yet?" he cried. "But I have told you a good deal; yes, and shown you a good deal. You have heard pretty nearly all that I have heard, and seen what I have seen; or at least," and his voice chilled as he spoke, "enough to make a good deal clear as noonday. The servants told you, I have no doubt, that the wretched boy Cradock had another seizure the night before last; he awoke me with cries in that voice you heard in the garden, and I went to him, and God forbid you should see what I saw that night. But all this is useless; my time here is drawing to a close; I must be back in town in three weeks, as I have a course of lectures to prepare, and need all my books about me. In a very few days it will be all over, and I shall no longer hint, and no longer be liable to ridicule as a madman and a quack. No, I shall speak plainly, and I shall be heard with such emotions as perhaps no other man has ever drawn from the breasts of his fellows."

He paused, and seemed to grow radiant with the joy of great and wonderful discovery.

"But all that is for the future, the near future certainly, but still the future," he went on at length. "There is something to be done yet; you will remember my telling you that my researches were not altogether devoid of peril? Yes, there is a certain amount of danger to be faced; I did not know how much when I spoke on the subject before, and to a certain extent I am still in the dark. But it will be a strange adventure, the last of all, the last demonstration in the chain."

He was walking up and down the room as he spoke, and I could hear in his voice the contending tones of exultation and despondence, or perhaps I should say awe, the awe of a man who goes forth on unknown waters, and I thought of his allusion to Columbus on the night he had laid his book before me. The evening was a little chilly, and a fire of logs had been lighted in the study where we were, and the remittent flame and the glow on the walls reminded me of the old days. I was sitting silent in an armchair by the fire, wondering over all I had heard, and still vainly speculating as to the secret springs concealed from me under all the phantasmagoria I had witnessed, when I became suddenly aware of a sensation that change of some sort had been at work in the room, and that there was something unfamiliar in its aspect. For some time I looked about me, trying in vain to localize the alteration that I knew had been made; the table by the window, the chairs, the faded settee were all as I had known them. Suddenly, as a sought-for recollection flashes into the mind, I knew what was amiss. I was facing the professor's desk, which stood on the other side of the fire, and above the desk was a grimy looking bust of Pitt, that I had never seen there before. And then I remembered the true position of this work of art; in the furthest corner by the door was an old cupboard, projecting into the room, and on the top of the cupboard, fifteen feet from the floor, the bust had been, and there no doubt it had delayed, accumulating dirt since the early years of the century.

I was utterly amazed, and sat silent still, in a confusion of thought. There was, so far as I knew, no such thing as a step-ladder in the house, for I had asked for one to make some alterations in the curtains of my room; and a tall man standing on a chair would have found it impossible to take down the bust. It had been placed not on the edge of the cupboard, but far back against the wall; and Professor Gregg was, if anything, under the average height.

"How on earth did you manage to get down Pitt?" I said at last.

The professor looked curiously at me, and seemed to hesitate a little.

"They must have found you a step-ladder, or perhaps the gardener brought in a short ladder from outside."

"No, I have had no ladder of any kind. Now, Miss Lally," he went on with an awkward simulation of jest, "there is a little puzzle for you; a problem in the manner of the inimitable Holmes; there are the facts, plain and patent; summon your acuteness to the solution of the puzzle. For Heaven's sake," he cried with a breaking voice, "say no more about it. I tell you, I never touched the thing," and he went out of the room with horror manifest on his face, and his hand shook and jarred the door behind him.

I looked round the room in vague surprise, not at all realizing what had happened, making vain and idle surmises by way of explanation, and wondering at the stirring of black waters by an idle word, and the trivial change of an ornament. "This is some petty business, some whim on which I have jarred," I reflected; "the professor is perhaps scrupulous and superstitious over trifles, and my question may have outraged unacknowledged fears, as though one killed a spider or spilled the salt before the very eyes of a practical Scotchwoman." I was immersed in these fond suspicions, and began to plume myself a little on my immunity from such empty fears, when the truth fell heavily as lead upon my heart, and I recognized with cold terror that some awful influence had been at work. The bust was simply inaccessible; without a ladder no one could have touched it.

I went out to the kitchen and spoke as quietly as I could to the housemaid.

"Who moved that bust from the top of the cupboard, Anne?" I said to her. "Professor Gregg says he has not touched it. Did you find an old step-ladder in one of the outhouses?"

The girl looked at me blankly.

"I never touched it," she said. "I found it where it is now the other morning when I dusted the room. I remember now, it, was Wednesday morning, because it was the morning after Cradock was taken bad in the night. My room is next to his, you know, miss," the girl went on piteously; "and it was awful to hear how he cried and called out names that I couldn't understand. It made me feel all afraid, and then master came, and I heard him speak, and he took down Cradock to the study and gave him something."

"And you found that bust moved the next morning?"

"Yes, miss, there was a queer sort of a smell in the study when I came down and opened the windows; a bad smell it was, and I wondered what it could be. Do you know, miss, I went a long time ago to the Zoo in London with my cousin Thomas Barker, one afternoon that I had off, when I was at Mrs. Prince's in Stanhope Gate, and we went into the snake-house to see the snakes, and it was just the same sort of a smell, very sick it made me feel, I remember, and I got Barker to take me out. And it was just the same kind of a smell in the study, as I was saying, and I was wondering what it could be from, when I see that bust with Pitt cut in it standing on the master's desk, and I thought to myself, now who has done that, and how have they done it? And when I came to dust the things, I looked at the bust, and I saw a great mark on it where the dust was gone, for I don't think it can have been touched with a duster for years and years, and it wasn't like finger-marks, but a large patch like, broad and spread out. So I passed my hand over it, without thinking what I was doing, and where that patch was it was all sticky and slimy, as if a snail had crawled over it. Very strange, isn't it, miss? and I wonder who can have done it, and how that mess was made."

The well-meant gabble of the servant touched me to the quick. I lay down upon my bed, and bit my lip that I should not cry out loud in the sharp anguish of my terror and bewilderment. Indeed, I was almost mad with dread; I believe that if it had been daylight I should have fled hot foot, forgetting all courage and all the debt of gratitude that was due to Professor Gregg, not caring whether my fate were that I must starve slowly so long as I might escape from the net of blind and panic fear that every day seemed to draw a little closer round me. If I knew, I thought, if I knew what there were to dread, I could guard against it; but here, in this lonely house, shut in on all sides by the olden woods and the vaulted hills, terror seems to spring inconsequent from every covert, and the flesh is aghast at the half-heard murmurs of horrible things. All in vain I strove to summon scepticism to my aid, and endeavored by cool common-sense to buttress my belief in a world of natural order, for the air that blew in at the open window was a mystic breath, and in the darkness I felt the silence go heavy and sorrowful as a mass of requiem, and I conjured images of strange shapes gathering fast amidst the reeds, beside the wash of the river.

In the morning, from the moment that I set foot in the breakfast-room I felt that the unknown plot was drawing to a crisis; the professor's face was firm and set, and he seemed hardly to hear our voices when we spoke.

"I am going out for rather a long walk," he said, when the meal was over. "You mustn't be expecting me, now, or thinking anything has happened if I don't turn up to dinner. I have been getting stupid lately, and I dare say a miniature walking tour will do me good. Perhaps I may even spend the night in some little inn, if I find any place that looks clean and comfortable."

I heard this, and knew by my experience of Professor Gregg's manner that it was no ordinary business or pleasure that impelled him. I knew not, nor even remotely guessed, where he was bound, nor had I the vaguest notion of his errand, but all the fear of the night before returned; and as he stood, smiling, on the terrace, ready to set out, I implored him to stay, and to forget all his dreams of the undiscovered continent.

"No, no, Miss Lally," he replied, still smiling, "it's too late now. Vestigia nulla retrorsum, you know, is the device of all true explorers, though I hope it won't be literally true in my ease. But, indeed, you are wrong to alarm yourself so; I look upon my little expedition as quite commonplace; no more exciting than a day with the geological hammers. There is a risk, of course, but so there is on the commonest excursion. I can afford to be jaunty; I am doing nothing so hazardous as 'Arry does a hundred times over in the course of every Bank Holiday. Well, then, you must look more cheerfully; and so good-by till to-morrow at latest."

He walked briskly up the road, and I saw him open the gate that marks the entrance of the wood, and then he vanished in the gloom of the trees.

All the day passed heavily with a strange darkness in the air, and again I felt as if imprisoned amidst the ancient woods, shut in an olden land of mystery and dread, and as if all was long ago and forgotten by the living outside. I hoped and dreaded, and when the dinner-hour came, I waited expecting to hear the professor's step in the hall, and his voice exulting at I knew not what triumph. I composed my face to welcome him gladly, but the night descended dark, and he did not come.

In the morning when the maid knocked at my door, I called out to her, and asked if her master had returned; and when she replied that his bedroom stood open and empty, I felt the cold clasp of despair. Still, I fancied he might have discovered genial company, and would return for luncheon, or perhaps in the afternoon, and I took the children for a walk in the forest, and tried my best to play and laugh with them, and to shut out the thoughts of mystery and veiled terror. Hour after hour I waited, and my thoughts grew darker; again the night came and found me watching, and at last, as I was making much ado to finish my dinner, I heard steps outside and the sound of a man's voice.

The maid came in and looked oddly at me.

"Please, miss," she began, "Mr. Morgan the gardener wants to speak to you for a minute, if you didn't mind."

"Show him in, please," I answered, and I set my lips tight.

The old man came slowly into the room, and the servant shut the door behind him.

"Sit down, Mr. Morgan," I said; "what is it that you want to say to me?"

"Well, miss, Mr. Gregg he gave me something for you yesterday morning, just before he went off; and he told me particular not to hand it up before eight o'clock this evening exactly, if so be as he wasn't back again home before, and if he should come home before I was just to return it to him in his own hands. So, you see, as Mr. Gregg isn't here yet, I suppose I'd better give you the parcel directly."

He pulled out something from his pocket, and gave it to me, half rising. I took it silently, and seeing that Morgan seemed doubtful as to what he was to do next, I thanked him and bade him good-night, and he went out. I was left alone in the room with the parcel in my hand,--a paper parcel neatly sealed and directed to me, with the instructions Morgan had quoted all written in the professor's large loose hand. I broke the seals with a choking at my heart, and found an envelope inside, addressed also, but open, and I took the letter out.

***

"MY DEAR MISS LALLY," it began, "To quote the old logic manual, the case of your reading this note is a case of my having made a blunder of some sort, and, I am afraid, a blunder that turns these lines into a farewell. It is practically certain that neither you nor anyone else will ever see me again. I have made my will with provision for this eventuality, and I hope you will consent to accept the small remembrance addressed to you, and my sincere thanks for the way in which you joined your fortunes to mine. The fate which has come upon me is desperate and terrible beyond the remotest dreams of man; but this fate you have a right to know--if you please. If you look in the left-hand drawer of my dressing-table, you will find the key of the escritoire, properly labelled. In the well of the escritoire is a large envelope sealed and addressed to your name. I advise you to throw it forthwith into the fire; you will sleep better of nights if you do so. But if you must know the history of what has happened, it is all written down for you to read."

***

The signature was firmly written below, and again I turned the page and read out the words one by one, aghast and white to the lips, my hands cold as ice, and sickness choking me. The dead silence of the room, and the thought of the dark woods and hills closing me in on every side, oppressed me, helpless and without capacity, and not knowing where to turn for counsel. At last I resolved that though knowledge should haunt my whole life and all the days to come, I must know the meaning of the strange terrors that had so long tormented me, rising gray, dim, and awful, like the shadows in the wood at dusk. I carefully carried out Professor Gregg's directions, and not without reluctance broke the seal of the envelope, and spread out his manuscript before me. That manuscript I always carry with me, and I see that I cannot deny your unspoken request to read it. This, then, was what I read that night, sitting at the desk, with a shaded lamp beside me.

The young lady who called herself Miss Lally then proceeded to recite:--

***

The Statement of William Gregg, F.R.S., etc.

It is many years since the first glimmer of the theory which is now almost, if not quite, reduced to fact dawned first on my mind. A somewhat extensive course of miscellaneous and obsolete reading had done a good deal to prepare the way, and, later, when I became somewhat of a specialist and immersed myself in the studies known as ethnological, I was now and then startled by facts that would not square with orthodox scientific opinion, and by discoveries that seemed to hint at something still hidden for all our research. More particularly I became convinced that much of the folk-lore of the world is but an exaggerated account of events that really happened, and I was especially drawn to consider the stories of the fairies, the good folk of the Celtic races. Here I thought I could detect the fringe of embroidery and exaggeration, the fantastic guise, the little people dressed in green and gold sporting in the flowers, and I thought I saw a distinct analogy between the name given to this race (supposed to be imaginary) and the description of their appearance and manners. Just as our remote ancestors called the dreaded beings "fair" and "good" precisely because they dreaded them, so they had dressed them up in charming forms, knowing the truth to be the very reverse. Literature, too, had gone early to work, and had lent a powerful hand in the transformation, so that the playful elves of Shakespeare are already far removed from the true original, and the real horror is disguised in a form of prankish mischief. But in the older tales, the stories that used to make men cross themselves as they sat round the burning logs, we tread a different stage; I saw a widely opposed spirit in certain histories of children and of men and women who vanished strangely from the earth. They would be seen by a peasant in the fields walking towards some green and rounded hillock, and seen no more on earth; and there are stories of mothers who have left a child quietly sleeping with the cottage door rudely barred with a piece of wood, and have returned, not to find the plump and rosy little Saxon, but a thin and wizened creature, with sallow skin and black piercing eyes, the child of another race. Then, again, there were myths darker still; the dread of witch and wizard, the lurid evil of the Sabbath, and the hint of demons who mingled with the daughters of men. And just as we have turned the terrible "fair folk" into a company of benignant, if freakish, elves, so we have hidden from us the black foulness of the witch and her companions under a popular diablerie of old women and broomsticks and a comic cat with tail on end. So the Greeks called the hideous furies benevolent ladies, and thus the northern nations have followed their example. I pursued my investigations, stealing odd hours from other and more imperative labors, and I asked myself the question: Supposing these traditions to be true, who were the demons who are reported to have attended the Sabbaths? I need not say that I laid aside what I may call the supernatural hypothesis of the middle ages, and came to the conclusion that fairies and devils were of one and the same race and origin; invention, no doubt, and the Gothic fancy of old days had done much in the way of exaggeration and distortion; yet I firmly believed that beneath all this imagery there was a black background of truth. As for some of the alleged wonders, I hesitated. While I should be very loth to receive any one specific instance of modern spiritualism as containing even a grain of the genuine, yet I was not wholly prepared to deny that human flesh may now and then, once perhaps in ten million cases, be the veil of powers which seem magical to us; powers which, so far from proceeding from the heights and leading men thither, are in reality survivals from the depths of being. The amoeba and the snail have powers which we do not possess; and I thought it possible that the theory of reversion might explain many things which seem wholly inexplicable. Thus stood my position; I saw good reason to believe that much of the tradition, a vast deal of the earliest and uncorrupted tradition of the so-called fairies, represented solid fact, and I thought that the purely supernatural element in these traditions, was to be accounted for on the hypothesis that a race which had fallen out of the grand march of evolution might have retained, as a survival, certain powers which would be to us wholly miraculous. Such was my theory as it stood conceived in my mind; and working with, this in view, I seemed to gather confirmation from every side, from the spoils of a tumulus or a barrow, from a local paper reporting an antiquarian meeting in the country, and from general literature of all kinds. Amongst other instances, I remember being struck by the phrase "articulate-speaking men" in Homer, as if the writer knew or had heard of men whose speech was so rude that it could hardly be termed articulate; and on my hypothesis of a race who had lagged far behind the rest, I could easily conceive that such a folk would speak a jargon but little removed from the inarticulate noises of brute-beasts.

Thus I stood, satisfied that my conjecture was at all events not far removed from fact, when a chance paragraph in a small country print one day arrested my attention. It was a short account of what was to all appearance the usual sordid tragedy of the village; a young girl unaccountably missing, and evil rumor blatant and busy with her reputation. Yet I could read between the lines that all this scandal was purely hypothetical, and in all probability invented to account for what was in any other manner unaccountable. A flight to London or Liverpool, or an undiscovered body lying with a weight about its neck in the foul depths of a woodland pool, of perhaps murder,--such were the theories of the wretched girl's neighbors. But as I idly scanned the paragraph, a flash of thought passed through me with the violence of an electric shock: What if the obscure and horrible race of the hills still survived, still remained haunting wild places, and barren hills, and now and then repeating the evil of Gothic legend, unchanged and unchangeable as the Turanian Shelta, or the Basques of Spain. I have said that the thought came with violence; and indeed I drew in my breath sharply, and clung with both hands to my elbow-chair, in a strange confusion of horror and elation. It was as if one of my confrères of physical science, roaming in a quiet English wood, had been suddenly stricken aghast by the presence of the slimy and loathsome terror of the ichthyosaurus, the original of the stories of the awful worms killed by valorous knights, or had seen the sun darkened by the pterodactyl, the dragon of tradition. Yet as a resolute explorer of knowledge, the thought of such a discovery threw me into a passion of joy, and I cut out the slip from the paper, and put it in a drawer in my old bureau, resolved that it should be but the first piece in a collection of the strangest significance. I sat long that evening dreaming of the conclusions I should establish, nor did cooler reflection at first dash my confidence. Yet as I began to put the case fairly, I saw that I might be building on an unstable foundation; the facts might possibly be in accordance with local opinion; and I regarded the affair with a mood of some reserve. Yet I resolved to remain perched on the look-out, and I hugged to myself the thought that I alone was watching and wakeful, while the great crowd of thinkers and searchers stood heedless and indifferent, perhaps letting the most prerogative facts pass by unnoticed.

Several years elapsed before I was enabled to add to the contents of the drawer; and the second find was in reality not a valuable one, for it was a mere repetition of the first, with only the variation of another and distant locality. Yet I gained something; for in the second case, as in the first, the tragedy took place in a desolate and lonely country, and so far my theory seemed justified. But the third piece was to me far more decisive. Again, amongst outland hills, far even from a main road of traffic, an old man was found done to death, and the instrument of execution was left beside him. Here, indeed, there was rumor and conjecture, for the deadly tool was a primitive stone axe, bound by gut to the wooden handle, and surmises the most extravagant and improbable were indulged in. Yet, as I thought with a kind of glee, the wildest conjectures went far astray; and I took the pains to enter into correspondence with the local doctor, who was called at the inquest. He, a man of some acuteness, was dumfoundered. "It will not do to speak of these things in country places, he wrote to me; but, frankly, Professor Gregg, there is some hideous mystery here. I have obtained possession of the stone axe, and have been so curious as to test its powers. I took it into the back-garden of my house one Sunday afternoon when my family and the servants were all out, and there, sheltered by the poplar hedges, I made my experiments. I found the thing utterly unmanageable. Whether there is some peculiar balance, some nice adjustment of weights, which require incessant practice, or whether an effectual blow can be struck only by a certain trick of the muscles, I do not know; but I assure you that I went into the house with but a sorry opinion of my athletic capacities. It was like an inexperienced man trying 'putting the hammer;' the force exerted seemed to return on oneself, and I found myself hurled backwards with violence, while the axe fell harmless to the ground. On another occasion I tried the experiment with a clever woodman of the place; but this man, who had handled his axe for forty years, could do nothing with the stone implement, and missed every stroke most ludicrously. In short, if it were not so supremely absurd, I should say that for four thousand years no one on earth could have struck an effective blow with the tool that undoubtedly was used to murder the old man." This, as may be imagined, was to me rare news; and afterwards, when I heard the whole story, and learned that the unfortunate old man had babbled tales of what might be seen at night on a certain wild hillside, hinting at unheard-of wonders, and that he had been found cold one morning on the very hill in question, my exultation was extreme, for I felt I was leaving conjecture far behind me. But the next step was of still greater importance. I had possessed for many years an extraordinary stone seal,--a piece of dull black stone, two inches long from the handle to the stamp, and the stamping end a rough hexagon an inch and a quarter in diameter. Altogether, it presented the appearance of an enlarged tobacco-stopper of an old-fashioned make. It had been sent to me by an agent in the East, who informed me that it had been found near the site of the ancient Babylon. But the characters engraved on the seal were to me an intolerable puzzle. Somewhat of the cuneiform pattern, there were yet striking differences, which I detected at the first glance, and all efforts to read the inscription on the hypothesis that the rules for deciphering the arrow-headed writing would apply proved futile. A riddle such as this stung my pride, and at odd moments I would take the Black Seal out of the cabinet, and scrutinize it with so much idle perseverance that every letter was familiar to my mind, and I could have drawn the inscription from memory without the slightest error. Judge then of my surprise, when I one day received from a correspondent in the west of England a letter and an enclosure that positively left me thunderstruck. I saw carefully traced on a large piece of paper the very characters of the Black Seal, without alteration of any kind, and above the inscription my friend had written: Inscription found on a limestone rock on the Grey Hills, Monmouthshire. Done in some red earth and quite recent. I turned to the letter. My friend wrote: "I send you the enclosed inscription with all due reserve. A shepherd who passed by the stone a week ago swears that there was then no mark of any kind. The characters, as I have noted, are formed by drawing some red earth over the stone, and are of an average height of one inch. They look to me like a kind of cuneiform character, a good deal altered, but this of course is impossible. It may be either a hoax or more probably some scribble of the gypsies, who are plentiful enough in this wild country. They have, as you are aware, many hieroglyphics which they use in communicating with one another. I happened to visit the stone in question two days ago in connection with a rather painful incident which has occurred here."

As may be supposed, I wrote immediately to my friend, thanking him for the copy of the inscription, and asking him in a casual manner, the history of the incident he mentioned. To be brief, I heard that a woman named Cradock, who had lost her husband a day before, had set out to communicate the sad news to a cousin who lived some five miles away. She took a short cut which led by the Gray Hills. Mrs. Cradock, who was then quite a young woman, never arrived at her relative's house. Late that night a farmer who had lost a couple of sheep, supposed to have wandered from the flock, was walking over the Gray Hills, with a lantern and his dog. His attention was attracted by a noise, which he described as a kind of wailing, mournful and pitiable to hear; and, guided by the sound, he found the unfortunate Mrs. Cradock crouched on the ground by the limestone rock, swaying her body to and fro, and lamenting and crying in so heart-rending a manner that the farmer was, as he says, at first obliged to stop his ears, or he would have run away. The woman allowed herself to be taken home, and a neighbor came to see to her necessities. All the night she never ceased her crying, mixing her lament with words of some unintelligible jargon, and when the doctor arrived he pronounced her insane. She lay on her bed for a week, now wailing, as people said, like one lost and damned for eternity, and now sunk in a heavy coma; it was thought that grief at the loss of her husband had unsettled her mind, and the medical man did not at one time expect her to live. I need not say that I was deeply interested in this story, and I made my friend write to me at intervals with all the particulars of the case. I heard then that in the course of six weeks the woman gradually recovered the use of her faculties and some months later she gave birth to a son, christened Jervase, who unhappily proved to be of weak intellect. Such were the facts known to the village; but to me while I whitened at the suggested thought of the hideous enormities that had doubtless been committed, all this was nothing short of conviction, and I incautiously hazarded a hint of something like the truth to some scientific friends. The moment the words had left my lips I bitterly regretted having spoken, and thus given away the great secret of my life, but with a good deal of relief mixed with indignation, I found my fears altogether misplaced, for my friends ridiculed me to my face, and I was regarded as a madman; and beneath a natural anger I chuckled to myself, feeling as secure amidst these blockheads, as if I had confided what I knew to the desert sands.

But now, knowing so much, I resolved I would know all, and I concentrated my efforts on the task of deciphering the inscription on the Black Seal. For many years I made this puzzle the sole object of my leisure moments; for the greater portion of my time was, of course, devoted to other duties, and it was only now and then that I could snatch a week of clear research. If I were to tell the full history of this curious investigation, this statement would be wearisome in the extreme, for it would contain simply the account of long and tedious failure. By what I knew already of ancient scripts I was well-equipped for the chase, as I always termed it to myself. I had correspondents amongst all the scientific men in Europe, and, indeed, in the world, and I could not believe that in these days any character, however ancient and however perplexed, could long resist the search-light I should bring to bear upon it. Yet, in point of fact, it was fully fourteen years before I succeeded. With every year my professional duties increased, and my leisure became smaller. This no doubt retarded me a good deal; and yet, when I look back on those years I am astonished at the vast scope of my investigation of the Black Seal. I made my bureau a centre, and from all the world and from all the ages I gathered transcripts of ancient writing. Nothing, I resolved, should pass me unawares, and the faintest hint should be welcomed and followed up. But as one covert after another was tried and proved empty of result, I began in the course of years to despair, and to wonder whether the Black Seal were the sole relic of some race that had vanished from the world and left no other trace of its existence,--had perished, in fine, as Atlantis is said to have done, in some great cataclysm, its secrets perhaps drowned beneath the ocean or moulded into the heart of the hills. The thought chilled my warmth a little, and though I still persevered, it was no longer with the same certainty of faith. A chance came to the rescue. I was staying in a considerable town in the north of England, and took the opportunity of going over the very creditable museum that had for some time been established in the place. The curator was one of my correspondents; and, as we were looking through one of the mineral cases, my attention was struck by a specimen, a piece of black stone some four inches square, the appearance of which reminded me in a measure of the Black Seal. I took it up carelessly, and was turning it over in my hand, when I saw, to my astonishment, that the under side was inscribed. I said, quietly enough, to my friend the curator that the specimen interested me, and that I should be much obliged if he would allow me to take it with me to my hotel for a couple of days. He, of course, made no objection, and I hurried to my rooms, and found that my first glance had not deceived me. There were two inscriptions; one in the regular cuneiform character, another in the character of the Black Seal, and I realized that my task was accomplished. I made an exact copy of the two inscriptions; and when I got to my London study, and had the Seal before me, I was able seriously to grapple with the great problem. The interpreting inscription on the museum specimen, though in itself curious enough, did not bear on my quest, but the transliteration made me master of the secret of the Black Seal. Conjecture, of course, had to enter into my calculations; there was here and there uncertainty about a particular ideograph, and one sign recurring again and again on the Seal baffled me for many successive nights. But at last the secret stood open before me in plain English, and I read the key of the awful transmutation of the hills. The last word was hardly written, when with fingers all trembling and unsteady I tore the scrap of paper into the minutest fragments, and saw them flame and blacken in the red hollow of the fire, and then I crushed the gray films that remained into finest powder. Never since then have I written those words; never will I write the phrases which tell me how man can be reduced to the slime from which he came, and be forced to put on the flesh of the reptile and the snake. There was now but one thing remaining. I knew; but I desired to see, and I was after some time able to take a house in the neighborhood of the Gray Hills, and not far from the cottage where Mrs. Cradock and her son Jervase resided. I need not go into a full and detailed account of the apparently inexplicable events which have occurred here, where I am writing this. I knew that I should find in Jervase Cradock something of the blood of the "Little People," and I found later that he had more than once encountered his kinsmen in lonely places in that lonely land. When I was summoned one day to the garden, and found him in a seizure speaking or hissing the ghastly jargon of the Black Seal, I am afraid that exultation prevailed over pity. I heard bursting from his lips the secrets of the underworld, and the word of dread, "Ishakshar," the signification of which I must be excused from giving.

But there is one incident I cannot pass over unnoticed. In the waste hollow of the night I awoke at the sound of those hissing syllables I knew so well; and on going to the wretched boy's room, I found him convulsed and foaming at the mouth, struggling on the bed as if he strove to escape the grasp of writhing demons. I took him down to my room and lit the lamp, while he lay twisting on the floor, calling on the power within his flesh to leave him. I saw his body swell and become distended as a bladder, while the face blackened before my eyes; and then at the crisis I did what was necessary according to the directions on the Seal, and putting all scruple on one side, I became a man of science, observant of what was passing. Yet the sight I had to witness was horrible, almost beyond the power of human conception and the most fearful fantasy; something pushed out from the body there on the floor, and stretched forth, a slimy wavering tentacle, across the room, and grasped the bust upon the cupboard, and laid it down on my desk.

When it was over, and I was left to walk up and down all the rest of the night, white and shuddering, with sweat pouring from my flesh, I vainly tried to reason with myself; I said, truly enough, that I had seen nothing really supernatural, that a snail pushing out his horns and drawing them in was but an instance on a smaller scale of what I had witnessed; and yet horror broke through all such reasonings and left me shattered and loathing myself for the share I had taken in the night's work.

There is little more to be said. I am going now to the final trial and encounter; for I have determined that there shall be nothing wanting, and I shall meet the "Little People" face to face. I shall have the Black Seal and the knowledge of its secrets to help me, and if I unhappily do not return from my journey, there is no need to conjure up here a picture of the awfulness of my fate.

Pausing a little at the end of Professor Gregg's statement, Miss Lally continued her tale in the following words:--

Such was the almost incredible story that the professor had left behind him. When I had finished reading it, it was late at night, but the next morning I took Morgan with me, and we proceeded to search the Gray Hills for some trace of the lost professor. I will not weary you with a description of the savage desolation of that tract of country, a tract of utterest loneliness, of bare green hills dotted over with gray limestone boulders, worn by the ravage of time into fantastic semblances of men and beasts. Finally, after many hours of weary searching, we found what I told you--the watch and chain, the purse, and the ring--wrapped in a piece of coarse parchment. When Morgan cut the gut that bound the parcel together, and I saw the professor's property, I burst into tears, but the sight of the dreaded characters of the Black Seal repeated on the parchment froze me to silent horror, and I think I understood for the first time the awful fate that had come upon my late employer.

I have only to add that Professor Gregg's lawyer treated my account of what had happened as a fairy tale, and refused even to glance at the documents I laid before him. It was he who was responsible for the statement that appeared in the public press, to the effect that Professor Gregg had been drowned, and that his body must have been swept into the open sea.

Miss Lally stopped speaking and looked at Mr. Phillipps, with a glance of some enquiry. He, for his part, was sunken in a deep revery of thought; and when he looked up and saw the bustle of the evening gathering in the square, men and women hurrying to partake of dinner, and crowds already besetting the music-halls, all the hum and press of actual life seemed unreal and visionary, a dream in the morning after an awakening.

"I thank you," he said at last, "for your most interesting story, interesting to me, because I feel fully convinced of its exact truth."

"Sir," said the lady, with some energy of indignation, "you grieve and offend me. Do you think I should waste my time and yours by concocting fictions on a bench in Leicester Square?"

"Pardon me, Miss Lally, you have a little misunderstood me. Before you began I knew that whatever you told would be told in good faith, but your experiences have a far higher value than that of bona fides. The most extraordinary circumstances in your account are in perfect harmony with the very latest scientific theories. Professor Lodge would, I am sure, value a communication from you extremely; I was charmed from the first by his daring hypothesis in explanation of the wonders of Spiritualism (so called), but your narrative puts the whole matter out of the range of mere hypothesis."

"Alas, sir, all this will not help me. You forget, I have lost my brother under the most startling and dreadful circumstances. Again, I ask you, did you not see him as you came here? His black whiskers, his spectacles, his timid glance to right and left; think, do not these particulars recall his face to your memory?"

"I am sorry to say I have never seen any one of the kind," said Phillipps, who had forgotten all about the missing brother. "But let me ask you a few questions. Did you notice whether Professor Gregg--"

"Pardon me, sir, I have stayed too long. My employers will be expecting me. I thank you for your sympathy. Good bye."

Before Mr. Phillipps had recovered from his amazement at this abrupt departure, Miss Lally had disappeared from his gaze, passing into the crowd that now thronged the approaches to the Empire. He walked home in a pensive frame of mind, and drank too much tea. At ten o'clock he had made his third brew, and had sketched out the outlines of a little work to be called Protoplasmic

INCIDENT OF THE PRIVATE BAR

Mr. Dyson often meditated at odd moments over the singular tale he had listened to at the Café de la Touraine. In the first place he cherished a profound conviction that the words of truth were scattered with a too niggardly and sparing hand over the agreeable history of Mr. Smith and the Black Gulf Cañon; and, secondly, there was the undeniable fact of the profound agitation of the narrator, and his gestures on the pavement, too violent to be simulated. The idea of a man going about London haunted by the fear of meeting a young man with spectacles struck Dyson as supremely ridiculous; he searched his memory for some precedent in romance, but without success; he paid visits at odd times to the little café, hoping to find Mr. Wilkins there; and he kept a sharp watch on the great generation of the spectacled men without much doubt that he would remember the face of the individual whom he had seen dart out of the Aerated Bread Shop. All his peregrinations and researches, however, seemed to lead to nothing of value, and Dyson needed all his warm conviction of his innate detective powers and his strong scent for mystery to sustain him in his endeavors. In fact, he had two affairs on hand; and every day, as he passed through streets crowded or deserted, and lurked in the obscure districts, and watched at corners, he was more than surprised to find that the affair of the gold coin persistently avoided him; while the ingenious Wilkins, and the young man with spectacles whom he dreaded, seemed to have vanished from the pavements.

He was pondering these problems one evening in a house of call in the Strand, and the obstinacy with which the persons he so ardently desired to meet hung back gave the modest tankard before him an additional touch of bitter. As it happened, he was alone in his compartment, and, without thinking, he uttered aloud the burden of his meditations. "How bizarre it all is!" he said, "a man walking the pavement with the dread of a timid-looking young man with spectacles continually hovering before his eyes. And there was some tremendous feeling at work, I could swear to that." Quick as thought, before he had finished the sentence, a head popped round the barrier, and was withdrawn again; and while Dyson was wondering what this could mean, the door of the compartment was swung open, and a smooth, clean-shaven, and smiling gentleman entered.

"You will excuse me, sir," he said politely, "for intruding on your thoughts, but you made a remark a minute ago."

"I did," said Dyson; "I have been puzzling over a foolish matter, and I thought aloud. As you heard what I said, and seem interested, perhaps you may be able to relieve my perplexity?"

"Indeed. I scarcely know; it is an odd coincidence. One has to be cautions. I suppose, sir, that you would have no repulsion in assisting the ends of justice."

"Justice," replied Dyson, "is a term of such wide meaning, that I too feel doubtful about giving an answer. But this place is not altogether fit for such a discussion; perhaps you would come to my rooms?"

"You are very kind; my name is Burton, but I am sorry to say I have not a card with me. Do you live near here?"

"Within ten minutes' walk."

Mr. Burton took out his watch and seemed to be making a rapid calculation.

"I have a train to catch," he said; "but after all, it is a late one. So, if you don't mind, I think I will come with you. I am sure we should have a little talk together. We turn up here?"

The theatres were filling as they crossed the Strand, the street seemed alive with voices, and Dyson looked fondly about him. The glittering lines of gas-lamps, with here and there the blinding radiance of an electric light, the hansoms that flashed to and fro with ringing bells, the laden buses, and the eager hurrying east and west of the foot passengers, made his most enchanting picture; and the graceful spire of St. Mary le Strand, on the one hand, and the last flush of sunset on the other, were to him a cause of thanksgiving, as the gorse blossom to Linnæus. Mr. Burton caught his look of fondness as they crossed the street.

"I see you can find the picturesque in London," he said. "To me this great town is as I see it is to you, the study and the love of life. Yet how few there are that can pierce the veils of apparent monotony and meanness! I have read in a paper which is said to have the largest circulation in the world, a comparison between the aspects of London and Paris, a comparison which should be positively laureat, as the great masterpiece of fatuous stupidity. Conceive if you can a human being of ordinary intelligence preferring the Boulevards to our London streets; imagine a man calling for the wholesale destruction of our most charming city, in order that the dull uniformity of that whited sepulchre called Paris should be reproduced here in London. Is it not positively incredible?"

"My dear sir," said Dyson, regarding Burton with a good deal of interest. "I agree most heartily with your opinions, but I really cannot share your wonder. Have you heard how much George Eliot received for 'Romola'? Do you know what the circulation of 'Robert Elsmere' was? Do you read 'Tit Bits' regularly? To me, on the contrary, it is constant matter both for wonder and thanksgiving that London was not boulevardized twenty years ago. I praise that exquisite jagged sky line that stands up against the pale greens and fading blues and flushing clouds of sunset, but I wonder even more than I praise. As for St. Mary le Strand, its preservation is a miracle, nothing more or less. A thing of exquisite beauty versus four buses abreast! Really, the conclusion is too obvious. Didn't you read the letter of the man who proposed that the whole mysterious system, the immemorial plan of computing Easter, should, be abolished off-hand because he doesn't like his son having his holidays as early as March 20th? But shall we be going on?"

They had lingered at the corner of a street on the north side of the Strand, enjoying the contrasts and the glamour of the scene. Dyson pointed the way with a gesture, and they strolled up the comparatively deserted streets, slanting a little to the right, and thus arriving at Dyson's lodging on the verge of Bloomsbury. Mr. Burton took a comfortable armchair by the open window, while Dyson lit the candles and produced the whiskey and soda and cigarettes.

"They tell me these cigarettes are very good," he said, "but I know nothing about it myself. I hold at last that there is only one tobacco, and that is shag. I suppose I could not tempt you to try a pipeful?"

Mr. Burton smilingly refused the offer, and picked out a cigarette from the box. When he had smoked it half through, he said with some hesitation:--

"It is really kind of you to have me here, Mr. Dyson; the fact is that the interests at issue are far too serious to be discussed in a bar, where, as you found for yourself, there may be listeners, voluntary or involuntary, on each side. I think the remark I heard you make was something about the oddity of an individual going about London in deadly fear of a young man with spectacles."

"Yes, that was it."

"Well, would you mind confiding to me the circumstances that gave rise to the reflection?"

"Not in the least; it was like this." And he ran over in brief outline the adventure in Oxford Street, dwelling on the violence of Mr. Wilkins's gestures, but wholly suppressing the tale told in the café. "He told me he lived in constant terror of meeting this man; and I left him when I thought he was cool enough to look after himself," said Dyson, ending his narrative.

"Really," said Mr. Burton. "And you actually saw this mysterious person."

"Yes."

"And could you describe him?"

"Well, he looked to me a youngish man, pale and nervous. He had small black side whiskers, and wore rather large spectacles."

"But this is simply marvellous! You astonish me. For I must tell you that my interest in the matter is this. I am not in the least in terror of meeting a dark young man with spectacles, but I shrewdly suspect a person of that description would much rather not meet me. And yet the account you give of the man tallies exactly. A nervous glance to right and left--is it not so? And, as you observed, he wears prominent spectacles, and has small black whiskers. There cannot be surely two people exactly identical--one a cause of terror, and the other, I should imagine, extremely anxious to get out of the way. But have you seen this man since?"

"No, I have not; and I have been looking out for him pretty keenly. But, of course, he may have left London, and England too for the matter of that."

Hardly, I think. Well, Mr. Dyson, it is only fair that I should explain my story, now that I have listened, to yours. I must tell you, then, that I am an agent for curiosities and precious things of all kinds. An odd employment, isn't it? Of course I wasn't brought up to the business; I gradually fell into it. I have always been fond of things queer and rare, and by the time I was twenty I had made half a dozen collections. It is not generally known how often farm laborers come upon rarities; you would be astonished if I told you what I have seen turned up by the plough. I lived in the country in those days, and I used to buy anything the men on the farms brought me; and I had the queerest set of rubbish, as my friends called my collection. But that's how I got the scent of the business, which means everything; and, later on, it struck me that I might very well turn my knowledge to account and add to my income. Since those early days I have been in most quarters of the world, and some very valuable things have passed through my hands, and I have had to engage in difficult and delicate negotiations. You have possibly heard of the Khan opal--called in the East 'The Stone of a Thousand and One Colors'? Well, perhaps the conquest of that stone was my greatest achievement. I call it myself the stone of the thousand and one lies, for I assure you that I had to invent a cycle of folk-lore before the Rajah who owned it would consent to sell the thing. I subsidized wandering story-tellers, who told tales in which the opal played a frightful part; I hired a holy man, a great ascetic, to prophesy against the thing in the language of Eastern symbolism; in short, I frightened the Rajah out of his wits. So you see there is room for diplomacy in the traffic I am engaged in. I have to be ever on my guard, and I have often been sensible that unless I watched every step and weighed every word my life would not last me much longer. Last April I became aware of the existence of a highly valuable antique gem. It was in Southern Italy, and in the possession of persons who were ignorant of its real value. It has always been my experience that it is precisely the ignorant who are most difficult to deal with. I have met farmers who were under the impression that a shilling of George I. was a find of almost incalculable value; and all the defeats I have sustained have been at the hands of people of this description. Reflecting on these facts, I saw that the acquisition of the gem I have mentioned would be an affair demanding the nicest diplomacy; I might possibly have got it by offering a sum approaching its real value, but I need not point out to you that such a proceeding would be most unbusinesslike. Indeed, I doubt whether it would have been successful, for the cupidity of such persons is aroused by a sum which seems enormous, and the low cunning which serves them in place of intelligence immediately suggests that the object for which such an amount is offered must be worth at least double. Of course, when it is a matter of an ordinary curiosity--an old jug, a carved chest, or a queer brass lantern--one does not much care; the cupidity of the owner defeats its object, the collector laughs, and goes away, for he is aware that such things are by no means unique. But this gem I fervently desired to possess; and as I did not see my way to giving more than a hundredth part of its value, I was conscious that all my, let us say, imaginative and diplomatic powers would have to be exerted. I am sorry to say that I came to the conclusion that I could not undertake to carry the matter through single-handed, and I determined to confide in my assistant, a young man named William Robbins, whom I judged to be by no means devoid of capacity. My idea was that Robbins should get himself up as a low-class dealer in precious stones; he could patter a little Italian, and would go to the town in question and manage to see the gem we were after, possibly by offering some trifling articles of jewelry for sale, but that I left to be decided, then my work was to begin, but I will not trouble you with a tale told twice over. In due course, then, Robbins went off to Italy with an assortment of uncut stones and a few rings, and some jewelry I bought in Birmingham, on purpose for his expedition. A week later I followed him, travelling leisurely, so that I was a fortnight later in arriving at our common destination. There was a decent hotel in the town, and on my inquiring of the landlord whether there were many strangers in the place, he told me very few; he had heard there was an Englishman staying in a small tavern, a pedlar he said, who sold beautiful trinkets very cheaply, and wanted to buy old rubbish. For five or six days I took life leisurely, and I must say I enjoyed myself. It was part of my plan to make the people think I was an enormously rich man; and I knew that such items as the extravagance of my meals, and the price of every bottle of wine I drank, would not be suffered, as Sancho Panza puts it, to rot in the landlord's breast. At the end of the week I was fortunate enough to make the acquaintance of Signor Melini, the owner of the gem I coveted, at the café, and with his ready hospitality and my geniality I was soon established as a friend of the house. On my third or fourth visit I managed to make the Italians talk about the English pedlar, who, they said, spoke a most detestable Italian. 'But that does not matter,' said the Signora Melini, 'for he has beautiful things, which he sells very very cheap.' 'I hope you may not find he has cheated you,' I said, 'for I must tell you that English people give these fellows a very wide berth. They usually make a great parade of the cheapness of their goods, which often turn out to be double the price of better articles in the shops,' They would not hear of this, and Signora Melini insisted on showing me the three rings and the bracelet she had bought of the pedlar. She told me the price she had paid; and after scrutinizing the articles carefully, I had to confess that she had made a bargain, and indeed Robbins had sold her the things at about fifty per cent below market value. I admired the trinkets as I gave them back to the lady, and I hinted that the pedlar must be a somewhat foolish specimen of his class. Two days later, as I was taking my vermouth at the café with Signor Melini, he led the conversation back to the pedlar, and mentioned casually that he had shown the man a little curiosity, for which he had made rather a handsome offer. 'My dear sir,' I said, 'I hope you will be careful. I told you that the travelling tradesman does not bear a very high reputation in England; and notwithstanding his apparent simplicity, this fellow may turn out to be an arrant cheat. May I ask you what is the nature of the curiosity you have shown him?' He told me it was a little thing, a pretty little stone with some figures cut on it: people said it was old. 'I should like to examine it,' I replied; 'as it happens I have, seen a good deal of these gems. We have a fine collection of them in our museum at London.' In due course I was shown the article, and I held the gem I so coveted between my fingers. I looked at it coolly, and put it down carelessly on the table. 'Would you mind telling me, signor,' I said, 'how much my fellow-countryman offered you for this?' 'Well,' he said, 'my wife says the man must be mad; he said he would give me twenty lire for it.'

"I looked at him quietly, and took up the gem and pretended to examine it in the light more carefully; I turned it over and over, and finally pulled out a magnifying glass from my pocket, and seemed to search every line in the cutting with minutest scrutiny. 'My dear sir,' I said at last, 'I am inclined to agree with Signora Melini. If this gem were genuine, it would be worth some money;

but as it happens to be a rather bad forgery, it is not worth twenty centesimi. It was sophisticated, I should imagine, some time in the last century, and by a very unskilful hand.' 'Then we had better get rid of it,' said Melini. 'I never thought it was worth anything myself. Of course I am sorry for the pedlar, but one must let a man know his own trade. I shall tell him we will take the twenty lire.' 'Excuse me,' I said, 'the man wants a lesson. It would be a charity to give him one. Tell him that you will not take anything under eighty lire, and I shall be much surprised if he does not close with you at once.'

"A day or two later I heard that the English pedlar had gone away, after debasing the minds of the country people with Birmingham art jewelry; for I admit that the gold sleeve links like kidney beans, the silver chains made apparently after the pattern of a dog-chain, and the initial brooches, have always been heavy on my conscience. I cannot acquit myself of having indirectly contributed to debauch the taste of a simple folk; but I hope that the end I had in view may finally outbalance this heavy charge. Soon afterwards, I paid a farewell visit at the Melinis, and the signor informed me with an oily chuckle that the plan I had suggested had been completely successful. I congratulated him on his bargain, and went away after expressing a wish that heaven might send many such pedlars in his path.

"Nothing of interest occurred on my return journey. I had arranged that Robbins was to meet me at a certain place on a certain day, and I went to the appointment full of the coolest confidence; the gem had been conquered, and I had only to reap the fruits of victory. I am sorry to shake that trust in our common human nature which I am sure you possess, but I am compelled to tell you that up to the present date I have never set eyes on my man Robbins, or on the antique gem in his custody. I have found out that he actually arrived in London, for he was seen three days before my arrival in England by a pawnbroker of my acquaintance consuming his favorite beverage, four ale, in the tavern where we met to-night. Since then he has not been heard of. I hope you will now pardon my curiosity as to the history and adventures of dark young men with spectacles. You will, I am sure, feel for me in my position; the savor of life has disappeared for me; it is a bitter thought that I have rescued one of the most perfect and exquisite specimens of antique art from the hands of ignorant, and indeed unscrupulous persons, only to deliver it into the keeping of a man who is evidently utterly devoid of the very elements of commercial morality."

"My dear sir," said Dyson, "you will allow me to compliment you on your style; your adventures have interested me exceedingly. But, forgive me, you just now used the word morality; would not some persons take exception to your own methods of business? I can conceive, myself, flaws of a moral kind being found in the very original conception you have described to me. I can imagine the Puritan shrinking in dismay from your scheme, pronouncing it unscrupulous, nay, dishonest."

Mr. Burton helped himself, very frankly, to some more whiskey.

"Your scruples entertain me," he said. "Perhaps you have not gone very deeply into these questions of ethics. I have been compelled to do so myself, just as I was forced to master a simple system of book-keeping. Without book-keeping, and still more without a system of ethics, it is impossible to conduct a business such as mine. But I assure you that I am often profoundly saddened as I pass through the crowded streets and watch the world at work by the thought of how few amongst all these hurrying individuals, black hatted, well dressed, educated we may presume sufficiently,--how few amongst them have any reasoned system of morality. Even you have not weighed the question; although you study life and affairs, and to a certain extent penetrate the veils and masks of the comedy of man, even you judge by empty conventions, and the false money which is allowed to pass current as sterling coin. Allow me to play the part of Socrates; I shall teach you nothing that you do not know. I shall merely lay aside the wrappings of prejudice and bad logic, and show you the real image which you possess in your soul. Come then. Do you allow that happiness is anything?"

"Certainly," said Dyson.

"And happiness is desirable or undesirable?"

"Desirable of course."

"And what shall we call the man who gives happiness? Is he not a philanthropist?"

"I think so."

"And such a person is praiseworthy, and the more praiseworthy in the proportion of the persons whom he makes happy?"

"By all means."

"So that he who makes a whole nation happy, is praiseworthy in the extreme, and the action by which he gives happiness is the highest virtue?"

"It appears so, O Burton," said Dyson, who found something very exquisite in the character of his visitor.

"Quite so; you find the several conclusions inevitable. Well, apply them to the story I have told, you. I conferred happiness on myself by obtaining (as I thought) possession of the gem; I conferred happiness on the Melinis by getting them eighty lire instead of an object for which they had not the slightest value, and I intended to confer happiness on the whole British nation by selling the thing to the British Museum, to say nothing of the happiness a profit of about nine thousand per cent would have conferred on me. I assure you I regard Robbins as an interferer with the cosmos and fair order of things. But that is nothing; you perceive that I am an apostle of the very highest morality; you have been forced to yield to argument."

"There certainly seems a great deal in what you advance," said Dyson. "I admit that I am a mere amateur of ethics, while you, as you say, have brought the most acute scrutiny to bear on these perplexed and doubtful questions. I can well understand your anxiety to meet the fallacious Robbins, and I congratulate myself on the chance which has made us acquainted. But you will pardon my seeming inhospitality, I see it is half past eleven, and I think you mentioned a train."

"A thousand thanks, Mr. Dyson, I have just time, I see. I will look you up some evening if I may. Good-night."

THE DECORATIVE IMAGINATION

In the course of a few weeks Dyson became accustomed, to the constant incursions of the ingenious Mr. Burton, who showed himself ready to drop in at all hours, not averse to refreshment, and a profound guide in the complicated questions of life. His visits at once terrified and delighted Dyson, who could no longer seat himself at his bureau secure from interruption while he embarked on literary undertakings, each one of which was to be a masterpiece. On the other hand, it was a vivid pleasure to be confronted with views so highly original; and if here and there Mr. Burton's reasonings seemed tinged with fallacy, yet Dyson freely yielded to the joy of strangeness, and never failed to give his visitor a frank and hearty welcome. Mr. Burton's first inquiry was always after the unprincipled Robbins, and he seemed to feel the stings of disappointment when Dyson told him that he had failed to meet this outrage on all morality, as Burton styled him, vowing that sooner or later he would take vengeance on such a shameless betrayal of trust.

One evening they had sat together for some time discussing the possibility of laying down for this present generation and our modern and intensely complicated order of society, some rules of social diplomacy, such as Lord Bacon gave to the courtiers of King James I. "It is a book to make," said Mr. Burton, "but who is there capable of making it? I tell you people are longing for such a book; it would bring fortune to its publisher. Bacon's Essays are exquisite, but they have now no practical application; the modern strategist can find but little use in a treatise 'De Re Militari,' written by a Florentine in the fifteenth century. Scarcely more dissimilar are the social conditions of Bacon's time and our own; the rules that he lays down so exquisitely for the courtier and diplomatist of James the First's age will avail us little in the rough-and-tumble struggle of to-day. Life, I am afraid, has deteriorated; it gives little play for fine strokes such as formerly advanced men in the state. Except in such businesses as mine, where a chance does occur now and then, it has all become, as I said, an affair of rough and tumble; men still desire to attain, it is true, but what is their moyen de parvenir? A mere imitation, and not a gracious one, of the arts of the soap-vender and the proprietor of baking powder. When I think of these things, my dear Dyson, I confess that I am tempted to despair of my century."

"You are too pessimistic, my dear fellow; you set up too high a standard. Certainly, I agree with you that the times are decadent in many ways. I admit a general appearance of squalor; it needs much philosophy to extract the wonderful and the beautiful from the Cromwell Road or the Nonconformist conscience. Australian wines of fine Burgundy character, the novels alike of the old women and the new women, popular journalism,--these things indeed make for depression. Yet we have our advantages. Before us is unfolded the greatest spectacle the world has ever seen,--the mystery of the innumerable unending streets, the strange adventures that must infallibly arise from so complicated a press of interests. Nay, I will say that he who has stood in the ways of a suburb and has seen them stretch before him all shining, void, and desolate at noonday, has not lived in vain. Such a sight is in reality more wonderful than any perspective of Bagdad or Grand Cairo. And, to set on one side the entertaining history of the gem which you told me, surely you must have had many singular adventures in your own career?"

"Perhaps not so many as you would think; a good deal--the larger part--of my business has been as commonplace as linen-drapery. But of course things happen now and then. It is ten years since I have established my agency, and I suppose that a house and estate agent who had been in trade for an equal time could tell you some queer stories. But I must give you a sample of my experiences some night.

"Why not to-night?" said Dyson. "This evening seems to me admirably adapted for an odd chapter. Look out into the street; you can catch a view of it, if you crane your neck from that chair of yours. Is it not charming? The double row of lamps growing closer in the distance, the hazy outline of the plane-tree in the square, and the lights of the hansoms swimming to and fro, gliding and vanishing; and above, the sky all clear and blue and shining. Come, let us have one of your cent nouvelles nouvelles."

"My dear Dyson, I am delighted to amuse you." With these words Mr. Burton prefaced the

NOVEL OF THE IRON MAID

I think the most extraordinary event which I can recall took place about five years ago. I was then still feeling my way; I had declared for business, and attended regularly at my office, but I had not succeeded in establishing a really profitable connection, and consequently I had a good deal of leisure time on my hands. I have never thought fit to trouble you with the details of my private life; they would be entirely devoid of interest. I must briefly say, however, that I had a numerous circle of acquaintance, and was never at a loss as to how to spend my evenings. I was so fortunate as to have friends in most of the ranks of the social order; there is nothing so unfortunate, to my mind, as a specialized circle, wherein a certain round of ideas is continually traversed and retraversed. I have always tried to find out new types and persons whose brains contained something fresh to me; one may chance to gain information even from the conversation of city men on an omnibus. Amongst my acquaintance I knew a young doctor who lived in a far outlying suburb, and I used often to brave the intolerably slow railway journey, to have the pleasure of listening to his talk. One night we conversed so eagerly together over our pipes and whiskey that the clock passed unnoticed, and when I glanced up I realized with a shock that I had just five minutes in which to catch the last tram. I made a dash for my hat and stick, and jumped out of the house and down the steps, and tore at full speed up the street. It was no good, however; there was a shriek of the engine whistle, and I stood there at the station door and saw far on the long dark line of the embankment a red light shine and vanish, and a porter came down and shut the door with a bang.

"How far to London?" I asked him.

"A good nine miles to Waterloo Bridge;" and with that he went off.

Before me was the long suburban street, its dreary distance marked by rows of twinkling lamps, and the air was poisoned by the faint sickly smell of burning bricks; it was not a cheerful prospect by any means, and I had to walk through nine miles of such streets, deserted as those of Pompeii. I knew pretty well what direction to take; so I set out wearily, looking at the stretch of lamps vanishing in perspective; and as I walked, street after street branched off to right and left,-- some far reaching to distances that seemed endless, communicating with, other systems of thoroughfare; and some mere protoplasmic streets, beginning in orderly fashion with serried two-storied houses, and ending suddenly in waste, and pits, and rubbish heaps, and fields whence the magic had departed. I have spoken of systems of thoroughfare, and I assure you that, walking alone through these silent places, I felt phantasy growing on me, and some glamour of the infinite. There was here. I felt, an immensity as in the outer void, of the universe. I passed from unknown to unknown, my way marked by lamps like stars, and on either band was an unknown world where myriads of men dwelt and slept, street leading into street, as it seemed to world's end. At first the road by which I was travelling was lined with houses of unutterable monotony,--a wall of gray brick pierced by two stories of windows, drawn close to the very pavement. But by degrees I noticed an improvement: there were gardens, and these grew larger. The suburban builder began to allow himself a wider scope; and for a certain distance each flight of steps was guarded by twin lions of plaster, and scents of flowers prevailed over the fume of heated bricks. The road began to climb a hill, and, looking up a side street, I saw the half moon rise over plane-trees, and there on the other side was as if a white cloud had fallen, and the air around it was sweetened as with incense; it was a may-tree in full bloom. I pressed on stubbornly, listening for the wheels and the clatter of some belated hansom; but into that land of men who go to the city in the morning and return in the evening, the hansom rarely enters, and I had resigned myself once more to the walk, when I suddenly became aware that some one was advancing to meet me along the walk. The man was strolling rather aimlessly; and though the time and the place would have allowed an unconventional style of dress, he was vested in the ordinary frock coat, black tie, and silk hat of civilization. We met each other under the lamp, and, as often happens in this great town, two casual passengers brought face to face found, each in the other an acquaintance.

"Mr. Mathias, I think?" I said.

"Quite so. And you are Frank Burton. You know you are a man with a Christian name, so I won't apologize for my familiarity. But may I ask where you are going?"

I explained the situation to him, saying I had traversed a region as unknown to me as the

173

darkest recesses of Africa. "I think I have only about five miles farther," I concluded.

"Nonsense; you must come home with me. My house is close by; in fact, I was just taking my evening walk when we met. Come along; I dare say you will find a makeshift bed easier than a five-mile walk."

I let him take my arm and lead me along, though I was a good deal surprised at so much geniality from a man who was, after all, a mere casual club acquaintance. I suppose I had not spoken to Mr. Mathias half-a-dozen times; he was a man who would sit silent in an armchair for hours, neither reading nor smoking, but now and again moistening his lips with his tongue and smiling queerly to himself. I confess he had never attracted me, and on the whole I should have preferred to continue my walk. But he took my arm and led me up a side street, and stopped at a door in a high wall. We passed through the still moonlit garden, beneath the black shadow of an old cedar, and into an old red brick house with many gables. I was tired enough, and I sighed with relief as I let myself fall into a great leather armchair. You know the infernal grit with which they strew the sidewalk in those suburban districts; it makes walking a penance, and I felt my four-mile tramp had made me more weary than ten miles on an honest country road. I looked about the room with some curiosity. There was a shaded lamp which threw a circle of brilliant light on a heap of papers lying on an old brass-bound secretaire of the last century; but the room was all vague and shadowy, and I could only see that it was long and low, and that it was filled with indistinct objects which might be furniture. Mr. Mathias sat down in a second armchair, and looked about him with that odd smile of his. He was a queer-looking man, clean-shaven, and white to the lips. I should think his age was something between fifty and sixty.

"Now I have got you here," he began, "I must inflict my hobby on you. You knew I was a collector? Oh, yes, I have devoted many years to collecting curiosities, which I think are really curious. But we must have a better light."

He advanced into the middle of the room, and lit a lamp which hung from the ceiling; and as the bright light flashed round the wick, from every corner and space there seemed to start a horror. Great wooden frames with complicated apparatus of ropes and pulleys stood against the wall; a wheel of strange shape had a place beside a thing that looked like a gigantic gridiron. Little tables glittered with bright steel instruments carelessly put down as if ready for use; a screw and vice loomed out, casting ugly shadows; and in another nook was a saw with cruel jagged teeth.

"Yes," said Mr. Mathias; "they are, as you suggest, instruments of torture,--of torture and death. Some--many, I may say--have been used; a few are reproductions after ancient examples. Those knives were used for flaying; that frame is a rack, and a very fine specimen. Look at this; it comes from Venice. You see that sort of collar, something like a big horse-shoe? Well, the patient, let us call him, sat down quite comfortably, and the horse-shoe was neatly fitted round his neck. Then the two ends were joined with a silken band, and the executioner began to turn a handle connected with the band. The horse-shoe contracted very gradually as the band tightened, and the turning continued till the man was strangled. It all took place quietly, in one of those queer garrets under the leads. But these things are all European; the Orientals are, of course, much more ingenious. These are the Chinese contrivances. You have heard of the 'heavy death'? It is my hobby, this sort of thing. Do you know, I often sit here, hour after hour, and meditate over the collection. I fancy I see the faces of the men who have suffered--faces lean with agony and wet with sweats of death--growing distinct out of the gloom, and I hear the echoes of their cries for mercy. But I must show you my latest acquisition. Come into the next room."

I followed Mr. Mathias out. The weariness of the walk, the late hour, and the strangeness of it all, made me feel like a man in a dream; nothing would have surprised me very much. The second room was as the first, crowded with ghastly instruments; but beneath the lamp was a wooden platform, and a figure stood on it. It was a large statue of a naked woman, fashioned in green bronze; the arms were stretched out, and there was a smile on the lips; it might well have been intended for a Venus, and yet there was about the thing an evil and a deadly look.

Mr. Mathias looked at it complacently. "Quite a work of art, isn't it?" he said. "It's made of bronze, as you see, but it has long had the name of the Iron Maid. I got it from Germany, and it was only unpacked this afternoon; indeed, I have not yet had time to open the letter of advice. You see that very small knob between the breasts? Well, the victim was bound to the Maid, the knob was pressed, and the arms slowly tightened round the neck. You can imagine the result."

As Mr. Mathias talked, he patted the figure affectionately. I had turned away, for I sickened at the sight of the man and his loathsome treasure. There was a slight click, of which I took no notice,--it was not much louder than the tick of a clock; and then I heard a sudden whir, the noise of machinery in motion, and I faced round. I have never forgotten the hideous agony on Mathias's face as those relentless arms tightened about his neck; there was a wild struggle as of a beast in the toils, and then a shriek that ended in a choking groan. The whirring noise had suddenly changed into a heavy droning. I tore with all my might at the bronze arms, and strove to wrench them apart, but I could do nothing. The head had slowly bent down, and the green lips were on the lips of Mathias.

Of course I had to attend at the inquest. The letter which had accompanied the figure was found unopened on the study table. The German firm of dealers cautioned their client to be most careful in touching the Iron Maid, as the machinery had been put in thorough working order.

For many revolving weeks Mr. Burton delighted Dyson by his agreeable conversation, diversified by anecdote, and interspersed with the narration of singular adventures. Finally, however, he vanished as suddenly as he had appeared, and on the occasion of his last visit he contrived to loot a copy of his namesake's Anatomy. Dyson, considering this violent attack on the rights of property, and certain glaring inconsistencies in the talk of his late friend, arrived at the conclusion that his stories were fabulous, and that the Iron Maid only existed in the sphere of a decorative imagination.

THE RECLUSE OF BAYSWATER

Amongst the many friends who were favored with the occasional pleasure of Mr. Dyson's society was Mr. Edgar Russell, realist and obscure struggler, who occupied a small back room on the second floor of a house in Abingdon Grove, Notting Hill. Turning off from the main street and walking a few paces onward, one was conscious of a certain calm, a drowsy peace, which made the feet inclined to loiter; and this was ever the atmosphere of Abingdon Grove. The houses stood a little back, with gardens where the lilac and laburnum and blood-red may blossomed gayly in their seasons, and there was a corner where an older house in another street had managed to keep a back garden of real extent; a walled-in garden whence there came a pleasant scent of greenness after the rains of early summer, where old elms held memories of the open fields, where there was yet sweet grass to walk on. The houses in Abingdon Grove belonged chiefly to the nondescript stucco period of thirty-five years ago, tolerably built with passable accommodation for moderate incomes; they had largely passed into the state of lodgings, and cards bearing the inscription "Furnished Apartments" were not infrequent over the doors. Here, then, in a house of sufficiently good appearance, Mr. Russell had established himself; for he looked upon the traditional dirt and squalor of Grub Street as a false and obsolete convention, and preferred, as he said, to live within sight of green leaves. Indeed, from his room one had a magnificent view of a long line of gardens, and a screen of poplars shut out the melancholy back premises of Wilton Street during the summer months. Mr. Russell lived chiefly on bread and tea, for his means were of the smallest; but when Dyson came to see him, he would send out the slavey for six-ale, and Dyson was always at liberty to smoke as much of his own tobacco as he pleased. The landlady had been so unfortunate as to have her drawing-room floor vacant for many months; a card had long proclaimed the void within; and Dyson, when he walked up the steps one evening in early autumn, had a sense that something was missing, and, looking at the fanlight, saw the appealing card had disappeared.

"You have let your first floor, have you?" he said, as he greeted Mr. Russell.

"Yes; it was taken about a fortnight ago by a lady."

"Indeed," said Dyson, always curious; "a young lady?"

"Yes, I believe so. She is a widow, and wears a thick crape veil. I have met her once or twice on the stairs and in the street, but I should not know her face."

"Well," said Dyson, when the beer had arrived, and the pipes were in full blast, "and what have you been doing? Do you find the work getting any easier?"

"Alas!" said the young man, with an expression of great gloom, "the life is a purgatory, and all but a hell. I write, picking out my words, weighing and balancing the force of every syllable, calculating the minutest effects that language can produce, erasing and rewriting, and spending a whole evening over a page of manuscript. And then in the morning when I read what I have written--Well, there is nothing to be done but to throw it in the waste-paper basket if the verso has been already written on, or to put it in the drawer if the other side happens to be clean. When I have written a phrase which undoubtedly embodies a happy turn of thought, I find it dressed up in feeble commonplace; and when the style is good, it serves only to conceal the baldness of superannuated fancies. I sweat over my work, Dyson,--every finished line means so much agony. I envy the lot of the carpenter in the side street who has a craft which he understands. When he gets an order for a table, he does not writhe with anguish; but if I were so unlucky as to get an order for a book, I think I should go mad."

"My dear fellow, you take it all too seriously. You should let the ink flow more readily. Above all, firmly believe, when you sit down to write, that you are an artist, and that whatever you are about is a masterpiece. Suppose ideas fail you, say; as I heard one of our most exquisite artists say, "It's of no consequence; the ideas are all there, at the bottom of that box of cigarettes." You, indeed, smoke tobacco, but the application is the same. Besides, you must have some happy moments, and these should be ample consolation."

"Perhaps you are right. But such moments are so few; and then there is the torture of a glorious conception matched, with execution beneath the standard of the Family Story Paper. For instance, I was happy for two hours a night or two ago; I lay awake and saw visions. But then the morning!"

"What was your idea?"

"It seemed to me a splendid one; I thought of Balzac and the 'Comédie Humaine,' of Zola and the Rougon-Macquart family. It dawned upon me that I would write the history of a street. Every house should form a volume. I fixed upon the street, I saw each house, and read, as clearly as in letters, the physiology and psychology of each. The little by-way stretched before me in its actual shape,--a street that I know and have passed down a hundred times; with some twenty houses, prosperous and mean, and lilac bushes in purple blossom; and yet it was at the same time a symbol, a via dolorosa of hopes cherished and disappointed, of years of monotonous existence without content or discontent, of tragedies and obscure sorrows; and on the door of one of those houses I saw the red stain of blood, and behind a window two shadows, blackened and faded, on the blind, as they swayed on tightened cords,--the shadows of a man and a woman hanging in a vulgar, gas-lit parlor. These were my fancies; but when pen touched paper, they shrivelled and vanished away,"

"Yes," said. Dyson, "there is a lot in that. I envy you the pains of transmuting vision into reality, and still more I envy you the day when you will look at your bookshelf and see twenty goodly books upon the shelves,--the series complete and done forever. Let me entreat you to have them bound in solid parchment, with gold lettering. It is the only real cover for a valiant book. When I look in at the windows of some choice shop, and see the bindings of Levant morocco, with pretty tools and panellings, and your sweet contrasts of red and green, I say to myself, 'These are not books, but bibelots.' A book bound so--a true book, mind you--is like a Gothic statue draped in brocade of Lyons."

"Alas!" said Russell, "we need not discuss the binding,--the books are not begun."

The talk went on as usual till eleven o'clock, when Dyson bade his friend good-night. He knew the way downstairs, and walked down by himself; but greatly to his surprise, as he crossed the first-floor landing, the door opened slightly, and a hand was stretched out, beckoning.

Dyson was not the man to hesitate under such circumstances. In a moment he saw himself involved in adventure; and, as he told himself, the Dysons had never disobeyed a lady's summons. Softly, then, with due regard for the lady's honor, he would have entered the room, when a low but clear voice spoke to him,--

"Go downstairs and open the door, and shut it again rather loudly. Then come up to me; and for heaven's sake, walk softly."

Dyson obeyed her commands,--not without some hesitation, for he was afraid of meeting the landlady or the maid on his return journey. But walking like a cat, and making each step he trod on crack loudly, he flattered himself that he had escaped observation; and as he gained the top of the stairs, the door opened wide before him, and he found himself in the lady's drawing-room, bowing awkwardly.

"Pray be seated, sir. Perhaps this chair will be the best; it was the favored chair of my landlady's deceased husband. I would ask you to smoke, but the odor would betray me. I know my proceedings must seem to you unconventional; but I saw you arrive this evening, and I do not think you would refuse to help a woman who is so unfortunate as I am."

Mr. Dyson looked shyly at the young lady before him. She was dressed in deep mourning; but the piquant smiling face and charming hazel eyes ill accorded with the heavy garments, and the mouldering surface of the crape.

"Madam," he said gallantly, "your instinct has served you well. We will not trouble, if you please, about the question of social conventions; the chivalrous gentleman knows nothing of such matters. I hope I may be privileged to serve you."

"You are very kind to me, but I knew it would be so. Alas, sir, I have had experience of life, and I am rarely mistaken. Yet man is too often so vile and so misjudging that I trembled even as I resolved to take this step, which, for all I knew, might prove to be both desperate and ruinous."

"With me you have nothing to fear," said Dyson. "I was nurtured in the faith of chivalry, and I have always endeavored to remember the proud traditions of my race. Confide in me then, and count upon my secrecy, and, if it prove possible, you may rely on my help."

"Sir, I will not waste your time, which I am sure is valuable, by idle parleyings. Learn, then, that I am a fugitive, and in hiding here. I place myself in your power; you have but to describe my features, and I fall into the hands of my relentless enemy."

Mr. Dyson wondered for a passing instant how this could be; but he only renewed his promise of silence, repeating that he would be the embodied spirit of dark concealment.

"Good," said the lady; "the Oriental fervor of your style is delightful. In the first place, I must disabuse your mind of the conviction that I am a widow. These gloomy vestments have been forced on me by strange circumstance; in plain language, I have deemed it expedient to go disguised. You have a friend, I think, in the house,--Mr. Russell? He seems of a coy and retiring nature."

"Excuse me, madam," said Dyson, "he is not coy, but he is a realist; and perhaps you are aware that no Carthusian monk can emulate the cloistral seclusion in which a realistic novelist loves to shroud himself. It is his way of observing human, nature."

"Well, well," said the lady; "all this, though deeply interesting is not germane to our affair. I must tell you my history."

With these words the young lady proceeded to relate the

NOVEL OF THE WHITE POWDER

My name is Leicester; my father. Major General Wyn Leicester, a distinguished officer of artillery, succumbed five years ago to a complicated liver complaint acquired in the deadly climate of India. A year later my only brother, Francis, came home after an exceptionally brilliant career at the University, and settled down with the resolution of a hermit to master what has been well called the great legend of the law. He was a man who seemed to live in utter indifference to everything that is called pleasure; and though he was handsomer than most men, and could talk as merrily and wittily as if he were a mere vagabond, he avoided society, and shut himself up in a large room at the top of the house to make himself a lawyer. Ten hours a day of hard reading was at first his allotted portion; from the first light in the east to the late afternoon he remained shut up with his books, taking a hasty half-hour's lunch with me as if he grudged the wasting of the moments, and going out for a short walk when it began to grow dusk. I thought that such relentless application must be injurious, and tried to cajole him from the crabbed text-books; but his ardor seemed to grow rather than diminish, and his daily tale of hours increased. I spoke to him seriously, suggesting some occasional relaxation, if it were but an idle afternoon with a harmless novel; but he laughed, and said that he read about feudal tenures when he felt in need of amusement, and scoffed at the notion of theatres, or a month's fresh confessed that he looked well, and seemed not to suffer from his labors; but I knew that such unnatural toil would take revenge at last, and I was not mistaken. A look of anxiety began to lurk about his eyes, and he seemed languid, and at last he avowed that he was no longer in perfect health; he was troubled, he said, with a sensation of dizziness, and awoke now and then of nights from fearful dreams, terrified and cold with icy sweats. "I am taking care of myself," he said; "so you must not trouble. I passed the whole of yesterday afternoon in idleness, leaning back in that comfortable chair you gave me, and scribbling nonsense on a sheet of paper. No, no; I will not overdo my work. I shall be well enough in a week or two, depend upon it."

Yet, in spite of his assurances, I could see that he grew no better, but rather worse; he would enter the drawing-room with a face all miserably wrinkled and despondent, and endeavor to look gayly when my eyes fell on him, and I thought such symptoms of evil omen, and was frightened sometimes at the nervous irritation of his movements, and at glances which I could not decipher. Much against his will, I prevailed on him to have medical advice, and with an ill grace he called in our old doctor.

Dr. Haberden cheered me after his examination of his patient.

"There is nothing really much amiss," he said to me. "No doubt he reads too hard, and eats hastily, and then goes back again to his books in too great a hurry; and the natural consequence is some digestive trouble, and a little mischief in the nervous system. But I think--I do, indeed, Miss Leicester--that we shall be able to set this all right. I have written him a prescription which ought to do great things. So you have no cause for anxiety."

My brother insisted on having the prescription made up by a chemist in the neighborhood; it was an odd old-fashioned shop, devoid of the studied coquetry and calculated glitter that make so gay a show on the counters and shelves of the modern apothecary; but Francis liked the old chemist, and believed in the scrupulous purity of his drugs. The medicine was sent in due course, and I saw that my brother took it regularly after lunch and dinner. It was an innocent-looking white powder, of which a little was dissolved, in a glass of cold water. I stirred it in, and it seemed to disappear, leaving the water clear and colorless. At first Francis seemed to benefit greatly; the weariness vanished from his face, and he became more cheerful than he had ever been since the time when he left school; he talked gayly of reforming himself, and avowed to me that he had wasted his time.

"I have given too many hours to law," he said, laughing; "I think you have saved me in the nick of time. Come, I shall be Lord Chancellor yet, but I must not forget life. You and I will have a holiday together before long; we will go to Paris and enjoy ourselves, and keep away from the

Bibliothèque Nationale."

I confessed myself delighted with the prospect.

"When shall we go?" I said. "I can start the day after to-morrow, if you like."

"Ah, that is perhaps a little too soon; after all, I do not know London yet, and I suppose a man ought to give the pleasures of his own country the first choice. But we will go off together in a week or two, so try and furbish up your French. I only know law French myself, and I am afraid that wouldn't do."

We were just finishing dinner, and he quaffed off his medicine with a parade of carousal as if it had been wine from some choicest bin.

"Has it any particular taste?" I said.

"No; I should not know I was not drinking water," and he got up from his chair, and began to pace up and down the room as if he were undecided as to what he should do next.

"Shall we have coffee in the drawing-room," I said, "or would you like to smoke?"

"No; I think I will take a turn, it seems a pleasant evening. Look at the afterglow; why, it is as if a great city were burning in flames, and down there between the dark houses it is raining blood fast, fast. Yes, I will go out. I may be in soon, but I shall take my key, so good-night, dear, if I don't see you again."

The door slammed behind him, and I saw him walk lightly down the street, swinging his malacca cane, and I felt grateful to Dr. Haberden for such an improvement.

I believe my brother came home very late that night; but he was in a merry mood the next morning.

"I walked on without thinking where I was going," he said, "enjoying the freshness of the air, and livened by the crowds as I reached more frequented quarters. And then I met an old college friend, Orford, in the press of the pavement, and then--well, we enjoyed ourselves. I have felt what it is to be young and a man, I find I have blood in my veins, as other men have. I made an appointment with Orford for to-night; there will be a little party of us at the restaurant. Yes, I shall enjoy myself for a week or two, and hear the chimes at midnight, and then we will go for our little trip together."

Such was the transmutation of my brother's character that in a few days he became a lover of pleasure, a careless and merry idler of western pavements, a hunter out of snug restaurants, and a fine critic of fantastic dancing; he grew fat before my eyes, and said no more of Paris, for he had clearly found his Paradise in London. I rejoiced, and yet wondered a little, for there was, I thought, something in his gayety that indefinitely displeased me, though I could not have defined my feeling. But by degrees there came a change; he returned still in the cold, hours of the morning, but I heard no more about his pleasures, and one morning as we sat at breakfast together, I looked suddenly into his eyes and saw a stranger before me.

"Oh, Francis!" I cried; "Oh, Francis, Francis, what have you done?" and rending sobs cut the words short, and I went weeping out of the room, for though I knew nothing, yet I knew all, and by some odd play of thought I remembered the evening when he first went abroad to prove his manhood, and the picture of the sunset sky glowed before me; the clouds like a city in burning flames, and the rain of blood. Yet I did battle with such thoughts, resolving that perhaps, after all, no great harm had been done, and in the evening at dinner I resolved to press him to fix a day for our holiday in Paris. We had talked easily enough, and my brother had just taken his medicine, which he had continued all the while. I was about to begin my topic, when the words forming in my mind vanished, and I wondered for a second what icy and intolerable weight oppressed my heart and suffocated me as with the unutterable horror of the coffin-lid nailed down on the living.

We had dined without candles, and the room had slowly grown from twilight to gloom, and the walls and corners were indistinct in the shadow. But from where I sat I looked out into the street; and as I thought of what I would say to Francis, the sky began to flush and shine, as it had done on a well-remembered evening, and in the gap between two dark masses that were houses an awful pageantry of flame appeared. Lurid whorls of writhed cloud, and utter depths burning, and gray masses like the fume blown from a smoking city, and an evil glory blazing far above shot with tongues of more ardent fire, and below as if there were a deep pool of blood. I looked down to where my brother sat facing me, and the words were shaped on my lips, when I saw his hand resting on the table. Between the thumb and forefinger of the closed hand, there was a mark, a small patch about the size of a sixpence, and somewhat of the color of a bad bruise. Yet, by some sense I cannot define, I knew that what I saw was no bruise at all. Oh, if human flesh could burn with flame, and if flame could be black as pitch, such was that before me! Without thought or fashioning of words, gray horror shaped within me at the sight, and in an inner cell it was known to be a brand. For a moment the stained sky became dark as midnight, and when the light returned to me, I was alone in the silent room, and soon after I heard my brother go out.

Late as it was, I put on my bonnet and went to Dr. Haberden, and in his great consulting-room, ill-lighted by a candle which the doctor brought in with him, with stammering lips, and a voice that would break in spite of my resolve, I told him all; from the day on which my brother began to take the medicine down to the dreadful thing I had seen scarcely half an hour before.

When I had done, the doctor looked at me for a minute with an expression of great pity on his face.

"My dear Miss Leicester," he said, "you have evidently been anxious about your brother; you have been worrying over him, I am sure. Come, now, is it not so?

"I have certainly been anxious," I said. "For the last week or two I have not felt at ease."

"Quite so; you know, of course, what a queer thing the brain is?"

"I understand what you mean; but I was not deceived. I saw what I have told you with my own eyes."

"Yes, yes, of course. But your eyes had been staring at that very curious sunset we had to-night. That is the only explanation. You will see it in the proper light to-morrow, I am sure. But, remember, I am always ready to give any help that is in my power; do not scruple to come to me, or to send for me if you are in any distress."

I went away but little comforted, all confusion and terror and sorrow, not knowing where to turn. When my brother and I met the next day, I looked quickly at him, and noticed, with a sickening at heart, that the right hand, the hand on which I had clearly seen the patch as of a black fire, was wrapped up with a handkerchief.

"What is the matter with your hand, Francis?" I said in a steady voice.

"Nothing of consequence. I cut a finger last night, and it bled rather awkwardly, so I did it up roughly to the best of my ability."

"I will do it neatly for you, if you like."

"No, thank you, dear, this will answer very well. Suppose we have breakfast; I am quite hungry."

We sat down, and I watched him. He scarcely ate or drank at all, but tossed his meat to the dog when he thought my eyes were turned away; and there was a look in his eyes that I had never yet seen, and the thought fled across my mind that it was a look that was scarcely human. I was firmly convinced that awful and incredible as was the thing I had seen the night before, yet it was no illusion, no glamour of bewildered sense, and in the course of the morning I went again to the doctor's house.

He shook his head with an air puzzled and incredulous, and seemed to reflect for a few minutes.

"And you say he still keeps up the medicine? But why? As I understand, all the symptoms he complained of have disappeared long ago; why should he go on taking the stuff when he is quite well? And by the bye where did he get it made up? At Sayce's? I never send any one there; the old man is getting careless. Suppose you come with me to the chemist's; I should like to have some talk with him."

We walked together to the shop. Old Sayce knew Dr. Haberden, and was quite ready to give any information.

"You have been sending that in to Mr. Leicester for some weeks, I think, on my prescription," said the doctor, giving the old man a pencilled scrap of paper.

The chemist put on his great spectacles with trembling uncertainty, and held up the paper with a shaking hand.

"Oh, yes," he said, "I have very little of it left; it is rather an uncommon drug, and I have had it in stock some time. I must get in some more, if Mr. Leicester goes on with it."

"Kindly let me have a look at the stuff," said Haberden; and the chemist gave him a glass bottle. He took out the stopper and smelt the contents, and looked strangely at the old man.

"Where did you get this?" he said, "and what is it? For one thing, Mr. Sayce, it is not what I prescribed. Yes, yes, I see the label is right enough, but I tell you this is not the drug."

"I have had it a long time," said the old man, in feeble terror. "I got it from Burbage's in the usual way. It is not prescribed often, and I have had it on the shelf for some years. You see there is very little left."

"You had better give it to me," said Haberden. "I am afraid something wrong has happened."

We went out of the shop in silence, the doctor carrying the bottle neatly wrapped in paper under his arm.

"Dr. Haberden," I said when we had walked a little way--"Dr. Haberden."

"Yes," he said, looking at me gloomily enough.

"I should like you to tell me what my brother has been taking twice a day for the last month or so."

"Frankly, Miss Leicester, I don't know. We will speak of this when we get to my house,"

We walked on quickly without another word till we reached Dr. Haberden's. He asked me to sit down, and began pacing up and down the room, his face clouded over, as I could see, with no common fears.

"Well," he said at length, "this is all very strange; it is only natural that you should feel alarmed, and I must confess that my mind is far from easy. We will put aside, if you please, what you told me last night and this morning, but the fact remains that for the last few weeks Mr. Leicester has been impregnating his system with a drug which is completely unknown to me. I tell you, it is not what I ordered; and what that stuff in the bottle really is remains to be seen."

He undid the wrapper, and cautiously tilted a few grains of the white powder on to a piece of paper, and peered curiously at it.

"Yes," he said, "it is like the sulphate of quinine, as you say; it is flaky. But smell it."

He held the bottle to me, and I bent over it. It was a strange sickly smell, vaporous and overpowering, like some strong anæsthetic.

"I shall have it analyzed," said Haberden. "I have a friend who has devoted his whole life to chemistry as a science. Then we shall have something to go upon. No, no, say no more about that other matter; I cannot listen to that, and take my advice and think no more about it yourself."

That evening my brother did not go out as usual after dinner.

"I have had my fling," he said with a queer laugh; "and I must go back to my old ways. A little law will be quite a relaxation after so sharp a dose of pleasure," and he grinned to himself, and soon after went up to his room. His hand was still all bandaged.

Dr. Haberden called a few days later.

"I have no special news to give you," he said. "Chambers is out of town, so I know no more about that stuff than you do. But I should like to see Mr. Leicester if he is in."

"He is in his room," I said; "I will tell him you are here."

"No, no, I will go up to him; we will have a little quiet talk together. I dare say that we have made a good deal of fuss about very little; for, after all, whatever the white powder may be, it seems to have done him good."

The doctor went upstairs, and standing in the hall I heard his knock, and the opening and shutting of the door; and then I waited in the silent house for an hour, and the stillness grew more and more intense as the hands of the clock crept round. Then there sounded from above the noise of a door shut sharply, and the doctor was coming down the stairs. His footsteps crossed the hall, and there was a pause at the door. I drew a long sick breath with difficulty, and saw my face white in a little mirror, and he came in and stood at the door. There was an unutterable horror shining in his eyes; he steadied himself by holding the back of a chair with one hand, and his lower lip trembled like a horse's, and he gulped and stammered unintelligible sounds before he spoke.

"I have seen that man," he began in a dry whisper. "I have been sitting in his presence for the last hour. My God! and I am alive and in my senses! I, who have dealt with death all my life, and have dabbled with the melting ruins of the earthly tabernacle. But not this! Oh, not this," and he covered his face with his hands as if to shut out the sight of something before him.

"Do not send for me again, Miss Leicester," he said with more composure. "I can do nothing in this house. Good-bye."

As I watched him totter down the steps and along the pavement towards his house, it seemed to me that he had aged by ten years since the morning.

My brother remained in his room. He called out to me in a voice I hardly recognized, that he was very busy, and would like his meals brought to his door and left there, and I gave the order to the servants. From that day it seemed as if the arbitrary conception we call time had been annihilated for me. I lived in an ever present sense of horror, going through the routine of the house mechanically, and only speaking a few necessary words to the servants. Now and then I went out and paced the streets for an hour or two and came home again; but whether I were without or within, my spirit delayed before the closed door of the upper room, and, shuddering, waited for it to open. I have said that I scarcely reckoned time, but I suppose it must have been a fortnight after Dr. Haberden's visit that I came home from my stroll a little refreshed and lightened. The air was sweet and pleasant, and the hazy form of green leaves, floating cloud-like in the square, and the smell of blossoms, had charmed my senses, and I felt happier and walked more briskly. As I delayed a moment at the verge of the pavement, waiting for a van to pass by before crossing over to the house, I happened to look up at the windows, and instantly there was the rush and swirl of deep cold waters in my ears, and my heart leapt up, and fell down, down as into a deep hollow, and I was amazed with a dread and terror without form or shape. I stretched out a hand blindly through folds of thick darkness, from the black and shadowy valley, and held myself from falling, while the stones beneath my feet rocked and swayed and tilted, and the sense of solid things seemed to sink away from under me. I had glanced up at the window of my brother's study, and at that moment the blind was drawn aside, and something that had life stared out into the world. Nay, I cannot say I saw a face or any human likeness; a living thing, two eyes of burning flame glared at me, and they were in the midst of something as formless as my fear, the symbol and presence of all evil and all hideous corruption. I stood shuddering and quaking as with the grip of ague, sick with unspeakable agonies of fear and loathing, and for five minutes I could not summon force or motion to my limbs. When I was within the door, I ran up the stairs to my brother's room, and knocked.

"Francis, Francis," I cried, "for heaven's sake answer me. What is the horrible thing in your room? Cast it out, Francis, cast it from you!"

I heard a noise as of feet shuffling slowly and awkwardly, and a choking, gurgling sound, as if some one was struggling to find utterance, and then the noise of a voice, broken and stifled, and words that I could scarcely understand.

"There is nothing here," the voice said, "Pray do not disturb me. I am not very well to-day."

I turned away, horrified and yet helpless. I could do nothing, and I wondered why Francis had lied to me, for I had seen the appearance beyond the glass too plainly to be deceived, though it was but the sight of a moment. And I sat still, conscious that there had been something else, something I had seen in the first flash of terror before those burning eyes had looked at me. Suddenly I remembered; as I lifted my face the blind was being drawn back, and I had had an instant's glance of the thing that was moving it, and in my recollection I knew that a hideous image was engraved forever on my brain. It was not a hand: there were no fingers that held the blind, but a black stump pushed it aside; the mouldering outline and the clumsy movement as of a beast's paw had glowed into my senses before the darkling waves of terror had overwhelmed me as I went down quick into the pit. My mind was aghast at the thought of this, and of the awful presence that dwelt with my brother in his room; I went to his door and cried to him again, but no answer came. That night one of the servants came up to me and told me in a whisper that for three days food had been regularly placed at the door and left untouched; the maid had knocked, but had received no answer; she had heard the noise of shuffling feet that I had noticed. Day after day went by, and still my brother's meals were brought to his door and left untouched; and though I knocked and called again and again, I could get no answer. The servants began to talk to me; it appeared they were as alarmed as I. The cook said that when my brother first shut himself up in his room, she used to hear him come out at night and go about the house; and once, she said, the hall door had opened and closed again, but for several nights she had heard no sound. The climax came at last. It was in the dusk of the evening, and I was sitting in the darkening dreary room when a terrible shriek jarred and rang harshly out of the silence, and I heard a frightened scurry of feet dashing down the stairs. I waited, and the servant maid staggered into the room and faced me, white and trembling.

"O Miss Helen," she whispered. "Oh, for the Lord's sake, Miss Helen, what has happened? Look at my hand, miss; look at that hand!" I drew her to the window, and saw there was a black wet stain upon her hand.

"I do not understand you," I said. "Will you explain to me?"

"I was doing your room just now," she began. "I was turning down the bedclothes, and all of a sudden there was something fell upon my hand wet, and I looked up, and the ceiling was black and dripping on me."

I looked bard at her, and bit my lip. "Come with me," I said. "Bring your candle with you."

The room I slept in was beneath my brother's, and as I went in I felt I was trembling. I looked up at the ceiling, and saw a patch, all black and wet and a dew of black drops upon it, and a pool of horrible liquor soaking into the white bedclothes.

I ran upstairs and knocked loudly.

"O Francis, Francis, my dear brother," I cried, "what has happened to you?"

And I listened. There was a sound of choking, and a noise like water bubbling and regurgitating, but nothing else, and I called louder, but no answer came.

In spite of what Dr. Haberden had said, I went to him, and with tears streaming down my cheeks, I told him of all that had happened, and he listened to me with a face set hard and grim.

"For your father's sake," he said at last, "I will go with you, though I can do nothing."

We went out together; the streets were dark and silent, and heavy with heat and a drought of many weeks. I saw the doctor's face white under the gas-lamps, and when we reached the house his hand was shaking. We did not hesitate, but went upstairs directly. I held the lamp, and he called out in a loud, determined voice:--

"Mr. Leicester, do you hear me? I insist on seeing you. Answer me at once."

There was no answer, but we both heard that choking noise I have mentioned.

"Mr. Leicester, I am waiting for you. Open the door this instant, or I shall break it down." And he called a third time in a voice that rang and echoed from the walls.

"Mr. Leicester! For the last time I order you to open the door."

"Ah!" he said, after a pause of heavy silence, "we are wasting time here. Will you be so kind as to get me a poker, or something of the kind?"

I ran into a little room at the back where odd articles were kept, and found a heavy adze-like tool that I thought might serve the doctor's purpose.

"Very good," he said, "that will do, I dare say. I give you notice, Mr. Leicester," he cried loudly at the keyhole, "that I am now about to break into your room."

Then I heard the wrench of the adze, and the woodwork split and cracked under it, and with a loud crash the door suddenly burst open; and for a moment we started back aghast at a fearful screaming cry, no human voice, but as the roar of a monster, that burst forth inarticulate and struck at us out of the darkness.

"Hold the lamp," said the doctor, and we went in and glanced quickly round the room. "There it is," said Dr. Haberden, drawing a quick breath; "look, in that corner."

I looked, and a pang of horror seized my heart as with a white-hot iron. There upon the floor was a dark and putrid mass, seething with corruption and hideous rottenness, neither liquid nor solid, but melting and changing before our eyes, and bubbling with unctuous oily bubbles like boiling pitch. And out of the midst of it shone two burning points like eyes, and I saw a writhing and stirring as of limbs, and something moved and lifted up that might have been an arm. The doctor took a step forward, and raised the iron bar and struck at the burning points, and drove in the weapon, and struck again and again in a fury of loathing. At last the thing was quiet.

***

A week or two later, when I had to some extent recovered from the terrible shock, Dr. Haberden came to see me.

"I have sold my practice," he began, "and to-morrow I am sailing on a long voyage. I do not know whether I shall ever return to England; in all probability I shall buy a little land in California, and settle there for the remainder of my life. I have brought you this packet, which you may open and read when you feel able to do so. It contains the report of Dr. Chambers on what I submitted to him. Good-bye, Miss Leicester, good-bye."

When he was gone, I opened the envelope; I could not wait, and proceeded to read the papers within. Here is the manuscript; and if you will allow me, I will read you the astounding story it contains.

"My dear Haberden," the letter began, "I have delayed inexcusably in answering your questions as to the white substance you sent me. To tell you the truth, I have hesitated for some time as to what course I should adopt, for there is a bigotry and an orthodox standard in physical science as in theology, and I knew that if I told you the truth I should offend rooted prejudices which I once held dear myself. However, I have determined to be plain with you, and first I must enter into a short personal explanation.

"You have known me, Haberden, for many years as a scientific man; you and I have often talked of our profession together, and discussed the hopeless gulf that opens before the feet of those who think to attain to truth by any means whatsoever, except the beaten way of experiment and observation, in the sphere of material things. I remember the scorn with which you have spoken to me of men of science who have dabbled a little in the unseen, and have timidly hinted that perhaps the senses are not, after all, the eternal, impenetrable bounds of all knowledge, the everlasting walls beyond which no human being has ever passed. We have laughed together heartily, and I think justly, at the "occult" follies of the day, disguised under various names,--the mesmerisms, spiritualisms, materializations, theosophies, all the rabble rant of imposture, with their machinery of poor tricks and feeble conjuring, the true back-parlor magic of shabby London streets. Yet, in spite of what I have said, I must confess to you that I am no materialist, taking the word of course in its usual signification. It is now many years since I have convinced myself, convinced myself a sceptic remember, that the old iron-bound theory is utterly and entirely false. Perhaps this confession will not wound you so sharply as it would have done twenty years ago; for I think you cannot have failed to notice that for some time hypotheses have been advanced by men of pure science which are nothing less than transcendental, and I suspect that most modern chemists and biologists of repute would not hesitate to subscribe the dictum of the old Schoolman, Omnia exeunt in mysterium, which means, I take it, that every branch of human knowledge if traced up to its source and final principles vanishes into mystery. I need not trouble you now with a detailed account of the painful steps which led me to my conclusions; a few simple experiments suggested a doubt as to my then standpoint, and a train of thought that rose from circumstances comparatively trifling brought me far. My old conception of the universe has been swept away, and I stand in a world that seems as strange and awful to me as the endless waves of the ocean seen for the first time, shining, from a Peak in Darien. Now I know that the walls of sense that seemed so impenetrable, that seemed to loom up above the heavens and to be founded below the depths, and to shut us in forevermore, are no such everlasting impassable barriers as we fancied, but thinnest and most airy veils that melt away before the seeker, and dissolve as the early mist of the morning about the brooks. I know that you never adopted the extreme materialistic position: you did not go about trying to prove a universal negative, for your logical sense withheld you from that crowning absurdity; yet I am sure that you will find all that I am saying strange and repellent to your habits of thought. Yet, Haberden, what I tell you is the truth, nay, to adopt our common language, the sole and scientific truth, verified by experience; and the universe is verily more splendid and more awful than we used to dream. The whole universe, my friend, is a tremendous sacrament; a mystic, ineffable force and energy, veiled by an outward form of matter; and man, and the sun and the other stars, and the flower of the grass, and the crystal in the test-tube, are each and every one as spiritual, as material, and subject to an inner working.

"You will perhaps wonder, Haberden, whence all this tends; but I think a little thought will make it clear. You will understand that from such a standpoint the whole view of things is changed, and what we thought incredible and absurd may be possible enough. In short, we must look at legend and belief with other eyes, and be prepared to accept tales that had become mere fables. Indeed, this is no such great demand. After all, modern science will concede as much, in a hypocritical manner. You must not, it is true, believe in witchcraft, but you may credit hypnotism; ghosts are out of date, but there is a good deal to be said for the theory of telepathy. Give a superstition a Greek name, and believe in it, should almost be a proverb.

"So much for my personal explanation. You sent me, Haberden, a phial, stoppered and sealed, containing a small quantity of a flaky white powder, obtained from a chemist who has been dispensing it to one of your patients. I am not surprised to hear that this powder refused to yield any results to your analysis. It is a substance which was known to a few many hundred years ago, but which I never expected to have submitted to me from the shop of a modern apothecary. There seems no reason to doubt the truth of the man's tale; he no doubt got, as he says, the rather uncommon salt you prescribed from the wholesale chemist's; and it has probably remained on his shelf for twenty years, or perhaps longer. Here what we call chance and coincidence begins to work; during all these years the salt in the bottle was exposed to certain recurring variations of temperature, variations probably ranging from 40° to 80°. And, as it happens, such changes, recurring year after year at irregular intervals, and with varying degrees of intensity and duration, have constituted a process, and a process so complicated and so delicate, that I question whether modern scientific apparatus directed with the utmost precision could produce the same result. The white powder you sent me is something very different from the drug you prescribed; it is the powder from which the wine of the Sabbath, the Vinum Sabbati was prepared. No doubt you have read of the Witches' Sabbath, and have laughed at the tales which terrified our ancestors; the black cats, and the broomsticks, and dooms pronounced against some old woman's cow. Since I have known the truth I have often reflected that it is on the whole a happy thing that such burlesque as this is believed, for it serves to conceal much that it is better should not be known generally. However, if you care to read the appendix to Payne Knight's monograph, you will find that the true Sabbath was something very different, though the writer has very nicely refrained from printing all he knew. The secrets of the true Sabbath were the secrets of remote times surviving into the Middle Ages, secrets of an evil science which existed long before Aryan man entered Europe. Men and women, seduced from their homes on specious pretences, were met by beings well qualified to assume, as they did assume, the part of devils, and taken by their guides to some, desolate and lonely place, known to the initiate by long tradition and unknown to all else. Perhaps it was a cave in some bare and wind-swept hill; perhaps some inmost recess of a great forest, and there the Sabbath was held. There, in the blackest hour of night, the Vinum Sabbati was prepared, and this evil graal was poured forth and offered to the neophytes, and they partook of an infernal sacrament; sumentes calicem principis inferorum, as an old author well expresses it. And suddenly, each one that had drunk found himself attended by a companion, a shape of glamour and unearthly allurement, beckoning him apart to share in joys more exquisite, more piercing than the thrill of any dream, to the consummation of the marriage of the Sabbath. It is hard to write of such things as these, and chiefly because that shape that allured with loveliness was no hallucination, but, awful as it is to express, the man himself. By the power of that Sabbath wine, a few grains of white powder thrown into a glass of water, the house of life was riven asunder, and the human trinity dissolved, and the worm which never dies, that which lies sleeping within us all, was made tangible and an external thing, and clothed with a garment of flesh. And then in the hour of midnight, the primal fall was repeated and represented, and the awful thing veiled in the mythos of the Tree in the Garden was done anew. Such was the nuptiæ Sabbati.

"I prefer to say no more; you, Haberden, know as well as I do that the most trivial laws of life are not to be broken with impunity; and for so terrible an act as this, in which the very inmost place of the temple was broken open and defiled, a terrible vengeance followed. What began with corruption ended also with corruption."

Underneath is the following in Dr. Haberden's writing:--

"The whole of the above is unfortunately strictly and entirely true. Your brother confessed all to me on that morning when I saw him in his room. My attention was first attracted to the bandaged hand, and I forced him to show it me. What I saw made me, a medical man of many years standing, grow sick with loathing; and the story I was forced to listen to was infinitely more frightful than I could have believed possible. It has tempted me to doubt the Eternal Goodness which can permit nature to offer such hideous possibilities; and if you had not with your own eyes seen the end, I should have said to you--disbelieve it all. I have not, I think, many more weeks to live, but you are young, and may forget all this.

"JOSEPH HABERDEN, M.D."

In the course of two or three months I heard that Dr. Haberden had died at sea, shortly after the ship left England.

Miss Leicester ceased speaking, and looked pathetically at Dyson, who could not refrain from exhibiting some symptoms of uneasiness.

He stuttered out some broken phrases expressive of his deep interest in her extraordinary history, and then said with a better grace--

"But, pardon me, Miss Leicester, I understood you were in some difficulty. You were kind enough to ask me to assist you in some way."

"Ah," she said, "I had forgotten that. My own present trouble seems of such little consequence in comparison with what I have told you. But as you are so good to me, I will go on. You will scarcely believe it, but I found that certain persons suspected, or rather pretended to suspect that I had murdered my brother. These persons were relatives of mine, and their motives were extremely sordid ones; but I actually found myself subject to the shameful indignity of being watched. Yes, sir, my steps were dogged when I went abroad, and at home I found myself exposed to constant if artful observation. With my high spirit this was more than I could brook, and I resolved to set my wits to work and elude the persons who were shadowing me. I was so fortunate as to succeed. I assumed this disguise, and for some time have lain snug and unsuspected. But of late I have reason to believe that the pursuer is on my track; unless I am greatly deceived, I saw yesterday the detective who is charged with the odious duty of observing my movements. You, sir, are watchful and keen-sighted; tell me, did you see any one lurking about this evening?"

"I hardly think so," said Dyson, "but perhaps you would give me some description of the detective in question."

"Certainly; he is a youngish man, dark, with dark whiskers. He has adopted spectacles of large size in the hope of disguising himself effectually, but he cannot disguise his uneasy manner, and the quick, nervous glances he casts to right and left."

This piece of description was the last straw for the unhappy Dyson, who was foaming with impatience to get out of the house, and would gladly have sworn eighteenth century oaths if propriety had not frowned on such a course.

"Excuse me, Miss Leicester," he said with cold politeness, "I cannot assist you."

"Ah!" she said sadly, "I have offended you in some way. Tell me what I have done, and I will ask you to forgive me."

"You are mistaken," said Dyson, grabbing his hat, but speaking with some difficulty; "you have done nothing. But, as I say, I cannot help you. Perhaps," he added, with some tinge of sarcasm, "my friend Russell might be of service."

"Thank you," she replied; "I will try him," and the lady went off into a shriek of laughter, which filled up Mr. Dyson's cup of scandal and confusion.

He left the house shortly afterwards, and had the peculiar delight of a five-mile walk, through streets which slowly changed from black to gray, and from gray to shining passages of glory for the sun to brighten. Here and there he met or overtook strayed revellers, but he reflected that no one could have spent the night in a more futile fashion than himself; and when he reached his home he had made resolves for reformation. He decided that he would abjure all Milesian and Arabian methods of entertainment, and subscribe to Mudie's for a regular supply of mild and innocuous romance.

STRANGE OCCURRENCE IN CLERKENWELL

Mr. Dyson had inhabited for some years a couple of rooms in a moderately quiet street in Bloomsbury, where, as he somewhat pompously expressed it, he held his finger on the pulse of life without being deafened with the thousand rumors of the main arteries of London. It was to him a source of peculiar, if esoteric gratification, that from the adjacent corner of Tottenham Court Road a hundred lines of omnibuses went to the four quarters of the town; he would dilate on the facilities for visiting Dalston, and dwell on the admirable line that knew extremest Ealing and the streets beyond Whitechapel. His rooms, which had been originally "furnished apartments," he had gradually purged of their more peccant parts; and though one would not find here the glowing splendors of his old chambers in the street off the Strand, there was something of severe grace about the appointments which did credit to his taste. The rugs were old, and of the true faded beauty; the etchings, nearly all of them proofs printed by the artist, made a good show with broad white margins and black frames, and there was no spurious black oak. Indeed, there was but little furniture of any kind: a plain and honest table, square and sturdy, stood in one corner; a seventeenth century settle fronted the hearth; and two wooden elbow-chairs, and a bookshelf of the Empire made up the equipment, with an exception worthy of note. For Dyson cared for none of these things. His place was at his own bureau, a quaint old piece of lacquered-work at which he would sit for hour after hour, with his back to the room, engaged in the desperate pursuit of literature, or, as he termed his profession, the chase of the phrase. The neat array of pigeon-holes and drawers teemed and overflowed with manuscript and note-books, the experiments and efforts of many years; and the inner well, a vast and cavernous receptacle, was stuffed with accumulated ideas. Dyson was a craftsman who gloved all the detail and the technique of his work intensely; and if, as has been hinted, he deluded himself a little with the name of artist, yet his amusements were eminently harmless, and, so far as can be ascertained, he (or the publishers) had chosen the good part of not tiring the world with printed matter.

Here, then, Dyson would shut himself up with his fancies, experimenting with words, and striving, as his friend the recluse of Bayswater strove, with the almost invincible problem of style, but always with a fine confidence, extremely different from the chronic depression of the realist. He had been almost continuously at work on some scheme that struck him as well-nigh magical in its possibilities since the night of his adventure with the ingenious tenant of the first floor in Abingdon Grove; and as he laid down the pen with a glow of triumph, he reflected that he had not viewed, the streets for five days in succession. With all the enthusiasm of his accomplished labor still working in his brain, he put away his papers, and went out, pacing the pavement at first in that rare mood of exultation which finds in every stone upon the way the possibilities of a masterpiece. It was growing late, and the autumn evening was drawing to a close amidst veils of haze and mist, and in the stilled air the voices, and the roaring traffic, and incessant feet seemed, to Dyson like the noise upon the stage when all the house is silent. In the square, the leaves rippled down as quick as summer rain, and the street beyond was beginning to flare with the lights in the butcher's shops and the vivid illumination of the green-grocer. It was a Saturday night, and the swarming populations of the slums were turning out in force; the battered women in rusty black had begun to paw the lumps of cagmag, and others gloated over unwholesome cabbages, and there was a brisk demand for four-ale. Dyson passed through these night-fires with some relief; he loved to meditate, but his thoughts were not as De Quincey's after his dose; he cared not two straws whether onions were dear or cheap, and would not have exulted if meat had fallen to twopence a pound. Absorbed in the wilderness of the tale he had been writing, weighing nicely the points of plot and construction, relishing the recollection of this and that happy phrase, and dreading failure here and there, he left the rush and the whistle of the gas-flares behind him, and began to touch upon pavements more deserted.

He had turned, without taking note, to the northward, and was passing through an ancient fallen street, where now notices of floors and offices to let hung out, but still about it there was the grace and the stiffness of the Age of Wigs; a broad roadway, a broad pavement, and on each side a grave line of houses with long and narrow windows flush with the walls, all of mellowed brick-work. Dyson walked with quick steps, as he resolved that short work must be made of a certain episode; but he was in that happy humor of invention, and another chapter rose in the inner chamber of his brain, and he dwelt on the circumstances he was to write down with curious pleasure. It was charming to have the quiet streets to walk in, and in his thought he made a whole district the cabinet of his studies, and vowed he would come again. Heedless of his course, he struck off to the east again, and soon found himself involved in a squalid network of gray two-storied houses, and then in the waste void and elements of brick-work, the passages and unmade roads behind great factory walls, encumbered with the refuse of the neighborhood, forlorn, ill-lighted, and desperate. A brief turn, and there rose before him the unexpected, a hill suddenly lifted from the level ground, its steep ascent marked by the lighted lamps, and eager as an explorer Dyson found his way to the place, wondering where his crooked paths had brought him. Here all was again decorous, but hideous in the extreme. The builder, some one lost in the deep gloom of the early 'twenties, had conceived the idea of twin villas in gray brick, shaped in a manner to recall the outlines of the Parthenon, each with its classic form broadly marked with raised bands of stucco. The name of the street was all strange, and for a further surprise, the top of the hill was crowned with an irregular plot of grass and fading trees, called a square, and here again the Parthenon-motive had persisted. Beyond the streets were curious, wild in their irregularities, here a row of sordid, dingy dwellings, dirty and disreputable in appearance, and there, without warning, stood a house genteel and prim with wire blinds and brazen knocker, as clean and trim as if it had been the doctor's house in some benighted little country town. These surprises and discoveries began to exhaust Dyson, and he hailed with delight the blazing windows of a public-house, and went in with the intention of testing the beverage provided for the dwellers in this region, as remote as Libya and Pamphylia and the parts about Mesopotamia. The babble of voices from within warned him that he was about to assist at the true parliament of the London workman, and he looked about him for that more retired entrance called private. When he had settled himself on an exiguous bench, and had ordered some beer, he began to listen to the jangling talk in the public bar beyond; it was a senseless argument, alternately furious and maudlin, with appeals to Bill and Tom, and mediæval survivals of speech, words that Chaucer wrote belched out with zeal and relish, and the din of pots jerked down and coppers rapped smartly on the zinc counter made a thorough bass for it all. Dyson was calmly smoking his pipe between the sips of beer, when an indefinite looking figure slid rather than walked into the compartment. The man started violently when he saw Dyson placidly sitting in the corner, and glanced keenly about him. He seemed to be on wires, controlled by some electric machine, for he almost bolted out of the door when the barman asked with what he could serve him, and his hand shivered as he took the glass. Dyson inspected him with a little curiosity; he was muffled up almost to the lips, and a soft felt hat was drawn down over his eyes; he looked as if he shrank from every glance, and a more raucous voice suddenly uplifted in the public bar seemed to find in him a sympathy that made him shake and quiver like a jelly. It was pitiable to see any one so thrilled with nervousness, and Dyson was about to address some trivial remark of casual inquiry to the man, when another person came into the compartment, and, laying a hand on his arm, muttered something in an undertone, and vanished as he came. But Dyson had recognized him as the smooth-tongued and smooth-shaven Burton, who had displayed so sumptuous a gift in lying; and yet he thought little of it, for his whole faculty of observation was absorbed in the lamentable and yet grotesque spectacle before him. At the first touch of the hand on his arm, the unfortunate man had wheeled round as if spun on a pivot, and shrank back with a low, piteous cry, as if some dumb beast were caught in the toils. The blood fled away from the wretch's face, and the skin became gray as if a shadow of death had passed in the air and fallen on it, and Dyson caught a choking whisper--

"Mr. Davies! For God's sake, have pity on me, Mr. Davies. On my oath, I say--" and his voice sank to silence as he heard the message, and strove in vain to bite his lip; and summon up to his aid some tinge of manhood. He stood there a moment, wavering as the leaves of an aspen, and then he was gone out into the street, as Dyson thought silently, with his doom upon his head. He had not been gone a minute when it suddenly flashed into Dyson's mind that he knew the man; it was undoubtedly the young man with spectacles for whom so many ingenious persons were searching; the spectacles indeed were missing, but the pale face, the dark whiskers, and the timid glances were enough to identify him, Dyson saw at once that by a succession of hazards he had unawares hit upon the scent of some desperate conspiracy, wavering as the track of a loathsome snake in and out of the highways and byways of the London cosmos; the truth was instantly pictured before him, and he divined that all unconscious and unheeding he had been privileged to see the shadows of hidden forms, chasing and hurrying, and grasping and vanishing across the bright curtain of common life, soundless and silent, or only babbling fables and pretences. For him in an instant the jargoning of voices, the garish splendor, and all the vulgar tumult of the public-house became part of magic; for here before his eyes a scene in this grim mystery play had been enacted, and he had seen human flesh grow gray with a palsy of fear; the very hell of cowardice and terror had gaped wide within an arm's breadth. In the midst of these reflections, the barman came up and stared at him as if to hint that he had exhausted his right to take his ease, and Dyson bought another lease of the seat by an order for more beer. As he pondered the brief glimpse of tragedy, he recollected that with his first start of haunted fear the young man with whiskers had drawn his hand swiftly from his great coat pocket, and that he had heard something fall to the ground; and pretending to have dropped his pipe, Dyson began to grope in the corner, searching with his fingers. He touched some thing, and drew it gently to him, and with one brief glance, as he put it quietly in his pocket, he saw it was a little old-fashioned note book, bound in faded green morocco.

He drank down his beer at a gulp, and left the place, overjoyed at his fortunate discovery, and busy with conjecture as to the possible importance of the find. By turns he dreaded to find perhaps mere blank leaves, or the labored follies of a betting-book, but the faded morocco cover seemed to promise better things, and hint at mysteries. He piloted himself with no little difficulty out of the sour and squalid quarter he had entered with a light heart, and emerging at Gray's Inn Road, struck off down Guilford Street, and hastened home, only anxious for a lighted candle and solitude.

Dyson sat down at his bureau, and placed the little book before him; it was an effort to open the leaves and dare disappointment. But in desperation at last he laid his finger between the pages at haphazard, and rejoiced to see a compact range of writing with a margin, and as it chanced, three words caught his glance, and stood out apart from the mass. Dyson read:

THE GOLD TIBERIUS,

and his face flushed with fortune and the lust of the hunter.

He turned at once to the first leaf of the pocket-book, and proceeded to read with rapt interest the

HISTORY OF THE YOUNG MAN WITH SPECTACLES

From the filthy and obscure lodging, situated, I verily believe, in one of the foulest slums of Clerkenwell, I indite this history of a life which, daily threatened, cannot last for very much longer. Every day, nay, every hour, I know too well my enemies are drawing their nets closer about me; even now, I am condemned to be a close prisoner in my squalid room, and I know that when I go out I shall go to my destruction. This history, if it chance to fall into good hands, may, perhaps, be of service in warning young men of the dangers and pitfalls that most surely must accompany any deviation from the ways of rectitude.

My name is Joseph Walters. When I came of age I found myself in possession of a small but sufficient income, and I determined that I would devote my life to scholarship. I do not mean the scholarship of these days; I had no intention of associating myself with men whose lives are spent in the unspeakably degrading occupation of "editing" classics, befouling the fair margins of the fairest books with idle and superfluous annotation, and doing their utmost to give a lasting disgust of all that is beautiful. An abbey church turned to the base use of a stable or a bake-house is a sorry sight; but more pitiable still is a masterpiece spluttered over with the commentator's pen, and his hideous mark "cf."

For my part I chose the glorious career of scholar in its ancient sense; I longed to possess encyclopædic learning, to grow old amongst books, to distil day by day, and year after year, the inmost sweetness of all worthy writings. I was not rich enough to collect a library, and I was therefore forced to betake myself to the Reading-Room of the British Museum.

O dim, far-lifted and mighty dome, Mecca of many minds, mausoleum of many hopes, sad house where all desires fail. For there men enter in with hearts uplifted, and dreaming minds, seeing in those exalted stairs a ladder to fame, in that pompous portico the gate of knowledge; and going in, find but vain vanity, and all but in vain. There, when the long streets are ringing, is silence, there eternal twilight, and the odor of heaviness. But there the blood flows thin and cold, and the brain burns adust; there is the hunt of shadows, and the chase of embattled phantoms; a striving against ghosts, and a war that has no victory. O dome, tomb of the quick; surely in thy galleries where no reverberant voice can call, sighs whisper ever, and mutterings of dead hopes; and there men's souls mount like moths towards the flame, and fall scorched and blackened beneath thee, O dim, far-lifted, and mighty dome.

Bitterly do I now regret the day when I took my place at a desk for the first time, and began my studies. I had not been an habitué of the place for many months, when I became acquainted with a serene and benevolent gentleman, a man somewhat past middle age, who nearly always occupied a desk next to mine. In the Reading-Room it takes little to make an acquaintance, a casual offer of assistance, a hint as to the search in the catalogue, and the ordinary politeness of men who constantly sit near each other; it was thus I came to know the man calling himself Dr. Lipsius. By degrees I grew to look for his presence, and to miss him when he was away, as was sometimes the case, and so a friendship sprang up between us. His immense range of learning was placed freely at my service; he would often astonish me by the way in which he would sketch out in a few minutes the bibliography of a given subject, and before long I had confided to him my ambitions.

"Ah," he said, "you should have been a German. I was like that myself when I was a boy. It is a wonderful resolve, an infinite career. 'I will know all things;' yes, it is a device indeed. But it means this--a life of labor without end, and a desire unsatisfied at last. The scholar has to die, and die saying, 'I know very little.'"

Gradually, by speeches such as these, Lipsius seduced me: he would praise the career, and at the same time hint that it was as hopeless as the search for the philosopher's stone, and so by artful suggestions, insinuated with infinite address, he by degrees succeeded in undermining all my principles. "After all," he used to say, "the greatest of all sciences, the key to all knowledge, is the science and art of pleasure. Rabelais was perhaps the greatest of all the encyclopædic scholars; and he, as you know, wrote the most remarkable book that has ever been written. And what does he teach men in this book? Surely, the joy of living. I need not remind you of the words, suppressed in most of the editions, the key of all the Rabelaisian mythology, of all the enigmas of his grand philosophy, Vivez joyeux. There you have all his learning; his work is the institutes of pleasure as the fine art; the finest art there is; the art of all arts. Rabelais had all science, but he had all life too. And we have gone a long way since his time. You are enlightened, I think; you do not consider all the petty rules and by-laws that a corrupt society has made for its own selfish convenience as the immutable decrees of the eternal."

Such were the doctrines that he preached; and it was by such insidious arguments, line upon line, here a little and there a little, that he at last succeeded in making me a man at war with the whole social system. I used to long for some opportunity to break the chains and to live a free life, to be my own rule and measure. I viewed existence with the eyes of a pagan, and Lipsius understood to perfection the art of stimulating the natural inclinations of a young man hitherto a hermit. As I gazed up at the great dome I saw it flushed with the flames and colors of a world of enticement, unknown to me, my imagination played me a thousand wanton tricks, and the forbidden drew me as surely as a loadstone draws on iron. At last my resolution was taken, and I boldly asked Lipsius to be my guide.

He told me to leave the Museum at my usual hour, half past four, to walk slowly along the northern pavement of Great Russell Street, and to wait at the corner of the street till I was addressed, and then to obey in all things the instructions of the person who came up to me. I carried out these directions, and stood at the corner looking about me anxiously, my heart beating fast, and my breath coming in gasps. I waited there for some time, and had begun to fear I had been made the object of a joke, when I suddenly became conscious of a gentleman who was looking at me with evident amusement from the opposite pavement of Tottenham Court Road. He came over, and raising his hat, politely begged me to follow him, and I did so without a word, wondering where we were going, and what was to happen. I was taken to a house of quiet and respectable aspect in a street lying to the north of Oxford Street, and my guide rang the bell, and a servant showed us into a large room, quietly furnished, on the ground floor. We sat there in silence for some time, and I noticed that the furniture, though unpretending, was extremely valuable. There were large oak-presses, two book-cases of extreme elegance, and in one corner a carved chest which must have been mediæval. Presently Dr. Lipsius came in and welcomed me with his usual manner, and after some desultory conversation, my guide left the room. Then an elderly man dropped in and began talking to Lipsius; and from their conversation I understood that my friend was a dealer in antiques; they spoke of the Hittite seal, and of the prospects of further discoveries, and later, when two or three more persons had joined us, there was an argument as to the possibility of a systematic exploration of the pre-celtic monuments in England I was; in fact, present at an archæological reception of an informal kind; and at nine o'clock, when the antiquaries were gone, I stared at Lipsius in a manner that showed I was puzzled, and sought an explanation.

"Now," he said, "we will go upstairs."

As we passed up the stairs, Lipsius lighting the way with a hand-lamp, I heard the sound of a jarring lock and bolts and bars shot on at the front door. My guide drew back a baize door, and we went down a passage, and I began to hear odd sounds, a noise of curious mirth, and then he pushed me through a second door, and my initiation began. I cannot write down what I witnessed that night; I cannot bear to recall what went on in those secret rooms fast shuttered and curtained so that no light should escape into the quiet street; they gave me red wine to drink, and a woman told me as I sipped it that it was wine of the Red Jar that Avallaunius had made. Another asked me how I liked the Wine of the Fauns, and I heard a dozen fantastic names, while the stuff boiled in my veins, and stirred, I think, something that had slept within me from the moment I was born. It seemed as if my self-consciousness deserted me; I was no longer a thinking agent, but at once subject and object. I mingled in the horrible sport and watched the mystery of the Greek groves and fountains enacted before me, saw the reeling dance, and heard the music calling as I sat beside my mate, and yet I was outside it all, and viewed my own part an idle spectator. Thus with strange rites they made me drink the cup, and when I woke up in the morning I was one of them, and had sworn to be faithful. At first I was shown the enticing side of things. I was bidden to enjoy myself and care for nothing but pleasure, and Lipsius himself indicated to me as the acutest enjoyment the spectacle of the terrors of the unfortunate persons who were from time to time decoyed into the evil house. But after a time it was pointed out to me that I must take my share in the work, and so I found myself compelled to be in my turn a seducer; and thus it is on my conscience that I have led many to the depths of the pit.

One day Lipsius summoned me to his private room, and told me that he had a difficult task to give me. He unlocked a drawer, and gave me a sheet of type-written paper, and had me read it. It was without place, or date, or signature, and ran as follows:--

"Mr. James Headley, F.S.A., will receive from his agent in Armenia, on the 12th inst., a unique coin, the gold Tiberius. It hears on the reverse a faun, with the legend VICTORIA. It is believed that this coin is of immense value. Mr. Headley will come up to town to show the coin to his friend, Professor Memys, of Chenies Street, Oxford Street, on some date between the 13th and the 18th."

Dr. Lipsius chuckled at my face of blank surprise when I laid down this singular communication.

"You will have a good chance of showing your discretion," he said. "This is not a common case; it requires great management and infinite tact. I am sure I wish I had a Panurge in my service, but we will see what you can do."

"But is it not a joke?" I asked him. "How can you know, or rather how can this correspondent of yours know that a coin has been despatched from Armenia to Mr. Headley? And how is it possible to fix the period in which Mr. Headley will take it into his head to come up to town? It seems to me a lot of guess work."

"My dear Mr. Walters," he replied; "we do not deal in guess work here. It would bore you if I went into all these little details, the cogs and wheels, if I may say so, which move the machine. Don't you think it is much more amusing to sit in front of the house and be astonished, than to be behind the scenes and see the mechanism? Better tremble at the thunder, believe me, than see the man rolling the cannon ball. But, after all, you needn't bother about the how and why; you have your share to do. Of course, I shall give you full instructions, but a great deal depends on the way the thing is carried out. I have often heard very young men maintain that style is everything in literature, and I can assure you that the same maxim holds good in our far more delicate profession. With us style is absolutely everything, and that is why we have friends like yourself."

I went away in some perturbation; he had no doubt designedly left everything in mystery, and I did not know what part I should have to play. Though I had assisted at scenes of hideous revelry, I was not yet dead to all echo of human feeling, and I trembled lest I should receive the order to be Mr. Headley's executioner.

A week later, it was on the sixteenth of the month, Dr. Lipsius made me a sign to come into his room.

"It is for to-night," he began. "Please to attend carefully to what I am going to say, Mr. Walters, and on peril of your life, for it is a dangerous matter,--on peril of your life I say, follow these instructions to the letter. You understand? Well, to-night at about half-past seven you will stroll quietly up the Hampstead Road till you come to Vincent Street. Turn down here and walk along, taking the third turning to your right, which is Lambert Terrace. Then follow the terrace, cross the road, and go along Hertford Street, and so into Lillington Square. The second turning you will come to in the square is called Sheen Street; but in reality it is more a passage between blank walls than a street. Whatever you do, take care to be at the corner of this street at eight o'clock precisely. You will walk along it, and just at the bend, where you lose sight of the square, you will find an old gentleman with white beard and whiskers. He will in all probability be abusing a cabman for having brought him to Sheen Street instead of Chenies Street. You will go up to him quietly and offer your services; he will tell you where he wants to go, and you will be so courteous as to offer to show him the way. I may say that Professor Memys moved, into Chenies Street a month ago; thus Mr. Headley has never been to see him there, and moreover he is very short-sighted, and knows little of the topography of London. Indeed he has quite lived the life of a learned hermit at Audley Hall.

"Well, need I say more to a man of your intelligence? You will bring him to this house; he will ring the bell, and a servant in quiet livery will let him in. Then your work will be done, and I am sure done well. You will leave Mr. Headley at the door, and simply continue your walk, and I shall hope to see you the next day. I really don't think there is anything more I can tell you."

These minute instructions I took care to carry out to the letter. I confess that I walked up the Tottenham Court Road by no means blindly, but with an uneasy sense that I was coming to a decisive point in my life. The noise and rumor of the crowded pavements were to me but dumb-show. I revolved again and again in ceaseless iteration the task that had been laid on me, and I questioned myself as to the possible results. As I got near the point of turning, I asked myself whether danger were not about my steps; the cold thought struck me that I was suspected and observed, and every chance foot-passenger who gave me a second glance seemed to me an officer of police. My time was running out, the sky had darkened, and I hesitated, half resolved to go no farther, but to abandon Lipsius and his friends forever. I had almost determined to take this course, when the conviction suddenly came to me that the whole thing was a gigantic joke, a fabrication of rank improbability. Who could have procured the information about the Armenian agent, I asked myself. By what means could Lipsius have known the particular day, and the very train that Mr. Headley was to take? How engage him to enter one special cab amongst the dozens waiting at Paddington? I vowed it a mere Milesian tale, and went forward merrily, and turned down Vincent Street, and threaded out the route that Lipsius had so carefully impressed upon me. The various streets he had named were all places of silence and an oppressive cheap gentility; it was dark, and I felt alone in the musty squares and crescents, where people pattered by at intervals, and the shadows were growing blacker. I entered Sheen Street, and found it, as Lipsius had said, more a passage than a street; it was a by-way, on one side a low wall and neglected gardens and grim backs of a line of houses, and on the other a timber yard. I turned the corner, and lost sight of the square, and then to my astonishment I saw the scene of which I had been told. A hansom cab had come to a stop beside the pavement, and an old man carrying a handbag was fiercely abusing the cabman, who sat on his perch the image of bewilderment.

"Yes, but I'm sure you said Sheen Street, and that's where I brought you," I heard him saying, as I came up, and the old gentleman boiled in a fury, and threatened police and suits at law.

The sight gave me a shock; and in an instant I resolved to go through with it. I strolled on, and without noticing the cabman, lifted my hat politely to old Mr. Headley.

"Pardon me, sir," I said, "but is there any difficulty? I see you are a traveller; perhaps the cabman has made a mistake. Can I direct you?"

The old fellow turned to me, and I noticed that he snarled and showed his teeth like an ill-tempered cur as he spoke.

"This drunken fool has brought me here," he said. "I told him to drive to Chenies Street, and he brings me to this infernal place. I won't pay him a farthing, and I meant to have given him a handsome sum. I am going to call for the police and give him in charge."

At this threat the cabman seemed to take alarm. He glanced round as if to make sure that no policeman was in sight and drove off grumbling loudly, and Mr. Headley grinned, savagely with satisfaction at having saved his fare, and put back one and sixpence into his pocket, the "handsome sum" the cabman had lost.

"My dear sir," I said, "I am afraid this piece of stupidity has annoyed you a great deal. It is a long way to Chenies Street, and you will have some difficulty in finding the place unless you know London pretty well."

"I know it very little," he replied. "I never come up except on important business, and I've never been to Chenies Street in my life."

"Really? I should be happy to show you the way. I have been for a stroll, and it will not at all inconvenience me to take you to your destination."

"I want to go to Professor Memys, at number 15. It's most annoying to me. I'm short-sighted, and I can never make out the numbers on the doors."

"This way if you please," I said, and we set out.

I did not find Mr. Headley an agreeable man; indeed, he grumbled the whole way. He informed me of his name, and I took care to say, "The well-known antiquary?" and thenceforth I was compelled to listen to the history of his complicated squabbles with publishers, who had treated him, as he said, disgracefully. The man was a chapter in the Irritability of Authors. He told me that he had been on the point of making the fortune of several firms, but had been compelled to abandon the design owing to their rank ingratitude. Besides these ancient histories of wrong and the more recent misadventure of the cabman, he had another grievous complaint to make. As he came along in the train, he had been sharpening a pencil, and the sudden jolt of the engine as it drew up at a station had driven the penknife against his face, inflicting a small triangular wound just on the cheek-bone, which he showed me. He denounced the railway company, and heaped imprecations on the head of the driver, and talked of claiming damages. Thus he grumbled all the way, not noticing in the least where he was going, and so inamiable did his conduct appear to me that I began to enjoy the trick I was playing on him.

Nevertheless my heart beat a little faster as we turned into the street where Lipsius was waiting. A thousand accidents, I thought, might happen. Some chance might bring one of Headley's friends to meet us; perhaps, though he knew not Chenies Street, he might know the street where I was taking him; in spite of his short-sight he might possibly make out the number, or in a sudden fit of suspicion he might make an inquiry of the policeman at the corner. Thus every step upon the pavement, as we drew nearer to the goal, was to me a pang and a terror, and every approaching passenger carried a certain threat of danger. I gulped down my excitement with an effort, and made shift to say pretty quietly:--

"No. 15, I think you said? That is the third house from this. If you will allow me, I will leave you now; I have been delayed a little, and my way lies on the other side of Tottenham Court Road."

He snarled out some kind of thanks, and I turned my back and walked swiftly in the opposite direction. A minute or two later, I looked round and saw Mr. Headley standing on the doorstep, and then the door opened and he went in. For my part I gave a sigh of relief, and hastened to get away from the neighborhood and endeavored to enjoy myself in merry company.

The whole of the next day I kept away from Lipsius. I felt anxious, but I did not know what had happened or what was happening, and a reasonable regard for my own safety told me that I should do well to remain quietly at home. My curiosity, however, to learn the end of the odd drama in which I had played a part stung me to the quick, and late in the evening I made up my mind to go and see how events had turned out. Lipsius nodded when I came in, and asked me if I could give him five minutes' talk. We went into his room, and he began to walk up and down, and I sat waiting for him to speak.

"My dear Mr. Walters," he said at length, "I congratulate you warmly. Your work was done in the most thorough and artistic manner. You will go far. Look."

He went to his escritoire and pressed a secret spring, and a drawer flew out, and he laid something on the table. It was a gold coin, and I took it up and examined it eagerly, and read the legend about the figure of the faun.

"Victoria," I said, smiling.

"Yes, it was a great capture, which we owe to you. I had great difficulty in persuading Mr. Headley that a little mistake had been made; that was how I put it. He was very disagreeable, and indeed ungentlemanly about it; didn't he strike you as a very cross old man?"

I held the coin, admiring the choice and rare design, clear cut as if from the mint; and I thought the fine gold glowed and burned like a lamp.

"And what finally became of Mr. Headley?" I said at last.

Lipsius smiled and shrugged his shoulders.

"What on earth does it matter?" he said. "He might be here, or there, or anywhere; but what possible consequence could it be? Besides, your question rather surprises me. You are an intelligent man, Mr. Walters. Just think it over, and I'm sure you won't repeat the question."

"My dear sir," I said, "I hardly think you are treating me fairly. You have paid me some handsome compliments on my share in the capture, and I naturally wish to know how the matter ended. From what I saw of Mr. Headley, I should think you must have had some difficulty with him."

He gave me no answer for the moment, but began again to walk up and down the room, apparently absorbed in thought.

"Well," he said at last, "I suppose there is something in what you say. We are certainly indebted to you. I have said, that I have a high opinion of your intelligence, Mr. Walters. Just look here, will you."

He opened a door communicating with another room and pointed.

There was a great box lying on the floor; a queer coffin-shaped thing. I looked at it and saw it was a mummy case like those in the British Museum, vividly painted in the brilliant Egyptian colors, with I knew not what proclamation of dignity or hopes of life immortal. The mummy, swathed about in the robes of death, was lying within, and the face had been uncovered.

"You are going to send this away?" I said, forgetting the question I had put.

"Yes; I have an order from a local museum. Look a little more closely, Mr. Walters."

Puzzled by his manner, I peered into the face, while he held up the lamp. The flesh was black with the passing of the centuries; but as I looked I saw upon the right cheek-bone a small triangular scar, and the secret of the mummy flashed upon me. I was looking at the dead body of the man whom I had decoyed into that house.

There was no thought or design of action in my mind. I held the accursed coin in my hand, burning me with a foretaste of hell, and I fled as I would have fled from pestilence and death, and dashed into the street in blind horror, not knowing where I went. I felt the gold coin grasped in my clenched list, and threw it away, I knew not where, and ran on and on through by-streets and dark ways, till at last I issued out into a crowded thoroughfare, and checked myself. Then, as consciousness returned, I realized my instant peril, and understood what would happen if I fell into the hands of Lipsius. I knew that I had put forth my finger to thwart a relentless mechanism rather than a man; my recent adventure with the unfortunate Mr. Headley had taught me that Lipsius had agents in all quarters, and I foresaw that if I fell into his hands, he would remain true to his doctrine of style, and cause me to die a death of some horrible and ingenious torture. I bent my whole mind to the task of outwitting him and his emissaries, three of whom I knew to have proved their ability for tracking down persons who for various reasons preferred to remain obscure. These servants of Lipsius were two men and a woman, and the woman was incomparably the most subtle and the most deadly. Yet I considered that I too had some portion of craft, and I took my resolve. Since then I have matched myself day by day and hour by hour against the ingenuity of Lipsius and his myrmidons. For a time I was successful; though they beat furiously after me in the covert of London, I remained perdu, and watched with some amusement their frantic efforts to recover the scent lost in two or three minutes. Every lure and wile was put forth to entice me from my hiding-place. I was informed by the medium of the public prints that what I had taken had been recovered, and meetings were proposed in which I might hope to gain a great deal without the slightest risk. I laughed at their endeavors, and began a little to despise the organization I had so dreaded, and ventured more abroad. Not once or twice, but several times, I recognized the two men who were charged with my capture, and I succeeded in eluding them easily at close quarters; and a little hastily I decided that I had nothing to dread, and that my craft was greater than theirs. But in the mean while, while I congratulated myself on my cunning, the third of Lipsius's emissaries was weaving her nets, and in an evil hour I paid a visit to an old friend, a literary man named Russell, who lived in a quiet street in Bayswater. The woman, as I found out too late, a day or two ago, occupied rooms in the same house, and I was followed and tracked down. Too late, as I have said, I recognized that I had made a fatal mistake, and that I was besieged. Sooner or later I shall find myself in the power of an enemy without pity; and so surely as I leave this house I shall go to receive doom. I hardly dare to guess how it will at last fall upon me. My imagination, always a vivid one, paints to me appalling pictures of the unspeakable torture which I shall probably endure; and I know that I shall die with Lipsius standing near and gloating over the refinements of my suffering and my shame.

Hours, nay, minutes, have become very precious to me. I sometimes pause in the midst of anticipating my tortures, to wonder whether even now I cannot hit upon some supreme stroke, some design of infinite subtlety, to free myself from the toils. But I find that the faculty of combination has left me. I am as the scholar in the old myth, deserted by the power which has helped, me hitherto. I do not know when the supreme moment will come, but sooner or later it is inevitable, and before long I shall receive sentence, and from the sentence to execution will not be long.

***

I cannot remain here a prisoner any longer. I shall go out to-night when the streets are full of crowds and clamors, and make a last effort to escape.

***

It was with profound astonishment that Dyson closed the little book, and thought of the strange series of incidents which had brought him into touch with the plots and counterplots connected with the Gold Tiberius. He had bestowed the coin carefully away, and he shuddered at the bare possibility of its place of deposit becoming known to the evil band who seemed to possess such extraordinary sources of information.

It had grown late while he read, and he put the pocket-book away, hoping with all his heart that the unhappy Walters might even at the eleventh hour escape the doom he dreaded.

ADVENTURE OF THE DESERTED RESIDENCE

"A wonderful story, as you say; an extraordinary sequence and play of coincidence. I confess that your expressions when you first showed me the Gold Tiberius were not exaggerated. But do you think that Walters has really some fearful fate to dread?"

"I cannot say. Who can presume to predict events when life itself puts on the robe of coincidence and plays at drama? Perhaps we have not yet reached the last chapter in the queer story. But, look, we are drawing near to the verge of London; there are gaps, you see, in the serried ranks of brick, and a vision of green fields beyond."

Dyson had persuaded the ingenious Mr. Phillipps to accompany him on one of those aimless walks to which he was himself so addicted. Starting from the very heart of London, they had made their way westward through the stony avenues, and were now just emerging from the red lines of an extreme suburb, and presently the half-finished road ended, a quiet lane began, and they were beneath the shade of elm-trees. The yellow autumn sunlight that had lit up the bare distance of the suburban street now filtered down through the boughs of the trees and shone on the glowing carpet of fallen leaves, and the pools of rain glittered and shot back the gleam of light. Over all the broad pastures there was peace and the happy rest of autumn before the great winds begin, and afar off, London lay all vague and immense amidst the veiling mist; here and there a distant window catching the sun and kindling with fire, and a spire gleaming high, and below the streets in shadow, and the turmoil of life. Dyson and Phillipps walked on in silence beneath the high hedges, till at a turn of the lane they saw a mouldering and ancient gate standing open, and the prospect of a house at the end of a moss-grown carriage drive.

"There is a survival for you," said Dyson; "it has come to its last days, I imagine. Look how the laurels have grown gaunt, and weedy, and black, and bare, beneath; look at the house, covered with yellow wash and patched with green damp. Why, the very notice-board which informs all and singular that the place is to be let has cracked and half fallen."

"Suppose we go in and see it," said Phillipps. "I don't think there is anybody about."

They turned up the drive, and walked slowly, towards this remnant of old days. It was a large straggling house, with curved wings at either end, and behind a series of irregular roofs and projections, showing that the place had been added to at divers dates; the two wings were roofed in cupola fashion, and at one side, as they came nearer, they could see a stable-yard, and a clock turret with a bell, and the dark masses of gloomy cedars. Amidst all the lineaments of dissolution, there was but one note of contrast: the sun was setting beyond the elm-trees, and all the west and the south were in flames, and on the upper windows of the house the glow shone reflected, and it seemed as if blood and fire were mingled. Before the yellow front of the mansion, stained, as Dyson had remarked, with gangrenous patches, green and blackening, stretched what once had been, no doubt, a well-kept lawn, but it was now rough and ragged, and nettles and great docks, and all manner of coarse weeds, struggled in the places of the flower-beds. The urns had fallen from their pillars beside the walk, and lay broken in shards upon the ground, and everywhere from grass-plot and path a fungoid growth had sprung up and multiplied, and lay dank and slimy like a festering sore upon the earth. In the middle of the rank grass of the lawn was a desolate fountain; the rim of the basin was crumbling and pulverized with decay, and within, the water stood stagnant, with green scum for the lilies that had once bloomed there; and rust had eaten into the bronze flesh of the Triton that stood in the middle, and the conch-shell he held was broken.

"Here," said Dyson, "one might moralize over decay and death. Here all the stage is decked out with the symbols of dissolution; the cedarn gloom and twilight hangs heavy around us, and everywhere within the pale dankness has found a harbor, and the very air is changed and brought to accord with the scene. To me, I confess, this deserted house is as moral as a graveyard, and I find something sublime in that lonely Triton, deserted in the midst of his water-pool. He is the last of the gods; they have left him and he remembers the sound of water falling on water, and the days that were sweet."

"I like your reflections extremely," said Phillipps, "but I may mention that the door of the house is open.".

"Let us go in then."

The door was just ajar, and they passed into the mouldy hall, and looked in at a room on one side. It was a large room, going far back, and the rich old red flock paper was peeling from the walls in long strips, and blackened with vague patches of rising damp; the ancient clay, the dank reeking earth rising up again, and subduing all the work of men's hands after the conquest of many years. And the floor was thick with the dust of decay, and the painted ceiling fading from all gay colors and light fancies of cupids in a career, and disfigured with sores of dampness, seemed transmuted into other work. No longer the amorini chased one another pleasantly, with limbs that sought not to advance, and hands that merely simulated the act of grasping at the wreathed flowers, but it appeared some savage burlesque of the old careless world and of its cherished conventions, and the dance of the loves had become a dance of Death; black pustules and festering sores swelled and clustered on fair limbs, and smiling faces showed corruption, and the fairy blood had boiled with the germs of foul disease; it was a parable of the leaven working, and worms devouring for a banquet the heart of the rose.

Strangely, under the painted ceiling, against the decaying walls, two old chairs still stood alone, the sole furniture of the empty place. High-backed, with curving arms and twisted legs, covered with faded gold leaf, and upholstered in tattered damask, they too were a part of the symbolism, and struck Dyson with surprise. "What have we here?" he said. "Who has sat in these chairs? Who, clad in peach-bloom satin, with lace ruffles and diamond buckles, all golden, a conté fleurettes to his companion? Phillipps, we are in another age. I wish I had some snuff to offer you, but failing that, I beg to offer you a seat, and we will sit and smoke tobacco. A horrid practice, but I am no pedant."

They sat down on the queer old chairs, and looked out of the dim and grimy panes to the ruined lawn, and the fallen urns, and the deserted Triton.

Presently Dyson ceased his imitation of eighteenth century airs; he no longer pulled forward imaginary ruffles, or tapped a ghostly snuff-box.

"It's a foolish fancy," he said at last, "but I keep thinking I hear a noise like some one groaning. Listen; no, I can't hear it now. There it is again! Did you notice it, Phillipps?

"No, I can't say I heard anything. But I believe that old places like this are like shells from the shore, ever echoing with noises. The old beams, mouldering piecemeal, yield a little and groan, and such a house as this I can fancy all resonant at night with voices, the voices of matter so slowly and so surely transformed into other shapes; the voice of the worm that gnaws at last the very heart of the oak; the voice of stone grinding on stone, and the voice of the conquest of time."

They sat still in the old armchairs and grew graver in the musty ancient air,--the air of a hundred years ago.

"I don't like the place," said Phillipps, after a long pause. "To me it seems, as if there were a sickly, unwholesome smell about it, a smell of something burning."

"You are right; there is an evil odor here. I wonder what it is! Hark! Did you hear that?"

A hollow sound, a noise of infinite sadness and infinite pain broke in upon the silence; and the two men looked fearfully at one another, horror and the sense of unknown things glimmering in their eyes.

"Come," said Dyson, "we must see into this," and they went into the hall and listened in the silence.

"Do you know," said Phillipps, "it seems absurd, but I could almost fancy that the smell is that of burning flesh."

They went up the hollow-sounding stairs, and the the odor became thick and noisome, stifling the breath; and a vapor, sickening as the smell of the chamber of death, choked them. A door was open and they entered the large upper room, and clung hard to one another, shuddering at the sight they saw.

A naked man was lying on the floor, his arms and legs stretched wide apart, and bound to pegs that had been hammered into the boards. The body was torn and mutilated in the most hideous fashion, scarred with the marks of red-hot irons, a shameful ruin of the human shape. But upon the middle of the body a fire of coals was smouldering; the flesh had been burned through. The man was dead, but the smoke of his torment mounted still, a black vapor.

"The young man with spectacles," said Mr. Dyson.

THE END

FAR OFF THINGS

LONDON: MARTIN SECKER
LONDON: MARTIN SECKER LTD. (1922)

DEDICATION
o ALFRED TURNER

This is a book, my dear Turner, which I had in my heart to write for many years. The thought of it came to me with that other thought that I was growing--rather, grown--old; that the curtain had definitely been rung down on all the days of my youth. And so I got into the way of looking back, of recalling the far gone times and suns of the 'seventies and early 'eighties when the scene of my life was being set. I made up my mind that I would write about it all--some day.

Some day would undoubtedly have been Never; if it had not been for you. I had not spoken of the projected book to you or anyone else; but one fine morning in 1915 you ordered me to write it! You were then, you will remember, editing the London Evening News, and as a reporter on your staff I had nothing to do but to obey. The book was written, appeared in the paper as "The Confessions of a Literary Man," and now reappears as "Far Off Things."

So far, good. I enjoyed writing the book enormously; and, I frankly confess, I enjoy reading it. In a word, I am not grumbling. But there is one little point that I do not mean to neglect. My complacent views as to "Far Off Things" may not be shared by other and, possibly, more competent judges. And what I want to impress on you is this: that if there is to be trouble, "you are going to have your share of it." You ordered the book to be written, you printed it in your paper, you have urged me to reprint it, not once or twice, but again and again.

Now, you remember Johnson on advising an author to print his book. "This author," said the Doctor, "when mankind are hunting him with a canister at his tail can say, 'I would not have published, had not Johnson, or Reynolds, or Musgrave, or some other good judge commended the work!'"

Now you see the purpose of this Epistle Dedicatory. It is to make it quite clear that, if there is to be any talk of canisters and tails, the order will run:

"Canisters for two!"

ARTHUR MACHEN

Chapter I

One night a year or so ago I was the guest of a famous literary society. This society, or club, it is well known, believes in celebrating literature--and all sorts of other things--in a thoroughly agreeable and human fashion. It meets not in any gloomy hall or lecture room, it has no gritty apparatus of blackboard, chalk, and bleared water-bottle. It summons its members and its guests to a well-known restaurant of the West End, it gives them red and white roses for their button-holes, and sets them down to an excellent dinner and good red wine at a gaily decked table, flower garlanded, luminous with many starry lamps.

Well, as I say, I found myself on a certain night a partaker of all this cheerfulness. I was one guest among many; there were explorers and ambassadors and great scientific personages and judges, and the author who has given the world the best laughter that it has enjoyed since Dickens died: in a word, I was in much more distinguished company than that to which I am accustomed. And after dinner the Persians (as I will call them) have a kindly and courteous custom of praising their guests; and to my astonishment and delight the speaker brought me into his oration and said the kindest and most glowing things imaginable about a translation I once made of the "Heptameron" of Margaret of Navarre. I was heartily pleased; I hold with Foker in "Pendennis" that every fellow likes a hand. Praise is grateful, especially when there has not been too much of it; but it is not to record my self-complacence that I have told this incident of the Persian banquet. As I sat at the board and heard the speaker's kindly compliments, I was visited for a twinkling part of a moment by a vision; by such a vision as they say comes to the spiritual eyes of drowning men as they sink through the green water. The scene about me was such as one will find nowhere else but in London. The multitude of lights, the decoration of the great room and the tables, above all the nature of the company and something in the very air of the place; all these were metropolitan in the sense in which the word is opposed to provincial. This is a subtlety which the provinces cannot understand, and it is natural enough that they are unable to do so. The big town in the Midlands or the North will tell you of its picture galleries, of its classical concerts, and of the serious books taken out in great numbers from its flourishing free libraries. It does not see, and, probably, will never see, that none of these things is to the point.

Well, from the heart of this London atmosphere I was suddenly transported in my vision to a darkling, solitary country lane as the dusk of a November evening closed upon it thirty long years before. And, as I think that the pure provincial can never understand the quiddity or essence of London, so I believe that for the born Londoner the country ever remains an incredible mystery. He knows that it is there--somewhere--but he has no true vision of it. In spite of himself he Londonises it, suburbanises it; he sticks a gas lamp or two in the lanes, dots some largish villas of red brick beside them, and extends the District or the Metropolitan to within easy distance of the dark wood. But here was I carried from luminous Oxford Street to the old deep lane in Gwent, which is on the borders of Wales. Nothing that a Londoner would call a town within eight miles, deep silence, deep stillness everywhere; hills and dark wintry woods growing dim in the twilight, the mountain to the west a vague, huge mass against a faint afterlight of the dead day, grey and heavy clouds massed over all the sky. I saw myself, a lad of twenty-one or thereabouts, strolling along this solitary lane on a daily errand, bound for a point about a mile from the rectory. Here a footpath over the fields crossed the road, and by the stile I would wait for the postman. I would hear him coming from far away, for he blew a horn as he walked, so that people in the scattered farms might come out with their letters if they had any. I lounged on the stile and waited, and when the postman came I would give him my packet--the day's portion of "copy" of that Heptameron translation that I was then making and sending to the publisher in York Street, Covent Garden. The postman would put the parcel in his bag, cross the road, and go striding off into the dim country beyond, finding his way on a track that no townsman could see, by field and wood and marshy places, crossing the Canthwr brook by a narrow plank, coming out somewhere on the Llanfrechfa road, and so entering at last Caerleon-on-Usk, the little silent, deserted village that was once the golden Isca of the Roman legions, that is golden for ever and immortal in the romances of King Arthur and the Graal and the Round Table.

So, in an instant's time, I journeyed from the lighted room in the big Oxford Street restaurant to the darkening lane in far-away Gwent, in far-away years. I gathered anew for that little while the savour of the autumnal wood beside which the boy of thirty years before was walking, and also the savour of his long-forgotten labours, of his old dreams of life and of letters. The speech and the dream came to an end: and the man on the other side of the table, who is probably the most skilful and witty writer of musical comedy "lyrics" in England, was saying that once on a time he had tried to write real poetry.

I shall always esteem it as the greatest piece of fortune that has fallen to me, that I was born in that noble, fallen Caerleon-on-Usk, in the heart of Gwent. My greatest fortune, I mean, from that point of view which I now more especially have in mind, the career of letters. For the older I grow the more firmly am I convinced that anything which I may have accomplished in literature is due to the fact that when my eyes were first opened in earliest childhood they had before them the vision of an enchanted land. As soon as I saw anything I saw Twyn Barlwm, that mystic tumulus, the memorial of peoples that dwelt in that region before the Celts left the Land of Summer. This guarded the southern limit of the great mountain wall in the west; a little northward was Mynydd Maen--the Mountain of the Stone--a giant, rounded billow; and still to the north mountains, and on fair, clear days one could see the pointed summit of the Holy Mountain by Abergavenny. It would shine, I remember, a pure blue in the far sunshine; it was a mountain peak in a fairy tale. And then to eastward the bedroom window of Llanddewi Rectory looked over hill and valley, over high woods, quivering with leafage like the beloved Zacynthus of Ulysses, away to the forest of Wentwood, to the church tower on the hill above Caerleon. Through a cleft one might see now and again a bright yellow glint of the Severn Sea, and the cliffs of Somerset beyond. And hardly a house in sight in all the landscape, look where you would. Here the gable of a barn, here a glint of a whitewashed farm-house, here blue wood smoke rising from an orchard grove, where an old cottage was snugly hidden; but only so much if you knew where to look. And of nights, when the dusk fell and the farmer went his rounds, you might chance to see his lantern glimmering a very spark on the hillside. This was all that showed in a vague, dark world; and the only sounds were the faint distant barking of the sheepdog and the melancholy cry of the owls from the border of the brake.

***

I believe that I have seen at all events the main streets of London at every hour of the day and night. I have viewed, for example, Leicester Square between four and five of a summer morning, and have marvelled at its dismal disarray and quite miserable shabbiness of aspect. With the pure morning sun shining upon its gay places in clear splendour they are infinitely more "shocking" than they can appear at night-time to the narrowest of provincials. The Strand is a solemn street at two in the morning, Holborn has a certain vastness and windiness about it as the sky grows from black to grey, and at six the residential quarters seem full of houses of mourning, their white blinds most strictly drawn.

And at one time I had almost as full a knowledge of my native country, though not so much with respect to the category of time as to that of place. I have, it is true, seen the sky above the dark stretch of Wentwood Forest redden to the dawn, and I have lost my way and strayed in a very maze of unknown brooks and hills and woods and wild lands in the blackest hours after midnight. But the habits of the country, unlike those of London, generally fail to give reason or excuse for night wanderings. If you stayed in friendly and hospitable company much after ten of the night, it was usually a case of the spare room, newly aired sheets, one pipe more, and so to bed. This at all events on nights that were very black or tempestuous with wind and rain; for on such nights it is difficult to make out the faint footpath from stile to stile, and only the surest sense of locality will enable one to strike the felled tree or the narrow plank that, hidden by a dense growth of alders, crosses the winding of the brook. But from very early years indeed I became an enchanted student of the daylight country, which, I think, for me never was illuminated by common daylight, but rather by suns that rose from the holy seas of faery and sank down behind magic hills. I was an only child, and as soon as I could walk beyond the limits of the fields and orchards about the rectory, my father would take me with him on such parish visitations as were fairly within the stretch and strength of short legs. Indeed, I began my peregrinations at a still earlier period, for I can remember a visit to the mill, that was paid when I was a passenger in a perambulator, and aged, I suppose, about three.

Later these travels became more frequent, and I have recollections, still fresh and pleasant, of sitting still in old farm-house kitchens while my father was about his ghostly business. Always, even in the full blaze of summer, there would be a glint of fire on the cavernous hearth and a faint blue spire of wood smoke mounting the huge hollow of the chimney. The smell of this wood smoke scented and sweetened the air, in which there was usually a hint of apples stored away in loft or cellar, somewhere behind one or other of the black tarred doors that opened from every wall in the long, low room, and here and there bevelled what should have been an angle. By the hearth stood a big curving settle on one side, on the other there was usually an armchair for the farmer's wife. One small window, with square leaded panes, with solid oaken mullions, looked out on the garden, and so thick were the walls--they were always heavily "battered," or sloped outward towards the ground--that there was a depth of at least three feet between the window panes and the inner wall of the room. There was whitewash within and without, renewed every spring, and it is one of the most beautiful circumstances in Gwent that this custom of whitewash prevails. To look up to a mountain side and to see the pure white of the walls of the farms and cottages established there, fronting great winds, but nestling too in a shelter of tossing trees, gives me even now the keenest pleasure. And if on a summer day one climbs up amidst those brave winds and looks down on all the rolling land of Gwent, it is dotted with these white farms, that shine radiant in the sunlight.

And these farm-house kitchens were floored with stone, which was so purely and exquisitely kept that people said "one could eat bread and butter off Mrs. Morgan's kitchen floor." Such a place was, and still is, my notion of comfort, of the material surroundings which are fit to house a man. Now and then, in these later days, my business--never my pleasure--calls me to our Hôtel Glorieux or our Hôtel Splendide; to the places where the rooms are fifty feet high, where the walls are marble, and mirrors and gilding, where there are flowery carpets and Louis Quinze chairs and the true American heat. I think then of the kitchens of Pantyreos and Penyrhaul, as Israel in exile remembered Syon.

But it is not in summer-time that it is best to remember these places, excellent though the thought of their coolness and refreshment may be. I like to think of them as set in a framework of late autumn or deep mid-winter. I will be more curious than De Quincey: no mere bitter wind or frost, not even snow will serve my turn, though each of these has its admirable uses.

But let me have a night late in November, let us say. Every leaf has long been down, save that the beech hedgerow in the sheltered forest road will keep its tawny copper all through the winter. Rain has been sweeping along the valleys for days past in giant misty pillars, the brooks are bank high with red, foaming water; down every steep field little hedgerow streams come pouring. In the farmyards the men go about their work clad in sacks, and if they may will shelter under penthouses and find work to do in the barns.

Give me a night in the midst of such weather, and then think of the farm atop the hill, to which two good miles of deep, wandering lane go climbing, and mix the rain with a great wind from the mountain: and then think of entering the place which I have described, set now for the old act of winter. The green shutters are close fastened without the window, the settle is curved about the hearth, and that great cavern is ablaze and glorious with heaped wood and coals, and the white walls golden with the light of the leaping flames. And those within can hear the rain dashing upon shutter and upon closed door, and the fire hisses now and again as stray drops fall down the chimney; and the great wind shakes the trees and goes roaring down the hillside to the valley and moans and mutters about the housetop.

A man will leave his place, snug in shelter, in the deepest glow of the fire, and go out for a moment and open but a little of the door in the porch and see all the world black and wild and wet, and then come back to the light and heat and thank God for his home, wondering whether any are still abroad on such a night of tempest.

Looking back on my native country as I first remember it, I have often regretted that I was not born say twenty or thirty years earlier. I should then have seen more of a singular social process, which I can only call the Passing of the Gentry. In my father's parish this had taken place very long before my day, or his either. Indeed, I am not quite sure that any armigerous families had ever inhabited Llanddewi; though I have a dim notion that certain old farm-houses were pointed out to me as having been "gentlemen's houses." But an adjoining parish had once held three very ancient families of small gentry. One was still in existence well within my recollection, another became extinct in the legitimate line soon after I was born, and the third had been merged in other and larger inheritances.

There were no Perrotts left, and their house had been "restored," and was occupied as a farm. I often sat under their memorials in the little church, and admired their arms, three golden pears, and their crest, a parrot; altogether a pretty example of heraldia cantans, or punning heraldry. Of the other two houses one was a pleasant, rambling, mouldering place, yellow-washed, verandahed, and on the whole more like a petit manoir in Touraine than a country house in England. The third mansion was a sixteenth-century house built in the L shape, and here dwelt in my childhood the last of the ancient gentry of the place.

Even he was descended from the old family in the female line. The old race had been named Meyrick, and they had given land in the thirteenth century that a light might burn before the altar of a neighbouring church for ever. The family affirmed that at one time they had owned all the land that could be seen from a certain high place near their house, and very possibly the tradition was a true one. They had remained faithful to the Latin Church through all the troubles--up to the year of Napoleon Buonaparte's sacring as Emperor by the Pope in Notre-Dame. And when the reigning squire of Lansoar heard the news he raged with fury, and saying, as the story goes, "Damn such a Pope as that!" left the Roman Church for ever. His grandson, whom I knew, always read the Bible in the Douay version and praised the Papists. Indeed, he used often to end up, addressing my father, "In fact they tell me that you're more than half a Roman Catholic yourself, and I like you none the worse for it!"

He was an extraordinary old man. In his youth he had been busy one morning packing up his portmanteau to go to Oxford. News came that his father was ruined; it was probably in the wild smash of speculation that brought down Sir Walter Scott. The young man quietly unpacked his portmanteau and took possession of the mill, not many yards from his own door. He ground corn for the farmers; he did well; he moved into Newport, and became, I think, an importer of Irish butter. Probably, also, he had his share in the industrial developments of Glamorganshire and Monmouthshire, then at the height of their prosperity. At any rate in twenty years or so the fortunes of the old house were redeemed. The drawing-room of Lansoar had been used as a barn for storing corn; in my day it was the most gracious and grave room that I have ever seen. The old family portraits were back on the walls, the old tapestried chairs were in their places, there was not a thing in the room less than a hundred years old, and the squire sat beside his hearth, looking--as I have found out since those days--exactly like Henry IV of France.

He had travelled a good deal in his time, and was supposed to have had his fancy taken by the clothes he had seen worn by the Heidelberg students. So he wore an odd sort of vestment striped with black and dull red, and gathered in with a belt of the same stuff. We called it a blouse, but it must have been something of the shape of a Norfolk jacket. In the evening he would put on a black velvet coat which, as he told me, he got from Poole's at the price of five guineas. Smoking he abominated, and it was never allowed at Lansoar, save when Mr. Williams of Llangibby was a guest.

The owner of Lansoar was in many ways a kindly and benevolent old gentleman, but I think we in the country were chiefly proud of his temper. It was said to be terrific, even in a land of furious, quickly-raised rages. People told how they had seen the old man's white moustache bristling up to his eyes; this was a sign that the fire was kindled. And, as I once heard him say, "the Meyricks always get white with love and hate." It was said that his sister was the only person who met him on something like equal terms. She was an ancient gentlewoman with a tremendous aquiline nose and was more like a marquise of 1793 going proudly to instant execution than can possibly be imagined. She and her brother differed--it was too mild a word, I am sure--so fiercely as to what were the true armorial bearings of the family that when these were to be emblazoned above the dining-room hearth a compromise had to be arranged, and two shields were painted, one on each side.

I am sorry that I was too young to observe Lansoar and its ways with intelligent interest. The people that lived there were of a race and sort that have now perished utterly out of the land; there never will be such people again. But I was banished from Lansoar for the last year or two of the old squire's life. I had left school and was at a loose end at home, and I heard I had fallen under heavy displeasure. It seemed that the descendant of the Meyricks had known a doctor who had lived in Paris on five shillings a week at the beginning of the nineteenth century; he wished to know why I was not living in London on five shillings a week in 1880. The answer would have been that I had neither five shillings nor five pence a week; but one did not answer Mr. James of Lansoar.

I am heartily sorry that the class which he represented has perished. I am sorry to think of all their houses scattered over Gwent; now mere memorials of something that is done for ever and ended. One came upon these houses in every other valley, on every other hillside, looking pleasantly towards the setting sun. They are noble old places, even though they are noble in a humble way; there are no Haddon Halls in Gwent. But these old homes of the small gentry of the borderland--now for the most part used as farm-houses--show their lineage in the dignity of their proportions, in the carved armorial bearings of their porches. The pride of race that belonged to the Morgans, Herberts, Meyricks that once lived in them has passed into their stones, and still shines there.

***

There is a great book that I am hoping to write one of these fine days. I have been hoping to write it, I may say, since 1898, or '99, and somewhere about the latter year I did write as many as a dozen pages. The magnum opus so far conducted did not wholly displease me, and yet it was not good enough to urge me forward in the task. And so it has languished ever since then, and I am afraid I have lost the MSS. that contained all that there was of it long ago. Seriously, of course, it would not have been a great book if it had been ever so prosperously continued and ended; but it would have been at least a curious book, and even now I feel conscious of warm desire at the thought of writing it--some day. For the idea of it came to me as follows:

I had been thinking at the old century end of the work that I had done in the fifteen years or so before, and it suddenly dawned upon me that this work, pretty good or pretty bad, or as it may be, had all been the expression of one formula, one endeavour. What I had been doing was this: I had been inventing tales in which and by which I had tried to realise my boyish impressions of that wonderful magic Gwent. Say that I had walked and wandered by unknown roads, and suddenly, after climbing a gentle hill, had seen before me for the first time the valley of the Usk, just above Newbridge. I think it was on one of those strange days of summer when the sky is at once grey and luminous that I achieved this adventure. There are no clouds in the upper air, the sky is simply covered with a veil which is, as I say, both grey and luminous, and there is no breath of wind, and every leaf is still.

But now and again as the day goes on the veil will brighten, and the sun almost appear; and then here and there in the woods it is as if white moons were descending. On such a day, then, I saw that wonderful and most lovely valley; the Usk, here purged of its muddy tidal waters, now like the sky, grey and silvery and luminous, winding in mystic esses, and the dense forest bending down to it, and the grey stone bridge crossing it. Down the valley in the distance was Caerleon-on-Usk; over the hill, somewhere in the lower slopes of the forest, Caerwent, also a Roman city, was buried in the earth, and gave up now and again strange relics--fragments of the temple of "Nodens, god of the depths." I saw the lonely house between the dark forest and the silver river, and years after I wrote "The Great God Pan," an endeavour to pass on the vague, indefinable sense of awe and mystery and terror that I had received.

This, then, was my process: to invent a story which would recreate those vague impressions of wonder and awe and mystery that I myself had received from the form and shape of the land of my boyhood and youth; and as I thought over this and meditated on the futility--or comparative futility--of the plot, however ingenious, which did not exist to express emotions of one kind or another, it struck me that it might be possible to reverse the process. Could one describe hills and valleys, woods and rivers, sunrise and sunset, buried temples and mouldering Roman walls so that a story should be suggested to the reader? Not, of course, a story of material incidents, not a story with a plot in the ordinary sense of the term, but an interior tale of the soul and its emotions; could such a tale be suggested in the way I have indicated? Such is to be the plan of the "great" book which is not yet written. I mention it here chiefly because I would lay stress on my doctrine that in the world of imagination the child is indeed father of the man, that the man is nothing more than the child with an improved understanding certainly, with all sorts of technical advantages in the way of information and in the arts of expression, but, on the other hand, with the disadvantages of a dimmed imaginative eye and a weakened vision. There have been a few men who have kept the awe and the surmise of earlier years and have added to those miraculous gifts the acquired accomplishments of age and instruction; and these are the only men who are entitled to the name of genius. I have said already that in my boyhood and youth I was a deep and learned student of the country about my home, and that I always saw it as a kind of fairyland. And, cross-examining my memory, I find that I have in no way exaggerated or overcoloured these early and earliest impressions. Fairyland is too precise a word; I would rather say that I saw everything in something of the spirit in which the first explorers gazed on the tropical luxuriance and strangeness of the South American forests, on the rock cities of Peru, on the unconjectured seas that burst upon them from that peak in Darien, on the wholly unimagined splendours of the Mexican monarchy. So it was with me as a child. I came into a strange country, and strange it ever remained to me, so that when I left it for ever there were still hills within sight and yet untrodden, lanes and paths of which I knew the beginning but not the end. For it is to be understood that country folk are in this respect like Londoners: that they have their customary tracks and ways which lead more or less to some end or other; it is only occasionally that either goes out determined not to find his way but to lose it, to stray for the very sake of straying. Thus I walked many times in Wentwood and became familiar with the Roman road that passes for some distance along the summit of that ancient forest, but only once, I think, did I set out from the yellow verge of the Severn and cross the level Moors--a belt of fen country that might well lie between Ely and Brandon; really, no doubt "y môr," the sea--and wonder for a while at the bastioned and battlemented ruins of Caldicot Castle, and so mount up by the outer hills and woods of the forest, through Caerwent, past the Foresters' Oaks, a grove of trees that were almost awful in the magnificence of their age and their decay, and so climb to the ridge and look down on the Usk and the more familiar regions to the west.

And, as you may judge, it was only the knowledge that one must not frighten one's family out of its wits and that camping out in forests without food or drink is highly inconvenient that kept me on this comparatively straight path. So all the while, as I paced an unknown way, yet more unknowns were beckoning to me on right and left. Paths full of promise allured me into green depths, the wildest heights urged me to attempt them, cottages in orchard dells seemed so isolated from all the world that they and theirs must be a part of enchantment. And so I crossed Wentwood, and felt not that I knew it, but that it was hardly to be known.

***

I have already mentioned, I think, that I was an only child. Add to this statement that I had no little cousins available as play-fellows, some of these being domiciled in Anglesea, others in London; that it was only by the merest chance and on the rarest occasions that I ever saw any children at all, and I have given some notion of the extreme solitude of my upbringing. I grew up, therefore, all alone so far as other children were concerned, and though I went to school, school did not seem to make much difference to my habit of mind. I was eleven years old at the time, and I suppose I was "set" to loneliness. I passed the term as a sort of interlude amongst strangers, and came home to my friendly lanes, to my deep and shadowy and secret valleys, as a man returns to his dear ones and his dear native fields after exile amongst aliens and outlanders.

I came back, then, again and again to solitude. There were no children's parties for me, no cricket, no football, and I was heartily glad of it, for I should have abhorred all these diversions with shudderings of body and spirit. My father and mother apart, I loved to be by myself, with unlimited leisure for mooning and loafing and roaming and wandering from lane to lane, from wood to wood. Constantly I seemed to be finding new, hitherto unsuspected tracks, to be emerging from deep lanes and climbing hills so far but seen from the distance, matters of surmise, and now trodden and found to be Darien peaks giving an outlook upon strange worlds of river and forest and bracken-covered slope. Wondering at these things, I never ceased to wonder; and even when I knew a certain path and became familiar with it I never lost my sense of its marvels, as they appeared to me.

I have read curious and perplexed commentaries on that place in Sir Thomas Browne in which he declares his life up to the period of the "Religio Medici" to have been "a miracle of thirty years, which to relate were not a history, but a piece of poetry." Dr. Johnson, summing up the known events of Browne's early life, finds therein nothing in the least miraculous; Southey says the miracle was the great writer's preservation from atheism; Leslie Stephen considers that the strangeness "consists rather in Browne's view of his own history than in any unusual phenomena." "View of his own history" seems a little vague; but however critical sagacity may determine the sense of the passage, I would very willingly adopt it to describe these early years of mine, spent in that rectory amongst the wild hills of Gwent. Of my private opinion, I think there can be little doubt that when Sir Thomas Browne used the word "miraculous" he was thinking not of miracles in the accepted sense as things done contrary to the generally observed laws of nature, but rather of his vision of the world, of his sense of a constant wonder latent in all things. Stevenson, I believe, had some sense of this doctrine as applied to landscape, at least, when he said that there were certain scenes--I forget how he particularised them--which demanded their stories, which cried out, as it were, to have tales indited to fit their singular aspects. This, I think I have shown, is a crude analysis. I should put it thus: this group of pines, this lonely shore, or whatever the scene may be, has made the soul thrill with an emotion intense but vague in the sense in which music is vague; and the man of letters does his best to realise--rather, perhaps, to actualise--this emotion by inventing a tale about the pines or the sands. Such at all events was my state through all the years of boyhood and of youth: everything to me was wonderful, everything visible was the veil of an invisible secret. Before an oddly shaped stone I was ready to fall into a sort of reverie or meditation, as if it had been a fragment of paradise or fairyland. There was a certain herb of the fields that grew plentifully in Gwent, that even now I cannot regard without a kind of reverence; it bears a spire of small yellow blossoms, and its leaves when crushed give out a very pungent, aromatic odour. This odour was to me a separate revelation or mystery, as if no one in the world had smelt it but myself, and I ceased not to admire even when a countryman told me that it was good for stone, if you gathered it "under the planet Juniper."

And here, may I say in passing, that in my opinion the country parson, with all the black-coated class, knows next to nothing of the true minds of the country folk. I feel certain that my father, if asked by a Royal Commission or some such valuable body, "What influence has astrology on your parishioners?" would have answered: "They have never heard of such a thing." In later years I have wondered as to the possible fields which extended beyond the bounds of our ignorance. I have wondered, for example, whether, by any possibility, there were waxen men, with pins in them, hidden in very secret nooks in any of the Llanddewi cottages.

But this is a mere side-issue. To return to my topic, to that attitude of the child-mind which almost says in its heart, "things are because they are wonderful," I am reminded of one of the secret societies with which I have had the pleasure of being connected. This particular society issued a little MS. volume of instructions to those who were to be initiated, and amongst these instructions was the note: "remember that nothing exists which is not God." "How can I possibly realise that?" I said to one of the members of the society. "When I read it I was looking at the tiles on each side of my fireplace in Gray's Inn, and they are of the beastliest design it is possible to imagine. I really cannot see anything of Divinity in those tiles." I do not remember how my objection was met; I don't think it was met. But, looking back, I believe that, as a child, I realised something of the spirit of the mystic injunction. Everywhere, through the darkness and the mists of the childish understanding, and yet by the light of the child's illumination, I saw latens deitas; the whole earth, down to the very pebbles, was but the veil of a quickening and adorable mystery. Hazlitt said that the man of genius spent his whole life in telling the world what he had known himself when he was eighteen. Waiving utterly--I am sorry to say--the title of man of genius, I would reaffirm Hazlitt's proposition on lower grounds. I would say that he who has any traffic with the affairs of the imagination has found out all the wisdom that he will ever know, in this life at all events, by the age of eighteen or thereabouts. And it is probable that Hazlitt, though he never dreamed of it, was but re-expressing those sentences in the Holy Gospels which deal with the intimate relationship between children and "the Kingdom of Heaven." In the popular conception, of course, both amongst priests and people, these texts are understood to refer to the innocence of childhood. But a little reflection will satisfy anyone that in the true sense of the word children are only innocent as a stone is innocent, as a stick is innocent; that is, they are incapable of committing the special offences which to our modern and utterly degraded system of popular ethics constitute the whole matter of morality and immorality. I remember a few years ago reading how an illustrious Primitive Methodist testified on the sacred mount of Primitive Methodism at some anniversary of the society. He said that his old grandmother had implored him when he was a boy never to drink, never to gamble, never to break the Sabbath, and, he concluded triumphantly, "I have never done any of these things."

"Therefore I am a good Christian" is the conclusion evidently suggested. This poor man, it may be said, knew no better, but I am much mistaken if the majority of our Anglican clergy would not accept his statement as a good confession of the faith. The New Testament for all these people has been written in vain; they will still believe that a good Christian is one who drinks a cup of cocoa at 9.30 and is in bed by ten sharp. And to such persons, of course, the texts which assert the necessity of becoming like little children if we would enter the Kingdom of Heaven are clear enough; it is a mere matter of early hours and plenty of cocoa--or, perhaps, of warm bread and milk. But, personally, I cannot at all symbolise with them. I look back to the time when the mountain and the tiny shining stone, the flower, and the brook were all alike signs and evidences of an ineffable mystery and beauty. I see myself all alone in the valley, under hanging woods, of a still summer evening, entranced, wondering what the secret was that was here almost told, and then, I am persuaded, I came near to the spirit of St. Thomas Aquinas: Adoro te devote latens Deitas.

***

There comes to me from very long ago the memory of a burning afternoon in the hot heart of July. I am not sure whether it was in the dry summer. This was in '68 or '69--I am not certain which--and it was notable for many things in my recollection. Firstly, the mountain caught fire. This sounds a terrific and unlikely statement, considered with relation to the temperate and reasonable geology of this land, which has known nothing for many æons of volcanoes or burning mountains. What had happened, of course, was that the heather and wild growth on the mountain had somehow been fired, and so all through that hot August I remember looking westward to the great mountain wall, and watching the dun fume that drifted along its highest places; looking with a certain dread, for there was something apocalyptic in the sight.

Another notable event was the failure of the water supply. The rectory stood almost on top of a long hill that mounted up from the valley of the Soar, there were no ponds or tanks in its curtilage and the drought of this year exhausted the water in the great butt that stood in the yard and received the streams from the roof in rainy weather. This, of course, was not drinking water; that we obtained always from a well deep in the brake, about a quarter of a mile from the house; and without contempt for other and more elaborate beverages, I may say that there are few draughts more delicious than cold well-water, dripping from the rock, and shaded in its hollow basin by the overhanging trees. Our London water is, I believe, perfectly wholesome, but it is absolutely tasteless, no doubt through the manifold purifications and purgations which it has undergone. But well-water has a savour and a character of its own, and the product of one well will often differ in a very marked degree from that of another. Before my day, oddly enough, we had in the county a connoisseur or gourmet of wells. He was a clergyman, and he had been heard to boast that he had tasted the water of every well in the forest of Wentwood. Our own well in the rectory brake was thought excellently of by good judges of clear cold water.

I think it was in this year of the burning mountain that the rectory paid a call on Mr. and Mrs. Roger Gibbon, of the Wern, on a blazing afternoon. They were very old people, and the stock of the Gibbons--I am not using their real name--was one of the most ancient and honoured in the land of Gwent. I suppose, indeed, that they would look on many dukes as parvenus of yesterday. Furthermore, this branch of the race was quite comfortable and well-to-do in money matters.

They received my father and my mother and myself with the heartiest kindness--they had known my father from his boyhood--and insisted on the necessity of some refreshment. So presently the maid came in with a tray and old Roger solemnly mixed for my father and mother, for his wife and himself, four reeking glasses of hot gin. I think that, all things considered, this was the very strangest refreshment ever offered. The old people swallowed their boiling spirit with relish, my parents took their dose with shuddering politeness, and the thermometer rose steadily. Roger and Caroline had been quarrelling about a carpet before we came, and after a decent interval the quarrel was resumed. Roger addressed himself to my mother.

"She would buy it too small. I told her it would be too small, and there it is, with three or four feet of the floor showing. And what do you think she says, Mrs. Machen? She says she will have the bare boards painted green to match the carpet. I say that's ridiculous, don't you think so? [Without waiting for an answer, and bellowing to deaf old Caroline.] There, Caroline, I told you what everyone would say. Mrs. Machen says it's ridiculous. The idea of painting the boards green!"

And the old man, turning to my father, told him in a lower voice and with considerable enjoyment of some home-made wine that his wife had concocted. She had stored it in a cupboard in their bedroom, and Roger told how he used to lie awake at night laughing as he listened to the bottles bursting, the old lady being much too deaf to hear the reports.

Old Gibbon was an expert shot, but he could never be persuaded to use the new-fangled percussion caps. He brought down his birds to the last by means of flint and steel. He was an enthusiastic fox hunter also, but he never hunted on horseback. Up to something past the middle of his life the Llangibby Hounds had been hunted afoot, the Rector of Llangibby being the master, and afoot Roger Gibbon followed them up to his old age. And so cunning had he become in matter of wind and scent and lie of the country that he rarely failed to be in at the death. I doubt whether he knew much of the world outside of a twenty-mile radius, Caerleon being taken as the centre of the circle. But when Roger Gibbon was quite an old man people told him that he ought to see London. So he went to London. He walked out of Paddington Station and saw London, as he thought; and, filled with a great horror and disgust and terror at what he had seen, he trotted back into the station, and paced the platform till the next train for the west started. He got into that train, and returned to the Wern and to the shelter and companionship of his hills and woods, and there abode till the ending of his long days.

It was strange how in those times people were fixed in the soil, so that for many miles round everybody knew everybody, or at least knew of everybody. It is all over, I suppose, and again I think it is a pity that it is over. It was a part of the old life of the friendly fires, and the friendly faces, and when, rarely enough, in this great desert of London, I meet a friend of those old days, I think we both feel as if we were surviving tribesmen of some sept that has been "literally annihilated" or "almost decimated"--to use our modern English.

One says: "Do you remember that walk over Mynydd Fawr to the Holy Well?" The other replies: "How good the beer at the Three Salmons tasted that day we walked all the way from Caerleon on the Old Usk Road." "Let me see; when was that?" "April, '83." And we look on one another and, lo, our heads have whitened and our eyes are beginning to grow dim.

But, as an instance of the fellowship and brotherhood that there was in the land of Gwent in the old days, here is a true story. I have told of fierce old Mr. James, of Lansoar, the ancient squire. Well, there had been a raging and tremendous quarrel between Mr. James and a neighbouring farmer called Williams, and as Williams was an honest and excellent and placable old man, there was not much doubt as to who was the aggressor. After years of hate, on one side at all events, a false rumour went about the county that Mr. James had lost all his money, in "Turkish Bonds," I think. Then did old Mr. Williams, the farmer, go up one night secretly to old Mr. James, the squire, and altogether heedless of the white face and the furious glance and the bristling moustache that greeted him, he offered all he had to his enemy.

May he remember me from his happy place.

Chapter II

By this time I hope that I have made a sort of picture of my conditions as they were up to the time that I left school at the age of seventeen. Solitude and woods and deep lanes and wonder; these were the chief elements of my life. One thing, however, I have so far omitted, that is the matter of books, which I will now consider.

And, firstly, I must record with deep thankfulness the circumstance that as soon as I could read I had the run of a thoroughly ill-selected library; or, rather, of a library that had not been selected at all. My father's collection, if that serious word may be applied to a hugger-mugger of books, had grown up anyhow and nohow, and in it the most revered stocks had mingled with the most frivolous. There were the Fathers, in the English version made by the Tractarians, and there was also no end of "yellowbacks" bought at Smith's bookstalls on railway journeys. There was a row of little Elzevir classics, "with the Sphere," bound in parchment that had grown golden with its two hundred and odd years; there was also Mr. Verdant Green in his tattered paper wrapper as my father had bought him at Oxford. Next to Verdant Green you might very likely find the Dialogues of Erasmus in seventeenth-century leather, and Borrow in his original boards--we read Borrow at Llanddewi long before there were any Borrovians--might hide an odd volume of "Martin Chuzzlewit" (in a "Railway Edition") which had tumbled to the back of the shelf. Hard by stood Copleston's "Prælectiones Academicæ," and close to it a complete set of Brontë books, including Mrs. Gaskell's "Life," all these in yellowish linen covers, being, I imagine, the first one-volume edition issued by the publishers. And here again Llanddewi in the woods may claim to have been in advance of its age, for we were devoted to the name of Brontë.

Suppose the weather did not beckon me, I would begin to go about the house on the search of books. I might have "Wuthering Heights" in my mind and be chasing that amazing volume very closely, and be, in fact, hot on the scent, when I would be brought up sharply by my grandfather's Hebrew grammar. I always loved the shape and show of the Hebrew character, and have meant to learn the language from 1877 onwards, but have not yet thoroughly mastered the alphabet. I once, indeed, got so advanced as to be able to spell out the Yiddish posters which cover the walls in the East End of London, and I remember being much amused when I had deciphered a most mystic, reverend-looking word and found that it read "Bishopsgyte." But I believe that in Yiddish the two "yods" represent the "a" sound.

Well, this Hebrew grammar would distract me from the hunt of Emily Brontë's masterpiece, and by the time I had decided that Monday would be soon enough for a serious beginning in Hebrew, while I meditated in the meanwhile on the beauty of the names of the four classes of accents--Emperors, Kings, Princes, and Dukes, I think--it was likely enough that I had got hold of Alison's "History of Europe," or "The Bible in Spain," or a book on Brasses. And by the time I had gloated over the horrors of the French Revolution as described in Alison, or had marvelled at Borrow in the character of a Protestant colporteur, or had admired the pictured brasses of Sir Robert de Septvans, Sir Roger de Trumpington--winnowing fans on the coat-armour of the one, trumpets on the shield of the other--and Abbot Delamere of St. Albans it was tea-time, and I probably spent the rest of the evening with a bound volume of "Chambers's Journal," "All the Year Round," "Cornhill," or "The Welcome Guest." These were always a great resource; and I particularly wish that I still possessed "The Welcome Guest," a popular weekly dating from the late 'fifties of last century. It was full of work by people who afterwards became famous, and now, again, are fading into forgetfulness. John Hollingshead we still remember, though it is only the elderly who can tell much now of "the sacred lamp of burlesque," which was kept burning at the Gaiety. Hollingshead was a contributor to "The Welcome Guest," so also were the Brothers Mayhew and the Brothers Brough, so on a great scale was George Augustus Sala, who wrote in it "Twice Round the Clock" and something that was called, I fancy, "Make Your Game or, the Adventures of the Stout Gentleman, the Thin Gentleman, and the Man with the Iron Chest." This was a "lively" account of a visit to the gaming tables then existing in Germany. The Stout Gentleman was one of the Mayhews, the Man with the Iron Chest was Sala himself; and I met the Thin Gentleman many years afterwards in a cock-loft in Catherine Street, where I was cataloguing books on magic and alchemy and the secret arts in general. The cock-loft was over the Vizetellys' publishing office, and the Thin Gentleman was old Mr. Vizetelly. We "larned" him to publish a translation of "La Terre" by sending him, an old man past seventy, to gaol for three months. He died soon afterwards; I forget whether his death took place before or after the very handsome and official and "respectable" reception and entertainment that were given to Zola on his visiting England.

I must say that I should like to see the old "Welcome Guest" volume again. I am afraid I should not admire its literature very much, for Sala, the chief contributor, had already acquired those vicious mannerisms which pleased the injudicious. He would speak of Billingsgate as a "piscatorial bourse," for instance. I am afraid I should find it all terribly old-fashioned. But I should like to hold the fat volume again and glance through its pages, for they would bring back to me the long winter evenings, and the rectory fire burning cheerfully, and the heavy red curtains drawn close over the windows, shutting out the night.

I must say that I found a great joy and resource in these old magazines. If one were in a mood averse from reading in the solid block, if the hour did not seem propitious for beginning once more "Pickwick" from the beginning, it was a delight to think of those bound volumes all in a row, and of the inexhaustible supply of mixed literature which they contained. For just as there was always the chance, and indeed the likelihood, of making new discoveries in the happy confusion of the Llanddewi library, so it was with these rows of "Household Words," "Chambers's," "All the Year Round," "Welcome Guest," and "Cornhill"; there was always the possibility of a find; some tale or essay hitherto overlooked or neglected might turn out to be full of matter and entertainment. And so the most unlikely events happened. You would expect to find good things of all sorts in a magazine edited by Charles Dickens, but you would hardly expect to find there the curious thing or the out-of-the-way thing. Still, it was in a volume of "Household Words" that I first read about alchemy in a short series of papers which (I have since recognised) were singularly well-informed and enlightened. I do not wish it to be understood that I myself have any strong convictions on the matter of turning inferior metals into superior, though I believe the later trend of science is certainly in favour of the theoretical possibility of such a process. Nor do I hold any distinct brief for the very fascinating doctrine which maintains, or would like to maintain, that the great alchemical books are really symbolical books; that while seeming to relate to lead and gold, to mercury and silver, they hide under these figures intimations as to a profound and ineffable transmutation of the spirit; that the experiment to which they relate is the Great Experiment of the mystics, which is the experiment of God. This, I say, is a fascinating theory; whether it have any truth in it I know not, and perhaps it is one of those questions of which Sir Thomas Browne speaks; questions difficult, indeed, and perplexed, but not beyond all conjecture. But, however this may be, I recollect that those articles in that old, half-calf bound volume of "Household Words," while not affirming this, that, or the other doctrine as to alchemy in so many distinct words, did suggest that a few of the old alchemists, at all events, were something more than blundering simpletons engaged on a quest which was a patent absurdity, which could only have been entertained by the besotted superstition of "the dark ages," which had this one claim to our attention inasmuch as the modern science of chemistry rose from the ashes of its foolish fires.

This is not the place for a discussion of the art of Thrice Great Hermes; the matter is cited here as an example of the odd and unexpected way in which my attention, I being some eight or nine years old, was directed to a singular and perplexing subject which has engaged my curiosity at intervals ever since. I see myself sitting on a stool by the rectory hearth, propping up "Household Words" against the fender, quite ravished by the story of Nicholas Flamel, who found by chance "The Book of Abraham the Jew," who journeyed all over Europe in search of one who would interpret its figures to him, who succeeded at last in the Operation of the Great Work, and was discovered by the King's Chamberlain living in great simplicity, eating cabbage soup with Pernelle, his wife. These fireside studies of mine must have been made forty-three or forty-four years ago, but I still think the story of Nicholas Flamel and Pernelle, his wife, an enchanting one. But then I re-read the tale of Aladdin and the Wonderful Lamp only the other day, and I am still thrilled and perplexed by that most singular and important fact; that the genie declared himself to be the servant of the Roc's Egg.

I am sorry to have to confess that the rectory shelves held no copy of "The Arabian Nights." I made up this deficiency soon after I went to school by buying an excellent edition, issued, I think, by Routledge for a shilling. This edition is now, the booksellers tell me, out of print, and it is a pity, for now if you want the book there is nothing between an edition obviously meant for the nursery, with gaudy plates, and Lane's version for thirty shillings. I speak not of Burton, for I found myself unable to read a couple of pages of his detestable English, made more terrible by the imitations of the rhymed prose of the original. I came upon something which went very much as follows:--

> Then followed the dawn of day, and the Princess finished her allotted say,
> Praise be to the Lord of Light alway, who faileth not to send the appointed ray----

and so on, at much greater length; highly ingenious, no doubt, and also infinitely foolish.

I remember once wasting hours--nay, days--in the effort to render Rabelais' "Verses written over the Great Gate of the Abbey of Thelème" into English, following as far as I could the rhyme system. Now, according to the French notion, "don" is a perfect rhyme to "pardon," and so Rabelais wrote:--

> Or donné par don,
> Ordonne pardon
> A cil qui le donne;
> Et bien guerdonne
> Tout mortel preudhom
> Or donné par don.

That is, the final sound of each line is almost identical with the final sound of every other line; and of this I made:--

> For given relief,
> Forgiven and lief
> The giver believe;
> And all men that live
> May gain the palm leaf
> For given relief.

Soon afterwards, while I was resting from this mighty effort, I read in Disraeli's "Curiosities of Literature" a quotation from Martial: Turpe est difficiles habere nugas--'Tis folly to sweat o'er a difficult trifle.' I was convinced of my sin. I suppose that the real translator when confronted by such puzzles contrives to think of an indirect rather than a direct solution. For example, the right way of getting the effect of the Arabic jingle into English might be sought by the path of alliteration; or possibly blank verse might give to the English reader something of the same kind of pleasure as that enjoyed by the Oriental in reading a prose which infringes on the region of poetry. And it may be that the queer music of Rabelais could be echoed, at least, in English by the use of assonance.

Here is, indeed, a diversion, but it has arisen, legitimately enough, from that shilling, paper wrapper volume of "The Arabian Nights" bought in 1875 or '76 or thereabouts. And another event of like importance was my seeing De Quincey's "Confessions of an English Opium Eater" at Pontypool Road Station. This also I instantly bought and as instantly loved, and still love very heartily. It always vexes me to detect, as I constantly do detect in modern critics, the subtle desire to run down De Quincey. The critic is afraid to make a frontal attack--the stress of these times will win pardon for the phrase--since he knows that he will be opposed by such splendours and such terrors--"an army with banners"--as the English language can scarce show elsewhere. He is quite aware, since he is, ex hypothesi, an able critic, that De Quincey deliberately used our tongue as if it had been a mighty organ in mightier cathedral, so that the very stones and the far-lifted vault and the hollow spaces of the towers re-echo and reverberate and thrill with tremendous fugal harmonies. And our critics are advised also that De Quincey was no mere player of clever tricks with the language; his was not the amusing Stevensonian method of counting the "l's" and estimating the value of medial "s's" and the terrifying effect of the final reiterated "r." There was none of this; he wrote in the great manner because he thought in the great manner. The critic cannot deny this; he must admit the beauty and pathos of the Ann episode and of the vision of Jerusalem; but still he will hint a fault and hesitate his dislike of this greater master. The reason is not far to seek. All realism is unpopular, and De Quincey was eminently a realist.

Now I know that I am touching here on a great question. I hope to debate it at length later on; for the moment I would merely say that I define realism as the depicting of eternal, inner realities-- the "things that really are" of Plato--as opposed to the description of transitory, external surfaces; the delusory masks and dominoes with which the human heart drapes and hides itself. But, all this apart, I cannot help dwelling on the manner in which I associate these early literary discoveries of mine with the places where they were made.

You may hear friends and lovers discussing after many years the manner of their first meeting; Daphnis as Darby will remind Chloe--now Joan--how they saw one another for the first time at the Smiths' garden-party, and one plate of their bread and butter tasted slightly of onions, and the curate achieved six faults running at lawn-tennis, and it came on to rain. So I can never take up De Quincey without thinking of the dismal platform at Pontypool Road, and the joy of coming home for the holidays, and the mountains all about me as I stood and waited for my father and the trap and read the first pages of the magic book. Those great mountains, and the drive home by the green arched lanes, abounding in flowers, and the very dear look of home amidst its orchards; all these are part and parcel of my joy in the "Confessions" for ever. And so again with another noble book; with one of the noblest of all books, as I have ever esteemed it. I am a very small boy; about seven or eight years old, I conceive, and my mother takes me with her to pay a call on Mrs. Gwyn, of Llanfrechfa Rectory. The ladies talk, and I, seeking quietly for something to entertain me, light in a low bookcase on a fat, dumpy little book. I suspect it was the oddity of the shape, the extreme squabness of the volume, that first took my fancy, and then I open the pages--and I have never really closed them. For the dumpy book was a translation of "The Ingenious Gentleman, Don Quixote de la Mancha"; and those are words that will thrill a lettered man as the opening notes of certain fugues of Bach will thrill a musician. I heard nothing of the amiable talk of the ladies. I was deep in the small print--alas! it would now blind my tired eyes--and when my mother rose to go I clung so desperately and piteously to the fat little book that the kind Mrs. Gwyn said she would lend it to me, and I might take it home. For which benevolence I am ever bound to pray for her good estate, or for her soul; as it may chance to be.

So, as Hereford Station spells for me, principally, "The Arabian Nights," as De Quincey is linked with domed mountains and green lanes and the return home: the Ingenious Gentleman advanced to greet me, mysteriously enough, in the drawing-room of the rectory of Llanfrechfa, and I shall always reckon Frechfa--the "freckled"--as among the most venerated of the Celtic saints.

***

For a long time, as it seems to me, I have been talking of discoveries of books; discoveries in our own Llanddewi shelves, in the shelves of neighbours, on railway bookstalls. We shall hear more of books by and by, of books found in very different places--Clare Market and the Strand of 1880 and back streets by Notting Hill Gate are even now looming before us--so for the present we may hear more of the conditions of that Gwent where I was a boy and a young man.

I have said that I was born just a little too late to witness the Passing of the Gentry. Few of them survived into my day, and I was too young to see with intelligence that which still remained to be seen of the old order. But one thing I do remember, that the gentry of those times, even when they were wealthy, lived with a simplicity that would astonish the people of to-day. Those who know "Martin Chuzzlewit" will remember how Tigg Montague, who was Montague Tigg, lunched luxuriously in the board room of his city office. The meal was brought in on a tray and consisted of "a pair of cold roast fowls, flanked by some potted meats and a cool salad." There was a bottle of champagne and a bottle of Madeira. This was the luncheon of vulgar and ostentatious luxury in the 'forties; compare it with the kind of midday meal that the modern Montague would eat at the Hôtel Splendide or the Hôtel Glorieux; the meal of the man who eats and drinks as much to impress others with his wealth as to gratify his own appetite.

Well, I have often seen "the old Lord Tredegar" eating his luncheon. My father and I would be in the coffee-room of the King's Head, Newport, waiting for the ostler to put in the pony. And there in one of the boxes sat the old lord--a very wealthy man--eating his luncheon; which was bread and cheese and a tankard of ale. And, oddly enough, on the one occasion on which I visited the Ham, the magnate thereof, Mr. Iltyd Nicholl, was enjoying a meal similar in every respect to that of Lord Tredegar--though I believe he had a little cold apple tart after his cheese. We, of the middle people, always dined at one on meat, pudding, and cheese; tea followed at five, an affair of bread and butter and jam, with, possibly, a caraway loaf. Hot buttered toast was distinctly festal. The day closed so far as meals were concerned with bread and cheese and beer at nine o'clock. On rare occasions, once in three years or so, a number of clergy who called themselves collectively the Ruridecanal Chapter came to hear a paper read and also to a dinner. This would probably consist of a salmon of Severn or Usk--which muddy waters breed incomparably the finest salmon in the world--of a saddle of Welsh mutton from the mountains, and of a rich sweet called, very lightly and unworthily, a trifle. There would be a dessert of almonds and raisins and, according to the season, home-grown apples and pears or greengages. These delicates would be displayed on a service which showed green vine-leaves in relief against a buff ground, bordered with deep purple and gold. It was hideous, and, I should think, Spode.

In the autumn my mother used to concoct a singular dish which she called fermety. It is more generally known as frumenty; you will find it mentioned in Washington Irving's "Christmas," where the squire makes his supper off it on Christmas Eve--no doubt because it was the traditional fasting dish for the Vigil of the Nativity. It was made, so far as I can remember, of the new wheat of the year, of milk, of eggs, of currants, of raisins, of sugar, and of spices, "all working up together in one delicious gravy." No doubt a very honourable dish and a most ancient and Christian pottage; but I am not quite sure that I should like it, if it were proffered to me now. Among the farmers a few of the elder people still breakfasted on cawl, a broth made of fat bacon and vegetables, and decorated, oddly enough, with marigold blossoms. And a fine old man whom I once met in a lane spoke violently against tea, as a corrupting thing and a very vain novelty. For women, he said, it might serve, but the breakfast for a man was a quart of cider with a toast. But most of the farming people breakfasted on rashers of bacon, cooked by being hung on hooks before the fire in a Dutch oven. With the bacon they ate potatoes, which were done in a very savoury manner. Take cold boiled potatoes, break into small pieces, fry (or rather, faites sauter) in bacon fat, then press into a shallow dish, pat to a smooth surface, and brown before the fire. This is a breakfast that goes very well with a keen mountain breath of a morning.

And I believe that cheese always formed part of the farmers' breakfast, as a kind of second or cold course. This was of their own making, and was of the kind called after Caerphilly, a little town with a huge ruinous castle in a hollow of giant hills. It is a white cheese of a creamy consistency and delicate flavour, and is to be commended for the making of Welsh rarebit. The farmers, as I say, ate it at breakfast, again at twelve o'clock dinner, after hot boiled fat bacon and beans or cabbage, and again at tea, where, to their tastes, it seemed to go very well with bread and butter--I find it hard to realise in London that bread and butter can be a choice delicacy--and a sweet, such as an open-work raspberry tart. And, of course, the Caerphilly cheese appeared again at supper, and with bread and onions it was always the hedgerow snack of the man in the fields.

And the cider of that land was good. It was a greenish yellow in colour, with a glint of gold in it if held up to the light, as it were a remembrance of the August and September suns that had shone mellow on the deep orchards of Gwent. It was of full body and flavour and strength, smooth on the palate, neither sweet nor sharp; and I do not think there was anyone in Llanddewi parish so poor as not to have a barrel or two in his cellar against Christmastide and snowy nights, though to be sure in years wherein apples were a scanty crop some of the smaller folk increased the bulk of their cider by strange expedients. Pears went to the mill always, and as a matter of course. In most of the orchards there were one or two big pear trees, and possibly the wisdom of the Gwentian ancients had concluded that a slight admixture of pears with the apples improved and mellowed the cider. But in scanty years, when the man with but a few trees saw bare boughs in autumn, he went to his garden, dug up a barrow load or two of parsnips and added them to his apples. I cannot say anything as to the resultant juice, since I never tasted it.

There was no wretched poverty in Llanddewi, because almost everybody had a little land of his own. Tenant farmers there were, of course, who held of Mr. John Hanbury, of Pontypool Park, lord of the manor of Edlogan; a manor named after a certain Edlogion who was a prince of the sixth century and the protector of Cybi Sant. But besides his tenants and those of other landlords there was a numerous race of small freeholders, who owned eighty, fifty, ten acres of land, and so down till you came to a holding of a house and a garden and a mere patch by the roadside. But with a garden and a patch of land a clever cottager of the old school could do a great deal. I remember an old man named Timothy who lived in a house very small and very ancient in the midst of the fields, far, even, from a by-road; and he thought in greengages as a Stock Exchange man thinks in shares.

For about his old cottage there were three or four, or maybe half a dozen, greengage trees that had been planted so long ago that they had grown almost to the dignity of timber, and spread wild branches high and low and far and wide, so that one might say that old Timothy lived in a grove or wood of greengage trees. So you may conceive how deeply the poor old man thought of these gages, beside which his little orchard of damsons and bullaces was of small account. A really plentiful crop, when the big boughs were heavy and drooping with rich green, sun-speckled fruit, meant to him abundance and luxury; and bare trees spelt on the other hand a bare winter and some pinching of poverty, though nothing beyond endurance. Timothy was a smallholder on the smallest scale, but there were many people of two, six, or twelve acres who did very well in their humble way--which I have always thought is the happy way, if one can attain to it. The man would work for a farmer in the day-time, and often be sturdy enough to do many things on his own estate on summer evenings; and all the day long his wife was busy with her pigs and bees and fowls, and perhaps with two or three cows. There was a good market for their produce at Pontypool, a town on the verge of the industrial district, for the colliers and the tinplate workers love to feed richly. I once saw a woman putting the last touches to a flat apple tart in a little tavern called Castell-y-bwch (Bucks' Castle) on the mountain side. She drew out the tart from the oven, prised open the lid of pastry, and inserted some half-pound of butter and half pound of moist Demerara sugar, and then put back the lid and replaced the pastry in the oven; so that apple juice, sugar, butter should fuse all together. That is a fair sample of hill cookery; other people of the hills would buy fresh butter at a high price, and give what they were asked for "green" Caerphilly cheese, still melting from the press; and they loved to plaster butter heavily on hot new bread and then crown all with an equal depth of golden honey. And they had a goodly appetite also for great fat salmon, caught in the yellow Usk water; and so the fishermen of Caerleon and the little farmers of such parishes as Llanddewi profited hugely by these mountain tastes.

Many years afterwards I lived for a short while on the Chiltern Hills. Here was a different tale. In a whole parish there was, I think, barely a single small holder; the little properties had all been bought up by the great landlords. There was no comfort about the tumbledown, leaky cottages which, in many cases, depended for their drinking water supply on dirty water-butts. None of the farm labourers had fowls or pigs or bees; the farmers, their employers, did not allow the men to keep pigs or fowls lest they should be tempted to steal corn and meal.

So the poorer folk were divided into two classes--the good-humoured wastrels, who "went on the parish" at the slightest provocation and without the slightest shame, and a few more prosperous, sour, ill-mannered boors, who were consumed with an acrid "Liberalism" and with a rancorous envy of anyone better off than themselves.

But at Llanddewi the small holder of land, so far from envying or hating the great landlord, took, as it were, a pride in him. I remember Mrs. Owen Tudor, owner of nine or ten rough acres of wild land in Llanddewi, being both grieved and angry when she heard that a great and ancient Gwentian house might be forced to sell a certain portion of their estates through the pressure of bad times in the early 'eighties. She, too, was a landowner--of rushes chiefly and alder copses and bracken--and of ancient, though unblazoned, family, and if the great Morgans suffered, so also did she suffer.

***

It comes to my mind that I must by no means forget Sir Walter Scott and all that he did for me. And to get at him it is necessary that we enter the drawing-room at Llanddewi. I was amused the other day to see in an old curiosity shop near Lincoln's Inn Fields amongst the rarities displayed small china jars or pots with a picture of two salmon against a background of leafage on the lid. I remember eating potted salmon out of just such jars as these, and now even in my lifetime they appear to have become curious. So, perhaps, if I describe a room which was furnished in 1864 that also may be found to be curious. I may note, by the way, that we always applied the word "parlour"--which properly means drawing-room, and is still, I think, used in that sense in the United States of America--to the dining-room, which was also our living room for general, everyday use. So Sir Walter Scott speaks of a "dining-parlour," and Mr. Pecksniff, entering Todgers's, of the "eating-parlour." And now the word only occurs in public-houses, in the phrase "parlour prices," and even that use is becoming obsolete.

But as for the Llanddewi drawing-room: the walls were covered with a white paper, on which was repeated at regular intervals a diamond-shaped design in pale, yellowish buff. The carpet was also white; on it, also at regular intervals, were bunches of very red roses and very green leaves. In the exact centre of the room was a round rosewood table standing on one leg, and consequently shaky. This was covered with a vivid green cloth, trimmed with a bright yellow border. In the centre of the cloth was a round mat, apparently made of scarlet and white tags or lengths of wool;

this supported the lamp of state. It was of white china and of alabastrous appearance, and it burned colza oil. One had to wind it up at intervals as if it had been a clock. In the sitting-room, before the coming of paraffin, we usually burned "composite" candles; two when we were by ourselves, four when there was company.

Over the drawing-room mantelpiece stood a large, high mirror in a florid gilt frame. Before it were two vases of cut-glass, with alternate facets of dull white and opaque green, of a green so evil and so bilious and so hideous that I marvel how the human mind can have conceived it. And yet my heart aches, too, when, as rarely happens, I see in rubbish shops in London back streets vases of like design and colour. Somewhere in the room was a smaller vase of Bohemian glass; its designs in "ground" glass against translucent ruby. This vase, I think, must have stood on the whatnot, a triangular pyramidal piece of furniture that occupied one corner and consisted of shelves getting smaller and smaller as they got higher.

Against one wall stood a cabinet, of inlaid wood, velvet lined, with glass doors. On the shelves were kept certain pieces of Nantgarw china, some old wine-glasses with high stems, and a collection of silver shoe-buckles and knee-buckles, and two stoneware jugs. The pictures--white mounts and gilt frames--were water-colours and chromo-lithographs. Against one of the window-panes hung a painting on glass, depicting a bouquet of flowers in an alabaster jar. There was a plaster cast in a round black frame, which I connect in my mind with the Crystal Palace and the Prince Consort, and an "Art Union," whatever that may be: it displayed a very fat little girl curled up apparently amidst wheat sheaves. A long stool in bead-work stood on the hearthrug before the fire; and a fire-screen, also in bead work, shaped like a banner, was suspended on a brass stand. On a bracket in one corner was the marble bust of Lesbia and her Sparrow; beneath it in a hanging bookcase the Waverley Novels, a brown row of golden books.

I can see myself now curled up in all odd corners of the rectory reading "Waverley," "Ivanhoe," "Rob Roy," "Guy Mannering," "Old Mortality," and the rest of them, curled up and entranced so that I was deaf and gave no answer when they called to me, and had to be roused to life--which meant tea--with a loud and repeated summons. But what can they say who have been in fairyland? Notoriously, it is impossible to give any true report of its ineffable marvels and delights. Happiness, said De Quincey, on his discovery of the paradise that he thought he had found in opium, could be sent down by the mail-coach; more truly I could announce my discovery that delight could be contained in small octavos and small type, in a bookshelf three feet long. I took Sir Walter to my heart with great joy, and roamed, enraptured, through his library of adventures and marvels as I roamed through the lanes and hollows, continually confronted by new enchantments and fresh pleasures. Perhaps I remember most acutely my first reading of "The Heart of Midlothian," and this for a good but external reason. I was suffering from the toothache of my life while I was reading it; from a toothache that lasted for a week and left me in a sort of low fever--as we called it then. And I remember very well as I sat, wretched and yet rapturous, by the fire, with a warm shawl about my face, my father saying with a grim chuckle that I would never forget my first reading of "The Heart of Midlothian." I never have forgotten it, and I have never forgotten that Sir Walter Scott's tales, with every deduction for their numerous and sometimes glaring faults, have the root of the matter in them. They are vital literature, they are of the heart of true romance. What is vital literature, what is true romance? Those are difficult questions which I once tried to answer, according to my lights, in a book called "Hieroglyphics"; here I will merely say that vital literature is something as remote as you can possibly imagine from the short stories of the late Guy de Maupassant.

The hanging bookcase in the drawing-room under the marble bust of Lesbia and her Sparrow is not only rich and golden in my memory from its being the habitation of the Waverley Novels. This had been treasure enough, indeed, to make the shelves for ever dear; but there was more than this. The bookcase held, besides Sir Walter's romances, my father's school and college prizes, dignified books in whole calf and in pigskin, adorned with the arms of Cowbridge School and Jesus College, Oxford, in rich gold. Here was the Judicious Hooker, whose judiciousness, I regret to say, I could never abide nor stomach; here that noble book, Parker's "Glossary of Gothic Architecture," in three volumes, one of text and two of beautifully executed plates; and here was an early volume of Tennyson.

Of these two last-named books I can scarcely say which is the more precious and eminent in my recollection. The one stands for my initiation into the spirit of Gothic, and I think that is one of the most magical of all initiations. More furious and frantic nonsense has been talked about "paganism" than about almost any other subject; it will only be necessary to think of Swinburne with his "world has grown grey" phrase to indicate what manner of nonsense I have in mind. But the fact is that the heart of paganism was not exactly contrite or broken, but certainly resigned, with an austere and stoical acceptance of fate, which is not without its beauty and its majesty. The nearest modern equivalent to the classic or pagan spirit is Calvinism--the Oedipus Tyrannus is nothing but the doctrine of predestination set to solemn music--and this austere spirit stamped itself on all the finest Greek art. It is somewhat softened in Plato, for Plato drew from the East by way of Pythagoras, but the beauty of Greek tragedy, architecture, sculpture, is essentially austere and severe. It is Calvinism in marble; and judgment and inexorable vengeance on guilty sinners are sung in choral odes.

Now winter has its splendours; but with what joy do we welcome the yearly miracle of spring. We and the whole earth exult together as though we had been delivered from prison, the hedgerows and the fields are glad, and the woods are filled with singing; and men's hearts are filled with an ineffable rapture. Israel once more has come out of Egypt, from the house of bondage. And all this is expressed in the Gothic, and much more than this. It is the art of the supreme exaltation, of the inebriation of the body and soul and spirit of man. It is not resigned to dwell calmly, stoically, austerely on the level plains of this earthly life, since its joy is in this, that it has stormed the battlements of heaven. And so its far-lifted vaults and its spires rush upward, and its pinnacles are like a wood of springing trees. And its hard stones, its strong-based pillars break out as it were into song, they blossom as the rose; all the secrets of the garden and the field and the wood have been delivered unto them. And not only is all this true of building. Take a common iron nail that is to be driven into a door. The Gothic smith would so deal with that nail that its head should become a little piece of joy and fantasy, a little portion of paradise. Nay, take the letter A, as the Romans gave it to us; a plain, well-built, business-like letter, admirably fulfilling its purpose, with no nonsense about it. Now look at a thirteenth-century illuminated manuscript and seek out this A. It has every kind of "nonsense" about it; of that nonsense that makes earth into heaven. It is not only that it glows with rich raised gold, that it is most imperially vested in blue and in scarlet, but its frigid form has relaxed into beauty; it is no longer a mere letter, it is as a wild rose-tree in a hedge. From it spring curves of infinite grace, which enclose the page of text, and hair-line branches break from the main stem and blossom out into flowers of paradise: so the wild roses, delicate, enchanting, sway and quiver over the green field in the month of June.

So much for the "Glossary"; now for the other volume, the little early Tennyson. My attention was directed to this in an odd manner. One of the masters at school had called me a "lotus-eater," and I was much pleased with the sound of the phrase, though the master did not mean to be complimentary, and I had no notion as to what a lotus-eater really was. But in the course of the next holidays, rummaging at random among the books at the rectory, as my custom was, I opened the Tennyson and found the poem of "The Lotos-Eaters" with the "Choric Song" annexed. I began to read that I might be instructed as to the exact nature of my crime. I read on, enchanted, and it was then, in my twelfth or thirteenth year, that I first delighted in poetry as poetry, for its own sake, apart from any story it might tell.

And here I find an extraordinary difficulty in "making a distinction," as the casuists say, between two very different kinds of literary pleasure. For some time I had enjoyed great literature in such books as "Don Quixote" and Sir Walter Scott's romances; but "The Lotos-Eaters"--which is also, I think, great literature--gave me a quite new and peculiar delight. Hitherto it had been the story which had charmed me; but now I found myself delighting in the music and melody of verse, in the "atmosphere" of the poem, in the "colour" of the words--to use terms of which I disapprove, but for which I can find no efficient substitutes. I suspect, indeed, that I found in Tennyson's poem the transmuted and golden image of my own solitary and meditative habit of mind; and this may have counted for something in the sum of my delight. The master, a cheery, excellent young man as I remember him, may have made a correct diagnosis; I had been a lotus-eater for years without knowing it, and so recognised Ulysses' entranced companions as my true comrades in dreams. It may have been so; but in any case I have always dated my inoculation with the specific virus of literature from my reading of those verses in the little calf-bound volume.

Chapter III

Some years ago I was asked by the editor of a well-known paper to write a short series of articles about London. The subject seems ambitious enough, and indeed London considered either physically or intellectually is so vast and mighty a world, that the study of any one--of even the smallest and least considerable--of its aspects may well be the task of a lifetime. But, so far as I can remember, my instructions were of the liberal and catholic kind. I mean, I was not required to write of the great city as the goal of the timber merchant or of the dealer in precious stones, or of the makers of chasubles, or of the fashioner of wigs, but rather to depict it as the end sought by all these, and by myriads more. And so I set about the task in my usual spirit, firmly convinced, that is, that better men had said all that there was to say on the matter brought before me, and yet resolved to do my best and to try to make something of the job in one way or another. So I set to work, and found, strangely enough, that though I was writing about London, I was also writing a mystical treatise, on a text which I will not divulge in this place. But for the beginning of my series I remember that I went back a good many years to the time when London began to call to me. I often speculate now in these later days as to how it would have been with me if this call had never come. For I have certain friends--very few of them--still living in Gwent and on its borders who have not heard the summons. The special family that I have in mind has lived in those regions for more centuries than I can tell. It would be a bold and learned Welsh herald who would trace them to their beginnings on the Celtic side, but on the Norman they go back to Sir Payne Turberville, the companion of Fitzhamon, and even in Wales a story of nine hundred years is a long story.

Well, coming down a little through the ages, the Rowlands that I knew--of course, their grandfather knew my grandfather--are still on the soil. Certainly a younger son has crossed the Severn, but the two others have not moved their habitations more than ten or twelve miles in the last fifty years. From half-way between Newport and Cardiff to Newport, from Newport to a mile east of Newport, then to four miles east of Newport, at last to three miles west of Cardiff: they will surely be laid in the land of their fathers at the end. So it might have been with me, perhaps, if it had not been for the blood of certain Scottish sailors intermingled with the stay-at-home stock of Gwent. But I often wonder, as I say, how it would have happened to me if I had found a home under the shadow of Twyn Barlwm instead of becoming a dweller in the tents of London. Tents, I say advisedly, for, with the rarest exceptions, Londoners have no homes. This was true in a great measure nearly two hundred years ago, when Dr. Johnson first came to London from Lichfield; it is now all but universally true.

But, anyhow, the call of London, partly external and partly internal, came to me, and for some months before I left the old land for the first time I was imagining London and making a picture of it in my mind, and longing for it. I turned up the old magazines and re-read Sala's "Twice Round the Clock." I came upon the strange phrase, "the City," in stories, and wondered what the City signified. And I began to have an appetite for London papers. For it should be understood that at Llanddewi Rectory a London paper was a thing of the rarest appearance. I think I can remember that when the Prince of Wales--afterwards King Edward VII, of happy memory--was dangerously ill, my father made some kind of arrangement--I cannot think what it could have been--by which he got the "Echo" of those days, not only on week days, but on Sunday afternoons. And in ordinary times, when we went into Newport on market days, we might possibly bring back a "Standard" or a "Telegraph," but likely enough not. We saw the "Western Mail" occasionally, the "Hereford Times" once a week; weekly also came the "Guardian," an excellent paper, but with more of Oxford, Pater, and Freeman, and Deans, and Dignitaries in it than of London or Londoners. Indeed, I remember how the news of the fall of Khartoum came to the rectory. I had been spending the evening with some friends across a few miles of midnight and black copse, and ragged field and wild, broken, and wandering brook land, and I remember that not a star was to be seen as I came home, wondering all the while if I ever should find my way. One of my friends had been in Newport that day, and had seen a paper, and so when I got back at last and found my father smoking his pipe by the fire, I announced the news in a tag of Apocalyptic Greek: Khartoum he polis he megale peptoke, peptoke; Khartoum the mighty city, has fallen, has fallen. And sometimes I wonder now in these days, when I am nearer to the heart of newspapers, whether our work in Fleet Street, with its anxious, flurried yell over the telephone, its tic-tac of tapes, its slither and rattle and clatter of linotypes, its frantic haste of men, its final roar and thunder of machinery ever gets itself delivered at last on a midnight hillside so queerly as the tragic news of Khartoum was delivered in the "parlour" of Llanddewi Rectory.

But the days came when above the clear voice of the brook in the hidden valley, above the murmur of the trees in the heart of the greenwood there sounded from beyond the hills to my heart a clearer voice, a mightier murmur. London called me, and all documents relating to this new unknown world became matters of the highest consequence and significance, and so London papers must by all means be obtained.

Far and long ago that spring and summer of 1880 now seem to me. It was then that London began to summon, and I was filled with an eager curiosity to know all about the new world which I was to visit.

As I have explained, the London paper made a very rare and occasional appearance at Llanddewi-among-the-Hills, and I don't think that any of us felt any aching need of it. But now for me "Standard" and "Telegraph" became mystic documents of the highest interest and most vital consequence; these were the charts to the Nova Terra Incognita; every line in them came from the heart of the mystery and was written by men who were learned in all the wisdom of London. London papers I must have; that was certain; so I set out to get them.

The nearest point at which these precious rarities were obtainable was Pontypool Road Station, about four miles distant from Llanddewi Rectory. It was the place where I had bought my copy of "De Quincey" some years earlier, and is now sacred to me on that account. But in this month of April thirty-five years ago I thought little of De Quincey or of his visions. Columbus, I suspect, while he watched the fitting of his caravel forgot any mere literary enthusiasms that he might have once possessed; for him there was but one object and that was the tremendous, marvellous, terrible venture into the unknown that he was soon to make. So it was with me; London loomed up before me, wonderful, mystical as Assyrian Babylon, as full of unheard-of things and great unveilings as any magic city in an Eastern tale. It loomed up with incredible pinnacles--to quote Tennyson on another city--and in its mighty shadow all lesser objects disappeared. De Quincey? After all he was not without value, since he spoke of Oxford Street; still, I wanted later news of the City of the Enchanters. So three or four times a week I walked the four miles to Pontypool Road, taking the short cut across the fields which leaves the by-way at Croeswen and brings one out on the high road from Newport to Abergavenny, somewhere about a mile from the station, near the lane which wanders through a very solitary country into Usk.

Pontypool Road Station lies, as I have said, under mountains, or rather under the huge domed hills which we in Gwent call mountains. It is one of the many meeting-points between the fields and the "works," and is always associated in my mind with a noise of clanking machinery and a reek of black oily smoke of rich flavour, which this generation would not recognise, since it is only to be imitated by blowing out a tallow candle that has long wanted snuffing; and now there are neither tallow candles nor snuffers. Here, then, of a "celestial" agent of W. H. Smith I bought my papers; usually the "Standard" and the "Daily Telegraph." The "Morning Post" was, I think, twopence in those days, and twopence was too much to give for a daily paper, and, moreover, we had a vague belief that the "Morning Post" was almost exclusively concerned with the social doings of the aristocracy, splendid matters, doubtless, but no affairs of mine. With these two papers, then, and once a week with a copy of "Truth," I would make my way out of the station, and along the high road till I came to the stile and the lonely path across the fields, and alone under a tree or in the shelter of a friendly hedge I would open my papers, cut their pages, and plunge into their garden of delights. One of my chief interests in these journals--perhaps my chiefest interest--was the theatre; and I am sure I cannot say why this was so. As far as I can remember I had up to this time witnessed three performances of stage plays, and of these three one was certainly not "legitimate," being a drama of the circus called "Dick Turpin's Ride to York." Its chief incidents were firing pistols and leaping over five-barred gates, and I must have been about seven when I saw it at Cardiff. Then in '76 I was at Dublin, and saw "Our Boys," and was very heartily bored, and finally in '78 or '79 I went with a school-fellow to the skating-rink at Hereford--I remember the former as well as the latter rinking mania--and enjoyed a touring company's rendering of "Pinafore." And, looking back, I believe that it was then that the delightful poison began to work; then when in that ramshackle barn of a place in the Hereford backstreet the curtain went up on the Saturday afternoon, and eight men dressed as sailors began to sing:--

We sail the ocean blue,
And our saucy ship's a beauty;
We're gallant men and true,
And attentive to our duty.

I remember that, young as I was, I could not help feeling that eight was a very small number for the male chorus. This circumstance confirms me in a belief which I have long entertained that Heaven meant me to be a stage-manager. True, I could never master simple addition, and a stage-manager has to keep accounts. Still, I should not have been the first stage-manager whose ledgers were filled with "comptes fantastiques."

But here I am under my tree or my hedge on a sunny morning of that Gwentian spring of so many years ago, eagerly opening the paper and turning to the theatrical advertisements in that part of the journal which I have in later years learned to call the "leader page." I read about Mr. Henry Irving at the Lyceum and Mr. Toole at the Folly--I do not think the vanished theatre was known as Toole's in those days. Mme. Modjeska and Mr. Forbes-Robertson were, I believe, at the Court, Dion Boucicault's play, "The Shaughraun," was running at the Adelphi--or, stay, was this old house of melodrama then the home of "The Danites"? In Wych Street, at the Opera Comique, was "The Pirates of Penzance"; "Madame Favart" enchanted at the Strand; "Les Cloches de Corneville" was at the Globe or the Olympic, I forget which. And, said each advertisement, "for cast see under the clock."

***

I was vividly interested in that phrase, "For cast see under the clock," which I read in the sibylline leaves of my London papers. The real meaning of the words never occurred to me; I conceived that somewhere, in some dimly-imagined central place of London, there was a great clock on a high square tower, and that this tower was so prominent an architectural feature as to be known all over London as "the clock." And at the base of this tower, so I proceeded in my fancy, there were displayed bills or posters, containing the casts of all the plays of all the theatres. I never found that mighty tower in London, but it was many years before it dawned on me that "the clock" was merely the pictured clock-face in the newspaper itself, under which the full casts were then printed.

As I have said, I cannot quite make out the sources of this intense interest of mine in the theatre. But I suspect that for the time I had got into that strange frame of mind to which Thackeray alluded when he asked a man if he were "fond of the play." Thackeray's friend replied, I think, to the effect that it depended on the play, whereupon Thackeray told him that he didn't understand in the least what the phrase "fond of the play" implied. Thackeray was right; for this attitude of mind is universal, not particular; and oddly enough, I believe it is very little related to any serious interest in the drama as a form of art. There is so vast a gulf between the theatre of to-day and that of thirty-five years ago that I do not know whether it is now possible for anybody to be "fond of the play" in the old sense; but if there be such people left, I am sure that they have not the faintest interest in the proposals to build and endow a national theatre. For to those in the happy state to which Thackeray alluded, the theatre was loved not for itself, but as a symbol of gaiety; I would almost say of metropolitanism as opposed to provincialism. I have known countrymen relating their adventures in London almost to wink as they included a visit to the Globe or the Strand in the list of their pleasures; the theatre represented to them the "chimes at midnight" mood.

Thackeray meant--do you like the mingled gas and orange odours of the theatre, do you like the sound of the orchestra tuning, the sight of the footlights suddenly lightening, can you project your self readily into the fantastic world disclosed by the rising curtain, and afterwards, do you like a midnight chop at Evans's, with Welsh rarebit to follow, and foaming tankards of brown stout, and then "something hot"; in fine, do you like to be out and about and in the midst of gaiety at hours of the night when your uncles and aunts and all quiet country people are abed and fast asleep? That is what Thackeray meant by his question, and I suppose that our modern, serious lovers of the drama would regard the man who was fond of the play in this sense as an utter reprobate, a stumbling-block and a stone of offence. But it was in that sense that I pored devoutly over everything relating to the theatre that I found in my newspapers, as I delayed in my walks home from Pontypool Road, not being able to refrain any longer.

Well, the day dawned at last for dreams to come true--or as true as they ever come. My father and I set out one fine Monday morning for Paddington, starting, I think, at about eleven o'clock from Newport, and getting to London by five in the afternoon. This was then the best train in the day; for the Severn Tunnel was not yet made, and we went all the way round by Gloucester. It was a six hours' journey, and now one can get from London to Newport in two hours and a half. At Westbourne Park we changed and got into the Underground system, and so came to the Temple Station on the Embankment. Thence it was a short walk to the private hotel in Surrey Street where my father had always stayed on his infrequent visits to town. I have forgotten the name of the hotel;--Bradshaw's office is built on the site of it--it was Williams's, or Smith's, or Evans's, or some such title, and as I believe was then the way, it was understood to be more or less the preserve of people from the west. I suppose there were other little hotels for parsons and small squires of the east and north and south; for all the streets that go down from the Strand to the river were then occupied by these private hotels and by lodging-houses. Craven Street, by Charing Cross, is the only one of these streets that has at all preserved the old manner, which, let me say, was a dingy and dim but on the whole a comfortable manner. Our hotel was just opposite the pit door of the old Strand Theatre, and in a former visit my father and mother, sitting at their window, had had the gratification of seeing Mrs. Swanborough sitting at her window over the way knitting busily. Now all our ladies, however smart, have become knitters, but if I had been writing these reminiscences a few years ago I should have asked: "Can you imagine a London manageress of these days sitting and knitting in her room at the theatre?"

We went out for a short stroll before eating, and for the first time I saw the Strand, and it instantly went to my head and to my heart, and I have never loved another street in quite the same way. My Strand is gone for ever; some of it is a wild rock-garden of purple flowers, some of it is imposing new buildings; but one way or another, the spirit is wholly departed. But on that June night in 1880 I walked up Surrey Street and stood on the Strand pavement and looked before me and to right and to left and gasped. No man has ever seen London; but at that moment I was very near to the vision--the theoria--of London.

After the astounding glimpse at the Strand we went back to the private hotel in Surrey Street and had something to eat. I am not sure, but I think the meal consisted of tea and ham and eggs, the latter beautifully poached. I know that my mind holds a recollection of this simple dish very admirably done in connection with Smith's, or whatever the place was called; and I believe it was eaten in the evening of our arrival. And I may say in passing that the hotel had a pleasant, well-worn, homely look about it; very plain, but extremely comfortable. I think that my bedroom carpet was threadbare and that the bed was a feather bed; at all events one slept sublimely there under the roof, under the London stars.

Then for the Strand again, now sunset flushed, beginning to twinkle with multitudinous lamps--I had hardly seen a lamp-lit street before--and so to the Opera Comique, where they were playing "The Pirates of Penzance." The Opera Comique was somewhere in Wych Street, which has gone the way of the streets of Babylon and Troy; purple blossoms and big hotels and other theatres that I know not grow now in the place where it once stood. We went to the upper boxes of the Opera Comique and enjoyed ourselves very well. I remember my father being especially pleased with the Pirate King's defence of his profession: "Compared with respectability it's almost honest," or words to that effect. But, oddly enough, I was a little disappointed. There was not the sense of gaiety that I had expected. For one thing the music reminded me of the classic glees and madrigals which I had heard discoursed by the Philharmonic Society at Hereford, where I was at school, and I did not want to be reminded of Hereford. And the female chorus hardly looked as thoughtless as I could have wished; it seemed to me that they might very well have come fresh from the rectory like myself. Of course, it was all very well to be ladylike, and so forth; but what I asked of the stage was careless devilry, the suggestion, at all events, of naughtiness. In fact, my attitude was perilously near to that of the Arkansas audiences as analysed by the Duke in "Huckleberry Finn": "What they wanted was low comedy--and maybe something ruther worse than low comedy." But I was not really quite so bad as the "Arkansaw lunkheads." We went on another night to "Les Cloches de Corneville," a most harmless production, I am sure; and that was what I wanted. I was enchanted from the rising of the curtain; there was the sunlit scene in Normandy, charming, smiling, and a whole row of pretty girls, evidently as thoughtless as the lightest heart could wish, dancing down to the footlights and singing:--

> *Just look at that,*
> *Just look at this,*
> *Don't you think we're not amiss?*
> *A glance give here,*
> *A glance give there,*
> *Tell us if you think we're dear.*

And--not one of these girls looked as if she could have come from any conceivable rectory. Decidedly, "Les Cloches de Corneville" was the comic opera for my money. What a pleasing thrill the scene afforded when the entire village, for some reason that I cannot well remember, dressed up as Crusaders and Crusaderesses, and came suddenly into the room of Gaspard, the miser, and the big bell began to toll and the gold was poured out in a torrent on the ground. "When the heir returneth, then shall ring the bell, so the legend runneth, so the old men tell"; in some such words was this grand peripeteia announced in the text. So the heir no doubt returned and married the extra pretty girl whose name I have forgotten--she was not Serpolette, I know, for Serpolette was comic, delightfully, impudently comic, but still comic, and so no mate for the hero. Serpolette, I think, having regard to the Unities, ought to have married the thin but amusing assistant of the Bailie; but I do not know whether this were so. But I am sure everybody was happy ever after, and of "Les Cloches" and other comic operas like it I say, in the words of Coleridge's friend: "Them's the jockeys for me!"

I have never been able to make up my mind as to the respective merits of "Les Cloches de Corneville" and "Madame Favart," which was running at the Strand. "Les Cloches" had the more coherent plot of the two, and the great scene of the miser and the crusaders was more effective in its stagey way than anything in "Madame Favart," but, then, Florence St. John was Madame Favart, and to old playgoers I need say no more. And Marius, a delightful French comedian, was in the cast; and there were those songs dear to memory: "Ave, my mother," "The Artless Thing," "To Age's Dull December," and

> *Pair of lovers meet,*
> *Stolen vows are sweet,*
> *Sighs, etcetera.*
> *Love is all in all,*
> *On a garden wall,*

Never heed papa.

This was sung by Marius, who had no voice in particular, but an infinite Gallic relish and unction and finish in everything that he did. The fourth piece that we went to in this wonderful week was "The Daughter of the Drum Major," at the Alhambra, then a theatre, with an extremely roomy, comfortable pit. This last piece made but little impression on me. From my recollection, it seems to have been more in the modern mode, that is, a mere excuse for showing off a "beauty chorus" without the little touch of thin, theatrical but pleasant romance that delighted me in the two other plays. But the poverty of the play was atoned for by the happy circumstance that before going to it we dined at the Cavour. And the Cavour in 1880 was exactly like the Cavour in 1915, save in this one matter, that on the earlier date there was included in the price of the dinner a bottle of violet wine.

***

Looking back through the years and comparing the London of the early 'eighties with the London of to-day, one circumstance emerges very clearly in my mind: that is, that the early London had an infinitely "smarter," wealthier air than the later. I say "air" advisedly, to make it clear that I knew nothing of the real interior life of the place, or of the resources of its rich inhabitants. I judged of London purely by its exterior aspects, as one may judge of a passing stranger in the street, and decide that he goes to an expensive tailor, without knowing anything of the condition of his banking account. So, I say that the outward show and lineaments of the London of 1880 were much more refulgent and splendid than those of the last few years. I was a good deal surprised when the truth of this first dawned on me some three or four years ago. For I believe that as a matter of fact the new London is a much wealthier, more luxurious, more extravagant place than the old. The rich people of to-day spend hundreds instead of tens, thousands for the hundreds of their fathers; the "pace" of the splendid has increased enormously in the last thirty-five years; and all the facilities for expending very large sums of money have also increased to a huge extent. So well was I convinced of all this when I fell to comparing the London of my boyhood with the London of my middle age that at first I thought that there must be a fallacy somewhere, and I was very willing to believe that those early impressions of mine were illusions, natural enough in a lad who had never seen any more splendid streets than those which the Newport and Cardiff of those days had to show, than the venerable, peaceful, ancient ways of Hereford, whose stillness was only broken by the deep, sweet chiming of the cathedral bells. But when, interested, I went into the facts of the question, I found that I had not been mistaken in my first view--i.e., that London was a smarter-looking place thirty years ago than at the present day, and this for several reasons.

To begin with, there is the trifling matter of men's dress. I do not know whether we have yet realised the fact that the frock coat is rapidly becoming "costume," verging, that is, towards the status of levee dress. Already, I believe, it is only worn on occasions of semi-state, at functions where the King is expected, at smart weddings, and so forth. Before long it will probably attain the singular twofold state of "evening dress," which is worn all day long by waiters and by what are conveniently called gentlemen after seven o'clock in the evening. So very likely the frock coat will soon be seen on the backs of the maître d'hôtel, the hotel manager, the shopwalker, the major-domo--if there be any majores-domo left--as a kind of uniform or livery, while it will also be the afternoon wear of dukes at great social functions. And so with the silk hat; it has not gone so far on the road of obsolescence as the frock coat, but, unless I mistake, it has entered on that sad way.

Here, then, is the point of contrast. Between 'eighty and 'ninety--and later still--practically every man in London went about his business and his pleasure with a high hat on his head. Every man, I say, above the rank of the mechanic; certainly all the clerkly class; Mr. Guppy and his friends were still faithful to this headdress; which, be it remembered, was once universal all over England, so that even smock-frocked farm labourers wore it. As for the London of pleasure, the West End, it would have been quite impossible to conceive a man of the faintest social pretensions being seen abroad in anything else. And now, I go up and down Piccadilly, Bond Street, the Row at the height of the London season, and see--a few silk hats and morning coats, it is true--but the majority of well-dressed men in "lounge" suits and grey soft hats and black and grey bowlers.

Now let it be clearly understood that I have no passion for black coats and shiny hats myself, nor for the dazzling white linen which has largely given way to soft, unstarched stuffs. But it is not to be denied that all those habits had a "smart" appearance, and that a pavement crowded with shiny black hats, shiny white cuffs and collars, and long black frock coats made a much more imposing show than the pavement of to-day, on which the men's dress is very much as they please. The modern men look extremely comfortable and well at their ease; but they do not scintillate in the old style. A soft grey hat does not flash back the rays of the sun.

Then, another point and a most important one: the coming of the motor. I suppose the kind of motor-impelled vehicle which one is likely to see in Hyde Park may very well have cost seven or eight or nine or ten times as much as the horse-drawn carriages which I remember going round and round so gay and so glorious. Well, I have watched the modern procession of motor-cars, and they are about as impressive as a career of light locomotive engines. It may indeed in course of time become fashionable to go up and down the Row in express locomotives capable of drawing their hundred coaches at a hundred miles an hour, but the effect would not be smart. Now, the old equipages were undeniably the last word of smartness; in themselves they were enough to tell the stranger that he had come to the very centre of the earth, of its riches and its splendours. There were the high-bred, high-spirited, high-stepping horses, in the first place, groomed to the last extreme of shiny, satiny perfection, tossing their heads proudly and champing their bits and doing the most wonderful things with their legs. The bright sunlight of those past London summers shone on their glossy coats, shone in the patent leather of the harness, shone and glittered on the plated bolts and buckles and ornaments. And the carriages were of graceful form, and the servants of those days sometimes wore gorgeous liveries; and scores of those brilliant equipages followed on one another in an unending dazzling procession. That was the old way; now there are some "Snorting Billies" that choke and snarl and splutter as they dodge furtively and meanly in and out of the Park, like mechanical rabbits bolting for their burrows.

While I contrast the London of my young days and the London of my old--or present--days, I would like it to be remembered that I am, so far, only contrasting the two cities from one point of view, the point of view of smartness. I have not been saying that 1880 London was more sensible than 1915 London; but merely that the former struck an outsider as a more brilliant place than the modern city. The fact is that I have the most cordial approval for all social pomps and splendours, so long as I am not required to take part therein. I hate wearing frock coats and silk hats and shiny shirts; but I am very well pleased to sit in the pit, as it were, and watch those exalted persons who are cast for the decorative parts going through their brilliant performances. And, after all, if a man finds that plate armour is uncomfortable, that is no reason why he should not delight in seeing other people wearing it, and wearing it with dignity. And in speaking of the Hyde Park and Rotten Row of the old days I mentioned that there were some gorgeous servants' liveries still left in 1880. And while we are on that matter, I may say that I have never sympathised at all with those persons who have found something mean and ridiculous in a manservant in purple and gold or in blue and crimson, unless, that is, the point be taken that only a splendid duty should be dignified with a splendid vestment, and in that objection I admit there is some force. Not that I agree for one moment that there is anything contemptible in "menial" service; but I am willing to allow that it may not be altogether seemly for a faithful fellow, whose business is to hold on behind a carriage and wait at dinner, to outshine a bishop in pontificals. But I suspect that the people who sneered at poor Jeames and his plush were not actuated by this reasonable motive, but rather by that vile "Liberal" objection to splendour as splendour. The man who found "Blazes" ridiculous would probably find the King in his Coronation robes equally ridiculous. And so you may go on, up the scale and down the scale; but the only logical alternative to splendour is Dr. Johnson's proposed suit of bull's hide--all beyond that is superfluity and vain show, according to the doctrine of the wretches who in times not long past sold antique civic ornaments, such as chains and maces, on the ground that the Mayor of Little Pedlington did not need such gauds to help him in his customary task of sentencing "drunks."

There is one more point in connection with the Row. Twenty-five years ago the appointed hour was five o'clock in the afternoon. Then people sat in the chairs and walked up and down and looked at the carriages, and I remember a friend observing to me this singularity, that though the place was public and open to anybody, still only those persons who were dressed in the regulation costume--frock coat and silk hat for men--ever came near the sacred ground. The people in lounge suits and bowler hats stood apart, and watched the show from some distance. Well, the hour of the Row is now in the morning; but there is a greater change. There are still "smart" people there; but there are also people who cannot by any possibility be described as smart, not even if they be judged by the very lax standards of these days.

In another matter the London of to-day is much less impressive in its outward show than the London of 1880; that is in the aspect of its principal streets. There are still excellent shops in Bond Street, Regent Street, and Piccadilly; but there is no longer in any of them that air of exclusiveness and expensiveness that I can remember, and this is particularly true of Regent Street. In 1880 you felt as soon as you turned up the Quadrant that anything you might buy therein would certainly be dear; the very stones and stucco exuded costliness and the essential attars of luxury. I feel convinced that the cigars of Regent Street were of a more curious aroma than cigars bought in any other street, that it was the very place wherein to purchase a great green flagon of rare scent as a present for a lady, that if you happened to want a Monte Cristo emerald this was the quarter wherein to search for it. That was my impression, but lest it should be mere fancy, a year or so ago I asked one of the older shopkeepers whether the street was quite what he and I remembered it. He said very emphatically it was not at all what it had been; and I feel sure that he was right, and that in a less degree the other principal shopping centres have declined from their former splendour.

And this for two reasons; first, the curious modern tendency of the best and most luxurious shops to scatter and disperse themselves abroad about the side streets of the West End, leaving gaps which are filled in most cases by dealers in cheaper wares. And secondly, the coming of the popular tea-shop has, in my opinion, done a very great deal to "unsmarten" the streets of which I am speaking. Let it not be understood for one moment that I would speak despitefully of cheap tea-shops; that would indeed be vilely thankless in one who has often made the principal meal of the day at an A.B.C.--large coffee, threepence; milk cake, twopence; butter, a penny--and has been grateful that for once in a way he has dined. But, it cannot be pretended that a milk cake is a costly or a curious dish, or that a plate of cold meat for sixpence or eightpence is an opimian banquet; and so, when I pass a popular tea-shop or eating-house, I feel that my dream of luxury and expense is broken; and that something of glitter and splendour has passed away from the West End of London.

***

I spent the years from the summer of 1880 to the winter of 1886 in a singular sort of apprenticeship to life and London and letters and to most other things. Sometimes I was in London; then for months at a time I was out of it, back again in my old haunts of Gwent. I had hot fits of desire for the town when I was forced to stay in the country; and then, settled, or apparently settled, in the heart of London, its immensities and its solitudes overwhelmed me, the faint, hot breath of its streets sickened me, so that my heart ached for the thought of the green wood by the valley of the Soar, and for the thought of friendly faces.

They say that in old Japan they had a wonderful and secret art of tempering their sword blades. Now the steel was placed in the white heat of the fire, now it was withdrawn and plunged into the water of an icy torrent; and then again the trial of the furnace. So heat and cold were alternated, according to an ancient and hidden tradition, till at last the craftsman obtained an exquisite and true and perfect blade, fit for the adorned scabbard of a great lord of Japan. When I think of those early years of mine I should be reminded of the process of the Japanese sword-craftsman--if only the heart were as tractable as steel. The Kabbalists, I believe, take the view--a gloomy one--that the innermost essence of man's spirit goes out from the world in much the same state as that in which it came into the world; and it is certainly true that some men seem incorrigible; neither fire nor ice will temper them aright.

During these early years of my London experience I lived under very varying conditions. I lived with families, and I lived alone; I lived in the suburbs and in the centre; I had enough to eat, and then narrowly escaped starvation. My first habitat was in the High Street of a southern suburb. My memory holds a picture of an ancient street of dignified red-brick houses, a Georgian church, and a stream of quite inky blackness. The old houses had old gardens behind them, green enough, but with a certain grime upon them that made them strange to eyes unused to this combination of soot and leafage. But it was quite easy in those days to get from the suburb to the open country.

Not that I desired any such excursions, for my notion of an ideal residence was then a lodging in one of the streets or courts or passages going down from the Strand to the Thames. This was a dream that I realised years afterwards, when many waters (not of the Thames) had passed over my head. It was well enough, and I used to go out and get my breakfast at the "chocolate as in Spain" shop at the west end of the Strand, on the north side. It was well enough, I say, but it was not absolute paradise. And, furthermore, and in an interior parenthesis, let me say that the chocolate at the old Strand shop was not as in Spain, though very decent chocolate. The Spanish service of chocolate--I encountered it when I was in Gascony--consists in this, first that the chocolate is made extremely strong and thick, and secondly that with it comes a goblet of ice-cold well-water, to be drunk after the chocolate, on the principle, I suppose, of the Scots who drink water, not with whisky, but after it.

Well, to return to the more or less--chiefly less--direct current of my tale, after my sojourn in the southern suburb came a return to the country, where I remained eight or nine months. It was during this exodus or hegira, I think, that I was excommunicated by old Mr. James, of Lansoar, because I was loafing at home instead of living on five shillings a week in London. But my long sojourn in Gwent was in fact due to a very dismal discovery having been made of me by certain persons called examiners. They found me utterly incapable of the simple rules of arithmetic; and hence I was debarred from the career which I had been contemplating. And here I would say that I am almost proud of myself for my quite extraordinary arithmetical incapacity. I am not merely dull and slow, but desperate. I am so wanting in the mere faculty of counting as to be curious, like those tribes of savages that can say "One, two, three, four, five ... many." There are people who make a living by exhibiting their arithmetical skill in the music-halls; someone writes on the blackboard a multiplication sum of fifteen figures multiplied by fifteen figures, and a second or two after the last figure is drawn the arithmetical artist utters the result. Well, I am at the opposite end of the scale, and I have sometimes wondered whether "Incompetent Machen" would not be quite a good turn. It would make anybody laugh to hear me doing a sum in simple addition. It is like "Forty-seven and nine, forty-seven and nine, forty-seven and nine." I ponder. Then a brilliant idea strikes me. I pretend the problem is "forty-seven and ten." I get the result, fifty-seven, deduct one and proceed.

Well, I came to London again in the summer of '81, thinking of another and quite a different career, which did not involve, on the face of it, that little difficulty of arithmetic. Again I was in a suburb, and again in an old one, but this time the quarter was in the far west. I stayed in Turnham Green, then a place of many amenities standing amongst fields and gardens and riparian lawns, which, long ago, have been buried beneath piles of cheap bricks and mortar, for a year and a half, and then again I altered my plans, or fate rather altered them for me. I started on a new tack and kept it for a month, and then somehow slid into a backwater, in which I was afloat and nothing more than afloat. Summoning this period into recollection, I find my position very much like to that of certain ancient and outworn barges, grass-grown, flower-grown, that I have come upon suddenly in improbable back alleys of water, in the midst of a maze of by-streets at Brentford; but, locally and literally, I was then living in a small room, a very small room, in Clarendon Road, Notting Hill Gate.

I have already stated that when I first came up to London I had no thought of literature as a career. Indeed, I never have thought of it as a career, but only as a destiny. Still, my meaning is that it in no wise dawned upon me as I travelled up from Newport to London in the early summer of 1880 that writing of any kind or sort was to be a great part of my life's business. And yet, before I had lived a month in the old red house by the inky stream, I was trying to write, in the intervals of a very different task, in an atmosphere which was utterly remote from literature of any kind. How was this? Partly, I suppose, because of the very large proportion of Celtic blood in my veins. It is quite true that the Celt--the Welsh Celt, at all events--has directly contributed very little to great literature. This I have always maintained, and always shall maintain; and I think all impartial judges will allow that if Welsh literature were annihilated at this moment the loss to the world's grand roll of masterpieces would be insignificant. I, speaking from the point of view of my own peculiar interests, I should be very sorry to miss my copy of the "Mabinogion," and there are certain stanzas of the poem called "Y Beddau"--"Vain is it to seek for the grave of Arthur"--which have a singular and enchanting and wizard music; but in neither case is there any question of a literary masterpiece.

Yet there is in Celtdom a certain literary feeling which does not exist in Anglo-Saxondom. It is diffused, no doubt, and appreciative rather than creative, and lacking in the sterner, critical spirit which is so necessary to all creative work; still it is there, and it is delighted with the rolling sound of the noble phrase. It perceives the music of words and the relation of that music to the world. I was taking a lesson in Welsh pronunciation some time ago, and uttered the phrase "yn oes oesodd"--from ages to ages. "That is right," said my Welsh friend, "speak it so that it makes a sound like the wind about the mountains." And, with or without the leave of the literary rationalists, I would say that the spirit of that sentence is very near to the heart of true literature.

So far then, as a man three-parts Celt, I was by nature inclined to the work of words, and there was, moreover, a feeble literary strain in my own family. There was a second cousin, or Welsh uncle, I am not certain which, who had composed a five-act heroic blank verse drama, called "Inez de Castro," which was almost, but not quite, represented by the famous Mrs. Somebody at the Lane in the early 'fifties. And then, more potent still, was the heredity of bookishness, the growing up among books that had accrued from grandfathers and uncles and cousins, all men who had lived all their days amongst books, and had sat over country hearths on mountain sides, reading this leathern Colloquies of Erasmus, this little Horace in mellow parchment, with the Sphere of Elzevir.

And then there was the old-fashioned grammar school education, of which it must be said, by friends and foes, that it is an education in words. One spent one's time, unconsciously, in weighing the values of words in English and Greek and Latin, in rendering one tongue into another, in estimating the exact sense of an English sentence before translating it into one or another of the old tongues. So that a boy who could do decent Latin prose must first have mastered the exact sense and significance of his English original, and then he must also have made himself understand to a certain extent, not only the logic but the polite habit of each language. I remember when I was a very small boy rendering "Put to the sword" literally into "Gladio positi." "Well," said my master, "there is no reason on earth why the Romans shouldn't have said 'gladio positi,' but as a matter of fact they did say 'ferro occisi'--killed with iron." And if one thinks of it, he who has mastered that little lesson has also mastered the larger lesson that literature is above logic, that there are matters in it which transcend plain common sense. And so, the long and the short of it was, that in 1880 I began to try to write.

Now I believe that one of the most tortuous and difficult questions that engages philosophy is the theory of cause and effect. I think, though I am not quite sure, that in one of Mr. Balfour's philosophical books this matter is treated, and the familiar case of a sportsman's pulling a trigger, firing a gun, and thereby bringing down a bird, is made an instance. What is the "cause" of the bird's death? Roughly speaking, of course, the pulling of the trigger; but roughly speaking is not the same thing as philosophically speaking; and if anyone be so simple as to conclude that roughly speaking means truly speaking and that philosophy is all nonsense, let me remind him that when he enjoys his after-dinner cigar in his arm-chair he is not conscious of the fact that he is being whirled through space, like a top, at the most terrific speed.

So, if I remember rightly, Mr. Balfour left the philosophical "cause" of the bird's death an open question, if not a question altogether beyond determination of human wit; and thus it is with the impulse that sends off a harmless young fellow on the career of letters. One can talk of the causes that impel a grain of corn to grow from the ground; sound seed, good soil, good farming; dry weather, wet weather, each in its season; but at the last the engendering of the green shoot remains a mystery. And so it is a mystery that near midsummer in 1880 I suddenly began to write horrible rubbish in a little manuscript book with a scarlet cover; rubbish that had rhymes to it.

But if ultimate causes lie beyond those flaming walls of the world that put bounds to all our inquisition, it is not so hard to trace those causes which are proximate. The bird dies because the shot hit it in a vital part, the corn sprouts because it is put into the ground--and I began to write because I bought a copy of Swinburne's "Songs Before Sunrise."

I forget how I heard of this name, which once loomed so fiery and strange a portent, which still, in the estimation of many excellent judges, stands for a great literary achievement. I know it was while I was down in the country, because I can remember one of our clergy, an Eton and Christchurch man, telling me gossip about the poet, who had in those early days retired from the world to Putney. It is to be supposed that I had read something concerning Swinburne in one of those wonderful London papers that came over our hills from another world, that might almost have fallen from the stars they were so wholly marvellous. But, somehow or other, I was possessed by an eager curiosity concerning this Swinburne, convinced in advance--I cannot remember how--that here I should surely find an unexpected, unsurmised treasure. And so, one hot, shiny afternoon, I came up from the old Georgian suburb by the black stream, crossed Hungerford Bridge, and made my way into the Strand; into that Strand which is as lost as Atlantis. And going eastward past many vanished things, past the rich odours of Messrs. Rimell's soap-boiling, I came to St. Mary-le-Strand, and the entrance of Holywell Street. At the southern corner of this street, facing the east end of the church, there stood Denny's bookshop, and, gold in my pocket, I went in with a bold appearance, and said, "Have you got Swinburne's 'Songs Before Sunrise'?" The shopman did not seem in the least astonished at my question. He said he had got the book, and produced it, and showed it me, and the very cover was such as I had never seen before, provocative, therefore, in a high degree. And so I bought the book and carried it out of Denny's into the sunlight in a great amazement.

For, be it remembered, one did not go into a provincial bookshop in that easy way and say, "Have you got this or that?" For the chances were about a thousand to one that they hadn't got it, and never would have it. It is odd, but I cannot remember exactly the nature of the stock of the average country bookseller; my impression is of Bibles, Prayer Books, Church Services, and Pitman's Shorthand Manuals. So, if you wanted a book in the county town, you did not say, "Have you got so-and-so?" but "Will you get me so-and-so?" and in four or five days you called and the book was ready. But I had a notion that in this wonderful London the bookshop would actually have the book that you wanted, there actually in presence, and waiting for you on its shelves. I had a notion, I say, but again, it seemed almost incredible that there should be such shops in the world, and so when the bookseller under St. Mary-le-Strand said "Yes," quite simply, and handed me the "Songs Before Sunrise" in two or three seconds, I was amazed and exultant too; the legend of London, though marvellous, was evidently a true one.

Now I have a friend who is very fond of preaching the doctrine of what he calls the cataclysm. He holds that we are all much bettered by an occasional earthquake, moral, mental or spiritual. He says that volcanoes which suddenly burst out from under our feet are the finest tonics in the world, that violent thunderstorms, cloud-bursts, and tornadoes clear our mental skies. The treatment is heroic, but my friend may be right; certainly that volume of "Songs Before Sunrise" was to me quite cataclysmic. First there was the literary manner of the book, which to me was wholly strange and new and wonderful, and then there was the tremendous boldness of it all, the denial of everything that I had been brought up to believe most sure and sacred; the book was positively strewn with the fragments of shattered altars and the torn limbs of kings and priests.

How do the lines go? I quote from memory, but they run something like this:--

Thou hast taken all, Galilæan, but these thou shalt not take;
The laurel, the doves and the pæan, the breasts of the nymph in the brake.

Clearly this was a terrible, a tremendous fellow, an earth-shaking, heaven-storming poet. And so between my endeavours to qualify for passing the preliminary examination of the Royal College of Surgeons, I began to write; I should think the most horrible drivel that ever has been written since rhymes first jingled. I can't remember, oddly enough, whether I tried to imitate Swinburne; I know one copy of verses was "inspired" by a picture called "Harmony," which I think was hung in the Academy of 1880. It depicted a mediæval maiden playing the organ, while a mediæval youth watched her in a dazed and love-stricken condition. This is positively the only one of these early horrors of mine, of which I have any recollection; my memory is purged of the rest of them, I am glad to say. I merely mention these things because they illustrate a very singular point in literary psychology; in universal psychology, for the matter of that. For I believe it is a rule that almost every literary career, certainly every literary career which is to be concerned with the imaginative side of literature, begins with the writing of verses. Nay, people who are to live lives quite remote from literature will often try to write poetry in their youth; and on the face of it, this is a great puzzle. For poetry, be it remembered, is the most "artificial" kind of literary composition, it is immeasurably the most difficult, it is by far the most remote from that which is commonly called life. Why, then, does the inexperienced beginner, devoid of all technical ability, invariably essay this most difficult technical task on his entry into the literary career?

The problem of the boy in the back room, not far from the dark stream of the Wandle, writing verses in the red notebook, is really one of the enigmas of the universe; it is rather a Chinese-box puzzle; riddle is within riddle.

For if we start at the beginning of things, or at what seems to us to be the beginning of things, we are met by the question as to why there should be any such thing as poetry in the universe. I need not say how much wider this question is than it seems; how it must be asked about all the arts, about fugues and cathedrals and romances and dances. It is an immense question; immense when one considers that with nine people out of ten the great criterion is, "Does it pay?" That is, will it result in a larger supply of fine champagne, four ale, roast legs of pork, and mousses royales to the population? Will this scheme of things enable Sir John to keep a fifth motor-car, or will it get Bill meat three times a day? That is, at last, the test by which we judge all things. It is an old and approved British test; by it Macaulay condemned the whole of Greek philosophy, because that philosophy did not lead up to the invention of the steam engine. Now, it is quite clear that poetry, speaking generally, pays neither the producer nor the consumer of it; it does not lead to motor-cars, beefsteaks, vintage clarets, or four ale. It is not even moral; not a single man has ever been induced to drink ginger-beer instead of beer by reading Keats.

I must pause for a moment; I fear that it may be thought that I am trying to be funny or--more injurious accusation!--trying to be clever. I am not trying to be either; I am stating the simple facts of the case. Hardly a month passes by without some indignant person pointing out in the Press that Engineering and Commercial Chemistry are infinitely more useful--i.e., lead to more beefsteaks--than Latin and Greek; and that when Oxford and Cambridge find out that obvious truth they may become of some service to the State. Indeed, it is only a few weeks ago since a gentleman wrote to a paper showing that military training was better for a boy--i.e., would make him the better soldier--than "silly old" Greek plays. And let me acknowledge that these contentions are perfectly true; just as it is perfectly true that fur coats are much warmer than Alcaics. So, I say, here is the problem: the common, widely accepted test of the right to existence of everything: does it pay, does it add to the physical comforts of life, is quite clearly opposed to the existence of poetry, and yet poetry exists. Therefore, either the poets and the lovers of poetry are mad, or else the common judgment is ... let us say, mistaken. I need scarcely say that I incline to the latter solution of the problem, and so qua human being, I am not ashamed of trying to write poetry by the Wandle, though I recognise, qua Arthur Machen, that I was, very decidedly, not born a poet.

For I firmly hold the doctrine that the natural, the arch-natural expression of man, so far as he is to be distinguished from pigs and dogs and goats, is in the arts, and through the arts and by the arts. It is not by reason, as reason is commonly understood, that man is distinguished from the other animals; but by art. I can quite well conceive the Black Ants sending the message "Hill 27 fell before the Red Ant attack early this afternoon," but I cannot conceive either Red or Black Ants writing odes or building miniature cathedrals. The arts, then, are man's difference, that which makes him to be what he is; and when he speaks through them he is using the utterance which is proper to him, as man. For, if we once set aside the "does it pay" nonsense, which is evidently nonsense and pestilent nonsense at that, we come clearly and freely to the truth that man is concerned with beauty, and with the ecstasy or rapture that proceeds from the creation of beauty and from the contemplation of it. And youth, as I think I have pointed out before, is the time of revelation. It is children who possess the "kingdom of heaven," to them are vouchsafed glimpses of that paradise which is the true home of man, and so it is that the boy with literature in his blood naturally makes his first efforts in the region of poetry, which is the heart and core of all literature.

The heart and core; for, as in the individual man, so in the whole history of men literature begins always with poetry, just as speech began with song. First, the magic incantation, sung about strange secret fires in hidden places by wild men, then the ballad or lyric, then Homer, then Herodotus, with the odours of the sanctuary of poetry still about him, though he has come down into the market-place of prose. And it is not necessary to go farther in time or space than the Northumberland of a few years ago to hear phrases common enough, things of everyday, set to enchanting melodies. I shall never forget how once in the years of my wandering I came one wet autumn afternoon to a little town called Morpeth. It struck me as a dingy place enough, "un petit trou de province, sale, noir, boueux," and my lodging was dingy, and musty too, in a house kept by an old invalid woman who moved about in a wheel chair and grumbled if a window were opened. But when it came to the question of the stroller's tea, the servant-maid, who came, I think, from the wild places of that land, said consolingly: "You need not trouble yourselves; you shall have your tea in half an hour." No doubt the girl was mortal, but she spoke the tongue of the immortals; her phrase about our tea was chanted to an exquisite melody that might have come from the Gradual-- or from fairyland.

The natural man, then, is a singer and a poet, and so we may say that all artists are in reality survivals from an earlier time, and so it is that even in these later days the lad, with something of the youth and true nature of his race restored to him for a brief hour, sits in solitary places and endeavours to exercise his birthright. Alas! he stutters deplorably in his speech as he delays by the Wandle, inditing verses; but it is thus that he would declare that he is a citizen of no mean city; he would fain say through those sorry rhymes, Civis coelestis sum.

Chapter IV

Well, I saw the first of Augustus Harris's autumn dramas at Drury Lane, heard the newsboys calling out the death of Miss Neilson one misty evening up and down the Strand, and went back to Gwent in the character of a bad penny; and so fell to writing of those autumn and winter nights, when all the house was still.

Poor wretch! For this is the misery of literature, that it has no technique in the sense that music and painting have each its own technique. The young painter and the young composer, having acquired a certain mechanical skill in the elements of their arts, have studios and schools which they can attend. They have masters who lead them in their several ways, or who tell them, if necessary, to abandon those ways with all convenient speed. But for the lad with letters on the brain there is no help, no guidance; nor is there the possibility of any direction in the literary path. Now and then people send me manuscripts, and ask for my opinion; I give it because I am weak, but I always tell them that in literature the other man's opinion is not worth twopence.

No; the only course is to go on stumbling and struggling and blundering like a man lost in a dense thicket on a dark night; a thicket, I say, of rebounding boughs that punish with the sting of a whip-lash, of thorns that most savagely lacerate the flesh--it is the flesh of the heart, alas! that they tear--of sharp rocks of agony and black pools of despair. Such is the obscure wood of the literary life; such, at least, it was to me. You struggle to find your way; but again and again you ask yourself whether, for you, there is any way. You think you have hit upon the lucky track at last. And lo! before your feet is the black pit. And such is not alone the adventure of little, ineffectual, struggling men. How old was glorious Cervantes, now serene for ever amongst the immortals, when he found his way to that village of La Mancha? Fifty, I think, or almost fifty. And he had been striving for years to write plays, and poetry, and short stories of passion and sentiment; and it was only the roar of applause that thundered up from the world when the Knight and the Squire were seen riding over the hill that convinced Cervantes that at last he had discovered his true path; if indeed he ever were convinced in his heart of the magnitude and majesty of the achievement of "Don Quixote."

And if these things are done with the great, what will be done with the little? If the clear-voiced rulers of the everlasting choir are to suffer so and agonise, what of miserable little Welshmen stammering and stuttering by the Wandle, in the obscure rectory amongst the hills, in waste places by Shepherd's Bush, in gloomy Great Russell Street, where the ghosts of dead, disappointed authors go sighing to and fro? For the fate of the little literary man there is no articulate speech that is sufficient; one must fall back on aoi or oimoi, or alas, or some such vague lament of unutterable woe.

Now one of the first agonies of the learner in letters is the discovery of the horrid gulf that yawns between the conception and the execution. Some years before this winter of 1880, when I was at school, I had read the tale of Owain in the Mabinogion, of the magic sudden storm, and of the singing of the birds after it. And going out for a walk one half-holiday with a school-fellow, just such a sudden storm, as it seemed to me, overtook us as we went down into a beautiful valley not far from Hereford; and after it there was a like joyful singing of birds in the trees. And somehow the magic atmosphere of the old tale, mingled with the enacting, as it were, of one of its chief circumstances, left on my mind a very strong and singular impression which, when the desire of literature came upon me, I yearned to put into words. I did so, in the blank verse form, and sent the "poem" to the "Gentleman's Magazine," and this I think was my first attempt to get into print. I need not say that my nonsense was returned to me, with thanks; but I wish I knew why I chose that particular magazine. It must have had some especial attraction for me, since ten years later I sent Sylvanus Urban a prose article, which he accepted and paid for at the appropriate eighteenth-century rate of a guinea a sheet; that is sixteen pages. But I must say in all fairness that Sylvanus warned me in advance of his rate of payment.

But that gulf between the idea as it glows warm and radiant in the author's heart, and its cold and faulty realisation in words is an early nightmare, and a late one, too. For the beginner, if he suffer from many terrible disappointments, has also the consolations of hope, fallacious though these may prove to be. This scheme that looked so well has certainly come to the saddest grief, but there may be better luck next time; if this road have led to nothing but a blank wall of failure, that way may rise from the valley and climb the hill and lead into a fair land. It is later in the life of the literary man, when he has tried all roads and made all the experiments, that his final sorrow comes upon him. He may not be forced to say, perhaps, that he has been a total failure; he may, indeed, be able to chronicle achievements of a minor kind, successes in the estimation of others. But now, with riper understanding, he perceives, as he did not perceive in the days of his youth, the depth of the gulf between the idea and the word, between the emotion that thrilled him to his very heart and soul, and the sorry page of print into which that emotion stands translated. He dreamed in fire; he has worked in clay.

I did not know (happily for myself) of these things in the ending of the year 1880; and so, when all the rectory was abed and asleep, I sat up by a dying fire writing a "poem" on a classic subject.

The classic "poem" was finished some time in the winter of 1880-81, and then I performed a bold action. I sent the manuscript--I can see it now, written in a sprawly hand on both sides of ordinary letter paper--to a Hereford stationer, and bade him print me one hundred copies thereof. He, strangely enough, did so, and I saw myself in print for the first time. I have been looking at my copy of this work, I should think the only copy in existence, and wondering whether I would quote a few lines from it. I have decided against this course. But, after all, I was only seventeen when I wrote "Eleusinia."

But the little pamphlet had its influence on my life. My relations decided, after reading it, that journalism was the career for me; a decision that then seemed to me both reasonable and pleasant, which now strikes me with amazement, nay with stupefaction. Since those days I have found out a good many things concerning both poetry and journalism; and looking over that old copy of "Eleusinia," I have meditated on what career I should advise for the author of that work if he were now to consult me. I give it up; I abandon the problem utterly. And yet, strange as it seems, strange most of all to me, my relations were justified after all. I did become a journalist, just thirty years afterwards. But by 1910, those who had arranged this destiny for me were long dead and delivered from all their troubles. I remember my father, who knew about as much of the matter as I did, sketching out my future career. I was to go to London to learn the business first of all, shorthand, of course, and all that sort of thing. A chief portion of the task, he said, half jocularly, would be to lurk in the entrance-halls of great houses and write down the names of distinguished guests on the nights of grand receptions. And then, eventually, some few hundreds would come to me, and with this I was to buy an interest in a small local paper, and so, I suppose, write leaders and live happily ever after. The programme has not been carried out literally. The few hundreds have been more agreeably spent long years ago, and my editor never sent me to get the names of distinguished guests at great houses--knowing, wise man, that I should make a sad mess of such a business. But one of my first "assignments" in journalism was to describe a Giant Apple. I chased after that apple from Bond Street to Covent Garden, from Covent Garden back to Bond Street, and wrote in my paper about its smiling face, wishing my poor father were alive to hear the story of my long-deferred entrance into the art and mystery of the journalist. He would have laughed consumedly; and from my dear remembrance of him, I think he would have found a quotation from Horace to meet the case. Once, I recollect, it turned out that the odd man at the rectory, supposed to be a bachelor, had abandoned a wife and twelve children--all of them small ones, for aught I know--somewhere in Gloucestershire. A policeman came for poor Robert, and my father was very sorry for the man, even though he were a sad dog, and a notorious toper of ale. But the rector thought of the phrase: "Raro antecedentem scelestum deseruit poena," and cheered up amazingly.

Well, on the strength of the verses about the Eleusinian mysteries, I am to be a journalist, and consequently, as it was thought in those days, I must learn shorthand, so that I may be able to write a hundred and fifty words in a minute. And here again comes a chapter as sad as that which I have written on my arithmetic. I never learnt shorthand effectively, because I was too stupid to learn it. The queer thing is that when I was quite a little boy at school this art of shorthand had a strange and mysterious attraction for me. Why? I am sure I don't know; why did the small boys of my generation love dark lanterns? Robert Louis Stevenson has written an enchanting essay on the fascination of this instrument of the mysteries; but I am not quite sure that even he has penetrated to the heart of the enigma. For I, though a lonely child, knew the joy of the dark lantern, and it was a great and exceeding joy. The glowing of heat that rose from its roof--corrugated, I think?--the rank smell of its oils were charms that somehow carried me over the borders of this common world into an exquisite region of wonder and surmise. And now I come to look back into days horribly distant--the shorthand question must wait for a while--I perceive that there was a perfect ritual, or ceremonial rather, of the Dark Lantern, the origins of which are as obscure to me as are the origins of other primitive mysteries. Of one thing only I am certain, and I speak with all due deference to the author of "The Golden Bough," not forgetting Miss Jane Harrison; the lantern service of my early boyhood had no reference whatever to the young crops or to the sprouting of the corn. As I lit the wick I did not say, "O Sun! shine thou also on the land and make it warm so that there may be many cabbages, so that green peas may not be lacking to the lamb which is equally nurtured by thy beams." Of course, I am quite willing to allow that, as a general rule, an anxiety about the spring crops fully explains the origin of all painting, all sculpture, all architecture, all poetry, all drama, all music, all religion, all romance: I admit that the Holy Gospels are really all about spring cabbage, that martyrdom and mass are spring cabbage, that Arthur is really arator, the ploughman; that Galahad, denoting the achievement and end of the great quest, is Caulahad, the cabbage god. I admit all this because it is so entirely reasonable and satisfactory, and, indeed, self-evident; but though all Frazerdom should rise up against me, I cannot allow that when I lit my dark lantern I was inviting the sun to help the crops.

There was some sort of obscure connection--I seem to remember--between Dark Lanterns and Masks. They were both properties in singular mysteries of a formless character which were enacted in dark shrubberies on dark nights, just before bed-time. It was well understood, I know, that these objects must be kept in secret places, and must not by any means be seen by the uninitiated; and the uninitiated were everybody besides myself. And here, I believe, I was following unconsciously, but most strictly, the rules of all primitive mysteries throughout the world. The Greeks of the historical period had become lax; they carried about the mystic fan of Iacchus in public procession. But amongst the Blackfellows of Australia, where the rites are much nearer to the original purity of their institution, the mystic fan is not seen, only heard. Therefore the Dark Lantern and the Mask were kept hidden in an obscure cranny of the coach-house, which was at the end of an overshadowed drive at some distance from the rectory. They were produced under the cover of the darkness, these sacramental instruments, clouds and stars and the dim boughs of trees and tangled undergrowth alone saw them. There were certain solemn words which accompanied the ostension of the objects, but they were in a language which I have long forgotten. But some day, when the turmoil has died down, when the clouds have cleared for the sunset and the apparition of the evening star, as I sit by a western shore awaiting the boat of Avalon, I shall write my last treatise, under the title of "The Dark Lantern and the Mask," libellus vere mysticus. And here I give notice to all good and lawful men that I am duly seized of the above title, so that they may abstain from intromitting with the same.

This digression of the dark lantern proceeded, naturally enough, from my speaking of shorthand. This art, I said, appealed to me when I was a boy, and its appeal was that of a kind of mystery writing, of a script not in common use. For my acquaintance did not lie in journalistic circles. I knew nobody who could write shorthand or understood anything about it, and so the three books of Pitman--"Teacher," "Manual," and "Reporter"--were three mystery books, so far as my small world was concerned. But now, in later years, having written that famous poem on the initiation of Eleusis, I was to be a journalist, and to be a journalist I must learn shorthand. And then I found Phonography a mystery indeed, and too great a mystery for me, since I could not attain to it. I muddled about with it for three or four years; I actually made some use of it in one of my queer employments, but I never wrote it decently. I was too fumble-fisted; try as I would, I could not form the characters with elegance or accuracy. My p's and b's would wobble and bend till they looked like f's and v's, if I tried to halve a letter I quartered it. A kindly reporter gave me a hint: "Don't bother about the thick and thin lines," he said, "I never do." And no doubt the skilled shorthand writer can play all manner of tricks with the system, but I was not a skilled writer, and I took the reporter's advice and made bad worse. My last shorthand lesson was taken in 1885, long after I had ceased to think of journalism as a profession. Indeed, I cannot now remember why I continued to waste my time over a craft that I could not master; but I suppose I thought the endeavour gave an air of respectability and solidity to my proceedings that they would have lacked without it. From June 1881 to December 1882 I was more or less vaguely bent on the journalist's career. I remember feeling somewhat discouraged during this period by reading an advertisement for a journalistic position in a London paper. The applicant could write shorthand at the rate of one hundred and fifty words a minute, he understood all about reporting, he was an expert at "leaderettes," and quite willing to take a turn at the case--all for thirty shillings a week. This did not seem promising, but I need not have disturbed myself; my journalistic days were not yet, nor for many years to come. In the meanwhile I read variously and became thoroughly familiar with Boswell's Johnson (in Mr. Percy Fitzgerald's edition). And one windy, gusty night, when the costers' flares in the back streets were burning with a rushing sound, I came upon a secondhand bookshop on the main road between Hammersmith and Turnham Green, and went in and found an odd volume of William Morris's "Earthly Paradise." Now followed the old trouble, and in a worse form. As Swinburne's "Songs Before Sunrise" had first set me versifying, so the "Earthly Paradise" reinforced the original virus. And now I had acquired some slight facility of a worthless sort, and so I began to imitate William Morris, and spent the odd hours of six good months in writing a sham-Greek tale in rhymed couplets; which I tore up thirty years ago. And then I discovered Herrick, and tried to imitate that inimitable writer; but this effort, though vain in itself, was not so wholly vain. For it brought me, as it were, into the seventeenth century, into an age which I have loved ever since with a peculiar devotion. Ten years later I went on pilgrimage to Dean Prior and Dean Churchtown, and in spite of the restored church, trod the lanes under the moor with reverence, since Herrick's feet had passed by those ways.

But now towards the end of the year 1882, after I had known London, on and off, for nearly two and a half years, all that feeling of its immense gaiety with which I had approached it in the first place was dropping from me. I began to realise, very gradually and by dismal degrees, that the gaieties of London were commodities that had to be bought with money, and that I had none. The theatre had ceased to charm me, and I am very sorry to say that it has never charmed me since; that is from the point of view of the man sitting in the pit. By the end of '82 I had quite definitely ceased to be "fond of the play."

For now London began to assume for me its terrible aspect. It was rather a goblin's castle than a city of delights; if indeed it had not become a place of punishment wherein I was condemned to hard labour through many dreary and hopeless years.

Chapter V

In that wonderful volume which is called the Grand Saint Graal we are told how the hermit Nasciens received a magic book from paradise. It was divided into portions, and one of these portions was intituled "Here Begin Terrors." I can find no words that might more fitly introduce the tale of my solitary life in London. I was only twenty; I was poor; I was desolate. And I frizzled all the time (or most of it) on the fire of my own futility; I longed to make literature, and I could only write nonsense.

I was employed for a time in a house of business in a street north of the Strand and parallel to it, which, I suppose, must have been Chandos Street. I know that it was still paved with cobblestones. My employers were publishers--the firm has for many years ceased to exist--and I was something or other in what is called the "editorial" department. But to the best of my belief publishing books was but a minor part of the energies of the house, and I should think a later growth. The real staple was wholesale stationery; there was an important "line" of copybooks, there was a great deal done with ornamental and decorated albums, and also with pictorial calendars. The Shakespeare calendar of the House is still in existence, or was in existence a year or two ago, and it bears the name of the vanished firm. Mr. (afterwards Sir) Walter Besant had been the "editor" of Messrs. Chandos and Co., but just before I made my first trial of business life he had resigned, and his place was taken by a very kindly literary gentleman, whose name I have forgotten. Afterwards he edited a series, if not several series, of anthologies, and was, I believe, appointed Professor of English Literature at some Indian seminary of learning. I do not know whether he is still alive. Well, it was my business to assist this gentleman. I think I was engaged as his "secretary," but I was known in the House as his "clurk." I am trying to recollect what I actually did to assist him.

My first job on the morning of my arrival I can remember. I made a copy of Mr. Gladstone's Latin version of the well-known hymn, "Rock of Ages": "Jesu, pro me perforatus," it began. And then I had to take down in shorthand and afterwards write in longhand a stern letter to somebody who had made a mistake in the name of King Alfred's grandmother. This error had occurred in one of a series of Board School history books that the firm was publishing; and this circumstance alone gave me a loathing and hatred for the whole business, since I thought then, and think still, that the name of King Alfred's grandmother is not of the faintest consequence to any reasonable being. It is the kind of fact which would interest a German deeply; he would spend years of his life to find out all about it; but such is not the occupation of a gentleman.

In the afternoon of that day we became a little livelier. My chief contributed a London letter to some Scottish paper--he came from the northern part of this island--and again my shorthand was required. The London letter was distinctly gay in its tone, it dealt in a cheerful spirit with some early incidents in the career of a certain admirable actress whose talents then engaged and delighted us. As I took it down it struck me as over worldly for the readers of the "Haddaneuk Herald," and sure enough my man reconsidered the matter and struck out the gaieties from the copy. And how did that famous shorthand of mine serve me? Not so vilely, considering all things. I had a quick memory then, and remembered many of the phrases that had been dictated, and I could read quite a lot of the characters that I had formed, and others gave me a vague sort of intimation of the sense; just as the neumes helped the church-singers of the earlier ages; they were quite useful if you knew the tune.

I search my memory for further details of my occupation with Chandos and Co. I think that the Shakespeare Calendar occupied me during odd hours for a week or more. This was January, and I was set to the preparation of the calendar for the next year. It was not a difficult task, and I was furnished with a sort of album, containing the Shakespeare calendars for the past six or seven years, and my only business was to make a new almanack out of these old elements. Thus January 1, 1884, gave the Shakespearean quotation that had been assigned to December 27, 1877; for January 2 I chose a motto that had pertained to February 6, 1882, and so forth. It was easy, but dull. And I was dull, too, or I would have invented Shakespearean lines that Shakespeare never wrote, and trusted to the all but universal ignorance of Shakespeare. I did something like that, when I was an older and a merrier man. I persuaded a friend of mine, a young fellow of literary tastes, that one of the most famous phrases ascribed to Shakespeare was in reality a gag, invented by Mr. F. R. Benson's stage manager. "Do you mean to say," said my friend, "that this Mr. Randle Ayrton invented 'a poor thing, but mine own'?" "Certainly," I replied. "Then," said he, "Ayrton must be a most wonderful man." And I wonder how many of my readers know exactly how the matter stands--without referring to the play?

And then what else did I do for my pound a week in Chandos Street? Chiefly, I think I took down and transcribed a daily report to the head office of the firm, which was in Belfast or Dundee or some such town. I don't remember in the least what it was about, whether it dealt with King Alfred's grandmother's name or with other matters. But I had to write about two quarto pages daily of this report, and put D 1 in the margin. I think D 1 meant Literary Department; but the whole thing was the terror of my life. For it had to be neatly written, with a fair and level margin on each side; and this I could by no means achieve. Again and again my D 1 was condemned as a ragged and untidy performance, and I had to copy it out all over again, as if I had been a careless schoolboy--as, indeed, I was from the firm's point of view.

And I sit in my corner, trying to write a round, clear, clerkly hand, trying to remember that of the two forms of the small "t" one was much to be preferred, trying to observe the rule that "today" must be written as one word, not two, and that for commercial purposes "draft" must be spelt with "f," not with "ugh"; and thinking of the nightingale in the thorn bush by the Soar, in the still valley.

Here I was, then, in Chandos Street, a peg of no particular shape at all in a perfectly round hole, feeling very miserable indeed. We were, I believe, somewhat cramped for room, and I had a desk in the album department. Here three very cheerful and kindly young fellows of about my own age did something with handsome albums. I don't know in the least what they did; so far as I could see they took albums out of tissue paper and put them back into tissue paper all day long. One of them, the senior of the room--he must have been three or four years older than any of us--was just about to make a real start in life. He used to tell me all about it when we were alone together for a minute or two, as sometimes happened. There was a young lady whom he was to marry in a few months' time, and he had made arrangements for setting up as a stationer in Harlesden, and he meant to push Chandos's stuff--albums and everything--and to do well and be happy. "Poor man, and then he died," to quote one of Dr. Johnson's muttered undertones. I do not know how far his short life at Harlesden was successful or felicitous. But as for me, I hated it all. It was not that the work was hard, but that I took no interest in it, and saw no reason why it should be done at all, or why anybody alive should do it. So I looked about me, and through the favour of a friend I got a little teaching of small children at twenty-five shillings a week. Then I gave notice to Messrs. Chandos. They were very kind; they offered me twenty-five shillings a week to stay, but I thanked them and said no. It was the business atmosphere of the place that I detested; I have always agreed with the small boy in "Nicholas Nickleby" who uttered the great maxim, "Never Perform Business." The teaching which followed was certainly not exciting, but I did not mind it. Indeed, having to teach Euclid, I found to my amazement that it was about something, and actually was a coherent and reasoned scheme of things, not a mere madhouse puzzle, as I had always imagined. But then my own geometrical instruction had been limited. It consisted simply in this: Fourteen Euclids were served out to fourteen small boys. The mathematical master then said: "Learn the Definitions, Axioms, and Postulates." That was my first and my last lesson in geometry; though I duly went through the accustomed books of Euclid, trying to learn by heart what was to me mere unmeaning gibberish.

At this time and for the next year and a half I was living in Clarendon Road, Notting Hill Gate--or Holland Park, to give the politer subdirection. I am sorry to say that I had not a garret, since the houses of that quarter, being comparatively modern, do not possess the sloping roofs which have seen the miseries of so many lettered men. Still, my room had its merits. It was, of course, at the top of the house, and it was much smaller than any monastic "cell" that I have ever seen. From recollection I should estimate its dimensions as ten feet by five. It held a bed, a washstand, a small table, and one chair; and so it was very fortunate that I had few visitors. Outside, on the landing, I kept my big wooden box with all my possessions--and these not many--in it. And there was a very notable circumstance about this landing. On the wall was suspended, lengthwise, a step-ladder by which one could climb through a trap door to the roof in case of fire, and so between the rungs or steps of this ladder I disposed my library. For anything I know, the books tasted as well thus housed as they did at a later period when I kept them in an eighteenth-century bookcase of noble dark mahogany, behind glass doors. There was no fireplace in my room, and I was often very cold. I would sit in my shabby old great-coat, reading or writing, and if I were writing I would every now and then stand up and warm my hands over the gas-jet, to prevent my fingers getting numb. I remember envying a man very much indeed on a certain night in late winter or early spring. It was a very cold night; there was a bitter north-easter blowing, and the wind seemed to pierce right through my old coat and to set my very bones shivering and aching. I had gone abroad, because I was weary of my den, because I was sick with reading and in no humour for writing, because I felt I must have some change, however slight. But it was an evil and a bitter blast, so I turned back after a little while, coming down one of the steep streets that lead from Notting Hill Gate Station to Clarendon Road. And half-way home I came upon a man encamped on the road by the pavement. He was watching over some barrows and tools and other instruments of street repair, and he sat in a sort of canvas wigwam, well sheltered from the wind that was chilling me to the heart. His coat, too, looked thick and heavy, and he had a warm comforter round his neck, and before him was a glowing, ardent brazier of red-hot coals. He held his hands and his nose over the radiant heat, and smoked a black clay pipe; and I think he had a can of beer beside him. I envied that man with all my heart; I don't think I have ever envied any man so much.

Occasionally I had applications for the loan of a book from my step-ladder library. These came from the lodgers on the ground floor, an Armenian and his wife, who annoyed the landlady by sleeping in cushions piled about the carpet and hanging their blankets in front of the doors and windows. It was the Armenian lady who had literary tastes, and her desire was always for "a story-book." I never saw her or her husband, but I often heard him calling Mary, the servant. He would stand at the top of the kitchen stairs and shout "Marry! Marry!" and then, reflectively, and after a short interval, "Damn that girl." He gave a fine, Oriental force to the common English "damn." Other lodgers that I remember were a young Greek and a chorus girl, mates for a single summer. They occupied the first floor and were succeeded by a family from Ireland. I have a confused notion that there was something a little queer about the head of this household. He was, I think, a major, and I know he was Evangelical. As I went down the stairs I heard him more than once uttering in loud, earnest tones the words, "Let us pray." This was startling; and one of his daughters would always shut the door of their room with a bang on these occasions, and that was startling, too.

The little table in my little room turned out to be a very useful piece of furniture. I not only read at it and wrote on it, but I used it as a larder. In the corner nearest the angle of the wall by the window I kept my provisions, that is to say, a loaf of bread and a canister of green tea. Morning and evening the landlady or "Marry" would bring me up a tray on which were a plate, a knife, a teapot, a cup and saucer, and a jug of hot water. With the aid of a kettle and a spirit lamp, which came, I think, from under that serviceable table--one may fairly say from the cellar--I made the hot water to boil and brewed a great pot of strong green tea.

In the first months of this life of mine an early dinner was added to the fees of my teaching; later, my pupils changed, and the dinner disappeared. I then used to spend the hour in the middle of the day in wanderings about Turnham Green and the waste places round Gunnersbury, making my meal on a large Captain's biscuit and a glass of beer. I varied this repast by taking it in various public-houses. In those days there were still pleasing and ancient taverns scattered along those western roads. One I remember in particular, a very old, tumbledown house, set at the edge of the market gardens, which then approached almost to Turnham Green. There was not a straight line about this old, old house, its roof-tree dipped and wavered, and the roof was of mellowed tiles, and one end of the place was quite overwhelmed by a huge billow of ivy. I used to think that highwaymen must have lurked in the little room where I took my biscuit and glass of ale; and the food and drink tasted much better on that account. The old tavern, and its leaning sheds and ragged outbuildings, its red roof and its green ivy; all are gone long ago. There is a row of raw houses where it stood, and I hate them. Sometimes I did not have any beer, either because I did not want any, or because it struck me as too great a luxury. Then I would buy a small bag of currant biscuits and take them to the region of the market gardens and devour them, sitting on a gate or sheltering behind a hedge. I don't know how it is, but these feasts are always connected in my mind with a grey and gloomy sky and a very cold wind, so that I shiver when I think of flat, square biscuits in which currants are embedded. But I have a reverence for them, too. There were, I confess, days of gross debauch. Once a week, or once a fortnight at the least, I went to a goodly and spacious and ancient tavern on the high road, and had a grilled chop, potatoes, bread, and beer; which came to one and a penny or one and twopence. Les Cotelettes de Mouton, Sauce Bénie the dish is called by the experts of the haute cuisine. I can recommend it. And in the evenings I sometimes exceeded, though not so violently. I would, nine evenings out of ten, buy my provision of bread at a shop at the bottom of the long main road, opposite or nearly opposite to Uxbridge Road Station. The shop kept a very choice kind of gingerbread, and I would buy a couple of bricks of this gingerbread, and munch them with a high relish as a supplement to the common bread.

As the spring of 1883 advanced, and the weather improved and the evenings lengthened, I began the habit of rambling abroad in the hope of finding something that could be called country. I would sometimes pursue Clarendon Road northward and get into all sorts of regions of which I never had any clear notion. They are obscure to me now, and a sort of nightmare. I see myself getting terribly entangled with a canal which seemed to cross my path in a manner contrary to the laws of reason. I turn a corner and am confronted with an awful cemetery, a terrible city of white gravestones and shattered marble pillars and granite urns, and every sort of horrid heathenry. This, I suppose, must have been Kensal Green: it added new terror to death. I think I came upon Kensal Green again and again; it was like the Malay, an enemy for months. I would break off by way of Portobello Road and entangle myself in Notting Hill, and presently I would come upon the goblin city; I might wander into the Harrow Road, but at last the ghost-stones would appal me. Maida Vale was treacherous, Paddington false--inevitably, it seemed, my path led me to the detested habitation of the dead.

Be it remembered that my horror at the sight of Kensal Green Cemetery was due to this, that, odd as it may seem to townsfolk, I had never seen a cemetery before. Well I knew the old graveyards of Gwent, solemn amongst the swelling hills, peaceful in the shadow of very ancient yews. I knew well these garths. There was Henllis, high up on the mountain side, in the place of roaring winds, under the faery dome of Twyn Barlwm. I had lingered there of autumn evenings while the sun set red over the mountains, and a drift of rain came with the gathering darkness, as the yew boughs beat upon the east window of the church. There were graves there with flourished inscriptions, deeply cut, and queer Welsh rhymes--dyma gareg dêg:--

Here's a rare stone--of death.
Beneath it lies
A rarer dust, that shall arise
By heavenly breath alone; and climb the skies--
We trust.

I knew the churchyard of Llanddewi, looking down the steep hillside into the chanting valley of the Soar, and Kemeys, between the Forest and the Usk, and Partrishw, in the heart of the wild mountains beyond Abergavenny. These places of the dead were solemn with old religion, and the tones of Dirige and De Profundis and Requiem Æternam sang still about them on their hills; but this white ghostly city of corruption--there was nothing but horror in it! Still, I see myself on these wanderings, beating to and fro in the stony wilderness, entangled, as I say, in the endless mazes of unknown streets. Now I would succeed in breaking away. I would pass that sad zone of destruction and disgrace that always lies just beyond the furthest points of the suburb. These are the places where the hedges are half ruined, half remaining, where the little winding brook is defiled, but not yet a drain, where one tree lies felled and withered, while its fellow is still all green. Here curbstones impinge on the fields, and show where new, rabid streets are to rush up the sweet hillside and capture it; here the well under the thorn is choked with a cartload of cheap bricks lately deposited. I would pass over these dismal regions and come, as I thought, into the fair open country, and then suddenly at the turn of the lane I would be confronted by red ranks of brand-new villas: this might be Harlesden or the outposts of Willesden.

I think that on the especial occasion that I have in mind the red row of houses must have been some portion or fragment of Harlesden. I remember that, like the cemetery, this impressed me as a wholly new and unforeseen horror, something as strange and terrible as the apparition of a rattlesnake or a boa-constrictor might be to an English child, wandering a little away into the orchard or the wood near the house. I had never lived in a world that might have prepared me for such things; in Gwent--in my day, at all events--there was no such phenomenon as this sudden and violent irruption of red brick in the midst of a green field; and thus when I came round the corner of a peaceful lane and saw in the midst of elms and meadows this staring spectacle, I was as aghast as Robinson Crusoe when he saw the track of the foot on the sand of his desert island.

... And here I would make a parenthesis, and say that so long as my writing habits had any concern with the imagination I never departed from the one formula. This not consciously; in fact, I have a secret doctrine to the effect that in literature no imaginative effects are achieved by logical predetermination. I have told, I think, how I was confronted suddenly and for the first time with the awe and solemnity and mystery of the valley of the Usk, and of the house called Bartholly hanging solitary between the deep forest and the winding esses of the river. This spectacle remained in my heart for years, and at last I transliterated it, clumsily enough, in the story of "The Great God Pan," which, as a friendly critic once said, "does at least make one believe in the devil, if it does nothing else." Here, of course, was my real failure; I translated awe, at worst awfulness, into evil; again, I say, one dreams in fire and works in clay. But, at all events, my method never altered. More legitimately than in the instance of "The Great God Pan" I made the horrid apparition of the crude new houses in the midst of green pastures the seed of my tale, "The Inmost Light," which was originally bound up with "The Great God Pan." And so the man in my story, resting in green fields, looked up and saw a face that chilled his blood gazing at him from the back of one of those red houses that once had frightened me, when I was a sorry lad of twenty, wandering about the verges of London. The doctor of my tale lived in Harlesden.

And if I may pursue this subject farther I would suggest that the whole matter of imaginative literature depends upon this faculty of seeing the universe, from the æonian pebble of the wayside to the raw suburban street as something new, unheard of, marvellous, finally, miraculous. The good people--amongst whom I naturally class myself--feel that everything is miraculous; they are continually amazed at the strangeness of the proportion of all things. The bad people, or scientists as they are sometimes called, maintain that nothing is properly an object of awe or wonder since everything can be explained. They are duly punished.

If we go more deeply into this text of Horror and Harlesden, it will become apparent, I think, that what is called genius is not only of many varying degrees of intensity, but also very distinctly of two parts or functions. There is the passive side of genius, that faculty which is amazed by the strange, mysterious, admirable spectacle of the world, which is enchanted and rapt out of our common airs by hints and omens of an adorable beauty everywhere latent beneath the veil of appearance. Now I think that every man or almost every man is born with the potentiality at all events of this function of genius. Os homini sublime dedit, coelumque tueri: man, as distinct from the other animals, carries his head on high so that he may look upon the heavens; and I think that we may say that this sentence has an interior as well as an exterior meaning. The beasts look downward, to the earth, not only in the letter but in the spirit; they are creatures of material sensation, living by far the greatest part of their lives in a world of hot and cold, hunger and thirst and satisfaction. Man, on the other hand, is by his nature designed to look upward, to gaze into the heavens that are all about him, to discern the eternal in things temporal. Or, as the Priestess of the Holy Bottle defines and distinguishes: the beasts are made to drink water, but men to drink wine. This, the receptive or passive part of genius, is, I say, given to every human being, at least potentially. We receive, each one of us, the magic bean, and if we will plant it it will undoubtedly grow and become our ladder to the stars and the cloud castles. Unfortunately the modern process, so oddly named civilisation, is as killing to this kind of gardening as the canker to the rose; and thus it is that if I want a really nice chair, I must either buy a chair that is from a hundred to a hundred and fifty years old, or else a careful copy or replica of such a chair. It may appear strange to Tottenham Court Road and the modern furniture trade; but it is none the less true that you cannot design so much as a nice arm-chair unless you have gone a little way at all events up the magic beanstalk.

Still, many of us have our portion of the passive or perceptive faculty of genius; we are moved by the wonder of the world; we know ourselves as citizens of an incredible city, we catch stray glimpses of faery Atlantis, drowned beneath the ocean of sense. But it is one thing to dream dreams; and quite another to interpret them, and in this active faculty of interpretation, or translation of the heavenly tongues into earthly speech, there are infinite degrees of excellence. And the masters in this craft of interpretation are few indeed. And the final conclusion--a sad one for me--is that if I could have "translated" the Horror of Harlesden competently I should have been a man of genius.

***

Still, I see myself all through that year 1883 tramping, loafing, strolling along interminable streets and roads lying to the north-west and the west of London, a shabby, sorry figure; and always alone. I remember walking to Hendon and back--this must have been on a whole holiday--and to this day I can't think how I found my way there, through what clues I struck from the north parts of Clarendon Road into the Harrow Road, and how I knew when to leave the Edgware Road and bend to the right. Anyhow, I got there and back, tired enough and glad of the half-loaf of bread that awaited me.

Then I became learned in Wormwood Scrubs and its possibilities. It was and is a very barren and bleak place itself, but in those days there was an attractive corner on the Acton side of the waste, that I was fond of contemplating. This was a sort of huddle of old cottages and barns and outhouses with a fringe of elms about them. It did my eyes good then as now to look on something that was old and worn with use and mellow; my eyes that were bleared and aching with the rawness and newness of multitudinous London. To me an old cottage, with its little latticed porch and its tangled garden patch, was veritable balm; I would gaze on such a place with refreshment and delight, as desert travellers must gaze on the cold pools and green leafage of an unexpected oasis. I used to light on these little, humble, pleasant retreats in my walks--there were many more of such cottages in the outskirts of London then than now--and make impossible plans for migrating from the urbanity of Clarendon Road into one of these hidden places, where there would be a garden for me to walk in, and perhaps a summer-house overgrown with white roses, and a little low room with oldish furniture. But I found no such place, and still went prowling in a kind of torment of the spirit by the highways and by-ways of the west. Acton used to do me good; it was then more like a country town than a modern suburb. On the right hand, as you came up from the Uxbridge Road under the railway bridge, there were then some grave and dignified houses of the early Georgian period, with broad lawns before them and big gardens behind them. On the left was the Priory, with spacious and park-like grounds and many greeny elms. Legends about the first Lord Lytton hung about the Priory, and it was whispered that the old lady who kept the lodge-gate had in her day written daring poetry, of the erotic kind. There are laundries and rows and rows of little houses now where the Priory stood; the Georgian houses on the other side of the road have all been pulled down. But I have a notion that the last time I went that way I saw a second-hand bookshop on the London side of the railway bridge, where in '83 I bought an old, odd volume of Cowley's poems.

The second-hand bookshop, which includes the bookstall, is one of the many things that I have dabbled in; but I have never been sworn to the hunt over the old shelves as to a devouring passion. I lack the great incentive: the love of rare books on account of their rarity. I have a great respect for the collector of such things, and I often envy him his sudden joys of discovery; it must be like finding a golden treasure in a rubbish heap; but I could never follow his example. Still, I often used to amuse myself by grubbing about the dusty shelves for an odd hour or two, turning over vast masses of insignificance--of insignificance for me, at all events--conning titles, diving into prefaces, glancing doubtfully over strange pages, wondering whether this or that or the other would bring me the best entertainment for the few shillings that I had to spend. In these new days the young man with a thirst for literature has his labours simplified; the classics of the world are ready for him, nicely printed, in a handy form, and at a low price. He has simply to go into a shop, put down his shilling, and get his book, and it is all over. This would never have done for me. When I bought a book I required and obtained a long drawn-out, deliberated pleasure; I considered that the possession of three-and-sixpence or five shillings entitled me to a whole afternoon's rich enjoyment. Just as ladies of the suburbs make arrangements--as I understand--to come up to town and do a little shopping, and have a delicate cress-sandwich or two in Regent Street, and then go to a matinée at the theatre, and have creamy cakes for tea before they start back for the red villas: so did I use to travel from Notting Hill Gate to Charing Cross, and stroll up Villiers Street, and walk along the Strand, relishing its savours, which never grew stale to me. For I do believe that the old Strand, before they destroyed it with their porphyries and their marbles and Babylonian fooleries and façades of all sorts, was the very finest street in all the world. I know quite well its manifest and manifold weaknesses and faults, if it were to be regarded from the point of view of a classical town-architect. There was no plan, no design about it, no uniformity; its houses were of all shapes, sizes, periods, and heights; it had no more been designed than a wild hedgerow has been designed. And there, exactly, was its infinite and subtle and curious charm. Nothing could be more urban or urbane than the Strand; and yet it had grown, as the green brake grows, as the cathedrals and the country houses of England grew from age to age, gathering beauty as they increased. The Strand was an altogether English street, and it was the very heart of London. In it, or beside it, were the theatres and the bookshops and the cookshops; to north and south odd passages and stairs and archways admitted the curious into the oddest places and quarters. You were weary of the traffic and the pattering feet? Then you could turn into New Inn or Clement's Inn and enjoy deep silence. You wanted to see the old hugger-mugger of the London back streets, dark taverns of the eighteenth century, where men had lain hidden from the hangman? Here was Clare Market for you. You had heard that "Elzevirs" were very rare and curious books, and would like to see an Elzevir? You would lose your opinion of their rarity, for you would see as many Elzevirs as any man could desire in Holywell Street, where I believe they were to be bought by the sack, as if they had been coals. And Elzevirs apart; the naughty prints and books of Holywell Street were as good as a play. For I believe that the Row had turned naughty somewhere in the early 'fifties; it had then got in its stocks--and had kept them. Here were the works of G. M. W. Reynolds in large volumes; "Mysteries of the Court of St. James," and such weariness. Here was the faded coloured engraving of a young female of extreme gaiety--with ringlets, and the appearance of the chambermaid in the once-famous print, "Sherry, sir." And with all the curiosity, and variety, and oddity and richness of the Strand, it had the while a manner of snug homeliness and cosiness and comfort about it which was quite inimitable. To be in the Strand was like drinking punch and reading Dickens. One felt it was such a warmhearted, hospitable street, if one only had a little money. Unfortunately, I was never on dining terms, as it were, with the Strand; but I always felt that if it only knew me it would have called me "old boy" and given me its choicest saddles of mutton and its oldest port, and I felt grateful. Somehow I always warmed my hands when I got into the Strand ... and they were often chilly enough.

Such, then, was my preparation for a book-foray in the heart of London, this relished, leisurely, savoury walk along the Strand; and then I might dive into Clare Market by Clement's Inn and look for mystery books in a certain shop that I knew there. I bought one of the most curious--I do not say the best--books in the world, Vaughan's "Lumen de Lumine" in a shop in Clare Market, and still I should be much obliged if someone would tell me what "Lumen de Lumine" is about. Or I might try Denny's, at the western end of Booksellers' Row, or like enough go grovelling round the shelves of Reeves and Turner, who were then in the southern bend of the Strand, opposite to St. Clement Dane's Church.

One dull afternoon, I remember, I ran to earth in this shop on a lower shelf a dim, brown elderly-looking book in cloth covers called "Ferrier's Institutes of Metaphysic." It repaid me many times over for the couple of shillings that I gave for it. I took Ferrier home in delight to the little room in Clarendon Road, and made a great deal of green tea, and found the dry bread of quite admirable flavour, and smoked pipes and read the new book far into the night. Before I went to bed Ferrier had quite convinced me of the truth of the proposition--which looked odd at first--that we can only be ignorant of that which we can know. This means, of course, that no man can be ignorant of the existence of four-sided triangles; which is evident enough. But as I fell asleep, I felt I had had a tremendous day.

***

I look back upon myself in that little room in Clarendon Road with some amazement. I come in from one of my long, prowling walks--I may have been to Hounslow to look for the Heath, or I may have been to Hampton Court--and make my meal of bread and tea, and then settle down to tobacco and literature. I find that my landlady turns off the gas at the meter at midnight, so I provide myself with carriage candles, which I fix up somehow on the table. I read on night after night. It may be Homer's "Odyssey," or it may be "Don Quixote"--to which I have been faithful ever since I found the book in the drawing-room of Llanfrechfa Rectory--it may be that singular magazine of oddities, Disraeli's "Curiosities of Literature," it may be Burton's "Anatomy of Melancholy"; a great refuge, this last, a world of literature in itself. Or I am reading Pepys for the first time, with ravishment, or Pomponius Mela "De Situ Orbis" in a noble Stephanus quarto, or Harris's "Hermes," or Hargrave Jennings on the Rosicrucians; this last one of the craziest and most entertaining of books, which had a little later an odd influence on my fortunes. It was a sad blow to me to find out afterwards, chiefly through the medium of A. E. Waite's "Real History of the Rosicrucians," that, as a cold matter of fact, there were no Rosicrucians. A Lutheran pastor who had read Paracelsus, wrote, early in the seventeenth century, a pamphlet describing a secret order which had no existence outside of his brain. Naturally enough, societies arose which imitated, so far as they could, the imaginary organisation described by the fantastic Johannes Valentinus Andrea; I should not be surprised, indeed, to be told that such societies are now in being in modern London;

but these orders are late "fakes"; the 'seventies and 'eighties of the last century saw their beginnings. There are no Rosicrucians--and there never were any.

Or I am reading Carlyle--"Sartor Resartus" or the Johnson and Burns and Walter Scott Essays--and I must say that I think a good many young men of this age would be all the better for a Carlyle course. For though Carlyle was not the prophet of full inspiration that the time just before my own imagined, though he exalted brute force into a place that belongs to the Divine Wisdom, though his original Calvinism hung like a dark and obscuring cloud over all his life, yet I know not any man of these days that is worthy to dust Carlyle's hat or to clean his pipe for him.

There is a passage in the Johnson essay telling how the poor, agonised, heroic doctor made for himself a boat of the transient driftwood and enduring iron, and sailed down Fleet Ditch, "the roaring mother of dead dogs," to the City that hath foundations; the phrases ring still in my heart, noble music; worthier stuff than the prophecies of to-day--or should I say of yesterday? These, so far as I can make out, bid us abstain from meat and beer and tobacco, and the State shall give us a pound a day and save our souls alive. This message does not ring in my heart a noble music; I think Carlyle would have called it "a damned potato gospel." I read Carlyle, then, in my little room, and find a strange encouragement and strength in him. His picture of life is of a bitter struggle, and so indeed I find it--at twenty. Man, in Carlyle, is a poor wretch in thin and ragged clothes, out on a blasted heath, with all the heavens and all the clouds crashing and pouring upon him; blackness over him, hailstorms and fire showers his portion in the world. Get into whatever kennel or doghole you can find, says Carlyle, and shelter yourself from the blast so long as you can keep it, and be thankful. I liked the doctrine then, and it still seems to me a very good philosophy.

So I read and meditated night after night, and I am amazed at the utter loneliness of it all, when I contrast this life of mine with the beginnings of other men of letters. These others have often gathered friends of all sorts, both useful and pleasant, at the University; they have come of well-known stocks, every step they take is eased for them, their way is pointed out, there are hands to help them over the rough and difficult places. Or, even if they have not been at Oxford or Cambridge, if they have not come of "kent folk," they know, somehow or other, young fellows of their own age, with whom they can engage in endless talk about letters over eternal pipes and ever-welling tankards. One informs another, one, consciously or unconsciously, charts the other's way for him. I am often made quite envious when I see and hear how a young man, fresh on the town, drops so easily, so pleasantly, so delightfully into a quite distinguished place in literature before he is twenty-five. He enters the world of letters as a perfectly well-bred man enters a room full of a great and distinguished company, knowing exactly what to say, and how to say it; everyone is charmed to see him; he is at home at once; and almost a classic in a year or two.

And I, all alone in my little room, friendless, desolate; conscious to my very heart of my stuttering awkwardness whenever I thought of attempting the great speech of literature; wandering, bewildered, in the world of imagination, not knowing whither I went, feeling my way like a blind man, stumbling like a blind man, like a blind man striking my head against the wall, for me no help, no friends, no counsel, no comfort.

Somehow or other, out of a welter of reading of the most miscellaneous and shapeless sort, out of long walks and long meditations, out of moonings and loafings by Brentford and the parts thereto adjacent, there rose up in the spring of 1883 the beginnings of something that had a vague resemblance to a book. I had finished that miserable "poem" which attempted the manner of William Morris, and from that time my attacks of verse-writing became brief and trifling, causing no uneasiness. And, this trouble happily over, I became immersed in the study of scholastic logic, and gave many days and nights to Whately's "Elements." I got Thomson also, and dallied with the quantification of the predicate, but I found such devices too new-fangled; what I wanted was the logic of the mediæval schools, and in this I took a singular and intense delight.

And here is a paradox, which may be worthy the consideration of the curious: that age which was above all the age of logic, was also the age of the most luxuriant and splendid imagination. The scholars and thinkers of the Middle Ages have been reproached with idolising the logical process to a point of utter extravagance, with treating the syllogism as a sort of divining rod by which all the treasures of the spiritual, intellectual, and physical worlds could be discovered and drawn up from the dark womb and chaos of things into the light of the sun. These reproaches, I think, have chiefly proceeded from people to whom exact thinking has proved unpleasant and unprofitable; but it is certainly true that the logical art was deeply and profoundly and constantly studied in the thirteenth century--which was the age of the marvellous imagery, the great magistry of the Gothic cathedrals, of the Arthurian romances, of Dante. Nay, it is interesting to note that Coleridge and De Quincey, two main agents of the "renascence of wonder" at the beginning of the nineteenth century, were both practised logicians. It would seem, therefore, that the dream and the syllogism have between them a certain secret alliance and bond, and so, naturally enough, two of the most extravagant dreams, "Alice in Wonderland," and "Alice Through the Looking-Glass," were the visions of a master of logic. As for the Snark, I can inform the inquisitive as to his true abode. He dwells in the place that is called Bocardo.

And so I steeped myself in these rare and entrancing studies, for such they seemed, and still seem to me. And thus I would sit on a bench on that bald, arid, detestable Shepherd's Bush Green, and be in reality, though not in actuality--let us for the moment adapt our discourse to the matter, and make the distinction--in cool, grey cloisters of the Middle Ages, walking in the silvery light with the Master of the Sentences, with the Angelic Doctor, listening to the high, interminable argument of the Schools. High, indeed, as dealing with immortal essences, not with monkeys' guts; interminable also in the manner of the cathedral rushing upwards to the stars which it cannot attain, of the old modes in which there are no true closes, but rather hints of undying melodies far beyond their endings; interminable, according to the dictum of one of these dark-robed Masters; omnia exeunt in mysterium. For there is a quest to which there is no term, nor bound, nor limit: pelagus vastissimum. Meditating these things, the jangling of the old horse trams might disturb me, and I would carry my quiddities to green fields by Hanger Hill, or to solitary places in Osterley Park, beyond Brentford, and so muse till the shadows came and sent me homeward under the twinkling, wavering lamps of those far-off days. Then for much tobacco, the disjunctive hypothetical syllogism and the strict rigour of the game. I am afraid very little of the old science has remained with me, but now and then I come with some amusement on distinguished personages engaged in what they suppose is argument. I see no arguments; but undistributed middle terms are thick as October leaves in Wentwood.

From such a soil, then, the thing that had certain resemblances to a book rose up and gradually took shape, so far as it ever had any shape. It came up out of my logic books and out of Burton's "Anatomy of Melancholy," and so it was called "The Anatomy of Tankards." For, having enough sense, even though I was only twenty, to know that I could not write a serious treatise concerning the high doctrines that entranced me, I wrote a grave burlesque of what I loved. I examined into the essence of the tankard, I sought deeply into its quiddity, I divided its properties from its accidents, and distinguished again between the separable and inseparable accidents. I showed philosophically and conclusively that if there were no tankards there would be no men, that is, no rational or civilised men. For the ancient Greeks truly taught that man was raised from the brutish to the spiritual state by Bacchus, the giver of the vine. By wine is man made divine; and a diviner, says Bacbuc: and since wine must be contained before it can be drunk, it is clear that without tankards man cannot become divine; that is, cannot be man at all, in the proper sense of the term. And so on, and so on, with an infinite deal of easy dictionary learning, with much twisting of my logic formulæ; it was all too elaborate, elephantine, prolonged; a little thing that might have been well enough in its way drawn out into a big thing, and so spoiled. Still, I was only twenty, and twenty is apt to worry its bone long after all the meat has disappeared.

But if I could only have written the real book--that is, the dreamed, intended book--and not the actual book! Then, I promise you, you should have had high fantasies; not only arguments that began with a pebble by the way and rose upward to the evening star, that deduced all the shining worlds in an ineffable sorites from one mere letter of the alphabet. You should not only have been in at the death when Achilles caught at last the tortoise and passed him by, spurning his body into that utter void where parallel straight lines meet; you should have had an English Rabelais.

I remember taking my thoughts of the book up to Ealing Common one autumn evening. The work was drawing to a close, and I stood meditating the matter, looking from the height down towards Brentford. There was a wild sunset, scarlet and green and gold, and as it were, gardens of Persian roses, far in the evening sky. I stood by an old twisted oak, and thought of my book as I would have made it, and sighed, and so went home and made it as I could.

Chapter VI

The kind of life that I have been trying to indicate lasted for about eighteen months, and then my pupils mysteriously disappeared. Mysteriously, I say, for I have completely forgotten what became of them, and by what ways they left me. At all events, they vanished, and I, being destitute, returned to Gwent and my old home. There they were almost as poor as poverty, but they were glad to see me. And I, waking in the morning to the brave breath from the mountain, wandering in the sunshine--it was summer-time--about the gardens and the orchards, revisiting the green, delicious heart of the twisted brake, listening once more to the water bubbling from the rock; I thought I had been translated from hell to paradise.

For, be it remembered, I have dealt gently with the days of Clarendon Road. I have spoken for the most part of the happier hours, of eager reading, of finding an enchanting book on dusty shelves, on the delights of the mind, on the capacity of changing dreary, common Shepherd's Bush into the cloistered walks of the Schools, on the joy of obtaining some kind of literary utterance. I have said little of the black days and the waste nights, of the desolation that would sometimes engulf me as it were with a deep flood. For many weeks at a time I never spoke to any human being; save to my pupils on Euclid and Cæsar, and this was a speech that was no speech. And being born, I believe, with at least the usual instincts of human fellowship and a great love of all genial interchanges of thought and opinion, this silence seared my spirit; to the interior sense I must have shown as something burnt and blasted with ice-winds and fires. Indeed, when I was released from this life in the manner that I have described, I came out, as it were, a prisoner from the black pit of his dungeon, all confused, trembling, and afraid, scarce able to bear the light of genial affection. For a long while I spoke but little, and then with difficulty; I was fast losing the habit of speech. Indeed, the eighteen months in Clarendon Road had been a very grave experience; but I think that what affected my relations most in my demeanour was this: for a long time I would cut myself a piece of dry bread at tea, and munch it mechanically, having forgotten all about the use of butter. This struck them as dreadful; one might be poor, but to eat dry bread was more than poverty; it was beggary. When my aunt first noticed this trick of mine, she pushed the butter dish towards me, saying in a disturbed voice that there was no need for that any more.

And for many days I was in a sort of swoon of delight. I had no desire for activities of any kind; I had all the happy languor of the convalescent about me. It was bliss to stroll gently in that delicious air, to watch the mists vanishing from the mountain-side in the morning, to see again the old white farms beneath Twyn Barlwm and Mynydd Maen gleaming in the sunlight, to lie in deep green shade and to feel that I was at home again; that my troubles were over. I did not fret myself by inquiring as to whether they would not begin again. Indeed, in this first passion of relief, I loved to imagine myself as dwelling for the rest of my days amidst friendly faces in a friendly land, and devoting, say, fifty years to healing the wounds of eighteen months. It is a sorry thing to be but twenty-one and to feel so.

But it is thus, I suppose, that the man of the imaginative cast of mind pays, and pays heavily, for whatever qualities he may possess, and it will always be a question whether the price exacted be not too dear and beyond all proportion to the value received. But the case, I apprehend, is this: Mr. Masefield has said, very finely, that literature is the art of presenting the world as it were in excess. To the lovers in Mr. Stephen Phillips's drama of "Paolo and Francesca" the earth appears a greener green, the heavens a bluer blue; all beautiful things are raised to a higher power by the fire of their passion; the whole world is alchemised. And this state, which is a result of love, is the condition of imaginative work in literature, and so the man who is to make romances sees everything and feels everything acutely, or, as Mr. Masefield says, excessively. Now there would be nothing amiss in this state of things if these exalted and intensified perceptions could be utilised when there was a question of making a book and then abrogated and laid aside with pen and ink and paper. Unluckily, however, this cannot be so managed; and too often the dealer in dreams finds that his magic magnifying glass is tight fixed to his eyes and cannot be moved. And thus a mere common bore or nuisance appears to him as dreadful as Nero or Heliogabalus, the possibility of missing a train is as tragical as "Hamlet," and the pettiest griefs swell into the hugest sorrows.

I, in truth, had suffered; I had been through a dreary and a dismal experience enough; but my pains had racked me to excess; the pinpricks, unpleasant in plain earnest, had become stabs of a poisoned dagger. And so I came back to Gwent as to Avalon; there to heal me of my grievous wounds. So, as I say, it was mercifully given to me to saunter under the apple trees in July and August weather, to watch the sun and the wind on the quivering woods, to wander alone, and yet how deeply consoled and medicined, by the winding Soar Valley. Now and again I recollected, as I hope we shall recollect earthly torments in Paradise, as things over and paid for, the interminable, cruel labyrinths of London. I saw myself again, a half-starved, unhappy, desolate wretch astray in those intolerable, friendless, stony mazes of Notting Hill and Paddington and Harrow Road; I came again by obscene, obscure paths to Kensal Green, the place of the whited sepulchres. Or the hideous raw row of suburban houses would suddenly confront me, surging up, a foul growth, from the green meadow, or the sick reek of the brickfields by Acton Vale blew in my nostrils. And the grim little room and solitude for the end of every journey!

I recollected these things, but though only days or weeks had been interposed between my happy state and my endurance of them they were as torments suffered in some remote æon. I said to myself, "I am as they that rest at last," and almost heard the words In Convertendo: with whatso in that psalm is after written.

***

Among the books that I kept in my step-ladder library in Clarendon Road I mentioned that queer piece of sham learning and entertaining extravagance "The Rosicrucians: Their Rites and Mysteries," by Hargrave (or Hargreave?) Jennings. I said that this odd volume had eventually a curious influence on my life; and this was as follows: I was reading Herodotus and that portion of Herodotus which treats of Egypt--I have long ago forgotten the Muse which names the book--and Herodotus, it will be remembered, was very deeply interested in the Mysteries of the Egyptian religion. In treating of these occult things of Osiris the historian mentions certain singular matters which were highly pertinent to Mr. Jennings's thesis--if Mr. Jennings could be said to have had anything so definite as a thesis. But "The Rosicrucians" contained no mention of that which Herodotus had seen when night was on the Nile, so I ventured to write to the ingenious author, pointing out the particular passage which, I thought, would interest him. Mr. Jennings did not answer my letter; he was odd to extremity in most things, but in this particular he conformed perfectly to all the literary men whom I encountered in my early days. I came into contact with four or five men of a certain reputation; or perhaps I should say I came within sight of them; and they could very easily have flung me a word or two of encouragement, which would have been very precious to me then. But I never had that word, and so was forced to go on and do my best without it; the better way, no doubt, but a hard way. But though the author of "The Rosicrucians" did not reply to my letter, he passed my name and address to another man, a young fellow who had just set up as a publisher, and was going to issue one of the astounding Jennings books. So Davenport, the publisher, sent me his catalogue of new and second-hand books, and I, on reading it, sent him the manuscript of my "Anatomy of Tankards."

Here a parenthesis, if not several parentheses. We are now in 1884, and I had finished the "Anatomy" in the autumn of 1883. Soon after it was ended I sent the MS. to a gentleman who was then but in a small way. He is now a very eminent publisher indeed, and loved so much by his authors--by some of them at all events--as to be known as "Uncle." Well, "Uncle" (though, alas! it was not fated that he should ever be uncle-in-letters of mine) sent back the MS. in due season with a letter that almost made up for any disappointment my first "boomerang" may have occasioned.

His letter delighted me, not because it was specially complimentary, nor because it gave evidence of a careful and critical reading of the rejected manuscript, but because it was almost a replica of the publisher's letter which introduces Mr. Tobias Smollett's admirable epistolary romance, "Humphry Clinker." My actual publisher so resembled Smollett's feigned bookseller in the manner of his letter that I should suppose the one had deliberately made the other his model, did I not know "Uncle" to be far too good a man to read such a book as "Humphry Clinker." I have not got my Smollett by me, I am sorry to say, so I cannot quote, but I may mention that both publishers made a very liberal use of the dash, or mark of parenthesis, and were curious in avoiding the word "I."

My letter ran somewhat as follows:--

"Dear Sir,
"Referring to your favour of the 17th ult., enclosing MS. of work, 'Anatomy of Tankards'-- have read MS. with interest--fear it would hardly command large sale--have had little encouragement to speculate lately--would recommend topic of more general public interest--hoping to have pleasure of hearing from you on some future occasion.
"Etc. etc."

I was delighted, only a few years ago, to find that "Uncle's" hand has not lost its epistolary cunning. A distinguished friend of mine had been good enough of his own motion--not with my knowledge--to write to this publisher suggesting that a book by me would ornament his catalogue. The publisher approached me by letter. I wrote to him briefly, saying that I was just finishing a romance. He wrote back: "Sorry you speak of a romance--fear there is very little sale for those old things--however," etc. etc.

I did not trouble to go into whatever might lie beyond the portals of "however." But note the phrase, "those old things." It seems to me more precious than gold that has passed the furnace.

But to return from this backwater of narrative; I found Mr. Davenport established in an old street in the quarter of Covent Garden. I got to know this street well afterwards, and to like it, too, for all its associations and circumstances. Over the way, opposite to Davenport's offices, was the house where they said De Quincey had written his great book; there were theatrical shops all tinsel and wigs and grease paints close at hand, and on market days the street was all apack with carts and waggons and clamorous with marketmen who are still a rough and primitive and jovial race. Indeed, the market overflowed into York Street and submerged it, and I have had to leap over an undergrowth of green, springing ferns established on the office steps. Mr. Davenport had written me a very agreeable letter, and we had a very agreeable interview. The book on his publication-list which had attracted my attention was called "Tavern Talk and Maltworms' Gossip," and an admirable little anthology it was, compiled (as I found out afterwards) by Davenport himself. I thought there was a certain congruity between this book and my "Anatomy of Tankards," hence the despatch of the manuscript to York Street. The publisher liked my book very much. He wanted to publish it badly; but there were certain preliminaries to be adjusted before this could be done, and I did not see how the obstacle could be surmounted. This conference took place at that singular hour of my career when my pupils seemed to melt away from me, as though they had been morning dew. I was just bound for the country, and the publisher agreed to hold the little matter of which I have spoken in suspense.

So I went westward, and there in Gwent there were kind people who had known my father all his days, and my grandfather before him, and so, for the sake of "the family," they helped me to arrange those "preliminaries." And, after all, perhaps it is fair enough that a man should pay his footing when he enters the craft.

***

So here was another element or elixir in the potion of my bliss, that I was drinking among those dearly-beloved hills and woods of Gwent. The bad old days were all over, and my torments were past; Clarendon Road and all its sad concatenations were like a black wrack of cloud seen far down on the horizon, as the sun rises splendid on a bright and happy day. I was come to the territory of Caerleon-on-Usk which was Avalon; and every herb of the fields and all the leaves of the wood, and the waters of all wells and streams were appointed for my healing. And my book was going to be published; I was to see myself in print, between covers--vegetable vellum they turned out to be--and I should be reviewed in London newspapers; and, not a doubt of it, be happy ever after.

Mr. Pecksniff, it will be remembered, spoke of the melancholy sweetness of youthful hopes. "I remember thinking once myself, in the days of my childhood, that pickled onions grew on trees, and that every elephant was born with an impregnable castle on his back. I have not found the fact to be so; far from it." Nor have I found "the fact" to be so. Still, these visions of fair print and title-pages and reviews are very pleasant in the green of youth, and they helped to make that summer of 1884 delightful for me. I "worked in" the thought of the coming proof-sheets--even the anticipation of a proof-sheet is almost too much joy at twenty-one--into my escape from hard bondage, into the summer sunlight, into the odours of the solemn woods at night, into the cool breath of the brook, into the twilight fires of the sky above Twyn Barlwm. They were brave days while they lasted.

And now and again I had gallant tramps over the country with my old friend Bill Rowlands. I saw Bill a couple of years ago, after an interval of a quarter of a century, and Bill wore a long black coat and a solemn collar, having been a clerk in holy orders for many years. But when I began to speak of the little tavern at Castell-y-Bwch there was a twinkle in Bill's eye, and at the mention of the chimes of Usk, we both laughed till we cried--and perhaps we did cry internally. But I said to Bill, "Now I am going to take you to the Café Royal; it's the best I can do for you. But I wish it were the Three Salmons at Usk!"--where, if I remember rightly, we had bread and cheese and a great deal of beer and hot brandy and water to follow.

But that was a great day. We had gone over hill and dale, through the depths of woods and over waste lands, finding footpaths in the most unsuspected places that we had never dreamed of. And I remember that these footpaths gave me a singular impression of travelling in time-- backwards, not forwards, as in Mr. Wells's enchantment. For the track of feet was but barely marked, and seemed on the point to fade away altogether, and the stiles that we climbed were of old, old oak, whitened and riven with age, and the outlets of these paths were into deep, forgotten lanes where no one came. And if one passed a house, it was roofless and ruinous; its gable-wall standing grey, with fifteenth-century corbel stones. The garden wall was fallen into a heap of stones, and the fruit trees were dead or straggled into wildness. So it seemed to me that we had fallen on old ways that were not of our day at all, and no one, perhaps, had been there for fifty or a hundred years, and if we saw anyone it would not be a man of our time. Bill, I am convinced, thought nothing of all this; his talk was of B.N.C. and mad tricks and all the mirth in the world, and I warmed the chilled hands of my spirit at his gaiety, as I had longed to warm my bodily hands at the watchman's brazier, glowing red in the cold London street. So Bill and I came at last into Caerleon, having succeeded by much extraordinary wandering in making five miles into ten, and at Caerleon we drank old ale at the Hanbury Arms, which is a mediæval hostelry, close to the Roman tower by the river. And then nothing would satisfy us but to go to Usk by the old road; again, ten miles instead of five, but with our "short cut" imposed upon it, a good fifteen miles.

The way goes over the river; on the right are King Arthur's Round Table and the relics of the Roman city wall of Isca Silurum, as the Second Augustan Legion, garrisoned at Caerleon, called the place. Then through the village, still known in my days as Caerleon-ultra-pontem, and so into that most wonderful, enchanted, delicious road that winds under the hillside, under deep Wentwood, above the solemn curves and esses of the river. We passed Bulmore, which does not mean a moor of bulls, but pwll mawr, the great pool, of the Usk river. It is a farmhouse now, but once a retired officer of the 2nd Augustan had his villa here, and his graveyard also: and here, I think, in the orchard, as they were planting some young trees, they found the stone inscribed: Ave, Julia, carissima conjux; in æternum vale. Hail, Julia, dearest wife; farewell for ever.

And here, to the best of my belief, Bill was telling me how an undergraduate friend of his at B.N.C., a schoolfellow of mine, found himself under the painful necessity of screwing up the Dean in his rooms; the screws employed being coffin-screws, headless, that is, and not to be extracted without enormous pains.

We went on our way by the river, and passed under Kemeys, a noble grey old house, with mullioned windows and Elizabethan chimneys. There is such a peace about this place, such a sweetness from the wood, such a refreshment from the water, so grave a repose upon it, that I translated to Kemeys one of my heroes, a clerk in Shepherd's Bush. This clerk had found out that all the bustle and activity of modern life are delusions and wild errors, and his reward was to be that he should end his days at Kemeys, sheltered from all turmoil and vanity, garnered from the evil world.

The peace of Kemeys was the peace of all the valley of the Usk, and what balms it exhibited to my spirit only those can know who have been bred in such places, and have experienced the jar and dust and racket of some great town, and then have returned to the old groves.

My friend Bill and I went swinging along the winding lane beside the winding river, and as we went the sound of pouring waters sang to us. For now the over-runnings of the wells of Wentwood came from the hill as rivulets, and about each stream its twisted thicket grew, accompanying it all down the steep, to the river below. We passed little Kemeys church, watching above the pools of the Usk, and then on the hillside, almost in the shadow of the forest, was Bartholly, that solitary house which awed me for years, so that I made my awe into a tale. And here was Newbridge, crossing a river that had now ceased to be tidal and yellow, and had become glassy clear, and so on northward, and it seemed into silences and solitudes that grew ever deeper and more solemn, more evidently declaring the great art-magic of God that has made all the world. The day drew on, the sun sank below wild unknown hills--neither of us had ever been this way before-- and the green world was dim for a while, and then was lighted up with the red flames of the afterglow. The evening redness appeared, and in those fires the ash tree became of immortal growth, the round hills rose above no earthly land, the winding river was a faery stream. Then, veil upon veil rising from the level, rising from the fountains in the wood, mists closing in upon us.

My friend Bill said we should never get to Usk at this rate; he felt sure that there must be a short cut across the fields. So we took the first stile that appeared and set out over country that was utterly unknown to us; and the marvel was that we ever got to Usk at all--or to anywhere for the matter of that. I have a confused recollection of walking for hours in a gathering darkness, through jungles and brakes of dark wood, climbing hills that rose fantastic as out of dreamland, going down into dusky valleys where white mist rose icy from the courses of the brooks, threading an uncertain way through quaking marshland, and the regions of the distance as vague as shapes of smoke.

The bells were ringing nine when we came out of this dim world into Usk, and to the lights and cheerfulness of the Three Salmons, to ale and to laughter. There was a wonderful old fellow, a Water Bailiff, making the mirth of that cheerful, ancient parlour; and he told us of the tricks he had played on poachers and fishermen till we roared again. He was a fellow of strange disguises; if one of his stories were to be believed he had caught the most famous salmon poacher of the Usk by assuming the gait and utterance of a calf seeking for its mother at midnight. The tale may have been true; it was certainly an excellent entertainment.

Such was one of our days; and again we would go wandering over the mountains to west and to northward; climbing up into great high wild places of yellow gorse and grey limestone rocks, stretching and mounting onward and still beyond, so that one said in one's heart "for ever and ever. Amen." High up there; the sunlight on that golden gorse, on the yellow lichens that encrusted the rocks ringed in old Druid circles, the great sweet wind that blew there, the heart of youth that rejoiced there, all the dear shining land of Gwent far below us, glorious; it is all an old song.

And there was a day on which we mounted over Mynydd Maen and came down into a valley in the very heart of the mountains, and walked there all the day, and in the evening returned again over the mountain at the southern end, winding under Twyn Barlwm as the twilight fell. It is only music, I think, that could image the wonder of the red sky over the faery dome, and the gathering dusk of the night as it fell on the rocks of that high land, on the streams rushing vehemently down into the darkness of the valley, on the lower woods, on the white farms, gleaming and then vanishing away. Only by music, if at all, can such things be expressed, since they are ineffable; not to be uttered in any literal or logical speech of men. And if one looks a little more closely into the nature of things it will become pretty plain, I think, that all that really matters and really exists is ineffable; that both the world without us--the tree and the brook and the hill--and the world within us do perpetually and necessarily transcend all our powers of utterance, whether to ourselves or to others. Night and day, sunrise and moonrise, and the noble assemblage of the stars, are continually exhibited to us, and we are forced to confess that not for one moment can we proclaim these appearances adequately. We stammer confusedly about them, much as a savage who had been taken through the National Gallery might stammer a few broken sentences, the applicability of which would be more or less dubious. "Woman--very bright round head," might be the Blackfellow's "description" of a famous Madonna; and a Turner would be summed up as "plenty clouds--one big tree." And in like manner we, confronted, not only with things remote and majestic, but with things familiar and near at hand, stutter a few lame sentences, endeavouring to describe what we have seen. And thus all literature can be but an approximation to the truth; not the "truth" of science, for that is a figment of the brain, a non-existent monster, like dragons, griffins, and basilisks; but to that truth which Keats perceived to be identical with beauty. And it is further evident that even this approximation to the truth of things is a matter of the utmost difficulty and not very far from a miracle, inasmuch as in a generation of men there are only two or three who achieve it, who in consequence are hailed as men of the highest genius.

Of course, there are persons for whom "truth" implies "even gilt-edged securities slumped heavily," or some such statement. To them, I tender my sincere apologies.

***

The proof-sheets of my book began to appear early in that autumn of '84; they made me rapturous reading. And while I was correcting them, with a vast sense of the importance and dignity of the task, Davenport, the publisher, was writing to me, asking if I had any ideas for new books, and throwing out suggestions of his own.

Now this was very pleasant, for it all tended to persuade me, in spite of any doubts and fears of mine, that I was really a literary man. I would read Davenport's letters again and again, and deliberate gravely with myself over the answering of them; I enjoyed this very much indeed. But the correspondence led to no practical result; because I could not then--or ever--perform the Indian mango trick. The expert conjurers of the East, as is well known--in magazine fiction--will put a seed into a flower pot, cover up for a second or two, and lo! there is a little plant. Again the concealment; the plant has grown, and so forth, till within the space of five minutes you can gather ripe mangoes from the tree that you saw sown. This is the mango trick of fiction; that of fact, as I have seen it, is about the dreariest and most ineffective piece of conjuring imaginable. But, as I say, I could never imitate those fabled Orientals. If Mr. Murray and Mr. Longman were to jostle one another on my doorstep, clamouring for a masterpiece, and offering Arabian terms, it would make no difference; if I had no book within me, I should not be able to produce one on demand. In practice, I have found that I take about ten years to grow these things; though I have one in my mind now that was first thought of in 1898-99 and is not yet begun.

So Mr. Davenport's letters produced no literature, interesting though they were; and I must say that a less sluggish mind would have found them stimulating in a high degree. But the literary publisher struck on cold iron; he suggested, I remember, a volume of scathing criticism--"like Mozley's Essays"--as likely to receive his most favourable attention. But, really, I could not think of anybody that I particularly wanted to scathe--now, perhaps, I could oblige a publisher in search of anathemas and Ernulphus curses--and I had not read Mozley, nor have I read him to this day. Then I, on my side, suggested a book to be called "A Quiet Life," this being, in fact, a description of the life that I was then gratefully and gladly leading. I sent a specimen chapter, and so far as I remember Davenport counselled me to defer the writing of that sort of book till I was eighty or thereabouts. I daresay he was right. Then my half-dozen copies of "The Anatomy of Tankards" reached me; and I believe that as soon as I saw the book printed and complete in its (vegetable) vellum boards I began to be ashamed of it. I think that this was hard lines, but the trick has been played on me again and again; and I do believe that a moderate, not excessive, dose of the good conceit of oneself is one of the chiefest boons that parents should beg from fairy godmothers for their offspring. For life is necessarily full of such buffetings and duckings, such kicks and blows and pummellings, that balms and elixirs and medicaments of healing are most urgently indicated, and there is nothing equal to this same rectified spirit of conceit. It may tend to make a man an ass, but it is better--or more agreeable, anyhow--to be an ass than to be miserable.

Then came the reviews, and they did me some good, for, as far as I remember them, they were kindly and indulgent. I think the critic of the "St. James's Gazette," then in its glory under the editorship of Greenwood, spoke of "this witty and humorous book," while he said, with absolute justice, that I had ruined the popularity of my parodies by their prolixity. Then the publisher, despairing, I suppose, of getting any ideas out of me, produced a notion of his own. He sent me three or four French texts of the "Heptameron," and bade me render it into the best English that I had within me; and so I did forthwith, for the sum of twenty pounds sterling. I wrote every night when the house was still, and every day I carried the roll of copy down the lane to meet the postman on his way to Caerleon-on-Usk.

And so my story has come round full circle. In the first of these chapters I told how the kindly speaker at the Persian Club, praising my version of the French classic, transported me in an instant from that shining banqueting hall in the heart of London, over the bridge of thirty years, into the shadows of the deep lane. Again it was the autumn evening, and the November twilight was passing into the gloom of night. There was a white ghost of the day in the sky far down in the west; but the bare woods were darkening under the leaden clouds; the familiar country grew into a wild land.

And I, with time to spare, walk slowly, meditatively down the hill, holding my manuscript, hoping that the day's portion has been well done. As I come to the stile there sounds faint through the rising of the melancholy night wind the note of the postman's horn. He has climbed the steep road that leads from Llandegveth village and is now two or three fields away.

It grows very dark; the waiting figure by the stile vanishes into the gloom. I can see it no more.

THE END

NOTE

"Far Off Things" was written in 1915, and, the work not being of an encyclopædic nature, no effort has been made to bring it up to date.

The book called "The Anatomy of Tankards" in the text was called in fact "The Anatomy of Tobacco." Simple-hearted American collectors are now willing to give four pounds for a copy of it.

Printed in Great Britain at The Mayflower Press, Plymouth. William Brendon & Son, Ltd.

THE HILL OF DREAMS

Originally Published in 1907

I

There was a glow in the sky as if great furnace doors were opened.

But all the afternoon his eyes had looked on glamour; he had strayed in fairyland. The holidays were nearly done, and Lucian Taylor had gone out resolved to lose himself, to discover strange hills and prospects that he had never seen before. The air was still, breathless, exhausted after heavy rain, and the clouds looked as if they had been molded of lead. No breeze blew upon the hill, and down in the well of the valley not a dry leaf stirred, not a bough shook in all the dark January woods.

About a mile from the rectory he had diverged from the main road by an opening that promised mystery and adventure. It was an old neglected lane, little more than a ditch, worn ten feet deep by its winter waters, and shadowed by great untrimmed hedges, densely woven together. On each side were turbid streams, and here and there a torrent of water gushed down the banks, flooding the lane. It was so deep and dark that he could not get a glimpse of the country through which he was passing, but the way went down and down to some unconjectured hollow.

Perhaps he walked two miles between the high walls of the lane before its descent ceased, but he thrilled with the sense of having journeyed very far, all the long way from the know to the unknown. He had come as it were into the bottom of a bowl amongst the hills, and black woods shut out the world. From the road behind him, from the road before him, from the unseen wells beneath the trees, rivulets of waters swelled and streamed down towards the center to the brook that crossed the lane. Amid the dead and wearied silence of the air, beneath leaden and motionless clouds, it was strange to hear such a tumult of gurgling and rushing water, and he stood for a while on the quivering footbridge and watched the rush of dead wood and torn branches and wisps of straw, all hurrying madly past him, to plunge into the heaped spume, the barmy froth that had gathered against a fallen tree.

Then he climbed again, and went up between limestone rocks, higher and higher, till the noise of waters became indistinct, a faint humming of swarming hives in summer. He walked some distance on level ground, till there was a break in the banks and a stile on which he could lean and look out. He found himself, as he had hoped, afar and forlorn; he had strayed into outland and occult territory. From the eminence of the lane, skirting the brow of a hill, he looked down into deep valleys and dingles, and beyond, across the trees, to remoter country, wild bare hills and dark wooded lands meeting the grey still sky. Immediately beneath his feet the ground sloped steep down to the valley, a hillside of close grass patched with dead bracken, and dotted here and there with stunted thorns, and below there were deep oak woods, all still and silent, and lonely as if no one ever passed that way. The grass and bracken and thorns and woods, all were brown and grey beneath the leaden sky, and as Lucian looked he was amazed, as though he were reading a wonderful story, the meaning of which was a little greater than his understanding. Then, like the hero of a fairy-book, he went on and on, catching now and again glimpses of the amazing country into which he had penetrated, and perceiving rather than seeing that as the day waned everything grew more grey and somber. As he advanced he heard the evening sounds of the farms, the low of the cattle, and the barking of the sheepdogs; a faint thin noise from far away. It was growing late, and as the shadows blackened he walked faster, till once more the lane began to descend, there was a sharp turn, and he found himself, with a good deal of relief, and a little disappointment, on familiar ground. He had nearly described a circle, and knew this end of the lane very well; it was not much more than a mile from home. He walked smartly down the hill; the air was all glimmering and indistinct, transmuting trees and hedges into ghostly shapes, and the walls of the White House Farm flickered on the hillside, as if they were moving towards him. Then a change came. First, a little breath of wind brushed with a dry whispering sound through the hedges, the few leaves left on the boughs began to stir, and one or two danced madly, and as the wind freshened and came up from a new quarter, the sapless branches above rattled against one another like bones. The growing breeze seemed to clear the air and lighten it. He was passing the stile where a path led to old Mrs.

Gibbon's desolate little cottage, in the middle of the fields, at some distance even from the lane, and he saw the light blue smoke of her chimney rise distinct above the gaunt greengage trees, against a pale band that was broadening along the horizon. As he passed the stile with his head bent, and his eyes on the ground, something white started out from the black shadow of the hedge, and in the strange twilight, now tinged with a flush from the west, a figure seemed to swim past him and disappear. For a moment he wondered who it could be, the light was so flickering and unsteady, so unlike the real atmosphere of the day, when he recollected it was only Annie Morgan, old Morgan's daughter at the White House. She was three years older than he, and it annoyed him to find that though she was only fifteen, there had been a dreadful increase in her height since the summer holidays. He had got to the bottom of the hill, and, lifting up his eyes, saw the strange changes of the sky. The pale band had broadened into a clear vast space of light, and above, the heavy leaden clouds were breaking apart and driving across the heaven before the wind. He stopped to watch, and looked up at the great mound that jutted out from the hills into mid-valley. It was a natural formation, and always it must have had something of the form of a fort, but its steepness had been increased by Roman art, and there were high banks on the summit which Lucian's father had told him were the vallum of the camp, and a deep ditch had been dug to the north to sever it from the hillside. On this summit oaks had grown, queer stunted-looking trees with twisted and contorted trunks, and writhing branches; and these now stood out black against the lighted sky. And then the air changed once more; the flush increased, and a spot like blood appeared in the pond by the gate, and all the clouds were touched with fiery spots and dapples of flame; here and there it looked as if awful furnace doors were being opened.

The wind blew wildly, and it came up through the woods with a noise like a scream, and a great oak by the roadside ground its boughs together with a dismal grating jar. As the red gained in the sky, the earth and all upon it glowed, even the grey winter fields and the bare hillsides crimsoned, the waterpools were cisterns of molten brass, and the very road glittered. He was wonder-struck, almost aghast, before the scarlet magic of the afterglow. The old Roman fort was invested with fire; flames from heaven were smitten about its walls, and above there was a dark floating cloud, like fume of smoke, and every haggard writhing tree showed as black as midnight against the black of the furnace.

When he got home he heard his mother's voice calling: "Here's Lucian at last. Mary, Master Lucian has come, you can get the tea ready." He told a long tale of his adventures, and felt somewhat mortified when his father seemed perfectly acquainted with the whole course of the lane, and knew the names of the wild woods through which he had passed in awe.

"You must have gone by the Darren, I suppose"--that was all he said. "Yes, I noticed the sunset; we shall have some stormy weather. I don't expect to see many in church tomorrow."

There was buttered toast for tea "because it was holidays." The red curtains were drawn, and a bright fire was burning, and there was the old familiar furniture, a little shabby, but charming from association. It was much pleasanter than the cold and squalid schoolroom; and much better to be reading Chambers's Journal than learning Euclid; and better to talk to his father and mother than to be answering such remarks as: "I say, Taylor, I've torn my trousers; how much do you charge for mending?" "Lucy, dear, come quick and sew this button on my shirt."

That night the storm woke him, and he groped with his hands amongst the bedclothes, and sat up, shuddering, not knowing where he was. He had seen himself, in a dream, within the Roman fort, working some dark horror, and the furnace doors were opened and a blast of flame from heaven was smitten upon him.

Lucian went slowly, but not discreditably, up the school, gaining prizes now and again, and falling in love more and more with useless reading and unlikely knowledge. He did his elegiacs and iambics well enough, but he preferred exercising himself in the rhymed Latin of the middle ages. He liked history, but he loved to meditate on a land laid waste, Britain deserted by the legions, the rare pavements riven by frost, Celtic magic still brooding on the wild hills and in the black depths of the forest, the rosy marbles stained with rain, and the walls growing grey. The masters did not encourage these researches; a pure enthusiasm, they felt, should be for cricket and football, the dilettanti might even play fives and read Shakespeare without blame, but healthy English boys should have nothing to do with decadent periods. He was once found guilty of recommending Villon to a school-fellow named Barnes. Barnes tried to extract unpleasantness from the text during preparation, and rioted in his place, owing to his incapacity for the language. The matter was a serious one; the headmaster had never heard of Villon, and the culprit gave up the name of his literary admirer without remorse. Hence, sorrow for Lucian, and complete immunity for the miserable illiterate Barnes, who resolved to confine his researches to the Old Testament, a book which the headmaster knew well. As for Lucian, he plodded on, learning his work decently, and sometimes doing very creditable Latin and Greek prose. His school-fellows thought him quite mad, and tolerated him, and indeed were very kind to him in their barbarous manner. He often remembered in after life acts of generosity and good nature done by wretches like Barnes, who had no care for old French nor for curious meters, and such recollections always moved him to emotion. Travelers tell such tales; cast upon cruel shores amongst savage races, they have found no little kindness and warmth of hospitality.

He looked forward to the holidays as joyfully as the rest of them. Barnes and his friend Duscot used to tell him their plans and anticipation; they were going home to brothers and sisters, and to cricket, more cricket, or to football, more football, and in the winter there were parties and jollities of all sorts. In return he would announce his intention of studying the Hebrew language, or perhaps Provençal, with a walk up a bare and desolate mountain by way of open-air amusement, and on a rainy day for choice. Whereupon Barnes would impart to Duscot his confident belief that old Taylor was quite cracked. It was a queer, funny life that of school, and so very unlike anything in Tom Brown. He once saw the headmaster patting the head of the bishop's little boy, while he called him "my little man," and smiled hideously. He told the tale grotesquely in the lower fifth room the same day, and earned much applause, but forfeited all liking directly by proposing a voluntary course of scholastic logic. One barbarian threw him to the ground and another jumped on him, but it was done very pleasantly. There were, indeed, some few of a worse class in the school, solemn sycophants, prigs perfected from tender years, who thought life already "serious," and yet, as the headmaster said, were "joyous, manly young fellows." Some of these dressed for dinner at home, and talked of dances when they came back in January. But this virulent sort was comparatively infrequent, and achieved great success in after life. Taking his school days as a whole, he always spoke up for the system, and years afterward he described with enthusiasm the strong beer at a roadside tavern, some way out of the town. But he always maintained that the taste for tobacco, acquired in early life, was the great life, was the great note of the English Public School.

Three years after Lucian's discovery of the narrow lane and the vision of the flaming fort, the August holidays brought him home at a time of great heat. It was one of those memorable years of English weather, when some Provençal spell seems wreathed round the island in the northern sea, and the grasshoppers chirp loudly as the cicadas, the hills smell of rosemary, and white walls of the old farmhouses blaze in the sunlight as if they stood in Arles or Avignon or famed Tarascon by Rhone.

Lucian's father was late at the station, and consequently Lucian bought the Confessions of an English Opium Eater which he saw on the bookstall. When his father did drive up, Lucian noticed that the old trap had had a new coat of dark paint, and that the pony looked advanced in years.

"I was afraid that I should be late, Lucian," said his father, "though I made old Polly go like anything. I was just going to tell George to put her into the trap when young Philip Harris came to me in a terrible state. He said his father fell down 'all of a sudden like' in the middle of the field, and they couldn't make him speak, and would I please to come and see him. So I had to go, though I couldn't do anything for the poor fellow. They had sent for Dr. Burrows, and I am afraid he will find it a bad case of sunstroke. The old people say they never remember such a heat before."

The pony jogged steadily along the burning turnpike road, taking revenge for the hurrying on the way to the station. The hedges were white with the limestone dust, and the vapor of heat palpitated over the fields. Lucian showed his Confessions to his father, and began to talk of the beautiful bits he had already found. Mr. Taylor knew the book well--had read it many years before. Indeed he was almost as difficult to surprise as that character in Daudet, who had one formula for all the chances of life, and when he saw the drowned Academician dragged out of the river, merely observed "J'ai vu tout ça." Mr. Taylor the parson, as his parishioners called him, had read the fine books and loved the hills and woods, and now knew no more of pleasant or sensational surprises. Indeed the living was much depreciated in value, and his own private means were reduced almost to vanishing point, and under such circumstances the great style loses many of its finer savors. He was very fond of Lucian, and cheered by his return, but in the evening he would be a sad man again, with his head resting on one hand, and eyes reproaching sorry fortune.

Nobody called out "Here's your master with Master Lucian; you can get tea ready," when the pony jogged up to the front door. His mother had been dead a year, and a cousin kept house. She was a respectable person called Deacon, of middle age, and ordinary standards; and, consequently, there was cold mutton on the table. There was a cake, but nothing of flour, baked in ovens, would rise at Miss Deacon's evocation. Still, the meal was laid in the beloved "parlor," with the view of hills and valleys and climbing woods from the open window, and the old furniture was still pleasant to see, and the old books in the shelves had many memories. One of the most respected of the armchairs had become weak in the castors and had to be artfully propped up, but Lucian found it very comfortable after the hard forms. When tea was over he went out and strolled in the garden and orchards, and looked over the stile down into the brake, where foxgloves and bracken and broom mingled with the hazel undergrowth, where he knew of secret glades and untracked recesses, deep in the woven green, the cabinets for many years of his lonely meditations. Every path about his home, every field and hedgerow had dear and friendly memories for him; and the odor of the meadowsweet was better than the incense steaming in the sunshine. He loitered, and hung over the stile till the far-off woods began to turn purple, till the white mists were wreathing in the valley.

Day after day, through all that August, morning and evening were wrapped in haze; day after day the earth shimmered in the heat, and the air was strange, unfamiliar. As he wandered in the lanes and sauntered by the cool sweet verge of the woods, he saw and felt that nothing was common or accustomed, for the sunlight transfigured the meadows and changed all the form of the earth. Under the violent Provençal sun, the elms and beeches looked exotic trees, and in the early morning, when the mists were thick, the hills had put on an unearthly shape.

The one adventure of the holidays was the visit to the Roman fort, to that fantastic hill about whose steep bastions and haggard oaks he had seen the flames of sunset writhing nearly three years before. Ever since that Saturday evening in January, the lonely valley had been a desirable place to him; he had watched the green battlements in summer and winter weather, had seen the heaped mounds rising dimly amidst the drifting rain, had marked the violent height swim up from the ice-white mists of summer evenings, had watched the fairy bulwarks glimmer and vanish in hovering April twilight. In the hedge of the lane there was a gate on which he used to lean and look down south to where the hill surged up so suddenly, its summit defined on summer evenings not only by the rounded ramparts but by the ring of dense green foliage that marked the circle of oak trees. Higher up the lane, on the way he had come that Saturday afternoon, one could see the white walls of Morgan's farm on the hillside to the north, and on the south there was the stile with the view of old Mrs. Gibbon's cottage smoke; but down in the hollow, looking over the gate, there was no hint of human work, except those green and antique battlements, on which the oaks stood in circle, guarding the inner wood.

The ring of the fort drew him with stronger fascination during that hot August weather. Standing, or as his headmaster would have said, "mooning" by the gate, and looking into that enclosed and secret valley, it seemed to his fancy as if there were a halo about the hill, an aureole that played like flame around it. One afternoon as he gazed from his station by the gate the sheer sides and the swelling bulwarks were more than ever things of enchantment; the green oak ring stood out against the sky as still and bright as in a picture, and Lucian, in spite of his respect for the law of trespass, slid over the gate. The farmers and their men were busy on the uplands with the harvest, and the adventure was irresistible. At first he stole along by the brook in the shadow of the alders, where the grass and the flowers of wet meadows grew richly; but as he drew nearer to the fort, and its height now rose sheer above him, he left all shelter, and began desperately to mount. There was not a breath of wind; the sunlight shone down on the bare hillside; the loud chirp of the grasshoppers was the only sound. It was a steep ascent and grew steeper as the valley sank away. He turned for a moment, and looked down towards the stream which now seemed to wind remote between the alders; above the valley there were small dark figures moving in the cornfield, and now and again there came the faint echo of a high-pitched voice singing through the air as on a wire. He was wet with heat; the sweat streamed off his face, and he could feel it trickling all over his body. But above him the green bastions rose defiant, and the dark ring of oaks promised coolness. He pressed on, and higher, and at last began to crawl up the vallum, on hands and knees, grasping the turf and here and there the roots that had burst through the red earth. And then he lay, panting with deep breaths, on the summit.

Within the fort it was all dusky and cool and hollow; it was as if one stood at the bottom of a great cup. Within, the wall seemed higher than without, and the ring of oaks curved up like a dark green vault. There were nettles growing thick and rank in the foss; they looked different from the common nettles in the lanes, and Lucian, letting his hand touch a leaf by accident, felt the sting burn like fire. Beyond the ditch there was an undergrowth, a dense thicket of trees, stunted and old, crooked and withered by the winds into awkward and ugly forms; beech and oak and hazel and ash and yew twisted and so shortened and deformed that each seemed, like the nettle, of no common kind. He began to fight his way through the ugly growth, stumbling and getting hard knocks from the rebound of twisted boughs. His foot struck once or twice against something harder than wood, and looking down he saw stones white with the leprosy of age, but still showing the work of the axe. And farther, the roots of the stunted trees gripped the foot-high relics of a wall; and a round heap of fallen stones nourished rank, unknown herbs, that smelt poisonous. The earth was black and unctuous, and bubbling under the feet, left no track behind. From it, in the darkest places where the shadow was thickest, swelled the growth of an abominable fungus, making the still air sick with its corrupt odor, and he shuddered as he felt the horrible thing pulped beneath his feet. Then there was a gleam of sunlight, and as he thrust the last boughs apart, he stumbled into the open space in the heart of the camp. It was a lawn of sweet close turf in the center of the matted brake, of clean firm earth from which no shameful growth sprouted, and near the middle of the glade was a stump of a felled yew-tree, left untrimmed by the woodman. Lucian thought it must have been made for a seat; a crooked bough through which a little sap still ran was a support for the back, and he sat down and rested after his toil. It was not really so comfortable a seat as one of the school forms, but the satisfaction was to find anything at all that would serve for a chair. He sat there, still panting after the climb and his struggle through the dank and jungle-like thicket, and he felt as if he were growing hotter and hotter; the sting of the nettle was burning his hand, and the tingling fire seemed to spread all over his body.

Suddenly, he knew that he was alone. Not merely solitary; that he had often been amongst the woods and deep in the lanes; but now it was a wholly different and a very strange sensation. He thought of the valley winding far below him, all its fields by the brook green and peaceful and still, without path or track. Then he had climbed the abrupt surge of the hill, and passing the green and swelling battlements, the ring of oaks, and the matted thicket, had come to the central space. And behind there were, he knew, many desolate fields, wild as common, untrodden, unvisited. He was utterly alone. He still grew hotter as he sat on the stump, and at last lay down at full length on the soft grass, and more at his ease felt the waves of heat pass over his body.

And then he began to dream, to let his fancies stray over half-imagined, delicious things, indulging a virgin mind in its wanderings. The hot air seemed to beat upon him in palpable waves, and the nettle sting tingled and itched intolerably; and he was alone upon the fairy hill, within the great mounds, within the ring of oaks, deep in the heart of the matted thicket. Slowly and timidly he began to untie his boots, fumbling with the laces, and glancing all the while on every side at the ugly misshapen trees that hedged the lawn. Not a branch was straight, not one was free, but all were interlaced and grew one about another; and just above ground, where the cankered stems joined the protuberant roots, there were forms that imitated the human shape, and faces and twining limbs that amazed him. Green mosses were hair, and tresses were stark in grey lichen; a twisted root swelled into a limb; in the hollows of the rotted bark he saw the masks of men. His eyes were fixed and fascinated by the simulacra of the wood, and could not see his hands, and so at last, and suddenly, it seemed, he lay in the sunlight, beautiful with his olive skin, dark haired, dark eyed, the gleaming bodily vision of a strayed faun.

Quick flames now quivered in the substance of his nerves, hints of mysteries, secrets of life passed trembling through his brain, unknown desires stung him. As he gazed across the turf and into the thicket, the sunshine seemed really to become green, and the contrast between the bright glow poured on the lawn and the black shadow of the brake made an odd flickering light, in which all the grotesque postures of stem and root began to stir; the wood was alive. The turf beneath him heaved and sank as with the deep swell of the sea. He fell asleep, and lay still on the grass, in the midst of the thicket.

He found out afterwards that he must have slept for nearly an hour. The shadows had changed when he awoke; his senses came to him with a sudden shock, and he sat up and stared at his bare limbs in stupid amazement. He huddled on his clothes and laced his boots, wondering what folly had beset him. Then, while he stood indecisive, hesitating, his brain a whirl of puzzled thought, his body trembling, his hands shaking; as with electric heat, sudden remembrance possessed him. A flaming blush shone red on his cheeks, and glowed and thrilled through his limbs. As he awoke, a brief and slight breeze had stirred in a nook of the matted boughs, and there was a glinting that might have been the flash of sudden sunlight across shadow, and the branches rustled and murmured for a moment, perhaps at the wind's passage.

He stretched out his hands, and cried to his visitant to return; he entreated the dark eyes that had shone over him, and the scarlet lips that had kissed him. And then panic fear rushed into his heart, and he ran blindly, dashing through the wood. He climbed the vallum, and looked out, crouching, lest anybody should see him. Only the shadows were changed, and a breath of cooler air mounted from the brook; the fields were still and peaceful, the black figures moved, far away, amidst the corn, and the faint echo of the high-pitched voices sang thin and distant on the evening wind. Across the stream, in the cleft on the hill, opposite to the fort, the blue wood smoke stole up a spiral pillar from the chimney of old Mrs. Gibbon's cottage. He began to run full tilt down the steep surge of the hill, and never stopped till he was over the gate and in the lane again. As he looked back, down the valley to the south, and saw the violent ascent, the green swelling bulwarks, and the dark ring of oaks; the sunlight seemed to play about the fort with an aureole of flame.

"Where on earth have you been all this time, Lucian?" said his cousin when he got home. "Why, you look quite ill. It is really madness of you to go walking in such weather as this. I wonder you haven't got a sunstroke. And the tea must be nearly cold. I couldn't keep your father waiting, you know."

He muttered something about being rather tired, and sat down to his tea. It was not cold, for the "cozy" had been put over the pot, but it was black and bitter strong, as his cousin expressed it. The draught was unpalatable, but it did him good, and the thought came with great consolation that he had only been asleep and dreaming queer, nightmarish dreams. He shook off all his fancies with resolution, and thought the loneliness of the camp, and the burning sunlight, and possibly the nettle sting, which still tingled most abominably, must have been the only factors in his farrago of impossible recollections. He remembered that when he had felt the sting, he had seized a nettle with thick folds of his handkerchief, and having twisted off a good length, and put it in his pocket to show his father. Mr. Taylor was almost interested when he came in from his evening stroll about the garden and saw the specimen.

"Where did you manage to come across that, Lucian?" he said. "You haven't been to Caermaen, have you?"

"No. I got it in the Roman fort by the common."

"Oh, the twyn. You must have been trespassing then. Do you know what it is?"

"No. I thought it looked different from the common nettles."

"Yes; it's a Roman nettle—arctic pilulifera. It's a rare plant. Burrows says it's to be found at Caermaen, but I was never able to come across it. I must add it to the flora of the parish."

Mr. Taylor had begun to compile a flora accompanied by a hortus siccus, but both stayed on high shelves dusty and fragmentary. He put the specimen on his desk, intending to fasten it in the book, but the maid swept it away, dry and withered, in a day or two.

Lucian tossed and cried out in his sleep that night, and the awakening in the morning was, in a measure, a renewal of the awakening in the fort. But the impression was not so strong, and in a plain room it seemed all delirium, a phantasmagoria. He had to go down to Caermaen in the afternoon, for Mrs. Dixon, the vicar's wife, had "commanded" his presence at tea. Mr. Dixon, though fat and short and clean shaven, ruddy of face, was a safe man, with no extreme views on anything. He "deplored" all extreme party convictions, and thought the great needs of our beloved Church were conciliation, moderation, and above all "amolgamation"—so he pronounced the word. Mrs. Dixon was tall, imposing, splendid, well fitted for the Episcopal order, with gifts that would have shone at the palace. There were daughters, who studied German Literature, and thought Miss Frances Ridley Havergal wrote poetry, but Lucian had no fear of them; he dreaded the boys. Everybody said they were such fine, manly fellows, such gentlemanly boys, with such a good manner, sure to get on in the world. Lucian had said "Bother!" in a very violent manner when the gracious invitation was conveyed to him, but there was no getting out of it. Miss Deacon did her best to make him look smart; his ties were all so disgraceful that she had to supply the want with a narrow ribbon of a sky-blue tint; and she brushed him so long and so violently that he quite understood why a horse sometimes bites and sometimes kicks the groom. He set out between two and three in a gloomy frame of mind; he knew too well what spending the afternoon with honest manly boys meant. He found the reality more lurid than his anticipation. The boys were in the field, and the first remark he heard when he got in sight of the group was:

"Hullo, Lucian, how much for the tie?" "Fine tie," another, a stranger, observed. "You bagged it from the kitten, didn't you?"

Then they made up a game of cricket, and he was put in first. He was l.b.w. in his second over, so they all said, and had to field for the rest of the afternoon. Arthur Dixon, who was about his own age, forgetting all the laws of hospitality, told him he was a beastly muff when he missed a catch, rather a difficult catch. He missed several catches, and it seemed as if he were always panting after balls, which, as Edward Dixon said, any fool, even a baby, could have stopped. At last the game broke up, solely from Lucian's lack of skill, as everybody declared. Edward Dixon, who was thirteen, and had a swollen red face and a projecting eye, wanted to fight him for spoiling the game, and the others agreed that he funked the fight in a rather dirty manner. The strange boy, who was called De Carti, and was understood to be faintly related to Lord De Carti of M'Carthytown, said openly that the fellows at his place wouldn't stand such a sneak for five minutes. So the afternoon passed off very pleasantly indeed, till it was time to go into the vicarage for weak tea, homemade cake, and unripe plums. He got away at last. As he went out at the gate, he heard De Carti's final observation:

"We like to dress well at our place. His governor must be beastly poor to let him go about like that. D'y' see his trousers are all ragged at heel? Is old Taylor a gentleman?"

It had been a very gentlemanly afternoon, but there was a certain relief when the vicarage was far behind, and the evening smoke of the little town, once the glorious capital of Siluria, hung haze-like over the ragged roofs and mingled with the river mist. He looked down from the height of the road on the huddled houses, saw the points of light start out suddenly from the cottages on the hillside beyond, and gazed at the long lovely valley fading in the twilight, till the darkness came and all that remained was the somber ridge of the forest. The way was pleasant through the solemn scented lane, with glimpses of dim country, the vague mystery of night overshadowing the woods and meadows. A warm wind blew gusts of odor from the meadowsweet by the brook, now and then bee and beetle span homeward through the air, booming a deep note as from a great organ far away, and from the verge of the wood came the "who-oo, who-oo, who-oo" of the owls, a wild strange sound that mingled with the whirr and rattle of the night-jar, deep in the bracken. The moon swam up through the films of misty cloud, and hung, a golden glorious lantern, in mid-air; and, set in the dusky hedge, the little green fires of the glowworms appeared. He sauntered slowly up the lane, drinking in the religion of the scene, and thinking the country by night as mystic and wonderful as a dimly-lit cathedral. He had quite forgotten the "manly young fellows" and their sports, and only wished as the land began to shimmer and gleam in the moonlight that he knew by some medium of words or color how to represent the loveliness about his way.

"Had a pleasant evening, Lucian?" said his father when he came in.

"Yes, I had a nice walk home. Oh, in the afternoon we played cricket. I didn't care for it much. There was a boy named De Carti there; he is staying with the Dixons. Mrs. Dixon whispered to me when we were going in to tea, 'He's a second cousin of Lord De Carti's,' and she looked quite grave as if she were in church."

The parson grinned grimly and lit his old pipe.

"Baron De Carti's great-grandfather was a Dublin attorney," he remarked. "Which his name was Jeremiah M'Carthy. His prejudiced fellow-citizens called him the Unjust Steward, also the Bloody Attorney, and I believe that 'to hell with M'Carthy' was quite a popular cry about the time of the Union."

Mr. Taylor was a man of very wide and irregular reading and a tenacious memory; he often used to wonder why he had not risen in the Church. He had once told Mr. Dixon a singular and drolatique anecdote concerning the bishop's college days, and he never discovered why the prelate did not bow according to his custom when the name of Taylor was called at the next visitation. Some people said the reason was lighted candles, but that was impossible, as the Reverend and Honorable Smallwood Stafford, Lord Beamys's son, who had a cure of souls in the cathedral city, was well known to burn no end of candles, and with him the bishop was on the best of terms. Indeed the bishop often stayed at Coplesey (pronounced "Copsey") Hall, Lord Beamys's place in the west.

Lucian had mentioned the name of De Carti with intention, and had perhaps exaggerated a little Mrs. Dixon's respectful manner. He knew such incidents cheered his father, who could never look at these subjects from a proper point of view, and, as people said, sometimes made the strangest remarks for a clergyman. This irreverent way of treating serious things was one of the great bonds between father and son, but it tended to increase their isolation. People said they would often have liked to asked Mr. Taylor to garden-parties, and tea-parties, and other cheap entertainments, if only he had not been such an extreme man and so queer. Indeed, a year before, Mr. Taylor had gone to a garden-party at the Castle, Caermaen, and had made such fun of the bishop's recent address on missions to the Portuguese, that the Gervases and Dixons and all who heard him were quite shocked and annoyed. And, as Mrs. Meyrick of Lanyravon observed, his black coat was perfectly green with age; so on the whole the Gervases did not like to invite Mr. Taylor again. As for the son, nobody cared to have him; Mrs. Dixon, as she said to her husband, really asked him out of charity.

"I am afraid he seldom gets a real meal at home," she remarked, "so I thought he would enjoy a good wholesome tea for once in a way. But he is such an unsatisfactory boy, he would only have one slice of that nice plain cake, and I couldn't get him to take more than two plums. They were really quite ripe too, and boys are usually so fond of fruit."

Thus Lucian was forced to spend his holidays chiefly in his own company, and make the best he could of the ripe peaches on the south wall of the rectory garden. There was a certain corner where the heat of that hot August seemed concentrated, reverberated from one wall to the other, and here he liked to linger of mornings, when the mists were still thick in the valleys, "mooning," meditating, extending his walk from the quince to the medlar and back again, beside the moldering walls of mellowed brick. He was full of a certain wonder and awe, not unmixed with a swell of strange exultation, and wished more and more to be alone, to think over that wonderful afternoon within the fort. In spite of himself the impression was fading; he could not understand that feeling of mad panic terror that drove him through the thicket and down the steep hillside; yet, he had experienced so clearly the physical shame and reluctance of the flesh; he recollected that for a few seconds after his awakening the sight of his own body had made him shudder and writhe as if it had suffered some profoundest degradation. He saw before him a vision of two forms; a faun with tingling and prickling flesh lay expectant in the sunlight, and there was also the likeness of a miserable shamed boy, standing with trembling body and shaking, unsteady hands. It was all confused, a procession of blurred images, now of rapture and ecstasy, and now of terror and shame, floating in a light that was altogether phantasmal and unreal. He dared not approach the fort again; he lingered in the road to Caermaen that passed behind it, but a mile away, and separated by the wild land and a strip of wood from the towering battlements. Here he was looking over a gate one day, doubtful and wondering, when he heard a heavy step behind him, and glancing round quickly saw it was old Morgan of the White House.

"Good afternoon, Master Lucian," he began. "Mr. Taylor pretty well, I suppose? I be goin' to the house a minute; the men in the fields are wantin' some more cider. Would you come and taste a drop of cider, Master Lucian? It's very good, sir, indeed."

Lucian did not want any cider, but he thought it would please old Morgan if he took some, so he said he should like to taste the cider very much indeed. Morgan was a sturdy, thick-set old man of the ancient stock; a stiff churchman, who breakfasted regularly on fat broth and Caerphilly cheese in the fashion of his ancestors; hot, spiced elder wine was for winter nights, and gin for festal seasons. The farm had always been the freehold of the family, and when Lucian, in the wake of the yeoman, passed through the deep porch by the oaken door, down into the long dark kitchen, he felt as though the seventeenth century still lingered on. One mullioned window, set deep in the sloping wall, gave all the light there was through quarries of thick glass in which there were whorls and circles, so that the lapping rose-branch and the garden and the fields beyond were distorted to the sight. Two heavy beams, oaken but whitewashed, ran across the ceiling; a little glow of fire sparkled in the great fireplace, and a curl of blue smoke fled up the cavern of the chimney. Here was the genuine chimney-corner of our fathers; there were seats on each side of the fireplace where one could sit snug and sheltered on December nights, warm and merry in the blazing light, and listen to the battle of the storm, and hear the flame spit and hiss at the falling snowflakes. At the back of the fire were great blackened tiles with raised initials and a date.--I.M., 1684.

"Sit down, Master Lucian, sit down, sir," said Morgan.

"Annie," he called through one of the numerous doors, "here's Master Lucian, the parson, would like a drop of cider. Fetch a jug, will you, directly?"

"Very well, father," came the voice from the dairy and presently the girl entered, wiping the jug she held. In his boyish way Lucian had been a good deal disturbed by Annie Morgan; he could see her on Sundays from his seat in church, and her skin, curiously pale, her lips that seemed as though they were stained with some brilliant pigment, her black hair, and the quivering black eyes, gave him odd fancies which he had hardly shaped to himself. Annie had grown into a woman in three years, and he was still a boy. She came into the kitchen, curtsying and smiling.

"Good-day, Master Lucian, and how is Mr. Taylor, sir?"

"Pretty well, thank you. I hope you are well."

"Nicely, sir, thank you. How nice your voice do sound in church, Master Lucian, to be sure. I was telling father about it last Sunday."

Lucian grinned and felt uncomfortable, and the girl set down the jug on the round table and brought a glass from the dresser. She bent close over him as she poured out the green oily cider, fragrant of the orchard; her hand touched his shoulder for a moment, and she said, "I beg your pardon, sir," very prettily. He looked up eagerly at her face; the black eyes, a little oval in shape, were shining, and the lips smiled. Annie wore a plain dress of some black stuff, open at the throat; her skin was beautiful. For a moment the ghost of a fancy hovered unsubstantial in his mind; and then Annie curtsied as she handed him the cider, and replied to his thanks with, "And welcome kindly, sir."

The drink was really good; not thin, nor sweet, but round and full and generous, with a fine yellow flame twinkling through the green when one held it up to the light. It was like a stray sunbeam hovering on the grass in a deep orchard, and he swallowed the glassful with relish, and had some more, warmly commending it. Mr. Morgan was touched.

"I see you do know a good thing, sir," he said. "Is, indeed, now, it's good stuff, though it's my own makin'. My old grandfather he planted the trees in the time of the wars, and he was a very good judge of an apple in his day and generation. And a famous grafter he was, to be sure. You will never see no swelling in the trees he grafted at all whatever. Now there's James Morris, Penyrhaul, he's a famous grafter, too, and yet them Redstreaks he grafted for me five year ago, they be all swollen-like below the graft already. Would you like to taste a Blemmin pippin, now, Master Lucian? there be a few left in the loft, I believe."

Lucian said he should like an apple very much, and the farmer went out by another door, and Annie stayed in the kitchen talking. She said Mrs. Trevor, her married sister, was coming to them soon to spend a few days.

"She's got such a beautiful baby," said Annie, "and he's quite sensible-like already, though he's only nine months old. Mary would like to see you, sir, if you would be so kind as to step in; that is, if it's not troubling you at all, Master Lucian. I suppose you must be getting a fine scholar now, sir?"

"I am doing pretty well, thank you," said the boy. "I was first in my form last term."

"Fancy! To think of that! D'you hear, father, what a scholar Master Lucian be getting?"

"He be a rare grammarian, I'm sure," said the farmer. "You do take after your father, sir; I always do say that nobody have got such a good deliverance in the pulpit."

Lucian did not find the Blenheim Orange as good as the cider, but he ate it with all the appearance of relish, and put another, with thanks, in his pocket. He thanked the farmer again when he got up to go; and Annie curtsied and smiled, and wished him good-day, and welcome, kindly.

Lucian heard her saying to her father as he went out what a nice-mannered young gentleman he was getting, to be sure; and he went on his way, thinking that Annie was really very pretty, and speculating as to whether he would have the courage to kiss her, if they met in a dark lane. He was quite sure she would only laugh, and say, "Oh, Master Lucian!"

For many months he had occasional fits of recollection, both cold and hot; but the bridge of time, gradually lengthening, made those dreadful and delicious images grow more and more indistinct, till at last they all passed into that wonderland which a youth looks back upon in amazement, not knowing why this used to be a symbol of terror or that of joy. At the end of each term he would come home and find his father a little more despondent, and harder to cheer even for a moment; and the wall paper and the furniture grew more and more dingy and shabby. The two cats, loved and ancient beasts, that he remembered when he was quite a little boy, before he went to school, died miserably, one after the other. Old Polly, the pony, at last fell down in the stable from the weakness of old age, and had to be killed there; the battered old trap ran no longer along the well-remembered lanes. There was long meadow grass on the lawn, and the trained fruit trees on the wall had got quite out of hand. At last, when Lucian was seventeen, his father was obliged to take him from school; he could no longer afford the fees. This was the sorry ending of many hopes, and dreams of a double-first, a fellowship, distinction and glory that the poor parson had long entertained for his son, and the two moped together, in the shabby room, one on each side of the sulky fire, thinking of dead days and finished plans, and seeing a grey future in the years that advanced towards them. At one time there seemed some chance of a distant relative coming forward to Lucian's assistance; and indeed it was quite settled that he should go up to London with certain definite aims. Mr. Taylor told the good news to his acquaintances--his coat was too green now for any pretence of friendship; and Lucian himself spoke of his plans to Burrows the doctor and Mr. Dixon, and one or two others. Then the whole scheme fell through, and the parson and his son suffered much sympathy. People, of course, had to say they were sorry, but in reality the news was received with high spirits, with the joy with which one sees a stone, as it rolls down a steep place, give yet another bounding leap towards the pool beneath. Mrs. Dixon heard the pleasant tidings from Mrs. Colley, who came in to talk about the Mothers' Meeting and the Band of Hope. Mrs. Dixon was nursing little Athelwig, or some such name, at the time, and made many affecting observations on the general righteousness with which the world was governed. Indeed, poor Lucian's disappointment seemed distinctly to increase her faith in the Divine Order, as if it had been some example in Butler's Analogy.

"Aren't Mr. Taylor's views very extreme?" she said to her husband the same evening.

"I am afraid they are," he replied. "I was quite grieved at the last Diocesan Conference at the way in which he spoke. The dear old bishop had given an address on Auricular Confession; he was forced to do so, you know, after what had happened, and I must say that I never felt prouder of our beloved Church."

Mr. Dixon told all the Homeric story of the conference, reciting the achievements of the champions, "deploring" this and applauding that. It seemed that Mr. Taylor had had the audacity to quote authorities which the bishop could not very well repudiate, though they were directly opposed to the "safe" Episcopal pronouncement.

Mrs. Dixon of course was grieved; it was "sad" to think of a clergyman behaving so shamefully.

"But you know, dear," she proceeded, "I have been thinking about that unfortunate Taylor boy and his disappointments, and after what you've just told me, I am sure it's some kind of judgment on them both. Has Mr. Taylor forgotten the vows he took at his ordination? But don't you think, dear, I am right, and that he has been punished: 'The sins of the fathers'?"

Somehow or other Lucian divined the atmosphere of threatenings and judgments, and shrank more and more from the small society of the countryside. For his part, when he was not "mooning" in the beloved fields and woods of happy memory, he shut himself up with books, reading whatever could be found on the shelves, and amassing a store of incongruous and obsolete knowledge. Long did he linger with the men of the seventeenth century; delaying the gay sunlit streets with Pepys, and listening to the charmed sound of the Restoration Revel; roaming by peaceful streams with Izaak Walton, and the great Catholic divines; enchanted with the portrait of Herbert the loving ascetic; awed by the mystic breath of Crashaw. Then the cavalier poets sang their gallant songs; and Herrick made Dean Prior magic ground by the holy incantation of a verse. And in the old proverbs and homely sayings of the time he found the good and beautiful English life, a time full of grace and dignity and rich merriment. He dived deeper and deeper into his books; he had taken all obsolescence to be his province; in his disgust at the stupid usual questions, "Will it pay?" "What good is it?" and so forth, he would only read what was uncouth and useless. The strange pomp and symbolism of the Cabala, with its hint of more terrible things; the Rosicrucian mysteries of Fludd, the enigmas of Vaughan, dreams of alchemists--all these were his delight. Such were his companions, with the hills and hanging woods, the brooks and lonely waterpools; books, the thoughts of books, the stirrings of imagination, all fused into one phantasy by the magic of the outland country. He held himself aloof from the walls of the fort; he was content to see the heaped mounds, the violent height with faerie bulwarks, from the gate in the lane, and to leave all within the ring of oaks in the mystery of his boyhood's vision. He professed to laugh at himself and at his fancies of that hot August afternoon, when sleep came to him within the thicket, but in his heart of hearts there was something that never faded--something that glowed like the red glint of a gypsy's fire seen from afar across the hills and mists of the night, and known to be burning in a wild land. Sometimes, when he was sunken in his books, the flame of delight shot up, and showed him a whole province and continent of his nature, all shining and aglow; and in the midst of the exultation and triumph he would draw back, a little afraid. He had become ascetic in his studious and melancholy isolation, and the vision of such ecstasies frightened him. He began to write a little; at first very tentatively and feebly, and then with more confidence. He showed some of his verses to his father, who told him with a sigh that he had once hoped to write--in the old days at Oxford, he added.

"They are very nicely done," said the parson; "but I'm afraid you won't find anybody to print them, my boy."

So he pottered on; reading everything, imitating what struck his fancy, attempting the effect of the classic meters in English verse, trying his hand at a masque, a Restoration comedy, forming impossible plans for books which rarely got beyond half a dozen lines on a sheet of paper; beset with splendid fancies which refused to abide before the pen. But the vain joy of conception was not altogether vain, for it gave him some armor about his heart.

The months went by, monotonous, and sometimes blotted with despair. He wrote and planned and filled the waste-paper basket with hopeless efforts. Now and then he sent verses or prose articles to magazines, in pathetic ignorance of the trade. He felt the immense difficulty of the career of literature without clearly understanding it; the battle was happily in a mist, so that the host of the enemy, terribly arrayed, was to some extent hidden. Yet there was enough of difficulty to appall; from following the intricate course of little nameless brooks, from hushed twilight woods, from the vision of the mountains, and the breath of the great wind, passing from deep to deep, he would come home filled with thoughts and emotions, mystic fancies which he yearned to translate into the written word. And the result of the effort seemed always to be bathos! Wooden sentences, a portentous stilted style, obscurity, and awkwardness clogged the pen; it seemed impossible to win the great secret of language; the stars glittered only in the darkness, and vanished away in clearer light. The periods of despair were often long and heavy, the victories very few and trifling; night after night he sat writing after his father had knocked out his last pipe, filling a page with difficulty in an hour, and usually forced to thrust the stuff away in despair, and go unhappily to bed, conscious that after all his labor he had done nothing. And these were moments when the accustomed vision of the land alarmed him, and the wild domed hills and darkling woods seemed symbols of some terrible secret in the inner life of that stranger--himself. Sometimes when he was deep in his books and papers, sometimes on a lonely walk, sometimes amidst the tiresome chatter of Caermaen "society," he would thrill with a sudden sense of awful hidden things, and there ran that quivering flame through his nerves that brought back the recollection of the matted thicket, and that earlier appearance of the bare black boughs enwrapped with flames. Indeed, though he avoided the solitary lane, and the sight of the sheer height, with its ring of oaks and molded mounds, the image of it grew more intense as the symbol of certain hints and suggestions. The exultant and insurgent flesh seemed to have its temple and castle within those olden walls, and he longed with all his heart to escape, to set himself free in the wilderness of London, and to be secure amidst the murmur of modern streets.

II

Lucian was growing really anxious about his manuscript. He had gained enough experience at twenty-three to know that editors and publishers must not be hurried; but his book had been lying at Messrs Beit's office for more than three months. For six weeks he had not dared to expect an answer, but afterwards life had become agonizing. Every morning, at post-time, the poor wretch nearly choked with anxiety to know whether his sentence had arrived, and the rest of the day was racked with alternate pangs of hope and despair. Now and then he was almost assured of success; conning over these painful and eager pages in memory, he found parts that were admirable, while again, his inexperience reproached him, and he feared he had written a raw and awkward book, wholly unfit for print. Then he would compare what he remembered of it with notable magazine articles and books praised by reviewers, and fancy that after all there might be good points in the thing; he could not help liking the first chapter for instance. Perhaps the letter might come tomorrow. So it went on; week after week of sick torture made more exquisite by such gleams of hope; it was as if he were stretched in anguish on the rack, and the pain relaxed and kind words spoken now and again by the tormentors, and then once more the grinding pang and burning agony. At last he could bear suspense no longer, and he wrote to Messrs Beit, inquiring in a humble manner whether the manuscript had arrived in safety. The firm replied in a very polite letter, expressing regret that their reader had been suffering from a cold in the head, and had therefore been unable to send in his report. A final decision was promised in a week's time, and the letter ended with apologies for the delay and a hope that he had suffered no inconvenience. Of course the "final decision" did not come at the end of the week, but the book was returned at the end of three weeks, with a circular thanking the author for his kindness in submitting the manuscript, and regretting that the firm did not see their way to producing it. He felt relieved; the operation that he had dreaded and deprecated for so long was at last over, and he would no longer grow sick of mornings when the letters were brought in. He took his parcel to the sunny corner of the garden, where the old wooden seat stood sheltered from the biting March winds. Messrs Beit had put in with the circular one of their short lists, a neat booklet, headed: Messrs Beit & Co.'s Recent Publications.

He settled himself comfortably on the seat, lit his pipe, and began to read: "A Bad Un to Beat: a Novel of Sporting Life, by the Honorable Mrs. Scudamore Runnymede, author of Yoicks, With the Mudshire Pack, The Sportleigh Stables, etc., etc., 3 vols. At all Libraries." The Press, it seemed, pronounced this to be a "charming book. Mrs. Runnymede has wit and humor enough to furnish forth half-a-dozen ordinary sporting novels." "Told with the sparkle and vivacity of a past-mistress in the art of novel writing," said the Review; while Miranda, of Smart Society, positively bubbled with enthusiasm. "You must forgive me, Aminta," wrote this young person, "if I have not sent the description I promised of Madame Lulu's new creations and others of that ilk. I must a tale unfold; Tom came in yesterday and began to rave about the Honorable Mrs. Scudamore Runnymede's last novel, A Bad Un to Beat. He says all the Smart Set are talking of it, and it seems the police have to regulate the crowd at Mudie's. You know I read everything Mrs. Runnymede writes, so I set out Miggs directly to beg, borrow or steal a copy, and I confess I burnt the midnight oil before I laid it down. Now, mind you get it, you will find it so awfully chic." Nearly all the novelists on Messrs Beit's list were ladies, their works all ran to three volumes, and all of them pleased the Press, the Review, and Miranda of Smart Society. One of these books, Millicent's Marriage, by Sarah Pocklington Sanders, was pronounced fit to lie on the school-room table, on the drawing-room bookshelf, or beneath the pillow of the most gently nurtured of our daughters. "This," the reviewer went on, "is high praise, especially in these days when we are deafened by the loud-voiced clamor of self-styled 'artists.' We would warn the young men who prate so persistently of style and literature, construction and prose harmonies, that we believe the English reading public will have none of them. Harmless amusement, a gentle flow of domestic interest, a faithful reproduction of the open and manly life of the hunting field, pictures of innocent and healthy English girlhood such as Miss Sanders here affords us; these are the topics that will always find a welcome in our homes, which remain bolted and barred against the abandoned artist and the scrofulous stylist."

He turned over the pages of the little book and chuckled in high relish; he discovered an honest enthusiasm, a determination to strike a blow for the good and true that refreshed and exhilarated. A beaming face, spectacled and whiskered probably, an expansive waistcoat, and a tender heart, seemed to shine through the words which Messrs Beit had quoted; and the alliteration of the final sentence; that was good too; there was style for you if you wanted it. The champion of the blushing cheek and the gushing eye showed that he too could handle the weapons of the enemy if he cared to trouble himself with such things. Lucian leant back and roared with indecent laughter till the tabby tom-cat who had succeeded to the poor dead beasts looked up reproachfully from his sunny corner, with a face like the reviewer's, innocent and round and whiskered. At last he turned to his parcel and drew out some half-dozen sheets of manuscript, and began to read in a rather desponding spirit; it was pretty obvious, he thought, that the stuff was poor and beneath the standard of publication. The book had taken a year and a half in the making; it was a pious attempt to translate into English prose the form and mystery of the domed hills, the magic of occult valleys, the sound of the red swollen brook swirling through leafless woods. Day-dreams and toil at nights had gone into the eager pages, he had labored hard to do his very best, writing and rewriting, weighing his cadences, beginning over and over again, grudging no patience, no trouble if only it might be pretty good; good enough to print and sell to a reading public which had become critical. He glanced through the manuscript in his hand, and to his astonishment, he could not help thinking that in its measure it was decent work. After three months his prose seemed fresh and strange as if it had been wrought by another man, and in spite of himself he found charming things, and impressions that were not commonplace. He knew how weak it all was compared with his own conceptions; he had seen an enchanted city, awful, glorious, with flame smitten about its battlements, like the cities of the Sangraal, and he had molded his copy in such poor clay as came to his hand; yet, in spite of the gulf that yawned between the idea and the work, he knew as he read that the thing accomplished was very far from a failure. He put back the leaves carefully, and glanced again at Messrs Beit's list. It had escaped his notice that A Bad Un to Beat was in its third three-volume edition. It was a great thing, at all events, to know in what direction to aim, if he wished to succeed. If he worked hard, he thought, he might some day win the approval of the coy and retiring Miranda of Smart Society; that modest maiden might in his praise interrupt her task of disinterested advertisement, her philanthropic counsels to "go to Jumper's, and mind you ask for Mr. C. Jumper, who will show you the lovely blue paper with the yellow spots at ten shillings the piece." He put down the pamphlet, and laughed again at the books and the reviewers: so that he might not weep. This then was English fiction, this was English criticism, and farce, after all, was but an ill-played tragedy.

The rejected manuscript was hidden away, and his father quoted Horace's maxim as to the benefit of keeping literary works for some time "in the wood." There was nothing to grumble at, though Lucian was inclined to think the duration of the reader's catarrh a little exaggerated. But this was a trifle; he did not arrogate to himself the position of a small commercial traveler, who expects prompt civility as a matter of course, and not at all as a favor. He simply forgot his old book, and resolved that he would make a better one if he could. With the hot fit of resolution, the determination not to be snuffed out by one refusal upon him, he began to beat about in his mind for some new scheme. At first it seemed that he had hit upon a promising subject; he began to plot out chapters and scribble hints for the curious story that had entered his mind, arranging his circumstances and noting the effects to be produced with all the enthusiasm of the artist. But after the first breath the aspect of the work changed; page after page was tossed aside as hopeless, the beautiful sentences he had dreamed of refused to be written, and his puppets remained stiff and wooden, devoid of life or motion. Then all the old despairs came back, the agonies of the artificer who strives and perseveres in vain; the scheme that seemed of amorous fire turned to cold hard ice in his hands. He let the pen drop from his fingers, and wondered how he could have ever dreamed of writing books. Again, the thought occurred that he might do something if he could only get away, and join the sad procession in the murmuring London streets, far from the shadow of those awful hills. But it was quite impossible; the relative who had once promised assistance was appealed to, and wrote expressing his regret that Lucian had turned out a "loafer," wasting his time in scribbling, instead of trying to earn his living. Lucian felt rather hurt at this letter, but the parson only grinned grimly as usual. He was thinking of how he signed a check many years before, in the days of his prosperity, and the check was payable to this didactic relative, then in but a poor way, and of a thankful turn of mind.

The old rejected manuscript had almost passed out of his recollection. It was recalled oddly enough. He was looking over the Reader, and enjoying the admirable literary criticisms, some three months after the return of his book, when his eye was attracted by a quoted passage in one of the notices. The thought and style both wakened memory, the cadences were familiar and beloved. He read through the review from the beginning; it was a very favorable one, and pronounced the volume an immense advance on Mr. Ritson's previous work. "Here, undoubtedly, the author has discovered a vein of pure metal," the reviewer added, "and we predict that he will go far." Lucian had not yet reached his father's stage, he was unable to grin in the manner of that irreverent parson. The passage selected for high praise was taken almost word for word from the manuscript now resting in his room, the work that had not reached the high standard of Messrs Beit & Co., who, curiously enough, were the publishers of the book reviewed in the Reader. He had a few shillings in his possession, and wrote at once to a bookseller in London for a copy of The Chorus in Green, as the author had oddly named the book. He wrote on June 21st and thought he might fairly expect to receive the interesting volume by the 24th; but the postman, true to his tradition, brought nothing for him, and in the afternoon he resolved to walk down to Caermaen, in case it might have come by a second post; or it might have been mislaid at the office; they forgot parcels sometimes, especially when the bag was heavy and the weather hot. This 24th was a sultry and oppressive day; a grey veil of cloud obscured the sky, and a vaporous mist hung heavily over the land, and fumed up from the valleys. But at five o'clock, when he started, the clouds began to break, and the sunlight suddenly streamed down through the misty air, making ways and channels of rich glory, and bright islands in the gloom. It was a pleasant and shining evening when, passing by devious back streets to avoid the barbarians (as he very rudely called the respectable inhabitants of the town), he reached the post-office; which was also the general shop.

"Yes, Mr. Taylor, there is something for you, sir," said the man. "Williams the postman forgot to take it up this morning," and he handed over the packet. Lucian took it under his arm and went slowly through the ragged winding lanes till he came into the country. He got over the first stile on the road, and sitting down in the shelter of a hedge, cut the strings and opened the parcel. The Chorus in Green was got up in what reviewers call a dainty manner: a bronze-green cloth, well-cut gold lettering, wide margins and black "old-face" type, all witnessed to the good taste of Messrs Beit & Co. He cut the pages hastily and began to read. He soon found that he had wronged Mr. Ritson--that old literary hand had by no means stolen his book wholesale, as he had expected. There were about two hundred pages in the pretty little volume, and of these about ninety were Lucian's, dovetailed into a rather different scheme with skill that was nothing short of exquisite. And Mr. Ritson's own work was often very good; spoilt here and there for some tastes by the "cataloguing" method, a somewhat materialistic way of taking an inventory of the holy country things; but, for that very reason, contrasting to a great advantage with Lucian's hints and dreams and note of haunting. And here and there Mr. Ritson had made little alterations in the style of the passages he had conveyed, and most of these alterations were amendments, as Lucian was obliged to confess, though he would have liked to argue one or two points with his collaborator and corrector. He lit his pipe and leant back comfortably in the hedge, thinking things over, weighing very coolly his experience of humanity, his contact with the "society" of the countryside, the affair of the The Chorus in Green, and even some little incidents that had struck him as he was walking through the streets of Caermaen that evening. At the post-office, when he was inquiring for his parcel, he had heard two old women grumbling in the street; it seemed, so far as he could make out, that both had been disappointed in much the same way. One was a Roman Catholic, hardened, and beyond the reach of conversion; she had been advised to ask alms of the priests, "who are always creeping and crawling about." The other old sinner was a Dissenter, and, "Mr. Dixon has quite enough to do to relieve good Church people."

Mrs. Dixon, assisted by Henrietta, was, it seemed, the lady high almoner, who dispensed these charities. As she said to Mrs. Colley, they would end by keeping all the beggars in the county, and they really couldn't afford it. A large family was an expensive thing, and the girls must have new frocks. "Mr. Dixon is always telling me and the girls that we must not demoralize the people by indiscriminate charity." Lucian had heard of these sage counsels, and through it them as he listened to the bitter complaints of the gaunt, hungry old women. In the back street by which he passed out of the town he saw a large "healthy" boy kicking a sick cat; the poor creature had just strength enough to crawl under an outhouse door; probably to die in torments. He did not find much satisfaction in thrashing the boy, but he did it with hearty good will. Further on, at the corner where the turnpike used to be, was a big notice, announcing a meeting at the school-room in aid of the missions to the Portuguese. "Under the Patronage of the Lord Bishop of the Diocese," was the imposing headline; the Reverend Merivale Dixon, vicar of Caermaen, was to be in the chair, supported by Stanley Gervase, Esq., J.P., and by many of the clergy and gentry of the neighborhood. Senhor Diabo, "formerly a Romanist priest, now an evangelist in Lisbon," would address the meeting. "Funds are urgently needed to carry on this good work," concluded the notice. So he lay well back in the shade of the hedge, and thought whether some sort of an article could not be made by vindicating the terrible Yahoos; one might point out that they were in many respects a simple and unsophisticated race, whose faults were the result of their enslaved position, while such virtues as they had were all their own. They might be compared, he thought, much to their advantage, with more complex civilizations. There was no hint of anything like the Beit system of publishing in existence amongst them; the great Yahoo nation would surely never feed and encourage a scabby Houyhnhnm, expelled for his foulness from the horse-community, and the witty dean, in all his minuteness, had said nothing of "safe" Yahoos. On reflection, however, he did not feel quite secure of this part of his defense; he remembered that the leading brutes had favorites, who were employed in certain simple domestic offices about their masters, and it seemed doubtful whether the contemplated vindication would not break down on this point. He smiled queerly to himself as he thought of these comparisons, but his heart burned with a dull fury. Throwing back his unhappy memory, he recalled all the contempt and scorn he had suffered; as a boy he had heard the masters murmuring their disdain of him and of his desire to learn other than ordinary school work. As a young man he had suffered the insolence of these wretched people about him; their cackling laughter at his poverty jarred and grated in his ears; he saw the acrid grin of some miserable idiot woman, some creature beneath the swine in intelligence and manners, merciless, as he went by with his eyes on the dust, in his ragged clothes. He and his father seemed to pass down an avenue of jeers and contempt, and contempt from such animals as these! This putrid filth, molded into human shape, made only to fawn on the rich and beslaver them, thinking no foulness too foul if it were done in honor of those in power and authority; and no refined cruelty of contempt too cruel if it were contempt of the poor and humble and oppressed; it was to this obscene and ghastly throng that he was something to be pointed at. And these men and women spoke of sacred things, and knelt before the awful altar of God, before the altar of tremendous fire, surrounded as they professed by Angels and Archangels and all the Company of Heaven; and in their very church they had one aisle for the rich and another for the poor. And the species was not peculiar to Caermaen; the rich business men in London and the successful brother author were probably amusing themselves at the expense of the poor struggling creature they had injured and wounded; just as the "healthy" boy had burst into a great laugh when the miserable sick cat cried out in bitter agony, and trailed its limbs slowly, as it crept away to die. Lucian looked into his own life and his own will; he saw that in spite of his follies, and his want of success, he had not been consciously malignant, he had never deliberately aided in oppression, or looked on it with enjoyment and approval, and he felt that when he lay dead beneath the earth, eaten by swarming worms, he would be in a purer company than now, when he lived amongst human creatures. And he was to call this loathsome beast, all sting and filth, brother! "I had rather call the devils my brothers, brother," he said in his heart, "I would fare better in hell." Blood was in his eyes, and as he looked up the sky seemed of blood, and the earth burned with fire.

The sun was sinking low on the mountain when he set out on the way again. Burrows, the doctor, coming home in his trap, met him a little lower on the road, and gave him a friendly good-night.

"A long way round on this road, isn't it?" said the doctor. "As you have come so far, why don't you try the short cut across the fields? You will find it easily enough; second stile on the left hand, and then go straight ahead."

He thanked Dr. Burrows and said he would try the short cut, and Burrows span on homeward. He was a gruff and honest bachelor, and often felt very sorry for the lad, and wished he could help him. As he drove on, it suddenly occurred to him that Lucian had an awful look on his face, and he was sorry he had not asked him to jump in, and to come to supper. A hearty slice of beef, with strong ale, whisky and soda afterwards, a good pipe, and certain Rabelaisian tales which the doctor had treasured for many years, would have done the poor fellow a lot of good, he was certain. He half turned round on his seat, and looked to see if Lucian were still in sight, but he had passed the corner, and the doctor drove on, shivering a little; the mists were beginning to rise from the wet banks of the river.

Lucian trailed slowly along the road, keeping a look out for the stile the doctor had mentioned. It would be a little of an adventure, he thought, to find his way by an unknown track; he knew the direction in which his home lay, and he imagined he would not have much difficulty in crossing from one stile to another. The path led him up a steep bare field, and when he was at the top, the town and the valley winding up to the north stretched before him. The river was stilled at the flood, and the yellow water, reflecting the sunset, glowed in its deep pools like dull brass. These burning pools, the level meadows fringed with shuddering reeds, the long dark sweep of the forest on the hill, were all clear and distinct, yet the light seemed to have clothed them with a new garment, even as voices from the streets of Caermaen sounded strangely, mounting up thin with the smoke. There beneath him lay the huddled cluster of Caermaen, the ragged and uneven roofs that marked the winding and sordid streets, here and there a pointed gable rising above its meaner fellows; beyond he recognized the piled mounds that marked the circle of the amphitheatre, and the dark edge of trees that grew where the Roman wall whitened and waxed old beneath the frosts and rains of eighteen hundred years. Thin and strange, mingled together, the voices came up to him on the hill; it was as if an outland race inhabited the ruined city and talked in a strange language of strange and terrible things. The sun had slid down the sky, and hung quivering over the huge dark dome of the mountain like a burnt sacrifice, and then suddenly vanished. In the afterglow the clouds began to writhe and turn scarlet, and shone so strangely reflected in the pools of the snake-like river, that one would have said the still waters stirred, the fleeting and changing of the clouds seeming to quicken the stream, as if it bubbled and sent up gouts of blood. But already about the town the darkness was forming; fast, fast the shadows crept upon it from the forest, and from all sides banks and wreaths of curling mist were gathering, as if a ghostly leaguer were being built up against the city, and the strange race who lived in its streets. Suddenly there burst out from the stillness the clear and piercing music of the réveillé, calling, recalling, iterated, reiterated, and ending with one long high fierce shrill note with which the steep hills rang. Perhaps a boy in the school band was practicing on his bugle, but for Lucian it was magic. For him it was the note of the Roman trumpet, tuba mirum spargens sonum, filling all the hollow valley with its command, reverberated in dark places in the far forest, and resonant in the old graveyards without the walls. In his imagination he saw the earthen gates of the tombs broken open, and the serried legion swarming to the eagles. Century by century they passed by; they rose, dripping, from the river bed, they rose from the level, their armor shone in the quiet orchard, they gathered in ranks and companies from the cemetery, and as the trumpet sounded, the hill fort above the town gave up its dead. By hundreds and thousands the ghostly battle surged about the standard, behind the quaking mist, ready to march against the moldering walls they had built so many years before.

He turned sharply; it was growing very dark, and he was afraid of missing his way. At first the path led him by the verge of a wood; there was a noise of rustling and murmuring from the trees as if they were taking evil counsel together. A high hedge shut out the sight of the darkening valley, and he stumbled on mechanically, without taking much note of the turnings of the track, and when he came out from the wood shadow to the open country, he stood for a moment quite bewildered and uncertain. A dark wild twilight country lay before him, confused dim shapes of trees near at hand, and a hollow below his feet, and the further hills and woods were dimmer, and all the air was very still. Suddenly the darkness about him glowed; a furnace fire had shot up on the mountain, and for a moment the little world of the woodside and the steep hill shone in a pale light, and he thought he saw his path beaten out in the turf before him. The great flame sank down to a red glint of fire, and it led him on down the ragged slope, his feet striking against ridges of ground, and falling from beneath him at a sudden dip. The bramble bushes shot out long prickly vines, amongst which he was entangled, and lower he was held back by wet bubbling earth. He had descended into a dark and shady valley, beset and tapestried with gloomy thickets; the weird wood noises were the only sounds, strange, unutterable mutterings, dismal, inarticulate. He pushed on in what he hoped was the right direction, stumbling from stile to gate, peering through mist and shadow, and still vainly seeking for any known landmark. Presently another sound broke upon the grim air, the murmur of water poured over stones, gurgling against the old misshapen roots of trees, and running clear in a deep channel. He passed into the chill breath of the brook, and almost fancied he heard two voices speaking in its murmur; there seemed a ceaseless utterance of words, an endless argument. With a mood of horror pressing on him, he listened to the noise of waters, and the wild fancy seized him that he was not deceived, that two unknown beings stood together there in the darkness and tried the balances of his life, and spoke his doom. The hour in the matted thicket rushed over the great bridge of years to his thought; he had sinned against the earth, and the earth trembled and shook for vengeance. He stayed still for a moment, quivering with fear, and at last went on blindly, no longer caring for the path, if only he might escape from the toils of that dismal shuddering hollow. As he plunged through the hedges the bristling thorns tore his face and hands; he fell amongst stinging-nettles and was pricked as he beat out his way amidst the gorse. He raced headlong, his head over his shoulder, through a windy wood, bare of undergrowth; there lay about the ground moldering stumps, the relics of trees that had thundered to their fall, crashing and tearing to earth, long ago; and from these remains there flowed out a pale thin radiance, filling the spaces of the sounding wood with a dream of light. He had lost all count of the track; he felt he had fled for hours, climbing and descending, and yet not advancing; it was as if he stood still and the shadows of the land went by, in a vision. But at last a hedge, high and straggling, rose before him, and as he broke through it, his feet slipped, and he fell headlong down a steep bank into a lane. He lay still, half-stunned, for a moment, and then rising unsteadily, he looked desperately into the darkness before him, uncertain and bewildered. In front it was black as a midnight cellar, and he turned about, and saw a glint in the distance, as if a candle were flickering in a farm-house window. He began to walk with trembling feet towards the light, when suddenly something pale started out from the shadows before him, and seemed to swim and float down the air. He was going down hill, and he hastened onwards, and he could see the bars of a stile framed dimly against the sky, and the figure still advanced with that gliding motion. Then, as the road declined to the valley, the landmark he had been seeking appeared. To his right there surged up in the darkness the darker summit of the Roman fort, and the streaming fire of the great full moon glowed through the bars of the wizard oaks, and made a halo shine about the hill. He was now quite close to the white appearance, and saw that it was only a woman walking swiftly down the lane; the floating movement was an effect due to the somber air and the moon's glamour. At the gate, where he had spent so many hours gazing at the fort, they walked foot to foot, and he saw it was Annie Morgan.

"Good evening, Master Lucian," said the girl, "it's very dark, sir, indeed."

"Good evening, Annie," he answered, calling her by her name for the first time, and he saw that she smiled with pleasure. "You are out late, aren't you?"

"Yes, sir; but I've been taking a bit of supper to old Mrs. Gibbon. She's been very poorly the last few days, and there's nobody to do anything for her."

Then there were really people who helped one another; kindness and pity were not mere myths, fictions of "society," as useful as Doe and Roe, and as non-existent. The thought struck Lucian with a shock; the evening's passion and delirium, the wild walk and physical fatigue had almost shattered him in body and mind. He was "degenerate," decadent, and the rough rains and blustering winds of life, which a stronger man would have laughed at and enjoyed, were to him "hail-storms and fire-showers." After all, Messrs Beit, the publishers, were only sharp men of business, and these terrible Dixons and Gervases and Colleys merely the ordinary limited clergy and gentry of a quiet country town; sturdier sense would have dismissed Dixon as an old humbug, Stanley Gervase, Esquire, J.P., as a "bit of a bounder," and the ladies as "rather a shoddy lot." But he was walking slowly now in painful silence, his heavy, lagging feet striking against the loose stones. He was not thinking of the girl beside him; only something seemed to swell and grow and swell within his heart; it was all the torture of his days, weary hopes and weary disappointment, scorn rankling and throbbing, and the thought "I had rather call the devils my brothers and live with them in hell." He choked and gasped for breath, and felt involuntary muscles working in his face, and the impulses of a madman stirring him; he himself was in truth the realization of the vision of Caermaen that night, a city with moldering walls beset by the ghostly legion. Life and the world and the laws of the sunlight had passed away, and the resurrection and kingdom of the dead began. The Celt assailed him, becoming from the weird wood he called the world, and his far-off ancestors, the "little people," crept out of their caves, muttering charms and incantations in hissing inhuman speech; he was beleaguered by desires that had slept in his race for ages.

"I am afraid you are very tired, Master Lucian. Would you like me to give you my hand over this rough bit?"

He had stumbled against a great round stone and had nearly fallen. The woman's hand sought his in the darkness; as he felt the touch of the soft warm flesh he moaned, and a pang shot through his arm to his heart. He looked up and found he had only walked a few paces since Annie had spoken; he had thought they had wandered for hours together. The moon was just mounting above the oaks, and the halo round the dark hill brightened. He stopped short, and keeping his hold of Annie's hand, looked into her face. A hazy glory of moonlight shone around them and lit up their eyes. He had not greatly altered since his boyhood; his face was pale olive in color, thin and oval; marks of pain had gathered about the eyes, and his black hair was already stricken with grey. But the eager, curious gaze still remained, and what he saw before him lit up his sadness with a new fire. She stopped too, and did not offer to draw away, but looked back with all her heart. They were alike in many ways; her skin was also of that olive color, but her face was sweet as a beautiful summer night, and her black eyes showed no dimness, and the smile on the scarlet lips was like a flame when it brightens a dark and lonely land.

"You are sorely tired, Master Lucian, let us sit down here by the gate."

It was Lucian who spoke next: "My dear, my dear." And their lips were together again, and their arms locked together, each holding the other fast. And then the poor lad let his head sink down on his sweetheart's breast, and burst into a passion of weeping. The tears streamed down his face, and he shook with sobbing, in the happiest moment that he had ever lived. The woman bent over him and tried to comfort him, but his tears were his consolation and his triumph. Annie was whispering to him, her hand laid on his heart; she was whispering beautiful, wonderful words, that soothed him as a song. He did not know what they meant.

"Annie, dear, dear Annie, what are you saying to me? I have never heard such beautiful words. Tell me, Annie, what do they mean?"

She laughed, and said it was only nonsense that the nurses sang to the children.

"No, no, you are not to call me Master Lucian any more," he said, when they parted, "you must call me Lucian; and I, I worship you, my dear Annie."

He fell down before her, embracing her knees, and adored, and she allowed him, and confirmed his worship. He followed slowly after her, passing the path which led to her home with a longing glance. Nobody saw any difference in Lucian when he reached the rectory. He came in with his usual dreamy indifference, and told how he had lost his way by trying the short cut. He said he had met Dr. Burrows on the road, and that he had recommended the path by the fields. Then, as dully as if he had been reading some story out of a newspaper, he gave his father the outlines of the Beit case, producing the pretty little book called The Chorus in Green. The parson listened in amazement.

"You mean to tell me that you wrote this book?" he said. He was quite roused.

"No; not all of it. Look; that bit is mine, and that; and the beginning of this chapter. Nearly the whole of the third chapter is by me."

He closed the book without interest, and indeed he felt astonished at his father's excitement. The incident seemed to him unimportant.

"And you say that eighty or ninety pages of this book are yours, and these scoundrels have stolen your work?"

"Well, I suppose they have. I'll fetch the manuscript, if you would like to look at it."

The manuscript was duly produced, wrapped in brown paper, with Messrs Beit's address label on it, and the post-office dated stamps.

"And the other book has been out a month." The parson, forgetting the sacerdotal office, and his good habit of grinning, swore at Messrs Beit and Mr. Ritson, calling them damned thieves, and then began to read the manuscript, and to compare it with the printed book.

"Why, it's splendid work. My poor fellow," he said after a while, "I had no notion you could write so well. I used to think of such things in the old days at Oxford; 'old Bill,' the tutor, used to praise my essays, but I never wrote anything like this. And this infernal ruffian of a Ritson has taken all your best things and mixed them up with his own rot to make it go down. Of course you'll expose the gang?"

Lucian was mildly amused; he couldn't enter into his father's feelings at all. He sat smoking in one of the old easy chairs, taking the rare relish of a hot grog with his pipe, and gazing out of his dreamy eyes at the violent old parson. He was pleased that his father liked his book, because he knew him to be a deep and sober scholar and a cool judge of good letters; but he laughed to himself when he saw the magic of print. The parson had expressed no wish to read the manuscript when it came back in disgrace; he had merely grinned, said something about boomerangs, and quoted Horace with relish. Whereas now, before the book in its neat case, lettered with another man's name, his approbation of the writing and his disapproval of the "scoundrels," as he called them, were loudly expressed, and, though a good smoker, he blew and puffed vehemently at his pipe.

"You'll expose the rascals, of course, won't you?" he said again.

"Oh no, I think not. It really doesn't matter much, does it? After all, there are some very weak things in the book; doesn't it strike you as 'young?' I have been thinking of another plan, but I haven't done much with it lately. But I believe I've got hold of a really good idea this time, and if I can manage to see the heart of it I hope to turn out a manuscript worth stealing. But it's so hard to get at the core of an idea--the heart, as I call it," he went on after a pause. "It's like having a box you can't open, though you know there's something wonderful inside. But I do believe I've a fine thing in my hands, and I mean to try my best to work it."

Lucian talked with enthusiasm now, but his father, on his side, could not share these ardors. It was his part to be astonished at excitement over a book that was not even begun, the mere ghost of a book flitting elusive in the world of unborn masterpieces and failures. He had loved good letters, but he shared unconsciously in the general belief that literary attempt is always pitiful, though he did not subscribe to the other half of the popular faith--that literary success is a matter of very little importance. He thought well of books, but only of printed books; in manuscripts he put no faith, and the paulo-post-futurum tense he could not in any manner conjugate. He returned once more to the topic of palpable interest.

"But about this dirty trick these fellows have played on you. You won't sit quietly and bear it, surely? It's only a question of writing to the papers."

"They wouldn't put the letter in. And if they did, I should only get laughed at. Some time ago a man wrote to the Reader, complaining of his play being stolen. He said that he had sent a little one-act comedy to Burleigh, the great dramatist, asking for his advice. Burleigh gave his advice and took the idea for his own very successful play. So the man said, and I daresay it was true enough. But the victim got nothing by his complaint. 'A pretty state of things,' everybody said. 'Here's a Mr. Tomson, that no one has ever heard of, bothers Burleigh with his rubbish, and then accuses him of petty larceny. Is it likely that a man of Burleigh's position, a playwright who can make his five thousand a year easily, would borrow from an unknown Tomson?' I should think it very likely, indeed," Lucian went on, chuckling, "but that was their verdict. No; I don't think I'll write to the papers."

"Well, well, my boy, I suppose you know your own business best. I think you are mistaken, but you must do as you like."

"It's all so unimportant," said Lucian, and he really thought so. He had sweeter things to dream of, and desired no communion of feeling with that madman who had left Caermaen some few hours before. He felt he had made a fool of himself, he was ashamed to think of the fatuity of which he had been guilty, such boiling hatred was not only wicked, but absurd. A man could do no good who put himself into a position of such violent antagonism against his fellow-creatures; so Lucian rebuked his heart, saying that he was old enough to know better. But he remembered that he had sweeter things to dream of; there was a secret ecstasy that he treasured and locked tight away, as a joy too exquisite even for thought till he was quite alone; and then there was that scheme for a new book that he had laid down hopelessly some time ago; it seemed to have arisen into life again within the last hour; he understood that he had started on a false tack, he had taken the wrong aspect of his idea. Of course the thing couldn't be written in that way; it was like trying to read a page turned upside down; and he saw those characters he had vainly sought suddenly disambushed, and a splendid inevitable sequence of events unrolled before him.

It was a true resurrection; the dry plot he had constructed revealed itself as a living thing, stirring and mysterious, and warm as life itself. The parson was smoking stolidly to all appearance, but in reality he was full of amazement at his own son, and now and again he slipped sly furtive glances towards the tranquil young man in the arm-chair by the empty hearth. In the first place, Mr. Taylor was genuinely impressed by what he had read of Lucian's work; he had so long been accustomed to look upon all effort as futile that success amazed him. In the abstract, of course, he was prepared to admit that some people did write well and got published and made money, just as other persons successfully backed an outsider at heavy odds; but it had seemed as improbable that Lucian should show even the beginnings of achievement in one direction as in the other. Then the boy evidently cared so little about it; he did not appear to be proud of being worth robbing, nor was he angry with the robbers.

He sat back luxuriously in the disreputable old chair, drawing long slow wreaths of smoke, tasting his whisky from time to time, evidently well at ease with himself. The father saw him smile, and it suddenly dawned upon him that his son was very handsome; he had such kind gentle eyes and a kind mouth, and his pale cheeks were flushed like a girl's. Mr. Taylor felt moved. What a harmless young fellow Lucian had been; no doubt a little queer and different from others, but wholly inoffensive and patient under disappointment. And Miss Deacon, her contribution to the evening's discussion had been characteristic; she had remarked, firstly, that writing was a very unsettling occupation, and secondly, that it was extremely foolish to entrust one's property to people of whom one knew nothing. Father and son had smiled together at these observations, which were probably true enough. Mr. Taylor at last left Lucian along; he shook hands with a good deal of respect, and said, almost deferentially:

"You mustn't work too hard, old fellow. I wouldn't stay up too late, if I were you, after that long walk. You must have gone miles out of your way."

"I'm not tired now, though. I feel as if I could write my new book on the spot"; and the young man laughed a gay sweet laugh that struck the father as a new note in his son's life.

He sat still a moment after his father had left the room. He cherished his chief treasure of thought in its secret place; he would not enjoy it yet. He drew up a chair to the table at which he wrote or tried to write, and began taking pens and paper from the drawer. There was a great pile of ruled paper there; all of it used, on one side, and signifying many hours of desperate scribbling, of heart-searching and rack of his brain; an array of poor, eager lines written by a waning fire with waning hope; all useless and abandoned. He took up the sheets cheerfully, and began in delicious idleness to look over these fruitless efforts. A page caught his attention; he remembered how he wrote it while a November storm was dashing against the panes; and there was another, with a queer blot in one corner; he had got up from his chair and looked out, and all the earth was white fairyland, and the snowflakes whirled round and round in the wind. Then he saw the chapter begun of a night in March: a great gale blew that night and rooted up one of the ancient yews in the churchyard. He had heard the trees shrieking in the woods, and the long wail of the wind, and across the heaven a white moon fled awfully before the streaming clouds. And all these poor abandoned pages now seemed sweet, and past unhappiness was transmuted into happiness, and the nights of toil were holy. He turned over half a dozen leaves and began to sketch out the outlines of the new book on the unused pages; running out a skeleton plan on one page, and dotting fancies, suggestions, hints on others. He wrote rapidly, overjoyed to find that loving phrases grew under his pen; a particular scene he had imagined filled him with desire; he gave his hand free course, and saw the written work glowing; and action and all the heat of existence quickened and beat on the wet page. Happy fancies took shape in happier words, and when at last he leant back in his chair he felt the stir and rush of the story as if it had been some portion of his own life. He read over what he had done with a renewed pleasure in the nimble and flowing workmanship, and as he put the little pile of manuscript tenderly in the drawer he paused to enjoy the anticipation of tomorrow's labor.

And then--but the rest of the night was given to tender and delicious things, and when he went up to bed a scarlet dawn was streaming from the east.

III

For days Lucian lay in a swoon of pleasure, smiling when he was addressed, sauntering happily in the sunlight, hugging recollection warm to his heart. Annie had told him that she was going on a visit to her married sister, and said, with a caress, that he must be patient. He protested against her absence, but she fondled him, whispering her charms in his ear till he gave in and then they said good-bye, Lucian adoring on his knees. The parting was as strange as the meeting, and that night when he laid his work aside, and let himself sink deep into the joys of memory, all the encounter seemed as wonderful and impossible as magic.

"And you really don't mean to do anything about those rascals?" said his father.

"Rascals? Which rascals? Oh, you mean Beit. I had forgotten all about it. No; I don't think I shall trouble. They're not worth powder and shot."

And he returned to his dream, pacing slowly from the medlar to the quince and back again. It seemed trivial to be interrupted by such questions; he had not even time to think of the book he had recommenced so eagerly, much less of this labor of long ago. He recollected without interest that it cost him many pains, that it was pretty good here and there, and that it had been stolen, and it seemed that there was nothing more to be said on the matter. He wished to think of the darkness in the lane, of the kind voice that spoke to him, of the kind hand that sought his own, as he stumbled on the rough way. So far, it was wonderful. Since he had left school and lost the company of the worthy barbarians who had befriended him there, he had almost lost the sense of kinship with humanity; he had come to dread the human form as men dread the hood of the cobra. To Lucian a man or a woman meant something that stung, that spoke words that rankled, and poisoned his life with scorn. At first such malignity shocked him: he would ponder over words and glances and wonder if he were not mistaken, and he still sought now and then for sympathy. The poor boy had romantic ideas about women; he believed they were merciful and pitiful, very kind to the unlucky and helpless. Men perhaps had to be different; after all, the duty of a man was to get on in the world, or, in plain language, to make money, to be successful; to cheat rather than to be cheated, but always to be successful; and he could understand that one who fell below this high standard must expect to be severely judged by his fellows. For example, there was young Bennett, Miss Spurry's nephew. Lucian had met him once or twice when he was spending his holidays with Miss Spurry, and the two young fellows compared literary notes together. Bennett showed some beautiful things he had written, over which Lucian had grown both sad and enthusiastic. It was such exquisite magic verse, and so much better than anything he ever hoped to write, that there was a touch of anguish in his congratulations. But when Bennett, after many vain prayers to his aunt, threw up a safe position in the bank, and betook himself to a London garret, Lucian was not surprised at the general verdict.

Mr. Dixon, as a clergyman, viewed the question from a high standpoint and found it all deplorable, but the general opinion was that Bennett was a hopeless young lunatic. Old Mr. Gervase went purple when his name was mentioned, and the young Dixons sneered very merrily over the adventure.

"I always thought he was a beastly young ass," said Edward Dixon, "but I didn't think he'd chuck away his chances like that. Said he couldn't stand a bank! I hope he'll be able to stand bread and water. That's all those littery fellows get, I believe, except Tennyson and Mark Twain and those sort of people."

Lucian of course sympathized with the unfortunate Bennett, but such judgments were after all only natural. The young man might have stayed in the bank and succeeded to his aunt's thousand a year, and everybody would have called him a very nice young fellow--"clever, too." But he had deliberately chosen, as Edward Dixon had said, to chuck his chances away for the sake of literature; piety and a sense of the main chance had alike pointed the way to a delicate course of wheedling, to a little harmless practicing on Miss Spurry's infirmities, to frequent compliances of a soothing nature, and the "young ass" had been blind to the direction of one and the other. It seemed almost right that the vicar should moralize, that Edward Dixon should sneer, and that Mr. Gervase should grow purple with contempt. Men, Lucian thought, were like judges, who may pity the criminal in their hearts, but are forced to vindicate the outraged majesty of the law by a severe sentence. He felt the same considerations applied to his own case; he knew that his father should have had more money, that his clothes should be newer and of a better cut, that he should have gone to the university and made good friends. If such had been his fortune he could have looked his fellow-men proudly in the face, upright and unashamed. Having put on the whole armor of a first-rate West End tailor, with money in his purse, having taken anxious thought for the morrow, and having some useful friends and good prospects; in such a case he might have held his head high in a gentlemanly and Christian community. As it was he had usually avoided the reproachful glance of his fellows, feeling that he deserved their condemnation. But he had cherished for a long time his romantic sentimentalities about women; literary conventions borrowed from the minor poets and pseudo-medievalists, or so he thought afterwards. But, fresh from school, wearied a little with the perpetual society of barbarian though worthy boys, he had in his soul a charming image of womanhood, before which he worshipped with mingled passion and devotion. It was a nude figure, perhaps, but the shining arms were to be wound about the neck of a vanquished knight; there was rest for the head of a wounded lover; the hands were stretched forth to do works of pity, and the smiling lips were to murmur not love alone, but consolation in defeat. Here was the refuge for a broken heart; here the scorn of men would but make tenderness increase; here was all pity and all charity with loving-kindness. It was a delightful picture, conceived in the "come rest on this bosom," and "a ministering angel thou" manner, with touches of allurement that made devotion all the sweeter. He soon found that he had idealized a little; in the affair of young Bennett, while the men were contemptuous the women were virulent. He had been rather fond of Agatha Gervase, and she, so other ladies said, had "set her cap" at him. Now, when he rebelled, and lost the goodwill of his aunt, dear Miss Spurry, Agatha insulted him with all conceivable rapidity. "After all, Mr. Bennett," she said, "you will be nothing better than a beggar; now, will you? You mustn't think me cruel, but I can't help speaking the truth. Write books!" Her expression filled up the incomplete sentence; she waggled with indignant emotion. These passages came to Lucian's ears, and indeed the Gervases boasted of "how well poor Agatha had behaved."

"Never mind, Gathy," old Gervase had observed. "If the impudent young puppy comes here again, we'll see what Thomas can do with the horse-whip."

"Poor dear child," Mrs. Gervase added in telling the tale, "and she was so fond of him too. But of course it couldn't go on after his shameful behavior."

But Lucian was troubled; he sought vainly for the ideal womanly, the tender note of "come rest on this bosom." Ministering angels, he felt convinced, do not rub red pepper and sulfuric acid into the wounds of suffering mortals.

Then there was the case of Mr. Vaughan, a squire in the neighborhood, at whose board all the aristocracy of Caermaen had feasted for years. Mr. Vaughan had a first-rate cook, and his cellar was rare, and he was never so happy as when he shared his good things with his friends. His mother kept his house, and they delighted all the girls with frequent dances, while the men sighed over the amazing champagne. Investments proved disastrous, and Mr. Vaughan had to sell the grey manor-house by the river. He and his mother took a little modern stucco villa in Caermaen, wishing to be near their dear friends. But the men were "very sorry; rough on you, Vaughan. Always thought those Patagonians were risky, but you wouldn't hear of it. Hope we shall see you before very long; you and Mrs. Vaughan must come to tea some day after Christmas."

"Of course we are all very sorry for them," said Henrietta Dixon. "No, we haven't called on Mrs. Vaughan yet. They have no regular servant, you know; only a woman in the morning. I hear old mother Vaughan, as Edward will call her, does nearly everything. And their house is absurdly small; it's little more than a cottage. One really can't call it a gentleman's house."

Then Mr. Vaughan, his heart in the dust, went to the Gervases and tried to borrow five pounds of Mr. Gervase. He had to be ordered out of the house, and, as Edith Gervase said, it was all very painful; "he went out in such a funny way," she added, "just like the dog when he's had a whipping. Of course it's sad, even if it is all his own fault, as everybody says, but he looked so ridiculous as he was going down the steps that I couldn't help laughing." Mr. Vaughan heard the ringing, youthful laughter as he crossed the lawn.

Young girls like Henrietta Dixon and Edith Gervase naturally viewed the Vaughans' comical position with all the high spirits of their age, but the elder ladies could not look at matters in this frivolous light.

"Hush, dear, hush," said Mrs. Gervase, "it's all too shocking to be a laughing matter. Don't you agree with me, Mrs. Dixon? The sinful extravagance that went on at Pentre always frightened me. You remember that ball they gave last year? Mr. Gervase assured me that the champagne must have cost at least a hundred and fifty shillings the dozen."

"It's dreadful, isn't it," said Mrs. Dixon, "when one thinks of how many poor people there are who would be thankful for a crust of bread?"

"Yes, Mrs. Dixon," Agatha joined in, "and you know how absurdly the Vaughans spoilt the cottagers. Oh, it was really wicked; one would think Mr. Vaughan wished to make them above their station. Edith and I went for a walk one day nearly as far as Pentre, and we begged a glass of water of old Mrs. Jones who lives in that pretty cottage near the brook. She began praising the Vaughans in the most fulsome manner, and showed us some flannel things they had given her at Christmas. I assure you, my dear Mrs. Dixon, the flannel was the very best quality; no lady could wish for better. It couldn't have cost less than half-a-crown a yard."

"I know, my dear, I know. Mr. Dixon always said it couldn't last. How often I have heard him say that the Vaughans were pauperizing all the common people about Pentre, and putting every one else in a most unpleasant position. Even from a worldly point of view it was very poor taste on their part. So different from the true charity that Paul speaks of."

"I only wish they had given away nothing worse than flannel," said Miss Colley, a young lady of very strict views. "But I assure you there was a perfect orgy, I can call it nothing else, every Christmas. Great joints of prime beef, and barrels of strong beer, and snuff and tobacco distributed wholesale; as if the poor wanted to be encouraged in their disgusting habits. It was really impossible to go through the village for weeks after; the whole place was poisoned with the fumes of horrid tobacco pipes."

"Well, we see how that sort of thing ends," said Mrs. Dixon, summing up judicially. "We had intended to call, but I really think it would be impossible after what Mrs. Gervase has told us. The idea of Mr. Vaughan trying to sponge on poor Mr. Gervase in that shabby way! I think meanness of that kind is so hateful."

It was the practical side of all this that astonished Lucian. He saw that in reality there was no high-flown quixotism in a woman's nature; the smooth arms, made he had thought for caressing, seemed muscular; the hands meant for the doing of works of pity in his system, appeared dexterous in the giving of "stingers," as Barnes might say, and the smiling lips could sneer with great ease. Nor was he more fortunate in his personal experiences. As has been told, Mrs. Dixon spoke of him in connection with "judgments," and the younger ladies did not exactly cultivate his acquaintance. Theoretically they "adored" books and thought poetry "too sweet," but in practice they preferred talking about mares and fox-terriers and their neighbors.

They were nice girls enough, very like other young ladies in other country towns, content with the teaching of their parents, reading the Bible every morning in their bedrooms, and sitting every Sunday in church amongst the well-dressed "sheep" on the right hand. It was not their fault if they failed to satisfy the ideal of an enthusiastic dreamy boy, and indeed, they would have thought his feigned woman immodest, absurdly sentimental, a fright ("never wears stays, my dear") and horrid.

At first he was a good deal grieved at the loss of that charming tender woman, the work of his brain. When the Miss Dixons went haughtily by with a scornful waggle, when the Miss Gervases passed in the wagonette laughing as the mud splashed him, the poor fellow would look up with a face of grief that must have been very comic; "like a dying duck," as Edith Gervase said. Edith was really very pretty, and he would have liked to talk to her, even about fox-terriers, if she would have listened. One afternoon at the Dixons' he really forced himself upon her, and with all the obtuseness of an enthusiastic boy tried to discuss the Lotus Eaters of Tennyson. It was too absurd. Captain Kempton was making signals to Edith all the time, and Lieutenant Gatwick had gone off in disgust, and he had promised to bring her a puppy "by Vick out of Wasp." At last the poor girl could bear it no longer:

"Yes, it's very sweet," she said at last. "When did you say you were going to London, Mr. Taylor?"

It was about the time that his disappointment became known to everybody, and the shot told. He gave her a piteous look and slunk off, "just like the dog when he's had a whipping," to use Edith's own expression. Two or three lessons of this description produced their due effect; and when he saw a male Dixon or Gervase approaching him he bit his lip and summoned up his courage. But when he descried a "ministering angel" he made haste and hid behind a hedge or took to the woods. In course of time the desire to escape became an instinct, to be followed as a matter of course; in the same way he avoided the adders on the mountain. His old ideals were almost if not quite forgotten; he knew that the female of the bête humaine, like the adder, would in all probability sting, and he therefore shrank from its trail, but without any feeling of special resentment. The one had a poisoned tongue as the other had a poisoned fang, and it was well to leave them both alone. Then had come that sudden fury of rage against all humanity, as he went out of Caermaen carrying the book that had been stolen from him by the enterprising Beit. He shuddered as he though of how nearly he had approached the verge of madness, when his eyes filled with blood and the earth seemed to burn with fire. He remembered how he had looked up to the horizon and the sky was blotched with scarlet; and the earth was deep red, with red woods and red fields. There was something of horror in the memory, and in the vision of that wild night walk through dim country, when every shadow seemed a symbol of some terrible impending doom. The murmur of the brook, the wind shrilling through the wood, the pale light flowing from the moldered trunks, and the picture of his own figure fleeing and fleeting through the shades; all these seemed unhappy things that told a story in fatal hieroglyphics. And then the life and laws of the sunlight had passed away, and the resurrection and kingdom of the dead began. Though his limbs were weary, he had felt his muscles grow strong as steel; a woman, one of the hated race, was beside him in the darkness, and the wild beast woke within him, ravening for blood and brutal lust; all the raging desires of the dim race from which he came assailed his heart. The ghosts issued out from the weird wood and from the caves in the hills, besieging him, as he had imagined the spiritual legion besieging Caermaen, beckoning him to a hideous battle and a victory that he had never imagined in his wildest dreams. And then out of the darkness the kind voice spoke again, and the kind hand was stretched out to draw him up from the pit. It was sweet to think of that which he had found at last; the boy's picture incarnate, all the passion and compassion of his longing, all the pity and love and consolation. She, that beautiful passionate woman offering up her beauty in sacrifice to him, she was worthy indeed of his worship. He remembered how his tears had fallen upon her breast, and how tenderly she had soothed him, whispering those wonderful unknown words that sang to his heart. And she had made herself defenseless before him, caressing and fondling the body that had been so despised. He exulted in the happy thought that he had knelt down on the ground before her, and had embraced her knees and worshipped. The woman's body had become his religion; he lay awake at night looking into the darkness with hungry eyes; wishing for a miracle, that the appearance of the so-desired form might be shaped before him. And when he was alone in quiet places in the wood, he fell down again on his knees, and even on his face, stretching out vain hands in the air, as if they would feel her flesh. His father noticed in those days that the inner pocket of his coat was stuffed with papers; he would see Lucian walking up and down in a secret shady place at the bottom of the orchard, reading from his sheaf of manuscript, replacing the leaves, and again drawing them out. He would walk a few quick steps, and pause as if enraptured, gazing in the air as if he looked through the shadows of the world into some sphere of glory, feigned by his thought. Mr. Taylor was almost alarmed at the sight; he concluded of course that Lucian was writing a book. In the first place, there seemed something immodest in seeing the operation performed under one's eyes; it was as if the "make-up" of a beautiful actress were done on the stage, in full audience; as if one saw the rounded calves fixed in position, the fleshings drawn on, the voluptuous outlines of the figure produced by means purely mechanical, blushes mantling from the paint-pot, and the golden tresses well secured by the wigmaker. Books, Mr. Taylor thought, should swim into one's ken mysteriously; they should appear all printed and bound, without apparent genesis; just as children are suddenly told that they have a little sister, found by mamma in the garden. But Lucian was not only engaged in composition; he was plainly rapturous, enthusiastic; Mr. Taylor saw him throw up his hands, and bow his head with strange gesture. The parson began to fear that his son was like some of those mad Frenchmen of whom he had read, young fellows who had a sort of fury of literature, and gave their whole lives to it, spending days over a page, and years over a book, pursuing art as Englishmen pursue money, building up a romance as if it were a business. Now Mr. Taylor held firmly by the "walking-stick" theory; he believed that a man of letters should have a real profession, some solid employment in life. "Get something to do," he would have liked to say, "and then you can write as much as you please. Look at Scott, look at Dickens and Trollope." And then there was the social point of view; it might be right, or it might be wrong, but there could be no doubt that the literary man, as such, was not thought much of in English society. Mr. Taylor knew his Thackeray, and he remembered that old Major Pendennis, society personified, did not exactly boast of his nephew's occupation. Even Warrington was rather ashamed to own his connection with journalism, and Pendennis himself laughed openly at his novel-writing as an agreeable way of making money, a useful appendage to the cultivation of dukes, his true business in life. This was the plain English view, and Mr. Taylor was no doubt right enough in thinking it good, practical common sense. Therefore when he saw Lucian loitering and sauntering, musing amorously over his manuscript, exhibiting manifest signs of that fine fury which Britons have ever found absurd, he felt grieved at heart, and more than ever sorry that he had not been able to send the boy to Oxford.

"B.N.C. would have knocked all this nonsense out of him," he thought. "He would have taken a double First like my poor father and made something of a figure in the world. However, it can't be helped." The poor man sighed, and lit his pipe, and walked in another part of the garden.

But he was mistaken in his diagnosis of the symptoms. The book that Lucian had begun lay unheeded in the drawer; it was a secret work that he was engaged on, and the manuscripts that he took out of that inner pocket never left him day or night. He slept with them next to his heart, and he would kiss them when he was quite alone, and pay them such devotion as he would have paid to her whom they symbolized. He wrote on these leaves a wonderful ritual of praise and devotion; it was the liturgy of his religion. Again and again he copied and recopied this madness of a lover; dallying all days over the choice of a word, searching for more exquisite phrases. No common words, no such phrases as he might use in a tale would suffice; the sentences of worship must stir and be quickened, they must glow and burn, and be decked out as with rare work of jewelry. Every part of that holy and beautiful body must be adored; he sought for terms of extravagant praise, he bent his soul and mind low before her, licking the dust under her feet, abased and yet rejoicing as a Templar before the image of Baphomet. He exulted more especially in the knowledge that there was nothing of the conventional or common in his ecstasy; he was not the fervent, adoring lover of Tennyson's poems, who loves with passion and yet with a proud respect, with the love always of a gentleman for a lady. Annie was not a lady; the Morgans had farmed their land for hundreds of years; they were what Miss Gervase and Miss Colley and the rest of them called common people. Tennyson's noble gentleman thought of their ladies with something of reticence; they imagined them dressed in flowing and courtly robes, walking with slow dignity; they dreamed of them as always stately, the future mistresses of their houses, mothers of their heirs. Such lovers bowed, but not too low, remembering their own honor, before those who were to be equal companions and friends as well as wives. It was not such conceptions as these that he embodied in the amazing emblems of his ritual; he was not, he told himself, a young officer, "something in the city," or a rising barrister engaged to a Miss Dixon or a Miss Gervase. He had not thought of looking out for a nice little house in a good residential suburb where they would have pleasant society; there were to be no consultations about wall-papers, or jocose whispers from friends as to the necessity of having a room that would do for a nursery. No glad young thing had leant on his arm while they chose the suite in white enamel, and china for "our bedroom," the modest salesman doing his best to spare their blushes. When Edith Gervase married she would get mamma to look out for two really good servants, "as we must begin quietly," and mamma would make sure that the drains and everything were right. Then her "girl friends" would come on a certain solemn day to see all her "lovely things." "Two dozen of everything!" "Look, Ethel, did you ever see such ducky frills?" "And that insertion, isn't it quite too sweet?" "My dear Edith, you are a lucky girl." "All the underlinen specially made by Madame Lulu!" "What delicious things!" "I hope he knows what a prize he is winning." "Oh! do look at those lovely ribbon-bows!" "You darling, how happy you must be." "Real Valenciennes!" Then a whisper in the lady's ear, and her reply, "Oh, don't, Nelly!" So they would chirp over their treasures, as in Rabelais they chirped over their cups; and every thing would be done in due order till the wedding-day, when mamma, who had strained her sinews and the commandments to bring the match about, would weep and look indignantly at the unhappy bridegroom. "I hope you'll be kind to her, Robert." Then in a rapid whisper to the bride: "Mind, you insist on Wyman's flushing the drains when you come back; servants are so careless and dirty too. Don't let him go about by himself in Paris. Men are so queer, one never knows. You have got the pills?" And aloud, after these secrets, "God bless you, my dear; good-bye! cluck, cluck, good-bye!"

There were stranger things written in the manuscript pages that Lucian cherished, sentences that burnt and glowed like "coals of fire which hath a most vehement flame." There were phrases that stung and tingled as he wrote them, and sonorous words poured out in ecstasy and rapture, as in some of the old litanies. He hugged the thought that a great part of what he had invented was in the true sense of the word occult: page after page might have been read aloud to the uninitiated without betraying the inner meaning. He dreamed night and day over these symbols, he copied and recopied the manuscript nine times before he wrote it out fairly in a little book which he made himself of a skin of creamy vellum. In his mania for acquirements that should be entirely useless he had gained some skill in illumination, or limning as he preferred to call it, always choosing the obscurer word as the obscurer arts. First he set himself to the severe practice of the text; he spent many hours and days of toil in struggling to fashion the serried columns of black letter, writing and rewriting till he could shape the massive character with firm true hand. He cut his quills with the patience of a monk in the scriptorium, shaving and altering the nib, lightening and increasing the pressure and flexibility of the points, till the pen satisfied him, and gave a stroke both broad and even. Then he made experiments in inks, searching for some medium that would rival the glossy black letter of the old manuscripts; and not till he could produce a fair page of text did he turn to the more entrancing labor of the capitals and borders and ornaments. He mused long over the Lombardic letters, as glorious in their way as a cathedral, and trained his hand to execute the bold and flowing lines; and then there was the art of the border, blossoming in fretted splendor all about the page. His cousin, Miss Deacon, called it all a great waste of time, and his father thought he would have done much better in trying to improve his ordinary handwriting, which was both ugly and illegible. Indeed, there seemed but a poor demand for the limner's art. He sent some specimens of his skill to an "artistic firm" in London; a verse of the "Maud," curiously emblazoned, and a Latin hymn with the notes pricked on a red stave. The firm wrote civilly, telling him that his work, though good, was not what they wanted, and enclosing an illuminated text. "We have great demand for this sort of thing," they concluded, "and if you care to attempt something in this style we should be pleased to look at it." The said text was "Thou, God, seest me." The letter was of a degraded form, bearing much the same relation to the true character as a "churchwarden gothic" building does to Canterbury Cathedral; the colours were varied. The initial was pale gold, the h pink, the o black, the u blue, and the first letter was somehow connected with a bird's nest containing the young of the pigeon, who were waited on by the female bird.

"What a pretty text," said Miss Deacon. "I should like to nail it up in my room. Why don't you try to do something like that, Lucian? You might make something by it."

"I sent them these," said Lucian, "but they don't like them much."

"My dear boy! I should think not! Like them! What were you thinking of to draw those queer stiff flowers all round the border? Roses? They don't look like roses at all events. Where do you get such ideas from?"

"But the design is appropriate; look at the words."

"My dear Lucian, I can't read the words; it's such a queer old-fashioned writing. Look how plain that text is; one can see what it's about. And this other one; I can't make it out at all."

"It's a Latin hymn."

"A Latin hymn? Is it a Protestant hymn? I may be old-fashioned, but Hymns Ancient and Modern is quite good enough for me. This is the music, I suppose? But, my dear boy, there are only four lines, and who ever heard of notes shaped like that: you have made some square and some diamond-shape? Why didn't you look in your poor mother's old music? It's in the ottoman in the drawing-room. I could have shown you how to make the notes; there are crotchets, you know, and quavers."

Miss Deacon laid down the illuminated Urbs Beata in despair; she felt convinced that her cousin was "next door to an idiot."

And he went out into the garden and raged behind a hedge. He broke two flower-pots and hit an apple-tree very hard with his stick, and then, feeling more calm, wondered what was the use in trying to do anything. He would not have put the thought into words, but in his heart he was aggrieved that his cousin liked the pigeons and the text, and did not like his emblematical roses and the Latin hymn. He knew he had taken great pains over the work, and that it was well done, and being still a young man he expected praise. He found that in this hard world there was a lack of appreciation; a critical spirit seemed abroad. If he could have been scientifically observed as he writhed and smarted under the strictures of "the old fool," as he rudely called his cousin, the spectacle would have been extremely diverting. Little boys sometimes enjoy a very similar entertainment; either with their tiny fingers or with mamma's nail scissors they gradually deprive a fly of its wings and legs. The odd gyrations and queer thin buzzings of the creature as it spins comically round and round never fail to provide a fund of harmless amusement. Lucian, indeed, fancied himself a very ill-used individual; but he should have tried to imitate the nervous organization of the flies, which, as mamma says, "can't really feel."

But now, as he prepared the vellum leaves, he remembered his art with joy; he had not labored to do beautiful work in vain. He read over his manuscript once more, and thought of the designing of the pages. He made sketches on furtive sheets of paper, and hunted up books in his father's library for suggestions. There were books about architecture, and medieval iron work, and brasses which contributed hints for adornment; and not content with mere pictures he sought in the woods and hedges, scanning the strange forms of trees, and the poisonous growth of great water-plants, and the parasite twining of honeysuckle and briony. In one of these rambles he discovered a red earth which he made into a pigment, and he found in the unctuous juice of a certain fern an ingredient which he thought made his black ink still more glossy. His book was written all in symbols, and in the same spirit of symbolism he decorated it, causing wonderful foliage to creep about the text, and showing the blossom of certain mystical flowers, with emblems of strange creatures, caught and bound in rose thickets. All was dedicated to love and a lover's madness, and there were songs in it which haunted him with their lilt and refrain. When the book was finished it replaced the loose leaves as his constant companion by day and night. Three times a day he repeated his ritual to himself, seeking out the loneliest places in the woods, or going up to his room; and from the fixed intentness and rapture of his gaze, the father thought him still severely employed in the questionable process of composition. At night he contrived to wake for his strange courtship; and he had a peculiar ceremony when he got up in the dark and lit his candle. From a steep and wild hillside, not far from the house, he had cut from time to time five large boughs of spiked and prickly gorse. He had brought them into the house, one by one, and had hidden them in the big box that stood beside his bed. Often he woke up weeping and murmuring to himself the words of one of his songs, and then when he had lit the candle, he would draw out the gorse-boughs, and place them on the floor, and taking off his nightgown, gently lay himself down on the bed of thorns and spines. Lying on his face, with the candle and the book before him, he would softly and tenderly repeat the praises of his dear, dear Annie, and as he turned over page after page, and saw the raised gold of the majuscules glow and flame in the candle-light, he pressed the thorns into his flesh. At such moments he tasted in all its acute savor the joy of physical pain; and after two or three experiences of such delights he altered his book, making a curious sign in vermilion on the margin of the passages where he was to inflict on himself this sweet torture. Never did he fail to wake at the appointed hour, a strong effort of will broke through all the heaviness of sleep, and he would rise up, joyful though weeping, and reverently set his thorny bed upon the floor, offering his pain with his praise. When he had whispered the last word, and had risen from the ground, his body would be all freckled with drops of blood; he used to view the marks with pride. Here and there a spine would be left deep in the flesh, and he would pull these out roughly, tearing through the skin. On some nights when he had pressed with more fervor on the thorns his thighs would stream with blood, red beads standing out on the flesh, and trickling down to his feet. He had some difficulty in washing away the bloodstains so as not to leave any traces to attract the attention of the servant; and after a time he returned no more to his bed when his duty had been accomplished. For a coverlet he had a dark rug, a good deal worn, and in this he would wrap his naked bleeding body, and lie down on the hard floor, well content to add an aching rest to the account of his pleasures. He was covered with scars, and those that healed during the day were torn open afresh at night; the pale olive skin was red with the angry marks of blood, and the graceful form of the young man appeared like the body of a tortured martyr. He grew thinner and thinner every day, for he ate but little; the skin was stretched on the bones of his face, and the black eyes burnt in dark purple hollows. His relations noticed that he was not looking well.

"Now, Lucian, it's perfect madness of you to go on like this," said Miss Deacon, one morning at breakfast. "Look how your hand shakes; some people would say that you have been taking brandy. And all that you want is a little medicine, and yet you won't be advised. You know it's not my fault; I have asked you to try Dr. Jelly's Cooling Powders again and again."

He remembered the forcible exhibition of the powders when he was a boy, and felt thankful that those days were over. He only grinned at his cousin and swallowed a great cup of strong tea to steady his nerves, which were shaky enough. Mrs. Dixon saw him one day in Caermaen; it was very hot, and he had been walking rather fast. The scars on his body burnt and tingled, and he tottered as he raised his hat to the vicar's wife. She decided without further investigation that he must have been drinking in public-houses.

"It seems a mercy that poor Mrs. Taylor was taken," she said to her husband. "She has certainly been spared a great deal. That wretched young man passed me this afternoon; he was quite intoxicated."

"How very said," said Mr. Dixon. "A little port, my dear?"

"Thank you, Merivale, I will have another glass of sherry. Dr. Burrows is always scolding me and saying I must take something to keep up my energy, and this sherry is so weak."

The Dixons were not teetotalers. They regretted it deeply, and blamed the doctor, who "insisted on some stimulant." However, there was some consolation in trying to convert the parish to total abstinence, or, as they curiously called it, temperance. Old women were warned of the sin of taking a glass of beer for supper; aged laborers were urged to try Cork-ho, the new temperance drink; an uncouth beverage, styled coffee, was dispensed at the reading-room. Mr. Dixon preached an eloquent "temperance" sermon, soon after the above conversation, taking as his text: Beware of the leaven of the Pharisees. In his discourse he showed that fermented liquor and leaven had much in common, that beer was at the present day "put away" during Passover by the strict Jews; and in a moving peroration he urged his dear brethren, "and more especially those amongst us who are poor in this world's goods," to beware indeed of that evil leaven which was sapping the manhood of our nation. Mrs. Dixon cried after church:

"Oh, Merivale, what a beautiful sermon! How earnest you were. I hope it will do good."

Mr. Dixon swallowed his port with great decorum, but his wife fuddled herself every evening with cheap sherry. She was quite unaware of the fact, and sometimes wondered in a dim way why she always had to scold the children after dinner. And so strange things sometimes happened in the nursery, and now and then the children looked queerly at one another after a red-faced woman had gone out, panting.

Lucian knew nothing of his accuser's trials, but he was not long in hearing of his own intoxication. The next time he went down to Caermaen he was hailed by the doctor.

"Been drinking again today?"

"No," said Lucian in a puzzled voice. "What do you mean?"

"Oh, well, if you haven't, that's all right, as you'll be able to take a drop with me. Come along in?"

Over the whisky and pipes Lucian heard of the evil rumors affecting his character.

"Mrs. Dixon assured me you were staggering from one side of the street to the other. You quite frightened her, she said. Then she asked me if I recommended her to take one or two ounces of spirit at bedtime for the palpitation; and of course I told her two would be better. I have my living to make here, you know. And upon my word, I think she wants it; she's always gurgling inside like waterworks. I wonder how old Dixon can stand it."

"I like 'ounces of spirit,'" said Lucian. "That's taking it medicinally, I suppose. I've often heard of ladies who have to 'take it medicinally'; and that's how it's done?"

"That's it. 'Dr Burrows won't listen to me': 'I tell him how I dislike the taste of spirits, but he says they are absolutely necessary for my constitution': 'my medical man insists on something at bedtime'; that's the style."

Lucian laughed gently; all these people had become indifferent to him; he could no longer feel savage indignation at their little hypocrisies and malignancies. Their voices uttering calumny, and morality, and futility had become like the thin shrill angry note of a gnat on a summer evening; he had his own thoughts and his own life, and he passed on without heeding.

"You come down to Caermaen pretty often, don't you?" said the doctor. "I've seen you two or three times in the last fortnight."

"Yes, I enjoy the walk."

"Well, look me up whenever you like, you know. I am often in just at this time, and a chat with a human being isn't bad, now and then. It's a change for me; I'm often afraid I shall lose my patients."

The doctor had the weakness of these terrible puns, dragged headlong into the conversation. He sometimes exhibited them before Mrs. Gervase, who would smile in a faint and dignified manner, and say:

"Ah, I see. Very amusing indeed. We had an old coachmen once who was very clever, I believe, at that sort of thing, but Mr. Gervase was obliged to send him away, the laughter of the other domestics was so very boisterous."

Lucian laughed, not boisterously, but good-humouredly, at the doctor's joke. He liked Burrows, feeling that he was a man and not an automatic gabbling machine.

"You look a little pulled down," said the doctor, when Lucian rose to go. "No, you don't want my medicine. Plenty of beef and beer will do you more good than drugs. I daresay it's the hot weather that has thinned you a bit. Oh, you'll be all right again in a month."

As Lucian strolled out of the town on his way home, he passed a small crowd of urchins assembled at the corner of an orchard. They were enjoying themselves immensely. The "healthy" boy, the same whom he had seen some weeks ago operating on a cat, seemed to have recognized his selfishness in keeping his amusements to himself. He had found a poor lost puppy, a little creature with bright pitiful eyes, almost human in their fond, friendly gaze. It was not a well-bred little dog; it was certainly not that famous puppy "by Vick out of Wasp"; it had rough hair and a foolish long tail which it wagged beseechingly, at once deprecating severity and asking kindness. The poor animal had evidently been used to gentle treatment; it would look up in a boy's face, and give a leap, fawning on him, and then bark in a small doubtful voice, and cower a moment on the ground, astonished perhaps at the strangeness, the bustle and animation. The boys were beside themselves with eagerness; there was quite a babble of voices, arguing, discussing, suggesting. Each one had a plan of his own which he brought before the leader, a stout and sturdy youth.

"Drown him! What be you thinkin' of, mun?" he was saying. "'Tain't no sport at all. You shut your mouth, gwaes. Be you goin' to ask your mother for the boiling-water? Is, Bob Williams, I do know all that: but where be you a-going to get the fire from? Be quiet, mun, can't you? Thomas Trevor, be this dog yourn or mine? Now, look you, if you don't all of you shut your bloody mouths, I'll take the dog 'ome and keep him. There now!"

He was a born leader of men. A singular depression and lowness of spirit showed itself on the boys' faces. They recognized that the threat might very possibly be executed, and their countenances were at once composed to humble attention. The puppy was still cowering on the ground in the midst of them: one or two tried to relieve the tension of their feelings by kicking him in the belly with their hobnail boots. It cried out with the pain and writhed a little, but the poor little beast did not attempt to bite or even snarl. It looked up with those beseeching friendly eyes at its persecutors, and fawned on them again, and tried to wag its tail and be merry, pretending to play with a straw on the road, hoping perhaps to win a little favor in that way.

The leader saw the moment for his master-stroke. He slowly drew a piece of rope from his pocket.

"What do you say to that, mun? Now, Thomas Trevor! We'll hang him over that there bough. Will that suit you, Bobby Williams?"

There was a great shriek of approval and delight. All was again bustle and animation. "I'll tie it round his neck?" "Get out, mun, you don't know how it be done." "Is, I do, Charley." "Now, let me, gwaes, now do let me." "You be sure he won't bite?" "He hain't mad, be he?" "Suppose we were to tie up his mouth first?"

The puppy still fawned and curried favor, and wagged that sorry tail, and lay down crouching on one side on the ground, sad and sorry in his heart, but still with a little gleam of hope; for now and again he tried to play, and put up his face, praying with those fond, friendly eyes. And then at last his gambols and poor efforts for mercy ceased, and he lifted up his wretched voice in one long dismal whine of despair. But he licked the hand of the boy that tied the noose.

He was slowly and gently swung into the air as Lucian went by unheeded; he struggled, and his legs twisted and writhed. The "healthy" boy pulled the rope, and his friends danced and shouted with glee. As Lucian turned the corner, the poor dangling body was swinging to and fro, the puppy was dying, but he still kicked a little.

Lucian went on his way hastily, and shuddering with disgust. The young of the human creature were really too horrible; they defiled the earth, and made existence unpleasant, as the pulpy growth of a noxious and obscene fungus spoils an agreeable walk. The sight of those malignant little animals with mouths that uttered cruelty and filthy, with hands dexterous in torture, and feet swift to run all evil errands, had given him a shock and broken up the world of strange thoughts in which he had been dwelling. Yet it was no good being angry with them: it was their nature to be very loathsome. Only he wished they would go about their hideous amusements in their own back gardens where nobody could see them at work; it was too bad that he should be interrupted and offended in a quiet country road. He tried to put the incident out of his mind, as if the whole thing had been a disagreeable story, and the visions amongst which he wished to move were beginning to return, when he was again rudely disturbed. A little girl, a pretty child of eight or nine, was coming along the lane to meet him. She was crying bitterly and looking to left and right, and calling out some word all the time.

"Jack, Jack, Jack! Little Jackie! Jack!"

Then she burst into tears afresh, and peered into the hedge, and tried to peep through a gate into a field.

"Jackie, Jackie, Jackie!"

She came up to Lucian, sobbing as if her heart would break, and dropped him an old-fashioned curtsy.

"Oh, please sir, have you seen my little Jackie?"

"What do you mean?" said Lucian. "What is it you've lost?"

"A little dog, please sir. A little terrier dog with white hair. Father gave me him a month ago, and said I might keep him. Someone did leave the garden gate open this afternoon, and he must 'a got away, sir, and I was so fond of him sir, he was so playful and loving, and I be afraid he be lost."

She began to call again, without waiting for an answer.

"Jack, Jack, Jack!"

"I'm afraid some boys have got your little dog," said Lucian. "They've killed him. You'd better go back home."

He went on, walking as fast as he could in his endeavor to get beyond the noise of the child's crying. It distressed him, and he wished to think of other things. He stamped his foot angrily on the ground as he recalled the annoyances of the afternoon, and longed for some hermitage on the mountains, far above the stench and the sound of humanity.

A little farther, and he came to Croeswen, where the road branched off to right and left. There was a triangular plot of grass between the two roads; there the cross had once stood, "the goodly and famous roode" of the old local chronicle. The words echoed in Lucian's ears as he went by on the right hand. "There were five steps that did go up to the first pace, and seven steps to the second pace, all of clene hewn ashler. And all above it was most curiously and gloriously wrought with thorowgh carved work; in the highest place was the Holy Roode with Christ upon the Cross having Marie on the one syde and John on the other. And below were six splendent and glisteringe archaungels that bore up the roode, and beneath them in their stories were the most fair and noble images of the xii Apostles and of divers other Saints and Martirs. And in the lowest storie there was a marvelous imagerie of divers Beasts, such as oxen and horses and swine, and little dogs and peacocks, all done in the finest and most curious wise, so that they all seemed as they were caught in a Wood of Thorns, the which is their torment of this life. And here once in the year was a marvelous solemn service, when the parson of Caermaen came out with the singers and all the people, singing the psalm Benedicite omnia opera as they passed along the road in their procession. And when they stood at the roode the priest did there his service, making certain prayers for the beasts, and then he went up to the first pace and preached a sermon to the people, shewing them that as our lord Jhu dyed upon the Tree of his deare mercy for us, so we too owe mercy to the beasts his Creatures, for that they are all his poor lieges and silly servants. And that like as the Holy Aungells do their suit to him on high, and the Blessed xii Apostles and the Martirs, and all the Blissful Saints served him aforetime on earth and now praise him in heaven, so also do the beasts serve him, though they be in torment of life and below men. For their spirit goeth downward, as Holy Writ teacheth us."

It was a quaint old record, a curious relic of what the modern inhabitants of Caermaen called the Dark Ages. A few of the stones that had formed the base of the cross still remained in position, grey with age, blotched with black lichen and green moss. The remainder of the famous rood had been used to mend the roads, to build pigsties and domestic offices; it had turned Protestant, in fact. Indeed, if it had remained, the parson of Caermaen would have had no time for the service; the coffee-stall, the Portuguese Missions, the Society for the Conversion of the Jews, and important social duties took up all his leisure. Besides, he thought the whole ceremony unscriptural.

Lucian passed on his way, wondering at the strange contrasts of the Middle Ages. How was it that people who could devise so beautiful a service believed in witchcraft, demoniacal possession and obsession, in the incubus and succubus, and in the Sabbath an in many other horrible absurdities? It seemed astonishing that anybody could even pretend to credit such monstrous tales, but there could be no doubt that the dread of old women who rode on broomsticks and liked black cats was once a very genuine terror.

A cold wind blew up from the river at sunset, and the scars on his body began to burn and tingle. The pain recalled his ritual to him, and he began to recite it as he walked along. He had cut a branch of thorn from the hedge and placed it next to his skin, pressing the spikes into the flesh with his hand till the warm blood ran down. He felt it was an exquisite and sweet observance for her sake; and then he thought of the secret golden palace he was building for her, the rare and wonderful city rising in his imagination. As the solemn night began to close about the earth, and the last glimmer of the sun faded from the hills, he gave himself anew to the woman, his body and his mind, all that he was, and all that he had.

IV

In the course of the week Lucian again visited Caermaen. He wished to view the amphitheatre more precisely, to note the exact position of the ancient walls, to gaze up the valley from certain points within the town, to imprint minutely and clearly on his mind the surge of the hills about the city, and the dark tapestry of the hanging woods. And he lingered in the museum where the relics of the Roman occupation had been stored; he was interested in the fragments of tessellated floors, in the glowing gold of drinking cups, the curious beads of fused and colored glass, the carved amber-work, the scent-flagons that still retained the memory of unctuous odors, the necklaces, brooches, hair-pins of gold and silver, and other intimate objects which had once belonged to Roman ladies. One of the glass flagons, buried in damp earth for many hundred years, had gathered in its dark grave all the splendors of the light, and now shone like an opal with a moonlight glamour and gleams of gold and pale sunset green, and imperial purple. Then there were the wine jars of red earthenware, the memorial stones from graves, and the heads of broken gods, with fragments of occult things used in the secret rites of Mithras. Lucian read on the labels where all these objects were found: in the churchyard, beneath the turf of the meadow, and in the old cemetery near the forest; and whenever it was possible he would make his way to the spot of discovery, and imagine the long darkness that had hidden gold and stone and amber. All these investigations were necessary for the scheme he had in view, so he became for some time quite a familiar figure in the dusty deserted streets and in the meadows by the river. His continual visits to Caermaen were a tortuous puzzle to the inhabitants, who flew to their windows at the sound of a step on the uneven pavements. They were at a loss in their conjectures; his motive for coming down three times a week must of course be bad, but it seemed undiscoverable. And Lucian on his side was at first a good deal put out by occasional encounters with members of the Gervase or Dixon or Colley tribes; he had often to stop and exchange a few conventional expressions, and such meetings, casual as they were, annoyed and distracted him. He was no longer infuriated or wounded by sneers of contempt or by the cackling laughter of the young people when they passed him on the road (his hat was a shocking one and his untidiness terrible), but such incidents were unpleasant just as the smell of a drain was unpleasant, and threw the strange mechanism of his thoughts out of fear for the time. Then he had been disgusted by the affair of the boys and the little dog; the loathsomeness of it had quite broken up his fancies. He had read books of modern occultism, and remembered some of the experiments described. The adept, it was alleged, could transfer the sense of consciousness from his brain to the foot or hand, he could annihilate the world around him and pass into another sphere. Lucian wondered whether he could not perform some such operation for his own benefit. Human beings were constantly annoying him and getting in his way, was it not possible to annihilate the race, or at all events to reduce them to wholly insignificant forms? A certain process suggested itself to his mind, a work partly mental and partly physical, and after two or three experiments he found to his astonishment and delight that it was successful. Here, he thought, he had discovered one of the secrets of true magic; this was the key to the symbolic transmutations of the Eastern tales. The adept could, in truth, change those who were obnoxious to him into harmless and unimportant shapes, not as in the letter of the old stories, by transforming the enemy, but by transforming himself. The magician puts men below him by going up higher, as one looks down on a mountain city from a loftier crag. The stones on the road and such petty obstacles do not trouble the wise man on the great journey, and so Lucian, when obliged to stop and converse with his fellow-creatures, to listen to their poor pretences and inanities, was no more inconvenienced than when he had to climb an awkward stile in the course of a walk. As for the more unpleasant manifestations of humanity; after all they no longer concerned him. Men intent on the great purpose did not suffer the current of their thoughts to be broken by the buzzing of a fly caught in a spider's web, so why should he be perturbed by the misery of a puppy in the hands of village boys? The fly, no doubt, endured its tortures; lying helpless and bound in those slimy bands, it cried out in its thin voice when the claws of the horrible monster fastened on it; but its dying agonies had never vexed the reverie of a lover. Lucian saw no reason why the boys should offend him more than the spider, or why he should pity the dog more than he pitied the fly. The talk of the men and women might be wearisome and inept and often malignant; but he could not imagine an alchemist at the moment of success, a general in the hour of victory, or a financier with a gigantic scheme of swindling well on the market being annoyed by the buzz of insects. The spider is, no doubt, a very terrible brute with a hideous mouth and hairy tiger-like claws when seen through the microscope; but Lucian had taken away the microscope from his eyes. He could now walk the streets of Caermaen confident and secure, without any dread of interruption, for at a moment's notice the transformation could be effected. Once Dr. Burrows caught him and made him promise to attend a bazaar that was to be held in aid of the Hungarian Protestants; Lucian assented the more willingly as he wished to pay a visit to certain curious mounds on a hill a little way out of the town, and he calculated on slinking off from the bazaar early in the afternoon. Lord Beamys was visiting Sir Vivian Ponsonby, a local magnate, and had kindly promised to drive over and declare the bazaar open. It was a solemn moment when the carriage drew up and the great man alighted. He was rather an evil-looking old nobleman, but the clergy and gentry, their wives and sons and daughters welcomed him with great and unctuous joy. Conversations were broken off in mid-sentence, slow people gaped, not realizing why their friends had so suddenly left them, the Meyricks came up hot and perspiring in fear lest they should be too late, Miss Colley, a yellow virgin of austere regard, smiled largely, Mrs. Dixon beckoned wildly with her parasol to the "girls" who were idly strolling in a distant part of the field, and the archdeacon ran at full speed. The air grew dark with bows, and resonant with the genial laugh of the archdeacon, the cackle of the younger ladies, and the shrill parrot-like voices of the matrons; those smiled who had never smiled before, and on some maiden faces there hovered that look of adoring ecstasy with which the old maidens graced their angels. Then, when all the due rites had been performed, the company turned and began to walk towards the booths of their small Vanity Fair. Lord Beamys led the way with Mrs. Gervase, Mrs. Dixon followed with Sir Vivian Ponsonby, and the multitudes that followed cried, saying, "What a dear old man!"--"Isn't it kind of him to come all this way?"--"What a sweet expression, isn't it?"--"I think he's an old love"--"One of the good old sort"--"Real English nobleman"--"Oh most correct, I assure you; if a girl gets into trouble, notice to quit at once"--"Always stands by the Church"-- "Twenty livings in his gift"--"Voted for the Public Worship Regulation Act"--"Ten thousand acres strictly preserved." The old lord was leering pleasantly and muttering to himself: "Some fine gals here. Like the looks of that filly with the pink hat. Ought to see more of her. She'd give Lotty points."

The pomp swept slowly across the grass: the archdeacon had got hold of Mr. Dixon, and they were discussing the misdeeds of some clergyman in the rural deanery.

"I can scarce credit it," said Mr. Dixon.

"Oh, I assure you, there can be no doubt. We have witnesses. There can be no question that there was a procession at Llanfihangel on the Sunday before Easter; the choir and minister went round the church, carrying palm branches in their hands."

"Very shocking."

"It has distressed the bishop. Martin is a hard-working man enough, and all that, but those sort of things can't be tolerated. The bishop told me that he had set his face against processions."

"Quite right: the bishop is perfectly right. Processions are unscriptural."

"It's the thin end of the wedge, you know, Dixon."

"Exactly. I have always resisted anything of the kind here."

"Right. Principiis obsta, you know. Martin is so imprudent. There's a way of doing things."

The "scriptural" procession led by Lord Beamys broke up when the stalls were reached, and gathered round the nobleman as he declared the bazaar open.

Lucian was sitting on a garden-seat, a little distance off, looking dreamily before him. And all that he saw was a swarm of flies clustering and buzzing about a lump of tainted meat that lay on the grass. The spectacle in no way interrupted the harmony of his thoughts, and soon after the opening of the bazaar he went quietly away, walking across the fields in the direction of the ancient mounds he desired to inspect.

All these journeys of his to Caermaen and its neighborhood had a peculiar object; he was gradually leveling to the dust the squalid kraals of modern times, and rebuilding the splendid and golden city of Siluria. All this mystic town was for the delight of his sweetheart and himself; for her the wonderful villas, the shady courts, the magic of tessellated pavements, and the hangings of rich stuffs with their intricate and glowing patterns. Lucian wandered all day through the shining streets, taking shelter sometimes in the gardens beneath the dense and gloomy ilex trees, and listening to the plash and trickle of the fountains. Sometimes he would look out of a window and watch the crowd and color of the market-place, and now and again a ship came up the river bringing exquisite silks and the merchandise of unknown lands in the Far East. He had made a curious and accurate map of the town he proposed to inhabit, in which every villa was set down and named. He drew his lines to scale with the gravity of a surveyor, and studied the plan till he was able to find his way from house to house on the darkest summer night. On the southern slopes about the town there were vineyards, always under a glowing sun, and sometimes he ventured to the furthest ridge of the forest, where the wild people still lingered, that he might catch the golden gleam of the city far away, as the light quivered and scintillated on the glittering tiles. And there were gardens outside the city gates where strange and brilliant flowers grew, filling the hot air with their odor, and scenting the breeze that blew along the streets. The dull modern life was far away, and people who saw him at this period wondered what was amiss; the abstraction of his glance was obvious, even to eyes not over-sharp. But men and women had lost all their power of annoyance and vexation; they could no longer even interrupt his thought for a moment. He could listen to Mr. Dixon with apparent attention, while he was in reality enraptured by the entreating music of the double flute, played by a girl in the garden of Avallaunius, for that was the name he had taken. Mr. Dixon was innocently discoursing archeology, giving a brief résumé of the view expressed by Mr. Wyndham at the last meeting of the antiquarian society.

"There can be no doubt that the temple of Diana stood there in pagan times," he concluded, and Lucian assented to the opinion, and asked a few questions which seemed pertinent enough. But all the time the flute notes were sounding in his ears, and the ilex threw a purple shadow on the white pavement before his villa. A boy came forward from the garden; he had been walking amongst the vines and plucking the ripe grapes, and the juice had trickled down over his breast. Standing beside the girl, unashamed in the sunlight, he began to sing one of Sappho's love songs. His voice was as full and rich as a woman's, but purged of all emotion; he was an instrument of music in the flesh. Lucian looked at him steadily; the white perfect body shone against the roses and the blue of the sky, clear and gleaming as marble in the glare of the sun. The words he sang burned and flamed with passion, and he was as unconscious of their meaning as the twin pipes of the flute. And the girl was smiling. The vicar shook hands and went on, well pleased with his remarks on the temple of Diana, and also with Lucian's polite interest.

"He is by no means wanting in intelligence," he said to his family. "A little curious in manner, perhaps, but not stupid."

"Oh, papa," said Henrietta, "don't you think he is rather silly? He can't talk about anything-- anything interesting, I mean. And he pretends to know a lot about books, but I heard him say the other day he had never read The Prince of the House of David or Ben-Hur. Fancy!"

The vicar had not interrupted Lucian. The sun still beat upon the roses, and a little breeze bore the scent of them to his nostrils together with the smell of grapes and vine-leaves. He had become curious in sensation, and as he leant back upon the cushions covered with glistening yellow silk, he was trying to analyze a strange ingredient in the perfume of the air. He had penetrated far beyond the crude distinctions of modern times, beyond the rough: "there's a smell of roses," "there must be sweetbriar somewhere." Modern perceptions of odor were, he knew, far below those of the savage in delicacy. The degraded black fellow of Australia could distinguish odors in a way that made the consumer of "damper" stare in amazement, but the savage's sensations were all strictly utilitarian. To Lucian as he sat in the cool porch, his feet on the marble, the air came laden with scents as subtly and wonderfully interwoven and contrasted as the harmonica of a great master. The stained marble of the pavement gave a cool reminiscence of the Italian mountain, the blood-red roses palpitating in the sunlight sent out an odor mystical as passion itself, and there was the hint of inebriation in the perfume of the trellised vines. Besides these, the girl's desire and the unripe innocence of the boy were as distinct as benzoin and myrrh, both delicious and exquisite, and exhaled as freely as the scent of the roses. But there was another element that puzzled him, an aromatic suggestion of the forest. He understood it at last; it was the vapor of the great red pines that grew beyond the garden; their spicy needles were burning in the sun, and the smell was as fragrant as the fume of incense blown from far. The soft entreaty of the flute and the swelling rapture of the boy's voice beat on the air together, and Lucian wondered whether there were in the nature of things any true distinction between the impressions of sound and scent and color. The violent blue of the sky, the song, and the odours seemed rather varied symbols of one mystery than distinct entities. He could almost imagine that the boy's innocence was indeed a perfume, and that the palpitating roses had become a sonorous chant.

In the curious silence which followed the last notes, when the boy and girl had passed under the purple ilex shadow, he fell into a reverie. The fancy that sensations are symbols and not realities hovered in his mind, and led him to speculate as to whether they could not actually be transmuted one into another. It was possible, he thought, that a whole continent of knowledge had been undiscovered; the energies of men having been expended in unimportant and foolish directions. Modern ingenuity had been employed on such trifles as locomotive engines, electric cables, and cantilever bridges; on elaborate devices for bringing uninteresting people nearer together; the ancients had been almost as foolish, because they had mistaken the symbol for the thing signified. It was not the material banquet which really mattered, but the thought of it; it was almost as futile to eat and take emetics and eat again as to invent telephones and high-pressure boilers. As for some other ancient methods of enjoying life, one might as well set oneself to improve calico printing at once.

"Only in the garden of Avallaunius," said Lucian to himself, "is the true and exquisite science to be found."

He could imagine a man who was able to live in one sense while he pleased; to whom, for example, every impression of touch, taste, hearing, or seeing should be translated into odor; who at the desired kiss should be ravished with the scent of dark violets, to whom music should be the perfume of a rose-garden at dawn.

When, now and again, he voluntarily resumed the experience of common life, it was that he might return with greater delight to the garden in the city of refuge. In the actual world the talk was of Nonconformists, the lodger franchise, and the Stock Exchange; people were constantly reading newspapers, drinking Australian Burgundy, and doing other things equally absurd. They either looked shocked when the fine art of pleasure was mentioned, or confused it with going to musical comedies, drinking bad whisky, and keeping late hours in disreputable and vulgar company. He found to his amusement that the profligate were by many degrees duller than the pious, but that the most tedious of all were the persons who preached promiscuity, and called their system of "pigging" the "New Morality."

He went back to the city lovingly, because it was built and adorned for his love. As the metaphysicians insist on the consciousness of the ego as the implied basis of all thought, so he knew that it was she in whom he had found himself, and through whom and for whom all the true life existed. He felt that Annie had taught him the rare magic which had created the garden of Avallaunius. It was for her that he sought strange secrets and tried to penetrate the mysteries of sensation, for he could only give her wonderful thoughts and a wonderful life, and a poor body stained with the scars of his worship.

It was with this object, that of making the offering of himself a worthy one, that he continually searched for new and exquisite experiences. He made lovers come before him and confess their secrets; he pried into the inmost mysteries of innocence and shame, noting how passion and reluctance strive together for the mastery. In the amphitheatre he sometimes witnessed strange entertainments in which such tales as Daphnis and Chloe and The Golden Ass were performed before him. These shows were always given at nighttime; a circle of torch-bearers surrounded the stage in the center, and above, all the tiers of seats were dark. He would look up at the soft blue of the summer sky, and at the vast dim mountain hovering like a cloud in the west, and then at the scene illumined by a flaring light, and contrasted with violent shadows. The subdued mutter of conversation in a strange language rising from bench after bench, swift hissing whispers of explanation, now and then a shout or a cry as the interest deepened, the restless tossing of the people as the end drew near, an arm lifted, a cloak thrown back, the sudden blaze of a torch lighting up purple or white or the gleam of gold in the black serried ranks; these were impressions that seemed always amazing. And above, the dusky light of the stars, around, the sweet-scented meadows, and the twinkle of lamps from the still city, the cry of the sentries about the walls, the wash of the tide filling the river, and the salt savor of the sea. With such a scenic ornament he saw the tale of Apuleius represented, heard the names of Fotis and Byrrhaena and Lucius proclaimed, and the deep intonation of such sentences as Ecce Veneris hortator et armiger Liber advenit ultro. The tale went on through all its marvelous adventures, and Lucian left the amphitheatre and walked beside the river where he could hear indistinctly the noise of voices and the singing Latin, and note how the rumor of the stage mingled with the murmur of the shuddering reeds and the cool lapping of the tide. Then came the farewell of the cantor, the thunder of applause, the crash of cymbals, the calling of the flutes, and the surge of the wind in the great dark wood.

At other times it was his chief pleasure to spend a whole day in a vineyard planted on the steep slope beyond the bridge. A grey stone seat had been placed beneath a shady laurel, and here he often sat without motion or gesture for many hours. Below him the tawny river swept round the town in a half circle; he could see the swirl of the yellow water, its eddies and miniature whirlpools, as the tide poured up from the south. And beyond the river the strong circuit of the walls, and within, the city glittered like a charming piece of mosaic. He freed himself from the obtuse modern view of towns as places where human beings live and make money and rejoice or suffer, for from the standpoint of the moment such facts were wholly impertinent. He knew perfectly well that for his present purpose the tawny sheen and shimmer of the tide was the only fact of importance about the river, and so he regarded the city as a curious work in jewelry. Its radiant marble porticoes, the white walls of the villas, a dome of burning copper, the flash and scintillation of tiled roofs, the quiet red of brickwork, dark groves of ilex, and cypress, and laurel, glowing rose-gardens, and here and there the silver of a fountain, seemed arranged and contrasted with a wonderful art, and the town appeared a delicious ornament, every cube of color owing its place to the thought and inspiration of the artificer. Lucian, as he gazed from his arbour amongst the trellised vines, lost none of the subtle pleasures of the sight; noting every nuance of color, he let his eyes dwell for a moment on the scarlet flash of poppies, and then on a glazed roof which in the glance of the sun seemed to spout white fire. A square of vines was like some rare green stone; the grapes were massed so richly amongst the vivid leaves, that even from far off there was a sense of irregular flecks and stains of purple running through the green. The laurel garths were like cool jade; the gardens, where red, yellow, blue and white gleamed together in a mist of heat, had the radiance of opal; the river was a band of dull gold. On every side, as if to enhance the preciousness of the city, the woods hung dark on the hills; above, the sky was violet, specked with minute feathery clouds, white as snowflakes. It reminded him of a beautiful bowl in his villa; the ground was of that same brilliant blue, and the artist had fused into the work, when it was hot, particles of pure white glass.

For Lucian this was a spectacle that enchanted many hours; leaning on one hand, he would gaze at the city glowing in the sunlight till the purple shadows grew down the slopes and the long melodious trumpet sounded for the evening watch. Then, as he strolled beneath the trellises, he would see all the radiant facets glimmering out, and the city faded into haze, a white wall shining here and there, and the gardens veiled in a dim glow of color. On such an evening he would go home with the sense that he had truly lived a day, having received for many hours the most acute impressions of beautiful color.

Often he spent the night in the cool court of his villa, lying amidst soft cushions heaped upon the marble bench. A lamp stood on the table at his elbow, its light making the water in the cistern twinkle. There was no sound in the court except the soft continual plashing of the fountain. Throughout these still hours he would meditate, and he became more than ever convinced that man could, if he pleased, become lord of his own sensations. This, surely, was the true meaning concealed under the beautiful symbolism of alchemy. Some years before he had read many of the wonderful alchemical books of the later Middle Ages, and had suspected that something other than the turning of lead into gold was intended. This impression was deepened when he looked into Lumen de Lumine by Vaughan, the brother of the Silurist, and he had long puzzled himself in the endeavor to find a reasonable interpretation of the hermetic mystery, and of the red powder, "glistening and glorious in the sun." And the solution shone out at last, bright and amazing, as he lay quiet in the court of Avallaunius. He knew that he himself had solved the riddle, that he held in his hand the powder of projection, the philosopher's stone transmuting all it touched to fine gold; the gold of exquisite impressions. He understood now something of the alchemical symbolism; the crucible and the furnace, the "Green Dragon," and the "Son Blessed of the Fire" had, he saw, a peculiar meaning. He understood, too, why the uninitiated were warned of the terror and danger through which they must pass; and the vehemence with which the adepts disclaimed all desire for material riches no longer struck him as singular. The wise man does not endure the torture of the furnace in order that he may be able to compete with operators in pork and company promoters; neither a steam yacht, nor a grouse-moor, nor three liveried footmen would add at all to his gratifications. Again Lucian said to himself:

"Only in the court of Avallaunius is the true science of the exquisite to be found."

He saw the true gold into which the beggarly matter of existence may be transmuted by spagyric art; a succession of delicious moments, all the rare flavors of life concentrated, purged of their lees, and preserved in a beautiful vessel. The moonlight fell green on the fountain and on the curious pavements, and in the long sweet silence of the night he lay still and felt that thought itself was an acute pleasure, to be expressed perhaps in terms of odor or color by the true artist.

And he gave himself other and even stranger gratifications. Outside the city walls, between the baths and the amphitheatre, was a tavern, a place where wonderful people met to drink wonderful wine. There he saw priests of Mithras and Isis and of more occult rites from the East, men who wore robes of bright colours, and grotesque ornaments, symbolizing secret things. They spoke amongst themselves in a rich jargon of colored words, full of hidden meanings and the sense of matters unintelligible to the uninitiated, alluding to what was concealed beneath roses, and calling each other by strange names. And there were actors who gave the shows in the amphitheatre, officers of the legion who had served in wild places, singers, and dancing girls, and heroes of strange adventure.

The walls of the tavern were covered with pictures painted in violent hues; blues and reds and greens jarring against one another and lighting up the gloom of the place. The stone benches were always crowded, the sunlight came in through the door in a long bright beam, casting a dancing shadow of vine leaves on the further wall. There a painter had made a joyous figure of the young Bacchus driving the leopards before him with his ivy-staff, and the quivering shadow seemed a part of the picture. The room was cool and dark and cavernous, but the scent and heat of the summer gushed in through the open door. There was ever a full sound, with noise and vehemence, there, and the rolling music of the Latin tongue never ceased.

"The wine of the siege, the wine that we saved," cried one.

"Look for the jar marked Faunus; you will be glad."

"Bring me the wine of the Owl's Face."

"Let us have the wine of Saturn's Bridge."

The boys who served brought the wine in dull red jars that struck a charming note against their white robes. They poured out the violet and purple and golden wine with calm sweet faces as if they were assisting in the mysteries, without any sign that they heard the strange words that flashed from side to side. The cups were all of glass; some were of deep green, of the color of the sea near the land, flawed and specked with the bubbles of the furnace. Others were of brilliant scarlet, streaked with irregular bands of white, and having the appearance of white globules in the molded stem. There were cups of dark glowing blue, deeper and more shining than the blue of the sky, and running through the substance of the glass were veins of rich gamboge yellow, twining from the brim to the foot. Some cups were of a troubled and clotted red, with alternating blotches of dark and light, some were variegated with white and yellow stains, some wore a film of rainbow colours, some glittered, shot with gold threads through the clear crystal, some were as if sapphires hung suspended in running water, some sparkled with the glint of stars, some were black and golden like tortoiseshell.

A strange feature was the constant and fluttering motion of hands and arms. Gesture made a constant commentary on speech; white fingers, whiter arms, and sleeves of all colours, hovered restlessly, appeared and disappeared with an effect of threads crossing and re-crossing on the loom. And the odor of the place was both curious and memorable; something of the damp cold breath of the cave meeting the hot blast of summer, the strangely mingled aromas of rare wines as they fell plashing and ringing into the cups, the drugged vapor of the East that the priests of Mithras and Isis bore from their steaming temples; these were always strong and dominant. And the women were scented, sometimes with unctuous and overpowering perfumes, and to the artist the experiences of those present were hinted in subtle and delicate nuances of odor.

They drank their wine and caressed all day in the tavern. The women threw their round white arms about their lover's necks, they intoxicated them with the scent of their hair, the priests muttered their fantastic jargon of Theurgy. And through the sonorous clash of voices there always seemed the ring of the cry:

"Look for the jar marked Faunus; you will be glad."

Outside, the vine tendrils shook on the white walls glaring in the sunshine; the breeze swept up from the yellow river, pungent with the salt sea savor.

These tavern scenes were often the subject of Lucian's meditation as he sat amongst the cushions on the marble seat. The rich sound of the voices impressed him above all things, and he saw that words have a far higher reason than the utilitarian office of imparting a man's thought. The common notion that language and linked words are important only as a means of expression he found a little ridiculous; as if electricity were to be studied solely with the view of "wiring" to people, and all its other properties left unexplored, neglected. Language, he understood, was chiefly important for the beauty of its sounds, by its possession of words resonant, glorious to the ear, by its capacity, when exquisitely arranged, of suggesting wonderful and indefinable impressions, perhaps more ravishing and farther removed from the domain of strict thought than the impressions excited by music itself. Here lay hidden the secret of the sensuous art of literature; it was the secret of suggestion, the art of causing delicious sensation by the use of words. In a way, therefore, literature was independent of thought; the mere English listener, if he had an ear attuned, could recognize the beauty of a splendid Latin phrase.

Here was the explanation of the magic of Lycidas. From the standpoint of the formal understanding it was an affected lament over some wholly uninteresting and unimportant Mr. King; it was full of nonsense about "shepherds" and "flocks" and "muses" and such stale stock of poetry; the introduction of St Peter on a stage thronged with nymphs and river gods was blasphemous, absurd, and, in the worst taste; there were touches of greasy Puritanism, the twang of the conventicle was only too apparent. And Lycidas was probably the most perfect piece of pure literature in existence; because every word and phrase and line were sonorous, ringing and echoing with music.

"Literature," he re-enunciated in his mind, "is the sensuous art of causing exquisite impressions by means of words."

And yet there was something more; besides the logical thought, which was often a hindrance, a troublesome though inseparable accident, besides the sensation, always a pleasure and a delight, besides these there were the indefinable inexpressible images which all fine literature summons to the mind. As the chemist in his experiments is sometimes astonished to find unknown, unexpected elements in the crucible or the receiver, as the world of material things is considered by some a thin veil of the immaterial universe, so he who reads wonderful prose or verse is conscious of suggestions that cannot be put into words, which do not rise from the logical sense, which are rather parallel to than connected with the sensuous delight. The world so disclosed is rather the world of dreams, rather the world in which children sometimes live, instantly appearing, and instantly vanishing away, a world beyond all expression or analysis, neither of the intellect nor of the senses. He called these fancies of his "Meditations of a Tavern," and was amused to think that a theory of letters should have risen from the eloquent noise that rang all day about the violet and golden wine.

"Let us seek for more exquisite things," said Lucian to himself. He could almost imagine the magic transmutation of the senses accomplished, the strong sunlight was an odor in his nostrils; it poured down on the white marble and the palpitating roses like a flood. The sky was a glorious blue, making the heart joyous, and the eyes could rest in the dark green leaves and purple shadow of the ilex. The earth seemed to burn and leap beneath the sun, he fancied he could see the vine tendrils stir and quiver in the heat, and the faint fume of the scorching pine needles was blown across the gleaming garden to the seat beneath the porch. Wine was before him in a cup of carved amber; a wine of the color of a dark rose, with a glint as of a star or of a jet of flame deep beneath the brim; and the cup was twined about with a delicate wreath of ivy. He was often loath to turn away from the still contemplation of such things, from the mere joy of the violent sun, and the responsive earth. He loved his garden and the view of the tessellated city from the vineyard on the hill, the strange clamor of the tavern, and white Fotis appearing on the torch-lit stage. And there were shops in the town in which he delighted, the shops of the perfume makers, and jewelers, and dealers in curious ware. He loved to see all things made for ladies' use, to touch the gossamer silks that were to touch their bodies, to finger the beads of amber and the gold chains which would stir above their hearts, to handle the carved hairpins and brooches, to smell odors which were already dedicated to love.

But though these were sweet and delicious gratifications, he knew that there were more exquisite things of which he might be a spectator. He had seen the folly of regarding fine literature from the standpoint of the logical intellect, and he now began to question the wisdom of looking at life as if it were a moral representation. Literature, he knew, could not exist without some meaning, and considerations of right and wrong were to a certain extent inseparable from the conception of life, but to insist on ethics as the chief interest of the human pageant was surely absurd. One might as well read Lycidas for the sake of its denunciation of "our corrupted Clergy," or Homer for "manners and customs." An artist entranced by a beautiful landscape did not greatly concern himself with the geological formation of the hills, nor did the lover of a wild sea inquire as to the chemical analysis of the water. Lucian saw a colored and complex life displayed before him, and he sat enraptured at the spectacle, not concerned to know whether actions were good or bad, but content if they were curious.

In this spirit he made a singular study of corruption. Beneath his feet, as he sat in the garden porch, was a block of marble through which there ran a scarlet stain. It began with a faint line, thin as a hair, and grew as it advanced, sending out offshoots to right and left, and broadening to a pool of brilliant red. There were strange lives into which he looked that were like the block of marble; women with grave sweet faces told him the astounding tale of their adventures, and how, they said, they had met the faun when they were little children. They told him how they had played and watched by the vines and the fountains, and dallied with the nymphs, and gazed at images reflected in the water pools, till the authentic face appeared from the wood. He heard others tell how they had loved the satyrs for many years before they knew their race; and there were strange stories of those who had longed to speak but knew not the word of the enigma, and searched in all strange paths and ways before they found it.

He heard the history of the woman who fell in love with her slave-boy, and tempted him for three years in vain. He heard the tale from the woman's full red lips, and watched her face, full of the ineffable sadness of lust, as she described her curious stratagems in mellow phrases. She was drinking a sweet yellow wine from a gold cup as she spoke, and the odor in her hair and the aroma of the precious wine seemed to mingle with the soft strange words that flowed like an unguent from a carven jar. She told how she bought the boy in the market of an Asian city, and had him carried to her house in the grove of fig-trees. "Then," she went on, "he was led into my presence as I sat between the columns of my court. A blue veil was spread above to shut out the heat of the sun, and rather twilight than light shone on the painted walls, and the wonderful colours of the pavement, and the images of Love and the Mother of Love. The men who brought the boy gave him over to my girls, who undressed him before me, one drawing gently away his robe, another stroking his brown and flowing hair, another praising the whiteness of his limbs, and another caressing him, and speaking loving words in his hear. But the boy looked sullenly at them all, striking away their hands, and pouting with his lovely and splendid lips, and I saw a blush, like the rosy veil of dawn, reddening his body and his cheeks. Then I made them bathe him, and anoint him with scented oils from head to foot, till his limbs shone and glistened with the gentle and mellow glow of an ivory statue. Then I said: 'You are bashful, because you shine alone amongst us all; see, we too will be your fellows.' The girls began first of all, fondling and kissing one another, and doing for each other the offices of waiting-maids. They drew out the pins and loosened the bands of their hair, and I never knew before that they were so lovely. The soft and shining tresses flowed down, rippling like sea-waves; some had hair golden and radiant as this wine in my cup, the faces of others appeared amidst the blackness of ebony; there were locks that seemed of burnished and scintillating copper, some glowed with hair of tawny splendor, and others were crowned with the brightness of the sardonyx. Then, laughing, and without the appearance of shame, they unfastened the brooches and bands which sustained their robes, and so allowed silk and linen to flow swiftly to the stained floor, so that one would have said there was a sudden apparition of the fairest nymphs. With many festive and jocose words they began to incite each other to mirth, praising the beauties that shone on every side, and calling the boy by a girl's name, they invited him to be their playmate. But he refused, shaking his head, and still standing dumb-founded and abashed, as if he saw a forbidden and terrible spectacle. Then I ordered the women to undo my hair and my clothes, making them caress me with the tenderness of the fondest lover, but without avail, for the foolish boy still scowled and pouted out his lips, stained with an imperial and glorious scarlet."

She poured out more of the topaz-colored wine in her cup, and Lucian saw it glitter as it rose to the brim and mirrored the gleam of the lamps. The tale went on, recounting a hundred strange devices. The woman told how she had tempted the boy by idleness and ease, giving him long hours of sleep, and allowing him to recline all day on soft cushions, that swelled about him, enclosing his body. She tried the experiment of curious odors: causing him to smell always about him the oil of roses, and burning in his presence rare gums from the East. He was allured by soft dresses, being clothed in silks that caressed the skin with the sense of a fondling touch. Three times a day they spread before him a delicious banquet, full of savor and odor and color; three times a day they endeavored to intoxicate him with delicate wine.

"And so," the lady continued, "I spared nothing to catch him in the glistening nets of love; taking only sour and contemptuous glances in return. And at last in an incredible shape I won the victory, and then, having gained a green crown, fighting in agony against his green and crude immaturity, I devoted him to the theatre, where he amused the people by the splendor of his death."

On another evening he heard the history of the man who dwelt alone, refusing all allurements, and was at last discovered to be the lover of a black statue. And there were tales of strange cruelties, of men taken by mountain robbers, and curiously maimed and disfigured, so that when they escaped and returned to the town, they were thought to be monsters and killed at their own doors. Lucian left no dark or secret nook of life unvisited; he sat down, as he said, at the banquet, resolved to taste all the savors, and to leave no flagon unvisited.

His relations grew seriously alarmed about him at this period. While he heard with some inner ear the suave and eloquent phrases of singular tales, and watched the lamp-light in amber and purple wine, his father saw a lean pale boy, with black eyes that burnt in hollows, and sad and sunken cheeks.

"You ought to try and eat more, Lucian," said the parson; "and why don't you have some beer?"

He was looking feebly at the roast mutton and sipping a little water; but he would not have eaten or drunk with more relish if the choicest meat and drink had been before him.

His bones seemed, as Miss Deacon said, to be growing through his skin; he had all the appearance of an ascetic whose body has been reduced to misery by long and grievous penance. People who chanced to see him could not help saying to one another: "How ill and wretched that Lucian Taylor looks!" They were of course quite unaware of the joy and luxury in which his real life was spent, and some of them began to pity him, and to speak to him kindly.

It was too late for that. The friendly words had as much lost their meaning as the words of contempt. Edward Dixon hailed him cheerfully in the street one day:

"Come in to my den, won't you, old fellow?" he said. "You won't see the pater. I've managed to bag a bottle of his old port. I know you smoke like a furnace, and I've got some ripping cigars. You will come, won't you! I can tell you the pater's booze is first rate."

He gently declined and went on. Kindness and unkindness, pity and contempt had become for him mere phrases; he could not have distinguished one from the other. Hebrew and Chinese, Hungarian and Pushtu would be pretty much alike to an agricultural laborer; if he cared to listen he might detect some general differences in sound, but all four tongues would be equally devoid of significance.

To Lucian, entranced in the garden of Avallaunius, it seemed very strange that he had once been so ignorant of all the exquisite meanings of life. Now, beneath the violet sky, looking through the brilliant trellis of the vines, he saw the picture; before, he had gazed in sad astonishment at the squalid rag which was wrapped about it.

V

And he was at last in the city of the unending murmuring streets, a part of the stirring shadow, of the amber-lighted gloom.

It seemed a long time since he had knelt before his sweetheart in the lane, the moon-fire streaming upon them from the dark circle of the fort, the air and the light and his soul full of haunting, the touch of the unimaginable thrilling his heart; and now he sat in a terrible "bed-sitting-room" in a western suburb, confronted by a heap and litter of papers on the desk of a battered old bureau.

He had put his breakfast-tray out on the landing, and was thinking of the morning's work, and of some very dubious pages that he had blackened the night before. But when he had lit his disreputable briar, he remembered there was an unopened letter waiting for him on the table; he had recognized the vague, staggering script of Miss Deacon, his cousin. There was not much news; his father was "just the same as usual," there had been a good deal of rain, the farmers expected to make a lot of cider, and so forth. But at the close of the letter Miss Deacon became useful for reproof and admonition.

"I was at Caermaen on Tuesday," she said, "and called on the Gervases and the Dixons. Mr. Gervase smiled when I told him you were a literary man, living in London, and said he was afraid you wouldn't find it a very practical career. Mrs. Gervase was very proud of Henry's success; he passed fifth for some examination, and will begin with nearly four hundred a year. I don't wonder the Gervases are delighted. Then I went to the Dixons, and had tea. Mrs. Dixon wanted to know if you had published anything yet, and I said I thought not. She showed me a book everybody is talking about, called the Dog and the Doctor. She says it's selling by thousands, and that one can't take up a paper without seeing the author's name. She told me to tell you that you ought to try to write something like it. Then Mr. Dixon came in from the study, and your name was mentioned again. He said he was afraid you had made rather a mistake in trying to take up literature as if it were a profession, and seemed to think that a place in a house of business would be more suitable and more practical. He pointed out that you had not had the advantages of a university training, and said that you would find men who had made good friends, and had the tone of the university, would be before you at every step. He said Edward was doing very well at Oxford. He writes to them that he knows several noblemen, and that young Philip Bullingham (son of Sir John Bullingham) is his most intimate friend; of course this is very satisfactory for the Dixons. I am afraid, my dear Lucian, you have rather overrated your powers. Wouldn't it be better, even now, to look out for some real work to do, instead of wasting your time over those silly old books? I know quite well how the Gervases and the Dixons feel; they think idleness so injurious for a young man, and likely to lead to bad habits. You know, my dear Lucian, I am only writing like this because of my affection for you, so I am sure, my dear boy, you won't be offended."

Lucian pigeon-holed the letter solemnly in the receptacle lettered "Barbarians." He felt that he ought to ask himself some serious questions: "Why haven't I passed fifth? why isn't Philip (son of Sir John) my most intimate friend? why am I an idler, liable to fall into bad habits?" but he was eager to get to his work, a curious and intricate piece of analysis. So the battered bureau, the litter of papers, and the thick fume of his pipe, engulfed him and absorbed him for the rest of the morning. Outside were the dim October mists, the dreary and languid life of a side street, and beyond, on the main road, the hum and jangle of the gliding trains. But he heard none of the uneasy noises of the quarter, not even the shriek of the garden gates nor the yelp of the butcher on his round, for delight in his great task made him unconscious of the world outside.

He had come by curious paths to this calm hermitage between Shepherd's Bush and Acton Vale. The golden weeks of the summer passed on in their enchanted procession, and Annie had not returned, neither had she written. Lucian, on his side, sat apart, wondering why his longing for her were not sharper. As he though of his raptures he would smile faintly to himself, and wonder whether he had not lost the world and Annie with it. In the garden of Avallaunius his sense of external things had grown dim and indistinct; the actual, material life seemed every day to become a show, a fleeting of shadows across a great white light. At last the news came that Annie Morgan had been married from her sister's house to a young farmer, to whom it appeared, she had been long engaged, and Lucian was ashamed to find himself only conscious of amusement, mingled with gratitude. She had been the key that opened the shut palace, and he was now secure on the throne of ivory and gold. A few days after he had heard the news he repeated the adventure of his boyhood; for the second time he scaled the steep hillside, and penetrated the matted brake. He expected violent disillusion, but his feeling was rather astonishment at the activity of boyish imagination. There was no terror nor amazement now in the green bulwarks, and the stunted undergrowth did not seem in any way extraordinary. Yet he did not laugh at the memory of his sensations, he was not angry at the cheat. Certainly it had been all illusion, all the heats and chills of boyhood, its thoughts of terror were without significance. But he recognized that the illusions of the child only differed from those of the man in that they were more picturesque; belief in fairies and belief in the Stock Exchange as bestowers of happiness were equally vain, but the latter form of faith was ugly as well as inept. It was better, he knew, and wiser, to wish for a fairy coach than to cherish longings for a well-appointed brougham and liveried servants.

He turned his back on the green walls and the dark oaks without any feeling of regret or resentment. After a little while he began to think of his adventures with pleasure; the ladder by which he had mounted had disappeared, but he was safe on the height. By the chance fancy of a beautiful girl he had been redeemed from a world of misery and torture, the world of external things into which he had come a stranger, by which he had been tormented. He looked back at a kind of vision of himself seen as he was a year before, a pitiable creature burning and twisting on the hot coals of the pit, crying lamentably to the laughing bystanders for but one drop of cold water wherewith to cool his tongue. He confessed to himself, with some contempt, that he had been a social being, depending for his happiness on the goodwill of others; he had tried hard to write, chiefly, it was true, from love of the art, but a little from a social motive. He had imagined that a written book and the praise of responsible journals would ensure him the respect of the county people. It was a quaint idea, and he saw the lamentable fallacies naked; in the first place, a painstaking artist in words was not respected by the respectable; secondly, books should not be written with the object of gaining the goodwill of the landed and commercial interests; thirdly and chiefly, no man should in any way depend on another.

From this utter darkness, from danger of madness, the ever dear and sweet Annie had rescued him. Very beautifully and fitly, as Lucian thought, she had done her work without any desire to benefit him, she had simply willed to gratify her own passion, and in doing this had handed to him the priceless secret. And he, on his side, had reversed the process; merely to make himself a splendid offering for the acceptance of his sweetheart, he had cast aside the vain world, and had found the truth, which now remained with him, precious and enduring.

And since the news of the marriage he found that his worship of her had by no means vanished; rather in his heart was the eternal treasure of a happy love, untarnished and spotless; it would be like a mirror of gold without alloy, bright and lustrous for ever. For Lucian, it was no defect in the woman that she was desirous and faithless; he had not conceived an affection for certain moral or intellectual accidents, but for the very woman. Guided by the self-evident axiom that humanity is to be judged by literature, and not literature by humanity, he detected the analogy between Lycidas and Annie. Only the dullard would object to the nauseous cant of the one, or to the indiscretions of the other. A sober critic might say that the man who could generalize Herbert and Laud, Donne and Herrick, Sanderson and Juxon, Hammond and Lancelot Andrewes into "our corrupted Clergy" must be either an imbecile or a scoundrel, or probably both. The judgment would be perfectly true, but as a criticism of Lycidas it would be a piece of folly. In the case of the woman one could imagine the attitude of the conventional lover; of the chevalier who, with his tongue in his cheek, "reverences and respects" all women, and coming home early in the morning writes a leading article on St English Girl. Lucian, on the other hand, felt profoundly grateful to the delicious Annie, because she had at precisely the right moment voluntarily removed her image from his way. He confessed to himself that, latterly, he had a little dreaded her return as an interruption; he had shivered at the thought that their relations would become what was so terribly called an "intrigue" or "affair." There would be all the threadbare and common stratagems, the vulgarity of secret assignations, and an atmosphere suggesting the period of Mr. Thomas Moore and Lord Byron and "segars." Lucian had been afraid of all this; he had feared lest love itself should destroy love.

He considered that now, freed from the torment of the body, leaving untasted the green water that makes thirst more burning, he was perfectly initiated in the true knowledge of the splendid and glorious love. There seemed to him a monstrous paradox in the assertion that there could be no true love without a corporal presence of the beloved; even the popular sayings of "Absence makes the heart grow fonder," and "familiarity breeds contempt," witnessed to the contrary. He thought, sighing, and with compassion, of the manner in which men are continually led astray by the cheat of the senses. In order that the unborn might still be added to the born, nature had inspired men with the wild delusion that the bodily companionship of the lover and the beloved was desirable above all things, and so, by the false show of pleasure, the human race was chained to vanity, and doomed to an eternal thirst for the non-existent.

Again and again he gave thanks for his own escape; he had been set free from a life of vice and sin and folly, from all the dangers and illusions that are most dreaded by the wise. He laughed as he remembered what would be the common view of the situation. An ordinary lover would suffer all the sting of sorrow and contempt; there would be grief for a lost mistress, and rage at her faithlessness, and hate in the heart; one foolish passion driving on another, and driving the man to ruin. For what would be commonly called the real woman he now cared nothing; if he had heard that she had died in her farm in Utter Gwent, he would have experienced only a passing sorrow, such as he might feel at the death of any one he had once known. But he did not think of the young farmer's wife as the real Annie; he did not think of the frost-bitten leaves in winter as the real rose. Indeed, the life of many reminded him of the flowers; perhaps more especially of those flowers which to all appearance are for many years but dull and dusty clumps of green, and suddenly, in one night, burst into the flame of blossom, and fill all the misty lawns with odor; till the morning. It was in that night that the flower lived, not through the long unprofitable years; and, in like manner, many human lives, he thought, were born in the evening and dead before the coming of day. But he had preserved the precious flower in all its glory, not suffering it to wither in the hard light, but keeping it in a secret place, where it could never be destroyed. Truly now, and for the first time, he possessed Annie, as a man possesses the gold which he has dug from the rock and purged of its baseness.

He was musing over these things when a piece of news, very strange and unexpected, arrived at the rectory. A distant, almost a mythical relative, known from childhood as "Cousin Edward in the Isle of Wight," had died, and by some strange freak had left Lucian two thousand pounds. It was a pleasure to give his father five hundred pounds, and the rector on his side forgot for a couple of days to lean his head on his hand. From the rest of the capital, which was well invested, Lucian found he would derive something between sixty and seventy pounds a year, and his old desires for literature and a refuge in the murmuring streets returned to him. He longed to be free from the incantations that surrounded him in the country, to work and live in a new atmosphere; and so, with many good wishes from his father, he came to the retreat in the waste places of London.

He was in high spirits when he found the square, clean room, horribly furnished, in the by-street that branched from the main road, and advanced in an unlovely sweep to the mud pits and the desolation that was neither town nor country. On every side monotonous grey streets, each house the replica of its neighbor, to the east an unexplored wilderness, north and west and south the brickfields and market-gardens, everywhere the ruins of the country, the tracks where sweet lanes had been, gangrened stumps of trees, the relics of hedges, here and there an oak stripped of its bark, white and haggard and leprous, like a corpse. And the air seemed always grey, and the smoke from the brickfields was grey.

At first he scarcely realized the quarter into which chance had led him. His only thought was of the great adventure of letters in which he proposed to engage, and his first glance round his "bed-sitting-room" showed him that there was no piece of furniture suitable for his purpose. The table, like the rest of the suite, was of bird's-eye maple; but the maker seemed to have penetrated the druidic secret of the rocking-stone, the thing was in a state of unstable equilibrium perpetually. For some days he wandered through the streets, inspecting the second-hand furniture shops, and at last, in a forlorn byway, found an old Japanese bureau, dishonored and forlorn, standing amongst rusty bedsteads, sorry china, and all the refuse of homes dead and desolate. The bureau pleased him in spite of its grime and grease and dirt. Inlaid mother-of-pearl, the gleam of lacquer dragons in red gold, and hints of curious design shone through the film of neglect and ill-usage, and when the woman of the shop showed him the drawers and well and pigeon-holes, he saw that it would be an apt instrument for his studies.

The bureau was carried to his room and replaced the "bird's-eye" table under the gas-jet. As Lucian arranged what papers he had accumulated: the sketches of hopeless experiments, shreds and tatters of stories begun but never completed, outlines of plots, two or three notebooks scribbled through and through with impressions of the abandoned hills, he felt a thrill of exaltation at the prospect of work to be accomplished, of a new world all open before him.

He set out on the adventure with a fury of enthusiasm; his last thought at night when all the maze of streets was empty and silent was of the problem, and his dreams ran on phrases, and when he awoke in the morning he was eager to get back to his desk. He immersed himself in a minute, almost a microscopic analysis of fine literature. It was no longer enough, as in the old days, to feel the charm and incantation of a line or a word; he wished to penetrate the secret, to understand something of the wonderful suggestion, all apart from the sense, that seemed to him the differentia of literature, as distinguished from the long follies of "character-drawing," "psychological analysis," and all the stuff that went to make the three-volume novel of commerce.

He found himself curiously strengthened by the change from the hills to the streets. There could be no doubt, he thought, that living a lonely life, interested only in himself and his own thoughts, he had become in a measure inhuman. The form of external things, black depths in woods, pools in lonely places, those still valleys curtained by hills on every side, sounding always with the ripple of their brooks, had become to him an influence like that of a drug, giving a certain peculiar color and outline to his thoughts. And from early boyhood there had been another strange flavor in his life, the dream of the old Roman world, those curious impressions that he had gathered from the white walls of Caermaen, and from the looming bastions of the fort. It was in reality the subconscious fancies of many years that had rebuilt the golden city, and had shown him the vine-trellis and the marbles and the sunlight in the garden of Avallaunius. And the rapture of love had made it all so vivid and warm with life, that even now, when he let his pen drop, the rich noise of the tavern and the chant of the theatre sounded above the murmur of the streets. Looking back, it was as much a part of his life as his schooldays, and the tessellated pavements were as real as the square of faded carpet beneath his feet.

But he felt that he had escaped. He could now survey those splendid and lovely visions from without, as if he read of opium dreams, and he no longer dreaded a weird suggestion that had once beset him, that his very soul was being molded into the hills, and passing into the black mirror of still waterpools. He had taken refuge in the streets, in the harbor of a modern suburb, from the vague, dreaded magic that had charmed his life. Whenever he felt inclined to listen to the old wood-whisper or to the singing of the fauns he bent more earnestly to his work, turning a deaf ear to the incantations.

In the curious labor of the bureau he found refreshment that was continually renewed. He experienced again, and with a far more violent impulse, the enthusiasm that had attended the writing of his book a year or two before, and so, perhaps, passed from one drug to another. It was, indeed, with something of rapture that he imagined the great procession of years all to be devoted to the intimate analysis of words, to the construction of the sentence, as if it were a piece of jewelry or mosaic.

Sometimes, in the pauses of the work, he would pace up and down his cell, looking out of the window now and again and gazing for an instant into the melancholy street. As the year advanced the days grew more and more misty, and he found himself the inhabitant of a little island wreathed about with the waves of a white and solemn sea. In the afternoon the fog would grow denser, shutting out not only sight but sound; the shriek of the garden gates, the jangling of the tram-bell echoed as if from a far way. Then there were days of heavy incessant rain; he could see a grey drifting sky and the drops plashing in the street, and the houses all dripping and saddened with wet.

He cured himself of one great aversion. He was no longer nauseated at the sight of a story begun and left unfinished. Formerly, even when an idea rose in his mind bright and wonderful, he had always approached the paper with a feeling of sickness and dislike, remembering all the hopeless beginnings he had made. But now he understood that to begin a romance was almost a separate and special art, a thing apart from the story, to be practiced with sedulous care. Whenever an opening scene occurred to him he noted it roughly in a book, and he devoted many long winter evenings to the elaboration of these beginnings. Sometimes the first impression would yield only a paragraph or a sentence, and once or twice but a splendid and sonorous word, which seemed to Lucian all dim and rich with unsurmised adventure. But often he was able to write three or four vivid pages, studying above all things the hint and significance of the words and actions, striving to work into the lines the atmosphere of expectation and promise, and the murmur of wonderful events to come.

In this one department of his task the labor seemed almost endless. He would finish a few pages and then rewrite them, using the same incident and nearly the same words, but altering that indefinite something which is scarcely so much style as manner, or atmosphere. He was astonished at the enormous change that was thus effected, and often, though he himself had done the work, he could scarcely describe in words how it was done. But it was clear that in this art of manner, or suggestion, lay all the chief secrets of literature, that by it all the great miracles were performed. Clearly it was not style, for style in itself was untranslatable, but it was that high theurgic magic that made the English Don Quixote, roughly traduced by some Jervas, perhaps the best of all English books. And it was the same element that made the journey of Roderick Random to London, so ostensibly a narrative of coarse jokes and common experiences and burlesque manners, told in no very choice diction, essentially a wonderful vision of the eighteenth century, carrying to one's very nostrils the aroma of the Great North Road, iron-bound under black frost, darkened beneath shuddering woods, haunted by highwaymen, with an adventure waiting beyond every turn, and great old echoing inns in the midst of lonely winter lands.

It was this magic that Lucian sought for his opening chapters; he tried to find that quality that gives to words something beyond their sound and beyond their meaning, that in the first lines of a book should whisper things unintelligible but all significant. Often he worked for many hours without success, and the grim wet dawn once found him still searching for hieroglyphic sentences, for words mystical, symbolic. On the shelves, in the upper part of his bureau, he had placed the books which, however various as to matter, seemed to have a part in this curious quality of suggestion, and in that sphere which might almost be called supernatural. To these books he often had recourse, when further effort appeared altogether hopeless, and certain pages in Coleridge and Edgar Allan Poe had the power of holding him in a trance of delight, subject to emotions and impressions which he knew to transcend altogether the realm of the formal understanding. Such lines as:

Bottomless vales and boundless floods,
And chasms, and caves, and Titan woods,

With forms that no man can discover
For the dews that drip all over;

had for Lucian more than the potency of a drug, lulling him into a splendid waking-sleep, every word being a supreme incantation. And it was not only his mind that was charmed by such passages, for he felt at the same time a strange and delicious bodily languor that held him motionless, without the desire or power to stir from his seat. And there were certain phrases in Kubla Khan that had such a magic that he would sometimes wake up, as it were, to the consciousness that he had been lying on the bed or sitting in the chair by the bureau, repeating a single line over and over again for two or three hours. Yet he knew perfectly well that he had not been really asleep; a little effort recalled a constant impression of the wall-paper, with its pink flowers on a buff ground, and of the muslin-curtained window, letting in the grey winter light. He had been some seven months in London when this odd experience first occurred to him. The day opened dreary and cold and clear, with a gusty and restless wind whirling round the corner of the street, and lifting the dead leaves and scraps of paper that littered the roadway into eddying mounting circles, as if a storm of black rain were to come. Lucian had sat late the night before, and rose in the morning feeling weary and listless and heavy-headed. While he dressed, his legs dragged him as with weights, and he staggered and nearly fell in bending down to the mat outside for his tea-tray. He lit the spirit lamp on the hearth with shaking, unsteady hands, and could scarcely pour out the tea when it was ready. A delicate cup of tea was one of his few luxuries; he was fond of the strange flavor of the green leaf, and this morning he drank the straw-colored liquid eagerly, hoping it would disperse the cloud of languor. He tried his best to coerce himself into the sense of vigor and enjoyment with which he usually began the day, walking briskly up and down and arranging his papers in order. But he could not free himself from depression; even as he opened the dear bureau a wave of melancholy came upon him, and he began to ask himself whether he were not pursuing a vain dream, searching for treasures that had no existence. He drew out his cousin's letter and read it again, sadly enough. After all there was a good deal of truth in what she said; he had "overrated" his powers, he had no friends, no real education. He began to count up the months since he had come to London; he had received his two thousand pounds in March, and in May he had said good-bye to the woods and to the dear and friendly paths. May, June, July, August, September, October, November, and half of December had gone by; and what had he to show? Nothing but the experiment, the attempt, futile scribblings which had no end nor shining purpose. There was nothing in his desk that he could produce as evidence of his capacity, no fragment even of accomplishment. It was a thought of intense bitterness, but it seemed as if the barbarians were in the right--a place in a house of business would have been more suitable. He leaned his head on his desk overwhelmed with the severity of his own judgment. He tried to comfort himself again by the thought of all the hours of happy enthusiasm he had spent amongst his papers, working for a great idea with infinite patience. He recalled to mind something that he had always tried to keep in the background of his hopes, the foundation-stone of his life, which he had hidden out of sight. Deep in his heart was the hope that he might one day write a valiant book; he scarcely dared to entertain the aspiration, he felt his incapacity too deeply, but yet this longing was the foundation of all his painful and patient effort. This he had proposed in secret to himself, that if he labored without ceasing, without tiring, he might produce something which would at all events be art, which would stand wholly apart from the objects shaped like books, printed with printers' ink, and called by the name of books that he had read. Giotto, he knew, was a painter, and the man who imitated walnut-wood on the deal doors opposite was a painter, and he had wished to be a very humble pupil in the class of the former. It was better, he thought, to fail in attempting exquisite things than to succeed in the department of the utterly contemptible; he had vowed he would be the dunce of Cervantes's school rather than top-boy in the academy of A Bad Un to Beat and Millicent's Marriage. And with this purpose he had devoted himself to laborious and joyous years, so that however mean his capacity, the pains should not be wanting. He tried now to rouse himself from a growing misery by the recollection of this high aim, but it all seemed hopeless vanity. He looked out into the grey street, and it stood a symbol of his life, chill and dreary and grey and vexed with a horrible wind. There were the dull inhabitants of the quarter going about their common business; a man was crying "mackerel" in a doleful voice, slowly passing up the street, and staring into the white-curtained "parlors," searching for the face of a purchaser behind the India-rubber plants, stuffed birds, and piles of gaudy gilt books that adorned the windows. One of the blistered doors over the way banged, and a woman came scurrying out on some errand, and the garden gate shrieked two melancholy notes as she opened it and let it swing back after her. The little patches called gardens were mostly untilled, uncared for, squares of slimy moss, dotted with clumps of coarse ugly grass, but here and there were the blackened and rotting remains of sunflowers and marigolds. And beyond, he knew, stretched the labyrinth of streets more or less squalid, but all grey and dull, and behind were the mud pits and the steaming heaps of yellowish bricks, and to the north was a great wide cold waste, treeless, desolate, swept by bitter wind. It was all like his own life, he said again to himself, a maze of unprofitable dreariness and desolation, and his mind grew as black and hopeless as the winter sky. The morning went thus dismally till twelve o'clock, and he put on his hat and great-coat. He always went out for an hour every day between twelve and one; the exercise was a necessity, and the landlady made his bed in the interval. The wind blew the smoke from the chimneys into his face as he shut the door, and with the acrid smoke came the prevailing odor of the street, a blend of cabbage-water and burnt bones and the faint sickly vapor from the brickfields. Lucian walked mechanically for the hour, going eastward, along the main road. The wind pierced him, and the dust was blinding, and the dreariness of the street increased his misery. The row of common shops, full of common things, the blatant public-houses, the Independent chapel, a horrible stucco parody of a Greek temple with a façade of hideous columns that was a nightmare, villas like smug Pharisees, shops again, a church in cheap Gothic, an old garden blasted and riven by the builder, these were the pictures of the way. When he got home again he flung himself on the bed, and lay there stupidly till sheer hunger roused him. He ate a hunch of bread and drank some water, and began to pace up and down the room, wondering whether there were no escape from despair. Writing seemed quite impossible, and hardly knowing what he did he opened his bureau and took out a book from the shelves. As his eyes fell on the page the air grew dark and heavy as night, and the wind wailed suddenly, loudly, terribly.

"By woman wailing for her Demon lover." The words were on his lips when he raised his eyes again. A broad band of pale clear light was shining into the room, and when he looked out of the window he saw the road all brightened by glittering pools of water, and as the last drops of the rain-storm starred these mirrors the sun sank into the wrack. Lucian gazed about him, perplexed, till his eyes fell on the clock above his empty hearth. He had been sitting, motionless, for nearly two hours without any sense of the passage of time, and without ceasing he had murmured those words as he dreamed an endless wonderful story. He experienced somewhat the sensations of Coleridge himself; strange, amazing, ineffable things seemed to have been presented to him, not in the form of the idea, but actually and materially, but he was less fortunate than Coleridge in that he could not, even vaguely, image to himself what he had seen. Yet when he searched his mind he knew that the consciousness of the room in which he sat had never left him; he had seen the thick darkness gather, and had heard the whirl of rain hissing through the air. Windows had been shut down with a crash, he had noted the pattering footsteps of people running to shelter, the landlady's voice crying to some one to look at the rain coming in under the door. It was like peering into some old bituminous picture, one could see at last that the mere blackness resolved itself into the likeness of trees and rocks and travelers. And against this background of his room, and the storm, and the noises of the street, his vision stood out illuminated, he felt he had descended to the very depths, into the caverns that are hollowed beneath the soul. He tried vainly to record the history of his impressions; the symbols remained in his memory, but the meaning was all conjecture.

The next morning, when he awoke, he could scarcely understand or realize the bitter depression of the preceding day. He found it had all vanished away and had been succeeded by an intense exaltation. Afterwards, when at rare intervals he experienced the same strange possession of the consciousness, he found this to be the invariable result, the hour of vision was always succeeded by a feeling of delight, by sensations of brightened and intensified powers. On that bright December day after the storm he rose joyously, and set about the labor of the bureau with the assurance of success, almost with the hope of formidable difficulties to be overcome. He had long busied himself with those curious researches which Poe had indicated in the Philosophy of Composition, and many hours had been spent in analyzing the singular effects which may be produced by the sound and resonance of words. But he had been struck by the thought that in the finest literature there were more subtle tones than the loud and insistent music of "never more," and he endeavored to find the secret of those pages and sentences which spoke, less directly, and less obviously, to the soul rather than to the ear, being filled with a certain grave melody and the sensation of singing voices. It was admirable, no doubt, to write phrases that showed at a glance their designed rhythm, and rang with sonorous words, but he dreamed of a prose in which the music should be less explicit, of names rather than notes. He was astonished that morning at his own fortune and facility; he succeeded in covering a page of ruled paper wholly to his satisfaction, and the sentences, when he read them out, appeared to suggest a weird elusive chanting, exquisite but almost imperceptible, like the echo of the plainsong reverberated from the vault of a monastic church.

He thought that such happy mornings well repaid him for the anguish of depression which he sometimes had to suffer, and for the strange experience of "possession" recurring at rare intervals, and usually after many weeks of severe diet. His income, he found, amounted to sixty-five pounds a year, and he lived for weeks at a time on fifteen shillings a week. During these austere periods his only food was bread, at the rate of a loaf a day; but he drank huge draughts of green tea, and smoked a black tobacco, which seemed to him a more potent mother of thought than any drug from the scented East. "I hope you go to some nice place for dinner," wrote his cousin; "there used to be some excellent eating-houses in London where one could get a good cut from the joint, with plenty of gravy, and a boiled potato, for a shilling. Aunt Mary writes that you should try Mr. Jones's in Water Street, Islington, whose father came from near Caermaen, and was always most comfortable in her day. I daresay the walk there would do you good. It is such a pity you smoke that horrid tobacco. I had a letter from Mrs. Dolly (Jane Diggs, who married your cousin John Dolly) the other day, and she said they would have been delighted to take you for only twenty-five shillings a week for the sake of the family if you had not been a smoker. She told me to ask you if you had ever seen a horse or a dog smoking tobacco. They are such nice, comfortable people, and the children would have been company for you. Johnnie, who used to be such a dear little fellow, has just gone into an office in the City, and seems to have excellent prospects. How I wish, my dear Lucian, that you could do something in the same way. Don't forget Mr. Jones's in Water Street, and you might mention your name to him."

Lucian never troubled Mr. Jones; but these letters of his cousin's always refreshed him by the force of contrast. He tried to imagine himself a part of the Dolly family, going dutifully every morning to the City on the bus, and returning in the evening for high tea. He could conceive the fine odor of hot roast beef hanging about the decorous house on Sunday afternoons, papa asleep in the dining-room, mamma lying down, and the children quite good and happy with their "Sundays books." In the evening, after supper, one read the Quiver till bedtime. Such pictures as these were to Lucian a comfort and a help, a remedy against despair. Often when he felt overwhelmed by the difficulty of the work he had undertaken, he thought of the alternative career, and was strengthened.

He returned again and again to that desire of a prose which should sound faintly, not so much with an audible music, but with the memory and echo of it. In the night, when the last tram had gone jangling by, and he had looked out and seen the street all wrapped about in heavy folds of the mist, he conducted some of his most delicate experiments. In that white and solitary midnight of the suburban street he experienced the curious sense of being on a tower, remote and apart and high above all the troubles of the earth. The gas lamp, which was nearly opposite, shone in a pale halo of light, and the houses themselves were merely indistinct marks and shadows amidst that palpable whiteness, shutting out the world and its noises. The knowledge of the swarming life that was so still, though it surrounded him, made the silence seem deeper than that of the mountains before the dawn; it was as if he alone stirred and looked out amidst a host sleeping at his feet. The fog came in by the open window in freezing puffs, and as Lucian watched he noticed that it shook and wavered like the sea, tossing up wreaths and drifts across the pale halo of the lamp, and, these vanishing, others succeeded. It was as if the mist passed by from the river to the north, as if it still passed by in the silence.

He would shut his window gently, and sit down in his lighted room with all the consciousness of the white advancing shroud upon him. It was then that he found himself in the mood for curious labors, and able to handle with some touch of confidence the more exquisite instruments of the craft. He sought for that magic by which all the glory and glamour of mystic chivalry were made to shine through the burlesque and gross adventures of Don Quixote, by which Hawthorne had lit his infernal Sabbath fires, and fashioned a burning aureole about the village tragedy of the Scarlet Letter. In Hawthorne the story and the suggestion, though quite distinct and of different worlds, were rather parallel than opposed to one another; but Cervantes had done a stranger thing. One read of Don Quixote, beaten, dirty, and ridiculous, mistaking windmills for giants, sheep for an army; but the impression was of the enchanted forest, of Avalon, of the San Graal, "far in the spiritual city." And Rabelais showed him, beneath the letter, the Tourainian sun shining on the hot rock above Chinon, on the maze of narrow, climbing streets, on the high-pitched, gabled roofs, on the grey-blue tourelles, pricking upward from the fantastic labyrinth of walls. He heard the sound of sonorous plain-song from the monastic choir, of gross exuberant gaiety from the rich vineyards; he listened to the eternal mystic mirth of those that halted in the purple shadow of the sorbier by the white, steep road. The gracious and ornate châteaux on the Loire and the Vienne rose fair and shining to confront the incredible secrets of vast, dim, far-lifted Gothic naves, that seemed ready to take the great deep, and float away from the mist and dust of earthly streets to anchor in the haven of the clear city that hath foundations. The rank tale of the garderobe, of the farm-kitchen, mingled with the reasoned, endless legend of the schools, with luminous Platonic argument; the old pomp of the Middle Ages put on the robe of a fresh life. There was a smell of wine and of incense, of June meadows and of ancient books, and through it all he hearkened, intent, to the exultation of chiming bells ringing for a new feast in a new land. He would cover pages with the analysis of these marvels, tracking the suggestion concealed beneath the words, and yet glowing like the golden threads in a robe of samite, or like that device of the old binders by which a vivid picture appeared on the shut edges of a book. He tried to imitate this art, to summon even the faint shadow of the great effect, rewriting a page of Hawthorne, experimenting and changing an epithet here and there, noting how sometimes the alteration of a trifling word would plunge a whole scene into darkness, as if one of those blood-red fires had instantly been extinguished. Sometimes, for severe practice, he attempted to construct short tales in the manner of this or that master. He sighed over these desperate attempts, over the clattering pieces of mechanism which would not even simulate life; but he urged himself to an infinite perseverance. Through the white hours he worked on amidst the heap and litter of papers; books and manuscripts overflowed from the bureau to the floor; and if he looked out he saw the mist still pass by, still passing from the river to the north.

It was not till the winter was well advanced that he began at all to explore the region in which he lived. Soon after his arrival in the grey street he had taken one or two vague walks, hardly noticing where he went or what he saw; but for all the summer he had shut himself in his room, beholding nothing but the form and color of words. For his morning walk he almost invariably chose the one direction, going along the Uxbridge Road towards Notting Hill, and returning by the same monotonous thoroughfare. Now, however, when the new year was beginning its dull days, he began to diverge occasionally to right and left, sometimes eating his luncheon in odd corners, in the bulging parlors of eighteenth-century taverns, that still fronted the surging sea of modern streets, or perhaps in brand new "publics" on the broken borders of the brickfields, smelling of the clay from which they had swollen. He found waste by-places behind railway embankments where he could smoke his pipe sheltered from the wind; sometimes there was a wooden fence by an old pear-orchard where he sat and gazed at the wet desolation of the market-gardens, munching a few currant biscuits by way of dinner. As he went farther afield a sense of immensity slowly grew upon him; it was as if, from the little island of his room, that one friendly place, he pushed out into the grey unknown, into a city that for him was uninhabited as the desert.

He came back to his cell after these purposeless wanderings always with a sense of relief, with the thought of taking refuge from grey. As he lit the gas and opened the desk of his bureau and saw the pile of papers awaiting him, it was as if he had passed from the black skies and the stinging wind and the dull maze of the suburb into all the warmth and sunlight and violent color of the south.

VI

It was in this winter after his coming to the grey street that Lucian first experienced the pains of desolation. He had all his life known the delights of solitude, and had acquired that habit of mind which makes a man find rich company on the bare hillside and leads him into the heart of the wood to meditate by the dark waterpools. But now in the blank interval when he was forced to shut up his desk, the sense of loneliness overwhelmed him and filled him with unutterable melancholy. On such days he carried about with him an unceasing gnawing torment in his breast; the anguish of the empty page awaiting him in his bureau, and the knowledge that it was worse than useless to attempt the work. He had fallen into the habit of always using this phrase "the work" to denote the adventure of literature; it had grown in his mind to all the austere and grave significance of "the great work" on the lips of the alchemists; it included every trifling and laborious page and the vague magnificent fancies that sometimes hovered below him. All else had become mere by-play, unimportant, trivial; the work was the end, and the means and the food of his life--it raised him up in the morning to renew the struggle, it was the symbol which charmed him as he lay down at night. All through the hours of toil at the bureau he was enchanted, and when he went out and explored the unknown coasts, the one thought allured him, and was the colored glass between his eyes and the world. Then as he drew nearer home his steps would quicken, and the more weary and grey the walk, the more he rejoiced as he thought of his hermitage and of the curious difficulties that awaited him there. But when, suddenly and without warning, the faculty disappeared, when his mind seemed a hopeless waste from which nothing could arise, then he became subject to a misery so piteous that the barbarians themselves would have been sorry for him. He had known some foretaste of these bitter and inexpressible griefs in the old country days, but then he had immediately taken refuge in the hills, he had rushed to the dark woods as to an anodyne, letting his heart drink in all the wonder and magic of the wild land. Now in these days of January, in the suburban street, there was no such refuge.

He had been working steadily for some weeks, well enough satisfied on the whole with the daily progress, glad to awake in the morning, and to read over what he had written on the night before. The new year opened with faint and heavy weather and a breathless silence in the air, but in a few days the great frost set in. Soon the streets began to suggest the appearance of a beleaguered city, the silence that had preceded the frost deepened, and the mist hung over the earth like a dense white smoke. Night after night the cold increased, and people seemed unwilling to go abroad, till even the main thoroughfares were empty and deserted, as if the inhabitants were lying close in hiding. It was at this dismal time that Lucian found himself reduced to impotence. There was a sudden break in his thought, and when he wrote on valiantly, hoping against hope, he only grew more aghast on the discovery of the imbecilities he had committed to paper. He ground his teeth together and persevered, sick at heart, feeling as if all the world were fallen from under his feet, driving his pen on mechanically, till he was overwhelmed. He saw the stuff he had done without veil or possible concealment, a lamentable and wretched sheaf of verbiage, worse, it seemed, than the efforts of his boyhood. He was not longer tautological, he avoided tautology with the infernal art of a leader-writer, filling his wind bags and mincing words as if he had been a trained journalist on the staff of the Daily Post. There seemed all the matter of an insufferable tragedy in these thoughts; that his patient and enduring toil was in vain, that practice went for nothing, and that he had wasted the labor of Milton to accomplish the tenth-rate. Unhappily he could not "give in"; the longing, the fury for the work burnt within him like a burning fire; he lifted up his eyes in despair.

It was then, while he knew that no one could help him, that he languished for help, and then, though he was aware that no comfort was possible, he fervently wished to be comforted. The only friend he had was his father, and he knew that his father would not even understand his distress. For him, always, the printed book was the beginning and end of literature; the agony of the maker, his despair and sickness, were as accursed as the pains of labor. He was ready to read and admire the work of the great Smith, but he did not wish to hear of the period when the great Smith had writhed and twisted like a scotched worm, only hoping to be put out of his misery, to go mad or die, to escape somehow from the bitter pains. And Lucian knew no one else. Now and then he read in the paper the fame of the great littérateurs; the Gypsies were entertaining the Prince of Wales, the Jolly Beggars were dining with the Lord Mayor, the Old Mumpers were mingling amicably and gorgeously with the leading members of the Stock Exchange. He was so unfortunate as to know none of these gentlemen, but it hardly seemed likely that they could have done much for him in any case. Indeed, in his heart, he was certain that help and comfort from without were in the nature of things utterly impossible, his ruin and grief were within, and only his own assistance could avail. He tried to reassure himself, to believe that his torments were a proof of his vocation, that the facility of the novelist who stood six years deep in contracts to produce romances was a thing wholly undesirable, but all the while he longed for but a drop of that inexhaustible fluency which he professed to despise.

He drove himself out from that dreary contemplation of the white paper and the idle pen. He went into the frozen and deserted streets, hoping that he might pluck the burning coal from his heart, but the fire was not quenched. As he walked furiously along the grim iron roads he fancied that those persons who passed him cheerfully on their way to friends and friendly hearths shrank from him into the mists as they went by. Lucian imagined that the fire of his torment and anguish must in some way glow visibly about him; he moved, perhaps, in a nimbus that proclaimed the blackness and the flames within. He knew, of course, that in misery he had grown delirious, that the well-coated, smooth-hatted personages who loomed out of the fog upon him were in reality shuddering only with cold, but in spite of common sense he still conceived that he saw on their faces an evident horror and disgust, and something of the repugnance that one feels at the sight of a venomous snake, half-killed, trailing its bleeding vileness out of sight. By design Lucian tried to make for remote and desolate places, and yet when he had succeeded in touching on the open country, and knew that the icy shadow hovering through the mist was a field, he longed for some sound and murmur of life, and turned again to roads where pale lamps were glimmering, and the dancing flame of firelight shone across the frozen shrubs. And the sight of these homely fires, the thought of affection and consolation waiting by them, stung him the more sharply perhaps because of the contrast with his own chills and weariness and helpless sickness, and chiefly because he knew that he had long closed an everlasting door between his heart and such felicities. If those within had come out and had called him by his name to enter and be comforted, it would have been quite unavailing, since between them and him there was a great gulf fixed. Perhaps for the first time he realized that he had lost the art of humanity for ever. He had thought when he closed his ears to the wood whisper and changed the fauns' singing for the murmur of the streets, the black pools for the shadows and amber light of London, that he had put off the old life, and had turned his soul to healthy activities, but the truth was that he had merely exchanged one drug for another. He could not be human, and he wondered whether there were some drop of the fairy blood in his body that made him foreign and a stranger in the world.

He did not surrender to desolation without repeated struggles. He strove to allure himself to his desk by the promise of some easy task; he would not attempt invention, but he had memoranda and rough jottings of ideas in his note-books, and he would merely amplify the suggestions ready to his hand. But it was hopeless, again and again it was hopeless. As he read over his notes, trusting that he would find some hint that might light up the dead fires, and kindle again that pure flame of enthusiasm, he found how desperately his fortune had fallen. He could see no light, no color in the lines he had scribbled with eager trembling fingers; he remembered how splendid all these things had been when he wrote them down, but now they were meaningless, faded into grey. The few words he had dashed on to the paper, enraptured at the thought of the happy hours they promised, had become mere jargon, and when he understood the idea it seemed foolish, dull, unoriginal. He discovered something at last that appeared to have a grain of promise, and determined to do his best to put it into shape, but the first paragraph appalled him; it might have been written by an unintelligent schoolboy. He tore the paper in pieces, and shut and locked his desk, heavy despair sinking like lead into his heart. For the rest of that day he lay motionless on the bed, smoking pipe after pipe in the hope of stupefying himself with tobacco fumes. The air in the room became blue and thick with smoke; it was bitterly cold, and he wrapped himself up in his great-coat and drew the counterpane over him. The night came on and the window darkened, and at last he fell asleep.

He renewed the effort at intervals, only to plunge deeper into misery. He felt the approaches of madness, and knew that his only hope was to walk till he was physically exhausted, so that he might come home almost fainting with fatigue, but ready to fall asleep the moment he got into bed. He passed the mornings in a kind of torpor, endeavoring to avoid thought, to occupy his mind with the pattern of the paper, with the advertisements at the end of a book, with the curious greyness of the light that glimmered through the mist into his room, with the muffled voices that rumbled now and then from the street. He tried to make out the design that had once colored the faded carpet on the floor, and wondered about the dead artist in Japan, the adorner of his bureau. He speculated as to what his thoughts had been as he inserted the rainbow mother-of-pearl and made that great flight of shining birds, dipping their wings as they rose from the reeds, or how he had conceived the lacquer dragons in red gold, and the fantastic houses in the garden of peach-trees. But sooner or later the oppression of his grief returned, the loud shriek and clang of the garden-gate, the warning bell of some passing bicyclist steering through the fog, the noise of his pipe falling to the floor, would suddenly awaken him to the sense of misery. He knew that it was time to go out; he could not bear to sit still and suffer. Sometimes she cut a slice of bread and put it in his pocket, sometimes he trusted to the chance of finding a public-house, where he could have a sandwich and a glass of beer. He turned always from the main streets and lost himself in the intricate suburban byways, willing to be engulfed in the infinite whiteness of the mist.

The roads had stiffened into iron ridges, the fences and trees were glittering with frost crystals, everything was of strange and altered aspect. Lucian walked on and on through the maze, now in a circle of shadowy villas, awful as the buried streets of Herculaneum, now in lanes dipping onto open country, that led him past great elm-trees whose white boughs were all still, and past the bitter lonely fields where the mist seemed to fade away into grey darkness. As he wandered along these unfamiliar and ghastly paths he became the more convinced of his utter remoteness from all humanity, he allowed that grotesque suggestion of there being something visibly amiss in his outward appearance to grow upon him, and often he looked with a horrible expectation into the faces of those who passed by, afraid lest his own senses gave him false intelligence, and that he had really assumed some frightful and revolting shape. It was curious that, partly by his own fault, and largely, no doubt, through the operation of mere coincidence, he was once or twice strongly confirmed in this fantastic delusion. He came one day into a lonely and unfrequented byway, a country lane falling into ruin, but still fringed with elms that had formed an avenue leading to the old manor-house. It was now the road of communication between two far outlying suburbs, and on these winter nights lay as black, dreary, and desolate as a mountain track. Soon after the frost began, a gentleman had been set upon in this lane as he picked his way between the corner where the bus had set him down, and his home where the fire was blazing, and his wife watched the clock. He was stumbling uncertainly through the gloom, growing a little nervous because the walk seemed so long, and peering anxiously for the lamp at the end of his street, when the two footpads rushed at him out of the fog. One caught him from behind, the other struck him with a heavy bludgeon, and as he lay senseless they robbed him of his watch and money, and vanished across the fields. The next morning all the suburb rang with the story; the unfortunate merchant had been grievously hurt, and wives watched their husbands go out in the morning with sickening apprehension, not knowing what might happen at night. Lucian of course was ignorant of all these rumors, and struck into the gloomy by-road without caring where he was or whither the way would lead him.

He had been driven out that day as with whips, another hopeless attempt to return to the work had agonised him, and existence seemed an intolerable pain. As he entered the deeper gloom, where the fog hung heavily, he began, half consciously, to gesticulate; he felt convulsed with torment and shame, and it was a sorry relief to clench his nails into his palm and strike the air as he stumbled heavily along, bruising his feet against the frozen ruts and ridges. His impotence was hideous, he said to himself, and he cursed himself and his life, breaking out into a loud oath, and stamping on the ground. Suddenly he was shocked at a scream of terror, it seemed in his very ear, and looking up he saw for a moment a woman gazing at him out of the mist, her features distorted and stiff with fear. A momentary convulsion twitched her arms into the ugly mimicry of a beckoning gesture, and she turned and ran for dear life, howling like a beast.

Lucian stood still in the road while the woman's cries grew faint and died away. His heart was chilled within him as the significance of this strange incident became clear. He remembered nothing of his violent gestures; he had not known at the time that he had sworn out loud, or that he was grinding his teeth with impotent rage. He only thought of that ringing scream, of the horrible fear on the white face that had looked upon him, of the woman's headlong flight from his presence. He stood trembling and shuddering, and in a little while he was feeling his face, searching for some loathsome mark, for the stigmata of evil branding his forehead. He staggered homewards like a drunken man, and when he came into the Uxbridge Road some children saw him and called after him as he swayed and caught at the lamp-post. When he got to his room he sat down at first in the dark. He did not dare to light the gas. Everything in the room was indistinct, but he shut his eyes as he passed the dressing-table, and sat in a corner, his face turned to the wall. And when at last he gathered courage and the flame leapt hissing from the jet, he crept piteously towards the glass, and ducked his head, crouching miserably, and struggling with his terrors before he could look at his own image.

To the best of his power he tried to deliver himself from these more grotesque fantasies; he assured himself that there was nothing terrific in his countenance but sadness, that his face was like the face of other men. Yet he could not forget that reflection he had seen in the woman's eyes, how the surest mirrors had shown him a horrible dread, her soul itself quailing and shuddering at an awful sight. Her scream rang and rang in his ears; she had fled away from him as if he offered some fate darker than death.

He looked again and again into the glass, tortured by a hideous uncertainty. His senses told him there was nothing amiss, yet he had had a proof, and yet, as he peered most earnestly, there was, it seemed, something strange and not altogether usual in the expression of the eyes. Perhaps it might be the unsteady flare of the gas, or perhaps a flaw in the cheap looking-glass, that gave some slight distortion to the image. He walked briskly up and down the room and tried to gaze steadily, indifferently, into his own face. He would not allow himself to be misguided by a word. When he had pronounced himself incapable of humanity, he had only meant that he could not enjoy the simple things of common life. A man was not necessarily monstrous, merely because he did not appreciate high tea, a quiet chat about the neighbors, and a happy noisy evening with the children. But with what message, then, did he appear charged that the woman's mouth grew so stark? Her hands had jerked up as if they had been pulled with frantic wires; she seemed for the instant like a horrible puppet. Her scream was a thing from the nocturnal Sabbath.

He lit a candle and held it close up to the glass so that his own face glared white at him, and the reflection of the room became an indistinct darkness. He saw nothing but the candle flame and his own shining eyes, and surely they were not as the eyes of common men. As he put down the light, a sudden suggestion entered his mind, and he drew a quick breath, amazed at the thought. He hardly knew whether to rejoice or to shudder. For the thought he conceived was this: that he had mistaken all the circumstances of the adventure, and had perhaps repulsed a sister who would have welcomed him to the Sabbath.

He lay awake all night, turning from one dreary and frightful thought to the other, scarcely dozing for a few hours when the dawn came. He tried for a moment to argue with himself when he got up; knowing that his true life was locked up in the bureau, he made a desperate attempt to drive the phantoms and hideous shapes from his mind. He was assured that his salvation was in the work, and he drew the key from his pocket, and made as if he would have opened the desk. But the nausea, the remembrances of repeated and utter failure, were too powerful. For many days he hung about the Manor Lane, half dreading, half desiring another meeting, and he swore he would not again mistake the cry of rapture, nor repulse the arms extended in a frenzy of delight. In those days he dreamed of some dark place where they might celebrate and make the marriage of the Sabbath, with such rites as he had dared to imagine.

It was perhaps only the shock of a letter from his father that rescued him from these evident approaches to madness. Mr. Taylor wrote how they had missed him at Christmas, how the farmers had inquired after him, of the homely familiar things that recalled his boyhood, his mother's voice, the friendly fireside, and the good old fashions that had nurtured him. He remembered that he had once been a boy, loving the cake and puddings and the radiant holly, and all the seventeenth-century mirth that lingered on in the ancient farmhouses. And there came to him the more holy memory of Mass on Christmas morning. How sweet the dark and frosty earth had smelt as he walked beside his mother down the winding lane, and from the stile near the church they had seen the world glimmering to the dawn, and the wandering lanthorns advancing across the fields. Then he had come into the church and seen it shining with candles and holly, and his father in pure vestments of white linen sang the longing music of the liturgy at the altar, and the people answered him, till the sun rose with the grave notes of the Paternoster, and a red beam stole through the chancel window.

The worst horror left him as he recalled the memory of these dear and holy things. He cast away the frightful fancy that the scream he had heard was a shriek of joy, that the arms, rigidly jerked out, invited him to an embrace. Indeed, the thought that he had longed for such an obscene illusion, that he had gloated over the recollection of that stark mouth, filled him with disgust. He resolved that his senses were deceived, that he had neither seen nor heard, but had for a moment externalized his own slumbering and morbid dreams. It was perhaps necessary that he should be wretched, that his efforts should be discouraged, but he would not yield utterly to madness.

Yet when he went abroad with such good resolutions, it was hard to resist an influence that seemed to come from without and within. He did not know it, but people were everywhere talking of the great frost, of the fog that lay heavy on London, making the streets dark and terrible, of strange birds that came fluttering about the windows in the silent squares. The Thames rolled out duskily, bearing down the jarring ice-blocks, and as one looked on the black water from the bridges it was like a river in a northern tale. To Lucian it all seemed mythical, of the same substance as his own fantastic thoughts. He rarely saw a newspaper, and did not follow from day to day the systematic readings of the thermometer, the reports of ice-fairs, of coaches driven across the river at Hampton, of the skating on the fens; and hence the iron roads, the beleaguered silence and the heavy folds of mist appeared as amazing as a picture, significant, appalling. He could not look out and see a common suburban street foggy and dull, nor think of the inhabitants as at work or sitting cheerfully eating nuts about their fires; he saw a vision of a grey road vanishing, of dim houses all empty and deserted, and the silence seemed eternal. And when he went out and passed through street after street, all void, by the vague shapes of houses that appeared for a moment and were then instantly swallowed up, it seemed to him as if he had strayed into a city that had suffered some inconceivable doom, that he alone wandered where myriads had once dwelt. It was a town as great as Babylon, terrible as Rome, marvelous as Lost Atlantis, set in the midst of a white wilderness surrounded by waste places. It was impossible to escape from it; if he skulked between hedges, and crept away beyond the frozen pools, presently the serried stony lines confronted him like an army, and far and far they swept away into the night, as some fabled wall that guards an empire in the vast dim East. Or in that distorting medium of the mist, changing all things, he imagined that he trod an infinite desolate plain, abandoned from ages, but circled and encircled with dolmen and menhir that loomed out at him, gigantic, terrible. All London was one grey temple of an awful rite, ring within ring of wizard stones circled about some central place, every circle was an initiation, every initiation eternal loss. Or perhaps he was astray for ever in a land of grey rocks. He had seen the light of home, the flicker of the fire on the walls; close at hand, it seemed, was the open door, and he had heard dear voices calling to him across the gloom, but he had just missed the path. The lamps vanished, the voices sounded thin and died away, and yet he knew that those within were waiting, that they could not bear to close the door, but waited, calling his name, while he had missed the way, and wandered in the pathless desert of the grey rocks. Fantastic, hideous, they beset him wherever he turned, piled up into strange shapes, pricked with sharp peaks, assuming the appearance of goblin towers, swelling into a vague dome like a fairy rath, huge and terrible. And as one dream faded into another, so these last fancies were perhaps the most tormenting and persistent; the rocky avenues became the camp and fortalice of some half-human, malignant race who swarmed in hiding, ready to bear him away into the heart of their horrible hills. It was awful to think that all his goings were surrounded, that in the darkness he was watched and surveyed, that every step but led him deeper and deeper into the labyrinth.

When, of an evening, he was secure in his room, the blind drawn down and the gas flaring, he made vigorous efforts toward sanity. It was not of his free will that he allowed terror to overmaster him, and he desired nothing better than a placid and harmless life, full of work and clear thinking. He knew that he deluded himself with imagination, that he had been walking through London suburbs and not through Pandemonium, and that if he could but unlock his bureau all those ugly forms would be resolved into the mist. But it was hard to say if he consoled himself effectually with such reflections, for the return to common sense meant also the return to the sharp pangs of defeat. It recalled him to the bitter theme of his own inefficiency, to the thought that he only desired one thing of life, and that this was denied him. He was willing to endure the austerities of a monk in a severe cloister, to suffer cold, to be hungry, to be lonely and friendless, to forbear all the consolation of friendly speech, and to be glad of all these things, if only he might be allowed to illuminate the manuscript in quietness. It seemed a hideous insufferable cruelty, that he should so fervently desire that which he could never gain.

He was led back to the old conclusion; he had lost the sense of humanity, he was wretched because he was an alien and a stranger amongst citizens. It seemed probable that the enthusiasm of literature, as he understood it, the fervent desire for the fine art, had in it something of the inhuman, and dissevered the enthusiast from his fellow-creatures. It was possible that the barbarian suspected as much, that by some slow process of rumination he had arrived at his fixed and inveterate impression, by no means a clear reasoned conviction; the average Philistine, if pressed for the reasons of his dislike, would either become inarticulate, ejaculating "faugh" and "pah" like an old-fashioned Scots Magazine, or else he would give some imaginary and absurd reason, alleging that all "littery men" were poor, that composers never cut their hair, that painters were rarely public-school men, that sculptors couldn't ride straight to hounds to save their lives, but clearly these imbecilities were mere afterthoughts; the average man hated the artist from a deep instinctive dread of all that was strange, uncanny, alien to his nature; he gibbered, uttered his harsh, semi-bestial "faugh," and dismissed Keats to his gallipots from much the same motives as usually impelled the black savages to dismiss the white man on an even longer journey.

Lucian was not especially interested in this hatred of the barbarian for the maker, except from this point, that it confirmed him in his belief that the love of art dissociated the man from the race. One touch of art made the whole world alien, but surely miseries of the civilized man cast amongst savages were not so much caused by dread of their ferocity as by the terror of his own thoughts; he would perhaps in his last despair leave his retreat and go forth to perish at their hands, so that he might at least die in company, and hear the sound of speech before death. And Lucian felt most keenly that in his case there was a double curse; he was as isolated as Keats, and as inarticulate as his reviewers. The consolation of the work had failed him, and he was suspended in the void between two worlds.

It was no doubt the composite effect of his failures, his loneliness of soul, and solitude of life, that had made him invest those common streets with such grim and persistent terrors. He had perhaps yielded to a temptation without knowing that he had been tempted, and, in the manner of De Quincey, had chosen the subtle in exchange for the more tangible pains. Unconsciously, but still of free will, he had preferred the splendor and the gloom of a malignant vision before his corporal pains, before the hard reality of his own impotence. It was better to dwell in vague melancholy, to stray in the forsaken streets of a city doomed from ages, to wander amidst forlorn and desperate rocks than to awake to a gnawing and ignoble torment, to confess that a house of business would have been more suitable and more practical, that he had promised what he could never perform. Even as he struggled to beat back the phantasmagoria of the mist, and resolved that he would no longer make all the streets a stage of apparitions, he hardly realized what he had done, or that the ghosts he had called might depart and return again.

He continued his long walks, always with the object of producing a physical weariness and exhaustion that would enable him to sleep of nights. But even when he saw the foggy and deserted avenues in their proper shape, and allowed his eyes to catch the pale glimmer of the lamps, and the dancing flame of the firelight, he could not rid himself of the impression that he stood afar off, that between those hearths and himself there was a great gulf fixed. As he paced down the footpath he could often see plainly across the frozen shrubs into the homely and cheerful rooms. Sometimes, late in the evening, he caught a passing glimpse of the family at tea, father, mother, and children laughing and talking together, well pleased with each other's company. Sometimes a wife or a child was standing by the garden gate peering anxiously through the fog, and the sight of it all, all the little details, the hideous but comfortable armchairs turned ready to the fire, maroon-red curtains being drawn close to shut out the ugly night, the sudden blaze and illumination as the fire was poked up so that it might be cheerful for father; these trivial and common things were acutely significant. They brought back to him the image of a dead boy--himself. They recalled the shabby old "parlor" in the country, with its shabby old furniture and fading carpet, and renewed a whole atmosphere of affection and homely comfort. His mother would walk to the end of the drive and look out for him when he was late (wandering then about the dark woodlands); on winter evenings she would make the fire blaze, and have his slippers warming by the hearth, and there was probably buttered toast "as a treat." He dwelt on all these insignificant petty circumstances, on the genial glow and light after the muddy winter lanes, on the relish of the buttered toast and the smell of the hot tea, on the two old cats curled fast asleep before the fender, and made them instruments of exquisite pain and regret. Each of these strange houses that he passed was identified in his mind with his own vanished home; all was prepared and ready as in the old days, but he was shut out, judged and condemned to wander in the frozen mist, with weary feet, anguished and forlorn, and they that would pass from within to help him could not, neither could he pass to them. Again, for the hundredth time, he came back to the sentence: he could not gain the art of letters and he had lost the art of humanity. He saw the vanity of all his thoughts; he was an ascetic caring nothing for warmth and cheerfulness and the small comforts of life, and yet he allowed his mind to dwell on such things. If one of those passers-by, who walked briskly, eager for home, should have pitied him by some miracle and asked him to come in, it would have been worse than useless, yet he longed for pleasures that he could not have enjoyed. It was as if he were come to a place of torment, where they who could not drink longed for water, where they who could feel no warmth shuddered in the eternal cold. He was oppressed by the grim conceit that he himself still slept within the matted thicket, imprisoned by the green bastions of the Roman fort. He had never come out, but a changeling had gone down the hill, and now stirred about the earth.

Beset by such ingenious terrors, it was not wonderful that outward events and common incidents should abet his fancies. He had succeeded one day in escaping from the mesh of the streets, and fell on a rough and narrow lane that stole into a little valley. For the moment he was in a somewhat happier mood; the afternoon sun glowed through the rolling mist, and the air grew clearer. He saw quiet and peaceful fields, and a wood descending in a gentle slope from an old farmstead of warm red brick. The farmer was driving the slow cattle home from the hill, and his loud halloo to his dog came across the land a cheerful mellow note. From another side a cart was approaching the clustered barns, hesitating, pausing while the great horses rested, and then starting again into lazy motion. In the well of the valley a wandering line of bushes showed where a brook crept in and out amongst the meadows, and, as Lucian stood, lingering, on the bridge, a soft and idle breath ruffled through the boughs of a great elm. He felt soothed, as by calm music, and wondered whether it would not be better for him to live in some such quiet place, within reach of the streets and yet remote from them. It seemed a refuge for still thoughts; he could imagine himself sitting at rest beneath the black yew tree in the farm garden, at the close of a summer day. He had almost determined that he would knock at the door and ask if they would take him as a lodger, when he saw a child running towards him down the lane. It was a little girl, with bright curls tossing about her head, and, as she came on, the sunlight glowed upon her, illuminating her brick-red frock and the yellow king-cups in her hat. She had run with her eyes on the ground, chirping and laughing to herself, and did not see Lucian till she was quite near him. She started and glanced into his eyes for a moment, and began to cry; he stretched out his hand, and she ran from him screaming, frightened no doubt by what was to her a sudden and strange apparition. He turned back towards London, and the mist folded him in its thick darkness, for on that evening it was tinged with black. It was only by the intensest strain of resolution that he did not yield utterly to the poisonous anodyne which was always at hand. It had been a difficult struggle to escape from the mesh of the hills, from the music of the fauns, and even now he was drawn by the memory of these old allurements. But he felt that here, in his loneliness, he was in greater danger, and beset by a blacker magic. Horrible fancies rushed wantonly into his mind; he was not only ready to believe that something in his soul sent a shudder through all that was simple and innocent, but he came trembling home one Saturday night, believing, or half-believing, that he was in communion with evil. He had passed through the clamorous and blatant crowd of the "high street," where, as one climbed the hill, the shops seemed all aflame, and the black night air glowed with the flaring gas-jets and the naphtha-lamps, hissing and wavering before the February wind. Voices, raucous, clamant, abominable, were belched out of the blazing public-houses as the doors swung to and fro, and above these doors were hideous brassy lamps, very slowly swinging in a violent blast of air, so that they might have been infernal thuribles, censing the people. Some man was calling his wares in one long continuous shriek that never stopped or paused, and, as a respond, a deeper, louder voice roared to him from across the road. An Italian whirled the handle of his piano-organ in a fury, and a ring of imps danced mad figures around him, danced and flung up their legs till the rags dropped from some of them, and they still danced on. A flare of naphtha, burning with a rushing noise, threw a light on one point of the circle, and Lucian watched a lank girl of fifteen as she came round and round to the flash. She was quite drunk, and had kicked her petticoats away, and the crowd howled laughter and applause at her. Her black hair poured down and leapt on her scarlet bodice; she sprang and leapt round the ring, laughing in Bacchic frenzy, and led the orgy to triumph. People were crossing to and fro, jostling against each other, swarming about certain shops and stalls in a dense dark mass that quivered and sent out feelers as if it were one writhing organism. A little farther a group of young men, arm in arm, were marching down the roadway chanting some music-hall verse in full chorus, so that it sounded like plainsong. An impossible hubbub, a hum of voices angry as swarming bees, the squeals of five or six girls who ran in and out, and dived up dark passages and darted back into the crowd; all these mingled together till his ears quivered. A young fellow was playing the concertina, and he touched the keys with such slow fingers that the tune wailed solemn into a dirge; but there was nothing so strange as the burst of sound that swelled out when the public-house doors were opened.

He walked amongst these people, looked at their faces, and looked at the children amongst them. He had come out thinking that he would see the English working class, "the best-behaved and the best-tempered crowd in the world," enjoying the simple pleasure of the Saturday night's shopping. Mother bought the joint for Sunday's dinner, and perhaps a pair of boots for father; father had an honest glass of beer, and the children were given bags of sweets, and then all these worthy people went decently home to their well-earned rest. De Quincey had enjoyed the sight in his day, and had studied the rise and fall of onions and potatoes. Lucian, indeed, had desired to take these simple emotions as an opiate, to forget the fine fret and fantastic trouble of his own existence in plain things and the palpable joy of rest after labor. He was only afraid lest he should be too sharply reproached by the sight of these men who fought bravely year after year against starvation, who knew nothing of intricate and imagined grief, but only the weariness of relentless labor, of the long battle for their wives and children. It would be pathetic, he thought, to see them content with so little, brightened by the expectation of a day's rest and a good dinner, forced, even then, to reckon every penny, and to make their children laugh with halfpence. Either he would be ashamed before so much content, or else he would be again touched by the sense of his inhumanity which could take no interest in the common things of life. But still he went to be at least taken out of himself, to be forced to look at another side of the world, so that he might perhaps forget a little while his own sorrows.

He was fascinated by what he saw and heard. He wondered whether De Quincey also had seen the same spectacle, and had concealed his impressions out of reverence for the average reader. Here there were no simple joys of honest toilers, but wonderful orgies, that drew out his heart to horrible music. At first the violence of sound and sight had overwhelmed him; the lights flaring in the night wind, the array of naphtha lamps, the black shadows, the roar of voices. The dance about the piano-organ had been the first sign of an inner meaning, and the face of the dark girl as she came round and round to the flame had been amazing in its utter furious abandon. And what songs they were singing all around him, and what terrible words rang out, only to excite peals of laughter. In the public-houses the workmen's wives, the wives of small tradesmen, decently dressed in black, were drinking their faces to a flaming red, and urging their husbands to drink more. Beautiful young women, flushed and laughing, put their arms round the men's necks and kissed them, and then held up the glass to their lips. In the dark corners, at the openings of side streets, the children were talking together, instructing each other, whispering what they had seen; a boy of fifteen was plying a girl of twelve with whisky, and presently they crept away. Lucian passed them as they turned to go, and both looked at him. The boy laughed, and the girl smiled quietly. It was above all in the faces around him that he saw the most astounding things, the Bacchic fury unveiled and unashamed. To his eyes it seemed as if these revelers recognized him as a fellow, and smiled up in his face, aware that he was in the secret. Every instinct of religion, of civilization even, was swept away; they gazed at one another and at him, absolved of all scruples, children of the earth and nothing more. Now and then a couple detached themselves from the swarm, and went away into the darkness, answering the jeers and laughter of their friends as they vanished.

On the edge of the pavement, not far from where he was standing, Lucian noticed a tall and lovely young woman who seemed to be alone. She was in the full light of a naphtha flame, and her bronze hair and flushed cheeks shone illuminate as she viewed the orgy. She had dark brown eyes, and a strange look as of an old picture in her face; and her eyes brightened with an urgent gleam. He saw the revelers nudging each other and glancing at her, and two or three young men went up and asked her to come for a walk. She shook her head and said "No thank you" again and again, and seemed as if she were looking for somebody in the crowd.

"I'm expecting a friend," she said at last to a man who proposed a drink and a walk afterwards; and Lucian wondered what kind of friend would ultimately appear. Suddenly she turned to him as he was about to pass on, and said in a low voice:

"I'll go for a walk with you if you like; you just go on, and I'll follow in a minute."

For a moment he looked steadily at her. He saw that the first glance has misled him; her face was not flushed with drink as he had supposed, but it was radiant with the most exquisite color, a red flame glowed and died on her cheek, and seemed to palpitate as she spoke. The head was set on the neck nobly, as in a statue, and about the ears the bronze hair strayed into little curls. She was smiling and waiting for his answer.

He muttered something about being very sorry, and fled down the hill out of the orgy, from the noise of roaring voices and the glitter of the great lamps very slowly swinging in the blast of wind. He knew that he had touched the brink of utter desolation; there was death in the woman's face, and she had indeed summoned him to the Sabbath. Somehow he had been able to refuse on the instant, but if he had delayed he knew he would have abandoned himself to her, body and soul. He locked himself in his room and lay trembling on the bed, wondering if some subtle sympathy had shown the woman her perfect companion. He looked in the glass, not expecting now to see certain visible and outward signs, but searching for the meaning of that strange glance that lit up his eyes. He had grown even thinner than before in the last few months, and his cheeks were wasted with hunger and sorrow, but there were still about his features the suggestion of a curious classic grace, and the look as of a faun who has strayed from the vineyards and olive gardens. He had broken away, but now he felt the mesh of her net about him, a desire for her that was a madness, as if she held every nerve in his body and drew him to her, to her mystic world, to the rosebush where every flower was a flame.

He dreamed all night of the perilous things he had refused, and it was loss to awake in the morning, pain to return to the world. The frost had broken and the fog had rolled away, and the grey street was filled with a clear grey light. Again he looked out on the long dull sweep of the monotonous houses, hidden for the past weeks by a curtain of mist. Heavy rain had fallen in the night, and the garden rails were still dripping, the roofs still dark with wet, all down the line the dingy white blinds were drawn in the upper windows. Not a soul walked the street; every one was asleep after the exertions of the night before; even on the main road it was only at intervals that some straggler paddled by. Presently a woman in a brown Ulster shuffled off on some errand, then a man in shirt-sleeves poked out his head, holding the door half-open, and stared up at a window opposite. After a few minutes he slunk in again, and three loafers came slouching down the street, eager for mischief or beastliness of some sort. They chose a house that seemed rather smarter than the rest, and, irritated by the neat curtains, the little grass plot with its dwarf shrub, one of the ruffians drew out a piece of chalk and wrote some words on the front door. His friends kept watch for him, and the adventure achieved, all three bolted, bellowing yahoo laughter. Then a bell began, tang, tang, tang, and here and there children appeared on their way to Sunday-school, and the chapel "teachers" went by with verjuice eyes and lips, scowling at the little boy who cried "Piper, piper!" On the main road many respectable people, the men shining and ill-fitted, the women hideously bedizened, passed in the direction of the Independent nightmare, the stuccoed thing with Doric columns, but on the whole life was stagnant. Presently Lucian smelt the horrid fumes of roast beef and cabbage; the early risers were preparing the one-o'clock meal, but many lay in bed and put off dinner till three, with the effect of prolonging the cabbage atmosphere into the late afternoon. A drizzly rain began as the people were coming out of church, and the mothers of little boys in velvet and little girls in foolishness of every kind were impelled to slap their offspring, and to threaten them with father. Then the torpor of beef and beer and cabbage settled down on the street; in some houses they snorted and read the Parish Magazine, in some they snored and read the murders and collected filth of the week; but the only movement of the afternoon was a second procession of children, now bloated and distended with food, again answering the summons of tang, tang, tang. On the main road the trams, laden with impossible people, went humming to and fro, and young men who wore bright blue ties cheerfully haw-hawed and smoked penny cigars. They annoyed the shiny and respectable and verjuice-lipped, not by the frightful stench of the cigars, but because they were cheerful on Sunday. By and by the children, having heard about Moses in the Bulrushes and Daniel in the Lion's Den, came straggling home in an evil humor. And all the day it was as if on a grey sheet grey shadows flickered, passing by.

And in the rose-garden every flower was a flame! He thought in symbols, using the Persian imagery of a dusky court, surrounded by white cloisters, gilded by gates of bronze. The stars came out, the sky glowed a darker violet, but the cloistered wall, the fantastic trellises in stone, shone whiter. It was like a hedge of may-blossom, like a lily within a cup of lapis-lazuli, like sea-foam tossed on the heaving sea at dawn. Always those white cloisters trembled with the lute music, always the garden sang with the clear fountain, rising and falling in the mysterious dusk. And there was a singing voice stealing through the white lattices and the bronze gates, a soft voice chanting of the Lover and the Beloved, of the Vineyard, of the Gate and the Way. Oh! the language was unknown; but the music of the refrain returned again and again, swelling and trembling through the white nets of the latticed cloisters. And every rose in the dusky air was a flame.

He had seen the life which he expressed by these symbols offered to him, and he had refused it; and he was alone in the grey street, with its lamps just twinkling through the dreary twilight, the blast of a ribald chorus sounding from the main road, a doggerel hymn whining from some parlor, to the accompaniment of the harmonium. He wondered why he had turned away from that woman who knew all secrets, in whose eyes were all the mysteries. He opened the desk of his bureau, and was confronted by the heap and litter of papers, lying in confusion as he had left them. He knew that there was the motive of his refusal; he had been unwilling to abandon all hope of the work. The glory and the torment of his ambition glowed upon him as he looked at the manuscript; it seemed so pitiful that such a single desire should be thwarted. He was aware that if he chose to sit down now before the desk he could, in a manner, write easily enough--he could produce a tale which would be formally well constructed and certain of favorable reception. And it would not be the utterly commonplace, entirely hopeless favorite of the circulating library; it would stand in those ranks where the real thing is skillfully counterfeited, amongst the books which give the reader his orgy of emotions, and yet contrive to be superior, and "art," in his opinion. Lucian had often observed this species of triumph, and had noted the acclamation that never failed the clever sham. Romola, for example, had made the great host of the serious, the portentous, shout for joy, while the real book, The Cloister and the Hearth, was a comparative failure.

He knew that he could write a Romola; but he thought the art of counterfeiting half-crowns less detestable than this shabby trick of imitating literature. He had refused definitely to enter the atelier of the gentleman who pleased his clients by ingeniously simulating the grain of walnut; and though he had seen the old oaken ambry kicked out contemptuously into the farmyard, serving perhaps the necessities of hens or pigs, he would not apprentice himself to the masters of veneer. He paced up and down the room, glancing now and again at his papers, and wondering if there were not hope for him. A great thing he could never do, but he had longed to do a true thing, to imagine sincere and genuine pages.

He was stirred again to this fury for the work by the event of the evening before, by all that had passed through his mind since the melancholy dawn. The lurid picture of that fiery street, the flaming shops and flaming glances, all its wonders and horrors, lit by the naphtha flares and by the burning souls, had possessed him; and the noises, the shriek and the whisper, the jangling rattle of the piano-organ, the long-continued scream of the butcher as he dabbled in the blood, the lewd litany of the singers, these seemed to be resolved into an infernal overture, loud with the expectation of lust and death. And how the spectacle was set in the cloud of dark night, a phantom play acted on that fiery stage, beneath those hideous brassy lamps, very slowly swinging in a violent blast. As all the medley of outrageous sights and sounds now fused themselves within his brain into one clear impression, it seemed that he had indeed witnessed and acted in a drama, that all the scene had been prepared and vested for him, and that the choric songs he had heard were but preludes to a greater act. For in that woman was the consummation and catastrophe of it all, and the whole stage waited for their meeting. He fancied that after this the voices and the lights died away, that the crowd sank swiftly into the darkness, and that the street was at once denuded of the great lamps and of all its awful scenic apparatus.

Again, he thought, the same mystery would be represented before him; suddenly on some dark and gloomy night, as he wandered lonely on a deserted road, the wind hurrying before him, suddenly a turn would bring him again upon the fiery stage, and the antique drama would be re-enacted. He would be drawn to the same place, to find that woman still standing there; again he would watch the rose radiant and palpitating upon her cheek, the argent gleam in her brown eyes, the bronze curls gilding the white splendor of her neck. And for the second time she would freely offer herself. He could hear the wail of the singers swelling to a shriek, and see the dusky dancers whirling round in a faster frenzy, and the naphtha flares tinged with red, as the woman and he went away into the dark, into the cloistered court where every flower was a flame, whence he would never come out.

His only escape was in the desk; he might find salvation if he could again hide his heart in the heap and litter of papers, and again be rapt by the cadence of a phrase. He threw open his window and looked out on the dim world and the glimmering amber lights. He resolved that he would rise early in the morning, and seek once more for his true life in the work.

But there was a strange thing. There was a little bottle on the mantelpiece, a bottle of dark blue glass, and he trembled and shuddered before it, as if it were a fetish.

VII

It was very dark in the room. He seemed by slow degrees to awake from a long and heavy torpor, from an utter forgetfulness, and as he raised his eyes he could scarcely discern the pale whiteness of the paper on the desk before him. He remembered something of a gloomy winter afternoon, of driving rain, of gusty wind: he had fallen asleep over his work, no doubt, and the night had come down.

He lay back in his chair, wondering whether it were late; his eyes were half closed, and he did not make the effort and rouse himself. He could hear the stormy noise of the wind, and the sound reminded him of the half-forgotten days. He thought of his boyhood, and the old rectory, and the great elms that surrounded it. There was something pleasant in the consciousness that he was still half dreaming; he knew he could wake up whenever he pleased, but for the moment he amused himself by the pretence that he was a little boy again, tired with his rambles and the keen air of the hills. He remembered how he would sometimes wake up in the dark at midnight, and listen sleepily for a moment to the rush of the wind straining and crying amongst the trees, and hear it beat upon the walls, and then he would fall to dreams again, happy in his warm, snug bed.

The wind grew louder, and the windows rattled. He half opened his eyes and shut them again, determined to cherish that sensation of long ago. He felt tired and heavy with sleep; he imagined that he was exhausted by some effort; he had, perhaps, been writing furiously without rest. He could not recollect at the instant what the work had been; it would be delightful to read the pages when he had made up his mind to bestir himself.

Surely that was the noise of boughs, swaying and grinding in the wind. He remembered one night at home when such a sound had roused him suddenly from a deep sweet sleep. There was a rushing and beating as of wings upon the air, and a heavy dreary noise, like thunder far away upon the mountain. He had got out of bed and looked from behind the blind to see what was abroad. He remembered the strange sight he had seen, and he pretended it would be just the same if he cared to look out now. There were clouds flying awfully from before the moon, and a pale light that made the familiar land look strange and terrible. The blast of wind came with a great shriek, and the trees tossed and bowed and quivered; the wood was scourged and horrible, and the night air was ghastly with a confused tumult, and voices as of a host. A huge black cloud rolled across the heaven from the west and covered up the moon, and there came a torrent of bitter hissing rain.

It was all a vivid picture to him as he sat in his chair, unwilling to wake. Even as he let his mind stray back to that night of the past years, the rain beat sharply on the window-panes, and though there were no trees in the grey suburban street, he heard distinctly the crash of boughs. He wandered vaguely from thought to thought, groping indistinctly amongst memories, like a man trying to cross from door to door in a darkened unfamiliar room. But, no doubt, if he were to look out, by some magic the whole scene would be displayed before him. He would not see the curve of monotonous two-storied houses, with here and there a white blind, a patch of light, and shadows appearing and vanishing, not the rain plashing in the muddy road, not the amber of the gas-lamp opposite, but the wild moonlight poured on the dearly loved country; far away the dim circle of the hills and woods, and beneath him the tossing trees about the lawn, and the wood heaving under the fury of the wind.

He smiled to himself, amidst his lazy meditations, to think how real it seemed, and yet it was all far away, the scenery of an old play long ended and forgotten. It was strange that after all these years of trouble and work and change he should be in any sense the same person as that little boy peeping out, half frightened, from the rectory window. It was as if looking in the glass one should see a stranger, and yet know that the image was a true reflection.

The memory of the old home recalled his father and mother to him, and he wondered whether his mother would come if he were to cry out suddenly. One night, on just such a night as this, when a great storm blew from the mountain, a tree had fallen with a crash and a bough had struck the roof, and he awoke in a fright, calling for his mother. She had come and had comforted him, soothing him to sleep, and now he shut his eyes, seeing her face shining in the uncertain flickering candle light, as she bent over his bed. He could not think she had died; the memory was but a part of the evil dreams that had come afterwards.

He said to himself that he had fallen asleep and dreamed sorrow and agony, and he wished to forget all the things of trouble. He would return to happy days, to the beloved land, to the dear and friendly paths across the fields. There was the paper, white before him, and when he chose to stir, he would have the pleasure of reading his work. He could not quite recollect what he had been about, but he was somehow conscious that he had been successful and had brought some long labor to a worthy ending. Presently he would light the gas, and enjoy the satisfaction that only the work could give him, but for the time he preferred to linger in the darkness, and to think of himself as straying from stile to stile through the scented meadows, and listening to the bright brook that sang to the alders.

It was winter now, for he heard the rain and the wind, and the swaying of the trees, but in those old days how sweet the summer had been. The great hawthorn bush in blossom, like a white cloud upon the earth, had appeared to him in twilight, he had lingered in the enclosed valley to hear the nightingale, a voice swelling out from the rich gloom, from the trees that grew around the well. The scent of the meadowsweet was blown to him across the bridge of years, and with it came the dream and the hope and the longing, and the afterglow red in the sky, and the marvel of the earth. There was a quiet walk that he knew so well; one went up from a little green byroad, following an unnamed brooklet scarce a foot wide, but yet wandering like a river, gurgling over its pebbles, with its dwarf bushes shading the pouring water. One went through the meadow grass, and came to the larch wood that grew from hill to hill across the stream, and shone a brilliant tender green, and sent vague sweet spires to the flushing sky. Through the wood the path wound, turning and dipping, and beneath, the brown fallen needles of last year were soft and thick, and the resinous cones gave out their odor as the warm night advanced, and the shadows darkened. It was quite still; but he stayed, and the faint song of the brooklet sounded like the echo of a river beyond the mountains. How strange it was to look into the wood, to see the tall straight stems rising, pillar-like, and then the dusk, uncertain, and then the blackness. So he came out from the larch wood, from the green cloud and the vague shadow, into the dearest of all hollows, shut in on one side by the larches and before him by high violent walls of turf, like the slopes of a fort, with a clear line dark against the twilight sky, and a weird thorn bush that grew large, mysterious, on the summit, beneath the gleam of the evening star.

And he retraced his wanderings in those deep old lanes that began from the common road and went away towards the unknown, climbing steep hills, and piercing the woods of shadows, and dipping down into valleys that seemed virgin, unexplored, secret for the foot of man. He entered such a lane not knowing where it might bring him, hoping he had found the way to fairyland, to the woods beyond the world, to that vague territory that haunts all the dreams of a boy. He could not tell where he might be, for the high banks rose steep, and the great hedges made a green vault above. Marvelous ferns grew rich and thick in the dark red earth, fastening their roots about the roots of hazel and beech and maple, clustering like the carven capitals of a cathedral pillar. Down, like a dark shaft, the lane dipped to the well of the hills, and came amongst the limestone rocks. He climbed the bank at last, and looked out into a country that seemed for a moment the land he sought, a mysterious realm with unfamiliar hills and valleys and fair plains all golden, and white houses radiant in the sunset light.

And he thought of the steep hillsides where the bracken was like a wood, and of bare places where the west wind sang over the golden gorse, of still circles in mid-lake, of the poisonous yew-tree in the middle of the wood, shedding its crimson cups on the dank earth. How he lingered by certain black waterpools hedged on every side by drooping wych-elms and black-stemmed alders, watching the faint waves widening to the banks as a leaf or a twig dropped from the trees.

And the whole air and wonder of the ancient forest came back to him. He had found his way to the river valley, to the long lovely hollow between the hills, and went up and up beneath the leaves in the warm hush of midsummer, glancing back now and again through the green alleys, to the river winding in mystic esses beneath, passing hidden glens receiving the streams that rushed down the hillside, ice-cold from the rock, passing the immemorial tumulus, the graves where the legionaries waited for the trumpet, the grey farmhouses sending the blue wreaths of wood smoke into the still air. He went higher and higher, till at last he entered the long passage of the Roman road, and from this, the ridge and summit of the wood, he saw the waves of green swell and dip and sink towards the marshy level and the gleaming yellow sea. He looked on the surging forest, and thought of the strange deserted city moldering into a petty village on its verge, of its encircling walls melting into the turf, of vestiges of an older temple which the earth had buried utterly.

It was winter now, for he heard the wail of the wind, and a sudden gust drove the rain against the panes, but he thought of the bee's song in the clover, of the foxgloves in full blossom, of the wild roses, delicate, enchanting, swaying on a long stem above the hedge. He had been in strange places, he had known sorrow and desolation, and had grown grey and weary in the work of letters, but he lived again in the sweetness, in the clear bright air of early morning, when the sky was blue in June, and the mist rolled like a white sea in the valley. He laughed when he recollected that he had sometimes fancied himself unhappy in those days; in those days when he could be glad because the sun shone, because the wind blew fresh on the mountain. On those bright days he had been glad, looking at the fleeting and passing of the clouds upon the hills, and had gone up higher to the broad dome of the mountain, feeling that joy went up before him.

He remembered how, a boy, he had dreamed of love, of an adorable and ineffable mystery which transcended all longing and desire. The time had come when all the wonder of the earth seemed to prefigure this alone, when he found the symbol of the Beloved in hill and wood and stream, and every flower and every dark pool discoursed a pure ecstasy. It was the longing for longing, the love of love, that had come to him when he awoke one morning just before the dawn, and for the first time felt the sharp thrill of passion.

He tried in vain to express to himself the exquisite joys of innocent desire. Even now, after troubled years, in spite of some dark cloud that overshadowed the background of his thought, the sweetness of the boy's imagined pleasure came like a perfume into his reverie. It was no love of a woman but the desire of womanhood, the Eros of the unknown, that made the heart tremble. He hardly dreamed that such a love could ever be satisfied, that the thirst of beauty could be slaked. He shrank from all contact of actuality, not venturing so much as to imagine the inner place and sanctuary of the mysteries. It was enough for him to adore in the outer court, to know that within, in the sweet gloom, were the vision and the rapture, the altar and the sacrifice.

He remembered, dimly, the passage of many heavy years since that time of hope and passion, but, perhaps, the vague shadow would pass away, and he could renew the boy's thoughts, the unformed fancies that were part of the bright day, of the wild roses in the hedgerow. All other things should be laid aside, he would let them trouble him no more after this winter night. He saw now that from the first he had allowed his imagination to bewilder him, to create a fantastic world in which he suffered, molding innocent forms into terror and dismay. Vividly, he saw again the black circle of oaks, growing in a haggard ring upon the bastions of the Roman fort. The noise of the storm without grew louder, and he thought how the wind had come up the valley with the sound of a scream, how a great tree had ground its boughs together, shuddering before the violent blast. Clear and distinct, as if he were standing now in the lane, he saw the steep slopes surging from the valley, and the black crown of the oaks set against the flaming sky, against a blaze and glow of light as if great furnace doors were opened. He saw the fire, as it were, smitten about the bastions, about the heaped mounds that guarded the fort, and the crooked evil boughs seemed to writhe in the blast of flame that beat from heaven. Strangely with the sight of the burning fort mingled the impression of a dim white shape floating up the dusk of the lane towards him, and he saw across the valley of years a girl's face, a momentary apparition that shone and vanished away.

Then there was a memory of another day, of violent summer, of white farmhouse walls blazing in the sun, and a far call from the reapers in the cornfields. He had climbed the steep slope and penetrated the matted thicket and lay in the heat, alone on the soft short grass that grew within the fort. There was a cloud of madness, and confusion of broken dreams that had no meaning or clue but only an indefinable horror and defilement. He had fallen asleep as he gazed at the knotted fantastic boughs of the stunted brake about him, and when he woke he was ashamed, and fled away fearing that "they" would pursue him. He did not know who "they" were, but it seemed as if a woman's face watched him from between the matted boughs, and that she summoned to her side awful companions who had never grown old through all the ages.

He looked up, it seemed, at a smiling face that bent over him, as he sat in the cool dark kitchen of the old farmhouse, and wondered why the sweetness of those red lips and the kindness of the eyes mingled with the nightmare in the fort, with the horrible Sabbath he had imagined as he lay sleeping on the hot soft turf. He had allowed these disturbed fancies, all this mad wreck of terror and shame that he had gathered in his mind, to trouble him for too long a time; presently he would light up the room, and leave all the old darkness of his life behind him, and from henceforth he would walk in the day.

He could still distinguish, though very vaguely, the pile of papers beside him, and he remembered, now, that he had finished a long task that afternoon, before he fell asleep. He could not trouble himself to recollect the exact nature of the work, but he was sure that he had done well; in a few minutes, perhaps, he would strike a match, and read the title, and amuse himself with his own forgetfulness. But the sight of the papers lying there in order made him think of his beginnings, of those first unhappy efforts which were so impossible and so hopeless. He saw himself bending over the table in the old familiar room, desperately scribbling, and then laying down his pen dismayed at the sad results on the page. It was late at night, his father had been long in bed, and the house was still. The fire was almost out, with only a dim glow here and there amongst the cinders, and the room was growing chilly. He rose at last from his work and looked out on a dim earth and a dark and cloudy sky.

Night after night he had labored on, persevering in his effort, even through the cold sickness of despair, when every line was doomed as it was made. Now, with the consciousness that he knew at least the conditions of literature, and that many years of thought and practice had given him some sense of language, he found these early struggles both pathetic and astonishing. He could not understand how he had persevered so stubbornly, how he had had the heart to begin a fresh page when so many folios of blotted, painful effort lay torn, derided, impossible in their utter failure. It seemed to him that it must have been a miracle or an infernal possession, a species of madness, that had driven him on, every day disappointed, and every day hopeful.

And yet there was a joyous side to the illusion. In these dry days that he lived in, when he had bought, by a long experience and by countless hours of misery, a knowledge of his limitations, of the vast gulf that yawned between the conception and the work, it was pleasant to think of a time when all things were possible, when the most splendid design seemed an affair of a few weeks. Now he had come to a frank acknowledgment; so far as he was concerned, he judged every book wholly impossible till the last line of it was written, and he had learnt patience, the art of sighing and putting the fine scheme away in the pigeon-hole of what could never be. But to think of those days! Then one could plot out a book that should be more curious than Rabelais, and jot down the outlines of a romance to surpass Cervantes, and design renaissance tragedies and volumes of contes, and comedies of the Restoration; everything was to be done, and the masterpiece was always the rainbow cup, a little way before him.

He touched the manuscript on the desk, and the feeling of the pages seemed to restore all the papers that had been torn so long ago. It was the atmosphere of the silent room that returned, the light of the shaded candle falling on the abandoned leaves. This had been painfully excogitated while the snowstorm whirled about the lawn and filled the lanes, this was of the summer night, this of the harvest moon rising like a fire from the tithebarn on the hill. How well he remembered those half-dozen pages of which he had once been so proud; he had thought out the sentences one evening, while he leaned on the foot-bridge and watched the brook swim across the road. Every word smelt of the meadowsweet that grew thick upon the banks; now, as he recalled the cadence and the phrase that had seemed so charming, he saw again the ferns beneath the vaulted roots of the beech, and the green light of the glowworm in the hedge.

And in the west the mountains swelled to a great dome, and on the dome was a mound, the memorial of some forgotten race, that grew dark and large against the red sky, when the sun set. He had lingered below it in the solitude, amongst the winds, at evening, far away from home; and oh, the labor and the vain efforts to make the form of it and the awe of it in prose, to write the hush of the vast hill, and the sadness of the world below sinking into the night, and the mystery, the suggestion of the rounded hillock, huge against the magic sky.

He had tried to sing in words the music that the brook sang, and the sound of the October wind rustling through the brown bracken on the hill. How many pages he had covered in the effort to show a white winter world, a sun without warmth in a grey-blue sky, all the fields, all the land white and shining, and one high summit where the dark pines towered, still in the still afternoon, in the pale violet air.

To win the secret of words, to make a phrase that would murmur of summer and the bee, to summon the wind into a sentence, to conjure the odor of the night into the surge and fall and harmony of a line; this was the tale of the long evenings, of the candle flame white upon the paper and the eager pen.

He remembered that in some fantastic book he had seen a bar or two of music, and, beneath, the inscription that here was the musical expression of Westminster Abbey. His boyish effort seemed hardly less ambitious, and he no longer believed that language could present the melody and the awe and the loveliness of the earth. He had long known that he, at all events, would have to be content with a far approach, with a few broken notes that might suggest, perhaps, the magistral everlasting song of the hill and the streams.

But in those far days the impossible was but a part of wonderland that lay before him, of the world beyond the wood and the mountain. All was to be conquered, all was to be achieved; he had but to make the journey and he would find the golden world and the golden word, and hear those songs that the sirens sang. He touched the manuscript; whatever it was, it was the result of painful labor and disappointment, not of the old flush of hope, but it came of weary days, of correction and re-correction. It might be good in its measure; but afterwards he would write no more for a time. He would go back again to the happy world of masterpieces, to the dreams of great and perfect books, written in an ecstasy.

Like a dark cloud from the sea came the memory of the attempt he had made, of the poor piteous history that had once embittered his life. He sighed and said alas, thinking of his folly, of the hours when he was shaken with futile, miserable rage. Some silly person in London had made his manuscript more saleable and had sold it without rendering an account of the profits, and for that he had been ready to curse humanity. Black, horrible, as the memory of a stormy day, the rage of his heart returned to his mind, and he covered his eyes, endeavoring to darken the picture of terror and hate that shone before him. He tried to drive it all out of his thought, it vexed him to remember these foolish trifles; the trick of a publisher, the small pomposities and malignancies of the country folk, the cruelty of a village boy, had inflamed him almost to the pitch of madness. His heart had burnt with fury, and when he looked up the sky was blotched, and scarlet as if it rained blood.

Indeed he had almost believed that blood had rained upon him, and cold blood from a sacrifice in heaven; his face was wet and chill and dripping, and he had passed his hand across his forehead and looked at it. A red cloud had seemed to swell over the hill, and grow great, and come near to him; he was but an ace removed from raging madness.

It had almost come to that; the drift and the breath of the scarlet cloud had well-nigh touched him. It was strange that he had been so deeply troubled by such little things, and strange how after all the years he could still recall the anguish and rage and hate that shook his soul as with a spiritual tempest.

The memory of all that evening was wild and troubled; he resolved that it should vex him no more, that now, for the last time, he would let himself be tormented by the past. In a few minutes he would rise to a new life, and forget all the storms that had gone over him.

Curiously, every detail was distinct and clear in his brain. The figure of the doctor driving home, and the sound of the few words he had spoken came to him in the darkness, through the noise of the storm and the pattering of the rain. Then he stood upon the ridge of the hill and saw the smoke drifting up from the ragged roofs of Caermaen, in the evening calm; he listened to the voices mounting thin and clear, in a weird tone, as if some outland folk were speaking in an unknown tongue of awful things.

He saw the gathering darkness, the mystery of twilight changing the huddled squalid village into an unearthly city, into some dreadful Atlantis, inhabited by a ruined race. The mist falling fast, the gloom that seemed to issue from the black depths of the forest, to advance palpably towards the walls, were shaped before him; and beneath, the river wound, snake-like, about the town, swimming to the flood and glowing in its still pools like molten brass. And as the water mirrored the afterglow and sent ripples and gouts of blood against the shuddering reeds, there came suddenly the piercing trumpet-call, the loud reiterated summons that rose and fell, that called and recalled, echoing through all the valley, crying to the dead as the last note rang. It summoned the legion from the river and the graves and the battlefield, the host floated up from the sea, the centuries swarmed about the eagles, the array was set for the last great battle, behind the leaguer of the mist.

He could imagine himself still wandering through the dim unknown, terrible country, gazing affrighted at the hills and woods that seemed to have put on an unearthly shape, stumbling amongst the briars that caught his feet. He lost his way in a wild country, and the red light that blazed up from the furnace on the mountains only showed him a mysterious land, in which he strayed aghast, with the sense of doom weighing upon him. The dry mutter of the trees, the sound of an unseen brook, made him afraid as if the earth spoke of his sin, and presently he was fleeing through a desolate shadowy wood, where a pale light flowed from the moldering stumps, a dream of light that shed a ghostly radiance.

And then again the dark summit of the Roman fort, the black sheer height rising above the valley, and the moonfire streaming around the ring of oaks, glowing about the green bastions that guarded the thicket and the inner place.

The room in which he sat appeared the vision, the trouble of the wind and rain without was but illusion, the noise of the waves in the seashell. Passion and tears and adoration and the glories of the summer night returned, and the calm sweet face of the woman appeared, and he thrilled at the soft touch of her hand on his flesh.

She shone as if she had floated down into the lane from the moon that swam between films of cloud above the black circle of the oaks. She led him away from all terror and despair and hate, and gave herself to him with rapture, showing him love, kissing his tears away, pillowing his cheek upon her breast.

His lips dwelt on her lips, his mouth upon the breath of her mouth, her arms were strained about him, and oh! she charmed him with her voice, with sweet kind words, as she offered her sacrifice. How her scented hair fell down, and floated over his eyes, and there was a marvelous fire called the moon, and her lips were aflame, and her eyes shone like a light on the hills.

All beautiful womanhood had come to him in the lane. Love had touched him in the dusk and had flown away, but he had seen the splendor and the glory, and his eyes had seen the enchanted light.

AVE ATQUE VALE

The old words sounded in his ears like the ending of a chant, and he heard the music's close. Once only in his weary hapless life, once the world had passed away, and he had known her, the dear, dear Annie, the symbol of all mystic womanhood.

The heaviness of languor still oppressed him, holding him back amongst these old memories, so that he could not stir from his place. Oddly, there seemed something unaccustomed about the darkness of the room, as if the shadows he had summoned had changed the aspect of the walls. He was conscious that on this night he was not altogether himself; fatigue, and the weariness of sleep, and the waking vision had perplexed him. He remembered how once or twice when he was a little boy startled by an uneasy dream, and had stared with a frightened gaze into nothingness, not knowing where he was, all trembling, and breathing quick, till he touched the rail of his bed, and the familiar outlines of the looking-glass and the chiffonier began to glimmer out of the gloom. So now he touched the pile of manuscript and the desk at which he had worked so many hours, and felt reassured, though he smiled at himself, and he felt the old childish dread, the longing to cry out for some one to bring a candle, and show him that he really was in his own room. He glanced up for an instant, expecting to see perhaps the glitter of the brass gas jet that was fixed on the wall, just beside his bureau, but it was too dark, and he could not rouse himself and make the effort that would drive the cloud and the muttering thoughts away.

He leant back again, picturing the wet street without, the rain driving like fountain spray about the gas lamp, the shrilling of the wind on those waste places to the north. It was strange how in the brick and stucco desert where no trees were, he all the time imagined the noise of tossing boughs, the grinding of the boughs together. There was a great storm and tumult in this wilderness of London, and for the sound of the rain and the wind he could not hear the hum and jangle of the trams, and the jar and shriek of the garden gates as they opened and shut. But he could imagine his street, the rain-swept desolate curve of it, as it turned northward, and beyond the empty suburban roads, the twinkling villa windows, the ruined field, the broken lane, and then yet another suburb rising, a solitary gas-lamp glimmering at a corner, and the plane tree lashing its boughs, and driving great showers against the glass.

It was wonderful to think of. For when these remote roads were ended one dipped down the hill into the open country, into the dim world beyond the glint of friendly fires. Tonight, how waste they were, these wet roads, edged with the red-brick houses, with shrubs whipped by the wind against one another, against the paling and the wall. There the wind swayed the great elms scattered on the sidewalk, the remnants of the old stately fields, and beneath each tree was a pool of wet, and a torment of raindrops fell with every gust. And one passed through the red avenues, perhaps by a little settlement of flickering shops, and passed the last sentinel wavering lamp, and the road became a ragged lane, and the storm screamed from hedge to hedge across the open fields. And then, beyond, one touched again upon a still remoter avant-garde of London, an island amidst the darkness, surrounded by its pale of twinkling, starry lights.

He remembered his wanderings amongst these outposts of the town, and thought how desolate all their ways must be tonight. They were solitary in wet and wind, and only at long intervals some one pattered and hurried along them, bending his eyes down to escape the drift of rain. Within the villas, behind the close-drawn curtains, they drew about the fire, and wondered at the violence of the storm, listening for each great gust as it gathered far away, and rocked the trees, and at last rushed with a huge shock against their walls as if it were the coming of the sea. He thought of himself walking, as he had often walked, from lamp to lamp on such a night, treasuring his lonely thoughts, and weighing the hard task awaiting him in his room. Often in the evening, after a long day's labor, he had thrown down his pen in utter listlessness, feeling that he could struggle no more with ideas and words, and he had gone out into driving rain and darkness, seeking the word of the enigma as he tramped on and on beneath these outer battlements of London.

Or on some grey afternoon in March or November he had sickened of the dull monotony and the stagnant life that he saw from his window, and had taken his design with him to the lonely places, halting now and again by a gate, and pausing in the shelter of a hedge through which the austere wind shivered, while, perhaps, he dreamed of Sicily, or of sunlight on the Provençal olives. Often as he strayed solitary from street to field, and passed the Syrian fig tree imprisoned in Britain, nailed to an ungenial wall, the solution of the puzzle became evident, and he laughed and hurried home eager to make the page speak, to note the song he had heard on his way.

Sometimes he had spent many hours treading this edge and brim of London, now lost amidst the dun fields, watching the bushes shaken by the wind, and now looking down from a height whence he could see the dim waves of the town, and a barbaric water tower rising from a hill, and the snuff-colored cloud of smoke that seemed blown up from the streets into the sky.

There were certain ways and places that he had cherished; he loved a great old common that stood on high ground, curtained about with ancient spacious houses of red brick, and their cedarn gardens. And there was on the road that led to this common a space of ragged uneven ground with a pool and a twisted oak, and here he had often stayed in autumn and looked across the mist and the valley at the great theatre of the sunset, where a red cloud like a charging knight shone and conquered a purple dragon shape, and golden lances glittered in a field of faërie green.

Or sometimes, when the unending prospect of trim, monotonous, modern streets had wearied him, he had found an immense refreshment in the discovery of a forgotten hamlet, left in a hollow, while all new London pressed and surged on every side, threatening the rest of the red roofs with its vulgar growth. These little peaceful houses, huddled together beneath the shelter of trees, with their bulging leaded windows and uneven roofs, somehow brought back to him the sense of the country, and soothed him with the thought of the old farm-houses, white or grey, the homes of quiet lives, harbors where, perhaps, no tormenting thoughts ever broke in.

For he had instinctively determined that there was neither rest nor health in all the arid waste of streets about him. It seemed as if in those dull rows of dwellings, in the prim new villas, red and white and staring, there must be a leaven working which transformed all to base vulgarity. Beneath the dull sad slates, behind the blistered doors, love turned to squalid intrigue, mirth to drunken clamor, and the mystery of life became a common thing; religion was sought for in the greasy piety and flatulent oratory of the Independent chapel, the stuccoed nightmare of the Doric columns. Nothing fine, nothing rare, nothing exquisite, it seemed, could exist in the weltering suburban sea, in the habitations which had risen from the stench and slime of the brickfields. It was as if the sickening fumes that steamed from the burning bricks had been sublimed into the shape of houses, and those who lived in these grey places could also claim kinship with the putrid mud.

Hence he had delighted in the few remains of the past that he could find still surviving on the suburb's edge, in the grave old houses that stood apart from the road, in the moldering taverns of the eighteenth century, in the huddled hamlets that had preserved only the glow and the sunlight of all the years that had passed over them. It appeared to him that vulgarity and greasiness and squalor had come with a flood, that not only the good but also the evil in man's heart had been made common and ugly, that a sordid scum was mingled with all the springs, of death as of life. It would be alike futile to search amongst these mean two-storied houses for a splendid sinner as for a splendid saint; the very vices of these people smelt of cabbage water and a pothouse vomit.

And so he had often fled away from the serried maze that encircled him, seeking for the old and worn and significant as an antiquary looks for the fragments of the Roman temple amidst the modern shops. In some way the gusts of wind and the beating rain of the night reminded him of an old house that had often attracted him with a strange indefinable curiosity. He had found it on a grim grey day in March, when he had gone out under a leaden-molded sky, cowering from a dry freezing wind that brought with it the gloom and the doom of far unhappy Siberian plains. More than ever that day the suburb had oppressed him; insignificant, detestable, repulsive to body and mind, it was the only hell that a vulgar age could conceive or make, an inferno created not by Dante but by the jerry-builder. He had gone out to the north, and when he lifted up his eyes again he found that he had chanced to turn up by one of the little lanes that still strayed across the broken fields. He had never chosen this path before because the lane at its outlet was so wholly degraded and offensive, littered with rusty tins and broken crockery, and hedged in with a paling fashioned out of scraps of wire, rotting timber, and bending worn-out rails. But on this day, by happy chance, he had fled from the high road by the first opening that offered, and he no longer groped his way amongst obscene refuse, sickened by the bloated bodies of dead dogs, and fetid odors from unclean decay, but the malpassage had become a peaceful winding lane, with warm shelter beneath its banks from the dismal wind. For a mile he had walked quietly, and then a turn in the road showed him a little glen or hollow, watered by such a tiny rushing brooklet as his own woods knew, and beyond, alas, the glaring foreguard of a "new neighborhood"; raw red villas, semi-detached, and then a row of lamentable shops.

But as he was about to turn back, in the hope of finding some other outlet, his attention was charmed by a small house that stood back a little from the road on his right hand. There had been a white gate, but the paint had long faded to grey and black, and the wood crumbled under the touch, and only moss marked out the lines of the drive. The iron railing round the lawn had fallen, and the poor flower-beds were choked with grass and a faded growth of weeds. But here and there a rosebush lingered amidst suckers that had sprung grossly from the root, and on each side of the hall door were box trees, untrimmed, ragged, but still green. The slate roof was all stained and livid, blotched with the drippings of a great elm that stood at one corner of the neglected lawn, and marks of damp and decay were thick on the uneven walls, which had been washed yellow many years before. There was a porch of trellis work before the door, and Lucian had seen it rock in the wind, swaying as if every gust must drive it down. There were two windows on the ground floor, one on each side of the door, and two above, with a blind space where a central window had been blocked up.

This poor and desolate house had fascinated him. Ancient and poor and fallen, disfigured by the slate roof and the yellow wash that had replaced the old mellow dipping tiles and the warm red walls, and disfigured again by spots and patches of decay; it seemed as if its happy days were for ever ended. To Lucian it appealed with a sense of doom and horror; the black streaks that crept upon the walls, and the green drift upon the roof, appeared not so much the work of foul weather and dripping boughs, as the outward signs of evil working and creeping in the lives of those within.

The stage seemed to him decked for doom, painted with the symbols of tragedy; and he wondered as he looked whether any one were so unhappy as to live there still. There were torn blinds in the windows, but he had asked himself who could be so brave as to sit in that room, darkened by the dreary box, and listen of winter nights to the rain upon the window, and the moaning of wind amongst the tossing boughs that beat against the roof.

He could not imagine that any chamber in such a house was habitable. Here the dead had lain, through the white blind the thin light had filtered on the rigid mouth, and still the floor must be wet with tears and still that great rocking elm echoed the groaning and the sobs of those who watched. No doubt, the damp was rising, and the odor of the earth filled the house, and made such as entered draw back, foreseeing the hour of death.

Often the thought of this strange old house had haunted him; he had imagined the empty rooms where a heavy paper peeled from the walls and hung in dark strips; and he could not believe that a light ever shone from those windows that stared black and glittering on the neglected lawn. But tonight the wet and the storm seemed curiously to bring the image of the place before him, and as the wind sounded he thought how unhappy those must be, if any there were, who sat in the musty chambers by a flickering light, and listened to the elm-tree moaning and beating and weeping on the walls.

And tonight was Saturday night; and there was about that phrase something that muttered of the condemned cell, of the agony of a doomed man. Ghastly to his eyes was the conception of any one sitting in that room to the right of the door behind the larger box tree, where the wall was cracked above the window and smeared with a black stain in an ugly shape.

He knew how foolish it had been in the first place to trouble his mind with such conceits of a dreary cottage on the outskirts of London. And it was more foolish now to meditate these things, fantasies, feigned forms, the issue of a sad mood and a bleak day of spring. For soon, in a few moments, he was to rise to a new life. He was but reckoning up the account of his past, and when the light came he was to think no more of sorrow and heaviness, of real or imagined terrors. He had stayed too long in London, and he would once more taste the breath of the hills, and see the river winding in the long lovely valley; ah! he would go home.

Something like a thrill, the thrill of fear, passed over him as he remembered that there was no home. It was in the winter, a year and a half after his arrival in town, that he had suffered the loss of his father. He lay for many days prostrate, overwhelmed with sorrow and with the thought that now indeed he was utterly alone in the world. Miss Deacon was to live with another cousin in Yorkshire; the old home was at last ended and done. He felt sorry that he had not written more frequently to his father: there were things in his cousin's letters that had made his heart sore. "Your poor father was always looking for your letters," she wrote, "they used to cheer him so much. He nearly broke down when you sent him that money last Christmas; he got it into his head that you were starving yourself to send it him. He was hoping so much that you would have come down this Christmas, and kept asking me about the plum-puddings months ago."

It was not only his father that had died, but with him the last strong link was broken, and the past life, the days of his boyhood, grew faint as a dream. With his father his mother died again, and the long years died, the time of his innocence, the memory of affection. He was sorry that his letters had gone home so rarely; it hurt him to imagine his father looking out when the post came in the morning, and forced to be sad because there was nothing. But he had never thought that his father valued the few lines that he wrote, and indeed it was often difficult to know what to say. It would have been useless to write of those agonizing nights when the pen seemed an awkward and outlandish instrument, when every effort ended in shameful defeat, or of the happier hours when at last wonder appeared and the line glowed, crowned and exalted. To poor Mr. Taylor such tales would have seemed but trivial histories of some Oriental game, like an odd story from a land where men have time for the infinitely little, and can seriously make a science of arranging blossoms in a jar, and discuss perfumes instead of politics. It would have been useless to write to the rectory of his only interest, and so he wrote seldom.

And then he had been sorry because he could never write again and never see his home. He had wondered whether he would have gone down to the old place at Christmas, if his father had lived. It was curious how common things evoked the bitterest griefs, but his father's anxiety that the plum-pudding should be good, and ready for him, had brought the tears into his eyes. He could hear him saying in a nervous voice that attempted to be cheerful: "I suppose you will be thinking of the Christmas puddings soon, Jane; you remember how fond Lucian used to be of plum-pudding. I hope we shall see him this December." No doubt poor Miss Deacon paled with rage at the suggestion that she should make Christmas pudding in July; and returned a sharp answer; but it was pathetic. The wind wailed, and the rain dashed and beat again and again upon the window. He imagined that all his thoughts of home, of the old rectory amongst the elms, had conjured into his mind the sound of the storm upon the trees, for, tonight, very clearly he heard the creaking of the boughs, the noise of boughs moaning and beating and weeping on the walls, and even a pattering of wet, on wet earth, as if there were a shrub near the window that shook off the raindrops, before the gust.

That thrill, as it were a shudder of fear, passed over him again, and he knew not what had made him afraid. There were some dark shadow on his mind that saddened him; it seemed as if a vague memory of terrible days hung like a cloud over his thought, but it was all indefinite, perhaps the last grim and ragged edge of the melancholy wrack that had swelled over his life and the bygone years. He shivered and tried to rouse himself and drive away the sense of dread and shame that seemed so real and so awful, and yet he could not grasp it. But the torpor of sleep, the burden of the work that he had ended a few hours before, still weighed down his limb and bound his thoughts. He could scarcely believe that he had been busy at his desk a little while ago, and that just before the winter day closed it and the rain began to fall he had laid down the pen with a sigh of relief, and had slept in his chair. It was rather as if he had slumbered deeply through a long and weary night, as if an awful vision of flame and darkness and the worm that dieth not had come to him sleeping. But he would dwell no more on the darkness; he went back to the early days in London when he had said farewell to the hills and to the waterpools, and had set to work in this little room in the dingy street.

How he had toiled and labored at the desk before him! He had put away the old wild hopes of the masterpiece conceived and executed in a fury of inspiration, wrought out in one white heat of creative joy; it was enough if by dint of long perseverance and singleness of desire he could at last, in pain and agony and despair, after failure and disappointment and effort constantly renewed, fashion something of which he need not be ashamed. He had put himself to school again, and had, with what patience he could command, ground his teeth into the rudiments, resolved that at last he would test out the heart of the mystery. They were good nights to remember, these; he was glad to think of the little ugly room, with its silly wall-paper and its "bird's-eye" furniture, lighted up, while he sat at the bureau and wrote on into the cold stillness of the London morning, when the flickering lamplight and the daystar shone together. It was an interminable labor, and he had always known it to be as hopeless as alchemy. The gold, the great and glowing masterpiece, would never shine amongst the dead ashes and smoking efforts of the crucible, but in the course of the life, in the interval between the failures, he might possibly discover curious things.

These were the good nights that he could look back on without any fear or shame, when he had been happy and content on a diet of bread and tea and tobacco, and could hear of some imbecility passing into its hundredth thousand, and laugh cheerfully--if only that last page had been imagined aright, if the phrases noted in the still hours rang out their music when he read them in the morning. He remembered the drolleries and fantasies that the worthy Miss Deacon used to write to him, and how he had grinned at her words of reproof, admonition, and advice. She had once instigated Dolly fils to pay him a visit, and that young prop of respectability had talked about the extraordinary running of Bolter at the Scurragh meeting in Ireland; and then, glancing at Lucian's books, had inquired whether any of them had "warm bits." He had been kind though patronizing, and seemed to have moved freely in the most brilliant society of Stoke Newington. He had not been able to give any information as to the present condition of Edgar Allan Poe's old school. It appeared eventually that his report at home had not been a very favorable one, for no invitation to high tea had followed, as Miss Deacon had hoped. The Dollys knew many nice people, who were well off, and Lucian's cousin, as she afterwards said, had done her best to introduce him to the beau monde of those northern suburbs.

But after the visit of the young Dolly, with what joy he had returned to the treasures which he had concealed from profane eyes. He had looked out and seen his visitor on board the tram at the street corner, and he laughed out loud, and locked his door. There had been moments when he was lonely, and wished to hear again the sound of friendly speech, but, after such an irruption of suburban futility, it was a keen delight, to feel that he was secure on his tower, that he could absorb himself in his wonderful task as safe and silent as if he were in mid-desert.

But there was one period that he dared not revive; he could no bear to think of those weeks of desolation and terror in the winter after his coming to London. His mind was sluggish, and he could not quite remember how many years had passed since that dismal experience; it sounded all an old story, but yet it was still vivid, a flaming scroll of terror from which he turned his eyes away. One awful scene glowed into his memory, and he could not shut out the sight of an orgy, of dusky figures whirling in a ring, of lurid naphtha flares blazing in the darkness, of great glittering lamps, like infernal thuribles, very slowly swaying in a violent blast of air. And there was something else, something which he could not remember, but it filled him with terror, but it slunk in the dark places of his soul, as a wild beast crouches in the depths of a cave.

Again, and without reason, he began to image to himself that old moldering house in the field. With what a loud incessant noise the wind must be clamoring about on this fearful night, how the great elm swayed and cried in the storm, and the rain dashed and pattered on the windows, and dripped on the sodden earth from the shaking shrubs beside the door. He moved uneasily on his chair, and struggled to put the picture out of his thoughts; but in spite of himself he saw the stained uneven walls, that ugly blot of mildew above the window, and perhaps a feeble gleam of light filtered through the blind, and some one, unhappy above all and for ever lost, sat within the dismal room. Or rather, every window was black, without a glimmer of hope, and he who was shut in thick darkness heard the wind and the rain, and the noise of the elm-tree moaning and beating and weeping on the walls.

For all his effort the impression would not leave him, and as he sat before his desk looking into the vague darkness he could almost see that chamber which he had so often imagined; the low whitewashed ceiling held up by a heavy beam, the smears of smoke and long usage, the cracks and fissures of the plaster. Old furniture, shabby, deplorable, battered, stood about the room; there was a horsehair sofa worn and tottering, and a dismal paper, patterned in a livid red, blackened and moldered near the floor, and peeled off and hung in strips from the dank walls. And there was that odor of decay, of the rank soil steaming, of rotting wood, a vapor that choked the breath and made the heart full of fear and heaviness.

Lucian again shivered with a thrill of dread; he was afraid that he had overworked himself and that he was suffering from the first symptoms of grave illness. His mind dwelt on confused and terrible recollections, and with a mad ingenuity gave form and substance to phantoms; and even now he drew a long breath, almost imagining that the air in his room was heavy and noisome, that it entered his nostrils with some taint of the crypt. And his body was still languid, and though he made a half motion to rise he could not find enough energy for the effort, and he sank again into the chair. At all events, he would think no more of that sad house in the field; he would return to those long struggles with letters, to the happy nights when he had gained victories.

He remembered something of his escape from the desolation and the worse than desolation that had obsessed him during that first winter in London. He had gone free one bleak morning in February, and after those dreary terrible weeks the desk and the heap and litter of papers had once more engulfed and absorbed him. And in the succeeding summer, of a night when he lay awake and listened to the birds, shining images came wantonly to him. For an hour, while the dawn brightened, he had felt the presence of an age, the resurrection of the life that the green fields had hidden, and his heart stirred for joy when he knew that he held and possessed all the loveliness that had so long moldered. He could scarcely fall asleep for eager and leaping thoughts, and as soon as his breakfast was over he went out and bought paper and pens of a certain celestial stationer in Notting Hill. The street was not changed as he passed to and fro on his errand. The rattling wagons jostled by at intervals, a rare hansom came spinning down from London, there sounded the same hum and jangle of the gliding trams. The languid life of the pavement was unaltered; a few people, un-classed, without salience or possible description, lounged and walked from east to west, and from west to east, or slowly dropped into the byways to wander in the black waste to the north, or perhaps go astray in the systems that stretched towards the river. He glanced down these by-roads as he passed, and was astonished, as always, at their mysterious and desert aspect. Some were utterly empty; lines of neat, appalling residences, trim and garnished as if for occupation, edging the white glaring road; and not a soul was abroad, and not a sound broke their stillness. It was a picture of the desolation of midnight lighted up, but empty and waste as the most profound and solemn hours before the day. Other of these by-roads, of older settlement, were furnished with more important houses, standing far back from the pavement, each in a little wood of greenery, and thus one might look down as through a forest vista, and see a way smooth and guarded with low walls and yet untrodden, and all a leafy silence. Here and there in some of these echoing roads a figure seemed lazily advancing in the distance, hesitating and delaying, as if lost in the labyrinth. It was difficult to say which were the more dismal, these deserted streets that wandered away to right and left, or the great main thoroughfare with its narcotic and shadowy life. For the latter appeared vast, interminable, grey, and those who traveled by it were scarcely real, the bodies of the living, but rather the uncertain and misty shapes that come and go across the desert in an Eastern tale, when men look up from the sand and see a caravan pass them, all in silence, without a cry or a greeting. So they passed and repassed each other on those pavements, appearing and vanishing, each intent on his own secret, and wrapped in obscurity. One might have sworn that not a man saw his neighbor who met him or jostled him, that here every one was a phantom for the other, though the lines of their paths crossed and recrossed, and their eyes stared like the eyes of live men. When two went by together, they mumbled and cast distrustful glances behind them as though afraid all the world was an enemy, and the pattering of feet was like the noise of a shower of rain. Curious appearances and simulations of life gathered at points in the road, for at intervals the villas ended and shops began in a dismal row, and looked so hopeless that one wondered who could buy. There were women fluttering uneasily about the greengrocers, and shabby things in rusty black touched and retouched the red lumps that an unshaven butcher offered, and already in the corner public there was a confused noise, with a tossing of voices that rose and fell like a Jewish chant, with the senseless stir of marionettes jerked into an imitation of gaiety. Then, in crossing a side street that seemed like grey mid-winter in stone, he trespassed from one world to another, for an old decayed house amidst its garden held the opposite corner. The laurels had grown into black skeletons, patched with green drift, the ilex gloomed over the porch, the deodar had blighted the flower-beds. Dark ivies swarmed over an elm-tree, and a brown clustering fungus sprang in gross masses on the lawn, showing where the roots of dead trees moldered. The blue verandah, the blue balcony over the door, had faded to grey, and the stucco was blotched with ugly marks of weather, and a dank smell of decay, that vapor of black rotten earth in old town gardens, hung heavy about the gates. And then a row of musty villas had pushed out in shops to the pavement, and the things in faded black buzzed and stirred about the limp cabbages, and the red lumps of meat.

It was the same terrible street, whose pavements he had trodden so often, where sunshine seemed but a gaudy light, where the fume of burning bricks always drifted. On black winter nights he had seen the sparse lights glimmering through the rain and drawing close together, as the dreary road vanished in long perspective. Perhaps this was its most appropriate moment, when nothing of its smug villas and skeleton shops remained but the bright patches of their windows, when the old house amongst its moldering shrubs was but a dark cloud, and the streets to the north and south seemed like starry wastes, beyond them the blackness of infinity. Always in the daylight it had been to him abhorred and abominable, and its grey houses and purlieus had been fungus-like sproutings, an efflorescence of horrible decay.

But on that bright morning neither the dreadful street nor those who moved about it appalled him. He returned joyously to his den, and reverently laid out the paper on his desk. The world about him was but a grey shadow hovering on a shining wall; its noises were faint as the rustling of trees in a distant wood. The lovely and exquisite forms of those who served the Amber Venus were his distinct, clear, and manifest visions, and for one amongst them who came to him in a fire of bronze hair his heart stirred with the adoration of love. She it was who stood forth from all the rest and fell down prostrate before the radiant form in amber, drawing out her pins in curious gold, her glowing brooches of enamel, and pouring from a silver box all her treasures of jewels and precious stones, chrysoberyl and sardonyx, opal and diamond, topaz and pearl. And then she stripped from her body her precious robes and stood before the goddess in the glowing mist of her hair, praying that to her who had given all and came naked to the shrine, love might be given, and the grace of Venus. And when at last, after strange adventures, her prayer was granted, then when the sweet light came from the sea, and her lover turned at dawn to that bronze glory, he saw beside him a little statuette of amber. And in the shrine, far in Britain where the black rains stained the marble, they found the splendid and sumptuous statue of the Golden Venus, the last fine robe of silk that the lady had dedicated falling from her fingers, and the jewels lying at her feet. And her face was like the lady's face when the sun had brightened it on that day of her devotion.

The bronze mist glimmered before Lucian's eyes; he felt as though the soft floating hair touched his forehead and his lips and his hands. The fume of burning bricks, the reek of cabbage water, never reached his nostrils that were filled with the perfume of rare unguents, with the breath of the violet sea in Italy. His pleasure was an inebriation, an ecstasy of joy that destroyed all the vile Hottentot kraals and mud avenues as with one white lightning flash, and through the hours of that day he sat enthralled, not contriving a story with patient art, but rapt into another time, and entranced by the urgent gleam in the lady's eyes.

The little tale of The Amber Statuette had at last issued from a humble office in the spring after his father's death. The author was utterly unknown; the author's Murray was a wholesale stationer and printer in process of development, so that Lucian was astonished when the book became a moderate success. The reviewers had been sadly irritated, and even now he recollected with cheerfulness an article in an influential daily paper, an article pleasantly headed: "Where are the disinfectants?"

And then--but all the months afterwards seemed doubtful, there were only broken revelations of the laborious hours renewed, and the white nights when he had seen the moonlight fade and the gaslight grow wan at the approach of dawn.

He listened. Surely that was the sound of rain falling on sodden ground, the heavy sound of great swollen drops driven down from wet leaves by the gust of wind, and then again the strain of boughs sang above the tumult of the air; there was a doleful noise as if the storm shook the masts of a ship. He had only to get up and look out of the window and he would see the treeless empty street, and the rain starring the puddles under the gas-lamp, but he would wait a little while.

He tried to think why, in spite of all his resolutions, a dark horror seemed to brood more and more over all his mind. How often he had sat and worked on just such nights as this, contented if the words were in accord though the wind might wail, though the air were black with rain. Even about the little book that he had made there seemed some taint, some shuddering memory that came to him across the gulf of forgetfulness. Somehow the remembrance of the offering to Venus, of the phrases that he had so lovingly invented, brought back again the dusky figures that danced in the orgy, beneath the brassy glittering lamps; and again the naphtha flares showed the way to the sad house in the fields, and the red glare lit up the mildewed walls and the black hopeless windows. He gasped for breath, he seemed to inhale a heavy air that reeked of decay and rottenness, and the odor of the clay was in his nostrils.

That unknown cloud that had darkened his thoughts grew blacker and engulfed him, despair was heavy upon him, his heart fainted with a horrible dread. In a moment, it seemed, a veil would be drawn away and certain awful things would appear.

He strove to rise from his chair, to cry out, but he could not. Deep, deep the darkness closed upon him, and the storm sounded far away. The Roman fort surged up, terrific, and he saw the writhing boughs in a ring, and behind them a glow and heat of fire. There were hideous shapes that swarmed in the thicket of the oaks; they called and beckoned to him, and rose into the air, into the flame that was smitten from heaven about the walls. And amongst them was the form of the beloved, but jets of flame issued from her breasts, and beside her was a horrible old woman, naked; and they, too, summoned him to mount the hill.

He heard Dr. Burrows whispering of the strange things that had been found in old Mrs. Gibbon's cottage, obscene figures, and unknown contrivances. She was a witch, he said, and the mistress of witches.

He fought against the nightmare, against the illusion that bewildered him. All his life, he thought, had been an evil dream, and for the common world he had fashioned an unreal red garment, that burned in his eyes. Truth and the dream were so mingled that now he could not divide one from the other. He had let Annie drink his soul beneath the hill, on the night when the moonfire shone, but he had not surely seen her exalted in the flame, the Queen of the Sabbath. Dimly he remembered Dr. Burrows coming to see him in London, but had he not imagined all the rest?

Again he found himself in the dusky lane, and Annie floated down to him from the moon above the hill. His head sank upon her breast again, but, alas, it was aflame. And he looked down, and he saw that his own flesh was aflame, and he knew that the fire could never be quenched.

There was a heavy weight upon his head, his feet were nailed to the floor, and his arms bound tight beside him. He seemed to himself to rage and struggle with the strength of a madman; but his hand only stirred and quivered a little as it lay upon the desk.

Again he was astray in the mist; wandering through the waste avenues of a city that had been ruined from ages. It had been splendid as Rome, terrible as Babylon, and for ever the darkness had covered it, and it lay desolate for ever in the accursed plain. And far and far the grey passages stretched into the night, into the icy fields, into the place of eternal gloom.

Ring within ring the awful temple closed around him; unending circles of vast stones, circle within circle, and every circle less throughout all ages. In the center was the sanctuary of the infernal rite, and he was borne thither as in the eddies of a whirlpool, to consummate his ruin, to celebrate the wedding of the Sabbath. He flung up his arms and beat the air, resisting with all his strength, with muscles that could throw down mountains; and this time his little finger stirred for an instant, and his foot twitched upon the floor.

Then suddenly a flaring street shone before him. There was darkness round about him, but it flamed with hissing jets of light and naphtha fires, and great glittering lamps swayed very slowly in a violent blast of air. A horrible music, and the exultation of discordant voices, swelled in his ears, and he saw an uncertain tossing crowd of dusky figures that circled and leapt before him. There was a noise like the chant of the lost, and then there appeared in the midst of the orgy, beneath a red flame, the figure of a woman. Her bronze hair and flushed cheeks were illuminate, and an argent light shone from her eyes, and with a smile that froze his heart her lips opened to speak to him. The tossing crowd faded away, falling into a gulf of darkness, and then she drew out from her hair pins of curious gold, and glowing brooches in enamel, and poured out jewels before him from a silver box, and then she stripped from her body her precious robes, and stood in the glowing mist of her hair, and held out her arms to him. But he raised his eyes and saw the mould and decay gaining on the walls of a dismal room, and a gloomy paper was dropping to the rotting floor. A vapor of the grave entered his nostrils, and he cried out with a loud scream; but there was only an indistinct guttural murmur in his throat.

And presently the woman fled away from him, and he pursued her. She fled away before him through midnight country, and he followed after her, chasing her from thicket to thicket, from valley to valley. And at last he captured her and won her with horrible caresses, and they went up to celebrate and make the marriage of the Sabbath. They were within the matted thicket, and they writhed in the flames, insatiable, for ever. They were tortured, and tortured one another, in the sight of thousands who gathered thick about them; and their desire rose up like a black smoke.

Without, the storm swelled to the roaring of an awful sea, the wind grew to a shrill long scream, the elm-tree was riven and split with the crash of a thunderclap. To Lucian the tumult and the shock came as a gentle murmur, as if a brake stirred before a sudden breeze in summer. And then a vast silence overwhelmed him.

A few minutes later there was a shuffling of feet in the passage, and the door was softly opened. A woman came in, holding a light, and she peered curiously at the figure sitting quite still in the chair before the desk. The woman was half dressed, and she had let her splendid bronze hair flow down, her cheeks were flushed, and as she advanced into the shabby room, the lamp she carried cast quaking shadows on the moldering paper, patched with marks of rising damp, and hanging in strips from the wet, dripping wall. The blind had not been drawn, but no light or glimmer of light filtered through the window, for a great straggling box tree that beat the rain upon the panes shut out even the night. The woman came softly, and as she bent down over Lucian an argent gleam shone from her brown eyes, and the little curls upon her neck were like golden work upon marble. She put her hand to his heart, and looked up, and beckoned to some one who was waiting by the door.

"Come in, Joe," she said. "It's just as I thought it would be: 'Death by misadventure'"; and she held up a little empty bottle of dark blue glass that was standing on the desk. "He would take it, and I always knew he would take a drop too much one of these days."

"What's all those papers that he's got there?"

"Didn't I tell you? It was crool to see him. He got it into 'is 'ead he could write a book; he's been at it for the last six months. Look 'ere."

She spread the neat pile of manuscript broadcast over the desk, and took a sheet at haphazard. It was all covered with illegible hopeless scribblings; only here and there it was possible to recognize a word.

"Why, nobody could read it, if they wanted to."

"It's all like that. He thought it was beautiful. I used to 'ear him jabbering to himself about it, dreadful nonsense it was he used to talk. I did my best to tongue him out of it, but it wasn't any good."

"He must have been a bit dotty. He's left you everything."

"Yes."

"You'll have to see about the funeral."

"There'll be the inquest and all that first."

"You've got evidence to show he took the stuff."

"Yes, to be sure I have. The doctor told him he would be certain to do for himself, and he was found two or three times quite silly in the streets. They had to drag him away from a house in Halden Road. He was carrying on dreadful, shaking at the gaite, and calling out it was 'is 'ome and they wouldn't let him in. I heard Dr. Manning myself tell 'im in this very room that he'd kill 'imself one of these days. Joe! Aren't you ashamed of yourself. I declare you're quite rude, and it's almost Sunday too. Bring the light over here, can't you?"

The man took up the blazing paraffin lamp, and set it on the desk, beside the scattered heap of that terrible manuscript. The flaring light shone through the dead eyes into the dying brain, and there was a glow within, as if great furnace doors were opened.

THE END

THE GREAT RETURN

PUBLISHED IN LONDON BY THE FAITH PRESS, AT THE FAITH HOUSE, 22, BUCKINGHAM STREET, STRAND, W.C. 1915

To D.P.M.

CHAPTER I - THE RUMOUR OF THE MARVELLOUS

There are strange things lost and forgotten in obscure corners of the newspaper. I often think that the most extraordinary item of intelligence that I have read in print appeared a few years ago in the London Press. It came from a well known and most respected news agency; I imagine it was in all the papers. It was astounding.

The circumstances necessary--not to the understanding of this paragraph, for that is out of the question--but, we will say, to the understanding of the events which made it possible, are these. We had invaded Thibet, and there had been trouble in the hierarchy of that country, and a personage known as the Tashai Lama had taken refuge with us in India. He went on pilgrimage from one Buddhist shrine to another, and came at last to a holy mountain of Buddhism, the name of which I have forgotten. And thus the morning paper.

His Holiness the Tashai Lama then ascended the Mountain and was transfigured.--Reuter.

That was all. And from that day to this I have never heard a word of explanation or comment on this amazing statement.

***

There was no more, it seemed, to be said. "Reuter," apparently, thought he had made his simple statement of the facts of the case, had thereby done his duty, and so it all ended. Nobody, so far as I know, ever wrote to any paper asking what Reuter meant by it, or what the Tashai Lama meant by it. I suppose the fact was that nobody cared two-pence about the matter; and so this strange event--if there were any such event--was exhibited to us for a moment, and the lantern show revolved to other spectacles.

This is an extreme instance of the manner in which the marvellous is flashed out to us and then withdrawn behind its black veils and concealments; but I have known of other cases. Now and again, at intervals of a few years, there appear in the newspapers strange stories of the strange doings of what are technically called poltergeists. Some house, often a lonely farm, is suddenly subjected to an infernal bombardment. Great stones crash through the windows, thunder down the chimneys, impelled by no visible hand. The plates and cups and saucers are whirled from the dresser into the middle of the kitchen, no one can say how or by what agency. Upstairs the big bedstead and an old chest or two are heard bounding on the floor as if in a mad ballet. Now and then such doings as these excite a whole neighbourhood; sometimes a London paper sends a man down to make an investigation. He writes half a column of description on the Monday, a couple of paragraphs on the Tuesday, and then returns to town. Nothing has been explained, the matter vanishes away; and nobody cares. The tale trickles for a day or two through the Press, and then instantly disappears, like an Australian stream, into the bowels of darkness. It is possible, I suppose, that this singular incuriousness as to marvellous events and reports is not wholly unaccountable. It may be that the events in question are, as it were, psychic accidents and misadventures. They are not meant to happen, or, rather, to be manifested. They belong to the world on the other side of the dark curtain; and it is only by some queer mischance that a corner of that curtain is twitched aside for an instant. Then--for an instant--we see; but the personages whom Mr. Kipling calls the Lords of Life and Death take care that we do not see too much. Our business is with things higher and things lower, with things different, anyhow; and on the whole we are not suffered to distract ourselves with that which does not really concern us. The Transfiguration of the Lama and the tricks of the poltergeist are evidently no affairs of ours; we raise an uninterested eyebrow and pass on--to poetry or to statistics.

***

Be it noted; I am not professing any fervent personal belief in the reports to which I have alluded. For all I know, the Lama, in spite of Reuter, was not transfigured, and the poltergeist, in spite of the late Mr. Andrew Lang, may in reality be only mischievous Polly, the servant girl at the farm. And to go farther: I do not know that I should be justified in putting either of these cases of the marvellous in line with a chance paragraph that caught my eye last summer; for this had not, on the face of it at all events, anything wildly out of the common. Indeed, I dare say that I should not have read it, should not have seen it, if it had not contained the name of a place which I had once visited, which had then moved me in an odd manner that I could not understand. Indeed, I am sure that this particular paragraph deserves to stand alone, for even if the poltergeist be a real poltergeist, it merely reveals the psychic whimsicality of some region that is not our region. There were better things and more relevant things behind the few lines dealing with Llantrisant, the little town by the sea in Arfonshire.

Not on the surface, I must say, for the cutting I have preserved it--reads as follows:--

LLANTRISANT.--*The season promises very favourably: temperature of the sea yesterday at noon, 65 deg. Remarkable occurrences are supposed to have taken place during the recent Revival. The lights have not been observed lately. "The Crown." "The Fisherman's Rest."*

The style was odd certainly; knowing a little of newspapers. I could see that the figure called, I think, tmesis, or cutting, had been generously employed; the exuberances of the local correspondent had been pruned by a Fleet Street expert. And these poor men are often hurried; but what did those "lights" mean? What strange matters had the vehement blue pencil blotted out and brought to naught?

That was my first thought, and then, thinking still of Llantrisant and how I had first discovered it and found it strange, I read the paragraph again, and was saddened almost to see, as I thought, the obvious explanation. I had forgotten for the moment that it was war-time, that scares and rumours and terrors about traitorous signals and flashing lights were current everywhere by land and sea; someone, no doubt, had been watching innocent farmhouse windows and thoughtless fanlights of lodging houses; these were the "lights" that had not been observed lately.

I found out afterwards that the Llantrisant correspondent had no such treasonous lights in his mind, but something very different. Still; what do we know? He may have been mistaken, "the great rose of fire" that came over the deep may have been the port light of a coasting-ship. Did it shine at last from the old chapel on the headland? Possibly; or possibly it was the doctor's lamp at Sarnau, some miles away. I have had wonderful opportunities lately of analysing the marvels of lying, conscious and unconscious; and indeed almost incredible feats in this way can be performed. If I incline to the less likely explanation of the "lights" at Llantrisant, it is merely because this explanation seems to me to be altogether congruous with the "remarkable occurrences" of the newspaper paragraph.

After all, if rumour and gossip and hearsay are crazy things to be utterly neglected and laid aside: on the other hand, evidence is evidence, and when a couple of reputable surgeons assert, as they do assert in the case of Olwen Phillips, Croeswen, Llantrisant, that there has been a "kind of resurrection of the body," it is merely foolish to say that these things don't happen. The girl was a mass of tuberculosis, she was within a few hours of death; she is now full of life. And so, I do not believe that the rose of fire was merely a ship's light, magnified and transformed by dreaming Welsh sailors.

***

But now I am going forward too fast. I have not dated the paragraph, so I cannot give the exact day of its appearance, but I think it was somewhere between the second and third week of June. I cut it out partly because it was about Llantrisant, partly because of the "remarkable occurrences." I have an appetite for these matters, though I also have this misfortune, that I require evidence before I am ready to credit them, and I have a sort of lingering hope that some day I shall be able to elaborate some scheme or theory of such things.

But in the meantime, as a temporary measure, I hold what I call the doctrine of the jig-saw puzzle. That is: this remarkable occurrence, and that, and the other may be, and usually are, of no significance. Coincidence and chance and unsearchable causes will now and again make clouds that are undeniable fiery dragons, and potatoes that resemble Eminent Statesmen exactly and minutely in every feature, and rocks that are like eagles and lions. All this is nothing; it is when you get your set of odd shapes and find that they fit into one another, and at last that they are but parts of a large design; it is then that research grows interesting and indeed amazing, it is then that one queer form confirms the other, that the whole plan displayed justifies, corroborates, explains each separate piece.

So, it was within a week or ten days after I had read the paragraph about Llantrisant and had cut it out that I got a letter from a friend who was taking an early holiday in those regions. "You will be interested," he wrote, "to hear that they have taken to ritualistic practices at Llantrisant. I went into the church the other day, and instead of smelling like a damp vault as usual, it was positively reeking with incense."

I knew better than that. The old parson was a firm Evangelical; he would rather have burnt sulphur in his church than incense any day. So I could not make out this report at all; and went down to Arfon a few weeks later determined to investigate this and any other remarkable occurrence at Llantrisant.

CHAPTER II - ODOURS OF PARADISE

I went down to Arfon in the very heat and bloom and fragrance of the wonderful summer that they were enjoying there. In London there was no such weather; it rather seemed as if the horror and fury of the war had mounted to the very skies and were there reigning. In the mornings the sun burnt down upon the city with a heat that scorched and consumed; but then clouds heavy and horrible would roll together from all quarters of the heavens, and early in the afternoon the air would darken, and a storm of thunder and lightning, and furious, hissing rain would fall upon the streets. Indeed, the torment of the world was in the London weather. The city wore a terrible vesture; within our hearts was dread; without we were clothed in black clouds and angry fire.

It is certain that I cannot show in any words the utter peace of that Welsh coast to which I came; one sees, I think, in such a change a figure of the passage from the disquiets and the fears of earth to the peace of paradise. A land that seemed to be in a holy, happy dream, a sea that changed all the while from olivine to emerald, from emerald to sapphire, from sapphire to amethyst, that washed in white foam at the bases of the firm, grey rocks, and about the huge crimson bastions that hid the western bays and inlets of the waters; to this land I came, and to hollows that were purple and odorous with wild thyme, wonderful with many tiny, exquisite flowers. There was benediction in centaury, pardon in eye-bright, joy in lady's slipper; and so the weary eyes were refreshed, looking now at the little flowers and the happy bees about them, now on the magic mirror of the deep, changing from marvel to marvel with the passing of the great white clouds, with the brightening of the sun. And the ears, torn with jangle and racket and idle, empty noise, were soothed and comforted by the ineffable, unutterable, unceasing murmur, as the tides swam to and fro, uttering mighty, hollow voices in the caverns of the rocks.

***

For three or four days I rested in the sun and smelt the savour of the blossoms and of the salt water, and then, refreshed, I remembered that there was something queer about Llantrisant that I might as well investigate. It was no great thing that I thought to find, for, it will be remembered, I had ruled out the apparent oddity of the reporter's-or commissioner's?--reference to lights, on the ground that he must have been referring to some local panic about signalling to the enemy; who had certainly torpedoed a ship or two off Lundy in the Bristol Channel. All that I had to go upon was the reference to the "remarkable occurrences" at some revival, and then that letter of Jackson's, which spoke of Llantrisant church as "reeking" with incense, a wholly incredible and impossible state of things. Why, old Mr. Evans, the rector, looked upon coloured stoles as the very robe of Satan and his angels, as things dear to the heart of the Pope of Rome. But as to incense! As I have already familiarly observed, I knew better.

But as a hard matter of fact, this may be worth noting: when I went over to Llantrisant on Monday, August 9th, I visited the church, and it was still fragrant and exquisite with the odour of rare gums that had fumed there.

Now I happened to have a slight acquaintance with the rector. He was a most courteous and delightful old man, and on my last visit he had come across me in the churchyard, as I was admiring the very fine Celtic cross that stands there. Besides the beauty of the interlaced ornament there is an inscription in Ogham on one of the edges, concerning which the learned dispute; it is altogether one of the more famous crosses of Celtdom. Mr. Evans, I say, seeing me looking at the cross, came up and began to give me, the stranger, a resume--somewhat of a shaky and uncertain resume, I found afterwards--of the various debates and questions that had arisen as to the exact meaning of the inscription, and I was amused to detect an evident but underlying belief of his own: that the supposed Ogham characters were, in fact, due to boys' mischief and weather and the passing of the ages. But then I happened to put a question as to the sort of stone of which the cross was made, and the rector brightened amazingly. He began to talk geology, and, I think, demonstrated that the cross or the material for it must have been brought to Llantrisant from the south-west coast of Ireland. This struck me as interesting, because it was curious evidence of the migrations of the Celtic saints, whom the rector, I was delighted to find, looked upon as good Protestants, though shaky on the subject of crosses; and so, with concessions on my part, we got on very well. Thus, with all this to the good, I was emboldened to call upon him.

I found him altered. Not that he was aged; indeed, he was rather made young, with a singular brightening upon his face, and something of joy upon it that I had not seen before, that I have seen on very few faces of men. We talked of the war, of course, since that is not to be avoided; of the farming prospects of the county; of general things, till I ventured to remark that I had been in the church, and had been surprised, to find it perfumed with incense.

"You have made some alterations in the service since I was here last? You use incense now?"

The old man looked at me strangely, and hesitated.

"No," he said, "there has been no change. I use no incense in the church. I should not venture to do so."

"But," I was beginning, "the whole church is as if High Mass had just been sung there, and--"

He cut me short, and there was a certain grave solemnity in his manner that struck me almost with awe.

"I know you are a railer," he said, and the phrase coming from this mild old gentleman astonished, me unutterably. "You are a railer and a bitter railer; I have read articles that you have written, and I know your contempt and your hatred for those you call Protestants in your derision; though your grandfather, the vicar of Caerleon-on-Usk, called himself Protestant and was proud of it, and your great-grand-uncle Hezekiah, ffeiriad coch yr Castletown--the Red Priest of Castletown--was a great man with the Methodists in his day, and the people flocked by their thousands when he administered the Sacrament. I was born and brought up in Glamorganshire, and old men have wept as they told me of the weeping and contrition that there was when the Red Priest broke the Bread and raised the Cup. But you are a railer, and see nothing but the outside and the show. You are not worthy of this mystery that has been done here."

I went out from his presence rebuked indeed, and justly rebuked; but rather amazed. It is curiously true that the Welsh are still one people, one family almost, in a manner that the English cannot understand, but I had never thought that this old clergyman would have known anything of my ancestry or their doings. And as for my articles and such-like, I knew that the country clergy sometimes read, but I had fancied my pronouncements sufficiently obscure, even in London, much more in Arfon.

But so it happened, and so I had no explanation from the rector of Llantrisant of the strange circumstance, that his church was full of incense and odours of paradise.

***

I went up and down the ways of Llantrisant wondering, and came to the harbour, which is a little place, with little quays where some small coasting trade still lingers. A brigantine was at anchor here, and very lazily in the sunshine they were loading it with anthracite; for it is one of the oddities of Llantrisant that there is a small colliery in the heart of the wood on the hillside. I crossed a causeway which parts the outer harbour from the inner harbour, and settled down on a rocky beach hidden under a leafy hill. The tide was going out, and some children were playing on the wet sand, while two ladies--their mothers, I suppose--talked together as they sat comfortably on their rugs at a little distance from me.

At first they talked of the war, and I made myself deaf, for of that talk one gets enough, and more than enough, in London. Then there was a period of silence, and the conversation had passed to quite a different topic when I caught the thread of it again. I was sitting on the further side of a big rock, and I do not think that the two ladies had noticed my approach. However, though they spoke of strange things, they spoke of nothing which made it necessary for me to announce my presence.

"And, after all," one of them was saying, "what is it all about? I can't make out what is come to the people."

This speaker was a Welshwoman; I recognised the clear, over-emphasised consonants, and a faint suggestion of an accent. Her friend came from the Midlands, and it turned out that they had only known each other for a few days. Theirs was a friendship of the beach and of bathing; such friendships are common, at small seaside places.

"There is certainly something odd about the people here. I have never been to Llantrisant before, you know; indeed, this is the first time we've been in Wales for our holidays, and knowing nothing about the ways of the people and not being accustomed to hear Welsh spoken, I thought, perhaps, it must be my imagination. But you think there really is something a little queer?"

"I can tell you this: that I have been in two minds whether I should not write to my husband and ask him to take me and the children away. You know where I am at Mrs. Morgan's, and the Morgans' sitting-room is just the other side of the passage, and sometimes they leave the door open, so that I can hear what they say quite plainly. And you see I understand the Welsh, though they don't know it. And I hear them saying the most alarming things!"

"What sort of things?

"Well, indeed, it sounds like some kind of a religious service, but it's not Church of England, I know that. Old Morgan begins it, and the wife and children answer. Something like; 'Blessed be God for the messengers of Paradise.' 'Blessed be His Name for Paradise in the meat and in the drink.' 'Thanksgiving for the old offering.' 'Thanksgiving for the appearance of the old altar,' 'Praise for the joy of the ancient garden.' 'Praise for the return of those that have been long absent.' And all that sort of thing. It is nothing but madness."

"Depend upon it," said the lady from the Midlands, "there's no real harm in it. They're Dissenters; some new sect, I dare say. You know some Dissenters are very queer in their ways."

"All that is like no Dissenters that I have ever known in all my life whatever," replied the Welsh lady somewhat vehemently, with a very distinct intonation of the land. "And have you heard them speak of the bright light that shone at midnight from the church?"

CHAPTER III - A SECRET IN A SECRET PLACE

Now here was I altogether at a loss and quite bewildered. The children broke into the conversation of the two ladies and cut it all short, just as the midnight lights from the church came on the field, and when the little girls and boys went back again to the sands whooping, the tide of talk had turned, and Mrs. Harland and Mrs. Williams were quite safe and at home with Janey's measles, and a wonderful treatment for infantile earache, as exemplified in the case of Trevor. There was no more to be got out of them, evidently, so I left the beach, crossed the harbour causeway, and drank beer at the "Fishermen's Rest" till it was time to climb up two miles of deep lane and catch the train for Penvro, where I was staying. And I went up the lane, as I say, in a kind of amazement; and not so much, I think, because of evidences and hints of things strange to the senses, such as the savour of incense where no incense had smoked for three hundred and fifty years and more, or the story of bright light shining from the dark, closed church at dead of night, as because of that sentence of thanksgiving "for paradise in meat and in drink."

For the sun went down and the evening fell as I climbed the long hill through the deep woods and the high meadows, and the scent of all the green things rose from the earth and from the heart of the wood, and at a turn of the lane far below was the misty glimmer of the still sea, and from far below its deep murmur sounded as it washed on the little hidden, enclosed bay where Llantrisant stands. And I thought, if there be paradise in meat and in drink, so much the more is there paradise in the scent of the green leaves at evening and in the appearance of the sea and in the redness of the sky; and there came to me a certain vision of a real world about us all the while, of a language that was only secret because we would not take the trouble to listen to it and discern it.

It was almost dark when I got to the station, and here were the few feeble oil lamps lit, glimmering in that lonely land, where the way is long from farm to farm. The train came on its way, and I got into it; and just as we moved from the station I noticed a group under one of those dim lamps. A woman and her child had got out, and they were being welcomed by a man who had been waiting for them. I had not noticed his face as I stood on the platform, but now I saw it as he pointed down the hill towards Llantrisant, and I think I was almost frightened.

He was a young man, a farmer's son, I would say, dressed in rough brown clothes, and as different from old Mr. Evans, the rector, as one man might be from another. But on his face, as I saw it in the lamplight, there was the like brightening that I had seen on the face of the rector. It was an illuminated face, glowing with an ineffable joy, and I thought it rather gave light to the platform lamp than received light from it. The woman and her child, I inferred, were strangers to the place, and had come to pay a visit to the young man's family. They had looked about them in bewilderment, half alarmed, before they saw him; and then his face was radiant in their sight, and it was easy to see that all their troubles were ended and over. A wayside station and a darkening country, and it was as if they were welcomed by shining, immortal gladness--even into paradise.

***

But though there seemed in a sense light all about my ways, I was myself still quite bewildered. I could see, indeed, that something strange had happened or was happening in the little town hidden under the hill, but there was so far no clue to the mystery, or rather, the clue had been offered to me, and I had not taken it, I had not even known that it was there; since we do not so much as see what we have determined, without judging, to be incredible, even though it be held up before our eyes. The dialogue that the Welsh Mrs. Williams had reported to her English friend might have set me on the right way; but the right way was outside all my limits of possibility, outside the circle of my thought. The palæontologist might see monstrous, significant marks in the slime of a river bank, but he would never draw the conclusions that his own peculiar science would seem to suggest to him; he would choose any explanation rather than the obvious, since the obvious would also be the outrageous--according to our established habit of thought, which we deem final.

***

The next day I took all these strange things with me for consideration to a certain place that I knew of not far from Penvro. I was now in the early stages of the jig-saw process, or rather I had only a few pieces before me, and--to continue the figure my difficulty was this: that though the markings on each piece seemed to have design and significance, yet I could not make the wildest guess as to the nature of the whole picture, of which these were the parts. I had clearly seen that there was a great secret; I had seen that on the face of the young farmer on the platform of Llantrisant station; and in my mind there was all the while the picture of him going down the dark, steep, winding lane that led to the town and the sea, going down through the heart of the wood, with light about him.

But there was bewilderment in the thought of this, and in the endeavour to match it with the perfumed church and the scraps of talk that I had heard and the rumour of midnight brightness; and though Penvro is by no means populous, I thought I would go to a certain solitary place called the Old Camp Head, which looks towards Cornwall and to the great deeps that roll beyond Cornwall to the far ends of the world; a place where fragments of dreams--they seemed such then--might, perhaps, be gathered into the clearness of vision.

It was some years since I had been to the Head, and I had gone on that last time and on a former visit by the cliffs, a rough and difficult path. Now I chose a landward way, which the county map seemed to justify, though doubtfully, as regarded the last part of the journey. So I went inland and climbed the hot summer by-roads, till I came at last to a lane which gradually turned turfy and grass-grown, and then on high ground, ceased to be. It left me at a gate in a hedge of old thorns; and across the field beyond there seemed to be some faint indications of a track. One would judge that sometimes men did pass by that way, but not often.

It was high ground but not within sight of the sea. But the breath of the sea blew about the hedge of thorns, and came with a keen savour to the nostrils. The ground sloped gently from the gate and then rose again to a ridge, where a white farmhouse stood all alone. I passed by this farmhouse, threading an uncertain way, followed a hedgerow doubtfully; and saw suddenly before me the Old Camp, and beyond it the sapphire plain of waters and the mist where sea and sky met. Steep from my feet the hill fell away, a land of gorse-blossom, red-gold and mellow, of glorious purple heather. It fell into a hollow that went down, shining with rich green bracken, to the glimmering sea; and before me and beyond the hollow rose a height of turf, bastioned at the summit with the awful, age-old walls of the Old Camp; green, rounded circumvallations, wall within wall, tremendous, with their myriad years upon them.

***

Within these smoothed, green mounds, looking across the shining and changing of the waters in the happy sunlight, I took out the bread and cheese and beer that I had carried in a bag, and ate and drank, and lit my pipe, and set myself to think over the enigmas of Llantrisant. And I had scarcely done so when, a good deal to my annoyance, a man came climbing up over the green ridges, and took up his stand close by, and stared out to sea. He nodded to me, and began with "Fine weather for the harvest" in the approved manner, and so sat down and engaged me in a net of talk. He was of Wales, it seemed, but from a different part of the country, and was staying for a few days with relations--at the white farmhouse which I had passed on my way. His tale of nothing flowed on to his pleasure and my pain, till he fell suddenly on Llantrisant and its doings. I listened then with wonder, and here is his tale condensed. Though it must be clearly understood that the man's evidence was only second-hand; he had heard it from his cousin, the farmer.

So, to be brief, it appeared that there had been a long feud at Llantrisant between a local solicitor, Lewis Prothero (we will say), and a farmer named James. There had been a quarrel about some trifle, which had grown more and more bitter as the two parties forgot the merits of the original dispute, and by some means or other, which I could not well understand, the lawyer had got the small freeholder "under his thumb." James, I think, had given a bill of sale in a bad season, and Prothero had bought it up; and the end was that the farmer was turned out of the old house, and was lodging in a cottage. People said he would have to take a place on his own farm as a labourer; he went about in dreadful misery, piteous to see. It was thought by some that he might very well murder the lawyer, if he met him.

They did meet, in the middle of the market-place at Llantrisant one Saturday in June. The farmer was a little black man, and he gave a shout of rage, and the people were rushing at him to keep him off Prothero.

"And then," said my informant, "I will tell you what happened. This lawyer, as they tell me, he is a great big brawny fellow, with a big jaw and a wide mouth, and a red face and red whiskers. And there he was in his black coat and his high hard hat, and all his money at his back, as you may say. And, indeed, he did fall down on his knees in the dust there in the street in front of Philip James, and every one could see that terror was upon him. And he did beg Philip James's pardon, and beg of him to have mercy, and he did implore him by God and man and the saints of paradise. And my cousin, John Jenkins, Penmawr, he do tell me that the tears were falling from Lewis Prothero's eyes like the rain. And he put his hand into his pocket and drew out the deed of Pantyreos, Philip James's old farm that was, and did give him the farm back and a hundred pounds for the stock that was on it, and two hundred pounds, all in notes of the bank, for amendment and consolation.

"And then, from what they do tell me, all the people did go mad, crying and weeping and calling out all manner of things at the top of their voices. And at last nothing would do but they must all go up to the churchyard, and there Philip James and Lewis Prothero they swear friendship to one another for a long age before the old cross, and everyone sings praises. And my cousin he do declare to me that there were men standing in that crowd that he did never see before in Llantrisant in all his life, and his heart was shaken within him as if it had been in a whirl-wind."

I had listened to all this in silence. I said then:

"What does your cousin mean by that? Men that he had never seen in Llantrisant? What men?"

"The people," he said very slowly, "call them the Fishermen."

And suddenly there came into my mind the "Rich Fisherman" who in the old legend guards the holy mystery of the Graal.

CHAPTER IV - THE RINGING OF THE BELL

So far I have not told the story of the things of Llantrisant, but rather the story of how I stumbled upon them and among them, perplexed and wholly astray, seeking, but yet not knowing at all what I sought; bewildered now and again by circumstances which seemed to me wholly inexplicable; devoid, not so much of the key to the enigma, but of the key to the nature of the enigma. You cannot begin to solve a puzzle till you know what the puzzle is about. "Yards divided by minutes," said the mathematical master to me long ago, "will give neither pigs, sheep, nor oxen." He was right; though his manner on this and on all other occasions was highly offensive. This is enough of the personal process, as I may call it; and here follows the story of what happened at Llantrisant last summer, the story as I pieced it together at last.

It all began, it appears, on a hot day, early in last June; so far as I can make out, on the first Saturday in the month. There was a deaf old woman, a Mrs. Parry, who lived by herself in a lonely cottage a mile or so from the town. She came into the market-place early on the Saturday morning in a state of some excitement, and as soon as she had taken up her usual place on the pavement by the churchyard, with her ducks and eggs and a few very early potatoes, she began to tell her neighbours about her having heard the sound of a great bell. The good women on each side smiled at one another behind Mrs. Parry's back, for one had to bawl into her ear before she could make out what one meant; and Mrs. Williams, Penycoed, bent over and yelled: "What bell should that be, Mrs. Parry? There's no church near you up at Penrhiw. Do you hear what nonsense she talks?" said Mrs. Williams in a low voice to Mrs. Morgan. "As if she could hear any bell, whatever."

"What makes you talk nonsense your self?" said Mrs. Parry, to the amazement of the two women. "I can hear a bell as well as you, Mrs. Williams, and as well as your whispers either."

And there is the fact, which is not to be disputed; though the deductions from it may be open to endless disputations; this old woman who had been all but stone deaf for twenty years--the defect had always been in her family--could suddenly hear on this June morning as well as anybody else. And her two old friends stared at her, and it was some time before they had appeased her indignation, and induced her to talk about the bell.

It had happened in the early morning, which was very misty. She had been gathering sage in her garden, high on a round hill looking over the sea. And there came in her ears a sort of throbbing and singing and trembling, "as if there were music coming out of the earth," and then something seemed to break in her head, and all the birds began to sing and make melody together, and the leaves of the poplars round the garden fluttered in the breeze that rose from the sea, and the cock crowed far off at Twyn, and the dog barked down in Kemeys Valley. But above all these sounds, unheard for so many years, there thrilled the deep and chanting note of the bell, "like a bell and a man's voice singing at once."

They stared again at her and at one another. "Where did it sound from?" asked one. "It came sailing across the sea," answered Mrs. Parry quite composedly, "and I did hear it coming nearer and nearer to the land."

"Well, indeed," said Mrs. Morgan, "it was a ship's bell then, though I can't make out why they would be ringing like that."

"It was not ringing on any ship, Mrs. Morgan," said Mrs. Parry.

"Then where do you think it was ringing?"

"Ym Mharadwys," replied Mrs. Parry. Now that means "in Paradise," and the two others changed the conversation quickly. They thought that Mrs. Parry had got back her hearing suddenly--such things did happen now and then--and that the shock had made her "a bit queer." And this explanation would no doubt have stood its ground, if it had not been for other experiences. Indeed, the local doctor who had treated Mrs. Parry for a dozen years, not for her deafness, which he took to be hopeless and beyond cure, but for a tiresome and recurrent winter cough, sent an account of the case to a colleague at Bristol, suppressing, naturally enough, the reference to Paradise. The Bristol physician gave it as his opinion that the symptoms were absolutely what mighty have been expected.

"You have here, in all probability," he wrote, "the sudden breaking down of an old obstruction in the aural passage, and I should quite expect this process to be accompanied by tinnitus of a pronounced and even violent character."

***

But for the other experiences? As the morning wore on and drew to noon, high market, and to the utmost brightness of that summer day, all the stalls and the streets were full of rumours and of awed faces. Now from one lonely farm, now from another, men and women came and told the story of how they had listened in the early morning with thrilling hearts to the thrilling music of a bell that was like no bell ever heard before. And it seemed that many people in the town had been roused, they knew not how, from sleep; waking up, as one of them said, as if bells were ringing and the organ playing, and a choir of sweet voices singing all together: "There were such melodies and songs that my heart was full of joy."

And a little past noon some fishermen who had been out all night returned, and brought a wonderful story into the town of what they had heard in the mist and one of them said he had seen something go by at a little distance from his boat. "It was all golden and bright," he said, "and there was glory about it." Another fisherman declared "there was a song upon the water that was like heaven."

And here I would say in parenthesis that on returning to town I sought out a very old friend of mine, a man who has devoted a lifetime to strange and esoteric studies. I thought that I had a tale that would interest him profoundly, but I found that he heard me with a good deal of indifference. And at this very point of the sailors' stories I remember saying: "Now what do you make of that? Don't you think it's extremely curious?" He replied: "I hardly think so. Possibly the sailors were lying; possibly it happened as they say. Well; that sort of thing has always been happening." I give my friend's opinion; I make no comment on it.

Let it be noted that there was something remarkable as to the manner in which the sound of the bell was heard--or supposed to be heard. There are, no doubt, mysteries in sound as in all else; indeed, I am informed that during one of the horrible outrages that have been perpetrated on London during this autumn there was an instance of a great block of workmen's dwellings in which the only person who heard the crash of a particular bomb falling was an old deaf woman, who had been fast asleep till the moment of the explosion. This is strange enough of a sound that was entirely in the natural (and horrible) order; and so it was at Llantrisant, where the sound was either a collective auditory hallucination or a manifestation of what is conveniently, if inaccurately, called the supernatural order.

For the thrill of the bell did not reach to all ears--or hearts. Deaf Mrs. Parry heard it in her lonely cottage garden, high above the misty sea; but then, in a farm on the other or western side of Llantrisant, a little child, scarcely three years old, was the only one out of a household of ten people who heard anything. He called out in stammering baby Welsh something that sounded like "Clychau fawr, clychau fawr"--the great bells, the great bells--and his mother wondered what he was talking about. Of the crews of half a dozen trawlers that were swinging from side to side in the mist, not more than four men had any tale to tell. And so it was that for an hour or two the man who had heard nothing suspected his neighbour who had heard marvels of lying; and it was some time before the mass of evidence coming from all manner of diverse and remote quarters convinced the people that there was a true story here. A might suspect B, his neighbour, of making up a tale; but when C, from some place on the hills five miles away, and D, the fisherman on the waters, each had a like report, then it was clear that something had happened.

***

And even then, as they told me, the signs to be seen upon the people were stranger than the tales told by them and among them. It has struck me that many people in reading some of the phrases that I have reported, will dismiss them with laughter as very poor and fantastic inventions; fishermen, they will say, do not speak of "a song like heaven" or of "a glory about it." And I dare say this would be a just enough criticism if I were reporting English fishermen; but, odd though it may be, Wales has not yet lost the last shreds of the grand manner. And let it be remembered also that in most cases such phrases are translated from another language, that is, from the Welsh.

So, they come trailing, let us say, fragments of the cloud of glory in their common speech; and so, on this Saturday, they began to display, uneasily enough in many cases, their consciousness that the things that were reported were of their ancient right and former custom. The comparison is not quite fair; but conceive Hardy's old Durbeyfield suddenly waking from long slumber to find himself in a noble thirteenth-century hall, waited on by kneeling pages, smiled on by sweet ladies in silken côtehardies.

So by evening time there had come to the old people the recollection of stories that their fathers had told them as they sat round the hearth of winter nights, fifty, sixty, seventy years; ago; stories of the wonderful bell of Teilo Sant, that had sailed across the glassy seas from Syon, that was called a portion of Paradise, "and the sound of its ringing was like the perpetual choir of the angels."

Such things were remembered by the old and told to the young that evening, in the streets of the town and in the deep lanes that climbed far hills. The sun went down to the mountain red with fire like a burnt offering, the sky turned violet, the sea was purple, as one told another of the wonder that had returned to the land after long ages.

CHAPTER V - THE ROSE OF FIRE

It was during the next nine days, counting from that Saturday early in June the first Saturday in June, as I believe--that Llantrisant and all the regions about became possessed either by an extraordinary set of hallucinations or by a visitation of great marvels.

This is not the place to strike the balance between the two possibilities. The evidence is, no doubt, readily available; the matter is open to systematic investigation.

But this may be said: The ordinary man, in the ordinary passages of his life, accepts in the main the evidence of his senses, and is entirely right in doing so. He says that he sees a cow, that he sees a stone wall, and that the cow and the stone wall are "there."

This is very well for all the practical purposes of life, but I believe that the metaphysicians are by no means so easily satisfied as to the reality of the stone wall and the cow. Perhaps they might allow that both objects are "there" in the sense that one's reflection is in a glass; there is an actuality, but is there a reality external to oneself? In any event, it is solidly agreed that, supposing a real existence, this much is certain--it is not in the least like our conception of it. The ant and the microscope will quickly convince us that we do not see things as they really are, even supposing that we see them at all. If we could "see" the real cow she would appear utterly incredible, as incredible as the things I am to relate.

Now, there is nothing that I know much more unconvincing than the stories of the red light on the sea. Several sailors, men on small coasting ships, who were working up or down the Channel on that Saturday night, spoke of "seeing" the red light, and it must be said that there is a very tolerable agreement in their tales. All make the time as between midnight of the Saturday and one o'clock on the Sunday morning. Two of those sailormen are precise as to the time of the apparition; they fix it by elaborate calculations of their own as occurring at 12.20 a.m. And the story?

A red light, a burning spark seen far away in the darkness, taken at the first moment of seeing for a signal, and probably an enemy signal. Then it approached at a tremendous speed, and one man said he took it to be the port light of some new kind of navy motor-boat which was developing a rate hitherto unheard of, a hundred or a hundred and fifty knots an hour. And then, in the third instant of the sight, it was clear that this was no earthly speed. At first a red spark in the farthest distance; then a rushing lamp; and then, as if in an incredible point of time, it swelled into a vast rose of fire that filled all the sea and all the sky and hid the stars and possessed the land. "I thought the end of the world had come," one of the sailors said.

And then, an instant more, and it was gone from them, and four of them say that there was a red spark on Chapel Head, where the old grey chapel of St. Teilo stands, high above the water, in a cleft of the limestone rocks.

And thus the sailors; and thus their tales are incredible; but they are not incredible. I believe that men of the highest eminence in physical science have testified to the occurrence of phenomena every whit as marvellous, to things as absolutely opposed to all natural order, as we conceive it; and it may be said that nobody minds them. "That sort of thing has always been happening," as my friend remarked to me. But the men, whether or no the fire had ever been without them, there was no doubt that it was now within them, for it burned in their eyes. They were purged as if they had passed through the Furnace of the Sages, governed with Wisdom that the alchemists know. They spoke without much difficulty of what they had seen, or had seemed to see, with their eyes, but hardly at all of what their hearts had known when for a moment the glory of the fiery rose had been about them.

For some weeks afterwards they were still, as it were, amazed; almost, I would say, incredulous. If there had been nothing more than the splendid and fiery appearance, showing and vanishing, I do believe that they themselves would have discredited their own senses and denied the truth of their own tales. And one does not dare to say whether they would not have been right. Men like Sir William Crookes and Sir Oliver Lodge are certainly to be heard with respect, and they bear witness to all manner of apparent eversions of laws which we, or most of us, consider far more deeply founded than the ancient hills. They may be justified; but in our hearts we do doubt. We cannot wholly believe in inner sincerity that the solid table did rise, without mechanical reason or cause, into the air, and so defy that which we name the "law of gravitation." I know what may be said on the other side; I know that there is no true question of "law" in the case; that the law of gravitation really means just this: that I have never seen a table rising without mechanical aid, or an apple, detached from the bough, soaring to the skies instead of falling to the ground. The so-called law is just the sum of common observation and nothing more; yet I say, in our hearts we do not believe that the tables rise; much less do we believe in the rose of fire that for a moment swallowed up the skies and seas and shores of the Welsh coast last June.

And the men who saw it would have invented fairy tales to account for it, I say again, if it had not been for that which was within them.

They said, all of them, and it was certain now that they spoke the truth, that in the moment of the vision, every pain and ache and malady in their bodies had passed away. One man had been vilely drunk on venomous spirit, procured at "Jobson's Hole" down by the Cardiff Docks. He was horribly ill; he had crawled up from his bunk for a little fresh air; and in an instant his horrors and his deadly nausea had left him. Another man was almost desperate with the raging hammering pain of an abscess on a tooth; he says that when the red flame came near he felt as if a dull, heavy blow had fallen on his jaw, and then the pain was quite gone; he could scarcely believe that there had been any pain there.

And they all bear witness to an extraordinary exaltation of the senses. It is indescribable, this; for they cannot describe it. They are amazed, again; they do not in the least profess to know what happened; but there is no more possibility of shaking their evidence than there is a possibility of shaking the evidence of a man who says that water is wet and fire hot.

"I felt a bit queer afterwards," said one of them, "and I steadied myself by the mast, and I can't tell how I felt as I touched it. I didn't know that touching a thing like a mast could be better than a big drink when you're thirsty, or a soft pillow when you're sleepy."

I heard other instances of this state of things, as I must vaguely call it, since I do not know what else to call it. But I suppose we can all agree that to the man in average health, the average impact of the external world on his senses is a matter of indifference. The average impact; a harsh scream, the bursting of a motor tyre, any violent assault on the aural nerves will annoy him, and he may say "damn." Then, on the other hand, the man who is not "fit" will easily be annoyed and irritated by someone pushing past him in a crowd, by the ringing of a bell, by the sharp closing of a book.

But so far as I could judge from the talk of these sailors, the average impact of the external world had become to them a fountain of pleasure. Their nerves were on edge, but an edge to receive exquisite sensuous impressions. The touch of the rough mast, for example; that was a joy far greater than is the joy of fine silk to some luxurious skins; they drank water and stared as if they had been fins gourmets tasting an amazing wine; the creak and whine of their ship on its slow way were as exquisite as the rhythm and song of a Bach fugue to an amateur of music.

And then, within; these rough fellows have their quarrels and strifes and variances and envyings like the rest of us; but that was all over between them that had seen the rosy light; old enemies shook hands heartily, and roared with laughter as they confessed one to another what fools they had been.

"I can't exactly say how it has happened or what has happened at all," said one, "but if you have all the world and the glory of it, how can you fight for fivepence?"

***

The church of Llantrisant is a typical example of a Welsh parish church, before the evil and horrible period of "restoration."

This lower world is a palace of lies, and of all foolish lies there is none more insane than a certain vague fable about the mediæval freemasons, a fable which somehow imposed itself upon the cold intellect of Hallam the historian. The story is, in brief, that throughout the Gothic period, at any rate, the art and craft of church building were executed by wandering guilds of "freemasons," possessed of various secrets of building and adornment, which they employed wherever they went. If this nonsense were true, the Gothic of Cologne would be as the Gothic of Colne, and the Gothic of Arles like to the Gothic of Abingdon. It is so grotesquely untrue that almost every county, let alone every country, has its distinctive style in Gothic architecture. Arfon is in the west of Wales; its churches have marks and features which distinguish them from the churches in the east of Wales.

The Llantrisant church has that primitive division between nave and chancel which only very foolish people decline to recognise as equivalent to the Oriental iconostasis and as the origin of the Western rood-screen. A solid wall divided the church into two portions; in the centre was a narrow opening with a rounded arch, through which those who sat towards the middle of the church could see the small, red-carpeted altar and the three roughly shaped lancet windows above it.

The "reading pew" was on the outer side of this wall of partition, and here the rector did his service, the choir being grouped in seats about him. On the inner side were the pews of certain privileged houses of the town and district.

On the Sunday morning the people were all in their accustomed places, not without a certain exultation in their eyes, not without a certain expectation of they knew not what. The bells stopped ringing, the rector, in his old-fashioned, ample surplice, entered the reading-desk, and gave out the hymn: "My God, and is Thy Table spread."

And, as the singing began, all the people who were in the pews within the wall came out of them and streamed through the archway into the nave. They took what places they could find up and down the church, and the rest of the congregation looked at them in amazement.

Nobody knew what had happened. Those whose seats were next to the aisle tried to peer into the chancel, to see what had happened or what was going on there. But somehow the light flamed so brightly from the windows above the altar, those being the only windows in the chancel, one small lancet in the south wall excepted, that no one could see anything at all.

"It was as if a veil of gold adorned with jewels was hanging there," one man said; and indeed there are a few odds and scraps of old painted glass left in the eastern lancets.

But there were few in the church who did not hear now and again voices speaking beyond the veil.

CHAPTER VI - OLWEN'S DREAM

The well-to-do and dignified personages who left their pews in the chancel of Llantrisant Church and came hurrying into the nave could give no explanation of what they had done. They felt, they said, that they had to go, and to go quickly; they were driven out, as it were, by a secret, irresistible command. But all who were present in the church that morning were amazed, though all exulted in their hearts; for they, like the sailors who saw the rose of fire on the waters, were filled with a joy that was literally ineffable, since they could not utter it or interpret it to themselves.

And they too, like the sailors, were transmuted, or the world was transmuted for them. They experienced what the doctors call a sense of bien être but a bien être raised, to the highest power. Old men felt young again, eyes that had been growing dim now saw clearly, and saw a world that was like Paradise, the same world, it is true, but a world rectified and glowing, as if an inner flame shone in all things, and behind all things.

And the difficulty in recording this state is this, that it is so rare an experience that no set language to express it is in existence. A shadow of its raptures and ecstasies is found in the highest poetry; there are phrases in ancient books telling of the Celtic saints that dimly hint at it; some of the old Italian masters of painting had known it, for the light of it shines in their skies and about the battlements of their cities that are founded on magic hills. But these are but broken hints.

It is not poetic to go to Apothecaries' Hall for similes. But for many years I kept by me an article from the Lancet or the British Medical Journal--I forget which--in which a doctor gave an account of certain experiments he had conducted with a drug called the Mescal Button, or Anhelonium Lewinii. He said that while under the influence of the drug he had but to shut his eyes, and immediately before him there would rise incredible Gothic cathedrals, of such majesty and splendour and glory that no heart had ever conceived. They seemed to surge from the depths to the very heights of heaven, their spires swayed amongst the clouds and the stars, they were fretted with admirable imagery. And as he gazed, he would presently become aware that all the stones were living stones, that they were quickening and palpitating, and then that they were glowing jewels, say, emeralds, sapphires, rubies, opals, but of hues that the mortal eye had never seen.

That description gives, I think, some faint notion of the nature of the transmuted world into which these people by the sea had entered, a world quickened and glorified and full of pleasures. Joy and wonder were on all faces; but the deepest joy and the greatest wonder were on the face of the rector. For he had heard through the veil the Greek word for "holy," three times repeated. And he, who had once been a horrified assistant at High Mass in a foreign church, recognised the perfume of incense that filled the place from end to end.

***

It was on that Sunday night that Olwen Phillips of Croeswen dreamed her wonderful dream. She was a girl of sixteen, the daughter of small farming people, and for many months she had been doomed to certain death. Consumption, which flourishes in that damp, warm climate, had laid hold of her; not only her lungs but her whole system was a mass of tuberculosis. As is common enough, she had enjoyed many fallacious brief recoveries in the early stages of the disease, but all hope had long been over, and now for the last few weeks she had seemed to rush vehemently to death. The doctor had come on the Saturday morning, bringing with him a colleague. They had both agreed that the girl's case was in its last stages. "She cannot possibly last more than a day or two," said the local doctor to her mother. He came again on the Sunday morning and found his patient perceptibly worse, and soon afterwards she sank into a heavy sleep, and her mother thought that she would never wake from it.

The girl slept in an inner room communicating with the room occupied by her father and mother. The door between was kept open, so that Mrs. Phillips could hear her daughter if she called to her in the night. And Olwen called to her mother that night, just as the dawn was breaking. It was no faint summons from a dying bed that came to the mother's ears, but a loud cry that rang through the house, a cry of great gladness. Mrs. Phillips started up from sleep in wild amazement, wondering what could have happened. And then she saw Olwen, who had not been able to rise from her bed for many weeks past, standing in the doorway in the faint light of the growing day. The girl called to her mother: "Mam! mam! It is all over. I am quite well again."

Mrs. Phillips roused her husband, and they sat up in bed staring, not knowing on earth, as they said afterwards, what had been done with the world. Here was their poor girl wasted to a shadow, lying on her death-bed, and the life sighing from her with every breath, and her voice, when she last uttered it, so weak that one had to put one's ear to her mouth. And here in a few hours she stood up before them; and even in that faint light they could see that she was changed almost beyond

315

knowing. And, indeed, Mrs. Phillips said that for a moment or two she fancied that the Germans must have come and killed them in their sleep, and so they were all dead together. But Olwen called, out again, so the mother lit a candle and got up and went tottering across the room, and there was Olwen all gay and plump again, smiling with shining eyes. Her mother led her into her own room, and set down the candle there, and felt her daughter's flesh, and burst into prayers and tears of wonder and delight, and thanksgivings, and held the girl again to be sure that she was not deceived. And then Olwen told her dream, though she thought it was not a dream.

She said she woke up in the deep darkness, and she knew the life was fast going from her. She could not move so much as a finger, she tried to cry out, but no sound came from her lips. She felt that in another instant the whole world would fall from her--her heart was full of agony. And as the last breath was passing her lips, she heard a very faint, sweet sound, like the tinkling of a silver bell. It came from far away, from over by Ty-newydd. She forgot her agony and listened, and even then, she says, she felt the swirl of the world as it came back to her. And the sound of the bell swelled and grew louder, and it thrilled all through her body, and the life was in it. And as the bell rang and trembled in her ears, a faint light touched the wall of her room and reddened, till the whole room was full of rosy fire. And then she saw standing before her bed three men in blood-coloured robes with shining faces. And one man held a golden bell in his hand. And the second man held up something shaped like the top of a table. It was like a great jewel, and it was of a blue colour, and there were rivers of silver and of gold running through it and flowing as quick streams flow, and there were pools in it as if violets had been poured out into water, and then it was green as the sea near the shore, and then it was the sky at night with all the stars shining, and then the sun and the moon came down and washed in it. And the third man held up high above this a cup that was like a rose on fire; "there was a great burning in it, and a dropping of blood in it, and a red cloud above it, and I saw a great secret. And I heard a voice that sang nine times, 'Glory and praise to the Conqueror of Death, to the Fountain of Life immortal.' Then the red light went from the wall, and it was all darkness, and the bell rang faint again by Capel Teilo, and then I got up and called to you."

The doctor came on the Monday morning with the death certificate in his pocket-book, and Olwen ran out to meet him. I have quoted his phrase in the first chapter of this record: "A kind of resurrection of the body." He made a most careful examination of the girl; he has stated that he found that every trace of disease had disappeared. He left on the Sunday morning a patient entering into the coma that precedes death, a body condemned utterly and ready for the grave. He met at the garden gate on the Monday morning a young woman in whom life sprang up like a fountain, in whose body life laughed and rejoiced as if it had been a river flowing from an unending well.

***

Now this is the place to ask one of those questions--there are many such--which cannot be answered. The question is as to the continuance of tradition; more especially as to the continuance of tradition among the Welsh Celts of today. On the one hand, such waves and storms have gone over them. The wave of the heathen Saxons went over them, then the wave of Latin mediævalism, then the waters of Anglicanism; last of all the flood of their queer Calvinistic Methodism, half Puritan, half pagan. It may well be asked whether any memory can possibly have survived such a series of deluges. I have said that the old people of Llantrisant had their tales of the Bell of Teilo Sant; but these were but vague and broken recollections. And then there is the name by which the "strangers" who were seen in the market-place were known; that is more precise. Students of the Graal legend know that the keeper of the Graal in the romances is the "King Fisherman," or the "Rich Fisherman"; students of Celtic hagiology know that it was prophesied before the birth of Dewi (or David) that he should be "a man of aquatic life," that another legend tells how a little child, destined to be a saint, was discovered on a stone in the river, how through his childhood a fish for his nourishment was found on that stone every day, while another saint, Ilar, if I remember, was expressly known as "The Fisherman." But has the memory of all this persisted in the church-going and chapel-going people of Wales at the present day? It is difficult to say. There is the affair of the Healing Cup of Nant Eos, or Tregaron Healing Cup, as it is also called. It is only a few years ago since it was shown to a wandering harper, who treated it lightly, and then spent a wretched night, as he said, and came back penitently and was left alone with the sacred vessel to pray over it, till "his mind was at rest." That was in 1887.

Then for my part--I only know modern Wales on the surface, I am sorry to say--I remember three or four years ago speaking to my temporary landlord of certain relics of Saint Teilo, which are supposed to be in the keeping of a particular family in that country. The landlord is a very jovial, merry fellow, and I observed with some astonishment that his ordinary, easy manner was completely altered as he said, gravely, "That will be over there, up by the mountain," pointing vaguely to the north. And he changed the subject, as a Freemason changes the subject.

There the matter lies, and its appositeness to the story of Llantrisant is this: that the dream of Olwen Phillips was, in fact, the Vision of the Holy Graal.

CHAPTER VII - THE MASS OF THE SANGRAAL

"FFEIRIADWYR Melcisidec! Ffeiriadwyr Melcisidec!" shouted the old Calvinistic Methodist deacon with the grey beard. "Priesthood of Melchizedek! Priesthood of Melchizedek!"

And he went on:

"The Bell that is like y glwys yr angel ym mharadwys--the joy of the angels in Paradise--is returned; the Altar that is of a colour that no men can discern is returned, the Cup that came from Syon is returned, the ancient Offering is restored, the Three Saints have come back to the church of the tri sant, the Three Holy Fishermen are amongst us, and their net is full. Gogoniant, gogoniant-- glory, glory!"

Then another Methodist began to recite in Welsh a verse from Wesley's hymn.

God still respects Thy sacrifice,
Its savour sweet doth always please;
The Offering smokes through earth and skies,
Diffusing life and joy and peace;
To these Thy lower courts it comes
And fills them with Divine perfumes.

The whole church was full, as the old books tell, of the odour of the rarest spiceries. There were lights shining within the sanctuary, through the narrow archway.

This was the beginning of the end of what befell at Llantrisant. For it was the Sunday after that night on which Olwen Phillips had been restored from death to life. There was not a single chapel of the Dissenters open in the town that day. The Methodists with their minister and their deacons and all the Nonconformists had returned on this Sunday morning to "the old hive." One would have said, a church of the Middle Ages, a church in Ireland today. Every seat--save those in the chancel --was full, all the aisles were full, the churchyard was full; everyone on his knees, and the old rector kneeling before the door into the holy place.

Yet they can say but very little of what was done beyond the veil. There was no attempt to perform the usual service; when the bells had stopped the old deacon raised his cry, and priest and people fell down on their knees as they thought they heard a choir within singing "Alleluya, alleluya, alleluya." And as the bells in the tower ceased ringing, there sounded the thrill of the bell from Syon, and the golden veil of sunlight fell across the door into the altar, and the heavenly voices began their melodies.

A voice like a trumpet cried from within the brightness.

Agyos, Agyos, Agyos.

And the people, as if an age-old memory stirred in them, replied:

Agyos yr Tâd, agyos yr Mab, agyos yr Yspryd Glan. Sant, sant, sant, Drindod sant vendigeid. Sanctus Arglwydd Dduw Sabaoth, Dominus Deus.

There was a voice that cried and sang from within the altar; most of the people had heard some faint echo of it in the chapels; a voice rising and falling and soaring in awful modulations that rang like the trumpet of the Last Angel. The people beat upon their breasts, the tears were like rain of the mountains on their cheeks; those that were able fell down flat on their faces before the glory of the veil. They said afterwards that men of the hills, twenty miles away, heard that cry and that singing, roaring upon them on the wind, and they fell down on their faces, and cried, "The offering is accomplished," knowing nothing of what they said.

There were a few who saw three come out of the door of the sanctuary, and stand for a moment on the pace before the door. These three were in dyed vesture, red as blood. One stood before two, looking to the west, and he rang the bell. And they say that all the birds of the wood, and all the waters of the sea, and all the leaves of the trees, and all the winds of the high rocks uttered their voices with the ringing of the bell. And the second and the third; they turned their faces one to another. The second held up the lost altar that they once called Sapphirus, which was like the changing of the sea and of the sky, and like the immixture of gold and silver. And the third heaved up high over the altar a cup that was red with burning and the blood of the offering.

And the old rector cried aloud then before the entrance:

Bendigeid yr Offeren yn oes oesoedd--blessed be the Offering unto the age of ages.

And then the Mass of the Sangraal was ended, and then began the passing out of that land of the holy persons and holy things that had returned to it after the long years. It seemed, indeed, to many that the thrilling sound of the bell was in their ears for days, even for weeks after that Sunday morning. But thenceforth neither bell nor altar nor cup was seen by anyone; not openly, that is, but only in dreams by day and by night. Nor did the people see Strangers again in the market of Llantrisant, nor in the lonely places where certain persons oppressed by great affliction and sorrow had once or twice encountered them.

***

But that time of visitation will never be forgotten by the people. Many things happened in the nine days that have not been set down in this record--or legend. Some of them were trifling matters, though strange enough in other times. Thus a man in the town who had a fierce dog that was always kept chained up found one day that the beast had become mild and gentle.

And this is odder: Edward Davies, of Lanafon, a farmer, was roused from sleep one night by a queer yelping and barking in his yard. He looked out of the window and saw his sheep-dog playing with a big fox; they were chasing each other by turns, rolling over and over one another, "cutting such capers as I did never see the like," as the astonished farmer put it. And some of the people said that during this season of wonder the corn shot up, and the grass thickened, and the fruit was multiplied on the trees in a very marvellous manner.

More important, it seemed, was the case of Williams, the grocer; though this may have been a purely natural deliverance. Mr. Williams was to marry his daughter Mary to a smart young fellow from Carmarthen, and he was in great distress over it. Not over the marriage itself, but because things had been going very badly with him for some time, and he could not see his way to giving anything like the wedding entertainment that would be expected of him. The wedding was to be on the Saturday--that was the day on which the lawyer, Lewis Prothero, and the farmer, Philip James, were reconciled--and this John Williams, without money or credit, could not think how shame would not be on him for the meagreness and poverty of the wedding feast. And then on the Tuesday came a letter from his brother, David Williams, Australia, from whom he had not heard for fifteen years. And David, it seemed, had been making a great deal of money, and was a bachelor, and here was with his letter a paper good for a thousand pounds: "You may as well enjoy it now as wait till I am dead." This was enough, indeed, one might say; but hardly an hour after the letter had come the lady from the big house (Plas Mawr) drove up in all her grandeur, and went into the shop and said, "Mr. Williams, your daughter Mary has always been a very good girl, and my husband and I feel that we must give her some little thing on her wedding, and we hope she'll be very happy." It was a gold watch worth fifteen pounds. And after Lady Watcyn, advances the old doctor with a dozen of port, forty years upon it, and a long sermon on how to decant it. And the old rector's old wife brings to the beautiful dark girl two yards of creamy lace, like an enchantment, for her wedding veil, and tells Mary how she wore it for her own wedding fifty years ago; and the squire, Sir Watcyn, as if his wife had not been already with a fine gift, calls from his horse, and brings out Williams and barks like a dog at him, "Goin' to have a weddin', eh, Williams? Can't have a weddin' without champagne, y' know; wouldn't be legal, don't y' know. So look out for a couple of cases." So Williams tells the story of the gifts; and certainly there was never so famous a wedding in Llantrisant before.

All this, of course, may have been altogether in the natural order; the "glow," as they call it, seems more difficult to explain. For they say that all through the nine days, and indeed after the time had ended, there never was a man weary or sick at heart in Llantrisant, or in the country round it. For if a man felt that his work of the body or the mind was going to be too much for his strength, then there would come to him of a sudden a warm glow and a thrilling all over him and he felt as strong as a giant, and happier than he had ever been in his life before, so that lawyer and hedger each rejoiced in the task that was before him, as if it were sport and play.

And much more wonderful than this or any other wonders was forgiveness, with love to follow it. There were meetings of old enemies in the market-place and in the street that made the people lift up their hands and declare that it was as if one walked the miraculous streets of Syon.

***

But as to the "phenomena," the occurrences for which, in ordinary talk, we should reserve the word "miraculous"? Well, what do we know? The question that I have already stated comes up again, as to the possible survival of old tradition in a kind of dormant, or torpid, semi-conscious state. In other words, did the people "see" and "hear" what they expected to see and hear? This point, or one similar to it, occurred in a debate between Andrew Lang and Anatole France as to the visions of Joan of Arc. M. France stated that when Joan saw St. Michael, she saw the traditional archangel of the religious art of her day, but to the best of my belief Andrew Lang proved that the visionary figure Joan described was not in the least like the fifteenth-century conception of St. Michael. So, in the case of Llantrisant, I have stated that there was a sort of tradition about the Holy Bell of Teilo Sant; and it is, of course, barely possible that some vague notion of the Graal Cup may have reached even Welsh country folks through Tennyson's Idylls. But so far I see no reason to suppose that these people had ever heard of the portable altar (called Sapphirus in William of Malmesbury) or of its changing colours "that no man could discern."

And then there are the other questions of the distinction between hallucination and vision, of the average duration of one and the other, and of the possibility of collective hallucination. If a number of people all see (or think they see) the same appearances, can this be merely hallucination? I believe there is a leading case on the matter, which concerns a number of people seeing the same appearance on a church wall in Ireland; but there is, of course, this difficulty, that one may be hallucinated and communicate his impression to the others, telepathically.

But at the last, what do we know?

THE ANGELS OF MONS
The Bowmen and Other Legends of the War
Originally Published in 1915

Introduction

I have been asked to write an introduction to the story of "The Bowmen", on its publication in book form together with three other tales of similar fashion. And I hesitate. This affair of "The Bowmen" has been such an odd one from first to last, so many queer complications have entered into it, there have been so many and so divers currents and cross-currents of rumour and speculation concerning it, that I honestly do not know where to begin. I propose, then, to solve the difficulty by apologising for beginning at all.

For, usually and fitly, the presence of an introduction is held to imply that there is something of consequence and importance to be introduced. If, for example, a man has made an anthology of great poetry, he may well write an introduction justifying his principle of selection, pointing out here and there, as the spirit moves him, high beauties and supreme excellencies, discoursing of the magnates and lords and princes of literature, whom he is merely serving as groom of the chamber. Introductions, that is, belong to the masterpieces and classics of the world, to the great and ancient and accepted things; and I am here introducing a short, small story of my own which appeared in _The Evening News_ about ten months ago.

I appreciate the absurdity, nay, the enormity of the position in all its grossness. And my excuse for these pages must be this: that though the story itself is nothing, it has yet had such odd and unforeseen consequences and adventures that the tale of them may possess some interest. And then, again, there are certain psychological morals to be drawn from the whole matter of the tale and its sequel of rumours and discussions that are not, I think, devoid of consequence; and so to begin at the beginning.

This was in last August, to be more precise, on the last Sunday of last August. There were terrible things to be read on that hot Sunday morning between meat and mass. It was in _The Weekly Dispatch_ that I saw the awful account of the retreat from Mons. I no longer recollect the details; but I have not forgotten the impression that was then on my mind, I seemed to see a furnace of torment and death and agony and terror seven times heated, and in the midst of the burning was the British Army. In the midst of the flame, consumed by it and yet aureoled in it, scattered like ashes and yet triumphant, martyred and for ever glorious. So I saw our men with a shining about them, so I took these thoughts with me to church, and, I am sorry to say, was making up a story in my head while the deacon was singing the Gospel.

This was not the tale of "The Bowmen". It was the first sketch, as it were, of "The Soldiers' Rest". I only wish I had been able to write it as I conceived it. The tale as it stands is, I think, a far better piece of craft than "The Bowmen", but the tale that came to me as the blue incense floated above the Gospel Book on the desk between the tapers: that indeed was a noble story--like all the stories that never get written. I conceived the dead men coming up through the flames and in the flames, and being welcomed in the Eternal Tavern with songs and flowing cups and everlasting mirth. But every man is the child of his age, however much he may hate it; and our popular religion has long determined that jollity is wicked. As far as I can make out modern Protestantism believes that Heaven is something like Evensong in an English cathedral, the service by Stainer and the Dean preaching. For those opposed to dogma of any kind--even the mildest--I suppose it is held that a Course of Ethical Lectures will be arranged.

Well, I have long maintained that on the whole the average church, considered as a house of preaching, is a much more poisonous place than the average tavern; still, as I say, one's age masters one, and clouds and bewilders the intelligence, and the real story of "The Soldiers' Rest", with its "sonus epulantium in æterno convivio", was ruined at the moment of its birth, and it was some time later that the actual story got written. And in the meantime the plot of "The Bowmen" occurred to me. Now it has been murmured and hinted and suggested and whispered in all sorts of quarters that before I wrote the tale I had heard something. The most decorative of these legends is also the most precise: "I know for a fact that the whole thing was given him in typescript by a lady-in-waiting." This was not the case; and all vaguer reports to the effect that I had heard some rumours or hints of rumours are equally void of any trace of truth.

Again I apologise for entering so pompously into the minutiæ of my bit of a story, as if it were the lost poems of Sappho; but it appears that the subject interests the public, and I comply with my instructions. I take it, then, that the origins of "The Bowmen" were composite. First of all, all ages and nations have cherished the thought that spiritual hosts may come to the help of earthly arms, that gods and heroes and saints have descended from their high immortal places to fight for their worshippers and clients. Then Kipling's story of the ghostly Indian regiment got in my head and got mixed with the mediævalism that is always there; and so "The Bowmen" was written. I was heartily disappointed with it, I remember, and thought it--as I still think it--an indifferent piece of work. However, I have tried to write for these thirty-five long years, and if I have not become practised in letters, I am at least a past master in the Lodge of Disappointment. Such as it was, "The Bowmen" appeared in _The Evening News_ of September 29th, 1914.

Now the journalist does not, as a rule, dwell much on the prospect of fame; and if he be an evening journalist, his anticipations of immortality are bounded by twelve o'clock at night at the latest; and it may well be that those insects which begin to live in the morning and are dead by sunset deem themselves immortal. Having written my story, having groaned and growled over it and printed it, I certainly never thought to hear another word of it. My colleague "The Londoner" praised it warmly to my face, as his kindly fashion is; entering, very properly, a technical caveat as to the language of the battle-cries of the bowmen. "Why should English archers use French terms?" he said. I replied that the only reason was this--that a "Monseigneur" here and there struck me as picturesque; and I reminded him that, as a matter of cold historical fact, most of the archers of Agincourt were mercenaries from Gwent, my native country, who would appeal to Mihangel and to saints not known to the Saxons--Teilo, Iltyd, Dewi, Cadwaladyr Vendigeid. And I thought that that was the first and last discussion of "The Bowmen". But in a few days from its publication the editor of _The Occult Review_ wrote to me. He wanted to know whether the story had any foundation in fact. I told him that it had no foundation in fact of any kind or sort; I forget whether I added that it had no foundation in rumour but I should think not, since to the best of my belief there were no rumours of heavenly interposition in existence at that time. Certainly I had heard of none. Soon afterwards the editor of _Light_ wrote asking a like question, and I made him a like reply. It seemed to me that I had stifled any "Bowmen" mythos in the hour of its birth.

A month or two later, I received several requests from editors of parish magazines to reprint the story. I--or, rather, my editor-- readily gave permission; and then, after another month or two, the conductor of one of these magazines wrote to me, saying that the February issue containing the story had been sold out, while there was still a great demand for it. Would I allow them to reprint "The Bowmen" as a pamphlet, and would I write a short preface giving the exact authorities for the story? I replied that they might reprint in pamphlet form with all my heart, but that I could not give my authorities, since I had none, the tale being pure invention. The priest wrote again, suggesting-- to my amazement--that I must be mistaken, that the main "facts" of "The Bowmen" must be true, that my share in the matter must surely have been confined to the elaboration and decoration of a veridical history. It seemed that my light fiction had been accepted by the congregation of this particular church as the solidest of facts; and it was then that it began to dawn on me that if I had failed in the art of letters, I had succeeded, unwittingly, in the art of deceit. This happened, I should think, some time in April, and the snowball of rumour that was then set rolling has been rolling ever since, growing bigger and bigger, till it is now swollen to a monstrous size.

It was at about this period that variants of my tale began to be told as authentic histories. At first, these tales betrayed their relation to their original. In several of them the vegetarian restaurant appeared, and St. George was the chief character. In one case an officer--name and address missing--said that there was a portrait of St. George in a certain London restaurant, and that a figure, just like the portrait, appeared to him on the battlefield, and was invoked by him, with the happiest results. Another variant--this, I think, never got into print--told how dead Prussians had been found on the battlefield with arrow wounds in their bodies. This notion amused me, as I had imagined a scene, when I was thinking out the story, in which a German general was to appear before the Kaiser to explain his failure to annihilate the English.

"All-Highest," the general was to say, "it is true, it is impossible to deny it. The men were killed by arrows; the shafts were found in their bodies by the burying parties."

I rejected the idea as over-precipitous even for a mere fantasy. I was therefore entertained when I found that what I had refused as too fantastical for fantasy was accepted in certain occult circles as hard fact.

Other versions of the story appeared in which a cloud interposed between the attacking

Germans and the defending British. In some examples the cloud served to conceal our men from the advancing enemy; in others, it disclosed shining shapes which frightened the horses of the pursuing German cavalry. St. George, it will he noted, has disappeared--he persisted some time longer in certain Roman Catholic variants--and there are no more bowmen, no more arrows. But so far angels are not mentioned; yet they are ready to appear, and I think that I have detected the machine which brought them into the story.

In "The Bowmen" my imagined soldier saw "a long line of shapes, with a shining about them." And Mr. A.P. Sinnett, writing in the May issue of _The Occult Review_, reporting what he had heard, states that "those who could see said they saw 'a row of shining beings' between the two armies." Now I conjecture that the word "shining" is the link between my tale and the derivative from it. In the popular view shining and benevolent supernatural beings are angels, and so, I believe, the Bowmen of my story have become "the Angels of Mons." In this shape they have been received with respect and credence everywhere, or almost everywhere.

And here, I conjecture, we have the key to the large popularity of the delusion--as I think it. We have long ceased in England to take much interest in saints, and in the recent revival of the cultus of St. George, the saint is little more than a patriotic figurehead. And the appeal to the saints to succour us is certainly not a common English practice; it is held Popish by most of our countrymen. But angels, with certain reservations, have retained their popularity, and so, when it was settled that the English army in its dire peril was delivered by angelic aid, the way was clear for general belief, and for the enthusiasms of the religion of the man in the street. And so soon as the legend got the title "The Angels of Mons" it became impossible to avoid it. It permeated the Press: it would not be neglected; it appeared in the most unlikely quarters--in _Truth_ and _Town Topics_, _The New Church Weekly_ (Swedenborgian) and _John Bull_. The editor of _The Church Times_ has exercised a wise reserve: he awaits that evidence which so far is lacking; but in one issue of the paper I noted that the story furnished a text for a sermon, the subject of a letter, and the matter for an article. People send me cuttings from provincial papers containing hot controversy as to the exact nature of the appearances; the "Office Window" of _The Daily Chronicle_ suggests scientific explanations of the hallucination; the _Pall Mall_ in a note about St. James says he is of the brotherhood of the Bowmen of Mons--this reversion to the bowmen from the angels being possibly due to the strong statements that I have made on the matter. The pulpits both of the Church and of Non-conformity have been busy: Bishop Welldon, Dean Hensley Henson (a disbeliever), Bishop Taylor Smith (the Chaplain-General), and many other clergy have occupied themselves with the matter. Dr. Horton preached about the "angels" at Manchester; Sir Joseph Compton Rickett (President of the National Federation of Free Church Councils) stated that the soldiers at the front had seen visions and dreamed dreams, and had given testimony of powers and principalities fighting for them or against them. Letters come from all the ends of the earth to the Editor of _The Evening News_ with theories, beliefs, explanations, suggestions. It is all somewhat wonderful; one can say that the whole affair is a psychological phenomenon of considerable interest, fairly comparable with the great Russian delusion of last August and September.

***

Now it is possible that some persons, judging by the tone of these remarks of mine, may gather the impression that I am a profound disbeliever in the possibility of any intervention of the super-physical order in the affairs of the physical order. They will be mistaken if they make this inference; they will be mistaken if they suppose that I think miracles in Judæa credible but miracles in France or Flanders incredible. I hold no such absurdities. But I confess, very frankly, that I credit none of the "Angels of Mons" legends, partly because I see, or think I see, their derivation from my own idle fiction, but chiefly because I have, so far, not received one jot or tittle of evidence that should dispose me to belief. It is idle, indeed, and foolish enough for a man to say: "I am sure that story is a lie, because the supernatural element enters into it;" here, indeed, we have the maggot writhing in the midst of corrupted offal denying the existence of the sun. But if this fellow be a fool--as he is-- equally foolish is he who says, "If the tale has anything of the supernatural it is true, and the less evidence the better;" and I am afraid this tends to be the attitude of many who call themselves occultists. I hope that I shall never get to that frame of mind. So I say, not that super-normal interventions are impossible, not that they have not happened during this war--I know nothing as to that point, one way or the other--but that there is not one atom of evidence (so far) to support the current stories of the angels of Mons. For, be it remarked, these stories are specific stories. They rest on the second, third, fourth, fifth hand stories told by "a soldier," by "an officer," by "a Catholic correspondent," by "a nurse," by any number of anonymous people. Indeed, names have been mentioned. A lady's name has been drawn, most unwarrantably as it appears to me, into the discussion, and I have no doubt that this lady has been subject to a good deal of pestering and annoyance. She has written to the Editor of _The Evening News_ denying all knowledge of the supposed miracle. The Psychical Research Society's expert confesses that no real evidence has been proffered to her Society on the matter. And then, to my amazement, she accepts as fact the proposition that some men on the battlefield have been "hallucinated," and proceeds to give the theory of sensory hallucination. She forgets that, by her own showing, there is no reason to suppose that anybody has been hallucinated at all. Someone (unknown) has met a nurse (unnamed) who has talked to a soldier (anonymous) who has seen angels. But _that_ is not evidence; and not even Sam Weller at his gayest would have dared to offer it as such in the Court of Common Pleas. So far, then, nothing remotely approaching proof has been offered as to any supernatural intervention during the Retreat from Mons. Proof may come; if so, it will be interesting and more than interesting.

But, taking the affair as it stands at present, how is it that a nation plunged in materialism of the grossest kind has accepted idle rumours and gossip of the supernatural as certain truth? The answer is contained in the question: it is precisely because our whole atmosphere is materialist that we are ready to credit anything--save the truth. Separate a man from good drink, he will swallow methylated spirit with joy. Man is created to be inebriated; to be "nobly wild, not mad." Suffer the Cocoa Prophets and their company to seduce him in body and spirit, and he will get himself stuff that will make him ignobly wild and mad indeed. It took hard, practical men of affairs, business men, advanced thinkers, Freethinkers, to believe in Madame Blavatsky and Mahatmas and the famous message from the Golden Shore: "Judge's plan is right; follow him and _stick_."

And the main responsibility for this dismal state of affairs undoubtedly lies on the shoulders of the majority of the clergy of the Church of England. Christianity, as Mr. W.L. Courtney has so admirably pointed out, is a great Mystery Religion; it is _the_ Mystery Religion. Its priests are called to an awful and tremendous hierurgy; its pontiffs are to be the pathfinders, the bridge-makers between the world of sense and the world of spirit. And, in fact, they pass their time in preaching, not the eternal mysteries, but a twopenny morality, in changing the Wine of Angels and the Bread of Heaven into gingerbeer and mixed biscuits: a sorry transubstantiation, a sad alchemy, as it seems to me.

The Bowmen

It was during the Retreat of the Eighty Thousand, and the authority of the Censorship is sufficient excuse for not being more explicit. But it was on the most awful day of that awful time, on the day when ruin and disaster came so near that their shadow fell over London far away; and, without any certain news, the hearts of men failed within them and grew faint; as if the agony of the army in the battlefield had entered into their souls.

On this dreadful day, then, when three hundred thousand men in arms with all their artillery swelled like a flood against the little English company, there was one point above all other points in our battle line that was for a time in awful danger, not merely of defeat, but of utter annihilation. With the permission of the Censorship and of the military expert, this corner may, perhaps, be described as a salient, and if this angle were crushed and broken, then the English force as a whole would be shattered, the Allied left would be turned, and Sedan would inevitably follow.

All the morning the German guns had thundered and shrieked against this corner, and against the thousand or so of men who held it. The men joked at the shells, and found funny names for them, and had bets about them, and greeted them with scraps of music-hall songs. But the shells came on and burst, and tore good Englishmen limb from limb, and tore brother from brother, and as the heat of the day increased so did the fury of that terrific cannonade. There was no help, it seemed. The English artillery was good, but there was not nearly enough of it; it was being steadily battered into scrap iron.

There comes a moment in a storm at sea when people say to one another, "It is at its worst; it can blow no harder," and then there is a blast ten times more fierce than any before it. So it was in these British trenches.

There were no stouter hearts in the whole world than the hearts of these men; but even they were appalled as this seven-times-heated hell of the German cannonade fell upon them and overwhelmed them and destroyed them. And at this very moment they saw from their trenches that a tremendous host was moving against their lines. Five hundred of the thousand remained, and as far as they could see the German infantry was pressing on against them, column upon column, a grey world of men, ten thousand of them, as it appeared afterwards.

There was no hope at all. They shook hands, some of them. One man improvised a new version of the battlesong, "Good-bye, good-bye to Tipperary," ending with "And we shan't get there". And they all went on firing steadily. The officers pointed out that such an opportunity for high-class, fancy shooting might never occur again; the Germans dropped line after line; the Tipperary humorist asked, "What price Sidney Street?" And the few machine guns did their best. But everybody knew it was of no use. The dead grey bodies lay in companies and battalions, as others came on and on and on, and they swarmed and stirred and advanced from beyond and beyond.

"World without end. Amen," said one of the British soldiers with some irrelevance as he took aim and fired. And then he remembered--he says he cannot think why or wherefore--a queer vegetarian restaurant in London where he had once or twice eaten eccentric dishes of cutlets made of lentils and nuts that pretended to be steak. On all the plates in this restaurant there was printed a figure of St. George in blue, with the motto, _Adsit Anglis Sanctus Geogius_--May St. George be a present help to the English. This soldier happened to know Latin and other useless things, and now, as he fired at his man in the grey advancing mass--300 yards away--he uttered the pious vegetarian motto. He went on firing to the end, and at last Bill on his right had to clout him cheerfully over the head to make him stop, pointing out as he did so that the King's ammunition cost money and was not lightly to be wasted in drilling funny patterns into dead Germans.

For as the Latin scholar uttered his invocation he felt something between a shudder and an electric shock pass through his body. The roar of the battle died down in his ears to a gentle murmur; instead of it, he says, he heard a great voice and a shout louder than a thunder-peal crying, "Array, array, array!"

His heart grew hot as a burning coal, it grew cold as ice within him, as it seemed to him that a tumult of voices answered to his summons. He heard, or seemed to hear, thousands shouting: "St. George! St. George!"

"Ha! messire; ha! sweet Saint, grant us good deliverance!"

"St. George for merry England!"

"Harow! Harow! Monseigneur St. George, succour us."

"Ha! St. George! Ha! St. George! a long bow and a strong bow."

"Heaven's Knight, aid us!"

And as the soldier heard these voices he saw before him, beyond the trench, a long line of shapes, with a shining about them. They were like men who drew the bow, and with another shout their cloud of arrows flew singing and tingling through the air towards the German hosts.

The other men in the trench were firing all the while. They had no hope; but they aimed just as if they had been shooting at Bisley. Suddenly one of them lifted up his voice in the plainest English, "Gawd help us!" he bellowed to the man next to him, "but we're blooming marvels! Look at those grey... gentlemen, look at them! D'ye see them? They're not going down in dozens, nor in 'undreds; it's thousands, it is. Look! look! there's a regiment gone while I'm talking to ye."

"Shut it!" the other soldier bellowed, taking aim, "what are ye gassing about!"

But he gulped with astonishment even as he spoke, for, indeed, the grey men were falling by the thousands. The English could hear the guttural scream of the German officers, the crackle of their revolvers as they shot the reluctant; and still line after line crashed to the earth.

All the while the Latin-bred soldier heard the cry: "Harow! Harow! Monseigneur, dear saint, quick to our aid! St. George help us!"

"High Chevalier, defend us!"

The singing arrows fled so swift and thick that they darkened the air; the heathen horde melted from before them.

"More machine guns!" Bill yelled to Tom.

"Don't hear them," Tom yelled back. "But, thank God, anyway; they've got it in the neck."

In fact, there were ten thousand dead German soldiers left before that salient of the English army, and consequently there was no Sedan. In Germany, a country ruled by scientific principles, the Great General Staff decided that the contemptible English must have employed shells containing an unknown gas of a poisonous nature, as no wounds were discernible on the bodies of the dead German soldiers. But the man who knew what nuts tasted like when they called themselves steak knew also that St. George had brought his Agincourt Bowmen to help the English.

The Soldiers' Rest

The soldier with the ugly wound in the head opened his eyes at last, and looked about him with an air of pleasant satisfaction.

He still felt drowsy and dazed with some fierce experience through which he had passed, but so far he could not recollect much about it. But--an agreeable glow began to steal about his heart-- such a glow as comes to people who have been in a tight place and have come through it better than they had expected. In its mildest form this set of emotions may be observed in passengers who have crossed the Channel on a windy day without being sick. They triumph a little internally, and are suffused with vague, kindly feelings.

The wounded soldier was somewhat of this disposition as he opened his eyes, pulled himself together, and looked about him. He felt a sense of delicious ease and repose in bones that had been racked and weary, and deep in the heart that had so lately been tormented there was an assurance of comfort--of the battle won. The thundering, roaring waves were passed; he had entered into the haven of calm waters. After fatigues and terrors that as yet he could not recollect he seemed now to be resting in the easiest of all easy chairs in a dim, low room.

In the hearth there was a glint of fire and a blue, sweet-scented puff of wood smoke; a great black oak beam roughly hewn crossed the ceiling. Through the leaded panes of the windows he saw a rich glow of sunlight, green lawns, and against the deepest and most radiant of all blue skies the wonderful far-lifted towers of a vast, Gothic cathedral--mystic, rich with imagery.

"Good Lord!" he murmured to himself. "I didn't know they had such places in France. It's just like Wells. And it might be the other day when I was going past the Swan, just as it might be past that window, and asked the ostler what time it was, and he says, 'What time? Why, summer-time'; and there outside it looks like summer that would last for ever. If this was an inn they ought to call it _The Soldiers' Rest_."

He dozed off again, and when he opened his eyes once more a kindly looking man in some sort of black robe was standing by him.

"It's all right now, isn't it?" he said, speaking in good English.

"Yes, thank you, sir, as right as can be. I hope to be back again soon."

"Well well; but how did you come here? Where did you get that?" He pointed to the wound on the soldier's forehead.

The soldier put his hand: up to his brow and looked dazed and puzzled.

"Well, sir," he said at last, "it was like this, to begin at the beginning. You know how we came over in August, and there we were in the thick of it, as you might say, in a day or two. An awful time it was, and I don't know how I got through it alive. My best friend was killed dead beside me as we lay in the trenches. By Cambrai, I think it was.

"Then things got a little quieter for a bit, and I was quartered in a village for the best part of a week. She was a very nice lady where I was, and she treated me proper with the best of everything. Her husband he was fighting; but she had the nicest little boy I ever knew, a little fellow of five, or six it might be, and we got on splendid. The amount of their lingo that kid taught me--'We, we' and 'Bong swot' and 'Commong voo potty we' and all--and I taught him English. You should have heard that nipper say "Arf a mo', old un!' It was a treat.

"Then one day we got surprised. There was about a dozen of us in the village, and two or three hundred Germans came down on us early one morning. They got us; no help for 'it. Before we could shoot.

"Well there we were. They tied our hands behind our backs, and smacked our faces and kicked us a bit, and we were lined up opposite the house where I'd been staying.

"And then that poor little chap broke away from his mother, and he run out and saw one of the Boshes, as we call them, fetch me one over the jaw with his clenched fist. Oh dear! oh dear! he might have done it a dozen times if only that little child hadn't seen him.

"He had a poor bit of a toy I'd bought him at the village shop; a toy gun it was. And out he came running, as I say, Crying out something in French like 'Bad man! bad man! don't hurt my Anglish or I shoot you'; and he pointed that gun at the German soldier. The German, he took his bayonet, and he drove it right through the poor little chap's throat."

The soldier's face worked and twitched and twisted itself into a sort of grin, and he sat grinding his teeth and staring at the man in the black robe. He was silent for a little. And then he found his voice, and the oaths rolled terrible, thundering from him, as he cursed that murderous wretch, and bade him go down and burn for ever in hell. And the tears were raining down his face, and they choked him at last.

"I beg your pardon, sir, I'm sure," he said, "especially you being a minister of some kind, I suppose; but I can't help it, he was such a dear little man."

The man in black murmured something to himself: "_Pretiosa in conspectu Domini mors innocentium ejus_"--Dear in the sight of the Lord is the death of His innocents. Then he put a hand very gently on the soldier's shoulder.

"Never mind," said he; "I've seen some service in my time, myself. But what about that wound?"

"Oh, that; that's nothing. But I'll tell you how I got it. It was just like this. The Germans had us fair, as I tell you, and they shut us up in a barn in the village; just flung us on the ground and left us to starve seemingly. They barred up the big door of the barn, and put a sentry there, and thought we were all right.

"There were sort of slits like very narrow windows in one of the walls, and on the second day it was, I was looking out of these slits down the street, and I could see those German devils were up to mischief. They were planting their machine-guns everywhere handy where an ordinary man coming up the street would never see them, but I see them, and I see the infantry lining up behind the garden walls. Then I had a sort of a notion of what was coming; and presently, sure enough, I could hear some of our chaps singing 'Hullo, hullo, hullo!' in the distance; and I says to myself, 'Not this time.'

"So I looked about me, and I found a hole under the wall; a kind of a drain I should think it was, and I found I could just squeeze through. And I got out and crept, round, and away I goes running down the street, yelling for all I was worth, just as our chaps were getting round the corner at the bottom. 'Bang, bang!' went the guns, behind me and in front of me, and on each side of me, and then--bash! something hit me on the head and over I went; and I don't remember anything more till I woke up here just now."

The soldier lay back in his chair and closed his eyes for a moment. When he opened them he saw that there were other people in the room besides the minister in the black robes. One was a man in a big black cloak. He had a grim old face and a great beaky nose. He shook the soldier by the hand.

"By God! sir," he said, "you're a credit to the British Army; you're a damned fine soldier and a good man, and, by God! I'm proud to shake hands with you."

And then someone came out of the shadow, someone in queer clothes such as the soldier had seen worn by the heralds when he had been on duty at the opening of Parliament by the King.

"Now, by _Corpus Domini_," this man said, "of all knights ye be noblest and gentlest, and ye be of fairest report, and now ye be a brother of the noblest brotherhood that ever was since this world's beginning, since ye have yielded dear life for your friends' sake."

The soldier did not understand what the man was saying to him. There were others, too, in strange dresses, who came and spoke to him. Some spoke in what sounded like French. He could not make it out; but he knew that they all spoke kindly and praised him.

"What does it all mean?" he said to the minister. "What are they talking about? They don't think I'd let down my pals?"

"Drink this," said the minister, and he handed the soldier a great silver cup, brimming with wine.

The soldier took a deep draught, and in that moment all his sorrows passed from him.

"What is it?" he asked?

"_Vin nouveau du Royaume_," said the minister. "New Wine of the Kingdom, you call it." And then he bent down and murmured in the soldier's ear.

"What," said the wounded man, "the place they used to tell us about in Sunday school? With such drink and such joy--"

His voice was hushed. For as he looked at the minister the fashion of his vesture was changed. The black robe seemed to melt away from him. He was all in armour, if armour be made of starlight, of the rose of dawn, and of sunset fires; and he lifted up a great sword of flame.

Full in the midst, his Cross of Red Triumphant Michael brandished,
And trampled the Apostate's pride.

The Monstrance

Then it fell out in the sacring of the Mass that right as the priest heaved up the Host there came a beam redder than any rose and smote upon it, and then it was changed bodily into the shape and fashion of a Child having his arms stretched forth, as he had been nailed upon the Tree.--Old Romance.

So far things were going very well indeed. The night was thick and black and cloudy, and the German force had come three-quarters of their way or more without an alarm. There was no challenge from the English lines; and indeed the English were being kept busy by a high shell-fire on their front. This had been the German plan; and it was coming off admirably. Nobody thought that there was any danger on the left; and so the Prussians, writhing on their stomachs over the ploughed field, were drawing nearer and nearer to the wood. Once there they could establish themselves comfortably and securely during what remained of the night; and at dawn the English left would be hopelessly enfiladed--and there would be another of those movements which people who really understand military matters call "readjustments of our line."

The noise made by the men creeping and crawling over the fields was drowned by the cannonade, from the English side as well as the German. On the English centre and right things were indeed very brisk; the big guns were thundering and shrieking and roaring, the machine-guns were keeping up the very devil's racket; the flares and illuminating shells were as good as the Crystal Palace in the old days, as the soldiers said to one another. All this had been thought of and thought out on the other side. The German force was beautifully organised. The men who crept nearer and nearer to the wood carried quite a number of machine guns in bits on their backs; others of them had small bags full of sand; yet others big bags that were empty. When the wood was reached the sand from the small bags was to be emptied into the big bags; the machine-gun parts were to be put together, the guns mounted behind the sandbag redoubt, and then, as Major Von und Zu pleasantly observed, "the English pigs shall to gehenna-fire quickly come."

The major was so well pleased with the way things had gone that he permitted himself a very low and guttural chuckle; in another ten minutes success would be assured. He half turned his head round to whisper a caution about some detail of the sandbag business to the big sergeant-major, Karl Heinz, who was crawling just behind him. At that instant Karl Heinz leapt into the air with a scream that rent through the night and through all the roaring of the artillery. He cried in a terrible voice, "The Glory of the Lord!" and plunged and pitched forward, stone dead. They said that his face as he stood up there and cried aloud was as if it had been seen through a sheet of flame.

"They" were one or two out of the few who got back to the German lines. Most of the Prussians stayed in the ploughed field. Karl Heinz's scream had frozen the blood of the English soldiers, but it had also ruined the major's plans. He and his men, caught all unready, clumsy with the burdens that they carried, were shot to pieces; hardly a score of them returned. The rest of the force were attended to by an English burying party. According to custom the dead men were searched before they were buried, and some singular relics of the campaign were found upon them, but nothing so singular as Karl Heinz's diary.

He had been keeping it for some time. It began with entries about bread and sausage and the ordinary incidents of the trenches; here and there Karl wrote about an old grandfather, and a big china pipe, and pinewoods and roast goose. Then the diarist seemed to get fidgety about his health. Thus:

April 17.--Annoyed for some days by murmuring sounds in my head. I trust I shall not become deaf, like my departed uncle Christopher.

April 20.--The noise in my head grows worse; it is a humming sound. It distracts me; twice I have failed to hear the captain and have been reprimanded.

April 22.--So bad is my head that I go to see the doctor. He speaks of tinnitus, and gives me an inhaling apparatus that shall reach, he says, the middle ear.

April 25.--The apparatus is of no use. The sound is now become like the booming of a great church bell. It reminds me of the bell at St. Lambart on that terrible day of last August.

April 26.--I could swear that it is the bell of St. Lambart that I hear all the time. They rang it as the procession came out of the church.

The man's writing, at first firm enough, begins to straggle unevenly over the page at this point. The entries show that he became convinced that he heard the bell of St. Lambart's Church ringing, though (as he knew better than most men) there had been no bell and no church at St. Lambart's since the summer of 1914. There was no village either--the whole place was a rubbish-heap.

Then the unfortunate Karl Heinz was beset with other troubles.

May 2.--I fear I am becoming ill. To-day Joseph Kleist, who is next to me in the trench, asked me why I jerked my head to the right so constantly. I told him to hold his tongue; but this shows that I am noticed. I keep fancying that there is something white just beyond the range of my sight on the right hand.

May 3.--This whiteness is now quite clear, and in front of me. All this day it has slowly passed before me. I asked Joseph Kleist if he saw a piece of newspaper just beyond the trench. He stared at me solemnly--he is a stupid fool--and said, "There is no paper."

May 4.--It looks like a white robe. There was a strong smell of incense to-day in the trench. No one seemed to notice it. There is decidedly a white robe, and I think I can see feet, passing very slowly before me at this moment while I write.

There is no space here for continuous extracts from Karl Heinz's diary. But to condense with severity, it would seem that he slowly gathered about himself a complete set of sensory hallucinations. First the auditory hallucination of the sound of a bell, which the doctor called tinnitus. Then a patch of white growing into a white robe, then the smell of incense. At last he lived in two worlds. He saw his trench, and the level before it, and the English lines; he talked with his comrades and obeyed orders, though with a certain difficulty; but he also heard the deep boom of St. Lambart's bell, and saw continually advancing towards him a white procession of little children, led by a boy who was swinging a censer. There is one extraordinary entry: "But in August those children carried no lilies; now they have lilies in their hands. Why should they have lilies?"

It is interesting to note the transition over the border line. After May 2 there is no reference in the diary to bodily illness, with two notable exceptions. Up to and including that date the sergeant knows that he is suffering from illusions; after that he accepts his hallucinations as actualities. The man who cannot see what he sees and hear what he hears is a fool. So he writes: "I ask who is singing 'Ave Maria Stella.' That blockhead Friedrich Schumacher raises his crest and answers insolently that no one sings, since singing is strictly forbidden for the present."

A few days before the disastrous night expedition the last figure in the procession appeared to those sick eyes.

The old priest now comes in his golden robe, the two boys holding each side of it. He is looking just as he did when he died, save that when he walked in St. Lambart there was no shining round his head. But this is illusion and contrary to reason, since no one has a shining about his head. I must take some medicine.

Note here that Karl Heinz absolutely accepts the appearance of the martyred priest of St. Lambart as actual, while he thinks that the halo must be an illusion; and so he reverts again to his physical condition.

The priest held up both his hands, the diary states, "as if there were something between them. But there is a sort of cloud or dimness over this object, whatever it may be. My poor Aunt Kathie suffered much from her eyes in her old age."

***

One can guess what the priest of St. Lambart carried in his hands when he and the little children went out into the hot sunlight to implore mercy, while the great resounding bell of St. Lambart boomed over the plain. Karl Heinz knew what happened then; they said that it was he who killed the old priest and helped to crucify the little child against the church door. The baby was only three years old. He died calling piteously for "mummy" and "daddy."

***

And those who will may guess what Karl Heinz saw when the mist cleared from before the monstrance in the priest's hands. Then he shrieked and died.

The Dazzling Light

The new head-covering is made of heavy steel, which has been specialty treated to increase its resisting power. The walls protecting the skull are particularly thick, and the weight of the helmet renders its use in open warfare out of the question. The rim is large, like that of the headpiece of Mambrino, and the soldier can at will either bring the helmet forward and protect his eyes or wear it so as to protect the base of the skull . . . Military experts admit that continuance of the present trench warfare may lead to those engaged in it, especially bombing parties and barbed wire cutters, being more heavily armoured than the knights, who fought at Bouvines and at Agincourt.--_The Times_, July 22, 1915

The war is already a fruitful mother of legends. Some people think that there are too many war legends, and a Croydon gentleman--or lady, I am not sure which--wrote to me quite recently telling me that a certain particular legend, which I will not specify, had become the "chief horror of the war." There may be something to be said for this point of view, but it strikes me as interesting that the old myth-making faculty has survived into these days, a relic of noble, far-off Homeric battles. And after all, what do we know? It does not do to be too sure that this, that, or the other hasn't happened and couldn't have happened.

What follows, at any rate, has no claim to be considered either as legend or as myth. It is merely one of the odd circumstances of these times, and I have no doubt it can easily be "explained away." In fact, the rationalistic explanation of the whole thing is patent and on the surface. There is only one little difficulty, and that, I fancy, is by no means insuperable. In any case this one knot or tangle may be put down as a queer coincidence and nothing more.

Here, then, is the curiosity or oddity in question. A young fellow, whom we will call for avoidance of all identification Delamere Smith-- he is now Lieutenant Delamere Smith--was spending his holidays on the coast of west South Wales at the beginning of the war. He was something or other not very important in the City, and in his leisure hours he smattered lightly and agreeably a little literature, a little art, a little antiquarianism. He liked the Italian primitives, he knew the difference between first, second, and third pointed, he had looked through Boutell's "Engraved Brasses." He had been heard indeed to speak with enthusiasm of the brasses of Sir Robert de Septvans and Sir Roger de Trumpington.

One morning--he thinks it must have been the morning of August 16, 1914--the sun shone so brightly into his room that he woke early, and the fancy took him that it would be fine to sit on the cliffs in the pure sunlight. So he dressed and went out, and climbed up Giltar Point, and sat there enjoying the sweet air and the radiance of the sea, and the sight of the fringe of creaming foam about the grey foundations of St. Margaret's Island. Then he looked beyond and gazed at the new white monastery on Caldy, and wondered who the architect was, and how he had contrived to make the group of buildings look exactly like the background of a mediæval picture.

After about an hour of this and a couple of pipes, Smith confesses that he began to feel extremely drowsy. He was just wondering whether it would be pleasant to stretch himself out on the wild thyme that scented the high place and go to sleep till breakfast, when the mounting sun caught one of the monastery windows, and Smith stared sleepily at the darting flashing light till it dazzled him. Then he felt "queer." There was an odd sensation as if the top of his head were dilating and contracting, and then he says he had a sort of shock, something between a mild current of electricity and the sensation of putting one's hand into the ripple of a swift brook.

Now, what happened next Smith cannot describe at all clearly. He knew he was on Giltar, looking across the waves to Caldy; he heard all the while the hollow, booming tide in the caverns of the rocks far below him, And yet he saw, as if in a glass, a very different country--a level fenland cut by slow streams, by long avenues of trimmed trees.

"It looked," he says, "as if it ought to have been a lonely country, but it was swarming with men; they were thick as ants in an anthill. And they were all dressed in armour; that was the strange thing about it.

"I thought I was standing by what looked as if it had been a farmhouse; but it was all battered to bits, just a heap of ruins and rubbish. All that was left was one tall round chimney, shaped very much like the fifteenth-century chimneys in Pembrokeshire. And thousands and tens of thousands went marching by.

"They were all in armour, and in all sorts of armour. Some of them had overlapping tongues of bright metal fastened on their clothes, others were in chain mail from head to foot, others were in heavy plate armour.

"They wore helmets of all shapes and sorts and sizes. One regiment had steel caps with wide trims, something like the old barbers' basins. Another lot had knights' tilting helmets on, closed up so that you couldn't see their faces. Most of them wore metal gauntlets, either of steel rings or plates, and they had steel over their boots. A great many had things like battle-maces swinging by their sides, and all these fellows carried a sort of string of big metal balls round their waist. Then a dozen regiments went by, every man with a steel shield slung over his shoulder. The last to go by were cross-bowmen."

In fact, it appeared to Delamere Smith that he watched the passing of a host of men in mediæval armour before him, and yet he knew--by the position of the sun and of a rosy cloud that was passing over the Worm's Head--that this vision, or whatever it was, only lasted a second or two. Then that slight sense of shock returned, and Smith returned to the contemplation of the physical phenomena of the Pembrokeshire coast--blue waves, grey St. Margaret's, and Caldy Abbey white in the sunlight.

It will be said, no doubt, and very likely with truth, that Smith fell asleep on Giltar, and mingled in a dream the thought of the great war just begun with his smatterings of mediæval battle and arms and armour. The explanation seems tolerable enough.

But there is the one little difficulty. It has been said that Smith is now Lieutenant Smith. He got his commission last autumn, and went out in May. He happens to speak French rather well, and so he has become what is called, I believe, an officer of liaison, or some such term. Anyhow, he is often behind the French lines.

He was home on short leave last week, and said:

"Ten days ago I was ordered to ----. I got there early in the morning, and had to wait a bit before I could see the General. I looked about me, and there on the left of us was a farm shelled into a heap of ruins, with one round chimney standing, shaped like the 'Flemish' chimneys in Pembrokeshire. And then the men in armour marched by, just as I had seen them--French regiments. The things like battle-maces were bomb-throwers, and the metal balls round the men's waists were the bombs. They told me that the cross-bows were used for bomb-shooting.

"The march I saw was part of a big movement; you will hear more of it before long."

The Bowmen And Other Noble Ghosts

By "The Londoner"

There was a journalist--and the _Evening News_ reader well knows the initials of his name--who lately sat down to write a story.

***

Of course his story had to be about the war; there are no other stories nowadays. And so he wrote of English soldiers who, in the dusk on a field of France, faced the sullen mass of the oncoming Huns. They were few against fearful odds, but, as they sent the breech-bolt home and aimed and fired, they became aware that others fought beside them. Down the air came cries to St. George and twanging of the bow-string; the old bowmen of England had risen at England's need from their graves in that French earth and were fighting for England.

***

He said that he made up that story by himself, that he sat down and wrote it out of his head. But others knew better. It must really have happened. There was, I remember, a clergyman of good credit who told him that he was clean mistaken; the archers had really and truly risen up to fight for England: the tale was all up and down the front.

For my part I had thought that he wrote out of his head; I had seen him at the detestable job of doing it. I myself have hated this business of writing ever since I found out that it was not so easy as it looks, and I can always spare a little sympathy for a man who is driving a pen to the task of putting words in their right places. Yet the clergyman persuaded me at last. Who am I that I should doubt the faith of a clerk in holy orders? It must have happened. Those archers fought for us, and the grey-goose feather has flown once again in English battle.

***

Since that day I look eagerly for the ghosts who must be taking their share in this world-war. Never since the world began was such a war as this: surely Marlborough and the Duke, Talbot and Harry of Monmouth, and many another shadowy captain must be riding among our horsemen. The old gods of war are wakened by this loud clamour of the guns.

***

All the lands are astir. It is not enough that Asia should be humming like an angry hive and the far islands in arms, Australia sending her young men and Canada making herself a camp. When we talk over the war news, we call up ancient names: we debate how Rome stands and what is the matter with Greece.

***

As for Greece, I have ceased to talk of her. If I wanted to say anything about Greece I should get down the Poetry Book and quote Lord Byron's fine old ranting verse. "The mountains look on Marathon--and Marathon looks on the sea." But "standing on the Persians' grave" Greece seems in the same humour that made Lord Byron give her up as a hopelessly flabby country.

***

"'Tis Greece, but living Greece no more" is as true as ever it was. That last telegram of the Kaiser must have done its soothing work. You remember how it ran: the Kaiser was too busy to make up new phrases. He telegraphed to his sister the familiar Potsdam sentence: "Woe to those who dare to draw the sword against me." I am sure that I have heard that before. And he added--delightful and significant postscript!--"My compliments to Tino."

***

And Tino--King Constantine of the Hellenes--understood. He is in bed now with a very bad cold, and like to stay in bed until the weather be more settled. But before going to bed he was able to tell a journalist that Greece was going quietly on with her proper business; it was her mission to carry civilisation to the world. Truly that was the mission of ancient Greece. What we get from Tino's modern Greece is not civilisation but the little black currants for plum-cake.

***

But Rome. Greece may be dead or in the currant trade. Rome is alive and immortal. Do not talk to me about Signor Giolitti, who is quite sure that the only things that matter in this new Italy, which is old Rome, are her commercial relations with Germany. Rome of the legions, our ancient mistress and conqueror, is alive to-day, and she cannot be for an ignoble peace. Here in my newspaper is the speech of a poet spoken in Rome to a shouting crowd: I will cut out the column and put it in the Poetry Book.

***

He calls to the living and to the dead: "I saw the fire of Vesta, O Romans, lit yesterday in the great steel works of Liguria, The fountain of Juturna, O Romans, I saw its water run to temper armour, to chill the drills that hollow out the bore of guns." This is poetry of the old Roman sort. I imagine that scene in Rome: the latest poet of Rome calling upon the Romans in the name of Vesta's holy fire, in the name of the springs at which the Great Twin Brethren washed their horses. I still believe in the power and the ancient charm of noble words. I do not think that Giolitti and the stockbrokers will keep old Rome off the old roads where the legions went.

Postscript

While this volume was passing through the press, Mr. Ralph Shirley, the Editor of "The Occult Review" called my attention to an article that is appearing in the August issue of his magazine, and was kind enough to let me see the advance proof sheets.

The article is called "The Angelic Leaders" It is written by Miss Phyllis Campbell. I have read it with great care.

Miss Campbell says that she was in France when the war broke out. She became a nurse, and while she was nursing the wounded she was informed that an English soldier wanted a "holy picture." She went to the man and found him to be a Lancashire Fusilier. He said that he was a Wesleyan Methodist, and asked "for a picture or medal (he didn't care which) of St. George... because he had seen him on a white horse, leading the British at Vitry-le-François, when the Allies turned"

This statement was corroborated by a wounded R.F.A. man who was present. He saw a tall man with yellow hair, in golden armour, on a white horse, holding his sword up, and his mouth open as if he was saying, "Come on, boys! I'll put the kybosh on the devils" This figure was bareheaded--as appeared later from the testimony of other soldiers--and the R.F.A. man and the Fusilier knew that he was St. George, because he was exactly like the figure of St. George on the sovereigns. "Hadn't they seen him with his sword on every 'quid' they'd ever had?"

From further evidence it seemed that while the English had seen the apparition of St. George coming out of a "yellow mist" or "cloud of light," to the French had been vouchsafed visions of St. Michael the Archangel and Joan of Arc. Miss Campbell says:--

> "Everybody has seen them who has fought through from Mons to Ypres;
> they all agree on them individually, and have no doubt at all as to
> the final issue of their interference"

Such are the main points of the article as it concerns the great legend of "The Angels of Mons." I cannot say that the author has shaken my incredulity--firstly, because the evidence is second-hand. Miss Campbell is perhaps acquainted with "Pickwick" and I would remind her of that famous (and golden) ruling of Stareleigh, J.: to the effect that you mustn't tell us what the soldier said; it's not evidence. Miss Campbell has offended against this rule, and she has not only told us what the soldier said, but she has omitted to give us the soldier's name and address.

If Miss Campbell proffered herself as a witness at the Old Bailey and said, "John Doe is undoubtedly guilty. A soldier I met told me that he had seen the prisoner put his hand into an old gentleman's pocket and take out a purse"--well, she would find that the stout spirit of Mr. Justice Stareleigh still survives in our judges.

The soldier must be produced. Before that is done we are not technically aware that he exists at all.

Then there are one or two points in the article itself which puzzle me. The Fusilier and the R.F.A. man had seen "St, George leading the British at Vitry-le-François, when the Allies turned." Thus the time of the apparition and the place of the apparition were firmly fixed in the two soldiers' minds.

Yet the very next paragraph in the article begins:--

"'Where was this ?' I asked. But neither of them could tell"

This is an odd circumstance. They knew, and yet they did not know; or, rather, they had forgotten a piece of information that they had themselves imparted a few seconds before.

Another point. The soldiers knew that the figure on the horse was St. George by his exact likeness to the figure of the saint on the English sovereign.

This, again, is odd. The apparition was of a bareheaded figure in golden armour. The St. George of the coinage is naked, except for a short cape flying from the shoulders, and a helmet. He is not bareheaded, and has no armour--save the piece on his head. I do not quite see how the soldiers were so certain as to the identity of the apparition.

Lastly, Miss Campbell declares that "everybody" who fought from Mons to Ypres saw the apparitions. If that be so, it is again odd that Nobody has come forward to testify at first hand to the most amazing event of his life. Many men have been back on leave from the front, we have many wounded in hospital, many soldiers have written letters home. And they have all combined, this great host, to keep silence as to the most wonderful of occurrences, the most inspiring assurance, the surest omen of victory.

It may be so, but--

Arthur Machen.

The Secret Glory

New York Alfred A Knopf Mcmxxii
COPYRIGHT, 1922, BY ALFRED A. KNOPF, INC.
Published August, 1922
Set up and printed by the Vail-Ballou Co., Binghamton, N. Y.
Paper furnished by W. F. Etherington & Co., New York, N. Y.
Bound by the H. Wolff Estate, New York, N. Y.
MANUFACTURED IN THE UNITED STATES OF AMERICA
TO VINCENT STARRETT

Note

One of the schoolmasters in "The Secret Glory" has views on the subject of football similar to those entertained by a well-known schoolmaster whose Biography appeared many years ago. That is the only link between the villain of invention and the good man of real life.

PREFACE

Some years ago I met my old master, Sir Frank Benson--he was Mr. F. R. Benson then--and he asked me in his friendly way what I had been doing lately.

"I am just finishing a book," I replied, "a book that everybody will hate."

"As usual," said the Don Quixote of our English stage--if I knew any nobler title to bestow upon him, I would, bestow it--"as usual; running your head against a stone wall!"

Well, I don't know about "as usual"; there may be something to be said for the personal criticism or there may not; but it has struck me that Sir Frank's remark is a very good description of "The Secret Glory," the book I had in mind as I talked to him. It is emphatically the history of an unfortunate fellow who ran his head against stone walls from the beginning to the end. He could think nothing and do nothing after the common fashion of the world; even when he "went wrong," he did so in a highly unusual and eccentric manner. It will be for the reader to determine whether he were a saint who had lost his way in the centuries or merely an undeveloped lunatic; I hold no passionate view on either side. In every age, there are people great and small for whom the times are out of joint, for whom everything is, somehow, wrong and askew. Consider Hamlet; an amiable man and an intelligent man. But what a mess he made of it! Fortunately, my hero--or idiot, which you will--was not called upon to intermeddle with affairs of State, and so only brought himself to grief: if it were grief; for the least chink of the door should be kept open, I am inclined to hold, for the other point of view. I have just been rereading Kipling's "The Miracle of Purun Bhagat," the tale of the Brahmin Prime Minister of the Native State in India, who saw all the world and the glory of it, in the West as well as in the East, and suddenly abjured all to become a hermit in the wood. Was he mad, or was he supremely wise? It is just a matter of opinion.

The origin and genesis of "The Secret Glory" were odd enough. Once on a time, I read the life of a famous schoolmaster, one of the most notable schoolmasters of these later days. I believe he was an excellent man in every way; but, somehow, that "Life" got on my nerves. I thought that the School Songs--for which, amongst other things, this master was famous--were drivel; I thought his views about football, regarded, not as a good game, but as the discipline and guide of life, were rot, and poisonous rot at that. In a word, the "Life" of this excellent man got my back up.

Very good. The year after, schoolmasters and football had ceased to engage my attention. I was deeply interested in a curious and minute investigation of the wonderful legend of the Holy Grail; or rather, in one aspect of that extraordinary complex. My researches led me to the connection of the Grail Legend with the vanished Celtic Church which held the field in Britain in the fifth and sixth and seventh centuries; I undertook an extraordinary and fascinating journey into a misty and uncertain region of Christian history. I must not say more here, lest--as Nurse says to the troublesome and persistent child--I "begin all over again"; but, indeed, it was a voyage on perilous seas, a journey to faery lands forlorn--and I would declare, by the way, my conviction that if there had been no Celtic Church, Keats could never have written those lines of tremendous evocation and incantation.

Again; very good. The year after, it came upon me to write a book. And I hit upon an original plan; or so I thought. I took my dislike of the good schoolmaster's "Life," I took my knowledge of Celtic mysteries--and combined my information.

Original, this plan! It was all thought of years before I was born. Do you remember the critic of the "Eatanswill Gazette"? He had to review for that admirable journal a work on Chinese Metaphysics. Mr. Pott tells the story of the article.

"He read up for the subject, at my desire, in the Encyclopædia Britannica ... he read for metaphysics under the letter M, and for China under the letter C, and combined his information!"

I

I

A heavy cloud passed swiftly away before the wind that came with the night, and far in a clear sky the evening star shone with pure brightness, a gleaming world set high above the dark earth and the black shadows in the lane. In the ending of October a great storm had blown from the west, and it was through the bare boughs of a twisted oak that Ambrose Meyrick saw the silver light of the star. As the last faint flash died in the sky he leaned against a gate and gazed upward; and then his eyes fell on the dull and weary undulations of the land, the vast circle of dun ploughland and grey meadow bounded by a dim horizon, dreary as a prison wall. He remembered with a start how late it must be; he should have been back an hour before, and he was still in the open country, a mile away at least from the outskirts of Lupton. He turned from the star and began to walk as quickly as he could along the lane through the puddles and the sticky clay, soaked with three weeks' heavy rain.

He saw at last the faint lamps of the nearest streets where the shoemakers lived and he tramped hurriedly through this wretched quarter, past its penny shops, its raw public-house, its rawer chapel, with twelve foundation-stones on which are written the names of the twelve leading Congregationalists of Lupton, past the squalling children whose mothers were raiding and harrying them to bed. Then came the Free Library, an admirable instance, as the Lupton Mercury declared, of the adaptation of Gothic to modern requirements. From a sort of tower of this building a great arm shot out and hung a round clock-face over the street, and Meyrick experienced another shock when he saw that it was even later than he had feared. He had to get to the other side of the town, and it was past seven already! He began to run, wondering what his fate would be at his uncle's hands, and he went by "our grand old parish church" (completely "restored" in the early 'forties), past the remains of the market-cross, converted most successfully, according to local opinion, into a drinking fountain for dogs and cattle, dodging his way among the late shoppers and the early loafers who lounged to and fro along the High Street.

He shuddered as he rang the bell at the Old Grange. He tried to put a bold face on it when the servant opened the door, and he would have gone straight down the hall into the schoolroom, but the girl stopped him.

"Master said you're to go to the study at once, Master Meyrick, as soon as ever you come in."

She was looking strangely at him, and the boy grew sick with dread. He was a "funk" through and through, and was frightened out of his wits about twelve times a day every day of his life. His uncle had said a few years before: "Lupton will make a man of you," and Lupton was doing its best. The face of the miserable wretch whitened and grew wet; there was a choking sensation in his throat, and he felt very cold. Nelly Foran, the maid, still looked at him with strange, eager eyes, then whispered suddenly:

"You must go directly, Master Meyrick, Master heard the bell, I know; but I'll make it up to you."

Ambrose understood nothing except the approach of doom. He drew a long breath and knocked at the study door, and entered on his uncle's command.

It was an extremely comfortable room. The red curtains were drawn close, shutting out the dreary night, and there was a great fire of coal that bubbled unctuously and shot out great jets of flame--in the schoolroom they used coke. The carpet was soft to the feet, and the chairs promised softness to the body, and the walls were well furnished with books. There were Thackeray, Dickens, Lord Lytton, uniform in red morocco, gilt extra; the Cambridge Bible for Students in many volumes, Stanley's Life of Arnold, Coplestone's Prælectiones Academicæ, commentaries, dictionaries, first editions of Tennyson, school and college prizes in calf, and, of course, a great brigade of Latin and Greek classics. Three of the wonderful and terrible pictures of Piranesi hung in the room; these Mr.

Horbury admired more for the subject-matter than for the treatment, in which he found, as he said, a certain lack of the aurea mediocritas--almost, indeed, a touch of morbidity. The gas was turned low, for the High Usher was writing at his desk, and a shaded lamp cast a bright circle of light on a mass of papers.

He turned round as Ambrose Meyrick came in. He had a high, bald forehead, and his fresh-coloured face was edged with reddish "mutton-chop" whiskers. There was a dangerous glint in his grey-green eyes, and his opening sentence was unpromising.

"Now, Ambrose, you must understand quite definitely that this sort of thing is not going to be tolerated any longer."

Perhaps it would not have fared quite so badly with the unhappy lad if only his uncle had not lunched with the Head. There was a concatenation accordingly, every link in which had helped to make Ambrose Meyrick's position hopeless. In the first place there was boiled mutton for luncheon, and this was a dish hateful to Mr. Horbury's palate. Secondly, the wine was sherry. Of this Mr. Horbury was very fond, but unfortunately the Head's sherry, though making a specious appeal to the taste, was in reality far from good and teemed with those fiery and irritating spirits which make the liver to burn and rage. Then Chesson had practically found fault with his chief assistant's work. He had not, of course, told him in so many words that he was unable to teach; he had merely remarked:

"I don't know whether you've noticed it, Horbury, but it struck me the other day that there was a certain lack of grip about those fellows of yours in the fifth. Some of them struck me as muddlers, if you know what I mean: there was a sort of vagueness, for example, about their construing in that chorus. Have you remarked anything of the kind yourself?"

And then, again, the Head had gone on:

"And, by the way, Horbury, I don't quite know what to make of your nephew, Meyrick. He was your wife's nephew, wasn't he? Yes. Well, I hardly know whether I can explain what I feel about the boy; but I can't help saying that there is something wrong about him. His work strikes me as good enough--in fact, quite above the form average--but, to use the musical term, he seems to be in the wrong key. Of course, it may be my fancy; but the lad reminds me of those very objectionable persons who are said to have a joke up their sleeve. I doubt whether he is taking the Lupton stamp; and when he gets up in the school I shall be afraid of his influence on the other boys."

Here, again, the master detected a note of blame; and by the time he reached the Old Grange he was in an evil humour. He hardly knew which he found the more offensive--Chesson's dish or his discourse. He was a dainty man in his feeding, and the thought of the great fat gigot pouring out a thin red stream from the gaping wound dealt to it by the Head mingled with his resentment of the indirect scolding which he considered that he had received, and on the fire just kindled every drop of that corrosive sherry was oil. He drank his tea in black silence, his rage growing fiercer for want of vent, and it is doubtful whether in his inmost heart he was altogether displeased when report was made at six o'clock that Meyrick had not come in. He saw a prospect--more than a prospect--of satisfactory relief.

Some philosophers have affirmed that lunatic doctors (or mental specialists) grow in time to a certain resemblance to their patients, or, in more direct language, become half mad themselves. There seems a good deal to be said for the position; indeed, it is probably a more noxious madness to swear a man into perpetual imprisonment in the company of maniacs and imbeciles because he sings in his bath and will wear a purple dressing-gown at dinner than to fancy oneself Emperor of China. However this may be, it is very certain that in many cases the schoolmaster is nothing more or less than a bloated schoolboy: the beasts are, radically, the same, but morbid conditions have increased the venom of the former's sting. Indeed, it is not uncommon for well-wishers to the great Public School System to praise their favourite masters in terms which admit, nay, glory in, this identity. Read the memorial tributes to departed Heads in a well-known and most respectable Church paper. "To the last he was a big boy at heart," writes Canon Diver of his friend, that illiterate old sycophant who brought up the numbers of the school to such a pitch by means of his conciliator policy to Jews, Turks, heretics and infidels that there was nothing for it but to make him a bishop. "I always thought he seemed more at home in the playing fields than in the sixth-form room.... He had all the English boy's healthy horror of anything approaching pose or eccentricity.... He could be a severe disciplinarian when severity seemed necessary, but everybody in the school knew that a well-placed 'boundary,' a difficult catch or a goal well won or well averted would atone for all but the most serious offences." There are many other points of resemblance between the average master and the average boy: each, for example, is intensely cruel, and experiences a quite abnormal joy in the infliction of pain. The baser boy tortures those animals which are not méchants. Tales have been told (they are hushed up by all true friends of the "System") of wonderful and exquisite orgies in lonely hollows of the moors, in obscure and hidden thickets: tales of a boy or two, a lizard or a toad, and the slow simmering heat of a bonfire. But these are the exceptional pleasures of the virtuosi; for the average lad there is plenty of fun to be got out of his feebler fellows, of whom there are generally a few even in the healthiest community. After all, the weakest must go to the wall, and if the bones of the weakest are ground in the process, that is their fault. When some miserable little wretch, after a year or two of prolonged and exquisite torture of body and mind, seeks the last escape of suicide, one knows how the Old Boys will come forward, how gallantly they will declare that the days at the "dear old school" were the happiest in their lives; how "the Doctor" was their father and the Sixth their nursing-mother; how the delights of the Mahomedans' fabled Paradise are but grey and weary sport compared with the joys of the happy fag, whose heart, as the inspired bard of Harrow tells us, will thrill in future years at the thought of the Hill. They write from all quarters, these brave Old Boys: from the hard-won Deanery, result of many years of indefatigable attack on the fundamental doctrines of the Christian faith; from the comfortable villa, the reward of commercial activity and acuteness on the Stock Exchange; from the courts and from the camps; from all the high seats of the successful; and common to them all is the convincing argument of praise. And we all agree, and say there is nothing like our great Public Schools, and perhaps the only dissentient voices are those of the father and mother who bury the body of a little child about whose neck is the black sign of the rope. But let them be comforted: the boy was no good at games, though his torments were not bad sport while he lasted.

Mr. Horbury was an old Luptonian; he was, in the words of Canon Diver, but "a big boy at heart," and so he gave orders that Meyrick was to be sent in the study directly he came in, and he looked at the clock on the desk before him with satisfaction and yet with impatience. A hungry man may long for his delayed dinner almost with a sense of fury, and yet at the back of his mind he cannot help being consoled by the thought of how wonderfully he will enjoy the soup when it appears at last. When seven struck, Mr. Horbury moistened his lips slightly. He got up and felt cautiously behind one of the bookshelves. The object was there, and he sat down again. He listened; there were footfalls on the drive. Ah! there was the expected ring. There was a brief interval, and then a knock. The fire was glowing with red flashes, and the wretched toad was secured.

"Now, Ambrose, you must understand quite definitely that this sort of thing isn't going to be tolerated any longer. This is the third time during this term that you have been late for lockup. You know the rules: six o'clock at latest. It is now twenty minutes past seven. What excuse have you to make? What have you been doing with yourself? Have you been in the Fields?"

"No, Sir."

"Why not? You must have seen the Resolution of the Sixth on the notice-board of the High School? You know what it promised any boy who shirked rocker? 'A good sound thrashing with tuds before the First Thirty.' I am afraid you will have a very bad time of it on Monday, after Graham has sent up your name to the Room."

There was a pause. Mr. Horbury looked quietly and lengthily at the boy, who stood white and sick before him. He was a rather sallow, ugly lad of fifteen. There was something of intelligence in his expression, and it was this glance that Chesson, the Headmaster, had resented. His heart beat against his breast, his breath came in gasps and the sweat of terror poured down his body. The master gazed at him, and at last spoke again.

"But what have you been doing? Where have you been all this time?"

"If you please, Sir, I walked over to Selden Abbey."

"To Selden Abbey? Why, it's at least six miles away! What on earth did you want to go to Selden Abbey for? Are you fond of old stones?"

"If you please, Sir, I wanted to see the Norman arches. There is a picture of them in Parker's Glossary."

"Oh, I see! You are a budding antiquarian, are you, Ambrose, with an interest in Norman arches--eh? I suppose we are to look forward to the time when your researches will have made Lupton famous? Perhaps you would like to lecture to the school on St. Paul's Cathedral? Pray, what are your views as to the age of Stonehenge?"

The wit was heavy enough, but the speaker's position gave a bitter sting to his lash. Mr. Horbury saw that every cut had told, and, without prejudice to more immediate and acuter pleasures, he resolved that such biting satire must have a larger audience. Indeed, it was a long time before Ambrose Meyrick heard the last of those wretched Norman arches. The method was absurdly easy. "Openings" presented themselves every day. For example, if the boy made a mistake in construing, the retort was obvious:

"Thank you, Meyrick, for your most original ideas on the force of the aorist. Perhaps if you studied your Greek Grammar a little more and your favourite Glossary of Architecture a little less, it would be the better. Write out 'Aorist means indefinite' five hundred times."

Or, again, perhaps the Classic Orders were referred to. Mr. Horbury would begin to instruct the form as to the difference between Ionic and Doric. The form listened with poor imitation of interest. Suddenly the master would break off:

"I beg your pardon. I was forgetting that we have a great architectural authority amongst us. Be so kind as to instruct us, Meyrick. What does Parker say? Or perhaps you have excogitated some theories of your own? I know you have an original mind, from the extraordinary quantities of your last copy of verse. By the way, I must ask you to write out 'The e in venio is short' five hundred times. I am sorry to interfere with your more important architectural studies, but I am afraid there is no help for it."

And so on; while the form howled with amusement.

But Mr. Horbury kept these gems for future and public use. For the moment he had more exciting work on hand. He burst out suddenly:

"The fact is, Ambrose Meyrick, you're a miserable little humbug! You haven't the honesty to say, fair and square, that you funked rocker and went loafing about the country, looking for any mischief you could lay your hands on. Instead of that you make up this cock-and-bull story of Selden Abbey and Norman arches--as if any boy in his senses ever knew or cared twopence about such things! I hope you haven't been spending the afternoon in some low public-house? There, don't speak! I don't want to hear any more lies. But, whatever you have been doing, you have broken the rules, and you must be taught that the rules have to be kept. Stand still!"

Mr. Horbury went to the bookshelf and drew out the object. He stood at a little distance behind Meyrick and opened proceedings with a savage cut at his right arm, well above the elbow. Then it was the turn of the left arm, and the master felt the cane bite so pleasantly into the flesh that he distributed some dozen cuts between the two arms. Then he turned his attention to the lad's thighs and finished up in the orthodox manner, Meyrick bending over a chair.

The boy's whole body was one mass of burning, stinging torture; and, though he had not uttered a sound during the process, the tears were streaming down his cheeks. It was not the bodily anguish, though that was extreme enough, so much as a far-off recollection. He was quite a little boy, and his father, dead long since, was showing him the western doorway of a grey church on a high hill and carefully instructing him in the difference between "billetty" and "chevronny."

"It's no good snivelling, you know, Ambrose. I daresay you think me severe, but, though you won't believe me now, the day will come when you will thank me from your heart for what I have just done. Let this day be a turning-point in your life. Now go to your work."

II

It was strange, but Meyrick never came in the after days and thanked his uncle for that sharp dose of physical and mental pain. Even when he was a man he dreamed of Mr. Horbury and woke up in a cold sweat, and then would fall asleep again with a great sigh of relief and gladness as he realised that he was no longer in the power of that "infernal old swine," "that filthy, canting, cruel brute," as he roughly called his old master.

The fact was, as some old Luptonians remarked, the two had never understood one another. With the majority of the boys the High Usher passed for a popular master enough. He had been a distinguished athlete in his time, and up to his last days at the school was a football enthusiast. Indeed, he organised a variety of the Lupton game which met with immense popularity till the Head was reluctantly compelled to stop it; some said because he always liked to drop bitter into Horbury's cup when possible; others--and with more probability on their side--maintained that it was in consequence of a report received from the school doctor to the effect that this new species of football was rapidly setting up an old species of heart disease in the weaker players.

However that might be, there could be no doubt as to Horbury's intense and deep-rooted devotion to the school. His father had been a Luptonian before him. He himself had gone from the school to the University, and within a year or two of taking his degree he had returned to Lupton to serve it as a master. It was the general opinion in Public School circles that the High Usher had counted for as much as Chesson, the Headmaster, if not for more, in the immense advance in prestige and popularity that the school had made; and everybody thought that when Chesson received the episcopal order Horbury's succession was a certainty. Unfortunately, however, there were wheels within wheels, and a total stranger was appointed, a man who knew nothing of the famous Lupton traditions, who (it was whispered) had been heard to say that "this athletic business" was getting a bit overdone. Mr. Horbury's friends were furious, and Horbury himself, it was supposed, was bitterly disappointed. He retreated to one of the few decent canonries which have survived the wave of agricultural depression; but those who knew him best doubted whether his ecclesiastical duties were an adequate consolation for the loss of that coveted Headmastership of Lupton.

To quote the memoir which appeared in the Guardian soon after his death, over some well-known initials:

"His friends were shocked when they saw him at the Residence. He seemed no longer the same man, he had aged more in six months, as some of them expressed themselves, than in the dozen years before. The old joyous Horbury, full of mirth, an apt master of word-play and logic-fence, was somehow 'dimmed,' to use the happy phrase of a former colleague, the Dean of Dorchester. Old Boys who remembered the sparkle of his wit, the zest which he threw into everything, making the most ordinary form-work better fun than the games at other schools, as one of them observed, missed something indefinable from the man whom they had loved so long and so well. One of them, who had perhaps penetrated as closely as any into the arcana of Horbury's friendship (a privilege which he will ever esteem as one of the greatest blessings of his life), tried to rouse him with an extravagant rumour which was then going the round of the popular Press, to the effect that considerable modifications were about to be introduced into the compulsory system of games at X., one of the greatest of our great Public Schools. Horbury flushed; the old light came into his eyes; his friend was reminded of the ancient war-horse who hears once more the inspiring notes of the trumpet. 'I can't believe it,' he said, and there was a tremor in his voice. 'They wouldn't dare. Not even Y. (the Headmaster of X.) would do such a scoundrelly thing as that. I won't believe it.' But the flush soon faded and his apathy returned. 'After all,' he said, 'I shouldn't wonder if it were so. Our day is past, I suppose, and for all I know they may be construing the Breviary and playing dominoes at X. in a few years' time.'

"I am afraid that those last years at Wareham were far from happy. He felt, I think, out of tune with his surroundings, and, pace the readers of the Guardian, I doubt whether he was ever quite at home in his stall. He confessed to one of his old associates that he doubted the wisdom of the whole Cathedral system. 'What,' he said, in his old characteristic manner, 'would St. Peter say if he could enter this building and see that gorgeous window in which he is represented with mitre, cope and keys?' And I do not think that he was ever quite reconciled to the daily recitation of the Liturgy, accompanied as it is in such establishments by elaborate music and all the pomp of the surpliced choir. 'Rome and water, Rome and water!' he has been heard to mutter under his breath as the procession swept up the nave, and before he died I think that he had the satisfaction of feeling that many in high places were coming round to his views.

"But to the very last he never forgot Lupton. A year or two before he died he wrote the great school song, 'Follow, follow, follow!' He was pleased, I know, when it appeared in the Luptonian, and a famous Old Boy informs me that he will never forget Horbury's delight when he was told that the song was already a great favourite in 'Chantry.' To many of your readers the words will be familiar; but I cannot resist quoting the first verse:

"I am getting old and grey and the hills seem far away,
And I cannot hear the horn that once proclaimed the morn
When we sallied forth upon the chase together;
For the years are gone--alack!--when we hastened on the track,
And the huntsman's whip went crack! as a signal to our pack
Riding in the sunshine and fair weather.
And yet across the ground
I seem to hear a sound,
A sound that comes up floating from the hollow;
And its note is very clear
As it echoes in my ear,
And the words are: 'Lupton, follow, follow, follow!'

Chorus.
"Lupton, follow away!
The darkness lies behind us, and before us is the day.
Follow, follow the sun,
The whole world's to be won,
So, Lupton, follow, follow, follow, follow away!

"An old pupil sang this verse to him on his death-bed, and I think, perhaps, that some at least of the readers of the Guardian will allow that George Horbury died 'fortified,' in the truest sense, 'with the rites of the Church'--the Church of a Great Aspiration."

Such was the impression that Mr. Horbury had evidently made upon some of his oldest friends; but Meyrick was, to the last, an infidel. He read the verses in the Guardian (he would never subscribe to the Luptonian) and jeered savagely at the whole sentiment of the memoir, and at the poetry, too.

"Isn't it incredible?" he would say. "Let's allow that the main purpose of the great Public Schools is to breed brave average boobies by means of rocker, sticker and mucker and the rest of it. Still, they do acknowledge that they have a sort of parergon--the teaching of two great literatures, two literatures that have moulded the whole of Western thought for more than two thousand years. And they pay an animal like this to teach these literatures--a swine that has not enough literature of any kind in him to save the soul of a louse! Look at those verses! Why, a decent fourth form boy would be ashamed to put his name to them!"

He was foolish to talk in this fashion. People merely said that it was evident he was one of the failures of the great Public School system; and the song was much admired in the right circles. A very well-turned idem Latine appeared in the Guardian shortly after the publication of the memoir, and the initials at the foot of the version were recognised as those of a literary dean.

And on that autumn evening, far away in the 'seventies, Meyrick, the boy, left Mr. Horbury's study in a white fury of grief and pain and rage. He would have murdered his master without the faintest compunction, nay, with huge delight. Psychologically, his frame of mind was quite interesting, though he was only a schoolboy who had just had a sound thrashing for breaking rules.

For the fact, of course, was that Horbury, the irritating influence of the Head's conversation and sherry apart, was by no means a bad fellow. He was for the moment savagely cruel, but then, most men are apt to be savagely cruel when they suffer from an inflamed liver and offensive superiors, more especially when there is an inferior, warranted defenceless, in their power. But, in the main, Horbury was a very decent specimen of his class--English schoolmaster--and Meyrick would never allow that. In all his reasoning about schools and schoolmasters there was a fatal flaw--he blamed both for not being what they never pretended to be. To use a figure that would have appealed to him, it was if one quarrelled with a plain, old-fashioned meeting-house because it was not in the least like Lincoln Cathedral. A chimney may not be a decorative object, but then it does not profess to be a spire or a pinnacle far in the spiritual city.

But Meyrick was always scolding meeting-houses because they were not cathedrals. He has been heard to rave for hours against useful, unpretentious chimney-pots because they bore no resemblance to celestial spires. Somehow or other, possibly by inheritance, possibly by the influence of his father's companionship, he had unconsciously acquired a theory of life which bore no relation whatever to the facts of it. The theory was manifest in his later years; but it must have been stubbornly, if vaguely, present in him all through his boyhood. Take, for instance, his comment on poor Canon Horbury's verses. He judged those, as we have seen, by the rules of the fine art of literature, and found them rubbish. Yet any old Luptonian would have told him that to hear the whole six hundred boys join in the chorus, "Lupton, follow away!" was one of the great experiences of life; from which it appears that the song, whatever its demerits from a literary point of view, fully satisfied the purpose for which is was written. In other words, it was an excellent chimney, but Meyrick still persisted in his easy and futile task of proving that it was not a bit like a spire. Then, again, one finds a fallacy of still huger extent in that major premiss of his: that the great Public Schools purpose to themselves as a secondary and minor object the imparting of the spirit and beauty of the Greek and Latin literatures. Now, it is very possible that at some distant period in the past this was an object, or even, perhaps, the object of the institutions in question. The Humanists, it may be conjectured, thought of school and University as places where Latin and Greek were to be learned, and to be learned with the object of enjoying the great thought and the great style of an antique world. One sees the spirit of this in Rabelais, for example. The Classics are a wonderful adventure; to learn to understand them is to be a spiritual Columbus, a discoverer of new seas and unknown continents, a drinker of new-old wine in a new-old land. To the student of those days a mysterious drowned Atlantis again rose splendid from the waves of the great deep. It was these things that Meyrick (unconsciously, doubtless) expected to find in his school life; it was for the absence of these things that he continued to scold the system in his later years; wherein, like Jim in Huckleberry Finn, he missed the point by a thousand miles.

The Latin and Greek of modern instruction are, of course, most curious and interesting survivals; no longer taught with any view of enabling students to enjoy and understand either the thought or beauty of the originals; taught rather in such a manner as to nauseate the learner for the rest of his days with the very notion of these lessons. Still, the study of the Classics survives, a curious and elaborate ritual, from which all sense and spirit have departed. One has only to recollect the form master's lessons in the Odyssey or the Bacchæ, and then to view modern Free-masons celebrating the Mystic Death and Resurrection of Hiram Abiff, the analogy is complete, for neither the master nor the Masons have the remotest notion of what they are doing. Both persevere in strange and mysterious actions from inveterate conservatism.

Meyrick was a lover of antiquity and a special lover of survivals, but he could never see that the round of Greek syntax, and Latin prose, of Elegiacs and verbs in [Greek: mi], with the mystery of the Oratio obliqua and the Optative, was one of the most strange and picturesque survivals of modern life. It is to be noted, by the way, that the very meaning of the word "scholar" has been radically changed. Thus a well-known authority points out that "Melancholy" Burton had no "scholarship" in the real sense of the word; he merely used his vast knowledge of ancient and modern literature to make one of the most entertaining and curious books that the world possesses. True "scholarship," in the modern sense, is to be sought for not in the Jacobean translators of the Bible, but in the Victorian revisers. The former made the greatest of English books out of their Hebrew and Greek originals; but the latter understood the force of the aorist. It is curious to reflect that "scholar" once meant a man of literary taste and knowledge.

Meyrick never mastered these distinctions, or, if he did so in later years, he never confessed to his enlightenment, but went on railing at the meeting-house, which, he still maintained, did pretend to be a cathedral. He has been heard to wonder why a certain Dean, who had pointed out the vast improvements that had been effected by the Revisers, did not employ a few young art students from Kensington to correct the infamous drawing of the fourteenth-century glass in his cathedral. He was incorrigible; he was always incorrigible, and thus, in his boyhood, on the dark November evening, he meditated the murder of his good master and uncle--for at least a quarter of an hour.

His father, he remembered, had always spoken of Gothic architecture as the most wonderful and beautiful thing in the world: a thing to be studied and loved and reverenced. His father had never so much as mentioned rocker, much less had he preached it as the one way by which an English boy must be saved. Hence, Ambrose maintained inwardly that his visit to Selden Abbey was deserving of reward rather than punishment, and he resented bitterly, the savage injustice (as he thought it) of his caning.

III

Yet Mr. Horbury had been right in one matter, if not in all. That evening was a turning-point in Meyrick's life. He had felt the utmost rage of the enemy, as it were, and he determined that he would be a funk no longer. He would not degenerate into the state of little Phipps, who had been bullied and "rockered" and beaten into such a deplorable condition that he fainted dead away while the Headmaster was operating on him for "systematic and deliberate lying." Phipps not only fainted, but, being fundamentally sensible, as Dr. Johnson expressed it, showed a strong disinclination to return to consciousness and the precious balms of the "dear old Head." Chesson was rather frightened, and the school doctor, who had his living to get, said, somewhat dryly, that he thought the lad had better go home for a week or two.

So Phipps went home in a state which made his mother cry bitterly and his father wonder whether the Public School system was not over-praised. But the old family doctor went about raging and swearing at the "scoundrels" who had reduced a child of twelve to a nervous wreck, with "neurasthenia cerebralis" well on its way. But Dr. Walford had got his education in some trumpery little academy, and did not understand or value the ethos of the great Public Schools.

Now, Ambrose Meyrick had marked the career of wretched Phipps with concern and pity. The miserable little creature had been brought by careful handling from masters and boys to such a pitch of neurotic perfection that it was only necessary to tap him smartly on the back or on the arm, and he would instantly burst into tears. Whenever anyone asked him the simplest question he suspected a cruel trap of some sort, and lied and equivocated and shuffled with a pitiable lack of skill. Though he was pitched by the heels into mucker about three times a week, that he might acquire the useful art of natation, he still seemed to grow dirtier and dirtier. His school books were torn to bits, his exercises made into darts; he had impositions for losing books and canings for not doing his work, and he lied and cried all the more.

Meyrick had never got to this depth. He was a sturdy boy, and Phipps had always been a weakly little animal; but, as he walked from the study to the schoolroom after his thrashing, he felt that he had been in some danger of descending on that sad way. He finally resolved that he would never tread it, and so he walked past the baize-lined doors into the room where the other boys were at work on prep, with an air of unconcern which was not in the least assumed.

Mr. Horbury was a man of considerable private means and did not care to be bothered with the troubles and responsibilities of a big House. But there was room and to spare in the Old Grange, so he took three boys besides his nephew. These three were waiting with a grin of anticipation, since the nature of Meyrick's interview with "old Horbury" was not dubious. But Ambrose strolled in with a "Hallo, you fellows!" and sat down in his place as if nothing had happened. This was intolerable.

"I say, Meyrick," began Pelly, a beefy boy with a red face, "you have been blubbing! Feel like writing home about it? Oh! I forgot. This is your home, isn't it? How many cuts? I didn't hear you howl."

The boy took no notice. He was getting out his books as if no one had spoken.

"Can't you answer?" went on the beefy one. "How many cuts, you young sneak?"

"Go to hell!"

The whole three stared aghast for a moment; they thought Meyrick must have gone mad. Only one, Bates the observant, began to chuckle quietly to himself, for he did not like Pelly. He who was always beefy became beefier; his eyes bulged out with fury.

"I'll give it you," he said and made for Ambrose, who was turning over the leaves of the Latin dictionary. Ambrose did not wait for the assault; he rose also and met Pelly half-way with a furious blow, well planted on the nose. Pelly took a back somersault and fell with a crash to the floor, where he lay for a moment half stunned. He rose staggering and looked about him with a pathetic, bewildered air; for, indeed, a great part of his little world had crumbled about his ears. He stood in the middle of the room, wondering what it meant, whether it was true indeed that Meyrick was no longer of any use for a little quiet fun. A horrible and incredible transmutation had, apparently, been effected in the funk of old. Pelly gazed wildly about him as he tried to staunch the blood that poured over his mouth.

"Foul blow!" ventured Rawson, a lean lad who liked to twist the arms of very little boys till they shrieked for mercy. The full inwardness of the incident had not penetrated to his brain; he saw without believing, in the manner of the materialist who denies the marvellous even when it is before his eyes.

"Foul blow, young Meyrick!"

The quiet student had gone back to his place and was again handling his dictionary. It was a hard, compact volume, rebound in strong boards, and the edge of these boards caught the unfortunate Rawson full across the eyes with extraordinary force. He put his face in his hands and blubbered quietly and dismally, rocking to and fro in his seat, hardly hearing the fluent stream of curses with which the quiet student inquired whether the blow he had just had was good enough for him.

Meyrick picked up his dictionary with a volley of remarks which would have done credit to an old-fashioned stage-manager at the last dress rehearsal before production.

"Hark at him," said Pelly feebly, almost reverently. "Hark at him." But poor Rawson, rocking to and fro, his head between his hands, went on blubbering softly and spoke no word.

Meyrick had never been an unobservant lad; he had simply made a discovery that evening that in Rome certain Roman customs must be adopted. The wise Bates went on doing his copy of Latin verse, chuckling gently to himself. Bates was a cynic. He despised all the customs and manners of the place most heartily and took the most curious care to observe them. He might have been the inventor and patentee of rocker, if one judged him by the fervour with which he played it. He entered his name for every possible event at the sports, and jumped the jumps and threw the hammer and ran the races as if his life depended on it. Once Mr. Horbury had accidentally over-head Bates saying something about "the honour of the House" which went to his heart. As for cricket, Bates played as if his sole ambition was to become a first-class professional. And he chuckled as he did his Latin verses, which he wrote (to the awe of other boys) "as if he were writing a letter"--that is, without making a rough copy. For Bates had got the "hang" of the whole system from rocker to Latin verse, and his copies were much admired. He grinned that evening, partly at the transmutation of Meyrick and partly at the line he was jotting down:

"Mira loquor, coelo resonans vox funditur alto."

In after life he jotted down a couple of novels which sold, as the journalists said, "like hot cakes." Meyrick went to see him soon after the first novel had gone into its thirtieth thousand, and Bates was reading "appreciations" and fingering a cheque and chuckling.

"Mira loquor, populo, resonans, cheque funditur alto," he said. "I know what schoolmasters and boys and the public want, and I take care they get it--sale espèce de sacrés cochons de N. de D.!"

The rest of prep. went off quite quietly. Pelly was slowly recovering from the shock that he had received and began to meditate revenge. Meyrick had got him unawares, he reflected. It was merely an accident, and he resolved to challenge Meyrick to fight and give him back the worst licking he had ever had in his life. He was beefy, but a bold fellow. Rawson, who was really a cruel coward and a sneak, had made up his mind that he wanted no more, and from time to time cast meek and propitiatory glances in Meyrick's direction.

At half-past nine they all went into their dining-room for bread and cheese and beer. At a quarter to ten Mr. Horbury appeared in cap and gown and read a chapter from St. Paul's Epistle to the Romans, with one or two singularly maundering and unhappy prayers. He stopped the boys as they were going up to their rooms.

"What's this, Pelly?" he said. "Your nose is all swollen. It's been bleeding, too, I see. What have you been doing to yourself? And you, Rawson, how do you account for your eyes being black? What's the meaning of all this?"

"Please, Sir, there was a very stiff bully down at rocker this afternoon, and Rawson and I got tokered badly."

"Were you in the bully, Bates?"

"No, Sir; I've been outside since the beginning of the term. But all the fellows were playing up tremendously, and I saw Rawson and Pelly had been touched when we were changing."

"Ah! I see. I'm very glad to find the House plays up so well. As for you, Bates, I hear you're the best outside for your age that we've ever had. Good night."

The three said "Thank you, Sir," as if their dearest wish had been gratified, and the master could have sworn that Bates flushed with pleasure at his word of praise. But the fact was that Bates had "suggested" the flush by a cunning arrangement of his features.

The boys vanished and Mr. Horbury returned to his desk. He was editing a selection called "English Literature for Lower Forms." He began to read from the slips that he had prepared:

> *"So all day long the noise of battle roll'd*
> *Among the mountains by the winter sea;*
> *Until King Arthur's table, man by man,*
> *Had fallen in Lyonnesse----"*

He stopped and set a figure by the last word, and then, on a blank slip, with a corresponding letter, he repeated the figure and wrote the note:

> *Lyonnesse--the Sicilly Isles.*

Then he took a third slip and wrote the question:

> *Give the ancient name of the Sicilly Isles.*

These serious labours employed him till twelve o'clock. He put the materials of his book away as the clock struck, and solemnly mixed himself his nightly glass of whisky and soda--in the daytime he never touched spirits--and bit the one cigar which he smoked in the twenty-four hours. The stings of the Head's sherry and of his conversation no longer burned within him; time and work and the bite of the cane in Meyrick's flesh had soothed his soul, and he set himself to dream, leaning back in his arm-chair, watching the cheerful fire.

He was thinking of what he would do when he succeeded to the Headmastership. Already there were rumours that Chesson had refused the Bishopric of St. Dubric's in order that he might be free to accept Dorchester, which, in the nature of things, must soon be vacant. Horbury had no doubt that the Headmastership would be his; he had influential friends who assured him that the trustees would not hesitate for an instant. Then he would show the world what an English Public School could be made. In five years, he calculated, he would double the numbers. He saw the coming importance of the modern side, and especially of science. Personally, he detested "stinks," but he knew what an effect he would produce with a great laboratory fitted with the very best appliances and directed by a highly qualified master. Then, again, an elaborate gymnasium must be built; there must be an engineer's shop, too, and a carpenter's as well. And people were beginning to complain that a Public School Education was of no use in the City. There must be a business master, an expert from the Stock Exchange who would see that this reproach was removed. Then he considered that a large number of the boys belonged to the land-owning class. Why should a country gentleman be at the mercy of his agent, forced for lack of technical knowledge to accept statements which he could not check? It was clear that the management of land and great estates must have its part in the scheme; and, again, the best-known of the Crammers must be bought on his own terms, so that the boys who wished to get into the Army or the Civil Service would be practically compelled to come to Lupton. Already he saw paragraphs in the Guardian and The Times--in all the papers--paragraphs which mentioned the fact that ninety-five per cent of the successful candidates for the Indian Civil Service had received their education at the foundation of "stout old Martin Rolle." Meanwhile, in all this flood of novelty, the old traditions should be maintained with more vigour than ever. The classics should be taught as they never had been taught. Every one of the masters on this side should be in the highest honours and, if possible, he would get famous men for the work--they should not merely be good, but also notorious scholars. Gee, the famous explorer in Crete, who had made an enormous mark in regions widely removed from the scholastic world by his wonderful book, Dædalus; or, The Secret of the Labyrinth, must come to Lupton at any price; and Maynard, who had discovered some most important Greek manuscripts in Egypt, he must have a form, too. Then there was Rendell, who had done so well with his Thucydides, and Davies, author of The Olive of Athene, a daring but most brilliant book which promised to upset the whole established theory of mythology--he would have such a staff as no school had ever dreamed of. "We shall have no difficulty about paying them," thought Horbury; "our numbers will go up by leaps and bounds, and the fees shall be five hundred pounds a year--and such terms will do us more good than anything."

He went into minute detail. He must take expert advice as to the advisability of the school farming on its own account, and so supplying the boys with meat, milk, bread, butter and vegetables at first cost. He believed it could be done; he would get a Scotch farmer from the Lowlands and make him superintendent at a handsome salary and with a share in the profits. There would be the splendid advertisement of "the whole dietary of the school supplied from the School Farms, under the supervision of Mr. David Anderson, formerly of Haddanneuk, the largest tenancy in the Duke of Ayr's estates." The food would be better and cheaper, too; but there would be no luxury. The "Spartan" card was always worth playing; one must strike the note of plain living in a luxurious age; there must be no losing of the old Public School severity. On the other hand, the boy's hands should be free to go into their own pockets; there should be no restraint here. If a boy chose to bring in Dindonneau aux truffes or Pieds de mouton à la Ste Menehould to help out his tea, that was his look-out. Why should not the school grant a concession to some big London firm, who would pay handsomely for the privilege of supplying the hungry lads with every kind of expensive dainty? The sum could be justly made a large one, as any competing shop could be promptly put out of bounds with reason or without it. On one side, confiserie; at the other counter, charcuterie; enormous prices could be charged to the wealthy boys of whom the school would be composed. Yet, on the other hand, the distinguished visitor--judge, bishop, peer or what not--would lunch at the Headmaster's house and eat the boys' dinner and go away saying it was quite the plainest and very many times the best meal he had ever tasted. There would be well-hung saddle of mutton, roasted and not baked; floury potatoes and cauliflower; apple pudding with real English cheese, with an excellent glass of the school beer, an honest and delicious beverage made of malt and hops in the well-found school brewery. Horbury knew enough of modern eating and drinking to understand that such a meal would be a choice rarity to nine rich people out of ten; and yet it was "Spartan," utterly devoid of luxury and ostentation.

Again, he passed from detail and minutiæ into great Napoleonic regions. A thousand boys at £500 a year; that would be an income for the school of five hundred thousand pounds! The profits would be gigantic, immense. After paying large, even extravagant, prices to the staff, after all building expenses had been deducted, he hardly dared to think how vast a sum would accrue year by year to the Trustees. The vision began to assume such magnificence that it became oppressive; it put on the splendours and delights of the hashish dream, which are too great and too piercing for mortal hearts to bear. And yet it was no mirage; there was not a step that could not be demonstrated, shown to be based on hard; matter-of-fact business considerations. He tried to keep back his growing excitement, to argue with himself that he was dealing in visions, but the facts were too obstinate. He saw that it would be his part to work the same miracle in the scholastic world as the great American storekeepers had operated in the world of retail trade. The principle was precisely the same: instead of a hundred small shops making comparatively modest and humdrum profits you had the vast emporium doing business on the gigantic scale with vastly diminished expenses and vastly increased rewards.

Here again was a hint. He had thought of America, and he knew that here was an inexhaustible gold mine, that no other scholastic prospector had even dreamed of. The rich American was notoriously hungry for everything that was English, from frock-coats to pedigrees. He had never thought of sending his son to an English Public School because he considered the system hopelessly behind the times. But the new translated Lupton would be to other Public Schools as a New York hotel of the latest fashion is to a village beer-shop. And yet the young millionaire would grow up in the company of the sons of the English gentlemen, imbibing the unique culture of English life, while at the same time he enjoyed all the advantages of modern ideas, modern science and modern business training. Land was still comparatively cheap at Lupton; the school must buy it quietly, indirectly, by degrees, and then pile after pile of vast buildings rose before his eyes. He saw the sons of the rich drawn from all the ends of the world to the Great School, there to learn the secret of the Anglo-Saxons.

Chesson was mistaken in that idea of his, which he thought daring and original, of establishing a distinct Jewish House where the food should be "Kosher." The rich Jew who desired to send his son to an English Public School was, in nine cases out of ten, anxious to do so precisely because he wanted to sink his son's connection with Jewry in oblivion. He had heard Chesson talk of "our Christian duty to the seed of Israel" in this connection. The man was clearly a fool. No, the more Jews the better, but no Jewish House. And no Puseyism either: broad, earnest religious teaching, with a leaning to moderate Anglicanism, should be the faith of Lupton. As to this Chesson was, certainly, sound enough. He had always made a firm stand against ecclesiasticism in any form. Horbury knew the average English parent of the wealthier classes thoroughly; he knew that, though he generally called himself a Churchman, he was quite content to have his sons prepared for confirmation by a confessed Agnostic. Certainly this liberty must not be narrowed when Lupton became cosmopolitan. "We will retain all the dignified associations which belong to the Established Church," he said to himself, "and at the same time we shall be utterly free from the taint of over-emphasising dogmatic teaching." He had a sudden brilliant idea. Everybody in Church circles was saying that the English bishops were terribly overworked, that it was impossible for the most strenuous men with the best intentions to supervise effectually the huge dioceses that had descended from the sparsely populated England of the Middle Ages. Everywhere there was a demand for suffragans and more suffragans. In the last week's Guardian there were three letters on the subject, one from a clergyman in their own diocese. The Bishop had been attacked by some rabid ritualistic person, who had pointed out that nine out of every ten parishes had not so much as seen the colour of his hood ever since his appointment ten years before. The Archdeacon of Melby had replied in a capital letter, scathing and yet humorous. Horbury turned to the paper on the table beside his chair and looked up the letter. "In the first place," wrote the Archdeacon, "your correspondent does not seem to have realised that the ethoes of the Diocese of Melby is not identical with that of sacerdotalism. The sturdy folk of the Midlands have not yet, I am thankful to say, forgotten the lessons of our great Reformation. They have no wish to see a revival of the purely mechanical religion of the Middle Ages--of the system of a sacrificing priesthood and of sacraments efficacious ex opere operato. Hence they do not regard the episcopate quite in the same light as your correspondent 'Senex,' who, it seems to me, looks upon a bishop as a sort of Christianised 'medicine-man,' endowed with certain mysterious thaumaturgic powers which have descended to him by an (imaginary) spiritual succession. This was not the view of Hooker, nor, I venture to say, has it ever been the view of the really representative divines of the Established Church of England.

"Still," the Archdeacon went on, "it must be admitted that the present diocese of Melby is unwieldy and, it may be fairly said, unworkable."

Then there followed the humorous anecdote of Sir Boyle Roche and the Bird, and finally the Archdeacon emitted the prayer that God in His own good time would put it into the hearts of our rulers in Church and State to give their good Bishop an episcopal curate.

Horbury got up from his chair and paced up and down the study; his excitement was so great that he could keep quiet no longer. His cigar had gone out long ago, and he had barely sipped the whisky and soda. His eyes glittered with excitement. Circumstances seemed positively to be playing into his hands; the dice of the world were being loaded in his favour. He was like Bel Ami at his wedding. He almost began to believe in Providence.

For he was sure it could be managed. Here was a general feeling that no one man could do the work of the diocese. There must be a suffragan, and Lupton must give the new Bishop his title. No other town was possible. Dunham had certainly been a see in the eighth century, but it was now little more than a village and a village served by a miserable little branch line; whereas Lupton was on the great main track of the Midland system, with easy connections to every part of the country. The Archdeacon, who was also a peer, would undoubtedly become the first Bishop of Lupton, and he should be the titular chaplain of the Great School! "Chaplain! The Right Reverend Lord Selwyn, Lord Bishop of Lupton." Horbury gasped; it was too magnificent, too splendid. He knew Lord Selwyn quite well and had no doubt as to his acceptance. He was a poor man, and there would be no difficulty whatever in establishing a modus. The Archdeacon was just the man for the place. He was no pedantic theologian, but a broad, liberal-minded man of the world. Horbury remembered, almost with ecstasy, that he had lectured all over the United States with immense success. The American Press had been enthusiastic, and the First Congregational Church of Chicago had implored Selwyn to accept its call, preach what he liked and pocket an honorarium of twenty-five thousand dollars a year. And, on the other hand, what could the most orthodox desire safer than a chaplain who was not only a bishop, but a peer of the realm? Wonderful! Here were the three birds--Liberalism, Orthodoxy and Reverence for the House of Lords--caught safe and secure in this one net.

The games? They should be maintained in all their glory, rather on an infinitely more splendid scale. Cricket and sticker (the Lupton hockey), rackets and fives, should be all encouraged; and more, Lupton should be the only school to possess a tennis court. The noble jeu de paume, the game of kings, the most aristocratic of all sports, should have a worthy home at Lupton. They would train champions; they would have both French and English markers skilled in the latest developments of the chemin de fer service. "Better than half a yard, I think," said Horbury to himself; "they will have to do their best to beat that."

But he placed most reliance on rocker. This was the Lupton football, a variant as distinctive in its way as the Eton Wall Game. People have thought that the name is a sort of portmanteau word, a combination of Rugger and Soccer; but in reality the title was derived from the field where the game used to be played in old days by the townsfolk. As in many other places, football at Lupton had been originally an excuse for a faction-fight between two parishes in the town--St. Michael's and St. Paul's-in-the-Fields. Every year, on Shrove Tuesday, the townsfolk, young and old, had proceeded to the Town Field and had fought out their differences with considerable violence. The field was broken land: a deep, sluggish stream crossed one angle of it, and in the middle there were quarries and jagged limestone rocks. Hence football was called in the town "playing rocks," for, indeed, it was considered an excellent point of play to hurl a man over the edge of the quarry on to the rocks beneath, and so late as 1830 a certain Jonas Simpson of St. Michael's had his spine broken in this way. However, as a boy from St. Paul's was drowned in the Wand the same day, the game was always reckoned a draw. It was from the peculiarities of this old English sport that the school had constructed its game. The Town Field had, of course, long been stolen from the townsfolk and built over; but the boys had, curiously enough, perpetuated the tradition of its peculiarities in a kind of football ritual. For, besides the two goals, one part of the field was marked by a line of low white posts: these indicated the course of a non-existent Wand brook, and in the line of these posts it was lawful to catch an opponent by the throat and choke him till he turned black in the face--the best substitute for drowning that the revisers of the game could imagine. Again: about the centre of the field two taller posts indicated the position of the quarries, and between these you might be hit or kicked full in the stomach without the smallest ground of complaint: the stroke being a milder version of the old fall on the rocks.

There were many other like amenities in rocker; and Horbury maintained it was by far the manliest variant of the game. For this pleasing sport he now designed a world-wide fame. Rocker should be played wherever the English flag floated: east and west, north and south; from Hong Kong to British Columbia; in Canada and New Zealand there should be the Temenoi of this great rite; and the traveller seeing the mystic enclosure--the two goals, the line of little posts marking "brooks" and the two poles indicating "quarries"--should know English soil as surely as by the Union Jack. The technical terms of rocker should become a part of the great Anglo-Saxon inheritance; the whole world should hear of "bully-downs" and "tokering," of "outsides" and "rammers." It would require working, but it was to be done: articles in the magazines and in the Press; perhaps a story of school life, a new Tom Brown must be written. The Midlands and the North must be shown that there was money in it, and the rest would be easy.

One thing troubled Horbury. His mind was full of the new and splendid buildings that were to be erected, but he was aware that antiquity still counted for something, and unfortunately Lupton could show very little that was really antique. Forty years before, Stanley, the first reforming Headmaster, had pulled down the old High School. There were prints of it: it was a half-timbered, fifteenth-century building, with a wavering roof-line and an overhanging upper story; there were dim, leaded windows and a grey arched porch--an ugly old barn, Stanley called it. Scott was called in and built the present High School, a splendid hall in red brick: French thirteenth-century, with Venetian detail; it was much admired. But Horbury was sorry that the old school had been destroyed; he saw for the first time that it might have been made a valuable attraction. Then again, Dowsing, who succeeded Stanley, had knocked the cloisters all to bits; there was only one side of the quadrangle left, and this had been boarded up and used as a gardeners' shed. Horbury did not know what to say of the destruction of the Cross that used to stand in the centre of the quad. No doubt Dowsing was right in thinking it superstitious; still, it might have been left as a curiosity and shown to visitors, just as the instruments of bygone cruelty--the rack and the Iron Maid--are preserved and exhibited to wondering sightseers. There was no real danger of any superstitious adoration of the Cross; it was, as a matter of fact, as harmless as the axe and block at the Tower of London; Dowsing had ruined what might have been an important asset in the exploitation of the school.

Still, perhaps the loss was not altogether irreparable. High School was gone and could not be recovered; but the cloisters might be restored and the Cross, too. Horbury knew that the monument in front of Charing Cross Railway Station was considered by many to be a genuine antique: why not get a good man to build them a Cross? Not like the old one, of course; that "Fair Roode with our Deare Ladie Saint Marie and Saint John," and, below, the stories of the blissful Saints and Angels--that would never do. But a vague, Gothic erection, with plenty of kings and queens, imaginary benefactors of the school, and a small cast-iron cross at the top: that could give no offence to anybody, and might pass with nine people out of ten as a genuine remnant of the Middle Ages. It could be made of soft stone and allowed to weather for a few years; then a coat of invisible anti-corrosive fluid would preserve carvings and imagery that would already appear venerable in decay. There was no need to make any precise statements: parents and the public might be allowed to draw their own conclusions.

Horbury was neglecting nothing. He was building up a great scheme in his mind, and to him it seemed that every detail was worth attending to, while at the same time he did not lose sight of the whole effect. He believed in finish: there must be no rough edges. It seemed to him that a school legend must be invented. The real history was not quite what he wanted, though it might work in with a more decorative account of Lupton's origins. One might use the Textus Receptus of Martin Rolle's Foundation--the bequest of land c. 1430 to build and maintain a school where a hundred boys should be taught grammar, and ten poor scholars and six priests should pray for the Founder's soul. This was well enough, but one might hint that Martin Rolle really refounded and re-endowed a school of Saxon origin, probably established by King Alfred himself in Luppa's Tun. Then, again, who could show that Shakespeare had not visited Lupton? His famous schoolboy, "creeping like snail unwillingly to school," might very possibly have been observed by the poet as he strolled by the banks of the Wand. Many famous men might have received their education at Lupton; it would not be difficult to make a plausible list of such. It must be done carefully and cautiously, with such phrases as "it has always been a tradition at Lupton that Sir Walter Raleigh received part of his education at the school"; or, again, "an earlier generation of Luptonians remembered the initials 'W. S. S. on A.' cut deeply in the mantel of old High School, now, unfortunately, demolished." Antiquarians would laugh? Possibly; but who cared about antiquarians? For the average man "Charing" was derived from "chère reine," and he loved to have it so, and Horbury intended to appeal to the average man. Though he was a schoolmaster he was no recluse, and he had marked the ways of the world from his quiet study in Lupton; hence he understood the immense value of a grain of quackery in all schemes which are meant to appeal to mortals. It was a deadly mistake to suppose that anything which was all quackery would be a success--a permanent success, at all events; it was a deadlier mistake still to suppose that anything quite devoid of quackery could pay handsomely. The average English palate would shudder at the flavour of aioli, but it would be charmed by the insertion of that petit point d'ail which turned mere goodness into triumph and laurelled perfection. And there was no need to mention the word "garlic" before the guests. Lupton was not going to be all garlic: it was to be infinitely the best scholastic dish that had ever been served--the ingredients should be unsurpassed and unsurpassable. But--King Alfred's foundation of a school at Luppa's Tun, and that "W. S. S. on A." cut deeply on the mantel of the vanished High School--these and legends like unto them, these would be the last touch, le petit point d'ail.

It was a great scheme, wonderful and glorious; and the most amazing thing about it was that it was certain to be realised. There was not a flaw from start to finish. The Trustees were certain to appoint him--he had that from a sure quarter--and it was but a question of a year or two, perhaps only of a month or two, before all this great and golden vision should be converted into hard and tangible fact. He drank off his glass of whisky and soda; it had become flat and brackish, but to him it was nectar, since it was flavoured with ecstasy.

He frowned suddenly as he went upstairs to his room. An unpleasant recollection had intruded for a moment on his amazing fantasy; but he dismissed the thought as soon as it arose. That was all over, there could be no possibility of trouble from that direction; and so, his mind filled with images, he fell asleep and saw Lupton as the centre of the whole world, like Jerusalem in the ancient maps.

A student of the deep things of mysticism has detected a curious element of comedy in the management of human concerns; and there certainly seems a touch of humour in the fact that on this very night, while Horbury was building the splendid Lupton of the future, the palace of his thought and his life was shattered for ever into bitter dust and nothingness. But so it was. The Dread Arrest had been solemnly recognised, and that wretched canonry at Wareham was irrevocably pronounced for doom. Fantastic were the elements of forces that had gone to the ordering of this great sentence: raw corn spirit in the guise of sherry, the impertinence (or what seemed such) of an elderly clergyman, a boiled leg of mutton, a troublesome and disobedient boy, and--another person.

II

I

He was standing in a wild, bare country. Something about it seemed vaguely familiar: the land rose and fell in dull and weary undulations, in a vast circle of dun ploughland and grey meadow, bounded by a dim horizon without promise or hope, dreary as a prison wall. The infinite melancholy of an autumn evening brooded heavily over all the world, and the sky was hidden by livid clouds.

It all brought back to him some far-off memory, and yet he knew that he gazed on that sad plain for the first time. There was a deep and heavy silence over all; a silence unbroken by so much as the fluttering of a leaf. The trees seemed of a strange shape, and strange were the stunted thorns dotted about the broken field in which he stood. A little path at his feet, bordered by the thorn bushes, wandered away to the left into the dim twilight; it had about it some indefinable air of mystery, as if it must lead one down into a mystic region where all earthly things are forgotten and lost for ever.

He sat down beneath the bare, twisted boughs of a great tree and watched the dreary land grow darker and yet darker; he wondered, half-consciously, where he was and how he had come to that place, remembering, faintly, tales of like adventure. A man passed by a familiar wall one day, and opening a door before unnoticed, found himself in a new world of unsurmised and marvellous experiences. Another man shot an arrow farther than any of his friends and became the husband of the fairy. Yet--this was not fairyland; these were rather the sad fields and unhappy graves of the underworld than the abode of endless pleasures and undying delights. And yet in all that he saw there was the promise of great wonder.

Only one thing was clear to him. He knew that he was Ambrose, that he had been driven from great and unspeakable joys into miserable exile and banishment. He had come from a far, far place by a hidden way, and darkness had closed about him, and bitter drink and deadly meat were given him, and all gladness was hidden from him. This was all he could remember; and now he was astray, he knew not how or why, in this wild, sad land, and the night descended dark upon him.

Suddenly there was, as it were, a cry far away in the shadowy silence, and the thorn bushes began to rustle before a shrilling wind that rose as the night came down. At this summons the heavy clouds broke up and dispersed, fleeting across the sky, and the pure heaven appeared with the last rose flush of the sunset dying from it, and there shone the silver light of the evening star. Ambrose's heart was drawn up to this light as he gazed: he saw that the star grew greater and greater; it advanced towards him through the air; its beams pierced to his soul as if they were the sound of a silver trumpet. An ocean of white splendour flowed over him: he dwelt within the star.

It was but for a moment; he was still sitting beneath the tree of the twisted branches. But the sky was now clear and filled with a great peace; the wind had fallen and a more happy light shone on the great plain. Ambrose was thirsty, and then he saw that beside the tree there was a well, half hidden by the arching roots that rose above it. The water was still and shining, as though it were a mirror of black marble, and marking the brim was a great stone on which were cut the letters:

"FONS VITAE IMMORTALIS."

He rose and, bending over the well, put down his lips to drink, and his soul and body were filled as with a flood of joy. Now he knew that all his days of exile he had borne with pain and grief a heavy, weary body. There had been dolours in every limb and achings in every bone; his feet had dragged upon the ground, slowly, wearily, as the feet of those who go in chains. But dim, broken spectres, miserable shapes and crooked images of the world had his eyes seen; for they were eyes bleared with sickness, darkened by the approach of death. Now, indeed, he clearly beheld the shining vision of things immortal. He drank great draughts of the dark, glittering water, drinking, it seemed, the light of the reflected stars; and he was filled with life. Every sinew, every muscle, every particle of the deadly flesh shuddered and quickened in the communion of that well-water. The nerves and veins rejoiced together; all his being leapt with gladness, and as one finger touched another, as he still bent over the well, a spasm of exquisite pleasure quivered and thrilled through his body. His heart throbbed with bliss that was unendurable; sense and intellect and soul and spirit were, as it were, sublimed into one white flame of delight. And all the while it was known to him that these were but the least of the least of the pleasures of the kingdom, but the overrunnings and base tricklings of the great supernal cup. He saw, without amazement, that, though the sun had set, the sky now began to flush and redden as if with the northern light. It was no longer the evening, no longer the time of the procession of the dusky night. The darkness doubtless had passed away in mortal hours while for an infinite moment he tasted immortal drink; and perhaps one drop of that water was endless life. But now it was the preparation for the day. He heard the words:

> *"Dies venit, dies Tua*
> *In qua reflorent omnia."*

They were uttered within his heart, and he saw that all was being made ready for a great festival. Over everything there was a hush of expectation; and as he gazed he knew that he was no longer in that weary land of dun ploughland and grey meadow, of the wild, bare trees and strange stunted thorn bushes. He was on a hillside, lying on the verge of a great wood; beneath, in the valley, a brook sang faintly under the leaves of the silvery willows; and beyond, far in the east, a vast wall of rounded mountain rose serene towards the sky. All about him was the green world of the leaves: odours of the summer night, deep in the mystic heart of the wood, odours of many flowers, and the cool breath rising from the singing stream mingled in his nostrils. The world whitened to the dawn, and then, as the light grew clear, the rose clouds blossomed in the sky and, answering, the earth seemed to glitter with rose-red sparks and glints of flame. All the east became as a garden of roses, red flowers of living light shone over the mountain, and as the beams of the sun lit up the circle of the earth a bird's song began from a tree within the wood. Then were heard the modulations of a final and exultant ecstasy, the chant of liberation, a magistral In Exitu; there was the melody of rejoicing trills, of unwearied, glad reiterations of choirs ever aspiring, prophesying the coming of the great feast, singing the eternal antiphon.

As the song aspired into the heights, so there aspired suddenly before him the walls and pinnacles of a great church set upon a high hill. It was far off, and yet as though it were close at hand he saw all the delicate and wonderful imagery cut in its stones. The great door in the west was a miracle: every flower and leaf, every reed and fern, were clustered in the work of the capitals, and in the round arch above moulding within moulding showed all the beasts that God has made. He saw the rose-window, a maze of fretted tracery, the high lancets of the fair hall, the marvellous buttresses, set like angels about this holy house, whose pinnacles were as a place of many springing trees. And high above the vast, far-lifted vault of the roof rose up the spire, golden in the light. The bells were ringing for the feast; he heard from within the walls the roll and swell and triumph of the organ:

> *O pius o bonus o placidus sonus hymnus eorum.*

He knew not how he had taken his place in this great procession, how, surrounded by ministrants in white, he too bore his part in endless litanies. He knew not through what strange land they passed in their fervent, admirable order, following their banners and their symbols that glanced on high before them. But that land stood ever, it seemed, in a clear, still air, crowned with golden sunlight; and so there were those who bore great torches of wax, strangely and beautifully adorned with golden and vermilion ornaments. The delicate flame of these tapers burned steadily in the still sunlight, and the glittering silver censers as they rose and fell tossed a pale cloud into the air. They delayed, now and again, by wayside shrines, giving thanks for unutterable compassions, and, advancing anew, the blessed company surged onward, moving to its unknown goal in the far blue mountains that rose beyond the plain. There were faces and shapes of awful beauty about him; he saw those in whose eyes were the undying lamps of heaven, about whose heads the golden hair was as an aureole; and there were they that above the girded vesture of white wore dyed garments, and as they advanced around their feet there was the likeness of dim flames.

The great white array had vanished and he was alone. He was tracking a secret path that wound in and out through the thickets of a great forest. By solitary pools of still water, by great oaks, worlds of green leaves, by fountains and streams of water, by the bubbling, mossy sources of the brooks he followed this hidden way, now climbing and now descending, but still mounting upward, still passing, as he knew, farther and farther from all the habitations of men. Through the green boughs now he saw the shining sea-water; he saw the land of the old saints, all the divisions of the land that men had given to them for God; he saw their churches, and it seemed as if he could hear, very faintly, the noise of the ringing of their holy bells. Then, at last, when he had crossed the Old Road, and had gone by the Lightning-struck Land and the Fisherman's Well, he found, between the forest and the mountain, a very ancient and little chapel; and now he heard the bell of the saint ringing clearly and so sweetly that it was as it were the singing of the angels. Within it was very dark and there was silence. He knelt and saw scarcely that the chapel was divided into two parts by a screen that rose up to the round roof. There was a glinting of shapes as if golden figures were painted on this screen, and through the joinings of its beams there streamed out thin needles of white splendour as if within there was a light greater than that of the sun at noonday. And the flesh began to tremble, for all the place was filled with the odours of Paradise, and he heard the ringing of the Holy Bell and the voices of the choir that out-sang the Fairy Birds of Rhiannon, crying and proclaiming:

"Glory and praise to the Conqueror of Death: to the Fountain of Life Unending."

Nine times they sang this anthem, and then the whole place was filled with blinding light. For a door in the screen had been opened, and there came forth an old man, all in shining white, on whose head was a gold crown. Before him went one who rang the bell; on each side there were young men with torches; and in his hands he bore the Mystery of Mysteries wrapped about in veils of gold and of all colours, so that it might not be discerned; and so he passed before the screen, and the light of heaven burst forth from that which he held. Then he entered in again by a door that was on the other side, and the Holy Things were hidden.

And Ambrose heard from within an awful voice and the words:

Woe and great sorrow are on him, for he hath looked unworthily into the Tremendous Mysteries, and on the Secret Glory which is hidden from the Holy Angels.

II

"Poetry is the only possible way of saying anything that is worth saying at all." This was an axiom that, in later years, Ambrose Meyrick's friends were forced to hear at frequent intervals. He would go on to say that he used the term poetry in its most liberal sense, including in it all mystic or symbolic prose, all painting and statuary that was worthy to be called art, all great architecture, and all true music. He meant, it is to be presumed, that the mysteries can only be conveyed by symbols; unfortunately, however, he did not always make it quite clear that this was the proposition that he intended to utter, and thus offence was sometimes given--as, for example, to the scientific gentleman who had been brought to Meyrick's rooms and went away early, wondering audibly and sarcastically whether "your clever friend" wanted to metrify biology and set Euclid to Bach's Organ Fugues.

However, the Great Axiom (as he called it) was the justification that he put forward in defence of the notes on which the previous section is based.

"Of course," he would say, "the symbolism is inadequate; but that is the defect of speech of any kind when you have once ventured beyond the multiplication table and the jargon of the Stock Exchange. Inadequacy of expression is merely a minor part of the great tragedy of humanity. Only an ass thinks that he has succeeded in uttering the perfect content of his thought without either excess or defect."

"Then, again," he might go on, "the symbolism would very likely be misleading to a great many people; but what is one to do? I believe many good people find Turner mad and Dickens tiresome. And if the great sometimes fail, what hope is there for the little? We cannot all be--well--popular novelists of the day."

Of course, the notes in question were made many years after the event they commemorate; they were the man's translation of all the wonderful and inexpressible emotions of the boy; and, as Meyrick puts it, many "words" (or symbols) are used in them which were unknown to the lad of fifteen.

"Nevertheless," he said, "they are the best words that I can find."

As has been said, the Old Grange was a large, roomy house; a space could easily have been found for half a dozen more boys if the High Usher had cared to be bothered with them. As it was, it was a favour to be at Horbury's, and there was usually some personal reason for admission. Pelly, for example, was the son of an old friend; Bates was a distant cousin; and Rawson's father was the master of a small Grammar School in the north with which certain ancestral Horburys were somehow connected. The Old Grange was a fine large Caroline house; it had a grave front of red brick, mellowed with age, tier upon tier of tall, narrow windows, flush with the walls, and a high-pitched, red-tiled roof. Above the front door was a rich and curious wooden pent-house, deeply carven; and within there was plenty of excellent panelling, and some good mantelpieces, added, it would seem, somewhere about the Adam period. Horbury had seen its solid and comfortable merits and had bought the freehold years before at a great bargain. The school was increasing rapidly even in those days, and he knew that before long more houses would be required. If he left Lupton he would be able to let the Old Grange easily--he might almost put it up for auction--and the rent would represent a return of fifty per cent on his investment. Many of the rooms were large; of a size out of all proportion to the boys' needs, and at a very trifling expense partitions might be made and the nine or ten available rooms be subdivided into studies for twenty or even twenty-five boys. Nature had gifted the High Usher with a careful, provident mind in all things, both great and small; and it is but fair to add that on his leaving Lupton for Wareham he found his anticipations more than justified. To this day Charles Horbury, his nephew, a high Government official, draws a comfortable income from his uncle's most prudent investment, and the house easily holds its twenty-five boys. Rainy, who took the place from Horbury, was an ingenious fellow and hit upon a capital plan for avoiding the expense of making new windows for some of the subdivided studies. After thoughtful consideration he caused the wooden partitions which were put up to stop short of the ceiling by four inches, and by this device the study with a window lighted the study that had none; and, as Rainy explained to some of the parents, a diffused light was really better for the eyes than a direct one.

In the old days, when Ambrose Meyrick was being made a man of, the four boys "rattled," as it were, in the big house. They were scattered about in odd corners, remote from each other, and it seemed from everybody else. Meyrick's room was the most isolated of any, but it was also the most comfortable in winter, since it was over the kitchen, to the extreme left of the house. This part, which was hidden from the road by the boughs of a great cedar, was an after-thought, a Georgian addition in grey brick, and rose only to two stories, and in the one furnished room out of the three or four over the kitchen and offices slept Ambrose. He wished his days could be as quiet and retired as his nights. He loved the shadows that were about his bed even on the brightest mornings in summer; for the cedar boughs were dense, and ivy had been allowed to creep about the panes of the window; so the light entered dim and green, filtered through the dark boughs and the ivy tendrils.

Here, then, after the hour of ten each night, he dwelt secure. Now and again Mr. Horbury would pay nocturnal surprise visits to see that all lights were out; but, happily, the stairs at the end of the passage, being old and badly fitted, gave out a succession of cracks like pistol shots if the softest foot was set on them. It was simple, therefore, on hearing the first of these reports, to extinguish the candle in the small secret lantern (held warily so that no gleam of light should appear from under the door) and to conceal the lantern under the bed-clothes. One wetted one's finger and pinched at the flame, so there was no smell of the expiring snuff, and the lantern slide was carefully drawn to guard against the possibility of suspicious grease-marks on the linen. It was perfect; and old Horbury's visits, which were rare enough, had no terrors for Ambrose.

So that night, while the venom of the cane still rankled in his body, though it had ceased to disturb his mind, instead of going to bed at once, according to the regulations, he sat for a while on his box seeking a clue in a maze of odd fancies and conceits. He took off his clothes and wrapped his aching body in the rug from the bed, and presently, blowing out the official paraffin lamp, he lit his candle, ready at the first warning creak on the stairs to douse the glim and leap between the sheets.

Odd enough were his first cogitations. He was thinking how very sorry he was to have hit Pelly that savage blow and to have endangered Rawson's eyesight by the hard boards of the dictionary! This was eccentric, for he had endured from those two young Apaches every extremity of unpleasantness for upwards of a couple of years. Pelly was not by any means an evil lad: he was stupid and beefy within and without, and the great Public School system was transmuting him, in the proper course and by the proper steps, into one of those Brave Average Boobies whom Meyrick used to rail against afterwards. Pelly, in all probability (his fortunes have not been traced), went into the Army and led the milder and more serious subalterns the devil's own life. In India he "lay doggo" with great success against some hill tribe armed with seventeenth-century muskets and rather barbarous knives; he seems to have been present at that "Conference of the Powers" described so brightly by Mr. Kipling. Promoted to a captaincy, he fought with conspicuous bravery in South Africa, winning the Victoria Cross for his rescue of a wounded private at the instant risk of his own life, and he finally led his troop into a snare set by an old farmer; a rabbit of average intelligence would have smelt and evaded it.

For Rawson one is sorry, but one cannot, in conscience, say much that is good, though he has been praised for his tact. He became domestic chaplain to the Bishop of Dorchester, whose daughter Emily he married.

But in those old days there was very little to choose between them, from Meyrick's point of view. Each had displayed a quite devilish ingenuity in the art of annoyance, in the whole cycle of jeers and sneers and "scores," as known to the schoolboy, and they were just proceeding to more active measures. Meyrick had borne it all meekly; he had returned kindly and sometimes quaint answers to the unceasing stream of remarks that were meant to wound his feelings, to make him look a fool before any boys that happened to be about. He had only countered with a mild: "What do you do that for, Pelly?" when the brave one smacked his head. "Because I hate sneaks and funks," Pelly had replied and Meyrick said no more. Rawson took a smaller size in victims when it was a question of physical torments; but he had invented a most offensive tale about Meyrick and had told it all over the school, where it was universally believed. In a word, the two had done their utmost to reduce him to a state of utter misery; and now he was sorry that he had punched the nose of one and bombarded the other with a dictionary!

The fact was that his forebearance had not been all cowardice; it is, indeed, doubtful whether he was in the real sense a coward at all. He went in fear, it is true, all his days, but what he feared was not the insult, but the intention, the malignancy of which the insult, or the blow, was the outward sign. The fear of a mad bull is quite distinct from the horror with which most people look upon a viper; it was the latter feeling which made Meyrick's life a burden to him. And again there was a more curious shade of feeling; and that was the intense hatred that he felt to the mere thought of "scoring" off an antagonist, of beating down the enemy. He was a much sharper lad than either Rawson or Pelly; he could have retorted again and again with crushing effect, but he held his tongue, for all such victories were detestable to him. And this odd sentiment governed all his actions and feelings; he disliked "going up" in form, he disliked winning a game, not through any acquired virtue, but by inherent nature. Poe would have understood Meyrick's feelings; but then the author of The Imp of the Perverse penetrated so deeply into the inmost secrets of humanity that Anglo-Saxon criticism has agreed in denouncing him as a wholly "inhuman" writer.

With Meyrick this mode of feeling had grown stronger by provocation; the more he was injured, the more he shrank from the thought of returning the injury. In a great measure the sentiment remained with him in later life. He would sally forth from his den in quest of fresh air on top of an omnibus and stroll peacefully back again rather than struggle for victory with the furious crowd. It was not so much that he disliked the physical contest: he was afraid of getting a seat! Quite naturally, he said that people who "pushed," in the metaphorical sense, always reminded him of the hungry little pigs fighting for the largest share of the wash; but he seemed to think that, whereas this course of action was natural in the little pigs, it was profoundly unnatural in the little men. But in his early boyhood he had carried this secret doctrine of his to its utmost limits; he had assumed, as it were, the rôle of the coward and the funk; he had, without any conscious religious motive certainly, but in obedience to an inward command, endeavoured to play the part of a Primitive Christian, of a religious, in a great Public School! Ama nesciri et pro nihilo æstimari. The maxim was certainly in his heart, though he had never heard it; but perhaps if he had searched the whole world over he could not have found a more impossible field for its exercise than this seminary, where the broad, liberal principles of Christianity were taught in a way that satisfied the Press, the public and the parents.

And he sat in his room and grieved over the fashion in which he had broken this discipline. Still, something had to be done: he was compelled to stay in this place, and he did not wish to be reduced to the imbecility of wretched little Phipps who had become at last more like a whimpering kitten with the mange than a human being. One had not the right to allow oneself to be made an idiot, so the principle had to be infringed--but externally only, never internally! Of that he was firmly resolved; and he felt secure in his recollection that there had been no anger in his heart. He resented the presence of Pelly and Rawson, certainly, but in the manner with which some people resent the presence of a cat, a mouse, or a black-beetle, as disagreeable objects which can't help being disagreeable objects. But his bashing of Pelly and his smashing of Rawson, his remarks (gathered from careful observation by the banks of the Lupton and Birmingham Canal); all this had been but the means to an end, the securing of peace and quiet for the future. He would not be murdered by this infernal Public School system either, after the fashion of Phipps--which was melancholy, or after the fashion of the rest--which was more melancholy still, since it is easier to recover from nervous breakdown than from suffusion of cant through the entire system, mental and spiritual. Utterly from his heart he abjured and renounced all the horrible shibboleths of the school, its sham enthusiasm, its "ethos," its "tone," its "loyal co-operation--masters and boys working together for the good of the whole school"--all its ridiculous fetish conventions and absurd observances, the joint contrivances of young fools and old knaves. But his resistance should be secret and not open, for a while; there should be no more "bashing" than was absolutely necessary.

And one thing he resolved upon--he would make all he could out of the place; he would work like a tiger and get all the Latin and Greek and French obtainable, in spite of the teaching and its imbecile pedantry. The school work must be done, so that trouble might be avoided, but here at night in his room he would really learn the languages they pottered over in form, wasting half their time in writing sham Ciceronian prose which would have made Cicero sick, and verse evil enough to cause Virgil to vomit. Then there was French, taught chiefly out of pompous eighteenth-century fooleries, with lists of irregular verbs to learn and Babylonish nonsense about the past participle, and many other rotten formulas and rules, giving to the whole tongue the air of a tiresome puzzle which had been dug up out of a prehistoric grave. This was not the French that he wanted; still, he could write out irregular verbs by day and learn the language at night. He wondered whether unhappy French boys had to learn English out of the Rambler, Blair's Sermons and Young's Night

Thoughts. For he had some sort of smattering of English literature which a Public School boy has no business to possess. So he went on with this mental tirade of his: one is not over-wise at fifteen. It is true enough, perhaps, that the French of the average English schoolboy is something fit to move only pity and terror; it may be true also that nobody except Deans and schoolmasters seems to bring away even the formulas and sacred teachings (such as the Optative mystery and the Doctrine of Dum) of the two great literatures. There is, doubtless, a good deal to be said on the subject of the Public Schoolman's knowledge of the history and literature of his own country; an infinite deal of comic stuff might be got out of his views and acquirements in the great science of theology--still let us say, Floreat!

Meyrick turned from his review of the wisdom of his elders and instructors to more intimate concerns. There were a few cuts of that vigorous cane which still stung and hurt most abominably, for skill or fortune had guided Mr. Horbury's hand so that he had been enabled here and there to get home twice in the same place, and there was one particular weal on the left arm where the flesh, purple and discoloured, had swelled up and seemed on the point of bursting. It was no longer with rage, but with a kind of rapture, that he felt the pain and smarting; he looked upon the ugly marks of the High Usher's evil humours as though they had been a robe of splendour. For he knew nothing of that bad sherry, nothing of the Head's conversation; he knew that when Pelly had come in quite as late it had only been a question of a hundred lines, and so he persisted in regarding himself as a martyr in the cause of those famous "Norman arches," which was the cause of that dear dead enthusiast, his father, who loved Gothic architecture and all other beautiful "unpractical" things with an undying passion. As soon as Ambrose could walk he had begun his pilgrimages to hidden mystic shrines; his father had led him over the wild lands to places known perhaps only to himself, and there, by the ruined stones, by the smooth hillock, had told the tale of the old vanished time, the time of the "old saints."

III

It was for this blessed and wonderful learning, he said to himself, that he had been beaten, that his body had been scored with red and purple stripes. He remembered his father's oft-repeated exclamation, "cythrawl Sais!" He understood that the phrase damned not Englishmen qua Englishmen, but Anglo-Saxonism--the power of the creed that builds Manchester, that "does business," that invents popular dissent, representative government, adulteration, suburbs, and the Public School system. It was, according to his father, the creed of "the Prince of this world," the creed that made for comfort, success, a good balance at the bank, the praise of men, the sensible and tangible victory and achievement; and he bade his little boy, who heard everything and understood next to nothing, fly from it, hate it and fight against it as he would fight against the devil--"and," he would add, "it is the only devil you are ever likely to come across."

And the little Ambrose had understood not much of all this, and if he had been asked--even at fifteen--what it all meant, he would probably have said that it was a great issue between Norman mouldings and Mr. Horbury, an Armageddon of Selden Abbey versus rocker. Indeed, it is doubtful whether old Nicholas Meyrick would have been very much clearer, for he forgot everything that might be said on the other side. He forgot that Anglo-Saxonism (save in the United States of America) makes generally for equal laws; that civil riot ("Labour" movements, of course, excepted) is more a Celtic than a Saxon vice; that the penalty of burning alive is unknown amongst Anglo-Saxons, unless the provocation be extreme; that Englishmen have substituted "Indentured Labour" for the old-world horrors of slavery; that English justice smites the guilty rich equally with the guilty poor; that men are no longer poisoned with swift and secret drugs, though somewhat unwholesome food may still be sold very occasionally. Indeed, the old Meyrick once told his rector that he considered a brothel a house of sanctity compared with a modern factory, and he was beginning to relate some interesting tales concerning the Three Gracious Courtesans of the Isle of Britain when the rector fled in horror--he came from Sydenham. And all this was a nice preparation for Lupton.

A wonderful joy, an ecstasy of bliss, swelled in Ambrose's heart as he assured himself that he was a witness, though a mean one, for the old faith, for the faith of secret and beautiful and hidden mysteries as opposed to the faith of rocker and sticker and mucker, and "the thought of the school as an inspiring motive in life"--the text on which the Head had preached the Sunday before. He bared his arms and kissed the purple swollen flesh and prayed that it might ever be so, that in body and mind and spirit he might ever be beaten and reviled and made ridiculous for the sacred things, that he might ever be on the side of the despised and the unsuccessful, that his life might ever be in the shadow--in the shadow of the mysteries.

He thought of the place in which he was, of the hideous school, the hideous town, the weary waves of the dun Midland scenery bounded by the dim, hopeless horizon; and his soul revisited the faery hills and woods and valleys of the West. He remembered how, long ago, his father had roused him early from sleep in the hush and wonder of a summer morning. The whole world was still and windless; all the magic odours of the night rose from the earth, and as they crossed the lawn the silence was broken by the enchanted song of a bird rising from a thorn tree by the gate. A high white vapour veiled the sky, and they only knew that the sun had risen by the brightening of this veil, by the silvering of the woods and the meadows and the water in the rejoicing brook. They crossed the road, and crossed the brook in the field beneath, by the old foot-bridge tremulous with age, and began to climb the steep hillside that one could see from the windows, and, the ridge of the hill once surmounted, the little boy found himself in an unknown land: he looked into deep, silent valleys, watered by trickling streams; he saw still woods in that dreamlike morning air; he saw winding paths that climbed into yet remoter regions. His father led him onward till they came to a lonely height--they had walked scarcely two miles, but to Ambrose it seemed a journey into another world--and showed him certain irregular markings in the turf.

And Nicholas Meyrick murmured:

"The cell of Iltyd is by the seashore,
The ninth wave washes its altar,
There is a fair shrine in the land of Morgan.

"The cell of Dewi is in the City of the Legions,
Nine altars owe obedience to it,
Sovereign is the choir that sings about it.

"The cell of Cybi is the treasure of Gwent,
Nine hills are its perpetual guardians,
Nine songs befit the memory of the saint."

"See," he said, "there are the Nine Hills." He pointed them out to the boy, telling him the tale of the saint and his holy bell, which they said had sailed across the sea from Syon and had entered the Severn, and had entered the Usk, and had entered the Soar, and had entered the Canthwr; and so one day the saint, as he walked beside the little brook that almost encompassed the hill in its winding course, saw the bell "that was made of metal that no man might comprehend," floating under the alders, and crying:

"Sant, sant, sant,
I sail from Syon
To Cybi Sant!"

"And so sweet was the sound of that bell," Ambrose's father went on, "that they said it was as the joy of angels ym Mharadwys, and that it must have come not from the earthly, but from the heavenly and glorious Syon."

And there they stood in the white morning, on the uneven ground that marked the place where once the Saint rang to the sacrifice, where the quickening words were uttered after the order of the Old Mass of the Britons.

"And then came the Yellow Hag of Pestilence, that destroyed the bodies of the Cymri; then the Red Hag of Rome, that caused their souls to stray; last is come the Black Hag of Geneva, that sends body and soul quick to hell. No honour have the saints any more."

Then they turned home again, and all the way Ambrose thought he heard the bell as it sailed the great deeps from Syon, crying aloud: "Sant, Sant, Sant!" And the sound seemed to echo from the glassy water of the little brook, as it swirled and rippled over the shining stones circling round those lonely hills.

So they made strange pilgrimages over the beloved land, going farther and farther afield as the boy grew older. They visited deep wells in the heart of the woods, where a few broken stones, perhaps, were the last remains of the hermitage. "Ffynnon Ilar Bysgootwr--the well of Saint Ilar the Fisherman," Nicholas Meyrick would explain, and then would follow the story of Ilar; how no man knew whence he came or who his parents were. He was found, a little child, on a stone in a river in Armorica, by King Alan, and rescued by him. And ever after they discovered on the stone in the river where the child had lain every day a great and shining fish lying, and on this fish Ilar was nourished. And so he came with a great company of the saints to Britain, and wandered over all the land.

"So at last Ilar Sant came to this wood, which people now call St. Hilary's wood because they have forgotten all about Ilar. And he was weary with his wandering, and the day was very hot; so he stayed by this well and began to drink. And there on that great stone he saw the shining fish, and so he rested, and built an altar and a church of willow boughs, and offered the sacrifice not only for the quick and the dead, but for all the wild beasts of the woods and the streams.

"And when this blessed Ilar rang his holy bell and began to offer, there came not only the Prince and his servants, but all the creatures of the wood. There, under the hazel boughs, you might see the hare, which flies so swiftly from men, come gently and fall down, weeping greatly on account of the Passion of the Son of Mary. And, beside the hare, the weasel and the pole-cat would lament grievously in the manner of penitent sinners; and wolves and lambs together adored the saint's hierurgy; and men have beheld tears streaming from the eyes of venomous serpents when Ilar Agios uttered 'Curiluson' with a loud voice--since the serpent is not ignorant that by its wickedness sorrow came to the whole world. And when, in the time of the holy ministry, it is necessary that frequent Alleluyas should be chanted and vociferated, the saint wondered what should be done, for as yet none in that place was skilled in the art of song. Then was a great miracle, since from all the boughs of the wood, from every bush and from every green tree, there resounded Alleluyas in enchanting and prolonged harmony; never did the Bishop of Rome listen to so sweet a singing in his church as was heard in this wood. For the nightingale and thrush and blackbird and blackcap, and all their companions, are gathered together and sing praises to the Lord, chanting distinct notes and yet concluding in a melody of most ravishing sweetness; such was the mass of the Fisherman. Nor was this all, for one day as the saint prayed beside the well he became aware that a bee circled round and round his head, uttering loud buzzing sounds, but not endeavouring to sting him. To be short; the bee went before Ilar, and led him to a hollow tree not far off, and straightway a swarm of bees issued forth, leaving a vast store of wax behind them. This was their oblation to the Most High, for from their wax Ilar Sant made goodly candles to burn at the Offering; and from that time the bee is holy, because his wax makes light to shine upon the Gifts."

This was part of the story that Ambrose's father read to him; and they went again to see the Holy Well. He looked at the few broken and uneven stones that were left to distinguish it from common wells; and there in the deep green wood, in the summer afternoon, under the woven boughs, he seemed to hear the strange sound of the saint's bell, to see the woodland creatures hurrying through the undergrowth that they might be present at the Offering. The weasel beat his little breast for his sins; the big tears fell down the gentle face of the hare; the adders wept in the dust; and all the chorus of the birds sang: "Alleluya, Alleluya, Alleluya!"

Once they drove a long way from the Wern, going towards the west, till they came to the Great Mountain, as the people called it. After they had turned from the high road they went down a narrow lane, and this led them with many windings to a lower ridge of the mountain, where the horse and trap were put up at a solitary tavern. Then they began to toil upward on foot, crossing many glistening and rejoicing streams that rushed out cold from the limestone rock, mounting up and up, through the wet land where the rare orchis grew amongst the rushes, through hazel brakes, through fields that grew wilder as they still went higher, and the great wind came down from the high dome above them. They turned, and all the shining land was unrolled before them; the white houses were bright in the sunlight, and there, far away, was the yellow sea and the two islands, and the coasts beyond.

Nicholas Meyrick pointed out a tuft of trees on a hill a long way off and told his son that the Wern was hidden beyond it; and then they began to climb once more, till they came at last to the line where the fields and hedges ended, and above there was only the wild mountain land. And on this verge stood an old farmhouse with strong walls, set into the rock, sheltered a little from the winds by a line of twisted beeches. The walls of the house were gleaming white, and by the porch there was a shrub covered with bright yellow flowers. Mr. Meyrick beat upon the oak door, painted black and studded with heavy nails. An old man, dressed like a farmer, opened it, and Ambrose noticed that his father spoke to him with something of reverence in his voice, as if he were some very great person. They sat down in a long room, but dimly lighted by the thick greenish glass in the quarried window, and presently the old farmer set a great jug of beer before them. They both drank heartily enough, and Mr. Meyrick said:

"Aren't you about the last to brew your own beer, Mr. Cradock?"

"Iss; I be the last of all. They do all like the muck the brewer sends better than cwrw dda."

"The whole world likes muck better than good drink, now."

"You be right, Sir. Old days and old ways of our fathers, they be gone for ever. There was a blasted preacher down at the chapel a week or two ago, saying--so they do tell me--that they would all be damned to hell unless they took to ginger-beer directly. Iss indeed now; and I heard that he should say that a man could do a better day's work on that rot-belly stuff than on good beer. Wass you ever hear of such a liarr as that?"

The old man was furious at the thought of these infamies and follies; his esses hissed through his teeth and his r's rolled out with fierce emphasis. Mr. Meyrick nodded his approval of this indignation.

"We have what we deserve," he said. "False preachers, bad drink, the talk of fools all the day long--even on the mountain. What is it like, do you think, in London?"

There fell a silence in the long, dark room. They could hear the sound of the wind in the beech trees, and Ambrose saw how the boughs were tossed to and fro, and he thought of what it must be like in winter nights, here, high upon the Great Mountain, when the storms swept up from the sea, or descended from the wilds of the north; when the shafts of rain were like the onset of an army, and the winds screamed about the walls.

"May we see It?" said Mr. Meyrick suddenly.

"I did think you had come for that. There be very few now that remember."

He went out, and returned carrying a bunch of keys. Then he opened a door in the room and warned "the young master" to take care of the steps. Ambrose, indeed, could scarcely see the way. His father led him down a short flight of uneven stone steps, and they were in a room which seemed at first quite dark, for the only light came from a narrow window high up in the wall, and across the glass there were heavy iron bars.

Cradock lit two tall candles of yellow wax that stood in brass candlesticks on a table; and, as the flame grew clear, Ambrose saw that he was opening a sort of aumbry constructed in the thickness of the wall. The door was a great slab of solid oak, three or four inches thick--as one could see when it was opened--and from the dark place within the farmer took an iron box and set it carefully upon the floor, Mr. Meyrick helping him. They were strong men, but they staggered under the weight of the chest; the iron seemed as thick as the door of the cupboard from which it was taken, and the heavy, antique lock yielded, with a grating scream, to the key. Inside it there was another box of some reddish metal, which, again, held a case of wood black with age; and from this, with reverent hands, the farmer drew out a veiled and splendid cup and set it on the table between the two candles. It was a bowl-like vessel of the most wonderful workmanship, standing on a short stem. All the hues of the world were mingled on it, all the jewels of the regions seemed to shine from it; and the stem and foot were encrusted with work in enamel, of strange and magical colours that shone and dimmed with alternating radiance, that glowed with red fires and pale glories, with the blue of the far sky, the green of the faery seas, and the argent gleam of the evening star. But before Ambrose had gazed more than a moment he heard the old man say, in pure Welsh, not in broken English, in a resonant and chanting voice:

"Let us fall down and adore the marvellous and venerable work of the Lord God Almighty."

To which his father responded:

"Agyos, Agyos, Agyos. Mighty and glorious is the Lord God Almighty, in all His works and wonderful operations. Curiluson, Curiluson, Curiluson."

They knelt down, Cradock in the midst, before the cup, and Ambrose and his father on either hand. The holy vessel gleamed before the boy's eyes, and he saw clearly its wonder and its beauty. All its surface was a marvel of the most delicate intertwining lines in gold and silver, in copper and in bronze, in all manner of metals and alloys; and these interlacing patterns in their brightness, in the strangeness of their imagery and ornament, seemed to enthral his eyes and capture them, as it were, in a maze of enchantment; and not only the eyes; for the very spirit was rapt and garnered into that far bright world whence the holy magic of the cup proceeded. Among the precious stones which were set into the wonder was a great crystal, shining with the pure light of the moon; about the rim of it there was the appearance of faint and feathery clouds, but in the centre it was a white splendour; and as Ambrose gazed he thought that from the heart of this jewel there streamed continually a shower of glittering stars, dazzling his eyes with their incessant motion and brightness. His body thrilled with a sudden ineffable rapture, his breath came and went in quick pantings; bliss possessed him utterly as the three crowned forms passed in their golden order. Then the interwoven sorcery of the vessel became a ringing wood of golden, and bronze, and silver trees; from every side resounded the clear summons of the holy bells and the exultant song of the faery birds; he no longer heard the low-chanting voices of Cradock and his father as they replied to one another in the forms of some antique liturgy. Then he stood by a wild seashore; it was a dark night, and there was a shrilling wind that sang about the peaks of the sharp rock, answering to the deep voices of the heaving sea. A white moon, of fourteen days old, appeared for a moment in the rift between two vast black clouds, and the shaft of light showed all the savage desolation of the shore-- cliffs that rose up into mountains, into crenellated heights that were incredible, whose bases were scourged by the torrents of hissing foam that were driven against them from the hollow-sounding sea. Then, on the highest of those awful heights, Ambrose became aware of walls and spires, of towers and battlements that must have touched the stars; and, in the midst of this great castle, there surged up the aspiring vault of a vast church, and all its windows were ablaze with a light so white and glorious that it was as if every pane were a diamond. And he heard the voices of a praising host, or the clamour of golden trumpets and the unceasing choir of the angels. And he knew that this place was the Sovereign Perpetual Choir, Cor-arbennic, into whose secret the deadly flesh may scarcely enter. But in the vision he lay breathless, on the floor before the gleaming wall of the sanctuary, while the shadows of the hierurgy were enacted; and it seemed to him that, for a moment of time, he saw in unendurable light the Mystery of Mysteries pass veiled before him, and the Image of the Slain and Risen.

For a brief while this dream was broken. He heard his father singing softly:

"Gogoniant y Tâd ac y Mab ac yr Yspryd Glân."

And the old man answered:

"Agya Trias eleeson ymas."

Then again his spirit was lost in the bright depths of the crystal, and he saw the ships of the saints, without oar or sail, afloat on the faery sea, seeking the Glassy Isle. All the whole company of the Blessed Saints of the Isle of Britain sailed on the adventure; dawn and sunset, night and morning, their illuminated faces never wavered; and Ambrose thought that at last they saw bright shores in the dying light of a red sun, and there came to their nostrils the scent of the deep apple-garths in Avalon, and odours of Paradise.

***

When he finally returned to the presence of earthly things he was standing by his father; while Cradock reverently wrapped the cup in the gleaming veils which covered it, saying as he did so, in Welsh:

"Remain in peace, O holy and divine cup of the Lord. Henceforth I know not whether I shall return to thee or not; but may the Lord vouchsafe me to see thee in the Church of the Firstborn which is in Heaven, on the Altar of the Sacrifice which is from age unto ages."

Ambrose went up the steps and out into the sunshine on the mountain side with the bewilderment of strange dreams, as a coloured mist, about him. He saw the old white walls, the yellow blossoms by the porch; above, the wild, high mountain wall; and, below, all the dear land of Gwent, happy in the summer air, all its woods and fields, its rolling hills and its salt verge, rich in a golden peace. Beside him the cold water swelled from the earth and trickled from the grey rock, and high in the air an exultant lark was singing. The mountain breeze was full of life and gladness, and the rustling and tossing of the woods, the glint and glimmer of the leaves beneath, made one think that the trees, with every creature, were merry on that day. And in that dark cell beneath many locks, beneath wood and iron, concealed in golden, glittering veils, lay hidden that glorious and awful cup, glass of wonderful vision, portal and entrance of the Spiritual Place.

His father explained to him something of that which he had seen. He told him that the vessel was the Holy Cup of Teilo sant, which he was said to have received from the Lord in the state of Paradise, and that when Teilo said Mass, using that Chalice, the choir of angels was present visibly; that it was a cup of wonders and mysteries, the bestower of visions and heavenly graces.

"But whatever you do," he said, "do not speak to anyone of what you have seen to-day, because if you do the mystery will be laughed at and blasphemed. Do you know that your uncle and aunt at Lupton would say that we were all mad together? That is because they are fools, and in these days most people are fools, and malignant fools too, as you will find out for yourself before you are much older. So always remember that you must hide the secrets that you have seen; and if you do not do so you will be sorry."

Mr. Meyrick told his son why old Cradock was to be treated with respect—indeed, with reverence.

"He is just what he looks," he said, "an old farmer with a small freehold up here on the mountain side; and, as you heard, his English is no better than that of any other farmer in this country. And, compared with Cradock, the Duke of Norfolk is a man of yesterday. He is of the tribe of Teilo the Saint; he is the last, in direct descent, of the hereditary keepers of the holy cup; and his race has guarded that blessed relic for thirteen hundred years. Remember, again, that to-day, on this mountain, you have seen great marvels which you must keep in silence."

Poor Ambrose! He suffered afterwards for his forgetfulness of his father's injunction. Soon after he went to Lupton one of the boys was astonishing his friends with a brilliant account of the Crown jewels, which he had viewed during the Christmas holidays. Everybody was deeply impressed, and young Meyrick, anxious to be agreeable in his turn, began to tell about the wonderful cup that he had once seen in an old farmhouse. Perhaps his manner was not convincing, for the boys shrieked with laughter over his description. A monitor who was passing asked to hear the joke, and, having been told the tale, clouted Ambrose over the head for an infernal young liar. This was a good lesson, and it served Ambrose in good stead when one of the masters having, somehow or other, heard the story, congratulated him in the most approved scholastic manner before the whole form on his wonderful imaginative gifts.

"I see the budding novelist in you, Meyrick," said this sly master. "Besant and Rice will be nowhere when you once begin. I suppose you are studying character just at present? Let us down gently, won't you? [To the delighted form.] We must be careful, mustn't we, how we behave? 'A chiel's amang us takin' notes,'" etc. etc.

But Meyrick held his tongue. He did not tell his form master that he was a beast, a fool and a coward, since he had found out that the truth, like many precious things, must often be concealed from the profane. A late vengeance overtook that foolish master. Long years after, he was dining at a popular London restaurant, and all through dinner he had delighted the ladies of his party by the artful mixture of brutal insolence and vulgar chaff with which he had treated one of the waiters, a humble-looking little Italian. The master was in the highest spirits at the success of his persiflage; his voice rose louder and louder, and his offensiveness became almost supernaturally acute. And then he received a heavy earthen casserole, six quails, a few small onions and a quantity of savoury but boiling juices full in the face. The waiter was a Neapolitan.

The hours of the night passed on, as Ambrose sat in his bedroom at the Old Grange, recalling many wonderful memories, dreaming his dreams of the mysteries, of the land of Gwent and the land of vision, just as his uncle, but a few yards away in another room of the house, was at the same time rapt into the world of imagination, seeing the new Lupton descending like a bride from the heaven of headmasters. But Ambrose thought of the Great Mountain, of the secret valleys, of the sanctuaries and hallows of the saints, of the rich carven work of lonely churches hidden amongst the hills and woods. There came into his mind the fragment of an old poem which he loved:

> *"In the darkness of old age let not my memory fail,*
> *Let me not forget to celebrate the beloved land of Gwent.*
> *If they imprison me in a deep place, in a house of pestilence,*
> *Still shall I be free, when I remember the sunshine upon Mynydd*

> *Maen.*
> *There have I listened to the singing of the lark, my soul has ascended with the song of the*
> little bird;
> *The great white clouds were the ships of my spirit, sailing to the haven of the Almighty.*
> *Equally to be held in honour is the site of the Great Mountain,*
> *Adorned with the gushing of many waters--*
> *Sweet is the shade of its hazel thickets,*
> *There a treasure is preserved, which I will not celebrate,*
> *It is glorious, and deeply concealed.*
> *If Teilo should return, if happiness were restored to the Cymri,*
> *Dewi and Dyfrig should serve his Mass; then a great marvel would be made visible.*
> *O blessed and miraculous work, then should my bliss be as the bliss of angels;*
> *I had rather behold this Offering than kiss the twin lips of dark*

> *Gwenllian.*
> *Dear my land of Gwent, O quam dilecta tabernacula!*
> *Thy rivers are like precious golden streams of Paradise,*
> *Thy hills are as the Mount Syon--*
> *Better a grave on Twyn Barlwm than a throne in the palace of the*
> *Saxons at Caer-Ludd."*

And then, by the face of contrast, he thought of the first verse of the great school song, "Rocker," one of the earliest of the many poems which his uncle had consecrated to the praise of the dear old school:

> *"Once on a time, in the books that bore me,*
> *I read that in olden days before me*
> *Lupton town had a wonderful game,*
> *It was a game with a noble story*
> *(Lupton town was then in its glory,*
> *Kings and Bishops had brought it fame).*
> *It was a game that you all must know,*
> *And 'rocker' they called it, long ago.*

> *Chorus.*

> *"Look out for 'brooks,' or you're sure to drown,*
> *Look out for 'quarries,' or else you're down--*
> *That was the way*
> *'Rocker' to play--*
> *Once on a day*
> *That was the way,*
> *Once on a day,*
> *That was the way that they used to play in Lupton town."*

Thinking of the two songs, he put out his light and, wearied, fell into a deep sleep.

IV

The British schoolboy, considered in a genial light by those who have made him their special study, has not been found to be either observant or imaginative. Or, rather, it would be well to say that his powers of observation, having been highly specialised within a certain limited tract of thought and experience (bounded mainly by cricket and football), are but faint without these bounds; while it is one of the chiefest works of the System to kill, destroy, smash and bring to nothing any powers of imagination he may have originally possessed. For if this were not done thoroughly, neither a Conservative nor a Liberal administration would be possible, the House of Commons itself would cease to exist, the Episcopus (var. Anglicanus) would go the way of the Great Bustard; a "muddling through somehow" (which must have been the brightest jewel in the British crown, wrung from King John by the barons) would become a lost art. And, since all these consequences would be clearly intolerable, the great Public Schools have perfected a very thorough system of destroying the imaginative toxin, and few cases of failure have been so far reported.

Still, there are facts which not even the densest dullards, the most complete boobies, can help seeing; and a good many of the boys found themselves wondering "what was the matter with Meyrick" when they saw him at Chapel on the Sunday morning. The news of his astounding violences both of act and word on the night before had not yet circulated generally. Bates was attending to that department, but hadn't had time to do much so far; and the replies of Pelly and Rawson to enquiries after black eyes and a potato-like nose were surly and misleading. Afterwards, when the tale was told, when Bates, having enlarged the incidents to folk-lore size, showed Pelly lying in a pool of his own blood, Rawson screaming as with the torments of the lost and Meyrick rolling out oaths--all original and all terrible--for the space of a quarter of an hour, then indeed the school was satisfied; it was no wonder if Meyrick did look a bit queer after the achievement of such an adventure. The funk of aforetime had found courage; the air of rapture was easily understood. It is probable that if, in the nature of things, it had been possible for an English schoolboy to meet St. Francis of Assisi, the boy would have concluded that the saint must have just made 200 not out in first-class cricket.

But Ambrose walked in a strange light; he had been admitted into worlds undreamed of, and from the first brightness of the sun, when he awoke in the morning in his room at the Grange, it was the material world about him, the walls of stone and brick, the solid earth, the sky itself, and the people who talked and moved and seemed alive--these were things of vision, unsubstantial shapes, odd and broken illusions of the mind. At half-past seven old Toby, the man-of-all-work at the old Grange banged at his door and let his clean boots fall with a crash on the boards after the usual fashion. He awoke, sat up in bed, staring about him. But what was this? The four walls covered with a foolish speckled paper, pale blue and pale brown, the white ceiling, the bare boards with the strip of carpet by the bedside: he knew nothing of all this. He was not horrified, because he knew that it was all non-existent, some plastic fantasy that happened to be presented for the moment to his brain. Even the big black wooden chest that held his books (Parker, despised by Horbury, among them) failed to appeal to him with any sense of reality; and the bird's-eye washstand and chest of drawers, the white water-jug with the blue band, were all frankly phantasmal. It reminded him of a trick he had sometimes played: one chose one's position carefully, shut an eye and, behold, a mean shed could be made to obscure the view of a mountain! So these walls and appurtenances made an illusory sort of intrusion into the true vision on which he gazed. That yellow washstand rising out of the shining wells of the undying, the speckled walls in the place of the great mysteries, a chest of drawers in the magic garden of roses--it had the air of a queer joke, and he laughed aloud to himself as he realized that he alone knew, that everybody else would say, "That is a white jug with a blue band," while he, and he only, saw the marvel and glory of the holy cup with its glowing metals, its interlacing myriad lines, its wonderful images, and its hues of the mountain and the stars, of the green wood and the faery sea where, in a sure haven, anchor the ships that are bound for

Avalon.

For he had a certain faith that he had found the earthly presentation and sacrament of the Eternal Heavenly Mystery.

He smiled again, with the quaint smile of an angel in an old Italian picture, as he realized more fully the strangeness of the whole position and the odd humours which would relieve to play a wonderful game of make-believe; the speckled walls, for instance, were not really there, but he was to behave just as if they were solid realities. He would presently rise and go through an odd pantomine of washing and dressing, putting on brilliant boots, and going down to various mumbo-jumbo ceremonies called breakfast, chapel and dinner, in the company of appearances to whom he would accord all the honours due to veritable beings. And this delicious phantasmagoria would go on and on day after day, he alone having the secret; and what a delight it would be to "play up" at rocker! It seemed to him that the solid-seeming earth, the dear old school and rocker itself had all been made to minister to the acuteness of his pleasure; they were the darkness that made the light visible, the matter through which form was manifested. For the moment he enclosed in the most secret place of his soul the true world into which he had been guided; and as he dressed he hummed the favourite school song, "Never mind!"

> *"If the umpire calls 'out' at your poor second over,*
> *If none of your hits ever turns out a 'rover,'*
> *If you fumble your fives and 'go rot' over sticker,*
> *If every hound is a little bit quicker;*
> *If you can't tackle rocker at all, not at all,*
> *And kick at the moon when you try for the ball,*
>
> *Never mind, never mind, never mind--if you fall,*
> *Dick falls before rising, Tom's short ere he's tall,*
>
> *Never mind!*
> *Don't be one of the weakest who go to the wall:*
>
> *Never mind!"*

Ambrose could not understand how Columbus could have blundered so grossly. Somehow or other he should have contrived to rid himself of his crew; he should have returned alone, with a dismal tale of failure, and passed the rest of his days as that sad and sorry charlatan who had misled the world with his mad whimsies of a continent beyond the waters of the Atlantic. If he had been given wisdom to do this, how great--how wonderful would his joys have been! They would have pointed at him as he paced the streets in his shabby cloak; the boys would have sung songs about him and his madness; the great people would have laughed contemptuously as he went by. And he would have seen in his heart all that vast far world of the west, the rich islands barred by roaring surf, a whole hemisphere of strange regions and strange people; he would have known that he alone possessed the secret of it. But, after all, Ambrose knew that his was a greater joy even than this; for the world that he had discovered was not far across the seas, but within him.

Pelly stared straight before him in savage silence all through breakfast; he was convinced that mere hazard had guided that crushing blow, and he was meditating schemes of complete and exemplary vengeance. He noticed nothing strange about Meyrick, nor would he have cared if he had seen the images of the fairies in his eyes. Rawson, on the other hand, was full of genial civility and good fellowship; it was "old chap" and "old fellow" every other word. But he was far from unintelligent, and, as he slyly watched Meyrick, he saw that there was something altogether unaccustomed and incomprehensible. Unknown lights burned and shone in the eyes, reflections of one knew not what; the expression was altered in some queer way that he could not understand. Meyrick had always been a rather ugly, dogged-looking fellow; his black hair and something that was not usual in the set of his features gave him an exotic, almost an Oriental appearance; hence a story of Rawson's to the effect that Meyrick's mother was a nigger woman in poor circumstances and of indifferent morality had struck the school as plausible enough.

But now the grimness of the rugged features seemed abolished; the face shone, as it were, with the light of a flame--but a flame of what fire? Rawson, who would not have put his observations into such terms, drew his own conclusions readily enough and imparted them to Pelly after Chapel.

"Look here, old chap," he said, "did you notice young Meyrick at breakfast?"

Pelly simply blasted Meyrick and announced his intention of giving him the worst thrashing he had ever had at an early date.

"Don't you try it on," said Rawson. "I had my eye on him all the time. He didn't see I was spotting him. He's cracked; he's dangerous. I shouldn't wonder if he were in a strait waistcoat in the County Lunatic Asylum in a week's time. My governor had a lot to do with lunatics, and he always says he can tell by the eyes. I'll swear Meyrick is raging mad."

"Oh, rot!" said Pelly. "What do you know about it?"

"Well, look out, old chap, and don't say I didn't give you the tip. Of course, you know a maniac is stronger than three ordinary men? The only thing is to get them down and crack their ribs. But you want at least half a dozen men before you can do it."

"Oh, shut up!"

So Rawson said no more, remaining quite sure that he had diagnosed Ambrose's symptoms correctly. He waited for the catastrophe with a dreadful joy, wondering whether Meyrick would begin by cutting old Horbury's throat with his own razor, or whether he would rather steal into Pelly's room at night and tear him limb from limb, a feat which, as a madman, he could, of course, accomplish with perfect ease. As a matter of fact, neither of these events happened. Pelly, a boy of the bulldog breed, smacked Ambrose's face a day or two later before a huge crowd of boys, and received in return such a terrific blow under the left ear that a formal fight in the Tom Brown manner was out of the question.

Pelly reached the ground and stayed there in an unconscious state for some while; and the other boys determined that it would be as well to leave Meyrick to himself. He might be cracked but he was undoubtedly a hard hitter. As for Pelly, like the sensible fellow that he was, he simply concluded that Meyrick was too good for him. He did not quite understand it; he dimly suspected the intrusion of some strange forces, but with such things he had nothing to do. It was a fair knock-out, and there was an end of it.

Bates had glanced up as Ambrose came into the dining-room on the Sunday morning. He saw the shining face, the rapturous eyes, and had silently wondered, recognising the presence of elements which transcended all his calculations.

Meanwhile the Lupton Sunday went on after its customary fashion. At eleven o'clock the Chapel was full of boys. There were nearly six hundred of them there, the big ones in frock-coats, with high, pointed collars, which made them look like youthful Gladstones. The younger boys wore broad, turn-down collars and had short, square jackets made somewhat in the Basque fashion. Young and old had their hair cut close to the scalp, and this gave them all a brisk but bullety appearance. The masters, in cassock, gown and hood, occupied the choir stalls. Mr. Horbury, the High Usher, clothed in a flowing surplice, was taking Morning Prayer, and the Head occupied a kind of throne by the altar.

The Chapel was not an inspiring building. It was the fourteenth century, certainly, but the fourteenth century translated by 1840, and, it is to be feared, sadly betrayed by the translators. The tracery of the windows was poor and shallow; the mouldings of the piers and arches faulty to a degree; the chancel was absurdly out of proportion, and the pitch-pine benches and stalls had a sticky look. There was a stained-glass window in memory of the Old Luptonians who fell in the Crimea. One wondered what the Woman of Samaria by the Well had to do either with Lupton or the Crimea. And the colouring was like that used in very common, cheap sweets.

The service went with a rush. The prayers, versicles and responses, and psalms were said, the officiant and the congregation rather pressing than pausing--often, indeed, coming so swiftly to cues that two or three words at the end of one verse or two or three at the beginning of the next would be lost in a confused noise of contending voices. But Venite and Te Deum and Benedictus were rattled off to frisky Anglicans with great spirit; sometimes the organ tooted, sometimes it bleated gently, like a flock of sheep; now one might have sworn that the music of penny whistles stole on the ear, and again, as the organist coupled up the full organ, using suddenly all the battery of his stops, a gas explosion and a Salvation Army band seemed to strive against one another. A well-known nobleman who had been to Chapel at Lupton was heard to say, with reference to this experience: "I am no Ritualist, heaven knows--but I confess I like a hearty service."

But it was, above all, the sermon that has made the Chapel a place of many memories. The Old Boys say--and one supposes that they are in earnest--that the tall, dignified figure of the Doctor, standing high above them all, his scarlet hood making a brilliant splash of colour against the dingy, bilious paint of the pale green walls, has been an inspiration to them in all quarters of the globe, in all manner of difficulties and temptations.

One man writes that in the midst of a complicated and dangerous deal on the Stock Exchange he remembered a sermon of Dr. Chesson's called in the printed volume, "Fighting the Good Fight."

"You have a phrase amongst you which I often hear," said the Head. "That phrase is 'Play the game,' and I wish to say that, though you know it not; though, it may be, the words are often spoken half in jest; still, they are but your modern, boyish rendering of the old, stirring message which I have just read to you.

"Fight the Good Fight.' 'Play the Game.' Remember the words in the storm and struggle, the anxiety and stress that may be--nay, must be--before you--etc., etc., etc."

"After the crisis was over," wrote the Stock Exchange man, "I was thankful that I had remembered those words."

"That voice sounding like a trumpet on the battle-field, bidding us all remember that Success was the prize of Effort and Endurance----" So writes a well-known journalist.

"I remembered what the Doctor said to us once about 'running the race,'" says a young soldier, recounting a narrow escape from a fierce enemy, "so I stuck to my orders."

Ambrose, on that Sunday morning, sat in his place, relishing acutely all the savours of the scene, consumed with inward mirth at the thought that this also professed to be a rite of religion. There was an aimless and flighty merriment about the chant to the Te Deum that made it difficult for him to control his laughter; and when he joined in the hymn "Pleasant are Thy courts above," there was an odd choke in his voice that made the boy next to him shuffle uneasily.

But the sermon!

It will be found on page 125 of the Lupton Sermons. It dealt with the Parable of the Talents, and showed the boys in what the sin of the man who concealed his Talent really consisted.

"I daresay," said the Head, "that many of the older amongst you have wondered what this man's sin really was. You may have read your Greek Testaments carefully, and then have tried to form in your minds some analogy to the circumstances of the parable--and it would not surprise me if you were to tell me that you had failed.

"What manner of man was this? I can imagine your saying one to another. I shall not be astonished if you confess that, for you at least, the question seems unanswerable.

"Yes; Unanswerable to you. For you are English boys, the sons of English gentlemen, to whom the atmosphere of casuistry, of concealment, of subtlety, is unknown; by whom such an atmosphere would be rejected with scorn. You come from homes where there is no shadow, no dark corner which must not be pried into. Your relations and your friends are not of those who hide their gifts from the light of day. Some of you, perhaps, have had the privilege of listening to the talk of one or other of the great statesmen who guide the doctrines of this vast Empire. You will have observed, I am sure, that in the world of politics there is no vain simulation of modesty, no feigned reluctance to speak of worthy achievement. All of you are members of this great community, of which each one of us is so proud, which we think of as the great inspiration and motive force of our lives. Here, you will say, there are no Hidden Talents, for the note of the English Public School (thank God for it!) is openness, frankness, healthy emulation; each endeavouring to do his best for the good of all. In our studies and in our games each desires to excel to carry off the prize. We strive for a corruptible crown, thinking that this, after all, is the surest discipline for the crown that is incorruptible. If a man say that he loveth God whom he hath not seen, and love not his brother whom he hath seen! Let your light shine before men. Be sure that we shall never win Heaven by despising earth.

"Yet that man hid his Talent in a napkin. What does the story mean? What message has it for us to-day?

"I will tell you.

"Some years ago during our summer holidays I was on a walking tour in a mountainous district in the north of England. The sky was of a most brilliant blue, the sun poured, as it were, a gospel of gladness on the earth. Towards the close of the day I was entering a peaceful and beautiful valley amongst the hills, when three sullen notes of a bell came down the breeze towards me. There was a pause. Again the three strokes, and for a third time this dismal summons struck my ears. I walked on in the direction of the sound, wondering whence it came and what it signified; and soon I saw before me a great pile of buildings, surrounded by a gloomy and lofty wall.

"It was a Roman Catholic monastery. The bell was ringing the Angelus, as it is called.

"I obtained admittance to this place and spoke to some of the unhappy monks. I should astonish you if I mentioned the names of some of the deluded men who had immured themselves in this prison-house. It is sufficient to say that among them were a soldier who had won distinction on the battle-field, an artist, a statesman and a physician of no mean repute.

"Now do you understand? Ah! a day will come--you know, I think, what that day is called-- when these poor men will have to answer the question: 'Where is the Talent that was given to you?'

"'Where was your sword in the hour of your country's danger?'

"'Where was your picture, your consecration of your art to the service of morality and humanity, when the doors of the great Exhibition were thrown open?'

"'Where was your silver eloquence, your voice of persuasion, when the strife of party was at its fiercest?'

"'Where was your God-given skill in healing when One of Royal Blood lay fainting on the bed of dire--almost mortal--sickness?'

"And the answer? 'I laid it up in a napkin.' And now, etc., etc."

Then the whole six hundred boys sang "O Paradise! O Paradise!" with a fervour and sincerity that were irresistible. The organ thundered till the bad glass shivered and rattled, and the service was over.

V

Almost the last words that Ambrose had heard after his wonderful awaking were odd enough, though at the time he took little note of them, since they were uttered amidst passionate embraces, amidst soft kisses on his poor beaten flesh. Indeed, if these words recurred to him afterwards, they never made much impression on his mind, though to most people they would seem of more serious import than much else that was uttered that night! The sentences ran something like this:

"The cruel, wicked brute! He shall be sorry all his days, and every blow shall be a grief to him. My dear! I promise you he shall pay for to-night ten times over. His heart shall ache for it till it stops beating."

There cannot be much doubt that this promise was kept to the letter. No one knew how wicked rumours concerning Mr. Horbury got abroad in Lupton, but from that very day the execution of the sentence began. In the evening the High Usher, paying a visit to a friend in town, took a short cut through certain dark, ill-lighted streets, and was suddenly horrified to hear his name shrieked out, coupled with a most disgusting accusation. His heart sank down in his breast; his face, he knew, was bloodless; and then he rushed forward to the malpassage whence the voice seemed to proceed.

There was nothing there. It was a horrid little alley, leading from one slum to another, between low walls and waste back-gardens, dismal and lampless. Horbury ran at top speed to the end of it, but there was nothing to be done. A few women were gossiping at their doors, a couple of men slouched past on their way to the beer-shop at the corner--that was all. He asked one of the women if she had seen anybody running, and she said no, civilly enough--and yet he fancied that she had leered at him.

He turned and went back home. He was not in the mood for paying visits. It was some time before he could compose his mind by assuring himself that the incident, though unpleasant, was not of the slightest significance. But from that day the nets were about his feet, and his fate was sealed.

Personally, he was subjected to no further annoyance, and soon forgot that unpleasant experience in the back-street. But it seems certain that from that Sunday onwards a cloud of calumny overshadowed the High Usher in all his ways. No one said anything definite, but everyone appeared to be conscious of something unpleasant when Horbury's name was mentioned. People looked oddly at one another, and the subject was changed.

One of the young masters, speaking to a colleague, did indeed allude casually to Horbury as Xanthias Phoceus. The other master, a middle-aged man, raised his eyebrows and shook his head without speaking. It is understood that these muttered slanders were various in their nature; but, as has been said, everything was indefinite, intangible as contagion--and as deadly to the master's worldly health.

That horrible accusation which had been screamed out of the alley was credited by some; others agreed with the young master; while a few had a terrible story of an idiot girl in a remote Derbyshire village. And the persistence of all these fables was strange.

It was four years before Henry Vibart Chesson, D. D., ascended the throne of St. Guthmund at Dorchester; and all through those four years the fountain of evil innuendo rose without ceasing. It is doubtful how far belief in the truth of these scandals was firm and settled, or how far they were in the main uttered and circulated by ill-natured people who disliked Horbury, but did not in their hearts believe him guilty of worse sins than pompousness and arrogance. The latter is the more probable opinion.

Of course, the deliberations of the Trustees were absolutely secret, and the report that the Chairman, the Marquis of Dunham, said something about Cæsar's wife is a report and nothing more. It is evident that the London press was absolutely in the dark as to the existence of this strange conspiracy of vengeance, since two of the chief dailies took the appointment of the High Usher to the Headmastership as a foregone conclusion, prophesying, indeed, a rule of phenomenal success. And then Millward, a Winchester man, understood to be rather unsound on some scholastic matters--"not quite the right man"; "just a little bit of a Jesuit"--received the appointment, and people did begin to say that there must be a screw loose somewhere. And Horbury was overwhelmed, and began to die.

The odd thing was that, save on that Sunday night, he never saw the enemy; he never suspected that there was an enemy; And as for the incident of the alley, after a little consideration

362

he treated it with contempt. It was only some drunken beast in the town who knew him by sight and wished to be offensive, in the usual fashion of drunken beasts.

And there was nothing else. Lupton society was much too careful to allow its suspicions to be known. A libel action meant, anyhow, a hideous scandal and might have no pleasant results for the libellers. Besides, no one wanted to offend Horbury, who was suspected of possessing a revengeful temper; and it had not dawned on the Lupton mind that the rumours they themselves were circulating would eventually ruin the High Usher's chances of the Headmastership. Each gossip heard, as it were, only his own mutter at the moment. He did not realize that when a great many people are muttering all at once an ugly noise of considerable volume is being produced.

It is true that a few of the masters were somewhat cold in their manner. They lacked the social gift of dissimulation, and could not help showing their want of cordiality. But Horbury, who noticed this, put it down to envy and disaffection, and resolved that the large powers given him by the Trustees should not be in vain so far as the masters in question were concerned.

Indeed, C. L. Wood, who was afterwards Headmaster of Marcester and died in Egypt a few years ago, had a curious story which in part relates to the masters in question, and perhaps throws some light on the extraordinary tale of Horbury's ruin.

Wood was an old Luptonian. He was a mighty athlete in his time, and his records for the Long Jump and Throwing the Cricket Ball have not been beaten at Lupton to this day. He had been one of the first boarders taken at the Old Grange. The early relations between Horbury and himself had been continued in later life, and Wood was staying with his former master at the time when the Trustee's decision was announced. It is supposed, indeed, that Horbury had offered him a kind of unofficial, but still important, position in the New Model; in fact, Wood confessed over his port that the idea was that he should be a kind of "Intelligence Department" to the Head. He did not seem very clear as to the exact scope of his proposed duties. We may certainly infer, however, that they would have been of a very confidential nature, for Wood had jotted down his recollections of that fatal morning somewhat as follows:

"I never saw Horbury in better spirits. Indeed, I remember thinking that he was younger than ever--younger than he was in the old days when he was a junior master and I was in the Third. Of course, he was always energetic; one could not disassociate the two notions of Horbury and energy, and I used to make him laugh by threatening to include the two terms in the new edition of my little book, Latin and English Synonyms. It did not matter whether he were taking the Fifth, or editing Classics for his boys, or playing rocker--one could not help rejoicing in the vivid and ebullient energy of the man. And perhaps this is one reason why shirkers and loafers dreaded him, as they certainly did.

"But during those last few days at Lupton his vitality had struck me as quite superhuman. As all the world knows, his succession to the Headmastership was regarded by everyone as assured, and he was, naturally and properly, full of the great task which he believed was before him. This is not the place to argue the merits or demerits of the scheme which had been maturing for many years in his brain.

"A few persons who, I cannot but think, have received very imperfect information on the subject, have denounced Horbury's views of the modern Public School as revolutionary. Revolutionary they certainly were, as an express engine is revolutionary compared to an ox-waggon. But those who think of the late Canon Horbury as indifferent to the good side of Public School traditions knew little of the real man. However, were his plans good or bad, they were certainly of vast scope, and on the first night of my visit he made me sit up with him till two o'clock while he expounded his ideas, some of which, as he was good enough to say, he trusted to me to carry out. He showed me the piles of MS. he had accumulated: hundreds of pages relating to the multiple departments of the great organisation which he was to direct, or rather to create; sheets of serried figures, sheaves of estimates which he had caused to be made out in readiness for immediate action.

"Nothing was neglected. I remember seeing a note on the desirability of compiling a 'Lupton Hymn Book' for use in the Chapel, and another on the question of forming a Botanical Garden, so that the school botany might be learned from 'the green life,' as he beautifully expressed it, not from dry letterpress and indifferent woodcuts. Then, I think, on a corner of the 'Botany Leaf' was a jotting--a mere hasty scrawl, waiting development and consideration: 'Should we teach Hindustani? Write to Tucker re the Moulvie Ahmed Khan.'

"I despair of giving the reader any conception of the range and minuteness of these wonderful memoranda. I remember saying to Horbury that he seemed to be able to use the microscope and the telescope at the same time. He laughed joyously, and told me to wait till he was really at work. 'You will have your share, I promise you,' he added. His high spirits were extraordinary and infectious. He was an excellent raconteur, and now and again, amidst his talk of the New Lupton which he was about to translate from the idea into substance, he told some wonderful stories which

I have not the heart to set down here. Tu ne quæsieris. I have often thought of those lines when I remember Horbury's intense happiness, the nervous energy which made the delay of a day or two seem almost intolerable. His brain and his fingers tingled, as it were, to set about the great work before him. He reminded me of a mighty host, awaiting but the glance of their general to rush forward with irresistible force.

"There was not a trace of misgiving. Indeed, I should have been utterly astonished if I had seen anything of the kind. He told me, indeed, that for some time past he had suspected the existence of a sort of cabal or clique against him. 'A. and X., B. and Y., M. and N., and, I think, Z., are in it,' he said, naming several of the masters. 'They are jealous, I suppose, and want to make things as difficult as they can. They are all cowards, though, and I don't believe one of them--except, perhaps, M.--would fail in obedience, or rather in subservience, when it comes to the point. But I am going to make short work of the lot.' And he told me his intention of ridding the school of these disaffected elements. 'The Trustees will back me up, I know,' he added, 'but we must try to avoid all unnecessary friction'; and he explained to me a plan he had thought of for eliminating the masters in question. 'It won't do to have half-hearted officers on our ship,' was the way in which he put it, and I cordially agreed with him.

"Possibly he may have underrated the force of the opposition which he treated so lightly; possibly he altogether misjudged the situation. He certainly regarded the appointment as already made, and this, of course, was, or appeared to be, the conviction of all who knew anything of Lupton and Horbury.

"I shall never forget the day on which the news came. Horbury made a hearty breakfast, opening letters, jotting down notes, talking of his plans as the meal proceeded. I left him for a while. I was myself a good deal excited, and I strolled up and down the beautiful garden at the Old Grange, wondering whether I should be able to satisfy such a chief who, the soul of energy himself, would naturally expect a like quality in his subordinates. I rejoined him in the course of an hour in the study, where he was as busy as ever--'snowed up,' as he expressed it, in a vast pile of papers and correspondence.

"He nodded genially and pointed to a chair, and a few minutes later a servant came in with a letter. She had just found it in the hall, she explained. I had taken a book and was reading. I noticed nothing till what I can only call a groan of intense anguish made me look up in amazement--indeed, in horror--and I was shocked to see my old friend, his face a ghastly white, his eyes staring into vacancy, and his expression one of the most terrible--the most terrible--that I have ever witnessed. I cannot describe that look. There was an agony of grief and despair, a glance of the wildest amazement, terror, as of an impending awful death, and with these the fiercest and most burning anger that I have ever seen on any human face. He held a letter clenched in his hand. I was afraid to speak or move.

"It was fully five minutes before he regained his self-control, and he did this with an effort which was in itself dreadful to contemplate--so severe was the struggle. He explained to me in a voice which faltered and trembled with the shock that he had received, that he had had very bad news--that a large sum of money which was absolutely necessary to the carrying out of his projects had been embezzled by some unscrupulous person, that he did not know what he should do. He fell back into his chair; in a few minutes he had become an old man.

"He did not seem upset, or even astonished, when, later in the day, a telegram announced that he had failed in the aim of his life--that a stranger was to bear rule in his beloved Lupton. He murmured something to the effect that it was no matter now. He never held up his head again."

This note is an extract from George Horbury: a Memoir. It was written by Dr. Wood for the use of a few friends and privately printed in a small edition of a hundred and fifty copies. The author felt, as he explains in his brief Foreword, that by restricting the sale to those who either knew Horbury or were especially interested in his work, he was enabled to dwell somewhat intimately on matters which could hardly have been treated in a book meant for the general public.

The extract that has been made from this book is interesting on two points. It shows that Horbury was quite unaware of what had been going on for four years before Chesson's resignation and that he had entirely misinterpreted the few and faint omens which had been offered him. He was preparing to break a sulky sentinel or two when all the ground of his fortalice was a very network of loaded mines! The other point is still more curious. It will be seen from Wood's story that the terrific effect that he describes was produced by a letter, received some hours before the news of the Trustees' decision arrived by telegram. "Later in the day" is the phrase in the Memoir; as a matter of fact, the final deliberation of the Lupton Trustees, held at Marshall's Hotel in Albemarle Street, began at eleven-thirty and was not over till one-forty-five. It is not likely that the result could have reached the Old Grange before two-fifteen; whereas the letter found in the hall must have been read by Horbury before ten o'clock. The invariable breakfast hour at the Old Grange was eight o'clock.

C. L. Wood says: "I rejoined him in the course of an hour," and the letter was brought in "a few minutes later." Afterwards, when the fatal telegram arrived, the Memoir notes that the unfortunate man was not "even astonished." It seems to follow almost necessarily from these facts that Horbury learnt the story of his ruin from the letter, for it has been ascertained that the High Usher's account of the contents of the letter was false from beginning to end. Horbury's most excellent and sagacious investments were all in the impeccable hands of "Witham's" (Messrs. Witham, Venables, Davenport and Witham), of Raymond Buildings, Gray's Inn, who do not include embezzlement in their theory and practice of the law; and, as a matter of fact, the nephew, Charles Horbury, came into a very handsome fortune on the death of his uncle--eighty thousand pounds in personality, with the Old Grange and some valuable ground rents in the new part of Lupton. It is as certain as anything can be that George Horbury never lost a penny by embezzlement or, indeed, in any other way.

One may surmise, then, the real contents of that terrible letter. In general, that is, for it is impossible to conjecture whether the writer told the whole story; one does not know, for example, whether Meyrick's name was mentioned or not: whether there was anything which carried the reader's mind to that dark evening in November when he beat the white-faced boy with such savage cruelty. But from Dr. Wood's description of the wretched man's appearance one understands how utterly unexpected was the crushing blow that had fallen upon him. It was a lightning flash from the sky at its bluest, and before that sudden and awful blast his whole life fell into deadly and evil ruin.

"He never held up his head again." He never lived again, one may say, unless a ceaseless wheel of anguish and anger and bitter and unavailing and furious regret can be called life. It was not a man, but a shell, full of gall and fire, that went to Wareham; but probably he was not the first of the Klippoth to be made a Canon.

As we have no means of knowing exactly what or how much that letter told him, one is not in a position to say whether he recognised the singularity--one might almost say, the eccentricity--with which his punishment was stage-managed. Nec deus intersit certainly; but a principle may be pushed too far, and a critic might point out that, putting avenging deities in their machines on one side, it was rather going to the other extreme to bring about the Great Catastrophe by means of bad sherry, a trying Headmaster, boiled mutton, a troublesome schoolboy and a servant-maid. Yet these were the agents employed; and it seems that we are forced to the conclusion that we do not altogether understand the management of the universe. The conclusion is a dangerous one, since we may be led by it, unless great care is exercised, into the worst errors of the Dark Ages.

There is the question, of course, of the truthfulness or falsity of the various slanders which had such a tremendous effect. The worst of them were lies--there can be little doubt of that--and for the rest, it may be hinted that the allusion of the young master to Xanthias Phoceus was not very far wide of the mark. Mrs. Horbury had been dead some years, and it is to be feared that there had been passages between the High Usher and Nelly Foran which public opinion would have condemned. It would be difficult to tell the whole story, but the girl's fury of revenge makes one apt to believe that she was exacting payment not only for Ambrose's wrongs, but for some grievous injury done to herself.

But before all these things could be brought to their ending, Ambrose Meyrick had to live in wonders and delights, to be initiated in many mysteries, to discover the meaning of that voice which seemed to speak within him, denouncing him because he had pried unworthily into the Secret which is hidden from the Holy Angels.

III

I

One of Ambrose Meyrick's favourite books was a railway timetable. He spent many hours in studying these intricate pages of figures, noting times of arrival and departure on a piece of paper, and following the turnings and intersections of certain lines on the map. In this way he had at last arrived at the best and quickest route to his native country, which he had not seen for five years. His father had died when he was ten years old.

This result once obtained, the seven-thirty to Birmingham got him in at nine-thirty-five; the ten-twenty for the west was a capital train, and he would see the great dome of Mynydd Mawr before one o'clock. His fancy led him often to a bridge which crossed the railway about a mile out of Lupton. East and west the metals stretched in a straight line, defying, it seemed, the wisdom of Euclid. He turned from the east and gazed westward, and when a red train went by in the right direction he would lean over the bridge and watch till the last flying carriage had vanished into the distance. He imagined himself in that train and thought of the joy of it, if the time ever came--for it seemed long--the joy in every revolution of the wheels, in every whistle of the engine; in the rush and in the rhythm of this swift flight from that horrible school and that horrible place.

Year after year went by and he had not revisited the old land of his father. He was left alone in the great empty house in charge of the servants during the holidays--except one summer when Mr. Horbury despatched him to a cousin of his who lived at Yarmouth.

The second year after his father's death there was a summer of dreadful heat. Day after day the sky was a glare of fire, and in these abhorred Midlands, far from the breath of the sea and the mountain breeze, the ground baked and cracked and stank to heaven. A dun smoke rose from the earth with the faint, sickening stench of a brick-field, and the hedgerows swooned in the heat and in the dust. Ambrose's body and soul were athirst with the desire of the hills and the woods; his heart cried out within him for the waterpools in the shadow of the forest; and in his ears continually he heard the cold water pouring and trickling and dripping from the grey rocks on the great mountain side. And he saw that awful land which God has no doubt made for manufacturers to prepare them for their eternal habitation, its weary waves burning under the glaring sky: the factory chimneys of Lupton vomiting their foul smoke; the mean red streets, each little hellway with its own stink; the dull road, choking in its dust. For streams there was the Wand, running like black oil between black banks, steaming here as boiling poisons were belched into it from the factory wall; there glittering with iridescent scum vomited from some other scoundrel's castle. And for the waterpools of the woods he was free to gaze at the dark green liquor in the tanks of the Sulphuric Acid factory, but a little way out of town. Lupton was a very rising place.

His body was faint with the burning heat and the foulness of all about him, and his soul was sick with loneliness and friendlessness and unutterable longing. He had already mastered his Bradshaw and had found out the bridge over the railway; and day after day he leaned over the parapet and watched the burning metals vanishing into the west, into the hot, thick haze that hung over all the land. And the trains sped away towards the haven of his desire, and he wondered if he should ever see again the dearly loved country or hear the song of the nightingale in the still white morning, in the circle of the green hills. The thought of his father, of the old days of happiness, of the grey home in the still valley, swelled in his heart and he wept bitterly, so utterly forsaken and wretched seemed his life.

It happened towards the end of that dreadful August that one night he had tossed all through the hours listening to the chiming bells, only falling into a fevered doze a little while before they called him. He woke from ugly and oppressive dreams to utter wretchedness; he crawled downstairs like an old man and left his breakfast untouched, for he could eat nothing. The flame of the sun seemed to burn in his brain; the hot smoke of the air choked him. All his limbs ached. From head to foot he was a body of suffering. He struggled out and tottered along the road to the bridge and gazed with dim, hopeless eyes along the path of desire, into the heavy, burning mist in the far distance. And then his heart beat quick, and he cried aloud in his amazed delight; for, in the shimmering glamour of the haze, he saw as in a mirror the vast green wall of the Great Mountain rise before him--not far, but as if close at hand. Nay, he stood upon its slope; his feet were in the sweet-smelling bracken; the hazel thicket was rustling beneath him in the brave wind, and the shining water poured cold from the stony rock. He heard the silver note of the lark, shrilling high and glad in the sunlight. He saw the yellow blossoms tossed by the breeze about the porch of the white house. He seemed to turn in this vision and before him the dear, long-remembered land appeared in its great peace and beauty: meadows and cornfield, hill and valley and deep wood between the mountains and the far sea. He drew a long breath of that quickening and glorious air, and knew that life had returned to him. And then he was gazing once more down the glittering railway into the mist; but strength and hope had replaced that deadly sickness of a moment before, and light and joy came back to his eyes.

The vision had doubtless been given to him in his sore and pressing need. It returned no more; not again did he see the fair height of Mynydd Mawr rise out of the mist. But from that day the station on the bridge was daily consecrated. It was his place of refreshment and hope in many seasons of evil and weariness. From this place he could look forward to the hour of release and return that must come at last. Here he could remind himself that the bonds of the flesh had been broken in a wonderful manner; that he had been set free from the jaws of hell and death.

Fortunately, few people came that way. It was but a by-road serving a few farms in the neighbourhood, and on the Sunday afternoon, in November, the Head's sermon over and dinner eaten, he betook himself to his tower, free to be alone for a couple of hours, at least.

He stood there, leaning on the wall, his face turned, as ever, to the west, and, as it were, a great flood of rapture overwhelmed him. He sank down, deeper, still deeper, into the hidden and marvellous places of delight. In his country there were stories of the magic people who rose all gleaming from the pools in lonely woods; who gave more than mortal bliss to those who loved them; who could tell the secrets of that land where flame was the most material substance; whose inhabitants dwelt in palpitating and quivering colours or in the notes of a wonderful melody. And in the dark of the night all legends had been fulfilled.

It was a strange thing, but Ambrose Meyrick, though he was a public schoolboy of fifteen, had lived all his days in a rapt innocence. It is possible that in school, as elsewhere, enlightenment, pleasant or unpleasant, only comes to those who seek for it--or one may say certainly that there are those who dwell under the protection of enchantments, who may go down into the black depths and yet appear resurgent and shining, without any stain or defilement of the pitch on their white robes. For these have ears so intent on certain immortal songs that they cannot hear discordant voices; their eyes are veiled with a light that shuts out the vision of evil. There are flames about these feet that extinguish the gross fires of the pit.

It is probable that all through those early years Ambrose's father had been charming his son's heart, drawing him forth from the gehenna-valley of this life into which he had fallen, as one draws forth a beast that has fallen into some deep and dreadful place. Various are the methods recommended. There is the way of what is called moral teaching, the way of physiology and the way of a masterly silence; but Mr. Meyrick's was the strange way of incantation. He had, in a certain manner, drawn the boy aside from that evil traffic of the valley, from the stench of the turmoil, from the blows and the black lechery, from the ugly fight in the poisonous smoke, from all the amazing and hideous folly that practical men call life, and had set him in that endless procession that for ever and for ever sings its litanies in the mountains, going from height to height on its great quest. Ambrose's soul had been caught in the sweet thickets of the woods; it had been bathed in the pure water of blessed fountains; it had knelt before the altars of the old saints, till all the earth was become a sanctuary, all life was a rite and ceremony, the end of which was the attainment of the mystic sanctity--the achieving of the Graal. For this--for what else?--were all things made. It was this that the little bird sang of in the bush, piping a few feeble, plaintive notes of dusky evenings, as if his tiny heart were sad that it could utter nothing better than such sorry praises. This also celebrated the awe of the white morning on the hills, the breath of the woods at dawn. This was figured in the red ceremony of sunset, when flames shone over the dome of the great mountain, and roses blossomed in the far plains of the sky. This was the secret of the dark places in the heart of the woods. This the mystery of the sunlight on the height; and every little flower, every delicate fern, and every reed and rush was entrusted with the hidden declaration of this sacrament. For this end, final and perfect rites had been given to men to execute; and these were all the arts, all the far-lifted splendour of the great cathedral; all rich carven work and all glowing colours; all magical utterance of word and tones: all these things were the witnesses that consented in the One Offering, in the high service of the Graal.

To this service also, together with songs and burning torches and dyed garments and the smoke of the bruised incense, were brought the incense of the bruised heart, the magic torches of virtue hidden from the world, the red dalmatics of those whose souls had been martyred, the songs of triumph and exultation chanted by them that the profane had crushed into the dust; holy wells and water-stoups were fountains of tears. So must the Mass be duly celebrated in Cor-arbennic when Cadwaladr returned, when Teilo Agyos lifted up again the Shining Cup.

Perhaps it was not strange that a boy who had listened to such spells as these should heed nothing of the foolish evils about him, the nastiness of silly children who, for want of wits, were "crushing the lilies into the dunghill." He listened to nothing of their ugly folly; he heard it not, understood it not, thought as little of it as of their everlasting chatter about "brooks" and "quarries" and "leg-hits" and "beaks from the off." And when an unseemly phrase did chance to fall on his ear it was of no more import or meaning than any or all of the stupid jargon that went on day after day, mixing itself with the other jargon about the optative and the past participle, the oratio obliqua and the verbs in [Greek: mi]. To him this was all one nothingness, and he would not have dreamed of connecting anything of it with the facts of life, as he understood life.

Hence it was that for him all that was beautiful and wonderful was a part of sanctity; all the glory of life was for the service of the sanctuary, and when one saw a lovely flower it was to be strewn before the altar, just as the bee was holy because by its wax the Gifts are illuminated. Where joy and delight and beauty were, there he knew by sure signs were the parts of the mystery, the glorious apparels of the heavenly vestments. If anyone had told him that the song of the nightingale was an unclean thing he would have stared in amazement, as though one had blasphemed the Sanctus. To him the red roses were as holy as the garments of the martyrs. The white lilies were pure and shining virtues; the imagery of the Song of Songs was obvious and perfect and unassailable, for in this world there was nothing common nor unclean. And even to him the great gift had been freely given.

So he stood, wrapt in his meditations and in his ecstasy, by the bridge over the Midland line from Lupton to Birmingham. Behind him were the abominations of Lupton: the chimneys vomiting black smoke faintly in honour of the Sabbath; the red lines of the workmen's streets advancing into the ugly fields; the fuming pottery kilns, the hideous height of the boot factory. And before him stretched the unspeakable scenery of the eastern Midlands, which seems made for the habitation of English Nonconformists--dull, monotonous, squalid, the very hedgerows cropped and trimmed, the trees looking like rows of Roundheads, the farmhouses as uninteresting as suburban villas. On a field near at hand a scientific farmer had recently applied an agreeable mixture consisting of superphosphate of lime, nitrate of soda and bone meal. The stink was that of a chemical works or a Texel cheese. Another field was just being converted into an orchard. There were rows of grim young apple trees planted at strictly mathematical intervals from one another, and grisly little graves had been dug between the apple trees for the reception of gooseberry bushes. Between these rows the farmer hoped to grow potatoes, so the ground had been thoroughly trenched. It looked sodden and unpleasant. To the right Ambrose could see how the operations on a wandering brook were progressing. It had moved in and out in the most wasteful and absurd manner, and on each bank there had grown a twisted brake of trees and bushes and rank water plants. There were wonderful red roses there in summer time. Now all this was being rectified. In the first place the stream had been cut into a straight channel with raw, bare banks, and then the rose bushes, the alders, the willows and the rest were being grubbed up by the roots and so much valuable land was being redeemed. The old barn which used to be visible on the left of the line had been pulled down for more than a year. It had dated perhaps from the seventeenth century. Its roof-tree had dipped and waved in a pleasant fashion, and the red tiles had the glow of the sun in their colours, and the half-timbered walls were not lacking in ruinous brace. It was a dilapidated old shed, and a neat-looking structure with a corrugated iron roof now stood in its place.

Beyond all was the grey prison wall of the horizon; but Ambrose no longer gazed at it with the dim, hopeless eyes of old. He had a Breviary among his books, and he thought of the words: Anima mea erepta est sicut passer de laqueo venantium, and he knew that in a good season his body would escape also. The exile would end at last.

He remembered an old tale which his father was fond of telling him--the story of Eos Amherawdur (the Emperor Nightingale). Very long ago, the story began, the greatest and the finest court in all the realms of faery was the court of the Emperor Eos, who was above all the kings of the Tylwydd Têg, as the Emperor of Rome is head over all the kings of the earth. So that even Gwyn ap Nudd, whom they now call lord over all the fair folk of the Isle of Britain, was but the man of Eos, and no splendour such as his was ever seen in all the regions of enchantment and faery. Eos had his court in a vast forest, called Wentwood, in the deepest depths of the green-wood between Caerwent and Caermaen, which is also called the City of the Legions; though some men say that we should rather name it the city of the Waterfloods. Here, then, was the Palace of Eos, built of the finest stones after the Roman manner, and within it were the most glorious chambers that eye has ever seen, and there was no end to the number of them, for they could not be counted. For the stones of the palace being immortal, they were at the pleasure of the Emperor. If he had willed, all the hosts of the world could stand in his greatest hall, and, if he had willed, not so much as an ant could enter into it, since it could not be discerned. But on common days they spread the Emperor's banquet in nine great halls, each nine times larger than any that are in the lands of the men of Normandi. And Sir Caw was the seneschal who marshalled the feast; and if you would count those under his command--go, count the drops of water that are in the Uske River. But if you would learn the splendour of this castle it is an easy matter, for Eos hung the walls of it with Dawn and Sunset. He lit it with the sun and moon. There was a well in it called Ocean. And nine churches of twisted boughs were set apart in which Eos might hear Mass; and when his clerks sang before him all the jewels rose shining out of the earth, and all the stars bent shining down from heaven, so enchanting was the melody. Then was great bliss in all the regions of the fair folk. But Eos was grieved because mortal ears could not hear nor comprehend the enchantment of their song. What, then, did he do? Nothing less than this. He divested himself of all his glories and of his kingdom, and transformed himself into the shape of a little brown bird, and went flying about the woods, desirous of teaching men the sweetness of the faery melody. And all the other birds said: "This is a contemptible stranger." The eagle found him not even worthy to be a prey; the raven and the magpie called him simpleton; the pheasant asked where he had got that ugly livery; the lark wondered why he hid himself in the darkness of the wood; the peacock would not suffer his name to be uttered. In short never was anyone so despised as was Eos by all the chorus of the birds. But wise men heard that song from the faery regions and listened all night beneath the bough, and these were the first who were bards in the Isle of Britain.

Ambrose had heard the song from the faery regions. He had heard it in swift whispers at his ear, in sighs upon his breast, in the breath of kisses on his lips. Never was he numbered amongst the despisers of Eos.

II

Mr. Horbury had suffered from one or two slight twinges of conscience for a few days after he had operated on his nephew. They were but very slight pangs, for, after all, it was a case of flagrant and repeated disobedience to rules, complicated by lying. The High Usher was quite sincere in scouting the notion of a boy's taking any interest in Norman architecture, and, as he said to himself, truly enough, if every boy at Lupton could come and go when and how he pleased, and choose which rules he would keep and which disobey--why, the school would soon be in a pretty state. Still, there was a very faint and indistinct murmur in his mind which suggested that Meyrick had received, in addition to his own proper thrashing, the thrashings due to the Head, his cook and his wine merchant. And Horbury was rather sorry, for he desired to be just according to his definition of justice--unless, indeed justice should be excessively inconvenient.

But these faint scruples were soon removed--turned, indeed, to satisfaction by the evident improvement which declared itself in Ambrose Meyrick's whole tone and demeanour. He no longer did his best to avoid rocker. He played, and played well and with relish. The boy was evidently all right at heart: he had only wanted a sharp lesson, and it was clear that, once a loafer, he was now on his way to be a credit to the school. And by some of those secret channels which are known to masters and to masters alone, rather more than a glimmering of the truth as to Rawson's black eyes and Pelly's disfigured nose was vouchsafed to Horbury's vision, and he was by no means displeased with his nephew. The two boys had evidently asked for punishment, and had got it. It served them right. Of course, if the swearing had been brought to his notice by official instead of by subterranean and mystic ways, he would have had to cane Meyrick a second time, since, by the Public School convention, an oath is a very serious offence--as bad as smoking, or worse; but, being far from a fool, under the circumstances he made nothing of it. Then the lad's school work was so very satisfactory. It had always been good, but it had become wonderfully good. That last Greek prose had shown real grip of the language. The High Usher was pleased. His sharp lesson had brought forth excellent results, and he foresaw the day when he would be proud of having taught a remarkably fine scholar.

With the boys Ambrose was becoming a general favourite. He learned not only to play rocker, he showed Pelly how he thought that blow under the ear should be dealt with. They all said he was a good fellow; but they could not make out why, without apparent reason, he would sometimes burst out into loud laughter. But he said it was something wrong with his inside--the doctors couldn't make it out--and this seemed rather interesting.

In after life he often looked back upon this period when, to all appearance, Lupton was "making a man" of him, and wondered at its strangeness. To boys and masters alike he was an absolutely normal schoolboy, busy with the same interests as the rest of them. There was certainly something rather queer in his appearance; but, as they said, generously enough, a fellow couldn't help his looks; and, that curious glint in the eyes apart, he seemed as good a Luptonian as any in the whole six hundred. Everybody thought that he had absolutely fallen into line; that he was absorbing the ethos of the place in the most admirable fashion, subduing his own individuality, his opinions, his habits, to the general tone of the community around him--putting off, as it were, the profane dust of his own spirit and putting on the mental frock of the brotherhood. This, of course, is one of the aims--rather, the great aim--of the system: this fashioning of very diverse characters into one common form, so that each great Public School has its type, which is easily recognisable in the grown-up man years after his school days are over. Thus, in far lands, in India and Egypt, in Canada and New Zealand, one recognises the brisk alertness of the Etonian, the exquisite politeness of Harrow, the profound seriousness of Rugby; while the note of Lupton may, perhaps, be called finality. The Old Luptonian no more thinks of arguing a question than does the Holy Father, and his conversation is a series of irreformable dogmas, and the captious person who questions any one article is made to feel himself a cad and an outsider.

Thus it has been related that two men who had met for the first time at a certain country house-party were getting on together capitally in the evening over their whisky and soda and cigars. Each held identical views of equal violence on some important topic--Home Rule or the Transvaal or Free Trade--and, as the more masterful of the two asserted that hanging was too good for Blank (naming a well-known statesman), the other would reply: "I quite agree with you: hanging is too good for Blank."

"He ought to be burned alive," said the one.

"That's about it: he ought to be burned at the stake," answered the other.

"Look at the way he treated Dash! He's a coward and a damned scoundrel!"

"Perfectly right. He's a damned cursed scoundrel!"

This was splendid, and each thought the other a charming companion. Unfortunately, however, the conversation, by some caprice, veered from the iniquities of Blank and glanced aside to cookery--possibly by the track of Irish stew, used metaphorically to express the disastrous and iniquitous policy of the great statesman with regard to Ireland. But, as it happened, there was not the same coincidence on the question of cookery as there had been on the question of Blank. The masterful man said:

"No cookery like English. No other race in the world can cook as we do. Look at French cookery--a lot of filthy, greasy messes."

Now, instead of assenting briskly and firmly as before the other man said: "Been much in France? Lived there?"

"Never set foot in the beastly country! Don't like their ways, and don't care to dine off snails and frogs swimming in oil."

The other man began then to talk of the simple but excellent meals he had relished in France-- the savoury croûte-au-pot, the bouilli--good eating when flavoured by a gherkin or two; velvety épinards au jus, a roast partridge, a salad, a bit of Roquefort and a bunch of grapes. But he had barely mentioned the soup when the masterful one wheeled round his chair and offered a fine view of his strong, well-knit figure--as seen from the back. He did not say anything--he simply took up the paper and went on smoking. The other men stared in amazement: the amateur of French cookery looked annoyed. But the host--a keen-eyed old fellow with a white moustache, turned to the enemy of frogs and snails and grease and said quite simply: "I say, Mulock, I never knew you'd been at Lupton."

Mulock gazed. The other men held their breath for a moment as the full force of the situation dawned on them, and then a wild scream of laughter shrilled from their throats. Yells and roars of mirth resounded in the room. Their delight was insatiable. It died for a moment for lack of breath, and then burst out anew in still louder, more uproarious clamour, till old Sir Henry Rawnsley, who was fat and short, could do nothing but choke and gasp and crow out a sound something between a wheeze and a chuckle. Mulock left the room immediately, and the house the next morning. He made some excuse to his host, but he told enquiring friends that, personally, he disliked bounders.

The story, true or false, illustrates the common view of the Lupton stamp.

"We try to teach the boys to know their own minds," said the Headmaster, and the endeavour seems to have succeeded in most cases. And, as Horbury noted in an article he once wrote on the Public School system, every boy was expected to submit himself to the process, to form and reform himself in accordance with the tone of the school.

"I sometimes compare our work with that of the metal founder," he says in the article in question. "Just as the metal comes to the foundry rudis indigestaque moles, a rough and formless mass, without the slightest suggestion of the shape which it must finally assume, so a boy comes to a great Public School with little or nothing about him to suggest the young man who, in eight or nine years' time, will say good-bye to the dear old school, setting his teeth tight, restraining himself from giving up to the anguish of this last farewell. Nay, I think that ours is the harder task, for the metal that is sent to the foundry has, I presume, been freed of its impurities; we have to deal rather with the ore--a mass which is not only shapeless, but contains much that is not metal at all, which must be burnt out and cast aside as useless rubbish. So the boy comes from his home, which may or may not have possessed valuable formative influences; which we often find has tended to create a spirit of individualism and assertiveness; which, in numerous cases, has left the boy under the delusion that he has come into the world to live his own life and think his own thoughts. This is the ore that we cast into our furnace. We burn out the dross and rubbish; we liquefy the stubborn and resisting metal till it can be run into the mould--the mould being the whole tone and feeling of a great community. We discourage all excessive individuality; we make it quite plain to the boy that he has come to Lupton, not to live his life, not to think his thoughts, but to live our life, to think our thoughts. Very often, as I think I need scarcely say, the process is a somewhat unpleasant one, but, sooner or later, the stubbornest metal yields to the cleansing, renewing, restoring fires of discipline and public opinion, and the shapeless mass takes on the shape of the Great School. Only the other day an old pupil came to see me and confessed that, for the whole of his first year at Lupton, he had been profoundly wretched. 'I was a dreamy young fool,' he said. 'My head was stuffed with all sorts of queer fancies, and I expect that if I hadn't come to Lupton I should have turned out an absolute loafer. But I hated it badly that first year. I loathed rocker--I did, really--and I thought the fellows were a lot of savages. And then I seemed to go into a kind of cloud. You see, Sir, I was losing my old self and hadn't got the new self in its place, and I couldn't make out what was happening. And then, quite suddenly, it all came out light and clear. I saw the purpose behind it all--how we were all working together, masters and boys, for the dear old school; how we were all "members one of another," as the Doctor said in Chapel; and that I had a part in this great work, too, though I was only a kid in the Third. It was like a flash of light: one minute I was only a poor little chap that nobody cared for and who didn't matter to anybody, and the next I saw that, in a way, I was as important as the Doctor himself--I was a part of the failure or success of it all. Do you know what I did, Sir? I had a book I thought a lot of--Poems and Tales of Edgar Allan Poe. It was my poor sister's book; she had died a year before when she was only seventeen, and she had written my name in it when she was dying--she knew I was fond of reading it. It was just the sort of thing I used to like--morbid fancies and queer poems, and I was always reading it when the fellows would let me alone. But when I saw what life really was, when the meaning of it all came to me, as I said just now, I took that book and tore it to bits, and it was like tearing myself up. But I knew that writing all that stuff hadn't done that American fellow much good, and I didn't see what good I should get by reading it. I couldn't make out to myself that it would fit in with the Doctor's plans of the spirit of the school, or that I should play up at rocker any better for knowing all about the "Fall of the House of Usher," or whatever it's called. I knew my poor sister would understand, so I tore it up, and I've gone straight ahead ever since--thanks to Lupton.' Like a refiner's fire. I remembered the dreamy, absent-minded child of fifteen years before; I could scarcely believe that he stood before--keen, alert, practical, living every moment of his life, a force, a power in the world, certain of successful achievement."

Such were the influences to which Ambrose Meyrick was being subjected, and with infinite success, as it seemed to everybody who watched him. He was regarded as a conspicuous instance of the efficacy of the system--he had held out so long, refusing to absorb the "tone," presenting an obstinate surface to the millstones which would, for his own good, have ground him to powder, not concealing very much his dislike of the place and of the people in it. And suddenly he had submitted with a good grace: it was wonderful! The masters are believed to have discussed the affair amongst themselves, and Horbury, who confessed or boasted that he had used sharp persuasion, got a good deal of kudos in consequence.

III

A few years ago a little book called Half-holidays attracted some attention in semi-scholastic, semi-clerical circles. It was anonymous, and bore the modest motto Crambe bis cocta; but those behind the scenes recognised it as the work of Charles Palmer, who was for many years a master at Lupton. His acknowledged books include a useful little work on the Accents and an excellent summary of Roman History from the Fall of the Republic to Romulus Augustulus. The Half-holidays contains the following amusing passage; there is not much difficulty in identifying the N. mentioned in it with Ambrose Meyrick.

"The cleverest dominie sometimes discovers"--the passage begins--"that he has been living in a fool's paradise, that he has been tricked by a quiet and persistent subtlety that really strikes one as almost devilish when one finds it exhibited in the person of an English schoolboy. A good deal of nonsense, I think, has been written about boys by people who in reality know very little about them; they have been credited with complexities of character, with feelings and aspirations and delicacies of sentiment which are quite foreign to their nature. I can quite believe in the dead cat trick of Stalky and his friends, but I confess that the incident of the British Flag leaves me cold and sceptical. Such refinement of perception is not the way of the boy--certainly not of the boy as I have known him. He is radically a simple soul, whose feelings are on the surface; and his deepest laid schemes and manoeuvres hardly call for the talents of a Sherlock Holmes if they are to be detected and brought to naught. Of course, a good deal of rubbish has been talked about the wonderful success of our English plan of leaving the boys to themselves without the everlasting supervision which is practised in French schools. As a matter of fact, the English schoolboy is under constant supervision; where in a French school one wretched usher has to look after a whole horde of boys, in an English school each boy is perpetually under the observation of hundreds of his fellows. In reality, each boy is an unpaid pion, a watchdog whose vigilance never relaxes. He is not aware of this; one need scarcely say that such a notion is far from his wildest thoughts. He thinks, and very rightly, doubtless, that he is engaged in maintaining the honour of the school, in keeping up the observance of the school tradition, in dealing sharply with slackers and loafers who would bring discredit on the place he loves so well. He is, no doubt, absolutely right in all this; none the less, he is doing the master's work unwittingly and admirably. When one thinks of this, and of the Compulsory System of Games, which ensures that every boy shall be in a certain place at a certain time, one sees, I think, that the phrase about our lack of supervision is a phrase and nothing more. There is no system of supervision known to human wit that approaches in thoroughness and minuteness the supervision under which every single boy is kept all through his life at an English Public School.

"Hence one is really rather surprised when, in spite of all these unpaid assistants, who are the whole school, one is thoroughly and completely taken in. I can only remember one such case, and I am still astonished at the really infernal ability with which the boy in question lived a double life under the very eyes of the masters and six hundred other boys. N., as I shall call him, was not in my House, and I can scarcely say how I came to watch his career with so much interest; but there was certainly something about him which did interest me a good deal. It may have been his appearance: he was an odd-looking boy--dark, almost swarthy, dreamy and absent in manner, and, for the first years of his school life, a quite typical loafer. Such boys, of course, are not common in a big school, but there are a few such everywhere. One never knows whether this kind will write a successful book, or paint a great picture, or go to the devil--from my observation I am sorry to say that the last career is the most usual. I need scarcely say that such boys meet with but little encouragement; it is not the type which the Public School exists to foster, and the boy who abandons himself to morbid introspection is soon made to feel pretty emphatically that he is matter in the wrong place. Of course, one may be crushing genius. If this ever happened it would be very unfortunate; still, in all communities the minority must suffer for the good of the majority, and, frankly, I have always been willing to run the risk. As I have hinted, the particular sort of boy I have in my mind turns out in nine cases out of ten to be not a genius, but that much more common type--a blackguard.

"Well, as I say, I was curious about N. I was sorry for him, too; both his parents were dead, and he was rather in the position of the poor fellows who have no home life to look forward to when the holidays are getting near. And his obstinacy astonished me; in most cases the pressure of public opinion will bring the slackest loafer to a sense of the error of his ways before his first term is ended; but N. seemed to hold out against us all with a sort of dreamy resistance that was most exasperating. I do not think he can have had a very pleasant time. His general demeanour suggested that of a sage who has been cast on an island inhabited by a peculiarly repulsive and degraded tribe of savages, and I need scarcely say that the other boys did their best to make him realise the extreme absurdity of such behaviour. He was clever enough at his work, but it was difficult to make him play games, and impossible to make him play up. He seemed to be looking through us at something else; and neither the boys nor the masters liked being treated as unimportant illusions. And then, quite suddenly, N. altered completely. I believe his housemaster, worn out of all patience, gave him a severe thrashing; at any rate, the change was instant and marvellous.

"I remember that a few days before N.'s transformation we had been discussing the question of the cane at the weekly masters' meeting. I had confessed myself a very half-hearted believer in the efficacy of the treatment. I forget the arguments that I used, but I know that I was strongly inclined to favour the 'Anti-baculist Party,' as the Head jocosely named it. But a few months later when N.'s housemaster pointed out N. playing up at football like a young demon, and then with a twinkle in his eye reminded me of the position I had taken up at the masters' meeting, there was nothing for it but to own that I had been in the wrong. The cane had certainly, in this case, proved itself a magic wand; the sometime loafer had been transformed by it into one of the healthiest and most energetic fellows in the whole school. It was a pleasure to watch him at the games, and I remember that his fast bowling was at once terrific in speed and peculiarly deadly in its accuracy.

"He kept up this deception, for deception it was, for three or four years. He was just going up to Oxford, and the whole school was looking forward to a career which we knew would be quite exceptional in its brilliance. His scholarship papers astonished the Balliol authorities. I remember one of the Fellows writing to our Head about them in terms of the greatest enthusiasm, and we all knew that N.'s bowling would get him into the University Eleven in his first term. Cricketers have not yet forgotten a certain performance of his at the Oval, when, as a poetic journalist observed, wickets fell before him as ripe corn falls before the sickle. N. disappeared in the middle of term. The whole school was in a ferment; masters and boys looked at one another with wild faces; search parties were sent out to scour the country; the police were communicated with; on every side one heard the strangest surmises as to what had happened. The affair got into the papers; most people thought it was a case of breakdown and loss of memory from overwork and mental strain. Nothing could be heard of N., till, at the end of a fortnight, his Housemaster came into our room looking, as I thought, puzzled and frightened.

"'I don't understand,' he said. 'I've had this by the second post. It's in N.'s handwriting. I can't make head or tail of it. It's some sort of French, I suppose.'

"He held out a paper closely written in N.'s exquisite, curious script, which always reminded me vaguely of some Oriental character. The masters shook their heads as the manuscript went from hand to hand, and one of them suggested sending for the French master. But, as it happened, I was something of a student of Old French myself, and I found I could make out the drift of the document that N. had sent his master.

"It was written in the manner and in the language of Rabelais. It was quite diabolically clever, and beyond all question the filthiest thing I have ever read. The writer had really exceeded his master in obscenity, impossible as that might seem: the purport of it all was a kind of nightmare vision of the school, the masters and the boys. Everybody and everything were distorted in the most horrible manner, seen, we might say, through an abominable glass, and yet every feature was easily recognisable; it reminded me of Swift's disgusting description of the Yahoos, over which one may shudder and grow sick, but which one cannot affect to misunderstand. There was a fantastic episode which I remember especially. One of us, an ambitious man, who for some reason or other had become unpopular with a few of his colleagues, was described as endeavouring to climb the school clock-tower, on the top of which a certain object was said to be placed. The object was defended, so the writer affirmed, by 'the Dark Birds of Night,' who resisted the master's approach in all possible and impossible manners. Even to indicate the way in which this extraordinary theme was treated would be utterly out of the question; but I shall never forget the description of the master's face, turned up towards the object of his quest, as he painfully climbed the wall. I have never read even in the most filthy pages of Rabelais, or in the savagest passages of Swift, anything which approached the revolting cruelty of those few lines. They were compounded of hell-fire and the Cloaca Maxima.

"I read out and translated a few of the least abominable sentences. I can hardly say whether the feeling of disgust or that of bewilderment predominated amongst us. One of my colleagues stopped me and said they had heard enough; we stared at one another in silence. The astounding ability, ferocity and obscenity of the whole thing left us quite dumbfounded, and I remember saying that if a volcano were suddenly to belch forth volumes of flame and filth in the middle of the playing fields I should scarcely be more astonished. And all this was the work of N., whose brilliant abilities in games and in the schools were to have been worth many thousands a year to X., as one of us put it! This was the boy that for the last four years we had considered as a great example of the formative influences of the school! This was the N. who we thought would have died for the honour of the school, who spoke as if he could never do enough to repay what X. had done for him! As I say, we looked at one another with faces of blank amazement and horror. At last somebody said that N. must have gone mad, and we tried to believe that it was so, for madness, awful calamity as it is, would be more endurable than sanity under such circumstances as these. I need scarcely say that this charitable hypothesis turned out to be quite unfounded: N. was perfectly sane; he was simply revenging himself for the suppression of his true feelings for the four last years of his school life. The 'conversion' on which we prided ourselves had been an utter sham; the whole of his life had been an elaborately organised hypocrisy maintained with unfailing and unflinching skill term after term and year after year. One cannot help wondering when one considers the inner life of this unhappy fellow. Every morning, I suppose, he woke up with curses in his soul; he smiled at us all and joined in the games with black rage devouring him. So far as one can say, he was quite sincere in his concealed opinions at all events. The hatred, loathing and contempt of the whole system of the place displayed in that extraordinary and terrible document struck me as quite genuine; and while I was reading it I could not help thinking of his eager, enthusiastic face as he joined with a will in the school songs; he seemed to inspire all the boys about him with something of his own energy and devotion. The apparition was a shocking one; I felt that for a moment I had caught a glimpse of a region that was very like hell itself.

"I remember that the French master contributed a characteristic touch of his own. Of course, the Headmaster had to be told of the matter, and it was arranged that M. and myself should collaborate in the unpleasant task of making a translation. M. read the horrible stuff through with an expression on his face that, to my astonishment, bordered on admiration, and when he laid down the paper he said:

"'Eh bien: Maître François est encore en vie, évidemment. C'est le vrai renouveau de la Renaissance; de la Renaissance en très mauvaise humeur, si vous voulez, mais de la Renaissance tout-de-même. Si, si; c'est de la crû véritable, je vous assure. Mais, notre bon N. est un Rabelais qui a habité une terre affreusement sèche.'

"I really think that to the Frenchman the terrible moral aspect of the case was either entirely negligible or absolutely non-existent; he simply looked on N.'s detestable and filthy performance as a little masterpiece in a particular literary genre. Heaven knows! One does not want to be a Pharisee; but as I saw M. grinning appreciatively over this dung-heap I could not help feeling that the collapse of France before Germany offered no insoluble problem to the historian.

"There is little more to be said as to this extraordinary and most unpleasant affair. It was all hushed up as much as possible. No further attempts to discover N.'s whereabouts were made. It was some months before we heard by indirect means that the wretched fellow had abandoned the Balliol Scholarship and the most brilliant prospects in life to attach himself to a company of greasy barnstormers--or 'Dramatic Artists,' as I suppose they would be called nowadays. I believe that his subsequent career has been of a piece with these beginnings; but of that I desire to say nothing."

The passage has been quoted merely in evidence of the great success with which Ambrose Meyrick adapted himself to his environment at Lupton. Palmer, the writer, who was a very well-meaning though intensely stupid person, has told the bare facts as he saw them accurately enough;

it need not be said that his inferences and deductions from the facts are invariably ridiculous. He was a well-educated man; but in his heart of hearts he thought that Rabelais, Maria Monk, Gay Life in Paris and La Terre all came to much the same thing.

IV

In an old notebook kept by Ambrose Meyrick in those long-past days there are some curious entries which throw light on the extraordinary experiences that befell him during the period which poor Palmer has done his best to illustrate. The following is interesting:

"I told her she must not come again for a long time. She was astonished and asked me why-- was I not fond of her? I said it was because I was so fond of her, that I was afraid that if I saw her often I could not live. I should pass away in delight because our bodies are not meant to live for long in the middle of white fire. I was lying on my bed in my dark room and she stood beside me. I looked up at her. The room was very dark and still. I could only just see her faintly, though she was so close to me that I could hear her breathing quite well. I thought of the white flowers that grew in the dark corners of the old garden at the Wern, by the great ilex tree. I used to go out on summer nights when the air was still and all the sky cloudy. One could hear the brook just a little, down beyond the watery meadow, and all the woods and hills were dim. One could not see the mountain at all. But I liked to stand by the wall and look into the darkest place, and in a little time those flowers would seem to grow out of the shadow. I could just see the white glimmer of them. She looked like the flowers to me, as I lay on the bed in my dark room.

"Sometimes I dream of wonderful things. It is just at the moment when one wakes up; one cannot say where one has been or what was so wonderful, but you know that you have lost everything in waking. For just that moment you knew everything and understood the stars and the hills and night and day and the woods and the old songs. They were all within you, and you were all light. But the light was music, and the music was violet wine in a great cup of gold, and the wine in the golden cup was the scent of a June night. I understood all this as she stood beside my bed in the dark and stretched out her hand and touched me on the breast.

"I knew a pool in an old, old grey wood a few miles from the Wern. I called it the grey wood because the trees were ancient oaks that they say must have grown there for a thousand years, and they have grown bare and terrible. Most of them are all hollow inside and some have only a few boughs left, and every year, they say, one leaf less grows on every bough. In the books they are called the Foresters' Oaks. If you stay under them you feel as if the old times must have come again. Among these trees there was a great yew, far older than the oaks, and beneath it a dark and shadowy pool. I had been for a long walk, nearly to the sea, and as I came back I passed this place and, looking into the pool, there was the glint of the stars in the water.

"She knelt by my bed in the dark, and I could just see the glinting of her eyes as she looked at me--the stars in the shadowy waterpool!

***

"I had never dreamed that there could be anything so wonderful in the whole world. My father had told me of many beautiful and holy and glorious things, of all the heavenly mysteries by which those who know live for ever, all the things which the Doctor and my uncle and the other silly clergymen in the Chapel ...[1] because they don't really know anything at all about them, only their names, so they are like dogs and pigs and asses who have somehow found their way into a beautiful room, full of precious and delicate treasures. These things my father told me of long ago, of the Great Mystery of the Offering.

"And I have learned the wonders of the old venerable saints that once were marvels in our land, as the Welch poem says, and of all the great works that shone around their feet as they went upon the mountains and sought the deserts of ocean. I have seen their marks and writings cut on the edges of the rocks. I know where Sagramnus lies buried in Wlad Morgan. And I shall not forget how I saw the Blessed Cup of Teilo Agyos drawn out from golden veils on Mynydd Mawr, when the stars poured out of the jewel, and I saw the sea of the saints and the spiritual things in Cor-arbennic. My father read out to me all the histories of Teilo, Dewi, and Iltyd, of their marvellous chalices and altars of Paradise from which they made the books of the Graal afterwards; and all these things are beautiful to me. But, as the Anointed Bard said: 'With the bodily lips I receive the drink of mortal vineyards; with spiritual understanding wine from the garths of the undying. May Mihangel intercede for me that these may be mingled in one cup; let the door between body and soul be thrown open. For in that day earth will have become Paradise, and the secret sayings of the bards shall be verified.' I always knew what this meant, though my father told me that many people

374

thought it obscure or, rather, nonsense. But it is just the same really as another poem by the same Bard, where he says:

"'My sin was found out, and when the old women on the bridge pointed at me I was ashamed;
I was deeply grieved when the boys shouted rebukes as I went from

Caer-Newydd.
How is it that I was not ashamed before the Finger of the Almighty?
I did not suffer agony at the rebuke of the Most High.
The fist of Rhys Fawr is more dreadful to me than the hand of God.'

"He means, I think, that our great loss is that we separate what is one and make it two; and then, having done so, we make the less real into the more real, as if we thought the glass made to hold wine more important than the wine it holds. And this is what I had felt, for it was only twice that I had known wonders in my body, when I saw the Cup of Teilo sant and when the mountains appeared in vision, and so, as the Bard says, the door is shut. The life of bodily things is hard, just as the wineglass is hard. We can touch it and feel it and see it always before us. The wine is drunk and forgotten; it cannot be held. I believe the air about us is just as substantial as a mountain or a cathedral, but unless we remind ourselves we think of the air as nothing. It is not hard. But now I was in Paradise, for body and soul were molten in one fire and went up in one flame. The mortal and the immortal vines were made one. Through the joy of the body I possessed the joy of the spirit. And it was so strange to think that all this was through a woman--through a woman I had seen dozens of times and had thought nothing of, except that she was pleasant-looking and that the colour of her hair, like copper, was very beautiful.

"I cannot understand it. I cannot feel that she is really Nelly Foran who opens the door and waits at table, for she is a miracle. How I should have wondered once if I had seen a stone by the roadside become a jewel of fire and glory! But if that were to happen, it would not be so strange as what happened to me. I cannot see now the black dress and the servant's cap and apron. I see the wonderful, beautiful body shining through the darkness of my room, the glimmering of the white flower in the dark, the stars in the forest pool.

"'O gift of the everlasting!
O wonderful and hidden mystery!
Many secrets have been vouchsafed to me.
I have been long acquainted with the wisdom of the trees;
Ash and oak and elm have communicated to me from my boyhood,
The birch and the hazel and all the trees of the green wood have not been dumb.
There is a caldron rimmed with pearls of whose gifts I am not ignorant.
I will speak little of it; its treasures are known to Bards.
Many went on the search of Caer-Pedryfan,
Seven alone returned with Arthur, but my spirit was present.
Seven are the apple trees in a beautiful orchard.
I have eaten of their fruit, which is not bestowed on Saxons.
I am not ignorant of a Head which is glorious and venerable.
It made perpetual entertainment for the warriors; their joys would have been immortal.
If they had not opened the door of the south, they could have feasted for ever,
Listening to the song of the Fairy Birds of Rhiannon.
Let not anyone instruct me concerning the Glassy Isle,
In the garments of the saints who returned from it were rich odours of Paradise.
All this I knew and yet my knowledge was ignorance,
For one day, as I walked by Caer-rhiu in the principal forest of

Gwent,
I saw golden Myfanwy, as she bathed in the brook Tarógi.
Her hair flowed about her. Arthur's crown had dissolved into a shining mist.
I gazed into her blue eyes as it were into twin heavens.
All the parts of her body were adornments and miracles.
O gift of the everlasting!
O wonderful and hidden mystery!
When I embraced Myfanwy a moment became immortality![12]

"And yet I daresay this 'golden Myfanwy' was what people call 'a common girl,' and perhaps she did rough, hard work, and nobody thought anything of her till the Bard found her bathing in the brook of Tarógi. The birds in the wood said, when they saw the nightingale: 'This is a contemptible stranger!'

"June 24. Since I wrote last in this book the summer has come. This morning I woke up very early, and even in this horrible place the air was pure and bright as the sun rose up and the long beams shone on the cedar outside the window. She came to me by the way they think is locked and fastened, and, just as the world is white and gold at the dawn, so was she. A blackbird began to sing beneath the window. I think it came from far, for it sang to me of morning on the mountain, and the woods all still, and a little bright brook rushing down the hillside between dark green alders, and air that must be blown from heaven.

> There is a bird that sings in the valley of the Soar.
> Dewi and Tegfeth and Cybi preside over that region;
> Sweet is the valley, sweet the sound of its waters.
>
> There is a bird that sings in the valley of the Soar;
> Its voice is golden, like the ringing of the saints' bells;
> Sweet is the valley, echoing with melodies.
>
> There is a bird that sings in the valley of the Soar;
> Tegfeth in the south won red martyrdom.
> Her song is heard in the perpetual choirs of heaven.
>
> There is a bird that sings in the valley of the Soar;
> Dewi in the west had an altar from Paradise.
> He taught the valleys of Britain to resound with Alleluia.
>
> There is a bird that sings in the valley of the Soar;
> Cybi in the north was the teacher of Princes.
> Through him Edlogan sings praise to heaven.
>
> There is a bird that sings in the valley of the Soar
> When shall I hear again the notes of its melody?
> When shall I behold once more Gwladys in that valley?[13]

"When I think of what I know, of the wonders of darkness and the wonders of dawn, I cannot help believing that I have found something which all the world has lost. I have heard some of the fellows talking about women. Their words and their stories are filthy, and nonsense, too. One would think that if monkeys and pigs could talk about their she-monkeys and sows, it would be just like that. I might have thought that, being only boys, they knew nothing about it, and were only making up nasty, silly tales out of their nasty, silly minds. But I have heard the poor women in the town screaming and scolding at their men, and the men swearing back; and when they think they are making love, it is the most horrible of all.

"And it is not only the boys and the poor people. There are the masters and their wives. Everybody knows that the Challises and the Redburns 'fight like cats,' as they say, and that the Head's daughter was 'put up for auction' and bought by the rich manufacturer from Birmingham--a horrible, fat beast, more than twice her age, with eyes like pig's. They called it a splendid match.

"So I began to wonder whether perhaps there are very few people in the world who know; whether the real secret is lost like the great city that was drowned in the sea and only seen by one or two. Perhaps it is more like those shining Isles that the saints sought for, where the deep apple orchards are, and all the delights of Paradise. But you had to give up everything and get into a boat without oar or sails if you wanted to find Avalon or the Glassy Isle. And sometimes the saints could stand on the rocks and see those Islands far away in the midst of the sea, and smell the sweet odours and hear the bells ringing for the feast, when other people could see and hear nothing at all.

"I often think now how strange it would be if it were found out that nearly everybody is like those who stood on the rocks and could only see the waves tossing and stretching far away, and the blue sky and the mist in the distance. I mean, if it turned out that we have all been in the wrong about everything; that we live in a world of the most wonderful treasures which we see all about us, but we don't understand, and kick the jewels into the dirt, and use the chalices for slop-pails and make the holy vestments into dish-cloths, while we worship a great beast--a monster, with the head of a monkey, the body of a pig and the hind legs of a goat, with swarming lice crawling all over it.

Suppose that the people that they speak of now as 'superstitious' and 'half-savages' should turn out to be in the right, and very wise, while we are all wrong and great fools! It would be something like the man who lived in the Bright Palace. The Palace had a hundred and one doors. A hundred of them opened into gardens of delight, pleasure-houses, beautiful bowers, wonderful countries, fairy seas, caves of gold and hills of diamonds, into all the most splendid places. But one door led into a cesspool, and that was the only door that the man ever opened. It may be that his sons and his grandsons have been opening that one door ever since, till they have forgotten that there are any others, so if anyone dares to speak of the ways to the garden of delight or the hills of gold he is called a madman, or a very wicked person.

"July 15. The other day a very strange thing happened. I had gone for a short walk out of the town before dinner on the Dunham road and came as far as the four ways where the roads cross. It is rather pretty for Lupton just there; there is a plot of grass with a big old elm tree in the middle of it, and round the tree is a rough sort of seat, where tramps and such people are often resting. As I came along I heard some sort of music coming from the direction of the tree; it was like fairies dancing, and then there were strange solemn notes like the priests' singing, and a choir answered in a deep, rolling swell of sound, and the fairies danced again; and I thought somehow of a grey church high on the cliff above a singing sea, and the Fair People outside dancing on the close turf, while the service was going on all the while. As I came nearer I heard the sea waves and the wind and the cry of the seagulls, and again the high, wonderful chanting, as if the fairies and the rocks and the waves and the wild birds were all subject to that which was being done within the church. I wondered what it could be, and then I saw there was an old ragged man sitting on the seat under the tree, playing the fiddle all to himself, and rocking from side to side. He stopped directly he saw me, and said:

"'Ah, now, would your young honour do yourself the pleasure of giving the poor old fiddler a penny or maybe two: for Lupton is the very hell of a town altogether, and when I play to dirty rogues the Reel of the Warriors, they ask for something about Two Obadiahs--the devil's black curse be on them! And it's but dry work playing to the leaf and the green sod--the blessing of the holy saints be on your honour now, this day, and for ever! 'Tis but a scarcity of beer that I have tasted for a long day, I assure your honour.'

"I had given him a shilling because I thought his music so wonderful. He looked at me steadily as he finished talking, and his face changed. I thought he was frightened, he stared so oddly. I asked him if he was ill.

"'May I be forgiven,' he said, speaking quite gravely, without that wheedling way he had when he first spoke. 'May I be forgiven for talking so to one like yourself; for this day I have begged money from one that is to gain Red Martyrdom; and indeed that is yourself.'

"He took off his old battered hat and crossed himself, and I stared at him, I was so amazed at what he said. He picked up his fiddle, and saying 'May you remember me in the time of your glory,' he walked quickly off, going away from Lupton, and I lost sight of him at the turn of the road. I suppose he was half crazy, but he played wonderfully."

Footnotes:

1. A highly Rabelaisian phrase is omitted.

2. Translated from the Welsh verses quoted in the notebook.

3. The following translation of these verses appeared in Poems from the Old Bards, by Taliesin, Bristol, 1812:

"In Soar's sweet valley, where the sound
Of holy anthems once was heard
From many a saint, the hills prolong
Only the music of the bird.

In Soar's sweet valley, where the brook
With many a ripple flows along,
Delicious prospects meet the eye,
The ear is charmed with Phil'mel's song.

In Soar's sweet valley once a Maid,
Despising worldly prospects gay,
Resigned her note in earthly choirs
Which now in Heaven must sound alway.

In Soar's sweet valley David preached;

His Gospel accents so beguiled
The savage Britons, that they turned
Their fiercest cries to music mild.

In Soar's sweet valley Cybi taught
To haughty Prince the Holy Law,
The way to Heaven he showed, and then
The subject tribes inspired with awe.

In Soar's sweet valley still the song
Of Phil'mel sounds and checks alarms.
But when shall I once more renew
Those heavenly hours in Gladys' arms?"

"Taliesin" was the pseudonym of an amiable clergyman, the Reverend Owen Thomas, for many years curate of Llantrisant. He died in 1820, at the great age of eighty-four. His original poetry in Welsh was reputed as far superior to his translations, and he made a very valuable and curious collection of "Cymric Antiquities," which remains in manuscript in the keeping of his descendants.

IV

I

The materials for the history of an odd episode in Ambrose Meyrick's life are to be found in a sort of collection he made under the title "Concerning Gaiety." The episode in question dates from about the middle of his eighteenth year.

"I do not know"--he says--"how it all happened. I had been leading two eager lives. On the outside I was playing games and going up in the school with a rush, and in the inside I was being gathered more and more into the sanctuaries of immortal things. All life was transfigured for me into a radiant glory, into a quickening and catholic sacrament; and, the fooleries of the school apart, I had more and more the sense that I was a participant in a splendid and significant ritual. I think I was beginning to be a little impatient with the outward signs: I think I had a feeling that it was a pity that one had to drink wine out of a cup, a pity that kernels seemed to imply shells. I wanted, in my heart, to know nothing but the wine itself flowing gloriously from vague, invisible fountains, to know the things 'that really are' in their naked beauty, without their various and elaborate draperies. I doubt whether Ruskin understood the motive of the monk who walked amidst the mountains with his eyes cast down lest he might see the depths and heights about him. Ruskin calls this a narrow asceticism; perhaps it was rather the result of a very subtle aestheticism. The monk's inner vision might be fixed with such rapture on certain invisible heights and depths, that he feared lest the sight of their visible counterparts might disturb his ecstasy. It is probable, I think, that there is a point where the ascetic principle and the aesthetic become one and the same. The Indian fakir who distorts his limbs and lies on spikes is at the one extreme, the men of the Italian Renaissance were at the other. In each case the true line is distorted and awry, for neither system attains either sanctity or beauty in the highest. The fakir dwells in surfaces, and the Renaissance artist dwelt in surfaces; in neither case is there the inexpressible radiance of the invisible world shining through the surfaces. A cup of Cellini's work is no doubt very lovely; but it is not beautiful in the same way as the old Celtic cups are beautiful.

"I think I was in some danger of going wrong at the time I am talking about. I was altogether too impatient of surfaces. Heaven forbid the notion that I was ever in danger of being in any sense of the word a Protestant; but perhaps I was rather inclined to the fundamental heresy on which Protestantism builds its objection to what is called Ritual. I suppose this heresy is really Manichee; it is a charge of corruption and evil made against the visible universe, which is affirmed to be not 'very good,' but 'very bad'--or, at all events, too bad to be used as the vehicle of spiritual truth. It is extraordinary by the way, that the thinking Protestant does not perceive that this principle damns all creeds and all Bibles and all teaching quite as effectually as it damns candles and chasubles--unless, indeed, the Protestant thinks that the logical understanding is a competent vehicle of Eternal Truth, and that God can be properly and adequately defined and explained in human speech. If he thinks that, he is an ass. Incense, vestments, candles, all ceremonies, processions, rites--all these things are miserably inadequate; but they do not abound in the horrible pitfalls, misapprehensions, errors which are inseparable from speech of men used as an expression of the Church. In a savage dance there may be a vast deal more of the truth than in many of the hymns in our hymn-books.

"After all, as Martinez said, we must even be content with what we have, whether it be censers or syllogisms, or both. The way of the censer is certainly the safer, as I have said; I suppose because the ruin of the external universe is not nearly so deep nor so virulent as the ruin of men. A flower, a piece of gold, no doubt approach their archetypes--what they were meant to be--much more nearly than man does; hence their appeal is purer than the speech or the reasoning of men.

"But in those days at Lupton my head was full of certain sentences which I had lit upon somewhere or other--I believe they must have been translations from some Eastern book. I knew about a dozen of these maxims; all I can remember now are:

"If you desire to be inebriated: abstain from wine."
"If you desire beauty: look not on beautiful things."
"If you desire to see: let your eyes be blindfolded."
"If you desire love: refrain from the Beloved."

"I expect the paradox of these sayings pleased me. One must allow that if one has the inborn appetite of the somewhat subtle, of the truth not too crudely and barely expressed, there is no such atmosphere as that of a Public School for sharpening this appetite to an edge of ravening, indiscriminate hunger. Think of our friend the Colonel, who is by way of being a fin gourmet; imagine him fixed in a boarding-house where the meals are a repeating cycle of Irish Stew, Boiled Rabbit, Cold Mutton and Salt Cod (without oyster or any other sause)! Then let him out and place him in the Café Anglais. With what a fierce relish would he set tooth into curious and sought-out dishes! It must be remembered that I listened every Sunday in every term to one of the Doctor's sermons, and it is really not strange that I gave an eager ear to the voice of Persian Wisdom--as I think the book was called. At any rate, I kept Nelly Foran at a distance for nine or ten months, and when I saw a splendid sunset I averted my eyes. I longed for a love purely spiritual, for a sunset of vision.

"I caught glimpses, too, I think, of a much more profound askesis than this. I suppose you have the askesis in its simplest, most rationalised form in the Case of Bill the Engine-driver--I forget in what great work of Theologia Moralis I found the instance; perhaps Bill was really Quidam in the original, and his occupation stated as that of Nauarchus. At all events, Bill is fond of four-ale; but he had perceived that two pots of this beverage consumed before a professional journey tended to make him rather sleepy, rather less alert, than he might be in the execution of his very responsible duties. Hence Bill, considering this, wisely contents himself with one pot before mounting on his cab. He has deprived himself of a sensible good in order that an equally sensible but greater good may be secured--in order that he and the passengers may run no risks on the journey. Next to this simple asceticism comes, I suppose, the ordinary discipline of the Church--the abandonment of sensible goods to secure spiritual ends, the turning away from the type to the prototype, from the sight of the eyes to the vision of the soul. For in the true asceticism, whatever its degree, there is always action to a certain end, to a perceived good. Does the self-tormenting fakir act from this motive? I don't know; but if he does not, his discipline is not asceticism at all, but folly, and impious folly, too. If he mortifies himself merely for the sake of mortifying himself; then he defiles and blasphemes the Temple. This in parenthesis.

"But, as I say, I had a very dim and distant glimpse of another region of the askesis. Mystics will understand me when I say that there are moments when the Dark Night of the Soul is seen to be brighter than her brightest day; there are moments when it is necessary to drive away even the angels that there may be place for the Highest. One may ascend into regions so remote from the common concerns of life that it becomes difficult to procure the help of analogy, even in the terms and processes of the Arts. But suppose a painter--I need not say that I mean an artist--who is visited by an idea so wonderful, so super-exalted in its beauty that he recognises his impotence; he knows that no pigments and no technique can do anything but grossly parody his vision. Well, he will show his greatness by not attempting to paint that vision: he will write on a bare canvass vidit anima sed non pinxit manus. And I am sure that there are many romances which have never been written. It was a highly paradoxical, even a dangerous philosophy that affirmed God to be rather Non-Ens than Ens; but there are moods in which one appreciates the thought.

"I think I caught, as I say, a distant vision of that Night which excels the Day in its splendour. It began with the eyes turned away from the sunset, with lips that refused kisses. Then there came a command to the heart to cease from longing for the dear land of Gwent, to cease from that aching desire that had never died for so many years for the sight of the old land and those hills and woods of most sweet and anguished memory. I remember once, when I was a great lout of sixteen, I went to see the Lupton Fair. I always liked the great booths and caravans and merry-go-rounds, all a blaze of barbaric green and red and gold, flaming and glowing in the middle of the trampled, sodden field against a background of Lupton and wet, grey autumn sky. There were country folk then who wore smock-frocks and looked like men in them, too. One saw scores of these brave fellows at the Fair: dull, good Jutes with flaxen hair that was almost white, and with broad pink faces. I liked to see them in the white robe and the curious embroidery; they were a note of wholesomeness, an embassage from the old English village life to our filthy 'industrial centre.' It was odd to see how they stared about them; they wondered, I think, at the beastliness of the place, and yet, poor fellows, they felt bound to admire the evidence of so much money. Yes, they were of Old England; they savoured of the long, bending, broad village street, the gable ends, the grave fronts of old mellow bricks, the thatched roofs here and there, the bulging window of the 'village shop,' the old church in decorous, somewhat dull perpendicular among the elms, and, above all, the old tavern--that excellent abode of honest mirth and honest beer, relic of the time when there were men, and men who lived. Lupton is very far removed from Hardy's land, and yet as I think of these country-folk in their smock-frocks all the essence of Hardy is distilled for me; I see the village street all white in snow, a light gleaming very rarely from an upper window, and presently, amid ringing bells, one hears the carol-singers begin:

> 'Remember Adam's fall,
> O thou man.'

"And I love to look at the whirl of the merry-go-rounds, at the people sitting with grave enjoyment on those absurd horses as they circle round and round till one's eyes were dazed. Drums beat and thundered, strange horns blew raucous calls from all quarters, and the mechanical music to which those horses revolved belched and blazed and rattled out its everlasting monotony, checked now and again by the shriek of the steam whistle, groaning into silence for a while: then the tune clanged out once more, and the horses whirled round and round.

"But on this Fair Day of which I am speaking I left the booths and the golden, gleaming merry-go-rounds for the next field, where horses were excited to brief madness and short energy. I had scarcely taken up my stand when a man close by me raised his voice to a genial shout as he saw a friend a little way off. And he spoke with the beloved accent of Gwent, with those tones that come to me more ravishing, more enchanting than all the music in the world. I had not heard them for years of weary exile! Just a phrase or two of common greeting in those chanting accents: the Fair passed away, was whirled into nothingness, its shouting voices, the charging of horses, drum and trumpet, clanging, metallic music--it rushed down into the abyss. There was the silence that follows a great peal of thunder; it was early morning and I was standing in a well-remembered valley, beside the blossoming thorn bush, looking far away to the wooded hills that kept the East, above the course of the shining river. I was, I say, a great lout of sixteen, but the tears flooded my eyes, my heart swelled with its longing.

"Now, it seemed, I was to quell such thoughts as these, to desire no more the fervent sunlight on the mountain, or the sweet scent of the dusk about the runnings of the brook. I had been very fond of 'going for walks'--walks of the imagination. I was afraid, I suppose, that unless by constant meditation I renewed the shape of the old land in my mind, its image might become a blurred and fading picture; I should forget little by little the ways of those deep, winding lanes that took courses that were almost subterranean over hill and vale, by woodside and waterside, narrow, cavernous, leaf-vaulted; cool in the greatest heats of summer. And the wandering paths that crossed the fields, that led one down into places hidden and remote, into still depths where no one save myself ever seemed to enter, that sometimes ended with a certain solemnity at a broken stile in a hedgerow grown into a thicket--within a plum tree returning to the savage life of the wood, a forest, perhaps, of blue lupins, and a great wild rose about the ruined walls of a house--all these ways I must keep in mind as if they were mysteries and great secrets, as indeed they were. So I strolled in memory through the Pageant of Gwent: 'lest I should forget the region of the flowers, lest I should become unmindful of the wells and the floods.'

"But the time came, as I say, when it was represented to me that all this was an indulgence which, for a season at least, must be pretermitted. With an effort I voided my soul of memory and desire and weeping; when the idols of doomed Twyn-Barlwm, and great Mynydd Maen, and the silver esses of the Usk appeared before me, I cast them out; I would not meditate white Caerleon shining across the river. I endured, I think, the severest pains. De Quincey, that admirable artist, that searcher into secrets and master of mysteries, has described my pains for me under the figure of the Opium Eater breaking the bonds of his vice. How often, when the abominations of Lupton, its sham energies, its sham morals, its sham enthusiasms, all its battalia of cant surged and beat upon me, have I been sorely tempted to yield, to suffer no more the press of folly, but to steal away by a secret path I knew, to dwell in a secure valley where the foolish could never trouble me. Sometimes

I 'fell,' as I drank deep then of the magic well-water, and went astray in the green dells and avenues of the wildwood. Still I struggled to refrain my heart from these things, to keep my spirit under the severe discipline of abstention; and with a constant effort I succeeded more and more.

"But there was a yet deeper depth in this process of catharsis. I have said that sometimes one must expel the angels that God may have room; and now the strict ordinance was given that I should sever myself from that great dream of Celtic sanctity that for me had always been the dream, the innermost shrine in which I could take refuge, the house of sovran medicaments where all the wounds of soul and body were healed. One does not wish to be harsh; we must admit, I suppose, that moderate, sensible Anglicanism must have something in it--since the absolute sham cannot very well continue to exist. Let us say, then, that it is highly favourable to a respectable and moral life, that it encourages a temperate and well-regulated spirit of devotion. It was certainly a very excellent and (according to her lights) devout woman who, in her version of the Anima Christi altered 'inebriate me' to 'purify me,' and it was a good cleric who hated the Vulgate reading, calix meus inebrians. My father had always instructed me that we must conform outwardly, and bear with Dearly Beloved Brethren; while we celebrated in our hearts the Ancient Mass of the Britons, and waited for Cadwaladr to return. I reverenced his teaching, I still reverence it, and agree that we must conform; but in my heart I have always doubted whether moderate Anglicanism be Christianity in any sense, whether it even deserves to be called a religion at all. I do not doubt, of course, that many truly religious people have professed it: I speak of the system, and of the atmosphere which emanates from it. And when the Public School ethos is added to this--well, the resultant teaching comes pretty much to the dogma that Heaven and the Head are strict allies. One must not degenerate into ecclesiastical controversy; I merely want to say that I never dreamed of looking for religion in our Chapel services. No doubt the Te Deum was still the Te Deum, but the noblest of hymns is degraded, obscured, defiled, made ridiculous, if you marry it to a tune that would disgrace a penny gaff. Personally, I think that the airs on the piano-organs are much more reverend compositions than Anglican chants, and I am sure that many popular hymn tunes are vastly inferior in solemnity to 'E Dunno where 'e are.

"No; the religion that led me and drew me and compelled me was that wonderful and doubtful mythos of the Celtic Church. It was the study--nay, more than the study, the enthusiasm--of my father's life; and as I was literally baptized with water from a Holy Well, so spiritually the great legend of the Saints and their amazing lives had tinged all my dearest aspirations, had become to me the glowing vestment of the Great Mystery. One may sometimes be deeply interested in the matter of a tale while one is wearied or sickened by the manner of it; one may have to embrace the bright divinity on the horrid lips of the serpent of Cos. Or, on the other hand, the manner--the style--may be admirable, and the matter a mere nothing but a ground for the embroidery. But for me the Celtic Mythos was the Perfect Thing, the King's Daughter: Omnis gloria ejus filiæ Regis ab, intus, in fimbriis aureis circumamicta varietatibus. I have learned much more of this great mystery since those days--I have seen, that is, how entirely, how absolutely my boyhood's faith was justified; but even then with but little knowledge I was rapt at the thought of this marvellous knight-errantry, of this Christianity which was not a moral code, with some sort of metaphorical Heaven held out as a reward for its due observance, but a great mystical adventure into the unknown sanctity. Imagine a Bishop of the Established Church getting into a boat without oar or sails! Imagine him, if you can, doing anything remotely analagous to such an action. Conceive the late Archbishop Tait going apart into the chapel at Lambeth for three days and three nights; then you may well conceive the people in the opposite bank being dazzled with the blinding supernatural light poured forth from the chapel windows. Of course, the end of the Celtic Church was ruin and confusion--but Don Quixote failed and fell, while Sancho Panza lived a fat, prosperous peasant. He inherited, I think, a considerable sum from the knight, and was, no doubt, a good deal looked up to in the village.

"Yes; the Celtic Church was the Company of the Great Errantry, of the Great Mystery, and, though all the history of it seems but a dim and shadowy splendour, its burning rose-red lamp yet glows for a few, and from my earliest childhood I was indoctrinated in the great Rite of Cor-arbennic. When I was still very young I had been humoured with the sight of a wonderful Relic of the Saints--never shall I forget that experience of the holy magic of sanctity. Every little wood, every rock and fountain, and every running stream of Gwent were hallowed for me by some mystical and entrancing legend, and the thought of this High Spiritual City and its Blessed Congregation could, in a moment, exercise and drive forth from me all the ugly and foolish and gibbering spectres that made up the life of that ugly and foolish place where I was imprisoned.

"Now, with a sorrowful farewell, I bade good-bye for a brief time (as I hoped it would be) to this golden legend; my heart was emptied of its treasures and its curious shows, and the lights on the altars were put out, and the images were strictly veiled. Hushed was the chanting in the Sovereign and Perpetual Choir, hidden were the High Hallows of the Saints, no more did I follow them to their cells in the wild hills, no more did I look from the rocks in the west and see them set forth for Avalon. Alas!

"A great silence seemed to fall upon me, the silence of the depths beneath the earth. And with the silence there was darkness. Only in a hidden place there was reserved the one taper--the Light of Conformity, of a perfect submission, that from the very excess of sorrow and deprivation drew its secret but quintessential joy. I am reminded, now that I look back upon this great purgation of the soul, of the story that I once read of the Arabic Alchemist. He came to the Caliph Haroun with a strange and extravagant proposal. Haroun sat in all his splendour, his viziers, his chamberlains, his great officers about him, in his golden court which displayed all the wonders and superfluities of the East. He gave judgment; the wicked were punished, the virtuous were rewarded; God's name was exalted, the Prophet was venerated. There came before the Commander of the Faithful a poor old man in the poor and ragged robes of a wandering poet; he was oppressed by the weight of his years, and his entrance was like the entrance of misery. So wretched was his appearance that one of the chamberlains, who was well acquainted with the poets, could not help quoting the well-known verses:

> *"'Between the main and a drop of rain the difference seen is nothing great.*
> *The sun so bright and the taper's light are alike and one save in pomp and state.*
> *In the grain of sand and in all the land what may ye arraign as disparate?*
> *A crust of bread and a King's board spread will hunger's lust alike abate.*
> *With the smallest blade or with host arrayed the Ruler may quench his gall and hate.*
> *A stone in a box and a quarry of rocks may be shown to be of an equal freight.*
> *With a sentence bold or with gold untold the lover may hold or capture his mate.*
> *The King and the Bard may alike be debarred from the fold of the*
> *Lord Compassionate.'"*

"The Commander of the Faithful praised God, the Merciful, the Compassionate, the King of the Day of Judgment, and caused the chamberlain to be handsomely rewarded. He then enquired of the old man for what reason he came before him, and the beggar (as, indeed, he seemed) informed the Caliph that he had for many years prosecuted his studies in magic, alchemy, astrology and geomancy and all other curious and surprising arts, in Spain, Grand Cairo, the land of the Moors, India, China, in various Cities of the Infidels; in fact, in every quarter of the world where magicians were to be found. In proof of his proficiency he produced a little box which he carried about him for the purpose of his geomantic operations and asked anyone who was willing to stand forth, that he might hear his whole life, past, present and future. The Caliph ordered one of his officers to submit himself to this ordeal, and the beggar having made the points in the sand, and having erected the figure according to the rules of the geomantic art, immediately informed the officer of all the most hidden transactions in which he had been engaged, including several matters which this officer thought had been secrets locked in his own breast. He also foretold his death in a year's time from a certain herb, and so it fell out, for he was strangled with a hempen cord by order of the Caliph. In the meantime, the Commander of the Faithful and all about him were astonished, and the Beggar Magician was ordered to proceed with his story. He spoke at great length, and everyone remarked the elegance and propriety of his diction, which was wanting in no refinement of classical eloquence. But the sum of his speech was this--that he had discovered the greatest wonder of the whole world, the name of which he declared was Asrar, and by this talisman he said that the Caliph might make himself more renowned than all the kings that had ever reigned on the earth, not excepting King Solomon, the son of David. This was the method of the operation which the beggar proposed. The Commander of the Faithful was to gather together all the wealth of his entire kingdom, omitting nothing that could possibly be discovered; and while this was being done the magician said that he would construct a furnace of peculiar shape in which all these splendours and magnificences and treasures of the world must be consumed in a certain fire of art, prepared with wisdom. And at last, he continued, after the operation had endured many days, the fire being all the while most curiously governed, there would remain but one drop no larger than a pearl, but glorious as the sun to the moon and all the starry heavens and the wonders of the compassionate; and with this drop the Caliph Haroun might heal all the sorrows of the universe. Both the Commander of the Faithful and all his viziers and officers were stupefied by this proposal, and most of the assemblage considered the beggar to be a madman. The Caliph, however, asked him to return the next day in order that his plans might receive more mature consideration.

"The beggar prostrated himself and went forth from the hall of audience, but he returned no more, nor could it be discovered that he had been seen again by anyone.

"'But one drop no larger than a pearl,' and 'where there is Nothing there is All.' I have often thought of those sentences in looking back on that time when, as Chesson said, I was one of those 'light-hearted and yet sturdy and reliable young fellows to whose hands the honour and safety of

England might one day be committed.' I cast all the treasures I possessed into the alembic; again and again they were rectified by the heat of the fire 'most curiously governed'; I saw the 'engendering of the Crow' black as pitch, the flight of the Dove with Silver Wings, and at last Sol rose red and glorious, and I fell down and gave thanks to heaven for this most wonderful gift, the 'Sun blessed of the Fire.' I had dispossessed myself of all, and I found that I possessed all; I had thrown away all the money in my purse, and I was richer than I had ever been; I had died, and I had found a new life in the land of the living.

"It is curious that I should now have to explain the pertinency of all that I have written to the title of this Note--concerning Gaiety. It should not be necessary. The chain of thought is almost painfully obvious. But I am afraid it is necessary.

"Well: I once read an interesting article in the daily paper. It was written apropos of some Shakespearean celebrations or other, and its purport was that modern England was ever so much happier than mediæval or Elizabethan England. It is possible that an acute logician might find something to say on this thesis; but my interest lay in the following passages, which I quote:

> *"'Merrie England,' with its maypoles and its Whitsun Ales, and its Shrove-tide jousts and junketings is dead for us, from the religious point of view. The England that has survived is, after all, a greater England still. It is Puritan England....*
> *The spirit has gone. Surely it is useless to revive the form. Wherefore should the May Queen be "holy, wise, and fair," if not to symbolise the Virgin Mary? And as for Shrove-tide, too, what point in jollity without a fast to follow?'*

"The article is not over-illuminating, but I think the writer had caught a glimpse of the truth that there is a deep relation between Mirth and Sanctity; that no real mirth is possible without the apprehension of the mysteries as its antecedent. The fast and the feast are complementary terms. He is right; there is no point in jollity unless there is a fast or something of the nature of a fast to follow--though, of course, there is nothing to hinder the most advanced thinker from drinking as much fusel-oil and raw Russian spirit as he likes. But the result of this course is not real mirth or jollity; it is perhaps more essentially dismal than a 'Tea' amongst the Protestant Dissenters. And, on the other hand, true gaiety is only possible to those who have fasted; and now perhaps it will be seen that I have been describing the preparations for a light-hearted festival.

"The cloud passed away from me, the restrictions and inhibitions were suddenly removed, and I woke up one morning in dancing, bubbling spirits, every drop of blood in my body racing with new life, my nerves tingling and thrilling with energy. I laughed as I awoke; I was conscious that I was to engage in a strange and fantastic adventure, though I had not the remotest notion of what it was to be."

II

Ambrose Meyrick's adventure was certainly of the fantastic order. His fame had long been established on a sure footing with his uncle and with everybody else, and Mr. Horbury had congratulated him with genuine enthusiasm on his work in the examinations--the Summer term was drawing to a close. Mr. Horbury was Ambrose's trustee, and he made no difficulty about signing a really handsome cheque for his nephew's holiday expenses and outfit. "There," he said "you ought to be able to do pretty well on that. Where do you think of going?"

Ambrose said that he had thought of North Devon, of tramping over Exmoor, visiting the Doone country, and perhaps of working down to Dartmoor.

"You couldn't do better. You ought to try your hand at fishing: wonderful sport in some of those streams. It mightn't come off at first, but with your eye and sense of distance you'll soon make a fine angler. If you do have a turn at the trout, get hold of some local man and make him give you a wrinkle or two. It's no good getting your flies from town. Now, when I was fishing in Hampshire---"

Mr. Horbury went on; but the devil of gaiety had already dictated a wonderful scheme to Ambrose, and that night he informed Nelly Foran that she must alter her plans; she was to come with him to France instead of spending a fortnight at Blackpool. He carried out this mad device with an ingenuity that poor Mr. Palmer would certainly have called "diabolical." In the first place, there was to be a week in London--for Nelly must have some clothes; and this week began as an experience of high delight. It was not devoid of terror, for masters might be abroad, and Ambrose did not wish to leave Lupton for some time. However, they neither saw nor were seen. Arriving at St. Pancras, the luggage was left in the station, and Ambrose, who had studied the map of London, stood for a while on the pavement outside Scott's great masterpiece of architecture and considered the situation with grave yet humorous deliberation. Nelly proved herself admirably worthy of the adventure; its monstrous audacity appealed to her, and she was in a state of perpetual subdued laughter for some days after their arrival. Meyrick looked about him and found that the Euston Road, being squalid and noisy, offered few attractions; and with sudden resolution he took the girl by the arm and steered into the heart of Bloomsbury. In this charmingly central and yet retired quarter they found rooms in a quiet byway which, oddly enough, looked on a green field; and under the pleasant style of Mr. and Mr. Lupton they partook of tea while the luggage was fetched by somebody--probably a husband--who came with a shock of red, untidy hair from the dark bowels of the basement. They screamed with mirth over the meal. Mr. Horbury had faults, but he kept a good table for himself, his boys and his servants; and the exotic, quaint flavour of the "bread" and "butter" seemed to these two young idiots exquisitely funny. And the queer, faint, close smell, too, of the whole house--it rushed out at one when the hall door was opened: it was heavy, and worth its weight in gold.

"I never know," Ambrose used to say afterwards, "whether to laugh or cry when I have been away for some time from town, and come back and smell that wonderful old London aroma. I don't believe it's so strong or so rare as it used to be; I have been disappointed once or twice in houses in quite shabby streets. It was there, of course, but--well, if it were a vintage wine I should say it was a second growth of a very poor year--Margaux, no doubt, but a Margaux of one of those very indifferent years in the early 'seventies. Or it may be like the smell of grease-paints; one doesn't notice it after a month or two. But I don't think it is.

"Still," he would go on, "I value what I can smell of it. It brings back to me that afternoon, that hot, choking afternoon of ever so many years ago. It was really tremendously hot--ninety-two degrees, I think I saw in the paper the next day--and when we got out at St. Pancras the wind came at one like a furnace blast. There was no sun visible; the sky was bleary--a sort of sickly, smoky yellow, and the burning wind came in gusts, and the dust hissed and rattled on the pavement. Do you know what a low public-house smells like in London on a hot afternoon? Do you know what London bitter tastes like on such a day--the publican being evidently careful of his clients' health, and aware of the folly of drinking cold beverages during a period of extreme heat? I do. Nelly, poor dear, had warm lemonade, and I had warm beer--warm chemicals, I mean. But the odour! Why doesn't some scientific man stop wasting his time over a lot of useless rubbish and discover a way of bottling the odour of the past?

"Ah! but if he did so, in a phial of rare crystal with a stopper as secure as the seal of Solimaun ben Daoud would I preserve one most precious scent, inscribing on the seal, within a perfect pentagram, the mystic legend 'No. 15, Little Russell Row.'"

The cat had come in with the tea-tray. He was a black cat, not very large, with a decent roundness of feature, and yet with a suggestion of sinewy skinniness about him--the Skinniness of the wastrel, not of the poor starveling. His bright green eyes had, as Ambrose observed, the wisdom of Egypt; on his tomb should be inscribed "The Justified in Sekht." He walked solemnly in front of the landlady, his body describing strange curves, his tail waving in the air, and his ears put back with an expression of intense cunning. He seemed delighted at "the let," and when Nelly stroked his back he gave a loud shriek of joy and made known his willingness to take a little refreshment.

They laughed so heartily over their tea that when the landlady came in to clear the things away they were still bubbling over with aimless merriment.

"I likes to see young people 'appy," she said pleasantly, and readily provided a latchkey in case they cared to come in rather late. She told them a good deal of her life: she had kept lodgings in Judd Street, near King's Cross--a nasty, noisy street, she called it--and she seemed to think the inhabitants a low lot. She had to do with all sorts, some good some bad, and the business wasn't what it had been in her mother's day.

They sat a little while on the sofa, hand in hand still consumed with the jest of their being there at all, and imagining grotesque entrances of Mr. Horbury or Dr. Chesson. Then they went out to wander about the streets, to see London easily, merrily, without bothering the Monument, or the British Museum, or Madame Tussaud's--finally, to get something to eat, they didn't know when or where or how, and they didn't in the least care! There was one "sight" they were not successful in avoiding: they had not journeyed far before the great portal of the British Museum confronted them, grandiose and gloomy. So, by the sober way of Great Russell Street, they made their way into Tottenham Court Road and, finally, into Oxford Street. The shops were bright and splendid, the pavement was crowded with a hurrying multitude, as it seemed to the country folk, though it was the dullest season of the year. It was a great impression--decidedly London was a wonderful place. Already Ambrose felt a curious sense of being at home in it; it was not beautiful, but it was on the immense scale; it did something more than vomit stinks into the air, poison into the water and rows of workmen's houses on the land. They wandered on, and then they had the fancy that they would like to explore the regions to the south; it was so impossible, as Ambrose said, to know where they would find themselves eventually. He carefully lost himself within a few minutes of Oxford Street. A few turnings to right and then to left; the navigation of strange alleys soon left them in the most satisfactory condition of bewilderment; the distinctions of the mariner's compass, its pedantry of east and west, north and south, were annihilated and had ceased to be; it was an adventure in a trackless desert, in the Australian bush, but on safer ground and in an infinitely more entertaining scene. At first they had passed through dark streets, Georgian and Augustan ways, gloomy enough, and half deserted; there were grave houses, with many stories of windows, now reduced to printing offices, to pickle warehouses, to odd crafts such as those of the metal assayer, the crucible maker, the engraver of seals, the fabricator of Boule. But how wonderful it was to see the actual place where those things were done! Ambrose had read of such arts, but had always thought of them as existing in a vague void--if some of them even existed at all in those days: but there in the windows were actual crucibles, strange-looking curvilinear pots of grey-yellowish ware, the veritable instruments of the Magnum Opus, inventions of Arabia. He was no longer astonished when a little farther he saw a harpsichord, which had only been a name to him, a beautiful looking thing, richly inlaid, with its date--1780--inscribed on a card above it. It was now utterly wonderland: he could very likely buy armour round the corner; and he had scarcely formed the thought when a very fine sixteenth-century suit, richly damascened, rose up before him, handsomely displayed between two black jacks. These were the comparatively silent streets; but they turned a corner, and what a change! All the roadway, not the pavement only, seemed full of a strolling, chatting, laughing mob of people: the women were bareheaded, and one heard nothing but the roll of the French "r," torrents of sonorous sound trolled out with the music of happy song. The papers in the shops were all French, ensigns on every side proclaimed "Vins Fins," "Beaune Supérieur": the tobacconists kept their tobacco in square blue, yellow and brown packets; "Charcuterie" made a brave and appetising show. And here was a "Café Restaurant: au château de Chinon." The name was enough; they could not dine elsewhere, and Ambrose felt that he was honouring the memory of the great Rabelais.

It was probably not a very good dinner. It was infinitely better than the Soho dinner of these days, for the Quarter had hardly begun to yield to the attack of Art, Intellect and the Suburbs which, between them, have since destroyed the character and unction of many a good cook-shop. Ambrose only remembered two dishes; the pieds de porc grillés and the salad. The former he thought both amusing and delicious, and the latter was strangely and artfully compounded of many herbs, of little vinegar, of abundant Provençal oil, with the chapon, or crust rubbed with garlic, reposing at the bottom of the bowl after Madame had "tormented" the ingredients--the salad was a dish from Fairyland. There be no such salads now in all the land of Soho.

"Let me celebrate, above all, the little red wine," says Ambrose in a brief dithyrambic note. "Not in any mortal vineyard did its father grape ripen; it was not nourished by the warmth of the visible sun, nor were the rains that made it swell common waters from the skies above us. Not even in the Chinonnais, sacred earth though that be, was the press made that caused its juices to be poured into the cuve, nor was the humming of its fermentation heard in any of the good cellars of the lower Touraine. But in that region which Keats celebrates when he sings the 'Mermaid Tavern' was this juice engendered--the vineyard lay low down in the south, among the starry plains where is the Terra Turonensis Celestis, that unimaginable country which Rabelais beheld in his vision where mighty Gargantua drinks from inexhaustible vats eternally, where Pantagruel is athirst for evermore, though he be satisfied continually. There, in the land of the Crowned Immortal Tosspots was that wine of ours vintaged, red with the rays of the Dog-star, made magical by the influence of Venus, fertilised by the happy aspect of Mercury. O rare, superabundant and most excellent juice, fruit of all fortunate stars, by thee were we translated, exalted into the fellowship of that Tavern of which the old poet writes: Mihi est propositum in Taberna mori!"

There were few English people in the Château de Chinon--indeed, it is doubtful whether there was more than one--the ménage Lupton excepted. This one compatriot happened to be a rather remarkable man--it was Carrol. He was not in the vanguard of anything; he knew no journalists and belonged to no clubs; he was not even acquainted in the most distant manner with a single person who could be called really influential or successful. He was an obscure literary worker, who published an odd volume every five or six years: now and then he got notices, when there was no press of important stuff in the offices, and sometimes a kindly reviewer predicted that he would come out all right in time, though he had still much to learn. About a year before he died, an intelligent reading public was told that one or two things of his were rather good; then, on his death, it was definitely discovered that the five volumes of verse occupied absolutely unique ground, that a supreme poet had been taken from us, a poet who had raised the English language into a fourth dimension of melody and magic. The intelligent reading public read him no more than they ever did, but they buy him in edition after edition, from large quarto to post octavo; they buy him put up into little decorated boxes; they buy him on Japanese vellum; they buy him illustrated by six different artists; they discuss no end of articles about him; they write their names in the Carrol Birthday Book; they set up the Carrol Calendar in their boudoirs; they have quotations from him in Westminster Abbey and St. Paul's Cathedral; they sing him in the famous Carrol Cycle of Song; and, last and best of all, a brilliant American playwright is talking even now of dramatising him. The Carrol Club, of course, is ancient history. Its membership is confined to the ranks of intellect and art; it invites to its dinners foreign princes, bankers, major-generals and other persons of distinction--all of whom, of course, are intensely interested in the master's book; and the record and praise of the Club are in all the papers. It is a pity that Carrol is dead. He would not have sworn: he would have grinned.

Even then, though he was not glorious, he was observant, and he left a brief note, a sort of thumb-nail sketch, of his impressions that night at the Château de Chinon.

"I was sitting in my old corner," he says, "wondering why the devil I wrote so badly on the whole, and what the devil I was going to do with the subject that I had tackled. The dinner was not so bad at the old Château in those days, though now they say the plate-glass is the best dish in the establishment. I liked the old place; it was dingy and low down and rather disreputable, I fancy, and the company was miscellaneous French with a dash of Italian. Nearly all of us knew each other, and there were regulars who sat in the same seat night after night. I liked it all. I liked the coarse tablecloths and the black-handled knives and the lead spoons and the damp, adhesive salt, and the coarse, strong, black pepper that one helped with a fork handle. Then there was Madame sitting on high, and I never saw an uglier woman nor a more good-natured. I was getting through my roast fowl and salad that evening, when two wonderful people came in, obviously from fairyland! I saw they had never been in such a place in all their lives before--I don't believe either of them had set foot in London until that day, and their wonder and delight and enjoyment of it all were so enormous that I had another helping of food and an extra half-bottle of wine. I enjoyed them, too, in their way, but I could see that their fowl and their wine were not a bit the same as mine. I once knew the restaurant they were really dining at--Grand Café de Paradis--some such name as that. He was an extraordinary looking chap, quite young, I should fancy, black hair, dark skin, and such burning eyes! I don't know why, but I felt he was a bit out of his setting, and I kept thinking how I should like to see him in a monk's robe. Madame was different. She was a lovely girl with amazing copper hair; dressed rather badly--of the people, I should imagine. But what a gaiety she had! I couldn't hear what they were saying, but one had to smile with sheer joy at the sight of her face--it positively danced with mirth, and a good musician could have set it to music, I am sure. There was something a little queer--too pronounced, perhaps--about the lower part of her face. Perhaps it would have been an odd tune, but I know I should have liked to hear it!"

Ambrose lit a black Caporal cigarette--he had bought a packet on his way. He saw an enticing bottle, of rotund form, paying its visits to some neighbouring tables, and the happy fools made the acquaintance of Benedictine.

"Oh, yes, it is all very well," Ambrose has been heard to say on being offered this agreeable and aromatic liqueur, "it's nice enough, I daresay. But you should have tasted the real stuff. I got it at a little cafe in Soho some years ago--the Château de Chinon. No, it's no good going there now, it's quite different. All the walls are plate-glass and gold; the head waiter is called Maître d'hôtel, and I am told it's quite the thing, both in southern and northern suburbs, to make up dinner parties at the Château--everything most correct, evening dress, fans, opera cloaks, 'Hide-seek' champagne, and stalls afterwards. One gets a glimpse of Bohemian life that way, and everybody says it's been such a queer evening, but quite amusing, too. But you can't get the real Benedictine there now.

"Where can you get it? Ah! I wish I knew. I never come across it. The bottle looks just the same, but it's quite a different flavour. The phylloxera may be responsible, of course, but I don't think it is. Perhaps the bottle that went round the table that night was like the powder in Jekyll and Hyde--its properties were the result of some strange accident. At all events, they were quite magical."

The two adventurers went forth into the maze of streets and lost themselves again. Heaven knows where they went, by what ways they wandered, as with wide-gleaming eyes, arm locked in arm, they gazed on an enchanted scene which they knew must be London and nothing else--what else could it be? Indeed, now and again, Ambrose thought he recognized certain features and monuments and public places of which he had read; but still! That wine of the Château was, by all mundane reckonings, of the smallest, and one little glass of Benedictine with coffee could not disturb the weakest head: yet was it London, after all?

What they saw was, doubtless, the common world of the streets and squares, the gay ways and the dull, the broad, ringing, lighted roads and the dark, echoing passages; yet they saw it all as one sees a mystery play, through a veil. But the veil before their eyes was a transmuting vision, and its substance was shot as if it were samite, with wonderful and admirable golden ornaments. In the Eastern Tales, people find themselves thus suddenly transported into an unknown magical territory, with cities that are altogether things of marvel and enchantment, whose walls are pure gold, lighted by the shining of incomparable jewels; and Ambrose declared later that never till that evening had he realized the extraordinary and absolute truth to nature of the Arabian Nights. Those who were present on a certain occasion will not soon forget his rejoinder to "a gentleman in the company" who said that for truth to nature he went to George Eliot.

"I was speaking of men and women, Sir," was the answer, "not of lice."

The gentleman in question, who was quite an influential man--some whisper that he was an editor--was naturally very much annoyed.

Still, Ambrose maintained his position. He would even affirm that for crude realism the Eastern Tales were absolutely unique.

"Of course," he said, "I take realism to mean absolute and essential truthfulness of description, as opposed to merely conventional treatment. Zola is a realist, not--as the imbeciles suppose-- because he described--well, rather minutely--many unpleasant sights and sounds and smells and emotions, but because he was a poet, a seer; because, in spite of his pseudo-philosophies, his cheap materialisms, he saw the true heart, the reality of things. Take La Terre; do you think it is 'realistic' because it describes minutely, and probably faithfully, the event of a cow calving? Not in the least; the local vet. who was called in could probably do all that as well, or better. It is 'realist' because it goes behind all the brutalities, all the piggeries and inhumanities, of those frightful people, and shows us the strange, mad, transcendent passion that lay behind all those things--the wild desire for the land--a longing that burned, that devoured, that inflamed, that drove men to hell and death as would a passion for a goddess who might never be attained. Remember how 'La Beauce' is personified, how the earth swells and quickens before one, how every clod and morsel of the soil cries for its service and its sacrifice and its victims--I call that realism.

"The Arabian Nights is also profoundly realistic, though both the subject-matter and the method of treatment--the technique--are very different from the subject-matter and the technique of Zola. Of course, there may be people who think that if you describe a pigsty well you are a 'realist,' and if you describe an altar well you are 'romantic.' ... I do not know that the mental processes of Crétins form a very interesting subject for discussion."

One may surmise, if one will, that the sudden violence of the change was a sufficient cause of exaltation. That detestable Lupton left behind; no town, but a collection of stink and poison factories and slave quarters; that more detestable school, more ridiculous than the Academy of Lagado; that most detestable routine, games, lessons and the Doctor's sermons--the transition was tremendous to the freedom of fabled London, of the unknown streets and unending multitudes.

Ambrose said he hesitated to talk of that walk, lest he should be thought an aimless liar. They strolled for hours seeing the most wonderful things, the most wonderful people; but he declared that the case was similar to that of the Benedictine--he could never discover again the regions that he had perambulated. Somewhere, he said, close to the Château de Chinon there must be a passage which had since been blocked up. By it was the entrance to Fairyland.

When at last they found Little Russell Row, the black cat was awaiting them with an expression which was pleased and pious, too; he had devoured the greater portion of that quarter-pound of dubious butter. Ambrose smoked black cigarettes in bed till the packet was finished.

III

It was an amazing week they spent in London. For a couple of days Nelly was busied in getting "things" and "odds and ends," and, to her credit, she dressed the part most admirably. She abjured all the imperial purples, the Mediterranean blues, the shrieking lilacs that her class usually affects, and appeared at last a model of neat gaiety.

In the meantime, while these shopping expeditions were in progress, while Nelly consulted with those tall, dark-robed, golden-haired and awful Elegances which preside over the last mysteries of the draper and milliner, Ambrose sat at home in Little Russell Row and worked out the outlines of some fantasies that had risen in his mind. It was, in fact, during these days that he made the notes which were afterwards expanded into the curious Defence of Taverns, a book which is now rare and sought after by collectors. It is supposed that it was this work that was in poor Palmer's mind when the earnest man referred with a sort of gloomy reticence to Meyrick's later career. He had, in all probability, not read a line of it; but the title was certainly not a very pleasing one, judged by ordinary scholastic standards. And it must be said that the critical reception of the book was not exactly encouraging. One paper wondered candidly why such a book was ever written or printed; another denounced the author in good, set terms as an enemy of the great temperance movement; while a third, a Monthly Reviewer, declared that the work made his blood boil. Yet even the severest moralists should have seen by the epigraph that the Apes and Owls and Antiques hid mysteries of some sort, since a writer whose purposes were really evil and intemperate would never have chosen such a motto as: Jalalúd-Din praised the behaviour of the Inebriated and drank water from the well. But the reviewers thought that this was unintelligible nonsense, and merely a small part of the writer's general purpose to annoy.

The rough sketch is contained in the first of the Note Books, which are still unpublished, and perhaps are likely to remain so. Meyrick jotted down his hints and ideas in the dingy "first floor front" of the Bloomsbury lodging-house, sitting at the rosewood "Davenport" which, to the landlady, seemed the last word in beautiful furniture.

The ménage rose late. What a relief it was to be free of the horrible bells that poisoned one's rest at Lupton, to lie in peace as long as one liked, smoking a matutinal cigarette or two to the accompaniment of a cup of tea! Nelly was acquiring the art of the cigarette-smoker by degrees. She did not like the taste at all at first, but the wild and daring deviltry of the practice sustained her, and she persevered. And while they thus wasted the best hours of the day, Ambrose would make to pass before the bottom of the bed a long procession of the masters, each uttering his characteristic word of horror and astonishment as he went by, each whirled away by some invisible power in the middle of a sentence. Thus would enter Chesson, fully attired in cassock, cap and gown:

"Meyrick! It is impossible? Are you not aware that such conduct as this is entirely inconsistent with the tone of a great Public School? Have the Games ..." But he was gone; his legs were seen vanishing in a whirlwind which bore him up the chimney.

Then Horbury rose out of the carpet:

"Plain living and clear thinking are the notes of the System. A Spartan Discipline--Meyrick! Do you call this a Spartan Discipline? Smoking tobacco and reposing with ..." He shot like an arrow after the Head.

"We discourage luxury by every means in our power. Boy! This is luxury! Boy, boy! You are like the later Romans, boy! Heliogabalus was accustomed ..." The chimney consumed Palmer also; and he gave place to another.

"Roughly speaking, a boy should be always either in school or playing games. He should never be suffered to be at a loose end. Is this your idea of playing games? I tell you, Meyrick ..."

The game amused Nelly, more from its accompanying "business" and facial expression than from any particular comprehension of the dialogue. Ambrose saw that she could not grasp all the comedy of his situations, so he invented an Idyll between the Doctor and a notorious and flamboyant barmaid at the "Bell." The fame of this lady ran great but not gracious through all Lupton. This proved a huge success; beginning as a mere episode, it gathered to itself a complicated network of incidents and adventures, of wild attempts and strange escapes, of stratagems and ambushes, of disguises and alarms. Indeed, as Ambrose instructed Nelly with great solemnity, the tale, at first an idyll, the simple, pastoral story of the loves of the Shepherd Chesson and the Nymph Bella, was rapidly becoming epical in its character. He talked of dividing it into twelve books! He enlarged very elaborately the Defeat of the Suitors. In this the dear old Head, disguised as a bookmaker, drugged the whisky of the young bloods who were accustomed to throng about the inner bar of the "Bell." There was quite a long passage describing the compounding of the patent draught from various herbs, the enormous cook at the Head's house enacting a kind of Canidia part, and helping in the concoction of the dose.

"Mrs. Belper," the Doctor would observe, "This is most gratifying. I had no idea that your knowledge of simples was so extensive. Do I understand you to affirm that those few leaves which you hold in your hand will produce marked symptoms?"

"Bless your dear 'art, Doctor Chesson, and if you'll forgive me for talking so to such a learned gentleman, and so good, I'm sure, but you'll find there's nothing in the world like it. Often and often have I 'eard my pore old mother that's dead and gone these forty year come Candlemas ..."

"Mrs. Belper, Mrs. Belper, I am surprised at you! Are you not aware that the Judicial Committee of the Privy Council has pronounced the observance of the festival you so lightly name to be of a highly superstitious nature? Your deceased mother, you were saying, will have entered into her reward forty years ago on February the second of next year? Is not this the case?"

"These forty years came Febbymas, I mean, and a good woman she was, and never have I seen a larger wart on the nose and her legs bad as bad for years and years!"

"These details, though, no doubt, of high personal interest, seem hardly germane to our present undertaking. However, Mrs. Belper, proceed in your remarks."

"And thank you kindly, Sir, and not forgetting you are a clergyman--but there! we can't all of us be everything. And my pore mother, as I was saying, Sir, she said, again and again, that if she'd been like some folks she'd a made a fortune in golden money from this very yarb I'm a-showing you, Sir."

"Dear me, Mrs. Belper! You interest me deeply. I have often thought how wrong it is of us to neglect, as undoubtedly we do neglect, the bounteous gifts of the kindly earth. Your lamented mother used this specific with remarkable success?"

"Lord a mercy, Doctor 'Chesson! elephants couldn't a stood against it, nor yet whales, being as how it's stronger than the strongest gunpowder that was ever brewed or blasted, and miles better than the nasty rubbidge you get in them doctors' shops, and a pretty penny they make you pay for it and no better than calomel, if you ask me, Sir. But be it the strongest of the strong, I'll take my Gospel oath it's weak to what my pore mother made, and that anybody in Much Moddle parish would tell you, for man, woman or child who took one of Mrs. Marjoram's Mixtures and got over it, remember it, he would, until his dying day. And my pore old mother, she was that funny--never was a cheerfuller woman, I do believe, and when Tom Copus, the lame fiddler, he got married, pore mother! though she could hardly walk, her legs was that bad, come she would, and if she didn't slip a little of the mixture into the beer when everybody was looking another way! Pore, dear soul! as she said herself afterwards, 'mirth becomes marriage,' and so to be sure it does, and merry they all were that day that didn't touch the beer, preferring spirits, which pore mother couldn't get at, being locked up--a nasty, mean trick, I call it, and always will."

"Enough, Mrs. Belper, enough! You have amply satisfied me as to the potency of the late Mrs. Marjoram's pharmacopoeia. We will, if you have no objection, Mrs. Belper, make the mixture--to use the words of Shakespeare--'slab and thick.'"

"And bless your kind 'art, Sir, and a good, kind master you've always been to me, if you 'aven't got enough 'ere to lay out all the Lupton town, call me a Dutchwoman, and that I never was, nor pore Belper neither."

"Certainly not, Mrs. Belper. The Dutch belong to a different branch of the great Teutonic stock, or, if identity had ever existed, the two races have long been differentiated. I think, Mrs. Belper, that the most eminent physicians have recognised the beneficial effects of a gentle laxative during the treacherous (though delightful) season of spring?"

"Law bless you, Sir, you're right, as you always are, or why, Doctor? As my pore mother used to say when she made up the mixture: 'Scour 'em out is the right way about!' And laugh she would as she pounded the stuff up till I really thought she would 'a busted, and shaking like the best blancmanges all the while."

"Mrs. Belper, you have removed a weight from my mind. You think, then, that I shall be freed from all unfair competition while I pay my addresses to my young friend, Miss Floyer?"

"As free you will be, Doctor Chesson, Sir, as the little birds in the air; for not one of them young fellers will stand on his feet for days, and groans and 'owls will be the best word that mortal man will speak, and bless you they will with their dying breath. So, Sir, you'll 'ave the sweet young lady, bless her dear 'art, all to yourself, and if it's twins, don't blame me!"

"Mrs. Belper, your construction, if I may say so, is somewhat proleptic in its character. Still, I am sure that your meaning is good. Ha! I hear the bell for afternoon school."

The Doctor's voice happened to be shrill and piercing, with something of the tone of the tooth-comb and tissue-paper; while the fat cook spoke in a suety, husky contralto. Ambrose reproduced these peculiarities with the gift of the born mimic, adding appropriate antic and gesture to grace the show, and Nelly's appreciation of its humours was intense.

Day by day new incidents and scenes were added. The Head, in the pursuit of his guilty passion, hid in the coal-cellar of the "Bell," and, rustling sounds being heard, evaded detection for a while by imitating the barks of a terrier in chase of a rat. Nelly liked to hear the "Wuff! wuff! wuff!" which was introduced at this point. She liked also the final catastrophe, when the odd man of the "Bell" burst into the bar and said: "Dang my eyes, if it ain't the Doctor! I seed his cap and gown as he run round and round the coals on all fours, a-growling 'orrible." To which the landlady rejoined: "Don't tell your silly lies here! How could he growl, him being a clergyman?" And all the loafers joined in the chorus: "That's right, Tom; why do you talk such silly lies as that--him being a clergyman?"

They laughed so loud and so merrily over their morning tea and these lunacies that the landlady doubted gravely as to their marriage lines. She cared nothing; they had paid what she asked, money down in advance, and, as she said: "Young gentlemen will have their fun with the young ladies--so what's the good of talking?"

Breakfast came at length. They gave the landlady a warning bell some half-hour in advance, so the odd food was, at all events, not cold. Afterwards Nelly sallied off on her shopping expeditions, which, as might have been expected, she enjoyed hugely, and Ambrose stayed alone, with his pen and ink and a fat notebook which had captured his eye in a stationer's window.

Under these odd circumstances, then, he laid the foundations of his rare and precious Defence of Taverns, which is now termed by those fortunate enough to possess copies as a unique and golden treatise. Though he added a good deal in later years and remodelled and rearranged freely, there is a certain charm of vigour and freshness about the first sketch which is quite delightful in its way. Take, for example, the description of the whole world overwhelmed with sobriety: a deadly absence of inebriation annulling and destroying all the works and thoughts of men, the country itself at point to perish of the want of good liquor and good drinkers. He shows how there is grave cause to dread that, by reason of this sad neglect of the Dionysiac Mysteries, humanity is fast falling backward from the great heights to which it had ascended, and is in imminent danger of returning to the dumb and blind and helpless condition of the brutes.

"How else," he says, "can one account for the stricken state in which all the animal world grows and is eternally impotent? To them, strange, vast and enormous powers and faculties have been given. Consider, for example, the curious equipments of two odd extremes in this sphere--the ant and the elephant. The ant, if one may say so, is very near to us. We have our great centres of industry, our Black Country and our slaves who, if not born black, become black in our service. And the ants, too, have their black, enslaved races who do their dirty work for them, and are, perhaps, congratulated on their privileges as sharing in the blessings of civilisation--though this may be a refinement. The ant slaves, I believe, will rally eagerly to the defence of the nest and the eggs, and they say that the labouring classes are Liberal to the core. Nay; we grow mushrooms by art, and so they. In some lands, I think, they make enormous nests which are the nuisance and terror of the country. We have Manchester and Lupton and Leeds, and many such places--one would think them altogether civilised.

"The elephant, again, has many gifts which we lack. Note the curious instinct (or intuition, rather) of danger. The elephant knows, for example, when a bridge is unsafe, and refuses to pass, where a man would go on to destruction. One might examine in the same way all the creatures, and find in them singular capacities.

"Yet--they have no art. They see--but they see not. They hear--and they hear not. The odour in their nostrils has no sweetness at all. They have made no report of all the wonders that they knew. Their houses are, sometimes, as ingenious as a Chemical Works, but never is there any beauty for beauty's sake.

"It is clear that their state is thus desolate, because of the heavy pall of sobriety that hangs over them all; and it scarcely seems to have occurred to our 'Temperance' advocates that when they urge on us the example and abstinence of the beasts they have advanced the deadliest of all arguments against their nostrum. The Laughing Jackass is a teetotaller, doubtless, but no sane man should desire to be a Laughing Jackass.

"But the history of the men who have attained, who have done the glorious things of the earth and have become for ever exalted is the history of the men who have quested the Cup. Dionysius, said the Greeks, civilised the world; and the Bacchic Mystery was, naturally, the heart and core of Greek civilisation.

"Note the similitudes of Vine and Vineyard in Old Testament.

"Note the Quest of the San Graal.

"Note Rabelais and La Dive Bouteille.

"Place yourself in imagination in a Gothic Cathedral of the thirteenth century and assist at High Mass. Then go to the nearest Little Bethel, and look, and listen. Consider the difference in the two buildings, in those who worship in one and listen and criticise in the other. You have the difference between the Inebriated and the Sober, displayed in their works. As Little Bethel is to Tintern, so is Sobriety to Inebriation.

"Modern civilisation has advanced in many ways? Yes. Bethel has a stucco front. This material was quite unknown to the builders of Tintern Abbey. Advanced? What is advancement? Freedom from excesses, from extravagances, from wild enthusiasms? Small Protestant tradesmen are free from all these things, certainly. But is the joy of Adulteration to be the last goal, the final Initiation of the Race of Men? Cælumque tueri--to sand the sugar?

"The Flagons of the Song of Songs did not contain ginger-beer.

"But the worst of it is we shall not merely descend to the beasts. We shall fall very far below the beasts. A black fellow is good, and a white fellow is good. But the white fellow who 'goes Fantee' does not become a negro--he becomes something infinitely worse, a horrible mass of the most putrid corruption.

"If we can clear our minds of the horrible cant of our 'civilisation,' if we can look at a modern 'industrial centre' with eyes purged of illusions, we shall have some notion of the awful horror to which we are descending in our effort to become as the ants and bees--creatures who know nothing of

CALIX INEBRIANS.

"I doubt if we can really make this effort. Blacks, Stinks, Desolations, Poisons, Hell's Nightmare generally have, I suspect, worked themselves into the very form and mould of our thoughts. We are sober, and perhaps the Tavern door is shut for ever against us.

"Now and then, perhaps, at rarer and still rarer intervals, a few of us will hear very faintly the far echoes of the holy madness within the closed door:

"When up the thyrse is raised, and when the sound
Of sacred orgies flies 'around, around.'
"Which is the Sonus Epulantium in Æterno Convivio.

"But this we shall not be able to discern. Very likely we shall take the noise of this High Choir for the horrid mirth of Hell. How strange it is that those who are pledged officially and ceremonially, as it were, to a Rite of Initiation which figures certainly a Feast, should in all their thoughts and words and actions be continually blaspheming and denying all the uses and ends of feastings and festivals.

"This is not the refusal of the species for the sake of enjoying perfectly the most beautiful and desirable genus; it is the renouncing of species and genus, the pronouncing of Good to be Evil. The Universal being denied, the Particular is degraded and defiled. What is called 'The Drink Curse' is the natural and inevitable result and sequence of the 'Protestant Reformation.' If the clear wells and fountains of the magic wood are buried out of sight, then men (who must have Drink) will betake them to the Slime Ponds and Poison Pools.

"In the Graal Books there is a curse--an evil enchantment--on the land of Logres because the mystery of the Holy Vessel is disregarded. The Knight sees the Dripping Spear and the Shining Cup pass before him, and says no word. He asks no question as to the end and meaning of this ceremony. So the land is blasted and barren and songless, and those who dwell in it are in misery.

"Every day of our lives we see the Graal carried before us in a wonderful order, and every day we leave the question unasked, the Mystery despised and neglected. Yet if we could ask that question, bowing down before these Heavenly and Glorious Splendours and Hallows--then every man should have the meat and drink that his soul desired; the hall would be filled with odours of Paradise, with the light of Immortality.

"In the books the Graal was at last taken away because of men's unworthiness. So it will be, I suppose. Even now, the Quester's adventure is a desperate one--few there be that find It.

"Ventilation and sanitation are well enough in their way. But it would not be very satisfactory to pass the day in a ventilated and sanitated Hell with nothing to eat or drink. If one is perishing of hunger and thirst, sanitation seems unimportant enough.

"How wonderful, how glorious it would be if the Kingdom of the Great Drinkers could be restored! If we could only sweep away all the might of the Sober Ones--the factory builders, the poison makers, the politicians, the manufacturers of bad books and bad pictures, together with Little Bethel and the morality of Mr. Mildmay, the curate (a series of negative propositions)--then imagine the Great Light of the Great Inebriation shining on every face, and not any work of man's hands, from a cathedral to a penknife, without the mark of the Tavern upon it! All the world a great festival; every well a fountain of strong drink; every river running with the New Wine; the Sangraal brought back from Sarras, restored to the awful shrine of Cor-arbennic, the Oracle of the Dive Bouteille once more freely given, the ruined Vineyard flourishing once more, girt about by shining, everlasting walls! Then we should hear the Old Songs again, and they would dance the Old Dances, the happy, ransomed people, Commensals and Compotators of the Everlasting Tavern."

The whole treatise, of which this extract is a fragment in a rudimentary and imperfect stage, is, of course, an impassioned appeal for the restoration of the quickening, exuberant imagination, not merely in art, but in all the inmost places of life. There is more than this, too. Here and there one can hear, as it were, the whisper and the hint of deeper mysteries, visions of a great experiment and a great achievement to which some men may be called. In his own words: "Within the Tavern there is an Inner Tavern, but the door of it is visible to few indeed."

In Ambrose's mind in the after years the stout notebook was dear, perhaps as a substitute for that aroma of the past in a phial which he has declared so desirable an invention. It stood, not so much for what was written in it as for the place and the circumstances in which it was written. It recalled Little Russell Row and Nelly, and the evenings at the Château de Chinon, where, night by night, they served still stranger, more delicious meats, and the red wine revealed more clearly its high celestial origin. One evening was diversified by an odd encounter.

A middle-aged man, sitting at an adjoining table, was evidently in want of matches, and Ambrose handed his box with the sympathetic smile which one smoker gives to another in such cases. The man--he had a black moustache and a small, pointed beard--thanked him in fluent English with a French accent, and they began to talk of casual things, veering, by degrees, in the direction of the arts. The Frenchman smiled at Meyrick's enthusiasm.

"What a life you have before you!" he said. "Don't you know that the populace always hates the artist--and kills him if it can? You are an artist and mystic, too. What a fate!

"Yes; but it is that applause, that réclame that comes after the artist is dead," he went on, replying to some objection of Ambrose's; "it is that which is the worst cruelty of all. It is fine for Burns, is it not, that his stupid compatriots have not ceased to utter follies about him for the last eighty years? Scotchmen? But they should be ashamed to speak his name! And Keats, and how many others in my country and in yours and in all countries? The imbeciles are not content to calumniate, to persecute, to make wretched the artist in his lifetime. They follow him with their praise to the grave--the grave that they have digged! Praise of the populace! Praise of a race of pigs! For, you see, while they are insulting the dead with their compliments they are at the same time insulting the living with their abuse."

He dropped into silence; from his expression he seemed to be cursing "the populace" with oaths too frightful to be uttered. He rose suddenly and turned to Ambrose.

"Artist--and mystic. Yes. You will probably be crucified. Good evening ... and a fine martyrdom to you!"

He was gone with a charming smile and a delightful bow to "Madame." Ambrose looked after him with a puzzled face; his last words had called up some memory that he could not capture; and then suddenly he recollected the old, ragged Irish fiddler, the player of strange fantasies under the tree in the outskirts of Lupton. He thought of his phrase about "red martyrdom"; it was an odd coincidence.

IV

The phrases kept recurring to his mind after they had gone out, and as they wandered through the lighted streets with all their strange and variegated show, with glittering windows and glittering lamps, with the ebb and flow of faces, the voices and the laughter, the surging crowds about the theatre doors, the flashing hansoms and the omnibuses lumbering heavily along to strange regions, such as Turnham Green and Castlenau, Cricklewood and Stoke Newington--why, they were as unknown as cities in Cathay!

It was a dim, hot night; all the great city smoked as with a mist, and a tawny moon rose through films of cloud far in the vista of the east. Ambrose thought with a sudden recollection that the moon, that world of splendour, was shining in a farther land, on the coast of the wild rocks, on the heaving sea, on the faery apple-garths in Avalon, where, though the apples are always golden, yet the blossoms of enchantment never fade, but hang for ever against the sky.

They were passing a half-lit street, and these dreams were broken by the sudden clanging, rattling music of a piano-organ. For a moment they saw the shadowy figures of the children as they flitted to and fro, dancing odd measures in the rhythm of the tune. Then they came into a long, narrow way with a church spire in the distance, and near the church they passed the "church-shop"--Roman, evidently, from the subjects and the treatment of the works of art on view. But it was strange! In the middle of the window was a crude, glaring statue of some saint. He was in bright red robes, sprinkled with golden stars; the blood rained down from a wound in his forehead, and with one hand he drew the scarlet vestment aside and pointed to the dreadful gash above his heart, and from this, again, the bloody drops fell thick. The colours stared and shrieked, and yet, through the bad, cheap art there seemed to shine a rapture that was very near to beauty; the thing expressed was so great that it had to a certain extent overcome the villainy of the expression.

They wandered vaguely, after their custom. Ambrose was silent; he was thinking of Avalon and "Red Martyrdom" and the Frenchman's parting salutation, of the vision in one of the old books, "the Man clothed in a robe redder and more shining than burning fire, and his feet and his hands and his face were of a like flame, and five angels in fiery vesture stood about him, and at the feet of the Man the ground was covered with a ruddy dew."

They passed under an old church tower that rose white in the moonlight above them. The air had cleared, the mist had floated away, and now the sky glowed violet, and the white stones of the classic spirit shone on high. From it there came suddenly a tumult of glad sound, exultant bells in ever-changing order, pealing out as if to honour some great victory, so that the mirth of the street below became but a trivial restless noise. He thought of some passage that he had read but could not distinctly remember: a ship was coming back to its haven after a weary and tempestuous voyage over many dreadful seas, and those on board saw the tumult in the city as their sails were sighted; heard afar the shouts of gladness from the rejoicing people; heard the bells from all the spires and towers break suddenly into triumphant chorus, sounding high above the washing of the waves.

Ambrose roused himself from his dreams. They had been walking in a circle and had returned almost to the street of the Château, though, their knowledge of the district being of an unscientific character, they were under the impression that they were a mile or so away from that particular point. As it happened, they had not entered this street before, and they were charmed at the sudden appearance of stained glass lighted up from within. The colour was rich and good; there were flourished scrolls and grotesques in the Renaissance manner, many emblazoned shields in ruby and gold and azure; and the centre-piece showed the Court of the Beer King--a jovial and venerable figure attended by a host of dwarfs and kobolds, all holding on high enormous mugs of beer. They went in boldly and were glad. It was the famous "Three Kings" in its golden and unreformed days, but this they knew not. The room was of moderate size, very low, with great dark beams in the white ceiling. White were the walls; on the plaster, black-letter texts with vermilion initials praised the drinker's art, and more kobolds, in black and red, loomed oddly in unsuspected corners. The lighting, presumably, was gas, but all that was visible were great antique lanterns depending from iron hooks, and through their dull green glass only a dim radiance fell upon the heavy oak tables and the drinkers. From the middle beam an enormous bouquet of fresh hops hung on high; there was a subdued murmur of talk, and now and then the clatter of the lid of a mug, as fresh beer was ordered. In one corner there was a kind of bar; behind it a couple of grim women--the kobolds apparently--performed their office; and above, on a sort of rack, hung mugs and tankards of all sizes and of all fantasies. There were plain mugs of creamy earthenware, mugs gaudily and oddly painted with garlanded goats, with hunting scenes, with towering castles, with flaming posies of flowers. Then some friend of the drunken, some sage who had pried curiously into the secrets of thirst, had made a series of wonders in glass, so shining and crystalline that to behold them was as if one looked into a well, for every glitter of the facets gave promise of satisfaction. There were the mugs, capacious and very deep, crowned for the most part not with mere plain lids of common use and make, but with tall spires in pewter, richly ornamented, evident survivals from the Middle Ages. Ambrose's eyes glistened; the place was altogether as he would have designed it. Nelly, too, was glad to sit down, for they had walked longer than usual. She was refreshed by a glass of some cool drink with a borage flower and a cherry floating in it, and Ambrose ordered a mug of beer.

It is not known how many of these krugs he emptied. It was, as has been noted, a sultry night, and the streets were dusty, and that glass of Benedictine after dinner rather evokes than dismisses the demon of thirst. Still, Munich beer is no hot and rebellious drink, so the causes of what followed must probably be sought for in other springs. Ambrose took a deep draught, gazed upward to the ceiling, and ordered another mug of beer for himself and some more of the cool and delicate and flowery beverage for Nelly. When the drink was set upon the board, he thus began, without title or preface:

"You must know, Nelly dear," he said, "that the marriage of Panurge, which fell out in due time (according to the oracle and advice of the Holy Bottle), was by no means a fortunate one. For, against all the counsel of Pantagruel and of Friar John, and indeed of all his friends, Panurge married in a fit of spleen and obstinacy the crooked and squinting daughter of the little old man who sold green sauce in the Rue Quincangrogne at Tours--you will see the very place in a few days, and then you will understand everything. You do not understand that? My child, that is impiety, since it accuses the Zeitgest, who is certainly the only god that ever existed, as you will see more fully demonstrated in Huxley and Spencer and all the leading articles in all the leading newspapers. Quod erat demonstrandum. To be still more precise: You must know that when I am dead, and a very great man indeed, many thousands of people will come from all the quarters of the globe--not forgetting the United States--to Lupton. They will come and stare very hard at the Old Grange, which will have an inscription about me on the wall; they will spend hours in High School; they will walk all round Playing Fields; they will cut little bits off 'brooks' and 'quarries.' Then they will view the Sulphuric Acid works, the Chemical Manure factory and the Free Library, and whatever other stink-pots and cesspools Lupton town may contain; they will finally enjoy the view of the Midland Railway Goods Station. Then they will say: 'Now we understand him; now one sees how he got all his inspiration in that lovely old school and the wonderful English country-side.' So you see that when I show you the Rue Quincangrogne you will perfectly understand this history. Let us drink; the world shall never be drowned again, so have no fear.

"Well, the fact remains that Panurge, having married this hideous wench aforesaid, was excessively unhappy. It was in vain that he argued with his wife in all known languages and in some that are unknown, for, as she said, she only knew two languages, the one of Touraine and the other of the Stick, and this second she taught Panurge per modum passionis--that is by beating him, and this so thoroughly that poor Pilgarlic was sore from head to foot. He was a worthy little fellow, but the greatest coward that ever breathed. Believe me, illustrious drinkers and most precious.... Nelly, never was man so wretched as this Panurge since Paradise fell from Adam. This is the true doctrine; I heard it when I was at Eleusis. You enquire what was the matter? Why, in the first place, this vile wretch whom they all called--so much did they hate her--La Vie Mortale, or Deadly Life, this vile wretch, I say: what do you think that she did when the last note of the fiddles had sounded and the wedding guests had gone off to the 'Three Lampreys' to kill a certain worm--the which worm is most certainly immortal, since it is not dead yet! Well, then, what did Madame Panurge?

Arthur Machen

Nothing but this: She robbed her excellent and devoted husband of all that he had. Doubtless you remember how, in the old days, Panurge had played ducks and drakes with the money that Pantagruel had given him, so that he borrowed on his corn while it was still in the ear, and before it was sown, if we enquire a little more closely. In truth, the good little man never had a penny to bless himself withal, for the which cause Pantagruel loved him all the more dearly. So that when the Dive Bouteille gave its oracle, and Panurge chose his spouse, Pantagruel showed how preciously he esteemed a hearty spender by giving him such a treasure that the goldsmiths who live under the bell of St. Gatien still talk of it before they dine, because by doing so their mouths water, and these salivary secretions are of high benefit to the digestion: read on this, Galen. If you would know how great and glorious this treasure was, you must go to the Library of the Archevêché at Tours, where they will show you a vast volume bound in pigskin, the name of which I have forgotten. But this book is nothing else than the list of all the wonders and glories of Pantagruel's wedding present to Panurge; it contains surprising things, I can tell you, for, in good coin of the realm alone, never was gift that might compare with it; and besides the common money there were ancient pieces, the very names of which are now incomprehensible, and incomprehensible they will remain till the coming of the Coqcigrues. There was, for instance, a great gold Sol, a world in itself, as some said truly, and I know not how many myriad myriad of Étoiles, all of the finest silver that was ever minted, and Anges-Gardiens, which the learned think must have been first coined at Angers, though others will have it that they were the same as our Angels; and, as for Roses de Paradis and Couronnes Immortelles, I believe he had as many of them as ever he would. Beauties and joys he was to keep for pocket-money; small change is sometimes great gain. And, as I say, no sooner had Panurge married that accursed daughter of the Rue Quincangrogne than she robbed him of everything, down to the last brass farthing. The fact is that the woman was a witch; she was also something else which I leave out for the present. But, if you will believe me, she cast such a spell upon Panurge that he thought himself an absolute beggar. Thus he would look at his Sol d'Or and say: 'What is the use of that? It is only a great bright lump: I can see it every day.' Then when they said, 'But how about those Anges-Gardiens?' he would reply, 'Where are they? Have you seen them? I never see them. Show them to me,' and so with all else; and all the while that villain of a woman beat, thumped and belaboured him so that the tears were always in his eyes, and they say you could hear him howling all over the world. Everybody said that he had made a pretty mess of it, and would come to a bad end.

"Luckily for him, this ... witch of a wife of his would sometimes doze off for a few minutes, and then he had a little peace, and he would wonder what had become of all the gay girls and gracious ladies that he had known in old times--for he had played the devil with the women in his day and could have taught Ovid lessons in arte amoris. Now, of course, it was as much as his life was worth to mention the very name of one of these ladies, and as for any little sly visits, stolen endearments, hidden embraces, or any small matters of that kind, it was good-bye, I shall see you next Nevermas. Nor was this all, but worse remains behind; and it is my belief that it is the thought of what I am going to tell you that makes the wind wail and cry of winter nights, and the clouds weep, and the sky look black; for in truth it is the greatest sorrow that ever was since the beginning of the world. I must out with it quick, or I shall never have done: in plain English, and as true as I sit here drinking good ale, not one drop or minim or drachm or pennyweight of drink had Panurge tasted since the day of his wedding! He had implored mercy, he had told her how he had served Gargantua and Pantagruel and had got into the habit of drinking in his sleep, and his wife had merely advised him to go to the devil--she was not going to let him so much as look at the nasty stuff. '"Touch not, taste not, smell not," is my motto,' said she. She gave him a blue ribbon, which she said would make up for it. 'What do you want with Drink?' said she. 'Go and do business instead, it's much better for you.'

"Sad, then, and sorry enough was the estate of poor Panurge. At last, so wretched did he become, that he took advantage of one of his wife's dozes and stole away to the good Pantagruel, and told him the whole story--and a very bad one it was--so that the tears rolled down Pantagruel's cheeks from sheer grief, and each teardrop contained exactly one hundred and eighteen gallons of aqueous fluid, according to the calculations of the best geometers. The great man saw that the case was a desperate one, and Heaven knew, he said, whether it could be mended or not; but certain it was that a business such as this could not be settled in a hurry, since it was not like a game at shove-ha'penny to be got over between two gallons of wine. He therefore counselled Panurge to have patience and bear with his wife for a few thousand years, and in the meantime they would see what could be done. But, lest his patience should wear out, he gave him an odd drug or medicine, prepared by the great artist of the Mountains of Cathay, and this he was to drop into his wife's glass--for though he might have no drink, she was drunk three times a day, and she would sleep all the longer, and leave him awhile in peace. This Panurge very faithfully performed, and got a little rest now and again, and they say that while that devil of a woman snored and snorted he was able,

394

by odd chances once or twice, to get hold of a drop of the right stuff--good old Stingo from the big barrel--which he lapped up as eagerly as a kitten laps cream. Others there be who declare that once or twice he got about his sad old tricks, while his ugly wife was sleeping in the sun; the women on the Maille make no secret of their opinion that his old mistress, Madame Sophia, was seen stealing in and out of the house as slyly as you please, and God knows what goes on when the door is shut. But the Tourainians were always sad gossips, and one must not believe all that one hears. I leave out the flat scandal-mongers who are bold enough to declare that he kept one mistress at Jerusalem, another at Eleusis, another in Egypt and about as many as are contained in the seraglio of the Grand Turk, scattered up and down in the towns and villages of Asia; but I do believe there was some kissing in dark corners, and a curtain hung across one room in the house could tell odd tales. Nevertheless, La Vie Mortale (a pest on her!) was more often awake than asleep, and when she was awake Panurge's case was worse than ever. For, you see, the woman was no piece of a fool, and she saw sure enough that something was going on. The Stingo in the barrel was lower than of rights, and more than once she had caught her husband looking almost happy, at which she beat the house about her ears. Then, another time, Madame Sophia dropped her ring, and again this sweet lady came one morning so strongly perfumed that she scented the whole place, and when La Vie woke up it smelt like a church. There was fine work then, I promise you; the people heard the bangs and curses and shrieks and groans as far as Amboise on the one side and Luynes on the other; and that year the Loire rose ten feet higher than the banks on account of Panurge's tears. As a punishment, she made him go and be industrial, and he built ten thousand stink-pot factories with twenty thousand chimneys, and all the leaves and trees and green grass and flowers in the world were blackened and died, and all the waters were poisoned so that there were no perch in the Loire, and salmon fetched forty sols the pound at Chinon market. As for the men and women, they became yellow apes and listened to a codger named Calvin, who told them they would all be damned eternally (except himself and his friends), and they found his doctrine very comforting, and probable too, since they had the sense to know that they were more than half damned already. I don't know whether Panurge's fate was worse on this occasion or on another when his wife found a book in his writing, full from end to end of poetry; some of it about the wonderful treasure that Pantagruel had given him, which he was supposed to have forgotten. Some of it verses to those old light-o'-loves of his, with a whole epic in praise of his mistress-in-chief, Sophia. Then, indeed, there was the very deuce to pay; it was bread and water, stripes and torment, all day long, and La Vie swore a great oath that if he ever did it again he should be sent to spend the rest of his life in Manchester, whereupon he fell into a swoon from horrid fright and lay like a log, so that everybody thought he was dead.

"All this while the great Pantagruel was not idle. Perceiving how desperate the matter was, he summoned the Thousand and First Great OEcumenical Council of all the sages of the wide world, and when the fathers had come, and had heard High Mass at St. Gatien's, the session was opened in a pavilion in the meadows by the Loire just under the Lanterne of Roche Corbon, whence this Council is always styled the great and holy Council of the Lantern. If you want to know where the place is you can do so very easily, for there is a choice tavern on the spot where the pavilion stood, and there you may have malelotte and friture and amber wine of Vouvray, better than in any tavern in Touraine. As for the history of the acts of this great Council, it is still a-writing, and so far only two thousand volumes in elephant folio have been printed sub signo Lucernæ cum permissu superiorum. However, as it is necessary to be brief, it may be said that the holy fathers of the Lantern, after having heard the whole case as it was exposed to them by the great clerks of Pantagruel, having digested all the arguments, looked into the precedents, applied themselves to the doctrine, explored the hidden wisdom, consulted the Canons, searched the Scriptures, divided the dogma, distinguished the distinctions and answered the questions, resolved with one voice that there was no help in the world for Panurge, save only this: he must forthwith achieve the most high, noble and glorious quest of the Sangraal, for no other way was there under heaven by which he might rid himself of that pestilent wife of his, La Vie Mortale.

"And on some other occasion," said Ambrose, "you may hear of the last voyage of Panurge to the Glassy Isle of the Holy Graal, of the incredible adventures that he achieved, of the dread perils through which he passed, of the great wonders and marvels and compassions of the way, of the manner in which he received the title Plentyn y Tonau, which signifies 'Child of the Waterfloods,' and how at last he gloriously attained the vision of the Sangraal, and was most happily translated out of the power of La Vie Mortale."

"And where is he now?" said Nelly, who had found the tale interesting but obscure.

"It is not precisely known--opinions vary. But there are two odd things: one is that he is exactly like that man in the red dress whose statue we saw in the shop window to-night; and the other is that from that day to this he has never been sober for a single minute.

V

Ambrose took a great draught from the mug and emptied it, and forthwith rapped the lid for a fresh supply. Nelly was somewhat nervous; she was afraid he might begin to sing, for there were extravagances in the history of Panurge which seemed to her to be of alcoholic source. However, he did not sing; he lapsed into silence, gazing at the dark beams, the hanging hops, the bright array of the tankards and the groups of drinkers dotted about the room. At a neighbouring table two Germans were making a hearty meal, chumping the meat and smacking their lips in a kind of heavy ecstasy. He had but little German, but he caught scraps of the conversation.

One man said:

"Heavenly swine cutlets!"

And the other answered:

"Glorious eating!"

"Nelly," said Ambrose, "I have a great inspiration!"

She trembled visibly.

"Yes; I have talked so much that I am hungry. We will have some supper."

They looked over the list of strange eatables and, with the waiter's help, decided on Leberwurst and potato-salad as light and harmless. With this they ate crescent loaves, sprinkled with caraway seeds: there was more Munich Lion-Brew and more flowery drink, with black coffee, a fine and a Maraschino to end all. For Nelly the kobolds began to perform a grotesque and mystic dance in the shadows, the glass tankards on the rack glittered strangely, the white walls with the red and black texts retreated into vast distances, and the bouquet of hops seemed suspended from a remote star. As for Ambrose, he was certainly not ebrius according to the Baron's definition; he was hardly ebriolus; but he was sensible, let us say, of a certain quickening of the fancy, of a more vivid and poignant enjoyment of the whole situation, of the unutterable gaiety of this mad escape from the conventions of Lupton.

"It was a Thursday night," said Ambrose in the after years, "and we were thinking of starting for Touraine either the next morning or on Saturday at latest. It will always be bright in my mind, that picture--the low room with the oak beams, the glittering tankards, the hops hanging from the ceiling, and Nelly sitting before me sipping the scented drink from a green glass. It was the last night of gaiety, and even then gaiety was mixed with odd patterns--the Frenchman's talk about martyrdom, and the statue of the saint pointing to the marks of his passion, standing in that dyed vesture with his rapt, exultant face; and then the song of final triumph and deliverance that rang out on the chiming bells from the white spire. I think the contrast of this solemn undertone made my heart all the lighter; I was in that odd state in which one delights to know that one is not being understood--so I told poor Nelly 'the story of Panurge's marriage to La Vie Mortale; I am sure she thought I was drunk!

"We went home in a hansom, and agreed that we would have just one cigarette and then go to bed. It was settled that we would catch the night boat to Dieppe on the next day, and we both laughed with joy at the thought of the adventure. And then--I don't know how it was--Nelly began to tell me all about herself. She had never said a word before; I had never asked her--I never ask anybody about their past lives. What does it matter? You know a certain class of plot--novelists are rather fond of using it--in which the hero's happiness is blasted because he finds out that the life of his wife or his sweetheart has not always been spotless as the snow. Why should it be spotless as the snow? What is the hero that he should be dowered with the love of virgins of Paradise? I call it cant--all that--and I hate it; I hope Angel Clare was eventually entrapped by a young person from Piccadilly Circus--she would probably be much too good for him! So, you see, I was hardly likely to have put any very searching questions to Nelly; we had other things to talk about.

"But this night I suppose she was a bit excited. It had been a wild and wonderful week. The transition from that sewage-pot in the Midlands to the Abbey of Theleme was enough to turn any head; we had laughed till we had grown dizzy. The worst of that miserable school discipline is that it makes one take an insane and quite disproportionate enjoyment in little things, in the merest trifles which ought really to be accepted as a matter of course. I assure you that every minute that I spent in bed after seven o'clock was to me a grain of Paradise, a moment of delight. Of course, it's ridiculous; let a man get up early or get up late, as he likes or as he finds best--and say no more about it. But at that wretched Lupton early rising was part of the infernal blether and blatter of the place, that made life there like a long dinner in which every dish has the same sauce. It may be a good sauce enough; but one is sick of the taste of it. According to our Bonzes there, getting up early on a winter's day was a high virtue which acquired merit. I believe I should have liked a hard chair to sit in of my own free will, if one of our old fools--Palmer--had not always been gabbling about the horrid luxury of some boys who had arm-chairs in their studies. Unless you were doing something or other to make yourself very uncomfortable, he used to say you were like the 'later Romans.' I am sure he believed that those lunatics who bathe in the Serpentine on Christmas Day would go straight to heaven!

"And there you are. I would awake at seven o'clock from persistent habit, and laugh as I realised that I was in Little Russell Row and not at the Old Grange. Then I would doze off again and wake up at intervals--eight, nine, ten--and chuckle to myself with ever-increasing enjoyment. It was just the same with smoking. I don't suppose I should have touched a cigarette for years if smoking had not been one of the mortal sins in our Bedlam Decalogue. I don't know whether smoking is bad for boys or not; I should think not, as I believe the Dutch--who are sturdy fellows-- begin to puff fat cigars at the age of six or thereabouts; but I do know that those pompous old boobies and blockheads and leather-skulls have discovered exactly the best way to make a boy think that a packet of Rosebuds represents the quintessence of frantic delight.

"Well, you see how it was, how Little Russell Row--the dingy, the stuffy, the dark retreat of old Bloomsbury--became the abode of miraculous joys, a bright portion of fairyland. Ah! it was a strong new wine that we tasted, and it went to our heads, and not much wonder. It all rose to its height on that Thursday night when we went to the 'Three Kings' and sat beneath the hop bush, drinking Lion-Brew and flowery drink as I talked extravagances concerning Panurge. It was time for the curtain to be rung down on our comedy.

"The one cigarette had become three or four when Nelly began to tell me her history; the wine and the rejoicing had got into her head also. She described the first things that she remembered: a little hut among wild hills and stony fields in the west of Ireland, and the great sea roaring on the shore but a mile away, and the wind and the rain always driving from across the waves. She spoke of the place as if she loved it, though her father and mother were as poor as they could be, and little was there to eat even in the old cabin. She remembered Mass in the little chapel, an old, old place hidden way in the most desolate part of the country, small and dark and bare enough except for the candles on the altar and a bright statue or two. St. Kieran's cell, they called it, and it was supposed that the Mass had never ceased to be said there even in the blackest days of persecution. Quite well she remembered the old priest and his vestments, and the gestures that he used, and how they all bowed down when the bell rang; she could imitate his quavering voice saying the Latin. Her own father, she said, was a learned man in his way, though it was not the English way. He could not read common print, or write; he knew nothing about printed books, but he could say a lot of the old Irish songs and stories by heart, and he had sticks on which he wrote poems on all sorts of things, cutting notches on the wood in Oghams, as the priest called them; and he could tell many wonderful tales of the saints and the people. It was a happy life altogether; they were as poor as poor could be, and praised God and wanted for nothing. Then her mother went into a decline and died, and her father never lifted up his head again, and she was left an orphan when she was nine years old. The priest had written to an aunt who lived in England, and so she found herself one black day standing on the platform of the station in a horrible little manufacturing village in Lancashire; everything was black--the sky and the earth, and the houses and the people; and the sound of their rough, harsh voices made her sick. And the aunt had married an Independent and turned Protestant, so she was black, too, Nelly thought. She was wretched for a long time, she said. The aunt was kind enough to her, but the place and the people were so awful. Mr. Deakin, the husband, said he couldn't encourage Popery in his house, so she had to go to the meeting-house on Sunday and listen to the nonsense they called 'religion'--all long sermons with horrible shrieking hymns. By degrees she forgot her old prayers, and she was taken to the Dissenters' Sunday School, where they learned texts and heard about King Solomon's Temple, and Jonadab the son of Rechab, and Jezebel, and the Judges. They seemed to think a good deal of her at the school; she had several prizes for Bible knowledge.

"She was sixteen when she first went out to service. She was glad to get away--nothing could be worse than Farnworth, and it might be better. And then there were tales to tell! I never have had a clearer light thrown on the curious and disgusting manners of the lower middle-class in England-- the class that prides itself especially on its respectability, above all, on what it calls 'Morality'--by which it means the observance of one particular commandment. You know the class I mean: the brigade of the shining hat on Sunday, of the neat little villa with a well-kept plot in front, of the consecrated drawing-room, of the big Bible well in evidence. It is more often Chapel than Church, this tribe, but it draws from both sources. It is above all things shiny--not only the Sunday hat, but the furniture, the linoleum, the hair and the very flesh which pertain to these people have an unwholesome polish on them; and they prefer their plants and shrubs to be as glossy as possible-- this gens lubrica.

"To these tents poor Nelly went as a slave; she dwelt from henceforth on the genteel outskirts of more or less prosperous manufacturing towns, and she soon profoundly regretted the frank grime and hideousness of Farnworth. A hedgehog is a rough and prickly fellow--better his prickles than the reptile's poisonous slime. The tales that yet await the novelist who has courage (what is his name, by the way?), who has the insight to see behind those Venetian blinds and white curtains, who has the word that can give him entrance through the polished door by the encaustic porch! What plots, what pictures, what characters are ready for his cunning hand, what splendid matter lies unknown, useless, and indeed offensive, which, in the artist's crucible, would be transmuted into golden and exquisite perfection. Do you know that I can never penetrate into the regions where these people dwell without a thrill of wonder and a great desire that I might be called to execute the masterpieces I have hinted at? Do you remember how Zola, viewing these worlds from the train when he visited London, groaned because he had no English, because he had no key to open the treasure-house before his eyes? He, of course, who was a great diviner, saw the infinite variety of romance that was concealed beneath those myriads of snug commonplace roofs: I wish he could have observed in English and recorded in French. He was a brave man, his defence of Dreyfus shows that; but, supposing the capacity, I do not think he was brave enough to tell the London suburbs the truth about themselves in their own tongue.

"Yes, I walk down these long ways on Sunday afternoons, when they are at their best. Sometimes, if you choose the right hour, you may look into one 'breakfast room'--an apartment half sunken in the earth--after another, and see in each one the table laid for tea, showing the charming order and uniformity that prevail. Tea in the drawing-room would be, I suppose, a desecration. I wonder what would happen if some chance guest were to refuse tea and to ask for a glass of beer, or even a brandy and soda? I suppose the central lake that lies many hundreds of feet beneath London would rise up, and the sinful town would be overwhelmed. Yes: consider these houses well; how demure, how well-ordered, how shining, as I have said; and then think of what they conceal.

"Generally speaking, you know, 'morality' (in the English suburban sense) has been a tolerably equal matter. I shouldn't imagine that those 'later Romans' that poor old Palmer was always bothering about were much better or worse than the earlier Babylonians; and London as a whole is very much the same thing in this respect as Pekin as a whole. Modern Berlin and sixteenth-century Venice might compete on equal terms--save that Venice, I am sure, was very picturesque, and Berlin, I have no doubt is very piggy. The fact is, of course (to use a simple analogy), man, by his nature, is always hungry and, that being the case, he will sometimes eat too much dinner and sometimes he will get his dinner in odd ways, and sometimes he will help himself to more or less unlawful snacks before breakfast and after supper. There it is, and there is an end of it. But suppose a society in which the fact of hunger was officially denied, in which the faintest hint at an empty stomach was considered the rankest, most abominable indecency, the most detestable offence against the most sacred religious feelings? Suppose the child severely reprimanded at the mere mention of bread and butter, whipped and shut up in a dark room for the offence of reading a recipe for making plum pudding; suppose, I say, a whole society organised on the strict official understanding that no decent person ever is or has been or can be conscious of the physical want of food; that breakfast, lunch, tea, dinner and supper are orgies only used by the most wicked and degraded wretches, destined to an awful and eternal doom? In such a world, I think, you would discover some very striking irregularities in diet. Facts are known to be stubborn things, but if their very existence is denied they become ferocious and terrible things. Coventry Patmore was angry, and with reason, when he heard that even at the Vatican the statues had received the order of the fig-leaf.

"Nelly went among these Manichees. She had been to the world beyond the Venetians, the white muslin curtains and the india-rubber plant, and she told me her report. They talk about the morality of the theatre, these swine! In the theatre--if there is anything of the kind--it is a case of a wastrel and a wanton who meet and part on perfectly equal terms, without deceit or false pretences. It is not a case of master creeping into a young girl's room at dead of night, with a Bible under his arm--the said Bible being used with grotesque skill to show that 'master's' wishes must be at once complied with under pain of severe punishment, not only in this world, but in the world to come. Every Sunday, you must remember, the girl has seen 'master' perhaps crouching devoutly in his pew, perhaps in the part of sidesman or even church-warden, more probably supplementing the gifts of the pastor at some nightmarish meeting-house. 'Master' offers prayer with wonderful fervour; he speaks to the Lord as man to man; in the emotional passages his voice gets husky, and everybody says how good he is. He is a deacon, a guardian of the poor (gracious title!), a builder and an earnest supporter of the British and Foreign Bible Society: in a word, he is of the great middle-class, the backbone of England and of the Protestant Religion. He subscribes to the excellent society which prosecutes booksellers for selling the Decameron of Boccaccio. He has from ten to fifteen children, all of whom were found by Mamma in the garden.

"'Mr. King was a horrible man,' said Nelly, describing her first place; 'he had a great greasy pale face with red whiskers, and a shiny bald head; he was fat, too, and when he smiled it made one feel sick. Soon after I got the place he came into the kitchen. Missus was away for three days, and the children were all in bed. He sat down by the hearth and asked whether I was saved, and did I love the Lord as I ought to, and if I ever had any bad thoughts about young men? Then he opened the Bible and read me nasty things from the Old Testament, and asked if I understood what it meant. I said I didn't know, and he said we must approach the Lord in prayer so that we might have grace to search the Scriptures together. I had to kneel down close to him, and he put his arm round my waist and began to pray, as he called it; and when we got up he took me on his knee and said he felt to me as if I were his own daughter.'

"There, that is enough of Mr. King. You can imagine what the poor child had to go through time after time. On prayer-meeting nights she used to put the chest of drawers against her bedroom door: there would be gentle, cautious pushes, and then a soft voice murmuring: 'My child, why is your heart so bad and stubborn?' I think we can conceive the general character of 'master' from these examples. 'Missus,' of course, requires a treatise to herself; her more frequent failings are child-torture, secret drinking and low amours with oily commercial travellers.

"Yes, it is a hideous world enough, isn't it? And isn't it a pleasant thought that you and I practically live under the government of these people? 'Master' is the 'man in the street,' the 'hard-headed, practical man of the world,' 'the descendant of the sturdy Puritans,' whose judgment is final on all questions from Poetics to Liturgiology. We hardly think that this picture will commend itself to the 'man in the street'--a course of action that is calculated to alienate practical men. Pleasant, isn't it? Suburbia locuta est: causa finita est.

"I suppose that, by nature, these people would not be so very much more depraved than the ordinary African black fellow. Their essential hideousness comes, I take it, from their essential and most abominable hypocrisy. You know how they are always prating about Bible Teaching--the 'simple morality of the Gospel,' and all that nauseous stuff? And what would be the verdict, in this suburban world, on a man who took no thought for the morrow, who regulated his life by the example of the lilies, who scoffed at the idea of saving money? You know perfectly well that his relations would have him declared a lunatic. There is the villainy. If you are continually professing an idolatrous and unctuous devotion to a body of teaching which you are also persistently and perpetually disregarding and disobeying in its plainest, most simple, most elementary injunctions, well, you will soon interest anglers in search of bait.

"Yes, such is the world behind the india-rubber plant into which Nelly entered. I believe she repelled the advances of 'master' with success. Her final undoing came from a different quarter, and I am afraid that drugs, not Biblical cajoleries, were the instruments used. She cried bitterly when she spoke of this event, but she said, too; 'I will kill him for it!' It was an ugly story, and a sad one, alas!--the saddest tale I ever listened to. Think of it: to come from that old cabin on the wild, bare hills, from the sound of the great sea, from the pure breath of the waves and the wet salt wind, to the stenches and the poisons of our 'industrial centres.' She came from parents who had nothing and possessed all things, to our civilisation which has everything, and lies on the dung-heap that it has made at the very gates of Heaven--destitute of all true treasures, full of sores and vermin and corruption. She was nurtured on the wonderful old legends of the saints and the fairies; she had listened to the songs that her father made and cut in Oghams; and we gave her the penny novelette and the works of Madame Chose. She had knelt before the altar, adoring the most holy sacrifice of the Mass; now she knelt beside 'master' while he approached the Lord in prayer, licking his fat white lips. I can imagine no more terrible transition.

"I do not know how or why it happened, but as I listened to Nelly's tale my eyes were opened to my own work and my own deeds, and I saw for the first time my wickedness. I should despair of explaining to anyone how utterly innocent I had been in intention all the while, how far I was from any deliberate design of guilt. In a sense, I was learned, and yet, in a sense, I was most ignorant; I had been committing what is, doubtless a grievous sin, under the impression that I was enjoying the greatest of all mysteries and graces and blessings--the great natural sacrament of human life.

"Did I not know I was doing wrong? I knew that if any of the masters found me with Nelly I should get into sad trouble. Certainly I knew that. But if any of the masters had caught me smoking a cigarette, or saying 'damn,' or going into a public-house to get a glass of beer, or using a crib, or reading Rabelais, I should have got into sad trouble also. I knew that I was sinning against the 'tone' of the great Public School; you may imagine how deeply I felt the guilt of such an offence as that! And, of course, I had heard the boys telling their foolish indecencies; but somehow their nasty talk and their filthy jokes were not in any way connected in my mind with my love of Nelly--no more, indeed, than midnight darkness suggests daylight, or torment symbolises pleasure. Indeed, there was a hint--a dim intuition--deep down in my consciousness that all was not well; but I knew of no reason for this; I held it a morbid dream, the fantasy of an imagination over-exalted, perhaps; I would not listen to a faint voice that seemed without sense or argument.

"And now that voice was ringing in my ears with the clear, resonant and piercing summons of a trumpet; I saw myself arraigned far down beside the pestilent horde of whom I have just spoken; and, indeed, my sin was worse than theirs, for I had been bred in light, and they in darkness. All heedless, without knowledge, without preparation, without receiving the mystic word, I had stumbled into the shrine, uninitiated I had passed beyond the veil and gazed upon the hidden mystery, on the secret glory that is concealed from the holy angels. Woe and great sorrow were upon me, as if a priest, devoutly offering the sacrifice, were suddenly to become aware that he was uttering, all inadvertently, hideous and profane blasphemies, summoning Satan in place of the Holy Spirit. I hid my face in my hands and cried out in my anguish.

"Do you know that I think Nelly was in a sense relieved when I tried to tell her of my mistake, as I called it; even though I said, as gently as I could, that it was all over. She was relieved, because for the first time she felt quite sure that I was altogether in my senses; I can understand it. My whole attitude must have struck her as bordering on insanity, for, of course, from first to last I had never for a moment taken up the position of the unrepentant but cheerful sinner, who knows that he is being a sad dog, but means to continue in his naughty way. She, with her evil experience, had thought the words I had sometimes uttered not remote from madness. She wondered, she told me, whether one night I might not suddenly take her throat in my hands and strangle her in a sudden frenzy. She hardly knew whether she dreaded such a death or longed for it.

"'You spoke so strangely,' she said; 'and all the while I knew we were doing wrong, and I wondered.'

"Of course, even after I had explained the matter as well as I could she was left to a large extent bewildered as to what my state of mind could have been; still, she saw that I was not mad, and she was relieved, as I have said.

"I do not know how she was first drawn to me--how it was that she stole that night to the room where I lay bruised and aching. Pity and desire and revenge, I suppose, all had their share. She was so sorry, she said, for me. She could see how lonely I was, how I hated the place and everybody about it, and she knew that I was not English. I think my wild Welsh face attracted her, too.

"Alas! that was a sad night, after all our laughter. We had sat on and on till the dawn began to come in through the drawn blinds. I told her that we must go to bed, or we should never get up the next day. We went into the bedroom, and there, sad and grey, the dawn appeared. There was a heavy sky covered with clouds and a straight, soft rain was pattering on the leaves of a great plane tree opposite; heavy drops fell into the pools in the road.

"It was still as on the mountain, filled with infinite sadness, and a sudden step clattering on the pavement of the square beyond made the stillness seem all the more profound. I stood by the window and gazed out at the weeping, dripping tree, the ever-falling rain and the motionless, leaden clouds--there was no breath of wind--and it was as if I heard the saddest of all music, tones of anguish and despair and notes that cried and wept. The theme was given out, itself wet, as it were, with tears. It was repeated with a sharper cry, a more piteous supplication; it was re-echoed with a bitter utterance, and tears fell faster as the raindrops fell plashing from the weeping tree. Inexorable in its sad reiterations, in its remorseless development, that music wailed and grew in its lamentation in my own heart; heavy it was, and without hope; heavy as those still, leaden clouds that hung motionless in heaven. No relief came to this sorrowing melody--rather a sharper note of anguish; and then for a moment, as if to embitter bitterness, sounded a fantastic, laughing air, a measure of jocund pipes and rushing violins, echoing with the mirth of dancing feet. But it was beaten into dust by the sentence of despair, by doom that was for ever, by a sentence pitiless, relentless; and, as a sudden breath shook the wet boughs of the plane tree and a torrent fell upon the road, so the last notes of that inner music were to me as a burst of hopeless weeping.

"I turned away from the window and looked at the dingy little room where we had laughed so well. It was a sad room enough, with its pale blue, stripy-patterned paper, its rickety old furniture and its feeble pictures. The only note of gaiety was on the dressing-table, where poor little Nelly had arranged some toys and trinkets and fantasies that she had bought for herself in the last few days. There was a silver-handled brush and a flagon of some scent that I liked, and a little brooch of olivines that had caught her fancy; and a powder-puff in a pretty gilt box. The sight of these foolish things cut me to the heart. But Nelly! She was standing by the bedside, half undressed, and she looked at me with the most piteous longing. I think that she had really grown fond of me. I suppose that I shall never forget the sad enchantment of her face, the flowing of her beautiful coppery hair about it; and the tears were wet on her cheeks. She half stretched out her bare arms to me and then let them fall. I had never known all her strange allurement before. I had refined and symbolised and made her into a sign of joy, and now before me she shone disarrayed--not a symbol, but a woman, in the new intelligence that had come to me, and I longed for her. I had just enough strength and no more."

EPILOGUE

It is unfortunate--or fortunate: that is a matter to be settled by the taste of the reader--that with this episode of the visit to London all detailed material for the life of Ambrose Meyrick comes to an end. Odd scraps of information, stray notes and jottings are all that is available, and the rest of Meyrick's life must be left in dim and somewhat legendary outline.

Personally, I think that this failure of documents is to be lamented. The four preceding chapters have, in the main, dealt with the years of boyhood, and therefore with a multitude of follies. One is inclined to wonder, as poor Nelly wondered, whether the lad was quite right in his head. It is possible that if we had fuller information as to his later years we might be able to dismiss him as decidedly eccentric, but well-meaning on the whole.

But, after all, I cannot be confident that he would get off so easily. Certainly he did not repeat the adventure of Little Russell Row, nor, so far as I am aware, did he address anyone besides his old schoolmaster in a Rabelaisian epistle. There are certain acts of lunacy which are like certain acts of heroism: they are hardly to be achieved twice by the same men.

But Meyrick continued to do odd things. He became a strolling player instead of becoming a scholar of Balliol. If he had proceeded to the University, he would have encountered the formative and salutary influence of Jowett. He wandered up and down the country for two or three years with the actors, and writes the following apostrophe to the memory of his old company.

"I take off my hat when I hear the old music, for I think of the old friends and the old days; of the theatre in the meadows by the sacred river, and the swelling song of the nightingales on sweet, spring nights. There is no doubt that we may safely hold with Plato his opinion, and safely may we believe that all brave earthly shows are but broken copies and dim lineaments of immortal things. Therefore, I hope and trust that I shall again be gathered unto the true Hathaway Company quæ sursum est, which is the purged and exalted image of the lower, which plays for ever a great mystery in the theatre of the meadows of asphodel, which wanders by the happy, shining streams, and drinks from an Eternal Cup in a high and blissful and everlasting Tavern. Ave, cara sodalitas, ave semper."

Thus does he translate into wild speech crêpe hair and grease paints, dirty dressing-rooms and dirtier lodgings. And when his strolling days were over he settled down in London, paying occasional visits to his old home in the west. He wrote three or four books which are curious and interesting in their way, though they will never be popular. And finally he went on a strange errand to the East; and from the East there was for him no returning.

It will be remembered that he speaks of a Celtic cup, which had been preserved in one family for many hundred years. On the death of the last "Keeper" this cup was placed in Meyrick's charge. He received it with the condition that it was to be taken to a certain concealed shrine in Asia and there deposited in hands that would know how to hide its glories for ever from the evil world.

He went on this journey into unknown regions, travelling by ragged roads and mountain passes, by the sandy wilderness and the mighty river. And he forded his way by the quaking and dubious track that winds in and out among the dangers and desolations of the Kevir--the great salt slough.

He came at last to the place appointed and gave the word and the treasure to those who know how to wear a mask and to keep well the things which are committed to them, and then set out on his journey back. He had reached a point not very far from the gates of West and halted for a day or two amongst Christians, being tired out with a weary pilgrimage. But the Turks or the Kurds--it does not matter which--descended on the place and worked their customary works, and so Ambrose was taken by them.

One of the native Christians, who had hidden himself from the miscreants, told afterwards how he saw "the stranger Ambrosian" brought out, and how they held before him the image of the Crucified that he might spit upon it and trample it under his feet. But he kissed the icon with great joy and penitence and devotion. So they bore him to a tree outside the village and crucified him there.

And after he had hung on the tree some hours, the infidels, enraged, as it is said, by the shining rapture of his face, killed him with their spears.

It was in this manner that Ambrose Meyrick gained Red Martyrdom and achieved the most glorious Quest and Adventure of the Sangraal.

THE END

THE INMOST LIGHT

I

One evening in autumn, when the deformities of London were veiled in faint, blue mist and its vistas and far-reaching streets seemed splendid, Mr. Charles Salisbury was slowly pacing down Rupert Street, drawing nearer to his favourite restaurant by slow degrees. His eyes were downcast in study of the pavement, and thus it was that as he passed in at the narrow door a man who had come up from the lower end of the street jostled against him.

"I beg your pardon--wasn't looking where I was going. Why, it's Dyson!"

"Yes, quite so. How are you, Salisbury?"

"Quite well. But where have you been, Dyson? I don't think I can have seen you for the last five years."

"No; I dare say not. You remember I was getting rather hard up when you came to my place at Charlotte Street?"

"Perfectly. I think I remember your telling me that you owed five weeks' rent, and that you had parted with your watch for a comparatively small sum."

"My dear Salisbury, your memory is admirable. Yes, I was hard up. But the curious thing is that soon after you saw me I became harder up. My financial state was described by a friend as 'stone broke.' I don't approve of slang, mind you, but such was my condition. But suppose we go in; there might be other people who would like to dine--it's a human weakness, Salisbury."

"Certainly; come along. I was wondering as I walked down whether the corner table were taken. It has a velvet back, you know."

"I know the spot; it's vacant. Yes, as I was saying, I became even harder up."

"What did you do then?" asked Salisbury, disposing of his hat, and settling down in the corner of the seat, with a glance of fond anticipation at the menu.

"What did I do? Why, I sat down and reflected. I had a good classical education, and a positive distaste for business of any kind; that was the capital with which I faced the world. Do you know, I have heard people describe olives as nasty! What lamentable philistinism! I have often thought, Salisbury, that I could write genuine poetry under the influence of olives and red wine. Let us have Chianti; it may not be very good, but the flasks are simply charming."

"It is pretty good here. We may as well have a big flask."

"Very good. I reflected, then, on my want of prospects, and I determined to embark in literature."

"Really, that was strange. You seem in pretty comfortable circumstances, though."

"Though! What a satire upon a noble profession. I am afraid, Salisbury, you haven't a proper idea of the dignity of an artist. You see me sitting at my desk,--or at least you can see me if you care to call,--with pen and ink, and simple nothingness before me, and if you come again in a few hours you will (in all probability) find a creation!"

"Yes, quite so. I had an idea that literature was not remunerative."

"You are mistaken; its rewards are great. I may mention, by the way, that shortly after you saw me I succeeded to a small income. An uncle died, and proved unexpectedly generous."

"Ah, I see. That must have been convenient."

"It was pleasant,--undeniably pleasant. I have always considered it in the light of an endowment of my researches. I told you I was a man of letters; it would, perhaps, be more correct to describe myself as a man of science."

"Dear me, Dyson, you have really changed very much in the last few years. I had a notion, don't you know, that you were a sort of idler about town, the kind of man one might meet on the north side of Piccadilly every day from May to July."

"Exactly. I was even then forming myself, though all unconsciously. You know my poor father could not afford to send me to the university. I used to grumble in my ignorance at not having completed my education. That was the folly of youth, Salisbury; my university was Piccadilly. There I began to study the great science which still occupies me."

"What science do you mean?"

"The science of the great city; the physiology of London; literally and metaphysically the greatest subject that the mind of man can conceive. What an admirable salmi this is; undoubtedly the final end of the pheasant. Yes, I feel sometimes positively overwhelmed with the thought of the vastness and complexity of London. Paris a man may get to understand thoroughly with a reasonable amount of study; but London is always a mystery. In Paris you may say, 'Here live the actresses, here the Bohemians, and the Ratés;' but it is different in London. You may point out a street, correctly enough, as the abode of washerwomen; but, in that second floor, a man may be studying Chaldee roots, and in the garret over the way a forgotten artist is dying by inches."

"I see you are Dyson, unchanged and unchangeable," said Salisbury, slowly sipping his Chianti. "I think you are misled by a too fervid imagination; the mystery of London exists only in your fancy. It seems to me a dull place enough. We seldom hear of a really artistic crime in London, whereas I believe Paris abounds in that sort of thing."

"Give me some more wine. Thanks. You are mistaken, my dear fellow, you are really mistaken. London has nothing to be ashamed of in the way of crime. Where we fail is for want of Homers, not Agamemnons. Carent quia vale sacro, you know."

"I recall the quotation. But I don't think I quite follow you."

"Well, in plain language, we have no good writers in London who make a specialty of that kind of thing. Our common reporter is a dull dog; every story that he has to tell is spoilt in the telling. His idea of horror and of what excites horror is so lamentably deficient. Nothing will content the fellow but blood, vulgar red blood, and when he can get it he lays it on thick, and considers that he has produced a telling story. It's a poor notion. And, by some curious fatality, it is the most commonplace and brutal murders which always attract the most attention and get written up the most. For instance, I dare say that you never heard of the Harlesden case?"

"No, no; I don't remember anything about it."

"Of course not. And yet the story is a curious one. I will tell it you over our coffee. Harlesden, you know, or I expect you don't know, is quite on the out-quarters of London; something curiously different from your fine old crusted suburb like Norwood or Hampstead, different as each of these is from the other. Hampstead, I mean, is where you look for the head of your great China house with his three acres of land and pine houses, though of late there is the artistic substratum; while Norwood is the home of the prosperous middle-class family who took the house 'because it was near the Palace,' and sickened of the Palace six months afterwards; but Harlesden is a place of no character. It's too new to have any character as yet. There are the rows of red houses and the rows of white houses and the bright green venetians, and the blistering doorways, and the little back-yards they call gardens, and a few feeble shops, and then, just as you think you're going to grasp the physiognomy of the settlement it all melts away."

"How the dickens is that? The houses don't tumble down before one's eyes I suppose."

"Well, no, not exactly that. But Harlesden as an entity disappears. Your street turns into a quiet lane, and your staring houses into elm trees, and the back gardens into green meadows. You pass instantly from town to country; there is no transition as in a small country town, no soft gradations of wider lawns and orchards, with houses gradually becoming less dense, but a dead stop. I believe the people who live there mostly go into the city. I have seen once or twice a laden 'bus bound thitherwards. But however that may be, I can't conceive a greater loneliness in a desert at midnight than there is there at midday. It is like a city of the dead; the streets are glaring and desolate, and as you pass it suddenly strikes you that this, too, is part of London. Well, a year or two ago there was a doctor living there; he had set up his brass plate and his red lamp at the very end of one of those shining streets, and from the back of the house the fields stretched away to the north. I don't know what his reason was in settling down in such an out-of-the-way place, perhaps Dr. Black, as we will call him, was a far-seeing man and looked ahead. His relations, so it appeared afterwards, had lost sight of him for many years and didn't even know he was a doctor, much less where he lived. However, there he was, settled in Harlesden, with some fragments of a practice, and an uncommonly pretty wife. People used to see them walking out together in the summer evenings soon after they came to Harlesden, and, so far as could be observed, they seemed a very affectionate couple. These walks went on through the autumn, and then ceased; but, of course, as the days grew dark and the weather cold, the lanes near Harlesden might be expected to lose many of their attractions. All through the winter nobody saw anything of Mrs. Black; the doctor used to reply to his patients' inquiries that she was a 'little out of sorts, would be better, no doubt, in the spring.' But the spring came, and the summer, and no Mrs. Black appeared, and at last people began to rumor and talk amongst themselves, and all sorts of queer things were said at 'high teas,' which you may possibly have heard are the only form of entertainment known in such suburbs. Dr. Black began to surprise some very odd looks cast in his direction, and the practice, such as it was, fell off before his eyes. In short, when the neighbours whispered about the matter, they whispered that Mrs.

Black was dead, and that the doctor had made away with her. But this wasn't the case; Mrs. Black was seen alive in June. It was a Sunday afternoon, one of those few exquisite days that an English climate offers, and half London had strayed out into the fields North, South, East, and West, to smell the scent of the white May, and to see if the wild roses were yet in blossom in the hedges. I had gone out myself early in the morning, and had had a long ramble, and somehow or other, as I was steering homeward, I found myself in this very Harlesden we have been talking about. To be exact, I had a glass of beer in the 'General Gordon,' the most flourishing house in the neighbourhood, and as I was wandering rather aimlessly about I saw an uncommonly tempting gap in a hedgerow, and resolved to explore the meadow beyond. Soft grass is very grateful to the feet after the infernal grit strewn on suburban sidewalks, and after walking about for some time, I thought I should like to sit down on a bank and have a smoke. While I was getting out my pouch, I looked up in the direction of the houses, and as I looked I felt my breath caught back, and my teeth began to chatter, and the stick I had in one hand snapped in two with the grip I gave it. It was as if I had had an electric current down my spine, and yet for some moment of time which seemed long, but which must have been very short, I caught myself wondering what on earth was the matter. Then I knew what had made my very heart shudder and my bones grind together in an agony. As I glanced up I had looked straight towards the last house in the row before me, and in an upper window of that house I had seen for some short fraction of a second a face. It was the face of a woman, and yet it was not human. You and I, Salisbury, have heard in our time, as we sat in our seats in church in sober English fashion, of a lust that cannot be satiated, and of a fire that is unquenchable, but few of us have any notion what these words mean. I hope you never may, for as I saw that face at the window, with the blue sky above me and the warm air playing in gusts about me, I knew I had looked into another world--looked through the window of a commonplace, brand-new house, and seen hell open before me. When the first shock was over, I thought once or twice that I should have fainted; my face streamed with a cold sweat, and my breath came and went in sobs, as if I had been half drowned. I managed to get up at last, and walked round to the street, and there I saw the name Dr. Black on the post by the front gate. As fate or my luck would have it, the door opened and a man came down the steps as I passed by. I had no doubt it was the doctor himself. He was of a type rather common in London,--long and thin with a pasty face and a dull black moustache. He gave me a look as we passed each other on the pavement, and though it was merely the casual glance which one foot-passenger bestows on another, I felt convinced in my mind that here was an ugly customer to deal with. As you may imagine I went my way a good deal puzzled and horrified, too, by what I had seen; for I had paid another visit to the 'General Gordon,' and had got together a good deal of the common gossip of the place about the Blacks. I didn't mention the fact that I had seen a woman's face in the window; but I heard that Mrs. Black had been much admired for her beautiful golden hair, and round what had struck me with such a nameless terror was a mist of flowing yellow hair, as it were an aureole of glory round the visage of a satyr. The whole thing bothered me in an indescribable manner; and when I got home I tried my best to think of the impression I had received as an illusion, but it was no use. I knew very well I had seen what I have tried to describe to you, and I was morally certain that I had seen Mrs. Black. And then there was the gossip of the place, the suspicion of foul play, which I knew to be false, and my own conviction that there was some deadly mischief or other going on in that bright red house at the corner of the Devon Road,--how to construct a theory of a reasonable kind out of these two elements. In short, I found myself in a world of mystery; I puzzled my head over it and filled up my leisure moments by gathering together odd threads of speculation, but I never moved a step toward any real solution, and as the summer days went on the matter seemed to grown misty and indistinct, shadowing some vague terror, like a nightmare of last month. I suppose it would before long have faded into the background of my brain--I should not have forgotten it, for such a thing could never be forgotten--but one morning as I was looking over the paper my eye was caught by a heading over some two dozen lines of small type. The words I had seen were simply, 'The Harlesden Case,' and I knew what I was going to read. Mrs. Black was dead. Black had called in another medical man to certify as to cause of death, and something or other had aroused the strange doctor's suspicions, and there had been an inquest and post-mortem. And the result? That, I will confess, did astonish me considerably; it was the triumph of the unexpected. The two doctors who made the autopsy were obliged to confess that they could not discover the faintest trace of any kind of foul play; their most exquisite tests and reagents failed to detect the presence of poison in the most infinitesimal quantity. Death, they found, had been caused by a somewhat obscure and scientifically interesting form of brain disease. The tissue of the brain and the molecules of the gray matter had undergone a most extraordinary series of changes; and the younger of the two doctors, who has some reputation, I believe, as a specialist in brain trouble, made some remarks in giving his evidence, which struck me deeply at the time, though I did not then grasp their full significance. He said: 'At the commencement of the examination I was astonished to find appearances of a character entirely new to me, notwithstanding my somewhat large experience. I need not specify these appearances at present; it will be sufficient for me to state that as I proceeded in my task I could scarcely believe that the brain before me was that of a human being at all.' There was some surprise at this statement, as you may imagine, and the coroner asked the doctor if he meant to say that the brain resembled that of an animal. 'No,' he replied, 'I should not put it in that way. Some of the appearances I noticed seemed to point in that direction, but others, and these were the more surprising, indicated a nervous organization of a wholly different character to that either of man or of the lower animals.' It was a curious thing to say, but of course the jury brought in a verdict of death from natural causes, and, so far as the public was concerned, the case came to an end. But after I had read what the doctor said, I made up my mind that I should like to know a good deal more, and I set to work on what seemed likely to prove an interesting investigation. I had really a good deal of trouble, but I was successful in a measure. Though--why, my dear fellow, I had no notion of the time. Are you aware that we have been here nearly four hours? The waiters are staring at us. Let's have the bill and be gone."

The two men went out in silence, and stood a moment in the cool air, watching the hurrying traffic of Coventry Street pass before them to the accompaniment of ringing bells of hansoms and the cries of the newsboys, the deep far murmur of London surging up ever and again from beneath these louder noises.

"It is a strange case, isn't it?" said Dyson, at length. "What do you think of it?"

"My dear fellow, I haven't heard the end, so I will reserve my opinion. When will you give me the sequel?"

"Come to my rooms some evening; say next Thursday. Here's the address. Good-night; I want to get down to the Strand."

Dyson hailed a passing hansom, and Salisbury turned northward to walk home to his lodgings.

II

Mr. Salisbury, as may have been gathered from the few remarks which he had found it possible to introduce in the course of the evening, was a young gentleman of a peculiarly solid form of intellect, coy and retiring before the mysterious and the uncommon, with a constitutional dislike of paradox. During the restaurant dinner he had been forced to listen in almost absolute silence to a strange tissue of improbabilities strung together with the ingenuity of a born meddler in plots and mysteries, and it was with a feeling of weariness that he crossed Shaftesbury Avenue, and dived into the recesses of Soho, for his lodgings were in a modest neighbourhood to the north of Oxford Street. As he walked he speculated on the probable fate of Dyson, relying on literature unbefriended by a thoughtful relative; and could not help concluding that so much subtlety united to a too vivid imagination would in all likelihood have been rewarded with a pair of Sandwich-boards or a super's banner. Absorbed in this train of thought, and admiring the perverse dexterity which could transmute the face of a sickly woman and a case of brain disease into the crude elements of romance, Salisbury strayed on through the dimly lighted streets, not noticing the gusty wind which drove sharply round corners and whirled the stray rubbish of the pavement into the air in eddies, while black clouds gathered over the sickly yellow moon. Even a stray drop or two of rain blown into his face did not rouse him from his meditations, and it was only when with a sudden rush the storm tore down upon the street that he began to consider the expediency of finding some shelter. The rain, driven by the wind, pelted down with the violence of a thunder-storm, dashing up from the stones and hissing through the air, and soon a perfect torrent of water coursed along the kennels and accumulated in pools over the choked-up drains. The few stray passengers who had been loafing rather than walking about the street, had scuttered away like frightened rabbits to some invisible places of refuge, and though Salisbury whistled loud and long for a hansom, no hansom appeared. He looked about him, as if to discover how far he might be from the haven of Oxford Street; but strolling carelessly along he had turned out of his way, and found himself in an unknown region, and one to all appearance devoid even of a public-house where shelter could be bought for the modest sum of twopence. The street lamps were few and at long intervals, and burned behind grimy glasses with the sickly light of oil lamps, and by this wavering light Salisbury could make out the shadowy and vast old houses of which the street was composed. As he passed along, hurrying, and shrinking from the full sweep of the rain, he noticed the innumerable bell-handles, with names that seemed about to vanish of old age graven on brass plates beneath them, and here and there a richly carved pent-house overhung the door, blackening with the grime of fifty years. The storm seemed to grow more and more furious; he was wet through, and a new hat had become a ruin, and still Oxford Street seemed as far off as ever. It was with deep relief that the dripping man caught sight of a dark archway which seemed to promise shelter from the rain if not from the wind. Salisbury took up his position in the dryest corner and looked about him; he was standing in a kind of passage contrived under part of a house, and behind him stretched a narrow footway leading between blank walls to regions unknown. He had stood there for some time, vainly endeavouring to rid himself of some of his superfluous moisture, and listening for the passing wheel of a hansom, when his attention was aroused by a loud noise coming from the direction of the passage behind, and growing louder as it drew nearer. In a couple of minutes he could make out the shrill, raucous voice of a woman, threatening and denouncing and making the very stones echo with her accents, while now and then a man grumbled and expostulated. Though to all appearance devoid of romance, Salisbury had some relish for street rows, and was, indeed, somewhat of an amateur in the more amusing phases of drunkenness; he therefore composed himself to listen and observe with something of the air of a subscriber to grand opera. To his annoyance, however, the tempest seemed suddenly to be composed, and he could hear nothing but the impatient steps of the woman and the slow lurch of the man as they came toward him. Keeping back in the shadow of the wall, he could see the two drawing nearer; the man was evidently drunk, and had much ado to avoid frequent collision with the wall as he tacked across from one side to the other, like some bark beating up against a wind. The woman was looking straight in front of her, with tears streaming from her eyes, but suddenly as they went by, the flame blazed up again, and she burst forth into a torrent of abuse, facing round upon her companion.

"You low rascal! You mean, contemptible cur!" she went on, after an incoherent storm of curses: "You think I'm to work and slave for you always, I suppose, while you're after that Green Street girl and drinking every penny you've got. But you're mistaken, Sam,--indeed, I'll bear it no longer. Damn you, you dirty thief, I've done with you and your master too, so you can go your own errands, and I only hope they'll get you into trouble."

The woman tore at the bosom of her dress, and taking something out that looked like paper, crumpled it up and flung it away. It fell at Salisbury's feet. She ran out and disappeared in the darkness, while the man lurched slowly into the street, grumbling indistinctly to himself in a perplexed tone of voice. Salisbury looked out after him, and saw him maundering along the pavement, halting now and then and swaying indecisively, and then starting off at some fresh tangent. The sky had cleared, and white fleecy clouds were fleeting across the moon, high in the heaven. The light came and went by turns as the clouds passed by, and, turning round as the clear white rays shone into the passage, Salisbury saw the little ball of crumpled paper which the woman had cast down. Oddly curious to know what it might contain, he picked it up and put it in his pocket, and set out afresh on his journey.

III

Salisbury was a man of habit. When he got home, drenched to the skin, his clothes hanging lank about him, and a ghastly dew besmearing his hat, his only thought was of his health, of which he took studious care. So, after changing his clothes and encasing himself in a warm dressing-gown he proceeded to prepare a sudorific in the shape of hot gin and water, warming the latter over one of those spirit lamps which mitigate the austerities of the modern hermit's life. By the time this preparation had been imbibed, and Salisbury's disturbed feelings had been soothed by a pipe of tobacco, he was able to get into bed in a happy state of vacuity, without a thought of his adventure in the dark archway, or of the weird fancies with which Dyson had seasoned his dinner. It was the same at breakfast the next morning, for Salisbury made a point of not thinking of anything until that meal was over; but when the cup and saucer were cleared away, and the morning pipe was lit, he remembered the little ball of paper, and began fumbling in the pockets of his wet coat. He did not remember into which pocket he had put it, and as he dived now into one, and now into another, he experienced a strange feeling of apprehension lest it should not be there at all, though he could not for the life of him have explained the importance he attached to what was in all probability mere rubbish. But he sighed with relief when his fingers touched the crumpled surface in an inside pocket, and he drew it out gently and laid it on the little desk by his easy chair with as much care as if it had been some rare jewel. Salisbury sat smoking and staring at his find for a few minutes, an odd temptation to throw the thing in the fire and have done with it struggling with as odd a speculation as to its possible contents and as to the reason why the infuriated woman should have flung a bit of paper from her with such vehemence. As might be expected, it was the latter feeling that conquered in the end, and yet it was with something like repugnance that he at last took the paper and unrolled it, and laid it out before him. It was a piece of common dirty paper, to all appearance torn out of a cheap exercise book, and in the middle were a few lines written in a queer cramped hand. Salisbury bent his head and stared eagerly at it for a moment, drawing a long breath, and then fell back in his chair gazing blankly before him, till at last with a sudden revulsion he burst into a peal of laughter, so long and loud and uproarious that the landlady's baby in the floor below awoke from sleep and echoed his mirth with hideous yells. But he laughed again and again, and took up the paper to read a second time what seemed such meaningless nonsense.

"Q. has had to go and see his friends in Paris," it began. "Traverse Handel S. 'Once around the grass, and twice around the lass, and thrice around the maple tree.'"

Salisbury took up the paper and crumpled it as the angry woman had done, and aimed it at the fire. He did not throw it there, however, but tossed it carelessly into the well of the desk, and laughed again. The sheer folly of the thing offended him, and he was ashamed of his own eager speculation, as one who pores over the high-sounding announcements in the agony column of the daily paper, and finds nothing but advertisement and triviality. He walked to the window, and stared out at the languid morning life of his quarter; the maids in slatternly print-dresses washing door-steps, the fishmonger and the butcher on their rounds, and the tradesmen standing at the doors of their small shops, drooping for lack of trade and excitement. In the distance a blue haze gave some grandeur to the prospect, but the view as a whole was depressing, and would have only interested a student of the life of London, who finds something rare and choice in its every aspect. Salisbury turned away in disgust, and settled himself in the easy chair, upholstered in a bright shade of green, and decked with yellow gimp, which was the pride and attraction of the apartments. Here he composed himself to his morning's occupation, the perusal of a novel that dealt with sport and love in a manner that suggested the collaboration of a stud-groom and a ladies' college. In an ordinary way, however, Salisbury would have been carried on by the interest of the story up to lunch time, but this morning he fidgeted in and out of his chair, took the book up and laid it down again, and swore at last to himself and at himself in mere irritation. In point of fact the jingle of the paper found in the archway had "got into his head," and do what he would he could not help muttering over and over, "Once around the grass, and twice around the lass, and thrice around the maple tree." It became a positive pain, like the foolish burden of a music-hall song, everlastingly quoted, and sung at all hours of the day and night, and treasured by the street boys as an unfailing resource for six months together. He went out into the streets, and tried to forget his enemy in the jostling of the crowds, and the roar and clatter of the traffic; but presently he would find himself stealing quietly aside and pacing some deserted byway, vainly puzzling his brains, and trying to fix some meaning to phrases that were meaningless. It was a positive relief when Thursday came, and he remembered that he had made an appointment to go and see Dyson; the flimsy reveries of the self-styled man of letters appeared entertaining when compared with this ceaseless iteration, this maze of thought from which there seemed no possibility of escape. Dyson's abode was in one of the quietest of the quiet streets that lead down from the Strand to the river, and when Salisbury passed from the narrow stairway into his friend's room, he saw that the uncle had been beneficent indeed. The floor glowed and flamed with all the colours of the east; it was, as Dyson pompously remarked, "a sunset in a dream," and the lamplight, the twilight of London streets, was shut out with strangely worked curtains, glittering here and there with threads of gold. In the shelves of an oak armoire stood jars and plates of old French china, and the black and white of etchings not to be found in the Haymarket or in Bond Street, stood out against the splendour of a Japanese paper. Salisbury sat down on the settle by the hearth, and sniffed the mingled fumes of incense and tobacco, wondering and dumb before all this splendour after the green rep and the oleographs, the gilt-framed mirror and the lustres of his own apartment.

"I am glad you have come," said Dyson. "Comfortable little room, isn't it? But you don't look very well, Salisbury. Nothing disagreed with you, has it?"

"No; but I have been a good deal bothered for the last few days. The fact is I had an odd kind of--of--adventure, I suppose I may call it, that night I saw you, and it has worried me a good deal. And the provoking part of it is that it's the merest nonsense--but, however, I will tell you all about it, by and by. You were going to let me have the rest of that odd story you began at the restaurant."

"Yes. But I am afraid, Salisbury, you are incorrigible. You are a slave to what you call matter of fact. You know perfectly well that in your heart you think the oddness in that case is of my making, and that it is all really as plain as the police reports. However, as I have begun, I will go on. But first we will have something to drink, and you may as well light your pipe."

Dyson went up to the oak cupboard, and drew from its depths a rotund bottle and two little glasses quaintly gilded.

"It's Benedictin," he said. "You'll have some, won't you?"

Salisbury assented, and the two men sat sipping and smoking reflectively for some minutes before Dyson began.

"Let me see," he said at last; "we were at the inquest, weren't we? No, we had done with that. Ah, I remember. I was telling you that on the whole I had been successful in my inquiries, investigation, or what ever you like to call it, into the matter. Wasn't that where I left off?"

"Yes, that was it. To be precise, I think 'though' was the last word you said on the matter."

"Exactly. I have been thinking it all over since the other night, and I have come to the conclusion that that 'though' is a very big 'though' indeed. Not to put too fine a point on it, I have had to confess that what I found out, or thought I found out, amounts in reality to nothing. I am as far away from the heart of the case as ever. However, I may as well tell you what I do know. You may remember my saying that I was impressed a good deal by some remarks of one of the doctors who gave evidence at the inquest. Well, I determined that my first step must be to try if I could get something more definite and intelligible out of that doctor. Somehow or other I managed to get an introduction to the man, and he gave me an appointment to come and see him. He turned out to be a pleasant, genial fellow; rather young and not in the least like the typical medical man, and he began the conference by offering me whiskey and cigars. I didn't think it worth while to beat about the bush, so I began by saying that part of his evidence at the Harlesden Inquest struck me as very peculiar, and I gave him the printed report, with the sentences in question underlined. He just glanced at the slip, and gave me a queer look. 'It struck you as peculiar, did it?' said he. 'Well, you must remember the Harlesden case was very peculiar. In fact, I think I may safely say that in some features it was unique--quite unique.' 'Quite so,' I replied, 'and that's exactly why it interests me, and why I want to know more about it. And I thought that if anybody could give me any information it would be you. What is your opinion of the matter?'

"It was a pretty downright sort of question, and my doctor looked rather taken aback.

"'Well,' he said, 'as I fancy your motive in inquiring into the question must be mere curiosity, I think I may tell you my opinion with tolerable freedom. So, Mr.--Mr. Dyson, if you want to know my theory, it is this: I believe that Dr. Black killed his wife.'

"'But the verdict,' I answered, 'the verdict was given from your own evidence.'

"'Quite so, the verdict was given in accordance with the evidence of my colleague and myself, and, under the circumstances, I think the jury acted very sensibly. In fact I don't see what else they could have done. But I stick to my opinion, mind you, and I say this also: I don't wonder at Black's doing what I firmly believe he did. I think he was justified.'

"'Justified! How could that be?' I asked. I was astonished, as you may imagine, at the answer I had got. The doctor wheeled round his chair, and looked steadily at me for a moment before he answered.

"'I suppose you are not a man of science yourself? No; then it would be of no use my going into detail. I have always been firmly opposed myself to any partnership between physiology and psychology. I believe that both are bound to suffer. No one recognizes more decidedly than I do the impassable gulf, the fathomless abyss that separates the world of consciousness from the sphere of matter. We know that every change of consciousness is accompanied by a rearrangement of the molecules in the gray matter; and that is all. What the link between them is, or why they occur together, we do not know, and most authorities believe that we never can know. Yet, I will tell you that as I did my work, the knife in my hand, I felt convinced, in spite of all theories, that what lay before me was not the brain of a dead woman; not the brain of a human being at all. Of course I saw the face; but it was quite placid, devoid of all expression. It must have been a beautiful face, no doubt; but I can honestly say that I would not have looked in that face when there was life behind it for a thousand guineas, no, nor for twice that sum.'

"'My dear sir,' I said, 'you surprise me extremely. You say that it was not the brain of a human being. What was it then?'

"'The brain of a devil.' He spoke quite coolly, and never moved a muscle. 'The brain of a devil,' he repeated, 'and I have no doubt that Black put a pillow over her mouth and kept it there for a few minutes. I don't blame him if he did. Whatever Mrs. Black was, she was not fit to stay in this world. Will you have anything more? No? Good-night, good-night.'

"It was a queer sort of opinion to get from a man of science, wasn't it? When he was saying that he would not have looked on that face when alive for a thousand guineas or two thousand guineas, I was thinking of the face I had seen, but I said nothing. I went again to Harlesden, and passed from one shop to another, making small purchases, and trying to find out whether there was anything about the Blacks which was not already common property; but there was very little to hear. One of the tradesmen to whom I spoke said he had known the dead woman well--she used to buy of him such quantities of grocery as were required for their small household, for they never kept a servant, but had a charwoman in occasionally, and she had not seen Mrs. Black for months before she died. According to this man, Mrs. Black was 'a nice lady,' always kind and considerate, so fond of her husband, and he of her, as everyone thought. And yet, to put the doctor's opinion on one side, I knew what I had seen. And then, after thinking it all over and putting one thing with another, it seemed to me that the only person likely to give me much assistance would be Black himself, and I made up my mind to find him. Of course he wasn't to be found in Harlesden; he had left, I was told, directly after the funeral. Everything in the house had been sold, and one fine day

Black got into the train with a small portmanteau, and went nobody knew where. It was a chance if he were ever heard of again, and it was by a mere chance that I came across him at last. I was walking one day along Gray's Inn Road, not bound for anywhere in particular, but looking about me, as usual, and holding on to my hat, for it was a gusty day in early March, and the wind was making the tree-tops in the Inn rock and quiver. I had come up from the Holborn end, and I had almost got to Theobald's Road, when I noticed a man walking in front of me, leaning on a stick and to all appearance very feeble. There was something about his look that made me curious, I don't know why; and I began to walk briskly, with the idea of overtaking him, when of a sudden his hat blew off, and came bounding along the pavement to my feet. Of course I rescued the hat, and gave it a glance as I went towards its owner. It was a biography in itself; a Piccadilly maker's name in the inside, but I don't think a beggar would have picked it out of the gutter. Then I looked up, and saw Dr. Black of Harlesden waiting for me. A queer thing, wasn't it? But, Salisbury, what a change! When I saw Dr. Black come down the steps of his house at Harlesden, he was an upright man, walking firmly with well-built limbs; a man, I should say, in the prime of his life. And now before me there crouched this wretched creature, bent and feeble, with shrunken cheeks, and hair that was whitening fast, and limbs that trembled and shook together, and misery in his eyes. He thanked me for bringing him his hat, saying, 'I don't think I should ever have got it, I can't run much now. A gusty day, sir, isn't it?' and with this he was turning away; but by little and little I contrived to draw him into the current of conversation, and we walked together eastward. I think the man would have been glad to get rid of me, but I didn't intend to let him go, and he stopped at last in front of a miserable house in a miserable street. It was, I verily believe, one of the most wretched quarters I have ever seen,--houses that must have been sordid and hideous enough when new, that had gathered foulness with every year, and now seemed to lean and totter to their fall. 'I live up there,' said Black, pointing to the tiles, 'not in the front,--in the back. I am very quiet there. I won't ask you to come in now, but perhaps some other day----'

"I caught him up at that, and told him I should be only too glad to come and see him. He gave me an odd sort of glance, as if he was wondering what on earth I or anybody else could care about him, and I left him fumbling with his latch-key. I think you will say I did pretty well, when I tell you that within a few weeks I had made myself an intimate friend of Black's. I shall never forget the first time I went to this room; I hope I shall never see such abject, squalid misery again. The foul paper, from which all pattern or trace of a pattern had long vanished, subdued and penetrated with the grime of the evil street, was hanging in mouldering pennons from the wall. Only at the end of the room was it possible to stand upright; and the sight of the wretched bed and the odour of corruption that pervaded the place made me turn faint and sick. Here I found him munching a piece of bread; he seemed surprised to find that I had kept my promise, but he gave me his chair, and sat on the bed while we talked. I used to go and see him often, and we had long conversations together, but he never mentioned Harlesden or his wife. I fancy that he supposed me ignorant of the matter, or thought that if I had heard of it, I should never connect the respectable Dr. Black of Harlesden with a poor garreteer in the backwoods of London. He was a strange man, and as we sat together smoking, I often wondered whether he were mad or sane, for I think the wildest dreams of Paracelsus and the Rosicrucians would appear plain and sober fact, compared with the theories I have heard him earnestly advance in that grimy den of his. I once ventured to hint something of the sort to him; I suggested that something he had said was in flat contradiction to all science and all experience. 'No, Dyson,' he answered, 'not all experience, for mine counts for something. I am no dealer in unproved theories; what I say I have proved for myself, and at a terrible cost. There is a region of knowledge of which you will never know, which wise men, seeing from afar off, shun like the plague, as well they may; but into that region I have gone. If you knew, if you could even dream of what may be done, of what one or two men have done, in this quiet world of ours, your very soul would shudder and faint within you. What you have heard from me has been but the merest husk and outer covering of true science,--that science which means death and that which is more awful than death to those who gain it. No, Dyson, when men say that there are strange things in the world, they little know the awe and the terror that dwell always within them and about them.'"

There was a sort of fascination about the man that drew me to him, and I was quite sorry to have to leave London for a month or two; I missed his odd talk. A few days after I came back to town I thought I would go and look him up; but when I gave the two rings at the bell that used to summon him, there was no answer. I rang and rang again, and was just turning to go away, when the door opened and a dirty woman asked me what I wanted. From her look I fancy she took me for a plain-clothes officer after one of her lodgers; but when I inquired if Mr. Black was in, she gave me a stare of another kind. 'There's no Mr. Black lives here,' she said. 'He's gone. He's dead this six weeks. I always thought he was a bit queer in his head, or else had been and got into some trouble or other. He used to go out every morning from ten till one, and one Monday morning we heard him come in and go into his room and shut the door, and a few minutes after, just as we was a-sitting down to our dinner, there was such a scream that I thought I should have gone right off. And then we heard a stamping, and down he came raging and cursing most dreadful, swearing he had been robbed of something that was worth millions. And then he just dropped down in the passage, and we thought he was dead. We got him up to his room, and put him on his bed, and I just sat there and waited, while my 'usband he went for the doctor. And there was the winder wide open, and a little tin box he had lying on the floor open and empty; but of course nobody could possible have got in at the winder, and as for him having anything that was worth anything, it's nonsense, for he was often weeks and weeks behind with his rent, and my 'usband he threatened often and often to turn him into the street, for, as he said, we've got a living to myke like other people, and of course that's true; but somehow I didn't like to do it, though he was an odd kind of a man, and I fancy had been better off. And then the doctor came and looked at him, and said as he couldn't do nothing, and that night he died as I was a-sitting by his bed; and I can tell you that, with one thing and another, we lost money by him, for the few bits of clothes as he had were worth next to nothing when they came to be sold.'

"I gave the woman half a sovereign for her trouble, and went home thinking of Dr. Black and the epitaph she had made him, and wondering at his strange fancy that he had been robbed. I take it that he had very little to fear on that score, poor fellow; but I suppose that he was really mad, and died in a sudden access of his mania. His landlady said that once or twice when she had had occasion to go into his room (to dun the poor wretch for his rent, most likely), he would keep her at the door for about a minute, and that when she came in she would find him putting away his tin box in the corner by the window. I suppose he had become possessed with the idea of some great treasure, and fancied himself a wealthy man in the midst of all his misery.

"Explicit, my tale is ended; and you see that though I knew Black I know nothing of his wife or of the history of her death. That's the Harlesden case, Salisbury, and I think it interests me all the more deeply because there does not seem the shadow of a possibility that I or anyone else will ever know more about it. What do you think of it?"

"Well, Dyson, I must say that I think you have contrived to surround the whole thing with a mystery of your own making. I go for the doctor's solution,--Black murdered his wife, being himself, in all probability, an undeveloped lunatic."

"What? Do you believe, then, that this woman was something too awful, too terrible, to be allowed to remain on the earth? You will remember that the doctor said it was the brain of a devil?"

"Yes, yes; but he was speaking, of course, metaphorically. It's really quite a simple matter, Dyson, if you only look at it like that."

"Ah, well, you may be right; but yet I am sure you are not. Well, well, it's no good discussing it anymore. A little more Benedictine? That's right; try some of this tobacco. Didn't you say that you had been bothered by something,--something which happened that night we dined together?"

"Yes, I have been worried, Dyson,--worried a great deal. I--But it's such a trivial matter, indeed, such an absurdity, that I feel ashamed to trouble you with it."

"Never mind; let's have it, absurd or not."

With many hesitations, and with much inward resentment of the folly of the thing, Salisbury told his tale, and repeated reluctantly the absurd intelligence and the absurder doggerel of the scrap of paper, expecting to hear Dyson burst out into a roar of laughter.

"Isn't it too bad that I should let myself be bothered by such stuff as that?" he asked, when he had stuttered out the jingle of once and twice and thrice.

Dyson had listened to it all gravely, even to the end, and meditated for a few minutes in silence.

"Yes," he said at length, "it was a curious chance, your taking shelter in that archway just as those two went by. But I don't know that I should call what was written on the paper nonsense; it is bizarre certainly, but I expect it has a meaning for somebody. Just repeat it again, will you? and I will write it down. Perhaps we might find a cipher of some sort, though I hardly think we shall."

Again had the reluctant lips of Salisbury to slowly stammer out the rubbish he abhorred, while Dyson jotted it down on a slip of paper.

"Look over it, will you?" he said, when it was done; "it may be important that I should have every word in its place. Is that all right?"

"Yes, that is an accurate copy. But I don't think you will get much out of it. Depend upon it, it is mere nonsense, a wanton scribble. I must be going now, Dyson. No, no more; that stuff of yours is pretty strong. Good-night."

"I suppose you would like to hear from me, if I did find out anything?"

"No, not I; I don't want to hear about the thing again. You may regard the discovery, if it is one as your own."

"Very well. Good-night."

IV

A good many hours after Salisbury had returned to the company of the green rep chairs, Dyson still sat at his desk, itself a Japanese romance, smoking many pipes, and meditating over his friend's story. The bizarre quality of the inscription which had annoyed Salisbury was to him an attraction; and now and again he took it up and scanned thoughtfully what he had written, especially the quaint jingle at the end. It was a token, a symbol, he decided, and not a cipher; and the woman who had flung it away was, in all probability, entirely ignorant of its meaning. She was but the agent of the "Sam" she had abused and discarded, and he, too, was again the agent of some one unknown,--possibly of the individual styled Q., who had been forced to visit his French friends. But what to make of "Traverse Handel S.?" Here was the root and source of the enigma, and not all the tobacco of Virginia seemed likely to suggest any clew here. It seemed almost hopeless; but Dyson regarded himself as the Wellington of mysteries, and went to bed feeling assured that sooner or later he would hit upon the right track. For the next few days he was deeply engaged in his literary labours,--labours which were a profound mystery even to the most intimate of his friends, who searched the railway bookstalls in vain for the result of so many hours spent at the Japanese bureau in company with strong tobacco and black tea. On this occasion Dyson confined himself to his room for four days, and it was with genuine relief that he laid down his pen and went out into the streets in quest of relaxation and fresh air. The gas lamps were being lighted, and the fifth edition of the evening papers was being howled through the streets; and Dyson, feeling that he wanted quiet, turned away from the clamorous Strand, and began to trend away to the northwest. Soon he found himself in streets that echoed to his foot-steps; and crossing a broad new throughfare, and verging still to the west, Dyson discovered that he had penetrated to the depths of Soho. Here again was life; rare vintages of France and Italy, at prices which seemed contemptibly small, allured the passer-by; here were cheeses, vast and rich; here olive oil, and here a grove of Rabelaisian sausages; while in a neighbouring shop the whole press of Paris appeared to be on sale. In the middle of the roadway a strange miscellany of nations sauntered to and fro; for there cab and hansom rarely ventured, and from window over window the inhabitants looked forth in pleased contemplation of the scene. Dyson made his way slowly along, mingling with the crowd on the cobblestones, listening to the queer babel of French and German and Italian and English, glancing now and again at the shop windows with their levelled batteries of bottles, and had almost gained the end of the street, when his attention was arrested by a small shop at the corner, a vivid contrast to its neighbours. It was the typical shop of the poor quarter, a shop entirely English. Here were vended tobacco and sweets, cheap pipes of clay and cherry wood; penny exercise-books and penholders jostled for precedence with comic songs, and story papers with appalling cuts showed that romance claimed its place beside the actualities of the evening paper, the bills of which fluttered at the doorway. Dyson glanced up at the name above the door, and stood by the kennel trembling; for a sharp pang, the pang of one who has made a discovery, had for a moment left him incapable of motion. The name over the little shop was Travers. Dyson looked up again, this time at the corner of the wall above the lamp-post, and read, in white letters on a blue ground, the words "Handel Street, W.C.," and the legend was repeated in fainter letters just below. He gave a little sigh of satisfaction, and without more ado walked boldly into the shop, and stared the fat man who was sitting behind the counter full in the face. The fellow rose to his feet and returned the stare a little curiously, and then began in stereotyped phrase,--

"What can I do for you, sir?"

Dyson enjoyed the situation, and a dawning perplexity on the man's face. He propped his stick carefully against the counter, and leaning over it, said slowly and impressively:

"Once around the grass, and twice around the lass, and thrice around the maple-tree."

Dyson had calculated on his words producing an effect, and he was not disappointed. The vendor of miscellanies gasped, open-mouthed, like a fish, and steadied himself against the counter. When he spoke, after a short interval, it was in a hoarse mutter, tremulous and unsteady.

"Would you mind saying that again, sir? I didn't quite catch it."

"My good man, I shall most certainly do nothing of the kind. You heard what I said perfectly well. You have got a clock in your shop, I see; an admirable timekeeper I have no doubt. Well, I give you a minute by your own clock."

The man looked about him in perplexed indecision, and Dyson felt that it was time to be bold.

"Look here, Travers, the time is nearly up. You have heard of Q., I think. Remember, I hold your life in my hands. Now!"

Dyson was shocked at the result of his own audacity. The man shrunk and shrivelled in terror, the sweat poured down a face of ashy white, and he held up his hands before him.

"Mr. Davies, Mr. Davies, don't say that, don't for Heaven's sake. I didn't know you at first, I didn't indeed. Good God! Mr. Davies, you wouldn't ruin me? I'll get it in a moment."

"You had better not lose any more time."

The man slunk piteously out of his shop, and went into a back parlour. Dyson heard his trembling fingers fumbling with a bunch of keys, and the creak of an opening box. He came back presently with a small package neatly tied up in brown paper in his hands, and, still full of terror, handed it to Dyson.

"I'm glad to be rid of it," he said. "I'll take no more jobs of this sort."

Dyson took the parcel and his stick, and walked out of the shop with a nod, turning round as he passed the door. Travers had sunk into his seat, his face still white with terror, with one hand over his eyes, and Dyson speculated a good deal as he walked rapidly away as to what queer chords those could be on which he had played so roughly. He hailed the first hansom he could see, and drove home, and when he had lit his hanging lamp, and laid his parcel on the table, he paused for a moment, wondering on what strange thing the lamplight would soon shine. He locked his door, and cut the strings, and unfolded the paper layer after layer, and came at last to a small wooden box, simply but solidly made. There was no lock, and Dyson had simply to raise the lid, and as he did so he drew a long breath and started back. The lamp seemed to glimmer feebly like a single candle, but the whole room blazed with light--and not with light alone but with a thousand colours, with all the glories of some painted window; and upon the walls of his room and on the familiar furniture, the glow flamed back and seemed to flow again to its source, the little wooden box. For there upon a bed of soft wool lay the most splendid jewel,--a jewel such as Dyson had never dreamed of, and within it shone the blue of far skies, and the green of the sea by the shore, and the red of the ruby, and deep violet rays, and in the middle of all it seemed aflame as if a fountain of fire rose up, and fell, and rose again with sparks like stars for drops. Dyson gave a long deep sigh, and dropped into his chair, and put his hands over his eyes to think. The jewel was like an opal, but from a long experience of the shop windows he knew there was no such thing as an opal one quarter or one eighth of its size. He looked at the stone again, with a feeling that was almost awe, and placed it gently on the table under the lamp, and watched the wonderful flame that shone and sparkled in its centre, and then turned to the box, curious to know whether it might contain other marvels. He lifted the bed of wool on which the opal had reclined, and saw beneath, no more jewels, but a little old pocket-book, worn and shabby with use. Dyson opened it at the first leaf, and dropped the book again appalled. He had read the name of the owner, neatly written in blue ink:--

STEVEN BLACK, M.D.,
  Oranmore,
  Devon Road,
  Harlesden.

It was several minutes before Dyson could bring himself to open the book a second time; he remembered the wretched exile in his garret and his strange talk, and the memory too of the face he had seen at the window, and of what the specialist had said surged up in his mind, and as he held his finger on the cover he shivered, dreading what might be written within. When at last he held it in his hand, and turned the pages, he found that the first two leaves were blank, but the third was covered with clear minute writing, and Dyson began to read with the light of the opal flaming in his eyes.

V

"Ever since I was a young man," the record began, "I devoted all my leisure and a good deal of time that ought to have been given to other studies to the investigation of curious and obscure branches of knowledge. What are commonly called the pleasures of life had never any attractions for me, and I lived alone in London, avoiding my fellow-students, and in my turn avoided by them as a man self-absorbed and unsympathetic. So long as I could gratify my desire of knowledge of a peculiar kind, knowledge of which the very existence is a profound secret to most men, I was intensely happy, and I have often spent whole nights sitting in the darkness of my room, and thinking of the strange world on the brink of which I trod. My professional studies, however, and the necessity of obtaining a degree, for some time forced my more obscure employment into the background, and soon after I had qualified I met Agnes, who became my wife. We took a new house in this remote suburb, and I began the regular routine of a sober practice, and for some months lived happily enough, sharing in the life about me, and only thinking at odd intervals of that occult science which had once fascinated my whole being. I had learnt enough of the paths I had begun to tread to know that they were beyond all expression difficult and dangerous, that to persevere meant in all probability the wreck of a life, and that they lead to regions so terrible that the mind of man shrinks appalled at the very thought. Moreover, the quiet and the peace I had enjoyed since my marriage had wiled me away to a great extent from places where I knew no peace could dwell. But suddenly,--I think, indeed, it was the work of a single night, as I lay awake on my bed gazing into the darkness,--suddenly, I say, the old desire, the former longing returned, and returned with a force that had been intensified ten times by its absence; and when the day dawned and I looked out of the window and saw with haggard eyes the sun rise in the East, I knew that my doom had been pronounced; that as I had gone far, so now I must go farther with steps that know no faltering. I turned to the bed where my wife was sleeping peacefully, and lay down again weeping bitter tears, for the sun had set on our happy life and had risen with a dawn of terror to us both. I will not set down here in minute detail what followed; outwardly I went about the day's labour as before, saying nothing to my wife. But she soon saw that I had changed. I spent my spare time in a room which I had fitted up as a laboratory, and often I crept upstairs in the gray dawn of the morning, when the light of many lamps still glowed over London; and each night I had stolen a step nearer to that great abyss which I was to bridge over, the gulf between the world of consciousness and the world of matter. My experiments were many and complicated in their nature, and it was some months before I realized whither they all pointed, and when this was borne in upon me in a moment's time, I felt my face whiten and my heart still within me. But the power to draw back, the power to stand before the doors that now opened wide before me and not to enter in, had long ago been absent; the way was closed, and I could only pass onward. My position was as utterly hopeless as that of the prisoner in an utter dungeon, whose only light is that of the dungeon above him; the doors were shut and escape was impossible. Experiment after experiment gave the same result, and I knew, and shrank even as the thought passed through my mind, that in the work I had to do there must be elements which no laboratory could furnish, which no scales could ever measure. In that work, from which even I doubted to escape with life, life itself must enter; from some human being there must be drawn that essence which men call the soul, and in its place (for in the scheme of the world there is no vacant chamber), in its place would enter in what the lips can hardly utter, what the mind cannot conceive without a horror more awful than the horror of death itself. And when I knew this, I knew also on whom this fate would fall; I looked into my wife's eyes. Even at that hour, if I had gone out and taken a rope and hanged myself I might have escaped, and she also, but in no other way. At last I told her all. She shuddered, and wept, and called on her dead mother for help, and asked me if I had no mercy, and I could only sigh. I concealed nothing from her; I told her what she would become, and what would enter in where her life had been; I told her of all the shame and of all the horror. You who will read this when I am dead,--if indeed I allow this record to survive--you who have opened the box and have seen what lies there, if you could understand what lies hidden in that opal! For one night my wife consented to what I asked of her, consented with the tears running down her beautiful face, and hot shame flushing red over her neck and breast, consented to undergo this for me. I threw open the window, and we looked together at the sky and the dark earth for the last time; it was a fine starlight night, and there was a pleasant breeze blowing, and I kissed her on her lips, and her tears ran down upon my face. That night she came down to my laboratory, and there, with shutters bolted and barred down, with curtains drawn thick and close so that the very stars might be shut out from the sight of that room, while the crucible hissed and boiled over the lamp, I did what had to be done, and led out what was no longer a woman. But on the table the opal flamed and sparkled with such light as no eyes of man have ever gazed on, and the rays of the flame that was within it flashed and glittered, and shone even to my heart. My wife had only asked one thing of me; that when there came at last what I had told her, I would kill her. I have kept that promise."

***

There was nothing more. Dyson let the little pocket-book fall, and turned and looked again at the opal with its flaming inmost light, and then, with unutterable irresistible horror surging up in his heart, grasped the jewel, and flung it on the ground, and trampled it beneath his heel. His face was white with terror as he turned away, and for a moment stood sick and trembling, and then with a start he leapt across the room and steadied himself against the door. There was an angry hiss, as of steam escaping under great pressure, and as he gazed, motionless, a volume of heavy yellow smoke was slowly issuing from the very centre of the jewel, and wreathing itself in snake-like coils above it. And then a thin white flame burst forth from the smoke, and shot up into the air and vanished; and on the ground there lay a thing like a cinder, black, and crumbling to the touch.

www.ingramcontent.com/pod-product-compliance
Lightning Source LLC
Chambersburg PA
CBHW030932020726
47498CB00001B/207